James Nic

THE COMPLETE
SHERLOCK HOLMES
SHORT STORIES

By Sir Arthur Conan Doyle

*The Adventures of Sherlock Holmes
*The Case-Book of Sherlock Holmes
*The Memoirs of Sherlock Holmes
*The Return of Sherlock Holmes
*His Last Bow
*The Hound of the Baskervilles
*The Sign of Four
*The Valley of Fear
 Sir Nigel
 The White Company
 Micah Clarke
 The Refugees
 Rodney Stone
 Uncle Bernac
 The Lost World
 The Tragedy of the Korosko
 Adventures of Gerard
 The Exploits of Brigadier Gerard

OMNIBUS VOLUMES

Great Stories of Sir Arthur Conan Doyle
The Conan Doyle Stories
The Sherlock Holmes Short Stories
The Sherlock Holmes Long Stories
The Historical Romances
The Complete Professor Challenger Stories
The Complete Napoleonic Stories

★ ★ ★ ★ ★

The Life of Sir Arthur Conan Doyle
    By John Dickson Carr

*Sherlock Holmes Stories

SHERLOCK HOLMES

HIS ADVENTURES. MEMOIRS. RETURN.
HIS LAST BOW & THE CASE-BOOK.

THE COMPLETE SHORT STORIES

By SIR ARTHUR CONAN DOYLE

LONDON
JOHN MURRAY, ALBEMARLE STREET, W.

First Edition in one volume
October 1928

Reprinted	.	. *October* *1928*
Reprinted	.	. *March 1929*
Reprinted	.	. *October 1929*
Reprinted	.	*September 1931*
Reprinted	.	. *June 1934*
Reprinted	.	*November 1937*
Reprinted	.	. *January 1942*
Reprinted	.	*December 1943*
Reprinted	.	. *May 1946*
Reprinted	.	. *May 1949*
Reprinted	.	*September 1950*
Reprinted	.	. *January 1952*
Reprinted	.	. *May 1953*
Reprinted	.	. *October 1956*
Reprinted	.	. *October 1959*

Made and printed in Great Britain by Butler & Tanner Ltd., Frome and London
and published by John Murray (Publishers) Ltd.

PREFACE

THIS book contains the whole series of stories concerning Sherlock Holmes apart from the four novels, " A Study in Scarlet," " The Sign of Four," " The Hound of the Baskervilles," " The Valley of Fear."

It begins with his first appearance in this form in " A Scandal in Bohemia " which came out in 1892, until he made his final exit in " Shoscombe Old Place " in 1927. As his methods and character became familiar to the public there was naturally less element of surprise, and the later stories suffered by comparison. As a witty critic remarked, " He may not have been killed when he fell over the cliff, but he was never quite the same man afterwards." I hope, however, that the reader who can now take them in any order will not find that the end shows any conspicuous falling off from the modest merits of the beginning.

ARTHUR CONAN DOYLE.

CROWBOROUGH,
1928.

CONTENTS

The Adventures of Sherlock Holmes

		PAGE
1	A SCANDAL IN BOHEMIA	3
2	THE RED-HEADED LEAGUE	29
3	A CASE OF IDENTITY	55
4	THE BOSCOMBE VALLEY MYSTERY	75
5	THE FIVE ORANGE PIPS	102
6	THE MAN WITH THE TWISTED LIP	124
7	THE BLUE CARBUNCLE	150
8	THE SPECKLED BAND	173
9	THE ENGINEER'S THUMB	201
10	THE NOBLE BACHELOR	224
11	THE BERYL CORONET	248
12	THE COPPER BEECHES	275

The Memoirs of Sherlock Holmes

13.	SILVER BLAZE	305
14.	THE YELLOW FACE	333
15.	THE STOCKBROKER'S CLERK	354
16.	THE " GLORIA SCOTT "	374
17.	THE MUSGRAVE RITUAL	396
18.	THE REIGATE SQUIRES	417
19.	THE CROOKED MAN	439
20.	THE RESIDENT PATIENT	458
21.	THE GREEK INTERPRETER	477
22.	THE NAVAL TREATY	498
23.	THE FINAL PROBLEM	536

The Return of Sherlock Holmes

| 24. | THE EMPTY HOUSE | 559 |
| 25. | THE NORWOOD BUILDER | 583 |

CONTENTS

		PAGE
26.	THE DANCING MEN .	610
27.	THE SOLITARY CYCLIST	639
28.	THE PRIORY SCHOOL .	661
29.	BLACK PETER .	696
30.	CHARLES AUGUSTUS MILVERTON .	720
31.	THE SIX NAPOLEONS .	739
32.	THE THREE STUDENTS	763
33.	THE GOLDEN PINCE-NEZ .	782
34.	THE MISSING THREE-QUARTER .	808
35.	THE ABBEY GRANGE .	833
36.	THE SECOND STAIN .	859

His Last Bow

37.	WISTERIA LODGE	891
38.	THE CARDBOARD BOX.	923
39.	THE RED CIRCLE	947
40.	THE BRUCE-PARTINGTON PLANS .	968
41.	THE DYING DETECTIVE .	1000
42.	THE DISAPPEARANCE OF LADY FRANCES CARFAX .	1018
43.	THE DEVIL'S FOOT .	1040
44.	HIS LAST BOW .	1068

The Case-Book of Sherlock Holmes

45.	THE ILLUSTRIOUS CLIENT .	1089
46.	THE BLANCHED SOLDIER .	1117
47.	THE MAZARIN STONE.	1140
48.	THE THREE GABLES .	1159
49.	THE SUSSEX VAMPIRE.	1178
50.	THE THREE GARRIDEBS .	1196
51.	THOR BRIDGE .	1215
52.	THE CREEPING MAN .	1243
53.	THE LION'S MANE .	1266
54.	THE VEILED LODGER .	1287
55.	SHOSCOMBE OLD PLACE .	1300
56.	THE RETIRED COLOURMAN .	1319

INDEX TO TITLES

	PAGE
ABBEY GRANGE, THE	833
BERYL CORONET, THE	248
BLACK PETER	696
BLANCHED SOLDIER, THE	1117
BLUE CARBUNCLE, THE	150
BOSCOMBE VALLEY MYSTERY, THE	75
BRUCE-PARTINGTON PLANS, THE	968
CARDBOARD BOX, THE	923
CASE OF IDENTITY, A	55
CHARLES AUGUSTUS MILVERTON	720
COPPER BEECHES, THE	275
CREEPING MAN, THE	1243
CROOKED MAN, THE	439
DANCING MEN, THE	610
DEVIL'S FOOT, THE	1040
DISAPPEARANCE OF LADY FRANCES CARFAX, THE . .	1018
DYING DETECTIVE, THE	1000
EMPTY HOUSE, THE	559
ENGINEER'S THUMB, THE	201
FINAL PROBLEM, THE	536
FIVE ORANGE PIPS, THE	102
" GLORIA SCOTT," THE	374

INDEX TO TITLES

	PAGE
GOLDEN PINCE-NEZ, THE	782
GREEK INTERPRETER, THE	477
HIS LAST BOW.	1068
ILLUSTRIOUS CLIENT, THE	1089
LION'S MANE, THE	1266
MAN WITH THE TWISTED LIP, THE	124
MAZARIN STONE, THE	1140
MISSING THREE-QUARTER, THE	808
MUSGRAVE RITUAL, THE	396
NAVAL TREATY, THE.	498
NOBLE BACHELOR, THE	224
NORWOOD BUILDER, THE	583
PRIORY SCHOOL, THE	661
RED CIRCLE, THE	947
RED-HEADED LEAGUE, THE	29
REIGATE SQUIRES, THE	417
RESIDENT PATIENT, THE	458
RETIRED COLOURMAN, THE	1319
SCANDAL IN BOHEMIA, A	3
SECOND STAIN, THE	859
SHOSCOMBE OLD PLACE	1300
SILVER BLAZE	305
SIX NAPOLEONS, THE	739
SOLITARY CYCLIST, THE	639
SPECKLED BAND, THE	173
STOCKBROKER'S CLERK, THE	354
SUSSEX VAMPIRE, THE	1178

INDEX TO TITLES

	PAGE
THOR BRIDGE	1215
THREE GABLES, THE	1159
THREE GARRIDEBS, THE	1196
THREE STUDENTS, THE	763
VEILED LODGER, THE	1287
WISTERIA LODGE	891
YELLOW FACE, THE	333

THE ADVENTURES OF
SHERLOCK HOLMES

I. *A Scandal in Bohemia*

I

TO Sherlock Holmes she is always *the* woman. I
have seldom heard him mention her under any
other name. In his eyes she eclipses and pre-
dominates the whole of her sex. It was not that he felt
any emotion akin to love for Irene Adler. All emotions,
and that one particularly, were abhorrent to his cold,
precise, but admirably balanced mind. He was, I take it,
the most perfect reasoning and observing machine that the
world has seen : but, as a lover, he would have placed
himself in a false position. He never spoke of the softer
passions, save with a gibe and a sneer. They were admirable things for the observer—excellent for drawing the veil
from men's motives and actions. But for the trained
reasoner to admit such intrusions into his own delicate and
finely adjusted temperament was to introduce a distracting
factor which might throw a doubt upon all his mental
results. Grit in a sensitive instrument, or a crack in one
of his own high-power lenses, would not be more disturbing than a strong emotion in a nature such as his.
And yet there was but one woman to him, and that woman
was the late Irene Adler, of dubious and questionable
memory.

I had seen little of Holmes lately. My marriage had
drifted us away from each other. My own complete
happiness, and the home-centred interests which rise up
around the man who first finds himself master of his own
establishment, were sufficient to absorb all my attention ;
while Holmes, who loathed every form of society with his

3

whole Bohemian soul, remained in our lodgings in Baker Street, buried among his old books, and alternating from week to week between cocaine and ambition, the drowsiness of the drug, and the fierce energy of his own keen nature. He was still, as ever, deeply attracted by the study of crime, and occupied his immense faculties and extraordinary powers of observation in following out those clues, and clearing up those mysteries, which had been abandoned as hopeless by the official police. From time to time I heard some vague account of his doings : of his summons to Odessa in the case of the Trepoff murder, of his clearing up of the singular tragedy of the Atkinson brothers at Trincomalee, and finally of the mission which he had accomplished so delicately and successfully for the reigning family of Holland. Beyond these signs of his activity, however, which I merely shared with all the readers of the daily press, I knew little of my former friend and companion.

One night—it was on the 20th of March, 1888—I was returning from a journey to a patient (for I had now returned to civil practice), when my way led me through Baker Street. As I passed the well-remembered door, which must always be associated in my mind with my wooing, and with the dark incidents of the Study in Scarlet, I was seized with a keen desire to see Holmes again, and to know how he was employing his extraordinary powers. His rooms were brilliantly lit, and, even as I looked up, I saw his tall spare figure pass twice in a dark silhouette against the blind. He was pacing the room swiftly, eagerly, with his head sunk upon his chest, and his hands clasped behind him. To me, who knew his every mood and habit, his attitude and manner told their own story. He was at work again. He had risen out of his drug-created dreams, and was hot upon the scent of some new problem. I rang the bell, and was shown up to the chamber which had formerly been in part my own.

His manner was not effusive. It seldom was ; but he was glad, I think, to see me. With hardly a word spoken,

4

but with a kindly eye, he waved me to an arm-chair, threw across his case of cigars, and indicated a spirit case and a gasogene in the corner. Then he stood before the fire, and looked me over in his singular introspective fashion.

" Wedlock suits you," he remarked. " I think, Watson, that you have put on seven and a half pounds since I saw you."

" Seven," I answered.

" Indeed, I should have thought a little more. Just a trifle more, I fancy, Watson. And in practice again, I observe. You did not tell me that you intended to go into harness."

' Then, how do you know ? "

" I see it, I deduce it. How do I know that you have been getting yourself very wet lately, and that you have a most clumsy and careless servant girl ? "

" My dear Holmes," said I, " this is too much. You would certainly have been burned had you lived a few centuries ago. It is true that I had a country walk on Thursday and came home in a dreadful mess ; but, as I have changed my clothes, I can't imagine how you deduce it. As to Mary Jane, she is incorrigible, and my wife has given her notice ; but there again I fail to see how you work it out."

He chuckled to himself and rubbed his long nervous hands together.

" It is simplicity itself," said he ; " my eyes tell me that on the inside of your left shoe, just where the firelight strikes it, the leather is scored by six almost parallel cuts. Obviously they have been caused by some one who has very carelessly scraped round the edges of the sole in order to remove crusted mud from it. Hence, you see, my double deduction that you had been out in vile weather, and that you had a particularly malignant boot-slitting specimen of the London slavey. As to your practice, if a gentleman walks into my rooms smelling of iodoform, with a black mark of nitrate of silver upon his right forefinger, and a bulge on the side of his top hat to show where he has secreted his stethoscope, I must be dull indeed if I do not pronounce him to be an active member of the medical profession."

I could not help laughing at the ease with which he explained his process of deduction. "When I hear you give your reasons," I remarked, "the thing always appears to me to be so ridiculously simple that I could easily do it myself, though at each successive instance of your reasoning I am baffled, until you explain your process. And yet I believe that my eyes are as good as yours."

"Quite so," he answered, lighting a cigarette, and throwing himself down into an arm-chair. "You see, but you do not observe. The distinction is clear. For example, you have frequently seen the steps which lead up from the hall to this room."

"Frequently."

"How often?"

"Well, some hundreds of times."

"Then how many are there?"

"How many! I don't know."

"Quite so! You have not observed. And yet you have seen. That is just my point. Now, I know that there are seventeen steps, because I have both seen and observed. By the way, since you are interested in these little problems, and since you are good enough to chronicle one or two of my trifling experiences, you may be interested in this." He threw over a sheet of thick pink-tinted note-paper which had been lying open upon the table. "It came by the last post," said he. "Read it aloud."

The note was undated, and without either signature or address.

"There will call upon you to-night, at a quarter to eight o'clock," it said, "a gentleman who desires to consult you upon a matter of the very deepest moment. Your recent services to one of the Royal Houses of Europe have shown that you are one who may safely be trusted with matters which are of an importance which can hardly be exagger-

6

ated. This account of you we have from all quarters received. Be in your chamber then at that hour, and do not take it amiss if your visitor wear a mask."

"This is indeed a mystery," I remarked. "What do you imagine that it means?"

"I have no data yet. It is a capital mistake to theorise before one has data. Insensibly one begins to twist facts to suit theories, instead of theories to suit facts. But the note itself. What do you deduce from it?"

I carefully examined the writing, and the paper upon which it was written.

"The man who wrote it was presumably well-to-do," I remarked, endeavouring to imitate my companion's processes. "Such paper could not be bought under half a crown a packet. It is peculiarly strong and stiff."

"Peculiar—that is the very word," said Holmes. "It is not an English paper at all. Hold it up to the light."

I did so, and saw a large E with a small g, a P, and a large G with a small t woven into the texture of the paper.

"What do you make of that?" asked Holmes.

"The name of the maker, no doubt; or his monogram, rather."

"Not at all. The G with the small t stands for 'Gesellschaft,' which is the German for 'Company.' It is a customary contraction like our 'Co.' P, of course, stands for 'Papier.' Now for the Eg. Let us glance at our Continental Gazetteer." He took down a heavy brown volume from his shelves. "Eglow, Eglonitz—here we are, Egria. It is in a German-speaking country—in Bohemia, not far from Carlsbad. 'Remarkable as being the scene of the death of Wallenstein, and for its numerous glass factories and paper mills.' Ha, ha, my boy, what do you make of that?" His eyes sparkled, and he sent up a great blue triumphant cloud from his cigarette.

"The paper was made in Bohemia," I said.

"Precisely. And the man who wrote the note is a German. Do you note the peculiar construction of the sentence—'This account of you we have from all quarters

7

received.' A Frenchman or Russian could not have written that. It is the German who is so uncourteous to his verbs. It only remains, therefore, to discover what is wanted by this German who writes upon Bohemian paper, and prefers wearing a mask to showing his face. And here he comes, if I am not mistaken, to resolve all our doubts."

As he spoke there was the sharp sound of horses' hoofs and grating wheels against the kerb, followed by a sharp pull at the bell. Holmes whistled.

" A pair by the sound," said he. " Yes," he continued, glancing out of the window. " A nice little brougham and a pair of beauties. A hundred and fifty guineas apiece. There's money in this case, Watson, if there is nothing else."

" I think that I had better go, Holmes."

" Not a bit, Doctor. Stay where you are. I am lost without my Boswell. And this promises to be interesting. It would be a pity to miss it."

" But your client——"

" Never mind him. I may want your help, and so may he. Here he comes. Sit down in that arm-chair, Doctor, and give us your best attention."

A slow and heavy step, which had been heard upon the stairs and in the passage, paused immediately outside the door. Then there was a loud and authoritative tap.

" Come in ! " said Holmes.

A man entered who could hardly have been less than six feet six inches in height, with the chest and limbs of a Hercules. His dress was rich with a richness which would, in England, be looked upon as akin to bad taste. Heavy bands of astrakhan were slashed across the sleeves and fronts of his double-breasted coat, while the deep blue cloak which was thrown over his shoulders was lined with flame-coloured silk, and secured at the neck with a brooch which consisted of a single flaming beryl. Boots which extended half-way up his calves, and which were trimmed at the tops with rich brown fur, completed the impression

8

of barbaric opulence which was suggested by his whole appearance. He carried a broad-brimmed hat in his hand, while he wore across the upper part of his face, extending down past the cheek-bones, a black vizard mask, which he had apparently adjusted that very moment, for his hand was still raised to it as he entered. From the lower part of the face he appeared to be a man of strong character, with a thick, hanging lip, and a long straight chin, suggestive of resolution pushed to the length of obstinacy.

"You had my note?" he asked, with a deep, harsh voice and a strongly marked German accent. "I told you that I would call." He looked from one to the other of us, as if uncertain which to address.

"Pray take a seat," said Holmes. "This is my friend and colleague, Dr. Watson, who is occasionally good enough to help me in my cases. Whom have I the honour to address?"

"You may address me as the Count von Kramm, a Bohemian nobleman. I understand that this gentleman, your friend, is a man of honour and discretion, whom I may trust with a matter of the most extreme importance. If not, I should much prefer to communicate with you alone."

I rose to go, but Holmes caught me by the wrist and pushed me back into my chair. "It is both, or none," said he. "You may say before this gentleman anything which you may say to me."

The Count shrugged his broad shoulders. "Then I must begin," said he, "by binding you both to absolute secrecy for two years, at the end of that time the matter will be of no importance. At present it is not too much to say that it is of such weight that it may have an influence upon European history."

"I promise," said Holmes.

"And I."

"You will excuse this mask," continued our strange visitor. "The august person who employs me wishes

9

his agent to be unknown to you, and I may confess at once that the title by which I have just called myself is not exactly my own."

" I was aware of it," said Holmes dryly.

" The circumstances are of great delicacy, and every precaution has to be taken to quench what might grow to be an immense scandal and seriously compromise one of the reigning families of Europe. To speak plainly, the matter implicates the great House of Ormstein, hereditary kings of Bohemia."

" I was also aware of that," murmured Holmes, settling himself down in his arm-chair, and closing his eyes.

Our visitor glanced with some apparent surprise at the languid, lounging figure of the man who had been no doubt depicted to him as the most incisive reasoner, and most energetic agent in Europe. Holmes slowly reopened his eyes, and looked impatiently at his gigantic client.

" If your Majesty would condescend to state your case," he remarked, " I should be better able to advise you."

The man sprang from his chair, and paced up and down the room in uncontrollable agitation. Then, with a gesture of desperation, he tore the mask from his face and hurled it upon the ground. " You are right," he cried, " I am the King. Why should I attempt to conceal it ? "

" Why, indeed ? " murmured Holmes. " Your Majesty had not spoken before I was aware that I was addressing Wilhelm Gottsreich Sigismond von Ormstein, Grand Duke of Cassel-Falstein, and hereditary King of Bohemia."

" But you can understand," said our strange visitor, sitting down once more and passing his hand over his high, white forehead, " you can understand that I am not accustomed to doing such business in my own person. Yet the matter was so delicate that I could not confide it to an agent without putting myself in his power. I have come *incognito* from Prague for the purpose of consulting you."

"Then, pray consult," said Holmes, shutting his eyes once more.

"The facts are briefly these : Some five years ago, during a lengthy visit to Warsaw, I made the acquaintance of the well-known adventuress Irene Adler. The name is no doubt familiar to you."

"Kindly look her up in my index, Doctor," murmured Holmes, without opening his eyes. For many years he had adopted a system of docketing all paragraphs concerning men and things, so that it was difficult to name a subject or a person on which he could not at once furnish information. In this case I found her biography sandwiched in between that of a Hebrew Rabbi and that of a staff-commander who had written a monograph upon the deep-sea fishes.

"Let me see," said Holmes. "Hum ! Born in New Jersey in the year 1858. Contralto—hum ! La Scala, hum ! Prima donna Imperial Opera of Warsaw—Yes ! Retired from operatic stage—ha ! Living in London—quite so ! Your Majesty, as I understand, became entangled with this young person, wrote her some compromising letters, and is now desirous of getting those letters back."

"Precisely so. But how——"

"Was there a secret marriage ?"

"None."

"No legal papers or certificates ?"

"None."

"Then I fail to follow Your Majesty. If this young person should produce her letters for blackmailing or other purposes, how is she to prove their authenticity ?"

"There is the writing."

"Pooh, pooh ! Forgery."

"My private note-paper."

"Stolen."

"My own seal."

"Imitated."

"My photograph."

" Bought."

" We were both in the photograph."

" Oh, dear ! That is very bad ! Your Majesty has indeed committed an indiscretion."

" I was mad—insane."

" You have compromised yourself seriously."

" I was only Crown Prince then. I was young. I am but thirty now."

" It must be recovered."

" We have tried and failed."

" Your Majesty must pay. It must be bought."

" She will not sell."

" Stolen, then."

" Five attempts have been made. Twice burglars in my pay ransacked her house. Once we diverted her luggage when she travelled. Twice she has been waylaid. There has been no result."

" No sign of it ? "

" Absolutely none."

Holmes laughed. " It is quite a pretty little problem," said he.

" But a very serious one to me," returned the King, reproachfully.

" Very, indeed. And what does she propose to do with the photograph ? "

" To ruin me."

" But how ? "

" I am about to be married."

" So I have heard."

" To Clotilde Lothman von Saxe-Meningen, second daughter of the King of Scandinavia. You may know the strict principles of her family. She is herself the very soul of delicacy. A shadow of a doubt as to my conduct would bring the matter to an end."

" And Irene Adler ? "

" Threatens to send them the photograph. And she will do it. I know that she will do it. You do not know her, but she has a soul of steel. She has the face of the most beautiful of women, and the mind of the most resolute of men. Rather than I should marry another woman, there are no lengths to which she would not go—none."

" You are sure that she has not sent it yet ? "

" I am sure."

" And why ? "

" Because she has said that she would send it on the day when the betrothal was publicly proclaimed. That will be next Monday."

" Oh, then, we have three days yet," said Holmes, with a yawn. " That is very fortunate, as I have one or two matters of importance to look into just at present. Your Majesty will, of course, stay in London for the present ? "

" Certainly. You will find me at the Langham, under the name of the Count von Kramm."

" Then I shall drop you a line to let you know how we progress."

" Pray do so. I shall be all anxiety."

" Then, as to money ? "

" You have *carte blanche*."

" Absolutely ? "

" I tell you that I would give one of the provinces of my kingdom to have that photograph."

" And for present expenses ? "

The King took a heavy chamois leather bag from under his cloak, and laid it on the table.

" There are three hundred pounds in gold, and seven hundred in notes," he said.

Holmes scribbled a receipt upon a sheet of his note-book, and handed it to him.

" And mademoiselle's address ? " he asked.

" Is Briony Lodge, Serpentine Avenue, St. John's Wood."

Holmes took a note of it. " One other question," said he. " Was the photograph a cabinet ? "

" It was."

" Then, good night, Your Majesty, and I trust that we

shall soon have some good news for you. And good
night, Watson," he added, as the wheels of the Royal
brougham rolled down the street. " If you will be good
enough to call to-morrow afternoon, at three o'clock, I
should like to chat this little matter over with you."

II

At three o'clock precisely I was at Baker Street, but
Holmes had not yet returned. The landlady informed
me that he had left the house shortly after eight o'clock
in the morning. I sat down beside the fire, however, with
the intention of awaiting him, however long he might be.
I was already deeply interested in his inquiry, for, though
it was surrounded by none of the grim and strange
features which were associated with the two crimes which
I have elsewhere recorded, still, the nature of the case and
the exalted station of his client gave it a character of its
own. Indeed, apart from the nature of the investigation
which my friend had on hand, there was something in his
masterly grasp of a situation, and his keen, incisive reasoning, which made it a pleasure to me to study his system of
work, and to follow the quick, subtle methods by which
he disentangled the most inextricable mysteries. So
accustomed was I to his invariable success that the very
possibility of his failing had ceased to enter into my
head.

It was close upon four before the door opened, and a
drunken-looking groom, ill-kempt and side-whiskered
with an inflamed face and disreputable clothes, walked
into the room. Accustomed as I was to my friend's
amazing powers in the use of disguises, I had to look
three times before I was certain that it was indeed he.
With a nod he vanished into the bedroom, whence he
emerged in five minutes tweed-suited and respectable, as
of old. Putting his hands into his pockets, he stretched
out his legs in front of the fire, and laughed heartily for
some minutes.

" Well, really ! " he cried, and then he choked ; and

14

laughed again until he was obliged to lie back, limp and helpless, in the chair.

" What is it ? "

" It's quite too funny. I am sure you could never guess how I employed my morning, or what I ended by doing."

" I can't imagine. I suppose that you have been watching the habits, and perhaps the house, of Miss Irene Adler."

" Quite so, but the sequel was rather unusual. I will tell you, however. I left the house a little after eight o'clock this morning, in the character of a groom out of work. There is a wonderful sympathy and freemasonry among horsey men. Be one of them, and you will know all that there is to know. I soon found Briony Lodge. It is a bijou villa, with a garden at the back, but built out in front right up to the road, two stories. Chubb lock to the door. Large sitting-room on the right side, well furnished, with long windows almost to the floor, and those preposterous English window fasteners which a child could open. Behind there was nothing remarkable, save that the passage window could be reached from the top of the coach-house. I walked round it and examined it closely from every point of view, but without noting anything else of interest.

" I then lounged down the street, and found, as I expected, that there was a mews in a lane which runs down by one wall of the garden. I lent the ostlers a hand in rubbing down their horses, and I received in exchange twopence, a glass of half-and-half, two fills of shag tobacco and as much information as I could desire about Miss Adler, to say nothing of half a dozen other people in the neighbourhood in whom I was not in the least interested, but whose biographies I was compelled to listen to."

" And what of Irene Adler ? " I asked.

" Oh, she has turned all the men's heads down in that part. She is the daintiest thing under a bonnet on this planet. So say the Serpentine Mews, to a man. She lives quietly, sings at concerts, drives out at five every day, and returns at seven sharp for dinner. Seldom goes out at other times, except when she sings. Has only one male visitor, but a good deal of him. He is dark, handsome, and dashing ; never calls less than once a day, and often twice. He is a Mr. Godfrey Norton, of the Inner Temple. See the advantages of a cabman as a confidant. They had driven him home a dozen times from Serpentine Mews, and knew all about him. When I had listened to all that they had to tell, I began to walk up and down near Briony Lodge once more, and to think over my plan of campaign.

" This Godfrey Norton was evidently an important factor in the matter. He was a lawyer. That sounded ominous. What was the relation between them, and what the object of his repeated visits ? Was she his client, his friend, or his mistress ? If the former, she had probably transferred the photograph to his keeping. If the latter, it was less likely. On the issue of this question depended whether I should continue my work at Briony Lodge, or turn my attention to the gentleman's chambers in the Temple. It was a delicate point, and it widened the field of my inquiry. I fear that I bore you with these details, but I have to let you see my little difficulties, if you are to understand the situation."

" I am following you closely," I answered.

" I was still balancing the matter in my mind when a hansom cab drove up to Briony Lodge, and a gentleman sprang out. He was a remarkably handsome man, dark, aquiline, and moustached—evidently the man of whom I had heard. He appeared to be in a great hurry, shouted to the cabman to wait, and brushed past the maid who opened the door with the air of a man who was thoroughly at home.

" He was in the house about half an hour, and I could catch glimpses of him, in the windows of the sitting-room, pacing up and down, talking excitedly and waving his arms. Of her I could see nothing. Presently he emerged, looking even more flurried than before. As he stepped up to the cab, he pulled a gold watch from his pocket and looked at it earnestly. ' Drive like the devil,' he shouted, ' first to Gross and Hankey's in Regent Street, and then to the church of St. Monica in the Edgware Road. Half a guinea if you do it in twenty minutes ! '

" Away they went, and I was just wondering whether I should not do well to follow them, when up the lane came a neat little landau, the coachman with his coat only half buttoned, and his tie under his ear, while all the tags of his harness were sticking out of the buckles. It hadn't pulled up before she shot out of the hall door and into it. I only caught a glimpse of her at the moment, but she was a lovely woman, with a face that a man might die for.

" ' The Church of St. Monica, John,' she cried, 'and half a sovereign if you reach it in twenty minutes.'

" This was quite too good to lose, Watson. I was just balancing whether I should run for it, or whether I should perch behind her landau, when a cab came through the street. The driver looked twice at such a shabby fare ; but I jumped in before he could object. ' The Church of St. Monica,' said I, ' and half a sovereign if you reach it in twenty minutes.' It was twenty-five minutes to twelve, and of course it was clear enough what was in the wind.

" My cabby drove fast. I don't think I ever drove faster, but the others were there before us. The cab and the landau with their steaming horses were in front of the door when I arrived. I paid the man and hurried into the church. There was not a soul there save the two whom I had followed, and a surpliced clergyman, who seemed to be expostulating with them. They were all three standing in a knot in front of the altar. I lounged up the side aisle like any other idler who has dropped into a church. Suddenly, to my surprise, the three at the altar faced round to me, and Godfrey Norton came running as hard as he could towards me.

" ' Thank God ! ' he cried. ' You'll do. Come ! Come ! '

" ' What then ? ' I asked.

" ' Come, man, come, only three minutes, or it won't be legal.'

" I was half dragged up to the altar, and before I knew where I was, I found myself mumbling responses which were whispered in my ear, and vouching for things of which I knew nothing, and generally assisting in the secure tying up of Irene Adler, spinster, to Godfrey Norton, bachelor. It was all done in an instant, and there was the gentleman thanking me on the one side and the lady on the other, while the clergyman beamed on me in front. It was the most preposterous position in which I ever found myself in my life, and it was the thought of it that started me laughing just now. It seems that there had been some informality about their licence, that the clergyman absolutely refused to marry them without a witness of some sort, and that my lucky appearance saved the bridegroom from having to sally out into the streets in search of a best man. The bride gave me a sovereign, and I mean to wear it on my watch-chain in memory of the occasion."

" This is a very unexpected turn of affairs," said I ; " and what then ? "

" Well, I found my plans very seriously menaced. It looked as if the pair might take an immediate departure, and so necessitate very prompt and energetic measures on my part. At the church door, however, they separated, he driving back to the Temple, and she to her own house. ' I shall drive out in the Park at five as usual,' she said as she left him. I heard no more. They drove away in different directions, and I went off to make my own arrangements."

" Which are ? "

" Some cold beef and a glass of beer," he answered, ringing the bell. " I have been too busy to think of food, and I am likely to be busier still this evening. By the way, Doctor, I shall want your co-operation."

" I shall be delighted."

" You don't mind breaking the law ? "

" Not in the least."

" Nor running a chance of arrest ? "

" Not in a good cause."

" Oh, the cause is excellent ! "

" Then I am your man."

" I was sure that I might rely on you."

" But what is it you wish ? "

" When Mrs. Turner has brought in the tray I will make it clear to you. Now," he said, as he turned hungrily on the simple fare that our landlady had provided, " I must discuss it while I eat, for I have not much time. It is nearly five now. In two hours we must be on the scene of action. Miss Irene, or Madame, rather, returns from her drive at seven. We must be at Briony Lodge to meet her."

" And what then ? "

" You must leave that to me. I have already arranged what is to occur. There is only one point on which I must insist. You must not interfere, come what may. You understand ? "

" I am to be neutral ? "

" To do nothing whatever. There will probably be some small unpleasantness. Do not join in it. It will end in my being conveyed into the house. Four or five minutes afterwards the sitting-room window will open. You are to station yourself close to that open window."

" Yes."

" You are to watch me, for I will be visible to you."

" Yes."

" And when I raise my hand—so—you will throw into the room what I give you to throw, and will, at the same time, raise the cry of fire. You quite follow me ? "

" Entirely."

" It is nothing very formidable," he said, taking a long cigar-shaped roll from his pocket. " It is an ordinary plumber's smoke rocket, fitted with a cap at either end to make it self-lighting. Your task is confined to that. When you raise your cry of fire, it will be taken up by

quite a number of people. You may then walk to the
end of the street, and I will rejoin you in ten minutes. I
hope that I have made myself clear ? "

" I am to remain neutral, to get near the window, to
watch you, and, at the signal, to throw in this object, then
to raise the cry of fire, and to await you at the corner of the
street."

" Precisely."

" Then you may entirely rely on me."

" That is excellent. I think perhaps it is almost time
that I prepared for the new rôle I have to play."

He disappeared into his bedroom, and returned in a
few minutes in the character of an amiable and simple-
minded Nonconformist clergyman. His broad black hat,
his baggy trousers, his white tie, his sympathetic smile,
and general look of peering and benevolent curiosity, were
such as Mr. John Hare alone could have equalled. It was
not merely that Holmes changed his costume. His
expression, his manner, his very soul seemed to vary with
every fresh part that he assumed. The stage lost a fine
actor, even as science lost an acute reasoner, when he
became a specialist in crime.

It was a quarter past six when we left Baker Street, and
it still wanted ten minutes to the hour when we found
ourselves in Serpentine Avenue. It was already dusk,
and the lamps were just being lighted as we paced up and
down in front of Briony Lodge, waiting for the coming of
its occupant. The house was just such as I had pictured
it from Sherlock Holmes's succinct description, but the
locality appeared to be less private than I expected. On
the contrary, for a small street in a quiet neighbourhood,
it was remarkably animated. There was a group of
shabbily-dressed men smoking and laughing in a corner,
a scissors-grinder with his wheel, two guardsmen who
were flirting with a nurse-girl, and several well-dressed
young men who were lounging up and down with cigars in
their mouths.

" You see," remarked Holmes, as we paced to and fro

in front of the house, "this marriage rather simplifies matters. The photograph becomes a double-edged weapon now. The chances are that she would be as averse to its being seen by Mr. Godfrey Norton, as our client is to its coming to the eyes of his Princess. Now the question is—Where are we to find the photograph?"

"Where, indeed?"

"It is most unlikely that she carries it about with her. It is cabinet size. Too large for easy concealment about a woman's dress. She knows that the King is capable of having her waylaid and searched. Two attempts of the sort have already been made. We may take it then that she does not carry it about with her."

"Where, then?"

"Her banker or her lawyer. There is that double possibility. But I am inclined to think neither. Women are naturally secretive, and they like to do their own secreting. Why should she hand it over to anyone else? She could trust her own guardianship, but she could not tell what indirect or political influence might be brought to bear upon a business man. Besides, remember that she had resolved to use it within a few days. It must be where she can lay her hands upon it. It must be in her own house."

"But it has twice been burgled."

"Pshaw! They did not know how to look."

"But how will you look?"

"I will not look."

"What then?"

"I will get her to show me."

"But she will refuse."

"She will not be able to. But I hear the rumble of wheels. It is her carriage. Now carry out my orders to the letter."

As he spoke, the gleam of the sidelights of a carriage came round the curve of the avenue. It was a smart little landau which rattled up to the door of Briony Lodge. As it pulled up, one of the loafing men at the corner dashed forward to open the door in the hope of earning a copper, but was elbowed away by another loafer who had rushed up with the same intention. A fierce quarrel broke out, which was increased by the two guardsmen, who took sides with one of the loungers, and by the scissors-grinder, who was equally hot upon the other side. A blow was struck, and in an instant the lady, who had stepped from her carriage, was the centre of a little knot of flushed and struggling men who struck savagely at each other with their fists and sticks. Holmes dashed into the crowd to protect the lady ; but just as he reached her, he gave a cry and dropped to the ground, with the blood running freely down his face. At his fall the guardsmen took to their heels in one direction and the loungers in the other, while a number of better dressed people who had watched the scuffle without taking part in it, crowded in to help the lady and to attend to the injured man. Irene Adler, as I will still call her, had hurried up the steps ; but she stood at the top with her superb figure outlined against the lights of the hall, looking back into the street.

" Is the poor gentleman much hurt ? " she asked.

" He is dead," cried several voices.

" No, no, there's life in him," shouted another. " But he'll be gone before you can get him to hospital."

" He's a brave fellow," said a woman. " They would have had the lady's purse and watch if it hadn't been for him. They were a gang, and a rough one, too. Ah, he's breathing now."

" He can't lie in the street. May we bring him in, marm ? "

" Surely. Bring him into the sitting-room. There is a comfortable sofa. This way, please ! "

Slowly and solemnly he was borne into Briony Lodge, and laid out in the principal room, while I still observed the proceedings from my post by the window. The lamps had been lit, but the blinds had not been drawn, so that I could see Holmes as he lay upon the couch. I do not know whether he was seized with compunction at that moment for the part he was playing, but I know that I never felt more heartily ashamed of myself in my life than when I saw the beautiful creature against whom I was conspiring, or the grace and kindliness with which she waited upon the injured man. And yet it would be the blackest treachery to Holmes to draw back now from the part which he had entrusted to me. I hardened my heart and took the smoke rocket from under my ulster. After all, I thought, we are not injuring her. We are but preventing her from injuring another.

Holmes had sat up upon the couch, and I saw him motion like a man who is in want of air. A maid rushed across and threw open the window. At the same instant I saw him raise his hand, and at the signal I tossed my rocket into the room with a cry of " Fire." The word was no sooner out of my mouth than the whole crowd of spectators, well dressed and ill—gentlemen, ostlers, and servant maids—joined in a general shriek of " Fire." Thick clouds of smoke curled through the room, and out at the open window. I caught a glimpse of rushing figures, and a moment later the voice of Holmes from within, assuring them that it was a false alarm. Slipping through the shouting crowd I made my way to the corner of the street, and in ten minutes was rejoiced to find my friend's arm in mine, and to get away from the scene of the uproar. He walked swiftly and in silence for some few minutes, until we had turned down one of the quiet streets which lead towards the Edgware Road.

" You did it very nicely, Doctor," he remarked. " Nothing could have been better. It is all right."

" You have the photograph ! "

" I know where it is."

" And how did you find out ? "

" She showed me, as I told you that she would."

" I am still in the dark."

" I do not wish to make a mystery," said he, laughing. " The matter was perfectly simple. You, of course, saw that every one in the street was an accomplice. They were all engaged for the evening."

" I guessed as much."

" Then, when the row broke out, I had a little moist red paint in the palm of my hand. I rushed forward, fell down, clapped my hand to my face, and became a piteous spectacle. It is an old trick."

" That also I could fathom."

" Then they carried me in. She was bound to have me in. What else could she do ? And into her sitting-room which was the very room which I suspected. It lay between that and her bedroom, and I was determined to see which. They laid me on a couch, I motioned for air, they were compelled to open the window and you had your chance."

" How did that help you ? "

" It was all-important. When a woman thinks that her house is on fire, her instinct is at once to rush to the thing which she values most. It is a perfectly overpowering impulse, and I have more than once taken advantage of it. In the case of the Darlington Substitution Scandal it was of use to me, and also in the Arnsworth Castle business. A married woman grabs at her baby—an un-married one reaches for her jewel box. Now it was clear to me that our lady of to-day had nothing in the house more precious to her than what we are in quest of. She would rush to secure it. The alarm of fire was admirably done. The smoke and shouting was enough to shake nerves of steel. She responded beautifully. The photo-graph is in a recess behind a sliding panel just above the right bell-pull. She was there in an instant, and I caught a glimpse of it as she half drew it out. When I cried out that it was a false alarm, she replaced it, glanced at the rocket, rushed from the room, and I have not seen her since. I rose, and, making my excuses, escaped from the house, I hesitated whether to attempt to secure the photo-graph at once ; but the coachman had come in, and as he was watching me narrowly, it seemed safer to wait. A little over-precipitance may ruin all."

" And now ? " I asked.

" Our quest is practically finished. I shall call with the King to-morrow, and with you, if you care to come with us. We will be shown into the sitting-room to wait for the lady, but it is probable that when she comes she may find neither us nor the photograph. It might be a satisfaction to His Majesty to regain it with his own hands."

" And when will you call ? "

" At eight in the morning. She will not be up, so that we shall have a clear field. Besides, we must be prompt, for this marriage may mean a complete change in her life and habits. I must wire to the King without delay."

We had reached Baker Street, and had stopped at the door. He was searching his pockets for the key, when some one passing said :

" Good night, Mister Sherlock Holmes."

There were several people on the pavement at the time, but the greeting appeared to come from a slim youth in an ulster who had hurried by.

" I've heard that voice before," said Holmes, staring down the dimly lit street. " Now, I wonder who the deuce that could have been."

III

I slept at Baker Street that night, and we were engaged upon our toast and coffee when the King of Bohemia rushed into the room.

" You have really got it ! " he cried, grasping Sherlock Holmes by either shoulder, and looking eagerly into his face.

" Not yet."

" But you have hopes ? "

" I have hopes."

" Then, come. I am all impatience to be gone."

" We must have a cab."

" No, my brougham is waiting."

" Then that will simplify matters."

We descended, and started off once more for Briony Lodge.

" Irene Adler is married," remarked Holmes

" Married ! When ? "

" Yesterday."

" But to whom ? "

" To an English lawyer named Norton."

" But she could not love him ? "

" I am in hopes that she does."

" And why in hopes ? "

" Because it would spare Your Majesty all fear of future annoyance. If the lady loves her husband, she does not love Your Majesty. If she does not love Your Majesty there is no reason why she should interfere with Your Majesty's plan."

" It is true. And yet—— ! Well ! I wish she had been of my own station ! What a queen she would have made ! " He relapsed into a moody silence which was not broken until we drew up in Serpentine Avenue.

The door of Briony Lodge was open, and an elderly woman stood upon the steps. She watched us with a sardonic eye as we stepped from the brougham.

" Mr. Sherlock Holmes, I believe ? " said she.

" I am Mr. Holmes," answered my companion, looking at her with a questioning and rather startled gaze.

" Indeed ! My mistress told me that you were likely to call. She left this morning with her husband, by the 5.15 train from Charing Cross, for the Continent."

" What ! " Sherlock Holmes staggered back, white with chagrin and surprise. " Do you mean that she has left England ? "

" Never to return."

" And the papers ? " asked the King hoarsely. " All is lost."

" We shall see." He pushed past the servant, and rushed into the drawing-room, followed by the King and myself. The furniture was scattered about in every direction, with dismantled shelves, and open drawers, as if the lady had hurriedly ransacked them before her flight. Holmes rushed at the bell-pull, tore back a small sliding shutter, and, plunging in his hand, pulled out a photograph and a letter. The photograph was of Irene Adler herself in evening dress, the letter was superscribed to " Sherlock Holmes, Esq. To be left till called for." My friend tore it open and we all three read it together. It was dated at midnight of the preceding night, and ran in this way :—

" MY DEAR MR. SHERLOCK HOLMES,—You really did it very well. You took me in completely. Until after the alarm of fire, I had not a suspicion. But then, when I found how I had betrayed myself, I began to think. I had been warned against you months ago. I had been told that if the King employed an agent, it would certainly be you. And your address had been given me. Yet, with all this, you made me reveal what you wanted to know. Even after I became suspicious, I found it hard to think evil of such a dear, kind old clergyman. But, you know, I have been trained as an actress myself. Male costume is nothing new to me. I often take advantage of the freedom which it gives. I sent John, the coachman, to watch you, ran upstairs, got into my walking clothes, as I call them, and came down just as you departed.

" Well, I followed you to your door, and so made sure that I was really an object of interest to the celebrated Mr. Sherlock Holmes. Then I, rather imprudently, wished you good night, and started for the Temple to see my husband.

" We both thought the best resource was flight when pursued by so formidable an antagonist ; so you will find the nest empty when you call to-morrow. As to the photograph, your client may rest in peace. I love and am loved by a better man than he. The King may do what he will without hindrance from one whom he has cruelly wronged. I keep it only to safeguard myself, and to preserve a weapon which will always secure me from any steps which he might take in the future. I leave a photograph which he might care to possess ; and I remain, dear Mr. Sherlock Holmes, very truly yours,

"IRENE NORTON, *née* ADLER."

"What a woman—oh, what a woman ! " cried the King of Bohemia, when we had all three read this epistle. "Did I not tell you how quick and resolute she was ? Would she not have made an admirable queen ? Is it not a pity she was not on my level ? "

"From what I have seen of the lady, she seems, indeed, to be on a very different level to Your Majesty," said Holmes, coldly. "I am sorry that I have not been able to bring Your Majesty's business to a more successful conclusion."

"On the contrary, my dear sir," cried the King. "Nothing could be more successful. I know that her word is inviolate. The photograph is now as safe as if it were in the fire."

"I am glad to hear Your Majesty say so."

"I am immensely indebted to you. Pray tell me in what way I can reward you. This ring——" He slipped an emerald snake ring from his finger and held it out upon the palm of his hand.

"Your Majesty has something which I should value even more highly," said Holmes.

"You have but to name it."

"This photograph ! "

The King stared at him in amazement.

"Irene's photograph ! " he cried. "Certainly, if you wish it."

"I thank Your Majesty. Then there is no more to be done in the matter. I have the honour to wish you a very good morning." He bowed, and, turning away without observing the hand which the King had stretched out to him, he set off in my company for his chambers.

And that was how a great scandal threatened to affect the kingdom of Bohemia, and how the best plans of Mr.

Sherlock Holmes were beaten by a woman's wit. He used to make merry over the cleverness of women, but I have not heard him do it of late. And when he speaks of Irene Adler, or when he refers to her photograph, it is always under the honourable title of *the* woman.

2. *The Red-Headed League*

I HAD called upon my friend, Mr. Sherlock Holmes, one day in the autumn of last year, and found him in deep conversation with a very stout, florid-faced, elderly gentleman, with fiery red hair. With an apology for my intrusion, I was about to withdraw, when Holmes pulled me abruptly into the room, and closed the door behind me.

"You could not possibly have come at a better time, my dear Watson," he said cordially.

"I was afraid that you were engaged."

"So I am. Very much so."

"Then I can wait in the next room."

"Not at all. This gentleman, Mr. Wilson, has been my partner and helper in many of my most successful cases, and I have no doubt that he will be of the utmost use to me in yours also."

The stout gentleman half rose from his chair, and gave a bob of greeting, with a quick little questioning glance from his small, fat-encircled eyes.

"Try the settee," said Holmes, relapsing into his arm-chair, and putting his finger-tips together, as was his custom when in judicial moods. "I know, my dear Watson, that you share my love of all that is bizarre and outside the conventions and humdrum routine of every-day life. You have shown your relish for it by the enthu-siasm which has prompted you to chronicle, and, if you will excuse my saying so, somewhat to embellish so many of my own little adventures."

"Your cases have indeed been of the greatest interest to me," I observed.

" You will remember that I remarked the other day, just before we went into the very simple problem presented by Miss Mary Sutherland, that for strange effects and extraordinary combinations we must go to life itself, which is always far more daring than any effort of the imagination."

" A proposition which I took the liberty of doubting."

" You did, Doctor, but none the less you must come round to my view, for otherwise I shall keep piling fact upon fact on you, until your reason breaks down under them and acknowledges me to be right. Now, Mr. Jabez Wilson here has been good enough to call upon me this morning, and to begin a narrative which promises to be one of the most singular which I have listened to for some time. You have heard me remark that the strangest and most unique things are very often connected not with the larger but with the smaller crimes, and occasionally, indeed, where there is room for doubt whether any positive crime has been committed. As far as I have heard, it is impossible for me to say whether the present case is an instance of crime or not, but the course of events is certainly among the most singular that I have ever listened to. Perhaps, Mr. Wilson, you would have the great kindness to recommence your narrative. I ask you not merely because my friend Dr. Watson has not heard the opening part, but also because the peculiar nature of the story makes me anxious to have every possible detail from your lips. As a rule, when I have heard some slight indication of the course of events I am able to guide myself by the thousands of other similar cases which occur to my memory. In the present instance I am forced to admit that the facts are, to the best of my belief, unique."

The portly client puffed out his chest with an appearance of some little pride, and pulled a dirty and wrinkled newspaper from the inside pocket of his greatcoat. As he glanced down the advertisement column, with his head thrust forward, and the paper flattened out upon his knee, I took a good look at the man, and endeavoured after the fashion of my companion to read the indications which might be presented by his dress or appearance.

I did not gain very much, however, by my inspection. Our visitor bore every mark of being an average commonplace British tradesman, obese, pompous, and slow. He wore rather baggy grey shepherds' check trousers, a not over-clean black frock-coat, unbuttoned in the front, and a drab waistcoat with a heavy brassy Albert chain, and a square pierced bit of metal dangling down as an ornament. A frayed top-hat, and a faded brown overcoat with a wrinkled velvet collar lay upon a chair beside him. Altogether, look as I would, there was nothing remarkable about the man save his blazing red head, and the expression of extreme chagrin and discontent upon his features.

Sherlock Holmes's quick eye took in my occupation and he shook his head with a smile as he noticed my questioning glances. " Beyond the obvious facts that he has at some time done manual labour, that he takes snuff, that he is a Freemason, that he has been in China, and that he has done a considerable amount of writing lately, I can deduce nothing else."

Mr. Jabez Wilson started up in his chair, with his forefinger upon the paper, but his eyes upon my companion.

" How, in the name of good fortune, did you know all that, Mr. Holmes ? " he asked. " How did you know, for example, that I did manual labour ? It's as true as gospel, and I began as a ship's carpenter."

" Your hands, my dear sir. Your right hand is quite a size larger than your left. You have worked with it, and the muscles are more developed."

" Well, the snuff, then, and the Freemasonry ? "

" I won't insult your intelligence by telling you how I read that, especially as, rather against the strict rules of your order, you use an arc and compass breastpin."

" Ah, of course, I forgot that. But the writing ? "

" What else can be indicated by that right cuff so very

shiny for five inches, and the left one with the smooth patch near the elbow where you rest it upon the desk."

" Well, but China ? "

" The fish which you have tattooed immediately above your right wrist could only have been done in China. I have made a small study of tattoo marks, and have even contributed to the literature of the subject. That trick of staining the fishes' scales of a delicate pink is quite peculiar to China. When, in addition, I see a Chinese coin hanging from your watch-chain, the matter becomes even more simple."

Mr. Jabez Wilson laughed heavily. " Well, I never ! " said he. " I thought at first you had done something clever, but I see that there was nothing in it after all."

" I begin to think, Watson," said Holmes, " that I make a mistake in explaining. ' Omne ignotum pro magnifico,' you know, and my poor little reputation, such as it is, will suffer shipwreck if I am so candid. Can you not find the advertisement, Mr. Wilson ? "

" Yes, I have got it now," he answered, with his thick, red finger planted half-way down the column. " Here it is. This is what began it all. You just read it for your-self, sir."

I took the paper from him and read as follows :—

" To the Red-Headed League.—On account of the bequest of the late Ezekiah Hopkins, of Lebanon, Penn., U.S.A., there is now another vacancy open which entitles a member of the League to a salary of four pounds a week for purely nominal services. All red-headed men who are sound in body and mind, and above the age of twenty-one years, are eligible. Apply in person on Monday, at eleven o'clock, to Duncan Ross, at the offices of the League, 7 Pope's Court, Fleet Street."

" What on earth does this mean ? " I ejaculated, after I had twice read over the extraordinary announcement.

Holmes chuckled, and wriggled in his chair, as was

his habit when in high spirits. "It is a little off the beaten track, isn't it?" said he. "And now, Mr. Wilson, off you go at scratch, and tell us all about yourself, your household, and the effect which this advertisement had upon your fortunes. You will first make a note, Doctor, of the paper and the date."

"It is *The Morning Chronicle*, of April 27, 1890. Just two months ago."

"Very good. Now, Mr. Wilson?"

"Well, it is just as I have been telling you, Mr. Sherlock Holmes," said Jabez Wilson, mopping his forehead, "I have a small pawnbroker's business at Coburg Square, near the City. It's not a very large affair, and of late years it has not done more than just give me a living. I used to be able to keep two assistants, but now I only keep one; and I would have a job to pay him, but that he is willing to come for half wages, so as to learn the business."

"What is the name of this obliging youth?" asked Sherlock Holmes.

"His name is Vincent Spaulding, and he's not such a youth either. It's hard to say his age. I should not wish a smarter assistant, Mr. Holmes; and I know very well that he could better himself, and earn twice what I am able to give him. But after all, if he is satisfied, why should I put ideas in his head?"

"Why, indeed? You seem most fortunate in having an employé who comes under the full market price. It is not a common experience among employers in this age. I don't know that your assistant is not as remarkable as your advertisement."

"Oh, he has his faults, too," said Mr. Wilson. "Never was such a fellow for photography. Snapping away with a camera when he ought to be improving his mind, and then diving down into the cellar like a rabbit into its hole to develop his pictures. That is his main fault; but on the whole, he's a good worker. There's no vice in him."

"He is still with you, I presume?"

" Yes, sir. He and a girl of fourteen, who does a bit of simple cooking, and keeps the place clean—that's all I have in the house, for I am a widower, and never had any family. We live very quietly, sir, the three of us ; and we keep a roof over our heads, and pay our debts, if we do nothing more.

" The first thing that put us out was that advertisement. Spaulding, he came down into the office just this day eight weeks with this very paper in his hand, and he says :

" ' I wish to the Lord, Mr. Wilson, that I was a red-headed man.'

" ' Why that ? ' I asks.

" ' Why,' says he, ' here's another vacancy on the League of the Red-headed Men. It's worth quite a little fortune to any man who gets it, and I understand that there are more vacancies than there are men, so that the trustees are at their wits' end what to do with the money. If my hair would only change colour, here's a nice little crib all ready for me to step into.'

" ' Why, what is it, then ? ' I asked. You see, Mr. Holmes, I am a very stay-at-home man, and, as my business came to me instead of my having to go to it, I was often weeks on end without putting my foot over the door-mat. In that way I didn't know much of what was going on outside, and I was always glad of a bit of news.

" ' Have you never heard of the League of the Red-headed Men ? ' he asked, with his eyes open.

" ' Never.'

" ' Why, I wonder at that, for you are eligible yourself for one of the vacancies.'

" ' And what are they worth ? ' I asked.

" ' Oh, merely a couple of hundred a year, but the work is slight, and it need not interfere much with one's other occupations.'

" Well, you can easily think that that made me prick up my ears, for the business has not been over good for some years, and an extra couple of hundred would have been very handy.

" ' Tell me all about it,' said I.

" ' Well,' said he, showing me the advertisement, ' you can see for yourself that the League has a vacancy, and there is the address where you should apply for particulars. As far as I can make out, the League was founded by an American millionaire, Ezekiah Hopkins, who was very peculiar in his ways. He was himself red-headed, and he had a great sympathy for all red-headed men ; so, when he died, it was found that he had left his enormous fortune in the hands of trustees, with instructions to apply the interest to the providing of easy berths to men whose hair is of that colour. From all I hear it is splendid pay, and very little to do.'

" ' But,' said I, ' there would be millions of red-headed men who would apply.'

" ' Not so many as you might think,' he answered. ' You see, it is really confined to Londoners, and to grown men. This American had started from London when he was young, and he wanted to do the old town a good turn. Then, again, I have heard it is no use your applying if your hair is light red, or dark red, or anything but real, bright, blazing, fiery red. Now, if you cared to apply, Mr. Wilson, you would just walk in ; but perhaps it would hardly be worth your while to put yourself out of the way for the sake of a few hundred pounds.'

" Now, it is a fact, gentlemen, as you may see for yourselves, that my hair is of a very full and rich tint, so that it seemed to me that, if there was to be any competition in the matter, I stood as good a chance as any man that I had ever met. Vincent Spaulding seemed to know so much about it that I thought he might prove useful, so I just ordered him to put up the shutters for the day, and to come right away with me. He was very willing to have a holiday, so we shut the business up, and started off for the address that was given us in the advertisement.

" I never hope to see such a sight as that again, Mr. Holmes. From north, south, east, and west every man who had a shade of red in his hair had tramped into the

35

City to answer the advertisement. Fleet Street was choked with red-headed folk, and Pope's Court looked like a coster's orange barrow. I should not have thought there were so many in the whole country as were brought together by that single advertisement. Every shade of colour they were—straw, lemon, orange, brick, Irish-setter, liver, clay ; but, as Spaulding said, there were not many who had the real vivid flame-coloured tint. When I saw how many were waiting, I would have given it up in despair ; but Spaulding would not hear of it. How he did it I could not imagine, but he pushed and pulled and butted until he got me through the crowd, and right up to the steps which led to the office. There was a double stream upon the stair, some going up in hope, and some coming back dejected ; but we wedged in as well as we could, and soon found ourselves in the office."

" Your experience has been a most entertaining one," remarked Holmes, as his client paused and refreshed his memory with a huge pinch of snuff. " Pray continue your very interesting statement."

" There was nothing in the office but a couple of wooden chairs and a deal table, behind which sat a small man, with a head that was even redder than mine. He said a few words to each candidate as he came up, and then he always managed to find some fault in them which would disqualify them. Getting a vacancy did not seem to be such a very easy matter after all. However, when our turn came, the little man was more favourable to me than to any of the others, and he closed the door as we entered, so that he might have a private word with us.

" ' This is Mr. Jabez Wilson,' said my assistant, ' and he is willing to fill a vacancy in the League.'

" ' And he is admirably suited for it,' the other an-swered. ' He has every requirement. I cannot recall when I have seen anything so fine.' He took a step back-wards, cocked his head on one side, and gazed at my hair until I felt quite bashful. Then suddenly he plunged forward, wrung my hand, and congratulated me warmly on my success.

"'It would be injustice to hesitate,' said he. 'You will, however, I am sure, excuse me for taking an obvious precaution.' With that he seized my hair in both his hands, and tugged until I yelled with the pain. 'There is water in your eyes,' said he, as he released me. 'I perceive that all is as it should be. But we have to be careful, for we have twice been deceived by wigs and once by paint. I could tell you tales of cobbler's wax which would disgust you with human nature.' He stepped over to the window, and shouted through it at the top of his voice that the vacancy was filled. A groan of disappointment came up from below, and the folk all trooped away in different directions, until there was not a red head to be seen except my own and that of the manager.

"'My name,' said he, 'is Mr. Duncan Ross, and I am myself one of the pensioners upon the fund left by our noble benefactor. Are you a married man, Mr. Wilson? Have you a family?'

"I answered that I had not.

"His face fell immediately.

"'Dear me!' he said gravely, 'that is very serious indeed! I am sorry to hear you say that. The fund was, of course, for the propagation and spread of the red-heads as well as for their maintenance. It is exceedingly unfortunate that you should be a bachelor.'

"My face lengthened at this, Mr. Holmes, for I thought that I was not to have the vacancy after all; but after thinking it over for a few minutes, he said that it would be all right.

"'In the case of another,' said he, 'the objection might be fatal, but we must stretch a point in favour of a man with such a head of hair as yours. When shall you be able to enter upon your new duties?'

"'Well, it is a little awkward, for I have a business already,' said I.

"'Oh, never mind about that, Mr. Wilson!' said Vincent Spaulding. ' I shall be able to look after that for you.'

" ' What would be the hours ? ' I asked.

" ' Ten to two.'

" Now a pawnbroker's business is mostly done of an evening, Mr. Holmes, especially Thursday and Friday evening, which is just before pay-day ; so it would suit me very well to earn a little in the mornings. Besides, I knew that my assistant was a good man, and that he would see to anything that turned up.

" ' That would suit me very well,' said I. ' And the pay ? '

" ' Is four pounds a week.'

" ' And the work ? '

" ' Is purely nominal.'

" ' What do you call purely nominal ? '

" ' Well, you have to be in the office, or at least in the building, the whole time. If you leave, you forfeit your whole position for ever. The will is very clear upon that point. You don't comply with the conditions if you budge from the office during that time.'

" ' It's only four hours a day, and I should not think of leaving,' said I.

" ' No excuse will avail,' said Mr. Duncan Ross, ' neither sickness, nor business, nor anything else. There you must stay, or you lose your billet.'

" ' And the work ? '

" ' Is to copy out the *Encyclopædia Britannica*. There is the first volume of it in that press. You must find your own ink, pens, and blotting-paper, but we provide this table and chair. Will you be ready to-morrow ? '

" ' Certainly,' I answered.

" ' Then, good-bye, Mr. Jabez Wilson, and let me congratulate you once more on the important position which you have been fortunate enough to gain.' He bowed me out of the room, and I went home with my assistant, hardly knowing what to say or do, I was so pleased at my own good fortune.

" ' Well, I thought over the matter all day, and by evening I was in low spirits again ; for I had quite persuaded myself that the whole affair must be some great hoax or fraud, though what its object might be I could not imagine. It seemed altogether past belief that anyone could make such a will, or that they would pay such a sum for doing anything so simple as copying out the *Encyclopædia Britannica*. Vincent Spaulding did what he could to cheer me up, but by bedtime I had reasoned myself out of the whole thing. However, in the morning I determined to have a look at it anyhow, so I bought a penny bottle of ink, and with a quill pen, and seven sheets of foolscap paper, I started off for Pope's Court.

" Well, to my surprise and delight everything was as right as possible. The table was set out ready for me, and Mr. Duncan Ross was there to see that I got fairly to work. He started me off upon the letter A, and then he left me ; but he would drop in from time to time to see that all was right with me. At two o'clock he bade me good day, complimented me upon the amount that I had written, and locked the door of the office after me.

" This went on day after day, Mr. Holmes, and on Saturday the manager came in and planked down four golden sovereigns for my week's work. It was the same next week, and the same the week after. Every morning I was there at ten, and every afternoon I left at two. By degrees Mr. Duncan Ross took to coming in only once of a morning, and then, after a time, he did not come in at all. Still, of course, I never dared to leave the room for an instant, for I was not sure when he might come, and the billet was such a good one, and suited me so well, that I would not risk the loss of it.

" Eight weeks passed away like this, and I had written about Abbots, and Archery, and Armour, and Architecture, and Attica, and hoped with diligence that I might get on to the B's before very long. It cost me something in foolscap, and I had pretty nearly filled a shelf with my writings. And then suddenly the whole business came to an end."

"To an end?"

"Yes, sir. And no later than this morning. I went to my work as usual at ten o'clock, but the door was shut and locked, with a little square of cardboard hammered on to the middle of the panel with a tack. Here it is, and you can read for yourself."

He held up a piece of white cardboard, about the size of a sheet of note-paper. It read in this fashion :—

"THE RED-HEADED LEAGUE IS DISSOLVED.
OCT. 9, 1890."

Sherlock Holmes and I surveyed this curt announcement and the rueful face behind it, until the comical side of the affair so completely over-topped every other consideration that we both burst out into a roar of laughter.

"I cannot see that there is anything very funny," cried our client, flushing up to the roots of his flaming head. "If you can do nothing better than laugh at me, I can go elsewhere."

"No, no," cried Holmes, shoving him back into the chair from which he had half risen. "I really wouldn't miss your case for the world. It is most refreshingly unusual. But there is, if you will excuse me saying so, something just a little funny about it. Pray what steps did you take when you found the card upon the door?"

"I was staggered, sir. I did not know what to do. Then I called at the offices round, but none of them seemed to know anything about it. Finally, I went to the landlord, who is an accountant living on the ground floor, and I asked him if he could tell me what had become of the Red-headed League. He said that he had never heard of any such body. Then I asked him who Mr. Duncan Ross was. He answered that the name was new to him.

"'Well,' said I, 'the gentleman at No. 4.'

"'What, the red-headed man?'

"'Yes.'

"'Oh,' said he, 'his name was William Morris. He was a solicitor, and was using my room as a temporary convenience until his new premises were ready. He moved out yesterday.'

"'Where could I find him?'

"'Oh, at his new offices. He did tell me the address. Yes, 17 King Edward Street, near St. Paul's.'

"I started off, Mr. Holmes, but when I got to that address it was a manufactory of artificial knee-caps, and no one in it had ever heard of either Mr. William Morris, or Mr. Duncan Ross."

"And what did you do then?" asked Holmes.

"I went home to Saxe-Coburg Square, and I took the advice of my assistant. But he could not help me in any way. He could only say that if I waited I should hear by post. But that was not quite good enough, Mr. Holmes. I did not wish to lose such a place without a struggle, so, as I had heard that you were good enough to give advice to poor folk who were in need of it, I came right away to you."

"And you did very wisely," said Holmes. "Your case is an exceedingly remarkable one, and I shall be happy to look into it. From what you have told me I think that it is possible that graver issues hang from it than might at first sight appear."

"Grave enough!" said Mr. Jabez Wilson. "Why, I have lost four pounds a week."

"As far as you are personally concerned," remarked Holmes, "I do not see that you have any grievance against this extraordinary league. On the contrary, you are, as I understand, richer by some thirty pounds, to say nothing of the minute knowledge which you have gained on every subject which comes under the letter A. You have lost nothing by them."

"No, sir. But I want to find out about them, and who they are, and what their object was in playing this prank —if it was a prank—upon me. It was a pretty expensive joke for them, for it cost them two-and-thirty pounds."

" We shall endeavour to clear up these points for you. And, first, one or two questions, Mr. Wilson. This assistant of yours who first called your attention to the advertisement—how long had he been with you ? "

" About a month then."

" How did he come ? "

" In answer to an advertisement."

" Was he the only applicant ? "

" No, I had a dozen."

" Why did you pick him ? "

" Because he was handy, and would come cheap."

" At half wages, in fact."

" Yes."

" What is he like, this Vincent Spaulding ? "

" Small, stout-built, very quick in his ways, no hair on his face, though he's not short of thirty. Has a white splash of acid upon his forehead."

Holmes sat up in his chair in considerable excitement.

" I thought as much," said he. " Have you ever observed that his ears are pierced for ear-rings ? "

" Yes, sir. He told me that a gipsy had done it for him when he was a lad."

" Hum ! " said Holmes, sinking back in deep thought. " He is still with you ? "

" Oh, yes, sir ; I have only just left him."

" And has your business been attended to in your absence ? "

" Nothing to complain of, sir. There's never very much to do of a morning."

" That will do, Mr. Wilson. I shall be happy to give you an opinion upon the subject in the course of a day or two. To-day is Saturday, and I hope that by Monday we may come to a conclusion."

" Well, Watson," said Holmes, when our visitor had left us, " what do you make of it all ? "

" I make nothing of it," I answered, frankly. " It is a most mysterious business."

" As a rule," said Holmes, " the more bizarre a thing

is the less mysterious it proves to be. It is your common-place, featureless crimes which are really puzzling, just as a commonplace face is the most difficult to identify. But I must be prompt over this matter."

"What are you going to do then?" I asked.

"To smoke," he answered. "It is quite a three-pipe problem, and I beg that you won't speak to me for fifty minutes." He curled himself up in his chair, with his thin knees drawn up to his hawk-like nose, and there he sat with his eyes closed and his black clay pipe thrusting out like the bill of some strange bird. I had come to the conclusion that he had dropped asleep, and indeed was nodding myself, when he suddenly sprang out of his chair with the gesture of a man who had made up his mind, and put his pipe down upon the mantelpiece.

"Sarasate plays at the St. James's Hall this afternoon," he remarked. "What do you think, Watson? Could your patients spare you for a few hours?"

"I have nothing to do to-day. My practice is never very absorbing."

"Then put on your hat, and come. I am going through the City first, and we can have some lunch on the way. I observe that there is a good deal of German music on the programme, which is rather more to my taste than Italian or French. It is introspective, and I want to introspect. Come along!"

We travelled by the Underground as far as Aldersgate; and a short walk took us to Saxe-Coburg Square, the scene of the singular story which we had listened to in the morning. It was a pokey, little, shabby-genteel place, where four lines of dingy two-storied brick houses looked out into a small railed-in enclosure, where a lawn of weedy grass and a few clumps of faded laurel bushes made a hard fight against a smoke-laden and uncongenial atmosphere. Three gilt balls and a brown board with "JABEZ WILSON" in white letters, upon a corner house, announced the place where our red-headed client carried on his business. Sherlock Holmes stopped in front of it

43

with his head on one side and looked it all over, with his eyes shining brightly between puckered lids. Then he walked slowly up the street and then down again to the corner, still looking keenly at the houses. Finally he returned to the pawnbroker's, and, having thumped vigorously upon the pavement with his stick two or three times, he went up to the door and knocked. It was instantly opened by a bright-looking, clean-shaven young fellow, who asked him to step in.

" Thank you," said Holmes, " I only wished to ask you how you would go from here to the Strand."

" Third right, fourth left," answered the assistant promptly, closing the door.

" Smart fellow, that," observed Holmes as we walked away. " He is, in my judgment, the fourth smartest man in London, and for daring I am not sure that he has not a claim to be third. I have known something of him before."

" Evidently," said I, " Mr. Wilson's assistant counts for a good deal in this mystery of the Red-headed League. I am sure that you inquired your way merely in order that you might see him."

" Not him."

" What then ? "

" The knees of his trousers."

" And what did you see ? "

" What I expected to see."

" Why did you beat the pavement ? "

" My dear Doctor, this is a time for observation, not for talk. We are spies in an enemy's country. We know something of Saxe-Coburg Square. Let us now explore the paths which lie behind it."

The road in which we found ourselves as we turned round the corner from the retired Saxe-Coburg Square presented as great a contrast to it as the front of a picture does to the back. It was one of the main arteries which convey the traffic of the City to the north and west. The roadway was blocked with the immense stream of commerce flowing in a double tide inwards and outwards, while the footpaths were black with the hurrying swarm of pedestrians. It was difficult to realize as we looked at the line of fine shops and stately business premises that they really abutted on the other side upon the faded and stagnant square which we had just quitted.

" Let me see," said Holmes, standing at the corner, and glancing along the line, " I should like just to remember the order of the houses here. It is a hobby of mine to have an exact knowledge of London. There is Mortimer's, the tobacconist, the little newspaper shop, the Coburg branch of the City and Suburban Bank, the Vegetarian Restaurant, and McFarlane's carriage-building depôt. That carries us right on to the other block. And now, Doctor, we've done our work, so it's time we had some play. A sandwich, and a cup of coffee, and then off to violin land, where all is sweetness, and delicacy, and harmony, and there are no red-headed clients to vex us with their conundrums."

My friend was an enthusiastic musician, being himself not only a very capable performer, but a composer of no ordinary merit. All the afternoon he sat in the stalls wrapped in the most perfect happiness, gently waving his long thin fingers in time to the music, while his gently smiling face and his languid, dreamy eyes were as unlike those of Holmes the sleuth-hound, Holmes the relentless, keen-witted, ready-handed criminal agent, as it was possible to conceive. In his singular character the dual nature alternately asserted itself, and his extreme exactness and astuteness represented, as I have often thought, the reaction against the poetic and contemplative mood which occasionally predominated in him. The swing of his nature took him from extreme languor to devouring energy ; and, as I knew well, he was never so truly formidable as when, for days on end, he had been lounging in his arm-chair amid his improvisations and his black-letter editions. Then it was that the lust of the chase would suddenly come upon him, and that his brilliant reasoning power would rise to the level of intuition, until those who were unacquainted with his methods would look askance at him as on a man whose knowledge was not that of other mortals. When I saw him that afternoon so enwrapped in the music at St. James's Hall I felt that an evil time might be coming upon those whom he had set himself to hunt down.

" You want to go home, no doubt, Doctor," he remarked, as we emerged.

" Yes, it would be as well."

" And I have some business to do which will take some hours. This business at Coburg Square is serious."

" Why serious ? "

" A considerable crime is in contemplation. I have every reason to believe that we shall be in time to stop it. But to-day being Saturday rather complicates matters. I shall want your help to-night."

" At what time ? "

" Ten will be early enough."

" I shall be at Baker Street at ten."

" Very well. And, I say, Doctor ! there may be some little danger, so kindly put your army revolver in your pocket." He waved his hand, turned on his heel, and disappeared in an instant among the crowd.

I trust that I am not more dense than my neighbours, but I was always oppressed with a sense of my own stupidity in my dealings with Sherlock Holmes. Here I had heard what he had heard, I had seen what he had seen, and yet from his words it was evident that he saw clearly not only what had happened, but what was about to happen, while to me the whole business was still confused and grotesque. As I drove home to my house in Kensington I thought over it all, from the extraordinary story of the red-headed copier of the *Encyclopædia* down to the visit to Saxe-Coburg Square, and the ominous words with which he had parted from me. What was this nocturnal expedition, and why should I go armed ? Where were we going, and what were we to do ? I had the hint from

Holmes that this smooth-faced pawnbroker's assistant was a formidable man—a man who might play a deep game. I tried to puzzle it out, but gave it up in despair, and set the matter aside until night should bring an explanation.

It was a quarter past nine when I started from home and made my way across the Park, and so through Oxford Street to Baker Street. Two hansoms were standing at the door, and, as I entered the passage, I heard the sound of voices from above. On entering his room, I found Holmes in animated conversation with two men, one of whom I recognized as Peter Jones, the official police agent ; while the other was a long, thin, sad-faced man, with a very shiny hat and oppressively respectable frock-coat.

" Ha ! our party is complete," said Holmes, buttoning up his pea-jacket, and taking his heavy hunting-crop from the rack. " Watson, I think you know Mr. Jones, of Scotland Yard ? Let me introduce you to Mr. Merry-weather, who is to be our companion in to-night's adventure."

" We're hunting in couples again, Doctor, you see," said Jones in his consequential way. " Our friend here is a wonderful man for starting a chase. All he wants is an old dog to help him to do the running down."

" I hope a wild goose may not prove to be the end of our chase," observed Mr. Merryweather gloomily.

" You may place considerable confidence in Mr. Holmes, sir," said the police agent loftily. " He has his own little methods, which are, if he won't mind my saying so, just a little too theoretical and fantastic, but he has the makings of a detective in him. It is not too much to say that once or twice, as in that business of the Sholto murder and the Agra treasure, he has been more nearly correct than the official force."

" Oh, if you say so, Mr. Jones, it is all right ! " said the stranger, with deference. " Still, I confess that I miss my rubber. It is the first Saturday night for seven-and-twenty years that I have not had my rubber."

47

"I think you will find," said Sherlock Holmes, "that you will play for a higher stake to-night than you have ever done yet, and that the play will be more exciting. For you, Mr. Merryweather, the stake will be some thirty thousand pounds; and for you, Jones, it will be the man upon whom you wish to lay your hands."

"John Clay, the murderer, thief, smasher, and forger. He's a young man, Mr. Merryweather, but he is at the head of his profession, and I would rather have my bracelets on him than on any criminal in London. He's a remarkable man, is young John Clay. His grandfather was a Royal Duke, and he himself has been to Eton and Oxford. His brain is as cunning as his fingers, and though we meet signs of him at every turn, we never know where to find the man himself. He'll crack a crib in Scotland one week, and be raising money to build an orphanage in Cornwall the next. I've been on his track for years, and have never set eyes on him yet."

"I hope that I may have the pleasure of introducing you to-night. I've had one or two little turns also with Mr. John Clay, and I agree with you that he is at the head of his profession. It is past ten, however, and quite time that we started. If you two will take the first hansom, Watson and I will follow in the second."

Sherlock Holmes was not very communicative during the long drive, and lay back in the cab humming the tunes which he had heard in the afternoon. We rattled through an endless labyrinth of gas-lit streets until we emerged into Farringdon Street.

"We are close there now," my friend remarked. "This fellow Merryweather is a bank director and personally interested in the matter. I thought it as well to have Jones with us also. He is not a bad fellow, though an absolute imbecile in his profession. He has one positive virtue. He is as brave as a bulldog, and as tenacious as a lobster if he gets his claws upon anyone. Here we are, and they are waiting for us."

We had reached the same crowded thoroughfare in

which we had found ourselves in the morning. Our cabs were dismissed, and, following the guidance of Mr. Merryweather, we passed down a narrow passage, and through a side door, which he opened for us. Within there was a small corridor, which ended in a very massive iron gate. This also was opened, and led down a flight of winding stone steps, which terminated at another formidable gate. Mr. Merryweather stopped to light a lantern, and then conducted us down a dark, earth-smelling passage, and so, after opening a third door, into a huge vault or cellar, which was piled all round with crates and massive boxes.

" You are not very vulnerable from above," Holmes remarked, as he held up the lantern and gazed about him.

" Nor from below," said Mr. Merryweather, striking his stick upon the flags which lined the floor. " Why, dear me, it sounds quite hollow ! " he remarked, looking up in surprise.

" I must really ask you to be a little more quiet," said Holmes severely. " You have already imperilled the whole success of our expedition. Might I beg that you would have the goodness to sit down upon one of those boxes, and not to interfere ? "

The solemn Mr. Merryweather perched himself upon a crate, with a very injured expression upon his face, while Holmes fell upon his knees upon the floor, and, with the lantern and a magnifying lens, began to examine minutely the cracks between the stones. A few seconds sufficed to satisfy him, for he sprang to his feet again, and put his glass in his pocket.

" We have at least an hour before us," he remarked, " for they can hardly take any steps until the good pawn-broker is safely in bed. Then they will not lose a minute, for the sooner they do their work the longer time they will have for their escape. We are at present, Doctor— as no doubt you have divined—in the cellar of the City branch of one of the principal London banks. Mr. Merryweather is the chairman of directors, and he will explain to you that there are reasons why the more daring criminals of London should take a considerable interest in this cellar at present."

" It is our French gold," whispered the director. " We have had several warnings that an attempt might be made upon it."

" Your French gold ? "

" Yes. We had occasion some months ago to strengthen our resources, and borrowed, for that purpose, thirty thousand napoleons from the Bank of France. It has become known that we have never had occasion to unpack the money, and that it is still lying in our cellar. The crate upon which I sit contains two thousand napoleons packed between layers of lead foil. Our reserve of bullion is much larger at present than is usually kept in a single branch office, and the directors have had misgivings upon the subject."

" Which were very well justified," observed Holmes. " And now it is time that we arranged our little plans. I expect that within an hour matters will come to a head. In the meantime, Mr. Merryweather, we must put the screen over that dark lantern."

" And sit in the dark ? "

" I am afraid so. I had brought a pack of cards in my pocket, and I thought that, as we were a *partie carrée*, you might have your rubber after all. But I see that the enemy's preparations have gone so far that we cannot risk the presence of a light. And, first of all, we must choose our positions. These are daring men, and, though we shall take them at a disadvantage they may do us some harm, unless we are careful. I shall stand behind this crate, and do you conceal yourself behind those. Then, when I flash a light upon them, close in swiftly. If they fire, Watson, have no compunction about shooting them down."

I placed my revolver, cocked, upon the top of the wooden case behind which I crouched. Holmes shot the slide across the front of his lantern, and left us in pitch darkness—such an absolute darkness as I have never before experienced. The smell of hot metal remained to assure us that the light was still there, ready to flash out at a moment's notice. To me, with my nerves worked up to a pitch of expectancy, there was something depressing and subduing in the sudden gloom, and in the cold, dank air of the vault.

"They have but one retreat," whispered Holmes. "That is back through the house into Saxe-Coburg Square. I hope that you have done what I asked you, Jones?"

"I have an inspector and two officers waiting at the front door."

"Then we have stopped all the holes. And now we must be silent and wait."

What a time it seemed! From comparing notes afterwards it was but an hour and a quarter, yet it appeared to me that the night must have almost gone, and the dawn be breaking above us. My limbs were weary and stiff, for I feared to change my position, yet my nerves were worked up to the highest pitch of tension, and my hearing was so acute that I could not only hear the gentle breathing of my companions, but I could distinguish the deeper, heavier in-breath of the bulky Jones from the thin sighing note of the bank director. From my position I could look over the case in the direction of the floor. Suddenly my eyes caught the glint of a light.

At first it was but a lurid spark upon the stone pavement. Then it lengthened out until it became a yellow line, and then, without any warning or sound, a gash seemed to open and a hand appeared, a white, almost womanly hand, which felt about in the centre of the little area of light. For a minute or more the hand, with its writhing fingers, protruded out of the floor. Then it was withdrawn as suddenly as it appeared, and all was dark again save the single lurid spark, which marked a chink between the stones.

Its disappearance, however, was but momentary.

With a rending, tearing sound, one of the broad, white stones turned over upon its side, and left a square, gaping hole, through which streamed the light of a lantern. Over the edge there peeped a clean-cut, boyish face, which looked keenly about it, and then, with a hand on either side of the aperture, drew itself shoulder high and waist high, until one knee rested upon the edge. In another instant he stood at the side of the hole, and was hauling after him a companion, lithe and small like himself, with a pale face and a shock of very red hair.

"It's all clear," he whispered. "Have you the chisel, and the bags. Great Scott! Jump, Archie, jump, and I'll swing for it!"

Sherlock Holmes had sprung out and seized the intruder by the collar. The other dived down the hole, and I heard the sound of rending cloth as Jones clutched at his skirts. The light flashed upon the barrel of a revolver, but Holmes's hunting-crop came down on the man's wrist, and the pistol clinked upon the stone floor.

"It's no use, John Clay," said Holmes blandly; "you have no chance at all."

"So I see," the other answered with the utmost coolness. "I fancy that my pal is all right, though I see you have got his coat-tails."

"There are three men waiting for him at the door," said Holmes.

"Oh, indeed. You seem to have done the thing very completely. I must compliment you."

"And I you," Holmes answered. "Your red-headed idea was very new and effective."

"You'll see your pal again presently," said Jones. "He's quicker at climbing down holes than I am. Just hold out while I fix the derbies."

"I beg that you will not touch me with your filthy hands," remarked our prisoner, as the handcuffs clattered upon his wrists. "You may not be aware that I have royal blood in my veins. Have the goodness also when you address me always to say 'sir' and 'please.'"

" All right," said Jones, with a stare and a snigger.
" Well, would you please, sir, march upstairs, where
we can get a cab to carry your highness to the police
station."

" That is better," said John Clay serenely. He made
a sweeping bow to the three of us, and walked quietly off
in the custody of the detective.

" Really, Mr. Holmes," said Mr. Merryweather, as
we followed them from the cellar, " I do not know how
the bank can thank you or repay you. There is no doubt
that you have detected and defeated in the most complete
manner one of the most determined attempts at bank
robbery that have ever come within my experience."

" I have had one or two little scores of my own to settle
with Mr. John Clay," said Holmes. " I have been at
some small expense over this matter, which I shall expect
the bank to refund, but beyond that I am amply repaid
by having had an experience which is in many ways
unique, and by hearing the very remarkable narrative of
the Red-headed League."

" You see, Watson," he explained in the early hours
of the morning, as we sat over a glass of whisky-and-soda
in Baker Street, " it was perfectly obvious from the first
that the only possible object of this rather fantastic business of the advertisement of the League, and the copying
of the *Encyclopædia*, must be to get this not over-bright
pawnbroker out of the way for a number of hours every
day. It was a curious way of managing it, but really it
would be difficult to suggest a better. The method was
no doubt suggested to Clay's ingenious mind by the
colour of his accomplice's hair. The four pounds a week
was a lure which must draw him, and what was it to them,
who were playing for thousands ? They put in the advertisement ; one rogue has the temporary office, the other
rogue incites the man to apply for it, and together they
manage to secure his absence every morning in the week.
From the time that I heard of the assistant having come

for half-wages, it was obvious to me that he had some strong motive for securing the situation."

" But how could you guess what the motive was ? "

" Had there been women in the house, I should have suspected a mere vulgar intrigue. That, however, was out of the question. The man's business was a small one, and there was nothing in his house which could account for such elaborate preparations and such an expenditure as they were at. It must then be something out of the house. What could it be ? I thought of the assistant's fondness for photography, and his trick of vanishing into the cellar. The cellar ! There was the end of this tangled clue. Then I made inquiries as to this mysterious assistant, and found that I had to deal with one of the coolest and most daring criminals in London. He was doing something in the cellar—something which took many hours a day for months on end. What could it be, once more ? I could think of nothing save that he was running a tunnel to some other building.

" So far I had got when we went to visit the scene of action. I surprised you by beating upon the pavement with my stick. I was ascertaining whether the cellar stretched out in front or behind. It was not in front. Then I rang the bell, and, as I hoped, the assistant answered it. We have had some skirmishes, but we had never set eyes on each other before. I hardly looked at his face. His knees were what I wished to see. You must yourself have remarked how worn, wrinkled and stained they were. They spoke of those hours of burrowing. The only remaining point was what they were burrowing for. I walked round the corner, saw that the City and Suburban Bank abutted on our friend's premises, and felt that I had solved my problem. When you drove home after the concert I called upon Scotland Yard, and upon the chairman of the bank directors, with the result that you have seen."

" And how could you tell that they would make their attempt to-night ? " I asked.

" Well, when they closed their League offices that was a sign that they cared no longer about Mr. Jabez Wilson's presence ; in other words, that they had completed their tunnel. But it was essential that they should use it soon, as it might be discovered, or the bullion might be removed. Saturday would suit them better than any other day, as it would give them two days for their escape. For all these reasons I expected them to come to-night."

" You reasoned it out beautifully," I exclaimed in unfeigned admiration. " It is so long a chain, and yet every link rings true."

" It saved me from ennui," he answered, yawning. " Alas, I already feel it closing in upon me ! My life is spent in one long effort to escape from the commonplaces of existence. These little problems help me to do so."

" And you are a benefactor of the race," said I.

He shrugged his shoulders. " Well, perhaps, after all, it is of some little use," he remarked. " ' *L'homme c'est rien—l'œuvre c'est tout*,' as Gustave Flaubert wrote to George Sand."

3. *A Case of Identity*

" MY dear fellow," said Sherlock Holmes, as we sat on either side of the fire in his lodgings at Baker Street, " life is infinitely stranger than anything which the mind of man could invent. We would not dare to conceive the things which are really mere commonplaces of existence. If we could fly out of that window hand in hand, hover over this great city, gently remove the roofs, and peep in at the queer things which are going on, the strange coincidences, the plannings, the cross-purposes, the wonderful chains of events, working through generations, and leading to the most *outré* results, it would make all fiction with its conventionalities and foreseen conclusions most stale and unprofitable."

" And yet I am not convinced of it," I answered.

" The cases which come to light in the papers are, as a rule, bald enough, and vulgar enough. We have in our police reports realism pushed to its extreme limits, and yet the result is, it must be confessed, neither fascinating nor artistic."

" A certain selection and discretion must be used in producing a realistic effect," remarked Holmes. " This is wanting in the police report, where more stress is laid perhaps upon the platitudes of the magistrate than upon the details, which to an observer contain the vital essence of the whole matter. Depend upon it there is nothing so unnatural as the commonplace."

I smiled and shook my head. " I can quite understand you thinking so," I said. " Of course, in your position of unofficial adviser and helper to everybody who is absolutely puzzled, throughout three continents, you are brought in contact with all that is strange and bizarre. But here "—I picked up the morning paper from the ground—" let us put it to a practical test. Here is the first heading upon which I come. ' A husband's cruelty to his wife.' There is half a column of print, but I know without reading it that it is all perfectly familiar to me. There is, of course, the other woman, the drink, the push, the blow, the bruise, the sympathetic sister or landlady. The crudest of writers could invent nothing more crude."

" Indeed, your example is an unfortunate one for your argument," said Holmes, taking the paper, and glancing his eye down it. " This is the Dundas separation case, and, as it happens, I was engaged in clearing up some small points in connection with it. The husband was a teetotaller, there was no other woman, and the conduct complained of was that he had drifted into the habit of winding up every meal by taking out his false teeth and hurling them at his wife, which you will allow is not an action likely to occur to the imagination of the average story-teller. Take a pinch of snuff, Doctor, and acknowledge that I have scored over you in your example."

He held out his snuff-box of old gold, with a great

amethyst in the centre of the lid. Its splendour was in such contrast to his homely ways and simple life that I could not help commenting upon it.

" Ah," said he, " I forgot that I had not seen you for some weeks. It is a little souvenir from the King of Bohemia in return for my assistance in the case of the Irene Adler papers."

" And the ring ? " I asked, glancing at a remarkable brilliant which sparkled upon his finger.

" It was from the reigning family of Holland, though the matter in which I served them was of such delicacy that I cannot confide it even to you, who have been good enough to chronicle one or two of my little problems."

" And have you any on hand just now ? " I asked with interest.

" Some ten or twelve, but none which presents any feature of interest. They are important, you understand, without being interesting. Indeed, I have found that it is usually in unimportant matters that there is a field for observation, and for the quick analysis of cause and effect which gives the charm to an investigation. The larger crimes are apt to be the simpler, for the bigger the crime, the more obvious, as a rule, is the motive. In these cases, save for one rather intricate matter which has been referred to me from Marseilles, there is nothing which presents any features of interest. It is possible, however, that I may have something better before very many minutes are over, for this is one of my clients, or I am much mistaken."

He had risen from his chair, and was standing between the parted blinds, gazing down into the dull, neutral-tinted London street. Looking over his shoulder I saw that on the pavement opposite there stood a large woman with a heavy fur boa round her neck, and a large curling red feather in a broad-brimmed hat which was tilted in a coquettish Duchess-of-Devonshire fashion over her ear. From under this great panoply she peeped up in a nervous, hesitating fashion at our windows, while her body oscillated backwards and forwards, and her fingers fidgeted with her glove buttons. Suddenly, with a plunge, as of the swimmer who leaves the bank, she hurried across the road, and we heard the sharp clang of the bell.

"I have seen those symptoms before," said Holmes, throwing his cigarette into the fire. "Oscillation upon the pavement always means an *affaire du cœur*. She would like advice, but is not sure that the matter is not too delicate for communication. And yet even here we may discriminate. When a woman has been seriously wronged by a man she no longer oscillates, and the usual symptom is a broken bell wire. Here we may take it that there is a love matter, but that the maiden is not so much angry as perplexed, or grieved. But here she comes in person to resolve our doubts."

As he spoke there was a tap at the door, and the boy in buttons entered to announce Miss Mary Sutherland, while the lady herself loomed behind his small black figure like a full-sailed merchantman behind a tiny pilot boat. Sherlock Holmes welcomed her with the easy courtesy for which he was remarkable, and having closed the door, and bowed her into an arm-chair, he looked over her in the minute and yet abstracted fashion which was peculiar to him.

"Do you not find," he said, "that with your short sight it is a little trying to do so much typewriting?"

"I did at first," she answered, "but now I know where the letters are without looking." Then, suddenly realizing the full purport of his words, she gave a violent start, and looked up with fear and astonishment upon her broad, good-humoured face. "You've heard about me, Mr. Holmes," she cried, "else how could you know all that?"

"Never mind," said Holmes, laughing, "it is my business to know things. Perhaps I have trained myself to see what others overlook. If not, why should you come to consult me?"

"I came to you, sir, because I heard of you from Mrs.

Etherege, whose husband you found so easy when the police and everyone had given him up for dead. Oh, Mr. Holmes, I wish you would do as much for me. I'm not rich, but still I have a hundred a year in my own right, besides the little that I make by the machine, and I would give it all to know what has become of Mr. Hosmer Angel."

"Why did you come away to consult me in such a hurry?" asked Sherlock Holmes, with his finger-tips together, and his eyes to the ceiling.

Again a startled look came over the somewhat vacuous face of Miss Mary Sutherland. "Yes, I did bang out of the house," she said, "for it made me angry to see the easy way in which Mr. Windibank—that is, my father—took it all. He would not go to the police, and he would not go to you, and so at last, as he would do nothing, and kept on saying that there was no harm done, it made me mad, and I just on with my things and came right away to you."

"Your father?" said Holmes. "Your stepfather, surely, since the name is different?"

"Yes, my stepfather. I call him father, though it sounds funny, too, for he is only five years and two months older than myself."

"And your mother is alive?"

"Oh, yes, mother is alive and well. I wasn't best pleased, Mr. Holmes, when she married again so soon after father's death, and a man who was nearly fifteen years younger than herself. Father was a plumber in the Tottenham Court Road, and he left a tidy business behind him, which mother carried on with Mr. Hardy, the foreman, but when Mr. Windibank came he made her sell the business, for he was very superior, being a traveller in wines. They got four thousand seven hundred for the goodwill and interest, which wasn't near as much as father could have got if he had been alive."

I had expected to see Sherlock Holmes impatient under this rambling and inconsequential narrative, but, on the contrary, he had listened with the greatest concentration of attention.

" Your own little income," he asked, " does it come out of the business ? "

" Oh, no, sir, it is quite separate, and was left me by my Uncle Ned in Auckland. It is in New Zealand Stock, paying 4½ per cent. Two thousand five hundred pounds was the amount, but I can only touch the interest."

" You interest me extremely," said Holmes. " And since you draw so large a sum as a hundred a year, with what you earn into the bargain, you no doubt travel a little and indulge yourself in every way. I believe that a single lady can get on very nicely upon an income of about sixty pounds."

" I could do with much less than that, Mr. Holmes, but you understand that as long as I live at home I don't wish to be a burden to them, and so they have the use of the money just while I am staying with them. Of course that is only just for the time. Mr. Windibank draws my interest every quarter, and pays it over to mother, and I find that I can do pretty well with what I earn at typewriting. It brings me twopence a sheet, and I can often do from fifteen to twenty sheets in a day."

" You have made your position very clear to me," said Holmes. " This is my friend, Dr. Watson, before whom you can speak as freely as before myself. Kindly tell us now all about your connection with Mr. Hosmer Angel."

A flush stole over Miss Sutherland's face, and she picked nervously at the fringe of her jacket. " I met him first at the gasfitters' ball," she said. " They used to send father tickets when he was alive, and then afterwards they remembered us, and sent them to mother. Mr. Windibank did not wish us to go. He never did wish us to go anywhere. He would get quite mad if I wanted so much as to join a Sunday school treat. But this time I was set on going, and I would go, for what right had he to prevent ? He said the folk were not fit for us to know, when all father's friends were to be there. And he said that I had nothing fit to wear, when I had my purple plush that I had never so much as taken out of the drawer. At last, when nothing else would do, he went off to France upon the business of the firm, but we went, mother and I, with Mr. Hardy, who used to be our foreman, and it was there I met Mr. Hosmer Angel."

"I suppose," said Holmes, "that when Mr. Windibank came back from France, he was very annoyed at your having gone to the ball."

"Oh, well, he was very good about it. He laughed, I remembered, and shrugged his shoulders, and said there was no use denying anything to a woman, for she would have her way."

"I see. Then at the gasfitters' ball you met, as I understand, a gentleman called Mr. Hosmer Angel."

"Yes, sir. I met him that night, and he called next day to ask if we had got home all safe, and after that we met him—that is to say, Mr. Holmes, I met him twice for walks, but after that father came back again, and Mr. Hosmer Angel could not come to the house any more."

"No?"

"Well, you know, father didn't like anything of the sort. He wouldn't have any visitors if he could help it, and he used to say that a woman should be happy in her own family circle. But then, as I used to say to mother, a woman wants her own circle to begin with, and I had not got mine yet."

"But how about Mr. Hosmer Angel? Did he make no attempt to see you?"

"Well, father was going off to France again in a week, and Hosmer wrote and said that it would be safer and better not to see each other until he had gone. We could write in the meantime, and he used to write every day. I took the letters in in the morning so there was no need for father to know."

"Were you engaged to the gentleman at this time?"

"Oh yes, Mr. Holmes. We were engaged after the

first walk that we took. Hosmer—Mr. Angel—was a
cashier in an office in Leadenhall Street—and——"

" What office ? "

" That's the worst of it, Mr. Holmes, I don't know."

" Where did he live then ? "

" He slept on the premises."

" And you don't know his address ? "

" No—except that it was Leadenhall Street."

" Where did you address your letters, then ? "

" To the Leadenhall Street Post Office, to be left till
called for. He said that if they were sent to the office
he would be chaffed by all the other clerks about having
letters from a lady, so I offered to typewrite them, like he
did his, but he wouldn't have that, for he said that when I
wrote them they seemed to come from me but when they
were typewritten he always felt that the machine had come
between us. That will just show you how fond he was of
me, Mr. Holmes, and the little things that he would think
of."

" It was most suggestive," said Holmes. " It has long
been an axiom of mine that the little things are infinitely
the most important. Can you remember any other little
things about Mr. Hosmer Angel ? "

" He was a very shy man, Mr. Holmes. He would
rather walk with me in the evening than in the daylight,
for he said that he hated to be conspicuous. Very retiring and gentlemanly he was. Even his voice was gentle.
He'd had the quinsy and swollen glands when he was
young, he told me, and it had left him with a weak throat,
and a hesitating, whispering fashion of speech. He was
always well-dressed, very neat and plain, but his eyes were
weak, just as mine are, and he wore tinted glasses against
the glare."

" Well, and what happened when Mr. Windibank,
your stepfather, returned to France ? "

" Mr. Hosmer Angel came to the house again, and proposed that we should marry before father came back. He
was in dreadful earnest, and made me swear, with my

hands on the Testament, that whatever happened I would always be true to him. Mother said he was quite right to make me swear, and that it was a sign of his passion. Mother was all in his favour from the first, and was even fonder of him than I was. Then, when they talked of marrying within the week, I began to ask about father ; but they both said never to mind about father, but just to tell him afterwards, and mother said she would make it all right with him. I didn't quite like that, Mr. Holmes. It seemed funny that I should ask his leave, as he was only a few years older than me ; but I didn't want to do anything on the sly, so I wrote to father at Bordeaux, where the Company has its French offices, but the letter came back to me on the very morning of the wedding."

" It missed him then ? "

" Yes, sir, for he had started to England just before it arrived."

" Ha ! that was unfortunate. Your wedding was arranged, then, for the Friday. Was it to be in church ? "

" Yes, sir, but very quietly. It was to be at St. Saviour's, near King's Cross, and we were to have breakfast afterwards at the St. Pancras Hotel. Hosmer came for us in a hansom, but as there were two of us, he put us both into it, and stepped himself into a four-wheeler which happened to be the only other cab in the street. We got to the church first, and when the four-wheeler drove up we waited for him to step out, but he never did, and when the cabman got down from the box and looked, there was no one there ! The cabman said he could not imagine what had become of him, for he had seen him get in with his own eyes. That was last Friday, Mr. Holmes, and I have never seen or heard anything since then to throw any light upon what became of him."

" It seems to me that you have been very shamefully treated," said Holmes.

" Oh no, sir ! He was too good and kind to leave me so. Why, all the morning he was saying to me that, whatever happened, I was to be true ; and that even if something quite unforeseen occurred to separate us, I was always to remember that I was pledged to him, and that he would claim his pledge sooner or later. It seemed strange talk for a wedding morning, but what has happened since gives a meaning to it."

"Most certainly it does. Your own opinion is, then, that some unforeseen catastrophe has occurred to him?"

"Yes, sir. I believe that he foresaw some danger, or else he would not have talked so. And then I think that what he foresaw happened."

"But you have no notion as to what it could have been?"

"None."

"One more question. How did your mother take the matter?"

"She was angry, and said that I was never to speak of the matter again."

"And your father? Did you tell him?"

"Yes, and he seemed to think, with me, that something had happened, and that I should hear of Hosmer again. As he said, what interest could anyone have in bringing me to the doors of the church, and then leaving me? Now, if he had borrowed my money, or if he had married me and got my money settled on him, there might be some reason; but Hosmer was very independent about money, and never would look at a shilling of mine. And yet what could have happened? And why could he not write? Oh, it drives me half mad to think of it! and I can't sleep a wink at night." She pulled a little handkerchief out of her muff, and began to sob heavily into it.

"I shall glance into the case for you," said Holmes, rising, "and I have no doubt that we shall reach some definite result. Let the weight of the matter rest upon me now, and do not let your mind dwell upon it further. Above all, try to let Mr. Hosmer Angel vanish from your memory, as he has done from your life."

"Then you don't think I'll see him again?"

"I fear not."

" Then what has happened to him ? "

" You will leave that question in my hands. I should like an accurate description of him, and any letters of his which you can spare."

" I advertised for him in last Saturday's *Chronicle*," said she. " Here is the slip, and here are four letters from him."

" Thank you. And your address ? "

" 31 Lyon Place, Camberwell."

" Mr. Angel's address you never had, I understand. Where is your father's place of business ? "

" He travels for Westhouse & Marbank, the great claret importers of Fenchurch Street."

" Thank you. You have made your statement very clearly. You will leave the papers here, and remember the advice which I have given you. Let the whole incident be a sealed book, and do not allow it to affect your life."

" You are very kind, Mr. Holmes, but I cannot do that. I shall be true to Hosmer. He shall find me ready when he comes back."

For all the preposterous hat and the vacuous face, there was something noble in the simple faith of our visitor which compelled our respect. She laid her little bundle of papers upon the table, and went her way, with a promise to come again whenever she might be summoned.

Sherlock Holmes sat silent for a few minutes with his finger-tips still pressed together, his legs stretched out in front of him, and his gaze directed upwards to the ceiling. Then he took down from the rack the old and oily clay pipe, which was to him as a counsellor, and, having lit it he leaned back in his chair, with the thick blue cloud-wreaths spinning up from him, and a look of infinite languor in his face.

" Quite an interesting study, that maiden," he observed. " I found her more interesting than her little problem, which, by the way, is rather a trite one. You will find parallel cases, if you consult my index, in Andover in '77, and there was something of the sort at The Hague last year. Old as is the idea, however, there were one or two details which were new to me. But the maiden herself was most instructive."

"You appeared to read a good deal upon her which was quite invisible to me," I remarked.

"Not invisible, but unnoticed, Watson. You did not know where to look, and so you missed all that was important. I can never bring you to realize the importance of sleeves, the suggestiveness of thumb-nails, or the great issues that may hang from a bootlace. Now what did you gather from that woman's appearance? Describe it."

"Well, she had a slate-coloured, broad-brimmed straw hat, with a feather of a brickish red. Her jacket was black, with black beads sewn upon it, and a fringe of little black jet ornaments. Her dress was brown, rather darker than coffee colour, with a little purple plush at the neck and sleeves. Her gloves were greyish, and were worn through at the right forefinger. Her boots I didn't observe. She had small, round, hanging gold ear-rings, and a general air of being fairly well to do, in a vulgar, comfortable, easy-going way."

Sherlock Holmes clapped his hands softly together and chuckled.

"'Pon my word, Watson, you are coming along wonderfully. You have really done very well indeed. It is true that you have missed everything of importance, but you have hit upon the method, and you have a quick eye for colour. Never trust to general impressions, my boy, but concentrate yourself upon details. My first glance is always at a woman's sleeve. In a man it is perhaps better first to take the knee of the trouser. As you observe, this woman had plush upon her sleeves, which is a most useful material for showing traces. The double line a little above the wrist, where the typewritist presses against the table, was beautifully defined. The sewing-machine, of the hand type, leaves a similar mark, but only on the left arm, and on the side of it farthest from the thumb, instead

of being right across the broadest part, as this was. I
then glanced at her face, and observing the dint of a pince-
nez at either side of her nose, I ventured a remark upon
short sight and typewriting, which seemed to surprise
her."

"It surprised me."

"But, surely, it was very obvious. I was then much
surprised and interested on glancing down to observe
that, though the boots which she was wearing were not
unlike each other, they were really odd ones, the one
having a slightly decorated toe-cap, and the other a plain
one. One was buttoned only in the two lower buttons
out of five, and the other at the first, third, and fifth.
Now, when you see that a young lady, otherwise neatly
dressed, has come away from home with odd boots, half
buttoned, it is no great deduction to say that she came
away in a hurry."

"And what else?" I asked, keenly interested, as I
always was, by my friend's incisive reasoning.

"I noted, in passing, that she had written a note before
leaving home, but after being fully dressed. You observed that her right glove was torn at the forefinger, but
you did not apparently see that both glove and finger were
stained with violet ink. She had written in a hurry, and
dipped her pen too deep. It must have been this morning, or the mark would not remain clear upon the finger.
All this is amusing, though rather elementary, but I must
go back to business, Watson. Would you mind reading
me the advertised description of Mr. Hosmer Angel?"

I held the little printed slip to the light. "Missing,"
it said, "on the morning of the 14th, a gentleman named
Hosmer Angel. About 5ft. 7in. in height; strongly built,
sallow complexion, black hair, a little bald in the centre,
bushy black side whiskers and moustache; tinted glasses,
slight infirmity of speech. Was dressed, when last seen,
in black frock-coat faced with silk, black waistcoat, gold
Albert chain, and grey Harris tweed trousers, with brown
gaiters over elastic-sided boots. Known to have been

employed in an office in Leadenhall Street. Anybody bringing," etc. etc.

" That will do," said Holmes. " As to the letters," he continued glancing over them, " they are very commonplace. Absolutely no clue in them to Mr. Angel, save that he quotes Balzac once. There is one remarkable point, however, which will no doubt strike you."

" They are typewritten," I remarked.

" Not only that, but the signature is typewritten. Look at the neat little ' Hosmer Angel ' at the bottom. There is a date you see, but no superscription, except Leadenhall Street, which is rather vague. The point about the signature is very suggestive—in fact, we may call it conclusive."

" Of what ? "

" My dear fellow, is it possible you do not see how strongly it bears upon the case."

" I cannot say that I do, unless it were that he wished to be able to deny his signature if an action for breach of promise were instituted."

" No, that was not the point. However, I shall write two letters which should settle the matter. One is to a firm in the City, the other is to the young lady's stepfather, Mr. Windibank, asking him whether he could meet us here at six o'clock to-morrow evening. It is just as well that we should do business with the male relatives. And now, Doctor, we can do nothing until the answers to those letters come, so we may put our little problem upon the shelf for the interim."

I had had so many reasons to believe in my friend's subtle powers of reasoning, and extraordinary energy in action, that I felt that he must have some solid grounds for the assured and easy demeanour with which he treated the singular mystery which he had been called upon to fathom. Only once had I known him to fail, in the case of the King of Bohemia and of the Irene Adler photograph, but when I looked back to the weird business of the Sign of Four, and the extraordinary circumstances connected with the Study in Scarlet, I felt that it would be a strange tangle indeed which he could not unravel.

I left him then, still puffing at his black clay pipe, with the conviction that when I came again on the next evening I would find that he held in his hands all the clues which would lead up to the identity of the disappearing bridegroom of Miss Mary Sutherland.

A professional case of great gravity was engaging my own attention at the time, and the whole of next day I was busy at the bedside of the sufferer. It was not until close upon six o'clock that I found myself free, and was able to spring into a hansom and drive to Baker Street, half afraid that I might be too late to assist at the *dénouement* of the little mystery. I found Sherlock Holmes alone, however, half asleep, with his long, thin form curled up in the recesses of his arm-chair. A formidable array of bottles and test-tubes, with the pungent cleanly smell of hydrochloric acid, told me that he had spent his day in the chemical work which was so dear to him.

" Well, have you solved it ? " I asked as I entered.

" Yes. It was the bisulphate of baryta."

" No, no, the mystery ! " I cried.

" Oh, that ! I thought of the salt that I have been working upon. There was never any mystery in the matter, though, as I said yesterday, some of the details are of interest. The only drawback is that there is no law, I fear, that can touch the scoundrel."

" Who was he, then, and what was his object in deserting Miss Sutherland ? "

The question was hardly out of my mouth, and Holmes had not yet opened his lips to reply, when we heard a heavy footfall in the passage, and a tap at the door.

" This is the girl's stepfather, Mr. James Windibank," said Holmes. " He has written to me to say that he would be here at six. Come in ! "

The man who entered was a sturdy middle-sized fellow, some thirty years of age, clean shaven, and sallow skinned, with a bland, insinuating manner, and a pair of wonderfully sharp and penetrating grey eyes. He shot a questioning glance at each of us, placed his shiny top-hat upon the sideboard, and, with a slight bow, sidled down into the nearest chair.

" Good evening, Mr. James Windibank," said Holmes. " I think that this typewritten letter is from you, in which you made an appointment with me for six o'clock ! "

" Yes, sir. I am afraid that I am a little late, but I am not quite my own master, you know. I am sorry that Miss Sutherland has troubled you about this little matter, for I think it is far better not to wash linen of this sort in public. It was quite against my wishes that she came, but she is a very excitable, impulsive girl, as you may have noticed, and she is not easily controlled when she has made up her mind on a point. Of course, I do not mind you so much, as you are not connected with the official police, but it is not pleasant to have a family misfortune like this noised abroad. Besides, it is a useless expense, for how could you possibly find this Hosmer Angel ? "

" On the contrary," said Holmes quietly ; " I have every reason to believe that I will succeed in discovering Mr. Hosmer Angel."

Mr. Windibank gave a violent start, and dropped his gloves. " I am delighted to hear it," he said.

" It is a curious thing," remarked Holmes, " that a typewriter has really quite as much individuality as a man's handwriting. Unless they are quite new, no two of them write exactly alike. Some letters get more worn than others, and some wear only on one side. Now, you remark in this note of yours, Mr. Windibank, that in every case there is some little slurring over of the ' e,' and a slight defect in the tail of the ' r.' There are fourteen other characteristics, but those are the more obvious."

" We do all our correspondence with this machine at the office, and no doubt it is a little worn," our visitor answered, glancing keenly at Holmes with his bright little eyes.

" And now I will show you what is really a very interesting study, Mr. Windibank," Holmes continued. " I think of writing another little monograph some of these days on the typewriter and its relation to crime. It is a subject to which I have devoted some little attention. I have here four letters which purport to come from the missing man. They are all typewritten. In each case, not only are the ' e's ' slurred and the ' r's ' tailless, but you will observe, if you care to use my magnifying lens, that the fourteen other characteristics to which I have alluded are there as well."

Mr. Windibank sprang out of his chair, and picked up his hat. " I cannot waste time over this sort of fantastic talk, Mr. Holmes," he said. " If you can catch the man, catch him, and let me know when you have done it."

" Certainly," said Holmes, stepping over and turning the key in the door. " I let you know, then, that I have caught him ! "

" What ! where ? " shouted Mr. Windibank, turning white to his lips, and glancing about him like a rat in a trap.

" Oh, it won't do—really it won't," said Holmes suavely. " There is no possible getting out of it, Mr. Windibank. It is quite too transparent, and it was a very bad compliment when you said it was impossible for me to solve so simple a question. That's right ! Sit down, and let us talk it over."

Our visitor collapsed into a chair with a ghastly face and a glitter of moisture on his brow. " It—it's not actionable," he stammered.

" I am very much afraid that it is not. But between ourselves, Windibank, it was as cruel, and selfish, and heartless a trick in a petty way as ever came before me. Now, let me just run over the course of events, and you will contradict me if I go wrong."

The man sat huddled up in his chair, with his head sunk upon his breast, like one who is utterly crushed. Holmes stuck his feet up on the corner of the mantelpiece, and leaning back with his hands in his pockets, began talking, rather to himself, as it seemed, than to us.

" The man married a woman very much older than himself for her money," said he, " and he enjoyed the use of the money of the daughter as long as she lived with them. It was a considerable sum for people in their position, and the loss of it would have made a serious difference. It was worth an effort to preserve it. The daughter was of a good, amiable disposition, but affectionate and warm-hearted in her ways, so that it was evident that with her fair personal advantages, and her little income, she would not be allowed to remain single long. Now her marriage would mean, of course, the loss of a hundred a year, so what does her stepfather do to prevent it ? He takes the obvious course of keeping her at home, and forbidding her to seek the company of people of her own age. But soon he found that that would not answer for ever. She became restive, insisted upon her rights, and finally announced her positive intention of going to a certain ball. What does her clever stepfather do then ? He conceives an idea more creditable to his head than to his heart. With the connivance and assistance of his wife he disguised himself, covered those keen eyes with tinted glasses, masked the face with a moustache and a pair of bushy whiskers, sunk that clear voice into an insinuating whisper, and, doubly secure on account of the girl's short sight, he appears as Mr. Hosmer Angel, and keeps off other lovers by making love himself."

" It was only a joke at first," groaned our visitor. " We never thought that she would have been so carried away."

" Very likely not. However that may be, the young lady was very decidedly carried away, and having quite made up her mind that her stepfather was in France, the suspicion of treachery never for an instant entered her mind. She was flattered by the gentleman's attentions, and the effect was increased by the loudly expressed admiration of her mother. Then Mr. Angel began to call, for it was obvious that the matter should be pushed as far as it would go, if a real effect were to be produced. There were meetings, and an engagement, which would finally secure the girl's affections from turning towards anyone else. But the deception could not be kept up for ever. These pretended journeys to France were rather cumbrous. The thing to do was clearly to bring the business to an end in such a dramatic manner that it would leave a permanent impression upon the young lady's mind, and prevent her from looking upon any other suitor for some time to come. Hence those vows of fidelity exacted upon a Testament, and hence also the allusions to a possibility of something happening on the very morning of the wedding. James Windibank wished Miss Sutherland to be so bound to Hosmer Angel, and so uncertain as to his fate, that for ten years to come, at any rate, she would not listen to another man. As far as the church door he brought her, and then, as he could go no further, he conveniently vanished away by the old trick of stepping in at one door of a four-wheeler, and out at the other. I think that that was the chain of events, Mr. Windibank ! "

Our visitor had recovered something of his assurance while Holmes had been talking, and he rose from his chair now with a cold sneer upon his pale face.

" It may be so, or it may not, Mr. Holmes," said he, " but if you are so very sharp you ought to be sharp enough to know that it is you who are breaking the law now, and not me. I have done nothing actionable from the first, but as long as you keep that door locked you lay yourself open to an action for assault and illegal constraint."

" The law cannot, as you say, touch you," said Holmes, unlocking and throwing open the door, " yet there never was a man who deserved punishment more. If the young lady has a brother or a friend he ought to lay a whip across your shoulders. By Jove ! " he continued, flushing up at the sight of the bitter sneer upon the man's face, " it is not part of my duties to my client, but here's a

73

hunting-crop handy, and I think I shall just treat myself to——" He took two swift steps to the whip, but before he could grasp it there was a wild clatter of steps upon the stairs, the heavy hall door banged, and from the window we could see Mr. James Windibank running at the top of his speed down the road.

"There's a cold-blooded scoundrel!" said Holmes, laughing, as he threw himself down into his chair once more. "That fellow will rise from crime to crime until he does something very bad, and ends on a gallows. The case has, in some respects, been not entirely devoid of interest."

"I cannot now entirely see all the steps of your reasoning," I remarked.

"Well, of course it was obvious from the first that this Mr. Hosmer Angel must have some strong object for his curious conduct, and it was equally clear that the only man who really profited by the incident, as far as we could see, was the stepfather. Then the fact that the two men were never together, but that the one always appeared when the other was away, was suggestive. So were the tinted spectacles and the curious voice, which both hinted at a disguise, as did the bushy whiskers. My suspicions were all confirmed by his peculiar action in typewriting his signature, which of course inferred that his handwriting was so familiar to her that she would recognize even the smallest sample of it. You see all these isolated facts, together with many minor ones, all pointed in the same direction."

"And how did you verify them?"

"Having once spotted my man, it was easy to get corroboration. I knew the firm for which this man worked. Having taken the printed description, I eliminated everything from it which could be the result of a disguise—the whiskers, the glasses, the voice, and I sent it to the firm, with a request that they would inform me whether it answered the description of any of their travellers. I had already noticed the peculiarities of the typewriter, and I wrote to the man himself at his business address, asking him if he would come here. As I expected, his reply was typewritten, and revealed the same trivial but characteristic defects. The same post brought me a letter from Westhouse & Marbank, of Fenchurch Street, to say that the description tallied in every respect with that of their employé, James Windibank. *Voilà tout !* "

" And Miss Sutherland ? "

" If I tell her she will not believe me. You may remember the old Persian saying, ' There is danger for him who taketh the tiger cub, and danger also for whoso snatches a delusion from a woman.' There is as much sense in Hafiz as in Horace, and as much knowledge of the world."

4. *The Boscombe Valley Mystery*

WE were seated at breakfast one morning, my wife and I, when the maid brought in a telegram. It was from Sherlock Holmes, and ran in this way :

" Have you a couple of days to spare ? Have just been wired for from the West of England in connection with Boscombe Valley tragedy. Shall be glad if you will come with me. Air and scenery perfect. Leave Paddington by the 11.15."

" What do you say, dear ? " said my wife, looking across at me. " Will you go ? "

" I really don't know what to say. I have a fairly long list at present."

" Oh, Anstruther would do your work for you. You have been looking a little pale lately. I think that the change would do you good, and you are always so interested in Mr. Sherlock Holmes' cases."

" I should be ungrateful if I were not, seeing what I gained through one of them," I answered. " But if I am to go I must pack at once, for I have only half an hour."

My experience of camp life in Afghanistan had at least had the effect of making me a prompt and ready traveller. My wants were few and simple, so that in less than the time stated I was in a cab with my valise, rattling away to Paddington Station. Sherlock Holmes was pacing up and down the platform, his tall, gaunt figure made even gaunter and taller by his long grey travelling-cloak and close-fitting cloth cap.

" It is really very good of you to come, Watson," said he. " It makes a considerable difference to me, having someone with me on whom I can thoroughly rely. Local aid is always either worthless or else biased. If you will keep the two corner seats I shall get the tickets."

We had the carriage to ourselves save for an immense litter of papers which Holmes had brought with him. Among these he rummaged and read, with intervals of note-taking and of meditation, until we were past Reading. Then he suddenly rolled them all into a gigantic ball, and tossed them up on to the rack.

" Have you heard anything of the case ? " he asked.

" Not a word. I have not seen a paper for some days."

" The London press has not had very full accounts. I have just been looking through all the recent papers in order to master the particulars. It seems, from what I gather, to be one of those simple cases which are so extremely difficult."

" That sounds a little paradoxical."

" But it is profoundly true. Singularity is almost invariably a clue. The more featureless and commonplace a crime is, the more difficult is it to bring it home. In this case, however, they have established a very serious case against the son of the murdered man."

" It is a murder, then ? "

" Well, it is conjectured to be so. I shall take nothing for granted until I have the opportunity of looking personally into it. I will explain the state of things to you, as far as I have been able to understand it, in a very few words.

" Boscombe Valley is a country district not very far from Ross, in Herefordshire. The largest landed proprietor in that part is a Mr. John Turner, who made his money in Australia, and returned some years ago to the old country. One of the farms which he held, that of Hatherley, was let to Mr. Charles McCarthy, who was also an ex-Australian. The men had known each other in the Colonies, so that it was not unnatural that when they came to settle down they should do so as near each other as possible. Turner was apparently the richer man, so McCarthy became his tenant, but still remained, it seems, upon terms of perfect equality, as they were frequently together. McCarthy had one son, a lad of eighteen, and Turner had an only daughter of the same age, but neither of them had wives living. They appear to have avoided the society of the neighbouring English families, and to have led retired lives, though both the McCarthys were fond of sport, and were frequently seen at the race meetings of the neighbourhood. McCarthy kept two servants—a man and a girl. Turner had a considerable household, some half-dozen at the least. That is as much as I have been able to gather about the families. Now for the facts.

" On June 3—that is, on Monday last—McCarthy left his house at Hatherley about three in the afternoon, and walked down to the Boscombe Pool, which is a small lake formed by the spreading out of the stream which runs down the Boscombe Valley. He had been out with his serving-man in the morning at Ross, and he had told the man that he must hurry, as he had an appointment of importance to keep at three. From that appointment he never came back alive.

" From Hatherley Farm-house to the Boscombe Pool is a quarter of a mile, and two people saw him as he passed over this ground. One was an old woman, whose name is not mentioned, and the other was William Crowder, a gamekeeper in the employ of Mr. Turner. Both these witnesses depose that Mr. McCarthy was walking alone.

The gamekeeper adds that within a few minutes of his seeing Mr. McCarthy pass he had seen his son, Mr. James McCarthy, going the same way with a gun under his arm. To the best of his belief, the father was actually in sight at the time, and the son was following him. He thought no more of the matter until he heard in the evening of the tragedy that had occurred.

" The two McCarthys were seen after the time when William Crowder, the gamekeeper, lost sight of them. The Boscombe Pool is thickly wooded round, with just a fringe of grass and of reeds round the edge. A girl of fourteen, Patience Moran, who is the daughter of the lodgekeeper of the Boscombe Valley Estate, was in one of the woods picking flowers. She states that while she was there she saw, at the border of the wood and close by the lake, Mr. McCarthy and his son, and that they appeared to be having a violent quarrel. She heard Mr. McCarthy the elder using very strong language to his son, and she saw the latter raise up his hand as if to strike his father. She was so frightened by their violence that she ran away, and told her mother when she reached home that she had left the two McCarthys quarrelling near Boscombe Pool, and that she was afraid that they were going to fight. She had hardly said the words when young Mr. McCarthy came running up to the lodge to say that he had found his father dead in the wood, and to ask for the help of the lodge-keeper. He was much excited, without either his gun or his hat, and his right hand and sleeve were observed to be stained with fresh blood. On following him they found the dead body of his father stretched out upon the grass beside the Pool. The head had been beaten in by repeated blows of some heavy and blunt weapon. The injuries were such as might very well have been inflicted by the butt-end of his son's gun, which was found lying on the grass within a few paces of the body. Under these circumstances the young man was instantly arrested, and a verdict of ' Wilful Murder ' having been returned at the inquest on

Tuesday, he was on Wednesday brought before the magistrates at Ross, who have referred the case to the next assizes. Those are the main facts of the case as they came out before the coroner and at the police-court."

" I could hardly imagine a more damning case," I remarked. " If ever circumstantial evidence pointed to a criminal it does so here."

" Circumstantial evidence is a very tricky thing," answered Holmes thoughtfully ; " it may seem to point very straight to one thing, but if you shift your own point of view a little, you may find it pointing in an equally uncompromising manner to something entirely different. It must be confessed, however, that the case looks exceedingly grave against the young man, and it is very possible that he is indeed the culprit. There are several people in the neighbourhood, however, and among them Miss Turner, the daughter of the neighbouring landowner, who believe in his innocence, and who have retained Lestrade, whom you may remember in connection with the Study in Scarlet, to work out the case in his interest. Lestrade, being rather puzzled, has referred the case to me, and hence it is that two middle-aged gentlemen are flying westward at fifty miles an hour, instead of quietly digesting their breakfasts at home."

" I am afraid," said I, " that the facts are so obvious that you will find little credit to be gained out of this case."

" There is nothing more deceptive than an obvious fact," he answered, laughing. " Besides, we may chance to hit upon some other obvious facts which may have been by no means obvious to Mr. Lestrade. You know me too well to think that I am boasting when I say that I shall either confirm or destroy his theory by means which he is quite incapable of employing, or even of understanding. To take the first example to hand, I very clearly perceive that in your bedroom the window is upon the right-hand side, and yet I question whether Mr. Lestrade would have noted even so self-evident a thing as that."

" How on earth—— ! "

" My dear fellow, I know you well. I know the military neatness which characterizes you. You shave every morning, and in this season you shave by the sunlight, but since your shaving is less and less complete as we get farther back on the left side, until it becomes positively slovenly as we get round the angle of the jaw, it is surely very clear that that side is less well illuminated than the other. I could not imagine a man of your habits looking at himself in an equal light, and being satisfied with such a result. I only quote this as a trivial example of observation and inference. Therein lies my *métier*, and it is just possible that it may be of some service in the investigation which lies before us. There are one or two minor points which were brought out in the inquest, and which are worth considering."

" What are they ? "

" It appears that his arrest did not take place at once, but after the return to Hatherley Farm. On the inspector of constabulary informing him that he was a prisoner, he remarked that he was not surprised to hear it, and that it was no more than his deserts. This observation of his had the natural effect of removing any traces of doubt which might have remained in the minds of the coroner's jury."

" It was a confession," I ejaculated.

" No, for it was followed by a protestation of innocence."

" Coming on the top of such a damning series of events, it was at least a most suspicious remark."

" On the contrary," said Holmes, " it is the brightest rift which I can at present see in the clouds. However innocent he might be, he could not be such an absolute imbecile as not to see that the circumstances were very black against him. Had he appeared surprised at his own arrest, or feigned indignation at it, I should have looked upon it as highly suspicious, because such surprise or anger would not be natural under the circumstances.

and yet might appear to be the best policy to a scheming man. His frank acceptance of the situation marks him as either an innocent man, or else as a man of considerable self-restraint and firmness. As to his remark about his deserts, it was also not unnatural if you consider that he stood by the dead body of his father, and that there is no doubt that he had that very day so far forgotten his filial duty as to bandy words with him, and even, according to the little girl whose evidence is so important, to raise his hand as if to strike him. The self-reproach and contrition which are displayed in his remark appear to me to be the signs of a healthy mind, rather than of a guilty one."

I shook my head. "Many men have been hanged on far slighter evidence," I remarked.

"So they have. And many men have been wrongfully hanged."

"What is the young man's own account of the matter?"

"It is, I am afraid, not very encouraging to his supporters, though there are one or two points in it which are suggestive. You will find it here, and may read it for yourself."

He picked out from his bundle a copy of the local Herefordshire paper, and having turned down the sheet, he pointed out the paragraph in which the unfortunate young man had given his own statement of what had occurred. I settled myself down in the corner of the carriage, and read it very carefully. It ran in this way:

"Mr. James McCarthy, the only son of the deceased, was then called, and gave evidence as follows: 'I had been away from home for three days at Bristol, and had only just returned upon the morning of last Monday, the 3rd. My father was absent from home at the time of my arrival, and I was informed by the maid that he had driven over to Ross with John Cobb, the groom. Shortly after my return I heard the wheels of his trap in the yard, and, looking out of my window, I saw him get out and walk rapidly out of the yard, though I was not aware in which direction he was going. I then took my gun, and strolled out in the direction of the Boscombe Pool, with the intention of visiting the rabbit warren which is upon the other side. On my way I saw William Crowder, the gamekeeper, as he has stated in his evidence ; but he is mistaken in thinking that I was following my father. I had no idea that he was in front of me. When about a hundred yards from the Pool I heard a cry of " Cooee ! " which was a usual signal between my father and myself. I then hurried forward, and found him standing by the Pool. He appeared to be much surprised at seeing me, and asked me rather roughly what I was doing there. A conversation ensued, which led to high words, and almost to blows, for my father was a man of a very violent temper. Seeing that his passion was becoming ungovernable, I left him, and returned towards Hatherley Farm. I had not gone more than one hundred and fifty yards, however, when I heard a hideous outcry behind me, which caused me to run back again. I found my father expiring on the ground, with his head terribly injured. I dropped my gun, and held him in my arms, but he almost instantly expired. I knelt beside him for some minutes, and then made my way to Mr. Turner's lodge-keeper, his house being the nearest, to ask for assistance. I saw no one near my father when I returned, and I have no idea how he came by his injuries. He was not a popular man, being somewhat cold and forbidding in his manners ; but he had, as far as I know, no active enemies. I know nothing further of the matter."

" The Coroner : Did your father make any statement to you before he died ?

" Witness : He mumbled a few words, but I could only catch some allusion to a rat.

" The Coroner : What did you understand by that ?

" Witness : It conveyed no meaning to me. I thought that he was delirious.

" The Coroner : What was the point upon which you and your father had this final quarrel ?

" Witness : I should prefer not to answer.

" The Coroner : I am afraid that I must press it.

" Witness : It is really impossible for me to tell you. I can assure you that it has nothing to do with the sad tragedy which followed.

" The Coroner : That is for the Court to decide. I need not point out to you that your refusal to answer will prejudice your case considerably in any future proceedings which may arise.

" Witness : I must still refuse.

" The Coroner : I understand that the cry of ' Cooee ' was a common signal between you and your father ?

" Witness : It was.

" The Coroner : How was it, then, that he uttered it before he saw you, and before he even knew that you had returned from Bristol ?

" Witness (with considerable confusion) : I do not know.

" A Juryman : Did you see nothing which aroused your suspicions when you returned on hearing the cry, and found your father fatally injured ?

" Witness : Nothing definite.

" The Coroner : What do you mean ?

" Witness : I was so disturbed and excited as I rushed out into the open, that I could think of nothing except my father. Yet I have a vague impression that as I ran forward something lay upon the ground to the left of me. It seemed to me to be something grey in colour, a coat of some sort, or a plaid perhaps. When I rose from my father I looked round for it, but it was gone.

" ' Do you mean that it disappeared before you went for help ? '

" ' Yes, it was gone.'

" ' You cannot say what it was ? '

" ' No, I had a feeling something was there.'

" ' How far from the body ? '

" ' A dozen yards or so.'

" ' And how far from the edge of the wood ? '

" ' About the same.'

" ' Then if it was removed it was while you were within a dozen yards of it ? '

" ' Yes, but with my back towards it.'

" This concluded the examination of the witness."

" I see," said I, as I glanced down the column, " that the coroner in his concluding remarks was rather severe upon young McCarthy. He calls attention, and with reason, to the discrepancy about his father having signalled to him before seeing him, also to his refusal to give details of his conversation with his father, and his singular account of his father's dying words. They are all, as he remarks, very much against the son."

Holmes laughed softly to himself, and stretched himself out upon the cushioned seat. " Both you and the coroner have been at some pains," said he, " to single out the very strongest points in the young man's favour. Don't you see that you alternately give him credit for having too much imagination and too little ? Too little, if he could not invent a cause of quarrel which would give him the sympathy of the jury ; too much, if he evolved from his own inner consciousness anything so *outré* as a dying reference to a rat, and the incident of the vanishing cloth. No, sir, I shall approach this case from the point of view that what this young man says is true, and we shall see whither that hypothesis will lead us. And now here is my pocket Petrarch, and not another word shall I say of this case until we are on the scene of action. We lunch at Swindon, and I see that we shall be there in twenty minutes."

It was nearly four o'clock when we at last, after passing through the beautiful Stroud Valley and over the broad gleaming Severn, found ourselves at the pretty little country town of Ross. A lean, ferret-like man, furtive and sly-looking, was waiting for us upon the platform. In spite of the light brown dust-coat and leather leggings which he wore in deference to his rustic surroundings, I had no difficulty in recognizing Lestrade, of Scotland

Yard. With him we drove to the " Hereford Arms,"
where a room had already been engaged for us.

" I have ordered a carriage," said Lestrade, as we sat
over a cup of tea. " I knew your energetic nature, and
that you would not be happy until you had been on the
scene of the crime."

" It was very nice and complimentary of you," Holmes
answered. " It is entirely a question of barometric
pressure."

Lestrade looked startled. " I do not quite follow," he
said.

" How is the glass ? Twenty-nine, I see. No wind,
and not a cloud in the sky. I have a caseful of cigarettes
here which need smoking, and the sofa is very much
superior to the usual country hotel abomination. I do
not think that it is probable that I shall use the carriage
to-night."

Lestrade laughed indulgently. " You have, no doubt,
already formed your conclusions from the newspapers,"
he said. " The case is as plain as a pikestaff, and the more
one goes into it the plainer it becomes. Still, of course,
one can't refuse a lady, and such a very positive one, too.
She had heard of you, and would have your opinion,
though I repeatedly told her that there was nothing which
you could do which I had not already done. Why, bless
my soul ! here is her carriage at the door."

He had hardly spoken before there rushed into the room
one of the most lovely young women that I have ever seen
in my life. Her violet eyes shining, her lips parted, a
pink flush upon her cheeks, all thought of her natural
reserve lost in her overpowering excitement and concern.

" Oh, Mr. Sherlock Holmes ! " she cried, glancing
from one to the other of us, and finally, with a woman's
quick intuition, fastening upon my companion, " I am
so glad that you have come. I have driven down to tell
you so. I know that James didn't do it. I know it, and
I want you to start upon your work knowing it, too.
Never let yourself doubt upon that point. We have

known each other since we were little children, and I know his faults as no one else does ; but he is too tender-hearted to hurt a fly. Such a charge is absurd to anyone who really knows him."

" I hope we may clear him, Miss Turner," said Sherlock Holmes. " You may rely upon my doing all that I can."

" But you have read the evidence. You have formed some conclusion ? Do you not see some loophole, some flaw ? Do you not yourself think that he is innocent ? "

" I think that it is very probable."

" There now ! " she cried, throwing back her head and looking defiantly at Lestrade. " You hear ! He gives me hope."

Lestrade shrugged his shoulders. " I am afraid that my colleague has been a little quick in forming his conclusions," he said.

" But he is right. Oh ! I know that he is right. James never did it. And about his quarrel with his father, I am sure that the reason why he would not speak about it to the coroner was because I was concerned in it."

" In what way ? " asked Holmes.

" It is no time for me to hide anything. James and his father had many disagreements about me. Mr. McCarthy was very anxious that there should be a marriage between us. James and I have always loved each other as brother and sister, but of course he is young and has seen very little of life yet, and—and—well, he naturally did not wish to do anything like that yet. So there were quarrels, and this, I am sure, was one of them."

" And your father ? " asked Holmes. " Was he in favour of such a union ? "

" No, he was averse to it also. No one but Mr. McCarthy was in favour of it." A quick blush passed over her fresh young face as Holmes shot one of his keen, questioning glances at her.

" Thank you for this information," said he. " May I see your father if I call to-morrow ? "

"I am afraid the doctor won't allow it."

"The doctor?"

"Yes, have you not heard? Poor father has never been strong for years back, but this has broken him down completely. He has taken to his bed, and Dr. Willows says that he is a wreck, and that his nervous system is shattered. Mr. McCarthy was the only man alive who had known dad in the old days in Victoria."

"Ha! In Victoria! That is important."

"Yes, at the mines."

"Quite so; at the gold mines, where, as I understand, Mr. Turner made his money."

"Yes, certainly."

"Thank you, Miss Turner. You have been of material assistance to me."

"You will tell me if you have any news to-morrow. No doubt you will go to the prison to see James. Oh, if you do, Mr. Holmes, do tell him that I know him to be innocent."

"I will, Miss Turner."

"I must go home now, for dad is very ill, and he misses me so if I leave him. Good-bye, and God help you in your undertaking." She hurried from the room as impulsively as she had entered, and we heard the wheels of her carriage rattle off down the street.

"I am ashamed of you, Holmes," said Lestrade with dignity, after a few minutes' silence. "Why should you raise up hopes which you are bound to disappoint? I am not over-tender of heart, but I call it cruel."

"I think that I see my way to clearing James McCarthy," said Holmes. "Have you an order to see him in prison?"

"Yes, but only for you and me."

"Then I shall reconsider my resolution about going out. We have still time to take a train to Hereford and see him to-night?"

"Ample."

"Then let us do so. Watson, I fear that you will

87

find it very slow, but I shall only be away a couple of hours."

I walked down to the station with them, and then wandered through the streets of the little town, finally returning to the hotel, where I lay upon the sofa and tried to interest myself in a yellow-backed novel. The puny plot of the story was so thin, however, when compared to the deep mystery through which we were groping, and I found my attention wander so constantly from the fiction to the fact, that I at last flung it across the room, and gave myself up entirely to a consideration of the events of the day. Supposing that this unhappy young man's story was absolutely true, then what hellish thing, what absolutely unforeseen and extraordinary calamity, could have occurred between the time when he parted from his father and the moment when, drawn back by his screams, he rushed into the glade ? It was something terrible and deadly. What could it be ? Might not the nature of the injuries reveal something to my medical instincts ? I rang the bell, and called for the weekly county paper, which contained a verbatim account of the inquest. In the surgeon's deposition it was stated that the posterior third of the left parietal bone and the left half of the occipital bone had been shattered by a heavy blow from a blunt weapon. I marked the spot upon my own head. Clearly such a blow must have been struck from behind. That was to some extent in favour of the accused, as when seen quarrelling he was face to face with his father. Still, it did not go for very much, for the older man might have turned his back before the blow fell. Still, it might be worth while to call Holmes' attention to it. Then there was the peculiar dying reference to a rat. What could that mean ? It could not be delirium. A man dying from a sudden blow does not commonly become delirious. No, it was more likely to be an attempt to explain how he met his fate. But what could it indicate ? I cudgelled my brains to find some possible explanation. And then the incident of the grey cloth, seen by young McCarthy.

If that were true, the murderer must have dropped some part of his dress, presumably his overcoat, in his flight, and must have had the hardihood to return and carry it away at the instant when the son was kneeling with his back turned not a dozen paces off. What a tissue of mysteries and improbabilities the whole thing was ! I did not wonder at Lestrade's opinion, and yet I had so much faith in Sherlock Holmes' insight that I could not lose hope as long as every fresh fact seemed to strengthen his conviction of young McCarthy's innocence.

It was late before Sherlock Holmes returned. He came back alone, for Lestrade was staying in lodgings in the town.

" The glass still keeps very high," he remarked, as he sat down. " It is of importance that it should not rain before we are able to go over the ground. On the other hand, a man should be at his very best and keenest for such nice work as that, and I did not wish to do it when fagged by a long journey. I have seen young McCarthy."

" And what did you learn from him ? "

" Nothing."

" Could he throw no light ? "

" None at all. I was inclined to think at one time that he knew who had done it, and was screening him or her, but I am convinced now that he is as puzzled as everyone else. He is not a very quick-witted youth, though comely to look at, and, I should think, sound at heart."

" I cannot admire his taste," I remarked, " if it is indeed a fact that he was averse to a marriage with so charming a young lady as this Miss Turner."

" Ah, thereby hangs a rather painful tale. This fellow is madly, insanely in love with her, but some two years ago, when he was only a lad, and before he really knew her, for she had been away five years at a boarding-school, what does the idiot do but get into the clutches of a barmaid in Bristol, and marry her at a registry office ! No one knows a word of the matter, but you can imagine how maddening it must be to him to be upbraided for not doing what he would give his very eyes to do, but what he knows to be absolutely impossible. It was sheer frenzy of this sort which made him throw his hands up into the air when his father, at their last interview, was goading him on to propose to Miss Turner. On the other hand, he had no means of supporting himself, and his father, who was by all accounts a very hard man, would have thrown him over utterly had he known the truth. It was with his barmaid wife that he had spent the last three days in Bristol, and his father did not know where he was. Mark that point. It is of importance. Good has come out of evil, however, for the barmaid, finding from the papers that he is in serious trouble, and likely to be hanged, has thrown him over utterly, and has written to him to say that she has a husband already in the Bermuda Dockyard, so that there is really no tie between them. I think that that bit of news has consoled young McCarthy for all that he has suffered."

"But if he is innocent, who has done it?"

"Ah! who? I would call your attention very particularly to two points. One is that the murdered man had an appointment with someone at the Pool, and that the someone could not have been his son, for his son was away, and he did not know when he would return. The second is that the murdered man was heard to cry 'Cooee!' before he knew that his son had returned. Those are the crucial points upon which the case depends. And now let us talk about George Meredith, if you please, and we shall leave minor points until to-morrow."

There was no rain, as Holmes had foretold, and the morning broke bright and cloudless. At nine o'clock Lestrade called for us with the carriage, and we set off for Hatherley Farm and the Boscombe Pool.

"There is serious news this morning," Lestrade observed. "It is said that Mr. Turner, of the Hall, is so ill that his life is despaired of."

"An elderly man, I presume?" said Holmes.

"About sixty; but his constitution has been shattered

by his life abroad, and he has been in failing health for some time. This business has had a very bad effect upon him. He was an old friend of McCarthy's, and, I may add, a great benefactor to him, for I have learned that he gave him Hatherley Farm rent free."

"Indeed! That is interesting," said Holmes.

"Oh, yes! In a hundred other ways he has helped him. Everybody about here speaks of his kindness to him."

"Really! Does it not strike you as a little singular that this McCarthy, who appears to have had little of his own, and to have been under such obligations to Turner, should still talk of marrying his son to Turner's daughter, who is, presumably, heiress to the estate, and that in such a very cocksure manner, as if it was merely a case of a proposal and all else would follow? It is the more strange since we know that Turner himself was averse to the idea. The daughter told us as much. Do you not deduce something from that?"

"We have got to the deductions and the inferences," said Lestrade, winking at me. "I find it hard enough to tackle facts, Holmes, without flying away after theories and fancies."

"You are right," said Holmes demurely; "you do find it very hard to tackle the facts."

"Anyhow, I have grasped one fact which you seem to find it difficult to get hold of," replied Lestrade with some warmth.

"And that is?"

"That McCarthy, senior, met his death from Mc-Carthy, junior, and that all theories to the contrary are the merest moonshine."

"Well, moonshine is a brighter thing than fog," said Holmes, laughing. "But I am very much mistaken if this is not Hatherley Farm upon the left."

"Yes, that is it." It was a widespread, comfortable-looking building, two-storied, slate-roofed, with great yellow blotches of lichen upon the grey walls. The drawn blinds and the smokeless chimneys, however, gave it a stricken look, as though the weight of this horror still lay heavy upon it. We called at the door, when the maid, at Holmes' request, showed us the boots which her master wore at the time of his death, and also a pair of the son's, though not the pair which he had then had. Having measured these very carefully from seven or eight different points, Holmes desired to be led to the courtyard, from which we all followed the winding track which led to Boscombe Pool.

Sherlock Holmes was transformed when he was hot upon such a scent as this. Men who had only known the quiet thinker and logician of Baker Street would have failed to recognize him. His face flushed and darkened. His brows were drawn into two hard, black lines, while his eyes shone out from beneath them with a steely glitter. His face was bent downwards, his shoulders bowed, his lips compressed, and the veins stood out like whip-cord in his long, sinewy neck. His nostrils seemed to dilate with a purely animal lust for the chase, and his mind was so absolutely concentrated upon the matter before him, that a question or remark fell unheeded upon his ears, or at the most only provoked a quick, impatient snarl in reply. Swiftly and silently he made his way along the track which ran through the meadows, and so by way of the woods to the Boscombe Pool. It was damp, marshy ground, as is all that district, and there were marks of many feet, both upon the path and amid the short grass which bounded it on either side. Sometimes Holmes would hurry on, sometimes stop dead, and once he made quite a little *détour* into the meadow. Lestrade and I walked behind him, the detective indifferent and contemptuous, while I watched my friend with the interest which sprang from the conviction that every one of his actions was directed towards a definite end.

The Boscombe Pool, which is a little reed-girt sheet of water some fifty yards across, is situated at the boundary between the Hatherley Farm and the private park of the wealthy Mr. Turner. Above the woods which lined it upon the farther side we could see the red jutting pinnacles which marked the site of the rich landowner's dwelling. On the Hatherley side of the Pool the woods grew very thick, and there was a narrow belt of sodden grass twenty paces across between the edge of the trees and the reeds which lined the lake. Lestrade showed us the exact spot at which the body had been found, and indeed, so moist was the ground, that I could plainly see the traces which had been left by the fall of the stricken man. To Holmes, as I could see by his eager face and peering eyes, very many other things were to be read upon the trampled grass. He ran round, like a dog who is picking up a scent, and then turned upon my companion.

" What did you go into the Pool for ? " he asked.

" I fished about with a rake. I thought there might be some weapon or other trace. But how on earth—— ? "

" Oh, tut, tut ! I have no time. That left foot of yours with its inward twist is all over the place. A mole could trace it, and there it vanishes among the reeds. Oh, how simple it would all have been had I been here before they came like a herd of buffalo, and wallowed all over it. Here is where the party with the lodge-keeper came, and they have covered all tracks for six or eight feet round the body. But here are three separate tracks of the same feet." He drew out a lens, and lay down upon his waterproof to have a better view, talking all the time rather to himself than to us. " These are young McCarthy's feet. Twice he was walking, and once he ran swiftly so that the soles are deeply marked, and the heels hardly visible. That bears out his story. He ran when he saw his father on the ground. Then here are the father's feet as he paced up and down. What is this, then ? It is the butt end of the gun as the son stood listening. And this ? Ha, ha ! What have we here ? Tip-toes, tip-toes ! Square, too, quite unusual boots ! They come, they go, they come again—of course that was for the cloak. Now where did they come from ? " He ran up and down, sometimes losing, sometimes finding the track, until we were well within the edge of the wood and under the shadow of a great beech, the largest tree in the neighbourhood. Holmes traced his way to the farther side of this, and lay down once more upon his face with a little cry of satisfaction. For a long time he remained there, turning over the leaves and dried sticks, gathering up what seemed to me to be dust into an envelope, and examining with his lens not only the ground, but even the bark of the tree as far as he could reach. A jagged stone was lying among the moss, and this also he carefully examined and retained. Then he followed a pathway through the wood until he came to the high-road, where all traces were lost.

" It has been a case of considerable interest," he remarked, returning to his natural manner. " I fancy that this grey house on the right must be the lodge. I think that I will go in and have a word with Moran, and perhaps write a little note. Having done that, we may drive back to our luncheon. You may walk to the cab, and I shall be with you presently."

It was about ten minutes before we regained our cab, and drove back into Ross, Holmes still carrying with him the stone which he had picked up in the wood.

" This may interest you, Lestrade," he remarked, holding it out. " The murder was done with it."

" I see no marks."

" There are none."

" How do you know, then ? "

" The grass was growing under it. It had only lain there a few days. There was no sign of a place whence it had been taken. It corresponds with the injuries. There is no sign of any other weapon."

" And the murderer ? "

" Is a tall man, left-handed, limps with the right leg, wears thick-soled shooting-boots and a grey cloak, smokes Indian cigars, uses a cigar-holder, and carries a blunt penknife in his pocket. There are several other indications, but these may be enough to aid us in our search."

Lestrade laughed. "I am afraid that I am still a sceptic," he said. "Theories are all very well, but we have to deal with a hard-headed British jury."

"*Nous verrons*," answered Holmes calmly. "You work your own method, and I shall work mine. I shall be busy this afternoon, and shall probably return to London by the evening train."

"And leave your case unfinished?"

"No, finished."

"But the mystery?"

"It is solved."

"Who was the criminal, then?"

"The gentleman I describe."

"But who is he?"

"Surely it would not be difficult to find out. This is not such a populous neighbourhood."

Lestrade shrugged his shoulders. "I am a practical man," he said, "and I really cannot undertake to go about the country looking for a left-handed gentleman with a game leg. I should become the laughing-stock of Scotland Yard."

"All right," said Holmes quietly. "I have given you the chance. Here are your lodgings. Good-bye. I shall drop you a line before I leave."

Having left Lestrade at his rooms we drove to our hotel, where we found lunch upon the table. Holmes was silent and buried in thought, with a pained expression upon his face, as one who finds himself in a perplexing position.

"Look here, Watson," he said, when the cloth was cleared; "just sit down in this chair and let me preach to you for a little. I don't quite know what to do, and I should value your advice. Light a cigar, and let me expound."

"Pray do so."

"Well, now, in considering this case there are two

points about young McCarthy's narrative which struck us both instantly, although they impressed me in his favour and you against him. One was the fact that his father should, according to his account, cry ' Cooee ! ' before seeing him. The other was his singular dying reference to a rat. He mumbled several words, you understand, but that was all that caught the son's ear. Now from this double point our research must commence, and we will begin it by presuming that what the lad says is absolutely true."

" What of this ' Cooee ! ' then ? "

" Well, obviously it could not have been meant for the son. The son, as far as he knew, was in Bristol. It was mere chance that he was within earshot. The ' Cooee ! ' was meant to attract the attention of whoever it was that he had the appointment with. But ' Cooee ' is a distinctly Australian cry, and one which is used between Australians. There is a strong presumption that the person whom McCarthy expected him to meet at Boscombe Pool was someone who had been in Australia."

" What of the rat, then ? "

Sherlock Holmes took a folded paper from his pocket and flattened it out on the table. " This is a map of the Colony of Victoria," he said. " I wired to Bristol for it last night." He put his hand over part of the map. " What do you read ? " he asked.

" ARAT," I read.

" And now ? " He raised his hand.

" BALLARAT."

" Quite so. That was the word the man uttered, and of which his son only caught the last two syllables. He was trying to utter the name of his murderer. So-and-so of Ballarat."

" It is wonderful ! " I exclaimed.

" It is obvious. And now, you see, I had narrowed the field down considerably. The possession of a grey garment was a third point which, granting the son's statement to be correct, was a certainty. We have come now out of mere vagueness to the definite conception of an Australian from Ballarat with a grey cloak."

" Certainly."

" And one who was at home in the district, for the Pool can only be approached by the farm or by the estate, where strangers could hardly wander."

" Quite so."

" Then comes our expedition of to-day. By an examination of the ground I gained the trifling details which I gave to that imbecile Lestrade, as to the personality of the criminal."

" But how did you gain them ? "

" You know my method. It is founded upon the observance of trifles."

" His height I know that you might roughly judge from the length of his stride. His boots, too, might be told from their traces."

" Yes, they were peculiar boots."

" But his lameness ? "

" The impression of his right foot was always less distinct than his left. He put less weight upon it. Why ? Because he limped—he was lame."

" But his left-handedness ? "

" You were yourself struck by the nature of the injury as recorded by the surgeon at the inquest. The blow was struck from immediately behind, and yet was upon the left side. Now, how can that be unless it were by a left-handed man ? He had stood behind that tree during the interview between the father and son. He had even smoked there. I found the ash of a cigar, which my special knowledge of tobacco ashes enabled me to pronounce as an Indian cigar. I have, as you know, devoted some attention to this, and written a little monograph on the ashes of 140 different varieties of pipe, cigar, and cigarette tobacco. Having found the ash, I then looked round and discovered the stump among the moss where he had tossed it. It was an Indian cigar, of the variety which are rolled in Rotterdam."

"And the cigar-holder?"

"I could see that the end had not been in his mouth. Therefore he used a holder. The tip had been cut off, not bitten off, but the cut was not a clean one, so I deduced a blunt penknife."

"Holmes," I said, "you have drawn a net round this man from which he cannot escape, and you have saved an innocent human life as truly as if you had cut the cord which was hanging him. I see the direction in which all this points. The culprit is——"

"Mr. John Turner," cried the hotel waiter, opening the door of our sitting-room, and ushering in a visitor.

The man who entered was a strange and impressive figure. His slow, limping step and bowed shoulders gave the appearance of decrepitude, and yet his hard, deep-lined, craggy features, and his enormous limbs showed that he was possessed of unusual strength of body and of character. His tangled beard, grizzled hair, and out-standing, drooping eyebrows combined to give an air of dignity and power to his appearance, but his face was of an ashen white, while his lips and the corners of his nostrils were tinged with a shade of blue. It was clear to me at a glance that he was in the grip of some deadly and chronic disease.

"Pray sit down on the sofa," said Holmes gently. "You had my note?"

"Yes, the lodge-keeper brought it up. You said that you wished to see me here to avoid scandal."

"I thought people would talk if I went to the Hall."

"And why did you wish to see me?" He looked across at my companion with despair in his weary eyes, as though his question were already answered.

"Yes," said Holmes, answering the look rather than the words. "It is so. I know all about McCarthy."

The old man sank his face in his hands. "God help me!" he cried. "But I would not have let the young man come to harm. I give you my word that I would have spoken out if it went against him at the Assizes."

"I am glad to hear you say so," said Holmes gravely.

"I would have spoken now had it not been for my dear girl. It would break her heart—it will break her heart when she hears that I am arrested."

"It may not come to that," said Holmes.

"What!"

"I am no official agent. I understand that it was your daughter who required my presence here, and I am acting in her interests. Young McCarthy must be got off, however."

"I am a dying man," said old Turner. "I have had diabetes for years. My doctor says it is a question whether I shall live a month. Yet I would rather die under my own roof than in a gaol."

Holmes rose and sat down at the table with his pen in his hand and a bundle of paper before him. "Just tell us the truth," he said. "I shall jot down the facts. You will sign it, and Watson here can witness it. Then I could produce your confession at the last extremity to save young McCarthy. I promise you that I shall not use it unless it is absolutely needed."

"It's as well," said the old man; "it's a question whether I shall live to the Assizes, so it matters little to me, but I should wish to spare Alice the shock. And now I will make the thing clear to you; it has been a long time in the acting, but will not take me long to tell.

"You didn't know this dead man, McCarthy. He was a devil incarnate. I tell you that. God keep you out of the clutches of such a man as he. His grip has been upon me these twenty years, and he has blasted my life. I'll tell you first how I came to be in his power.

"It was in the early 'sixties at the diggings. I was a young chap then, hot-blooded and reckless, ready to turn my hand to anything; I got among bad companions, took to drink, had no luck with my claim, took to the bush, and, in a word, became what you would call over here a highway robber. There were six of us, and we had a wild, free life of it, sticking up a station from time to time, or stopping the wagons on the road to the diggings. Black Jack of Ballarat was the name I went under, and our party is still remembered in the colony as the Ballarat Gang.

" One day a gold convoy came down from Ballarat to Melbourne, and we lay in wait for it and attacked it. There were six troopers and six of us, so it was a close thing, but we emptied four of their saddles at the first volley. Three of our boys were killed, however, before we got the swag. I put my pistol to the head of the wagon-driver, who was this very man McCarthy. I wish to the Lord that I had shot him then, but I spared him, though I saw his wicked little eyes fixed on my face, as though to remember every feature. We got away with the gold, became wealthy men, and made our way over to England without being suspected. There I parted from my old pals, and determined to settle down to a quiet and respectable life. I bought this estate, which chanced to be in the market, and I set myself to do a little good with my money, to make up for the way in which I had earned it. I married, too, and though my wife died young, she left me my dear little Alice. Even when she was just a baby her wee hand seemed to lead me down the right path as nothing else had ever done. In a word, I turned over a new leaf, and did my best to make up for the past. All was going well when McCarthy laid his grip upon me.

" I had gone up to town about an investment, and I met him in Regent Street with hardly a coat to his back or a boot to his foot.

" ' Here we are, Jack,' says he, touching me on the arm ; ' we'll be as good as a family to you. There's two of us, me and my son, and you can have the keeping of us. If you don't—it's a fine, law-abiding country is England, and there's always a policeman within hail.'

" Well, down they came to the West Country, there was no shaking them off, and there they have lived rent free on my best land ever since. There was no rest for me, no peace, no forgetfulness ; turn where I would, there was his cunning, grinning face at my elbow. It grew worse as Alice grew up, for he soon saw I was more afraid of her knowing my past than of the police. Whatever he wanted he must have, and whatever it was I gave him without question, land, money, houses, until at last he asked for a thing which I could not give. He asked for Alice.

" His son, you see, had grown up, and so had my girl, and as I was known to be in weak health, it seemed a fine stroke to him that his lad should step into the whole property. But there I was firm. I would not have his cursed stock mixed with mine ; not that I had any dislike to the lad, but his blood was in him, and that was enough. I stood firm. McCarthy threatened. I braved him to do his worst. We were to meet at the Pool midway between our houses to talk it over.

" When I went down there I found him talking with his son, so I smoked a cigar, and waited behind a tree until he should be alone. But as I listened to his talk all that was black and bitter in me seemed to come uppermost. He was urging his son to marry my daughter with as little regard for what she might think as if she were a slut from off the streets. It drove me mad to think that I and all that I held most dear should be in the power of such a man as this. Could I not snap the bond ? I was already a dying and a desperate man. Though clear of mind and fairly strong of limb, I knew that my own fate was sealed. But my memory and my girl ! Both could be saved, if I could but silence that foul tongue. I did it, Mr. Holmes. I would do it again. Deeply as I have sinned, I have led a life of martyrdom to atone for it. But that my girl should be entangled in the same meshes which held me was more than I could suffer. I struck him down with no more compunction than if he had been some foul and venomous beast. His cry brought back his son ; but I had gained the cover of the wood, though I was forced to go back to fetch the cloak which I had dropped in my flight. That is the true story, gentlemen, of all that occurred."

"Well, it is not for me to judge you," said Holmes, as the old man signed the statement which had been drawn out. "I pray that we may never be exposed to such a temptation."

"I pray not, sir. And what do you intend to do ?"

"In view of your health, nothing. You are yourself aware that you will soon have to answer for your deed at a higher court than the Assizes. I will keep your confession, and, if McCarthy is condemned, I shall be forced to use it. If not, it shall never be seen by mortal eye ; and your secret, whether you be alive or dead, shall be safe with us."

"Farewell ! then," said the old man solemnly. "Your own death-beds, when they come, will be the easier for the thought of the peace which you have given to mine." Tottering and shaking in all his giant frame, he stumbled slowly from the room.

"God help us !" said Holmes, after a long silence. "Why does Fate play such tricks with poor helpless worms ? I never hear of such a case as this that I do not think of Baxter's words, and say : ' There, but for the grace of God, goes Sherlock Holmes.' "

James McCarthy was acquitted at the Assizes, on the strength of a number of objections which had been drawn out by Holmes, and submitted to the defending counsel. Old Turner lived for seven months after our interview, but he is now dead ; and there is every prospect that the son and daughter may come to live happily together, in ignorance of the black cloud which rests upon their past.

5. *The Five Orange Pips*

WHEN I glance over my notes and records of the Sherlock Holmes cases between the years '82 and '90, I am faced by so many which present strange and interesting features, that it is no easy matter to know which to choose and which to leave. Some, however, have already gained publicity through the papers, and others have not offered a field for those peculiar qualities which my friend possessed in so high a degree, and which it is the object of these papers to illustrate. Some, too, have baffled his analytical skill, and would be, as narratives, beginnings without an ending, while others have been but partially cleared up, and have their explanations founded rather upon conjecture and surmise than on that absolute logical proof which was so dear to him. There is, however, one of these last which was so remarkable in its details and so startling in its results, that I am tempted to give some account of it, in spite of the fact that there are points in connection with it which never have been, and probably never will be, entirely cleared up.

The year '87 furnished us with a long series of cases of greater or less interest, of which I retain the records. Among my headings under this one twelve months, I find an account of the adventure of the Paradol Chamber, of the Amateur Mendicant Society, who held a luxurious club in the lower vault of a furniture warehouse, of the facts connected with the loss of the British barque *Sophy Anderson*, of the singular adventures of the Grice Patersons in the island of Uffa, and finally of the Camberwell poisoning case. In the latter, as may be remembered, Sherlock Holmes was able, by winding up the dead man's watch, to prove that it had been wound up two hours ago, and that therefore the deceased had gone to bed within that time—a deduction which was of the greatest importance in clearing up the case. All these I may sketch out at some future date, but none of them present such singular features as the strange train of circumstances which I have now taken up my pen to describe.

It was in the latter days of September, and the equinoctial gales had set in with exceptional violence. All day the wind had screamed and the rain had beaten against the windows, so that even here in the heart of great, hand-made London we were forced to raise our minds for the instant from the routine of life, and to recognize the presence of those great elemental forces which shriek at mankind through the bars of his civilization, like untamed beasts in a cage. As evening drew in the storm grew louder and louder, and the wind cried and sobbed like a child in the chimney. Sherlock Holmes sat moodily at one side of the fireplace cross-indexing his records of crime, whilst I at the other was deep in one of Clark Russell's fine sea stories, until the howl of the gale from without seemed to blend with the text, and the splash of the rain to lengthen out into the long swash of the sea waves. My wife was on a visit to her aunt's, and for a few days I was a dweller once more in my old quarters at Baker Street.

" Why," said I, glancing up at my companion, " that was surely the bell ? Who could come to-night ? Some friend of yours, perhaps ? "

" Except yourself I have none," he answered. " I do not encourage visitors."

" A client, then ? "

" If so, it is a serious case. Nothing less would bring a man out on such a day, and at such an hour. But I take it that it is more likely to be some crony of the landlady's."

Sherlock Holmes was wrong in his conjecture, however, for there came a step in the passage, and a tapping at the door. He stretched out his long arm to turn the lamp away from himself and towards the vacant chair upon which a new-comer must sit. " Come in ! " said he.

The man who entered was young, some two-and-twenty at the outside, well groomed and trimly clad, with something of refinement and delicacy in his bearing. The streaming umbrella which he held in his hand, and his long shining waterproof told of the fierce weather through which he had come. He looked about him anxiously in the glare of the lamp, and I could see that his face was pale and his eyes heavy, like those of a man who is weighed down with some great anxiety.

" I owe you an apology," he said, raising his golden pince-nez to his eyes. " I trust that I am not intruding. I fear that I have brought some traces of the storm and the rain into your snug chamber."

" Give me your coat and umbrella," said Holmes. " They may rest here on the hook, and will be dry presently. You have come up from the south-west, I see."

" Yes, from Horsham."

" That clay and chalk mixture which I see upon your toe-caps is quite distinctive."

" I have come for advice."

" That is easily got."

" And help."

" That is not always so easy."

" I have heard of you, Mr. Holmes. I heard from Major Prendergast how you saved him in the Tankerville Club Scandal."

" Ah, of course. He was wrongfully accused of cheating at cards."

" He said that you could solve anything."

" He said too much."

" That you are never beaten."

" I have been beaten four times—three times by men and once by a woman."

" But what is that compared with the number of your successes ? "

" It is true that I have been generally successful."

" Then you may be so with me."

" I beg that you will draw your chair up to the fire, and favour me with some details as to your case."

" It is no ordinary one."

" None of those which come to me are. I am the last court of appeal."

" And yet I question, sir, whether, in all your experience, you have ever listened to a more mysterious and inexplicable chain of events than those which have happened in my own family."

"You fill me with interest," said Holmes. "Pray give us the essential facts from the commencement, and I can afterwards question you as to those details which seem to me to be most important."

The young man pulled his chair up, and pushed his wet feet out towards the blaze.

"My name," said he, "is John Openshaw, but my own affairs have, so far as I can understand it, little to do with this awful business. It is a hereditary matter, so in order to give you an idea of the facts, I must go back to the commencement of the affair.

"You must know that my grandfather had two sons— my uncle Elias and my father Joseph. My father had a small factory at Coventry, which he enlarged at the time of the invention of bicycling. He was the patentee of the Openshaw unbreakable tire, and his business met with such success that he was able to sell it, and to retire upon a handsome competence.

"My uncle Elias emigrated to America when he was a young man, and became a planter in Florida, where he was reported to have done very well. At the time of the war he fought in Jackson's army, and afterwards under Hood, where he rose to be a colonel. When Lee laid down his arms my uncle returned to his plantation, where he remained for three or four years. About 1869 or 1870 he came back to Europe, and took a small estate in Sussex, near Horsham. He had made a very considerable fortune in the States, and his reason for leaving them was his aversion to the negroes, and his dislike of the Republican policy in extending the franchise to them. He was a singular man, fierce and quick-tempered, very foul-mouthed when he was angry, and of a most retiring disposition. During all the years that he lived at Horsham I doubt if ever he set foot in the town. He had a garden and two or three fields round his house, and there he would take his exercise, though very often for weeks on end he would never leave his room. He drank a great deal of brandy, and smoked very heavily, but he would see no society, and did not want any friends, not even his own brother.

" He didn't mind me, in fact he took a fancy to me, for at the time when he saw me first I was a youngster of twelve or so. That would be in the year 1878, after he had been eight or nine years in England. He begged my father to let me live with him, and he was very kind to me in his way. When he was sober he used to be fond of playing backgammon and draughts with me, and he would make me his representative both with the servants and with the tradespeople, so that by the time that I was sixteen I was quite master of the house. I kept all the keys, and could go where I liked and do what I liked, so long as I did not disturb him in his privacy. There was one singular exception, however, for he had a single room, a lumber-room up among the attics, which was invariably locked, and which he would never permit either me or anyone else to enter. With a boy's curiosity I have peeped through the keyhole, but I was never able to see more than such a collection of old trunks and bundles as would be expected in such a room.

" One day—it was in March, 1883—a letter with a foreign stamp lay upon the table in front of the Colonel's plate. It was not a common thing for him to receive letters, for his bills were all paid in ready money, and he had no friends of any sort. ' From India ! ' said he, as he took it up, ' Pondicherry postmark ! What can this be ? ' Opening it hurriedly, out there jumped five little dried orange pips, which pattered down upon his plate. I began to laugh at this, but the laugh was struck from my lips at the sight of his face. His lip had fallen, his eyes were protruding, his skin the colour of putty, and he glared at the envelope which he still held in his trembling hand. ' K. K. K.,' he shrieked, and then : ' My God, my God, my sins have overtaken me.'

" ' What is it, uncle ? ' I cried.

" ' Death,' said he, and rising from the table he retired to his room, leaving me palpitating with horror. I took up the envelope, and saw scrawled in red ink upon the inner flap, just above the gum, the letter K three times repeated. There was nothing else save the five dried pips. What could be the reason of his overpowering terror ? I left the breakfast-table, and as I ascended the stairs I met him coming down with an old rusty key, which must have belonged to the attic, in one hand, and a small brass box, like a cash box, in the other.

" ' They may do what they like, but I'll checkmate them still,' said he, with an oath. ' Tell Mary that I shall want a fire in my room to-day, and send down to Fordham, the Horsham lawyer.'

" I did as he ordered, and when the lawyer arrived I was asked to step up to the room. The fire was burning brightly, and in the grate there was a mass of black, fluffy ashes, as of burned paper, while the brass box stood open and empty beside it. As I glanced at the box I noticed, with a start, that upon the lid were printed the treble K which I had read in the morning upon the envelope.

" ' I wish you, John,' said my uncle, ' to witness my will. I leave my estate, with all its advantages and all its disadvantages to my brother, your father, whence it will, no doubt, descend to you. If you can enjoy it in peace, well and good ! If you find you cannot, take my advice, my boy, and leave it to your deadliest enemy. I am sorry to give you such a two-edged thing, but I can't say what turn things are going to take. Kindly sign the paper where Mr. Fordham shows you.'

" I signed the paper as directed, and the lawyer took it away with him. The singular incident made, as you may think, the deepest impression upon me, and I pondered over it, and turned it every way in my mind without being able to make anything of it. Yet I could not shake off the vague feeling of dread which it left behind it, though the sensation grew less keen as the weeks passed, and nothing happened to disturb the usual routine of our lives. I could see a change in my uncle, however. He drank more than ever, and he was less inclined for any sort of society. Most of his time he would spend in his room, with the door locked upon the inside, but sometimes he would emerge in a sort of drunken frenzy and would burst out of the house and tear about the garden with a revolver in his hand, screaming out that he was afraid of no man, and that he was not to be cooped up, like a sheep in a pen, by man or devil. When these hot fits were over, however, he would rush tumultuously in at the door, and lock and bar it behind him, like a man who can brazen it out no longer against the terror which lies at the roots of his soul. At such times I have seen his face even on a cold day, glisten with moisture as though it were new raised from a basin.

" Well, to come to an end of the matter, Mr. Holmes, and not to abuse your patience, there came a night when he made one of those drunken sallies from which he never came back. We found him, when we went to search for him, face downwards in a little green-scummed pool, which lay at the foot of the garden. There was no sign of any violence, and the water was but two feet deep, so that the jury, having regard to his known eccentricity, brought in a verdict of suicide. But I, who knew how he winced from the very thought of death, had much ado to persuade myself that he had gone out of his way to meet it. The matter passed, however, and my father entered into possession of the estate, and of some fourteen thousand pounds, which lay to his credit at the bank."

" One moment," Holmes interposed. " Your statement is, I foresee, one of the most remarkable to which I have ever listened. Let me have the date of the reception by your uncle of the letter, and the date of his supposed suicide."

" The letter arrived on March the 10th, 1883. His death was seven weeks later, upon the night of the 2nd of May."

" Thank you. Pray proceed."

" When my father took over the Horsham property, he, at my request, made a careful examination of the attic, which had been always locked up. We found the brass box there, although its contents had been destroyed. On the inside of the cover was a paper label, with the initials K. K. K. repeated upon it, and ' Letters, memoranda, receipts and a register ' written beneath. These, we presume, indicated the nature of the papers which had been destroyed by Colonel Openshaw. For the rest, there was nothing of much importance in the attic, save a great many scattered papers and notebooks bearing upon my uncle's life in America. Some of them were of the war time, and showed that he had done his duty well, and had borne the repute of being a brave soldier. Others were of a date during the reconstruction of the Southern States, and were mostly concerned with politics, for he had evidently taken a strong part in opposing the carpet-bag politicians who had been sent down from the North.

" Well, it was the beginning of '84, when my father came to live at Horsham, and all went as well as possible with us until the January of '85. On the fourth day after the New Year I heard my father give a sharp cry of surprise as we sat together at the breakfast-table. There he was, sitting with a newly opened envelope in one hand and five dried orange pips in the outstretched palm of the other one. He had always laughed at what he called my cock-and-bull story about the Colonel, but he looked very puzzled and scared now that the same thing had come upon himself.

" ' Why, what on earth does this mean, John ? ' he stammered.

" My heart had turned to lead. ' It is K. K. K.,' said I.

" He looked inside the envelope. ' So it is,' he cried. ' Here are the very letters. But what is this written above them ? '

" ' Put the papers on the sundial,' I read, peeping over his shoulder.

" ' What papers ? What sundial ? ' he asked.

" ' The sundial in the garden. There is no other,' said I ; ' but the papers must be those that are destroyed.'

" ' Pooh ! ' said he, gripping hard at his courage. ' We are in a civilized land here, and we can't have tomfoolery of this kind. Where does the thing come from ? '

" ' From Dundee,' I answered, glancing at the post-mark.

" ' Some preposterous practical joke,' said he. ' What have I to do with sundials and papers ? I shall take no notice of such nonsense.'

" ' I should certainly speak to the police,' I said.

" ' And be laughed at for my pains. Nothing of the sort.'

" ' Then let me do so.'

" ' No, I forbid you. I won't have a fuss made over such nonsense.'

" It was in vain to argue with him, for he was a very obstinate man. I went about, however, with a heart which was full of forebodings.

" On the third day after the coming of the letter my father went from home to visit an old friend of his, Major Freebody, who is in command of one of the forts upon Portsdown Hill. I was glad that he should go, for it seemed to me that he was farther from danger when he was away from home. In that, however, I was in error. Upon the second day of his absence I received a telegram from the Major, imploring me to come at once. My father had fallen over one of the deep chalk-pits which abound in the neighbourhood, and was lying senseless, with a shattered skull. I hurried to him, but he passed away without having ever recovered his consciousness. He had, as it appears, been returning from Fareham in the twilight, and as the country was unknown to him, and the chalk-pit unfenced, the jury had no hesitation in bringing in a verdict of ' Death from accidental causes.' Carefully as I examined every fact connected with his death, I was unable to find anything which could suggest the idea of murder. There were no signs of violence, no footmarks, no robbery, no record of strangers having been seen upon the roads And yet I need not tell you that my mind was far from at ease, and that I was wellnigh certain that some foul plot had been woven round him.

" In this sinister way I came into my inheritance. You will ask me why I did not dispose of it ? I answer because I was well convinced that our troubles were in some way dependent upon an incident in my uncle's life, and that the danger would be as pressing in one house as in another.

" It was in January, '85, that my poor father met his end, and two years and eight months have elapsed since then. During that time I have lived happily at Horsham, and I had begun to hope that this curse had passed away from the family, and that it had ended with the last generation. I had begun to take comfort too soon, however ; yesterday morning the blow fell in the very shape in which it had come upon my father."

The young man took from his waistcoat a crumpled envelope, and, turning to the table, he shook out upon it five little dried orange pips.

" This is the envelope," he continued. " The post-mark is London—eastern division. Within are the very words which were upon my father's last message. ' K. K. K.' ; and then ' Put the papers on the sundial.' "

" What have you done ? " asked Holmes.

" Nothing."

" Nothing ? "

" To tell the truth "—he sank his face into his thin, white hands—" I have felt helpless. I have felt like one of those poor rabbits when the snake is writhing towards it. I seem to be in the grasp of some resistless, inexorable evil, which no foresight and no precautions can guard against."

" Tut ! Tut ! " cried Sherlock Holmes. " You must act, man, or you are lost. Nothing but energy can save you. This is no time for despair."

" I have seen the police."

" Ah ? "

" But they listened to my story with a smile. I am convinced that the inspector has formed the opinion that the letters are all practical jokes, and that the deaths of my relations were really accidents, as the jury stated, and were not to be connected with the warnings."

Holmes shook his clenched hands in the air. " Incredible imbecility ! " he cried.

" They have, however, allowed me a policeman, who may remain in the house with me."

" Has he come with you to-night ? "

" No. His orders were to stay in the house."

Again Holmes raved in the air.

" Why did you come to me ? " he said ; " and, above all, why did you not come at once ? "

" I did not know. It was only to-day that I spoke to Major Prendergast about my trouble, and was advised by him to come to you."

" It is really two days since you had the letter. We should have acted before this. You have no further evidence, I suppose, than that which you have placed before us—no suggestive detail which might help us."

" There is one thing," said John Openshaw. He rummaged in his coat pocket, and drawing out a piece of discoloured, blue-tinted paper, he laid it out upon the table. " I have some remembrance," said he, " that on the day when my uncle burned the papers I observed that the small, unburned margins which lay amid the ashes were of this particular colour. I found this single sheet upon the floor of his room, and I am inclined to think that it may be one of the papers which had, perhaps, fluttered out from among the others, and in that way have escaped destruction. Beyond the mention of pips, I do not see that it helps us much. I think myself that it is a page from some private diary. The writing is undoubtedly my uncle's."

Holmes moved the lamp, and we both bent over the sheet of paper, which showed by its ragged edge that it had indeed been torn from a book. It was headed " March, 1869," and beneath were the following enigmatical notices :

" 4th. Hudson came. Same old platform.

" 7th. Set the pips on McCauley, Paramore, and Swain of St. Augustine.

" 9th. McCauley cleared.

" 10th. John Swain cleared.

" 12th. Visited Paramore. All well."

" Thank you ! " said Holmes, folding up the paper and returning it to our visitor. " And now you must on no account lose another instant. We cannot spare time even to discuss what you have told me. You must get home instantly, and act."

" What shall I do ? "

" There is but one thing to do. It must be done at once. You must put this piece of paper which you have shown us into the brass box which you have described. You must also put in a note to say that all the other papers were burned by your uncle, and that this is the only one which remains. You must assert that in such words as will carry conviction with them. Having done this, you must at once put the box out upon the sundial, as directed. Do you understand ? "

" Entirely."

" Do not think of revenge, or anything of the sort, at present. I think that we may gain that by means of the law ; but we have our web to weave, while theirs is already woven. The first consideration is to remove the pressing danger which threatens you. The second is to clear up the mystery, and to punish the guilty parties."

" I thank you," said the young man, rising, and pulling on his overcoat. " You have given me fresh life and hope. I shall certainly do as you advise."

" Do not lose an instant. And, above all, take care of yourself in the meanwhile, for I do not think that there can be a doubt that you are threatened by a very real and imminent danger. How do you go back ? "

" By train from Waterloo."

" It is not yet nine. The streets will be crowded, so I

trust that you may be in safety. And yet you cannot guard yourself too closely."

" I am armed."

" That is well. To-morrow I shall set to work upon your case."

" I shall see you at Horsham, then ? "

" No, your secret lies in London. It is there that I shall seek it."

" Then I shall call upon you in a day, or in two days, with news as to the box and the papers. I shall take your advice in every particular." He shook hands with us, and took his leave. Outside the wind still screamed, and the rain splashed and pattered against the windows. This strange, wild story seemed to have come to us from amid the mad elements—blown in upon us like a sheet of seaweed in a gale—and now to have been reabsorbed by them once more.

Sherlock Holmes sat for some time in silence with his head sunk forward, and his eyes bent upon the red glow of the fire. Then he lit his pipe, and leaning back in his chair he watched the blue smoke rings as they chased each other up to the ceiling.

" I think, Watson," he remarked at last, " that of all our cases we have had none more fantastic than this."

" Save, perhaps, the Sign of Four."

" Well, yes. Save, perhaps, that. And yet this John Openshaw seems to me to be walking amid even greater perils than did the Sholtos."

" But have you," I asked, " formed any definite conception as to what these perils are ? "

" There can be no question as to their nature," he answered.

" Then what are they ? Who is this K. K. K., and why does he pursue this unhappy family ? "

Sherlock Holmes closed his eyes, and placed his elbows upon the arms of his chair, with his finger-tips together. " The ideal reasoner," he remarked, " would, when he has once been shown a single fact in all its bearings, deduce from it not only all the chain of events which led up to it, but also all the results which would follow from it. As Cuvier could correctly describe a whole animal by the contemplation of a single bone, so the observer who has thoroughly understood one link in a series of incidents, should be able accurately to state all the other ones, both before and after. We have not yet grasped the results which the reason alone can attain to. Problems may be solved in the study which have baffled all those who have sought a solution by the aid of their senses. To carry the art, however, to its highest pitch, it is necessary that the reasoner should be able to utilize all the facts which have come to his knowledge, and this in itself implies, as you will readily see, a possession of all knowledge, which, even in these days of free education and encyclopædias, is a somewhat rare accomplishment. It is not so impossible, however, that a man should possess all knowledge which is likely to be useful to him in his work, and this I have endeavoured in my case to do. If I remember rightly, you on one occasion, in the early days of our friendship, defined my limits in a very precise fashion."

" Yes," I answered, laughing. " It was a singular document. Philosophy, astronomy, and politics were marked at zero, I remember. Botany variable, geology profound as regards the mudstains from any region within fifty miles of town, chemistry eccentric, anatomy unsystematic, sensational literature and crime records unique, violin player, boxer, swordsman, lawyer, and self-poisoner by cocaine and tobacco. Those, I think, were the main points of my analysis."

Holmes grinned at the last item. " Well," he said, " I say now, as I said then, that a man should keep his little brain attic stocked with all the furniture that he is likely to use, and the rest he can put away in the lumber-room of his library, where he can get it if he wants it. Now, for such a case as the one which has been submitted to us to-night, we need certainly to muster all our resources. Kindly hand me down the letter K of the American Encyclopædia which stands upon the shelf beside you. Thank you. Now let us consider the situation, and see what may be deduced from it. In the first place, we may start with a strong presumption that Colonel Openshaw had some very strong reason for leaving America. Men at his time of life do not change all their habits, and exchange willingly the charming climate of Florida for the lonely life of an English provincial town. His extreme love of solitude in England suggests the idea that he was in fear of someone or something, so we may assume as a working hypothesis that it was fear of someone or something which drove him from America. As to what it was he feared, we can only deduce that by considering the formidable letters which were received by himself and his successors. Did you remark the postmarks of those letters ? "

" The first was from Pondicherry, the second from Dundee, and the third from London."

" From East London. What do you deduce from that ? "

" They are all seaports. That the writer was on board a ship."

" Excellent. We have already a clue. There can be no doubt that the probability—the strong probability—is that the writer was on board of a ship. And now let us consider another point. In the case of Pondicherry seven weeks elapsed between the threat and its fulfilment, in Dundee it was only some three or four days. Does that suggest anything ? "

" A greater distance to travel."

" But the letter had also a greater distance to come."

" Then I do not see the point."

" There is at least a presumption that the vessel in which the man or men are is a sailing ship. It looks as if they always sent their singular warning or token before them when starting upon their mission. You see how quickly the deed followed the sign when it came from Dundee. If they had come from Pondicherry in a steamer they would have arrived almost as soon as their letter. But as a matter of fact seven weeks elapsed. I think that those seven weeks represented the difference between the mail boat which brought the letter, and the sailing vessel which brought the writer."

" It is possible."

" More than that. It is probable. And now you see the deadly urgency of this new case, and why I urged young Openshaw to caution. The blow has always fallen at the end of the time which it would take the senders to travel the distance. But this one comes from London, and therefore we cannot count upon delay."

" Good God ! " I cried. " What can it mean, this relentless persecution ? "

" The papers which Openshaw carried are obviously of vital importance to the person or persons in the sailing ship. I think that it is quite clear that there must be more than one of them. A single man could not have carried out two deaths in such a way as to deceive a coroner's jury. There must have been several in it, and they must have been men of resource and determination. Their papers they mean to have, be the holder of them who it may. In this way you see K. K. K. ceases to be the initials of an individual, and becomes the badge of a society."

" But of what society ? "

" Have you never—" said Sherlock Holmes, bending forward and sinking his voice—" have you never heard of the Ku Klux Klan ? "

" I never have."

Holmes turned over the leaves of the book upon his knee. " Here it is," said he presently, " ' Ku Klux Klan. A name derived from a fanciful resemblance to the sound produced by cocking a rifle. This terrible secret society was formed by some ex-Confederate soldiers in the Southern States after the Civil War, and it rapidly formed local branches in different parts of the country, notably in Tennessee, Louisiana, the Carolinas, Georgia, and Florida. Its power was used for political purposes, principally for the terrorizing of the negro voters, and the murdering or driving from the country of those who were opposed to its views. Its outrages were usually preceded by a warning sent to the marked man in some fantastic but generally recognized shape—a sprig of oak leaves in some parts, melon seeds or orange pips in others. On receiving this the victim might either openly abjure his former ways, or might fly from the country. If he braved the matter out, death would unfailingly come upon him, and usually in some strange and unforeseen manner. So perfect was the organization of the society, and so systematic its methods, that there is hardly a case upon record where any man succeeded in braving it with impunity, or in which any of its outrages were traced home to the perpetrators. For some years the organization flourished, in spite of the efforts of the United States Government, and of the better classes of the community in the South. Eventually, in the year 1869, the movement rather suddenly collapsed, although there have been sporadic outbreaks of the same sort since that date.'

" You will observe," said Holmes, laying down the volume, " that the sudden breaking up of the society was coincident with the disappearance of Openshaw from America with their papers. It may well have been cause and effect. It is no wonder that he and his family have some of the more implacable spirits upon their track. You can understand that this register and diary may implicate some of the first men in the South, and that there may be many who will not sleep easy at night until it is recovered."

" Then the page which we have seen——"

" Is such as we might expect. It ran, if I remember right, ' sent the pips to A, B, and C '—that is, sent the society's warning to them. Then there are successive entries that A and B cleared, or left the country, and finally that C was visited, with, I fear, a sinister result for C. Well, I think, Doctor, that we may let some light into this dark place, and I believe that the only chance young Openshaw has in the meantime is to do what I have told him. There is nothing more to be said or to be done to-night, so hand me over my violin and let us try to forget for half an hour the miserable weather, and the still more miserable ways of our fellow-men."

It had cleared in the morning, and the sun was shining with a subdued brightness through the dim veil which hangs over the great city. Sherlock Holmes was already at breakfast when I came down.

" You will excuse me for not waiting for you," said he ; " I have, I foresee, a very busy day before me in looking into this case of young Openshaw's."

" What steps will you take ? " I asked.

" It will very much depend upon the results of my first inquiries. I may have to go down to Horsham after all."

" You will not go there first ? "

" No, I shall commence with the City. Just ring the bell, and the maid will bring up your coffee."

As I waited, I lifted the unopened newspaper from the table and glanced my eye over it. It rested upon a heading which sent a chill to my heart.

" Holmes," I cried, " you are too late."

" Ah ! " said he, laying down his cup, " I feared as much. How was it done ? " He spoke calmly, but I could see that he was deeply moved.

" My eye caught the name of Openshaw, and the heading ' Tragedy near Waterloo Bridge.' Here is the account : ' Between nine and ten last night Police-constable Cook, of the H Division, on duty near Waterloo Bridge, heard a cry for help and a splash in the water. The night, however, was extremely dark and stormy, so that, in spite of the help of several passers-by, it was quite impossible to effect a rescue. The alarm, however, was given, and, by the aid of the water police, the body was eventually recovered. It proved to be that of a young gentleman whose name, as it appears from an envelope which was found in his pocket, was John Openshaw, and whose residence is near Horsham. It is conjectured that he may have been hurrying down to catch the last train from Waterloo Station, and that in his haste and the extreme darkness, he missed his path, and walked over the edge of one of the small landing-places for river steamboats. The body exhibited no traces of violence, and there can be no doubt that the deceased had been the victim of an unfortunate accident, which should have the effect of calling the attention of the authorities to the condition of the riverside landing-stages.' "

We sat in silence for some minutes, Holmes more depressed and shaken than I had ever seen him.

" That hurts my pride, Watson," he said at last. " It is a petty feeling, no doubt, but it hurts my pride. It becomes a personal matter with me now, and, if God sends me health, I shall set my hand upon this gang. That he should come to me for help, and that I should send him away to his death—— ! " He sprang from his chair, and paced about the room in uncontrollable agitation, with a flush upon his sallow cheeks, and a nervous clasping and unclasping of his long, thin hands.

" They must be cunning devils," he exclaimed at last. " How could they have decoyed him down there ? The Embankment is not on the direct line to the station. The bridge, no doubt, was too crowded, even on such a night, for their purpose. Well, Watson, we shall see who will win in the long run. I am going out now ! "

" To the police ? "

" No ; I shall be my own police. When I have spun the web they may take the flies, but not before."

All day I was engaged in my professional work, and it was late in the evening before I returned to Baker Street. Sherlock Holmes had not come back yet. It was nearly ten o'clock before he entered, looking pale and worn. He walked up to the sideboard, and, tearing a piece from the loaf, he devoured it voraciously, washing it down with a long draught of water.

" You are hungry," I remarked.

" Starving. It had escaped my memory. I have had nothing since breakfast."

" Nothing ? "

" Not a bite. I had no time to think of it."

" And how have you succeeded ? "

" Well."

" You have a clue ? "

" I have them in the hollow of my hand. Young Openshaw shall not remain long unavenged. Why, Watson, let us put their own devilish trade-mark upon them. It is well thought of ! "

" What do you mean ? "

He took an orange from the cupboard, and tearing it to pieces, he squeezed out the pips upon the table. Of these he took five, and thrust them into an envelope. On the inside of the flap he wrote, " S.H. for J.C." Then he sealed it and addressed it to " Captain James Calhoun, Barque *Lone Star*, Savannah, Georgia."

" That will await him when he enters port," said he, chuckling. " It may give him a sleepless night. He will find it as sure a precursor of his fate as Openshaw did before him."

" And who is this Captain Calhoun ? "

" The leader of the gang. I shall have the others, but he first."

" How did you trace it, then ? "

He took a large sheet of paper from his pocket, all covered with dates and names.

" I have spent the whole day," said he, " over Lloyd's registers and the files of old papers, following the future career of every vessel which touched at Pondicherry in January and in February in '83. There were thirty-six ships of fair tonnage which were reported there during those months. Of these, the *Lone Star* instantly attracted my attention, since, although it was reported as having cleared from London, the name is that which is given to one of the States of the Union."

" Texas, I think."

" I was not and am not sure which ; but I knew that the ship must have an American origin."

" What then ? "

" I searched the Dundee records, and when I found that the barque *Lone Star* was there in January, '85, my suspicion became a certainty. I then inquired as to vessels which lay at present in the port of London."

" Yes ? "

" The *Lone Star* had arrived here last week. I went down to the Albert dock, and found that she had been taken down the river by the early tide this morning, homeward bound to Savannah. I wired to Gravesend, and learned that she had passed some time ago, and as the wind is easterly, I have no doubt that she is now past the Goodwins, and not very far from the Isle of Wight."

" What will you do, then ? "

" Oh, I have my hand upon him. He and the two mates are, as I learn, the only native-born Americans in the ship. The others are Finns and Germans. I also know that they were all three away from the ship last night. I had it from the stevedore, who has been loading their cargo. By the time their sailing ship reaches Savannah the mail boat will have carried this letter, and the cable will have informed the police of Savannah that these three gentlemen are badly wanted here upon a charge of murder."

There is ever a flaw, however, in the best laid of human plans, and the murderers of John Openshaw were never to receive the orange pips which would show them that another, as cunning and as resolute as themselves, was upon their track. Very long and severe were the equinoctial gales that year. We waited long for news of the *Lone Star* of Savannah, but none ever reached us. We did at last hear that somewhere far out in the Atlantic a shattered sternpost of a boat was seen swinging in the trough of a wave, with the letters " L. S." carved upon it, and that is all which we shall ever know of the fate of the *Lone Star*.

6. *The Man with the Twisted Lip*

ISA WHITNEY, brother of the late Elias Whitney, D.D., Principal of the Theological College of St. George's, was much addicted to opium. The habit grew upon him, as I understand, from some foolish freak when he was at college, for having read De Quincey's description of his dreams and sensations, he had drenched his tobacco with laudanum in an attempt to produce the same effects. He found, as so many more have done, that the practice is easier to attain than to get rid of, and for many years he continued to be a slave to the drug, an object of mingled horror and pity to his friends and relatives. I can see him now, with yellow, pasty face, drooping lids and pin-point pupils, all huddled in a chair, the wreck and ruin of a noble man.

One night—it was in June, '89—there came a ring to my bell, about the hour when a man gives his first yawn, and glances at the clock. I sat up in my chair, and my wife laid her needlework down in her lap and made a little face of disappointment.

" A patient ! " said she. " You'll have to go out."

I groaned, for I was newly come back from a weary day.

We heard the door open, a few hurried words, and then quick steps upon the linoleum. Our own door flew open, and a lady, clad in some dark-coloured stuff with a black veil, entered the room.

" You will excuse my calling so late," she began, and then, suddenly losing her self-control, she ran forward, threw her arms about my wife's neck, and sobbed upon her shoulder. " Oh ! I'm in such trouble ! " she cried ; " I do so want a little help."

" Why," said my wife, pulling up her veil, " it is Kate Whitney. How you startled me, Kate ! I had not an idea who you were when you came in."

" I didn't know what to do, so I came straight to you."

That was always the way. Folk who were in grief came to my wife like birds to a lighthouse.

" It was very sweet of you to come. Now, you must have some wine and water, and sit here comfortably and tell us all about it. Or should you rather that I sent James off to bed ? "

" Oh, no, no. I want the Doctor's advice and help too. It's about Isa. He has not been home for two days. I am so frightened about him ! "

It was not the first time that she had spoken to us of her husband's trouble, to me as a doctor, to my wife as an old friend and school companion. We soothed and comforted her by such words as we could find. Did she know where her husband was ? Was it possible that we could bring him back to her ?

It seemed that it was. She had the surest information that of late he had, when the fit was on him, made use of an opium den in the furthest east of the City. Hitherto his orgies had always been confined to one day, and he had come back, twitching and shattered, in the evening. But now the spell had been upon him eight-and-forty hours, and he lay there, doubtless, among the dregs of the docks, breathing in the poison or sleeping off the effects. There he was to be found, she was sure of it, at the " Bar of Gold," in Upper Swandam Lane. But what was she to do ? How could she, a young and timid woman, make her way into such a place, and pluck her husband out from among the ruffians who surrounded him ?

There was the case, and of course there was but one way out of it. Might I not escort her to this place ? And, then, as a second thought, why should she come at all ? I was Isa Whitney's medical adviser, and as such I had influence over him. I could manage it better if I were alone. I promised her on my word that I would send him home in a cab within two hours if he were indeed at the address which she had given me. And so in ten minutes I had left my arm-chair and cheery sitting-room behind me, and was speeding eastward in a hansom on a strange errand, as it seemed to me at the time, though the future only could show how strange it was to be.

But there was no great difficulty in the first stage of my adventure. Upper Swandam Lane is a vile alley lurking behind the high wharves which line the north side of the river to the east of London Bridge. Between a slop shop and a gin shop, approached by a steep flight of steps leading down to a black gap like the mouth of a cave, I found the den of which I was in search. Ordering my cab to wait, I passed down the steps, worn hollow in the centre by the ceaseless tread of drunken feet, and by the light of a flickering oil lamp above the door I found the latch and made my way into a long, low room, thick and heavy with the brown opium smoke, and terraced with wooden berths, like the forecastle of an emigrant ship.

Through the gloom one could dimly catch a glimpse of bodies lying in strange fantastic poses, bowed shoulders, bent knees, heads thrown back and chins pointing upwards, with here and there a dark, lack-lustre eye turned upon the new-comer. Out of the black shadows there glimmered little red circles of light, now bright, now faint, as the burning poison waxed or waned in the bowls of the metal pipes. The most lay silent, but some muttered to themselves, and others talked together in a strange, low, monotonous voice, their conversation coming in gushes, and then suddenly tailing off into silence, each mumbling out his own thoughts, and paying little heed to the words of his neighbour. At the further end was a small brazier of burning charcoal, beside which on a three-legged wooden stool there sat a tall, thin old man, with his jaw resting upon his two fists, and his elbows upon his knees, staring into the fire.

As I entered, a sallow Malay attendant had hurried up with a pipe for me and a supply of the drug, beckoning me to an empty berth.

"Thank you, I have not come to stay," said I. "There is a friend of mine here, Mr. Isa Whitney, and I wish to speak with him."

There was a movement and an exclamation from my right, and, peering through the gloom, I saw Whitney, pale, haggard, and unkempt, staring out at me.

"My God! It's Watson," said he. He was in a pitiable state of reaction, with every nerve in a twitter. "I say, Watson, what o'clock is it?"

"Nearly eleven."

"Of what day?"

"Of Friday, June 19."

"Good heavens! I thought it was Wednesday. It *is* Wednesday. What d'you want to frighten a chap for?" He sank his face on to his arms, and began to sob in a high treble key.

"I tell you that it is Friday, man. Your wife has been waiting this two days for you. You should be ashamed of yourself!"

"So I am. But you've got mixed, Watson, for I have only been here a few hours, three pipes, four pipes—I forget how many. But I'll go home with you. I wouldn't frighten Kate—poor little Kate. Give me your hand! Have you a cab?"

"Yes, I have one waiting."

"Then I shall go in it. But I must owe something. Find what I owe, Watson. I am all off colour. I can do nothing for myself."

I walked down the narrow passage between the double row of sleepers, holding my breath to keep out the vile, stupefying fumes of the drug, and looking about for the manager. As I passed the tall man who sat by the brazier I felt a sudden pluck at my skirt, and a low voice whispered, "Walk past me, and then look back at me." The words fell quite distinctly upon my ear. I glanced down. They could only have come from the old man at my side, and yet he sat now as absorbed as ever, very thin, very wrinkled, bent with age, an opium pipe dangling down from between his knees, as though it had dropped in sheer lassitude from his fingers. I took two steps forward and looked back. It took all my self-control to prevent me from breaking out into a cry of astonishment. He had turned his back so that none could see him but I. His form had filled out, his wrinkles were gone, the dull eyes had regained their fire, and there, sitting by the fire, and grinning at my surprise, was none other than Sherlock Holmes. He made a slight motion to me to approach him, and instantly, as he turned his face half round to the company once more, subsided into a doddering, loose-lipped senility.

" Holmes ! " I whispered, " what on earth are you doing in this den ? "

" As low as you can," he answered, " I have excellent ears. If you would have the great kindness to get rid of that sottish friend of yours, I should be exceedingly glad to have a little talk with you."

" I have a cab outside."

" Then pray send him home in it. You may safely trust him, for he appears to be too limp to get into any mischief. I should recommend you also to send a note by the cabman to your wife to say that you have thrown in your lot with me. If you will wait outside, I shall be with you in five minutes."

It was difficult to refuse any of Sherlock Holmes' requests, for they were always so exceedingly definite, and put forward with such an air of mastery. I felt, however, that when Whitney was once confined in the cab, my mission was practically accomplished ; and for the rest, I could not wish anything better than to be associated with my friend in one of those singular adventures which were the normal condition of his existence. In a few minutes I had written my note, paid Whitney's bill, led him out to the cab, and seen him driven through the darkness. In a very short time a decrepit figure had emerged from the opium den, and I was walking down the street with Sherlock Holmes. For two streets he shuffled along with a bent back and an uncertain foot. Then, glancing quickly round, he straightened himself out and burst into a hearty fit of laughter.

" I suppose, Watson," said he, " that you imagine that I have added opium-smoking to cocaine injections and all the other little weaknesses on which you have favoured me with your medical views."

" I was certainly surprised to find you there."

" But not more so than I to find you."

" I came to find a friend."

" And I to find an enemy ! "

" An enemy ? "

" Yes, one of my natural enemies, or, shall I say, my natural prey. Briefly, Watson, I am in the midst of a very remarkable inquiry, and I have hoped to find a clue in the incoherent ramblings of these sots, as I have done before now. Had I been recognized in that den my life would not have been worth an hour's purchase, for I have used it before now for my own purposes, and the rascally Lascar who runs it has sworn vengeance upon me. There is a trap-door at the back of that building, near the corner of Paul's Wharf, which could tell some strange tales of what has passed through it upon the moonless nights."

" What ! You do not mean bodies ? "

" Aye, bodies, Watson. We should be rich men if we had a thousand pounds for every poor devil who has been done to death in that den. It is the vilest murder-trap on the whole river-side, and I fear Neville St. Clair has entered it never to leave it more. But our trap should be here ! " He put his two forefingers between his teeth and whistled shrilly, a signal which was answered by a similar whistle from the distance, followed shortly by the rattle of wheels and the clink of horse's hoofs.

" Now, Watson," said Holmes, as a tall dog-cart dashed up through the gloom, throwing out two golden tunnels of yellow light from its side-lanterns, " you'll come with me, won't you ? "

" If I can be of use."

" Oh, a trusty comrade is always of use. And a chronicler still more so. My room at the Cedars is a double-bedded one."

" The Cedars ? "

" Yes ; that is Mr. St. Clair's house. I am staying there while I conduct the inquiry."

" Where is it, then ? "

" Near Lee, in Kent. We have a seven-mile drive before us."

" But I am all in the dark."

" Of course you are. You'll know all about it presently. Jump up here ! All right, John, we shall not need you. Here's half-a-crown. Look out for me to-morrow about eleven. Give her her head ! So long, then ! "

He flicked the horse with his whip, and we dashed away through the endless succession of sombre and deserted streets, which widened gradually, until we were flying across a broad balustraded bridge, with the murky river flowing sluggishly beneath us. Beyond lay another broad wilderness of bricks and mortar, its silence broken only by the heavy, regular footfall of the policeman, or the songs and shouts of some belated party of revellers. A dull wrack was drifting slowly across the sky, and a star or two twinkled dimly here and there through the rifts of the clouds. Holmes drove in silence, with his head sunk upon his breast, and the air of a man who is lost in thought, whilst I sat beside him curious to learn what this new quest might be which seemed to tax his powers so sorely, and yet afraid to break in upon the current of his thoughts. We had driven several miles, and were beginning to get to the fringe of the belt of suburban villas, when he shook himself, shrugged his shoulders, and lit up his pipe with the air of a man who has satisfied himself that he is acting for the best.

" You have a grand gift of silence, Watson," said he. " It makes you quite invaluable as a companion. 'Pon my word, it is a great thing for me to have someone to talk to, for my own thoughts are not over-pleasant. I was wondering what I should say to this dear little woman to-night when she meets me at the door."

" You forget that I know nothing about it."

" I shall just have time to tell you the facts of the case before we get to Lee. It seems absurdly simple, and yet, somehow, I can get nothing to go upon. There's plenty of thread, no doubt, but I can't get the end of it in my hand. Now, I'll state the case clearly and concisely to you, Watson, and maybe you may see a spark where all is dark to me."

" Proceed, then."

" Some years ago—to be definite, in May, 1884—there came to Lee a gentleman, Neville St. Clair by name, who appeared to have plenty of money. He took a large villa, laid out the grounds very nicely, and lived generally in good style. By degrees he made friends in the neighbour-hood, and in 1887 he married the daughter of a local brewer, by whom he has now had two children. He had no occupation, but was interested in several companies, and went into town as a rule in the morning, returning by the 5.14 from Cannon Street every night. Mr. St. Clair is now 37 years of age, is a man of temperate habits, a good husband, a very affectionate father, and a man who is popular with all who know him. I may add that his whole debts at the present moment, as far as we have been able to ascertain, amount to £88 10s., while he has £220 standing to his credit in the Capital and Counties Bank. There is no reason, therefore, to think that money troubles have been weighing upon his mind.

" Last Monday Mr. Neville St. Clair went into town rather earlier than usual, remarking before he started that he had two important commissions to perform, and that he would bring his little boy home a box of bricks. Now, by the merest chance his wife received a telegram upon this same Monday, very shortly after his departure, to the effect that a small parcel of considerable value which she had been expecting was waiting for her at the offices of the Aberdeen Shipping Company. Now, if you are well up in your London, you will know that the office of the company is in Fresno Street, which branches out of Upper

Swandam Lane, where you found me to-night. Mrs. St. Clair had her lunch, started for the City, did some shopping, proceeded to the company's office, got her packet, and found herself exactly at 4.35 walking through Swandam Lane on her way back to the station. Have you followed me so far ? "

" It is very clear."

" If you remember, Monday was an exceedingly hot day, and Mrs. St. Clair walked slowly, glancing about in the hope of seeing a cab, as she did not like the neighbourhood in which she found herself. While she walked in this way down Swandam Lane she suddenly heard an ejaculation or cry, and was struck cold to see her husband looking down at her, and, as it seemed to her, beckoning to her from a second-floor window. The window was open, and she distinctly saw his face, which she describes as being terribly agitated. He waved his hands frantically to her, and then vanished from the window so suddenly that it seemed to her that he had been plucked back by some irresistible force from behind. One singular point which struck her quick feminine eye was that, although he wore some dark coat, such as he had started to town in, he had on neither collar nor necktie.

" Convinced that something was amiss with him, she rushed down the steps—for the house was none other than the opium den in which you found me to-night— and, running through the front room, she attempted to ascend the stairs which led to the first floor. At the foot of the stairs, however, she met this Lascar scoundrel, of whom I have spoken, who thrust her back, and, aided by a Dane, who acts as assistant there, pushed her out into the street. Filled with the most maddening doubts and fears, she rushed down the lane, and, by rare good fortune, met, in Fresno Street, a number of constables with an inspector, all on their way to their beat. The inspector and two men accompanied her back, and, in spite of the continued resistance of the proprietor, they made their way to the room in which Mr. St. Clair had last been seen.

There was no sign of him there. In fact, in the whole of that floor there was no one to be found, save a crippled wretch of hideous aspect, who, it seems, made his home there. Both he and the Lascar stoutly swore that no one else had been in the front room during that afternoon. So determined was their denial that the inspector was staggered, and had almost come to believe that Mrs. St. Clair had been deluded when, with a cry, she sprang at a small deal box which lay upon the table, and tore the lid from it. Out there fell a cascade of children's bricks. It was the toy which he had promised to bring home.

" This discovery, and the evident confusion which the cripple showed, made the inspector realize that the matter was serious. The rooms were carefully examined, and results all pointed to an abominable crime. The front room was plainly furnished as a sitting-room, and led into a small bedroom, which looked out upon the back of one of the wharves. Between the wharf and the bedroom window is a narrow strip, which is dry at low tide, but is covered at high tide with at least four and a half feet of water. The bedroom window was a broad one, and opened from below. On examination traces of blood were to be seen upon the window-sill, and several scattered drops were visible upon the wooden floor of the bedroom. Thrust away behind a curtain in the front room were all the clothes of Mr. Neville St. Clair, with the exception of his coat. His boots, his socks, his hat, and his watch—all were there. There were no signs of violence upon any of these garments, and there were no other traces of Mr. Neville St. Clair. Out of the window he must apparently have gone, for no other exit could be discovered, and the ominous blood-stains upon the sill gave little promise that he could save himself by swimming, for the tide was at its very highest at the moment of the tragedy.

" And now as to the villains who seemed to be immediately implicated in the matter. The Lascar was known to be a man of the vilest antecedents, but as by Mrs. St.

Clair's story he was known to have been at the foot of the stair within a few seconds of her husband's appearance at the window, he could hardly have been more than an accessory to the crime. His defence was one of absolute ignorance, and he protested that he had no knowledge as to the doings of Hugh Boone, his lodger, and that he could not account in any way for the presence of the missing gentleman's clothes.

" So much for the Lascar manager. Now for the sinister cripple who lives upon the second floor of the opium den, and who was certainly the last human being whose eyes rested upon Neville St. Clair. His name is Hugh Boone, and his hideous face is one which is familiar to every man who goes much to the City. He is a professional beggar, though in order to avoid the police regulations he pretends to a small trade in wax vestas. Some little distance down Threadneedle Street upon the left-hand side there is, as you may have remarked, a small angle in the wall. Here it is that the creature takes his daily seat, cross-legged, with his tiny stock of matches on his lap, and as he is a piteous spectacle a small rain of charity descends into the greasy leather cap which lies upon the pavement before him. I have watched this fellow more than once, before ever I thought of making his professional acquaintance, and I have been surprised at the harvest which he has reaped in a short time. His appearance, you see, is so remarkable that no one can pass him without observing him. A shock of orange hair, a pale face disfigured by a horrible scar, which, by its contraction, has turned up the outer edge of his upper lip, a bull-dog chin, and a pair of very penetrating dark eyes, which present a singular contrast to the colour of his hair, all mark him out from amid the common crowd of mendicants, and so, too, does his wit, for he is ever ready with a reply to any piece of chaff which may be thrown at him by the passers-by. This is the man whom we now learn to have been the lodger at the opium den, and to have been the last man to see the gentleman of whom we are in quest."

"But a cripple!" said I. "What could he have done single-handed against a man in the prime of life?"

"He is a cripple in the sense that he walks with a limp; but, in other respects, he appears to be a powerful and well-nurtured man. Surely your medical experience would tell you, Watson, that weakness in one limb is often compensated for by exceptional strength in the others."

"Pray continue your narrative."

"Mrs. St. Clair had fainted at the sight of the blood upon the window, and she was escorted home in a cab by the police, as her presence could be of no help to them in their investigations. Inspector Barton, who had charge of the case, made a very careful examination of the premises, but without finding anything which threw any light upon the matter. One mistake had been made in not arresting Boone instantly, as he was allowed some few minutes during which he might have communicated with his friend the Lascar, but this fault was soon remedied, and he was seized and searched, without anything being found which could incriminate him. There were, it is true, some bloodstains upon his right shirt-sleeve, but he pointed to his ring finger, which had been cut near the nail, and explained that the bleeding came from there, adding that he had been to the window not long before, and that the stains which had been observed there came doubtless from the same source. He denied strenuously having ever seen Mr. Neville St. Clair, and swore that the presence of the clothes in his room was as much a mystery to him as to the police. As to Mrs. St. Clair's assertion, that she had actually seen her husband at the window, he declared that she must have been either mad or dreaming. He was removed, loudly protesting, to the police station, while the inspector remained upon the premises in the hope that the ebbing tide might afford some fresh clue.

"And it did, though they hardly found upon the mud-bank what they had feared to find. It was Neville St. Clair's coat, and not Neville St. Clair, which lay uncovered as the tide receded. And what do you think they found in the pockets ? "

" I cannot imagine."

" No, I don't think you will guess. Every pocket stuffed with pennies and halfpennies—four hundred and twenty-one pennies, and two hundred and seventy halfpennies. It was no wonder that it had not been swept away by the tide. But a human body is a different matter. There is a fierce eddy between the wharf and the house. It seemed likely enough that the weighted coat had remained when the stripped body had been sucked away into the river."

" But I understand that all the other clothes were found in the room. Would the body be dressed in a coat alone ? "

" No, sir, but the facts might be met speciously enough. Suppose that this man Boone had thrust Neville St. Clair through the window, there is no human eye which could have seen the deed. What would he do then ? It would of course instantly strike him that he must get rid of the tell-tale garments. He would seize the coat then, and be in the act of throwing it out when it would occur to him that it would swim and not sink. He has little time, for he had heard the scuffle downstairs when the wife tried to force her way up, and perhaps he has already heard from his Lascar confederate that the police are hurrying up the street. There is not an instant to be lost. He rushes to some secret hoard, where he has accumulated the fruits of his beggary, and he stuffs all the coins upon which he can lay his hands into the pockets to make sure of the coat's sinking. He throws it out, and would have done the same with the other garments had not he heard the rush of steps below, and only just had time to close the window when the police appeared."

" It certainly sounds feasible."

" Well, we will take it as a working hypothesis for want of a better. Boone, as I have told you, was arrested and taken to the station, but it could not be shown that there had ever before been anything against him. He had for years been known as a professional beggar, but his life appeared to have been a very quiet and innocent one. There the matter stands at present, and the questions which have to be solved, what Neville St. Clair was doing in the opium den, what happened to him when there, where is he now, and what Hugh Boone had to do with his disappearance, are all as far from a solution as ever. I confess that I cannot recall any case within my experience which looked at the first glance so simple, and yet which presented such difficulties."

Whilst Sherlock Holmes had been detailing this singular series of events we had been whirling through the outskirts of the great town until the last straggling houses had been left behind, and we rattled along with a country hedge upon either side of us. Just as he finished, however, we drove through two scattered villages, where a few lights still glimmered in the windows.

"We are on the outskirts of Lee," said my companion. "We have touched on three English counties in our short drive, starting in Middlesex, passing over an angle of Surrey, and ending in Kent. See that light among the trees? That is the Cedars, and beside that lamp sits a woman whose anxious ears have already, I have little doubt, caught the clink of our horse's feet."

"But why are you not conducting the case from Baker Street?" I asked.

"Because there are many inquiries which must be made out here. Mrs. St. Clair has most kindly put two rooms at my disposal, and you may rest assured that she will have nothing but a welcome for my friend and colleague. I hate to meet her, Watson, when I have no news of her husband. Here we are. Whoa, there, whoa!"

We had pulled up in front of a large villa which stood within its own grounds. A stable-boy had run out to the horse's head, and, springing down, I followed Holmes up the small, winding gravel drive which led to the house. As we approached the door flew open, and a little blonde woman stood in the opening, clad in some sort of light *mousseline-de-soie*, with a touch of fluffy pink chiffon at her neck and wrists. She stood with her figure outlined against the flood of light, one hand upon the door, one half raised in eagerness, her body slightly bent, her head and face protruded, with eager eyes and parted lips, a standing question.

" Well ? " she cried, " well ? " And then, seeing that there were two of us, she gave a cry of hope which sank into a groan as she saw that my companion shook his head and shrugged his shoulders.

" No good news ? "

" None."

" No bad ? "

" No."

" Thank God for that. But come in. You must be weary, for you have had a long day."

" This is my friend, Dr. Watson. He has been of most vital use to me in several of my cases, and a lucky chance has made it possible for me to bring him out and associate him with this investigation."

" I am delighted to see you," said she, pressing my hand warmly. " You will, I am sure, forgive anything which may be wanting in our arrangements, when you consider the blow which has come so suddenly upon us."

" My dear madam," said I, " I am an old campaigner, and if I were not, I can very well see that no apology is needed. If I can be of any assistance, either to you or to my friend here, I shall be indeed happy."

" Now, Mr. Sherlock Holmes," said the lady as we entered a well-lit dining-room, upon the table of which a cold supper had been laid out. " I should very much like to ask you one or two plain questions, to which I beg that you will give a plain answer."

" Certainly, madam."

" Do not trouble about my feelings. I am not hysterical, nor given to fainting. I simply wish to hear your real, real opinion."

"Upon what point?"

"In your heart of hearts, do you think that Neville is alive?"

Sherlock Holmes seemed to be embarrassed by the question. "Frankly now!" she repeated, standing upon the rug, and looking keenly down at him, as he leaned back in a basket chair.

"Frankly, then, madam, I do not."

"You think that he is dead?"

"I do."

"Murdered?"

"I don't say that. Perhaps."

"And on what day did he meet his death?"

"On Monday."

"Then perhaps, Mr. Holmes, you will be good enough to explain how it is that I have received this letter from him to-day?"

Sherlock Holmes sprang out of his chair as if he had been galvanized.

"What!" he roared.

"Yes, to-day." She stood smiling, holding up a little slip of paper in the air.

"May I see it?"

"Certainly."

He snatched it from her in his eagerness, and smoothing it out upon the table, he drew over the lamp, and examined it intently. I had left my chair, and was gazing at it over his shoulder. The envelope was a very coarse one, and was stamped with the Gravesend postmark, and with the date of that very day, or rather of the day before, for it was considerably after midnight.

"Coarse writing!" murmured Holmes. "Surely this is not your husband's writing, madam."

"No, but the enclosure is."

"I perceive also that whoever addressed the envelope had to go and inquire as to the address."

"How can you tell that?"

"The name, you see, is in perfectly black ink, which has

dried itself. The rest is of the greyish colour which shows that blotting-paper has been used. If it had been written straight off, and then blotted, none would be of a deep black shade. This man has written the name, and there has then been a pause before he wrote the address, which can only mean that he was not familiar with it. It is, of course, a trifle, but there is nothing so important as trifles. Let us now see the letter ! Ha ! there has been an enclosure here ! "

" Yes, there was a ring. His signet ring."

" And you are sure that this is your husband's hand ? "

" One of his hands."

" One ? "

" His hand when he wrote hurriedly. It is very unlike his usual writing, and yet I know it well."

" ' Dearest, do not be frightened. All will come well. There is a huge error which it may take some little time to rectify. Wait in patience.—Neville.' Written in pencil upon a fly-leaf of a book, octavo size, no watermark. Posted to-day in Gravesend by a man with a dirty thumb. Ha ! And the flap has been gummed, if I am not very much in error, by a person who had been chewing tobacco. And you have no doubt that it is your husband's hand, madam ? "

" None. Neville wrote those words."

" And they were posted to-day at Gravesend. Well, Mrs. St. Clair, the clouds lighten, though I should not venture to say that the danger is over."

" But he must be alive, Mr. Holmes."

" Unless this is a clever forgery to put us on the wrong scent. The ring, after all, proves nothing. It may have been taken from him."

" No, no ; it is, it is, it is his very own writing ! "

" Very well. It may, however, have been written on Monday, and only posted to-day."

" That is possible."

" If so, much may have happened between."

" Oh, you must not discourage me, Mr. Holmes. I

know that all is well with him. There is so keen a sympathy between us that I should know if evil came upon him. On the very day that I saw him last he cut himself in the bedroom, and yet I in the dining-room rushed upstairs instantly with the utmost certainty that something had happened. Do you think that I would respond to such a trifle, and yet be ignorant of his death ? "

" I have seen too much not to know that the impression of a woman may be more valuable than the conclusion of an analytical reasoner. And in this letter you certainly have a very strong piece of evidence to corroborate your view. But if your husband is alive and able to write letters, why should he remain away from you ? "

" I cannot imagine. It is unthinkable."

" And on Monday he made no remarks before leaving you ? "

" No."

" And you were surprised to see him in Swandam Lane ? "

" Very much so."

" Was the window open ? "

" Yes."

" Then he might have called to you ? "

" He might."

" He only, as I understand, gave an inarticulate cry ? "

" Yes."

" A call for help, you thought ? "

" Yes. He waved his hands."

" But it might have been a cry of surprise. Astonishment at the unexpected sight of you might cause him to throw up his hands."

" It is possible."

" And you thought he was pulled back."

" He disappeared so suddenly."

" He might have leaped back. You did not see anyone else in the room."

" No, but this horrible man confessed to having been there, and the Lascar was at the foot of the stairs."

"Quite so. Your husband, as far as you could see, had his ordinary clothes on?"

"But without his collar or tie. I distinctly saw his bare throat."

"Had he ever spoken of Swandam Lane?"

"Never."

"Had he ever shown any signs of having taken opium?"

"Never."

"Thank you, Mrs. St. Clair. Those are the principal points about which I wished to be absolutely clear. We shall now have a little supper and then retire, for we may have a very busy day to-morrow."

A large and comfortable double-bedded room had been placed at our disposal, and I was quickly between the sheets, for I was weary after my night of adventure. Sherlock Holmes was a man, however, who when he had an unsolved problem upon his mind would go for days, and even for a week, without rest, turning it over, rearranging his facts, looking at it from every point of view, until he had either fathomed it, or convinced himself that his data were insufficient. It was soon evident to me that he was now preparing for an all-night sitting. He took off his coat and waistcoat, put on a large blue dressing-gown, and then wandered about the room collecting pillows from his bed, and cushions from the sofa and arm-chairs. With these he constructed a sort of Eastern divan, upon which he perched himself cross-legged, with an ounce of shag tobacco and a box of matches laid out in front of him. In the dim light of the lamp I saw him sitting there, an old brier pipe between his lips, his eyes fixed vacantly upon the corner of the ceiling, the blue smoke curling up from him, silent, motionless, with the light shining upon his strong-set aquiline features. So he sat as I dropped off to sleep, and so he sat when a sudden ejaculation caused me to wake up, and I found the summer sun shining into the apartment. The pipe was still between his lips, the smoke still curled upwards, and the room was full of a dense tobacco haze, but nothing remained of the heap of shag which I had seen upon the previous night.

" Awake, Watson ? " he asked.

" Yes."

" Game for a morning drive ? "

" Certainly."

" Then dress. No one is stirring yet, but I know where the stable-boy sleeps, and we shall soon have the trap out." He chuckled to himself as he spoke, his eyes twinkled, and he seemed a different man to the sombre thinker of the previous night.

As I dressed I glanced at my watch. It was no wonder that no one was stirring. It was twenty-five minutes past four. I had hardly finished when Holmes returned with the news that the boy was putting in the horse.

" I want to test a little theory of mine," said he, pulling on his boots. " I think, Watson, that you are now standing in the presence of one of the most absolute fools in Europe. I deserve to be kicked from here to Charing Cross. But I think I have the key of the affair now."

" And where is it ? " I asked, smiling.

" In the bath-room," he answered. " Oh, yes, I am not joking," he continued, seeing my look of incredulity. " I have just been there, and I have taken it out, and I have got it in this Gladstone bag. Come on, my boy, and we shall see whether it will not fit the lock."

We made our way downstairs as quickly as possible ; and out into the bright morning sunshine. In the road stood our horse and trap, with the half-clad stable-boy waiting at the head. We both sprang in, and away we dashed down the London road. A few country carts were stirring, bearing in vegetables to the metropolis, but the lines of villas on either side were as silent and lifeless as some city in a dream.

" It has been in some points a singular case," said Holmes, flicking the horse on into a gallop. " I confess that I have been as blind as a mole, but it is better to learn wisdom late, than never to learn it at all."

In town, the earliest risers were just beginning to look sleepily from their windows as we drove through the streets of the Surrey side. Passing down the Waterloo Bridge Road we crossed over the river, and dashing up Wellington Street wheeled sharply to the right, and found ourselves in Bow Street. Sherlock Holmes was well known to the Force, and the two constables at the door saluted him. One of them held the horse's head while the other led us in.

"Who is on duty?" asked Holmes.

"Inspector Bradstreet, sir."

"Ah, Bradstreet, how are you?" A tall, stout official had come down the stone-flagged passage, in a peaked cap and frogged jacket. "I wish to have a word with you, Bradstreet."

"Certainly, Mr. Holmes. Step into my room here."

It was a small office-like room, with a huge ledger upon the table, and a telephone projecting from the wall. The inspector sat down at his desk.

"What can I do for you, Mr. Holmes?"

"I called about that beggar-man, Boone—the one who was charged with being concerned in the disappearance of Mr. Neville St. Clair, of Lee."

"Yes. He was brought up and remanded for further inquiries."

"So I heard. You have him here?"

"In the cells."

"Is he quiet?"

"Oh, he gives no trouble. But he is a dirty scoundrel."

"Dirty?"

"Yes, it is all we can do to make him wash his hands, and his face is as black as a tinker's. Well, when once his case has been settled he will have a regular prison bath; and I think, if you saw him, you would agree with me that he needed it."

"I should like to see him very much."

"Would you? That is easily done. Come this way. You can leave your bag."

" No, I think I'll take it."

" Very good. Come this way, if you please." He led us down a passage, opened a barred door, passed down a winding stair, and brought us to a whitewashed corridor with a line of doors on each side.

" The third on the right is his," said the inspector. " Here it is ! " He quietly shot back a panel in the upper part of the door, and glanced through.

" He is asleep," said he. " You can see him very well."

We both put our eyes to the grating. The prisoner lay with his face towards us, in a very deep sleep, breathing slowly and heavily. He was a middle-sized man, coarsely clad as became his calling, with a coloured shirt protruding through the rent in his tattered coat. He was, as the inspector had said, extremely dirty, but the grime which covered his face could not conceal its repulsive ugliness. A broad weal from an old scar ran across it from eye to chin, and by its contraction had turned up one side of the upper lip, so that three teeth were exposed in a perpetual snarl. A shock of very bright red hair grew low over his eyes and forehead.

" He's a beauty, isn't he ? " said the inspector.

" He certainly needs a wash," remarked Holmes. " I had an idea that he might, and I took the liberty of bringing the tools with me." He opened his Gladstone bag as he spoke, and took out, to my astonishment, a very large bath sponge.

" He ! he ! You are a funny one," chuckled the inspector.

" Now, if you will have the great goodness to open that door very quietly, we will soon make him cut a much more respectable figure."

" Well, I don't know why not," said the inspector. " He doesn't look a credit to the Bow Street cells, does he ? " He slipped his key into the lock, and we all very quietly entered the cell. The sleeper half turned, and then settled down once more into a deep slumber.

Holmes stooped to the water jug, moistened his sponge, and then rubbed it twice vigorously across and down the prisoner's face.

"Let me introduce you," he shouted, "to Mr. Neville St. Clair, of Lee, in the county of Kent."

Never in my life have I seen such a sight. The man's face peeled off under the sponge like the bark from a tree. Gone was the coarse brown tint! Gone, too, the horrid scar which had seamed it across, and the twisted lip which had given the repulsive sneer to the face! A twitch brought away the tangled red hair, and there, sitting up in his bed, was a pale, sad-faced, refined-looking man, black-haired and smooth-skinned, rubbing his eyes, and staring about him with sleepy bewilderment. Then suddenly realizing the exposure, he broke into a scream, and threw himself down with his face to the pillow.

"Great heaven!" cried the inspector, "it is, indeed, the missing man. I know him from the photograph."

The prisoner turned with the reckless air of a man who abandons himself to his destiny. "Be it so," said he. "And pray what am I charged with?"

"With making away with Mr. Neville St.—— Oh, come, you can't be charged with that, unless they make a case of attempted suicide of it," said the inspector, with a grin. "Well, I have been twenty-seven years in the Force, but this really takes the cake."

"If I am Mr. Neville St. Clair, then it is obvious that no crime has been committed, and that, therefore, I am illegally detained."

"No crime, but a very great error has been committed," said Holmes. "You would have done better to have trusted your wife."

"It was not the wife, it was the children," groaned the prisoner. "God help me, I would not have them ashamed of their father. My God! What an exposure! What can I do?"

Sherlock Holmes sat down beside him on the couch, and patted him kindly on the shoulder.

" If you leave it to a court of law to clear the matter up," said he, " of course you can hardly avoid publicity. On the other hand, if you convince the police authorities that there is no possible case against you, I do not know that there is any reason that the details should find their way into the papers. Inspector Bradstreet would, I am sure, make notes upon anything which you might tell us, and submit it to the proper authorities. The case would then never go into court at all."

" God bless you ! " cried the prisoner passionately. " I would have endured imprisonment, aye, even execution, rather than have left my miserable secret as a family blot to my children.

" You are the first who have ever heard my story. My father was a schoolmaster in Chesterfield, where I received an excellent education. I travelled in my youth, took to the stage, and finally became a reporter on an evening paper in London. One day my editor wished to have a series of articles upon begging in the metropolis, and I volunteered to supply them. There was the point from which all my adventures started. It was only by trying begging as an amateur that I could get the facts upon which to base my articles. When an actor I had, of course, learned all the secrets of making up, and had been famous in the green-room for my skill. I took advantage now of my attainments. I painted my face, and to make myself as pitiable as possible I made a good scar and fixed one side of my lip in a twist by the aid of a small slip of flesh-coloured plaster. Then with a red head of hair, and an appropriate dress, I took my station in the busiest part of the City, ostensibly as a match-seller, but really as a beggar. For seven hours I plied my trade, and when I returned home in the evening I found, to my surprise, that I had received no less than twenty-six shillings and fourpence.

" I wrote my articles, and thought little more of the matter until, some time later, I backed a bill for a friend, and had a writ served upon me for £25. I was at my wits' end where to get the money, but a sudden idea came to me. I begged a fortnight's grace from the creditor, asked for a holiday from my employers, and spent the time in begging in the City under my disguise. In ten days I had the money, and had paid the debt.

"Well, you can imagine how hard it was to settle down to arduous work at two pounds a week, when I knew that I could earn as much in a day by smearing my face with a little paint, laying my cap on the ground, and sitting still. It was a long fight between my pride and the money, but the dollars won at last, and I threw up reporting, and sat day after day in the corner which I had first chosen, inspiring pity by my ghastly face and filling my pockets with coppers. Only one man knew my secret. He was the keeper of a low den in which I used to lodge in Swandam Lane, where I could every morning emerge as a squalid beggar, and in the evenings transform myself into a well-dressed man about town. This fellow, a Lascar, was well paid by me for his rooms, so that I knew that my secret was safe in his possession.

"Well, very soon I found that I was saving considerable sums of money. I do not mean that any beggar in the streets of London could earn seven hundred pounds a year—which is less than my average takings—but I had exceptional advantages in my power of making up, and also in a facility in repartee, which improved by practice, and made me quite a recognized character in the City. All day a stream of pennies, varied by silver, poured in upon me, and it was a very bad day upon which I failed to take two pounds.

"As I grew richer I grew more ambitious, took a house in the country, and eventually married, without anyone having a suspicion as to my real occupation. My dear wife knew that I had business in the City. She little knew what.

"Last Monday I had finished for the day, and was dressing in my room above the opium den, when I looked out of the window, and saw, to my horror and astonishment, that my wife was standing in the street, with her eyes fixed full upon me. I gave a cry of surprise, threw up my arms to cover my face, and rushing to my confidant, the Lascar, entreated him to prevent anyone from coming up to me. I heard her voice downstairs, but I knew that she could not ascend. Swiftly I threw off my clothes, pulled on those of a beggar, and put on my pigments and wig. Even a wife's eyes could not pierce so complete a disguise. But then it occurred to me that there might be a search in the room and that the clothes might betray me. I threw open the window, re-opening by my violence a small cut which I had inflicted upon myself in the bedroom that morning. Then I seized my coat, which was weighted by the coppers which I had just transferred to it from the leather bag in which I carried my takings. I hurled it out of the window, and it disappeared into the Thames. The other clothes would have followed, but at that moment there was a rush of constables up the stairs, and a few minutes after I found, rather, I confess, to my relief, that instead of being identified as Mr. Neville St. Clair, I was arrested as his murderer.

"I do not know that there is anything else for me to explain. I was determined to preserve my disguise as long as possible, and hence my preference for a dirty face. Knowing that my wife would be terribly anxious, I slipped off my ring, and confided it to the Lascar at a moment when no constable was watching me, together with a hurried scrawl, telling her that she had no cause to fear."

"That note only reached her yesterday," said Holmes.

"Good God! What a week she must have spent."

"The police have watched this Lascar," said Inspector Bradstreet, "and I can quite understand that he might find it difficult to post a letter unobserved. Probably he handed it to some sailor customer of his, who forgot all about it for some days."

"That was it," said Holmes, nodding approvingly, " I

have no doubt of it. But have you never been prosecuted for begging ? "

" Many times ; but what was a fine to me ? "

" It must stop here, however," said Bradstreet. " If the police are to hush this thing up, there must be no more of Hugh Boone."

" I have sworn it by the most solemn oaths which a man can take."

" In that case I think that it is probable that no further steps may be taken. But if you are found again, then all must come out. I am sure, Mr. Holmes, that we are very much indebted to you for having cleared the matter up. I wish I knew how you reach your results."

" I reached this one," said my friend, " by sitting upon five pillows and consuming an ounce of shag. I think, Watson, that if we drive to Baker Street we shall just be in time for breakfast."

7. *The Blue Carbuncle*

I HAD called upon my friend Sherlock Holmes upon the second morning after Christmas, with the intention of wishing him the compliments of the season. He was lounging upon the sofa in a purple dressing-gown, a pipe-rack within his reach upon the right, and a pile of crumpled morning papers, evidently newly studied, near at hand. Beside the couch was a wooden chair, and on the angle of the back hung a very seedy and disreputable hard felt hat, much the worse for wear, and cracked in several places. A lens and a forceps lying upon the seat of the chair suggested that the hat had been suspended in this manner for the purpose of examination.

" You are engaged," said I ; " perhaps I interrupt you."

" Not at all. I am glad to have a friend with whom I can discuss my results. The matter is a perfectly trivial one " (he jerked his thumb in the direction of the old hat), " but there are points in connection with it which are not entirely devoid of interest, and even of instruction."

I seated myself in his arm-chair, and warmed my hands before his crackling fire, for a sharp frost had set in, and the windows were thick with the ice crystals. "I suppose," I remarked, "that, homely as it looks, this thing has some deadly story linked on to it—that it is the clue which will guide you in the solution of some mystery, and the punishment of some crime."

"No, no. No crime," said Sherlock Holmes, laughing. "Only one of those whimsical little incidents which will happen when you have four million human beings all jostling each other within the space of a few square miles. Amid the action and reaction of so dense a swarm of humanity, every possible combination of events may be expected to take place, and many a little problem will be presented which may be striking and bizarre without being criminal. We have already had experience of such."

"So much so," I remarked, "that, of the last six cases which I have added to my notes, three have been entirely free of any legal crime."

"Precisely. You allude to my attempt to recover the Irene Adler papers, to the singular case of Miss Mary Sutherland, and to the adventure of the man with the twisted lip. Well, I have no doubt that this small matter will fall into the same innocent category. You know Peterson, the commissionaire?"

"Yes."

"It is to him that this trophy belongs."

"It is his hat."

"No, no; he found it. Its owner is unknown. I beg that you will look upon it, not as a battered billycock, but as an intellectual problem. And, first as to how it came here. It arrived upon Christmas morning, in company with a good fat goose, which is, I have no doubt, roasting at this moment in front of Peterson's fire. The facts are these. About four o'clock on Christmas morning, Peterson, who, as you know, is a very honest fellow, was returning from some small jollification, and was making his way homewards down Tottenham Court Road. In front of him he saw, in the gaslight, a tallish man, walking with a slight stagger, and carrying a white goose slung over his shoulder. As he reached the corner of Goodge Street a row broke out between this stranger and a little knot of roughs. One of the latter knocked off the man's hat, on which he raised his stick to defend himself, and, swinging it over his head, smashed the shop window behind him. Peterson had rushed forward to protect the stranger from his assailants, but the man, shocked at having broken the window and seeing an official-looking person in uniform rushing towards him, dropped his goose, took to his heels, and vanished amid the labyrinth of small streets which lie at the back of Tottenham Court Road. The roughs had also fled at the appearance of Peterson, so that he was left in possession of the field of battle, and also of the spoils of victory in the shape of this battered hat and a most unimpeachable Christmas goose."

" Which surely he restored to their owner ? "

" My dear fellow, there lies the problem. It is true that ' For Mrs. Henry Baker ' was printed upon a small card which was tied to the bird's left leg, and it is also true that the initials ' H. B.' are legible upon the lining of this hat ; but, as there are some thousands of Bakers, and some hundreds of Henry Bakers in this city of ours, it is not easy to restore lost property to any one of them."

" What, then, did Peterson do ? "

" He brought round both hat and goose to me on Christmas morning, knowing that even the smallest problems are of interest to me. The goose we retained until this morning, when there were signs that, in spite of the slight frost, it would be well that it should be eaten without unnecessary delay. Its finder has carried it off therefore to fulfil the ultimate destiny of a goose, while I continue to retain the hat of the unknown gentleman who lost his Christmas dinner."

" Did he not advertise ? "

" No."

" Then, what clue could you have as to his identity ? "

" Only as much as we can deduce."

" From his hat ? "

" Precisely."

" But you are joking. What can you gather from this old battered felt ? "

" Here is my lens. You know my methods. What can you gather yourself as to the individuality of the man who has worn this article ? "

I took the tattered object in my hands, and turned it over rather ruefully. It was a very ordinary black hat of the usual round shape, hard and much the worse for wear. The lining had been of red silk, but was a good deal discoloured. There was no maker's name ; but, as Holmes had remarked, the initials " H. B." were scrawled upon one side. It was pierced in the brim for a hat-securer, but the elastic was missing. For the rest, it was cracked, exceedingly dusty, and spotted in several places, although there seemed to have been some attempt to hide the discoloured patches by smearing them with ink.

" I can see nothing," said I, handing it back to my friend.

" On the contrary, Watson, you can see everything. You fail, however, to reason from what you see. You are too timid in drawing your inferences."

" Then, pray tell me what it is that you can infer from this hat ? "

He picked it up, and gazed at it in the peculiar introspective fashion which was characteristic of him. " It is perhaps less suggestive than it might have been," he remarked, " and yet there are a few inferences which are very distinct, and a few others which represent at least a strong balance of probability. That the man was highly intellectual is of course obvious upon the face of it, and also that he was fairly well-to-do within the last three years, although he has now fallen upon evil days. He had foresight, but has less now than formerly, pointing to a moral retrogression, which, when taken with the decline of his fortunes, seems to indicate some evil influence, probably drink, at work upon him. This may account also for the obvious fact that his wife has ceased to love him."

" My dear Holmes ! "

" He has, however, retained some degree of self-respect," he continued, disregarding my remonstrance. " He is a man who leads a sedentary life, goes out little, is out of training entirely, is middle-aged, has grizzled hair which he has had cut within the last few days, and which he anoints with lime-cream. These are the more patent facts which are to be deduced from his hat. Also, by the way, that it is extremely improbable that he has gas laid on in his house."

" You are certainly joking, Holmes."

" Not in the least. Is it possible that even now when I give you these results you are unable to see how they are attained ? "

" I have no doubt that I am very stupid ; but I must confess that I am unable to follow you. For example, how did you deduce that this man was intellectual ? "

For answer Holmes clapped the hat upon his head. It came right over the forehead and settled upon the bridge of his nose. " It is a question of cubic capacity," said he : " a man with so large a brain must have something in it."

" The decline of his fortunes, then ? "

" This hat is three years old. These flat brims curled at the edge came in then. It is a hat of the very best quality. Look at the band of ribbed silk, and the excellent lining. If this man could afford to buy so expensive a hat three years ago, and has had no hat since, then he has assuredly gone down in the world."

" Well, that is clear enough, certainly. But how about the foresight, and the moral retrogression ? "

Sherlock Holmes laughed. " Here is the foresight," said he, putting his finger upon the little disc and loop of the hat-securer. " They are never sold upon hats. If this man ordered one, it is a sign of a certain amount of foresight, since he went out of his way to take this precaution against the wind. But since we see that he has broken the elastic, and has not troubled to replace it, it is obvious that he has less foresight now than formerly, which is a distinct proof of a weakening nature. On the other hand, he has endeavoured to conceal some of these stains upon the felt by daubing them with ink, which is a sign that he has not entirely lost his self-respect."

"Your reasoning is certainly plausible."

"The further points, that he is middle-aged, that his hair is grizzled, that it has been recently cut, and that he uses lime-cream, are all to be gathered from a close examination of the lower part of the lining. The lens discloses a large number of hair-ends, clean cut by the scissors of the barber. They all appear to be adhesive, and there is a distinct odour of lime-cream. This dust, you will observe, is not the gritty, grey dust of the street, but the fluffy brown dust of the house, showing that it has been hung up indoors most of the time; while the marks of moisture upon the inside are proof positive that the wearer perspired very freely, and could, therefore, hardly be in the best of training."

"But his wife—you said that she had ceased to love him."

"This hat has not been brushed for weeks. When I see you, my dear Watson, with a week's accumulation of dust upon your hat, and when your wife allows you to go out in such a state, I shall fear that you also have been unfortunate enough to lose your wife's affection."

"But he might be a bachelor."

"Nay, he was bringing home the goose as a peace-offering to his wife. Remember the card upon the bird's leg."

"You have an answer to everything. But how on earth do you deduce that the gas is not laid on in the house?"

"One tallow stain, or even two, might come by chance;

but, when I see no less than five, I think that there can be little doubt that the individual must be brought into frequent contact with burning tallow—walks upstairs at night probably with his hat in one hand and a guttering candle in the other. Anyhow, he never got tallow stains from a gas jet. Are you satisfied ? "

" Well, it is very ingenious," said I, laughing ; " but since, as you said just now, there has been no crime committed, and no harm done save the loss of a goose, all this seems to be rather a waste of energy."

Sherlock Holmes had opened his mouth to reply, when the door flew open, and Peterson the commissionaire rushed into the compartment with flushed cheeks and the face of a man who is dazed with astonishment.

" The goose, Mr. Holmes ! The goose, sir ! " he gasped.

" Eh ! What of it, then ? Has it returned to life, and flapped off through the kitchen window ? " Holmes twisted himself round upon the sofa to get a fairer view of the man's excited face.

" See here, sir ! See what my wife found in its crop ! " He held out his hand, and displayed upon the centre of the palm a brilliantly scintillating blue stone, rather smaller than a bean in size, but of such purity and radiance that it twinkled like an electric point in the dark hollow of his hand.

Sherlock Holmes sat up with a whistle. " By Jove, Peterson," said he, " this is treasure-trove indeed ! I suppose you know what you have got ? "

" A diamond, sir ! A precious stone ! It cuts into glass as though it were putty."

" It's more than a precious stone. It's *the* precious stone."

" Not the Countess of Morcar's blue carbuncle ? " I ejaculated.

" Precisely so. I ought to know its size and shape, seeing that I have read the advertisement about it in *The Times* every day lately. It is absolutely unique, and its value can only be conjectured, but the reward offered of a thousand pounds is certainly not within a twentieth part of the market price."

" A thousand pounds ! Great Lord of mercy ! " The commissionaire plumped down into a chair, and stared from one to the other of us.

" That is the reward, and I have reason to know that there are sentimental considerations in the background which would induce the Countess to part with half of her fortune if she could but recover the gem."

" It was lost, if I remember aright, at the Hotel Cosmopolitan," I remarked.

" Precisely so, on the twenty-second of December, just five days ago. John Horner, a plumber, was accused of having abstracted it from the lady's jewel-case. The evidence against him was so strong that the case has been referred to the Assizes. I have some account of the matter here, I believe." He rummaged amid his newspapers, glancing over the dates, until at last he smoothed one out, doubled it over, and read the following paragraph :

" Hotel Cosmopolitan Jewel Robbery. John Horner, 26, plumber, was brought up upon the charge of having upon the 22nd inst., abstracted from the jewel-case of the Countess of Morcar the valuable gem known as the blue carbuncle. James Ryder, upper-attendant at the hotel, gave his evidence to the effect that he had shown Horner up to the dressing-room of the Countess of Morcar upon the day of the robbery, in order that he might solder the second bar of the grate, which was loose. He had remained with Horner some little time but had finally been called away. On returning he found that Horner had disappeared, that the bureau had been forced open, and that the small morocco casket in which, as it afterwards transpired, the Countess was accustomed to keep her jewel, was lying empty upon the dressing-table. Ryder instantly gave the alarm, and Horner was arrested the same evening ; but the stone could not be found either upon his person or in his rooms. Catherine Cusack, maid to the Countess, deposed to having heard Ryder's cry of dismay on discovering the robbery, and to having rushed into the room, where she found matters were as described by the last witness. Inspector Bradstreet, B Division, gave evidence as to the arrest of Horner, who struggled frantically, and protested his innocence in the strongest terms. Evidence of a previous conviction for robbery having been given against the prisoner, the magistrate refused to deal summarily with the offence, but referred it to the Assizes. Horner, who had shown signs of intense emotion during the proceedings, fainted away at the conclusion, and was carried out of court."

"Hum! So much for the police-court," said Holmes thoughtfully, tossing aside his paper. "The question for us now to solve is the sequence of events leading from a rifled jewel-case at one end to the crop of a goose in Tottenham Court Road at the other. You see, Watson, our little deductions have suddenly assumed a much more important and less innocent aspect. Here is the stone; the stone came from the goose, and the goose came from Mr. Henry Baker, the gentleman with the bad hat and all the other characteristics with which I have bored you. So now we must set ourselves very seriously to finding this gentleman, and ascertaining what part he has played in this little mystery. To do this, we must try the simplest means first, and these lie undoubtedly in an advertisement in all the evening papers. If this fail, I shall have recourse to other methods."

"What will you say?"

"Give me a pencil, and that slip of paper. Now, then: 'Found at the corner of Goodge Street, a goose and a black felt hat. Mr. Henry Baker can have the same by applying at 6.30 this evening at 221B Baker Street.' That is clear and concise."

"Very. But will he see it?"

"Well, he is sure to keep an eye on the papers, since, to a poor man, the loss was a heavy one. He was clearly so scared by his mischance in breaking the window, and by the approach of Peterson, that he thought of nothing but flight ; but since then he must have bitterly regretted the impulse which caused him to drop his bird. Then, again, the introduction of his name will cause him to see it, for every one who knows him will direct his attention to it. Here you are, Peterson, run down to the advertising agency, and have this put in the evening papers."

" In which, sir ? "

" Oh, in the *Globe, Star, Pall Mall, St. James's Gazette, Evening News, Standard, Echo,* and any others that occur to you."

" Very well, sir. And this stone ? "

" Ah, yes, I shall keep the stone. Thank you. And, I say, Peterson, just buy a goose on your way back, and leave it here with me, for we must have one to give to this gentleman in place of the one which your family is now devouring."

When the commissionaire had gone, Holmes took up the stone and held it against the light. " It's a bonny thing," said he. " Just see how it glints and sparkles. Of course it is a nucleus and focus of crime. Every good stone is. They are the devil's pet baits. In the larger and older jewels every facet may stand for a bloody deed. This stone is not yet twenty years old. It was found in the banks of the Amoy River in Southern China, and is remarkable in having every characteristic of the carbuncle, save that it is blue in shade, instead of ruby red. In spite of its youth, it has already a sinister history. There have been two murders, a vitriol-throwing, a suicide, and several robberies brought about for the sake of this forty-grain weight of crystallized charcoal. Who would think that so pretty a toy would be a purveyor to the gallows and the prison ? I'll lock it up in my strong-box now, and drop a line to the Countess to say that we have it."

" Do you think this man Horner is innocent ? "

" I cannot tell."

" Well, then, do you imagine that this other one, Henry Baker, had anything to do with the matter ? "

" It is, I think, much more likely that Henry Baker is an absolutely innocent man, who had no idea that the bird which he was carrying was of considerably more value than if it were made of solid gold. That, however, I shall determine by a very simple test, if we have an answer to our advertisement."

" And you can do nothing until then ? "

" Nothing."

" In that case I shall continue my professional round. But I shall come back in the evening at the hour you have mentioned, for I should like to see the solution of so tangled a business."

" Very glad to see you. I dine at seven. There is a woodcock, I believe. By the way, in view of recent occurrences, perhaps I ought to ask Mrs. Hudson to examine its crop."

I had been delayed at a case, and it was a little after half-past six when I found myself in Baker Street once more. As I approached the house I saw a tall man in a Scotch bonnet, with a coat which was buttoned up to his chin, waiting outside in the bright semicircle which was thrown from the fanlight. Just as I arrived, the door was opened, and we were shown up together to Holmes' room.

" Mr. Henry Baker, I believe," said he, rising from his arm-chair, and greeting his visitor with the easy air of geniality which he could so readily assume. " Pray take this chair by the fire, Mr. Baker. It is a cold night, and I observe that your circulation is more adapted for summer than for winter. Ah, Watson, you have just come at the right time. Is that your hat, Mr. Baker ? "

" Yes, sir, that is undoubtedly my hat."

He was a large man, with rounded shoulders, a massive head, and a broad, intelligent face, sloping down to a pointed beard of grizzled brown. A touch of red in nose and cheeks, with a slight tremor of his extended hand, recalled Holmes' surmise as to his habits. His rusty black frock-coat was buttoned right up in front, with the collar turned up, and his lank wrists protruded from his sleeves without a sign of cuff or shirt. He spoke in a low staccato fashion, choosing his words with care, and gave the impression generally of a man of learning and letters who had had ill-usage at the hands of fortune.

" We have retained these things for some days," said Holmes, " because we expected to see an advertisement from you giving your address. I am at a loss to know now why you did not advertise."

Our visitor gave a rather shamefaced laugh. " Shillings have not been so plentiful with me as they once were," he remarked. " I had no doubt that the gang of roughs who assaulted me had carried off both my hat and the bird. I did not care to spend more money in a hopeless attempt at recovering them."

" Very naturally. By the way, about the bird—we were compelled to eat it."

" To eat it ! " Our visitor half rose from his chair in his excitement.

" Yes ; it would have been no use to anyone had we not done so. But I presume that this other goose upon the sideboard, which is about the same weight and perfectly fresh, will answer your purpose equally well ? "

" Oh, certainly, certainly ! " answered Mr. Baker, with a sigh of relief.

" Of course, we still have the feathers, legs, crop, and so on of your own bird, if you so wish——"

The man burst into a hearty laugh. " They might be useful to me as relics of my adventure," said he, " but beyond that I can hardly see what use the *disjecta membra* of my late acquaintance are going to be to me. No, sir, I think that, with your permission, I will confine my attentions to the excellent bird which I perceive upon the sideboard."

Sherlock Holmes glanced sharply across at me with a slight shrug of his shoulders.

" There is your hat, then, and there your bird," said he. " By the way, would it bore you to tell me where you got the other one from ? I am somewhat of a fowl fancier, and I have seldom seen a better-grown goose."

" Certainly, sir," said Baker, who had risen and tucked his newly gained property under his arm. " There are a few of us who frequent the Alpha Inn near the Museum—we are to be found in the Museum itself during the day, you understand. This year our good host, Windigate by name, instituted a goose-club, by which, on consideration of some few pence every week, we were to receive a bird at Christmas. My pence were duly paid, and the rest is familiar to you. I am much indebted to you, sir, for a Scotch bonnet is fitted neither to my years nor my gravity." With a comical pomposity of manner he bowed solemnly to both of us, and strode off upon his way.

" So much for Mr. Henry Baker," said Holmes, when he had closed the door behind him. " It is quite certain that he knows nothing whatever about the matter. Are you hungry, Watson ? "

" Not particularly."

" Then I suggest that we turn our dinner into a supper, and follow up this clue while it is still hot."

" By all means."

It was a bitter night, so we drew on our ulsters and wrapped cravats about our throats. Outside, the stars were shining coldly in a cloudless sky, and the breath of the passers-by blew out into smoke like so many pistol shots. Our footfalls rang out crisply and loudly as we swung through the doctors' quarter, Wimpole Street, Harley Street, and so through Wigmore Street into Oxford Street. In a quarter of an hour we were in Bloomsbury at the Alpha Inn, which is a small public-house at the corner of one of the streets which runs down into Holborn. Holmes pushed open the door of the private bar, and ordered two glasses of beer from the ruddy-faced, white-aproned landlord.

" Your beer should be excellent if it is as good as your geese," he said.

" My geese ! " The man seemed surprised.

" Yes. I was speaking only half an hour ago to Mr. Henry Baker, who was a member of your goose-club."

" Ah ! yes, I see. But you see, sir, them's not *our* geese."

" Indeed ! Whose, then ? "

" Well, I get the two dozen from a salesman in Covent Garden."

" Indeed ! I know some of them. Which was it ? "

" Breckinridge is his name."

" Ah ! I don't know him. Well, here's your good health, landlord, and prosperity to your house. Good night."

" Now for Mr. Breckinridge," he continued, buttoning up his coat, as we came out into the frosty air. " Remember, Watson, that though we have so homely a thing as a goose at one end of this chain, we have at the other a man who will certainly get seven years' penal servitude, unless we can establish his innocence. It is possible that our inquiry may but confirm his guilt ; but, in any case, we have a line of investigation which has been missed by the police, and which a singular chance has placed in our hands. Let us follow it out to the bitter end. Faces to the south, then, and quick march ! "

We passed across Holborn, down Endell Street, and so through a zigzag of slums to Covent Garden Market. One of the largest stalls bore the name of Breckinridge upon it, and the proprietor, a horsy-looking man, with a sharp face and trim side-whiskers, was helping a boy to put up the shutters.

" Good evening. It's a cold night," said Holmes.

The salesman nodded, and shot a questioning glance at my companion.

" Sold out of geese, I see," continued Holmes, pointing at the bare slabs of marble.

" Let you have five hundred to-morrow morning."

" That's no good."

" Well, there are some on the stall with the gas flare."

" Ah, but I was recommended to you."

" Who by ? "

" The landlord of the ' Alpha.' "

" Ah, yes ; I sent him a couple of dozen."

" Fine birds they were, too. Now where did you get them from ? "

To my surprise the question provoked a burst of anger from the salesman.

" Now then, mister," said he, with his head cocked and his arms akimbo, " what are you driving at ? Let's have it straight, now."

" It is straight enough. I should like to know who sold you the geese which you supplied to the ' Alpha.' "

" Well, then, I shan't tell you. So now ! "

" Oh, it is a matter of no importance ; but I don't know why you should be so warm over such a trifle."

" Warm ! You'd be as warm, maybe, if you were as pestered as I am. When I pay good money for a good article there should be an end of the business ; but it's ' Where are the geese ? ' and ' Who did you sell the geese to ? ' and ' What will you take for the geese ? ' One would think they were the only geese in the world, to hear the fuss that is made over them."

" Well, I have no connection with any other people who have been making inquiries," said Holmes carelessly. " If you won't tell us the bet is off, that is all. But I'm always ready to back my opinion on a matter of fowls, and I have a fiver on it that the bird I ate is country bred."

" Well, then, you've lost your fiver, for it's town bred," snapped the salesman.

" It's nothing of the kind."

" I say it is."

" I don't believe you."

" D'you think you know more about fowls than I, who have handled them ever since I was a nipper ? I tell you, all those birds that went to the ' Alpha ' were town bred."

" You'll never persuade me to believe that."

" Will you bet, then ? "

" It's merely taking your money, for I know that I am

right. But I'll have a sovereign on with you, just to teach you not to be obstinate."

The salesman chuckled grimly. " Bring me the books, Bill," said he.

The small boy brought round a small thin volume and a great greasy-backed one, laying them out together beneath the hanging lamp.

" Now then, Mr. Cocksure," said the salesman, " I thought that I was out of geese, but before I finish you'll find that there is still one left in my shop. You see this little book ? "

" Well ? "

" That's the list of the folk from whom I buy. D'you see ? Well, then, here on this page are the country folk, and the numbers after their names are where their accounts are in the big ledger. Now, then ! You see this other page in red ink ? Well, that is a list of my town suppliers. Now, look at that third name. Just read it out to me."

" Mrs. Oakshott, 117 Brixton Road—249," read Holmes.

" Quite so. Now turn that up in the ledger."

Holmes turned to the page indicated. " Here you are, ' Mrs. Oakshott, 117 Brixton Road, egg and poultry supplier.' "

" Now, then, what's the last entry ? "

" ' December 22. Twenty-four geese at 7s. 6d.' "

" Quite so. There you are. And underneath ? "

" ' Sold to Mr. Windigate of the " Alpha " at 12s.' "

" What have you to say now ? "

Sherlock Holmes looked deeply chagrined. He drew a sovereign from his pocket and threw it down upon the slab, turning away with the air of a man whose disgust is too deep for words. A few yards off he stopped under a lamp-post, and laughed in the hearty, noiseless fashion which was peculiar to him.

" When you see a man with whiskers of that cut and the ' Pink 'Un ' protruding out of his pocket, you can always draw him by a bet," said he. " I dare say that if I had put a hundred pounds down in front of him that man would not have given me such complete information as was drawn from him by the idea that he was doing me on a wager. Well, Watson, we are, I fancy, nearing the end of our quest, and the only point which remains to be determined is whether we should go on to this Mrs. Oakshott to-night, or whether we should reserve it for to-morrow. It is clear from what that surly fellow said that there are others besides ourselves who are anxious about the matter, and I should——"

His remarks were suddenly cut short by a loud hubbub which broke out from the stall which we had just left. Turning round we saw a little rat-faced fellow standing in the centre of the circle of yellow light which was thrown by the swinging lamp, while Breckinridge the salesman, framed in the door of his stall, was shaking his fists fiercely at the cringing figure.

" I've had enough of you and your geese," he shouted. " I wish you were all at the devil together. If you come pestering me any more with your silly talk I'll set the dog at you. You bring Mrs. Oakshott here and I'll answer her, but what have you to do with it ? Did I buy the geese off you ? "

" No ; but one of them was mine all the same," whined the little man.

" Well, then, ask Mrs. Oakshott for it."

" She told me to ask you."

" Well, you can ask the King of Proosia, for all I care. I've had enough of it. Get out of this ! " He rushed fiercely forward, and the inquirer flitted away into the darkness.

" Ha, this may save us a visit to Brixton Road," whispered Holmes. " Come with me, and we will see what is to be made of this fellow." Striding through the scattered knots of people who lounged round the flaring stalls, my companion speedily overtook the little man and touched him upon the shoulder. He sprang round, and I could see in the gaslight that every vestige of colour had been driven from his face.

" Who are you, then ? What do you want ? " he asked in a quavering voice.

" You will excuse me," said Holmes blandly, " but I could not help overhearing the questions which you put to the salesman just now. I think that I could be of assistance to you."

" You ? Who are you ? How could you know anything of the matter ? "

" My name is Sherlock Holmes. It is my business to know what other people don't know."

" But you can know nothing of this ? "

" Excuse me, I know everything of it. You are endeavouring to trace some geese which were sold by Mrs. Oakshott, of Brixton Road, to a salesman named Breckinridge, by him in turn to Mr. Windigate, of the ' Alpha,' and by him to his club, of which Mr. Henry Baker is a member."

" Oh, sir, you are the very man whom I have longed to meet," cried the little fellow, with outstretched hands and quivering fingers. " I can hardly explain to you how interested I am in this matter."

Sherlock Holmes hailed a four-wheeler which was passing. " In that case we had better discuss it in a cosy room rather than in this wind-swept market-place," said he. " But pray tell me, before we go further, who it is that I have the pleasure of assisting."

The man hesitated for an instant. " My name is John Robinson," he answered, with a sidelong glance.

" No, no ; the real name," said Holmes sweetly. " It is always awkward doing business with an *alias*."

A flush sprang to the white cheeks of the stranger. " Well, then," said he, " my real name is James Ryder."

" Precisely so. Head attendant at the Hotel Cosmopolitan. Pray step into the cab, and I shall soon be able to tell you everything which you would wish to know."

The little man stood glancing from one to the other of us with half-frightened, half-hopeful eyes, as one who is not sure whether he is on the verge of a windfall or of a catastrophe. Then he stepped into the cab, and in half an hour we were back in the sitting-room at Baker Street. Nothing had been said during our drive, but the high, thin breathings of our new companion, and the claspings and unclaspings of his hands, spoke of the nervous tension within him.

" Here we are ! " said Holmes cheerily, as we filed into the room. " The fire looks very seasonable in this weather. You look cold, Mr. Ryder. Pray take the basket chair. I will just put on my slippers before we settle this little matter of yours. Now, then ! You want to know what became of those geese ? "

" Yes, sir."

" Or rather, I fancy, of that goose. It was one bird, I imagine, in which you were interested—white, with a black bar across the tail."

Ryder quivered with emotion. " Oh, sir," he cried, " can you tell me where it went to ? "

" It came here."

" Here ? "

" Yes, and a most remarkable bird it proved. I don't wonder that you should take an interest in it. It laid an egg after it was dead—the bonniest, brightest little blue egg that ever was seen. I have it here in my museum."

Our visitor staggered to his feet, and clutched the mantelpiece with his right hand. Holmes unlocked his strong-box, and held up the blue carbuncle, which shone out like a star, with a cold, brilliant, many-pointed radiance. Ryder stood glaring with a drawn face, uncertain whether to claim or to disown it.

" The game's up, Ryder," said Holmes quietly. " Hold up, man, or you'll be into the fire. Give him an arm back into his chair, Watson. He's not got blood enough to go in for felony with impunity. Give him a dash of brandy. So ! Now he looks a little more human. What a shrimp it is, to be sure ! "

For a moment he had staggered and nearly fallen, but the brandy brought a tinge of colour into his cheeks, and he sat staring with frightened eyes at his accuser.

" I have almost every link in my hands, and all the proofs which I could possibly need, so there is little which you need tell me. Still, that little may as well be cleared up to make the case complete. You had heard, Ryder, of this blue stone of the Countess of Morcar's ? "

" It was Catherine Cusack who told me of it," said he, in a crackling voice.

" I see. Her ladyship's waiting-maid. Well, the temptation of sudden wealth so easily acquired was too much for you, as it has been for better men before you ; but you were not very scrupulous in the means you used. It seems to me, Ryder, that there is the making of a very pretty villain in you. You knew that this man Horner, the plumber, had been concerned in some such matter before, and that suspicion would rest the more readily upon him. What did you do, then ? You made some small job in my lady's room—you and your confederate Cusack—and you managed that he should be the man sent for. Then, when he had left, you rifled the jewel-case, raised the alarm, and had this unfortunate man arrested. You then——"

Ryder threw himself down suddenly upon the rug, and clutched at my companion's knees. " For God's sake, have mercy ! " he shrieked. " Think of my father ! Of my mother ! It would break their hearts. I never went wrong before ! I never will again. I swear it. I'll swear it on a Bible. Oh, don't bring it into court ! For Christ's sake, don't ! "

" Get back into your chair ! " said Holmes sternly. " It is very well to cringe and crawl now, but you thought little enough of this poor Horner in the dock for a crime of which he knew nothing."

" I will fly, Mr. Holmes. I will leave the country, sir. Then the charge against him will break down."

" Hum ! We will talk about that. And now let us hear a true account of the next act. How came the stone into the goose, and how came the goose into the open market ? Tell us the truth, for there lies your only hope of safety."

Ryder passed his tongue over his parched lips. " I will

tell you it just as it happened, sir," said he. " When Horner had been arrested, it seemed to me that it would be best for me to get away with the stone at once, for I did not know at what moment the police might not take it into their heads to search me and my room. There was no place about the hotel where it would be safe. I went out, as if on some commission, and I made for my sister's house. She had married a man named Oakshott, and lived in Brixton Road, where she fattened fowls for the market. All the way there every man I met seemed to me to be a policeman or a detective, and for all that it was a cold night, the sweat was pouring down my face before I came to the Brixton Road. My sister asked me what was the matter, and why I was so pale ; but I told her that I had been upset by the jewel robbery at the hotel. Then I went into the back-yard, and smoked a pipe, and wondered what it would be best to do.

" I had a friend once called Maudsley, who went to the bad, and has just been serving his time in Pentonville. One day he had met me, and fell into talk about the ways of thieves and how they could get rid of what they stole. I knew that he would be true to me, for I knew one or two things about him, so I made up my mind to go right on to Kilburn, where he lived, and take him into my confidence. He would show me how to turn the stone into money. But how to get to him in safety ? I thought of the agonies I had gone through in coming from the hotel. I might at any moment be seized and searched, and there would be the stone in my waistcoat pocket. I was leaning against the wall at the time, and looking at the geese which were waddling about round my feet, and suddenly an idea came into my head which showed me how I could beat the best detective that ever lived.

" My sister had told me some weeks before that I might have the pick of her geese for a Christmas present, and I knew that she was always as good as her word. I would take my goose now, and in it I would carry my stone to Kilburn. There was a little shed in the yard, and behind this I drove one of the birds, a fine big one, white, with a barred tail. I caught it and, prising its bill open, I thrust the stone down its throat as far as my finger could reach. The bird gave a gulp, and I felt the stone pass along its gullet and down into its crop. But the creature flapped and struggled, and out came my sister to know what was the matter. As I turned to speak to her the brute broke loose, and fluttered off among the others.

" ' Whatever were you doing with that bird, Jem ? ' says she.

" ' Well,' said I, ' you said you'd give me one for Christmas, and I was feeling which was the fattest.'

" ' Oh,' says she, ' we've set yours aside for you. Jem's bird, we call it. It's the big, white one over yonder. There's twenty-six of them, which makes one for you, and one for us, and two dozen for the market.'

" ' Thank you, Maggie,' says I ; ' but if it is all the same to you I'd rather have that one I was handling just now.'

" ' The other is a good three pound heavier,' she said, ' and we fattened it expressly for you.'

" ' Never mind. I'll have the other, and I'll take it now,' said I.

" ' Oh, just as you like,' said she, a little huffed. ' Which is it you want, then ? '

" ' That white one, with the barred tail, right in the middle of the flock.'

" ' Oh, very well. Kill it and take it with you.'

" Well, I did what she said, Mr. Holmes, and I carried the bird all the way to Kilburn. I told my pal what I had done, for he was a man that it was easy to tell a thing like that to. He laughed until he choked, and we got a knife and opened the goose. My heart turned to water, for there was no sign of the stone, and I knew that some terrible mistake had occurred. I left the bird, rushed back to my sister's, and hurried into the back-yard. There was not a bird to be seen there.

" ' Where are they all, Maggie ? ' I cried.

" ' Gone to the dealer's.'

" ' Which dealer's ? '

" ' Breckinridge, of Covent Garden.'

" ' But was there another with a barred tail ? ' I asked,
' the same as the one I chose ? '

" ' Yes, Jem, there were two barred-tailed ones, and I
could never tell them apart.'

" Well, then, of course, I saw it all, and I ran off as hard
as my feet would carry me to this man Breckinridge ; but
he had sold the lot at once, and not one word would he tell
me as to where they had gone. You heard him yourselves
to-night. Well, he has always answered me like that.
My sister thinks that I am going mad. Sometimes I think
that I am myself. And now—and now I am myself a
branded thief, without ever having touched the wealth for
which I sold my character. God help me ! God help
me ! " He burst into convulsive sobbing, with his face
buried in his hands.

There was a long silence, broken only by his heavy
breathing, and by the measured tapping of Sherlock
Holmes' finger-tips upon the edge of the table. Then my
friend rose, and threw open the door.

" Get out ! " said he.

" What, sir ! Oh, Heaven bless you ! "

" No more words. Get out ! "

And no more words were needed. There was a rush, a
clatter upon the stairs, the bang of a door, and the crisp
rattle of running footfalls from the street.

" After all, Watson," said Holmes, reaching up his hand
for his clay pipe, " I am not retained by the police to supply
their deficiencies. If Horner were in danger it would be
another thing, but this fellow will not appear against him,
and the case must collapse. I suppose that I am commut-
ing a felony, but it is just possible that I am saving a soul.
This fellow will not go wrong again. He is too terribly
frightened. Send him to gaol now, and you make him a
gaolbird for life. Besides, it is the season of forgiveness.
Chance has put in our way a most singular and whimsical
problem, and its solution is its own reward. If you will

have the goodness to touch the bell, Doctor, we will begin
another investigation, in which also a bird will be the chief
feature."

8. *The Speckled Band*

IN glancing over my notes of the seventy odd cases in
which I have during the last eight years studied the
methods of my friend Sherlock Holmes, I find many
tragic, some comic, a large number merely strange, but
none commonplace ; for, working as he did rather for the
love of his art than for the acquirement of wealth, he
refused to associate himself with any investigation which
did not tend towards the unusual, and even the fantastic.
Of all these varied cases, however, I cannot recall any
which presented more singular features than that which
was associated with the well-known Surrey family of the
Roylotts of Stoke Moran. The events in question occurred
in the early days of my association with Holmes, when we
were sharing rooms as bachelors, in Baker Street. It is
possible that I might have placed them upon record before,
but a promise of secrecy was made at the time, from which
I have only been freed during the last month by the untimely death of the lady to whom the pledge was given.
It is perhaps as well that the facts should now come to
light, for I have reasons to know there are widespread
rumours as to the death of Dr. Grimesby Roylott which
tend to make the matter even more terrible than the truth.

It was early in April, in the year '83, that I woke one
morning to find Sherlock Holmes standing, fully dressed,
by the side of my bed. He was a late riser as a rule, and,
as the clock on the mantelpiece showed me that it was only
a quarter past seven, I blinked up at him in some surprise,
and perhaps just a little resentment, for I was myself
regular in my habits.

" Very sorry to knock you up, Watson," said he, " but
it's the common lot this morning. Mrs. Hudson has been
knocked up, she retorted upon me, and I on you."

" What is it, then ? A fire ? "

" No, a client. It seems that a young lady has arrived in a considerable state of excitement, who insists upon seeing me. She is waiting now in the sitting-room. Now, when young ladies wander about the metropolis at this hour of the morning, and knock sleepy people up out of their beds, I presume that it is something very pressing which they have to communicate. Should it prove to be an interesting case, you would, I am sure, wish to follow it from the outset. I thought at any rate that I should call you, and give you the chance."

" My dear fellow, I would not miss it for anything."

I had no keener pleasure than in following Holmes in his professional investigations, and in admiring the rapid deductions, as swift as intuitions, and yet always founded on a logical basis, with which he unravelled the problems which were submitted to him. I rapidly threw on my clothes, and was ready in a few minutes to accompany my friend down to the sitting-room. A lady dressed in black and heavily veiled, who had been sitting in the window, rose as we entered.

" Good morning, madam," said Holmes cheerily. " My name is Sherlock Holmes. This is my intimate friend and associate, Dr. Watson, before whom you can speak as freely as before myself. Ha, I am glad to see that Mrs. Hudson has had the good sense to light the fire. Pray draw up to it, and I shall order you a cup of hot coffee, for I observe that you are shivering."

" It is not cold which makes me shiver," said the woman in a low voice, changing her seat as requested.

" What then ? "

" It is fear, Mr. Holmes. It is terror." She raised her veil as she spoke, and we could see that she was indeed in a pitiable state of agitation, her face all drawn and grey, with restless, frightened eyes, like those of some hunted animal. Her features and figure were those of a woman of thirty, but her hair was shot with premature grey, and her expression was weary and haggard. Sherlock Holmes ran her over with one of his quick, all-comprehensive glances.

"You must not fear," said he soothingly, bending forward and patting her forearm. "We shall soon set matters right, I have no doubt. You have come in by train this morning, I see."

"You know me, then?"

"No, but I observe the second half of a return ticket in the palm of your left glove. You must have started early, and yet you had a good drive in a dog-cart, along heavy roads, before you reached the station."

The lady gave a violent start, and stared in bewilderment at my companion.

"There is no mystery, my dear madam," said he, smiling. "The left arm of your jacket is spattered with mud in no less than seven places. The marks are perfectly fresh. There is no vehicle save a dog-cart which throws up mud in that way, and then only when you sit on the left-hand side of the driver."

"Whatever your reasons may be, you are perfectly correct," said she. "I started from home before six, reached Leatherhead at twenty past, and came in by the first train to Waterloo. Sir, I can stand this strain no longer, I shall go mad if it continues. I have no one to turn to—none, save only one, who cares for me, and he, poor fellow, can be of little aid. I have heard of you, Mr. Holmes; I have heard of you from Mrs. Farintosh, whom you helped in the hour of her sore need. It was from her that I had your address. Oh, sir, do you not think you could help me too, and at least throw a little light through the dense darkness which surrounds me? At present it is out of my power to reward you for your services, but in a month or two I shall be married, with the control of my own income, and then at least you shall not find me ungrateful."

Holmes turned to his desk, and unlocking it, drew out a small case-book which he consulted.

"Farintosh," said he. "Ah, yes, I recall the case; it

was concerned with an opal tiara. I think it was before your time, Watson. I can only say, madam, that I shall be happy to devote the same care to your case as I did to that of your friend. As to reward, my profession is its reward ; but you are at liberty to defray whatever expenses I may be put to, at the time which suits you best. And now I beg that you will lay before us everything that may help us in forming an opinion upon the matter."

" Alas ! " replied our visitor. " The very horror of my situation lies in the fact that my fears are so vague, and my suspicions depend so entirely upon small points, which might seem trivial to another, that even he to whom of all others I have a right to look for help and advice looks upon all that I tell him about it as the fancies of a nervous woman. He does not say so, but I can read it from his soothing answers and averted eyes. But I have heard, Mr. Holmes, that you can see deeply into the manifold wickedness of the human heart. You may advise me how to walk amid the dangers which encompass me."

" I am all attention, madam."

" My name is Helen Stoner, and I am living with my stepfather, who is the last survivor of one of the oldest Saxon families in England, the Roylotts of Stoke Moran, on the western border of Surrey."

Holmes nodded his head. " The name is familiar to me," said he.

" The family was at one time among the richest in England, and the estate extended over the borders into Berkshire in the north, and Hampshire in the west. In the last century, however, four successive heirs were of a dissolute and wasteful disposition, and the family ruin was eventually completed by a gambler, in the days of the Regency. Nothing was left save a few acres of ground and the two-hundred-year-old house, which is itself crushed under a heavy mortgage. The last squire dragged out his existence there, living the horrible life of an aristocratic pauper ; but his only son, my stepfather, seeing that he must adapt himself to the new conditions, obtained an advance from a relative, which enabled him to take a medical degree, and went out to Calcutta, where, by his professional skill and his force of character, he established a large practice. In a fit of anger, however, caused by some robberies which had been perpetrated in the house, he beat his native butler to death, and narrowly escaped a capital sentence. As it was, he suffered a long term of imprisonment, and afterwards returned to England a morose and disappointed man.

" When Dr. Roylott was in India he married my mother, Mrs. Stoner, the young widow of Major-General Stoner, of the Bengal Artillery. My sister Julia and I were twins, and we were only two years old at the time of my mother's re-marriage. She had a considerable sum of money, not less than a thousand a year, and this she bequeathed to Dr. Roylott entirely whilst we resided with him, with a provision that a certain annual sum should be allowed to each of us in the event of our marriage. Shortly after our return to England my mother died—she was killed eight years ago in a railway accident near Crewe. Dr. Roylott then abandoned his attempts to establish himself in practice in London, and took us to live with him in the ancestral house at Stoke Moran. The money which my mother had left was enough for all our wants, and there seemed no obstacle to our happiness.

" But a terrible change came over our stepfather about this time. Instead of making friends and exchanging visits with our neighbours, who had at first been overjoyed to see a Roylott of Stoke Moran back in the old family seat, he shut himself up in his house, and seldom came out save to indulge in ferocious quarrels with whoever might cross his path. Violence of temper approaching to mania has been hereditary in the men of the family, and in my stepfather's case it had, I believe, been intensified by his long residence in the tropics. A series of disgraceful brawls took place, two of which ended in the police-court, until at last he became the terror of the village, and the folks would fly at his approach, for he is a man of immense strength, and absolutely uncontrollable in his anger.

" Last week he hurled the local blacksmith over a parapet into a stream and it was only by paying over all the money that I could gather together that I was able to avert another public exposure. He had no friends at all save the wandering gipsies, and he would give these vagabonds leave to encamp upon the few acres of bramble-covered land which represent the family estate, and would accept in return the hospitality of their tents, wandering away with them sometimes for weeks on end. He has a passion also for Indian animals, which are sent over to him by a correspondent, and he has at this moment a cheetah and a baboon, which wander freely over his grounds, and are feared by the villagers almost as much as their master.

" You can imagine from what I say that my poor sister Julia and I had no great pleasure in our lives. No servant would stay with us, and for a long time we did all the work of the house. She was but thirty at the time of her death, and yet her hair had already begun to whiten, even as mine has."

" Your sister is dead, then ? "

" She died just two years ago, and it is of her death that I wish to speak to you. You can understand that, living the life which I have described, we were little likely to see anyone of our own age and position. We had, however, an aunt, my mother's maiden sister, Miss Honoria Westphail, who lives near Harrow, and we were occasionally allowed to pay short visits at this lady's house. Julia went there at Christmas two years ago, and met there a half-pay Major of Marines, to whom she became engaged. My stepfather learned of the engagement when my sister returned, and offered no objection to the marriage ; but within a fortnight of the day which had been fixed for the wedding, the terrible event occurred which has deprived me of my only companion."

Sherlock Holmes had been leaning back in his chair with his eyes closed, and his head sunk in a cushion, but he half opened his lids now, and glanced across at his visitor.

"Pray be precise as to details," said he.

"It is easy for me to be so, for every event of that dreadful time is seared into my memory. The manor house is, as I have already said, very old, and only one wing is now inhabited. The bedrooms in this wing are on the ground floor, the sitting-rooms being in the central block of the buildings. Of these bedrooms, the first is Dr. Roylott's, the second my sister's, and the third my own. There is no communication between them, but they all open out into the same corridor. Do I make myself plain?"

"Perfectly so."

"The windows of the three rooms open out upon the lawn. That fatal night Dr. Roylott had gone to his room early, though we knew that he had not retired to rest, for my sister was troubled by the smell of the strong Indian cigars which it was his custom to smoke. She left her room, therefore, and came into mine, where she sat for some time, chatting about her approaching wedding. At eleven o'clock she rose to leave me, but she paused at the door and looked back.

"'Tell me, Helen,' said she, 'have you ever heard any-one whistle in the dead of the night?'

"'Never,' said I.

"'I suppose that you could not possibly whistle your-self in your sleep?'

"'Certainly not. But why?'

"'Because during the last few nights I have always, about three in the morning, heard a low clear whistle. I am a light sleeper, and it has awakened me. I cannot tell where it came from—perhaps from the next room, perhaps from the lawn. I thought that I would just ask you whether you had heard it.'

"'No, I have not. It must be those wretched gipsies in the plantation.'

"'Very likely. And yet if it were on the lawn I won-der that you did not hear it also.'

"'Ah, but I sleep more heavily than you.'

"'Well, it is of no great consequence, at any rate,' she smiled back at me, closed my door, and a few moments later I heard her key turn in the lock."

"Indeed," said Holmes. "Was it your custom always to lock yourselves in at night?"

"Always."

"And why?"

"I think that I mentioned to you that the Doctor kept a cheetah and a baboon. We had no feeling of security unless our doors were locked."

"Quite so. Pray proceed with your statement."

"I could not sleep that night. A vague feeling of impending misfortune impressed me. My sister and I, you will recollect, were twins, and you know how subtle are the links which bind two souls which are so closely allied. It was a wild night. The wind was howling outside, and the rain was beating and splashing against the windows. Suddenly, amidst all the hubbub of the gale, there burst forth the wild scream of a terrified woman. I knew that it was my sister's voice. I sprang from my bed, wrapped a shawl round me, and rushed into the corridor. As I opened my door I seemed to hear a low whistle, such as my sister described, and a few moments later a clanging sound, as if a mass of metal had fallen. As I ran down the passage my sister's door was unlocked, and revolved slowly upon its hinges. I stared at it horror-stricken, not knowing what was about to issue from it. By the light of the corridor lamp I saw my sister appear at the opening, her face blanched with terror, her hands groping for help, her whole figure swaying to and fro like that of a drunkard. I ran to her and threw my arms round her, but at that moment her knees seemed to give way and she fell to the ground. She writhed as one who is in terrible pain, and her limbs were dreadfully convulsed. At first I thought that she had not recognized me, but as I bent over her she suddenly shrieked out in a voice which I shall never forget, 'O, my God! Helen! It was the band! The speckled band ! ' There was something else which she would fain have said, and she stabbed with her finger into the air in the direction of the Doctor's room, but a fresh convulsion seized her and choked her words. I rushed out, calling loudly for my stepfather, and I met him hastening from his room in his dressing-gown. When he reached my sister's side she was unconscious, and though he poured brandy down her throat, and sent for medical aid from the village, all efforts were in vain, for she slowly sank and died without having recovered her consciousness. Such was the dreadful end of my beloved sister."

"One moment," said Holmes ; "are you sure about this whistle and metallic sound ? Could you swear to it ? "

"That was what the county coroner asked me at the inquiry. It is my strong impression that I heard it, and yet among the crash of the gale, and the creaking of an old house, I may possibly have been deceived."

"Was your sister dressed ? "

"No, she was in her nightdress. In her right hand was found the charred stump of a match, and in her left a matchbox."

"Showing that she had struck a light and looked about her when the alarm took place. That is important. And what conclusions did the coroner come to ? "

"He investigated the case with great care, for Dr. Roylott's conduct had long been notorious in the county, but he was unable to find any satisfactory cause of death. My evidence showed that the door had been fastened upon the inner side, and the windows were blocked by old-fashioned shutters with broad iron bars, which were secured every night. The walls were carefully sounded, and were shown to be quite solid all round, and the flooring was also thoroughly examined, with the same result. The chimney is wide, but is barred up by four large staples. It is certain, therefore, that my sister was quite alone when she met her end. Besides, there were no marks of any violence upon her."

"How about poison ? "

" The doctors examined her for it, but without success."

" What do you think that this unfortunate lady died of, then ? "

" It is my belief that she died of pure fear and nervous shock, though what it was which frightened her I cannot imagine."

" Were there gipsies in the plantation at the time ? "

" Yes, there are nearly always some there."

" Ah, and what did you gather from this allusion to a band—a speckled band ? "

" Sometimes I have thought that it was merely the wild talk of delirium, sometimes that it may have referred to some band of people, perhaps to these very gipsies in the plantation. I do not know whether the spotted handkerchiefs which so many of them wear over their heads might have suggested the strange adjective which she used."

Holmes shook his head like a man who is far from being satisfied.

" These are very deep waters," said he ; " pray go on with your narrative."

" Two years have passed since then, and my life has been until lately lonelier than ever. A month ago, however, a dear friend, whom I have known for many years, has done me the honour to ask my hand in marriage. His name is Armitage—Percy Armitage—the second son of Mr. Armitage, of Crane Water, near Reading. My stepfather has offered no opposition to the match, and we are to be married in the course of the spring. Two days ago some repairs were started in the west wing of the building, and my bedroom wall has been pierced, so that I have had to move into the chamber in which my sister died, and to sleep in the very bed in which she slept. Imagine, then, my thrill of terror when last night, as I lay awake, thinking over her terrible fate, I suddenly heard in the silence of the night the low whistle which had been the herald of her own death. I sprang up and lit the lamp, but nothing was to be seen in the room. I was too shaken to go to bed again, however, so I dressed, and as soon as it was daylight I slipped down, got a dog-cart at the Crown Inn, which is opposite, and drove to Leatherhead, from whence I have come on this morning, with the one object of seeing you and asking your advice."

" You have done wisely," said my friend. " But have you told me all ? "

" Yes, all."

" Miss Stoner, you have not. You are screening your stepfather."

" Why, what do you mean ? "

For answer Holmes pushed back the frill of black lace which fringed the hand that lay upon our visitor's knee. Five little livid spots, the marks of four fingers and a thumb, were printed upon the white wrist.

" You have been cruelly used," said Holmes.

The lady coloured deeply, and covered over her injured wrist. " He is a hard man," she said, " and perhaps he hardly knows his own strength."

There was a long silence, during which Holmes leaned his chin upon his hands and stared into the crackling fire.

" This is very deep business," he said at last. " There are a thousand details which I should desire to know before I decide upon our course of action. Yet we have not a moment to lose. If we were to come to Stoke Moran to-day, would it be possible for us to see over these rooms without the knowledge of your stepfather ? "

" As it happens, he spoke of coming into town to-day upon some most important business. It is probable that he will be away all day, and that there would be nothing to disturb you. We have a housekeeper now, but she is old and foolish, and I could easily get her out of the way."

" Excellent. You are not averse to this trip, Watson ? "

" By no means."

" Then we shall both come. What are you going to do yourself ? "

" I have one or two things which I would wish to do now that I am in town. But I shall return by the twelve o'clock train, so as to be there in time for your coming."

" And you may expect us early in the afternoon. I have myself some small business matters to attend to. Will you not wait and breakfast ? "

" No, I must go. My heart is lightened already since I have confided my trouble to you. I shall look forward to seeing you again this afternoon." She dropped her thick black veil over her face, and glided from the room.

" And what do you think of it all, Watson ? " asked Sherlock Holmes, leaning back in his chair.

" It seems to me to be a most dark and sinister business."

" Dark enough and sinister enough."

" Yet if the lady is correct in saying that the flooring and walls are sound, and that the door, window, and chimney are impassable, then her sister must have been undoubtedly alone when she met her mysterious end."

" What becomes, then, of these nocturnal whistles, and what of the very peculiar words of the dying woman ? "

" I cannot think."

" When you combine the ideas of whistles at night, the presence of a band of gipsies who are on intimate terms with this old doctor, the fact that we have every reason to believe that the doctor has an interest in preventing his stepdaughter's marriage, the dying allusion to a band, and finally, the fact that Miss Helen Stoner heard a metallic clang, which might have been caused by one of those metal bars which secured the shutters falling back into their place, I think there is good ground to think that the mystery may be cleared along those lines."

" But what, then, did the gipsies do ? "

" I cannot imagine."

" I see many objections to any such a theory."

" And so do I. It is precisely for that reason that we are going to Stoke Moran this day. I want to see whether the objections are fatal, or if they may be explained away. But what, in the name of the devil ! "

The ejaculation had been drawn from my companion by the fact that our door had been suddenly dashed open, and that a huge man framed himself in the aperture. His costume was a peculiar mixture of the professional and of the agricultural, having a black top-hat, a long frock-coat, and a pair of high gaiters, with a hunting-crop swinging in his hand. So tall was he that his hat actually brushed the cross-bar of the doorway, and his breadth seemed to span it across from side to side. A large face, seared with a thousand wrinkles, burned yellow with the sun, and marked with every evil passion, was turned from one to the other of us, while his deep-set, bile-shot eyes, and the high thin fleshless nose, gave him somewhat the resemblance to a fierce old bird of prey.

" Which of you is Holmes ? " asked this apparition.

" My name, sir, but you have the advantage of me," said my companion quietly.

" I am Dr. Grimesby Roylott, of Stoke Moran."

" Indeed, Doctor," said Holmes blandly. " Pray take a seat."

" I will do nothing of the kind. My stepdaughter has been here. I have traced her. What has she been saying to you ? "

" It is a little cold for the time of the year," said Holmes.

" What has she been saying to you ? " screamed the old man furiously.

" But I have heard that the crocuses promise well," continued my companion imperturbably.

" Ha ! You put me off, do you ? " said our new visitor, taking a step forward, and shaking his hunting-crop. " I know you, you scoundrel ! I have heard of you before You are Holmes the meddler."

My friend smiled.

" Holmes the busybody ! "

His smile broadened.

" Holmes the Scotland Yard jack-in-office."

Holmes chuckled heartily. " Your conversation is most entertaining," said he. " When you go out close the door, for there is a decided draught."

" I will go when I have had my say. Don't you dare to meddle with my affairs. I know that Miss Stoner has been here——I traced her ! I am a dangerous man to fall foul of ! See here." He stepped swiftly forward, seized the poker, and bent it into a curve with his huge brown hands.

" See that you keep yourself out of my grip," he snarled, and hurling the twisted poker into the fireplace, he strode out of the room.

" He seems a very amiable person," said Holmes, laughing. " I am not quite so bulky, but if he had remained I might have shown him that my grip was not much more feeble than his own." As he spoke he picked up the steel poker, and with a sudden effort straightened it out again.

" Fancy his having the insolence to confound me with the official detective force ! This incident gives zest to our investigation, however, and I only trust that our little friend will not suffer from her imprudence in allowing this brute to trace her. And now, Watson, we shall order breakfast, and afterwards I shall walk down to Doctors' Commons, where I hope to get some data which may help us in this matter."

It was nearly one o'clock when Sherlock Holmes returned from his excursion. He held in his hand a sheet of blue paper, scrawled over with notes and figures.

" I have seen the will of the deceased wife," said he. " To determine its exact meaning I have been obliged to work out the present prices of the investments with which it is concerned. The total income, which at the time of the wife's death was little short of £1,100, is now through the fall in agricultural prices not more than £750. Each daughter can claim an income of £250, in case of marriage. It is evident, therefore, that if both girls had married this beauty would have had a mere pittance, while even one of them would cripple him to a serious extent. My morning's work has not been wasted, since it has proved that he has the very strongest motives for standing in the way of anything of the sort. And now, Watson, this is too serious for dawdling, especially as the old man is aware that we are interesting ourselves in his affairs, so if you are ready we shall call a cab and drive to Waterloo. I should be very much obliged if you would slip your revolver into your pocket. An Eley's No. 2 is an excellent argument with gentlemen who can twist steel pokers into knots. That and a tooth-brush are, I think, all that we need."

At Waterloo we were fortunate in catching a train for Leatherhead, where we hired a trap at the station inn, and drove for four or five miles through the lovely Surrey lanes. It was a perfect day, with a bright sun and a few fleecy clouds in the heavens. The trees and wayside hedges were just throwing out their first green shoots, and the air was full of the pleasant smell of the moist earth. To me at least there was a strange contrast between the sweet promise of the spring and this sinister quest upon which we were engaged. My companion sat in front of the trap, his arms folded, his hat pulled down over his eyes, and his chin sunk upon his breast, buried in the deepest thought. Suddenly, however, he started, tapped me on the shoulder, and pointed over the meadows.

" Look there ! " said he.

A heavily timbered park stretched up in a gentle slope, thickening into a grove at the highest point. From amidst the branches there jutted out the grey gables and high roof-tree of a very old mansion.

" Stoke Moran ? " said he.

" Yes, sir, that be the house of Dr. Grimesby Roylott," remarked the driver.

" There is some building going on there," said Holmes ; " that is where we are going."

" There's the village," said the driver, pointing to a cluster of roofs some distance to the left ; " but if you want to get to the house, you'll find it shorter to go over this stile, and so by the footpath over the fields. There it is, where the lady is walking."

" And the lady, I fancy, is Miss Stoner," observed Holmes, shading his eyes. " Yes, I think we had better do as you suggest."

We got off, paid our fare, and the trap rattled back on its way to Leatherhead.

" I thought it as well," said Holmes, as we climbed the stile, " that this fellow should think we had come here as architects, or on some definite business. It may stop his gossip. Good afternoon, Miss Stoner. You see that we have been as good as our word."

Our client of the morning had hurried forward to meet us with a face which spoke her joy. " I have been waiting so eagerly for you," she cried, shaking hands with us warmly. " All has turned out splendidly. Dr. Roylott has gone to town, and it is unlikely that he will be back before evening."

" We have had the pleasure of making the Doctor's acquaintance," said Holmes, and in a few words he sketched out what had occurred. Miss Stoner turned white to the lips as she listened.

" Good heavens ! " she cried, " he has followed me, then."

" So it appears."

" He is so cunning that I never know when I am safe from him. What will he say when he returns ? "

" He must guard himself, for he may find that there is someone more cunning than himself upon his track. You must lock yourself from him to-night. If he is violent, we shall take you away to your aunt's at Harrow. Now, we must make the best use of our time, so kindly take us at once to the rooms which we are to examine."

The building was of grey, lichen-blotched stone, with a high central portion, and two curving wings, like the claws of a crab, thrown out on each side. In one of these wings the windows were broken, and blocked with wooden boards, while the roof was partly caved in, a picture of ruin. The central portion was in little better repair, but the right-hand block was comparatively modern, and the blinds in the windows, with the blue smoke curling up from the chimneys, showed that this was where the family resided. Some scaffolding had been erected against the end wall, and the stonework had been broken into, but there were no signs of any workmen at the moment of our visit. Holmes walked slowly up and down the ill-trimmed lawn, and examined with deep attention the outsides of the windows.

" This, I take it, belongs to the room in which you used to sleep, the centre one to your sister's, and the one next to the main building to Dr. Roylott's chamber ? "

" Exactly so. But I am now sleeping in the middle one."

" Pending the alterations, as I understand. By the way, there does not seem to be any very pressing need for repairs at that end wall."

" There were none. I believe that it was an excuse to move me from my room."

" Ah ! that is suggestive. Now, on the other side of this narrow wing runs the corridor from which these three rooms open. There are windows in it, of course ? "

" Yes, but very small ones. Too narrow for anyone to pass through."

" As you both locked your doors at night, your rooms were unapproachable from that side. Now, would you have the kindness to go into your room, and to bar your shutters."

Miss Stoner did so, and Holmes, after a careful examination through the open window, endeavoured in every way to force the shutter open, but without success. There was no slit through which a knife could be passed to raise the bar. Then with his lens he tested the hinges, but they were of solid iron, built firmly into the massive masonry. " Hum ! " said he, scratching his chin in some perplexity, " my theory certainly presents some difficulties. No one could pass these shutters if they were bolted. Well, we shall see if the inside throws any light upon the matter."

A small side-door led into the whitewashed corridor from which the three bedrooms opened. Holmes refused to examine the third chamber, so we passed at once to the second, that in which Miss Stoner was now sleeping, and in which her sister had met her fate. It was a homely little room, with a low ceiling and a gaping fireplace, after the fashion of old country houses. A brown chest of drawers stood in one corner, a narrow white-counterpaned bed in another, and a dressing-table on the left-hand side of the window. These articles, with two small wicker-work chairs, made up all the furniture in the room, save for a square of Wilton carpet in the centre. The boards round and the panelling of the walls were brown, worm-eaten oak, so old and discoloured that it may have dated from the original building of the house. Holmes drew one of the chairs into a corner and sat silent, while his eyes travelled round and round and up and down, taking in every detail of the apartment.

" Where does that bell communicate with ? " he asked at last, pointing to a thick bell-rope which hung down beside the bed, the tassel actually lying upon the pillow.

" It goes to the housekeeper's room."

" It looks newer than the other things ? "

" Yes, it was only put there a couple of years ago."

" Your sister asked for it, I suppose ? "

" No, I never heard of her using it. We used always to get what we wanted for ourselves."

" Indeed, it seemed unnecessary to put so nice a bell-pull there. You will excuse me for a few minutes while I satisfy myself as to this floor." He threw himself down upon his face with his lens in his hand, and crawled swiftly backwards and forwards, examining minutely the cracks between the boards. Then he did the same with the woodwork with which the chamber was panelled. Finally he walked over to the bed and spent some time in staring at it, and in running his eye up and down the wall. Finally he took the bell-rope in his hand and gave it a brisk tug.

" Why, it's a dummy," said he.

" Won't it ring ? "

" No, it is not even attached to a wire. This is very interesting. You can see now that it is fastened to a hook just above where the little opening of the ventilator is."

" How very absurd ! I never noticed that before."

" Very strange ! " muttered Holmes, pulling at the rope. " There are one or two very singular points about this room. For example, what a fool a builder must be to open a ventilator in another room, when, with the same trouble, he might have communicated with the outside air ! "

" That is also quite modern," said the lady.

" Done about the same time as the bell-rope," remarked Holmes.

" Yes, there were several little changes carried out about that time."

" They seem to have been of a most interesting character—dummy bell-ropes, and ventilators which do not ventilate. With your permission, Miss Stoner, we shall now carry our researches into the inner apartment."

Dr. Grimesby Roylott's chamber was larger than that of his stepdaughter, but was as plainly furnished. A camp bed, a small wooden shelf full of books, mostly of a technical character, an arm-chair beside the bed, a plain wooden chair against the wall, a round table, and a large iron safe were the principal things which met the eye. Holmes walked slowly round and examined each and all of them with the keenest interest.

" What's in here ? " he asked, tapping the safe.

" My stepfather's business papers."

" Oh ! you have seen inside, then ? "

" Only once, some years ago. I remember that it was full of papers."

" There isn't a cat in it, for example ? "

" No. What a strange idea ! "

" Well, look at this ! " He took up a small saucer of milk which stood on the top of it.

" No ; we don't keep a cat. But there is a cheetah and a baboon."

" Ah, yes, of course ! Well, a cheetah is just a big cat, and yet a saucer of milk does not go very far in satisfying its wants, I daresay. There is one point which I should wish to determine." He squatted down in front of the wooden chair, and examined the seat of it with the greatest attention.

" Thank you. That is quite settled," said he, rising and putting his lens in his pocket. " Hullo ! here is something interesting ! "

The object which had caught his eye was a small dog lash hung on one corner of the bed. The lash, however, was curled upon itself, and tied so as to make a loop of whipcord.

" What do you make of that, Watson ? "

" It's a common enough lash. But I don't know why it should be tied."

" That is not quite so common, is it ? Ah, me ! it's a wicked world, and when a clever man turns his brain to crime it is the worst of all. I think that I have seen enough now, Miss Stoner, and, with your permission, we shall walk out upon the lawn."

I had never seen my friend's face so grim, or his brow so dark, as it was when we turned from the scene of this investigation. We had walked several times up and down the lawn, neither Miss Stoner nor myself liking to break in upon his thoughts before he roused himself from his reverie.

" It is very essential, Miss Stoner," said he, " that you should absolutely follow my advice in every respect."

" I shall most certainly do so."

" The matter is too serious for any hesitation. Your life may depend upon your compliance."

" I assure you that I am in your hands."

" In the first place, both my friend and I must spend the night in your room."

Both Miss Stoner and I gazed at him in astonishment.

" Yes, it must be so. Let me explain. I believe that that is the village inn over there ? "

" Yes, that is the ' Crown.' "

" Very good. Your windows would be visible from there ? "

" Certainly."

" You must confine yourself to your room, on pretence of a headache, when your stepfather comes back. Then when you hear him retire for the night, you must open the shutters of your window, undo the hasp, put your lamp there as a signal to us, and then withdraw with everything which you are likely to want into the room which you used to occupy. I have no doubt that, in spite of the repairs, you could manage there for one night."

" Oh, yes, easily."

" The rest you will leave in our hands."

" But what will you do ? "

" We shall spend the night in your room, and we shall investigate the cause of this noise which has disturbed you."

" I believe, Mr. Holmes, that you have already made up your mind," said Miss Stoner, laying her hand upon my companion's sleeve.

" Perhaps I have."

" Then for pity's sake tell me what was the cause of my sister's death."

" I should prefer to have clearer proofs before I speak."

" You can at least tell me whether my own thought is correct, and if she died from some sudden fright."

" No, I do not think so. I think that there was probably some more tangible cause. And now, Miss Stoner, we must leave you, for if Dr. Roylott returned and saw us, our journey would be in vain. Good-bye, and be brave, for if you will do what I have told you, you may rest assured that we shall soon drive away the dangers that threaten you."

Sherlock Holmes and I had no difficulty in engaging a bedroom and sitting-room at the Crown Inn. They were on the upper floor, and from our window we could command a view of the avenue gate, and of the inhabited wing of Stoke Moran Manor House. At dusk we saw Dr. Grimesby Roylott drive past, his huge form looming up beside the little figure of the lad who drove him. The boy had some slight difficulty in undoing the heavy iron gates, and we heard the hoarse roar of the Doctor's voice, and saw the fury with which he shook his clenched fists at him. The trap drove on, and a few minutes later we saw a sudden light spring up among the trees as the lamp was lit in one of the sitting-rooms.

" Do you know, Watson," said Holmes, as we sat together in the gathering darkness, " I have really some scruples as to taking you to-night. There is a distinct element of danger."

" Can I be of assistance ? "

" Your presence might be invaluable."

" Then I shall certainly come."

" It is very kind of you."

" You speak of danger. You have evidently seen more in these rooms than was visible to me."

" No, but I fancy that I may have deduced a little more. I imagine that you saw all that I did."

" I saw nothing remarkable save the bell-rope, and what purpose that could answer I confess is more than I can imagine."

" You saw the ventilator, too ? "

" Yes, but I do not think that it is such a very unusual thing to have a small opening between two rooms. It was so small that a rat could hardly pass through."

" I knew that we should find a ventilator before ever we came to Stoke Moran."

" My dear Holmes ! "

" Oh, yes, I did. You remember in her statement she said that her sister could smell Dr. Roylott's cigar. Now, of course that suggests at once that there must be a communication between the two rooms. It could only be a small one, or it would have been remarked upon at the coroner's inquiry. I deduced a ventilator."

" But what harm can there be in that ? "

" Well, there is at least a curious coincidence of dates. A ventilator is made, a cord is hung, and a lady who sleeps in the bed dies. Does not that strike you ? "

" I cannot as yet see any connection."

" Did you observe anything very peculiar about that bed ? "

" No."

" It was clamped to the floor. Did you ever see a bed fastened like that before ? "

" I cannot say that I have."

" The lady could not move her bed. It must always be in the same relative position to the ventilator and to the rope—for so we may call it, since it was clearly never meant for a bell-pull."

" Holmes," I cried, " I seem to see dimly what you are hitting at. We are only just in time to prevent some subtle and horrible crime."

" Subtle enough and horrible enough. When a doctor does go wrong he is the first of criminals. He has nerve and he has knowledge. Palmer and Pritchard were among the heads of their profession. This man strikes even deeper, but I think, Watson, that we shall be able to strike deeper still. But we shall have horrors enough before the night is over : for goodness' sake let us have a quiet pipe, and turn our minds for a few hours to something more cheerful."

About nine o'clock the light among the trees was extinguished, and all was dark in the direction of the Manor House. Two hours passed slowly away, and then, suddenly, just at the stroke of eleven, a single bright light shone out right in front of us.

" That is our signal," said Holmes, springing to his feet ; " it comes from the middle window."

As we passed out he exchanged a few words with the landlord, explaining that we were going on a late visit to an acquaintance, and that it was possible that we might spend the night there. A moment later we were out on the dark road, a chill wind blowing in our faces, and one yellow light twinkling in front of us through the gloom to guide us on our sombre errand.

There was little difficulty in entering the grounds, for

unrepaired breaches gaped in the old park wall. Making our way among the trees, we reached the lawn, crossed it, and were about to enter through the window, when out from a clump of laurel bushes there darted what seemed to be a hideous and distorted child, who threw itself on the grass with writhing limbs, and then ran swiftly across the lawn into the darkness.

" My God ! " I whispered, " did you see it ? "

Holmes was for the moment as startled as I. His hand closed like a vice upon my wrist in his agitation. Then he broke into a low laugh, and put his lips to my ear.

" It is a nice household," he murmured, " that is the baboon."

I had forgotten the strange pets which the Doctor affected. There was a cheetah, too ; perhaps we might find it upon our shoulders at any moment. I confess that I felt easier in my mind when, after following Holmes' example and slipping off my shoes, I found myself inside the bedroom. My companion noiselessly closed the shutters, moved the lamp on to the table, and cast his eyes round the room. All was as we had seen it in the day-time. Then creeping up to me and making a trumpet of his hand, he whispered into my ear again so gently that it was all that I could do to distinguish the words :

" The least sound would be fatal to our plans."

I nodded to show that I had heard.

" We must sit without a light. He would see it through the ventilator."

I nodded again.

" Do not go to sleep ; your very life may depend upon it. Have your pistol ready in case we should need it. I will sit on the side of the bed, and you in that chair."

I took out my revolver and laid it on the corner of the table.

Holmes had brought up a long thin cane, and this he placed upon the bed beside him. By it he laid the box of matches and the stump of a candle. Then he turned down the lamp and we were left in darkness.

How shall I ever forget that dreadful vigil ? I could not hear a sound, not even the drawing of a breath, and yet I knew that my companion sat open-eyed, within a few feet of me, in the same state of nervous tension in which I was myself. The shutters cut off the least ray of light, and we waited in absolute darkness. From outside came the occasional cry of a night-bird, and once at our very window a long drawn, cat-like whine, which told us that the cheetah was indeed at liberty. Far away we could hear the deep tones of the parish clock, which boomed out every quarter of an hour. How long they seemed, those quarters ! Twelve o'clock, and one, and two, and three, and still we sat waiting silently for whatever might befall.

Suddenly there was the momentary gleam of a light up in the direction of the ventilator, which vanished immediately, but was succeeded by a strong smell of burning oil and heated metal. Someone in the next room had lit a dark lantern. I heard a gentle sound of movement, and then all was silent once more, though the smell grew stronger. For half an hour I sat with straining ears. Then suddenly another sound became audible—a very gentle, soothing sound, like that of a small jet of steam escaping continually from a kettle. The instant that we heard it, Holmes sprang from the bed, struck a match, and lashed furiously with his cane at the bell-pull.

" You see it, Watson ? " he yelled. " You see it ? "

But I saw nothing. At the moment when Holmes struck the light I heard a low, clear whistle, but the sudden glare flashing into my weary eyes made it impossible for me to tell what it was at which my friend lashed so savagely. I could, however, see that his face was deadly pale, and filled with horror and loathing.

He had ceased to strike, and was gazing up at the ventilator, when suddenly there broke from the silence of the night the most horrible cry to which I have ever listened. It swelled up louder and louder, a hoarse yell of pain and fear and anger all mingled in the one dreadful shriek. They say that away down in the village, and even in the distant parsonage, that cry raised the sleepers from their beds. It struck cold to our hearts, and I stood gazing at Holmes, and he at me, until the last echoes of it had died away into the silence from which it rose.

" What can it mean ? " I gasped.

" It means that it is all over," Holmes answered. " And perhaps, after all, it is for the best. Take your pistol, and we shall enter Dr. Roylott's room."

With a grave face he lit the lamp, and led the way down the corridor. Twice he struck at the chamber door without any reply from within. Then he turned the handle and entered, I at his heels, with the cocked pistol in my hand.

It was a singular sight which met our eyes. On the table stood a dark lantern with the shutter half open, throwing a brilliant beam of light upon the iron safe, the door of which was ajar. Beside this table, on the wooden chair, sat Dr. Grimesby Roylott, clad in a long grey dressing-gown, his bare ankles protruding beneath, and his feet thrust into red heelless Turkish slippers. Across his lap lay the short stock with the long lash which we had noticed during the day. His chin was cocked upwards, and his eyes were fixed in a dreadful rigid stare at the corner of the ceiling. Round his brow he had a peculiar yellow band, with brownish speckles, which seemed to be bound tightly round his head. As we entered he made neither sound nor motion.

" The band ! the speckled band ! " whispered Holmes.

I took a step forward. In an instant his strange head-gear began to move, and there reared itself from among his hair the squat diamond-shaped head and puffed neck of a loathsome serpent.

" It is a swamp adder ! " cried Holmes—" the deadliest snake in India. He has died within ten seconds of being bitten. Violence does, in truth, recoil upon the violent, and the schemer falls into the pit which he digs for another. Let us thrust this creature back into its den, and we can then remove Miss Stoner to some place of shelter, and let the county police know what has happened."

As he spoke he drew the dog whip swiftly from the dead man's lap, and throwing the noose round the reptile's neck, he drew it from its horrid perch, and, carrying it at arm's length, threw it into the iron safe, which he closed upon it.

Such are the true facts of the death of Dr. Grimesby Roylott, of Stoke Moran. It is not necessary that I should prolong a narrative which has already run to too great a length, by telling how we broke the sad news to the terrified girl, how we conveyed her by the morning train to the care of her good aunt at Harrow, of how the slow process of official inquiry came to the conclusion that the Doctor met his fate while indiscreetly playing with a dangerous pet. The little which I had yet to learn of the case was told me by Sherlock Holmes as we travelled back next day.

" I had," said he, " come to an entirely erroneous conclusion, which shows, my dear Watson, how dangerous it always is to reason from insufficient data. The presence of the gipsies, and the use of the word ' band,' which was used by the poor girl, no doubt, to explain the appearance which she had caught a horrid glimpse of by the light of her match, were sufficient to put me upon an entirely wrong scent. I can only claim the merit that I instantly reconsidered my position when, however, it became clear to me that whatever danger threatened an occupant of the room could not come either from the window or the door. My attention was speedily drawn, as I have already remarked to you, to this ventilator, and to the bell-rope which hung down to the bed. The discovery that this was a dummy, and that the bed was clamped to the floor, instantly gave rise to the suspicion that the rope was there as a bridge for something passing through the hole, and coming to the bed. The idea of a snake instantly occurred to me, and when I coupled it with my knowledge that the Doctor was furnished with a supply of creatures from India, I felt that I was probably on the right track. The idea of using a form of poison which could not possibly be discovered by any chemical test was just such a one as would occur to a clever and ruthless man who had had an Eastern training. The rapidity with which such a poison would take effect would also, from his point of view, be an advantage. It would be a sharp-eyed coroner indeed who could distinguish the two little dark punctures which would show where the poison fangs had done their work. Then I thought of the whistle. Of course, he must recall the snake before the morning light revealed it to the victim. He had trained it, probably by the use of the milk which we saw, to return to him when summoned. He would put it through the ventilator at the hour that he thought best, with the certainty that it would crawl down the rope, and land on the bed. It might or might not bite the occupant, perhaps she might escape every night for a week, but sooner or later she must fall a victim.

" I had come to these conclusions before ever I had entered his room. An inspection of his chair showed me that he had been in the habit of standing on it, which, of course, would be necessary in order that he should reach the ventilator. The sight of the safe, the saucer of milk, and the loop of whipcord were enough to finally dispel any doubts which may have remained. The metallic clang heard by Miss Stoner was obviously caused by her father hastily closing the door of his safe upon its terrible occupant. Having once made up my mind, you know the steps which I took in order to put the matter to the proof. I heard the creature hiss, as I have no doubt that you did also, and I instantly lit the light and attacked it."

" With the result of driving it through the ventilator."

" And also with the result of causing it to turn upon its master at the other side. Some of the blows of my cane came home, and roused its snakish temper, so that it flew upon the first person it saw. In this way I am no doubt indirectly responsible for Dr. Grimesby Roylott's death, and I cannot say that it is likely to weigh very heavily upon my conscience."

9. *The Engineer's Thumb*

OF all the problems which have been submitted to my friend Mr. Sherlock Holmes for solution during the years of our intimacy, there were only two which I was the means of introducing to his notice, that of Mr. Hatherley's thumb and that of Colonel Warburton's madness. Of these the latter may have afforded a finer field for an acute and original observer, but the other was so strange in its inception and so dramatic in its details, that it may be the more worthy of being placed upon record, even if it gave my friend fewer openings for those deductive methods of reasoning by which he achieved such remarkable results. The story has, I believe, been told more than once in the newspapers, but, like all such narratives, its effect is much less striking when set forth *en bloc* in a single half-column of print than when the facts slowly evolve before your own eyes and the mystery clears gradually away as each new discovery furnishes a step which leads on to the complete truth. At the time the circumstances made a deep impression upon me, and the lapse of two years has hardly served to weaken the effect.

It was in the summer of '89, not long after my marriage, that the events occurred which I am now about to summarize. I had returned to civil practice, and had finally abandoned Holmes in his Baker Street rooms, although I continually visited him, and occasionally even persuaded him to forgo his Bohemian habits so far as to come and visit us. My practice had steadily increased, and as I happened to live at no very great distance from Paddington Station, I got a few patients from among the officials.

One of these whom I had cured of a painful and lingering disease, was never weary of advertising my virtues, and of endeavouring to send me on every sufferer over whom he might have any influence.

One morning, at a little before seven o'clock, I was awakened by the maid tapping at the door, to announce that two men had come from Paddington, and were waiting in the consulting-room. I dressed hurriedly, for I knew by experience that railway cases were seldom trivial, and hastened downstairs. As I descended, my old ally, the guard, came out of the room, and closed the door tightly behind him.

" I've got him here," he whispered, jerking his thumb over his shoulder ; " he's all right."

" What is it, then ? " I asked, for his manner suggested that it was some strange creature which he had caged up in my room.

" It's a new patient," he whispered. " I thought I'd bring him round myself ; then he couldn't slip away. There he is, all safe and sound. I must go now, Doctor, I have my dooties, just the same as you." And off he went, this trusty tout, without even giving me time to thank him.

I entered my consulting-room, and found a gentleman seated by the table. He was quietly dressed in a suit of heather tweed, with a soft cloth cap, which he had laid down upon my books. Round one of his hands he had a handkerchief wrapped, which was mottled all over with bloodstains. He was young, not more than five-and-twenty, I should say, with a strong masculine face ; but he was exceedingly pale, and gave me the impression of a man who was suffering from some strong agitation, which it took all his strength of mind to control.

" I am sorry to knock you up so early, Doctor," said he. " But I have had a very serious accident during the night. I came in by train this morning, and on inquiring at Paddington as to where I might find a doctor a worthy fellow very kindly escorted me here. I gave the maid a card, but I see that she has left it upon the side table."

I took it up and glanced at it. " Mr. Victor Hatherley, hydraulic engineer, 16A Victoria Street (3rd floor)." That was the name, style, and abode of my morning visitor. " I regret that I have kept you waiting," said I, sitting down in my library chair. " You are fresh from a night journey, I understand, which is in itself a monotonous occupation."

" Oh, my night could not be called monotonous," said he, and laughed. He laughed very heartily, with a high ringing note, leaning back in his chair, and shaking his sides. All my medical instincts rose up against that laugh.

" Stop it ! " I cried. " Pull yourself together ! " and I poured out some water from a carafe.

It was useless, however. He was off in one of those hysterical outbursts which come upon a strong nature when some great crisis is over and gone. Presently he came to himself once more, very weary and blushing hotly.

" I have been making a fool of myself," he gasped.

" Not at all. Drink this ! " I dashed some brandy into the water, and the colour began to come back to his bloodless cheeks.

" That's better ! " said he. " And now, Doctor, perhaps you would kindly attend to my thumb, or rather to the place where my thumb used to be."

He unwound the handkerchief and held out his hand. It gave even my hardened nerves a shudder to look at it. There were four protruding fingers and a horrid red spongy surface where the thumb should have been. It had been hacked or torn right out from the roots.

" Good heavens ! " I cried, " this is a terrible injury. It must have bled considerably."

" Yes, it did. I fainted when it was done ; and I think that I must have been senseless for a long time. When I came to, I found that it was still bleeding, so I tied one end of my handkerchief very tightly round the wrist, and braced it up with a twig."

" Excellent ! You should have been a surgeon."

" It is a question of hydraulics, you see, and came within my own province."

" This has been done," said I, examining the wound, " by a very heavy and sharp instrument."

" A thing like a cleaver," said he.

" An accident, I presume ? "

" By no means."

" What, a murderous attack ! "

" Very murderous indeed."

" You horrify me."

I sponged the wound, cleaned it, dressed it ; and, finally, covered it over with cotton wadding and carbolized bandages. He lay back without wincing, though he bit his lip from time to time.

" How is that ? " I asked, when I had finished.

" Capital ! Between your brandy and your bandage, I feel a new man. I was very weak, but I have had a good deal to go through."

" Perhaps you had not better speak of the matter. It is evidently trying to your nerves."

" Oh, no ; not now. I shall have to tell my tale to the police ; but, between ourselves, if it were not for the convincing evidence of this wound of mine, I should be surprised if they believed my statement, for it is a very extraordinary one, and I have not much in the way of proof with which to back it up. And, even if they believe me, the clues which I can give them are so vague that it is a question whether justice will be done."

" Ha ! " cried I, " if it is anything in the nature of a problem which you desire to see solved, I should strongly recommend you to come to my friend Mr. Sherlock Holmes before you go to the official police."

" Oh, I have heard of that fellow," answered my visitor, " and I should be very glad if he would take the matter up, though of course I must use the official police as well. Would you give me an introduction to him ? "

" I'll do better. I'll take you round to him myself."

"I should be immensely obliged to you."

"We'll call a cab and go together. We shall just be in time to have a little breakfast with him. Do you feel equal to it?"

"Yes. I shall not feel easy until I have told my story."

"Then my servant will call a cab, and I shall be with you in an instant." I rushed upstairs, explained the matter shortly to my wife, and in five minutes was inside a hansom, driving with my new acquaintance to Baker Street.

Sherlock Holmes was, as I expected, lounging about his sitting-room in his dressing-gown, reading the agony column of *The Times*, and smoking his before-breakfast pipe, which was composed of all the plugs and dottles left from his smokes of the day before, all carefully dried and collected on the corner of the mantelpiece. He received us in his quietly genial fashion, ordered fresh rashers and eggs, and joined us in a hearty meal. When it was concluded he settled our new acquaintance upon the sofa, placed a pillow beneath his head, and laid a glass of brandy and water within his reach.

"It is easy to see that your experience has been no common one, Mr. Hatherley," said he. "Pray lie down there and make yourself absolutely at home. Tell us what you can, but stop when you are tired, and keep up your strength with a little stimulant."

"Thank you," said my patient, "but I have felt another man since the doctor bandaged me, and I think that your breakfast has completed the cure. I shall take up as little of your valuable time as possible, so I shall start at once upon my peculiar experiences."

Holmes sat in his big arm-chair, with the weary, heavy-lidded expression which veiled his keen and eager nature, while I sat opposite to him, and we listened in silence to the strange story which our visitor detailed to us.

"You must know," said he, "that I am an orphan and a bachelor, residing alone in lodgings in London. By profession I am a hydraulic engineer, and have had considerable experience of my work during the seven years that I was apprenticed to Venner & Matheson, the well-known firm of Greenwich. Two years ago, having served my time, and having also come into a fair sum of money through my poor father's death, I determined to start in business for myself, and took professional chambers in Victoria Street.

"I suppose that everyone finds his first independent start in business a dreary experience. To me it has been exceptionally so. During two years I have had three consultations and one small job, and that is absolutely all that my profession has brought me. My gross takings amount to twenty-seven pounds ten. Every day, from nine in the morning until four in the afternoon, I waited in my little den, until at last my heart began to sink, and I came to believe that I should never have any practice at all.

"Yesterday, however, just as I was thinking of leaving the office, my clerk entered to say there was a gentleman waiting who wished to see me upon business. He brought up a card, too, with the name of ' Colonel Lysander Stark ' engraved upon it. Close at his heels came the Colonel himself, a man rather over the middle size but of an exceeding thinness. I do not think that I have ever seen so thin a man. His whole face sharpened away into nose and chin, and the skin of his cheeks was drawn quite tense over his outstanding bones. Yet this emaciation seemed to be his natural habit, and due to no disease, for his eye was bright, his step brisk, and his bearing assured. He was plainly but neatly dressed, and his age, I should judge, would be nearer forty than thirty.

"' Mr. Hatherley ? ' said he, with something of a German accent. ' You have been recommended to me, Mr. Hatherley, as being a man who is not only proficient in his profession, but is also discreet and capable of preserving a secret.'

"I bowed, feeling as flattered as any young man would at such an address. ' May I ask who it was who gave me so good a character ? ' I asked.

" ' Well, perhaps it is better that I should not tell you just at this moment. I have it from the same source that you are both an orphan and a bachelor, and are residing alone in London.'

" ' That is quite correct,' I answered, ' but you will excuse me if I say that I cannot see how all this bears upon my professional qualifications. I understood that it was on a professional matter that you wished to speak to me ? '

" ' Undoubtedly so. But you will find that all I say is really to the point. I have a professional commission for you, but absolute secrecy is quite essential—*absolute* secrecy, you understand, and of course we may expect that more from a man who is alone than from one who lives in the bosom of his family.'

" ' If I promise to keep a secret,' said I, ' you may absolutely depend upon my doing so.'

" He looked very hard at me as I spoke, and it seemed to me that I had never seen so suspicious and questioning an eye.

" ' You do promise, then ? ' said he at last.

" ' Yes, I promise.'

" ' Absolute and complete silence, before, during, and after ? No reference to the matter at all, either in word or writing ? '

" ' I have already given you my word.'

" ' Very good.' He suddenly sprang up, and darting like lightning across the room he flung open the door. The passage outside was empty.

" ' That's all right,' said he, coming back. ' I know that clerks are sometimes curious as to their masters' affairs. Now we can talk in safety.' He drew up his chair very close to mine, and began to stare at me again with the same questioning and thoughtful look.

" A feeling of repulsion and of something akin to fear had begun to rise within me at the strange antics of this fleshless man. Even my dread of losing a client could not restrain me from showing my impatience.

207

" ' I beg that you will state your business, sir,' said I ;
' my time is of value.' Heaven forgive me for that last
sentence, but the words came to my lips.

" ' How would fifty guineas for a night's work suit
you ? ' he asked.

" ' Most admirably.'

" ' I say a night's work, but an hour's would be nearer
the mark. I simply want your opinion about a hydraulic
stamping machine which has got out of gear. If you
show us what is wrong we shall soon set it right ourselves.
What do you think of such a commission as that ? '

" ' The work appears to be light, and the pay muni-
ficent.'

" ' Precisely so. We shall want you to come to-night
by the last train.'

" ' Where to ? '

" ' To Eyford, in Berkshire. It is a little place near the
borders of Oxfordshire, and within seven miles of Reading. There is a train from Paddington which would
bring you in there at about eleven fifteen.'

" ' Very good.'

" ' I shall come down in a carriage to meet you.'

" ' There is a drive, then ? '

" ' Yes, our little place is quite out in the country. It
is a good seven miles from Eyford station.'

" ' Then we can hardly get there before midnight. I
suppose there would be no chance of a train back. I
should be compelled to stop the night.'

" ' Yes, we could easily give you a shakedown.'

" ' That is very awkward. Could I not come at some
more convenient hour ? '

" ' We have judged it best that you should come late.
It is to recompense you for any inconvenience that we
are paying you, a young and unknown man, a fee which
would buy an opinion from the very heads of your profession. Still, of course, if you would like to draw out
of the business, there is plenty of time to do so.'

" I thought of the fifty guineas, and of how very useful

they would be to me. ' Not at all,' said I ; ' I shall be very happy to accommodate myself to your wishes. I should like, however, to understand a little more clearly what it is that you wish me to do.'

" ' Quite so. It is very natural that the pledge of secrecy which we have exacted from you should have aroused your curiosity. I have no wish to commit you to anything without your having it all laid before you. I suppose that we are absolutely safe from eavesdroppers ? '

" ' Entirely.'

" ' Then the matter stands thus. You are probably aware that fuller's earth is a valuable product, and that it is only found in one or two places in England ? '

" ' I have heard so.'

" ' Some little time ago I bought a small place—a very small place—within ten miles of Reading. I was fortunate enough to discover that there was a deposit of fuller's earth in one of my fields. On examining it, however, I found that this deposit was a comparatively small one, and that it formed a link between two very much larger ones upon the right and the left—both of them, however, in the grounds of my neighbours. These good people were absolutely ignorant that their land contained that which was quite as valuable as a gold mine. Naturally, it was to my interest to buy their land before they discovered its true value ; but, unfortunately, I had no capital by which I could do this. I took a few of my friends into the secret, however, and they suggested that we should quietly and secretly work our own little deposit, and that in this way we should earn the money which would enable us to buy the neighbouring fields. This we have now been doing for some time, and in order to help us in our operations we erected a hydraulic press. This press, as I have already explained, has got out of order, and we wish your advice upon the subject. We guard our secret very jealously, however, and if it once became known that we had hydraulic engineers coming to our little house, it would soon rouse inquiry, and then, if the facts came out, it would be good-bye to any chance of getting these fields and carrying out our plans. That is why I have made you promise me that you will not tell a human being that you are going to Eyford to-night. I hope that I make it all plain?'

"'I quite follow you,' said I. 'The only point which I could not quite understand, was what use you could make of a hydraulic press in excavating fuller's earth, which, as I understand, is dug out like gravel from a pit.'

"'Ah!' said he carelessly, 'we have our own process. We compress the earth into bricks, so as to remove them without revealing what they are. But that is a mere detail. I have taken you fully into my confidence now, Mr. Hatherley, and I have shown you how I trust you.' He rose as he spoke. 'I shall expect you, then, at Eyford, at 11.15.'

"'I shall certainly be there.'

"'And not a word to a soul.' He looked at me with a last long, questioning gaze, and then, pressing my hand in a cold, dank grasp, he hurried from the room.

"Well, when I came to think it all over in cool blood I was very much astonished, as you may both think, at this sudden commission which had been entrusted to me. On the one hand, of course, I was glad, for the fee was at least tenfold what I should have asked had I set a price upon my own services, and it was possible that this order might lead to other ones. On the other hand, the face and manner of my patron had made an unpleasant impression upon me, and I could not think that his explanation of the fuller's earth was sufficient to explain the necessity for my coming at midnight, and his extreme anxiety lest I should tell anyone of my errand. However, I threw all my fears to the winds, ate a hearty supper, drove to Paddington, and started off, having obeyed to the letter the injunction as to holding my tongue.

"At Reading I had to change not only my carriage but my station. However, I was in time for the last train to Eyford, and I reached the little dim-lit station after eleven o'clock. I was the only passenger who got out there, and there was no one upon the platform save a single sleepy porter with a lantern. As I passed out through the wicket-gate, however, I found my acquaintance of the morning waiting in the shadow upon the other side. Without a word he grasped my arm and hurried me into a carriage, the door of which was standing open. He drew up the windows on either side, tapped on the woodwork, and away we went as hard as the horse could go."

" One horse ? " interjected Holmes.

" Yes, only one."

" Did you observe the colour ? "

" Yes, I saw it by the sidelights when I was stepping into the carriage. It was a chestnut."

" Tired-looking or fresh ? "

" Oh, fresh and glossy."

" Thank you. I am sorry to have interrupted you. Pray continue your most interesting statement."

" Away we went then, and we drove for at least an hour. Colonel Lysander Stark had said that it was only seven miles, but I should think, from the rate that we seemed to go, and the time that we took, that it must have been nearer twelve. He sat at my side in silence all the time, and I was aware, more than once when I glanced in his direction, that he was looking at me with great intensity. The country roads seemed to be not very good in that part of the world, for we lurched and jolted terribly. I tried to look out of the windows to see something of where we were, but they were made of frosted glass, and I could make out nothing save an occasional blurr of a passing light. Now and then I hazarded some remark to break the monotony of the journey, but the Colonel answered only in monosyllables, and the conversation soon flagged. At last, however, the bumping of the road was exchanged for the crisp smoothness of a gravel drive and the carriage came to a stand. Colonel Lysander Stark sprang out, and, as I followed after him, pulled me swiftly into a porch which gaped in front of us. We stepped, as it were, right out of the carriage and into the hall, so that I failed to catch the most fleeting glance of the front of the house. The instant that I had crossed the threshold the door slammed heavily behind us, and I heard faintly the rattle of the wheels as the carriage drove away.

" It was pitch dark inside the house, and the Colonel fumbled about looking for matches, and muttering under his breath. Suddenly a door opened at the other end of the passage, and a long, golden bar of light shot out in our direction. It grew broader, and a woman appeared with a lamp in her hand, which she held above her head, pushing her face forward and peering at us. I could see that she was pretty, and from the gloss with which the light shone upon her dark dress I knew that it was a rich material. She spoke a few words in a foreign tongue in a tone as though asking a question, and when my companion answered in a gruff monosyllable she gave such a start that the lamp nearly fell from her hand. Colonel Stark went up to her, whispered something in her ear, and then, pushing her back into the room from whence she had come, he walked towards me again with the lamp in his hand.

" ' Perhaps you will have the kindness to wait in this room for a few minutes,' said he, throwing open another door. It was a quiet little plainly furnished room, with a round table in the centre, on which several German books were scattered. Colonel Stark laid down the lamp on the top of a harmonium beside the door. ' I shall not keep you waiting an instant,' said he, and vanished into the darkness.

" I glanced at the books upon the table, and in spite of my ignorance of German, I could see that two of them were treatises on science, the others being volumes of poetry. Then I walked across to the window, hoping that I might catch some glimpse of the country-side, but an oak shutter, heavily barred, was folded across it. It was a wonderfully silent house. There was an old clock ticking loudly somewhere in the passage, but otherwise everything was deadly still. A vague feeling of uneasiness began to steal over me. Who were these German people, and what were they doing, living in this strange, out-of-the-way place? And where was the place? I was ten miles or so from Eyford, that was all I knew, but whether north, south, east, or west, I had no idea. For that matter, Reading, and possibly other large towns, were within that radius, so the place might not be so secluded after all. Yet it was quite certain from the absolute stillness that we were in the country. I paced up and down the room humming a tune under my breath to keep up my spirits, and feeling that I was thoroughly earning my fifty-guinea fee.

"Suddenly, without any preliminary sound in the midst of the utter stillness, the door of my room swung slowly open. The woman was standing in the aperture, the darkness of the hall behind her, the yellow light from my lamp beating upon her eager and beautiful face. I could see at a glance that she was sick with fear, and the sight sent a chill to my own heart. She held up one shaking finger to warn me to be silent, and she shot a few whispered words of broken English at me, her eyes glancing back, like those of a frightened horse, into the gloom behind her.

"'I would go,' said she, trying hard, as it seemed to me, to speak calmly; 'I would go. I should not stay here. There is no good for you to do.'

"'But, madam,' said I, 'I have not yet done what I came for. I cannot possibly leave until I have seen the machine.'

"'It is not worth your while to wait,' she went on. 'You can pass through the door; no one hinders.' And then, seeing that I smiled and shook my head, she suddenly threw aside her constraint, and made a step forward, with her hands wrung together. 'For the love of Heaven!' she whispered, 'get away from here before it is too late!'

"But I am somewhat headstrong by nature, and the

213

more ready to engage in an affair when there is some obstacle in the way. I thought of my fifty-guinea fee, of my wearisome journey, and of the unpleasant night which seemed to be before me. Was it all to go for nothing ? Why should I slink away without having carried out my commission, and without the payment which was my due ? This woman might, for all I knew, be a monomaniac. With a stout bearing, therefore, though her manner had shaken me more than I cared to confess, I still shook my head, and declared my intention of remaining where I was. She was about to renew her entreaties when a door slammed overhead, and the sound of several footsteps were heard upon the stairs. She listened for an instant, threw up her hands with a despairing gesture, and vanished as suddenly and noiselessly as she had come.

" The new-comers were Colonel Lysander Stark, and a short thick man with a chinchilla beard growing out of the creases of his double chin, who was introduced to me as Mr. Ferguson.

" ' This is my secretary and manager,' said the Colonel. ' By the way, I was under the impression that I left this door shut just now. I fear that you have felt the draught.'

" ' On the contrary,' said I, ' I opened the door myself, because I felt the room to be a little close.'

" He shot one of his suspicious glances at me. ' Perhaps we had better proceed to business, then,' said he. ' Mr. Ferguson and I will take you up to see the machine.'

" ' I had better put my hat on, I suppose.'

" ' Oh no, it is in the house.'

" ' What, do you dig fuller's earth in the house ? '

" ' No, no. This is only where we compress it. But never mind that ! All we wish you to do is to examine the machine and to let us know what is wrong with it.'

" We went upstairs together, the Colonel first with the lamp, the fat manager and I behind him. It was a labyrinth of an old house, with corridors, passages, narrow winding staircases, and little low doors, the thresholds of which were hollowed out by the generations who had crossed them. There were no carpets, and no signs of any furniture above the ground floor, while the plaster was peeling off the walls, and the damp was breaking through in green, unhealthy blotches. I tried to put on as unconcerned an air as possible, but I had not forgotten the warnings of the lady, even though I disregarded them, and I kept a keen eye upon my two companions. Ferguson appeared to be a morose and silent man, but I could see from the little that he said that he was at least a fellow-countryman.

"Colonel Lysander Stark stopped at last before a low door, which he unlocked. Within was a small square room, in which the three of us could hardly get at one time. Ferguson remained outside, and the Colonel ushered me in.

"'We are now,' said he, 'actually within the hydraulic press, and it would be a particularly unpleasant thing for us if anyone were to turn it on. The ceiling of this small chamber is really the end of the descending piston, and it comes down with the force of many tons upon this metal floor. There are small lateral columns of water outside which receive the force, and which transmit and multiply it in the manner which is familiar to you. The machine goes readily enough, but there is some stiffness in the working of it and it has lost a little of its force. Perhaps you will have the goodness to look it over, and to show us how we can set it right.'

"I took the lamp from him, and I examined the machine very thoroughly. It was indeed a gigantic one, and capable of exercising enormous pressure. When I passed outside, however, and pressed down the levers which controlled it, I knew at once by the whishing sound that there was a slight leakage, which allowed a regurgitation of water through one of the side-cylinders. An examination showed that one of the india-rubber bands which was round the head of a driving-rod had shrunk so as not quite to fill the socket along which it worked. This was clearly the cause of the loss of power, and I pointed it out to my companions, who followed my remarks very carefully, and asked several practical questions as to how they should proceed to set it right. When I had made it clear to them, I returned to the main chamber of the machine, and took a good look at it to satisfy my own curiosity. It was obvious at a glance that the story of the fuller's earth was the merest fabrication, for it would be absurd to suppose that so powerful an engine could be designed for so inadequate a purpose. The walls were of wood, but the floor consisted of a large iron trough, and when I came to examine it I could see a crust of metallic deposit all over it. I had stooped and was scraping at this to see exactly what it was, when I heard a muttered exclamation in German, and saw the cadaverous face of the Colonel looking down at me.

" ' What are you doing there ? ' he asked.

" I felt angry at having been tricked by so elaborate a story as that which he had told me. ' I was admiring your fuller's earth,' said I ; ' I think that I should be better able to advise you as to your machine if I knew what the exact purpose was for which it was used.'

" The instant that I uttered the words I regretted the rashness of my speech. His face set hard, and a baleful light sprang up in his grey eyes.

" ' Very well,' said he, ' you shall know all about the machine.' He took a step backward, slammed the little door, and turned the key in the lock. I rushed towards it and pulled at the handle, but it was quite secure, and did not give in the least to my kicks and shoves. ' Hallo ! ' I yelled. ' Hallo ! Colonel ! Let me out ! '

" And then suddenly in the silence I heard a sound which sent my heart into my mouth. It was the clank of the levers, and the swish of the leaking cylinder. He had set the engine at work. The lamp still stood upon the floor where I had placed it when examining the trough. By its light I saw that the black ceiling was coming down upon me, slowly, jerkily, but, as none knew better than myself, with a force which must within a minute grind me to a shapeless pulp. I threw myself, screaming, against the door, and dragged with my nails at the lock. I implored the Colonel to let me out, but the remorseless clanking of the levers drowned my cries. The ceiling was only a foot or two above my head, and with my hand upraised I could feel its hard rough surface. Then it flashed through my mind that the pain of my death would depend very much upon the position in which I met it. If I lay on my face the weight would come upon my spine, and I shuddered to think of that dreadful snap. Easier the other way, perhaps, and yet had I the nerve to lie and look up at that deadly black shadow wavering down upon me? Already I was unable to stand erect, when my eye caught something which brought a gush of hope back to my heart.

" I have said that though floor and ceiling were of iron, the walls were of wood. As I gave a last hurried glance around, I saw a thin line of yellow light between two of the boards, which broadened and broadened as a small panel was pushed backwards. For an instant I could hardly believe that here was indeed a door which led away from death. The next I threw myself through, and lay half fainting upon the other side. The panel had closed again behind me, but the crash of the lamp, and a few moments afterwards the clang of the two slabs of metal, told me how narrow had been my escape.

" I was recalled to myself by a frantic plucking at my wrist, and I found myself lying upon the stone floor of a narrow corridor, while a woman bent over me and tugged at me with her left hand, while she held a candle in her right. It was the same good friend whose warning I had so foolishly rejected.

" ' Come! Come!' she cried breathlessly. ' They will be here in a moment. They will see that you are not there. Oh, do not waste the so precious time, but come!'

" This time, at least, I did not scorn her advice. I staggered to my feet, and ran with her along the corridor and down a winding stair. The latter led to another broad passage, and, just as we reached it we heard the sound of running feet and the shouting of two voices—one answering the other—from the floor on which we were, and from the one beneath. My guide stopped, and looked about her like one who is at her wits' end. Then she threw open a door which led into a bedroom, through the window of which the moon was shining brightly.

" ' It is your only chance,' said she. ' It is high, but it may be that you can jump it.'

" As she spoke a light sprang into view at the further end of the passage, and I saw the lean figure of Colonel Lysander Stark rushing forward with a lantern in one hand, and a weapon like a butcher's cleaver in the other. I rushed across the bedroom, flung open the window, and looked out. How quiet and sweet and wholesome the garden looked in the moonlight, and it could not be more than thirty feet down. I clambered out upon the sill, but I hesitated to jump, until I should have heard what passed between my saviour and the ruffian who pursued me. If she were ill-used, then at any risk I was determined to go back to her assistance. The thought had hardly flashed through my mind before he was at the door, pushing his way past her ; but she threw her arms round him, and tried to hold him back.

" ' Fritz ! Fritz ! ' she cried in English, ' remember your promise after the last time. You said it should not be again. He will be silent ! Oh, he will be silent ! '

" ' You are mad, Elise ! ' he shouted, struggling to break away from her. ' You will be the ruin of us. He has seen too much. Let me pass, I say ! ' He dashed her to one side, and, rushing to the window, cut at me with his heavy weapon. I had let myself go, and was hanging with my fingers in the window slot and my hands across the sill, when his blow fell. I was conscious of a dull pain, my grip loosened, and I fell into the garden below.

" I was shaken, but not hurt by the fall ; so I picked myself up, and rushed off among the bushes as hard as I could run, for I understood that I was far from being out of danger yet. Suddenly, however, as I ran, a deadly dizziness and sickness came over me. I glanced down at my hand, which was throbbing painfully, and then, for the first time, saw that my thumb had been cut off, and that the blood was pouring from my wound. I endeavoured to tie my handkerchief round it, but there came a sudden buzzing in my ears, and next moment I fell in a dead faint among the rose-bushes.

" How long I remained unconscious I cannot tell. It must have been a very long time, for the moon had sunk and a bright morning was breaking when I came to myself. My clothes were all sodden with dew, and my coat-sleeve was drenched with blood from my wounded thumb. The smarting of it recalled in an instant all the particulars of my night's adventure, and I sprang to my feet with the feeling that I might hardly yet be safe from my pursuers. But, to my astonishment, when I came to look round me neither house nor garden were to be seen. I had been lying in an angle of the hedge close by the highroad, and just a little lower down was a long building, which proved, upon my approaching it, to be the very station at which I had arrived upon the previous night. Were it not for the ugly wound upon my hand, all that had passed during those dreadful hours might have been an evil dream.

" Half dazed, I went into the station, and asked about the morning train There would be one to Reading in less than an hour. The same porter was on duty, I found, as had been there when I arrived. I inquired from him whether he had ever heard of Colonel Lysander Stark. The name was strange to him. Had he observed a carriage the night before waiting for me ? No, he had not. Was there a police station anywhere near ? There was one about three miles off.

" It was too far for me to go, weak and ill as I was. I determined to wait until I got back to town before telling my story to the police. It was a little past six when I arrived, so I went first to have my wound dressed, and then the doctor was kind enough to bring me along here.

I put the case into your hands, and shall do exactly what you advise."

We both sat in silence for some little time after listening to this extraordinary narrative. Then Sherlock Holmes pulled down from the shelf one of the ponderous commonplace books in which he placed his cuttings.

" Here is an advertisement which will interest you," said he. " It appeared in all the papers about a year ago. Listen to this :—' Lost on the 9th inst., Mr. Jeremiah Hayling, aged 26, a hydraulic engineer. Left his lodgings at ten o'clock at night, and has not been heard of since. Was dressed in,' etc. etc. Ha ! That represents the last time that the Colonel needed to have his machine overhauled, I fancy."

" Good heavens ! " cried my patient. " Then that explains what the girl said."

" Undoubtedly. It is quite clear that the Colonel was a cool and desperate man, who was absolutely determined that nothing should stand in the way of his little game, like those out-and-out pirates who will leave no survivor from a captured ship. Well, every moment now is precious, so, if you feel equal to it, we shall go down to Scotland Yard at once as a preliminary to starting for Eyford."

Some three hours or so afterwards we were all in the train together, bound from Reading to the little Berkshire village. There were Sherlock Holmes, the hydraulic engineer, Inspector Bradstreet of Scotland Yard, a plain-clothes man, and myself. Bradstreet had spread an ordnance map of the country out upon the seat, and was busy with his compasses drawing a circle with Eyford for its centre.

" There you are," said he. " That circle is drawn at a radius of ten miles from the village. The place we want must be somewhere near that line. You said ten miles, I think, sir ? "

" It was an hour's good drive."

" And you think that they brought you back all that way when you were unconscious ? "

" They must have done so. I have a confused memory, too, of having been lifted and conveyed somewhere."

" What I cannot understand," said I, " is why they should have spared you when they found you lying fainting in the garden. Perhaps the villain was softened by the woman's entreaties."

" I hardly think that likely. I never saw a more inexorable face in my life."

" Oh, we shall soon clear up all that," said Bradstreet. " Well, I have drawn my circle, and I only wish I knew at what point upon it the folk that we are in search of are to be found."

" I think I could lay my finger on it," said Holmes quietly.

" Really, now ! " cried the inspector, " you have formed your opinion ! Come now, we shall see who agrees with you. I say it is south, for the country is more deserted there."

" And I say east," said my patient.

" I am for west," remarked the plain-clothes man. " There are several quiet little villages up there."

" And I am for north," said I ; " because there are no hills there, and our friend says that he did not notice the carriage go up any."

" Come," said the inspector, laughing ; " it's a very pretty diversity of opinion. We have boxed the compass among us. Who do you give your casting vote to ? "

" You are all wrong."

" But we can't *all* be."

" Oh, yes, you can. This is my point," he placed his finger on the centre of the circle. " This is where we shall find them."

" But the twelve-mile drive ? " gasped Hatherley.

" Six out and six back. Nothing simpler. You say yourself that the horse was fresh and glossy when you got in. How could it be that, if it had gone twelve miles over heavy roads ? "

" Indeed it is a likely ruse enough," observed Bradstreet thoughtfully. " Of course there can be no doubt as to the nature of this gang."

" None at all," said Holmes. " They are coiners on a large scale, and have used the machine to form the amalgam which has taken the place of silver."

" We have known for some time that a clever gang was at work," said the inspector. " They have been turning out half-crowns by the thousand. We even traced them as far as Reading, but could get no further ; for they had covered their traces in a way that showed that they were very old hands. But now, thanks to this lucky chance, I think that we have got them right enough."

But the inspector was mistaken, for those criminals were not destined to fall into the hands of justice. As we rolled in Eyford station we saw a gigantic column of smoke which streamed up from behind a small clump of trees in the neighbourhood, and hung like an immense ostrich feather over the landscape.

" A house on fire ? " asked Bradstreet, as the train steamed off again on its way.

" Yes, sir," said the stationmaster.

" When did it break out ? "

" I hear that it was during the night, sir, but it has got worse, and the whole place is in a blaze."

" Whose house is it ? "

" Dr. Becher's."

" Tell me," broke in the engineer, " is Dr. Becher a German, very thin, with a long sharp nose ? "

The stationmaster laughed heartily. " No, sir, Dr. Becher is an Englishman, and there isn't a man in the parish who has a better lined waistcoat. But he has a gentleman staying with him, a patient as I understand, who is a foreigner, and he looks as if a little good Berkshire beef would do him no harm."

The stationmaster had not finished his speech before we were all hastening in the direction of the fire. The road topped a low hill, and there was a great widespread whitewashed building in front of us, spouting fire at every chink and window, while in the garden in front three fire-engines were vainly striving to keep the flames under.

" That's it ! " cried Hatherley, in intense excitement. " There is the gravel drive, and there are the rose-bushes where I lay. That second window is the one that I jumped from."

" Well, at least," said Holmes, " you have had your revenge upon them. There can be no question that it was your oil lamp which, when it was crushed in the press, set fire to the wooden walls, though no doubt they were too excited in the chase after you to observe it at the time. Now keep your eyes open in this crowd for your friends of last night, though I very much fear that they are a good hundred miles off by now."

And Holmes' fears came to be realized, for from that day to this no word has ever been heard either of the beautiful woman, the sinister German, or the morose Englishman. Early that morning a peasant had met a cart, containing several people and some very bulky boxes, driving rapidly in the direction of Reading, but there all traces of the fugitives disappeared, and even Holmes' ingenuity failed to discover the least clue to their whereabouts.

The firemen had been much perturbed at the strange arrangements which they found within, and still more so by discovering a newly-severed human thumb upon a window-sill of the second floor. About sunset, however, their efforts were at last successful, and they subdued the flames, but not before the roof had fallen in, and the whole place reduced to such absolute ruin that, save some twisted cylinders and iron piping, not a trace remained of the machinery which had cost our unfortunate acquaintance so dearly. Large masses of nickel and of tin were discovered stored in an outhouse, but no coins were to be found, which may have explained the presence of those bulky boxes which have been already referred to.

How our hydraulic engineer had been conveyed from the garden to the spot where he recovered his senses might

have remained for ever a mystery were it not for the soft
mould, which told us a very plain tale. He had evidently
been carried down by two persons, one of whom had
remarkably small feet, and the other unusually large ones.
On the whole, it was most probable that the silent Englishman, being less bold or less murderous than his companion, had assisted the woman to bear the unconscious
man out of the way of danger.

" Well," said our engineer ruefully, as we took our
seats to return to London, " it has been a pretty business
for me ! I have lost my thumb, and I have lost a fifty-
guinea fee, and what have I gained ? "

" Experience," said Holmes, laughing. " Indirectly it
may be of value, you know ; you have only to put it into
words to gain the reputation of being excellent company
for the remainder of your existence."

10. *The Noble Bachelor*

THE Lord St. Simon marriage, and its curious
termination, have long since ceased to be a
subject of interest in those exalted circles in
which the unfortunate bridegroom moves. Fresh scandals have eclipsed it, and their more piquant details have
drawn the gossips away from this four-year-old drama.
As I have reason to believe, however, that the full facts
have never been revealed to the general public, and as my
friend Sherlock Holmes had a considerable share in clearing the matter up, I feel that no memoir of him would be
complete without some little sketch of this remarkable
episode.

It was a few weeks before my own marriage, during
the days when I was still sharing rooms with Holmes in
Baker Street, that he came home from an afternoon stroll
to find a letter on the table waiting for him. I had remained indoors all day, for the weather had taken a sudden
turn to rain, with high autumnal winds, and the jezail
bullet which I had brought back in one of my limbs as a

relic of my Afghan campaign, throbbed with dull persistency. With my body in one easy chair and my legs upon another, I had surrounded myself with a cloud of newspapers, until at last, saturated with the news of the day, I tossed them all aside and lay listless, watching the huge crest and monogram upon the envelope upon the table, and wondering lazily who my friend's noble correspondent could be.

" Here is a very fashionable epistle," I remarked as he entered. " Your morning letters, if I remember right, were from a fishmonger and a tide-waiter."

" Yes, my correspondence has certainly the charm of variety," he answered, smiling, " and the humbler are usually the more interesting. This looks like one of those unwelcome social summonses which call upon a man either to be bored or to lie."

He broke the seal, and glanced over the contents.

" Oh, come, it may prove to be something of interest after all."

" Not social, then ? "

" No, distinctly professional."

" And from a noble client ? "

" One of the highest in England."

" My dear fellow, I congratulate you."

" I assure you, Watson, without affectation, that the status of my client is a matter of less moment to me than the interest of his case. It is just possible, however, that that also may not be wanting in this new investigation. You have been reading the papers diligently of late, have you not ? "

" It looks like it," said I ruefully, pointing to a huge bundle in the corner. " I have had nothing else to do."

" It is fortunate, for you will perhaps be able to post me up. I read nothing except the criminal news and the agony column. The latter is always instructive. But if you have followed recent events so closely you must have read about Lord St. Simon and his wedding ? "

" Oh, yes, with the deepest interest."

" That is well. The letter which I hold in my hand is from Lord St. Simon. I will read it to you, and in return you must turn over these papers and let me have whatever bears upon the matter. This is what he says :

" ' MY DEAR MR. SHERLOCK HOLMES,—Lord Backwater tells me that I may place implicit reliance upon your judgment and discretion. I have determined, therefore, to call upon you, and to consult you in reference to the very painful event which has occurred in connection with my wedding. Mr. Lestrade, of Scotland Yard, is acting already in the matter, but he assures me that he sees no objection to your co-operation, and that he even thinks that it might be of some assistance. I will call at four o'clock in the afternoon, and should you have any other engagement at that time, I hope you will postpone it, as this is a matter of paramount importance.—Yours faithfully,

' ROBERT ST. SIMON.'

" It is dated from Grosvenor Mansions, written with a quill pen, and the noble lord has had the misfortune to get a smear of ink upon the outer side of his right little finger," remarked Holmes, as he folded up the epistle.

" He says four o'clock. It is three now. He will be here in an hour."

" Then I have just time, with your assistance, to get clear upon the subject. Turn over those papers, and arrange the extracts in their order of time, while I take a glance as to who our client is." He picked a red-covered volume from a line of books of reference beside the mantelpiece. " Here he is," said he, sitting down and flattening it out upon his knee. " ' Robert Walsingham de Vere St. Simon, second son of the Duke of Balmoral '—Hum ! ' Arms : Azure, three caltrops in chief over a fess sable. Born in 1846.' He's forty-one years of age, which is mature for marriage. Was Under-Secretary for the Colonies in a late Administration. The Duke, his father, was at one time Secretary for Foreign Affairs. They inherit Plantagenet blood by direct descent, and Tudor on the distaff side. Ha! Well, there is nothing very instructive in all this. I think I must turn to you, Watson, for something more solid."

" I have very little difficulty in finding what I want," said I, " for the facts are quite recent, and the matter struck me as remarkable. I feared to refer them to you, however, as I knew that you had an inquiry on hand, and that you disliked the intrusion of other matters."

" Oh, you mean the little problem of the Grosvenor Square furniture van. That is quite cleared up now— though, indeed, it was obvious from the first. Pray give me the results of your newspaper selections."

" Here is the first notice which I can find. It is in the personal column of the *Morning Post*, and dates, as you see, some weeks back. ' A marriage has been arranged,' it says, ' and will, if rumour is correct, very shortly take place, between Lord Robert St. Simon, second son of the Duke of Balmoral, and Miss Hatty Doran, the only daughter of Aloysius Doran, Esq., of San Francisco, Cal., U.S.A.' That is all."

" Terse and to the point," remarked Holmes, stretching his long, thin legs towards the fire.

" There was a paragraph amplifying this in one of the society papers of the same week. Ah, here it is. ' There will soon be a call for protection in the marriage market, for the present free-trade principle appears to tell heavily against our home product. One by one the management of the noble houses of Great Britain is passing into the hands of our fair cousins from across the Atlantic. An important addition has been made during the last week to the list of prizes which have been borne away by these charming invaders. Lord St. Simon, who has shown himself for over twenty years proof against the little god's arrows, has now definitely announced his approaching marriage with Miss Hatty Doran, the fascinating daughter of a Californian millionaire. Miss Doran, whose graceful figure and striking face attracted much attention at the Westbury House festivities, is an only child, and it is currently reported that her dowry will run to considerably over the six figures, with expectancies for the future. As it is an open secret that the Duke of Balmoral has been compelled to sell his pictures within the last few years, and as Lord St. Simon has no property of his own, save the small estate of Birchmoor, it is obvious that the Californian heiress is not the only gainer by an alliance which will enable her to make the easy and common transition from a Republican lady to a British title.' "

" Anything else ? " asked Holmes, yawning.

" Oh yes ; plenty. Then there is another note in the *Morning Post* to say that the marriage would be an absolutely quiet one, that it would be at St. George's, Hanover Square, that only half a dozen intimate friends would be invited, and that the party would return to the furnished house at Lancaster Gate which has been taken by Mr. Aloysius Doran. Two days later—that is, on Wednesday last—there is a curt announcement that the wedding had taken place, and that the honeymoon would be passed at Lord Backwater's place, near Petersfield. Those are all the notices which appeared before the disappearance of the bride."

" Before the what ? " asked Holmes, with a start.

" The vanishing of the lady."

" When did she vanish, then ? "

" At the wedding breakfast."

" Indeed. This is more interesting than it promised to be ; quite dramatic, in fact."

" Yes ; it struck me as being a little out of the common."

" They often vanish before the ceremony, and occasionally during the honeymoon ; but I cannot call to mind anything quite so prompt as this. Pray let me have the details."

" I warn you that they are very incomplete."

" Perhaps we may make them less so."

" Such as they are, they are set forth in a single article of a morning newspaper of yesterday, which I will read to you. It is headed, ' Singular Occurrence at a Fashionable Wedding ' :

" ' The family of Lord Robert St. Simon has been thrown into the greatest consternation by the strange and painful episodes which have taken place in connection with his wedding. The ceremony, as shortly announced in the papers of yesterday, occurred on the previous morning ; but it is only now that it has been possible to confirm the strange rumours which have been so persistently floating about. In spite of the attempts of the friends to hush the matter up, so much public attention has now been drawn to it that no good purpose can be served by affecting to disregard what is a common subject for conversation.

" ' The ceremony, which was performed at St. George's, Hanover Square, was a very quiet one, no one being present save the father of the bride, Mr. Aloysius Doran, the Duchess of Balmoral, Lord Backwater, Lord Eustace and Lady Clara St. Simon (the younger brother and sister of the bridegroom), and Lady Alicia Whittington. The whole party proceeded afterwards to the house of Mr. Aloysius Doran, at Lancaster Gate, where breakfast had been prepared. It appears that some little trouble had been caused by a woman, whose name has not been ascertained, who endeavoured to force her way into the house after the bridal party, alleging that she had some claim upon Lord St. Simon. It was only after a painful and prolonged scene that she was ejected by the butler and the footman. The bride, who had fortunately entered the house before this unpleasant interruption, had sat down to breakfast with the rest, when she complained of a sudden indisposition, and retired to her room. Her prolonged absence having caused some comment, her father followed her ; but learned from her maid that she had only come up to her chamber for an instant, caught up an ulster and bonnet, and hurried down to the passage.

One of the footmen declared that he had seen a lady leave the house thus apparelled ; but had refused to credit that it was his mistress, believing her to be with the company. On ascertaining that his daughter had disappeared, Mr. Aloysius Doran, in conjunction with the bridegroom, instantly put themselves into communication with the police, and very energetic inquiries are being made, which will probably result in a speedy clearing up of this very singular business. Up to a late hour last night, however, nothing had transpired as to the whereabouts of the missing lady. There are rumours of foul play in the matter, and it is said that the police have caused the arrest of the woman who had caused the original disturbance, in the belief that, from jealousy or some other motive, she may have been concerned in the strange disappearance of the bride.' "

" And is that all ? "

" Only one little item in another of the morning papers, but it is a suggestive one."

" And it is ? "

" That Miss Flora Millar, the lady who had caused the disturbance, has actually been arrested. It appears that she was formerly a *danseuse* at the Allegro, and that she had known the bridegroom for some years. There are no further particulars, and the whole case is in your hands now—so far as it has been set forth in the public press."

" And an exceedingly interesting case it appears to be. I would not have missed it for worlds. But there is a ring at the bell, Watson, and as the clock makes it a few minutes after four, I have no doubt that this will prove to be our noble client. Do not dream of going, Watson, for I very much prefer having a witness, if only as a check to my own memory."

" Lord Robert St. Simon," announced our page-boy, throwing open the door. A gentleman entered, with a pleasant, cultured face, high-nosed and pale, with something perhaps of petulance about the mouth, and with the steady, well-opened eye of a man whose pleasant lot it had ever been to command and to be obeyed. His manner was brisk, and yet his general appearance gave an undue impression of age, for he had a slight forward stoop, and a little bend of the knees as he walked. His hair, too, as he swept off his curly brimmed hat, was grizzled round the edges, and thin upon the top. As to his dress, it was careful to the verge of foppishness, with high collar, black frock-coat, white waistcoat, yellow gloves, patent-leather shoes, and light-coloured gaiters. He advanced slowly into the room, turning his head from left to right, and swinging in his right hand the cord which held his golden eye-glasses.

" Good day, Lord St. Simon," said Holmes, rising and bowing. " Pray take the basket chair. This is my friend and colleague, Dr. Watson. Draw up a little to the fire, and we shall talk this matter over."

" A most painful matter to me, as you can most readily imagine, Mr. Holmes. I have been cut to the quick. I understand you have already managed several delicate cases of this sort, sir, though I presume that they were hardly from the same class of society."

" No, I am descending."

" I beg pardon ? "

" My last client of the sort was a king."

" Oh, really ! I had no idea. And which king ? "

" The King of Scandinavia."

" What ! Had he lost his wife ? "

" You can understand," said Holmes suavely, " that I extend to the affairs of my other clients the same secrecy which I promise to you in yours."

" Of course ! Very right ! very right ! I'm sure I beg pardon. As to my own case, I am ready to give you any information which may assist you in forming an opinion."

" Thank you. I have already learned all that is in the public prints, nothing more. I presume that I may take it as correct—this article, for example, as to the disappearance of the bride."

Lord St. Simon glanced over it. " Yes, it is correct, as far as it goes."

" But it needs a great deal of supplementing before anyone could offer an opinion. I think that I may arrive at my facts most directly by questioning you."

" Pray do so."

" When did you first meet Miss Hatty Doran ? "

" In San Francisco, a year ago."

" You were travelling in the States ? "

" Yes."

" Did you become engaged then ? "

" No."

" But you were on a friendly footing ? "

" I was amused by her society, and she could see that I was amused."

" Her father is very rich ? "

" He is said to be the richest man on the Pacific Slope."

" And how did he make his money ? "

" In mining. He had nothing a few years ago. Then he struck gold, invested it, and came up by leaps and bounds."

" Now, what is your own impression as to the young lady's—your wife's character ? "

The nobleman swung his glasses a little faster and stared down into the fire. " You see, Mr. Holmes," said he, " my wife was twenty before her father became a rich man. During that time she ran free in a mining camp, and wandered through woods or mountains, so that her education has come from nature rather than from the schoolmaster. She is what we call in England a tomboy, with a strong nature, wild and free, unfettered by any sort of traditions. She is impetuous—volcanic, I was about to say. She is swift in making up her mind, and fearless in carrying out her resolutions. On the other hand, I would not have given her the name which I have the honour to bear " (he gave a little stately cough) " had I not thought her to be at bottom a noble woman. I believe she is capable of heroic self-sacrifice, and that anything dishonourable would be repugnant to her."

" Have you her photograph ? "

" I brought this with me." He opened a locket, and showed us the full face of a very lovely woman. It was not a photograph, but an ivory miniature, and the artist had brought out the full effect of the lustrous black hair, the large dark eyes, and the exquisite mouth. Holmes gazed long and earnestly at it. Then he closed the locket and handed it back to Lord St. Simon.

" The young lady came to London, then, and you renewed your acquaintance ? "

" Yes, her father brought her over for this last London season. I met her several times, became engaged to her, and have now married her."

" She brought, I understand, a considerable dowry."

" A fair dowry. Not more than is usual in my family."

" And this, of course, remains to you, since the marriage is a *fait accompli* ? "

" I really have made no inquiries on the subject."

" Very naturally not. Did you see Miss Doran on the day before the wedding ? "

" Yes."

" Was she in good spirits ? "

" Never better. She kept talking of what we should do in our future lives."

" Indeed. That is very interesting. And on the morning of the wedding ? "

" She was as bright as possible—at least, until after the ceremony."

" And did you observe any change in her then ? "

" Well, to tell the truth, I saw then the first signs that I had ever seen that her temper was just a little sharp. The incident, however, was too trivial to relate, and can have no possible bearing upon the case."

" Pray let us have it, for all that."

" Oh, it is childish. She dropped her bouquet as we went towards the vestry. She was passing the front pew

233

at the time, and it fell over into the pew. There was a moment's delay, but the gentleman in the pew handed it up to her again, and it did not appear to be the worse for the fall. Yet, when I spoke to her of the matter, she answered me abruptly ; and in the carriage, on our way home, she seemed absurdly agitated over this trifling cause."

" Indeed. You say that there was a gentleman in the pew. Some of the general public were present, then ? "

" Oh, yes. It is impossible to exclude them when the church is open."

" This gentleman was not one of your wife's friends ? "

" No, no ; I call him a gentleman by courtesy, but he was quite a common-looking person. I hardly noticed his appearance. But really I think that we are wandering rather far from the point."

" Lady St. Simon, then, returned from the wedding in a less cheerful frame of mind than she had gone to it. What did she do on re-entering her father's house ? "

" I saw her in conversation with her maid."

" And who is her maid ? "

" Alice is her name. She is an American, and came from California with her."

" A confidential servant ? "

" A little too much so. It seemed to me that her mistress allowed her to take great liberties. Still, of course, in America they look upon these things in a different way."

" How long did she speak to this Alice ? "

" Oh, a few minutes. I had something else to think of."

" You did not overhear what they said ? "

" Lady St. Simon said something about ' jumping a claim.' She was accustomed to use slang of the kind. I have no idea what she meant."

" American slang is very expressive sometimes. And what did your wife do when she had finished speaking to her maid ? "

" She walked into the breakfast-room."

" On your arm ? "

" No, alone. She was very independent in little matters like that. Then, after we had sat down for ten minutes or so, she rose hurriedly, muttered some words of apology, and left the room. She never came back."

" But this maid Alice, as I understand, deposes that she went to her room, covered her bride's dress with a long ulster, put on a bonnet, and went out."

" Quite so. And she was afterwards seen walking into Hyde Park in company with Flora Millar, a woman who is now in custody, and who had already made a disturbance at Mr. Doran's house that morning."

" Ah, yes. I should like a few particulars as to this young lady, and your relations to her."

Lord St. Simon shrugged his shoulders, and raised his eyebrows. " We have been on a friendly footing for some years—I may say on a *very* friendly footing. She used to be at the Allegro. I have not treated her ungenerously, and she has no just cause of complaint against me, but you know what women are, Mr. Holmes. Flora was a dear little thing, but exceedingly hot-headed, and devotedly attached to me. She wrote me dreadful letters when she heard that I was to be married, and to tell the truth the reason why I had the marriage celebrated so quietly was that I feared lest there might be a scandal in the church. She came to Mr. Doran's door just after we returned, and she endeavoured to push her way in, uttering very abusive expressions towards my wife, and even threatening her, but I had foreseen the possibility of something of the sort, and I had given instructions to the servants, who soon pushed her out again. She was quiet when she saw that there was no good in making a row."

" Did your wife hear all this ? "

" No, thank goodness, she did not."

" And she was seen walking with this very woman afterwards ? "

" Yes. That is what Mr. Lestrade, of Scotland Yard,

looks upon as so serious.   It is thought that Flora decoyed my wife out, and laid some terrible trap for her."

" Well, it is a possible supposition."

" You think so, too ? "

" I did not say a probable one.   But you do not yourself look upon this as likely ? "

" I do not think Flora would hurt a fly."

" Still, jealousy is a strange transformer of characters. Pray what is your own theory as to what took place ? "

" Well, really, I came to seek a theory, not to propound one.   I have given you all the facts.   Since you ask me, however, I may say that it has occurred to me as possible that the excitement of this affair, the consciousness that she had made so immense a social stride, had the effect of causing some little nervous disturbance in my wife."

" In short, that she had become suddenly deranged ? "

" Well, really, when I consider that she has turned her back—I will not say upon me, but upon so much that many have aspired to without success—I can hardly explain it in any other fashion."

" Well, certainly that is also a conceivable hypothesis," said Holmes, smiling.   " And now, Lord St. Simon, I think that I have nearly all my data.   May I ask whether you were seated at the breakfast-table so that you could see out of the window ? "

" We could see the other side of the road, and the Park."

" Quite so.   Then I do not think that I need detain you any longer.   I shall communicate with you."

" Should you be fortunate enough to solve this problem," said our client, rising.

" I have solved it."

" Eh ?   What was that ? "

" I say that I have solved it."

" Where, then, is my wife ? "

" That is a detail which I shall speedily supply."

Lord St. Simon shook his head.   " I am afraid that it will take wiser heads than yours or mine," he remarked, and bowing in a stately, old-fashioned manner, he departed.

"It is very good of Lord St. Simon to honour my head by putting it on a level with his own," said Sherlock Holmes, laughing. "I think that I shall have a whisky and soda and a cigar after all this cross-questioning. I had formed my conclusions as to the case before our client came into the room."

"My dear Holmes!"

"I have notes of several similar cases, though none, as I remarked before, which were quite as prompt. My whole examination served to turn my conjecture into a certainty. Circumstantial evidence is occasionally very convincing, as when you find a trout in the milk, to quote Thoreau's example."

"But I have heard all that you have heard."

"Without, however, the knowledge of pre-existing cases which serves me so well. There was a parallel instance in Aberdeen some years back, and something on very much the same lines at Munich the year after the Franco-Prussian War. It is one of these cases—but hallo, here is Lestrade! Good afternoon, Lestrade! You will find an extra tumbler upon the sideboard, and there are cigars in the box."

The official detective was attired in a pea-jacket and cravat, which gave him a decidedly nautical appearance, and he carried a black canvas bag in his hand. With a short greeting he seated himself, and lit the cigar which had been offered to him.

"What's up, then?" asked Holmes, with a twinkle in his eye. "You look dissatisfied."

"And I feel dissatisfied. It is this infernal St. Simon marriage case. I can make neither head nor tail of the business."

"Really! You surprise me."

"Who ever heard of such a mixed affair? Every clue seems to slip through my fingers. I have been at work upon it all day."

"And very wet it seems to have made you," said Holmes, laying his hand upon the arm of the pea-jacket.

"Yes, I have been dragging the Serpentine."

"In Heaven's name, what for?"

"In search of the body of Lady St. Simon."

Sherlock Holmes leaned back in his chair and laughed heartily.

"Have you dragged the basin of the Trafalgar Square fountain?" he asked.

"Why? What do you mean?"

"Because you have just as good a chance of finding this lady in the one as in the other."

Lestrade shot an angry glance at my companion. "I suppose you know all about it," he snarled.

"Well, I have only just heard the facts, but my mind is made up."

"Oh, indeed! Then you think that the Serpentine plays no part in the matter?"

"I think it very unlikely."

"Then perhaps you will kindly explain how it is that we found this in it?" He opened his bag as he spoke, and tumbled on to the floor a wedding dress of watered silk, a pair of white satin shoes, and a bride's wreath and veil, all discoloured and soaked in water. "There," said he, putting a new wedding-ring upon the top of the pile. "There is a little nut for you to crack, Master Holmes."

"Oh, indeed," said my friend, blowing blue rings into the air. "You dragged them from the Serpentine?"

"No. They were found floating near the margin by a park-keeper. They were identified as her clothes, and it seemed to me that if the clothes were there the body would not be far off."

"By the same brilliant reasoning, every man's body is to be found in the neighbourhood of his wardrobe. And pray what did you hope to arrive at through this?"

"At some evidence implicating Flora Millar in the disappearance."

"I am afraid you will find it difficult."

"Are you indeed, now ? " cried Lestrade, with some bitterness. " I am afraid, Holmes, that you are not very practical with your deductions and your inferences. You have made two blunders in as many minutes. This dress does implicate Miss Flora Millar."

" And how ? "

" In the dress is a pocket. In the pocket is a card-case. In the card-case is a note. And here is the very note." He slapped it down upon the table in front of him. " Listen to this. ' You will see me when all is ready. Come at once. F. H. M.' Now my theory all along has been that Lady St. Simon was decoyed away by Flora Millar, and that she, with confederates no doubt, was responsible for her disappearance. Here, signed with her initials, is the very note which was no doubt quietly slipped into her hand at the door, and which lured her within their reach."

" Very good, Lestrade," said Holmes, laughing. " You really are very fine indeed. Let me see it." He took up the paper in a listless way, but his attention instantly became riveted, and he gave a little cry of satisfaction. " This is indeed important," said he.

" Ha, you find it so ? "

" Extremely so. I congratulate you warmly."

Lestrade rose in his triumph and bent his head to look. " Why," he shrieked, " you're looking on the wrong side."

" On the contrary, this is the right side."

" The right side ? You're mad ! Here is the note written in pencil over here."

" And over here is what appears to be a fragment of a hotel bill, which interests me deeply."

" There's nothing in it. I looked at it before," said Lestrade. " ' Oct. 4th, rooms 8s., breakfast 2s. 6d., cocktail 1s., lunch 2s. 6d., glass sherry 8d.' I see nothing in that."

" Very likely not. It is most important all the same. As to the note, it is important also, or at least the initials are, so I congratulate you again."

" I've wasted time enough," said Lestrade, rising, " I

believe in hard work, and not in sitting by the fire spinning fine theories. Good day, Mr. Holmes, and we shall see which gets to the bottom of the matter first." He gathered up the garments, thrust them into the bag, and made for the door.

"Just one hint to you, Lestrade," drawled Holmes, before his rival vanished; "I will tell you the true solution of the matter. Lady St. Simon is a myth. There is not, and there never has been, any such person."

Lestrade looked sadly at my companion. Then he turned to me, tapped his forehead three times, shook his head solemnly, and hurried away.

He had hardly shut the door behind him, when Holmes rose and put on his overcoat. "There is something in what the fellow says about outdoor work," he remarked, "so I think, Watson, that I must leave you to your papers for a little."

It was after five o'clock when Sherlock Holmes left me, but I had no time to be lonely, for within an hour there arrived a confectioner's man with a very large flat box. This he unpacked with the help of a youth whom he had brought with him, and presently, to my very great astonishment, a quite epicurean little cold supper began to be laid out upon our humble lodging-house mahogany. There were a couple of brace of cold woodcock, a pheasant, a *pâté-de-foie-gras* pie, with a group of ancient and cobwebby bottles. Having laid out all these luxuries, my two visitors vanished away, like the genii of the Arabian Nights, with no explanation save that the things had been paid for, and were ordered to this address.

Just before nine o'clock Sherlock Holmes stepped briskly into the room. His features were gravely set, but there was a light in his eye which made me think that he had not been disappointed in his conclusions.

"They have laid the supper, then," he said, rubbing his hands.

"You seem to expect company. They have laid for five."

"Yes, I fancy we may have some company dropping in," said he. "I am surprised that Lord St. Simon has not already arrived. Ha! I fancy that I hear his step now upon the stairs."

It was indeed our visitor of the morning who came bustling in, dangling his glasses more vigorously than ever, and with a very perturbed expression upon his aristocratic features.

"My messenger reached you, then?" asked Holmes.

"Yes, and I must confess that the contents startled me beyond measure. Have you good authority for what you say?"

"The best possible."

Lord St. Simon sank into a chair, and passed his hand over his forehead.

"What will the Duke say," he murmured, "when he hears that one of the family has been subjected to such a humiliation?"

"It is the purest accident. I cannot allow that there is any humiliation."

"Ah, you look on these things from another standpoint."

"I fail to see that anyone is to blame. I can hardly see how the lady could have acted otherwise, though her abrupt method of doing it was undoubtedly to be regretted. Having no mother, she had no one to advise her at such a crisis."

"It was a slight, sir, a public slight," said Lord St. Simon, tapping his fingers upon the table.

"You must make allowance for this poor girl, placed in so unprecedented a position."

"I will make no allowance. I am very angry indeed, and I have been shamefully used."

"I think I heard a ring," said Holmes. "Yes, there are steps on the landing. If I cannot persuade you to take a lenient view of the matter, Lord St. Simon, I have brought an advocate here who may be more successful." He opened the door and ushered in a lady and gentleman.

" Lord St. Simon," said he, " allow me to introduce you to Mr. and Mrs. Francis Hay Moulton. The lady, I think, you have already met."

At the sight of these new-comers our client had sprung from his seat, and stood very erect, with his eyes cast down and his hand thrust into the breast of his frock-coat, a picture of offended dignity. The lady had taken a quick step forward and had held out her hand to him, but he still refused to raise his eyes. It was as well for his resolution, perhaps, for her pleading face was one which it was hard to resist.

" You're angry, Robert," said she. " Well, I guess you have every cause to be."

" Pray make no apology to me," said Lord St. Simon bitterly.

" Oh, yes, I know that I treated you real bad, and that I should have spoken to you before I went ; but I was kind of rattled, and from the time when I saw Frank here again, I just didn't know what I was doing or saying. I only wonder that I didn't fall down and do a faint right there before the altar."

" Perhaps, Mrs. Moulton, you would like my friend and me to leave the room while you explain this matter ? "

" If I may give an opinion," remarked the strange gentleman, " we've had just a little too much secrecy over this business already. For my part, I should like all Europe and America to hear the rights of it." He was a small, wiry, sunburned man, with a sharp face and alert manner.

" Then I'll tell our story right away," said the lady. " Frank here and I met in '81, in McQuire's camp, near the Rockies, where Pa was working a claim. We were engaged to each other, Frank and I ; but then one day father struck a rich pocket, and made a pile, while poor Frank here had a claim that petered out and came to nothing. The richer Pa grew, the poorer was Frank ; so at last Pa wouldn't hear of our engagement lasting any longer, and he took me away to 'Frisco. Frank wouldn't throw up his hand, though ; so he followed me there, and he saw me without Pa knowing anything about it. It would only have made him mad to know, so we just fixed it all up for ourselves. Frank said that he would go and make his pile, too, and never come back to claim me until he had as much as Pa. So then I promised to wait for him to the end of time, and pledged myself not to marry anyone else while he lived. 'Why shouldn't we be married right away, then,' said he, ' and then I will feel sure of you ; and I won't claim to be your husband until I come back.' Well, we talked it over, and he had fixed it all up so nicely, with a clergyman all ready in waiting, that we just did it right there ; and then Frank went off to seek his fortune and I went back to Pa.

" The next that I heard of Frank was that he was in Montana, and then he went prospecting into Arizona, and then I heard of him from New Mexico. After that came a long newspaper story about how a miners' camp had been attacked by Apache Indians, and there was my Frank's name among the killed. I fainted dead away, and I was very sick for months after. Pa thought I had a decline, and took me to half the doctors in 'Frisco. Not a word of news came for a year or more, so that I never doubted that Frank was really dead. Then Lord St. Simon came to 'Frisco, and we came to London, and a marriage was arranged, and Pa was very pleased, but I felt all the time that no man on this earth would ever take the place in my heart that had been given to my poor Frank.

" Still, if I had married Lord St. Simon, of course I'd have done my duty by him. We can't command our love, but we can our actions. I went to the altar with him with the intention that I would make him just as good a wife as it was in me to be. But you may imagine what I felt when, just as I came to the altar rails, I glanced back and saw Frank standing looking at me out of the first pew. I thought it was his ghost at first ; but, when I looked again, there he was still, with a kind of question in his eyes as if to ask me whether I were glad or sorry to see him. I wonder I didn't drop. I know that everything was turning round, and the words of the clergyman were just like the buzz of a bee in my ear. I didn't know what to do. Should I stop the service and make a scene in the church? I glanced at him again, and he seemed to know what I was thinking, for he raised his fingers to his lips to tell me to be still. Then I saw him scribble on a piece of paper, and I knew he was writing me a note. As I passed his pew on the way out I dropped my bouquet over to him, and he slipped the note into my hand when he returned me the flowers. It was only a line asking me to join him when he made the sign to me to do so. Of course I never doubted for a moment that my first duty now was to him, and I determined to do just whatever he might direct.

"When I got back I told my maid, who had known him in California, and had always been his friend. I ordered her to say nothing, but to get a few things packed and my ulster ready. I know I ought to have spoken to Lord St. Simon, but it was dreadful hard before his mother and all those great people. I just made up my mind to run away, and explain afterwards. I hadn't been at the table ten minutes before I saw Frank out of the window at the other side of the road. He beckoned to me, and then began walking into the Park. I slipped out, put on my things, and followed him. Some woman came talking something or other about Lord St. Simon to me—seemed to me from the little I heard as if he had a little secret of his own before marriage also—but I managed to get away from her, and soon overtook Frank. We got into a cab together, and away we drove to some lodgings he had taken in Gordon Square, and that was my true wedding after all those years of waiting. Frank had been a prisoner among the Apaches, had escaped, came on to 'Frisco, found that I had given him up for dead and had gone to England, followed me there, and had come upon me at last on the very morning of my second wedding."

"I saw it in a paper," explained the American. "It

gave the name and the church, but not where the lady lived."

"Then we had a talk as to what we should do, and Frank was all for openness, but I was so ashamed of it all that I felt as if I would like to vanish away and never see any of them again, just sending a line to Pa, perhaps, to show him that I was alive. It was awful to me to think of all those lords and ladies sitting round that breakfast-table, and waiting for me to come back. So Frank took my wedding clothes and things, and made a bundle of them so that I should not be traced, and dropped them away somewhere where no one should find them. It is likely that we should have gone on to Paris to-morrow, only that this good gentleman, Mr. Holmes, came round to us this evening, though how he found us is more than I can think, and he showed us very clearly and kindly that I was wrong and that Frank was right, and that we should put ourselves in the wrong if we were so secret. Then he offered to give us a chance of talking to Lord St. Simon alone, and so we came right away round to his rooms at once. Now, Robert, you have heard all, and I am very sorry if I have given you pain, and I hope that you do not think very meanly of me."

Lord St. Simon had by no means relaxed his rigid attitude, but had listened with a frowning brow and a compressed lip to this long narrative.

"Excuse me," he said, "but it is not my custom to discuss my most intimate personal affairs in this public manner."

"Then you won't forgive me? You won't shake hands before I go?"

"Oh, certainly, if it would give you any pleasure." He put out his hand and coldly grasped that which she extended to him.

"I had hoped," suggested Holmes, "that you would have joined us in a friendly supper."

"I think that there you ask a little too much," responded his lordship. "I may be forced to acquiesce in these recent developments, but I can hardly be expected to make merry over them. I think that, with your permission, I will now wish you all a very good night." He included us all in a sweeping bow, and stalked out of the room.

"Then I trust that you at least will honour me with your company," said Sherlock Holmes. "It is always a joy to me to meet an American, Mr. Moulton, for I am one of those who believe that the folly of a monarch and the blundering of a Minister in fargone years will not prevent our children from being some day citizens of the same world-wide country under a flag which shall be a quartering of the Union Jack with the Stars and Stripes."

"The case has been an interesting one," remarked Holmes, when our visitors had left, "because it serves to show very clearly how simple the explanation may be of an affair which at first sight seems to be almost inexplicable. Nothing could be more inexplicable. Nothing could be more natural than the sequence of events as narrated by this lady, and nothing stranger than the result when viewed, for instance, by Mr. Lestrade of Scotland Yard."

"You were not yourself at fault, then?"

"From the first, two facts were very obvious to me, the one that the lady had been quite willing to undergo the wedding ceremony, the other that she had repented of it within a few minutes of returning home. Obviously something had occurred during the morning, then, to cause her to change her mind. What could that something be? She could not have spoken to anyone when she was out, for she had been in the company of the bridegroom. Had she seen someone, then? If she had, it must be someone from America, because she had spent so short a time in this country that she could hardly have allowed anyone to acquire so deep an influence over her that the mere sight of him would induce her to change her plans so completely. You see we have already arrived, by a process of exclusion, at the idea that she might have seen an American. Then who could this American be, and why should he possess so much influence over her ? It might be a lover ; it might be a husband. Her young womanhood had, I knew, been spent in rough scenes, and under strange conditions. So far had I got before I ever heard Lord St. Simon's narrative. When he told us of a man in a pew, of the change in the bride's manner, of so transparent a device of obtaining a note as the dropping of a bouquet, of her resort to her confidential maid, and of her very significant allusion to claim-jumping, which in miners' parlance means taking possession of that which another person has a prior claim to, the whole situation became absolutely clear. She had gone off with a man, and the man was either a lover or was a previous husband, the chances being in favour of the latter."

" And how in the world did you find them ? "

" It might have been difficult, but friend Lestrade held information in his hands the value of which he did not himself know. The initials were of course of the highest importance, but more valuable still was it to know that within a week he had settled his bill at one of the most select London hotels."

" How did you deduce the select ? "

" By the select prices. Eight shillings for a bed and eightpence for a glass of sherry, pointed to one of the most expensive hotels. There are not many in London which charge at that rate. In the second one which I visited in Northumberland Avenue, I learned by an inspection of the book that Francis H. Moulton, an American gentleman, had left only the day before, and on looking over the entries against him, I came upon the very items which I had seen in the duplicate bill. His letters were to be forwarded to 226 Gordon Square, so thither I travelled, and being fortunate enough to find the loving couple at home, I ventured to give them some paternal advice, and to point out to them that it would be better in every way that they should make their position a little clearer, both to the general public and to Lord St. Simon in particular. I invited them to meet him here, and, as you see, I made him keep the appointment."

"But with no very good results," I remarked. "His conduct was certainly not very gracious."

"Ah! Watson," said Holmes, smiling, "perhaps you would not be very gracious either, if, after all the trouble of wooing and wedding, you found yourself deprived in an instant of wife and of fortune. I think that we may judge Lord St. Simon very mercifully, and thank our stars that we are never likely to find ourselves in the same position. Draw your chair up, and hand me my violin, for the only problem which we have still to solve is how to while away these bleak autumnal evenings."

11. *The Beryl Coronet*

"HOLMES," said I, as I stood one morning in our bow-window looking down the street, "here is a madman coming along. It seems rather sad that his relatives should allow him to come out alone."

My friend rose lazily from his arm-chair, and stood with his hands in the pockets of his dressing-gown, looking over my shoulder. It was a bright, crisp February morning, and the snow of the day before still lay deep upon the ground, shimmering brightly in the wintry sun. Down the centre of Baker Street it had been ploughed into a brown crumbly band by the traffic, but at either side and on the heaped-up edges of the footpaths it still lay as white as when it fell. The grey pavement had been cleaned and scraped, but was still dangerously slippery, so that there were fewer passengers than usual. Indeed, from the direction of the Metropolitan station no one was coming save the single gentleman whose eccentric conduct had drawn my attention.

He was a man of about fifty, tall, portly, and imposing, with a massive, strongly marked face and a commanding figure. He was dressed in a sombre yet rich style, in black frock-coat, shining hat, neat brown gaiters, and well-cut pearl-grey trousers. Yet his actions were in absurd contrast to the dignity of his dress and features, for he was running hard, with occasional little springs, such as a weary man gives who is little accustomed to set any tax upon his legs. As he ran he jerked his hands up and down, waggled his head, and writhed his face into the most extraordinary contortions.

" What on earth can be the matter with him ? " I asked. " He is looking up at the numbers of the houses."

" I believe that he is coming here," said Holmes, rubbing his hands.

" Here ? "

" Yes ; I rather think he is coming to consult me professionally. I think that I recognize the symptoms. Ha ! did I not tell you ? " As he spoke, the man, puffing and blowing, rushed at our door, and pulled at our bell until the whole house resounded with the clanging.

A few moments later he was in our room, still puffing, still gesticulating, but with so fixed a look of grief and despair in his eyes that our smiles were turned in an instant to horror and pity. For a while he could not get his words out, but swayed his body and plucked at his hair like one who has been driven to the extreme limits of his reason. Then, suddenly springing to his feet, he beat his head against the wall with such force that we both rushed upon him, and tore him away to the centre of the room. Sherlock Holmes pushed him down into the easy chair, and, sitting beside him, patted his hand, and chatted with him in the easy, soothing tones which he knew so well how to employ.

" You have come to me to tell me your story, have you not ? " said he. " You are fatigued with your haste. Pray wait until you have recovered yourself, and then I shall be most happy to look into any little problem which you may submit to me."

The man sat for a minute or more with a heaving chest, fighting against his emotion. Then he passed his handkerchief over his brow, set his lips tight, and turned his face towards us.

"No doubt you think me mad ? " said he.

"I see that you have had some great trouble," responded Holmes.

"God knows I have !—a trouble which is enough to unseat my reason, so sudden and so terrible is it. Public disgrace I might have faced, although I am a man whose character has never yet borne a stain. Private affliction also is the lot of every man ; but the two coming together, and in so frightful a form, have been enough to shake my very soul. Besides, it is not I alone. The very noblest in the land may suffer, unless some way be found out of this horrible affair."

"Pray compose yourself, sir," said Holmes, "and let me have a clear account of who you are, and what it is that has befallen you."

"My name," answered our visitor, "is probably familiar to your ears. I am Alexander Holder, of the banking firm of Holder & Stevenson, of Threadneedle Street."

The name was indeed well known to us, as belonging to the senior partner in the second largest private banking concern in the City of London. What could have happened, then, to bring one of the foremost citizens of London to this most pitiable pass ? We waited, all curiosity, until with another effort he braced himself to tell his story.

"I feel that time is of value," said he, "that is why I hastened here when the police inspector suggested that I should secure your co-operation. I came to Baker Street by the Underground, and hurried from there on foot, for the cabs go slowly through this snow. That is why I was so out of breath, for I am a man who takes very little exercise. I feel better now, and I will put the facts before you as shortly and yet as clearly as I can.

"It is, of course, well known to you, that in a successful banking business as much depends upon our being able to find remunerative investments for our funds, as upon our increasing our connection and the number of our depositors. One of our most lucrative means of laying out money is in the shape of loans, where the security is unimpeachable. We have done a good deal in this direction during the last few years, and there are many noble families to whom we have advanced large sums upon the security of their pictures, libraries, or plate.

" Yesterday morning I was seated in my office at the Bank, when a card was brought in to me by one of the clerks. I started when I saw the name, for it was that of none other than—well, perhaps even to you I had better say no more than that it was a name which is a household word all over the earth—one of the highest, noblest, most exalted names in England. I was overwhelmed by the honour, and attempted, when he entered, to say so, but he plunged at once into business with the air of a man who wishes to hurry quickly through a disagreeable task.

" ' Mr. Holder,' said he, ' I have been informed that you are in the habit of advancing money.'

" ' The firm do so when the security is good,' I answered.

" ' It is absolutely essential to me,' said he, ' that I should have fifty thousand pounds at once. I could of course borrow so trifling a sum ten times over from my friends, but I much prefer to make it a matter of business, and to carry out that business myself. In my position you can readily understand that it is unwise to place oneself under obligations.'

" ' For how long, may I ask, do you want this sum ? ' I asked.

" ' Next Monday I have a large sum due to me, and I shall then most certainly repay what you advance, with whatever interest you think it right to charge. But it is very essential to me that the money should be paid at once.'

" ' I should be happy to advance it without further parley from my own private purse,' said I, ' were it not that the strain would be rather more than it could bear. If, on the other hand, I am to do it in the name of the firm, then in justice to my partner I must insist that, even in your case, every business-like precaution should be taken.'

" ' I should much prefer to have it so,' said he, raising up a square, black morocco case which he had laid beside his chair. ' You have doubtless heard of the Beryl coronet ? '

" ' One of the most precious public possessions of the Empire,' said I.

" ' Precisely.' He opened the case, and there, embedded in soft, flesh-coloured velvet, lay the magnificent piece of jewellery which he had named. ' There are thirty-nine enormous beryls,' said he, ' and the price of the gold chasing is incalculable. The lowest estimate would put the worth of the coronet at double the sum which I have asked. I am prepared to leave it with you as my security.'

" I took the precious case into my hands and looked in some perplexity from it to my illustrious client.

" ' You doubt its value ? ' he asked.

" ' Not at all. I only doubt—'

" ' The propriety of my leaving it. You may set your mind at rest about that. I should not dream of doing so were it not absolutely certain that I should be able in four days to reclaim it. It is a pure matter of form. Is the security sufficient ? '

" ' Ample.'

" ' You understand, Mr. Holder, that I am giving you a strong proof of the confidence which I have in you, founded upon all that I have heard of you. I rely upon you not only to be discreet and to refrain from all gossip upon the matter, but, above all, to preserve this coronet with every possible precaution, because I need not say that a great public scandal would be caused if any harm were to befall it. Any injury to it would be almost as serious as its complete loss, for there are no beryls in the world to match these, and it would be impossible to replace them. I leave it with you, however, with every confidence, and I shall call for it in person on Monday morning.'

" Seeing that my client was anxious to leave, I said no more ; but, calling for my cashier, I ordered him to pay over fifty thousand-pound notes. When I was alone once more, however, with the precious case lying upon the table in front of me, I could not but think with some misgivings of the immense responsibility which it entailed upon me. There could be no doubt that, as it was a national possession, a horrible scandal would ensue if any misfortune should occur to it. I already regretted having ever consented to take charge of it. However, it was too late to alter the matter now, so I locked it up in my private safe, and turned once more to my work.

" When evening came, I felt that it would be an imprudence to leave so precious a thing in the office behind me. Bankers' safes had been forced before now, and why should not mine be ? If so, how terrible would be the position in which I should find myself ! I determined, therefore, that for the next few days I would always carry the case backwards and forwards with me, so that it might never be really out of my reach. With this intention, I called a cab, and drove out to my house at Streatham, carrying the jewel with me. I did not breathe freely until I had taken it upstairs, and locked it in the bureau of my dressing-room.

" And now a word as to my household, Mr. Holmes, for I wish you to thoroughly understand the situation. My groom and my page sleep out of the house, and may be set aside altogether. I have three maid-servants who have been with me a number of years, and whose absolute reliability is quite above suspicion. Another, Lucy Parr, the second waiting-maid, has only been in my service a few months. She came with an excellent character, however, and has always given me satisfaction. She is a very pretty girl, and has attracted admirers who have occasionally hung about the place. That is the only drawback which we have found to her, but we believe her to be a thoroughly good girl in every way.

" So much for the servants. My family itself is so small that it will not take me long to describe it. I am a widower, and have an only son, Arthur. He has been a disappointment to me, Mr. Holmes, a grievous disappointment. I have no doubt that I am myself to blame. People tell me that I have spoiled him. Very likely I have. When my dear wife died I felt that he was all I had to love. I could not bear to see the smile fade even for a moment from his face. I have never denied him a wish. Perhaps it would have been better for both of us had I been sterner, but I meant it for the best.

" It was naturally my intention that he should succeed me in my business, but he was not of a business turn. He was wild, wayward, and, to speak the truth, I could not trust him in the handling of large sums of money. When he was young he became a member of an aristocratic club, and there, having charming manners, he was soon the intimate of a number of men with long purses and expensive habits. He learned to play heavily at cards and to squander money on the turf, until he had again and again to come to me and implore me to give him an advance upon his allowance, that he might settle his debts of honour. He tried more than once to break away from the dangerous company which he was keeping, but each time the influence of his friend Sir George Burnwell was enough to draw him back again.

" And, indeed, I could not wonder that such a man as Sir George Burnwell should gain an influence over him, for he has frequently brought him to my house, and I have found myself that I could hardly resist the fascination of his manner. He is older than Arthur, a man of the world to his finger-tips, one who has been everywhere, seen everything, a brilliant talker, and a man of great personal beauty. Yet when I think of him in cold blood, far away from the glamour of his presence, I am convinced from his cynical speech, and the look which I have caught in his eyes, that he is one who should be deeply distrusted. So I think, and so, too, thinks my little Mary, who has a woman's quick insight into character.

" And now there is only she to be described. She is my niece ; but when my brother died five years ago and left

her alone in the world I adopted her, and have looked upon
her ever since as my daughter. She is a sunbeam in my
house—sweet, loving, beautiful, a wonderful manager and
housekeeper, yet as tender and quiet and gentle as a woman
could be. She is my right hand. I do not know what I
could do without her. In only one matter has she ever
gone against my wishes. Twice my boy has asked her to
marry him, for he loves her devotedly, but each time she
has refused him. I think that if anyone could have drawn
him into the right path it would have been she, and that
his marriage might have changed his whole life ; but now,
alas ! it is too late—for ever too late !

"Now, Mr. Holmes, you know the people who live under
my roof, and I shall continue with my miserable story.

"When we were taking coffee in the drawing-room that
night, after dinner, I told Arthur and Mary my experience,
and of the precious treasure which we had under our roof,
suppressing only the name of my client. Lucy Parr, who
had brought in the coffee, had, I am sure, left the room ;
but I cannot swear that the door was closed. Mary and
Arthur were much interested, and wished to see the famous
coronet, but I thought it better not to disturb it.

"'Where have you put it ?' asked Arthur.

"'In my own bureau.'

"'Well, I hope to goodness the house won't be burgled
during the night,' said he.

"'It is locked up,' I answered.

"'Oh, any old key will fit that bureau. When I was a
youngster I have opened it myself with the key of the box-
room cupboard.'

"He often had a wild way of talking, so that I thought
little of what he said. He followed me to my room, however, that night with a very grave face.

"'Look here, dad,' said he, with his eyes cast down.
Can you let me have two hundred pounds ?'

"'No, I cannot !' I answered sharply. 'I have been
far too generous with you in money matters.'

"'You have been very kind,' said he ; 'but I must

255

have this money, or else I can never show my face inside the club again.'

" ' And a very good thing, too ! ' I cried.

" ' Yes, but you would not have me leave it a dishonoured man,' said he. ' I could not bear the disgrace. I must raise the money in some way, and if you will not let me have it, then I must try other means.'

" I was very angry, for this was the third demand during the month. ' You shall not have a farthing from me,' I cried, on which he bowed and left the room without another word.

" When he was gone I unlocked my bureau, made sure that my treasure was safe, and locked it again. Then I started to go round the house to see that all was secure—a duty which I usually leave to Mary, but which I thought it well to perform myself that night. As I came down the stairs I saw Mary herself at the side-window of the hall, which she closed and fastened as I approached.

" ' Tell me, dad,' said she, looking, I thought, a little disturbed, ' did you give Lucy, the maid, leave to go out to-night ? '

" ' Certainly not.'

" ' She came in just now by the back door. I have no doubt that she has only been to the side-gate to see someone, but I think that it is hardly safe, and should be stopped.'

" ' You must speak to her in the morning, or I will, if you prefer it. Are you sure that everything is fastened ? '

" ' Quite sure, dad.'

" ' Then, good night.' I kissed her, and went to my bedroom, where I was soon asleep.

" I am endeavouring to tell you everything, Mr. Holmes, which may have any bearing upon the case, but I beg that you will question me upon any point which I do not make clear."

" On the contrary, your statement is singularly lucid."

" I come to a part of my story now in which I should wish to be particularly so. I am not a very heavy sleeper, and the anxiety in my mind tended, no doubt, to make me even less so than usual. About two in the morning, then, I was awakened by some sound in the house. It had ceased ere I was wide awake, but it had left an impression behind it as though a window had gently closed somewhere. I lay listening with all my ears. Suddenly, to my horror, there was a distinct sound of footsteps moving softly in the next room. I slipped out of bed, all palpitating with fear, and peeped round the corner of my dressing-room door.

" ' Arthur ! ' I screamed, ' you villain ! you thief ! How dare you touch that coronet ? '

" The gas was half up, as I had left it, and my unhappy boy, dressed only in his shirt and trousers, was standing beside the light, holding the coronet in his hands. He appeared to be wrenching at it, or bending it with all his strength. At my cry he dropped it from his grasp, and turned as pale as death. I snatched it up and examined it. One of the gold corners, with three of the beryls in it, was missing.

" ' You blackguard ! ' I shouted, beside myself with rage. ' You have destroyed it ! You have dishonoured me for ever ! Where are the jewels you have stolen ? '

" ' Stolen ! ' he cried.

" ' Yes, you thief ! ' I roared, shaking him by the shoulder.

" ' There are none missing. There cannot be any missing,' said he.

" ' There are three missing. And you know where they are. Must I call you a liar as well as a thief ? Did I not see you trying to tear off another piece ? '

" ' You have called me names enough,' said he ; ' I will not stand it any longer. I shall not say another word about this business since you have chosen to insult me. I will leave your house in the morning, and make my own way in the world.'

" ' You shall leave it in the hands of the police ! ' I cried, half mad with grief and rage. ' I shall have this matter probed to the bottom.'

" ' You shall learn nothing from me,' said he, with a passion such as I should not have thought was in his nature. ' If you choose to call the police, let them find what they can.'

" By this time the whole house was astir, for I had raised my voice in my anger. Mary was the first to rush into my room, and at the sight of the coronet and of Arthur's face, she read the whole story, and, with a scream, fell down senseless on the ground. I sent the housemaid for the police, and put the investigation into their hands at once. When the inspector and a constable entered the house, Arthur, who had stood sullenly with his arms folded, asked me whether it was my intention to charge him with theft. I answered that it had ceased to be a private matter, but had become a public one, since the ruined coronet was national property. I was determined that the law should have its way in everything.

" ' At least,' said he, ' you will not have me arrested at once. It would be to your advantage as well as mine if I might leave the house for five minutes.'

" ' That you may get away, or perhaps that you may conceal what you have stolen,' said I. And then realizing the dreadful position in which I was placed, I implored him to remember that not only my honour, but that of one who was far greater than I, was at stake ; and that he threatened to raise a scandal which would convulse the nation. He might avert it all if he would but tell me what he had done with the three missing stones.

" ' You may as well face the matter,' said I ; ' you have been caught in the act, and no confession could make your guilt more heinous. If you but make such reparation as is in your power, by telling us where the beryls are, all shall be forgiven and forgotten.'

" ' Keep your forgiveness for those who ask for it,' he answered, turning away from me with a sneer. I saw that he was too hardened for any words of mine to influence him. There was but one way for it. I called in the inspector, and gave him into custody. A search was made at once, not only of his person, but of his room, and of every portion of the house where he could possibly have concealed the gems ; but no trace of them could be found, nor would the wretched boy open his mouth for all our persuasions and our threats. This morning he was removed to a cell, and I, after going through all the police formalities, have hurried round to you, to implore you to use your skill in unravelling the matter. The police have openly confessed that they can at present make nothing of it. You may go to any expense which you think necessary. I have already offered a reward of a thousand pounds. My God, what shall I do ! I have lost my honour, my gems, and my son in cne night. Oh, what shall I do ! "

He put a hand on either side of his head, and rocked himself to and fro, droning to himself like a child whose grief has got beyond words.

Sherlock Holmes sat silent for some few minutes, with his brows knitted and his eyes fixed upon the fire.

" Do you receive much company ? " he asked.

" None, save my partner with his family, and an occasional friend of Arthur's. Sir George Burnwell has been several times lately. No one else, I think."

" Do you go out much in society ? "

" Arthur does. Mary and I stay at home. We neither of us care for it."

" That is unusual in a young girl."

" She is of a quiet nature. Besides, she is not so very young. She is four-and-twenty."

" This matter, from what you say, seems to have been a shock to her also."

" Terrible ! She is even more affected than I."

" You have neither of you any doubt as to your son's guilt ? "

" How can we have, when I saw him with my own eyes with the coronet in his hands ? "

" I hardly consider that a conclusive proof. Was the remainder of the coronet at all injured ? "

" Yes, it was twisted."

" Do you not think, then, that he might have been trying to straighten it ? "

" God bless you ! You are doing what you can for him and for me. But it is too heavy a task. What was he doing there at all ? If his purpose were innocent, why did he not say so ? "

" Precisely. And if he were guilty, why did he not invent a lie ? His silence appears to me to cut both ways. There are several singular points about the case. What did the police think of the noise which awoke you from your sleep ? "

" They considered that it might be caused by Arthur's closing his bedroom door."

" A likely story ! As if a man bent on felony would slam the door so as to awake a household. What did they say, then, of the disappearance of these gems ? "

" They are still sounding the planking and probing the furniture in the hope of finding them."

" Have they thought of looking outside the house ? "

" Yes, they have shown extraordinary energy. The whole garden has already been minutely examined."

" Now, my dear sir," said Holmes, " is it not obvious to you now that this matter really strikes very much deeper than either you or the police were at first inclined to think ? It appeared to you to be a simple case ; to me it seems exceedingly complex. Consider what is involved by your theory. You suppose that your son came down from his bed, went, at great risk, to your dressing-room, opened your bureau, took out your coronet, broke off by main force a small portion of it, went off to some other place, concealed three gems out of the thirty-nine, with such skill that nobody can find them, and then returned with the other thirty-six into the room in which he exposed himself to the greatest danger of being discovered. I ask you now, is such a theory tenable ? "

" But what other is there ? " cried the banker with a gesture of despair. " If his motives were innocent, why does he not explain them ? "

" It is our task to find that out," replied Holmes, " so now, if you please, Mr. Holder, we will set off for Streatham together and devote an hour to glancing a little more closely into details."

My friend insisted upon my accompanying them in their expedition, which I was eager enough to do, for my curiosity and sympathy were deeply stirred by the story to which we had listened. I confess that the guilt of the banker's son appeared to me to be as obvious as it did to his unhappy father, but still I had such faith in Holmes' judgment that I felt that there must be some grounds for hope as long as he was dissatisfied with the accepted explanation. He hardly spoke a word the whole way out to the southern suburb, but sat with his chin upon his breast, and his hat drawn over his eyes, sunk in the deepest thought. Our client appeared to have taken fresh heart at the little glimpse of hope which had been presented to him, and he even broke into a desultory chat with me over his business affairs. A short railway journey, and a shorter walk, brought us to Fairbank, the modest residence of the great financier.

Fairbank was a good-sized square house of white stone, standing back a little from the road. A double carriage sweep, with a snow-clad lawn, stretched down in front to the two large iron gates which closed the entrance. On the right side was a small wooden thicket which led into a narrow path between two neat hedges stretching from the road to the kitchen door, and forming the tradesmen's entrance. On the left ran a lane which led to the stables, and was not itself within the grounds at all, being a public, though little used, thoroughfare. Holmes left us standing at the door, and walked slowly all round the house, across the front, down the tradesmen's path, and so round by the garden behind into the stable lane. So long was he that Mr. Holder and I went into the dining-room, and waited by the fire until he should return. We were sitting there in silence when the door opened, and a young lady came in. She was rather above the middle height, slim, with dark hair and eyes, which seemed the darker against the absolute pallor of her skin. I do not think that I have ever seen such deadly paleness in a woman's face. Her lips, too, were bloodless, but her eyes were flushed with crying. As she swept silently into the room she impressed me with a greater sense of her grief than the banker had done in the morning, and it was the more striking in her as she was evidently a woman of strong character, with immense capacity for self-restraint. Disregarding my presence, she went straight to her uncle, and passed her hand over his head with a sweet womanly caress.

"You have given orders that Arthur should be liberated, have you not, dad?" she asked.

"No, no, my girl, the matter must be probed to the bottom."

"But I am so sure that he is innocent. You know what women's instincts are. I know that he has done no harm, and that you will be sorry for having acted so harshly."

"Why is he silent, then, if he is innocent?"

"Who knows? Perhaps because he was so angry that you should suspect him."

"How could I help suspecting him, when I actually saw him with the coronet in his hand?"

"Oh, but he had only picked it up to look at it. Oh, do, do take my word for it that he is innocent. Let the matter drop, and say no more. It is so dreadful to think of our dear Arthur in prison!"

"I shall never let it drop until the gems are found—never, Mary! Your affection for Arthur blinds you as to the awful consequences to me. Far from hushing the thing up, I have brought a gentleman down from London to inquire more deeply into it."

"This gentleman?" she asked, facing round to me.

"No, his friend. He wished us to leave him alone. He is round in the stable lane now."

"The stable lane?" She raised her dark eyebrows. "What can he hope to find there? Ah, this, I suppose, is he. I trust, sir, that you will succeed in proving, what

I feel sure is the truth, that my cousin Arthur is innocent of this crime."

" I fully share your opinion, and, I trust with you, that we may prove it," returned Holmes, going back to the mat to knock the snow from his shoes. " I believe I have the honour of addressing Miss Mary Holder. Might I ask you a question or two ? "

" Pray do, sir, if it may help to clear this horrible affair up."

" You heard nothing yourself last night ? "

" Nothing, until my uncle here began to speak loudly. I heard that, and I came down."

" You shut up the windows and doors the night before. Did you fasten all the windows ? "

" Yes."

" Were they all fastened this morning ? "

" Yes."

" You have a maid who has a sweetheart ? I think that you remarked to your uncle last night that she had been out to see him ? "

" Yes, and she was the girl who waited in the drawing-room, and who may have heard uncle's remarks about the coronet."

" I see. You infer that she may have gone out to tell her sweetheart, and that the two may have planned the robbery."

" But what is the good of all these vague theories," cried the banker impatiently, " when I have told you that I saw Arthur with the coronet in his hands ? "

" Wait a little, Mr. Holder. We must come back to that. About this girl, Miss Holder. You saw her return by the kitchen door, I presume ? "

" Yes ; when I went to see if the door was fastened for the night I met her slipping in. I saw the man, too, in the gloom."

" Do you know him ? "

" Oh, yes ; he is the greengrocer who brings our vegetables round. His name is Francis Prosper."

263

"He stood," said Holmes, "to the left of the door—that is to say, farther up the path than is necessary to reach the door?"

"Yes, he did."

"And he is a man with a wooden leg?"

Something like fear sprang up in the young lady's expressive black eyes. "Why, you are like a magician," said she. "How do you know that?" She smiled, but there was no answering smile in Holmes' thin, eager face.

"I should be very glad now to go upstairs," said he. "I shall probably wish to go over the outside of the house again. Perhaps I had better take a look at the lower windows before I go up."

He walked swiftly round from one to the other, pausing only at the large one which looked from the hall on to the stable lane. This he opened, and made a very careful examination of the sill with his powerful magnifying lens. "Now we shall go upstairs," said he, at last.

The banker's dressing-room was a plainly furnished little chamber with a grey carpet, a large bureau, and a long mirror. Holmes went to the bureau first, and looked hard at the lock.

"Which key was used to open it?" he asked.

"That which my son himself indicated—that of the cupboard of the lumber-room."

"Have you it here?"

"That is it on the dressing-table."

Sherlock Holmes took it up and opened the bureau.

"It is a noiseless lock," said he. "It is no wonder that it did not wake you. This case, I presume, contains the coronet. We must have a look at it." He opened the case, and, taking out the diadem, he laid it upon the table. It was a magnificent specimen of the jeweller's art, and the thirty-six stones were the finest that I have ever seen. At one side of the coronet was a crooked cracked edge, where a corner holding three gems had been torn away.

"Now, Mr. Holder," said Holmes; "here is the corner

which corresponds to that which has been so unfortunately lost. Might I beg that you will break it off."

The banker recoiled in horror. " I should not dream of trying," said he.

" Then I will." Holmes suddenly bent his strength upon it, but without result. " I feel it give a little," said he ; " but, though I am exceptionally strong in the fingers, it would take me all my time to break it. An ordinary man could not do it. Now, what do you think would happen if I did break it, Mr. Holder ? There would be a noise like a pistol shot. Do you tell me that all this happened within a few yards of your bed, and that you heard nothing of it ? "

" I do not know what to think. It is all dark to me."

" But perhaps it may grow lighter as we go. What do you think, Miss Holder ? "

" I confess that I still share my uncle's perplexity."

" Your son had no shoes or slippers on when you saw him ? "

" He had nothing on save only his trousers and shirt."

" Thank you. We have certainly been favoured with extraordinary luck during this inquiry, and it will be entirely our own fault if we do not succeed in clearing the matter up. With your permission, Mr. Holder, I shall now continue my investigations outside."

He went alone, at his own request, for he explained that any unnecessary footmarks might make his task more difficult. For an hour or more he was at work, returning at last with his feet heavy with snow and his features as inscrutable as ever.

" I think that I have seen now all that there is to see, Mr. Holder," said he ; " I can serve you best by returning to my rooms."

" But the gems, Mr. Holmes. Where are they ? "

" I cannot tell."

The banker wrung his hands. " I shall never see them again ! " he cried. " And my son ? You give me hopes ? "

" My opinion is in no way altered."

" Then for God's sake what was this dark business which was acted in my house last night ? "

" If you can call upon me at my Baker Street rooms to-morrow morning between nine and ten I shall be happy to do what I can to make it clearer. I understand that you give me *carte blanche* to act for you, provided only that I get back the gems, and that you place no limit on the sum I may draw."

" I would give my fortune to have them back."

" Very good. I shall look into the matter between this and then. Good-bye ; it is just possible that I may have to come over here again before evening."

It was obvious to me that my companion's mind was now made up about the case, although what his conclusions were was more than I could even dimly imagine. Several times during our homeward journey I endeavoured to sound him upon that point, but he always glided away to some other topic, until at last I gave it over in despair. It was not yet three when we found ourselves in our room once more. He hurried to his chamber, and was down again in a few minutes dressed as a common loafer. With his collar turned up, his shiny seedy coat, his red cravat, and his worn boots, he was a perfect sample of the class.

" I think that this should do," said he, glancing into the glass above the fireplace. " I only wish that you could come with me, Watson, but I fear that it won't do. I may be on the trail in this matter, or I may be following a will-o'-the-wisp, but I shall soon know which it is. I hope that I may be back in a few hours." He cut a slice of beef from the joint upon the sideboard, sandwiched it between two rounds of bread, and, thrusting this rude meal into his pocket, he started off upon his expedition.

I had just finished my tea when he returned, evidently in excellent spirits, swinging an old elastic-sided boot in his hand. He chucked it down into a corner and helped himself to a cup of tea.

" I only looked in as I passed," said he. " I am going right on."

" Where to ? "

" Oh, to the other side of the West End. It may be some time before I get back. Don't wait up for me in case I should be late."

" How are you getting on ? "

" Oh, so-so. Nothing to complain of. I have been out to Streatham since I saw you last, but I did not call at the house. It is a very sweet little problem, and I would not have missed it for a good deal. However, I must not sit gossiping here, but must get these disreputable clothes off and return to my highly respectable self."

I could see by his manner that he had stronger reasons for satisfaction than his words alone would imply. His eyes twinkled, and there was even a touch of colour upon his sallow cheeks. He hastened upstairs, and a few minutes later I heard the slam of the hall door, which told me that he was off once more upon his congenial hunt.

I waited until midnight, but there was no sign of his return, so I retired to my room. It was no uncommon thing for him to be away for days and nights on end when he was hot upon a scent, so that his lateness caused me no surprise. I do not know at what hour he came in, but when I came down to breakfast in the morning, there he was with a cup of coffee in one hand and the paper in the other, as fresh and trim as possible.

" You will excuse my beginning without you, Watson," said he ; " but you remember that our client has rather an early appointment this morning."

" Why, it is after nine now," I answered. " I should not be surprised if that were he. I thought I heard a ring."

It was, indeed, our friend the financier. I was shocked by the change which had come over him, for his face, which was naturally of a broad and massive mould, was now pinched and fallen in, while his hair seemed to be at least a shade whiter. He entered with a weariness and lethargy which was even more painful than his violence of the morning before, and he dropped heavily into the armchair which I pushed forward for him.

"I do not know what I have done to be so severely tried," said he. "Only two days ago I was a happy and prosperous man, without a care in the world. Now I am left to a lonely and dishonoured age. One sorrow comes close upon the heels of another. My niece Mary has deserted me."

"Deserted you?"

"Yes. Her bed this morning had not been slept in, her room was empty, and a note lay for me upon the hall table. I had said to her last night, in sorrow and not in anger, that if she had married my boy all might have been well with him. Perhaps it was thoughtless of me to say so. It is to that remark that she refers in this note: 'MY DEAREST UNCLE—I feel that I have brought this trouble upon you, and that if I had acted differently this terrible misfortune might never have occurred. I cannot, with this thought in my mind, ever again be happy under your roof, and I feel that I must leave you for ever. Do not worry about my future, for that is provided for; and, above all, do not search for me, for it will be fruitless labour, and an ill service to me. In life or in death, I am ever your loving— MARY.' What could she mean by that note, Mr. Holmes? Do you think it points to suicide?"

"No, no, nothing of the kind. It is perhaps the best possible solution. I trust, Mr. Holder, that you are nearing the end of your troubles."

"Ha! You say so! You have heard something, Mr. Holmes; you have learned something! Where are the gems?"

"You would not think a thousand pounds apiece an excessive sum for them?"

"I would pay ten."

"That would be unnecessary. Three thousand will cover the matter. And there is a little reward, I fancy. Have you your cheque-book? Here is a pen. Better make it out for four thousand pounds."

With a dazed face the banker made out the required cheque. Holmes walked over to his desk, took out a little

triangular piece of gold with three gems in it, and threw it
down upon the table.

With a shriek of joy our client clutched it up.

"You have it!" he gasped. "I am saved! I am
saved!"

The reaction of joy was as passionate as his grief had
been, and he hugged his recovered gems to his bosom.

"There is one other thing you owe, Mr. Holder," said
Sherlock Holmes, rather sternly.

"Owe!" He caught up a pen. "Name the sum,
and I will pay it."

"No, the debt is not to me. You owe a very humble
apology to that noble lad, your son, who has carried himself in this matter as I should be proud to see my own son
do, should I ever chance to have one."

"Then it was not Arthur who took them?"

"I told you yesterday, and I repeat to-day, that it was
not."

"You are sure of it! Then let us hurry to him at once,
to let him know that the truth is known."

"He knows it already. When I had cleared it all up I
had an interview with him, and finding that he would not
tell me the story, I told it to him, on which he had to confess that I was right, and to add the very few details which
were not yet quite clear to me. Your news of this morning, however, may open his lips."

"For Heaven's sake tell me, then, what is this extraordinary mystery!"

"I will do so, and I will show you the steps by which
I reached it. And let me say to you, first, what it is hardest
for me to say and for you to hear. There has been an
understanding between Sir George Burnwell and your
niece, Mary. They have now fled together."

"My Mary? Impossible!"

"It is, unfortunately, more than possible; it is certain.
Neither you nor your son knew the true character of this
man when you admitted him into your family circle. He
is one of the most dangerous men in England—a ruined

gambler, an absolutely desperate villain ; a man without heart or conscience. Your niece knew nothing of such men. When he breathed his vows to her, as he had done to a hundred before her, she flattered herself that she alone had touched his heart. The devil knows best what he said, but at last she became his tool, and was in the habit of seeing him nearly every evening."

" I cannot, and I will not, believe it ! " cried the banker with an ashen face.

" I will tell you, then, what occurred in your house that night. Your niece, when you had, as she thought, gone to your room, slipped down and talked to her lover through the window which leads into the stable lane. His foot-marks had pressed right through the snow, so long had he stood there. She told him of the coronet. His wicked lust for gold kindled at the news, and he bent her to his will. I have no doubt that she loved you, but there are women in whom the love of a lover extinguishes all other loves, and I think that she must have been one. She had hardly listened to his instructions when she saw you coming downstairs, on which she closed the window rapidly, and told you about one of the servants' escapade with her wooden-legged lover, which was all perfectly true.

" Your boy, Arthur, went to bed after his interview with you, but he slept badly on account of his uneasiness about his club debts. In the middle of the night he heard a soft tread pass his door, so he rose, and looking out, was surprised to see his cousin walking very stealthily along the passage, until she disappeared into your dressing-room. Petrified with astonishment the lad slipped on some clothes, and waited there in the dark to see what would come of this strange affair. Presently she emerged from the room again, and in the light of the passage lamp your son saw that she carried the precious coronet in her hands. She passed down the stairs, and he, thrilling with horror, ran along and slipped behind the curtain near your door, whence he could see what passed in the hall beneath. He saw her stealthily open the window, hand out the coronet to someone in the gloom, and then closing it once more hurry back to her room, passing quite close to where he stood hid behind the curtain.

" As long as she was on the scene he could not take any action without a horrible exposure of the woman whom he loved. But the instant she was gone he realized how crushing a misfortune this would be for you, and how all-important it was to set it right. He rushed down, just as he was, in his bare feet, opened the window, sprang out into the snow, and ran down the lane, where he could see a dark figure in the moonlight. Sir George Burnwell tried to get away, but Arthur caught him, and there was a struggle between them, your lad tugging at one side of the coronet, and his opponent at the other. In the scuffle, your son struck Sir George, and cut him over the eye. Then something suddenly snapped, and your son, finding that he had the coronet in his hands, rushed back, closed the window, ascended to your room, and had just observed that the coronet had been twisted in the struggle and was endeavouring to straighten it, when you appeared upon the scene."

" Is it possible ? " gasped the banker.

" You then roused his anger by calling him names at a moment when he felt that he had deserved your warmest thanks. He could not explain the true state of affairs without betraying one who certainly deserved little enough consideration at his hands. He took the more chivalrous view, however, and preserved her secret."

" And that was why she shrieked and fainted when she saw the coronet," cried Mr. Holder. " Oh, my God ! what a blind fool I have been. And his asking to be allowed to go out for five minutes ! The dear fellow wanted to see if the missing piece were at the scene of the struggle. How cruelly I have misjudged him ! "

" When I arrived at the house," continued Holmes, " I at once went very carefully round it to observe if there were any traces in the snow which might help me. I knew that none had fallen since the evening before, and also that there had been a strong frost to preserve impressions. I passed along the tradesmen's path, but found it all trampled down and indistinguishable. Just beyond it, however, at the far side of the kitchen door, a woman had stood and talked with a man, whose round impression on one side showed that he had a wooden leg. I could even tell that they had been disturbed, for the woman had run back swiftly to the door, as was shown by the deep toe and light heel-marks, while Wooden-leg had waited a little, and then had gone away. I thought at the time that this might be the maid and her sweetheart, of whom you had already spoken to me, and inquiry showed it was so. I passed round the garden without seeing anything more than random tracks, which I took to be the police ; but when I got into the stable lane a very long and complex story was written in the snow in front of me.

" There was a double line of tracks of a booted man, and a second double line which I saw with delight belonged to a man with naked feet. I was at once convinced from what you had told me that the latter was your son. The first had walked both ways, but the other had run swiftly, and, as his tread was marked in places over the depression of the boot, it was obvious that he had passed after the other. I followed them up, and found that they led to the hall window, where Boots had worn all the snow away while waiting. Then I walked to the other end, which was a hundred yards or more down the lane. I saw where Boots had faced round, where the snow was cut up, as though there had been a struggle, and, finally, where a few drops of blood had fallen, to show me that I was not mistaken. Boots had then run down the lane, and another little smudge of blood showed that it was he who had been hurt. When he came to the high-road at the other end, I found that the pavement had been cleared, so there was an end to that clue.

" On entering the house, however, I examined, as you remember, the sill and framework of the hall window with my lens, and I could at once see that someone had passed out. I could distinguish the outline of an instep where the wet foot had been placed in coming in. I was then beginning to be able to form an opinion as to what had occurred. A man had waited outside the window, some-one had brought him the gems ; the deed had been over-seen by your son, he had pursued the thief, had struggled with him, they had each tugged at the coronet, their united strength causing injuries which neither alone could have effected. He had returned with the prize, but had left a fragment in the grasp of his opponent. So far I was clear. The question now was, who was the man, and who was it brought him the coronet ?

" It is an old maxim of mine that when you have ex-cluded the impossible, whatever remains, however improb-able, must be the truth. Now, I knew that it was not you who had brought it down, so there only remained your niece and the maids. But if it were the maids, why should your son allow himself to be accused in their place ? There could be no possible reason. As he loved his cousin, however, there was an excellent explanation why he should retain her secret—the more so as the secret was a disgrace-ful one. When I remembered that you had seen her at that window, and how she had fainted on seeing the coro-net again, my conjecture became a certainty.

" And who could it be who was her confederate ? A lover evidently, for who else could outweigh the love and grati-tude which she must feel to you ? I knew that you went out little, and that your circle of friends was a very limited one. But among them was Sir George Burnwell. I had heard of him before as being a man of evil reputation among women. It must have been he who wore those boots, and retained the missing gems. Even though he knew that Arthur had discovered him, he might still flatter himself that he was safe, for the lad could not say a word without compromising his own family.

" Well, your own good sense will suggest what measures I took next. I went in the shape of a loafer to Sir George's house, managed to pick up an acquaintance with his valet, learned that his master had cut his head the night before, and finally, at the expense of six shillings, made all sure by buying a pair of his cast-off shoes. With these I journeyed down to Streatham, and saw that they exactly fitted the tracks."

" I saw an ill-dressed vagabond in the lane yesterday evening," said Mr. Holder.

" Precisely. It was I. I found that I had my man, so I came home and changed my clothes. It was a delicate part which I had to play then, for I saw that a prosecution must be avoided to avert scandal, and I knew that so astute a villain would see that our hands were tied in the matter. I went and saw him. At first, of course, he denied everything. But when I gave him every particular that had occurred, he tried to bluster, and took down a life-preserver from the wall. I knew my man, however, and I clapped a pistol to his head before he could strike. Then he became a little more reasonable. I told him that we would give him a price for the stones he held—a thousand pounds apiece. That brought out the first signs of grief he had shown. ' Why, dash it all ! ' said he, ' I've let them go at six hundred for the three ! ' I soon managed to get the address of the receiver who had them, on promising him that there would be no prosecution. Off I set to him, and after much chaffering I got our stones at a thousand apiece. Then I looked in upon your son, told him that all was right, and eventually got to my bed about two o'clock, after what I may call a really hard day's work."

" A day which has saved England from a great public scandal," said the banker, rising. " Sir, I cannot find words to thank you, but you shall not find me ungrateful for what you have done. Your skill has indeed exceeded all that I have ever heard of it. And now I must fly to my dear boy to apologize to him for the wrong which I have done him. As to what you tell me of poor Mary, it goes to my heart. Not even your skill can inform me where she is now."

" I think that we may safely say," returned Holmes,

" that she is wherever Sir George Burnwell is. It is equally certain, too, that whatever her sins are, they will soon receive a more than sufficient punishment."

12. *The Copper Beeches*

" TO the man who loves art for its own sake," remarked Sherlock Holmes, tossing aside the advertisement sheet of the *Daily Telegraph*, " it is frequently in its least important and lowliest manifestations that the keenest pleasure is to be derived. It is pleasant to me to observe, Watson, that you have so far grasped this truth that in these little records of our cases which you have been good enough to draw up, and, I am bound to say, occasionally to embellish, you have given prominence not so much to the many *causes célèbres* and sensational trials in which I have figured, but rather to those incidents which may have been trivial in themselves, but which have given room for those faculties of deduction and of logical synthesis which I have made my special province."

" And yet," said I, smiling, " I cannot quite hold myself absolved from the charge of sensationalism which has been urged against my records."

" You have erred, perhaps," he observed, taking up a glowing cinder with the tongs, and lighting with it the long cherrywood pipe which was wont to replace his clay when he was in a disputatious rather than a meditative mood— " you have erred, perhaps, in attempting to put colour and life into each of your statements, instead of confining yourself to the task of placing upon record that severe reasoning from cause to effect which is really the only notable feature about the thing."

" It seems to me that I have done you full justice in the matter," I remarked with some coldness, for I was repelled by the egotism which I had more than once observed to be a strong factor in my friend's singular character.

" No, it is not selfishness or conceit," said he, answer-

ing, as was his wont, my thoughts rather than my words.
" If I claim full justice for my art, it is because it is an
impersonal thing—a thing beyond myself. Crime is common. Logic is rare. Therefore it is upon the logic rather
than upon the crime that you should dwell. You have
degraded what should have been a course of lectures into a
series of tales."

It was a cold morning of the early spring, and we sat
after breakfast on either side of a cheery fire in the old
room in Baker Street. A thick fog rolled down between
the lines of dun-coloured houses, and the opposing windows loomed like dark, shapeless blurs, through the heavy
yellow wreaths. Our gas was lit, and shone on the white
cloth, and glimmer of china and metal, for the table had
not been cleared yet. Sherlock Holmes had been silent
all the morning, dipping continuously into the advertisement columns of a succession of papers, until at last, having apparently given up his search, he had emerged in no
very sweet temper to lecture me upon my literary short-
comings.

" At the same time," he remarked, after a pause, during
which he had sat puffing at his long pipe and gazing down
into the fire, " you can hardly be open to a charge of
sensationalism, for out of these cases which you have been
so kind as to interest yourself in, a fair proportion do not
treat of crime, in its legal sense, at all. The small matter
in which I endeavoured to help the King of Bohemia, the
singular experience of Miss Mary Sutherland, the problem
connected with the man with the twisted lip, and the incident of the noble bachelor, were all matters which are outside the pale of the law. But in avoiding the sensational, I
fear that you may have bordered on the trivial."

" The end may have been so," I answered, " but the
methods I hold to have been novel and of interest."

" Pshaw, my dear fellow, what do the public, the great
unobservant public, who could hardly tell a weaver by his
tooth or a compositor by his left thumb, care about the
finer shades of analysis and deduction ! But, indeed, if

you are trivial, I cannot blame you, for the days of the great cases are past. Man, or at least criminal man, has lost all enterprise and originality. As to my own little practice, it seems to be degenerating into an agency for recovering lost lead pencils and giving advice to young ladies from boarding-schools. I think that I have touched bottom at last, however. This note I had this morning marks my zero point, I fancy. Read it ! " He tossed a crumpled letter across to me.

It was dated from Montague Place upon the preceding evening, and ran thus :

" DEAR MR. HOLMES,—I am very anxious to consult you as to whether I should or should not accept a situation which has been offered to me as governess. I shall call at half-past ten to-morrow, if I do not inconvenience you.—Yours faithfully,

" VIOLET HUNTER."

" Do you know the young lady ? " I asked.

" Not I."

" It is half-past ten now."

" Yes, and I have no doubt that is her ring."

" It may turn out to be of more interest than you think. You remember that the affair of the blue carbuncle, which appeared to be a mere whim at first, developed into a serious investigation. It may be so in this case also."

" Well, let us hope so ! But our doubts will very soon be solved, for here, unless I am much mistaken, is the person in question."

As he spoke the door opened, and a young lady entered the room. She was plainly but neatly dressed, with a bright, quick face, freckled like a plover's egg, and with the brisk manner of a woman who has had her own way to make in the world.

" You will excuse my troubling you, I am sure," said she, as my companion rose to greet her ; " but I have had a very strange experience, and as I have no parents or relations of any sort from whom I could ask advice, I thought

277

that perhaps you would be kind enough to tell me what I should do."

" Pray take a seat, Miss Hunter. I shall be happy to do anything that I can to serve you."

I could see that Holmes was favourably impressed by the manner and speech of his new client. He looked her over in his searching fashion, and then composed himself with his lids drooping and his finger-tips together to listen to her story.

" I have been a governess for five years," said she, " in the family of Colonel Spence Munro, but two months ago the Colonel received an appointment at Halifax, in Nova Scotia, and took his children over to America with him, so that I found myself without a situation. I advertised and I answered advertisements, but without success. At last the little money which I had saved began to run short, and I was at my wits' end as to what I should do.

" There is a well-known agency for governesses in the West End called Westaway's, and there I used to call about once a week in order to see whether anything had turned up which might suit me. Westaway was the name of the founder of the business, but it is really managed by Miss Stoper. She sits in her own little office, and the ladies who are seeking employment wait in an ante-room, and are then shown in one by one, when she consults her ledgers, and sees whether she has anything which would suit them.

" Well, when I called last week I was shown into the little office as usual, but I found that Miss Stoper was not alone. A prodigiously stout man with a very smiling face, and a great heavy chin which rolled down in fold upon fold over his throat, sat at her elbow with a pair of glasses on his nose, looking very earnestly at the ladies who entered. As I came in he gave quite a jump in his chair, and turned quickly to Miss Stoper :

" ' That will do,' said he ; ' I could not ask for anything better. Capital ! Capital ! ' He seemed quite enthusiastic and rubbed his hands together in the most genial fashion. He was such a comfortable-looking man that it was quite a pleasure to look at him.

" ' You are looking for a situation, miss ? ' he asked.

" ' Yes, sir.'

" ' As governess ? '

" ' Yes, sir.'

" ' And what salary do you ask ? '

" ' I had four pounds a month in my last place with Colonel Spence Munro.'

" ' Oh, tut, tut ! sweating—rank sweating ! ' he cried, throwing his fat hands out into the air like a man who is in a boiling passion. ' How could anyone offer so pitiful a sum to a lady with such attractions and accomplishments ? '

" ' My accomplishments, sir, may be less than you imagine,' said I. ' A little French, a little German, music and drawing——'

" ' Tut, tut ! ' he cried. ' This is all quite beside the question. The point is, have you or have you not the bearing and deportment of a lady ? There it is in a nut-shell. If you have not, you are not fitted for the rearing of a child who may some day play a considerable part in the history of the country. But if you have, why, then how could any gentleman ask you to condescend to accept anything under the three figures ? Your salary with me, madam, would commence at a hundred pounds a year.'

" You may imagine, Mr. Holmes, that to me, destitute as I was, such an offer seemed almost too good to be true. The gentleman, however, seeing perhaps the look of incredulity upon my face, opened a pocket-book and took out a note.

" ' It is also my custom,' said he, smiling in the most pleasant fashion until his eyes were just two shining slits, amid the white creases of his face, ' to advance to my young ladies half their salary beforehand, so that they may meet any little expenses of their journey and their ward-robe.'

" It seemed to me that I had never met so fascinating and so thoughtful a man. As I was already in debt to my tradesmen, the advance was a great convenience, and yet there was something unnatural about the whole transaction which made me wish to know a little more before I quite committed myself.

" ' May I ask where you live, sir ? ' said I.

" ' Hampshire. Charming rural place. The Copper Beeches, five miles on the far side of Winchester. It is the most lovely country, my dear young lady, and the dearest old country house.'

" ' And my duties, sir ? I should be glad to know what they would be.'

" ' One child—one dear little romper just six years old. Oh, if you could see him killing cockroaches with a slipper ! Smack ! smack ! smack ! Three gone before you could wink ! ' He leaned back in his chair and laughed his eyes into his head again.

" I was a little startled at the nature of the child's amusement, but the father's laughter made me think that perhaps he was joking.

" ' My sole duties, then,' I asked, ' are to take charge of a single child ? '

" ' No, no, not the sole, not the sole, my dear young lady,' he cried. ' Your duty would be, as I am sure your good sense would suggest, to obey any little commands which my wife might give, provided always that they were such commands as a lady might with propriety obey. You see no difficulty, heh ? '

" ' I should be happy to make myself useful.'

" ' Quite so. In dress now, for example ! We are faddy people, you know—faddy, but kind-hearted. If you were asked to wear any dress which we might give you, you would not object to our little whim. Heh ? '

" ' No,' said I, considerably astonished at his words.

" ' Or to sit here, or sit there, that would not be offensive, to you ? '

" ' Oh, no.'

" ' Or to cut your hair quite short before you come to us ? '

" I could hardly believe my ears. As you may observe, Mr. Holmes, my hair is somewhat luxuriant, and of a rather peculiar tint of chestnut. It has been considered artistic. I could not dream of sacrificing it in this off-hand fashion.

" ' I am afraid that that is quite impossible,' said I. He had been watching me eagerly out of his small eyes, and I could see a shadow pass over his face as I spoke.

" ' I am afraid that it is quite essential,' said he. ' It is a little fancy of my wife's, and ladies' fancies, you know, madam, ladies' fancies must be consulted. And so you won't cut your hair ? '

" ' No, sir, I really could not,' I answered firmly.

" ' Ah, very well ; then that quite settles the matter. It is a pity, because in other respects you would really have done very nicely. In that case, Miss Stoper, I had best inspect a few more of your young ladies.'

" The manageress had sat all this while busy with her papers without a word to either of us, but she glanced at me now with so much annoyance upon her face that I could not help suspecting that she had lost a handsome commission through my refusal.

" ' Do you desire your name to be kept upon the books ? ' she asked.

" ' If you please, Miss Stoper.'

" ' Well, really, it seems rather useless, since you refuse the most excellent offers in this fashion,' said she sharply. ' You can hardly expect us to exert ourselves to find another such opening for you. Good day to you, Miss Hunter.' She struck a gong upon the table, and I was shown out by the page.

" Well, Mr. Holmes, when I got back to my lodgings and found little enough in the cupboard, and two or three bills upon the table, I began to ask myself whether I had not done a very foolish thing. After all, if these people had strange fads, and expected obedience on the most extraordinary matters, they were at least ready to pay for their eccentricity. Very few governesses in England are getting a hundred a year. Besides, what use was my hair to me ? Many people are improved by wearing it short, and perhaps I should be among the number. Next day I was inclined to think that I had made a mistake, and by the day after I was sure of it. I had almost overcome my pride, so far as to go back to the agency and inquire whether the place was still open, when I received this letter from the gentleman himself. I have it here, and I will read it to you :

" THE COPPER BEECHES, NEAR WINCHESTER.

" DEAR MISS HUNTER,—Miss Stoper has very kindly given me your address, and I write from here to ask you whether you have reconsidered your decision. My wife is very anxious that you should come, for she has been much attracted by my description of you. We are willing to give thirty pounds a quarter, or £120 a year, so as to recompense you for any little inconvenience which our fads may cause you. They are not very exacting after all. My wife is fond of a particular shade of electric blue, and would like you to wear such a dress indoors in the morning. You need not, however, go to the expense of purchasing one, as we have one belonging to my dear daughter Alice (now in Philadelphia) which would, I should think, fit you very well. Then, as to sitting here or there, or amusing yourself in any manner indicated, that need cause you no inconvenience. As regards your hair, it is no doubt a pity, especially as I could not help remarking its beauty during our short interview, but I am afraid that I must remain firm upon this point, and I only hope that the increased salary may recompense you for the loss. Your duties, as far as the child is concerned, are very light. Now do try to come, and I shall meet you with the dogcart at Winchester. Let me know your train.—Yours faithfully,

" JEPHRO RUCASTLE.

" That is the letter which I have just received, Mr.
282

Holmes, and my mind is made up that I will accept it. I thought, however, that before taking the final step, I should like to submit the whole matter to your consideration."

"Well, Miss Hunter, if your mind is made up, that settles the question," said Holmes, smiling.

"But you would not advise me to refuse?"

"I confess that it is not the situation which I should like to see a sister of mine apply for."

"What is the meaning of it all, Mr. Holmes?"

"Ah, I have no data. I cannot tell. Perhaps you have yourself formed some opinion?"

"Well, there seems to me to be only one possible solution. Mr. Rucastle seemed to be a very kind, good-natured man. Is it not possible that his wife is a lunatic, that he desires to keep the matter quiet for fear she should be taken to an asylum, and that he humours her fancies in every way in order to prevent an outbreak."

"That is a possible solution—in fact, as matters stand, it is the most probable one. But in any case it does not seem to be a nice household for a young lady."

"But the money, Mr. Holmes, the money!"

"Well, yes, of course, the pay is good—too good. That is what makes me uneasy. Why should they give you £120 a year, when they could have their pick for £40? There must be some strong reason behind."

"I thought that if I told you the circumstances you would understand afterwards if I wanted your help. I should feel so much stronger if I felt that you were at the back of me."

"Oh, you may carry that feeling away with you. I assure you that your little problem promises to be the most interesting which has come my way for some months. There is something distinctly novel about some of the features. If you should find yourself in doubt or in danger——"

"Danger! What danger do you foresee?"

Holmes shook his head gravely. "It would cease to be

a danger if we could define it," said he. " But at any time, day or night, a telegram would bring me down to your help."

" That is enough." She rose briskly from her chair with the anxiety all swept from her face. " I shall go down to Hampshire quite easy in my mind now. I shall write to Mr. Rucastle at once, sacrifice my poor hair to-night, and start for Winchester to-morrow." With a few grateful words to Holmes she bade us both good night, and bustled off upon her way.

" At least," said I, as we heard her quick, firm step descending the stairs, " she seems to be a young lady who is very well able to take care of herself."

" And she would need to be," said Holmes gravely ; " I am much mistaken if we do not hear from her before many days are past."

It was not very long before my friend's prediction was fulfilled. A fortnight went by, during which I frequently found my thoughts turning in her direction, and wondering what strange side-alley of human experience this lonely woman had strayed into. The unusual salary, the curious conditions, the light duties, all pointed to something abnormal, though whether a fad or a plot, or whether the man were a philanthropist or a villain, it was quite beyond my powers to determine. As to Holmes, I observed that he sat frequently for half an hour on end, with knitted brows and an abstracted air, but he swept the matter away with a wave of his hand when I mentioned it. " Data ! data ! data ! " he cried impatiently. " I can't make bricks without clay." And yet he would always wind up by muttering that no sister of his should ever have accepted such a situation.

The telegram which we eventually received came late one night, just as I was thinking of turning in, and Holmes was settling down to one of those all-night researches which he frequently indulged in, when I would leave him stooping over a retort and a test-tube at night, and find him in the same position when I came down to breakfast in the morning. He opened the yellow envelope, and then, glancing at the message, threw it across to me.

"Just look up the trains in Bradshaw," said he, and turned back to his chemical studies.

The summons was a brief and urgent one.

"Please be at the Black Swan Hotel at Winchester at midday to-morrow," it said. "Do come! I am at my wits' end.

"HUNTER."

"Will you come with me?" asked Holmes, glancing up.

"I should wish to."

"Just look it up, then."

"There is a train at half-past nine," said I, glancing over my Bradshaw. "It is due at Winchester at 11.30."

"That will do very nicely. Then perhaps I had better postpone my analysis of the acetones, as we may need to be at our best in the morning."

By eleven o'clock the next day we were well upon our way to the old English capital. Holmes had been buried in the morning papers all the way down, but after we had passed the Hampshire border he threw them down, and began to admire the scenery. It was an ideal spring day, a light blue sky, flecked with little fleecy white clouds drifting across from west to east. The sun was shining very brightly, and yet there was an exhilarating nip in the air, which set an edge to a man's energy. All over the country-side, away to the rolling hills around Aldershot, the little red and grey roofs of the farm-steadings peeped out from amidst the light green of the new foliage.

"Are they not fresh and beautiful?" I cried, with all the enthusiasm of a man fresh from the fogs of Baker Street.

But Holmes shook his head gravely.

"Do you know, Watson," said he, "that it is one of the

curses of a mind with a turn like mine that I must look at
everything with reference to my own special subject. You
look at these scattered houses, and you are impressed by
their beauty. I look at them, and the only thought which
comes to me is a feeling of their isolation, and of the
impunity with which crime may be committed there."

" Good heavens ! " I cried. " Who would associate
crime with these dear old homesteads ? "

" They always fill me with a certain horror. It is my
belief, Watson, founded upon my experience, that the
lowest and vilest alleys in London do not present a more
dreadful record of sin than does the smiling and beautiful
country-side."

" You horrify me ! "

" But the reason is very obvious. The pressure of
public opinion can do in the town what the law cannot
accomplish. There is no lane so vile that the scream of a
tortured child, or the thud of a drunkard's blow, does not
beget sympathy and indignation among the neighbours,
and then the whole machinery of justice is ever so close
that a word of complaint can set it going, and there is but a
step between the crime and the dock. But look at these
lonely houses, each in its own fields, filled for the most part
with poor ignorant folk who know little of the law. Think
of the deeds of hellish cruelty, the hidden wickedness
which may go on, year in, year out, in such places, and
none the wiser. Had this lady who appeals to us for help
gone to live in Winchester, I should never have had a fear
for her. It is the five miles of country which makes
the danger. Still, it is clear that she is not personally
threatened."

" No. If she can come to Winchester to meet us she
can get away."

" Quite so. She has her freedom."

" What *can* be the matter, then ? Can you suggest no
explanation ? "

" I have devised seven separate explanations, each of
which would cover the facts as far as we know them. But

which of these is correct can only be determined by the fresh information which we shall no doubt find waiting for us. Well, there is the tower of the Cathedral, and we shall soon learn all that Miss Hunter has to tell."

The " Black Swan " is an inn of repute in the High Street, at no distance from the station, and there we found the young lady waiting for us. She had engaged a sitting-room, and our lunch awaited us upon the table.

" I am so delighted that you have come," she said earnestly, " it is so kind of you both ; but indeed I do not know what I should do. Your advice will be altogether invaluable to me."

" Pray tell us what has happened to you."

" I will do so, and I must be quick, for I have promised Mr. Rucastle to be back before three. I got his leave to come into town this morning, though he little knew for what purpose."

" Let us have everything in its due order." Holmes thrust his long thin legs out towards the fire, and composed himself to listen.

" In the first place, I may say that I have met, on the whole, with no actual ill-treatment from Mr. and Mrs. Rucastle. It is only fair to them to say that. But I cannot understand them, and I am not easy in my mind about them."

" What can you not understand ? "

" Their reasons for their conduct. But you shall have it all just as it occurred. When I came down Mr. Rucastle met me here, and drove me in his dog-cart to Copper Beeches. It is, as he said, beautifully situated, but it is not beautiful in itself, for it is a large square block of a house, whitewashed, but all stained and streaked with damp and bad weather. There are grounds round it, woods on three sides, and on the fourth a field which slopes down to the Southampton high-road, which curves past about a hundred yards from the front door. This ground in front belongs to the house, but the woods all round are part of Lord Southerton's preserves. A clump of copper beeches immediately in front of the hall door has given its name to the place.

" I was driven over by my employer, who was as amiable as ever, and was introduced by him that evening to his wife and the child. There was no truth, Mr. Holmes, in the conjecture which seemed to us to be probable in your rooms at Baker Street. Mrs. Rucastle is not mad. I found her to be a silent, pale-faced woman, much younger than her husband, not more than thirty, I should think, while he can hardly be less than forty-five. From their conversation I have gathered that they have been married about seven years, that he was a widower, and that his only child by the first wife was the daughter who has gone to Philadelphia. Mr. Rucastle told me in private that the reason why she had left them was that she had an unreasoning aversion to her stepmother. As the daughter could not have been less than twenty, I can quite imagine that her position must have been uncomfortable with her father's young wife.

" Mrs. Rucastle seemed to me to be colourless in mind as well as in feature. She impressed me neither favourably nor the reverse. She was a nonentity. It was easy to see that she was passionately devoted both to her husband and to her little son. Her light grey eyes wandered continually from one to the other, noting every little want and forestalling it if possible. He was kind to her also in his bluff boisterous fashion, and on the whole they seemed to be a happy couple. And yet she had some secret sorrow, this woman. She would often be lost in deep thought, with the saddest look upon her face. More than once I have surprised her in tears. I have thought sometimes that it was the disposition of her child which weighed upon her mind, for I have never met so utterly spoilt and so ill-natured a little creature. He is small for his age, with a head which is quite disproportionately large. His whole life appears to be spent in an alternation between savage fits of passion and gloomy intervals of sulking. Giving pain to any creature weaker than himself seems to be his one idea of amusement, and he shows quite remarkable talent in planning the capture of mice, little birds, and insects. But I would rather not talk about the creature, Mr. Holmes, and, indeed, he has little to do with my story."

" I am glad of all details," remarked my friend, " whether they seem to you to be relevant or not."

" I shall try not to miss anything of importance. The one unpleasant thing about the house, which struck me at once, was the appearance and conduct of the servants. There are only two, a man and his wife. Toller, for that's his name, is a rough, uncouth man, with grizzled hair and whiskers, and a perpetual smell of drink. Twice since I have been with them he has been quite drunk, and yet Mr. Rucastle seemed to take no notice of it. His wife is a very tall and strong woman with a sour face, as silent as Mrs. Rucastle, and much less amiable. They are a most unpleasant couple, but fortunately I spend most of my time in the nursery and my own room, which are next to each other in one corner of the building.

" For two days after my arrival at the Copper Beeches my life was very quiet ; on the third, Mrs. Rucastle came down just after breakfast and whispered something to her husband.

" ' Oh yes,' said he, turning to me, ' we are very much obliged to you, Miss Hunter, for falling in with our whims so far as to cut your hair. I assure you that it has not detracted in the tiniest iota from your appearance. We shall now see how the electric blue dress will become you. You will find it laid out upon the bed in your room, and if you would be so good as to put it on we should both be extremely obliged.'

" The dress which I found waiting for me was of a peculiar shade of blue. It was of excellent material, a sort of beige, but it bore unmistakable signs of having been worn before. It could not have been a better fit if I had been measured for it. Both Mr. and Mrs. Rucastle expressed a delight at the look of it which seemed quite exaggerated in its vehemence. They were waiting for me in the drawing-room, which is a very large room, stretching along the entire front of the house, with three long windows reaching down to the floor. A chair had been placed close to the central window, with its back turned towards it. In this I was asked to sit, and then Mr. Rucastle, walking up and down on the other side of the room, began to tell me a series of the funniest stories that I have ever listened to. You cannot imagine how comical he was, and I laughed until I was quite weary. Mrs. Rucastle, however, who has evidently no sense of humour, never so much as smiled, but sat with her hands in her lap, and a sad, anxious look upon her face. After an hour or so, Mr. Rucastle suddenly remarked that it was time to commence the duties of the day, and that I might change my dress, and go to little Edward in the nursery.

" Two days later this same performance was gone through under exactly similar circumstances. Again I changed my dress, again I sat in the window, and again I laughed very heartily at the funny stories of which my employer had an immense repertoire, and which he told inimitably. Then he handed me a yellow-backed novel, and, moving my chair a little sideways, that my own shadow might not fall upon the page, he begged me to read aloud to him. I read for about ten minutes, beginning in the heart of a chapter, and then suddenly, in the middle of a sentence, he ordered me to cease and change my dress.

" You can easily imagine, Mr. Holmes, how curious I became as to what the meaning of this extraordinary performance could possibly be. They were always very careful, I observed, to turn my face away from the window, so that I became consumed with the desire to see what was going on behind my back. At first it seemed to be impossible, but I soon devised a means. My hand mirror had been broken, so a happy thought seized me, and I concealed a little of the glass in my handkerchief. On the next occasion, in the midst of my laughter, I put my handkerchief up to my eyes, and was able with a little management to see all that there was behind me. I confess that I was disappointed. There was nothing.

"At least, that was my first impression. At the second glance, however, I perceived that there was a man standing in the Southampton road, a small bearded man in a grey suit, who seemed to be looking in my direction. The road is an important highway, and there are usually people there. This man, however, was leaning against the railings which bordered our field, and was looking earnestly. I lowered my handkerchief, and glanced at Mrs. Rucastle to find her eyes fixed upon me with a most searching gaze. She said nothing, but I am convinced that she had divined that I had a mirror in my hand, and had seen what was behind me. She rose at once.

"'Jephro,' said she, 'there is an impertinent fellow upon the road there who stares up at Miss Hunter.'

"'No friend of yours, Miss Hunter?' he asked.

"'No; I know no one in these parts.'

"'Dear me! How very impertinent! Kindly turn round, and motion him to go away.'

"'Surely it would be better to take no notice?'

"'No, no, we should have him loitering here always. Kindly turn round, and wave him away like that.'

"I did as I was told, and at the same instant Mrs. Rucastle drew down the blind. That was a week ago, and from that time I have not sat again in the window, nor have I worn the blue dress, nor seen the man in the road."

"Pray continue," said Holmes. "Your narrative promises to be a most interesting one."

"You will find it rather disconnected, I fear, and there may prove to be little relation between the different incidents of which I speak. On the very first day that I was at Copper Beeches, Mr. Rucastle took me to a small outhouse which stands near the kitchen door. As we approached it I heard the sharp rattling of a chain, and the sound as of a large animal moving about.

"'Look in here!' said Mr. Rucastle, showing me a slit between two planks. 'Is he not a beauty?'

" I looked through, and was conscious of two glowing eyes, and of a vague figure huddled up in the darkness.

" ' Don't be frightened,' said my employer, laughing at the start which I had given. ' It's only Carlo, my mastiff. I call him mine, but really old Toller, my groom, is the only man who can do anything with him. We feed him once a day, and not too much then, so that he is always as keen as mustard. Toller lets him loose every night, and God help the trespasser whom he lays his fangs upon. For goodness' sake don't you ever on any pretext set your foot over the threshold at night, for it is as much as your life is worth.'

" The warning was no idle one, for two nights later I happened to look out of my bedroom window about two o'clock in the morning. It was a beautiful moonlight night, and the lawn in front of the house was silvered over and almost as bright as day. I was standing wrapt in the peaceful beauty of the scene, when I was aware that something was moving under the shadow of the copper beeches. As it emerged into the moonshine I saw what it was. It was a giant dog, as large as a calf, tawny-tinted, with hanging jowl, black muzzle, and huge projecting bones. It walked slowly across the lawn and vanished into the shadow upon the other side. That dreadful silent sentinel sent a chill to my heart, which I do not think that any burglar could have done.

" And now I have a very strange experience to tell you. I had, as you know, cut off my hair in London, and I had placed it in a great coil at the bottom of my trunk. One evening, after the child was in bed, I began to amuse myself by examining the furniture of my room, and by rearranging my own little things. There was an old chest of drawers in the room, the two upper ones empty and open, the lower one locked. I had filled the two first with my linen, and as I had still much to pack away, I was naturally annoyed at not having the use of the third drawer. It struck me that it might have been fastened by a mere oversight, so I took out my bunch of keys and tried to open it. The very first key fitted to perfection, and I drew the drawer open. There was only one thing in it, but I am sure that you would never guess what it was. It was my coil of hair.

"I took it up and examined it. It was of the same peculiar tint, and the same thickness. But then the impossibility of the thing obtruded itself upon me. How *could* my hair have been locked in the drawer? With trembling hands I undid my trunk, turned out the contents, and drew from the bottom my own hair. I laid the two tresses together, and I assure you they were identical. Was it not extraordinary? Puzzle as I would, I could make nothing at all of what it meant. I returned the strange hair to the drawer, and I said nothing of the matter to the Rucastles, as I felt that I had put myself in the wrong by opening a drawer which they had locked.

"I am naturally observant as you may have remarked, Mr. Holmes, and I soon had a pretty good plan of the whole house in my head. There was one wing, however, which appeared not to be inhabited at all. A door which faced that which led into the quarters of the Tollers opened into this suite, but it was invariably locked. One day, however, as I ascended the stair, I met Mr. Rucastle coming out through this door, his keys in his hand, and a look on his face which made him a very different person to the round jovial man to whom I was accustomed. His cheeks were red, his brow was all crinkled with anger, and the veins stood out at his temples with passion. He locked the door, and hurried past me without a word or a look.

"This aroused my curiosity; so when I went out for a walk in the grounds with my charge, I strolled round to the side from which I could see the windows of this part of the house. There were four of them in a row, three of which were simply dirty, while the fourth was shuttered up. They were evidently all deserted. As I strolled up and down, glancing at them occasionally, Mr. Rucastle came out to me, looking as merry and jovial as ever.

"' Ah!' said he, ' you must not think me rude if I

passed you without a word, my dear young lady. I was preoccupied with business matters.'

" I assured him that I was not offended. ' By the way,' said I, ' you seem to have quite a suite of spare rooms up there, and one of them has the shutters up.'

" ' Photography is one of my hobbies,' said he. ' I have made my dark-room up there. But, dear me ! what an observant young lady we have come upon. Who would have believed it ? Who would have ever believed it ? " He spoke in a jesting tone, but there was no jest in his eyes as he looked at me. I read suspicion there, and annoyance, but no jest.

" Well, Mr. Holmes, from the moment that I understood that there was something about that suite of rooms which I was not to know, I was all on fire to go over them. It was not mere curiosity, though I have my share of that. It was more a feeling of duty—a feeling that some good might come from my penetrating to this place. They talk of woman's instinct ; perhaps it was woman's instinct which gave me that feeling. At any rate, it was there ; and I was keenly on the look-out for any chance to pass the forbidden door.

" It was only yesterday that the chance came. I may tell you that, besides Mr. Rucastle, both Toller and his wife find something to do in these deserted rooms, and I once saw him carrying a large black linen bag with him through the door. Recently he has been drinking hard, and yesterday evening he was very drunk ; and, when I came upstairs, there was the key in the door. I have no doubt at all that he had left it there. Mr. and Mrs. Rucastle were both downstairs, and the child was with them, so that I had an admirable opportunity. I turned the key gently in the lock, opened the door, and slipped through.

" There was a little passage in front of me, unpapered and uncarpeted, which turned at a right angle at the farther end. Round this corner were three doors in a line, the first and third of which were open. They each led into an empty room, dusty and cheerless, with two windows in the one, and one in the other, so thick with dirt that the evening light glimmered dimly through them. The centre door was closed, and across the outside of it had been fastened one of the broad bars of an iron bed, padlocked at one end to a ring in the wall, and fastened at the other with stout cord. The door itself was locked as well, and the key was not there. This barricaded door corresponded clearly with the shuttered window outside, and yet I could see by the glimmer from beneath it that the room was not in darkness. Evidently there was a skylight which let in light from above. As I stood in the passage gazing at this sinister door, and wondering what secret it might veil, I suddenly heard the sound of steps within the room, and saw a shadow pass backwards and forwards against the little slit of dim light which shone out from under the door. A mad, unreasoning terror rose up in me at the sight, Mr. Holmes. My overstrung nerves failed me suddenly, and I turned and ran—ran as though some dreadful hand were behind me, clutching at the skirt of my dress. I rushed down the passage, through the door, and straight into the arms of Mr. Rucastle, who was waiting outside.

"'So,' said he, smiling, ' it was you, then. I thought it must be when I saw the door open.'

"'Oh, I am so frightened ! ' I panted.

"' My dear young lady ! my dear young lady ! '—you cannot think how caressing and soothing his manner was— ' and what has frightened you, my dear young lady ? '

" But his voice was just a little too coaxing. He overdid it. I was keenly on my guard against him.

"' I was foolish enough to go into the empty wing,' I answered. ' But it is so lonely and eerie in this dim light that I was frightened and ran out again. Oh, it is so dreadfully still in there ! '

"' Only that ? ' said he, looking at me keenly.

"' Why, what do you think ? ' I asked.

"' Why do you think that I lock this door ? '

295

" ' I am sure that I do not know.'

" ' It is to keep people out who have no business there. Do you see ? ' He was still smiling in the most amiable manner.

" ' I am sure if I had known——'

" ' Well, then, you know now. And if you ever put your foot over that threshold again——' here in an instant the smile hardened into a grin of rage, and he glared down at me with the face of a demon, ' I'll throw you to the mastiff.'

" I was so terrified that I do not know what I did. I suppose that I must have rushed past him into my room. I remember nothing until I found myself lying on my bed trembling all over. Then I thought of you, Mr. Holmes. I could not live there longer without some advice. I was frightened of the house, of the man, of the woman, of the servants, even of the child. They were all horrible to me. If I could only bring you down all would be well. Of course I might have fled from the house, but my curiosity was almost as strong as my fears. My mind was soon made up. I would send you a wire. I put on my hat and cloak, went down to the office, which is about half a mile from the house, and then returned, feeling very much easier. A horrible doubt came into my mind as I approached the door lest the dog might be loose, but I remembered that Toller had drunk himself into a state of insensibility that evening, and I knew that he was the only one in the household who had any influence with the savage creature, or who would venture to set him free. I slipped in in safety, and lay awake half the night in my joy at the thought of seeing you. I had no difficulty in getting leave to come into Winchester this morning, but I must be back before three o'clock, for Mr. and Mrs. Rucastle are going on a visit, and will be away all the evening, so that I must look after the child. Now I have told you all my adventures, Mr. Holmes, and I should be very glad if you could tell me what it all means, and, above all, what I should do."

Holmes and I had listened spellbound to this extraordinary story. My friend rose now, and paced up and down the room, his hands in his pockets, and an expression of the most profound gravity upon his face.

" Is Toller still drunk ? " he asked.

" Yes. I heard his wife tell Mrs. Rucastle that she could do nothing with him."

" That is well. And the Rucastles go out to-night ? "

" Yes."

" Is there a cellar with a good strong lock ? "

" Yes, the wine cellar."

" You seem to me to have acted all through this matter like a brave and sensible girl, Miss Hunter. Do you think that you could perform one more feat ? I should not ask it of you if I did not think you a quite exceptional woman."

" I will try. What is it ? "

" We shall be at the Copper Beeches by seven o'clock, my friend and I. The Rucastles will be gone by that time, and Toller will, we hope, be incapable. There only remains Mrs. Toller, who might give the alarm. If you could send her into the cellar, on some errand, and then turn the key upon her, you would facilitate matters immensely."

" I will do it."

" Excellent ! We shall then look thoroughly into the affair. Of course there is only one feasible explanation. You have been brought there to personate someone, and the real person is imprisoned in this chamber. That is obvious. As to who this prisoner is, I have no doubt that it is the daughter, Miss Alice Rucastle, if I remember right, who was said to have gone to America. You were chosen, doubtless, as resembling her in height, figure, and the colour of your hair. Hers had been cut off, very possibly in some illness through which she has passed, and so, of course, yours had to be sacrificed also. By a curious chance you came upon her tresses. The man in the road was, undoubtedly, some friend of hers—possibly her fiancé

—and no doubt as you wore the girl's dress, and were so like her, he was convinced from your laughter, whenever he saw you, and afterwards from your gesture, that Miss Rucastle was perfectly happy, and that she no longer desired his attentions. The dog is let loose at night to prevent him from endeavouring to communicate with her. So much is fairly clear. The most serious point in the case is the disposition of the child."

" What on earth has that to do with it ? " I ejaculated.

" My dear Watson, you as a medical man are continually gaining light as to the tendencies of a child by the study of the parents. Don't you see that the converse is equally valid. I have frequently gained my first real insight into the character of parents by studying their children. This child's disposition is abnormally cruel, merely for cruelty's sake, and whether he derives this from his smiling father, as I should suspect, or from his mother, it bodes evil for the poor girl who is in their power."

" I am sure that you are right, Mr. Holmes," cried our client. " A thousand things come back to me which make me certain that you have hit it. Oh, let us lose not an instant in bringing help to this poor creature."

" We must be circumspect, for we are dealing with a very cunning man. We can do nothing until seven o'clock. At that hour we shall be with you, and it will not be long before we solve the mystery."

We were as good as our word, for it was just seven when we reached the Copper Beeches, having put up our trap at a wayside public-house. The group of trees, with their dark leaves shining like burnished metal in the light of the setting sun, were sufficient to mark the house even had Miss Hunter not been standing smiling on the door-step.

" Have you managed it ? " asked Holmes.

A loud thudding noise came from somewhere downstairs. " That is Mrs. Toller in the cellar," said she. " Her husband lies snoring on the kitchen rug. Here are his keys, which are the duplicates of Mr. Rucastle's."

" You have done well indeed ! " cried Holmes, with enthusiasm. " Now lead the way, and we shall soon see the end of this black business."

We passed up the stair, unlocked the door, followed on down a passage, and found ourselves in front of the barricade which Miss Hunter had described. Holmes cut the cord and removed the transverse bar. Then he tried the various keys in the lock, but without success. No sound came from within, and at the silence Holmes' face clouded over.

" I trust that we are not too late," said he. " I think, Miss Hunter, that we had better go in without you. Now, Watson, put your shoulder to it, and we shall see whether we cannot make our way in."

It was an old rickety door and gave at once before our united strength. Together we rushed into the room. It was empty. There was no furniture save a little pallet bed, a small table, and a basketful of linen. The skylight above was open, and the prisoner gone.

" There has been some villainy here," said Holmes ; " this beauty has guessed Miss Hunter's intentions, and has carried his victim off."

" But how ? "

" Through the skylight. We shall soon see how he managed it." He swung himself up on to the roof. " Ah, yes," he cried, " here's the end of a long light ladder against the eaves. That is how he did it."

" But it is impossible," said Miss Hunter, " the ladder was not there when the Rucastles went away."

" He has come back and done it. I tell you that he is a clever and dangerous man. I should not be very much surprised if this were he whose step I hear now upon the stair. I think, Watson, that it would be as well for you to have your pistol ready."

The words were hardly out of his mouth before a man appeared at the door of the room, a very fat and burly man, with a heavy stick in his hand. Miss Hunter screamed and shrunk against the wall at the sight of him, but Sherlock Holmes sprang forward and confronted him.

"You villain," said he, "where's your daughter?"

The fat man cast his eyes round, and then up at the open skylight.

"It is for me to ask you that," he shrieked, "you thieves! Spies and thieves! I have caught you, have I? You are in my power. I'll serve you!" He turned and clattered down the stairs as hard as he could go.

"He's gone for the dog!" cried Miss Hunter.

"I have my revolver," said I.

"Better close the front door," cried Holmes, and we all rushed down the stairs together. We had hardly reached the hall when we heard the baying of a hound, and then a scream of agony, with a horrible worrying sound which it was dreadful to listen to. An elderly man with a red face and shaking limbs came staggering out at a side-door.

"My God!" he cried. "Someone has loosed the dog. It's not been fed for two days. Quick, quick, or it'll be too late!"

Holmes and I rushed out, and round the angle of the house, with Toller hurrying behind us. There was the huge famished brute, its black muzzle buried in Rucastle's throat, while he writhed and screamed upon the ground. Running up, I blew its brains out, and it fell over with its keen white teeth still meeting in the great creases of his neck. With much labour we separated them, and carried him, living but horribly mangled, into the house. We laid him upon the drawing-room sofa, and having despatched the sobered Toller to bear the news to his wife, I did what I could to relieve his pain. We were all assembled round him when the door opened, and a tall, gaunt woman entered the room.

"Mrs. Toller!" cried Miss Hunter.

"Yes, miss. Mr. Rucastle let me out when he came back before he went up to you. Ah, miss, it is a pity you didn't let me know what you were planning, for I would have told you that your pains were wasted."

"Ha!" said Holmes, looking keenly at her. "It is

clear that Mrs. Toller knows more about this matter than anyone else."

" Yes, sir, I do, and I am ready enough to tell what I know."

" Then pray sit down, and let us hear it, for there are several points on which I must confess that I am still in the dark."

" I will soon make it clear to you," said she ; " and I'd have done so before now if I could ha' got out from the cellar. If there's police-court business over this, you'll remember that I was the one that stood your friend, and that I was Miss Alice's friend too.

" She was never happy at home, Miss Alice wasn't, from the time that her father married again. She was slighted like, and had no say in anything ; but it never really became bad for her until after she met Mr. Fowler at a friend's house. As well as I could learn, Miss Alice had rights of her own by will, but she was so quiet and patient, she was, that she never said a word about them, but just left everything in Mr. Rucastle's hands. He knew he was safe with her ; but when there was a chance of a husband coming forward, who would ask for all that the law could give him, then her father thought it time to put a stop on it. He wanted her to sign a paper so that whether she married or not, he could use her money. When she wouldn't do it, he kept on worrying her until she got brain fever, and for six weeks was at death's door. Then she got better at last, all worn to a shadow, and with her beautiful hair cut off ; but that didn't make no change in her young man, and he stuck to her as true as man could be."

" Ah," said Holmes, " I think that what you have been good enough to tell us makes the matter fairly clear, and that I can deduce all that remains. Mr. Rucastle, then, I presume, took to this system of imprisonment ? "

" Yes, sir."

" And brought Miss Hunter down from London in order to get rid of the disagreeable persistence of Mr. Fowler."

" That was it, sir."

" But Mr. Fowler, being a persevering man, as a good seaman should be, blockaded the house, and, having met you, succeeded by certain arguments, metallic or otherwise, in convincing you that your interests were the same as his."

" Mr. Fowler was a very kind-spoken, free-handed gentleman," said Mrs. Toller serenely.

" And in this way he managed that your good man should have no want of drink, and that a ladder should be ready at the moment when your master had gone out."

" You have it, sir, just as it happened."

" I am sure we owe you an apology, Mrs. Toller," said Holmes, " for you have certainly cleared up everything which puzzled us. And here comes the country surgeon and Mrs. Rucastle, so I think, Watson, that we had best escort Miss Hunter back to Winchester, as it seems to me that our *locus standi* now is rather a questionable one."

And thus was solved the mystery of the sinister house with the copper beeches in front of the door. Mr. Rucastle survived, but was always a broken man, kept alive solely through the care of his devoted wife. They still live with their old servants, who probably know so much of Rucastle's past life that he finds it difficult to part from them. Mr. Fowler and Miss Rucastle were married, by special licence, in Southampton the day after their flight, and he is now the holder of a Government appointment in the Island of Mauritius. As to Miss Violet Hunter, my friend Holmes, rather to my disappointment, manifested no further interest in her when once she had ceased to be the centre of one of his problems, and she is now the head of a private school at Walsall, where I believe that she has met with considerable success.

THE MEMOIRS OF
SHERLOCK HOLMES

13. *Silver Blaze*

"I AM afraid, Watson, that I shall have to go," said Holmes, as we sat down together to our breakfast one morning.

"Go! Where to?"

"To Dartmoor—to King's Pyland."

I was not surprised. Indeed, my only wonder was that he had not already been mixed up in this extraordinary case, which was the one topic of conversation through the length and breadth of England. For a whole day my companion had rambled about the room with his chin upon his chest and his brows knitted, charging and re-charging his pipe with the strongest black tobacco, and absolutely deaf to any of my questions or remarks. Fresh editions of every paper had been sent up by our newsagent only to be glanced over and tossed down into a corner. Yet, silent as he was, I knew perfectly well what it was over which he was brooding. There was but one problem before the public which could challenge his powers of analysis, and that was the singular disappearance of the favourite for the Wessex Cup, and the tragic murder of its trainer. When, therefore, he suddenly announced his intention of setting out for the scene of the drama, it was only what I had both expected and hoped for.

"I should be most happy to go down with you if I should not be in the way," said I.

"My dear Watson, you would confer a great favour upon me by coming. And I think that your time will not be mis-spent, for there are points about this case which promise to make it an absolutely unique one. We

305

have, I think, just time to catch our train at Paddington, and I will go further into the matter upon our journey. You would oblige me by bringing with you your very excellent field-glass."

And so it happened that an hour or so later I found myself in the corner of a first-class carriage, flying along, *en route* for Exeter, while Sherlock Holmes, with his sharp, eager face framed in his ear-flapped travelling-cap, dipped rapidly into the bundle of fresh papers which he had procured at Paddington. We had left Reading far behind us before he thrust the last of them under the seat, and offered me his cigar-case.

" We are going well," said he, looking out of the window, and glancing at his watch. " Our rate at present is fifty-three and a half miles an hour."

" I have not observed the quarter-mile posts," said I.

" Nor have I. But the telegraph posts upon this line are sixty yards apart, and the calculation is a simple one. I presume that you have already looked into this matter of the murder of John Straker and the disappearance of Silver Blaze ? "

" I have seen what the *Telegraph* and the *Chronicle* have to say."

" It is one of those cases where the art of the reasoner should be used rather for the sifting of details than for the acquiring of fresh evidence. The tragedy has been so uncommon, so complete, and of such personal import-ance to so many people that we are suffering from a plethora of surmise, conjecture, and hypothesis. The difficulty is to detach the framework of fact—of absolute, undeniable fact—from the embellishments of theorists and reporters. Then, having established ourselves upon this sound basis, it is our duty to see what inferences may be drawn, and which are the special points upon which the whole mystery turns. On Tuesday evening I received telegrams, both from Colonel Ross, the owner of the horse, and from Inspector Gregory, who is looking after the case, inviting my co-operation."

"Tuesday evening!" I exclaimed. "And this is Thursday morning. Why did you not go down yesterday?"

"Because I made a blunder, my dear Watson—which is, I am afraid, a more common occurrence than anyone would think who only knew me through your memoirs. The fact is that I could not believe it possible that the most remarkable horse in England could long remain concealed, especially in so sparsely inhabited a place as the north of Dartmoor. From hour to hour yesterday I expected to hear that he had been found, and that his abductor was the murderer of John Straker. When, however, another morning had come and I found that, beyond the arrest of young Fitzroy Simpson, nothing had been done, I felt that it was time for me to take action. Yet in some ways I feel that yesterday has not been wasted."

"You have formed a theory then?"

"At least I have a grip of the essential facts of the case. I shall enumerate them to you, for nothing clears up a case so much as stating it to another person, and I can hardly expect your co-operation if I do not show you the position from which we start."

I lay back against the cushions, puffing at my cigar, while Holmes, leaning forward, with his long thin forefinger checking off the points upon the palm of his left hand, gave me a sketch of the events which had led to our journey.

"Silver Blaze," said he, "is from the Isonomy stock, and holds as brilliant a record as his famous ancestor. He is now in his fifth year, and has brought in turn each of the prizes of the turf to Colonel Ross, his fortunate owner. Up to the time of the catastrophe he was first favourite for the Wessex Cup, the betting being three to one on. He has always, however, been a prime favourite with the racing public, and has never yet disappointed them, so that even at short odds enormous sums of money have been laid upon him. It is obvious, therefore, that there were many people who had the strongest interest in preventing Silver Blaze from being there at the fall of the flag next Tuesday.

"This fact was, of course, appreciated at King's Pyland, where the Colonel's training stable is situated. Every precaution was taken to guard the favourite. The trainer, John Straker, is a retired jockey, who rode in Colonel Ross's colours before he became too heavy for the weighing-chair. He has served the Colonel for five years as jockey, and for seven as trainer, and has always shown himself to be a zealous and honest servant. Under him were three lads, for the establishment was a small one, containing only four horses in all. One of these lads sat up each night in the stable, while the others slept in the loft. All three bore excellent characters. John Straker, who is a married man, lived in a small villa about two hundred yards from the stables. He has no children, keeps one maid-servant, and is comfortably off. The country round is very lonely, but about half a mile to the north there is a small cluster of villas which have been built by a Tavistock contractor for the use of invalids and others who may wish to enjoy the pure Dartmoor air. Tavistock itself lies two miles to the west, while across the moor, also about two miles distant, is the larger training establishment of Capleton, which belongs to Lord Backwater, and is managed by Silas Brown. In every other direction the moor is a complete wilderness, inhabited only by a few roaming gipsies. Such was the general situation last Monday night, when the catastrophe occurred.

"On that evening the horses had been exercised and watered as usual, and the stables were locked up at nine o'clock. Two of the lads walked up to the trainer's house, where they had supper in the kitchen, while the third, Ned Hunter, remained on guard. At a few minutes after nine the maid, Edith Baxter, carried down to the stables his supper, which consisted of a dish of curried mutton. She took no liquid, as there was a water-tap in the stables, and it was the rule that the lad on duty should drink

308

nothing else. The maid carried a lantern with her, as it was very dark, and the path ran across the open moor.

" Edith Baxter was within thirty yards of the stables when a man appeared out of the darkness and called to her to stop. As he stepped into the circle of yellow light thrown by the lantern she saw that he was a person of gentlemanly bearing, dressed in a grey suit of tweed with a cloth cap. He wore gaiters, and carried a heavy stick with a knob to it. She was most impressed, however, by the extreme pallor of his face and by the nervousness of his manner. His age, she thought, would be rather over thirty than under it.

" ' Can you tell me where I am ? ' he asked. ' I had almost made up my mind to sleep on the moor when I saw the light of your lantern.'

" ' You are close to the King's Pyland training stables,' she said.

" ' Oh, indeed ! What a stroke of luck ! ' he cried. ' I understand that a stable boy sleeps there alone every night. Perhaps that is his supper which you are carrying to him. Now I am sure that you would not be too proud to earn the price of a new dress, would you ? ' He took a piece of white paper folded up out of his waistcoat pocket. ' See that the boy has this to-night, and you shall have the prettiest frock that money can buy.'

" She was frightened by the earnestness of his manner, and ran past him to the window through which she was accustomed to hand the meals. It was already open, and Hunter was seated at the small table inside. She had begun to tell him of what had happened, when the stranger came up again.

" ' Good evening,' said he, looking through the window, ' I wanted to have a word with you.' The girl has sworn that as he spoke she noticed the corner of the little paper packet protruding from his closed hand.

" ' What business have you here ? ' asked the lad.

" ' It's business that may put something into your pocket,' said the other. ' You've two horses in for the

Wessex Cup—Silver Blaze and Bayard. Let me have the straight tip, and you won't be a loser. Is it a fact that at the weights Bayard could give the other a hundred yards in five furlongs, and that the stable have put their money on him ? '

" ' So you're one of those damned touts,' cried the lad. ' I'll show you how we serve them in King's Pyland.' He sprang up and rushed across the stable to unloose the dog. The girl fled away to the house, but as she ran she looked back, and saw that the stranger was leaning through the window. A minute later, however, when Hunter rushed out with the hound he was gone, and though the lad ran all round the buildings he failed to find any trace of him."

" One moment ! " I asked. " Did the stable boy, when he ran out with the dog, leave the door unlocked behind him ? "

" Excellent, Watson ; excellent ! " murmured my companion. " The importance of the point struck me so forcibly, that I sent a special wire to Dartmoor yesterday to clear the matter up. The boy locked the door before he left it. The window, I may add, was not large enough for a man to get through.

" Hunter waited until his fellow-grooms had returned, when he sent a message up to the trainer and told him what had occurred. Straker was excited at hearing the account, although he does not seem to have quite realized its true significance. It left him, however, vaguely uneasy, and Mrs. Straker, waking at one in the morning, found that he was dressing. In reply to her inquiries, he said that he could not sleep on account of his anxiety about the horses, and that he intended to walk down to the stables to see that all was well. She begged him to remain at home, as she could hear the rain pattering against the windows, but in spite of her entreaties he pulled on his large mackintosh and left the house.

" Mrs. Straker awoke at seven in the morning, to find that her husband had not yet returned. She dressed herself hastily, called the maid, and set off for the stables.

The door was open ; inside, huddled together upon a chair, Hunter was sunk in a state of absolute stupor, the favourite's stall was empty, and there were no signs of his trainer.

" The two lads who slept in the chaff-cutting loft above the harness-room were quickly roused. They had heard nothing during the night, for they are both sound sleepers. Hunter was obviously under the influence of some powerful drug ; and, as no sense could be got out of him, he was left to sleep it off while the two lads and the two women ran out in search of the absentees. They still had hopes that the trainer had for some reason taken out the horse for early exercise, but on ascending the knoll near the house, from which all the neighbouring moors were visible, they not only could see no signs of the favourite, but they perceived something which warned them that they were in the presence of a tragedy.

" About a quarter of a mile from the stables, John Straker's overcoat was flapping from a furze bush. Immediately beyond there was a bowl-shaped depression in the moor, and at the bottom of this was found the dead body of the unfortunate trainer. His head had been shattered by a savage blow from some heavy weapon, and he was wounded in the thigh, where there was a long, clean cut, inflicted evidently by some very sharp instrument. It was clear, however, that Straker had defended himself vigorously against his assailants, for in his right hand he held a small knife, which was clotted with blood up to the handle, while in his left he grasped a red and black silk cravat, which was recognized by the maid as having been worn on the preceding evening by the stranger who had visited the stables.

" Hunter, on recovering from his stupor, was also quite positive as to the ownership of the cravat. He was equally certain that the same stranger had, while standing at the window, drugged his curried mutton, and so deprived the stables of their watchman.

" As to the missing horse, there were abundant proofs

in the mud which lay at the bottom of the fatal hollow, that he had been there at the time of the struggle. But from that morning he has disappeared; and although a large reward has been offered, and all the gipsies of Dartmoor are on the alert, no news has come of him. Finally an analysis has shown that the remains of his supper, left by the stable lad, contain an appreciable quantity of powdered opium, while the people of the house partook of the same dish on the same night without any ill effect.

"Those are the main facts of the case stripped of all surmise and stated as baldly as possible. I shall now recapitulate what the police have done in the matter.

"Inspector Gregory, to whom the case has been committed, is an extremely competent officer. Were he but gifted with imagination he might rise to great heights in his profession. On his arrival he promptly found and arrested the man upon whom suspicion naturally rested. There was little difficulty in finding him, for he was thoroughly well known in the neighbourhood. His name, it appears, was Fitzroy Simpson. He was a man of excellent birth and education, who had squandered a fortune upon the turf, and who lived now by doing a little quiet and genteel bookmaking in the sporting clubs of London. An examination of his betting-book shows that bets to the amount of five thousand pounds had been registered by him against the favourite.

"On being arrested he volunteered the statement that he had come down to Dartmoor in the hope of getting some information about the King's Pyland horses, and also about Desborough, the second favourite, which was in charge of Silas Brown, at the Capleton stables. He did not attempt to deny that he had acted as described upon the evening before, but declared that he had no sinister designs, and had simply wished to obtain first-hand information. When confronted with the cravat he turned very pale, and was utterly unable to account for its presence in the hand of the murdered man. His wet clothing showed that he had been out in the storm of the night before, and his stick, which was a Penang lawyer, weighted with lead, was just such a weapon as might, by repeated blows, have inflicted the terrible injuries to which the trainer had succumbed.

"On the other hand, there was no wound upon his person, while the state of Straker's knife would show that one, at least, of his assailants must bear his mark upon him. There you have it all in a nutshell, Watson, and if you can give me any light I shall be infinitely obliged to you."

I had listened with the greatest interest to the statement which Holmes, with characteristic clearness, had laid before me. Though most of the facts were familiar to me, I had not sufficiently appreciated their relative importance, nor their connection with each other.

"Is it not possible," I suggested, "that the incised wound upon Straker may have been caused by his own knife in the convulsive struggles which follow any brain injury ? "

"It is more than possible ; it is probable," said Holmes. "In that case, one of the main points in favour of the accused disappears."

"And yet," said I, "even now I fail to understand what the theory of the police can be."

"I am afraid that whatever theory we state has very grave objections to it," returned my companion. "The police imagine, I take it, that this Fitzroy Simpson, having drugged the lad, and having in some way obtained a duplicate key, opened the stable door, and took out the horse, with the intention, apparently, of kidnapping him altogether. His bridle is missing, so that Simpson must have put it on. Then, having left the door open behind him, he was leading the horse away over the moor, when he was either met or overtaken by the trainer. A row naturally ensued, Simpson beat out the trainer's brains with his heavy stick without receiving any injury from the small knife which Straker used in self-defence, and then the thief either led the horse on to some secret hiding-place, or else it may have bolted during the struggle, and be now wandering out on the moors. That is the case as it appears to the police, and improbable as it is, all other explanations are more improbable still. However, I shall very quickly test the matter when I am once upon the spot, and until then I really cannot see how we can get much further than our present position."

It was evening before we reached the little town of Tavistock, which lies, like the boss of a shield, in the middle of the huge circle of Dartmoor. Two gentlemen were awaiting us at the station ; the one a tall fair man with lion-like hair and beard, and curiously penetrating light blue eyes, the other a small alert person, very neat and dapper, in a frock-coat and gaiters, with trim little side-whiskers and an eye-glass. The latter was Colonel Ross, the well-known sportsman, the other Inspector Gregory, a man who was rapidly making his name in the English detective service.

"I am delighted that you have come down, Mr. Holmes," said the Colonel. "The Inspector here has done all that could possibly be suggested ; but I wish to leave no stone unturned in trying to avenge poor Straker, and in recovering my horse."

"Have there been any fresh developments ? " asked Holmes.

"I am sorry to say that we have made very little progress," said the Inspector. "We have an open carriage outside, and as you would no doubt like to see the place before the light fails, we might talk it over as we drive."

A minute later we were all seated in a comfortable landau and were rattling through the quaint old Devonshire town. Inspector Gregory was full of his case, and poured out a stream of remarks, while Holmes threw in an occasional question or interjection. Colonel Ross leaned back with his arms folded and his hat tilted over his eyes, while I listened with interest to the dialogue of the two detectives. Gregory was formulating his theory, which was almost exactly what Holmes had foretold in the train.

" The net is drawn pretty close round Fitzroy Simpson," he remarked, " and I believe myself that he is our man. At the same time, I recognize that the evidence is purely circumstantial, and that some new development may upset it."

" How about Straker's knife ? "

" We have quite come to the conclusion that he wounded himself in his fall."

" My friend Dr. Watson made that suggestion to me as we came down. If so, it would tell against this man Simpson."

" Undoubtedly. He has neither a knife nor any sign of a wound. The evidence against him is certainly very strong. He had a great interest in the disappearance of the favourite, he lies under the suspicion of having poisoned the stable boy, he was undoubtedly out in the storm, he was armed with a heavy stick, and his cravat was found in the dead man's hand. I really think we have enough to go before a jury."

Holmes shook his head. " A clever counsel would tear it all to rags," said he. " Why should he take the horse out of the stable ? If he wished to injure it, why could he not do it there ? Has a duplicate key been found in his possession ? What chemist sold him the powdered opium ? Above all, where could he, a stranger to the district, hide a horse, and such a horse as this ? What is his own explanation as to the paper which he wished the maid to give to the stable boy ? "

" He says that it was a ten-pound note. One was found in his purse. But your other difficulties are not so formidable as they seem. He is not a stranger to the district. He has twice lodged at Tavistock in the summer. The opium was probably brought from London. The key, having served its purpose, would be hurled away. The horse may lie at the bottom of one of the pits or old mines upon the moor."

315

" What does he say about the cravat ? "

" He acknowledges that it is his, and declares that he had lost it. But a new element has been introduced into the case which may account for his leading the horse from the stable."

Holmes pricked up his ears.

" We have found traces which show that a party of gipsies encamped on Monday night within a mile of the spot where the murder took place. On Tuesday they were gone. Now, presuming that there was some understanding between Simpson and these gipsies, might he not have been leading the horse to them when he was overtaken, and may they not have him now ? "

" It is certainly possible."

" The moor is being scoured for these gipsies. I have also examined every stable and outhouse in Tavistock, and for a radius of ten miles."

" There is another training stable quite close, I understand ? "

" Yes, and that is a factor which we must certainly not neglect. As Desborough, their horse, was second in the betting, they had an interest in the disappearance of the favourite. Silas Brown, the trainer, is known to have had large bets upon the event, and he was no friend to poor Straker. We have, however, examined the stables, and there is nothing to connect him with the affair."

" And nothing to connect this man Simpson with the interests of the Capleton stable ? "

" Nothing at all."

Holmes leaned back in the carriage and the conversation ceased. A few minutes later our driver pulled up at a neat little red-brick villa with overhanging eaves, which stood by the road. Some distance off, across a paddock, lay a long grey-tiled outbuilding. In every other direction the low curves of the moor, bronze-coloured from the fading ferns, stretched away to the skyline, broken only by the steeples of Tavistock, and by a cluster of houses away to the westward, which marked the Capleton stables.

We all sprang out with the exception of Holmes, who continued to lean back with his eyes fixed upon the sky in front of him, entirely absorbed in his own thoughts. It was only when I touched his arm that he roused himself with a violent start and stepped out of the carriage.

"Excuse me," said he, turning to Colonel Ross, who had looked at him in some surprise. "I was day-dreaming." There was a gleam in his eyes and a suppressed excitement in his manner which convinced me, used as I was to his ways, that his hand was upon a clue, though I could not imagine where he had found it.

"Perhaps you would prefer at once to go on to the scene of the crime, Mr. Holmes?" said Gregory.

"I think that I should prefer to stay here a little and go into one or two questions of detail. Straker was brought back here, I presume?"

"Yes, he lies upstairs. The inquest is to-morrow."

"He has been in your service some years, Colonel Ross?"

"I have always found him an excellent servant."

"I presume that you made an inventory of what he had in his pockets at the time of his death, Inspector?"

"I have the things themselves in the sitting-room, if you would care to see them."

"I should be very glad."

We all filed into the front room, and sat round the central table, while the Inspector unlocked a square tin box and laid a small heap of things before us. There was a box of vestas, two inches of tallow candle, an A.D.P. briar-root pipe, a pouch of sealskin with half an ounce of long-cut cavendish, a silver watch with a gold chain, five sovereigns in gold, an aluminium pencil-case, a few papers, and an ivory-handled knife with a very delicate inflexible blade marked Weiss & Co., London.

"This is a very singular knife," said Holmes, lifting it up and examining it minutely. "I presume, as I see blood-stains upon it, that it is the one which was found in

317

the dead man's grasp. Watson, this knife is surely in your line."

" It is what we call a cataract knife," said I.

" I thought so. A very delicate blade devised for very delicate work. A strange thing for a man to carry with him upon a rough expedition, especially as it would not shut in his pocket."

" The tip was guarded by a disc of cork which we found beside his body," said the Inspector. " His wife tells us that the knife had lain for some days upon the dressing-table, and that he had picked it up as he left the room. It was a poor weapon, but perhaps the best that he could lay his hand on at the moment."

" Very possible. How about these papers ? "

" Three of them are receipted hay-dealers' accounts. One of them is a letter of instructions from Colonel Ross. This other is a milliner's account for thirty-seven pounds fifteen, made out by Madame Lesurier, of Bond Street, to William Darbyshire. Mrs. Straker tells us that Darby-shire was a friend of her husband's, and that occasionally his letters were addressed here."

" Madame Darbyshire had somewhat expensive tastes," remarked Holmes, glancing down the account. " Twenty-two guineas is rather heavy for a single costume. How-ever, there appears to be nothing more to learn, and we may now go down to the scene of the crime."

As we emerged from the sitting-room a woman who had been waiting in the passage took a step forward and laid her hand upon the Inspector's sleeve. Her face was hag-gard, and thin, and eager ; stamped with the print of a recent horror.

" Have you got them ? Have you found them ? " she panted.

" No, Mrs. Straker ; but Mr. Holmes, here, has come from London to help us, and we shall do all that is possible."

" Surely I met you in Plymouth, at a garden-party, some little time ago, Mrs. Straker," said Holmes.

" No, sir ; you are mistaken."

" Dear me ; why, I could have sworn to it. You wore a costume of dove-coloured silk with ostrich feather trimming."

" I never had such a dress, sir," answered the lady.

" Ah ; that quite settles it," said Holmes ; and, with an apology, he followed the Inspector outside. A short walk across the moor took us to the hollow in which the body had been found. At the brink of it was the furze bush upon which the coat had been hung.

" There was no wind that night, I understand," said Holmes.

" None ; but very heavy rain."

" In that case the overcoat was not blown against the furze bushes, but placed there."

" Yes, it was laid across the bush."

" You fill me with interest. I perceive that the ground has been trampled up a good deal. No doubt many feet have been there since Monday night."

" A piece of matting has been laid here at the side, and we have all stood upon that."

" Excellent."

" In this bag I have one of the boots which Straker wore, one of Fitzroy Simpson's shoes, and a cast horseshoe of Silver Blaze."

" My dear Inspector, you surpass yourself ! "

Holmes took the bag, and descending into the hollow he pushed the matting into a more central position. Then stretching himself upon his face and leaning his chin upon his hands he made a careful study of the trampled mud in front of him.

" Halloa ! " said he, suddenly, " what's this ? "

It was a wax vesta, half burned, which was so coated with mud that it looked at first like a little chip of wood.

" I cannot think how I came to overlook it," said the Inspector, with an expression of annoyance.

" It was invisible, buried in the mud. I only saw it because I was looking for it."

" What ! You expected to find it ? "

" I thought it not unlikely." He took the boots from the bag and compared the impressions of each of them with marks upon the ground. Then he clambered up to the rim of the hollow and crawled about among the ferns and bushes.

" I am afraid that there are no more tracks," said the Inspector. " I have examined the ground very carefully for a hundred yards in each direction."

" Indeed ! " said Holmes, rising, " I should not have the impertinence to do it again after what you say. But I should like to take a little walk over the moors before it grows dark, that I may know my ground to-morrow, and I think that I shall put this horseshoe into my pocket for luck."

Colonel Ross, who had shown some signs of impatience at my companion's quiet and systematic method of work, glanced at his watch.

" I wish you would come back with me, Inspector," said he. " There are several points on which I should like your advice, and especially as to whether we do not owe it to the public to remove our horse's name from the entries for the Cup."

" Certainly not," cried Holmes, with decision ; " I should let the name stand."

The Colonel bowed. " I am very glad to have had your opinion, sir," said he. " You will find us at poor Straker's house when you have finished your walk, and we can drive together into Tavistock."

He turned back with the Inspector, while Holmes and I walked slowly across the moor. The sun was beginning to sink behind the stables of Capleton, and the long sloping plain in front of us was tinged with gold, deepening into rich, ruddy brown where the faded ferns and brambles caught the evening light. But the glories of the landscape were all wasted upon my companion, who was sunk in the deepest thought.

" It's this way, Watson," he said, at last. " We may

leave the question of who killed John Straker for the instant, and confine ourselves to finding out what has become of the horse. Now, supposing that he broke away during or after the tragedy, where could he have gone to? The horse is a very gregarious creature. If left to himself, his instincts would have been either to return to King's Pyland or go over to Capleton. Why should he run wild upon the moor? He would surely have been seen by now. And why should gipsies kidnap him? These people always clear out when they hear of trouble, for they do not wish to be pestered by the police. They could not hope to sell such a horse. They would run a great risk and gain nothing by taking him. Surely that is clear."

"Where is he, then?"

"I have already said that he must have gone to King's Pyland or to Capleton. He is not at King's Pyland, therefore he is at Capleton. Let us take that as a working hypothesis, and see what it leads us to. This part of the moor, as the Inspector remarked, is very hard and dry. But it falls away towards Capleton, and you can see from here that there is a long hollow over yonder, which must have been very wet on Monday night. If our supposition is correct, then the horse must have crossed that, and there is the point where we should look for his tracks."

We had been walking briskly during this conversation, and a few more minutes brought us to the hollow in question. At Holmes' request I walked down the bank to the right, and he to the left, but I had not taken fifty paces before I heard him give a shout, and saw him waving his hand to me. The track of a horse was plainly outlined in the soft earth in front of him, and the shoe which he took from his pocket exactly fitted the impression.

"See the value of imagination," said Holmes. "It is the one quality which Gregory lacks. We imagined what might have happened, acted upon the supposition, and find ourselves justified. Let us proceed."

We crossed the marshy bottom and passed over a

quarter of a mile of dry, hard turf. Again the ground sloped and again we came on the tracks. Then we lost them for half a mile, but only to pick them up once more quite close to Capleton. It was Holmes who saw them first, and he stood pointing with a look of triumph upon his face. A man's track was visible beside the horse's.

" The horse was alone before," I cried.

" Quite so. It was alone before. Halloa ! what is this ?"

The double track turned sharp off and took the direction of King's Pyland. Holmes whistled, and we both followed along after it. His eyes were on the trail, but I happened to look a little to one side, and saw to my surprise the same tracks coming back again in the opposite direction.

" One for you, Watson," said Holmes, when I pointed it out ; " you have saved us a long walk which would have brought us back on our own traces. Let us follow the return track."

We had not to go far. It ended at the paving of asphalt which led up to the gates of the Capleton stables. As we approached a groom ran out from them.

" We don't want any loiterers about here," said he.

" I only wished to ask a question," said Holmes, with his finger and thumb in his waistcoat pocket. " Should I be too early to see your master, Mr. Silas Brown, if I were to call at five o'clock to-morrow morning ? "

" Bless you, sir, if anyone is about he will be, for he is always the first stirring. But here he is, sir, to answer your questions for himself. No, sir, no ; it's as much as my place is worth to let him see me touch your money. Afterwards, if you like."

As Sherlock Holmes replaced the half-crown which he had drawn from his pocket, a fierce-looking elderly man strode out from the gate with a hunting-crop swinging in his hand.

" What's this, Dawson ? " he cried. " No gossiping ! Go about your business ! And you—what the devil do you want here ? "

"Ten minutes' talk with you, my good sir," said
Holmes, in the sweetest of voices.

"I've no time to talk to every gadabout. We want no
strangers here. Be off, or you may find a dog at your
heels."

Holmes leaned forward and whispered something in the
trainer's ear. He started violently and flushed to the
temples.

"It's a lie!" he shouted. "An infernal lie!"

"Very good! Shall we argue about it here in public,
or talk it over in your parlour?"

"Oh, come in if you wish to."

Holmes smiled. "I shall not keep you more than a
few minutes, Watson," he said. "Now, Mr. Brown, I
am quite at your disposal."

It was quite twenty minutes, and the reds had all faded
into greys before Holmes and the trainer reappeared.
Never have I seen such a change as had been brought
about in Silas Brown in that short time. His face was
ashy pale, beads of perspiration shone upon his brow, and
his hands shook until the hunting-crop wagged like a
branch in the wind. His bullying, overbearing manner
was all gone too, and he cringed along at my companion's
side like a dog with its master.

"Your instructions will be done. It shall be done,"
said he.

"There must be no mistake," said Holmes, looking
round at him. The other winced as he read the menace
in his eyes.

"Oh, no, there shall be no mistake. It shall be there.
Should I change it first or not?"

Holmes thought a little and then burst out laughing.
"No, don't," said he. "I shall write to you about it.
No tricks now or——"

"Oh, you can trust me, you can trust me!"

"You must see to it on the day as if it were your
own."

"You can rely upon me."

" Yes, I think I can. Well, you shall hear from me tomorrow." He turned upon his heel, disregarding the trembling hand which the other held out to him, and we set off for King's Pyland.

" A more perfect compound of the bully, coward and sneak than Master Silas Brown I have seldom met with," remarked Holmes, as we trudged along together.

" He has the horse, then ? "

" He tried to bluster out of it, but I described to him so exactly what his actions had been upon that morning, that he is convinced that I was watching him. Of course, you observed the peculiarly square toes in the impressions, and that his own boots exactly corresponded to them. Again, of course, no subordinate would have dared to have done such a thing. I described to him how when, according to his custom, he was the first down, he perceived a strange horse wandering over the moor ; how he went out to it, and his astonishment at recognizing from the white forehead which has given the favourite its name that chance had put in his power the only horse which could beat the one upon which he had put his money. Then I described how his first impulse had been to lead him back to King's Pyland, and how the devil had shown him how he could hide the horse until the race was over, and how he had led it back and concealed it at Capleton. When I told him every detail he gave it up, and thought only of saving his own skin."

" But his stables had been searched."

" Oh, an old horse-faker like him has many a dodge."

" But are you not afraid to leave the horse in his power now, since he has every interest in injuring it ? "

" My dear fellow, he will guard it as the apple of his eye. He knows that his only hope of mercy is to produce it safe."

" Colonel Ross did not impress me as a man who would be likely to show much mercy in any case."

" The matter does not rest with Colonel Ross. I follow my own methods, and tell as much or as little as I choose

That is the advantage of being unofficial. I don't know whether you observed it, Watson, but the Colonel's manner has been just a trifle cavalier to me. I am inclined now to have a little amusement at his expense. Say nothing to him about the horse."

" Certainly not, without your permission."

" And, of course, this is all quite a minor case compared with the question of who killed John Straker."

" And you will devote yourself to that ? "

" On the contrary, we both go back to London by the night train."

I was thunderstruck by my friend's words. We had only been a few hours in Devonshire, and that he should give up an investigation which he had begun so brilliantly was quite incomprehensible to me. Not a word more could I draw from him until we were back at the trainer's house. The Colonel and the Inspector were awaiting us in the parlour.

" My friend and I return to town by the midnight express," said Holmes. " We have had a charming little breath of your beautiful Dartmoor air."

The Inspector opened his eyes, and the Colonel's lips curled in a sneer.

" So you despair of arresting the murderer of poor Straker," said he.

Holmes shrugged his shoulders. " There are certainly grave difficulties in the way," said he. " I have every hope, however, that your horse will start upon Tuesday, and I beg that you will have your jockey in readiness. Might I ask for a photograph of Mr. John Straker ? "

The Inspector took one from an envelope in his pocket and handed it to him.

" My dear Gregory, you anticipate all my wants. If I might ask you to wait here for an instant, I have a question which I should like to put to the maid."

" I must say that I am rather disappointed in our London consultant," said Colonel Ross, bluntly, as my friend left the room. "I do not see that we are any further than when he came."

"At least, you have his assurance that your horse will run," said I.

"Yes, I have his assurance," said the Colonel, with a shrug of his shoulders. "I should prefer to have the horse."

I was about to make some reply in defence of my friend, when he entered the room again.

"Now, gentlemen," said he, "I am quite ready for Tavistock."

As we stepped into the carriage one of the stable lads held the door open for us. A sudden idea seemed to occur to Holmes, for he leaned forward and touched the lad upon the sleeve.

"You have a few sheep in the paddock," he said. "Who attends to them?"

"I do, sir."

"Have you noticed anything amiss with them of late?"

"Well, sir, not of much account; but three of them have gone lame, sir."

I could see that Holmes was extremely pleased, for he chuckled and rubbed his hands together.

"A long shot, Watson; a very long shot!" said he, pinching my arm. "Gregory, let me recommend to your attention this singular epidemic among the sheep. Drive on, coachman!"

Colonel Ross still wore an expression which showed the poor opinion which he had formed of my companion's ability, but I saw by the Inspector's face that his attention had been keenly aroused.

"You consider that to be important?" he asked.

"Exceedingly so."

"Is there any other point to which you would wish to draw my attention?"

"To the curious incident of the dog in the night-time."

"The dog did nothing in the night-time."

" That was the curious incident," remarked Sherlock Holmes.

Four days later Holmes and I were again in the train bound for Winchester, to see the race for the Wessex Cup. Colonel Ross met us, by appointment, outside the station, and we drove in his drag to the course beyond the town. His face was grave and his manner was cold in the extreme.

" I have seen nothing of my horse," said he.

" I suppose that you would know him when you saw him ? " asked Holmes.

The Colonel was very angry. " I have been on the turf for twenty years, and never was asked such a question as that before," said he. " A child would know Silver Blaze with his white forehead and his mottled off foreleg."

" How is the betting ? "

" Well, that is the curious part of it. You could have got fifteen to one yesterday, but the price has become shorter and shorter, until you can hardly get three to one now."

" Hum ! " said Holmes. " Somebody knows something, that is clear ! "

As the drag drew up in the enclosure near the grandstand, I glanced at the card to see the entries. It ran :

Wessex Plate. 50 sovs. each, h ft, with 1,000 sovs. added, for four- and five-year olds. Second £300. Third £200. New course (one mile and five furlongs).

    1. Mr. Heath Newton's The Negro (red cap, cinnamon jacket).

    2. Colonel Wardlaw's Pugilist (pink cap, blue and black jacket).

    3. Lord Backwater's Desborough (yellow cap and sleeves).

    4. Colonel Ross's Silver Blaze (black cap, red jacket).

    5. Duke of Balmoral's Iris (yellow and black stripes).

    6. Lord Singleford's Rasper (purple cap, black sleeves).

" We scratched our other one and put all hopes on your word," said the Colonel. " Why, what is that ? Silver Blaze favourite ? "

" Five to four against Silver Blaze ! " roared the ring. " Five to four against Silver Blaze ! Fifteen to five against Desborough ! Five to four on the field ! "

" There are the numbers up," I cried. " They are all six there."

" All six there ! Then my horse is running," cried the Colonel, in great agitation. " But I don't see him. My colours have not passed."

" Only five have passed. This must be he."

As I spoke a powerful bay horse swept out from the weighing enclosure and cantered past us, bearing on its back the well-known black and red of the Colonel.

" That's not my horse," cried the owner. " That beast has not a white hair upon its body. What is this that you have done, Mr. Holmes ? "

" Well, well, let us see how he gets on," said my friend, imperturbably. For a few minutes he gazed through my field-glass. " Capital ! An excellent start ! " he cried suddenly. " There they are, coming round the curve ! "

From our drag we had a superb view as they came up the straight. The six horses were so close together that a carpet could have covered them, but half-way up the yellow of the Capleton stable showed to the front. Before they reached us, however, Desborough's bolt was shot, and the Colonel's horse, coming away with a rush, passed the post a good six lengths before its rival, the Duke of Balmoral's Iris making a bad third.

" It's my race anyhow," gasped the Colonel, passing his hand over his eyes. " I confess that I can make neither head nor tail of it. Don't you think that you have kept up your mystery long enough, Mr. Holmes ? "

" Certainly, Colonel. You shall know everything. Let us all go round and have a look at the horse together. Here he is," he continued, as we made our way into the weighing enclosure where only owners and their friends find admittance. " You have only to wash his face and his leg in spirits of wine and you will find that he is the same old Silver Blaze as ever."

" You take my breath away ! "

" I found him in the hands of a faker, and took the liberty of running him just as he was sent over."

" My dear sir, you have done wonders. The horse looks very fit and well. It never went better in its life. I owe you a thousand apologies for having doubted your ability. You have done me a great service by recovering my horse. You would do me a greater still if you could lay your hands on the murderer of John Straker."

" I have done so," said Holmes, quietly.

The Colonel and I stared at him in amazement. " You have got him ! Where is he, then ? "

" He is here."

" Here ! Where ? "

" In my company at the present moment."

The Colonel flushed angrily. " I quite recognize that I am under obligations to you, Mr. Holmes," said he, " but I must regard what you have just said as either a very bad joke or an insult."

Sherlock Holmes laughed. " I assure you that I have not associated you with the crime, Colonel," said he ; " the real murderer is standing immediately behind you ! "

He stepped past and laid his hand upon the glossy neck of the thoroughbred.

" The horse ! " cried both the Colonel and myself.

" Yes, the horse. And it may lessen his guilt if I say that it was done in self-defence, and that John Straker was a man who was entirely unworthy of your confidence. But there goes the bell ; and as I stand to win a little on this next race, I shall defer a more lengthy explanation until a more fitting time."

We had the corner of a Pullman car to ourselves that evening as we whirled back to London, and I fancy that the journey was a short one to Colonel Ross as well as to myself, as we listened to our companion's narrative of the events which had occurred at the Dartmoor training stables upon that Monday night, and the means by which he had unravelled them.

" I confess," said he, " that any theories which I had formed from the newspaper reports were entirely erroneous. And yet there were indications there, had they not been overlaid by other details which concealed their true import. I went to Devonshire with the conviction that Fitzroy Simpson was the true culprit, although, of course, I saw that the evidence against him was by no means complete.

" It was while I was in the carriage, just as we reached the trainer's house, that the immense significance of the curried mutton occurred to me. You may remember that I was distrait, and remained sitting after you had all alighted. I was marvelling in my own mind how I could possibly have overlooked so obvious a clue."

" I confess," said the Colonel, " that even now I cannot see how it helps us."

" It was the first link in my chain of reasoning. Powdered opium is by no means tasteless. The flavour is not disagreeable, but it is perceptible. Were it mixed with any ordinary dish, the eater would undoubtedly detect it, and would probably eat no more. A curry was exactly the medium which would disguise this taste. By no possible supposition could this stranger, Fitzroy Simpson, have caused curry to be served in the trainer's family that night, and it is surely too monstrous a coincidence to suppose that he happened to come along with powdered opium upon the very night when a dish happened to be served which would disguise the flavour. That is unthinkable. Therefore Simpson becomes eliminated from the case, and our attention centres upon Straker and his wife, the only two people who could have chosen curried mutton for supper that night. The opium was added after the dish was set aside for the stable boy, for the others had the same for supper with no ill effects. Which of them, then, had access to that dish without the maid seeing them ?

" Before deciding that question I had grasped the significance of the silence of the dog, for one true inference invariably suggests others. The Simpson incident had shown me that a dog was kept in the stables, and yet, though someone had been in and had fetched out a horse, he had not barked enough to arouse the two lads in the loft. Obviously the midnight visitor was someone whom the dog knew well.

" I was already convinced, or almost convinced, that John Straker went down to the stables in the dead of the night and took out Silver Blaze. For what purpose ? For a dishonest one, obviously, or why should he drug his own stable boy ? And yet I was at a loss to know why. There have been cases before now where trainers have made sure of great sums of money by laying against their own horses, through agents, and then prevented them from winning by fraud. Sometimes it is a pulling jockey. Sometimes it is some surer and subtler means. What was it here ? I hoped that the contents of his pockets might help me to form a conclusion.

" And they did so. You cannot have forgotten the singular knife which was found in the dead man's hand, a knife which certainly no sane man would choose for a weapon. It was, as Dr. Watson told us, a form of knife which is used for the most delicate operations known in surgery. And it was to be used for a delicate operation that night. You must know, with your wide experience of turf matters, Colonel Ross, that it is possible to make a slight nick upon the tendons of a horse's ham, and to do it subcutaneously so as to leave absolutely no trace. A horse so treated would develop a slight lameness which would be put down to a strain in exercise or a touch of rheumatism, but never to foul play."

" Villain ! Scoundrel ! " cried the Colonel.

" We have here the explanation of why John Straker wished to take the horse out on to the moor. So spirited a creature would have certainly roused the soundest of sleepers when it felt the prick of the knife. It was absolutely necessary to do it in the open air."

" I have been blind ! " cried the Colonel. " Of course, that was why he needed the candle, and struck the match."

" Undoubtedly. But in examining his belongings, I was fortunate enough to discover, not only the method of the crime, but even its motives. As a man of the world, Colonel, you know that men do not carry other people's bills about in their pockets. We have most of us quite enough to do to settle our own. I at once concluded that Straker was leading a double life, and keeping a second establishment. The nature of the bill showed that there was a lady in the case, and one who had expensive tastes. Liberal as you are with your servants, one hardly expects that they can buy twenty-guinea walking dresses for their women. I questioned Mrs. Straker as to the dress without her knowing it, and having satisfied myself that it had never reached her, I made a note of the milliner's address, and felt that by calling there with Straker's photograph, I could easily dispose of the mythical Darbyshire.

" From that time on all was plain. Straker had led out the horse to a hollow where his light would be invisible. Simpson, in his flight, had dropped his cravat, and Straker had picked it up with some idea, perhaps, that he might use it in securing the horse's leg. Once in the hollow he had got behind the horse, and had struck a light, but the creature, frightened at the sudden glare, and with the strange instinct of animals feeling that some mischief was intended, had lashed out, and the steel shoe had struck Straker full on the forehead. He had already, in spite of the rain, taken off his overcoat in order to do his delicate task, and so, as he fell, his knife gashed his thigh. Do I make it clear ? "

" Wonderful ! " cried the Colonel. " Wonderful ! You might have been there."

" My final shot was, I confess, a very long one. It

struck me that so astute a man as Straker would not
undertake this delicate tendon-nicking without a little
practice. What could he practise on ? My eyes fell
upon the sheep, and I asked a question which, rather to
my surprise, showed that my surmise was correct."

"You have made it perfectly clear, Mr. Holmes."

"When I returned to London I called upon the milliner, who at once recognized Straker as an excellent customer, of the name of Darbyshire, who had a very dashing
wife with a strong partiality for expensive dresses. I have
no doubt that this woman had plunged him over head and
ears in debt, and so led him into this miserable plot."

"You have explained all but one thing," cried the
Colonel. "Where was the horse ? "

"Ah, it bolted and was cared for by one of your neighbours. We must have an amnesty in that direction, I
think. This is Clapham Junction, if I am not mistaken,
and we shall be in Victoria in less than ten minutes. If
you care to smoke a cigar in our rooms, Colonel, I shall
be happy to give you any other details which might
interest you."

14. *The Yellow Face*

IN publishing these short sketches, based upon the
numerous cases which my companion's singular
gifts have made me the listener to, and eventually
the actor in some strange drama, it is only natural that
I should dwell rather upon his successes than upon his
failures. And this is not so much for the sake of his reputation, for indeed it was when he was at his wits' end that
his energy and his versatility were most admirable, but
because where he failed it happened so often that no one
else succeeded, and that the tale was left for ever without
a conclusion. Now and again, however, it chanced that
even when he erred the truth was still discovered. I have
notes of some half-dozen cases of the kind, of which the
affair of the second stain, and that which I am now about

to recount are the two which present the strongest features of interest.

Sherlock Holmes was a man who seldom took exercise for exercise's sake. Few men were capable of greater muscular effort, and he was undoubtedly one of the finest boxers of his weight that I have ever seen ; but he looked upon aimless bodily exertion as a waste of energy, and he seldom bestirred himself save where there was some professional object to be served. Then he was absolutely untiring and indefatigable. That he should have kept himself in training under such circumstances is remarkable, but his diet was usually of the sparest, and his habits were simple to the verge of austerity. Save for the occasional use of cocaine he had no vices, and he only turned to the drug as a protest against the monotony of existence when cases were scanty and the papers uninteresting.

One day in early spring he had so far relaxed as to go for a walk with me in the Park, where the first faint shoots of green were breaking out upon the elms, and the sticky spearheads of the chestnuts were just beginning to burst into their five-fold leaves. For two hours we rambled about together, in silence for the most part, as befits two men who know each other intimately. It was nearly five before we were back in Baker Street once more.

" Beg pardon, sir," said our page-boy, as he opened the door ; " there's been a gentleman here asking for you, sir."

Holmes glanced reproachfully at me. " So much for afternoon walks ! " said he. " Has this gentleman gone, then ? "

" Yes, sir."

" Didn't you ask him in ? "

" Yes, sir ; he came in."

" How long did he wait ? "

" Half an hour, sir. He was a very restless gentleman, sir, a-walkin' and a-stampin' all the time he was here. I was waitin' outside the door, sir, and I could hear him.

334

At last he goes out into the passage and he cries : ' Is that man never goin' to come ? ' Those were his very words, sir. ' You'll only need to wait a little longer,' says I. ' Then I'll wait in the open air, for I feel half choked,' says he. ' I'll be back before long,' and with that he ups and he outs, and all I could say wouldn't hold him back."

" Well, well, you did your best," said Holmes, as we walked into our room. " It's very annoying though, Watson. I was badly in need of a case, and this looks, from the man's impatience, as if it were of importance. Halloa ! that's not your pipe on the table ! He must have left his behind him. A nice old briar, with a good long stem of what the tobacconists call amber. I wonder how many real amber mouthpieces there are in London. Some people think a fly in it is a sign. Why, it is quite a branch of trade, the putting of sham flies into the sham amber. Well, he must have been disturbed in his mind to leave a pipe behind him which he evidently values highly."

" How do you know that he values it highly ? " I asked.

" Well, I should put the original cost of the pipe at seven-and-sixpence. Now it has, you see, been twice mended : once in the wooden stem and once in the amber. Each of these mends, done, as you observe, with silver bands, must have cost more than the pipe did originally. The man must value the pipe highly when he prefers to patch it up rather than buy a new one with the same money."

" Anything else ? " I asked, for Holmes was turning the pipe about in his hand and staring at it in his peculiar pensive way.

He held it up and tapped on it with his long, thin forefinger as a professor might who was lecturing on a bone.

" Pipes are occasionally of extraordinary interest," said he. " Nothing has more individuality save, perhaps, watches and bootlaces. The indications here, however, are neither very marked nor very important. The owner is obviously a muscular man, left-handed, with an excellent set of teeth, careless in his habits, and with no need to practise economy."

My friend threw out the information in a very off-hand way, but I saw that he cocked his eye at me to see if I had followed his reasoning.

" You think a man must be well-to-do if he smokes a seven-shilling pipe ? " said I.

" This is Grosvenor mixture at eightpence an ounce," Holmes answered, knocking a little out on his palm. " As he might get an excellent smoke for half the price, he has no need to practise economy."

" And the other points ? "

" He has been in the habit of lighting his pipe at lamps and gas-jets. You can see that it is quite charred all down one side. Of course, a match could not have done that. Why should a man hold a match to the side of his pipe ? But you cannot light it at a lamp without getting the bowl charred. And it is on the right side of the pipe. From that I gather that he is a left-handed man. You hold your own pipe to the lamp, and see how naturally you, being right-handed, hold the left side to the flame. You might do it once the other way, but not as a constancy. This has always been held so. Then he has bitten through his amber. It takes a muscular, energetic fellow, and one with a good set of teeth, to do that. But if I am not mistaken I hear him upon the stair, so we shall have something more interesting than his pipe to study."

An instant later our door opened, and a tall young man entered the room. He was well but quietly dressed in a dark-grey suit, and carried a brown wide-awake in his hand. I should have put him at about thirty, though he was really some years older.

" I beg your pardon," said he, with some embarrassment ; " I suppose I should have knocked. Yes, of course I should have knocked. The fact is that I am a little upset, and you must put it all down to that." He

336

passed his hand over his forehead like a man who is half dazed, and then fell, rather than sat, down upon a chair.

" I can see that you have not slept for a night or two," said Holmes, in his easy, genial way. " That tries a man's nerves more than work, and more even than pleasure. May I ask how I can help you ? "

" I wanted your advice, sir. I don't know what to do, and my whole life seems to have gone to pieces."

" You wish to employ me as a consulting detective ? "

" Not that only. I want your opinion as a judicious man—as a man of the world. I want to know what I ought to do next. I hope to God you'll be able to tell me."

He spoke in little, sharp, jerky outbursts, and it seemed to me that to speak at all was very painful to him, and that his will all through was overriding his inclinations.

" It's a very delicate thing," said he. " One does not like to speak of one's domestic affairs to strangers. It seems dreadful to discuss the conduct of one's wife with two men whom I have never seen before. It's horrible to have to do it. But I've got to the end of my tether, and I must have advice."

" My dear Mr. Grant Munro——" began Holmes.

Our visitor sprang from his chair. " What ! " he cried. " You know my name ? "

" If you wish to preserve your *incognito*," said Holmes, smiling, " I should suggest that you cease to write your name upon the lining of your hat, or else that you turn the crown towards the person whom you are addressing. I was about to say that my friend and I have listened to many strange secrets in this room, and that we have had the good fortune to bring peace to many troubled souls. I trust that we may do as much for you. Might I beg you, as time may prove to be of importance, to furnish me with the facts of your case without further delay ? "

Our visitor again passed his hand over his forehead as if he found it bitterly hard. From every gesture and expression I could see that he was a reserved, self-contained man, with a dash of pride in his nature, more likely to hide his wounds than to expose them. Then suddenly, with a fierce gesture of his closed hand, like one who throws reserve to the winds, he began.

" The facts are these, Mr. Holmes," said he. " I am a married man, and have been so for three years. During that time my wife and I have loved each other as fondly, and lived as happily, as any two that ever were joined. We have not had a difference, not one, in thought, or word, or deed. And now, since last Monday, there has suddenly sprung up a barrier between us, and I find that there is something in her life and in her thoughts of which I know as little as if she were the woman who brushes by me in the street. We are estranged, and I want to know why.

" Now there is one thing I want to impress upon you before I go any further, Mr. Holmes : Effie loves me. Don't let there be any mistake about that. She loves me with her whole heart and soul, and never more than now. I know it, I feel it. I don't want to argue about that. A man can tell easily enough when a woman loves him. But there's this secret between us, and we can never be the same until it is cleared."

" Kindly let me have the facts, Mr. Munro," said Holmes, with some impatience.

" I'll tell you what I know about Effie's history. She was a widow when I met her first, though quite young— only twenty-five. Her name then was Mrs. Hebron. She went out to America when she was young and lived in the town of Atlanta, where she married this Hebron, who was a lawyer with a good practice. They had one child, but the yellow fever broke out badly in the place, and both husband and child died of it. I have seen his death certificate. This sickened her of America, and she came back to live with a maiden aunt at Pinner, in Middlesex. I may mention that her husband had left her comfortably off, and that she had a capital of about four thousand five hundred pounds, which had been so well invested by him that it returned an average of 7 per cent. She had only been six months at Pinner when I met her ; we fell in love with each other, and we married a few weeks afterwards.

" I am a hop merchant myself, and as I have an income of seven or eight hundred, we found ourselves comfortably off, and took a nice eighty-pound-a-year villa at Norbury. Our little place was very countrified, considering that it is so close to town. We had an inn and two houses a little above us, and a single cottage at the other side of the field which faces us, and except those there were no houses until you get half-way to the station. My business took me into town at certain seasons, but in summer I had less to do, and then in our country home my wife and I were just as happy as could be wished. I tell you that there never was a shadow between us until this accursed affair began.

" There's one thing I ought to tell you before I go further. When we married, my wife made over all her property to me—rather against my will, for I saw how awkward it would be if my business affairs went wrong. However, she would have it so, and it was done. Well, about six weeks ago she came to me.

" ' Jack,' said she, ' when you took my money you said that if ever I wanted any I was to ask you for it.'

" ' Certainly,' said I, ' it's all your own.'

" ' Well,' said she, ' I want a hundred pounds.'

" I was a bit staggered at this, for I had imagined it was simply a new dress or something of the kind that she was after.

" ' What on earth for ? ' I asked.

" ' Oh,' said she, in her playful way, ' you said that you were only my banker, and bankers never ask questions, you know.'

" ' If you really mean it, of course you shall have the money,' said I.

" ' Oh, yes, I really mean it.'

" ' And you won't tell me what you want it for ? '

" ' Some day, perhaps, but not just at present, Jack.'

" So I had to be content with that, though it was the first time that there had ever been any secret between us. I gave her a cheque, and I never thought any more of the matter. It may have nothing to do with what came afterwards, but I thought it only right to mention it.

" Well, I told you just now that there is a cottage not far from our house. There is just a field between us, but to reach it you have to go along the road and then turn down a lane. Just beyond it is a nice little grove of Scotch firs, and I used to be very fond of strolling down there, for trees are always neighbourly kinds of things. The cottage had been standing empty this eight months, and it was a pity, for it was a pretty two-storied place, with an old-fashioned porch and honeysuckle about it. I have stood many a time and thought what a neat little homestead it would make.

" Well, last Monday evening I was taking a stroll down that way, when I met an empty van coming up the lane, and saw a pile of carpets and things lying about on the grass-plot beside the porch. It was clear that the cottage had at last been let. I walked past it, and then stopping, as an idle man might, I ran my eye over it, and wondered what sort of folk they were who had come to live so near us. And as I looked I suddenly became aware that a face was watching me out of one of the upper windows.

" I don't know what there was about that face, Mr. Holmes, but it seemed to send a chill right down my back. I was some little way off, so that I could not make out the features, but there was something unnatural and inhuman about the face. That was the impression I had, and I moved quickly forwards to get a nearer view of the person who was watching me. But as I did so the face suddenly disappeared, so suddenly that it seemed to have been plucked away into the darkness of the room. I stood for five minutes thinking the business over, and trying to analyse my impressions. I could not tell if the face was that of a man or a woman. But the colour was what

impressed me most. It was of a livid dead yellow, and
with something set and rigid about it, which was shock-
ingly unnatural. So disturbed was I, that I determined to
see a little more of the new inmates of the cottage. I
approached and knocked at the door, which was instantly
opened by a tall, gaunt woman, with a harsh, forbidding
face.

" ' What may you be wantin' ? ' she asked, in a northern
accent.

" ' I am your neighbour over yonder,' said I, nodding
towards my house. ' I see that you have only just moved
in, so I thought that if I could be of any help to you in
any——'

" ' Aye, we'll just ask ye when we want ye,' said she,
and shut the door in my face. Annoyed at the churlish
rebuff, I turned my back and walked home. All the
evening, though I tried to think of other things, my mind
would still turn to the apparition at the window and the
rudeness of the woman. I determined to say nothing
about the former to my wife, for she is a nervous, highly
strung woman, and I had no wish that she should share
the unpleasant impression which had been produced upon
myself. I remarked to her, however, before I fell asleep
that the cottage was now occupied, to which she returned
no reply.

" I am usually an extremely sound sleeper. It has been
a standing jest in the family that nothing could ever wake
me during the night ; and yet somehow on that particular night, whether it may have been the slight excitement produced by my little adventure or not, I know not,
but I slept much more lightly than usual. Half in my
dreams I was dimly conscious that something was going
on in the room, and gradually became aware that my
wife had dressed herself and was slipping on her mantle
and her bonnet. My lips were parted to murmur out
some sleepy words of surprise or remonstrance at this
untimely preparation, when suddenly my half-opened
eyes fell upon her face, illuminated by the candle-light,

and astonishment held me dumb. She wore an expression such as I had never seen before—such as I should have thought her incapable of assuming. She was deadly pale, and breathing fast, glancing furtively towards the bed, as she fastened her mantle, to see if she had disturbed me. Then, thinking that I was still asleep, she slipped noiselessly from the room, and an instant later I heard a sharp creaking, which could only come from the hinges of the front door. I sat up in bed and rapped my knuckles against the rail to make certain that I was truly awake. Then I took my watch from under the pillow. It was three in the morning. What on this earth could my wife be doing out on the country road at three in the morning ?

" I had sat for about twenty minutes turning the thing over in my mind and trying to find some possible explanation. The more I thought the more extraordinary and inexplicable did it appear. I was still puzzling over it when I heard the door gently close again and her footsteps coming up the stairs.

" ' Where in the world have you been, Effie ? ' I asked, as she entered.

" She gave a violent start and a kind of gasping cry when I spoke, and that cry and start troubled me more than all the rest, for there was something indescribably guilty about them. My wife had always been a woman of a frank, open nature, and it gave me a chill to see her slinking into her own room, and crying out and wincing when her own husband spoke to her.

" ' You awake, Jack ? ' she cried, with a nervous laugh. ' Why, I thought that nothing could awaken you.'

" ' Where have you been ? ' I asked, more sternly.

" ' I don't wonder that you are surprised,' said she, and I could see that her fingers were trembling as she undid the fastenings of her mantle. ' Why, I never remember having done such a thing in my life before. The fact is, that I felt as though I were choking, and had a perfect longing for a breath of fresh air. I really think that I

342

should have fainted if I had not gone out. I stood at the door for a few minutes, and now I am quite myself again.'

" All the time that she was telling me this story she never once looked in my direction, and her voice was quite unlike her usual tones. It was evident to me that she was saying what was false. I said nothing in reply, but turned my face to the wall, sick at heart, with my mind filled with a thousand venomous doubts and suspicions. What was it that my wife was concealing from me ? Where had she been during that strange expedition ? I felt that I should have no peace until I knew, and yet I shrank from asking her again after once she had told me what was false. All the rest of the night I tossed and tumbled, framing theory after theory, each more unlikely than the last.

" I should have gone to the City that day, but I was too perturbed in my mind to be able to pay attention to business matters. My wife seemed to be as upset as myself, and I could see from the little questioning glances which she kept shooting at me, that she understood that I disbelieved her statement, and that she was at her wits' ends what to do. We hardly exchanged a word during breakfast, and immediately afterwards I went out for a walk, that I might think the matter over in the fresh morning air.

" I went as far as the Crystal Palace, spent an hour in the grounds, and was back in Norbury by one o'clock. It happened that my way took me past the cottage, and I stopped for an instant to look at the windows and to see if I could catch a glimpse of the strange face which had stared out at me on the day before. As I stood there imagine my surprise, Mr. Holmes, when the door suddenly opened and my wife walked out !

" I was struck dumb with astonishment at the sight of her, but my emotions were nothing to those which showed themselves upon her face when our eyes met. She seemed for an instant to wish to shrink back inside the house again, and then, seeing how useless all concealment must be, she came forward with a very white face and frightened eyes which belied the smile upon her lips.

" ' Oh, Jack ! ' she said, ' I have just been in to see if I can be of any assistance to our new neighbours. Why do you look at me like that, Jack ? You are not angry with me ? '

" ' So,' said I, ' this is where you went during the night ? '

" ' What do you mean ? ' she cried.

" ' You came here. I am sure of it. Who are these people that you should visit them at such an hour ? '

" ' I have not been here before.'

" ' How can you tell me what you know is false ? ' I cried. ' Your very voice changes as you speak. When have I ever had a secret from you ? I shall enter that cottage, and I shall probe the matter to the bottom.'

" ' No, no, Jack, for God's sake ! ' she gasped, in incontrollable emotion. Then as I approached the door, she seized my sleeve and pulled me back with convulsive strength.

" ' I implore you not to do this, Jack,' she cried. ' I swear that I will tell you everything some day, but nothing but misery can come of it if you enter that cottage.' Then, as I tried to shake her off, she clung to me in a frenzy of entreaty.

" ' Trust me, Jack ! ' she cried. ' Trust me only this once. You will never have cause to regret it. You know that I would not have a secret from you if it were not for your own sake. Our whole lives are at stake on this. If you come home with me all will be well. If you force your way into that cottage, all is over between us.'

" There was such earnestness, such despair, in her manner that her words arrested me, and I stood irresolute before the door.

" ' I will trust you on one condition, and on one condition only,' said I at last. ' It is that this mystery comes to an end from now. You are at liberty to preserve your secret, but you must promise me that there shall be no more nightly visits, no more doings which are kept from my knowledge. I am willing to forget those which are passed if you will promise that there shall be no more in the future.'

" ' I was sure that you would trust me,' she cried, with a great sigh of relief. ' It shall be just as you wish. Come away, oh, come away up to the house ! ' Still plucking at my sleeve she led me away from the cottage. As we went I glanced back, and there was that yellow, livid face watching us out of the upper window. What link could there be between that creature and my wife ? Or how could the coarse, rough woman whom I had seen the day before be connected with her ? It was a strange puzzle, and yet I knew that my mind could never know ease again until I had solved it.

" For two days after this I stayed at home, and my wife appeared to abide loyally by our engagement, for, as far as I know, she never stirred out of the house. On the third day, however, I had ample evidence that her solemn promise was not enough to hold her back from this secret influence which drew her away from her husband and her duty.

" I had gone into town on that day, but I returned by the 2.40 instead of the 3.36, which is my usual train. As I entered the house the maid ran into the hall with a startled face.

" ' Where is your mistress ? ' I asked.

" ' I think that she has gone out for a walk,' she answered.

" My mind was instantly filled with suspicion. I rushed upstairs to make sure that she was not in the house. As I did so I happened to glance out of one of the upper windows, and saw the maid with whom I had just been speaking running across the field in the direction of the cottage. Then, of course, I saw exactly what it all meant. My wife had gone over there and had asked the servant to call her if I should return. Tingling with anger, I rushed down and strode across, determined to end the matter once and for ever. I saw my wife and the maid hurrying back together along the lane, but I did not stop to speak with them. In the cottage lay the secret which was casting a shadow over my life. I vowed that, come what might, it should be a secret no longer. I did not even knock when I reached it, but turned the handle and rushed into the passage.

" It was all still and quiet upon the ground-floor. In the kitchen a kettle was singing on the fire, and a large black cat lay coiled up in a basket, but there was no sign of the woman whom I had seen before. I ran into the other room, but it was equally deserted. Then I rushed up the stairs, but only to find two other rooms empty and deserted at the top. There was no one at all in the whole house. The furniture and pictures were of the most common and vulgar description, save in the one chamber at the window of which I had seen the strange face. That was comfortable and elegant, and all my suspicions rose into a fierce, bitter blaze when I saw that on the mantelpiece stood a full-length photograph of my wife, which had been taken at my request only three months ago.

" I stayed long enough to make certain that the house was absolutely empty. Then I left it, feeling a weight at my heart such as I had never had before. My wife came out into the hall as I entered my house, but I was too hurt and angry to speak with her, and pushing past her I made my way into my study. She followed me, however, before I could close the door.

" ' I am sorry that I broke my promise, Jack,' said she, ' but if you knew all the circumstances I am sure you would forgive me.'

" ' Tell me everything, then,' said I.

" ' I cannot, Jack, I cannot ! ' she cried.

" ' Until you tell me who it is that has been living in that cottage, and who it is to whom you have given that photograph, there can never be any confidence between us,' said I, and breaking away from her I left the house. That was yesterday, Mr. Holmes, and I have not seen her since, nor do I know anything more about this strange business. It is the first shadow that has come between us, and it has so shaken me that I do not know what I should do for the best. Suddenly this morning it occurred to me that you were the man to advise me, so I have hurried to you now, and I place myself unreservedly in your hands. If there is any point which I have not made clear, pray question me about it. But above all tell me quickly what I have to do, for this misery is more than I can bear."

Holmes and I had listened with the utmost interest to this extraordinary statement, which had been delivered in the jerky, broken fashion of a man who is under the influence of extreme emotion. My companion sat silent now for some time, with his chin upon his hand, lost in thought.

" Tell me," said he at last, " could you swear that this was a man's face which you saw at the window ? "

" Each time that I saw it I was some distance away from it, so that it is impossible for me to say."

" You appear, however, to have been disagreeably impressed by it."

" It seemed to be of an unnatural colour, and to have a strange rigidity about the features. When I approached, it vanished with a jerk."

" How long is it since your wife asked you for a hundred pounds ? "

" Nearly two months."

" Have you ever seen a photograph of her first husband ? "

" No ; there was a great fire at Atlanta very shortly after his death, and all her papers were destroyed."

" And yet she had a certificate of death. You say that you saw it ? "

" Yes, she got a duplicate after the fire."

" Did you ever meet anyone who knew her in America ? "

" No."

347

" Did she ever talk of revisiting the place ? "

" No."

" Or get letters from it ? "

" Not to my knowledge."

" Thank you. I should like to think over the matter a little now. If the cottage is permanently deserted we may have some difficulty ; if on the other hand, as I fancy is more likely, the inmates were warned of your coming, and left before you entered yesterday, then they may be back now, and we should clear it all up easily. Let me advise you, then, to return to Norbury and to examine the windows of the cottage again. If you have reason to believe that it is inhabited do not force your way in, but send a wire to my friend and me. We shall be with you within an hour of receiving it, and we shall then very soon get to the bottom of the business."

" And if it is still empty ? "

" In that case I shall come out to-morrow and talk it over with you. Good-bye, and above all things do not fret until you know that you really have a cause for it."

" I am afraid that this is a bad business, Watson," said my companion, as he returned after accompanying Mr. Grant Munro to the door. " What do you make of it ? "

" It had an ugly sound," I answered.

" Yes. There's blackmail in it, or I am much mistaken."

" And who is the blackmailer ? "

" Well, it must be this creature who lives in the only comfortable room in the place, and has her photograph above his fireplace. Upon my word, Watson, there is something very attractive about that livid face at the window, and I would not have missed the case for worlds."

" You have a theory ? "

" Yes, a provisional one. But I shall be surprised if it does not turn out to be correct. This woman's first husband is in that cottage."

" Why do you think so ? "

" How else can we explain her frenzied anxiety that

348

her second one should not enter it ? The facts, as I read them, are something like this : This woman was married in America. Her husband developed some hateful qualities, or, shall we say, that he contracted some loathsome disease, and became a leper or an imbecile. She fled from him at last, returned to England, changed her name, and started her life, as she thought, afresh. She had been married three years, and believed that her position was quite secure—having shown her husband the death certificate of some man whose name she had assumed—when suddenly her whereabouts was discovered by her first husband, or, we may suppose, by some unscrupulous woman who had attached herself to the invalid. They write to the wife and threaten to come and expose her. She asks for a hundred pounds and endeavours to buy them off. They come in spite of it, and when the husband mentions casually to the wife that there are new-comers in the cottage, she knows in some way that they are her pursuers. She waits until her husband is asleep, and then she rushes down to endeavour to persuade them to leave her in peace. Having no success, she goes again next morning, and her husband meets her, as he has told us, as she came out. She promises him then not to go there again, but two days afterwards, the hope of getting rid of those dreadful neighbours is too strong for her, and she makes another attempt, taking down with her the photograph which had probably been demanded from her. In the midst of this interview the maid rushes in to say that the master has come home, on which the wife, knowing that he would come straight down to the cottage, hurries the inmates out at the back door, into that grove of fir trees probably which was mentioned as standing near. In this way he finds the place deserted. I shall be very much surprised, however, if it is still so when he reconnoitres it this evening. What do you think of my theory ? "

" It is all surmise."

" But at least it covers all the facts. When new facts

come to our knowledge which cannot be covered by it, it will be time enough to reconsider it. At present we can do nothing until we have a fresh message from our friend at Norbury."

But we had not very long to wait. It came just as we had finished our tea. " The cottage is still tenanted," it said. " Have seen the face again at the window. I'll meet the seven o'clock train, and take no steps until you arrive."

He was waiting on the platform when we stepped out, and we could see in the light of the station lamps that he was very pale, and quivering with agitation.

" They are still there, Mr. Holmes," said he, laying his hand upon my friend's sleeve. " I saw lights in the cottage as I came down. We shall settle it now, once and for all."

" What is your plan, then ? " asked Holmes, as we walked down the dark, tree-lined road.

" I am going to force my way in and see for myself who is in the house. I wish you both to be there as witnesses."

" You are quite determined to do this, in spite of your wife's warning that it is better that you should not solve the mystery ? "

" Yes, I am determined."

" Well, I think that you are in the right. Any truth is better than indefinite doubt. We had better go up at once. Of course, legally, we are putting ourselves hopelessly in the wrong, but I think that it is worth it."

It was a very dark night and a thin rain began to fall as we turned from the high-road into a narrow lane, deeply rutted, with edges on either side. Mr. Grant Munro pushed impatiently forward, however, and we stumbled after him as best we could.

" There are the lights of my house," he murmured, pointing to a glimmer among the trees, " and here is the cottage which I am going to enter."

We turned a corner in the lane as he spoke, and there

was the building close beside us. A yellow bar falling across the black foreground showed that the door was not quite closed, and one window in the upper story was brightly illuminated. As we looked we saw a dark blur moving across the blind.

"There is that creature," cried Grant Munro ; " you can see for yourselves that someone is there. Now follow me, and we shall soon know all."

We approached the door, but suddenly a woman appeared out of the shadow and stood in the golden track of the lamp-light. I could not see her face in the darkness, but her arms were thrown out in an attitude of entreaty.

"For God's sake, don't, Jack ! " she cried. " I had a presentiment that you would come this evening. Think better of it, dear ! Trust me again, and you will never have cause to regret it."

" I have trusted you too long, Effie ! " he cried, sternly. " Leave go of me ! I must pass you. My friends and I are going to settle this matter once and for ever." He pushed her to one side and we followed closely after him. As he threw the door open an elderly woman ran out in front of him and tried to bar his passage, but he thrust her back, and an instant afterwards we were all upon the stairs. Grant Munro rushed into the lighted room at the top, and we entered it at his heels.

It was a cosy, well-furnished apartment, with two candles burning upon the table and two upon the mantel-piece. In the corner, stooping over a desk, there sat what appeared to be a little girl. Her face was turned away as we entered, but we could see that she was dressed in a red frock, and that she had long white gloves on. As she whisked round to us I gave a cry of surprise and horror. The face which she turned towards us was of the strangest livid tint, and the features were absolutely devoid of any expression. An instant later the mystery was explained. Holmes, with a laugh, passed his hand behind the child's ear, a mask peeled off from her countenance, and there was a little coal-black negress with all her white teeth flashing in amusement at our amazed faces. I burst out laughing out of sympathy with her merriment, but Grant Munro stood staring, with his hand clutching at his throat.

" My God ! " he cried, " what can be the meaning of this ? "

" I will tell you the meaning of it," cried the lady, sweeping into the room with a proud, set face. " You have forced me against my own judgment to tell you, and now we must both make the best of it. My husband died at Atlanta. My child survived."

" Your child ! "

She drew a large silver locket from her bosom. " You have never seen this open."

" I understood that it did not open."

She touched a spring, and the front hinged back. There was a portrait within of a man, strikingly handsome and intelligent, but bearing unmistakable signs upon his features of his African descent.

" That is John Hebron, of Atlanta," said the lady, " and a nobler man never walked the earth. I cut myself off from my race in order to wed him ; but never once while he lived did I for one instant regret it. It was our misfortune that our only child took after his people rather than mine. It is often so in such matches, and little Lucy is darker far than ever her father was. But, dark or fair, she is my own dear little girlie, and her mother's pet." The little creature ran across at the words and nestled up against the lady's dress.

" When I left her in America," she continued, " it was only because her health was weak, and the change might have done her harm. She was given to the care of a faithful Scotchwoman who had once been our servant. Never for an instant did I dream of disowning her as my child. But when chance threw you in my way, Jack, and I learned to love you, I feared to tell you about my child. God forgive me, I feared that I should lose you, and I had not the courage to tell you. I had to choose between you, and in my weakness I turned away from my own little girl. For three years I have kept her existence a secret from you, but I heard from the nurse, and I knew that all was well with her. At last, however, there came an overwhelming desire to see the child once more. I struggled against it, but in vain. Though I knew the danger I determined to have the child over, if it were but for a few weeks. I sent a hundred pounds to the nurse, and I gave her instructions about this cottage, so that she might come as a neighbour without my appearing to be in any way connected with her. I pushed my precautions so far as to order her to keep the child in the house during the daytime, and to cover up her little face and hands, so that even those who might see her at the window should not gossip about there being a black child in the neighbourhood. If I had been less cautious I might have been more wise, but I was half crazy with fear lest you should learn the truth.

" It was you who told me first that the cottage was occupied. I should have waited for the morning, but I could not sleep for excitement, and so at last I slipped out, knowing how difficult it is to awaken you. But you saw me go, and that was the beginning of my troubles. Next day you had my secret at your mercy, but you nobly refrained from pursuing your advantage. Three days later, however, the nurse and child only just escaped from the back door as you rushed in at the front one. And now to-night you at last know all, and I ask you what is to become of us, my child and me ? " She clasped her hands and waited for an answer.

It was a long two minutes before Grant Munro broke the silence, and when his answer came it was one of which I love to think. He lifted the little child, kissed her, and then, still carrying her, he held his other hand out to his wife, and turned towards the door.

" We can talk it over more comfortably at home," said he. " I am not a very good man, Effie, but I think that

I am a better one than you have given me credit for being."

Holmes and I followed them down to the lane, and my friend plucked at my sleeve as we came out. " I think," said he, " that we shall be of more use in London than in Norbury."

Not another word did he say of the case until late that night when he was turning away, with his lighted candle, for his bedroom.

" Watson," said he, " if it should ever strike you that I am getting a little over-confident in my powers, or giving less pains to a case than it deserves, kindly whisper ' Norbury ' in my ear, and I shall be infinitely obliged to you."

15. *The Stockbroker's Clerk*

SHORTLY after my marriage I had bought a connection in the Paddington district. Old Mr. Farquhar, from whom I purchased it, had at one time an excellent general practice, but his age, and an affliction of the nature of St. Vitus' dance from which he suffered, had very much thinned it. The public, not unnaturally, goes upon the principle that he who would heal others must himself be whole, and looks askance at the curative powers of the man whose own case is beyond the reach of his drugs. Thus, as my predecessor weakened his practice declined, until when I purchased it from him it had sunk from twelve hundred to little more than three hundred a year. I had confidence, however, in my own youth and energy, and was convinced that in a very few years the concern would be as flourishing as ever.

For three months after taking over the practice I was kept very closely at work, and saw little of my friend Sherlock Holmes, for I was too busy to visit Baker Street, and he seldom went anywhere himself save upon professional business. I was surprised, therefore, when one morning in June, as I sat reading the *British Medical Journal* after breakfast, I heard a ring at the bell followed by the high, somewhat strident, tones of my old companion's voice.

"Ah, my dear Watson," said he, striding into the room, "I am very delighted to see you. I trust that Mrs. Watson has entirely recovered from all the little excitements connected with our adventure of the ' Sign of Four ' ? "

"Thank you, we are both very well," said I, shaking him warmly by the hand.

"And I hope also," he continued, sitting down in the rocking-chair, "that the cares of medical practice have not entirely obliterated the interest which you used to take in our little deductive problems."

"On the contrary," I answered ; "it was only last night that I was looking over my old notes and classifying some of our past results."

"I trust that you don't consider your collection closed ? "

"Not at all. I should wish nothing better than to have some more of such experiences."

"To-day, for example ? "

"Yes ; to-day, if you like."

"And as far off as Birmingham ? "

"Certainly, if you wish it."

"And the practice ? "

"I do my neighbour's when he goes. He is always ready to work off the debt."

"Ha ! Nothing could be better ! " said Holmes, leaning back in his chair and looking keenly at me from under his half-closed lids. "I perceive that you have been unwell lately. Summer colds are always a little trying."

"I was confined to the house by a severe chill for three days last week. I thought, however, that I had cast off every trace of it."

"So you have. You look remarkably robust."

"How, then, did you know of it ? "

"My dear fellow, you know my methods."

"You deduced it, then ? "

"Certainly."

" And from what ? "

" From your slippers."

I glanced down at the new patent leathers which I was wearing. " How on earth—— ? " I began, but Holmes answered my question before it was asked.

" Your slippers are new," he said. " You could not have had them more than a few weeks. The soles which you are at this moment presenting to me are slightly scorched. For a moment I thought they might have got wet and been burned in the drying. But near the instep there is a small circular wafer of paper with the shopman's hieroglyphics upon it. Damp would of course have removed this. You had then been sitting with your feet outstretched to the fire, which a man would hardly do even in so wet a June as this if he were in his full health."

Like all Holmes' reasoning, the thing seemed simplicity itself when it was once explained. He read the thought upon my features, and his smile had a tinge of bitterness.

" I am afraid that I rather give myself away when I explain," said he. " Results without causes are much more impressive. You are ready to come to Birmingham, then ? "

" Certainly. What is the case ? "

" You shall hear it all in the train. My client is outside in a four-wheeler. Can you come at once ? "

" In an instant." I scribbled a note to my neighbour, rushed upstairs to explain the matter to my wife, and joined Holmes upon the doorstep.

" Your neighbour is a doctor ? " said he, nodding at the brass plate.

" Yes. He bought a practice, as I did."

" An old-established one ? "

" Just the same as mine. Both have been ever since the houses were built."

" Ah, then you got hold of the better of the two."

" I think I did. But how do you know ? "

" By the steps, my boy. Yours are worn three inches

deeper than his. But this gentleman in the cab is my client, Mr. Hall Pycroft. Allow me to introduce you to him. Whip your horse up, cabby, for we have only just time to catch our train."

The man whom I found myself facing was a well-built, fresh-complexioned young fellow with a frank, honest face and a slight, crisp, yellow moustache. He wore a very shiny top-hat and a neat suit of sober black, which made him look what he was—a smart young City man, of the class who have been labelled Cockneys, but who give us our crack Volunteer regiments, and who turn out more fine athletes and sportsmen than any body of men in these islands. His round, ruddy face was naturally full of cheeriness, but the corners of his mouth seemed to me to be pulled down in a half-comical distress. It was not, however, until we were all in a first-class carriage and well started upon our journey to Birmingham, that I was able to learn what the trouble was which had driven him to Sherlock Holmes.

" We have a clear run here of seventy minutes," Holmes remarked. " I want you, Mr. Hall Pycroft, to tell my friend your very interesting experience exactly as you have told it to me, or with more detail if possible. It will be of use to me to hear the succession of events again. It is a case, Watson, which may prove to have something in it, or may prove to have nothing, but which at least presents those unusual and *outré* features which are as dear to you as they are to me. Now, Mr. Pycroft, I shall not interrupt you again."

Our young companion looked at me with a twinkle in his eye.

" The worst of the story is," said he, " that I show myself up as such a confounded fool. Of course, it may work out all right, and I don't see that I could have done otherwise ; but if I have lost my crib and get nothing in exchange, I shall feel what a soft Johnny I have been. I'm not very good at telling a story, Dr. Watson, but it is like this with me.

"I used to have a billet at Coxon & Woodhouse, of Drapers' Gardens, but they were let in early in the spring through the Venezuelan loan, as no doubt you remember, and came a nasty cropper. I had been with them five years, and old Coxon gave me a ripping good testimonial when the smash came ; but, of course, we clerks were all turned adrift, the twenty-seven of us. I tried here and tried there, but there were lots of other chaps on the same lay as myself, and it was a perfect frost for a long time. I had been taking three pounds a week at Coxon's, and I had saved about seventy of them, but I soon worked my way through that and out at the other end. I was fairly at the end of my tether at last, and could hardly find the stamps to answer the advertisements or the envelopes to stick them to. I had worn out my boots padding up office stairs, and I seemed just as far from getting a billet as ever.

"At last I saw a vacancy at Mawson & Williams', the great stockbroking firm in Lombard Street. I dare say E.C. is not much in your line, but I can tell you that this is about the richest house in London. The advertisement was to be answered by letter only. I sent in my testimonial and application, but without the least hope of getting it. Back came an answer by return saying that if I would appear next Monday I might take over my new duties at once, provided that my appearance was satisfactory. No one knows how these things are worked. Some people say the manager just plunges his hand into the heap and takes the first that comes. Anyhow, it was my innings that time, and I don't ever wish to feel better pleased. The screw was a pound a week rise, and the duties just about the same as at Coxon's.

"And now I come to the queer part of the business. I was in diggings out Hampstead way—17 Potter's Terrace, was the address. Well, I was sitting doing a smoke that very evening after I had been promised the appointment, when up came my landlady with a card which had ' Arthur Pinner, financial agent,' printed upon it. I had never heard the name before, and could not imagine what he wanted with me, but of course I asked her to show him up. In he walked—a middle-sized, dark-haired, dark-eyed, black-bearded man, with a touch of the sheeny about his nose. He had a brisk kind of way with him and spoke sharply, like a man that knew the value of time.

" ' Mr. Hall Pycroft, I believe ? ' said he.

" ' Yes, sir,' I answered, and pushed a chair towards him.

" ' Lately engaged at Coxon & Woodhouse's ? '

" ' Yes, sir.'

" ' And now on the staff of Mawson's ? '

" ' Quite so.'

" ' Well,' said he. ' The fact is that I have heard some really extraordinary stories about your financial ability. You remember Parker who used to be Coxon's manager ? He can never say enough about it.'

" Of course I was pleased to hear this. I had always been pretty smart in the office, but I had never dreamed that I was talked about in the City in this fashion.

" ' You have a good memory ? ' said he.

" ' Pretty fair,' I answered, modestly.

" ' Have you kept in touch with the market while you have been out of work ? ' he asked.

" ' Yes ; I read the Stock Exchange List every morning.'

" ' Now, that shows real application ! ' he cried. ' That is the way to prosper ! You won't mind my testing you, will you ? Let me see ! How are Ayrshires ? '

" ' One hundred and five, to one hundred and five and a quarter.'

" ' And New Zealand Consolidated ? '

" ' A hundred and four.'

" ' And British Broken Hills ? '

" ' Seven to seven and six.'

" ' Wonderful ! ' he cried, with his hands up. ' This quite fits in with all that I had heard. My boy, my boy, you are very much too good to be a clerk at Mawson's ! '

" This outburst rather astonished me, as you can think. 'Well,' said I, ' other people don't think quite so much of me as you seem to do, Mr. Pinner. I had a hard enough fight to get this berth, and I am very glad to have it.'

" ' Pooh, man, you should soar above it. You are not in your true sphere. Now I'll tell you how it stands with me. What I have to offer is little enough when measured by your ability, but when compared with Mawson's it is light to dark. Let me see! When do you go to Mawson's ? '

" ' On Monday.'

" ' Ha ! ha ! I think I would risk a little sporting flutter that you don't go there at all.'

" ' Not go to Mawson's ? '

" ' No, sir. By that day you will be business manager of the Franco-Midland Hardware Company, Limited, with one hundred and thirty-four branches in the towns and villages of France, not counting one in Brussels and one in San Remo.'

" This took my breath away. ' I never heard of it,' said I.

" ' Very likely not. It has been kept very quiet, for the capital was all privately subscribed, and it is too good a thing to let the public into. My brother, Harry Pinner, is promoter, and joins the board after allotment as managing director. He knew that I was in the swim down here, and he asked me to pick up a good man cheap— a young, pushing man with plenty of snap about him. Parker spoke of you, and that brought me here to-night. We can only offer you a beggarly five hundred to start with——'

" ' Five hundred a year !' I shouted.

" ' Only that at the beginning, but you are to have an overriding commission of 1 per cent on all business done by your agents, and you may take my word for it that this will come to more than your salary.'

" ' But I know nothing about hardware.'

" ' Tut, my boy, you know about figures.'

" My head buzzed, and I could hardly sit still in the chair. But suddenly a little chill of doubt came over me.

" ' I must be frank with you,' said I. ' Mawson only gives me two hundred, but Mawson is safe. Now, really, I know so little about your company that——'

" ' Ah, smart, smart ! ' he cried, in a kind of ecstasy of delight. ' You are the very man for us ! You are not to be talked over, and quite right too. Now here's a note for a hundred pounds ; and if you think that we can do business you may just slip it into your pocket as an advance upon your salary.'

" ' That is very handsome,' said I. ' When shall I take over my new duties ? '

" ' Be in Birmingham to-morrow at one,' said he. ' I have a note in my pocket here which you will take to my brother. You will find him at 126B Corporation Street, where the temporary offices of the company are situated. Of course he must confirm your engagement, but between ourselves it will be all right.'

" ' Really, I hardly know how to express my gratitude, Mr. Pinner,' said I.

" ' Not at all, my boy. You have only got your deserts. There are one or two small things—mere formalities— which I must arrange with you. You have a bit of paper beside you there. Kindly write upon it, " I am perfectly willing to act as business manager to the Franco-Midland Hardware Company, Limited, at a minimum salary of £500." '

" I did as he asked, and he put the paper in his pocket.

" ' There is one other detail,' said he. ' What do you intend to do about Mawson's ? '

" I had forgotten all about Mawson's in my joy.

" ' I'll write and resign,' said I.

" ' Precisely what I don't want you to do. I had a row over you with Mawson's manager. I had gone up to ask him about you, and he was very offensive—accused me of coaxing you away from the service of the firm, and that sort of thing. At last I fairly lost my temper. " If you want good men you should pay them a good price," said I. " He would rather have our small price than your big one," said he. " I'll lay you a fiver," said I, " that when he has my offer you will never so much as hear from him again." " Done ! " said he. " We picked him out of the gutter, and he won't leave us so easily." Those were his very words.'

" ' The impudent scoundrel ! ' I cried. ' I've never so much as seen him in my life. Why should I consider him in any way ? I shall certainly not write if you would rather that I didn't.'

" ' Good ! That's a promise ! ' said he, rising from his chair. ' Well, I am delighted to have got so good a man for my brother. Here is your advance of a hundred pounds, and here is the letter. Make a note of the address, 126B Corporation Street, and remember that one o'clock to-morrow is your appointment. Good night, and may you have all the fortune that you deserve.'

" That's just about all that passed between us as near as I can remember it. You can imagine, Dr. Watson, how pleased I was at such an extraordinary piece of good fortune. I sat up half the night hugging myself over it, and next day I was off to Birmingham in a train that would take me in plenty of time for my appointment. I took my things to an hotel in New Street, and then I made my way to the address which had been given me.

" It was a quarter of an hour before my time, but I thought that would make no difference. 126B was a passage between two large shops which led to a winding stone stair, from which there were many flats, let as offices to companies or professional men. The names of the occupants were painted up at the bottom on the wall, but there was no such name as the Franco-Midland Hardware Company, Limited. I stood for a few minutes with my heart in my boots, wondering whether the whole thing was an elaborate hoax or not, when up came a man and addressed me. He was very like the chap that I had seen the night before, the same figure and voice, but he was clean shaven and his hair was lighter.

" ' Are you Mr. Hall Pycroft ? ' he asked.

" ' Yes,' said I.

" ' Ah ! I was expecting you, but you are a trifle before your time. I had a note from my brother this morning, in which he sang your praises very loudly.'

" ' I was just looking for the offices when you came.'

" ' We have not got our name up yet, for we only secured these temporary premises last week. Come up with me and we will talk the matter over.'

" I followed him to the top of a very lofty stair, and there right under the slates were a couple of empty and dusty little rooms, uncarpeted and uncurtained, into which he led me. I had thought of a great office with shining tables and rows of clerks such as I was used to, and I dare say I stared rather straight at the two deal chairs and one little table, which, with a ledger and a waste-paper basket, made up the whole furniture.

" ' Don't be disheartened, Mr. Pycroft,' said my new acquaintance, seeing the length of my face. ' Rome was not built in a day, and we have lots of money at our backs, though we don't cut much dash yet in offices. Pray sit down and let me have your letter.'

" I gave it to him, and he read it over very carefully.

" ' You seem to have made a vast impression upon my brother Arthur,' said he, ' and I know that he is a pretty shrewd judge. He swears by London, you know, and I by Birmingham, but this time I shall follow his advice. Pray consider yourself definitely engaged.'

" ' What are my duties ? ' I asked.

" ' You will eventually manage the great depôt in Paris, which will pour a flood of English crockery into the shops of one hundred and thirty-four agents in France. The purchase will be completed in a week, and meanwhile you will remain in Birmingham and make yourself useful.'

" ' How ? '

" For answer he took a big red book out of a drawer. ' This is a directory of Paris,' said he, ' with the trades after the names of the people. I want you to take it home with you, and to mark off all the hardware sellers with their addresses. It would be of the greatest use to me to have them.'

" ' Surely, there are classified lists ? ' I suggested.

" ' Not reliable ones. Their system is different to ours. Stick at it and let me have the lists by Monday, at twelve. Good day, Mr. Pycroft ; if you continue to show zeal and intelligence, you will find the company a good master.'

" I went back to the hotel with the big book under my arm, and with very conflicting feelings in my breast. On the one hand I was definitely engaged, and had a hundred pounds in my pocket. On the other, the look of the offices, the absence of name on the wall, and other of the points which would strike a business man, had left a bad impression as to the position of my employers. However, come what might, I had my money, so I settled down to my task. All Sunday I was kept hard at work, and yet by Monday I had only got as far as H. I went round to my employer, found him in the same dismantled kind of room, and was told to keep at it until Wednesday, and then come again. On Wednesday it was still unfinished, so I hammered away until Friday—that is, yesterday. Then I brought it round to Mr. Harry Pinner.

" ' Thank you very much,' said he. ' I fear that I underrated the difficulty of the task. This list will be of very material assistance to me.'

" ' It took some time,' said I.

" ' And now,' said he, ' I want you to make a list of the furniture shops, for they all sell crockery.'

" ' Very good.'

" ' And you can come up to-morrow evening at seven, and let me know how you are getting on. Don't overwork yourself. A couple of hours at Day's Music-Hall in the evening would do you no harm after your labours.' He laughed as he spoke, and I saw with a thrill that his second tooth upon the left-hand side had been very badly stuffed with gold."

Sherlock Holmes rubbed his hands with delight, and I stared in astonishment at our client.

"You may well look surprised, Dr. Watson, but it is this way," said he. "When I was speaking to the other chap in London at the time that he laughed at my not going to Mawson's, I happened to notice that his tooth was stuffed in this very identical fashion. The glint of the gold in each case caught my eye, you see. When I put that with the voice and figure being the same, and only those things altered which might be changed by a razor or a wig, I could not doubt that it was the same man. Of course, you expect two brothers to be alike, but not that they should have the same tooth stuffed in the same way. He bowed me out and I found myself in the street, hardly knowing whether I was on my head or my heels. Back I went to my hotel, put my head in a basin of cold water, and tried to think it out. Why had he sent me from London to Birmingham; why had he got there before me; and why had he written a letter from himself to himself? It was altogether too much for me, and I could make no sense of it. And then suddenly it struck me that what was dark to me might be very light to Mr. Sherlock Holmes. I had just time to get up to town by the night train, to see him this morning, and to bring you both back with me to Birmingham."

There was a pause after the stockbroker's clerk had concluded his surprising experience. Then Sherlock Holmes cocked his eye at me, leaning back on the cushions with a pleased and yet critical face, like a connoisseur who had just taken his first sip of a comet vintage.

"Rather fine, Watson, is it not?" said he. "There are points in it which please me. I think you will agree with me that an interview with Mr. Arthur Harry Pinner in the temporary offices of the Franco-Midland Hardware Company, Limited, would be a rather interesting experience for both of us."

" But how can we do it ? " I asked.

" Oh, easily enough," said Hall Pycroft, cheerily.
" You are two friends of mine who are in want of a
billet, and what could be more natural than that I should
bring you both round to the managing director ? "

" Quite so ! Of course ! " said Holmes. " I should
like to have a look at the gentleman and see if I can make
anything of his little game. What qualities have you,
my friend, which would make your services so valuable ?
or is it possible that——" He began biting his nails
and staring blankly out of the window, and we hardly
drew another word from him until we were in New
Street.

At seven o'clock that evening we were walking, the
three of us, down Corporation Street to the company's
offices.

" It is of no use our being at all before our time,'
said our client. " He only comes there to see me apparently, for the place is deserted up to the very hour he
names."

" That is suggestive," remarked Holmes.

" By Jove, I told you so ! " cried the clerk. " That's
he walking ahead of us there."

He pointed to a smallish, blond, well-dressed man,
who was bustling along the other side of the road. As
we watched him he looked across at a boy who was
bawling out the latest edition of the evening paper, and,
running over among the cabs and 'buses, he bought one
from him. Then clutching it in his hand he vanished
through a doorway.

" There he goes ! " cried Hall Pycroft. " Those are
the company's offices into which he has gone. Come
with me and I'll fix it up as easily as possible."

Following his lead we ascended five stories, until we
found ourselves outside a half-opened door, at which our
client tapped. A voice within bade us " Come in," and
we entered a bare, unfurnished room, such as Hall Pycroft

had described. At the single table sat the man whom we had seen in the street, with his evening paper spread out in front of him, and as he looked up at us it seemed to me that I had never looked upon a face which bore such marks of grief, and of something beyond grief—of a horror such as comes to few men in a lifetime. His brow glistened with perspiration, his cheeks were of the dull dead white of a fish's belly, and his eyes were wild and staring. He looked at his clerk as though he failed to recognize him, and I could see, by the astonishment depicted upon our conductor's face, that this was by no means the usual appearance of his employer.

"You look ill, Mr. Pinner," he exclaimed.

"Yes, I am not very well," answered the other, making obvious efforts to pull himself together, and licking his dry lips before he spoke. "Who are these gentlemen whom you have brought with you?"

"One is Mr. Harris, of Bermondsey, and the other is Mr. Price, of this town," said our clerk, glibly. "They are friends of mine, and gentlemen of experience, but they have been out of a place for some little time, and they hoped that perhaps you might find an opening for them in the company's employment."

"Very possibly! Very possibly!" cried Mr. Pinner, with a ghastly smile. "Yes, I have no doubt that we shall be able to do something for you. What is your particular line, Mr. Harris?"

"I am an accountant," said Holmes.

"Ah, yes, we shall want something of the sort. And you, Mr. Price?"

"A clerk," said I.

"I have every hope that the company may accommodate you. I will let you know about it as soon as we come to any conclusion. And now I beg that you will go. For God's sake, leave me to myself!"

These last words were shot out of him, as though the constraint which he was evidently setting upon himself had suddenly and utterly burst asunder. Holmes and I glanced at each other, and Hall Pycroft took a step towards the table.

" You forget, Mr. Pinner, that I am here by appointment to receive some directions from you," said he.

" Certainly, Mr. Pycroft, certainly," the other answered in a calmer tone. " You may wait here a moment, and there is no reason why your friends should not wait with you. I will be entirely at your service in three minutes, if I might trespass upon your patience so far." He rose with a very courteous air, and bowing to us he passed out through a door at the farther end of the room, which he closed behind him.

" What now ? " whispered Holmes. " Is he giving us the slip ? "

" Impossible," answered Pycroft.

" Why so ? "

" That door leads into an inner room."

" There is no exit ? "

" None."

" Is it furnished ? "

" It was empty yesterday."

" Then what on earth can he be doing ? There is something which I don't understand in this matter. If ever a man was three parts mad with terror, that man's name is Pinner. What can have put the shivers on him ? "

" He suspects that we are detectives," I suggested.

" That's it," said Pycroft.

Holmes shook his head. " He did not turn pale. He *was* pale when we entered the room," said he. " It is just possible that——"

His words were interrupted by a sharp rat-tat from the direction of the inner door.

" What the deuce is he knocking at his own door for ? " cried the clerk.

Again and much louder came the rat-tat-tat. We all gazed expectantly at the closed door. Glancing at Holmes I saw his face turn rigid, and he leaned forward in intense excitement. Then suddenly came a low gurgling, gargling sound and a brisk drumming upon woodwork. Holmes sprang frantically across the room and pushed at the door. It was fastened on the inner side. Following his example, we threw ourselves upon it with all our weight. One hinge snapped, then the other, and down came the door with a crash. Rushing over it, we found ourselves in the inner room.

It was empty.

But it was only for a moment that we were at fault. At one corner, the corner nearest the room which we had left, there was a second door. Holmes sprang to it and pulled it open. A coat and waistcoat were lying on the floor, and from a hook behind the door, with his own braces round his neck, was hanging the managing director of the Franco-Midland Hardware Company. His knees were drawn up, his head hung at a dreadful angle to his body, and the clatter of his heels against the door made the noise which had broken in upon our conversation. In an instant I had caught him round the waist and held him up, while Holmes and Pycroft untied the elastic bands which had disappeared between the livid creases of skin. Then we carried him into the other room, where he lay with a slate-coloured face, puffing his purple lips in and out with every breath—a dreadful wreck of all that he had been but five minutes before.

"What do you think of him, Watson?" asked Holmes.

I stooped over him and examined him. His pulse was feeble and intermittent, but his breathing grew longer, and there was a little shivering of his eyelids which showed a thin white slit of ball beneath.

"It has been touch and go with him," said I, "but he'll live now. Just open that window and hand me the water carafe." I undid his collar, poured the cold water over his face, and raised and sank his arms until he drew a long natural breath.

"It's only a question of time now," said I, as I turned away from him.

Holmes stood by the table with his hands deep in his trousers pockets and his chin upon his breast.

" I suppose we ought to call the police in now," said he ; " and yet I confess that I like to give them a complete case when they come."

" It's a blessed mystery to me," cried Pycroft, scratching his head. " Whatever they wanted to bring me all the way up here for, and then——"

" Pooh ! All that is clear enough," said Holmes impatiently. " It is this last sudden move."

" You understand the rest, then ? "

" I think that is fairly obvious. What do you say, Watson ? "

I shrugged my shoulders.

" I must confess that I am out of my depths," said I.

" Oh, surely, if you consider the events at first they can only point to one conclusion."

" What do you make of them ? "

" Well, the whole thing hinges upon two points. The first is the making of Pycroft write a declaration by which he entered the service of this preposterous company. Do you not see how very suggestive that is ? "

" I am afraid I miss the point."

" Well, why did they want him to do it ? Not as a business matter, for these arrangements are usually verbal, and there was no earthly business reason why this should be an exception. Don't you see, my young friend, that they were very anxious to obtain a specimen of your handwriting, and had no other way of doing it ? "

" And why ? "

" Quite so. Why ? When we answer that, we have made some progress with our little problem. Why ? There can be only one adequate reason. Someone wanted to learn to imitate your writing, and had to procure a specimen of it first. And now if we pass on to the second point, we find that each throws light upon the other. That point is the request made by Pinner that you should not resign your place, but should leave the manager of this important business in the full expectation that a Mr. Hall Pycroft, whom he had never seen, was about to enter the office upon the Monday morning."

" My God ! " cried our client, " what a blind beetle I have been ! "

" Now you see the point about the handwriting. Suppose that someone turned up in your place who wrote a completely different hand from that in which you had applied for the vacancy, of course the game would have been up. But in the interval the rogue learnt to imitate you, and his position was therefore secure, as I presume that nobody in the office had ever set eyes upon you ? "

" Not a soul," groaned Hall Pycroft.

" Very good. Of course, it was of the utmost importance to prevent you from thinking better of it, and also to keep you from coming into contact with anyone who might tell you that your double was at work in Mawson's office. Therefore they gave you a handsome advance on your salary, and ran you off to the Midlands, where they gave you enough work to do to prevent your going to London, where you might have burst their little game up. That is all plain enough."

" But why should this man pretend to be his own brother ? "

" Well, that is pretty clear also. There are evidently only two of them in it. The other is personating you at the office. This one acted as your engager, and then found that he could not find you an employer without admitting a third person into his plot. That he was most unwilling to do. He changed his appearance as far as he could, and trusted that the likeness, which you could not fail to observe, would be put down to a family resemblance. But for the happy chance of the gold stuffing your suspicions would probably have never been aroused."

Hall Pycroft shook his clenched hands in the air. " Good Lord ! " he cried. " While I have been fooled in this way, what has this other Hall Pycroft been doing at Mawson's? What should we do, Mr. Holmes? Tell me what to do!"

"We must wire to Mawson's."

"They shut at twelve on Saturdays."

"Never mind; there may be some door-keeper or attendant——"

"Ah, yes; they keep a permanent guard there on account of the value of the securities that they hold. I remember hearing it talked of in the City."

"Very good, we shall wire to him, and see if all is well, and if a clerk of your name is working there. That is clear enough, but what is not so clear is why at sight of us one of the rogues should instantly walk out of the room and hang himself."

"The paper!" croaked a voice behind us. The man was sitting up, blanched and ghastly, with returning reason in his eyes, and hands which rubbed nervously at the broad red band which still encircled his throat.

"The paper! Of course!" yelled Holmes, in a paroxysm of excitement. "Idiot that I was! I thought so much of our visit that the paper never entered my head for an instant. To be sure, the secret must lie there." He flattened it out on the table, and a cry of triumph burst from his lips.

"Look at this, Watson!" he cried. "It is a London paper, an early edition of the *Evening Standard*. Here is what we want. Look at the headlines—'Crime in the City. Murder at Mawson & Williams'. Gigantic Attempted Robbery; Capture of the Criminal.' Here, Watson, we are all equally anxious to hear it, so kindly read it aloud to us."

It appeared from its position in the paper to have been the one event of importance in town, and the account of it ran in this way:

"A desperate attempt at robbery, culminating in the death of one man and the capture of the criminal, occurred this afternoon in the City. For some time back Mawson

& Williams, the famous financial house, have been the guardians of securities which amount in the aggregate to a sum of considerably over a million sterling. So conscious was the manager of the responsibility which devolved upon him in consequence of the great interests at stake, that safes of the very latest construction have been employed, and an armed watchman has been left day and night in the building. It appears that last week a new clerk, named Hall Pycroft, was engaged by the firm. This person appears to have been none other than Beddington, the famous forger and cracksman, who, with his brother, has only recently emerged from a five years' spell of penal servitude. By some means, which are not yet clear, he succeeded in winning, under a false name, this official position in the office, which he utilized in order to obtain mouldings of various locks and a thorough knowledge of the position of the strong-room and the safes.

" It is customary at Mawson's for the clerks to leave at midday on Saturday. Sergeant Tuson, of the City Police, was somewhat surprised therefore to see a gentleman with a carpet bag come down the steps at twenty minutes past one. His suspicions being aroused, the sergeant followed the man, and with the aid of Constable Pollock succeeded, after a most desperate resistance, in arresting him. It was at once clear that a daring and gigantic robbery had been committed. Nearly a hundred thousand pounds' worth of American railway bonds, with a large amount of scrip in other mines and companies, were discovered in the bag. On examining the premises the body of the unfortunate watchman was found doubled up and thrust into the largest of the safes, where it would not have been discovered until Monday morning had it not been for the prompt action of Sergeant Tuson. The man's skull had been shattered by a blow from a poker, delivered from behind. There could be no doubt that Beddington had obtained entrance by pretending that he had left something behind him, and having murdered the watchman, rapidly rifled the large safe, and then made off with his booty. His brother, who usually works with him, has not appeared in this job, as far as can at present be ascertained, although the police are making energetic inquiries as to his whereabouts."

"Well, we may save the police some little trouble in that direction," said Holmes, glancing at the haggard figure huddled up by the window. "Human nature is a strange mixture, Watson. You see that even a villain and a murderer can inspire such affection that his brother turns to suicide when he learns that his neck is forfeited. However, we have no choice as to our action. The doctor and I will remain on guard, Mr. Pycroft, if you will have the kindness to step out for the police."

16. *The " Gloria Scott "*

"I HAVE some papers here," said my friend, Sherlock Holmes, as we sat one winter's night on either side of the fire, "which I really think, Watson, it would be worth your while to glance over. These are the documents in the extraordinary case of the *Gloria Scott*, and this is the message which struck Justice of the Peace Trevor dead with horror when he read it."

He had picked from a drawer a little tarnished cylinder, and, undoing the tape, he handed me a short note scrawled upon a half sheet of slate-grey paper.

"The supply of game for London is going steadily up," it ran. "Head-keeper Hudson, we believe, has been now told to receive all orders for fly-paper, and for preservation of your hen pheasant's life."

As I glanced up from reading this enigmatical message I saw Holmes chuckling at the expression upon my face.

"You look a little bewildered," said he.

"I cannot see how such a message as this could inspire horror. It seems to me to be rather grotesque than otherwise."

"Very likely. Yet the fact remains that the reader,

who was a fine, robust old man, was knocked clean down by it, as if it had been the butt-end of a pistol."

" You arouse my curiosity," said I. " But why did you say just now that there were very particular reasons why I should study this case ? "

" Because it was the first in which I was ever engaged."

I had often endeavoured to elicit from my companion what had first turned his mind in the direction of criminal research, but I had never caught him before in a communicative humour. Now he sat forward in his armchair, and spread out the documents upon his knees. Then he lit his pipe and sat for some time smoking and turning them over.

" You never heard me talk of Victor Trevor ? " he asked. " He was the only friend I made during the two years that I was at college. I was never a very sociable fellow, Watson, always rather fond of moping in my rooms and working out my own little methods of thought, so that I never mixed much with the men of my year. Bar fencing and boxing I had few athletic tastes, and then my line of study was quite distinct from that of the other fellows, so that we had no points of contact at all. Trevor was the only man I knew, and that only through the accident of his bull-terrier freezing on to my ankle one morning as I went down to chapel.

" It was a prosaic way of forming a friendship, but it was effective. I was laid by the heels for ten days, and Trevor used to come in to inquire after me. At first it was only a minute's chat, but soon his visits lengthened, and before the end of the term we were close friends. He was a hearty, full-blooded fellow, full of spirit and energy, the very opposite to me in most respects ; but we found we had some subjects in common, and it was a bond of union when I learned that he was as friendless as I. Finally, he invited me down to his father's place at Donnithorpe, in Norfolk, and I accepted his hospitality for a month of the long vacation.

" Old Trevor was evidently a man of some wealth and consideration, a J.P. and a landed proprietor. Donnithorpe is a little hamlet just to the north of Langmere, in the country of the Broads. The house was an old-fashioned, wide-spread, oak-beamed, brick building, with a fine lime-lined avenue leading up to it. There was excellent wild-duck shooting in the fens, remarkably good fishing, a small but select library, taken over, as I understood, from a former occupant, and a tolerable cook, so that it would be a fastidious man who could not put in a pleasant month there.

" Trevor senior was a widower, and my friend was his only son. There had been a daughter, I heard, but she had died of diphtheria while on a visit to Birmingham. The father interested me extremely. He was a man of little culture, but with a considerable amount of rude strength both physically and mentally. He knew hardly any books, but he had travelled far, had seen much of the world, and had remembered all that he had learned. In person he was a thick-set, burly man, with a shock of grizzled hair, a brown, weather-beaten face, and blue eyes which were keen to the verge of fierceness. Yet he had a reputation for kindness and charity on the country-side, and was noted for the leniency of his sentences from the bench.

" One evening, shortly after my arrival, we were sitting over a glass of port after dinner, when young Trevor began to talk about those habits of observation and inference which I had already formed into a system, although I had not yet appreciated the part which they were to play in my life. The old man evidently thought that his son was exaggerating in his description of one or two trivial feats which I had performed.

" ' Come now, Mr. Holmes,' said he, laughing good-humouredly, ' I'm an excellent subject, if you can deduce anything from me.'

" ' I fear there is not very much,' I answered. ' I might suggest that you have gone about in fear of some personal attack within the last twelve months.'

" The laugh faded from his lips, and he stared at me in great surprise.

" ' Well, that's true enough,' said he. ' You know, Victor,' turning to his son, ' when we broke up that poaching gang, they swore to knife us ; and Sir Edward Hoby has actually been attacked. I've always been on my guard since then, though I have no idea how you know it.'

" ' You have a very handsome stick,' I answered. ' By the inscription, I observed that you had not had it more than a year. But you have taken some pains to bore the head of it and pour melted lead into the hole, so as to make it a formidable weapon. I argued that you would not take such precautions unless you had some danger to fear.'

" ' Anything else ? ' he asked, smiling.

" ' You have boxed a good deal in your youth.'

" ' Right again. How did you know it ? Is my nose knocked a little out of the straight ? '

" ' No,' said I. ' It is your ears. They have the peculiar flattening and thickening which marks the boxing man.'

" ' Anything else ? '

" ' You have done a great deal of digging, by your callosities.'

" ' Made all my money at the gold-fields.'

" ' You have been in New Zealand.'

" ' Right again.'

" ' You have visited Japan.'

" ' Quite true.'

" ' And you have been most intimately associated with someone whose initials were J. A., and whom you afterwards were eager to entirely forget.'

" Mr. Trevor stood slowly up, fixed his large blue eyes on me with a strange, wild stare, and then pitched forward on his face among the nutshells which strewed the cloth, in a dead faint.

" You can imagine, Watson, how shocked both his son and I were. His attack did not last long, however, for

377

when we undid his collar and sprinkled the water from one of the finger-glasses over his face, he gave a gasp or two and sat up.

"' Ah boys!' said he, forcing a smile. 'I hope I haven't frightened you. Strong as I look, there is a weak place in my heart, and it does not take much to knock me over. I don't know how you manage this, Mr. Holmes, but it seems to me that all the detectives of fact and of fancy would be children in your hands. That's your line of life, sir, and you may take the word of a man who has seen something of the world.'

"And that recommendation, with the exaggerated estimate of my ability with which he prefaced it, was, if you will believe me, Watson, the very first thing which ever made me feel that a profession might be made out of what had up to that time been the merest hobby. At the moment, however, I was too much concerned at the sudden illness of my host to think of anything else.

"' I hope that I have said nothing to pain you,' said I.

"' Well, you certainly touched upon rather a tender point. Might I ask how you know and how much you know?' He spoke now in a half-jesting fashion, but a look of terror still lurked at the back of his eyes.

"' It is simplicity itself,' said I. 'When you bared your arm to draw that fish into the boat, I saw that " J. A." had been tattooed in the bend of the elbow. The letters were still legible, but it was perfectly clear from their blurred appearance, and from the staining of the skin round them, that efforts had been made to obliterate them. It was obvious, then, that those initials had once been very familiar to you, and that you had afterwards wished to forget them.'

"' What an eye you have!' he cried, with a sigh of relief. 'It is just as you say. But we won't talk of it. Of all ghosts the ghosts of our old loves are the worst. Come into the billiard-room and have a quiet cigar.'

"From that day, amid all his cordiality, there was

378

always a touch of suspicion in Mr. Trevor's manner towards me. Even his son remarked it. ' You've given the governor such a turn,' said he, ' that he'll never be sure again of what you know and what you don't know.' He did not mean to show it, I am sure, but it was so strongly in his mind that it peeped out at every action. At last I became so convinced that I was causing him uneasiness that I drew my visit to a close. On the very day, however, before I left, an incident occurred which proved in the sequel to be of importance.

" We were sitting out upon the lawn on garden chairs, the three of us, basking in the sun and admiring the view across the Broads, when the maid came out to say that there was a man at the door who wanted to see Mr. Trevor.

" ' What is his name ? ' asked my host.

" ' He would not give any.'

" ' What does he want, then ? '

" ' He says that you know him, and that he only wants a moment's conversation.'

" ' Show him round here.' An instant afterwards there appeared a little weazened fellow, with a cringing manner and a shambling style of walking. He wore an open jacket, with a splotch of tar on the sleeve, a red and black check shirt, dungaree trousers, and heavy boots badly worn. His face was thin and brown and crafty, with a perpetual smile upon it, which showed an irregular line of yellow teeth, and his crinkled hands were half closed in a way that is distinctive of sailors. As he came slouching across the lawn I heard Mr. Trevor make a sort of hiccoughing noise in his throat, and, jumping out of his chair, he ran into the house. He was back in a moment, and I smelt a strong reek of brandy as he passed me.

" ' Well, my man,' said he, ' what can I do for you ? '

" The sailor stood looking at him with puckered eyes, and with the same loose-lipped smile upon his face.

" ' You don't know me ? ' he asked.

379

" ' Why, dear me, it is surely Hudson ! ' said Mr. Trevor, in a tone of surprise.

" ' Hudson it is, sir,' said the seaman. ' Why, it's thirty year and more since I saw you last. Here you are in your house, and me still picking my salt meat out of the harness cask.'

" ' Tut, you will find that I have not forgotten old times,' cried Mr. Trevor, and, walking towards the sailor, he said something in a low voice. ' Go into the kitchen,' he continued out loud, ' and you will get food and drink. I have no doubt that I shall find you a situation.'

" ' Thank you, sir,' said the seaman, touching his forelock. ' I'm just off a two-yearer in an eight-knot tramp, short handed at that, and I wants a rest. I thought I'd get it either with Mr. Beddoes or with you.'

" ' Ah ! ' cried Mr. Trevor, ' you know where Mr. Beddoes is ? '

" ' Bless you, sir, I know where all my old friends are,' said the fellow, with a sinister smile, and slouched off after the maid to the kitchen. Mr. Trevor mumbled something to us about having been shipmates with the man when he was going back to the diggings, and then, leaving us on the lawn, he went indoors. An hour later, when we entered the house we found him stretched dead drunk upon the dining-room sofa. The whole incident left a most ugly impression upon my mind, and I was not sorry next day to leave Donnithorpe behind me, for I felt that my presence must be a source of embarrassment to my friend.

" All this occurred during the first month of the long vacation. I went up to my London rooms, where I spent seven weeks working out a few experiments in organic chemistry. One day, however, when the autumn was far advanced and the vacation drawing to a close, I received a telegram from my friend imploring me to return to Donnithorpe, and saying that he was in great need of my advice and assistance. Of course I dropped everything and set out for the north once more.

"He met me with the dog-cart at the station, and I saw at a glance that the last two months had been very trying ones for him. He had grown thin and careworn, and had lost the loud, cheery manner for which he had been remarkable.

"'The governor is dying,' were the first words he said.

"'Impossible!' I cried. 'What is the matter?'

"'Apoplexy. Nervous shock. He's been on the verge all day. I doubt if we shall find him alive.'

"I was, as you may think, Watson, horrified at this unexpected news.

"'What has caused it?' I asked.

"'Ah, that is the point. Jump in, and we can talk it over while we drive. You remember that fellow who came upon the evening before you left us?'

"'Perfectly.'

"'Do you know who it was that we let into the house that day?'

"'I have no idea.'

"'It was the Devil, Holmes!' he cried.

"I stared at him in astonishment.

"'Yes; it was the Devil himself. We have not had a peaceful hour since—not one. The governor has never held up his head from that evening, and now the life has been crushed out of him, and his heart broken all through this accursed Hudson.'

"'What power had he, then?'

"'Ah, that is what I would give so much to know. The kindly, charitable, good old governor! How could he have fallen into the clutches of such a ruffian? But I am so glad that you have come, Holmes. I trust very much to your judgment and discretion, and I know that you will advise me for the best.'

"We were dashing along the smooth, white country road, with the long stretch of Broads in front of us glimmering in the red light of the setting sun. From a grove upon our left I could already see the high chimneys and the flag-staff which marked the squire's dwelling.

" ' My father made the fellow gardener,' said my companion, ' and then, as that did not satisfy him, he was promoted to be butler. The house seemed to be at his mercy, and he wandered about and did what he chose in it. The maids complained of his drunken habits and his vile language. The dad raised their wages all round to recompense them for the annoyance. The fellow would take the boat and my father's best gun and treat himself to little shooting parties. And all this with such a sneering, leering, insolent face, that I would have knocked him down twenty times over if he had been a man of my own age. I tell you, Holmes, I have had to keep a tight hold upon myself all this time, and now I am asking myself whether, if I had let myself go a little more, I might not have been a wiser man.

" ' Well, matters went from bad to worse with us, and this animal, Hudson, became more and more intrusive, until at last, on his making some insolent reply to my father in my presence one day, I took him by the shoulder and turned him out of the room. He slunk away with a livid face, and two venomous eyes which uttered more threats than his tongue could do. I don't know what passed between the poor dad and him after that, but the dad came to me next day and asked me whether I would mind apologizing to Hudson. I refused, as you can imagine, and asked my father how he could allow such a wretch to take such liberties with himself and his household.

" ' " Ah, my boy," said he, " it is all very well to talk, but you don't know how I am placed. But you shall know, Victor. I'll see that you shall know, come what may ! You wouldn't believe harm of your poor old father, would you, lad ? " He was very much moved, and shut himself up in the study all day, where I could see through the window that he was writing busily.

" ' That evening there came what seemed to be a grand release, for Hudson told us that he was going to leave us. He walked into the dining-room as we sat after dinner and announced his intention in the thick voice of a half-drunken man.

" ' " I've had enough of Norfolk," said he, " I'll run down to Mr. Beddoes, in Hampshire. He'll be as glad to see me as you were, I dare say."

" ' " You're not going away in an unkind spirit, Hudson, I hope ? " said my father, with a tameness which made my blood boil.

" ' " I've not had my 'pology," said he, sulkily, glancing in my direction.

" ' " Victor, you will acknowledge that you have used this worthy fellow rather roughly ? " said the dad, turning to me.

" ' " On the contrary, I think that we have both shown extraordinary patience towards him," I answered.

" ' " Oh, you do, do you ? " he snarled. ' Very good, mate. We'll see about that ! " He slouched out of the room, and half an hour afterwards left the house, leaving my father in a state of pitiable nervousness. Night after night I heard him pacing his room, and it was just as he was recovering his confidence that the blow did at last fall.'

" ' And how ? ' I asked, eagerly.

" ' In a most extraordinary fashion. A letter arrived for my father yesterday evening, bearing the Fording-bridge postmark. My father read it, clapped both his hands to his head, and began running round the room in little circles like a man who has been driven out of his senses. When I at last drew him down on to the sofa, his mouth and eyelids were all puckered on one side, and I saw that he had a stroke. Dr. Fordham came over at once, and we put him to bed ; but the paralysis has spread, he has shown no sign of returning consciousness, and I think that we shall hardly find him alive.'

" ' You horrify me, Trevor ! ' I cried. ' What, then, could have been in this letter to cause so dreadful a result ? '

" ' Nothing. There lies the inexplicable part of it.

The message was absurd and trivial. Ah, my God, it is as I feared ! '

" As he spoke we came round the curve of the avenue, and saw in the fading light that every blind in the house had been drawn down. As we dashed up to the door, my friend's face convulsed with grief, a gentleman in black emerged from it.

" ' When did it happen, doctor ? ' asked Trevor.

" ' Almost immediately after you left.'

" ' Did he recover consciousness ? '

" ' For an instant before the end.'

" ' Any message for me ? '

" ' Only that the papers were in the back drawer of the Japanese cabinet.'

" My friend ascended with the doctor to the chamber of death, while I remained in the study, turning the whole matter over and over in my head, and feeling as sombre as ever I had done in my life. What was the past of this Trevor : pugilist, traveller, and gold-digger ? and how had he placed himself in the power of this acid-faced seaman ? Why, too, should he faint at an allusion to the half-effaced initials upon his arm, and die of fright when he had a letter from Fordingbridge ? Then I remembered that Fordingbridge was in Hampshire, and that this Mr. Beddoes, whom the seaman had gone to visit, and presumably to blackmail, had also been mentioned as living in Hampshire. The letter, then, might either come from Hudson, the seaman, saying that he had betrayed the guilty secret which appeared to exist, or it might come from Beddoes, warning an old confederate that such a betrayal was imminent. So far it seemed clear enough. But, then, how could the letter be trivial and grotesque as described by the son ? He must have misread it. If so, it must have been one of those ingenious secret codes which mean one thing while they seem to mean another. I must see this letter. If there were a hidden meaning in it, I was confident that I could pluck it forth. For an hour I sat pondering over it in the gloom, until at last a weeping maid brought in a lamp, and close at her heels came my friend Trevor, pale but composed, with these very papers which lie upon my knee held in his grasp. He sat down opposite to me, drew the lamp to the edge of the table, and handed me a short note scribbled, as you see, upon a single sheet of grey paper. ' The supply of game for London is going steadily up,' it ran. ' Head-keeper Hudson, we believe, has been now told to receive all orders for fly-paper and for preservation of your hen pheasant's life.'

" I dare say my face looked as bewildered as yours did just now when first I read this message. Then I re-read it very carefully. It was evidently as I had thought, and some second meaning must be buried in this strange combination of words. Or could it be that there was a pre-arranged significance to such phrases as ' fly-paper ' and ' hen pheasant ' ? Such a meaning would be arbitrary, and could not be deduced in any way. And yet I was loath to believe that this was the case, and the presence of the word ' Hudson ' seemed to show that the subject of the message was as I had guessed, and that it was from Beddoes rather than the sailor. I tried it backwards, but the combination, ' Life pheasant's hen,' was not encouraging. Then I tried alternate words, but neither ' The of for ' nor ' supply game London ' promised to throw any light upon it. Then in an instant the key of the riddle was in my hands, and I saw that every third word beginning with the first would give a message which might well drive old Trevor to despair.

" It was short and terse, the warning, as I now read it to my companion :

" ' The game is up. Hudson has told all. Fly for your life.'

" Victor Trevor sank his face into his shaking hands. ' It must be that, I suppose,' said he. ' This is worse than death, for it means disgrace as well. But what is the meaning of these " head-keepers " and " hen pheasants " ? '

" ' It means nothing to the message, but it might mean a good deal to us if we had no other means of discovering the sender. You see that he has begun by writing, " The . . . game . . . is," and so on. Afterwards he had, to fulfil the prearranged cipher, to fill in any two words in each space. He would naturally use the first words which came to his mind, and if there were so many which referred to sport among them, you may be tolerably sure that he is either an ardent shot or interested in breeding. Do you know anything of this Beddoes ? '

" ' Why, now that you mention it,' said he, ' I remember that my poor father used to have an invitation from him to shoot over his preserves every autumn.'

" ' Then it is undoubtedly from him that the note comes,' said I. ' It only remains for us to find out what this secret was which the sailor Hudson seems to have held over the heads of these two wealthy and respected men.'

" ' Alas, Holmes, I fear that it is one of sin and shame ! ' cried my friend. ' But from you I shall have no secrets. Here is the statement which was drawn up by my father when he knew that the danger from Hudson had become imminent. I found it in the Japanese cabinet, as he told the doctor. Take it and read it to me, for I have neither the strength nor the courage to do it myself.'

" These are the very papers, Watson, which he handed to me, and I will read them to you as I read them in the old study that night to him. They are endorsed outside as you see : ' Some particulars of the voyage of the barque *Gloria Scott*, from her leaving Falmouth on the 8th October, 1855, to her destruction in N. lat. 15° 20', W. long. 25° 14', on November 6th.' It is in the form of a letter, and runs in this way :

" My dear, dear son,—Now that approaching disgrace begins to darken the closing years of my life, I can write with all truth and honesty that it is not the terror of the law, it is not the loss of my position in the county, nor is it my fall in the eyes of all who have known me, which cuts me to the heart ; but it is the thought that you should come to blush for me—you who love me, and who have seldom, I hope, had reason to do other than respect me. But if the blow falls which is for ever hanging over me, then I should wish you to read this that you may know straight from me how far I have been to blame. On the other hand, if all should go well (which may kind God Almighty grant !), then if by any chance this paper should be still undestroyed, and should fall into your hands, I conjure you by all you hold sacred, by the memory of your dear mother, and by the love which has been between us, to hurl it into the fire, and to never give one thought to it again.

" If, then, your eye goes on to read this line, I know that I shall already have been exposed and dragged from my home, or, as is more likely—for you know that my heart is weak—be lying with my tongue sealed for ever in death. In either case the time for suppression is past, and every word which I tell you is the naked truth ; and this I swear as I hope for mercy.

" My name, dear lad, is not Trevor. I was James Armitage in my younger days, and you can understand now the shock that it was to me a few weeks ago when your college friend addressed me in words which seemed to imply that he had surmised my secret. As Armitage it was that I entered a London banking house, and as Armitage I was convicted of breaking my country's laws, and was sentenced to transportation. Do not think very harshly of me, laddie. It was a debt of honour, so-called, which I had to pay, and I used money which was not my own to do it, in the certainty that I could replace it before there could be any possibility of its being missed. But the most dreadful ill-luck pursued me. The money which I had reckoned upon never came to hand, and a premature examination of accounts exposed my deficit. The case might have been dealt leniently with, but the laws were more harshly administered thirty years ago than now, and on my twenty-third birthday I found myself chained as a felon with thirty-seven other convicts in the 'tween-decks of the barque *Gloria Scott*, bound for Australia.

" It was the year '55, when the Crimean War was at its height, and the old convict ships had been largely used as transports in the Black Sea. The Government was compelled therefore to use smaller and less suitable vessels for sending out their prisoners. The *Gloria Scott* had been in the Chinese tea trade, but she was an old-fashioned, heavy-bowed, broad-beamed craft, and the new clippers had cut her out. She was a 500-ton boat, and besides her thirty-eight gaol-birds, she carried twenty-six of a crew, eighteen soldiers, a captain, three mates, a doctor, a chaplain, and four warders. Nearly a hundred souls were in her, all told, when we set sail from Falmouth.

" The partitions between the cells of the convicts, instead of being of thick oak, as is usual in convict ships, were quite thin and frail. The man next to me upon the aft side was one whom I had particularly noticed when we were led down to the quay. He was a young man with a clear, hairless face, a long thin nose, and rather nutcracker jaws. He carried his head very jauntily in the air, had a swaggering style of walking, and was above all else remarkable for his extraordinary height. I don't think any of our heads would come up to his shoulder, and I am sure that he could not have measured less than six and a half feet. It was strange among so many sad and weary faces to see one which was full of energy and resolution. The sight of it was to me like a fire in a snowstorm. I was glad then to find that he was my neighbour, and gladder still when, in the dead of the night, I heard a whisper close to my ear, and found that he had managed to cut an opening in the board which separated us.

" ' Halloa, chummy ! ' said he, ' what's your name, and what are you here for ? '

" I answered him, and asked in turn who I was talking with.

" ' I'm Jack Prendergast,' said he, ' and, by God,

388

you'll learn to bless my name before you've done with me ! '

" I remembered hearing of his case, for it was one which had made an immense sensation throughout the country, some time before my own arrest. He was a man of good family and of great ability, but of incurably vicious habits, who had, by an ingenious system of fraud, obtained huge sums of money from the leading London merchants.

" ' Ah, ah ! You remember my case ? ' said he, proudly.

" ' Very well indeed.'

" ' Then maybe you remember something queer about it ? '

" ' What was that, then ? '

" ' I'd had nearly a quarter of a million, hadn't I ? '

" ' So it was said.'

" ' But none was recovered, eh ? '

" ' No.'

" ' Well, where d'ye suppose the balance is ? ' he asked.

" ' I have no idea,' said I.

" ' Right between my finger and thumb,' he cried. ' By God, I've got more pounds to my name than you have hairs on your head. And if you've money, my son, and know how to handle it and spread it, you can do *anything* ! Now, you don't think it likely that a man who could do anything is going to wear his breeches out sitting in the stinking hold of a rat-gutted, beetle-ridden, mouldy old coffin of a China coaster ? No, sir, such a man will look after himself, and will look after his chums. You may lay to that ! You hold on to him, and you may kiss the Book that he'll haul you through.'

" That was his style of talk, and at first I thought it meant nothing, but after a while, when he had tested me and sworn me in with all possible solemnity, he let me understand that there really was a plot to gain command of the vessel. A dozen of the prisoners had hatched it before they came aboard ; Prendergast was the leader, and his money was the motive power.

" ' I'd a partner,' said he, ' a rare good man, as true as a stock to a barrel. He's got the dibbs, he has, and where do you think he is at this moment ? Why, he's the chaplain of this ship—the chaplain, no less ! He came aboard with a black coat and his papers right, and money enough in his box to buy the thing right up from keel to maintruck. The crew are his, body and soul. He could buy 'em at so much a gross with a cash discount, and he did it before ever they signed on. He's got two of the warders and Mercer the second mate, and he'd get the captain himself if he thought him worth it.'

" ' What are we to do, then ? ' I asked.

" ' What do you think ? ' said he. ' We'll make the coats of some of these soldiers redder than ever the tailor did.'

" ' But they are armed,' said I.

" ' And so shall we be, my boy. There's a brace of pistols for every mother's son of us, and if we can't carry this ship, with the crew at our back, it's time we were all sent to a young Misses' boarding school. You speak to your mate on the left to-night, and see if he is to be trusted.'

" I did so, and found my other neighbour to be a young fellow in much the same position as myself, whose crime had been forgery. His name was Evans, but he afterwards changed it, like myself, and he is now a rich and prosperous man in the South of England. He was ready enough to join the conspiracy, as the only means of saving ourselves, and before we had crossed the Bay there were only two of the prisoners who were not in the secret. One of these was of weak mind, and we did not dare to trust him, and the other was suffering from jaundice, and could not be of any use to us.

" From the beginning there was really nothing to prevent us taking possession of the ship. The crew were a set of ruffians, specially picked for the job. The sham chaplain came into our cells to exhort us, carrying a black bag, supposed to be full of tracts ; and so often did he come that by the third day we had each stowed away at the foot of our bed a file, a brace of pistols, a pound of powder, and twenty slugs. Two of the warders were agents of Prendergast, and the second mate was his right-hand man. The captain, the two mates, two warders, Lieutenant Martin, his eighteen soldiers, and the doctor were all that we had against us. Yet, safe as it was, we determined to neglect no precaution, and to make our attack suddenly at night. It came, however, more quickly than we expected, and in this way :

" One evening, about the third week after our start, the doctor had come down to see one of the prisoners, who was ill, and, putting his hand down on the bottom of his bunk, he felt the outline of the pistols. If he had been silent he might have blown the whole thing ; but he was a nervous little chap, so he gave a cry of surprise and turned so pale, that the man knew what was up in an instant and seized him. He was gagged before he could give the alarm, and tied down upon the bed. He had unlocked the door that led to the deck, and we were through it in a rush. The two sentries were shot down, and so was a corporal who came running to see what was the matter. There were two more soldiers at the door of the state-room, and their muskets seemed not to be loaded, for they never fired upon us, and they were shot while trying to fix their bayonets. Then we rushed on into the captain's cabin, but as we pushed open the door there was an explosion from within, and there he lay with his head on the chart of the Atlantic, which was pinned upon the table, while the chaplain stood, with a smoking pistol in his hand, at his elbow. The two mates had both been seized by the crew, and the whole business seemed to be settled.

" The state-room was next the cabin, and we flocked in there and flopped down on the settees all speaking together, for we were just mad with the feeling that we were free once more. There were lockers all round, and Wilson, the sham chaplain, knocked one of them in, and pulled out a dozen of brown sherry. We cracked off the necks of the bottles, poured the stuff out into tumblers, and were just tossing them off, when in an instant, without warning, there came the roar of muskets in our ears, and the saloon was so full of smoke that we could not see across the table. When it cleared away again the place was a shambles. Wilson and eight others were wriggling on the top of each other on the floor, and the blood and brown sherry on that table turn me sick now when I think of it. We were so cowed by the sight that I think we should have given the job up if it had not been for Prendergast. He bellowed like a bull and rushed for the door with all that were left alive at his heels. Out we ran, and there on the poop were the lieutenant and ten of his men. The swing skylights above the saloon table had been a bit open, and they had fired on us through the slit. We got on them before they could load, and they stood to it like men, but we had the upper hand of them, and in five minutes it was all over. My God! was there ever a slaughter-house like that ship? Prendergast was like a raging devil, and he picked the soldiers up as if they had been children and threw them overboard, alive or dead. There was one sergeant that was horribly wounded, and yet kept on swimming for a surprising time, until some-one in mercy blew out his brains. When the fighting was over there was no one left of our enemies except just the warders, the mates, and the doctor.

" It was over them that the great quarrel arose. There were many of us who were glad enough to win back our freedom, and yet who had no wish to have murder on our souls. It was one thing to knock the soldiers over with their muskets in their hands, and it was another to stand by while men were being killed in cold blood. Eight of us, five convicts and three sailors, said that we would not see it done. But there was no moving Prendergast and those who were with him. Our only chance of safety lay in making a clean job of it, said he, and he would not leave a tongue with power to wag in a witness-box. It nearly came to our sharing the fate of the prisoners, but at last he said that if we wished we might take a boat and go. We jumped at the offer, for we were already sick of these bloodthirsty doings, and we saw that there would be worse before it was done. We were given a suit of sailor's togs each, a barrel of water, two casks, one of junk and one of biscuits, and a compass. Prendergast threw us over a chart, told us that we were shipwrecked mariners whose ship had foundered in lat. 15° N. and long. 25° W., and then cut the painter and let us go.

" And now I come to the most surprising part of my story, my dear son. The seamen had hauled the foreyard aback during the rising, but now as we left them they brought it square again, and, as there was a light wind from the north and east, the barque began to draw slowly away from us. Our boat lay, rising and falling, upon the long, smooth rollers, and Evans and I, who were the most educated of the party, were sitting in the sheets working out our position and planning what coast we should make for. It was a nice question, for the Cape de Verds was about 500 miles to the north of us, and the African coast about 700 miles to the east. On the whole, as the wind was coming round to north, we thought that Sierra Leone might be best, and turned our head in that direction, the barque being at that time nearly hull down on our starboard quarter. Suddenly as we looked at her we saw a dense black cloud of smoke shoot up from her, which hung like a monstrous tree upon the skyline. A few seconds later a roar like thunder burst upon our ears, and as the smoke thinned away there was no sign left of the *Gloria Scott*. In an instant we swept the boat's head round again, and pulled with all our strength for the place where the haze, still trailing over the water, marked the scene of this catastrophe.

" It was a long hour before we reached it, and at first we feared that we had come too late to save anyone. A splintered boat and a number of crates and fragments of spars rising and falling on the waves showed us where the vessel had foundered, but there was no sign of life, and we had turned away in despair when we heard a cry for help, and saw at some distance a piece of wreckage with a man lying stretched across it. When we pulled him aboard the boat he proved to be a young seaman of the name of Hudson, who was so burned and exhausted that he could give us no account of what had happened until the following morning.

" It seemed that after we had left, Prendergast and his gang had proceeded to put to death the five remaining prisoners : the two warders had been shot and thrown overboard, and so also had the third mate. Prendergast then descended into the 'tween-decks, and with his own hands cut the throat of the unfortunate surgeon. There only remained the first mate, who was a bold and active man. When he saw the convict approaching him with the bloody knife in his hand, he kicked off his bonds, which he had somehow contrived to loosen, and rushing down the deck he plunged into the afterhold.

" A dozen convicts who descended with their pistols in search of him found him with a match-box in his hand seated beside an open powder barrel, which was one of a hundred carried on board, and swearing that he would blow all hands up if he were in any way molested. An instant later the explosion occurred, though Hudson thought it was caused by the misdirected bullet of one of the convicts rather than the mate's match. Be the cause what it may, it was the end of the *Gloria Scott*, and of the rabble who held command of her.

" Such, in a few words, my dear boy, is the history of this terrible business in which I was involved. Next day we were picked up by the brig *Hotspur*, bound for Australia, whose captain found no difficulty in believing that we were the survivors of a passenger ship which had foundered. The transport ship, *Gloria Scott*, was set down by the Admiralty as being lost at sea, and no word has ever leaked out as to her true fate. After an excellent voyage the *Hotspur* landed us at Sydney, where Evans and I changed our names and made our way to the diggings, where among the crowds who were gathered from all nations, we had no difficulty in losing our former identities.

" The rest I need not relate. We prospered, we travelled, we came back as rich colonials to England, and we bought country estates. For more than twenty years we have led peaceful and useful lives, and we hoped that our past was for ever buried. Imagine, then, my feelings when in the seaman who came to us I recognized instantly the man who had been picked off the wreck ! He had tracked us down somehow, and had set himself to live upon our fears. You will understand now how it was that I strove to keep peace with him, and you will in some measure sympathize with me in the fears which fill me, now that he has gone from me to his other victim with threats upon his tongue.

" Underneath is written, in a hand so shaky as to be hardly legible, ' Beddoes writes in cipher to say that H. has told all. Sweet Lord, have mercy on our souls ! '

" That was the narrative which I read that night to young Trevor, and I think, Watson, that under the circumstances it was a dramatic one. The good fellow was heartbroken at it, and went out to the Terai tea planting, where I hear that he is doing well. As to the sailor and Beddoes, neither of them was ever heard of again after that day on which the letter of warning was written. They both disappeared utterly and completely. No complaint had been lodged with the police, so that Beddoes had mistaken a threat for a deed. Hudson had been seen lurking about, and it was believed by the police that he had done away with Beddoes, and had fled. For myself, I believe that the truth was exactly the opposite. I think it is most probable that Beddoes, pushed to desperation, and believing himself to have been already betrayed, had revenged himself upon Hudson, and had fled from the country with as much money as he could lay his hands on. Those are the facts of the case, Doctor, and if they are of any use to your collection, I am sure that they are very heartily at your service."

17. *The Musgrave Ritual*

AN anomaly which often struck me in the character of my friend Sherlock Holmes was that, although in his methods of thought he was the neatest and most methodical of mankind, and although also he affected a certain quiet primness of dress, he was none the less in his personal habits one of the most untidy men that ever drove a fellow-lodger to distraction. Not that I am in the least conventional in that respect myself. The rough-and-tumble work in Afghanistan, coming on the top of a natural Bohemianism of disposition, has made me rather more lax than befits a medical man. But with me there is a limit, and when I find a man who keeps his cigars in the coal-scuttle, his tobacco in the toe-end of a Persian slipper, and his unanswered correspondence transfixed by a jack-knife into the very centre of his wooden mantelpiece, then I begin to give myself virtuous airs. I have always held, too, that pistol practice should distinctly be an open-air pastime ; and when Holmes in one of his queer humours would sit in an arm-chair, with his hair-trigger and a hundred Boxer cartridges, and proceed to adorn the opposite wall with a patriotic V.R. done in bullet-pocks, I felt strongly that neither the atmosphere nor the appearance of our room was improved by it.

Our chambers were always full of chemicals and of criminal relics, which had a way of wandering into unlikely positions, and of turning up in the butter-dish, or in even less desirable places. But his papers were my great crux. He had a horror of destroying documents, especially those which were connected with his past cases, and yet it was only once in every year or two that he would muster energy to docket and arrange them, for as I have mentioned somewhere in these incoherent memoirs,

the outbursts **of** passionate energy when he performed the remarkable feats with which his name is associated were followed by reactions of lethargy, during which he would lie about with his violin and his books, hardly moving, save from the sofa to the table. Thus month after month his papers accumulated, until every corner of the room was stacked with bundles of manuscript which were on no account to be burned, and which could not be put away save by their owner.

One winter's night, as we sat together by the fire, I ventured to suggest to him that as he had finished pasting extracts into his commonplace book he might employ the next two hours in making our room a little more habitable. He could not deny the justice of my request, so with a rather rueful face he went off to his bedroom, from which he returned presently pulling a large tin box behind him. This he placed in the middle of the floor, and squatting down upon a stool in front of it he threw back the lid. I could see that it was already a third full of bundles of paper tied up with red tape into separate packages.

"There are cases enough here, Watson," said he, looking at me with mischievous eyes. "I think that if you knew all that I had in this box you would ask me to pull some out instead of putting others in."

"These are the records of your early work, then ?" I asked. "I have often wished that I had notes of those cases."

"Yes, my boy ; these were all done prematurely, before my biographer had come to glorify me." He lifted bundle after bundle in a tender, caressing sort of way. "They are not all successes, Watson," said he, "but there are some pretty little problems among them. Here's the record of the Tarleton murders, and the case of Vamberry, the wine merchant, and the adventure of the old Russian woman, and the singular affair of the aluminium crutch, as well as a full account of Ricoletti of the club foot and his abominable wife. And here—ah, now ! this really is something a little *recherché*."

He dived his arm down to the bottom of the chest, and brought up a small wooden box, with a sliding lid, such as children's toys are kept in. From within he produced a crumpled piece of paper, an old-fashioned brass key, a peg of wood with a ball of string attached to it, and three rusty old discs of metal.

" Well, my boy, what do you make of this lot ? " he asked, smiling at my expression.

" It is a curious collection."

" Very curious, and the story that hangs round it will strike you as being more curious still."

" These relics have a history, then ? "

" So much so that they *are* history."

" What do you mean by that ? "

Sherlock Holmes picked them up one by one, and laid them along the edge of the table. Then he re-seated himself in his chair, and looked them over with a gleam of satisfaction in his eyes.

" These," said he, " are all that I have left to remind me of the episode of the Musgrave Ritual."

I had heard him mention the case more than once, though I had never been able to gather the details.

" I should be so glad," said I, " if you would give me an account of it."

" And leave the litter as it is ? " he cried, mischievously. " Your tidiness won't bear much strain, after all, Watson. But I should be glad that you should add this case to your annals, for there are points in it which make it quite unique in the criminal records of this or, I believe, of any other country. A collection of my trifling achievements would certainly be incomplete which contained no account of this very singular business.

" You may remember how the affair of the *Gloria Scott*, and my conversation with the unhappy man whose fate I told you of, first turned my attention in the direction of the profession which has become my life's work. You see me now when my name has become known far and wide, and when I am generally recognized both by the public and by the official force as being a final court of appeal in doubtful cases. Even when you knew me first, at the time of the affair which you have commemorated in ' A Study in Scarlet,' I had already established a considerable, though not a very lucrative, connection. You can hardly realize, then, how difficult I found it at first, and how long I had to wait before I succeeded in making any headway.

"When I first came up to London I had rooms in Montague Street, just round the corner from the British Museum, and there I waited, filling in my too abundant leisure time by studying all those branches of science which might make me more efficient. Now and again cases came in my way, principally through the introduction of old fellow-students, for during my last years at the university there was a good deal of talk there about myself and my methods. The third of these cases was that of the Musgrave Ritual, and it is to the interest which was aroused by that singular chain of events, and the large issues which proved to be at stake, that I trace my first stride towards the position which I now hold.

"Reginald Musgrave had been in the same college as myself, and I had some slight acquaintance with him. He was not generally popular among the undergraduates, though it always seemed to me that what was set down as pride was really an attempt to cover extreme natural diffidence. In appearance he was a man of an exceedingly aristocratic type, thin, high-nosed, and large-eyed, with languid and yet courtly manners. He was indeed a scion of one of the very oldest families in the kingdom, though his branch was a cadet one which had separated from the Northern Musgraves some time in the sixteenth century, and had established itself in Western Sussex, where the manor house of Hurlstone is perhaps the oldest inhabited building in the county. Something of his birthplace seemed to cling to the man, and I never looked at his pale, keen face, or the poise of his head, without associating him with grey archways and mullioned windows and all the venerable wreckage of a feudal keep. Now and again we drifted into talk, and I can remember that more than once he expressed a keen interest in my methods of observation and inference.

"For four years I had seen nothing of him, until one morning he walked into my room in Montague Street. He had changed little, was dressed like a young man of fashion—he was always a bit of a dandy—and preserved the same quiet, suave manner which had formerly distinguished him.

"'How has all gone with you, Musgrave?' I asked, after we had cordially shaken hands.

"'You probably heard of my poor father's death,' said he. 'He was carried off about two years ago. Since then I have, of course, had the Hurlstone estates to manage, and as I am member for my district as well, my life has been a busy one; but I understand, Holmes, that you are turning to practical ends those powers with which you used to amaze us.'

"'Yes,' said I, 'I have taken to living by my wits.'

"'I am delighted to hear it, for your advice at present would be exceedingly valuable to me. We have had some very strange doings at Hurlstone, and the police have been able to throw no light upon the matter. It is really the most extraordinary and inexplicable business.'

"You can imagine with what eagerness I listened to him, Watson, for the very chance for which I had been panting during all those months of inaction seemed to have come within my reach. In my inmost heart I believed that I could succeed where others failed, and now I had the opportunity to test myself.

"'Pray let me have the details,' I cried.

"Reginald Musgrave sat down opposite to me, and lit the cigarette which I had pushed towards him.

"'You must know,' said he, 'that though I am a bachelor I have to keep up a considerable staff of servants at Hurlstone, for it is a rambling old place, and takes a good deal of looking after. I preserve, too, and in the pheasant months I usually have a house-party, so that it would not do to be short-handed. Altogether there are eight maids, the cook, the butler, two footmen, and a boy. The garden and the stables, of course, have a separate staff.

" ' Of these servants the one who had been longest in our service was Brunton, the butler. He was a young schoolmaster out of place when he was first taken up by my father, but he was a man of great energy and character, and he soon became quite invaluable in the household. He was a well-grown, handsome man, with a splendid forehead, and though he has been with us for twenty years he cannot be more than forty now. With his personal advantages and his extraordinary gifts, for he can speak several languages and play nearly every musical instrument, it is wonderful that he should have been satisfied so long in such a position, but I suppose that he was comfortable and lacked energy to make any change. The butler of Hurlstone is always a thing that is remembered by all who visit us.

" ' But this paragon has one fault. He is a bit of a Don Juan, and you can imagine that for a man like him it is not a very difficult part to play in a quiet country district.

" ' When he was married it was all right, but since he has been a widower we have had no end of trouble with him. A few months ago we were in hopes that he was about to settle down again, for he became engaged to Rachel Howells, our second housemaid, but he has thrown her over since then and taken up with Janet Tregellis, the daughter of the head gamekeeper. Rachel, who is a very good girl, but of an excitable Welsh temperament, had a sharp touch of brain fever, and goes about the house now —or did until yesterday—like a black-eyed shadow of her former self. That was our first drama at Hurlstone, but a second one came to drive it from our minds, and it was prefaced by the disgrace and dismissal of butler Brunton.

" ' This is how it came about. I have said that the man was intelligent, and this very intelligence has caused his ruin, for it seems to have led to an insatiable curiosity about things which did not in the least concern him. I had no idea of the lengths to which this would carry him until the merest accident opened my eyes to it.

" ' I have said that the house is a rambling one. One night last week—on Thursday night, to be more exact—I found that I could not sleep, having foolishly taken a cup of strong *café noir* after my dinner. After struggling against it until two in the morning I felt that it was quite hopeless, so I rose and lit the candle with the intention of continuing a novel which I was reading. The book, however, had been left in the billiard-room, so I pulled on my dressing-gown and started off to get it.

" ' In order to reach the billiard-room I had to descend a flight of stairs, and then to cross the head of the passage which led to the library and the gun-room. You can imagine my surprise when as I looked down this corridor I saw a glimmer of light coming from the open door of the library. I had myself extinguished the lamp and closed the door before coming to bed. Naturally, my first thought was of burglars. The corridors at Hurlstone have their walls largely decorated with trophies of old weapons. From one of these I picked a battle-axe, and then, leaving my candle behind me, I crept on tiptoe down the passage and peeped in at the open door.

" ' Brunton, the butler, was in the library. He was sitting, fully dressed, in an easy chair, with a slip of paper, which looked like a map, upon his knee, and his forehead sunk forward upon his hand in deep thought. I stood, dumb with astonishment, watching him from the darkness. A small taper on the edge of the table shed a feeble light, which sufficed to show me that he was fully dressed. Suddenly, as I looked, he rose from his chair, and walking over to a bureau at the side, he unlocked it and drew out one of the drawers. From this he took a paper, and, returning to his seat, he flattened it out beside the taper on the edge of the table, and began to study it with minute attention. My indignation at this calm examination of our family documents overcame me so far that I took a step forward, and Brunton looking up saw me standing in the doorway. He sprang to his feet, his face turned livid with fear, and he thrust into his breast the chart-like paper which he had been originally studying.

"'"So!" said I, "this is how you repay the trust which we have reposed in you! You will leave my service to-morrow."

"'He bowed with the look of a man who is utterly crushed, and slunk past me without a word. The taper was still on the table, and by its light I glanced to see what the paper was which Brunton had taken from the bureau. To my surprise it was nothing of any importance at all, but simply a copy of the questions and answers in the singular old observance called the Musgrave Ritual. It is a sort of ceremony peculiar to our family, which each Musgrave for centuries past has gone through upon his coming of age—a thing of private interest, and perhaps of some little importance to the archæologist, like our own blazonings and charges, but of no practical use whatever.

"'"We had better come back to the paper afterwards," said I.

"'"If you think it really necessary," he answered, with some hesitation.

"'To continue my statement, however, I re-locked the bureau, using the key which Brunton had left, and I had turned to go, when I was surprised to find that the butler had returned and was standing before me.

"'"Mr. Musgrave, sir," he cried, in a voice which was hoarse with emotion, "I can't bear disgrace, sir. I've always been proud above my station in life, and disgrace would kill me. My blood will be on your head, sir—it will, indeed—if you drive me to despair. If you cannot keep me after what has passed, then for God's sake let me give you notice and leave in a month, as if of my own free will. I could stand that, Mr. Musgrave, but not to be cast out before all the folk that I know so well."

" ' " You don't deserve much consideration, Brunton,"
I answered. " Your conduct has been most infamous.
However, as you have been a long time in the family, I
have no wish to bring public disgrace upon you. A
month, however, is too long. Take yourself away in a
week, and give what reason you like for going.''

" ' " Only a week, sir ? '' he cried in a despairing voice.
" A fortnight—say at least a fortnight.''

" ' " A week,'' I repeated, " and you may consider
yourself to have been very leniently dealt with.''

" ' He crept away, his face sunk upon his breast, like a
broken man, while I put out the light and returned to my
room.

" ' For two days after this Brunton was most assiduous
in his attention to his duties. I made no allusion to
what had passed, and waited with some curiosity to see
how he would cover his disgrace. On the third morning,
however, he did not appear, as was his custom, after
breakfast to receive my instructions for the day. As I
left the dining-room I happened to meet Rachel Howells,
the maid. I have told you that she had only recently
recovered from an illness, and was looking so wretchedly
pale and wan that I remonstrated with her for being at
work.

" ' " You should be in bed,'' I said. " Come back to
your duties when you are stronger.''

" ' She looked at me with so strange an expression that
I began to suspect that her brain was affected.

" ' " I am strong enough, Mr. Musgrave,'' said she.

" ' " We will see what the doctor says,'' I answered.
" You must stop work now, and when you go downstairs
just say that I wish to see Brunton.''

" ' " The butler is gone,'' said she.

" ' " Gone ! Gone where ? ''

" ' " He is gone. No one has seen him. He is not in
his room. Oh, yes, he is gone—he is gone ! '' She fell
back against the wall with shriek after shriek of laughter,
while I, horrified at this sudden hysterical attack, rushed

to the bell to summon help. The girl was taken to her room, still screaming and sobbing, while I made inquiries about Brunton. There was no doubt about it that he had disappeared. His bed had not been slept in ; he had been seen by no one since he had retired to his room the night before ; and yet it was difficult to see how he could have left the house, as both windows and doors were found to be fastened in the morning. His clothes, his watch, and even his money were in his room—but the black suit which he usually wore was missing. His slippers, too, were gone, but his boots were left behind. Where, then, could butler Brunton have gone in the night, and what could have become of him now ?

" ' Of course we searched the house from cellar to garret, but there was no trace of him. It is as I have said a labyrinth of an old house, especially the original wing, which is now practically uninhabited, but we ransacked every room and attic without discovering the least sign of the missing man. It was incredible to me that he could have gone away leaving all his property behind him, and yet where could he be ? I called in the local police, but without success. Rain had fallen on the night before, and we examined the lawn and the paths all round the house, but in vain. Matters were in this state when a new development quite drew our attention away from the original mystery.

" ' For two days Rachel Howells had been so ill, some-times delirious, sometimes hysterical, that a nurse had been employed to sit up with her at night. On the third night after Brunton's disappearance, the nurse, finding her patient sleeping nicely, had dropped into a nap in the arm-chair, when she woke in the early morning to find the bed empty, the window open, and no signs of the invalid. I was instantly aroused, and with the two foot-men started off at once in search of the missing girl. It was not difficult to tell the direction which she had taken, for, starting from under her window, we could follow her footmarks easily across the lawn to the edge of the mere, where they vanished, close to the gravel path which leads out of the grounds. The lake there is 8 feet deep, and you can imagine our feelings when we saw that the trail of the poor demented girl came to an end at the edge of it.

"'Of course, we had the drags at once, and set to work to recover the remains ; but no trace of the body could we find. On the other hand, we brought to the surface an object of a most unexpected kind. It was a linen bag, which contained within it a mass of old rusted and discoloured metal and several dull-coloured pieces of pebble or glass. This strange find was all that we could get from the mere, and although we made every possible search and inquiry yesterday, we know nothing of the fate either of Rachel Howells or Richard Brunton. The county police are at their wits' end, and I have come up to you as a last resource.'

"You can imagine, Watson, with what eagerness I listened to this extraordinary sequence of events, and endeavoured to piece them together, and to devise some common thread upon which they might all hang.

"The butler was gone. The maid was gone. The maid had loved the butler, but had afterwards had cause to hate him. She was of Welsh blood, fiery and passionate. She had been terribly excited immediately after his disappearance. She had flung into the lake a bag containing some curious contents. These were all factors which had to be taken into consideration, and yet none of them got quite to the heart of the matter. What was the starting-point of this chain of events ? There lay the end of this tangled line.

"'I must see that paper, Musgrave,' said I, 'which this butler of yours thought it worth his while to consult, even at the risk of the loss of his place.'

"'It is rather an absurd business, this Ritual of ours,' he answered, 'but it has at least the saving grace of antiquity to excuse it. I have a copy of the questions and answers here, if you care to run your eye over them.'

" He handed me the very paper which I have here, Watson, and this is the strange catechism to which each Musgrave had to submit when he came to man's estate. I will read you the questions and answers as they stand :

" ' Whose was it ?

" ' His who is gone.

" ' Who shall have it ?

" ' He who will come.

" ' What was the month ?

" ' The sixth from the first.

" ' Where was the sun ?

" ' Over the oak.

" ' Where was the shadow ?

" ' Under the elm.

" ' How was it stepped ?

" ' North by ten and by ten, east by five and by five, south by two and by two, west by one and by one, and so under.

" ' What shall we give for it ?

" ' All that is ours.

" ' Why should we give it ?

" ' For the sake of the trust.'

" ' The original has no date, but is in the spelling of the middle of the seventeenth century,' remarked Musgrave. ' I am afraid, however, that it can be of little help to you in solving this mystery.'

" ' At least,' said I, ' it gives us another mystery, and one which is even more interesting than the first. It may be that the solution of the one may prove to be the solution of the other. You will excuse me, Musgrave, if I say that your butler appears to me to have been a very clever man, and to have had a clearer insight than ten generations of his masters.'

" ' I hardly follow you,' said Musgrave. ' The paper seems to me of no practical importance.'

" ' But to me it seems immensely practical, and I fancy that Brunton took the same view. He had probably seen it before that night on which you caught him.'

" ' It is very possible. We took no pains to hide it.'

" ' He simply wished, I should imagine, to refresh his memory upon that last occasion. He had, as I understand, some sort of map or chart which he was comparing with the manuscript, and which he thrust into his pocket when you appeared ? '

" ' That is true. But what could he have to do with this old family custom of ours, and what does this rigmarole mean ? '

" ' I don't think that we should have much difficulty in determining that,' said I. ' With your permission we will take the first train down to Sussex and go a little more deeply into the matter upon the spot.'

" The same afternoon saw us both at Hurlstone. Possibly you have seen pictures and read descriptions of the famous old building, so I will confine my account of it to saying that it is built in the shape of an L, the long arm being the more modern portion, and the shorter the ancient nucleus from which the other has developed. Over the low, heavy-lintelled door, in the centre of this old part, is chiselled the date 1607, but experts are agreed that the beams and stonework are really much older than this. The enormously thick walls and tiny windows of this part had in the last century driven the family into building the new wing, and the old one was used now as a storehouse and a cellar when it was used at all. A splendid park, with fine old timber, surrounded the house, and the lake, to which my client had referred, lay close to the avenue, about two hundred yards from the building.

" I was already firmly convinced, Watson, that there were not three separate mysteries here, but one only, and that if I could read the Musgrave Ritual aright, I should hold in my hand the clue which would lead me to the truth concerning both the butler Brunton, and the maid Howells. To that, then, I turned all my energies. Why should this servant be so anxious to master this old formula ? Evidently because he saw something in it which had escaped all those generations of country squires, and from which he expected some personal advantage. What was it, then, and how had it affected his fate ?

" It was perfectly obvious to me on reading the Ritual that the measurements must refer to some spot to which the rest of the document alluded, and that if we could find that spot we should be in a fair way towards knowing what the secret was which the old Musgraves had thought it necessary to embalm in so curious a fashion. There were two guides given us to start with, an oak and an elm. As to the oak, there could be no question at all. Right in front of the house, upon the left-hand side of the drive, there stood a patriarch among oaks, one of the most magnificent trees that I have ever seen.

" ' That was there when your Ritual was drawn up ? ' said I, as we drove past it.

" ' It was there at the Norman Conquest, in all probability,' he answered. ' It has a girth of 23 feet.'

" Here was one of my fixed points secured.

" ' Have you any old elms ? ' I asked.

" ' There used to be a very old one over yonder, but it was struck by lightning ten years ago, and we cut down the stump.'

" ' You can see where it used to be ? '

" ' Oh, yes.'

" ' There are no other elms ? '

" ' No old ones, but plenty of beeches.'

" ' I should like to see where it grew.'

" We had driven up in a dog-cart, and my client led me away at once, without our entering the house, to the scar on the lawn where the elm had stood. It was nearly midway between the oak and the house. My investigation seemed to be progressing.

" ' I suppose it is impossible to find out how high the elm was ? ' I asked.

" ' I can give you it at once. It was 64 feet.'

" ' How do you come to know it ? ' I asked in surprise.

" ' When my old tutor used to give me an exercise in

trigonometry it always took the shape of measuring heights. When I was a lad I worked out every tree and building on the estate.'

"This was an unexpected piece of luck. My data were coming more quickly than I could have reasonably hoped.

"'Tell me,' I asked, 'did your butler ever ask you such a question?'

"Reginald Musgrave looked at me in astonishment. 'Now that you call it to my mind,' he answered, 'Brunton *did* ask me about the height of the tree some months ago, in connection with some little argument with the groom.'

"This was excellent news, Watson, for it showed me that I was on the right road. I looked up at the sun. It was low in the heavens, and I calculated that in less than an hour it would lie just above the topmost branches of the old oak. One condition mentioned in the Ritual would then be fulfilled. And the shadow of the elm must mean the further end of the shadow, otherwise the trunk would have been chosen as the guide. I had then to find where the far end of the shadow would fall when the sun was just clear of the oak."

"That must have been difficult, Holmes, when the elm was no longer there."

"Well, at least, I knew that if Brunton could do it, I could also. Besides, there was no real difficulty. I went with Musgrave to his study and whittled myself this peg, to which I tied this long string, with a knot at each yard. Then I took two lengths of a fishing-rod, which came to just 6 feet, and I went back with my client to where the elm had been. The sun was just grazing the top of the oak. I fastened the rod on end, marked out the direction of the shadow, and measured it. It was 9 feet in length.

"Of course, the calculation was now a simple one. If a rod of 6 feet threw a shadow of 9 feet, a tree of 64 feet would throw one of 96 feet, and the line of one would of course be the line of the other. I measured out the distance, which brought me almost to the wall of the house, and I thrust a peg into the spot. You can imagine my exultation, Watson, when within 2 inches of my peg I saw a conical depression in the ground. I knew that it was the mark made by Brunton in his measurements, and that I was still upon his trail.

" From this starting-point I proceeded to step, having first taken the cardinal points by my pocket compass. Ten steps with each foot took me along parallel with the wall of the house, and again I marked my spot with a peg. Then I carefully paced off five to the east and two to the south. It brought me to the very threshold of the old door. Two steps to the west meant now that I was to go two paces down the stone-flagged passage, and this was the place indicated by the Ritual.

" Never have I felt such a cold chill of disappointment, Watson. For a moment it seemed to me that there must be some radical mistake in my calculations. The setting sun shone full upon the passage floor, and I could see that the old foot-worn grey stones, with which it was paved, were firmly cemented together, and had certainly not been moved for many a long year. Brunton had not been at work here. I tapped upon the floor, but it sounded the same all over, and there was no sign of any crack or crevice. But fortunately Musgrave, who had begun to appreciate the meaning of my proceedings, and who was now as excited as myself, took out his manuscript to check my calculations.

" ' And under,' he cried : ' you have omitted the " and under." '

" I had thought that it meant that we were to dig, but now, of course, I saw at once that I was wrong. ' There is a cellar under this, then ? ' I cried.

" ' Yes, and as old as the house. Down here, through this door.'

" We went down a winding stone stair, and my companion, striking a match, lit a large lantern which stood on a barrel in the corner. In an instant it was obvious that

411

we had at last come upon the true place, and that we had not been the only people to visit the spot recently.

" It had been used for the storage of wood, but the billets, which had evidently been littered over the floor, were now piled at the sides so as to leave a clear space in the middle. In this space lay a large and heavy flagstone, with a rusted iron ring in the centre, to which a thick shepherd's check muffler was attached.

" ' By Jove ! ' cried my client, ' that's Brunton's muffler. I have seen it on him, and could swear to it. What has the villain been doing here ? '

" At my suggestion a couple of the county police were summoned to be present, and I then endeavoured to raise the stone by pulling on the cravat. I could only move it slightly, and it was with the aid of one of the constables that I succeeded at last in carrying it to one side. A black hole yawned beneath, into which we all peered, while Musgrave, kneeling at the side, pushed down the lantern.

" A small chamber about 7 feet deep and 4 feet square lay open to us. At one side of this was a squat, brass-bound, wooden box, the lid of which was hinged upwards, with this curious, old-fashioned key projecting from the lock. It was furred outside by a thick layer of dust, and damp and worms had eaten through the wood so that a crop of living fungi was growing on the inside of it. Several discs of metal—old coins apparently—such as I hold here, were scattered over the bottom of the box, but it contained nothing else.

" At the moment, however, we had not thought for the old chest, for our eyes were riveted upon that which crouched beside it. It was the figure of a man, clad in a suit of black, who squatted down upon his hams with his forehead sunk upon the edge of the box and his two arms thrown out on each side of it. The attitude had drawn all the stagnant blood to his face, and no man could have recognized that distorted, liver-coloured countenance ; but his height, his dress, and his hair were all sufficient to show my client, when we had drawn the body up, that it was indeed his missing butler. He had been dead some days, but there was no wound or bruise upon his person to show how he had met his dreadful end. When his body had been carried from the cellar we found ourselves still confronted with a problem which was almost as formidable as that with which we had started.

" I confess that so far, Watson, I had been disappointed in my investigation. I had reckoned upon solving the matter when once I had found the place referred to in the Ritual ; but now I was there, and was apparently as far as ever from knowing what it was which the family had concealed with such elaborate precautions. It is true that I had thrown a light upon the fate of Brunton, but now I had to ascertain how that fate had come upon him, and what part had been played in the matter by the woman who had disappeared. I sat down upon a keg in the corner and thought the whole matter carefully over.

" You know my methods in such cases, Watson : I put myself in the man's place, and having first gauged his intelligence, I try to imagine how I should myself have proceeded under the same circumstances. In this case the matter was simplified by Brunton's intelligence being quite first rate, so that it was unnecessary to make any allowance for personal equation, as the astronomers have dubbed it. He knew that something valuable was concealed. He had spotted the place. He found that the stone which covered it was just too heavy for a man to move unaided. What would he do next ? He could not get help from outside, even if he had someone whom he could trust, without the unbarring of doors, and considerable risk of detection. It was better, if he could, to have his helpmate inside the house. But whom could he ask ? This girl had been devoted to him. A man always finds it hard to realize that he may have finally lost a woman's love, however badly he may have treated her. He would try by a few attentions to make his peace with the girl Howells, and then would engage her as his accomplice. Together they would come at night to the cellar, and their united force would suffice to raise the stone. So far I could follow their actions as if I had actually seen them.

" But for two of them, and one a woman, it must have been heavy work, the raising of that stone. A burly Sussex policeman and I had found it no light job. What would they do to assist them ? Probably what I should have done myself. I rose and examined carefully the different billets of wood which were scattered round the floor. Almost at once I came upon what I expected. One piece, about 3 feet in length, had a marked indentation at one end, while several were flattened at the sides as if they had been compressed by some considerable weight. Evidently as they had dragged the stone up they had thrust the chunks of wood into the chink, until at last, when the opening was large enough to crawl through, they would hold it open by a billet placed lengthwise, which might very well become indented at the lower end, since the whole weight of the stone would press it down on to the edge of the other slab. So far I was still on safe ground.

" And now, how was I to proceed to reconstruct this midnight drama ? Clearly only one could get into the hole, and that one was Brunton. The girl must have waited above. Brunton then unlocked the box, handed up the contents, presumably—since they were not to be found—and then—and then what happened ?

" What smouldering fire of vengeance had suddenly sprung into flame in this passionate Celtic woman's soul when she saw the man who had wronged her—wronged her perhaps far more than we suspected—in her power ? Was it a chance that the wood had slipped and that the stone had shut Brunton into what had become his sepulchre ? Had she only been guilty of silence as to his fate ? Or had some sudden blow from her hand dashed the support away and sent the slab crashing down into its place. Be that as it might, I seemed to see that

414

woman's figure, still clutching at her treasure-trove, and
flying wildly up the winding stair with her ears ringing perhaps with the muffled screams from behind her,
and with the drumming of frenzied hands against the
slab of stone which was choking her faithless lover's life
out.

" Here was the secret of her blanched face, her shaken
nerves, her peals of hysterical laughter on the next
morning. But what had been in the box ? What had
she done with that ? Of course, it must have been the
old metal and pebbles which my client had dragged from
the mere. She had thrown them in there at the first
opportunity, to remove the last trace of her crime.

" For twenty minutes I had sat motionless thinking
the matter out. Musgrave still stood with a very pale
face swinging his lantern and peering down into the hole.

" ' These are coins of Charles I,' said he, holding out
the few which had been left in the box. ' You see we
were right in fixing our date for the Ritual.'

" ' We may find something else of Charles I,' I cried,
as the probable meaning of the first two questions of the
Ritual broke suddenly upon me. ' Let me see the contents of the bag you fished from the mere.'

" We ascended to his study, and he laid the *débris*
before me. I could understand his regarding it as of
small importance when I looked at it, for the metal was
almost black, and the stones lustreless and dull. I
rubbed one of them on my sleeve, however, and it glowed
afterwards like a spark, in the dark hollow of my hand.
The metal-work was in the form of a double-ring, but
it had been bent and twisted out of its original shape.

" ' You must bear in mind,' said I, ' that the Royal
party made head in England even after the death of the
King, and that when they at last fled they probably left
many of their most precious possessions buried behind
them, with the intention of returning for them in more
peaceful times.'

" ' My ancestor, Sir Ralph Musgrave, was a prominent

415

Cavalier, and the right-hand man of Charles II in his wanderings,' said my friend.

"'Ah, indeed!' I answered. 'Well, now, I think that really should give us the last link that we wanted. I must congratulate you on coming into possession, though in rather a tragic manner, of a relic which is of great intrinsic value, but even of greater importance as an historical curiosity.'

"'What is it, then?' he gasped in astonishment.

"'It is nothing less than the ancient crown of the Kings of England.'

"'The crown!'

"'Precisely. Consider what the Ritual says. How does it run? "Whose was it?" "His who is gone." That was after the execution of Charles. Then, "Who shall have it?" "He who will come." That was Charles II, whose advent was already foreseen. There can, I think, be no doubt that this battered and shapeless diadem once encircled the brows of the Royal Stuarts.'

"'And how came it in the pond?'

"'Ah, that is a question which will take some time to answer,' and with that I sketched out the whole long chain of surmise and of proof which I had constructed. The twilight had closed in and the moon was shining brightly in the sky before my narrative was finished.

"'And how was it, then, that Charles did not get his crown when he returned?' asked Musgrave, pushing back the relic into its linen bag.

"'Ah, there you lay your finger upon the one point which we shall probably never be able to clear up. It is likely that the Musgrave who held the secret died in the interval, and by some oversight left this guide to his descendant without explaining the meaning of it. From that day to this it has been handed down from father to son, until at last it came within reach of a man who tore its secret out of it and lost his life in the venture.'

"And that's the story of the Musgrave Ritual, Watson. They have the crown down at Hurlstone—though they had some legal bother, and a considerable sum to pay before they were allowed to retain it. I am sure that if you mentioned my name they would be happy to show it to you. Of the woman nothing was ever heard, and the probability is that she got away out of England, and carried herself, and the memory of her crime, to some land beyond the seas."

18. *The Reigate Squires*

IT was some time before the health of my friend, Mr. Sherlock Holmes, recovered from the strain caused by his immense exertions in the spring of '87. The whole question of the Netherland-Sumatra Company and of the colossal schemes of Baron Maupertuis is too recent in the minds of the public, and too intimately concerned with politics and finance, to be a fitting subject for this series of sketches. It led, however, in an indirect fashion to a singular and complex problem, which gave my friend an opportunity of demonstrating the value of a fresh weapon among the many with which he waged his lifelong battle against crime.

On referring to my notes, I see that it was on the 14th of April that I received a telegram from Lyons, which informed me that Holmes was lying ill in the Hotel Dulong. Within twenty-four hours I was in his sick-room, and was relieved to find that there was nothing formidable in his symptoms. His iron constitution, how-ever, had broken down under the strain of an investigation which had extended over two months, during which period he had never worked less than fifteen hours a day, and had more than once, as he assured me, kept to his task for five days at a stretch. The triumphant issue of his labours could not save him from reaction after so terrible an exertion, and at a time when Europe was ringing with his name, and when his room was literally ankle-deep with congratulatory telegrams, I found him a prey to the blackest depression. Even the knowledge that he had succeeded where the police of three countries had failed, and that he had outmanœuvred at every point the most accomplished swindler in Europe, was insufficient to rouse him from his nervous prostration.

Three days later we were back in Baker Street together, but it was evident that my friend would be much the better for a change, and the thought of a week of springtime in the country was full of attractions to me also. My old friend Colonel Hayter, who had come under my professional care in Afghanistan, had now taken a house near Reigate, in Surrey, and had frequently asked me to come down to him upon a visit. On the last occasion he had remarked that if my friend would only come with me, he would be glad to extend his hospitality to him also. A little diplomacy was needed, but when Holmes understood that the establishment was a bachelor one, and that he would be allowed the fullest freedom, he fell in with my plans, and a week after our return from Lyons, we were under the Colonel's roof. Hayter was a fine old soldier, who had seen much of the world, and he soon found, as I had expected, that Holmes and he had plenty in common.

On the evening of our arrival we were sitting in the Colonel's gun-room after dinner, Holmes stretched upon the sofa, while Hayter and I looked over his little armoury of firearms.

"By the way," said he, suddenly, "I'll take one of these pistols upstairs with me in case we have an alarm."

"An alarm!" said I.

"Yes, we've had a scare in this part lately. Old Acton, who is one of our county magnates, had his house broken into last Monday. No great damage done, but the fellows are still at large."

"No clue?" asked Holmes, cocking his eye at the Colonel.

"None as yet. But the affair is a petty one, one of our little country crimes, which must seem too small for your attention, Mr. Holmes, after this great international affair."

Holmes waved away the compliment, though his smile showed that it had pleased him.

"Was there any feature of interest?"

"I fancy not. The thieves ransacked the library, and got very little for their pains. The whole place was turned upside down, drawers burst open and presses ransacked, with the result that an odd volume of Pope's 'Homer,' two plated candlesticks, an ivory letter-weight, a small oak barometer, and a ball of twine are all that have vanished."

"What an extraordinary assortment!" I exclaimed.

"Oh, the fellows evidently grabbed hold of anything they could get."

Holmes grunted from the sofa.

"The county police ought to make something of that," said he. "Why, it is surely obvious that——"

But I held up a warning finger.

"You are here for a rest, my dear fellow. For Heaven's sake, don't get started on a new problem when your nerves are all in shreds."

Holmes shrugged his shoulders with a glance of comic resignation towards the Colonel, and the talk drifted away into less dangerous channels.

It was destined, however, that all my professional caution should be wasted, for next morning the problem obtruded itself upon us in such a way that it was impossible to ignore it, and our country visit took a turn which neither of us could have anticipated. We were at breakfast when the Colonel's butler rushed in with all his propriety shaken out of him.

"Have you heard the news, sir?" he gasped. "At the Cunninghams', sir!"

"Burglary?" cried the Colonel, with his coffee-cup in mid-air.

"Murder!"

The Colonel whistled. "By Jove!" said he, "who's killed, then? The J.P. or his son?"

"Neither, sir. It was William, the coachman. Shot through the heart, sir, and never spoke again."

" Who shot him, then ? "

" The burglar, sir. He was off like a shot and got clean away. He'd just broke in at the pantry window when William came on him and met his end in saving his master's property."

" What time ? "

" It was last night, sir, somewhere about twelve."

" Ah, then, we'll step over presently," said the Colonel, coolly settling down to his breakfast again. " It's a baddish business," he added, when the butler had gone. " He's our leading squire about here, is old Cunningham, and a very decent fellow, too. He'll be cut up over this, for the man has been in his service for years, and was a good servant. It's evidently the same villains who broke into Acton's."

" And stole that very singular collection ? " said Holmes, thoughtfully.

" Precisely."

" Hum ! It may prove the simplest matter in the world ; but, all the same, at first glance this is just a little curious, is it not ? A gang of burglars acting in the country might be expected to vary the scene of their operations, and not to crack two cribs in the same district within a few days. When you spoke last night of taking precautions, I remember that it passed through my mind that this was probably the last parish in England to which the thief or thieves would be likely to turn their attention ; which shows that I have still much to learn."

" I fancy it's some local practitioner," said the Colonel. " In that case, of course, Acton's and Cunningham's are just the places he would go for, since they are far the largest about here."

" And richest ? "

" Well, they ought to be ; but they've had a law-suit for some years which has sucked the blood out of both of them, I fancy. Old Acton has some claim on half Cunningham's estate, and the lawyers have been at it with both hands."

"If it's a local villain, there should not be much difficulty in running him down," said Holmes, with a yawn. "All right, Watson, I don't intend to meddle."

"Inspector Forrester, sir," said the butler, throwing open the door.

The official, a smart, keen-faced young fellow, stepped into the room. "Good morning, Colonel," said he. "I hope I don't intrude, but we hear that Mr. Holmes, of Baker Street, is here."

The Colonel waved his hand towards my friend, and the Inspector bowed.

"We thought that perhaps you would care to step across, Mr. Holmes."

"The Fates are against you, Watson," said he, laughing. "We were chatting about the matter when you came in, Inspector. Perhaps you can let us have a few details." As he leaned back in his chair in the familiar attitude, I knew that the case was hopeless.

"We had no clue in the Acton affair. But here we have plenty to go on, and there's no doubt it is the same party in each case. The man was seen."

"Ah!"

"Yes, sir. But he was off like a deer after the shot that killed poor William Kirwan was fired. Mr. Cunningham saw him from the bedroom window, and Mr. Alec Cunningham saw him from the back passage. It was a quarter to twelve when the alarm broke out. Mr. Cunningham had just got into bed, and Mister Alec was smoking a pipe in his dressing-gown. They both heard William, the coachman, calling for help, and Mister Alec he ran down to see what was the matter. The back door was open, and as he came to the foot of the stairs he saw two men wrestling together outside. One of them fired a shot, the other dropped, and the murderer rushed across the garden and over the hedge. Mr. Cunningham, looking out of his bedroom window, saw the fellow as he gained the road, but lost sight of him at once. Mister Alec stopped to see if he could help the dying man, and so the villain got clean away. Beyond the fact that he was a middle-sized man, and dressed in some dark stuff, we have no personal clue, but we are making energetic inquiries, and if he is a stranger we shall soon find him out."

"What was this William doing there? Did he say anything before he died?"

"Not a word. He lives at the lodge with his mother, and as he was a very faithful fellow, we imagine that he walked up to the house with the intention of seeing that all was right there. Of course, this Acton business has put everyone on their guard. The robber must have just burst open the door—the lock has been forced—when William came upon him."

"Did William say anything to his mother before going out?"

"She is very old and deaf, and we can get no information from her. The shock has made her half-witted, but I understand that she was never very bright. There is one very important circumstance, however. Look at this!"

He took a small piece of torn paper from a notebook and spread it out upon his knee.

"This was found between the finger and thumb of the dead man. It appears to be a fragment torn from a larger sheet. You will observe that the hour mentioned upon it is the very time at which the poor fellow met his

fate. You see that his murderer might have torn the rest of the sheet from him or he might have taken this fragment from the murderer. It reads almost as though it was an appointment."

Holmes took up the scrap of paper, a facsimile of which is here reproduced.

"Presuming that it is an appointment," continued the Inspector, "it is, of course, a conceivable theory that this William Kirwan, although he had the reputation of being an honest man, may have been in league with the thief. He may have met him there, may even have helped him to break in the door, and then they may have fallen out between themselves."

" This writing is of extraordinary interest," said Holmes, who had been examining it with intense concentration. " These are much deeper waters than I had thought." He sank his head upon his hands, while the Inspector smiled at the effect which his case had had upon the famous London specialist.

" Your last remark," said Holmes, presently, " as to the possibility of there being an understanding between the burglar and the servant, and this being a note of appointment from one to the other, is an ingenious and not entirely an impossible supposition. But this writing opens up——" He sank his head into his hands again and remained for some minutes in the deepest thought. When he raised his face I was surprised to see that his cheek was tinged with colour, and his eyes as bright as before his illness. He sprang to his feet with all his old energy.

" I'll tell you what ! " said he. " I should like to have a quiet little glance into the details of this case. There is something in it which fascinates me extremely. If you will permit me, Colonel, I will leave my friend, Watson, and you, and I will step round with the Inspector to test the truth of one or two little fancies of mine. I will be with you again in half an hour."

An hour and a half had elapsed before the Inspector returned alone.

" Mr. Holmes is walking up and down in the field outside," said he. " He wants us all four to go up to the house together."

" To Mr. Cunningham's ? "

" Yes, sir."

" What for ? "

The Inspector shrugged his shoulders. " I don't quite

know, sir. Between ourselves, I think Mr. Holmes has not quite got over his illness yet. He's been behaving very queerly, and he is very much excited."

" I don't think you need alarm yourself," said I. " I have usually found that there was method in his madness.'

" Some folk might say there was madness in his method," muttered the Inspector. " But he's all on fire to start, Colonel, so we had best go out, if you are ready."

We found Holmes pacing up and down in the field, his chin sunk upon his breast, and his hands thrust into his trouser pockets.

" The matter grows in interest," said he. " Watson, your country trip has been a distinct success. I have had a charming morning."

" You have been up to the scene of the crime, I understand ? " said the Colonel.

" Yes ; the Inspector and I have made quite a little reconnaissance together."

" Any success ? "

" Well, we have seen some very interesting things. I'll tell you what we did as we walk. First of all we saw the body of this unfortunate man. He certainly died from a revolver wound, as reported."

" Had you doubted it, then ? "

" Oh, it is as well to test everything. Our inspection was not wasted. We then had an interview with Mr. Cunningham and his son, who were able to point out the exact spot where the murderer had broken through the garden hedge in his flight. That was of great interest."

" Naturally."

" Then we had a look at this poor fellow's mother. We could get no information from her, however, as she is very old and feeble."

" And what is the result of your investigations ? "

" The conviction that the crime is a very peculiar one. Perhaps our visit now may do something to make it less obscure. I think that we are both agreed, Inspector, that the fragment of paper in the dead man's hand, bearing, as it does, the very hour of his death written upon it, is of extreme importance."

"It should give a clue, Mr. Holmes."

"It *does* give a clue. Whoever wrote that note was the man who brought William Kirwan out of his bed at that hour. But where is the rest of that sheet of paper?"

"I examined the ground carefully in the hope of finding it," said the Inspector.

"It was torn out of the dead man's hand. Why was someone so anxious to get possession of it? Because it incriminated him. And what would he do with it? Thrust it into his pocket most likely, never noticing that a corner of it had been left in the grip of the corpse. If we could get the rest of that sheet, it is obvious that we should have gone a long way towards solving the mystery."

"Yes, but how can we get at the criminal's pocket before we catch the criminal."

"Well, well, it was worth thinking over. Then there is another obvious point. The note was sent to William. The man who wrote it could not have taken it, otherwise of course he might have delivered his own message by word of mouth. Who brought the note, then? Or did it come through the post?"

"I have made inquiries," said the Inspector. "William received a letter by the afternoon post yesterday. The envelope was destroyed by him."

"Excellent!" cried Holmes, clapping the Inspector on the back. "You've seen the postman. It is a pleasure to work with you. Well, here is the lodge, and if you will come up, Colonel, I will show you the scene of the crime."

We passed the pretty cottage where the murdered man had lived, and walked up an oak-lined avenue to the fine old Queen Anne house, which bears the date of Malplaquet upon the lintel of the door. Holmes and the Inspector led us round it until we came to the side gate, which is separated by a stretch of garden from the hedge which lines the road. A constable was standing at the kitchen door.

" Throw the door open, officer," said Holmes. " Now it was on those stairs that young Mr. Cunningham stood and saw the two men struggling just where we are. Old Mr. Cunningham was at that window—the second on the left—and he saw the fellow get away just to the left of that bush. So did the son. They are both sure of it on account of the bush. Then Mister Alec ran out and knelt beside the wounded man. The ground is very hard, you see, and there are no marks to guide us."

As he spoke two men came down the garden path, from round the angle of the house. The one was an elderly man, with a strong, deep-lined, heavy-eyed face ; the other a dashing young fellow, whose bright, smiling expression and showy dress were in strange contrast with the business which had brought us there.

" Still at it, then ? " said he to Holmes. " I thought you Londoners were never at fault. You don't seem to be so very quick after all."

" Ah ! you must give us a little time," said Holmes, good-humouredly.

" You'll want it," said young Alec Cunningham. " Why, I don't see that we have any clue at all."

" There's only one," answered the Inspector. " We thought that if we could only find—— Good heavens ! Mr. Holmes, what is the matter ? "

My poor friend's face had suddenly assumed the most dreadful expression. His eyes rolled upwards, his features writhed in agony, and with a suppressed groan he dropped on his face upon the ground. Horrified at the suddenness and severity of the attack, we carried him into the kitchen, where he lay back in a large chair and breathed heavily for some minutes. Finally, with a shamefaced apology for his weakness, he rose once more.

" Watson would tell you that I have only just recovered from a severe illness," he explained. " I am liable to these sudden nervous attacks."

426

" Shall I send you home in my trap ? " asked old Cunningham.

" Well, since I am here there is one point on which I should like to feel sure. We can very easily verify it."

" What is it ? "

" Well, it seems to me that it is just possible that the arrival of this poor fellow William was not before but after the entrance of the burglar into the house. You appear to take it for granted that although the door was forced the robber never got in."

" I fancy that is quite obvious," said Mr. Cunningham, gravely. " Why, my son Alec had not yet gone to bed, and he would certainly have heard anyone moving about."

" Where was he sitting ? "

" I was sitting smoking in my dressing-room."

" Which window is that ? "

" The last on the left, next my father's."

" Both your lamps were lit, of course ? "

" Undoubtedly."

" There are some very singular points here," said Holmes, smiling. " Is it not extraordinary that a burglar —and a burglar who had had some previous experience —should deliberately break into a house at a time when he could see from the lights that two of the family were still afoot ? "

" He must have been a cool hand."

" Well, of course, if the case were not an odd one we should not have been driven to ask you for an explanation," said Mister Alec. " But as to your idea that the man had robbed the house before William tackled him, I think it a most absurd notion. Shouldn't we have found the place disarranged and missed the things which he had taken ? "

" It depends on what the things were," said Holmes. " You must remember that we are dealing with a burglar who is a very peculiar fellow, and who appears to work on lines of his own. Look, for example, at the queer lot of things which he took from Acton's—what was it ?—a ball of string, a letter-weight, and I don't know what other odds and ends ! "

" Well, we are quite in your hands, Mr. Holmes," said old Cunningham. " Anything which you or the Inspector may suggest will most certainly be done."

" In the first place," said Holmes, " I should like you to offer a reward—coming from yourself, for the officials may take a little time before they would agree upon the sum, and these things cannot be done too promptly. I have jotted down the form here, if you would not mind signing it. Fifty pounds was quite enough, I thought."

" I would willingly give five hundred," said the J.P., taking the slip of paper and the pencil which Holmes handed to him. " This is not quite correct, however," he added, glancing over the document.

" I wrote it rather hurriedly."

" You see you begin : ' Whereas, at about a quarter to one on Tuesday morning, an attempt was made '—and so on. It was at a quarter to twelve, as a matter of fact."

I was pained at the mistake, for I knew how keenly Holmes would feel any slip of the kind. It was his speciality to be accurate as to fact, but his recent illness had shaken him, and this one little incident was enough to show me that he was still far from being himself. He was obviously embarrassed for an instant, while the Inspector raised his eyebrows and Alec Cunningham burst into a laugh. The old gentleman corrected the mistake, however, and handed the paper back to Holmes.

" Get it printed as soon as possible," he said. " I think your idea is an excellent one."

Holmes put the slip of paper carefully away in his pocket-book.

" And now," said he, " it would really be a good thing that we should all go over the house together, and make certain that this rather erratic burglar did not, after all, carry anything away with him."

Before entering, Holmes made an examination of the door which had been forced. It was evident that a chisel or strong knife had been thrust in, and the lock forced back with it. We could see the marks in the wood where it had been pushed in.

"You don't use bars, then?" he asked.

"We have never found it necessary."

"You don't keep a dog?"

"Yes; but he is chained on the other side of the house."

"When do the servants go to bed?"

"About ten."

"I understand that William was usually in bed also at that hour?"

"Yes."

"It is singular that on this particular night he should have been up. Now, I should be very glad if you would have the kindness to show us over the house, Mr. Cunningham."

A stone-flagged passage, with the kitchens branching away from it, led by a wooden staircase directly to the first floor of the house. It came out upon the landing opposite to a second more ornamental stair which led up from the front hall. Out of this landing opened the drawing-room and several bedrooms, including those of Mr. Cunningham and his son. Holmes walked slowly, taking keen note of the architecture of the house. I could tell from his expression that he was on a hot scent, and yet I could not in the least imagine in what direction his inferences were leading him.

"My good sir," said Mr. Cunningham, with some impatience, "this is surely very unnecessary. That is my room at the end of the stairs, and my son's is the one beyond it. I leave it to your judgment whether it was possible for the thief to have come up here without disturbing us."

"You must try round and get on a fresh scent, I fancy," said the son, with a rather malicious smile.

"Still, I must ask you to humour me a little further. I should like, for example, to see how far the windows of the bedrooms command the front. This, I understand, is your son's room "—he pushed open the door—" and that, I presume, is the dressing-room in which he sat smoking when the alarm was given. Where does the window of that look out to ? " He stepped across the bedroom, pushed open the door, and glanced round the other chamber.

" I hope you are satisfied now ? " said Mr. Cunningham, testily.

" Thank you ; I think I have seen all that I wished."

" Then, if it is really necessary, we can go into my room."

" If it is not too much trouble."

The J.P. shrugged his shoulders, and led the way into his own chamber, which was a plainly furnished and commonplace room. As we moved across it in the direction of the window, Holmes fell back until he and I were the last of the group. Near the foot of the bed was a small square table, on which stood a dish of oranges and a carafe of water. As we passed it, Holmes, to my unutterable astonishment, leaned over in front of me and deliberately knocked the whole thing over. The glass smashed into a thousand pieces, and the fruit rolled about into every corner of the room.

" You've done it now, Watson," said he, coolly. " A pretty mess you've made of the carpet."

I stooped in some confusion and began to pick up the fruit, understanding that for some reason my companion desired me to take the blame upon myself. The others did the same, and set the table on its legs again.

" Holloa ! " cried the Inspector, " where's he got to ? " Holmes had disappeared.

" Wait here an instant," said young Alec Cunningham. " The fellow is off his head, in my opinion. Come with me, father, and see where he has got to ! "

They rushed out of the room, leaving the Inspector, the Colonel, and me, staring at each other.

" 'Pon my word, I am inclined to agree with Mister

Alec," said the official. "It may be the effect of this illness, but it seems to me that——"

His words were cut short by a sudden scream of "Help! Help! Murder!" With a thrill I recognized the voice as that of my friend. I rushed madly from the room on to the landing. The cries, which had sunk down into a hoarse, inarticulate shouting, came from the room which we had first visited. I dashed in, and on into the dressing-room beyond. The two Cunninghams were bending over the prostrate figure of Sherlock Holmes, the younger clutching his throat with both hands, while the elder seemed to be twisting one of his wrists. In an instant the three of us had torn them away from him, and Holmes staggered to his feet, very pale, and evidently greatly exhausted.

"Arrest these men, Inspector!" he gasped.

"On what charge?"

"That of murdering their coachman, William Kirwan!"

The Inspector stared about him in bewilderment. "Oh, come now, Mr. Holmes," said he at last; "I am sure you don't really mean to——"

"Tut, man; look at their faces!" cried Holmes, curtly.

Never, certainly, have I seen a plainer confession of guilt upon human countenances. The older man seemed numbed and dazed, with a heavy, sullen expression upon his strongly marked face. The son, on the other hand, had dropped all that jaunty, dashing style which had characterized him, and the ferocity of a dangerous wild beast gleamed in his dark eyes and distorted his handsome features. The Inspector said nothing, but, stepping to the door, he blew his whistle. Two of his constables came at the call.

"I have no alternative, Mr. Cunningham," said he. "I trust that this may all prove to be an absurd mistake; but you can see that—— Ah, would you? Drop it!"

He struck out with his hand, and a revolver, which the

431

younger man was in the act of cocking, clattered down upon the floor.

"Keep that," said Holmes, quickly putting his foot upon it. "You will find it useful at the trial. But this is what we really wanted." He held up a little crumpled piece of paper.

"The remainder of the sheet?" cried the Inspector.

"Precisely."

"And where was it?"

"Where I was sure it must be. I'll make the whole matter clear to you presently. I think, Colonel, that you and Watson might return now, and I will be with you again in an hour at the furthest. The Inspector and I must have a word with the prisoners; but you will certainly see me back at luncheon-time."

Sherlock Holmes was as good as his word, for about one o'clock he rejoined us in the Colonel's smoking-room. He was accompanied by a little, elderly gentleman, who was introduced to me as the Mr. Acton whose house had been the scene of the original burglary.

"I wished Mr. Acton to be present while I demonstrated this small matter to you," said Holmes, "for it is natural that he should take a keen interest in the details. I am afraid, my dear Colonel, that you must regret the hour that you took in such a stormy petrel as I am."

"On the contrary," answered the Colonel, warmly, "I consider it the greatest privilege to have been permitted to study your methods of working. I confess that they quite surpass my expectations, and that I am utterly unable to account for your result. I have not yet seen the vestige of a clue."

"I am afraid that my explanation may disillusionize you, but it has always been my habit to hide none of my methods, either from my friend Watson or from anyone who might take an intelligent interest in them. But first, as I am rather shaken by the knocking about which I had in the dressing-room, I think that I shall help myself to a dash of your brandy, Colonel. My strength has been rather tried of late."

" I trust you had no more of those nervous attacks."

Sherlock Holmes laughed heartily. " We will come to that in its turn," said he. " I will lay an account of the case before you in its due order, showing you the various points which guided me in my decision. Pray interrupt me if there is any inference which is not perfectly clear to you.

" It is of the highest importance in the art of detection to be able to recognize out of a number of facts which are incidental and which vital. Otherwise your energy and attention must be dissipated instead of being concentrated. Now, in this case there was not the slightest doubt in my mind from the first that the key of the whole matter must be looked for in the scrap of paper in the dead man's hand.

" Before going into this I would draw your attention to the fact that if Alec Cunningham's narrative were correct, and if the assailant after shooting William Kirwan had *instantly* fled, then it obviously could not be he who tore the paper from the dead man's hand. But if it was not he, it must have been Alec Cunningham himself, for by the time the old man had descended several servants were upon the scene. The point is a simple one, but the Inspector had overlooked it because he had started with the supposition that these county magnates had had nothing to do with the matter. Now, I make a point of never having any prejudices and of following docilely wherever fact may lead me, and so in the very first stage of the investigation I found myself looking a little askance at the part which had been played by Mr. Alec Cunningham.

" And now I made a very careful examination of the corner of paper which the Inspector had submitted to us. It was at once clear to me that it formed part of a very remarkable document. Here it is. Do you not now observe something very suggestive about it ? "

433

" It has a very irregular look," said the Colonel.

" My dear sir," cried Holmes, " there cannot be tne least doubt in the world that it has been written by two persons doing alternate words. When I draw your attention to the strong t's of ' at ' and ' to ' and ask you to compare them with the weak ones of ' quarter ' and ' twelve,' you will instantly recognize the fact. A very brief analysis of those four words would enable you to say with the utmost confidence that the ' learn ' and the ' maybe ' are written in the stronger hand, and the ' what ' in the weaker."

" By Jove, it's as clear as day ! " cried the Colonel. " Why on earth should two men write a letter in such a fashion ? "

" Obviously the business was a bad one, and one of the men who distrusted the other was determined that, whatever was done, each should have an equal hand in it. Now, of the two men it is clear that the one who wrote the ' at ' and ' to ' was the ringleader."

" How do you get at that ? "

" We might deduce it from the mere character of the one hand as compared with the other. But we have more assured reasons than that for supposing it. If you examine this scrap with attention you will come to the conclusion that the man with the stronger hand wrote all his words first, leaving blanks for the other to fill up. These blanks were not always sufficient, and you can see that the second man had a squeeze to fit his ' quarter ' in between the ' at ' and the ' to,' showing that the latter were already written. The man who wrote all his words first is undoubtedly the man who planned this affair."

" Excellent ! " cried Mr. Acton.

" But very superficial," said Holmes. " We come now, however, to a point which is of importance. You may not be aware that the deduction of a man's age from his writing is one which has been brought to considerable accuracy by experts. In normal cases one can place a man in his true decade with tolerable confidence. I say normal cases, because ill-health and physical weakness reproduce the signs of old age, even when the invalid is a youth. In this case, looking at the bold, strong hand of the one, and the rather broken-backed appearance of the other, which still retains its legibility, although the t's have begun to lose their crossings, we can say that the one was a young man, and the other was advanced in years without being positively decrepit."

" Excellent ! " cried Mr. Acton again.

" There is a further point, however, which is subtler and of greater interest. There is something in common between these hands. They belong to men who are blood-relatives. It may be most obvious to you in the Greek e's, but to me there are many small points which indicate the same thing. I have no doubt at all that a family mannerism can be traced in these two specimens of writing. I am only, of course, giving you the leading results now of my examination of the paper. There were twenty-three other deductions which would be of more interest to experts than to you. They all tended to deepen the impression upon my mind that the Cunninghams, father and son, had written this letter.

" Having got so far, my next step was, of course, to examine into the details of the crime and to see how far they would help us. I went up to the house with the Inspector, and saw all that was to be seen. The wound upon the dead man was, as I was able to determine with absolute confidence, caused by a shot from a revolver fired at a distance of something over four yards. There was no powder-blackening on the clothes. Evidently, therefore, Alec Cunningham had lied when he said that the two men were struggling when the shot was fired. Again, both father and son agreed as to the place where the man escaped into the road. At that point, however, as it happens, there is a broadish ditch, moist at the bottom. As there were no indications of boot-marks about this ditch, I was absolutely sure not only that the Cunninghams had again lied, but that there had never been any unknown man upon the scene at all.

" And now I had to consider the motive of this singular crime. To get at this I endeavoured first of all to solve the reason of the original burglary at Mr. Acton's. I understood from something which the Colonel told us that a lawsuit had been going on between you, Mr. Acton, and the Cunninghams. Of course, it instantly occurred to me that they had broken into your library with the intention of getting at some document which might be of importance in the case."

" Precisely so," said Mr. Acton ; " there can be no possible doubt as to their intentions. I have the clearest claim upon half their present estate, and if they could have found a single paper—which, fortunately, was in the strong box of my solicitors—they would undoubtedly have crippled our case."

" There you are ! " said Holmes, smiling. " It was a dangerous, reckless attempt, in which I seemed to trace the influence of young Alec. Having found nothing, they tried to divert suspicion by making it appear to be an ordinary burglary, to which end they carried off whatever they could lay their hands upon. That is all clear enough, but there was much that was still obscure. What I wanted above all was to get the missing part of that note. I was certain that Alec had torn it out of the dead man's hand, and almost certain that he must have thrust it into the pocket of his dressing-gown. Where else could he have put it ? The only question was whether it was still there. It was worth an effort to find out, and for that object we all went up to the house.

" The Cunninghams joined us, as you doubtless remember, outside the kitchen door. It was, of course, of the very first importance that they should not be reminded of the existence of this paper, otherwise they would naturally destroy it without delay. The Inspector was about to tell them the importance which was attached to it when, by the luckiest chance in the world, I tumbled down in a sort of fit and so changed the conversation."

" Good heavens ! " cried the Colonel, laughing. " Do you mean to say all our sympathy was wasted and your fit an imposture ? "

" Speaking professionally, it was admirably done," cried I, looking in amazement at this man who was for ever confounding me with some new phase of his astuteness.

" It is an art which is often useful," said he. " When I recovered I managed by a device, which had, perhaps, some little merit of ingenuity, to get old Cunningham to write the word ' twelve,' so that I might compare it with the ' twelve ' upon the paper."

" Oh, what an ass I have been ! " I exclaimed.

" I could see that you were commiserating with me over my weakness," said Holmes, laughing. " I was sorry to cause you the sympathetic pain which I know that you felt. We then went upstairs together, and having entered the room, and seen the dressing-gown hanging up behind the door, I contrived by upsetting a table to engage their attention for the moment and slipped back to examine the pockets. I had hardly got the paper, however, which was as I had expected, in one of them, when the two Cunninghams were on me, and would, I verily believe, have murdered me then and there but for your prompt and friendly aid. As it is, I feel that young man's grip on my throat now, and the father has twisted my wrist round in the effort to get the paper out of my hand. They saw that I must know all about it, you see, and the sudden change from absolute security to complete despair made them perfectly desperate.

" I had a little talk with old Cunningham afterwards as to the motive of the crime. He was tractable enough, though his son was a perfect demon, ready to blow out his own or anybody else's brains if he could have got to his revolver. When Cunningham saw that the case against him was so strong he lost all heart, and made a clean breast of everything. It seems that William had secretly followed his two masters on the night when they made their raid upon Mr. Acton's, and, having thus got them into his power, proceeded under threats of exposure to levy blackmail upon them. Mister Alec, however, was a dangerous man to play games of that sort with. It was a stroke of positive genius on his part to see in the burglary scare, which was convulsing the country-side, an opportunity of plausibly getting rid of the man whom he feared. William was decoyed up and shot ; and, had they only got the whole of the note, and paid a little more attention to detail in their accessories, it is very possible that suspicion might never have been aroused."

" And the note ? " I asked.

Sherlock Holmes placed the subjoined paper before us.

" It is very much the sort of thing that I expected," said he. " Of course, we do not yet know what the relations may have been between Alec Cunningham, William Kirwan, and Annie Morrison. The result shows that the trap was skilfully baited. I am sure that you cannot fail to be delighted with the traces of heredity shown in the p's and in the tails of the g's. The absence of the i-dots in the old man's writing is also most characteristic. Watson, I think our quiet rest in the country has been a distinct success, and I shall certainly return, much invigorated, to Baker Street to-morrow."

19. *The Crooked Man*

ONE summer night, a few months after my marriage, I was seated by my own hearth smoking a last pipe and nodding over a novel, for my day's work had been an exhausting one. My wife had already gone upstairs, and the sound of the locking of the hall door some time before told me that the servants had also retired. I had risen from my seat and was knocking out the ashes of my pipe, when I suddenly heard the clang of the bell.

I looked at the clock. It was a quarter to twelve. This could not be a visitor at so late an hour. A patient, evidently, and possibly an all-night sitting. With a wry face I went out into the hall and opened the door. To my astonishment, it was Sherlock Holmes who stood upon my step.

" Ah, Watson," said he, " I hoped that I might not be too late to catch you."

" My dear fellow, pray come in."

" You look surprised, and no wonder ! Relieved, too, I fancy ! Hum ! you still smoke the Arcadia mixture of your bachelor days, then ! There's no mistaking that fluffy ash upon your coat. It's easy to tell that you've been accustomed to wear a uniform, Watson ; you'll never pass as a pure-bred civilian as long as you keep that habit of carrying your handkerchief in your sleeve. Could you put me up to-night ? "

" With pleasure."

" You told me that you had bachelor quarters for one, and I see that you have no gentleman visitor at present. Your hat-stand proclaims as much."

" I shall be delighted if you will stay."

" Thank you. I'll fill a vacant peg, then. Sorry to see that you've had the British workman in the house. He's a token of evil. Not the drains, I hope ? "

" No, the gas."

439

"Ah! He has left two nail marks from his boot upon your linoleum just where the light strikes it. No, thank you, I had some supper at Waterloo, but I'll smoke a pipe with you with pleasure."

I handed him my pouch, and he seated himself opposite to me, and smoked for some time in silence. I was well aware that nothing but business of importance could have brought him to me at such an hour, so I waited patiently until he should come round to it.

"I see that you are professionally rather busy just now," said he, glancing very keenly across at me.

"Yes, I've had a busy day," I answered. "It may seem very foolish in your eyes," I added, "but really I don't know how you deduced it."

Holmes chuckled to himself.

"I have the advantage of knowing your habits, my dear Watson," said he. "When your round is a short one you walk, and when it is a long one you use a hansom. As I perceive that your boots, although used, are by no means dirty, I cannot doubt that you are at present busy enough to justify the hansom."

"Excellent!" I cried.

"Elementary," said he. "It is one of those instances where the reasoner can produce an effect which seems remarkable to his neighbour, because the latter has missed the one little point which is the basis of the deduction. The same may be said, my dear fellow, for the effect of some of these little sketches of yours, which is entirely meretricious, depending as it does upon your retaining in your own hands some factors in the problem which are never imparted to the reader. Now, at present I am in the position of these same readers, for I hold in this hand several threads of one of the strangest cases which ever perplexed a man's brain, and yet I lack the one or two which are needful to complete my theory. But I'll have them, Watson, I'll have them!" His eyes kindled and a slight flush sprang into his thin cheeks. For an instant the veil had lifted upon his keen, intense nature, but for an instant only. When I glanced again his face had resumed that Red Indian composure which had made so many regard him as a machine rather than a man.

"The problem presents features of interest," said he; "I may even say very exceptional features of interest. I have already looked into the matter, and have come, as I think, within sight of my solution. If you could accompany me in that last step, you might be of considerable service to me."

"I should be delighted."

"Could you go as far as Aldershot to-morrow?"

"I have no doubt Jackson would take my practice."

"Very good. I want to start by the 11.10 from Waterloo."

"That would give me time."

"Then, if you are not too sleepy, I will give you a sketch of what has happened and of what remains to be done."

"I was sleepy before you came. I am quite wakeful now."

"I will compress the story as far as may be done without omitting anything vital to the case. It is conceivable that you may even have read some account of the matter. It is the supposed murder of Colonel Barclay, of the Royal Mallows, at Aldershot, which I am investigating."

"I have heard nothing of it."

"It has not excited much attention yet, except locally. The facts are only two days old. Briefly they are these:

"The Royal Mallows is, as you know, one of the most famous Irish regiments in the British Army. It did wonders both in the Crimea and the Mutiny, and has since that time distinguished itself upon every possible occasion. It was commanded up to Monday night by James Barclay, a gallant veteran, who started as a full private, was raised to commissioned rank for his bravery at the time of the Mutiny, and so lived to command the regiment in which he had once carried a musket.

"Colonel Barclay had married at the time when he was

a sergeant, and his wife, whose maiden name was Miss Nancy Devoy, was the daughter of a former colour-sergeant in the same corps. There was, therefore, as can be imagined, some little social friction when the young couple (for they were still young) found themselves in their new surroundings. They appear, however, to have quickly adapted themselves, and Mrs. Barclay has always, I understand, been as popular with the ladies of the regiment as her husband was with his brother officers. I may add that she was a woman of great beauty, and that even now, when she has been married for upwards of thirty years, she is still of a striking appearance.

"Colonel Barclay's family life appears to have been a uniformly happy one. Major Murphy, to whom I owe most of my facts, assures me that he has never heard of any misunderstanding between the pair. On the whole, he thinks that Barclay's devotion to his wife was greater than his wife's to Barclay. He was acutely uneasy if he were absent from her for a day. She, on the other hand, though devoted and faithful, was less obtrusively affectionate. But they were regarded in the regiment as the very model of a middle-aged couple. There was absolutely nothing in their mutual relations to prepare people for the tragedy which was to follow.

"Colonel Barclay himself seems to have had some singular traits in his character. He was a dashing, jovial old soldier in his usual mood, but there were occasions on which he seemed to show himself capable of considerable violence and vindictiveness. This side of his nature, however, appears never to have been turned towards his wife. Another fact which had struck Major Murphy, and three out of five of the other officers with whom I conversed, was the singular sort of depression which came upon him at times. As the Major expressed it, the smile had often been struck from his mouth, as if by some invisible hand, when he has been joining in the gaieties and chaff of the mess table. For days on end, when the mood was on him, he had been sunk in the deepest gloom.

This and a certain tinge of superstition were the only unusual traits in his character which his brother officers had observed. The latter peculiarity took the form of a dislike to being left alone, especially after dark. This puerile feature in a nature which was conspicuously manly had often given rise to comment and conjecture.

"The first battalion of the Royal Mallows (which is the old 117th) has been stationed at Aldershot for some years. The married officers live out of barracks, and the Colonel has during all this time occupied a villa called Lachine, about half a mile from the North Camp. The house stands in its own grounds, but the west side of it is not more than thirty yards from the high-road. A coachman and two maids form the staff of servants. These, with their master and mistress, were the sole occupants of Lachine, for the Barclays had no children, nor was it usual for them to have resident visitors.

"Now for the events at Lachine between nine and ten on the evening of last Monday.

"Mrs. Barclay was, it appears, a member of the Roman Catholic Church, and had interested herself very much in the establishment of the Guild of St. George, which was formed in connection with the Watt Street Chapel for the purpose of supplying the poor with cast-off clothing. A meeting of the Guild had been held that evening at eight, and Mrs. Barclay had hurried over her dinner in order to be present at it. When leaving the house, she was heard by the coachman to make some commonplace remark to her husband, and to assure him that she would be back before long. She then called for Miss Morrison, a young lady who lives in the next villa, and the two went off together to their meeting. It lasted forty minutes, and at a quarter-past nine Mrs. Barclay returned home, having left Miss Morrison at her door as she passed.

"There is a room which is used as a morning-room at Lachine. This faces the road, and opens by a large glass folding door on to the lawn. The lawn is thirty yards across, and is only divided from the highway by a low

443

wall with an iron rail above it. It was into this room
that Mrs. Barclay went upon her return. The blinds
were not down, for the room was seldom used in the
evening, but Mrs. Barclay herself lit the lamp and then
rang the bell, asking Jane Stewart, the housemaid, to
bring her a cup of tea, which was quite contrary to her
usual habits. The Colonel had been sitting in the dining-
room, but hearing that his wife had returned, he joined
her in the morning-room. The coachman saw him cross
the hall, and enter it. He was never seen again alive.

"The tea which had been ordered was brought up at
the end of ten minutes, but the maid, as she approached
the door, was surprised to hear the voices of her master
and mistress in furious altercation. She knocked without receiving any answer, and even turned the handle, but
only to find that the door was locked upon the inside.
Naturally enough, she ran down to tell the cook, and the
two women with the coachman came up into the hall and
listened to the dispute which was still raging. They all
agree that only two voices were to be heard, those of
Barclay and his wife. Barclay's remarks were subdued
and abrupt, so that none of them were audible to the
listeners. The lady's, on the other hand, were most
bitter, and when she raised her voice, could be plainly
heard. ' You coward ! ' she repeated over and over again.
' What can be done now ? Give me back my life. I will
never so much as breathe the same air as you again !
You coward ! You coward ! ' Those were scraps of her
conversation, ending in a sudden dreadful cry in the man's
voice, with a crash, and a piercing scream from the woman.
Convinced that some tragedy had occurred, the coachman
rushed to the door and strove to force it, while scream
after scream issued from within. He was unable, however, to make his way in, and the maids were too distracted with fear to be of any assistance to him. A sudden
thought struck him, however, and he ran through the
hall door and round to the lawn, upon which the long
French windows opened. One side of the window was

open, which I understand was quite usual in the summer-time, and he passed without difficulty into the room. His mistress had ceased to scream, and was stretched insensible upon a couch, while with his feet tilted over the side of an arm-chair, and his head upon the ground near the corner of the fender, was lying the unfortunate soldier, stone dead, in a pool of his own blood.

"Naturally the coachman's first thought, on finding that he could do nothing for his master, was to open the door. But here an unexpected and singular difficulty presented itself. The key was not on the inner side of the door, nor could he find it anywhere in the room. He went out again, therefore, through the window, and having obtained the help of a policeman and of a medical man, he returned. The lady, against whom naturally the strongest suspicion rested, was removed to her room, still in a state of insensibility. The Colonel's body was then placed upon the sofa, and a careful examination made of the scene of the tragedy.

"The injury from which the unfortunate veteran was suffering was found to be a ragged cut, some two inches long, at the back part of his head, which had evidently been caused by a violent blow from a blunt weapon. Nor was it difficult to guess what that weapon may have been. Upon the floor, close to the body, was lying a singular club of hard carved wood with a bone handle. The Colonel possessed a varied collection of weapons brought from the different countries in which he had fought, and it is conjectured by the police that this club was among his trophies. The servants deny having seen it before, but among the numerous curiosities in the house it is possible that it may have been overlooked. Nothing else of importance was discovered in the room by the police, save the inexplicable fact that neither upon Mrs. Barclay's person, nor upon that of the victim, nor in any part of the room was the missing key to be found. The door had eventually to be opened by a locksmith from Aldershot.

" That was the state of things, Watson, when upon the Tuesday morning I, at the request of Major Murphy, went down to Aldershot to supplement the efforts of the police. I think you will acknowledge that the problem was already one of interest, but my observations soon made me realize that it was in truth much more extraordinary than would at first sight appear.

" Before examining the room I cross-questioned the servants, but only succeeded in eliciting the facts which I have already stated. One other detail of interest was remembered by Jane Stewart, the housemaid. You will remember that on hearing the sound of the quarrel she descended and returned with the other servants. On that first occasion, when she was alone, she says that the voices of her master and mistress were sunk so low that she could hear hardly anything, and judged by their tones, rather than their words, that they had fallen out. On my pressing her, however, she remembered that she heard the word ' David ' uttered twice by the lady. The point is of the utmost importance as guiding us towards the reason of the sudden quarrel. The Colonel's name, you remember, was James.

" There was one thing in the case which had made the deepest impression both upon the servants and the police. This was the contortion of the Colonel's face. It had set, according to their account, into the most dreadful expression of fear and horror which a human countenance is capable of assuming. More than one person fainted at the mere sight of him, so terrible was the effect. It was quite certain that he had foreseen his fate, and that it had caused him the utmost horror. This, of course, fitted in well enough with the police theory, if the Colonel could have seen his wife making a murderous attack upon him. Nor was the fact of the wound being on the back of his head a fatal objection to this, as he might have turned to avoid the blow. No information could be got from the lady herself, who was temporarily insane from an acute attack of brain fever.

"From the police I learned that Miss Morrison, who, you remember, went out that evening with Mrs. Barclay, denied having any knowledge of what it was which had caused the ill-humour in which her companion had returned.

"Having gathered these facts, Watson, I smoked several pipes over them, trying to separate those which were crucial from others which were merely incidental. There could be no question that the most distinctive and suggestive point in the case was the singular disappearance of the door-key. A most careful search had failed to discover it in the room. Therefore, it must have been taken from it. But neither the Colonel nor the Colonel's wife could have taken it. That was perfectly clear. Therefore a third person must have entered the room. And that third person could only have come in through the window. It seemed to me that a careful examination of the room and the lawn might possibly reveal some traces of this mysterious individual. You know my methods, Watson. There was not one of them which I did not apply to the inquiry. And it ended by my discovering traces, but very different ones from those which I had expected. There had been a man in the room, and he had crossed the lawn coming from the road. I was able to obtain five very clear impressions of his footmarks— one on the roadway itself, at the point where he had climbed the low wall, two on the lawn, and two very faint ones upon the stained boards near the window where he had entered. He had apparently rushed across the lawn, for his toe-marks were much deeper than his heels. But it was not the man who surprised me. It was his companion."

"His companion!"

Holmes pulled a large sheet of tissue paper out of his pocket and carefully unfolded it upon his knee.

"What do you make of that?" he asked.

The paper was covered with tracings of the footmarks of some small animal. It had five well-marked footpads, an indication of long nails, and the whole print might be nearly as large as a dessert-spoon.

" It's a dog," said I.

" Did ever you hear of a dog running up a curtain ? I found distinct traces that this creature had done so."

" A monkey, then ? "

" But it is not the print of a monkey."

" What can it be, then ? "

" Neither dog, nor cat, nor monkey, nor any creature that we are familiar with. I have tried to reconstruct it from the measurements. Here are four prints where the beast has been standing motionless. You see that it is no less than fifteen inches from forefoot to hind. Add to that the length of neck and head, and you get a creature not much less than two feet long—probably more if there is any tail. But now observe this other measurement. The animal has been moving, and we have the length of its stride. In each case it is only about three inches. You have an indication, you see, of a long body with very short legs attached to it. It has not been considerate enough to leave any of its hair behind it. But its general shape must be what I have indicated, and it can run up a curtain and is carnivorous."

" How do you deduce that ? "

" Because it ran up the curtain. A canary's cage was hanging in the window, and its aim seems to have been to get at the bird."

" Then what was the beast ? "

" Ah, if I could give it a name it might go a long way towards solving the case. On the whole it was probably some creature of the weasel or stoat tribe—and yet it is larger than any of these that I have seen."

" But what had it to do with the crime ? "

" That also is still obscure. But we have learned a good deal, you perceive. We know that a man stood in the road looking at the quarrel between the Barclays—the blinds were up and the room lighted. We know also that he ran across the lawn, entered the room, accompanied by a strange animal, and that he either struck the Colonel, or, as is equally possible, that the Colonel fell down from sheer fright at the sight of him, and cut his head on the corner of the fender. Finally, we have the curious fact that the intruder carried away the key with him when he left."

" Your discoveries seem to have left the business more obscure than it was before," said I.

" Quite so. They undoubtedly showed that the affair was much deeper than was at first conjectured. I thought the matter over, and I came to the conclusion that I must approach the case from another aspect. But really, Watson, I am keeping you up, and I might just as well tell you all this on our way to Aldershot to-morrow."

" Thank you, you've gone rather too far to stop."

" It was quite certain that when Mrs. Barclay left the house at half-past seven she was on good terms with her husband. She was never, as I think I have said, ostentatiously affectionate, but she was heard by the coachman chatting with the Colonel in a friendly fashion. Now, it was equally certain that immediately on her return she had gone to the room in which she was least likely to see her husband, had flown to tea, as an agitated woman will, and, finally, on his coming in to her, had broken into violent recriminations. Therefore, something had occurred between seven-thirty and nine o'clock which had completely altered her feelings towards him. But Miss Morrison had been with her during the whole of that hour and a half. It was absolutely certain, therefore, in spite of her denial, that she must know something of the matter.

" My first conjecture was that possibly there had been some passages between this young woman and the old soldier, which the former had now confessed to the wife. That would account for the angry return and also for the girl's denial that anything had occurred. Nor would it be entirely incompatible with most of the words overheard. But there was the reference to David, and there

449

was the known affection of the Colonel for his wife to weigh against it, to say nothing of the tragic intrusion of this other man, which might, of course, be entirely disconnected with what had gone before. It was not easy to pick one's steps, but on the whole I was inclined to dismiss the idea that there had been anything between the Colonel and Miss Morrison, but more than ever convinced that the young lady held the clue as to what it was which had turned Mrs. Barclay to hatred of her husband. I took the obvious course, therefore, of calling upon Miss Morrison, of explaining to her that I was perfectly certain that she held the facts in her possession, and of assuring her that her friend, Mrs. Barclay, might find herself in the dock upon a capital charge unless the matter were cleared up.

" Miss Morrison is a little, ethereal slip of a girl, with timid eyes and blonde hair, but I found her by no means wanting in shrewdness and common sense. She sat thinking for some time after I had spoken, and then turning to me with a brisk air of resolution, she broke into a remarkable statement, which I will condense for your benefit.

" ' I promised my friend that I would say nothing of the matter, and a promise is a promise,' said she. ' But if I can really help her when so serious a charge is made against her, and when her own mouth, poor darling, is closed by illness, then I think I am absolved from my promise. I will tell you exactly what happened on Monday evening.

" ' We were returning from the Watt Street Mission, about a quarter to nine o'clock. On our way we had to pass through Hudson Street, which is a very quiet thoroughfare. There is only one lamp in it upon the left-hand side, and as we approached this lamp I saw a man coming towards us with his back very bent, and something like a box slung over one of his shoulders. He appeared to be deformed, for he carried his head low, and walked with his knees bent. We were passing him when he raised his face to look at us in the circle of light thrown by the lamp, and as he did so he stopped and screamed out in a dreadful voice, " My God, it's Nancy ! " Mrs. Barclay turned as white as death, and would have fallen down had the dreadful-looking creature not caught hold of her. I was going to call for the police, but she, to my surprise, spoke quite civilly to the fellow.

" ' " I thought you had been dead this thirty years, Henry," said she, in a shaking voice.

" ' " So I have,' said he, and it was awful to hear the tones that he said it in. He had a very dark, fearsome face, and a gleam in his eyes that comes back to me in my dreams. His hair and whiskers were shot with grey, and his face was all crinkled and puckered like a withered apple.

" ' " Just walk on a little way, dear," said Mrs. Barclay. " I want to have a word with this man. There is nothing to be afraid of." She tried to speak boldly, but she was still deadly pale, and could hardly get her words out for the trembling of her lips.

" ' I did as she asked me, and they talked together for a few minutes. Then she came down the street with her eyes blazing, and I saw the crippled wretch standing by the lamp-post and shaking his clenched fists in the air, as if he were mad with rage. She never said a word until we were at the door here, when she took me by the hand and begged me to tell no one what had happened. " It is an old acquaintance of mine who has come down in the world," said she. When I promised her that I would say nothing she kissed me, and I have never seen her since. I have told you now the whole truth, and if I withheld it from the police it is because I did not realize then the danger in which my dear friend stood. I know that it can only be to her advantage that everything should be known.'

" There was her statement, Watson, and to me, as you can imagine, it was like a light on a dark night. Everything which had been disconnected before began at once to assume its true place, and I had a shadowy presentiment of the whole sequence of events. My next step obviously was to find the man who had produced such a remarkable impression upon Mrs. Barclay. If he were still in Aldershot it should not be a very difficult matter. There are not such a very great number of civilians, and a deformed man was sure to have attracted attention. I spent a day in the search, and by evening—this very evening, Watson—I had run him down. The man's name is Henry Wood, and he lives in lodgings in the same street in which the ladies met him. He has only been five days in the place. In the character of a registration agent I had a most interesting gossip with his landlady. The man is by trade a conjurer and performer, going round the canteens, after nightfall, and giving a little entertainment at each. He carries some creature about with him in his box, about which the landlady seemed to be in considerable trepidation, for she had never seen an animal like it. He uses it in some of his tricks, according to her account. So much the woman was able to tell me, and also that it was a wonder the man lived, seeing how twisted he was, and that he spoke in a strange tongue sometimes, and that for the last two nights she had heard him groaning and weeping in his bedroom. He was all right as far as money went, but in his deposit he had given her what looked like a bad florin. She showed it to me, Watson, and it was an Indian rupee.

" So now, my dear fellow, you see exactly how we stand and why it is I want you. It is perfectly plain that after the ladies parted from this man he followed them at a distance, that he saw the quarrel between husband and wife through the window, that he rushed in, and that the creature which he carried in his box got loose. That is all very certain. But he is the only person in this world who can tell us exactly what happened in that room."

" And you intend to ask him ? "

" Most certainly—but in the presence of a witness."

" And I am the witness ? "

" If you will be so good. If he can clear the matter up,

well and good. If he refuses, we have no alternative but to apply for a warrant."

"But how do you know he will be there when we return ? "

"You may be sure that I took some precautions. I have one of my Baker Street boys mounting guard over him who would stick to him like a burr, go where he might. We shall find him in Hudson Street to-morrow, Watson ; and meanwhile I should be the criminal myself if I kept you out of bed any longer."

It was midday when we found ourselves at the scene of the tragedy, and, under my companion's guidance, we made our way at once to Hudson Street. In spite of his capacity for concealing his emotions I could easily see that Holmes was in a state of suppressed excitement, while I was myself tingling with that half-sporting, half-intellectual pleasure which I invariably experienced when I associated myself with him in his investigations.

"This is the street," said he, as he turned into a short thoroughfare lined with plain two-storied brick houses— "Ah ! here is Simpson to report."

"He's in all right, Mr. Holmes," cried a small street Arab, running up to us.

"Good, Simpson ! " said Holmes, patting him on the head. "Come along, Watson. This is the house." He sent in his card with a message that he had come on important business, and a moment later we were face to face with the man whom we had come to see. In spite of the warm weather he was crouching over a fire, and the little room was like an oven. The man sat all twisted and huddled in his chair in a way which gave an indescribable impression of deformity, but the face which he turned towards us, though worn and swarthy, must at some time have been remarkable for its beauty. He looked suspiciously at us now out of yellow-shot bilious eyes, and, without speaking or rising, he waved towards two chairs.

"Mr. Henry Wood, late of India, I believe ? " said

Holmes, affably. " I've come over this little matter of Colonel Barclay's death."

" What should I know about that ? "

" That's what I wanted to ascertain. You know, I suppose, that unless the matter is cleared up, Mrs. Barclay, who is an old friend of yours, will in all probability be tried for murder ? "

The man gave a violent start.

" I don't know who you are," he cried, " nor how you come to know what you do know, but will you swear that this is true that you tell me ? "

" Why, they are only waiting for her to come to her senses to arrest her."

" My God ! Are you in the police yourself ? "

" No."

" What business is it of yours, then ? "

" It's every man's business to see justice done."

" You can take my word that she is innocent."

" Then you are guilty ? "

" No, I am not."

" Who killed Colonel James Barclay, then ? "

" It was a just Providence that killed him. But mind you this, that if I had knocked his brains out, as it was in my heart to do, he would have had no more than his due from my hands. If his own guilty conscience had not struck him down, it is likely enough that I might have had his blood upon my soul. You want me to tell the story ? Well, I don't know why I shouldn't, for there's no cause for me to be ashamed of it.

" It was in this way, sir. You see me now with my back like a camel and my ribs all awry, but there was a time when Corporal Henry Wood was the smartest man in the 117th Foot. We were in India then, in cantonments, at a place we'll call Bhurtee. Barclay, who died the other day, was sergeant in the same company as myself, and the belle of the regiment—aye, and the finest girl that ever had the breath of life between her lips—was Nancy Devoy, the daughter of the colour-sergeant.

There were two men who loved her, and one whom she loved ; and you'll smile when you look at this poor thing huddled before the fire, and hear me say that it was for my good looks that she loved me.

" Well, though I had her heart her father was set upon her marrying Barclay. I was a harum-scarum, reckless lad, and he had had an education, and was already marked for the sword-belt. But the girl held true to me, and it seemed that I would have had her, when the Mutiny broke out, and all Hell was loose in the country.

" We were shut up in Bhurtee, the regiment of us, with half a battery of artillery, a company of Sikhs, and a lot of civilians and women-folk. There were ten thousand rebels round us, and they were as keen as a set of terriers round a rat cage. About the second week of it our water gave out, and it was a question whether we could communicate with General Neill's column, which was moving up-country. It was our only chance, for we could not hope to fight our way out with all the women and children, so I volunteered to go out and warn General Neill of our danger. My offer was accepted, and I talked it over with Sergeant Barclay, who was supposed to know the ground better than any other man, and who drew up a route by which I might get through the rebel lines. At ten o'clock the same night I started off upon my journey. There were a thousand lives to save, but it was of only one that I was thinking when I dropped over the wall that night.

" My way ran down a dried-up water-course, which we hoped would screen me from the enemy's sentries, but as I crept round the corner of it I walked right into six of them, who were crouching down in the dark, waiting for me. In an instant I was stunned with a blow, and bound hand and foot. But the real blow was to my heart and not to my head, for as I came to and listened to as much as I could understand of their talk, I heard enough to tell me that my comrade, the very man who had arranged the way I was to take, had betrayed me by means of a native servant into the hands of the enemy.

" Well, there's no need for me to dwell on that part of it. You know now what James Barclay was capable of. Bhurtee was relieved by Neill next day, but the rebels took me away with them in their retreat, and it was many a long year before I ever saw a white face again. I was tortured, and tried to get away, and was captured and tortured again. You can see for yourselves the state in which I was left. Some of them that fled into Nepaul took me with them, and then afterwards I was up past Darjeeling. The hill-folk up there murdered the rebels who had me, and I became their slave for a time until I escaped, but instead of going south I had to go north, until I found myself among the Afghans. There I wandered about for many a year, and at last came back to the Punjab, where I lived mostly among the natives, and picked up a living by the conjuring tricks that I had learned. What use was it for me, a wretched cripple, to go back to England, or to make myself known to my old comrades ? Even my wish for revenge would not make me do that. I had rather that Nancy and my old pals should think of Harry Wood as having died with a straight back, than see him living and crawling with a stick like a chimpanzee. They never doubted that I was dead, and I meant that they never should. I heard that Barclay had married Nancy, and that he was rapidly rising in the regiment, but even that did not make me speak.

" But when one gets old, one has a longing for home. For years I've been dreaming of the bright green fields and the hedges of England. At last I determined to see them before I died. I saved enough to bring me across, and then I came here where the soldiers are, for I know their ways, and how to amuse them, and so earn enough to keep me."

" Your narrative is most interesting," said Sherlock Holmes. " I have already heard of your meeting with Mrs. Barclay and your mutual recognition. You then, as I understand, followed her home and saw through the window an altercation between her husband and her, in which she doubtless cast his conduct to you in his teeth. Your own feelings overcame you, and you ran across the lawn and broke in upon them."

" I did, sir, and at the sight of me he looked as I have never seen a man look before, and over he went with his head on the fender. But he was dead before he fell. I read death on his face as plain as I can read that text over the fire. The bare sight of me was like a bullet through his guilty heart."

" And then ? "

" Then Nancy fainted, and I caught up the key of the door from her hand, intending to unlock it and get help. But as I was doing it it seemed to me better to leave it alone and get away, for the thing might look black against me, and anyway my secret would be out if I were taken. In my haste I thrust the key into my pocket, and dropped my stick while I was chasing Teddy, who had run up the curtain. When I got him into his box, from which he had slipped, I was off as fast as I could run."

" Who's Teddy ? " asked Holmes.

The man leaned over and pulled up the front of a kind of hutch in the corner. In an instant out there slipped a beautiful reddish-brown creature, thin, and lithe, with the legs of a stoat, a long thin nose, and a pair of the finest red eyes that ever I saw in an animal's head.

" It's a mongoose ! " I cried.

" Well, some call them that, and some call them ich-neumon," said the man. " Snake-catcher is what I call them, and Teddy is amazing quick on cobras. I have one here without the fangs, and Teddy catches it every night to please the folk in the canteen. Any other point, sir ? "

" Well, we may have to apply to you again if Mrs. Barclay should prove to be in serious trouble."

" In that case, of course, I'd come forward."

" But if not, there is no object of raking up this scandal against a dead man, foully as he has acted. You have, at least, the satisfaction of knowing that for thirty years of his life his conscience bitterly reproached him for his wicked deed. Ah, there goes Major Murphy on the other side of the street. Good-bye, Wood ; I want to learn if anything has happened since yesterday."

We were in time to overtake the Major before he reached the corner.

" Ah, Holmes," he said, " I suppose you have heard that all this fuss has come to nothing ? "

" What, then ? "

" The inquest is just over. The medical evidence showed conclusively that death was due to apoplexy. You see, it was quite a simple case after all."

" Oh, remarkably superficial," said Holmes, smiling. " Come, Watson, I don't think we shall be wanted in Aldershot any more."

" There's one thing," said I, as we walked down to the station ; " if the husband's name was James, and the other was Henry, what was this talk about David ? "

" That one word, my dear Watson, should have told me the whole story had I been the ideal reasoner which you are so fond of depicting. It was evidently a term of reproach."

" Of reproach ? "

" Yes, David strayed a little now and then, you know, and on one occasion in the same direction as Sergeant James Barclay. You remember the small affair of Uriah and Bathsheba ? My Biblical knowledge is a trifle rusty, I fear, but you will find the story in the first or second of Samuel."

20. *The Resident Patient*

IN glancing over the somewhat incoherent series of memoirs with which I have endeavoured to illustrate a few of the mental peculiarities of my friend, Mr. Sherlock Holmes, I have been struck by the difficulty which I have experienced in picking out examples which shall in every way answer my purpose. For in those cases in which Holmes has performed some *tour-de-force* of analytical reasoning, and has demonstrated the value of his peculiar methods of investigation, the facts themselves have often been so slight or so commonplace that I could not feel justified in laying them before the public. On the other hand, it has frequently happened that he has been concerned in some research where the facts have been of the most remarkable and dramatic character, but where the share which he has himself taken in determining their causes has been less pronounced than I, as his biographer, could wish. The small matter which I have chronicled under the heading of " A Study in Scarlet," and that other later one connected with the loss of the *Gloria Scott*, may serve as examples of this Scylla and Charybdis which are for ever threatening his historian. It may be that, in the business of which I am now about to write, the part which my friend played is not sufficiently accentuated ; and yet the whole train of circumstances is so remarkable that I cannot bring myself to omit it entirely from this series.

It had been a close, rainy day in October. " Unhealthy weather, Watson," said my friend. But the evening has brought a breeze with it. What do you say to a ramble through London ? "

I was weary of our little sitting-room, and gladly acquiesced. For three hours we strolled about together, watching the ever-changing kaleidoscope of life as it ebbs and flows through Fleet Street and the Strand. Holmes' characteristic talk, with its keen observance of detail and subtle power of inference, held me amused and enthralled.

It was ten o'clock before we reached Baker Street again. A brougham was waiting at our door.

" Hum ! A doctor's—general practitioner, I perceive," said Holmes. " Not been long in practice, but has had a good deal to do. Come to consult us, I fancy ! Lucky we came back ! "

I was sufficiently conversant with Holmes' methods to

be able to follow his reasoning, and to see that the nature and state of the various medical instruments in the wicker basket which hung in the lamp-light inside the brougham had given him the data for his swift deduction. The light in our window above showed that this late visit was indeed intended for us. With some curiosity as to what could have sent a brother medico to us at such an hour, I followed Holmes into our sanctum.

A pale, taper-faced man with sandy whiskers rose up from a chair by the fire as we entered. His age may not have been more than three- or four-and-thirty, but his haggard expression and unhealthy hue told of a life which had sapped his strength and robbed him of his youth. His manner was nervous and shy, like that of a sensitive gentleman, and the thin white hand which he laid on the mantelpiece as he rose was that of an artist rather than of a surgeon. His dress was quiet and sombre, a black frock-coat, dark trousers, and a touch of colour about his neck-tie.

"Good evening, Doctor," said Holmes, cheerily; "I am glad to see that you have only been waiting a very few minutes."

"You spoke to my coachman, then?"

"No, it was the candle on the side-table that told me. Pray resume your seat and let me know how I can serve you."

"My name is Doctor Percy Trevelyan," said our visitor, "and I live at 403 Brook Street."

"Are you not the author of a monograph upon obscure nervous lesions?" I asked.

His pale cheeks flushed with pleasure at hearing that his work was known to me.

"I so seldom hear of the work that I thought it was quite dead," said he. "My publishers give me a most discouraging account of its sale. You are yourself, I presume, a medical man?"

"A retired Army surgeon."

"My own hobby has always been nervous disease. I

460

should wish to make it an absolute speciality, but, of course, a man must take what he can get at first. This, however, is beside the question, Mr. Sherlock Holmes, and I quite appreciate how valuable your time is. The fact is that a very singular train of events has occurred recently at my house in Brook Street, and to-night they came to such a head that I felt it was quite impossible for me to wait another hour before asking for your advice and assistance."

Sherlock Holmes sat down and lit his pipe. "You are very welcome to both," said he. "Pray let me have a detailed account of what the circumstances are which have disturbed you."

"One or two of them are so trivial," said Dr. Trevelyan, "that really I am almost ashamed to mention them. But the matter is so inexplicable, and the recent turn which it has taken is so elaborate, that I shall lay it all before you, and you shall judge what is essential and what is not.

"I am compelled, to begin with, to say something of my own college career. I am a London University man, you know, and I am sure you will not think that I am unduly singing my own praises if I say that my student career was considered by my professors to be a very promising one. After I had graduated I continued to devote myself to research, occupying a minor position in King's College Hospital, and I was fortunate enough to excite considerable interest by my research into the pathology of catalepsy, and finally to win the Bruce Pinkerton prize and medal by the monograph on nervous lesions to which your friend has just alluded. I should not go too far if I were to say that there was a general impression at that time that a distinguished career lay before me.

"But the one great stumbling-block lay in my want of capital. As you will readily understand, a specialist who aims high is compelled to start in one of a dozen streets in the Cavendish Square quarter, all of which entail enormous rents and furnishing expenses. Besides this

461

preliminary outlay, he must be prepared to keep himself for some years, and to hire a presentable carriage and horse. To do this was quite beyond my power, and I could only hope that by economy I might in ten years' time save enough to enable me to put up my plate. Suddenly, however, an unexpected incident opened up quite a new prospect to me.

" This was a visit from a gentleman of the name of Blessington, who was a complete stranger to me. He came up into my room one morning, and plunged into business in an instant.

" ' You are the same Percy Trevelyan who has had so distinguished a career and won a great prize lately ? ' said he. I bowed.

" ' Answer me frankly,' he continued, ' for you will find it to your interest to do so. You have all the cleverness which makes a successful man. Have you the tact ? '

" I could not help smiling at the abruptness of the question.

" ' I trust that I have my share,' I said.

" ' Any bad habits ? Not drawn towards drink, eh ? '

" ' Really, sir ! ' I cried.

" ' Quite right ! That's all right ! But I was bound to ask. With all these qualities why are you not in practice ? '

" I shrugged my shoulders.

" ' Come, come ! ' said he, in his bustling way. It's the old story. More in your brains than in your pocket, eh ? What would you say if I were to start you in Brook Street ? '

" I stared at him in astonishment.

" ' Oh, it's for my sake, not for yours,' he cried. ' I'll be perfectly frank with you, and if it suits you it will suit me very well. I have a few thousands to invest, d'ye see, and I think I'll sink them in you.'

" ' But why ? ' I gasped.

" ' Well, it's just like any other speculation, and safer than most.'

" ' What am I to do, then ? '

" ' I'll tell you. I'll take the house, furnish it, pay the maids, and run the whole place. All you have to do is to wear out your chair in the consulting-room. I'll let you have pocket-money and everything. Then you hand over to me three-quarters of what you earn, and you keep the other quarter for yourself.'

" This was the strange proposal, Mr. Holmes, with which the man Blessington approached me. I won't weary you with the account of how we bargained and negotiated. It ended in my moving into the house next Lady Day, and starting in practice on very much the same conditions as he had suggested. He came himself to live with me in the character of a resident patient. His heart was weak, it appears, and he needed constant medical supervision. He turned the two best rooms on the first floor into a sitting-room and bedroom for himself. He was a man of singular habits, shunning company and very seldom going out. His life was irregular, but in one respect he was regularity itself. Every evening at the same hour he walked into the consulting-room, examined the books, put down five and threepence for every guinea that I had earned, and carried the rest off to the strong box in his own room.

" I may say with confidence that he never had occasion to regret his speculation. From the first it was a success. A few good cases and the reputation which I had won in the hospital brought me rapidly to the front, and during the last year or two I have made him a rich man.

" So much, Mr. Holmes, for my past history and my relations with Mr. Blessington. It only remains for me now to tell you what has occurred to bring me here to-night.

" Some weeks ago Mr. Blessington came down to me in, as it seemed to me, a state of considerable agitation. He spoke of some burglary which, he said, had been committed in the West End, and he appeared, I remember, to be quite unnecessarily excited about it, declaring that a day should not pass before we should add stronger bolts to our windows and doors. For a week he continued to be in a peculiar state of restlessness, peering continually out of the windows, and ceasing to take the short walk which had usually been the prelude to his dinner. From his manner it struck me that he was in mortal dread of something or somebody, but when I questioned him upon the point he became so offensive that I was compelled to drop the subject. Gradually as time passed his fears appeared to die away, and he had renewed his former habits, when a fresh event reduced him to the pitiable state of prostration in which he now lies.

"What happened was this. Two days ago I received the letter which I now read to you. Neither address nor date is attached to it.

"'A Russian nobleman who is now resident in England,' it runs, 'would be glad to avail himself of the professional assistance of Dr. Percy Trevelyan. He has been for some years a victim to cataleptic attacks, on which, as is well known, Dr. Trevelyan is an authority. He proposes to call at about a quarter-past six to-morrow evening, if Dr. Trevelyan will make it convenient to be at home.'

"This letter interested me deeply, because the chief difficulty in the study of catalepsy is the rareness of the disease. You may believe, then, that I was in my consulting-room when at the appointed hour, the page showed in the patient.

"He was an elderly man, thin, demure, and commonplace—by no means the conception one forms of a Russian nobleman. I was much more struck by the appearance of his companion. This was a tall young man, surprisingly handsome, with a dark, fierce face, and the limbs and chest of a Hercules. He had his hand under the other's arm as they entered, and helped him to a chair with a tenderness which one would hardly have expected from his appearance.

"'You will excuse my coming in, Doctor,' said he to

me, speaking English with a slight lisp. 'This is my father, and his health is a matter of the most overwhelming importance to me.'

" I was touched by this filial anxiety. ' You would, perhaps, care to remain during the consultation ? ' said I.

" ' Not for the world,' he cried, with a gesture of horror. ' It is more painful to me than I can express. If I were to see my father in one of those dreadful seizures, I am convinced that I should never survive it. My own nervous system is an exceptionally sensitive one. With your permission I will remain in the waiting-room while you go into my father's case.'

" To this, of course, I assented, and the young man withdrew. The patient and I then plunged into a discussion of his case, of which I took exhaustive notes. He was not remarkable for intelligence, and his answers were frequently obscure, which I attributed to his limited acquaintance with our language. Suddenly, however, as I sat writing he ceased to give any answer at all to my inquiries, and on my turning towards him I was shocked to see that he was sitting bolt upright in his chair, staring at me with a perfectly blank and rigid face. He was again in the grip of his mysterious malady.

" My first feeling, as I have just said, was one of pity and horror. My second, I fear, was rather one of professional satisfaction. I made notes of my patient's pulse and temperature, tested the rigidity of his muscles, and examined his reflexes. There was nothing markedly abnormal in any of these conditions, which harmonized with my former experiences. I had obtained good results in such cases by the inhalation of nitrite of amyl, and the present seemed an admirable opportunity of testing its virtues. The bottle was downstairs in my laboratory, so, leaving my patient seated in his chair, I ran down to get it. There was some little delay in finding it—five minutes, let us say—and then I returned. Imagine my amazement to find the room empty and the patient gone !

" Of course, my first act was to run into the waiting-room. The son had gone also. The hall door had been closed, but not shut. My page who admits patients is a new boy, and by no means quick. He waits downstairs, and runs up to show patients out when I ring the consulting-room bell. He had heard nothing, and the affair remained a complete mystery. Mr. Blessington came in from his walk shortly afterwards, but I did not say anything to him upon the subject, for to tell the truth, I have got in the way of late of holding as little communication with him as possible.

"Well, I never thought that I should see anything more of the Russian and his son, so you can imagine my amazement when at the very same hour this evening they both came marching into my consulting-room, just as they had done before.

"'I feel that I owe you a great many apologies for my abrupt departure yesterday, Doctor,' said my patient.

"'I confess that I was very much surprised at it,' said I.

"'Well, the fact is,' he remarked, 'that when I recover from these attacks my mind is always very clouded as to all that has gone before. I woke up in a strange room, as it seemed to me, and made my way out into the street in a sort of dazed way when you were absent.'

"'And I,' said the son, 'seeing my father pass the door of the waiting-room, naturally thought that the consultation had come to an end. It was not until we had reached home that I began to realize the true state of affairs.'

"'Well,' said I, laughing, 'there is no harm done, except that you puzzled me terribly; so if you, sir, would kindly step into the waiting-room, I shall be happy to continue our consultation, which was brought to so abrupt an ending.'

"For half an hour or so I discussed the old gentleman's symptoms with him, and then, having prescribed for him, I saw him go off on the arm of his son.

" I have told you that Mr. Blessington generally chose this hour of the day for his exercise. He came in shortly afterwards and passed upstairs. An instant later I heard him running down, and he burst into my consulting-room like a man who is mad with panic.

" ' Who has been in my room ? ' he cried.

" ' No one,' said I.

" ' It's a lie ! ' he yelled. ' Come up and look.'

" I passed over the grossness of his language, as he seemed half out of his mind with fear. When I went upstairs with him he pointed to several footprints upon the light carpet.

" ' D'you mean to say those are mine ? ' he cried.

" They were certainly very much larger than any which he could have made, and were evidently quite fresh. It rained hard this afternoon, as you know, and my patients were the only people who called. It must have been the case, then, that the man in the waiting-room had for some unknown reason, while I was busy with the other, ascended to the room of my resident patient. Nothing had been touched or taken, but there were the footprints to prove that the intrusion was an undoubted fact.

" Mr. Blessington seemed more excited over the matter than I should have thought possible, though, of course, it was enough to disturb anybody's peace of mind. He actually sat crying in an arm-chair, and I could hardly get him to speak coherently. It was his suggestion that I should come round to you, and of course I at once saw the propriety of it, for certainly the incident is a very singular one, though he appears to completely overrate its importance. If you would only come back with me in my brougham, you would at least be able to soothe him, though I can hardly hope that you will be able to explain this remarkable occurrence."

Sherlock Holmes had listened to this long narrative with an intentness which showed me that his interest was keenly aroused. His face was as impassive as ever, but his lids had drooped more heavily over his eyes, and his smoke had curled up more thickly from his pipe to emphasize each curious episode in the doctor's tale. As our visitor concluded Holmes sprang up without a word, handed me my hat, picked up his own from the table, and followed Dr. Trevelyan to the door. Within a quarter of an hour we had been dropped at the door of the physician's residence in Brook Street, one of those sombre, flat-faced houses which one associates with a West End practice. A small page admitted us, and we began at once to ascend the broad, well-carpeted stair.

But a singular interruption brought us to a standstill. The light at the top was suddenly whisked out, and from the darkness came a reedy, quavering voice.

" I have a pistol," it cried ; " I give you my word that I'll fire if you come any nearer."

" This really grows outrageous, Mr. Blessington," cried Dr. Trevelyan.

" Oh, then it is you, Doctor ? " said the voice, with a great heave of relief. " But those other gentlemen, are they what they pretend to be ? "

We were conscious of a long scrutiny out of the darkness.

" Yes, yes, it's all right," said the voice at last. " You can come up, and I am sorry if my precautions have annoyed you."

He re-lit the stair gas as he spoke, and we saw before us a singular-looking man, whose appearance, as well as his voice, testified to his jangled nerves. He was very fat, but had apparently at some time been much fatter, so that the skin hung about his face in loose pouches, like the cheeks of a bloodhound. He was of a sickly colour, and his thin, sandy hair seemed to bristle up with the intensity of his emotion. In his hand he held a pistol, but he thrust it into his pocket as we advanced.

" Good evening, Mr. Holmes," said he ; " I am sure I am very much obliged to you for coming round. No one ever needed your advice more than I do. I suppose that Dr. Trevelyan has told you of this most unwarrantable intrusion into my rooms ? "

" Quite so," said Holmes. " Who are these two men, Mr. Blessington, and why do they wish to molest you ? "

" Well, well," said the resident patient, in a nervous fashion, " of course it is hard to say that. You can hardly expect me to answer that, Mr. Holmes."

" Do you mean that you don't know ? "

" Come in here, if you please. Just have the kindness to step in here."

He led the way into his bedroom, which was large and comfortably furnished.

" You see that ? " said he, pointing to a big black box at the end of his bed. " I have never been a very rich man, Mr. Holmes—never made but one investment in my life, as Dr. Trevelyan would tell you. But I don't believe in bankers. I would never trust a banker, Mr. Holmes. Between ourselves, what little I have is in that box, so you can understand what it means to me when unknown people force themselves into my rooms."

Holmes looked at Blessington in his questioning way, and shook his head.

" I cannot possibly advise you if you try to deceive me," said he.

" But I have told you everything."

Holmes turned on his heel with a gesture of disgust. " Good night, Dr. Trevelyan," said he.

" And no advice for me ? " cried Blessington, in a breaking voice.

" My advice to you, sir, is to speak the truth."

A minute later we were in the street and walking for home. We had crossed Oxford Street, and were half-way down Harley Street before I could get a word from my companion.

" Sorry to bring you out on such a fool's errand, Watson," he said, at last. " It is an interesting case, too, at the bottom of it."

" I can make little of it," I confessed.

" Well, it is quite evident that there are two men— more, perhaps, but at least two—who are determined for

469

some reason to get at this fellow Blessington. I have no doubt in my mind that both on the first and on the second occasion that young man penetrated to Blessington's room, while his confederate, by an ingenious device, kept the doctor from interfering."

" And the catalepsy ! "

" A fraudulent imitation, Watson, though I should hardly dare to hint as much to our specialist. It is a very easy complaint to imitate. I have done it myself."

" And then ? "

" By the purest chance Blessington was out on each occasion. Their reason for choosing so unusual an hour for a consultation was obviously to ensure that there should be no other patient in the waiting-room. It just happened, however, that this hour coincided with Blessington's constitutional, which seems to show that they were not very well acquainted with his daily routine. Of course if they had been merely after plunder they would at least have made some attempt to search for it. Besides, I can read in a man's eye when it is his own skin that he is frightened for. It is inconceivable that this fellow could have made two such vindictive enemies as these appear to be without knowing of it. I hold it, therefore, to be certain that he does know who these men are, and that for reasons of his own he suppresses it. It is just possible that to-morrow may find him in a more communicative mood."

" Is there not one alternative," I suggested, " grotesquely improbable, no doubt, but still just conceivable ? Might the whole story of the cataleptic Russian and his son be a concoction of Dr. Trevelyan's, who has, for his own purposes, been in Blessington's rooms ? "

I saw in the gaslight that Holmes wore an amused smile at this brilliant departure of mine.

" My dear fellow," said he, " it was one of the first solutions which occurred to me, but I was soon able to corroborate the doctor's tale. This young man has left prints upon the stair carpet which made it quite superduous for me to ask to see those which he had made in the room. When I tell you that his shoes were square-toed, instead of being pointed like Blessington's, and were quite an inch and a third longer than the doctor's, you will acknowledge that there can be no doubt as to his individuality. But we may sleep on it now, for I shall be surprised if we do not hear something further from Brook Street in the morning."

Sherlock Holmes' prophecy was soon fulfilled, and in a dramatic fashion. At half-past seven next morning, in the first dim glimmer of daylight, I found him standing by my bedside in his dressing-gown.

" There's a brougham waiting for us, Watson," said he.

" What's the matter, then ? "

" The Brook Street business."

" Any fresh news ? "

" Tragic, but ambiguous," said he pulling up the blind. " Look at this—a sheet from a notebook with ' For God's sake, come at once—P. T.' scrawled upon it in pencil. Our friend the doctor was hard put to it when he wrote this. Come along, my dear fellow, for it's an urgent call."

In a quarter of an hour or so we were back at the physician's house. He came running out to meet us with a face of horror.

" Oh, such a business ! " he cried, with his hands to his temples.

" What, then ? "

" Blessington has committed suicide ! "

Holmes whistled.

" Yes, he hanged himself during the night ! "

We had entered, and the doctor had preceded us into what was evidently his waiting-room.

" I really hardly know what I am doing," he cried. " The police are already upstairs. It has shaken me most dreadfully."

" When did you find it out ? "

" He has a cup of tea taken in to him early every

471

morning. When the maid entered about seven, there the unfortunate fellow was hanging in the middle of the room. He had tied his cord to the hook on which the heavy lamp used to hang, and he had jumped off from the top of the very box that he showed us yesterday."

Holmes stood for a moment in deep thought.

" With your permission," said he at last, " I should like to go upstairs and look into the matter." We both ascended, followed by the doctor.

It was a dreadful sight which met us as we entered the bedroom door. I have spoken of the impression of flabbiness which this man Blessington conveyed. As he dangled from the hook it was exaggerated and intensified until he was scarce human in his appearance. The neck was drawn out like a plucked chicken's, making the rest of him seem the more obese and unnatural by the contrast. He was clad only in his long night-dress, and his swollen ankles and ungainly feet protruded starkly from beneath it. Beside him stood a smart-looking police inspector, who was taking notes in a pocket-book.

" Ah, Mr. Holmes," said he, as my friend entered. " I am delighted to see you."

" Good morning, Lanner," answered Holmes. " You won't think me an intruder, I am sure. Have you heard of the events which led up to this affair ? "

" Yes, I heard something of them."

" Have you formed any opinion ? "

" As far as I can see, the man has been driven out of his senses by fright. The bed has been well slept in, you see. There's his impression deep enough. It's about five in the morning, you know, that suicides are most common. That would be about his time for hanging himself. It seems to have been a very deliberate affair."

" I should say that he has been dead about three hours, judging by the rigidity of the muscles," said I.

" Noticed anything peculiar about the room ? " asked Holmes.

" Found a screwdriver and some screws on the wash-hand stand. Seems to have smoked heavily during the night, too. Here are four cigar-ends that I picked out of the fire-place."

" Hum ! " said Holmes. " Have you got his cigar-holder ? "

" No, I have seen none."

" His cigar-case, then ? "

" Yes, it was in his coat pocket."

Holmes opened it and smelled the single cigar which it contained.

" Oh, this is a Havana, and these others are cigars of the peculiar sort which are imported by the Dutch from their East Indian colonies. They are usually wrapped in straw, you know, and are thinner for their length than any other brand." He picked up the four ends and examined them with his pocket lens.

" Two of these have been smoked from a holder and two without," said he. " Two have been cut by a not very sharp knife, and two have had the ends bitten off by a set of excellent teeth. This is no suicide, Mr. Lanner. It is a very deeply planned and cold-blooded murder."

" Impossible ! " cried the Inspector.

" And why ? "

" Why should anyone murder a man in so clumsy a fashion as by hanging him ? "

" That is what we have to find out."

" How could they get in ? "

" Through the front door."

" It was barred in the morning."

" Then it was barred after them."

" How do you know ? "

" I saw their traces. Excuse me a moment, and I may be able to give you some further information about it."

He went over to the door, and turning the lock he examined it in his methodical fashion. Then he took out the key, which was on the inside, and inspected that also. The bed, the carpet, the chairs, the mantelpiece, the dead body, and the rope were each in turn examined, until at last he professed himself satisfied, and with my aid and that of the Inspector cut down the wretched object, and laid it reverently under a sheet.

"How about this rope ? " he asked.

"It is cut off this," said Dr. Trevelyan, drawing a large coil from under the bed. "He was morbidly nervous of fire, and always kept this beside him, so that he might escape by the window in case the stairs were burning."

"That must have saved them trouble," said Holmes, thoughtfully. "Yes, the actual facts are very plain, and I shall be surprised if by the afternoon I cannot give you the reasons for them as well. I will take this photograph of Blessington which I see upon the mantelpiece, as it may help me in my inquiries."

"But you have told us nothing," cried the doctor.

"Oh, there can be no doubt as to the sequence of events," said Holmes. "There were three of them in it : the young man, the old man, and a third to whose identity I have no clue. The first two, I need hardly remark, are the same who masqueraded as the Russian Count and his son, so we can give a very full description of them. They were admitted by a confederate inside the house. If I might offer you a word of advice, Inspector, it would be to arrest the page, who, as I understand, has only recently come into your service, Doctor."

"The young imp cannot be found," said Dr. Trevelyan ; "the maid and the cook have just been searching for him."

Holmes shrugged his shoulders.

"He has played a not unimportant part in this drama," said he. "The three men having ascended the stair, which they did on tiptoe, the elder man first, the younger man second, and the unknown man in the rear——"

"My dear Holmes ! " I ejaculated.

"Oh, there could be no question as to the superimposing of the footmarks. I had the advantage of learning which was which last night. They ascended then to Mr. Blessington's room, the door of which they found to be locked. With the help of a wire, however, they forced round the key. Even without the lens, you will perceive, by the scratches on this ward, where the pressure was applied.

"On entering the room, their first proceeding must have been to gag Mr. Blessington. He may have been asleep, or he may have been so paralysed with terror as to have been unable to cry out. These walls are thick, and it is conceivable that his shriek, if he had time to utter one, was unheard.

"Having secured him, it is evident to me that a consultation of some sort was held. Probably it was something in the nature of a judicial proceeding. It must have lasted for some time, for it was then that these cigars were smoked. The older man sat in that wicker chair : it was he who used the cigar-holder. The younger man sat over yonder ; he knocked his ash off against the chest of drawers. The third fellow paced up and down. Blessington, I think, sat upright in the bed, but of that I cannot be absolutely certain.

"Well, it ended by their taking Blessington and hanging him. The matter was so pre-arranged that it is my belief that they brought with them some sort of block or pulley which might serve as a gallows. That screwdriver and those screws were, as I conceive, for fixing it up. Seeing the hook, however, they naturally saved themselves the trouble. Having finished their work they made off, and the door was barred behind them by their confederate."

We had all listened with the deepest interest to this sketch of the night's doings, which Holmes had deduced from signs so subtle and minute, that even when he had pointed them out to us, we could scarcely follow him in his reasonings. The Inspector hurried away on the instant to make inquiries about the page, while Holmes and I returned to Baker Street for breakfast.

"I'll be back by three," said he when we had finished our meal. "Both the Inspector and the doctor will meet me here at that hour, and I hope by that time to have cleared up any little obscurity which the case may still present."

Our visitors arrived at the appointed time, but it was a quarter to four before my friend put in an appearance. From his expression as he entered, however, I could see that all had gone well with him.

" Any news, Inspector ? "

" We have got the boy, sir."

" Excellent, and I have got the men."

" You have got them ! " we cried all three.

" Well, at least I have got their identity. This so-called Blessington is, as I expected, well known at head-quarters, and so are his assailants. Their names are Biddle, Hayward, and Moffat."

" The Worthingdon bank gang," cried the Inspector.

" Precisely," said Holmes.

" Then Blessington must have been Sutton ? "

" Exactly," said Holmes.

" Why, that makes it as clear as crystal," said the Inspector.

But Trevelyan and I looked at each other in bewilderment.

" You must surely remember the great Worthingdon bank business," said Holmes ; " five men were in it, these four and a fifth called Cartwright. Tobin, the caretaker, was murdered, and the thieves got away with seven thousand pounds. This was in 1875. They were all five arrested, but the evidence against them was by no means conclusive. This Blessington or Sutton, who was the worst of the gang, turned informer. On his evidence Cartwright was hanged, and the other three got fifteen years apiece. When they got out the other day, which was some years before their full term, they set themselves, as you perceive, to hunt down the traitor and to avenge the death of their comrade upon him. Twice they tried to get at him and failed ; a third time, you see, it came off. Is there anything further which I can explain, Dr. Trevelyan ? "

" I think you have made it all remarkably clear," said the doctor. " No doubt the day on which he was so perturbed was the day when he read of their release in the newspapers."

" Quite so. His talk about a burglary was the merest blind."

" But why could he not tell you this ? "

" Well, my dear sir, knowing the vindictive character of his old associates, he was trying to hide his own identity from everybody as long as he could. His secret was a shameful one, and he could not bring himself to divulge it. However, wretch as he was, he was still living under the shield of British law, and I have no doubt, Inspector, that you will see that, though that shield may fail to guard, the sword of justice is still there to avenge."

Such were the singular circumstances in connection with the resident patient and the Brook Street doctor. From that night nothing has been seen of the three murderers by the police, and it is surmised at Scotland Yard that they were among the passengers of the ill-fated steamer *Norah Creina*, which was lost some years ago with all hands upon the Portuguese coast, some leagues to the north of Oporto. The proceedings against the page broke down for want of evidence, and the " Brook Street Mystery," as it was called, has never, until now, been fully dealt with in any public print.

21. *The Greek Interpreter*

DURING my long and intimate acquaintance with Mr. Sherlock Holmes I had never heard him refer to his relations, and hardly ever to his own early life. This reticence upon his part had increased the somewhat inhuman effect which he produced upon me, until sometimes I found myself regarding him as an isolated phenomenon, a brain without a heart, as deficient in human sympathy as he was pre-eminent in intelligence. His aversion to women, and his disinclination to form new friendships, were both typical of his unemotional character, but not more so than his complete suppression of every reference to his own people. I had come to believe that he was an orphan with no relatives living, but one day, to my very great surprise, he began to talk to me about his brother.

It was after tea on a summer evening, and the conversation, which had roamed in a desultory, spasmodic fashion from golf clubs to the causes of the change in the obliquity of the ecliptic, came round at last to the question of atavism and hereditary aptitudes. The point under discussion was how far any singular gift in an individual was due to his ancestry, and how far to his own early training.

" In your own case," said I, " from all that you have told me it seems obvious that your faculty of observation and your peculiar facility for deduction are due to your own systematic training."

" To some extent," he answered, thoughtfully. " My ancestors were country squires, who appear to have led much the same life as is natural to their class. But, none the less, my turn that way is in my veins, and may have come with my grandmother, who was the sister of Vernet, the French artist. Art in the blood is liable to take the strangest forms."

" But how do you know that it is hereditary ? "

" Because my brother Mycroft possesses it in a larger degree than I do."

This was news to me, indeed. If there were another man with such singular powers in England, how was it that neither police nor public had heard of him ? I put the question, with a hint that it was my companion's modesty which made him acknowledge his brother as his superior. Holmes laughed at my suggestion.

" My dear Watson," said he. " I cannot agree with those who rank modesty among the virtues. To the logician all things should be seen exactly as they are, and to under-estimate oneself is as much a departure from truth as to exaggerate one's own powers. When I say, therefore, that Mycroft has better powers of observation than I, you may take it that I am speaking the exact and literal truth."

" Is he your junior ? "

" Seven years my senior."

" How comes it that he is unknown ? "

" Oh, he is very well known in his own circle."

" Where, then ? "

" Well, in the Diogenes Club, for example."

I had never heard of the institution, and my face must have proclaimed as much, for Sherlock Holmes pulled out his watch.

" The Diogenes Club is the queerest club in London, and Mycroft one of the queerest men. He's always there from a quarter to five till twenty to eight. It's six now, so if you care for a stroll this beautiful evening I shall be very happy to introduce you to two curiosities."

Five minutes later we were in the street, walking towards Regent Circus.

" You wonder," said my companion, " why it is that Mycroft does not use his powers for detective work. He is incapable of it."

" But I thought you said——! "

" I said that he was my superior in observation and deduction. If the art of the detective began and ended in reasoning from an arm-chair, my brother would be the greatest criminal agent that ever lived. But he has no ambition and no energy. He would not even go out of his way to verify his own solutions, and would rather be considered wrong than take the trouble to prove himself right. Again and again I have taken a problem to him and have received an explanation which has afterwards proved to be the correct one. And yet he was absolutely incapable of working out the practical points which must be gone into before a case could be laid before a judge or jury."

" It is not his profession, then ? "

" By no means. What is to me a means of livelihood is to him the merest hobby of a dilettante. He has an extraordinary faculty for figures, and audits the books in some of the Government departments. Mycroft lodges in Pall Mall, and he walks round the corner into White-hall every morning and back every evening. From year's end to year's end he takes no other exercise, and is seen nowhere else, except only in the Diogenes Club, which is just opposite his rooms."

" I cannot recall the name."

" Very likely not. There are many men in London, you know, who, some from shyness, some from misan-thropy have no wish for the company of their fellows. Yet they are not averse to comfortable chairs and the latest periodicals. It is for the convenience of these that the Diogenes Club was started, and it now contains the most unsociable and unclubbable men in town. No member is permitted to take the least notice of any other one. Save in the Strangers' Room, no talking is, under any circumstances, permitted, and three offences, if brought to the notice of the committee, render the talker liable to expulsion. My brother was one of the founders, and I have myself found it a very soothing atmosphere."

We had reached Pall Mall as we talked, and were walk-ing down it from the St. James's end. Sherlock Holmes stopped at a door some little distance from the Carlton, and, cautioning me not to speak, he led the way into the hall. Through the glass panelling I caught a glimpse of a large and luxurious room in which a considerable number of men were sitting about and reading papers, each in his own little nook. Holmes showed me into a small chamber which looked out on to Pall Mall, and then, leaving me for a minute, he came back with a companion who I knew could only be his brother.

Mycroft Holmes was a much larger and stouter man than Sherlock. His body was absolutely corpulent, but his face, though massive, had preserved something of the sharpness of expression which was so remarkable in that of his brother. His eyes, which were of a peculiarly light watery grey, seemed to always retain that far-away, intro-spective look which I had only observed in Sherlock's when he was exerting his full powers.

" I am glad to meet you, sir," said he, putting out a broad, flat hand, like the flipper of a seal. " I hear of Sherlock everywhere since you became his chronicler. By the way, Sherlock, I expected to see you round last week to consult me over that Manor House case. I thought you might be a little out of your depth."

" No, I solved it," said my friend, smiling.

" It was Adams, of course ? "

" Yes, it was Adams."

" I was sure of it from the first." The two sat down together in the bow-window of the club. " To anyone who wishes to study mankind this is the spot," said Mycroft. " Look at the magnificent types ! Look at these two men who are coming towards us, for example."

" The billiard-marker and the other ? "

" Precisely. What do you make of the other ? "

The two men had stopped opposite the window. Some chalk marks over the waistcoat pocket were the only signs of billiards which I could see in one of them. The other was a very small, dark fellow, with his hat pushed back and several packages under his arm.

" An old soldier, I perceive," said Sherlock.

" And very recently discharged," remarked the brother.

" Served in India, I see."

" And a non-commissioned officer."

" Royal Artillery, I fancy," said Sherlock.

" And a widower."

" But with a child."

" Children, my dear boy, children."

" Come," said I, laughing, " this is a little too much."

" Surely," answered Holmes, " it is not hard to say that a man with that bearing, expression of authority, and sun-baked skin is a soldier, is more than a private, and is not long from India."

" That he has not left the service long is shown by his still wearing his ' ammunition boots,' as they are called," observed Mycroft.

" He has not the cavalry stride, yet he wore his hat on one side, as is shown by the lighter skin on that side of his brow. His weight is against his being a sapper. He is in the artillery."

" Then, of course, his complete mourning shows that he has lost someone very dear. The fact that he is doing his own shopping looks as though it were his wife. He has been buying things for children, you perceive. There is a rattle, which shows that one of them is very young. The wife probably died in child-bed. The fact that he has a picture-book under his arm shows that there is another child to be thought of."

I began to understand what my friend meant when he said that his brother possessed even keener faculties than he did himself. He glanced across at me and smiled. Mycroft took snuff from a tortoiseshell box and brushed away the wandering grains from his coat with a large, red silk handkerchief.

" By the way, Sherlock," said he, " I have had something quite after your own heart—a most singular problem —submitted to my judgment. I really had not the energy to follow it up, save in a very incomplete fashion, but it gave me a basis for some very pleasing speculations. If you would care to hear the facts——"

" My dear Mycroft, I should be delighted."

The brother scribbled a note upon a leaf of his pocket-book, and, ringing the bell, he handed it to the waiter.

" I have asked Mr. Melas to step across," said he. " He lodges on the floor above me, and I have some slight acquaintance with him, which led him to come to me in his perplexity. Mr. Melas is a Greek by extraction, as I understand, and he is a remarkable linguist. He earns his living partly as interpreter in the law courts, partly by acting as guide to any wealthy Orientals who may visit the Northumberland Avenue hotels. I think I will leave him to tell his own very remarkable experience in his own fashion."

A few minutes later we were joined by a short, stout man, whose olive face and coal-black hair proclaimed his Southern origin, though his speech was that of an educated Englishman. He shook hands eagerly with Sherlock Holmes, and his dark eyes sparkled with pleasure when he understood that the specialist was anxious to hear his story.

"I do not believe that the police credit me—on my word I do not," said he, in a wailing voice. "Just because they have never heard of it before, they think that such a thing cannot be. But I know that I shall never be easy in my mind until I know what has become of my poor man with the sticking-plaster upon his face."

"I am all attention," said Sherlock Holmes.

"This is Wednesday evening," said Mr. Melas ; "well, then it was on Monday night—only two days ago, you understand—that all this happened. I am an interpreter, as, perhaps, my neighbour there has told you. I interpret all languages—or nearly all—but as I am a Greek by birth, and with a Grecian name, it is with that particular tongue that I am principally associated. For many years I have been the chief Greek interpreter in London, and my name is very well known in the hotels.

"It happens, not unfrequently, that I am sent for at strange hours, by foreigners who get into difficulties, or by travellers who arrive late and wish my services. I was not surprised, therefore, on Monday night when a Mr. Latimer, a very fashionably dressed young man, came up to my rooms and asked me to accompany him in a cab, which was waiting at the door. A Greek friend had come to see him upon business, he said, and, as he could speak nothing but his own tongue, the services of an interpreter were indispensable. He gave me to understand that his house was some little distance off, in Kensington, and he seemed to be in a great hurry, bustling me rapidly into the cab when we had descended into the street.

" I say into the cab, but I soon became doubtful as to whether it was not a carriage in which I found myself. It was certainly more roomy than the ordinary four-wheeled disgrace to London, and the fittings, though frayed, were of rich quality. Mr. Latimer seated himself opposite to me, and we started off through Charing Cross and up the Shaftesbury Avenue. We had come out upon Oxford Street, and I had ventured some remark as to this being a roundabout way to Kensington, when my words were arrested by the extraordinary conduct of my companion.

" He began by drawing a most formidable-looking bludgeon loaded with lead from his pocket, and switched it backwards and forwards several times, as if to test its weight and strength. Then he placed it, without a word, upon the seat beside him. Having done this, he drew up the windows on each side, and I found to my astonishment that they were covered with paper so as to prevent my seeing through them.

" ' I am sorry to cut off your view, Mr. Melas,' said he. ' The fact is that I have no intention that you should see what the place is to which we are driving. It might possibly be inconvenient to me if you could find your way there again.'

" As you can imagine, I was utterly taken aback by such an address. My companion was a powerful, broad-shouldered young fellow, and, apart from the weapon, I should not have had the slightest chance in a struggle with him.

" ' This is very extraordinary conduct, Mr. Latimer,' I stammered. ' You must be aware that what you are doing is quite illegal.'

" ' It is somewhat of a liberty, no doubt,' said he, ' but we'll make it up to you. But I must warn you, however, Mr. Melas, that if at any time to-night you attempt to raise an alarm or do anything which is against my interests, you will find it a very serious thing. I beg you to remember that no one knows where you are, and that whether you are in this carriage or in my house, you are equally in my power.'

" His words were quiet, but he had a rasping way of saying them which was very menacing. I sat in silence, wondering what on earth could be his reason for kidnapping me in this extraordinary fashion. Whatever it might be, it was perfectly clear that there was no possible use in my resisting, and that I could only wait to see what might befall.

" For nearly two hours we drove without my having the least clue as to where we were going. Sometimes the rattle of the stones told of a paved causeway, and at others our smooth, silent course suggested asphalt, but save this variation in sound there was nothing at all which could in the remotest way help me to form a guess as to where we were. The paper over each window was impenetrable to light, and a blue curtain was drawn across the glass-work in front. It was a quarter past seven when we left Pall Mall, and my watch showed me that it was ten minutes to nine when we at last came to a standstill. My companion let down the window and I caught a glimpse of a low, arched doorway with a lamp burning above it. As I was hurried from the carriage it swung open, and I found myself inside the house, with a vague impression of a lawn and trees on each side of me as I entered. Whether these were private grounds, however, or *bona-fide* country was more than I could possibly venture to say.

" There was a coloured gas-lamp inside, which was turned so low that I could see little save that the hall was of some size and hung with pictures. In the dim light I could make out that the person who had opened the door was a small, mean-looking, middle-aged man with rounded shoulders. As he turned towards us the glint of the light showed me that he was wearing glasses.

" ' Is this Mr. Melas, Harold ? ' said he.

" ' Yes.'

" ' Well done ! Well done ! No ill-will, Mr. Melas, I hope, but we could not get on without you. If you deal fair with us you'll not regret it ; but if you try any tricks, God help you ! '

" He spoke in a jerky, nervous fashion, and with some giggling laughs in between, but somehow he impressed me with fear more than the other.

" ' What do you want with me ? ' I asked.

" ' Only to ask a few questions of a Greek gentleman who is visiting us, and to let us have the answers. But say no more than you are told to say, or '—here came the nervous giggle again—' you had better never have been born.'

" As he spoke he opened a door and showed the way into a room which appeared to be very richly furnished— but again the only light was afforded by a single lamp half turned down. The chamber was certainly large, and the way in which my feet sank into the carpet as I stepped across it told me of its richness. I caught glimpses of velvet chairs, a high, white marble mantelpiece, and what seemed to be a suit of Japanese armour at one side of it. There was a chair just under the lamp, and the elderly man motioned that I should sit in it. The younger had left us, but he suddenly returned through another door, leading with him a gentleman clad in some sort of loose dressing-gown, who moved slowly towards us. As he came into the circle of dim light which enabled me to see him more clearly, I was thrilled with horror at his appearance. He was deadly pale and terribly emaciated, with the protruding, brilliant eyes of a man whose spirit is greater than his strength. But what shocked me more than any signs of physical weakness was that his face was grotesquely criss-crossed with sticking-plaster, and that one large pad of it was fastened over his mouth.

" ' Have you the slate, Harold ? ' cried the older man, as this strange being fell rather than sat down into a chair. ' Are his hands loose ? Now then, give him the pencil. You are to ask the questions, Mr. Melas, and he will write the answers. Ask him first of all whether he is prepared to sign the papers.'

"The man's eyes flashed fire.

"'Never,' he wrote in Greek upon the slate.

"'On no conditions?' I asked at the bidding of our tyrant.

"'Only if I see her married in my presence by a Greek priest whom I know.'

"The man giggled in his venomous way.

"'You know what awaits you, then?'

"'I care nothing for myself.'

"These are samples of the questions and answers which made up our strange, half-spoken, half-written conversation. Again and again I had to ask him whether he would give in and sign the document. Again and again I had the same indignant reply. But soon a happy thought came to me. I took to adding on little sentences of my own to each question—innocent ones at first, to test whether either of our companions knew anything of the matter, and then, as I found that they showed no sign, I played a more dangerous game. Our conversation ran something like this:

"'You can do no good by this obstinacy. *Who are you?*'

"'I care not. *I am a stranger in London.*'

"'Your fate will be on your own head. *How long have you been here?*'

"'Let it be so. *Three weeks.*'

"'The property can never be yours. *What ails you?*'

"'It shall not go to villains. *They are starving me.*'

"'You shall go free if you sign. *What house is this?*'

"'I will never sign. *I do not know.*'

"'You are not doing her any service. *What is your name?*'

"'Let me hear her say so. *Kratides.*'

"'You shall see her if you sign. *Where are you from?*'

"'Then I shall never see her. *Athens.*'

"Another five minutes, Mr. Holmes, and I should have wormed out the whole story under their very noses. My very next question might have cleared the matter up, but at that instant the door opened and a woman stepped into the room. I could not see her clearly enough to know more than that she was tall and graceful, with black hair, and clad in some sort of loose white gown.

"'Harold!' said she, speaking English with a broken accent, 'I could not stay away longer. It is so lonely up there with only—oh, my God, it is Paul!'

"These last words were in Greek, and at the same instant the man, with a convulsive effort, tore the plaster from his lips, and screaming out 'Sophy! Sophy!' rushed into the woman's arms. Their embrace was but for an instant, however, for the younger man seized the woman and pushed her out of the room, while the elder easily overpowered his emaciated victim, and dragged him away through the other door. For a moment I was left alone in the room, and I sprang to my feet with some vague idea that I might in some way get a clue to what this house was in which I found myself. Fortunately, however, I took no steps, for, looking up, I saw that the older man was standing in the doorway, with his eyes fixed upon me.

"'That will do, Mr. Melas,' said he. 'You perceive that we have taken you into our confidence over some very private business. We should not have troubled you only that our friend who speaks Greek and who began these negotiations has been forced to return to the East. It was quite necessary for us to find someone to take his place, and we were fortunate in hearing of your powers.'

"I bowed.

"'There are five sovereigns here,' said he, walking up to me, 'which will, I hope, be a sufficient fee. But remember,' he added, tapping me lightly on the chest and giggling, 'if you speak to a human soul about this —one human soul mind—well, may God have mercy upon your soul!'

" I cannot tell you the loathing and horror with which this insignificant-looking man inspired me. I could see him better now as the lamp-light shone upon him. His features were peeky and sallow, and his little, pointed beard was thready and ill-nourished. He pushed his face forward as he spoke, and his lips and eyelids were continually twitching, like a man with St. Vitus's dance. I could not help thinking that his strange, catchy little laugh was also a symptom of some nervous malady. The terror of his face lay in his eyes, however, steel grey, and glistening coldly, with a malignant, inexorable cruelty in their depths.

" 'We shall know if you speak of this,' said he. 'We have our own means of information. Now, you will find the carriage waiting, and my friend will see you on your way.'

" I was hurried through the hall, and into the vehicle, again obtaining that momentary glimpse of trees and a garden. Mr. Latimer followed closely at my heels, and took his place opposite to me without a word. In silence we again drove for an interminable distance, with the windows raised, until at last, just after midnight, the carriage pulled up.

" 'You will get down here, Mr. Melas,' said my companion. 'I am sorry to leave you so far from your house, but there is no alternative. Any attempt upon your part to follow the carriage can only end in injury to yourself.'

" He opened the door as he spoke, and I had hardly time to spring out when the coachman lashed the horse, and the carriage rattled away. I looked round me in astonishment. I was on some sort of a heathy common, mottled over with dark clumps of furze bushes. Far away stretched a line of houses, with a light here and there in the upper windows. On the other side I saw the red signal lamps of a railway.

" The carriage which had brought me was already out of sight. I stood gazing round and wondering where on earth I might be, when I saw someone coming towards me in the darkness. As he came up to me I made out that it was a railway porter.

" ' Can you tell me what place this is ? ' I asked.

" ' Wandsworth Common,' said he.

" ' Can I get a train into town ? '

" ' If you walk on a mile or so, to Clapham Junction,' said he, ' you'll just be in time for the last to Victoria.'

" So that was the end of my adventure, Mr. Holmes. I do not know where I was nor whom I spoke with, nor anything, save what I have told you. But I know that there is foul play going on, and I want to help that unhappy man if I can. I told the whole story to Mr. Mycroft Holmes next morning, and, subsequently, to the police."

We all sat in silence for some little time after listening to this extraordinary narrative. Then Sherlock looked across at his brother.

" Any steps ? " he asked.

Mycroft picked up the *Daily News*, which was lying on a side-table.

" ' Anybody supplying any information as to the whereabouts of a Greek gentleman named Paul Kratides, from Athens, who is unable to speak English, will be rewarded. A similar reward paid to anyone giving information about a Greek lady whose first name is Sophy. X 2473.' That was in all the dailies. No answer."

" How about the Greek Legation ? "

" I have inquired. They know nothing."

" A wire to the head of the Athens police, then."

" Sherlock has all the energy of the family," said Mycroft, turning to me. " Well, you take up the case by all means, and let me know if you do any good."

" Certainly," answered my friend, rising from his chair. " I'll let you know, and Mr. Melas also. In the meantime, Mr. Melas, I should certainly be on my guard if I were you, for, of course, they must know through these advertisements that you have betrayed them."

As we walked home together Holmes stopped at a telegraph office and sent off several wires.

" You see, Watson," he remarked, " our evening has been by no means wasted. Some of my most interesting cases have come to me in this way through Mycroft. The problem which we have just listened to, although it can admit of but one explanation, has still some distinguishing features."

" You have hopes of solving it ? "

" Well, knowing as much as we do, it will be singular indeed if we fail to discover the rest. You must yourself have formed some theory which will explain the facts to which we have listened."

" In a vague way, yes."

" What was your idea, then ? "

" It seemed to me to be obvious that this Greek girl had been carried off by the young Englishman named Harold Latimer."

" Carried off from where ? "

" Athens, perhaps."

Sherlock Holmes shook his head. " This young man could not talk a word of Greek. The lady could talk English fairly well. Inference, that she had been in England some little time, but he had not been in Greece."

" Well, then, we will presume that she had come on a visit to England, and that this Harold had persuaded her to fly with him."

" That is the more probable."

" Then the brother—for that, I fancy, must be the relationship—comes over from Greece to interfere. He imprudently puts himself into the power of the young man and his older associate. They seize him and use violence towards him in order to make him sign some papers to make over the girl's fortune—of which he may be trustee—to them. This he refuses to do. In order to negotiate with him, they have to get an interpreter, and they pitch upon this Mr. Melas, having used some other one before. The girl is not told of the arrival of her brother, and finds it out by the merest accident."

"Excellent, Watson," cried Holmes. "I really fancy that you are not far from the truth. You see that we hold all the cards, and we have only to fear some sudden act of violence on their part. If they give us time we must have them."

"But how can we find where this house lies?"

"Well, if our conjecture is correct, and the girl's name is, or was, Sophy Kratides, we should have no difficulty in tracing her. That must be our main hope, for the brother, of course, is a complete stranger. It is clear that some time has elapsed since this Harold established these relations with the girl—some weeks at any rate—since the brother in Greece has had time to hear of it, and come across. If they have been living in the same place during this time, it is probable that we shall have some answer to Mycroft's advertisement."

We had reached our house in Baker Street whilst we had been talking, Holmes ascended the stairs first, and as he opened the door of our room he gave a start of surprise. Looking over his shoulder I was equally astonished. His brother Mycroft was sitting smoking in the arm-chair.

"Come in, Sherlock! Come in, sir," said he, blandly, smiling at our surprised faces. "You don't expect such energy from me, do you, Sherlock? But somehow this case attracts me."

"How did you get here?"

"I passed you in a hansom."

"There has been some new development?"

"I had an answer to my advertisement."

"Ah!"

"Yes; it came within a few minutes of your leaving."

"And to what effect?"

Mycroft Holmes took out a sheet of paper.

"Here it is," said he, "written with a J pen on royal cream paper by a middle-aged man with a weak constitution. ' Sir,' he says, ' in answer to your advertisement of to-day's date, I beg to inform you that I know the young lady in question very well. If you should care to call upon me, I could give you some particulars as to her painful history. She is living at present at The Myrtles, Beckenham.—Yours faithfully, J. DAVENPORT.'

"He writes from Lower Brixton," said Mycroft Holmes. "Do you not think that we might drive to him now, Sherlock, and learn these particulars ? "

"My dear Mycroft, the brother's life is more valuable than the sister's story. I think we should call at Scotland Yard for Inspector Gregson, and go straight out to Beckenham. We know that a man is being done to death, and every hour may be vital."

"Better pick up Mr. Melas upon our way," I suggested ; "we may need an interpreter."

"Excellent ! " said Sherlock Holmes. "Send the boy for a four-wheeler, and we shall be off at once." He opened the table-drawer as he spoke, and I noticed that he slipped his revolver into his pocket. "Yes," said he, in answer to my glance, "I should say from what we have heard that we are dealing with a particularly dangerous gang."

It was almost dark before we found ourselves in Pall Mall, at the rooms of Mr. Melas. A gentleman had just called for him, and he was gone.

"Can you tell me where ? " asked Mycroft Holmes.

"I don't know, sir," answered the woman who had opened the door. "I only know that he drove away with the gentleman in a carriage."

"Did the gentleman give a name ? "

"No, sir."

"He wasn't a tall, handsome, dark young man ? "

"Oh, no, sir ; he was a little gentleman, with glasses, thin in the face, but very pleasant in his ways, for he was laughing all the time that he was talking."

"Come along ! " cried Sherlock Holmes, abruptly. "This grows serious ! " he observed, as we drove to Scotland Yard. " These men have got hold of Melas again. He is a man of no physical courage, as they are well aware from their experience the other night. This villain was able to terrorize him the instant that he got into his presence. No doubt they want his professional services ; but, having used him, they may be inclined to punish him for what they will regard as his treachery."

Our hope was that by taking train we might get to Beckenham as soon as, or sooner than, the carriage. On reaching Scotland Yard, however, it was more than an hour before we could get Inspector Gregson and comply with the legal formalities which would enable us to enter the house. It was a quarter to ten before we reached London Bridge, and half-past before the four of us alighted on the Beckenham platform. A drive of half a mile brought us to The Myrtles—a large, dark house, standing back from the road in its own grounds. Here we dismissed our cab, and made our way up the drive together.

" The windows are all dark," remarked the Inspector. " The house seems deserted."

" Our birds are flown and the nest empty," said Holmes.

" Why do you say so ? "

" A carriage heavily loaded with luggage has passed out during the last hour."

The Inspector laughed. " I saw the wheel-tracks in the light of the gate-lamp, but where does the luggage come in ? "

" You may have observed the same wheel-tracks going the other way. But the outward-bound ones were very much deeper—so much so that we can say for a certainty that there was a very considerable weight on the carriage."

" You get a trifle beyond me there," said the Inspector, shrugging his shoulders. " It will not be an easy door to force. But we will try if we cannot make someone hear us."

He hammered loudly at the knocker and pulled at the

bell, but without any success. Holmes had slipped away, but he came back in a few minutes.

" I have a window open," said he.

" It is a mercy that you are on the side of the Force, and not against it, Mr. Holmes," remarked the Inspector, as he noted the clever way in which my friend had forced back the catch. " Well, I think that, under the circumstances, we may enter without waiting for an invitation."

One after the other we made our way into a large apartment, which was evidently that in which Mr. Melas had found himself. The Inspector had lit his lantern, and by its light we could see the two doors, the curtain, the lamp and the suit of Japanese mail as he had described them. On the table stood two glasses, an empty brandy bottle, and the remains of a meal.

" What is that ? " asked Holmes, suddenly.

We all stood still and listened. A low, moaning sound was coming from somewhere above our heads. Holmes rushed to the door and out into the hall. The dismal noise came from upstairs. He dashed up, the Inspector and I at his heels, while his brother, Mycroft, followed as quickly as his great bulk would permit.

Three doors faced us upon the second floor, and it was from the central of these that the sinister sounds were issuing, sinking sometimes into a dull mumble and rising again into a shrill whine. It was locked, but the key was on the outside. Holmes flung open the door and rushed in, but he was out again in an instant with his hand to his throat.

" It's charcoal ! " he cried. " Give it time. It will clear."

Peering in, we could see that the only light in the room came from a dull, blue flame, which flickered from a small brass tripod in the centre. It threw a livid, unnatural circle upon the floor, while in the shadows beyond, we saw the vague loom of two figures, which crouched against the wall. From the open door there reeked a horrible, poisonous exhalation, which set us gasping and coughing.

Holmes rushed to the top of the stairs to draw in the fresh air, and then, dashing into the room, he threw up the window and hurled the brazen tripod out into the garden.

"We can enter in a minute," he gasped, darting out again. "Where is a candle? I doubt if we could strike a match in that atmosphere. Hold the light at the door and we shall get them out, Mycroft. Now!"

With a rush we got to the poisoned men and dragged them out on to the landing. Both of them were blue-lipped and insensible, with swollen, congested faces and protruding eyes. Indeed, so distorted were their features that, save for his black beard and stout figure, we might have failed to recognize in one of them the Greek interpreter who had parted from us only a few hours before at the Diogenes Club. His hands and feet were securely strapped together and he bore over one eye the mark of a violent blow. The other, who was secured in a similar fashion, was a tall man in the last stage of emaciation, with several strips of sticking-plaster arranged in a grotesque pattern over his face. He had ceased to moan as we laid him down, and a glance showed me that for him, at least, our aid had come too late. Mr. Melas, however, still lived, and in less than an hour, with the aid of ammonia and brandy, I had the satisfaction of seeing him open his eyes, and of knowing that my hand had drawn him back from the dark valley in which all paths meet.

It was a simple story which he had to tell, and one which did but confirm our own deductions. His visitor on entering his rooms had drawn a life-preserver from his sleeve, and had so impressed him with the fear of instant and inevitable death, that he had kidnapped him for the second time. Indeed, it was almost mesmeric the effect which this giggling ruffian had produced upon the unfortunate linguist, for he could not speak of him save with trembling hands and a blanched cheek. He had been taken swiftly to Beckenham, and had acted as interpreter in a second interview, even more dramatic than the

first, in which the two Englishmen had menaced their prisoner with instant death if he did not comply with their demands. Finally, finding him proof against every threat, they had hurled him back into his prison, and after reproaching Melas with his treachery, which appeared from the newspaper advertisements, they had stunned him with a blow from a stick, and he remembered nothing more until he found us bending over him.

And this was the singular case of the Grecian Interpreter, the explanation of which is still involved in some mystery. We were able to find out, by communicating with the gentleman who had answered the advertisement, that the unfortunate young lady came of a wealthy Grecian family, and that she had been on a visit to some friends in England. While there she had met a young man named Harold Latimer, who had acquired an ascendancy over her, and had eventually persuaded her to fly with him. Her friends, shocked at the event, had contented themselves with informing her brother at Athens, and had then washed their hands of the matter. The brother, on his arrival in England, had imprudently placed himself in the power of Latimer and of his associate, whose name was Wilson Kemp—a man of the foulest antecedents. These two, finding, that through his ignorance of the language, he was helpless in their hands, had kept him a prisoner, and had endeavoured, by cruelty and starvation, to make him sign away his own and his sister's property. They had kept him in the house without the girl's knowledge, and the plaster over the face had been for the purpose of making recognition difficult in case she should ever catch a glimpse of him. Her feminine perceptions, however, had instantly seen through the disguise when, on the occasion of the interpreter's first visit, she had seen him for the first time. The poor girl, however, was herself a prisoner, for there was no one about the house except the man who acted as coachman and his wife, both of whom were tools of the conspirators. Finding that their secret was out and that their prisoner was

not to be coerced, the two villains, with the girl, had fled away at a few hours' notice from the furnished house which they had hired, having first, as they thought, taken vengeance both upon the man who had defied and the one who had betrayed them.

Months afterwards a curious newspaper cutting reached us from Buda-Pesth. It told how two Englishmen who had been travelling with a woman had met with a tragic end. They had each been stabbed, it seems, and the Hungarian police were of opinion that they had quarrelled and had inflicted mortal injuries upon each other. Holmes, however, is, I fancy, of a different way of thinking, and he holds to this day that if one could find the Grecian girl one might learn how the wrongs of herself and her brother came to be avenged.

22. *The Naval Treaty*

THE July which immediately succeeded my marriage was made memorable by three cases of interest in which I had the privilege of being associated with Sherlock Holmes, and of studying his methods. I find them recorded in my notes under the headings of " The Adventure of the Second Stain," " The Adventure of the Naval Treaty," and " The Adventure of the Tired Captain." The first of these, however, deals with interests of such importance, and implicates so many of the first families in the kingdom, that for many years it will be impossible to make it public. No case, however, in which Holmes was ever engaged has illustrated the value of his analytical methods so clearly or has impressed those who were associated with him so deeply. I still retain an almost verbatim report of the interview in which he demonstrated the true facts of the case to Monsieur Dubuque, of the Paris police, and Fritz von Waldbaum, the well-known specialist of Dantzig, both of whom had wasted their energies upon what

proved to be side-issues. The new century will have come, however, before the story can be safely told. Meanwhile, I pass on to the second upon my list, which promised also, at one time, to be of national importance, and was marked by several incidents which give it a quite unique character.

During my school-days I had been intimately associated with a lad named Percy Phelps, who was of much the same age as myself, though he was two classes ahead of me. He was a very brilliant boy, and carried away every prize which the school had to offer, finishing his exploits by winning a scholarship, which sent him on to continue his triumphant career at Cambridge. He was, I remember, extremely well connected and even when we were all little boys together, we knew that his mother's brother was Lord Holdhurst, the great Conservative politician. This gaudy relationship did him little good at school ; on the contrary, it seemed rather a piquant thing to us to chevy him about the playground and hit him over the shins with a wicket. But it was another thing when he came out into the world. I heard vaguely that his abilities and the influence which he commanded had won him a good position at the Foreign Office, and then he passed completely out of my mind until the following letter recalled his existence :

"BRIARBRAE, WOKING.

"MY DEAR WATSON,—I have no doubt that you can remember ' Tadpole ' Phelps, who was in the fifth form when you were in the third. It is possible even that you may have heard that, through my uncle's influence, I obtained a good appointment at the Foreign Office, and that I was in a situation of trust and honour until a horrible misfortune came suddenly to blast my career.

" There is no use writing the details of that dreadful event. In the event of your acceding to my request, it is probable that I shall have to narrate them to you. I have only just recovered from nine weeks of brain fever, and am still exceedingly weak. Do you think that you could bring your friend, Mr. Holmes, down to see me ? I should like to have his opinion of the case, though the authorities assure me that nothing more can be done. Do try to bring him down, and as soon as possible. Every minute seems an hour while I live in this horrible suspense. Assure him that, if I have not asked his advice sooner, it was not because I did not appreciate his talents, but because I have been off my head ever since the blow fell. Now I am clear again, though I dare not think of it too much for fear of a relapse. I am still so weak that I have to write, as you see, by dictating. Do try and bring him.

" Your old schoolfellow,
" PERCY PHELPS."

There was something that touched me as I read this letter, something pitiable in the reiterated appeals to bring Holmes. So moved was I that, even if it had been a difficult matter, I should have tried it ; but, of course, I knew well that Holmes loved his art so, that he was ever as ready to bring his aid as his client could be to receive it. My wife agreed with me that not a moment should be lost in laying the matter before him, and so, within an hour of breakfast-time, I found myself back once more in the old rooms in Baker Street.

Holmes was seated at his side-table clad in his dressing-gown and working hard over a chemical investigation. A large curved retort was boiling furiously in the bluish flame of a Bunsen burner, and the distilled drops were condensing into a two-litre measure. My friend hardly glanced up as I entered, and I, seeing that his investigation must be of importance, seated myself in an arm-chair and waited. He dipped into this bottle or that, drawing out a few drops of each with his glass pipette, and finally brought a test-tube containing a solution over to the table. In his right hand he had a slip of litmus-paper.

"You come at a crisis, Watson," said he. " If this

paper remains blue, all is well. If it turns red, it means a man's life." He dipped it into the test-tube, and it flushed at once into a dull, dirty crimson. "Hum! I thought as much!" he cried. "I shall be at your service in one instant, Watson. You will find tobacco in the Persian slipper." He turned to his desk and scribbled off several telegrams, which were handed over to the page-boy. Then he threw himself down in the chair opposite, and drew up his knees until his fingers clasped round his long, thin shins.

"A very commonplace little murder," said he. "You've got something better, I fancy. You are the stormy petrel of crime, Watson. What is it?"

I handed him the letter, which he read with the most concentrated attention.

"It does not tell us very much, does it?" he remarked, as he handed it back to me.

"Hardly anything."

"And yet the writing is of interest."

"But the writing is not his own."

"Precisely. It is a woman's."

"A man's surely!" I cried.

"No, a woman's; and a woman of rare character. You see, at the commencement of an investigation, it is something to know that your client is in close contact with someone who for good or evil has an exceptional nature. My interest is already awakened in the case. If you are ready, we will start at once for Woking and see this diplomatist who is in such evil case, and the lady to whom he dictates his letters."

We were fortunate enough to catch an early train at Waterloo, and in a little under an hour we found ourselves among the fir-woods and the heather of Woking. Briar-brae proved to be a large detached house standing in exten-sive grounds, within a few minutes' walk of the station. On sending in our cards we were shown into an elegantly appointed drawing-room, where we were joined in a few minutes by a rather stout man, who received us with much hospitality. His age may have been nearer forty than thirty, but his cheeks were so ruddy and his eyes so merry, that he still conveyed the impression of a plump and mischievous boy.

" I am so glad that you have come," said he, shaking our hands with effusion. " Percy has been inquiring for you all the morning. Ah, poor old chap, he clings to any straw. His father and mother asked me to see you, for the mere mention of the subject is very painful to them."

" We have had no details yet," observed Holmes. " I perceive that you are not yourself a member of the family."

Our acquaintance looked surprised, and then glancing down he began to laugh.

" Of course you saw the ' J. H.' monogram on my locket," said he. " For a moment I thought you had done something clever. Joseph Harrison is my name, and as Percy is to marry my sister Annie, I shall at least be a relation by marriage. You will find my sister in his room, for she has nursed him hand-and-foot these two months back. Perhaps we had better go in at once, for I know how impatient he is."

The chamber into which we were shown was on the same floor as the drawing-room. It was furnished partly as a sitting- and partly as a bedroom, with flowers arranged daintily in every nook and corner. A young man, very pale and worn, was lying upon a sofa near the open window, through which came the rich scent of the garden and the balmy summer air. A woman was sitting beside him, and rose as we entered.

" Shall I leave, Percy ? " she asked.

He clutched her hand to detain her. " How are you, Watson ? " said he, cordially. " I should never have known you under that moustache, and I daresay you would not be prepared to swear to me. This, I presume, is your celebrated friend, Mr. Sherlock Holmes ? "

I introduced him in a few words, and we both sat down. The stout young man had left us, but his sister still remained, with her hand in that of the invalid. She was a striking-looking woman, a little short and thick for symmetry, but with a beautiful olive complexion, large, dark Italian eyes, and a wealth of deep black hair. Her rich tints made the white face of her companion the more worn and haggard by the contrast.

" I won't waste your time," said he, raising himself upon the sofa. " I'll plunge into the matter without further preamble. I was a happy and successful man, Mr. Holmes, and on the eve of being married, when a sudden and dreadful misfortune wrecked all my prospects in life.

" I was, as Watson may have told you, in the Foreign Office, and through the influence of my uncle, Lord Holdhurst, I rose rapidly to a responsible position. When my uncle became Foreign Minister in this Administration he gave me several missions of trust, and as I always brought them to a successful conclusion, he came at last to have the utmost confidence in my ability and tact.

" Nearly ten weeks ago—to be more accurate, on the 23rd of May—he called me into his private room and, after complimenting me upon the good work which I had done, informed me that he had a new commission of trust for me to execute.

" ' This,' said he, taking a grey roll of paper from his bureau, ' is the original of that secret treaty between England and Italy, of which, I regret to say, some rumours have already got into the public Press. It is of enormous importance that nothing further should leak out. The French or Russian Embassies would pay an immense sum to learn the contents of these papers. They should not leave my bureau were it not that it is absolutely necessary to have them copied. You have a desk in your office ? '

" ' Yes, sir.'

" ' Then take the treaty and lock it up there. I shall give directions that you may remain behind when the others go, so that you may copy it at your leisure, without fear of being overlooked. When you have finished, re-lock both the original and the draft in the desk, and hand them over to me personally to-morrow morning.'

" I took the papers and——"

" Excuse me an instant," said Holmes ; " were you alone during this conversation ? "

" Absolutely."

" In a large room ? "

" Thirty feet each way."

" In the centre ? "

" Yes, about it."

" And speaking low ? "

" My uncle's voice is always remarkably low. I hardly spoke at all."

" Thank you," said Holmes, shutting his eyes ; " pray go on."

" I did exactly what he had indicated, and waited until the other clerks had departed. One of them in my room, Charles Gorot, had some arrears of work to make up, so I left him there and went out to dine. When I returned he was gone. I was anxious to hurry my work, for I knew that Joseph, the Mr. Harrison whom you saw just now, was in town, and that he would travel down to Woking by the eleven o'clock train, and I wanted if possible to catch it.

" When I came to examine the treaty I saw at once that it was of such importance that my uncle had been guilty of no exaggeration in what he had said. Without going into details, I may say that it defined the position of Great Britain towards the Triple Alliance, and fore-shadowed the policy which this country would pursue in the event of the French fleet gaining a complete ascendency over that of Italy in the Mediterranean. The questions treated in it were purely naval. At the end were the signatures of the high dignitaries who had signed it. I glanced my eyes over it, and then settled down to my task of copying.

" It was a long document, written in the French language, and containing twenty-six separate articles. I copied as quickly as I could, but at nine o'clock I had only done nine articles, and it seemed hopeless for me to attempt to catch my train. I was feeling drowsy and stupid, partly from my dinner and also from the effects of a long day's work. A cup of coffee would clear my brain. A commissionaire remains all night in a little lodge at the foot of the stairs, and is in the habit of making coffee at his spirit-lamp for any of the officials who may be working overtime. I rang the bell, therefore, to summon him.

"To my surprise, it was a woman who answered the summons, a large, coarse-faced, elderly woman, in an apron. She explained that she was the commissionaire's wife, who did the charing, and I gave her the order for the coffee.

"I wrote two more articles, and then, feeling more drowsy than ever, I rose and walked up and down the room to stretch my legs. My coffee had not yet come, and I wondered what the cause of the delay could be. Opening the door, I started down the corridor to find out. There was a straight passage dimly lit which led from the room in which I had been working, and was the only exit from it. It ended in a curving staircase, with the commissionaire's lodge in the passage at the bottom. Half-way down this staircase is a small landing, with another passage running into it at right angles. The second one leads, by means of a second small stair, to a side-door used by servants, and also as a short cut by clerks when coming from Charles Street.

"Here is a rough chart of the place."

"Thank you. I think that I quite follow you," said Sherlock Holmes.

"It is of the utmost importance that you should notice this point. I went down the stairs and into the hall, where I found the commissionaire fast asleep in his box, with the kettle boiling furiously upon the spirit-lamp, for the water was spurting over the floor. I had put out my hand and was about to shake the man, who was still sleeping soundly, when a bell over his head rang loudly, and he woke with a start.

Labels in chart: landing, commissionaire, HALL, STREET, Main door, CLERKS ROOM, Side door, LANE

"HERE IS A ROUGH CHART OF THE PLACE."

" ' Mr. Phelps, sir ! ' said he, looking at me in bewilderment.

" ' I came down to see if my coffee was ready.'

" ' I was boiling the kettle when I fell asleep, sir.' He looked at me and then up at the still quivering bell, with an ever-growing astonishment upon his face.

" ' If you was here, sir, then who rang the bell ? ' he asked.

" ' The bell ! ' I said. ' What bell is it ? '

" ' It's the bell of the room you were working in.'

" A cold hand seemed to close round my heart. Someone, then, was in that room where my precious treaty lay upon the table. I ran frantically up the stairs and along the passage. There was no one in the corridor, Mr. Holmes. There was no one in the room. All was exactly as I left it, save only that the papers committed to my care had been taken from the desk on which they lay. The copy was there and the original was gone."

Holmes sat up in his chair and rubbed his hands. I could see that the problem was entirely to his heart. "Pray, what did you do then ? " he murmured.

" I recognized in an instant that the thief must have come up the stairs from the side-door. Of course I must have met him if he had come the other way."

506

" You were satisfied that he could not have been concealed in the room all the time, or in the corridor which you have just described as dimly lighted ? "

" It is absolutely impossible. A rat could not conceal himself either in the room or the corridor. There is no cover at all."

" Thank you. Pray proceed."

" The commissionaire, seeing by my pale face that something was to be feared, had followed me upstairs. Now we both rushed along the corridor and down the steep steps which led to Charles Street. The door at the bottom was closed but unlocked. We flung it open and rushed out. I can distinctly remember that as we did so there came three chimes from a neighbouring church. It was a quarter to ten."

" That is of enormous importance," said Holmes, making a note upon his shirt cuff.

" The night was very dark, and a thin, warm rain was falling. There was no one in Charles Street, but a great traffic was going on, as usual, in Whitehall, at the extremity. We rushed along the pavement, bareheaded as we were, and at the far corner we found a policeman standing.

" ' A robbery has been committed,' I gasped. ' A document of immense value has been stolen from the Foreign Office. Has anyone passed this way ? '

" ' I have been standing here for a quarter of an hour, sir,' said he ; ' only one person has passed during that time—a woman, tall and elderly, with a Paisley shawl.'

" ' Ah, that is only my wife,' cried the commissionaire. ' Has no one else passed ? '

" ' No one.'

" ' Then it must be the other way that the thief took,' cried the fellow, tugging at my sleeve.

" But I was not satisfied, and the attempts which he made to draw me away increased my suspicions.

" ' Which way did the woman go ? ' I cried.

" ' I don't know, sir. I noticed her pass, but I had no

special reason for watching her. She seemed to be in a hurry.'

" ' How long ago was it ? '

" ' Oh, not very many minutes.'

" ' Within the last five ? '

" ' Well, it could not be more than five.'

" ' You're only wasting your time, sir, and every minute now is of importance,' cried the commissionaire. ' Take my word for it that my old woman has nothing to do with it, and come down to the other end of the street. Well, if you won't, I will,' and with that he rushed off in the other direction.

" But I was after him in an instant and caught him by the sleeve.

" ' Where do you live ? ' said I.

" ' No. 16 Ivy Lane, Brixton,' he answered ; ' but don't let yourself be drawn away upon a false scent, Mr. Phelps. Come to the other end of the street, and let us see if we can hear of anything.'

" Nothing was to be lost by following his advice. With the policeman we both hurried down, but only to find the street full of traffic, many people coming and going, but all only too eager to get to a place of safety upon so wet a night. There was no lounger who could tell us who had passed.

" Then we returned to the office, and searched the stairs and the passage without result. The corridor which led to the room was laid down with a kind of creamy linoleum, which shows an impression very easily. We examined it very carefully, but found no outline of any footmark."

" Had it been raining all the evening ? "

" Since about seven."

" How is it, then, that the woman who came into the room about nine left no traces with her muddy boots ? "

" I am glad you raise the point. It occurred to me at the time. The charwomen are in the habit of taking off their boots at the commissionaire's office, and putting on list slippers."

"That is very clear. There were no marks, then, though the night was a wet one? The chain of events is certainly one of extraordinary interest. What did you do next?"

"We examined the room also. There was no possibility of a secret door, and the windows are quite thirty feet from the ground. Both of them were fastened on the inside. The carpet prevents any possibility of a trap-door, and the ceiling is of the ordinary whitewashed kind. I will pledge my life that whoever stole my papers could only have come through the door."

"How about the fireplace?"

"They use none. There is a stove. The bell-rope hangs from the wire just to the right of my desk. Whoever rang it must have come right up to the desk to do it. But why should any criminal wish to ring the bell? It is a most insoluble mystery."

"Certainly the incident was unusual. What were your next steps? You examined the room, I presume, to see if the intruder had left any traces—any cigar-end, or dropped glove, or hairpin, or other trifle?"

"There was nothing of the sort."

"No smell?"

"Well, we never thought of that."

"Ah, a scent of tobacco would have been worth a great deal to us in such an investigation."

"I never smoke myself, so I think I should have observed it if there had been any smell of tobacco. There was absolutely no clue of any kind. The only tangible fact was that the commissionaire's wife—Mrs. Tangey was the name—had hurried out of the place. He could give no explanation save that it was about the time when the woman always went home. The policeman and I agreed that our best plan would be to seize the woman before she could get rid of the papers, presuming that she had them.

"The alarm had reached Scotland Yard by this time, and Mr. Forbes, the detective, came round at once and took up the case with a great deal of energy. We hired a hansom, and in half an hour we were at the address which had been given to us. A young woman opened the door, who proved to be Mrs. Tangey's eldest daughter. Her mother had not come back yet, and we were shown into the front room to wait.

" About ten minutes later a knock came at the door, and here we made the one serious mistake for which I blame myself. Instead of opening the door ourselves we allowed the girl to do so. We heard her say, ' Mother, there are two men in the house waiting to see you,' and an instant afterwards we heard the patter of feet rushing down the passage. Forbes flung open the door, and we both ran into the back room or kitchen, but the woman had got there before us. She stared at us with defiant eyes, and then suddenly recognizing me, an expression of absolute astonishment came over her face.

" ' Why, if it isn't Mr. Phelps, of the office ! ' she cried.

" ' Come, come, who did you think we were when you ran away from us ? ' asked my companion.

" ' I thought you were the brokers,' said she. ' We've had some trouble with a tradesman.'

" ' That's not quite good enough,' answered Forbes. ' We have reason to believe that you have taken a paper of importance from the Foreign Office, and that you ran in here to dispose of it. You must come back with us to Scotland Yard to be searched.'

" It was in vain that she protested and resisted. A four-wheeler was brought, and we all three drove back in it. We had first made an examination of the kitchen, and especially of the kitchen fire, to see whether she might have made away with the papers during the instant that she was alone. There were no signs, however, of any ashes or scraps. When we reached Scotland Yard she was handed over at once to the female searcher. I waited in an agony of suspense until she came back with her report. There were no signs of the papers.

" Then for the first time, the horror of my situation

came in its full force upon me. Hitherto I had been acting, and action had numbed thought. I had been so confident of regaining the treaty at once that I had not dared to think of what would be the consequence if I failed to do so. But now there was nothing more to be done, and I had leisure to realize my position. It was horrible ! Watson there would tell you that I was a nervous, sensitive boy at school. It is my nature. I thought of my uncle and of his colleagues in the Cabinet, of the shame which I had brought upon him, upon myself, upon everyone connected with me. What though I was the victim of an extraordinary accident ? No allowance is made for accidents where diplomatic interests are at stake. I was ruined ; shamefully, hopelessly ruined. I don't know what I did. I fancy I must have made a scene. I have a dim recollection of a group of officials who crowded round me endeavouring to soothe me. One of them drove down with me to Waterloo and saw me into the Woking train. I believe that he would have come all the way had it not been that Dr. Ferrier, who lives near me, was going down by that very train. The doctor most kindly took charge of me, and it was well he did so, for I had a fit in the station, and before we reached home I was practically a raving maniac.

" You can imagine the state of things here when they were roused from their beds by the doctor's ringing, and found me in this condition. Poor Annie here and my mother were broken-hearted. Dr. Ferrier had just heard enough from the detective at the station to be able to give an idea of what had happened, and his story did not mend matters. It was evident to all that I was in for a long illness, so Joseph was bundled out of this cheery bed-room, and it was turned into a sick-room for me. Here I have lain, Mr. Holmes, for over nine weeks, uncon-scious, and raving with brain fever. If it had not been for Miss Harrison here and for the doctor's care I should not be speaking to you now. She has nursed me by day, and a hired nurse has looked after me by night, for in my mad fits I was capable of anything. Slowly my reason has cleared, but it is only during the last three days that my memory has quite returned. Sometimes I wish that it never had. The first thing I did was to wire to Mr. Forbes, who had the case in hand. He came out and assured me that, though everything has been done, no trace of a clue has been discovered. The commissionaire and his wife have been examined in every way without any light being thrown upon the matter. The suspicions of the police then rested upon young Gorot, who, as you may remember, stayed overtime in the office that night. His remaining behind and his French name were really the only two points which could suggest suspicion; but as a matter of fact, I did not begin work until he had gone, and his people are of Huguenot extraction, but as English in sympathy and tradition as you and I are. Nothing was found to implicate him in any way, and there the matter dropped. I turn to you, Mr. Holmes, as absolutely my last hope. If you fail me, then my honour as well as my position are for ever forfeited."

The invalid sank back upon his cushions, tired out by this long recital, while his nurse poured him out a glass of some stimulating medicine. Holmes sat silently with his head thrown back and his eyes closed in an attitude which might seem listless to a stranger, but which I knew betokened the most intense absorption.

"Your statement has been so explicit," said he at last, "that you have really left me very few questions to ask. There is one of the very utmost importance, however. Did you tell anyone that you had this special task to perform?"

"No one."

"Not Miss Harrison here, for example?"

"No. I had not been back to Woking between getting the order and executing the commission."

"And none of your people had by chance been to see you?"

" None."

" Did any of them know their way about in the office ? "

" Oh, yes ; all of them had been shown over it."

" Still, of course, if you said nothing to anyone about the treaty, these inquiries are irrelevant."

" I said nothing."

" Do you know anything of the commissionaire ? "

" Nothing, except that he is an old soldier."

" What regiment ? "

" Oh, I have heard—Coldstream Guards."

" Thank you. I have no doubt I can get details from Forbes. The authorities are excellent at amassing facts, though they do not always use them to advantage. What a lovely thing a rose is ! "

He walked past the couch to the open window, and held up the drooping stalk of a moss rose, looking down at the dainty blend of crimson and green. It was a new phase of his character to me, for I had never before seen him show any keen interest in natural objects.

" There is nothing in which deduction is so necessary as in religion," said he, leaning with his back against the shutters. " It can be built up as an exact science by the reasoner. Our highest assurance of the goodness of Providence seems to me to rest in the flowers. All other things, our powers, our desires, our food, are really necessary for our existence in the first instance. But this rose is an extra. Its smell and its colour are an embellishment of life, not a condition of it. It is only goodness which gives extras, and so I say again that we have much to hope from the flowers."

Percy Phelps and his nurse looked at Holmes during this demonstration with surprise and a good deal of disappointment written upon their faces. He had fallen into a reverie, with the moss rose between his fingers. It had lasted some minutes before the young lady broke in upon it.

" Do you see any prospect of solving this mystery, Mr. Holmes ? " she asked, with a touch of asperity in her voice.

" Oh, the mystery ! " he answered, coming back with a start to the realities of life. " Well, it would be absurd to deny that the case is a very abstruse and complicated one ; but I can promise you that I will look into the matter and let you know any points which may strike me."

" Do you see any clue ? "

" You have furnished me with seven, but of course I must test them before I can pronounce upon their value."

" You suspect someone ? "

" I suspect myself——"

" What ? "

" Of coming to conclusions too rapidly."

" Then go to London and test your conclusions."

" Your advice is very excellent, Miss Harrison," said Holmes, rising. " I think, Watson, we cannot do better. Do not allow yourself to indulge in false hopes, Mr. Phelps. The affair is a very tangled one."

" I shall be in a fever until I see you again," cried the diplomatist.

" Well, I'll come out by the same train to-morrow, though it's more than likely that my report will be a negative one."

" God bless you for promising to come," cried our client. " It gives me fresh life to know that something is being done. By the way, I have had a letter from Lord Holdhurst."

" Ha ! What did he say ? "

" He was cold, but not harsh. I dare say my severe illness prevented him from being that. He repeated that the matter was of the utmost importance, and added that no steps would be taken about my future—by which he means, of course, my dismissal—until my health was restored and I had an opportunity of repairing my misfortune."

" Well, that was reasonable and considerate," said Holmes. " Come, Watson, for we have a good day's work before us in town."

Mr. Joseph Harrison drove us down to the station, and

we were soon whirling up in a Portsmouth train. Holmes was sunk in profound thought, and hardly opened his mouth until we had passed Clapham Junction.

" It's a very cheering thing to come into London by any of these lines which run high and allow you to look down upon the houses like this."

I thought he was joking, for the view was sordid enough, but he soon explained himself.

" Look at those big, isolated clumps of buildings rising up above the slates, like brick islands in a lead-coloured sea."

" The Board schools."

" Lighthouses, my boy! Beacons of the future! Capsules, with hundreds of bright little seeds in each, out of which will spring the wiser, better England of the future. I suppose that man Phelps does not drink?"

" I should not think so."

" Nor should I. But we are bound to take every possibility into account. The poor devil has certainly got himself into very deep water, and it's a question whether we shall ever be able to get him ashore. What did you think of Miss Harrison?"

" A girl of strong character."

" Yes, but she is a good sort, or I am mistaken. She and her brother are the only children of an ironmaster somewhere up Northumberland way. Phelps got engaged to her when travelling last winter, and she came down to be introduced to his people, with her brother as escort. Then came the smash, and she stayed on to nurse her lover, while brother Joseph, finding himself pretty snug, stayed on too. I've been making a few independent inquiries, you see. But to-day must be a day of inquiries."

" My practice——" I began.

" Oh, if you find your own cases more interesting than mine——" said Holmes, with some asperity.

" I was going to say that my practice could get along very well for a day or two, since it is the slackest time in the year."

" Excellent," said he, recovering his good humour. " Then we'll look into this matter together. I think that we should begin by seeing Forbes. He can probably tell us all the details we want, until we know from what side the case is to be approached."

" You said you had a clue."

" Well, we have several, but we can only test their value by further inquiry. The most difficult crime to track is the one which is purposeless. Now, this is not purposeless. Who is it that profits by it ? There is the French Ambassador, there is the Russian, there is whoever might sell it to either of these, and there is Lord Holdhurst."

" Lord Holdhurst ! "

" Well, it is just conceivable that a statesman might find himself in a position where he was not sorry to have such a document accidentally destroyed."

" Not a statesman with the honourable record of Lord Holdhurst."

" It is a possibility, and we cannot afford to disregard it. We shall see the noble lord to-day, and find out if he can tell us anything. Meanwhile, I have already set inquiries upon foot."

" Already ? "

" Yes, I sent wires from Woking station to every evening paper in London. This advertisement will appear in each of them."

He handed over a sheet torn from the notebook. On it was scribbled in pencil :

" £10 Reward.—The number of the cab which dropped a fare at or about the door of the Foreign Office in Charles Street, at a quarter to ten in the evening of May 23rd. Apply 221B Baker Street."

" You are confident that the thief came in a cab ? "

" If not, there is no harm done. But if Mr. Phelps is correct in stating that there is no hiding-place either in the room or the corridors, then the person must have come from outside. If he came from outside on so wet a night, and yet left no trace of damp upon the linoleum, which was examined within a few minutes of his passing, then it is exceedingly probable that he came in a cab. Yes, I think that we may safely deduce a cab."

" It sounds plausible."

" That is one of the clues of which I spoke. It may lead us to something. And then, of course, there is the bell—which is the most distinctive feature of the case. Why should the bell ring ? Was it the thief that did it out of bravado ? Or was it someone who was with the thief who did it in order to prevent the crime ? Or was it an accident ? Or was it——? " He sank back into the state of intense and silent thought from which he had emerged, but it seemed to me, accustomed as I was to his every mood, that some new possibility had dawned suddenly upon him.

It was twenty-past three when we reached our terminus, and after a hasty luncheon at the buffet we pushed on at once to Scotland Yard. Holmes had already wired to Forbes, and we found him waiting to receive us : a small, foxy man, with a sharp but by no means amiable expression. He was decidedly frigid in his manner to us, especially when he heard the errand upon which we had come.

" I've heard of your methods before now, Mr. Holmes," said he, tartly. " You are ready enough to use all the information that the police can lay at your disposal, and then you try to finish the case yourself and bring discredit upon them."

" On the contrary," said Holmes ; " out of my last fifty-three cases my name has only appeared in four, and the police have had all the credit in forty-nine. I don't blame you for not knowing this ; for you are young and inexperienced ; but if you wished to get on in your new duties you will work with me, and not against me."

" I'd be very glad of a hint or two," said the detective, changing his manner. " I've certainly had no credit from the case so far."

" What steps have you taken ? "

" Tangey, the commissionaire, has been shadowed. He left the Guards with a good character, and we can find nothing against him. His wife is a bad lot, though. I fancy she knows more about this than appears."

" Have you shadowed her ? "

" We have set one of our women on to her. Mrs. Tangey drinks, and our woman has been with her twice when she was well on, but she could get nothing out of her."

" I understand that they have had brokers in the house ? "

" Yes, but they were paid off."

" Where did the money come from ? "

" That was all right. His pension was due ; they have not shown any sign of being in funds."

" What explanation did she give of having answered the bell when Mr. Phelps rang for the coffee ? "

" She said that her husband was very tired and she wished to relieve him."

" Well, certainly that would agree with his being found, a little later, asleep in his chair. There is nothing against them, then, but the woman's character. Did you ask her why she hurried away that night ? Her haste attracted the attention of the police-constable."

" She was later than usual, and wanted to get home."

" Did you point out to her that you and Mr. Phelps, who started at least twenty minutes after her, got there before her ? "

" She explains that by the difference between a 'bus and a hansom."

" Did she make it clear why, on reaching her house, she ran into the back kitchen ? "

" Because she had the money there with which to pay off the brokers."

" She has at least an answer for everything. Did you ask her whether in leaving she met anyone or saw anyone loitering about Charles Street ? "

" She saw no one but the constable."

"Well, you seem to have cross-examined her pretty thoroughly. What else have you done ? "

" The clerk, Gorot, has been shadowed all these nine weeks, but without result. We can show nothing against him."

" Anything else ? "

" Well, we have nothing else to go upon—no evidence of any kind."

" Have you formed any theory about how that bell rang ? "

" Well, I must confess that it beats me. It was a cool hand, whoever it was, to go and give the alarm like that."

" Yes, it was a queer thing to do. Many thanks to you for what you have told me. If I can put the man into your hands you shall hear from me. Come along, Watson ! "

" Where are we going to now ? " I asked, as we left the office.

" We are now going to interview Lord Holdhurst, the Cabinet Minister and future Premier of England."

We were fortunate in finding that Lord Holdhurst was still in his chambers at Downing Street, and on Holmes sending in his card we were instantly shown up. The statesman received us with that old-fashioned courtesy for which he is remarkable, and seated us on the two luxurious easy chairs on either side of the fireplace. Standing on the rug between us, with his slight, tall figure, his sharp-featured, thoughtful face, and his curling hair prematurely tinged with grey, he seemed to represent that not too common type, a nobleman who is in truth noble.

" Your name is very familiar to me, Mr. Holmes," said he, smiling. " And, of course, I cannot pretend to be ignorant of the object of your visit. There has only been one occurrence in these offices which could call for your attention. In whose interest are you acting, may I ask ? "

" In that of Mr. Percy Phelps," answered Holmes.

" Ah, my unfortunate nephew ! You can understand that our kinship makes it the more impossible for me to screen him in any way. I fear that the incident must have a very prejudicial effect upon his career."

" But if the document is found ? "

" Ah, that, of course, would be different."

" I had one or two questions which I wished to ask you, Lord Holdhurst."

" I shall be happy to give you any information in my power."

" Was it in this room that you gave your instructions as to the copying of the document ? "

" It was."

" Then you could hardly have been overheard ? "

" It is out of the question."

" Did you ever mention to anyone that it was your intention to give out the treaty to be copied ? "

" Never."

" You are certain of that ? "

" Absolutely."

" Well, since you never said so, and Mr. Phelps never said so, and nobody else knew anything of the matter, then the thief's presence in the room was purely accidental. He saw his chance and he took it."

The statesman smiled. " You take me out of my province there," said he.

Holmes considered for a moment. " There is another very important point which I wish to discuss with you," said he. " You feared, as I understand, that very grave results might follow from the details of this treaty becoming known ? "

A shadow passed over the expressive face of the statesman. " Very grave results, indeed."

" And have they occurred ? "

" Not yet."

" If the treaty had reached, let us say, the French or Russian Foreign Office, you would expect to hear of it ? "

" I should," said Lord Holdhurst, with a wry face.

" Since nearly ten weeks have elapsed, then, and nothing has been heard, it is not unfair to suppose that for some reason the treaty has not reached them ? "

Lord Holdhurst shrugged his shoulders.

" We can hardly suppose, Mr. Holmes, that the thief took the treaty in order to frame it and hang it up."

" Perhaps he is waiting for a better price."

" If he waits a little longer he will get no price at all. The treaty will cease to be a secret in a few months."

" That is most important," said Holmes. " Of course it is a possible supposition that the thief has had a sudden illness——"

" An attack of brain fever, for example ? " asked the statesman, flashing a swift glance at him.

" I did not say so," said Holmes, imperturbably. " And now, Lord Holdhurst, we have already taken up too much of your valuable time, and we shall wish you good day."

" Every success to your investigation, be the criminal who it may," answered the nobleman, as he bowed us out at the door.

" He's a fine fellow," said Holmes, as we came out into Whitehall. " But he has a struggle to keep up his position. He is far from rich, and has many calls. You noticed, of course, that his boots had been re-soled ? Now, Watson, I won't detain you from your legitimate work any longer. I shall do nothing more to-day, unless I have an answer to my cab advertisement. But I should be extremely obliged to you if you would come down with me to Woking to-morrow, by the same train which we took to-day."

I met him accordingly next morning, and we travelled down to Woking together. He had had no answer to his advertisement, he said, and no fresh light had been thrown upon the case. He had, when he so willed it, the utter immobility of countenance of a Red Indian, and I could not gather from his appearance whether he was satisfied or not with the position of the case. His conversation, I remember, was about the Bertillon system of measurements, and he expressed his enthusiastic admiration of the French savant.

We found our client still under the charge of his devoted nurse, but looking considerably better than before. He rose from the sofa and greeted us without difficulty when we entered.

" Any news ? " he asked, eagerly.

" My report, as I expected, is a negative one," said Holmes. " I have seen Forbes, and I have seen your uncle, and I have set one or two trains of inquiry upon foot which may lead to something."

" You have not lost heart, then ? "

" By no means."

" God bless you for saying that ! " cried Miss Harrison. " If we keep our courage and our patience, the truth must come out."

" We have more to tell you than you have for us," said Phelps, re-seating himself upon the couch.

" I hoped you might have something."

" Yes, we have had an adventure during the night, and one which might have proved to be a serious one." His expression grew very grave as he spoke, and a look of something akin to fear sprang up in his eyes. " Do you know," said he, " that I begin to believe that I am the unconscious centre of some monstrous conspiracy, and that my life is aimed at as well as my honour ? "

" Ah ! " cried Holmes.

" It sounds incredible, for I have not, as far as I know, an enemy in the world. Yet from last night's experience I can come to no other conclusion."

" Pray let me hear it."

" You must know that last night was the very first night that I have ever slept without a nurse in the room. I was so much better that I thought I could dispense with one. I had a night-light burning, however. Well, about two in the morning I had sunk into a light sleep, when I was suddenly aroused by a slight noise. It was like the sound which a mouse makes when it is gnawing a plank, and I lay listening to it for some time under the impression that it must come from that cause. Then it grew louder, and suddenly there came from the window a sharp metallic snick. I sat up in amazement. There could be no doubt what the sounds were now. The faint ones had been caused by someone forcing an instrument through the slit between the sashes, and the second by the catch being pressed back.

"There was a pause then for about ten minutes, as if the person were waiting to see whether the noise had awoken me. Then I heard a gentle creaking as the window was very slowly opened. I could stand it no longer, for my nerves are not what they used to be. I sprang out of bed and flung open the shutters. A man was crouching at the window. I could see little of him, for he was gone like a flash. He was wrapped in some sort of cloak, which came across the lower part of his face. One thing only I am sure of, and that is that he had some weapon in his hand. It looked to me like a long knife. I distinctly saw the gleam of it as he turned to run."

"This is most interesting," said Holmes. "Pray, what did you do then?"

"I should have followed him through the open window if I had been stronger. As it was, I rang the bell and roused the house. It took me some little time, for the bell rings in the kitchen, and the servants all sleep upstairs. I shouted, however, and that brought Joseph down, and he roused the others. Joseph and the groom found marks on the flower-bed outside the window, but the weather has been so dry lately that they found it hopeless to follow the trail across the grass. There's a place, however, on the wooden fence which skirts the road which shows signs, they tell me, as if someone had got over and had snapped the top of the rail in doing so. I have said nothing to the local police yet, for I thought I had best have your opinion first."

This tale of our client's appeared to have an extraordinary effect upon Sherlock Holmes. He rose from his chair and paced about the room in uncontrollable excitement.

" Misfortunes never come singly," said Phelps, smiling, though it was evident that his adventure had somewhat shaken him.

" You have certainly had your share," said Holmes. " Do you think you could walk round the house with me ? "

" Oh, yes, I should like a little sunshine. Joseph will come too."

" And I also," said Miss Harrison.

" I am afraid not," said Holmes, shaking his head. " I think I must ask you to remain sitting exactly where you are."

The young lady resumed her seat with an air of displeasure. Her brother, however, had joined us, and we set off all four together. We passed round the lawn to the outside of the young diplomatist's window. There were, as he had said, marks upon the flower-bed, but they were hopelessly blurred and vague. Holmes stooped over them for an instant, and then rose, shrugging his shoulders.

" I don't think anyone could make much of this," said he. " Let us go round the house and see why this particular room was chosen by the burglar. I should have thought those larger windows of the drawing-room and dining-room would have had more attractions for him."

" They are more visible from the road," suggested Mr. Joseph Harrison.

" Ah, yes, of course. There is a door here which he might have attempted. What is it for ? "

" It is the side-entrance for tradespeople. Of course, it is locked at night."

" Have you ever had an alarm like this before ? "

" Never," said our client.

" Do you keep plate in the house, or anything to attract burglars ? "

" Nothing of value."

Holmes strolled round the house with his hands in his pockets, and a negligent air which was unusual with him.

" By the way," said he to Joseph Harrison, " you found some place, I understand, where the fellow scaled the fence. Let us have a look at that."

The young man led us to a spot where the top of one of the wooden rails had been cracked. A small fragment of the wood was hanging down. Holmes pulled it off and examined it critically.

" Do you think that was done last night ? It looks rather old, does it not ? "

" Well, possibly so."

" There are no marks of anyone jumping down upon the other side. No, I fancy we shall get no help here. Let us go back to the bedroom and talk the matter over."

Percy Phelps was walking very slowly, leaning upon the arm of his future brother-in-law. Holmes walked swiftly across the lawn, and we were at the open window of the bedroom long before the others came up.

" Miss Harrison," said Holmes, speaking with the utmost intensity of manner, " you must stay where you are all day. Let nothing prevent you from staying where you are all day. It is of most vital importance."

" Certainly, if you wish it, Mr. Holmes," said the girl, in astonishment.

" When you go to bed lock the door of this room on the outside and keep the key. Promise to do this."

" But Percy ? "

" He will come to London with us."

" And I am to remain here ? "

" It is for his sake. You can serve him ! Quick ! Promise ! "

She gave a nod of assent just as the other two came up.

" Why do you sit moping there, Annie ? " cried her brother. " Come out into the sunshine ! "

" No, thank you, Joseph. I have a slight headache, and this room is deliciously cool and soothing."

" What do you propose now, Mr. Holmes ? " asked our client.

" Well, in investigating this minor affair we must not lose sight of our main inquiry. It would be a very great help to me if you could come up to London with us."

" At once ? "

" Well, as soon as you conveniently can. Say in an hour."

" I feel quite strong enough, if I can really be of any help."

" The greatest possible."

" Perhaps you would like me to stay there to-night."

" I was just going to propose it."

" Then if my friend of the night comes to revisit me, he will find the bird flown. We are all in your hands, Mr. Holmes, and you must tell us exactly what you would like done. Perhaps you would prefer that Joseph came with us, so as to look after me ? "

" Oh, no ; my friend Watson is a medical man, you know, and he'll look after you. We'll have our lunch here, if you will permit us, and then we shall all three set off for town together."

It was arranged as he suggested, though Miss Harrison excused herself from leaving the bedroom, in accordance with Holmes' suggestion. What the object of my friend's manœuvres was I could not conceive, unless it were to keep the lady away from Phelps, who, rejoiced by his returning health and by the prospect of action, lunched with us in the dining-room. Holmes had a still more startling surprise for us, however, for after accompanying us down to the station and seeing us into our carriage, he calmly announced that he had no intention of leaving Woking.

" There are one or two small points which I should

desire to clear up before I go," said he. "Your absence,
Mr. Phelps, will in some ways rather assist me. Watson,
when you reach London you would oblige me by driving
at once to Baker Street with our friend here, and remaining with him until I see you again. It is fortunate that
you are old schoolfellows, as you must have much to talk
over. Mr. Phelps can have the spare bedroom to-night,
and I shall be with you in time for breakfast, for there is
a train which will take me into Waterloo at eight."

"But how about our investigation in London?" asked
Phelps, ruefully.

"We can do that to-morrow. I think that just at
present I can be of more immediate use here."

"You might tell them at Briarbrae that I hope to be
back to-morrow night," cried Phelps, as we began to
move from the platform.

"I hardly expect to go back to Briarbrae," answered
Holmes, and waved his hand to us cheerily as we shot out
from the station.

Phelps and I talked it over on our journey, but neither
of us could devise a satisfactory reason for this new
development.

"I suppose he wants to find out some clue as to the
burglary last night, if a burglar it was. For myself, I
don't believe it was an ordinary thief."

"What is your idea, then?"

"Upon my word, you may put it down to my weak
nerves or not, but I believe there is some deep political
intrigue going on around me, and that, for some reason
that passes my understanding, my life is aimed at by the
conspirators. It sounds high-flown and absurd, but consider the facts! Why should a thief try to break in at a
bedroom window, where there could be no hope of any
plunder, and why should he come with a long knife in his
hand?"

"You are sure it was not a housebreaker's jemmy?"

"Oh, no; it was a knife. I saw the flash of the blade
quite distinctly."

"But why on earth should you be pursued with such animosity?"

"Ah! that is the question."

"Well, if Holmes takes the same view, that would account for his action, would it not? Presuming that your theory is correct, if he can lay his hands upon the man who threatened you last night, he will have gone a long way towards finding who took the naval treaty. It is absurd to suppose that you have two enemies, one of whom robs you while the other threatens your life."

"But Mr. Holmes said that he was not going to Briarbrae."

"I have known him for some time," said I, "but I never knew him do anything yet without a very good reason," and with that our conversation drifted off into other topics.

But it was a weary day for me. Phelps was still weak after his long illness, and his misfortunes made him querulous and nervous. In vain I endeavoured to interest him in Afghanistan, in India, in social questions, in anything which might take his mind out of the groove. He would always come back to his lost treaty; wondering, guessing, speculating, as to what Holmes was doing, what steps Lord Holdhurst was taking, what news we should have in the morning. As the evening wore on his excitement became quite painful.

"You have implicit faith in Holmes?" he asked.

"I have seen him do some remarkable things."

"But he never brought light into anything quite so dark as this?"

"Oh, yes; I have known him solve questions which presented fewer clues than yours."

"But not where such large interests are at stake?"

"I don't know that. To my certain knowledge he has acted on behalf of three of the reigning Houses of Europe in very vital matters."

"But you know him well, Watson. He is such an inscrutable fellow, that I never quite know what to make of him. Do you think he is hopeful ? Do you think he expects to make a success of it ? "

" He has said nothing."

" That is a bad sign."

" On the contrary, I have noticed that when he is off the trail he generally says so. It is when he is on a scent, and is not quite absolutely sure yet that it is the right one, that he is most taciturn. Now, my dear fellow, we can't help matters by making ourselves nervous about them, so let me implore you to go to bed, and so be fresh for whatever may await us to-morrow."

I was able at last to persuade my companion to take my advice, though I knew from his excited manner that there was not much hope of sleep for him. Indeed, his mood was infectious, for I lay tossing half the night myself, brooding over this strange problem, and inventing a hundred theories, each of which was more impossible than the last. Why had Holmes remained at Woking ? Why had he asked Miss Harrison to stay in the sick-room all day ? Why had he been so careful not to inform the people at Briarbrae that he intended to remain near them ? I cudgelled my brains until I fell asleep in the endeavour to find some explanation which would cover all these facts.

It was seven o'clock when I awoke, and I set off at once for Phelps' room, to find him haggard and spent after a sleepless night. His first question was whether Holmes had arrived yet.

" He'll be here when he promised," said I, " and not an instant sooner or later."

And my words were true, for shortly after eight a hansom dashed up to the door and our friend got out of it. Standing in the window, we saw that his left hand was swathed in a bandage and that his face was very grim and pale. He entered the house, but it was some little time before he came upstairs.

" He looks like a beaten man," cried Phelps.

I was forced to confess that he was right. " After all,"

said I, " the clue of the matter lies probably here in town."

Phelps gave a groan.

" I don't know how it is," said he, " but I had hoped for so much from his return. But surely his hand was not tied up like that yesterday ? What can be the matter ? "

" You are not wounded, Holmes ? " I asked, as my friend entered the room.

" Tut, it is only a scratch through my own clumsiness," he answered, nodding his good morning to us. " This case of yours, Mr. Phelps, is certainly one of the darkest which I have ever investigated."

" I feared that you would find it beyond you."

" It has been a most remarkable experience."

" That bandage tells of adventures," said I. " Won't you tell us what has happened ? "

" After breakfast, my dear Watson. Remember that I have breathed thirty miles of Surrey air this morning. I suppose there has been no answer to my cabman advertisement ? Well, well, we cannot expect to score every time."

The table was all laid, and, just as I was about to ring, Mrs. Hudson entered with the tea and coffee. A few minutes later she brought in the covers, and we all drew up to the table, Holmes ravenous, I curious, and Phelps in the gloomiest state of depression.

" Mrs. Hudson has risen to the occasion," said Holmes, uncovering a dish of curried chicken. " Her cuisine is a little limited, but she has as good an idea of breakfast as a Scotchwoman. What have you there, Watson ? "

" Ham and eggs," I answered.

" Good ! What are you going to take, Mr. Phelps : curried fowl, eggs, or will you help yourself ? "

" Thank you, I can eat nothing," said Phelps.

" Oh, come ! Try the dish before you."

" Thank you, I would really rather not."

" Well, then," said Holmes, with a mischievous

twinkle, " I suppose that you have no objection to helping me ? "

Phelps raised the cover, and as he did so he uttered a scream, and sat there staring with a face as white as the plate upon which he looked. Across the centre of it was lying a little cylinder of blue-grey paper. He caught it up, devoured it with his eyes, and then danced madly about the room, pressing it to his bosom and shrieking out in his delight. Then he fell back into an arm-chair, so limp and exhausted with his own emotions that we had to pour brandy down his throat to keep him from fainting.

" There ! there ! " said Holmes, soothingly, patting him upon the shoulder. " It was too bad to spring it on you like this ; but Watson here will tell you that I never can resist a touch of the dramatic."

Phelps seized his hand and kissed it. " God bless you ! " he cried ; " you have saved my honour."

" Well, my own was at stake, you know," said Holmes. " I assure you, it is just as hateful to me to fail in a case as it can be to you to blunder over a commission."

Phelps thrust away the precious document into the innermost pocket of his coat.

" I have not the heart to interrupt your breakfast any further, and yet I am dying to know how you got it and where it was."

Sherlock Holmes swallowed a cup of coffee and turned his attention to the ham and eggs. Then he rose, lit his pipe, and settled himself down into his chair.

" I'll tell you what I did first, and how I came to do it afterwards," said he. " After leaving you at the station I went for a charming walk through some admirable Surrey scenery to a pretty little village called Ripley, where I had my tea at an inn, and took the precaution of filling my flask and of putting a paper of sandwiches in my pocket. There I remained until evening, when I set off for Woking again and found myself in the high-road outside Briarbrae just after sunset.

" Well, I waited until the road was clear—it is never a

very frequented one at any time, I fancy—and then I clambered over the fence into the grounds."

" Surely the gate was open ? " ejaculated Phelps.

" Yes ; but I have a peculiar taste in these matters. I chose the place where the three fir trees stand, and behind their screen I got over without the least chance of anyone in the house being able to see me. I crouched down among the bushes on the other side, and crawled from one to the other—witness the disreputable state of my trouser knees—until I had reached the clump of rhododendrons just opposite to your bedroom window. There I squatted down and awaited developments.

" The blind was not down in your room, and I could see Miss Harrison sitting there reading by the table. It was a quarter past ten when she closed her book, fastened the shutters, and retired. I heard her shut the door, and felt quite sure that she had turned the key in the lock."

" The key ? " ejaculated Phelps.

" Yes, I had given Miss Harrison instructions to lock the door on the outside and take the key with her when she went to bed. She carried out every one of my injunctions to the letter, and certainly without her co-operation you would not have that paper in your coat pocket. She departed then, the lights went out, and I was left squatting in the rhododendron bush.

" The night was fine, but still it was a very weary vigil. Of course, it has the sort of excitement about it that the sportsman feels when he lies beside the watercourse and waits for the big game. It was very long, though—almost as long, Watson, as when you and I waited in that deadly room when we looked into the little problem of the ' Speckled Band.' There was a church clock down at Woking which struck the quarters, and I thought more than once that it had stopped. At last, however, about two in the morning, I suddenly heard the gentle sound of a bolt being pushed back, and the creaking of a key. A moment later the servants' door was opened and Mr. Joseph Harrison stepped out into the moonlight."

" Joseph ! " ejaculated Phelps.

" He was bare-headed, but he had a black cloak thrown over his shoulder, so that he could conceal his face in an instant if there were any alarm. He walked on tiptoe under the shadow of the wall, and when he reached the window, he worked a long-bladed knife through the sash and pushed back the catch. Then he flung open the window and, putting his knife through the crack in the shutters, he thrust the bar up and swung them open.

" From where I lay I had a perfect view of the inside of the room and of every one of his movements. He lit the two candles which stand upon the mantelpiece, and then he proceeded to turn back the corner of the carpet in the neighbourhood of the door. Presently he stooped and picked out a square piece of board, such as is usually left to enable plumbers to get at the joints of the gas pipes. This one covered, as a matter of fact, the T-joint which gives off the pipe which supplies the kitchen under-neath. Out of this hiding-place he drew that little cylinder of paper, pushed down the board, rearranged the carpet, blew out the candles, and walked straight into my arms as I stood waiting for him outside the window.

" Well, he has rather more viciousness than I gave him credit for, has Master Joseph. He flew at me with his knife, and I had to grass him twice, and got a cut over the knuckles, before I had the upper hand of him. He looked ' murder ' out of the only eye he could see with when we had finished, but he listened to reason and gave up the papers. Having got them I let my man go, but I wired full particulars to Forbes this morning. If he is quick enough to catch his bird, well and good ! But if, as I shrewdly suspect, he finds the nest empty before he gets there, why, all the better for the Government. I fancy that Lord Holdhurst, for one, and Mr. Percy Phelps, for another would very much rather that the affair never got so far as a police-court."

" My God ! " gasped our client. " Do you tell me that

during these long ten weeks of agony, the stolen papers were within the very room with me all the time ? "

" So it was."

" And Joseph ! Joseph a villain and a thief ! "

" Hum ! I am afraid Joseph's character is a rather deeper and more dangerous one than one might judge from his appearance. From what I have heard from him this morning, I gather that he has lost heavily in dabbling with stocks, and that he is ready to do anything on earth to better his fortunes. Being an absolutely selfish man, when a chance presented itself he did not allow either his sister's happiness or your reputation to hold his hand."

Percy Phelps sank back in his chair. " My head whirls," said he ; " your words have dazed me."

" The principal difficulty in your case," remarked Holmes, in his didactic fashion, " lay in the fact of there being too much evidence. What was vital was overlaid and hidden by what was irrelevant. Of all the facts which were presented to us, we had to pick just those which we deemed to be essential, and then piece them together in their order, so as to reconstruct this very remarkable chain of events. I had already begun to suspect Joseph, from the fact that you had intended to travel home with him that night, and that therefore it was a likely enough thing that he should call for you—knowing the Foreign Office well—upon his way. When I heard that someone had been so anxious to get into the bedroom, in which no one but Joseph could have concealed anything—you told us in your narrative how you had turned Joseph out when you arrived with the doctor—my suspicions all changed to certainties, especially as the attempt was made on the first night upon which the nurse was absent, showing that the intruder was well acquainted with the ways of the house."

" How blind I have been ! "

" The facts of the case, as far as I have worked them out, are these : This Joseph Harrison entered the office through the Charles Street door, and knowing his way he walked straight into your room the instant after you left it. Finding no one there he promptly rang the bell, and at the instant that he did so his eyes caught the paper upon the table. A glance showed him that chance had put in his way a State document of immense value, and in a flash he had thrust it into his pocket and was gone. A few minutes elapsed, as you remember, before the sleepy commissionaire drew your attention to the bell, and those were just enough to give the thief time to make his escape.

" He made his way to Woking by the first train, and, having examined his booty and assured himself that it really was of immense value, he concealed it in what he thought was a very safe place, with the intention of taking it out again in a day or two, and carrying it to the French Embassy, or wherever he thought that a long price was to be had. Then came your sudden return. He, without a moment's warning, was bundled out of his room, and from that time onwards there were always at least two of you there to prevent him from regaining his treasure. The situation to him must have been a maddening one. But at last he thought he saw his chance. He tried to steal in, but was baffled by your wakefulness. You may remember that you did not take your usual draught that night."

" I remember."

" I fancy that he had taken steps to make that draught efficacious, and that he quite relied upon your being unconscious. Of course, I understood that he would repeat the attempt whenever it could be done with safety. Your leaving the room gave him the chance he wanted. I kept Miss Harrison in it all day, so that he might not anticipate us. Then, having given him the idea that the coast was clear, I kept guard as I have described. I already knew that the papers were probably in the room, but I had no desire to rip up all the planking and skirting in search of them. I let him take them, therefore, from the hiding-place, and so saved myself an infinity of trouble. Is there any other point which I can make clear ? "

" Why did he try the window on the first occasion," I asked, " when he might have entered by the door ? "

" In reaching the door he would have to pass seven bedrooms. On the other hand, he could get out on to the lawn with ease. Anything else ? "

" You do not think," asked Phelps, " that he had any murderous intention ? The knife was only meant as a tool."

" It may be so," answered Holmes, shrugging his shoulders. " I can only say for certain that Mr. Joseph Harrison is a gentleman to whose mercy I should be extremely unwilling to trust."

23. *The Final Problem*

IT is with a heavy heart that I take up my pen to write these the last words in which I shall ever record the singular gifts by which my friend Mr. Sherlock Holmes was distinguished. In an incoherent and, as I deeply feel, an entirely inadequate fashion, I have endeavoured to give some account of my strange experiences in his company from the chance which first brought us together at the period of the " Study in Scarlet," up to the time of his interference in the matter of the " Naval Treaty "—an interference which had the unquestionable effect of preventing a serious international complication. It was my intention to have stopped there, and to have said nothing of that event which has created a void in my life which the lapse of two years has done little to fill. My hand has been forced, however, by the recent letters in which Colonel James Moriarty defends the memory of his brother, and I have no choice but to lay the facts before the public exactly as they occurred. I alone know the absolute truth of the matter, and I am satisfied that the time has come when no good purpose is to be served by its suppression. As far as I know, there have been only three accounts in the public Press : that in the *Journal de Genève* upon May 6th, 1891, the Reuter's despatch in the English papers upon May 7th, and finally the recent letters to which I have alluded. Of these the first and second were extremely condensed, while the last is, as I shall now show, an absolute perversion of the facts. It lies with me to tell for the first time what really took place between Professor Moriarty and Mr. Sherlock Holmes.

It may be remembered that after my marriage, and my subsequent start in private practice, the very intimate relations which had existed between Holmes and myself became to some extent modified. He still came to me from time to time when he desired a companion in his investigations, but these occasions grew more and more seldom, until I find that in the year 1890 there were only three cases of which I retain any record. During the winter of that year and the early spring of 1891, I saw in the papers that he had been engaged by the French Government upon a matter of supreme importance, and I received two notes from Holmes, dated from Narbonne and from Nîmes, from which I gathered that his stay in France was likely to be a long one. It was with some surprise, therefore, that I saw him walk into my consulting-room upon the evening of the 24th of April. It struck me that he was looking even paler and thinner than usual.

" Yes, I have been using myself up rather too freely," he remarked, in answer to my look rather than to my words ; " I have been a little pressed of late. Have you any objection to my closing your shutters ? "

The only light in the room came from the lamp upon the table at which I had been reading. Holmes edged his way round the wall, and flinging the shutters together, he bolted them securely.

" You are afraid of something ? " I asked.

" Well, I am."

" Of what ? "

537

" Of air-guns."

" My dear Holmes, what do you mean ? "

" I think that you know me well enough, Watson, to understand that I am by no means a nervous man. At the same time, it is stupidity rather than courage to refuse to recognize danger when it is close upon you. Might I trouble you for a match ? " He drew in the smoke of his cigarette as if the soothing influence was grateful to him.

" I must apologize for calling so late," said he, " and I must further beg you to be so unconventional as to allow me to leave your house presently by scrambling over your back garden wall."

" But what does it all mean ? " I asked.

He held out his hand, and I saw in the light of the lamp that two of his knuckles were burst and bleeding.

" It's not an airy nothing, you see," said he, smiling. " On the contrary, it is solid enough for a man to break his hand over. Is Mrs. Watson in ? "

" She is away upon a visit."

" Indeed ! You are alone ? "

" Quite."

" Then it makes it the easier for me to propose that you should come away with me for a week on to the Continent."

" Where ? "

" Oh, anywhere. It's all the same to me."

There was something very strange in all this. It was not Holmes' nature to take an aimless holiday, and something about his pale, worn face told me that his nerves were at their highest tension. He saw the question in my eyes, and, putting his finger-tips together and his elbows upon his knees, he explained the situation.

" You have probably never heard of Professor Moriarty ? " said he.

" Never."

" Aye, there's the genius and the wonder of the thing ! " he cried. " The man pervades London, and no one has heard of him. That's what puts him on a pinnacle in the records of crime. I tell you, Watson, in all seriousness, that if I could beat that man, if I could free society of him, I should feel that my own career had reached its summit, and I should be prepared to turn to some more placid line in life. Between ourselves, the recent cases in which I have been of assistance to the Royal Family of Scandinavia, and to the French Republic, have left me in such a position that I could continue to live in the quiet fashion which is most congenial to me, and to concentrate my attention upon my chemical researches. But I could not rest, Watson, I could not sit quiet in my chair, if I thought that such a man as Professor Moriarty were walking the streets of London unchallenged."

"What has he done, then?"

"His career has been an extraordinary one. He is a man of good birth and excellent education, endowed by Nature with a phenomenal mathematical faculty. At the age of twenty-one he wrote a treatise upon the Binomial Theorem, which has had a European vogue. On the strength of it, he won the Mathematical Chair at one of our smaller Universities, and had, to all appearance, a most brilliant career before him. But the man had hereditary tendencies of the most diabolical kind. A criminal strain ran in his blood, which, instead of being modified, was increased and rendered infinitely more dangerous by his extraordinary mental powers. Dark rumours gathered round him in the University town, and eventually he was compelled to resign his Chair and to come down to London, where he set up as an Army coach. So much is known to the world, but what I am telling you now is what I have myself discovered.

"As you are aware, Watson, there is no one who knows the higher criminal world of London so well as I do. For years past I have continually been conscious of some power behind the malefactor, some deep organizing power which for ever stands in the way of the law, and throws its shield over the wrong-doer. Again and again in cases of the most varying sorts—forgery cases, robberies, murders—I have felt the presence of this force, and I have deduced its action in many of those undiscovered crimes in which I have not been personally consulted. For years I have endeavoured to break through the veil which shrouded it, and at last the time came when I seized my thread and followed it, until it led me, after a thousand cunning windings, to ex-Professor Moriarty of mathematical celebrity.

" He is the Napoleon of crime, Watson. He is the organizer of half that is evil and of nearly all that is undetected in this great city. He is a genius, a philosopher, an abstract thinker. He has a brain of the first order. He sits motionless, like a spider in the centre of its web, but that web has a thousand radiations, and he knows well every quiver of each of them. He does little himself. He only plans. But his agents are numerous and splendidly organized. Is there a crime to be done, a paper to be abstracted, we will say, a house to be rifled, a man to be removed—the word is passed to the Professor, the matter is organized and carried out. The agent may be caught. In that case money is found for his bail or his defence. But the central power which uses the agent is never caught—never so much as suspected. This was the organization which I deduced, Watson, and which I devoted my whole energy to exposing and breaking up.

" But the Professor was fenced round with safeguards so cunningly devised that, do what I would, it seemed impossible to get evidence which could convict in a court of law. You know my powers, my dear Watson, and yet at the end of three months I was forced to confess that I had at last met an antagonist who was my intellectual equal. My horror at his crimes was lost in my admiration at his skill. But at last he made a trip—only a little, little trip—but it was more than he could afford, when I was so close upon him. I had my chance, and, starting from that point, I have woven my net round him until now it is all ready to close. In three days, that is to say on Monday next, matters will be ripe, and the Professor, with all the principal members of his gang, will be in the hands of the police. Then will come the greatest criminal trial of the century, the clearing up of over forty mysteries, and the rope for all of them—but if we move at all prematurely, you understand, they may slip out of our hands even at the last moment.

" Now, if I could have done this without the knowledge of Professor Moriarty, all would have been well. But he was too wily for that. He saw every step which I took to draw my toils round him. Again and again he strove to break away, but I as often headed him off. I tell you, my friend, that if a detailed account of that silent contest could be written, it would take its place as the most brilliant bit of thrust-and-parry work in the history of detection. Never have I risen to such a height, and never have I been so hard pressed by an opponent. He cut deep, and yet I just undercut him. This morning the last steps were taken, and three days only were wanted to complete the business. I was sitting in my room thinking the matter over, when the door opened and Professor Moriarty stood before me.

" My nerves are fairly proof, Watson, but I must confess to a start when I saw the very man who had been so much in my thoughts standing there on my threshold. His appearance was quite familiar to me. He is extremely tall and thin, his forehead domes out in a white curve, and his two eyes are deeply sunken in his head. He is clean-shaven, pale, and ascetic-looking, retaining something of the professor in his features. His shoulders are rounded from much study, and his face protrudes forward, and is for ever slowly oscillating from side to side in a curiously reptilian fashion. He peered at me with great curiosity in his puckered eyes.

" ' You have less frontal development than I should have expected,' said he at last. ' It is a dangerous habit to finger loaded firearms in the pocket of one's dressing-gown.'

" The fact is that upon his entrance I had instantly recognized the extreme personal danger in which I lay. The only conceivable escape for him lay in silencing my tongue. In an instant I had slipped the revolver from the drawer into my pocket, and was covering him through the cloth. At his remark I drew the weapon out and laid it cocked upon the table. He still smiled and blinked, but there was something about his eyes which made me feel very glad that I had it there.

" ' You evidently don't know me,' said he.

" ' On the contrary,' I answered, ' I think it is fairly evident that I do. Pray take a chair. I can spare you five minutes if you have anything to say.'

" ' All that I have to say has already crossed your mind,' said he.

" ' Then possibly my answer has crossed yours,' I replied.

" ' You stand fast ? '

" ' Absolutely.'

" He clapped his hand into his pocket, and I raised the pistol from the table. But he merely drew out a memo-randum-book in which he had scribbled some dates.

" ' You crossed my path on the 4th of January,' said he. ' On the 23rd you incommoded me ; by the middle of February I was seriously inconvenienced by you ; at the end of March I was absolutely hampered in my plans ; and now, at the close of April, I find myself placed in such a position through your continual persecution that I am in positive danger of losing my liberty. The situation is becoming an impossible one.'

" ' Have you any suggestion to make ? ' I asked.

" ' You must drop it, Mr. Holmes,' said he, swaying his face about. ' You really must, you know.'

" ' After Monday,' said I.

" ' Tut, tut ! ' said he. ' I am quite sure that a man of your intelligence will see that there can be but one out-come to this affair. It is necessary that you should withdraw. You have worked things in such a fashion that we have only one resource left. It has been an intellectual treat to me to see the way in which you have grappled with this affair, and I say, unaffectedly, that it would be a grief to me to be forced to take any extreme measure. You smile, sir, but I assure you that it really would.'

" ' Danger is part of my trade,' I remarked.

" ' This is not danger,' said he. ' It is inevitable destruction. You stand in the way not merely of an individual, but of a mighty organization, the full extent of which you, with all your cleverness, have been unable to realize. You must stand clear, Mr. Holmes, or be trodden under foot.'

" ' I am afraid,' said I, rising, ' that in the pleasure of this conversation I am neglecting business of importance which awaits me elsewhere.'

" He rose also and looked at me in silence, shaking his head sadly.

" ' Well, well,' said he at last. ' It seems a pity, but I have done what I could. I know every move of your game. You can do nothing before Monday. It has been a duel between you and me, Mr. Holmes. You hope to place me in the dock. I tell you that I will never stand in the dock. You hope to beat me. I tell you that you will never beat me. If you are clever enough to bring destruction upon me, rest assured that I shall do as much to you.'

" ' You have paid me several compliments, Mr. Moriarty,' said I. ' Let me pay you one in return when I say that if I were assured of the former eventuality I would, in the interests of the public, cheerfully accept the latter.'

" ' I can promise you the one but not the other,' he snarled, and so turned his rounded back upon me and went peering and blinking out of the room.

" That was my singular interview with Professor Moriarty. I confess that it left an unpleasant effect upon my mind. His soft, precise fashion of speech leaves a conviction of sincerity which a mere bully could not produce. Of course, you will say : ' Why not take police precautions against him ? ' The reason is that I am well convinced that it is from his agents the blow would fall. I have the best of proofs that it would be so."

" You have already been assaulted ? "

" My dear Watson, Professor Moriarty is not a man who lets the grass grow under his feet. I went out about midday to transact some business in Oxford Street. As I passed the corner which leads from Bentinck Street on to the Welbeck Street crossing a two-horse van furiously driven whizzed round and was on me like a flash. I sprang for the footpath and saved myself by the fraction of a second. The van dashed round from Marylebone Lane and was gone in an instant. I kept to the pavement after that, Watson, but as I walked down Vere Street a brick came down from the roof of one of the houses, and was shattered to fragments at my feet. I called the police and had the place examined. There were slates and bricks piled upon the roof preparatory to some repairs, and they would have me believe that the wind had toppled over one of these. Of course I knew better, but I could prove nothing. I took a cab after that and reached my brother's rooms in Pall Mall, where I spent the day. Now I have come round to you, and on my way I was attacked by a rough with a bludgeon. I knocked him down, and the police have him in custody ; but I can tell you with the most absolute confidence that no possible connection will ever be traced between the gentleman upon whose front teeth I have barked my knuckles and the retiring mathematical coach, who is, I dare say, working out problems upon a blackboard ten miles away. You will not wonder, Watson, that my first act on entering your rooms was to close your shutters, and that I have been compelled to ask your permission to leave the house by some less conspicuous exit than the front door."

I had often admired my friend's courage, but never more than now, as he sat quietly checking off a series of incidents which must have combined to make up a day of horror.

" You will spend the night here ? " I said.

" No, my friend ; you might find me a dangerous guest. I have my plans laid, and all will be well. Matters have gone so far now that they can move without my help as far as the arrest goes, though my presence is necessary for a conviction. It is obvious, therefore, that I cannot do better than get away for the few days which remain before the police are at liberty to act. It would be a great pleasure to me, therefore, if you could come on to the Continent with me."

" The practice is quiet," said I, " and I have an accommodating neighbour. I should be glad to come."

" And to start to-morrow morning ? "

" If necessary."

" Oh yes, it is most necessary. Then these are your instructions, and I beg, my dear Watson, that you will obey them to the letter, for you are now playing a double-handed game with me against the cleverest rogue and the most powerful syndicate of criminals in Europe. Now listen ! You will despatch whatever luggage you intend to take by a trusty messenger unaddressed to Victoria to-night. In the morning you will send for a hansom, desiring your man to take neither the first nor the second which may present itself. Into this hansom you will jump, and you will drive to the Strand end of the Low-ther Arcade, handing the address to the cabman upon a slip of paper, with a request that he will not throw it away. Have your fare ready, and the instant that your cab stops, dash through the Arcade, timing yourself to reach the other side at a quarter-past nine. You will find a small brougham waiting close to the kerb, driven by a fellow with a heavy black cloak tipped at the collar with red. Into this you will step, and you will reach Victoria in time for the Continental express."

" Where shall I meet you ? "

" At the station. The second first-class carriage from
the front will be reserved for us."

" The carriage is our rendezvous, then ? "

" Yes."

It was in vain that I asked Holmes to remain for the
evening. It was evident to me that he thought he might
bring trouble to the roof he was under, and that that was
the motive which impelled him to go. With a few hurried words as to our plans for the morrow he rose and came
out with me into the garden, clambering over the wall
which leads into Mortimer Street, and immediately
whistling for a hansom, in which I heard him drive away.

In the morning I obeyed Holmes' injunctions to the
letter. A hansom was procured with such precautions as
would prevent its being one which was placed ready for us,
and I drove immediately after breakfast to the Lowther
Arcade, through which I hurried at the top of my speed.
A brougham was waiting with a very massive driver
wrapped in a dark cloak, who, the instant that I had
stepped in, whipped up the horse and rattled off to
Victoria Station. On my alighting there he turned the
carriage, and dashed away without so much as a look in
my direction.

So far all had gone admirably. My luggage was waiting for me, and I had no difficulty in finding the carriage
in which Holmes had indicated, the less so as it was the
only one in the train which was marked " Engaged."
My only source of anxiety now was the non-appearance
of Holmes. The station clock marked only seven minutes
from the time when we were due to start. In vain I
searched among the groups of travellers and leave-takers
for the lithe figure of my friend. There was no sign of
him. I spent a few minutes in assisting a venerable
Italian priest, who was endeavouring to make a porter
understand, in his broken English, that his luggage was
to be booked through to Paris. Then, having taken
another look round, I returned to my carriage, where
I found that the porter, in spite of the ticket, had given

me my decrepit Italian friend as a travelling companion. It was useless for me to explain to him that his presence was an intrusion, for my Italian was even more limited than his English, so I shrugged my shoulders resignedly and continued to look out anxiously for my friend. A chill of fear had come over me, as I thought that his absence might mean that some blow had fallen during the night. Already the doors had all been shut and the whistle blown, when——

" My dear Watson," said a voice, " you have not even condescended to say good morning."

I turned in incontrollable astonishment. The aged ecclesiastic had turned his face towards me. For an instant the wrinkles were smoothed away, the nose drew away from the chin, the lower lip ceased to protrude and the mouth to mumble, the dull eyes regained their fire, the drooping figure expanded. The next the whole frame collapsed, and Holmes had gone as quickly as he had come.

" Good heavens ! " I cried. " How you startled me ! "

" Every precaution is still necessary," he whispered. " I have reason to think that they are hot upon our trail. Ah, there is Moriarty himself."

The train had already begun to move as Holmes spoke. Glancing back I saw a tall man pushing his way furiously through the crowd and waving his hand as if he desired to have the train stopped. It was too late, however, for we were rapidly gathering momentum, and an instant later had shot clear of the station.

" With all our precautions, you see that we have cut it rather fine," said Holmes, laughing. He rose, and throwing off the black cassock and hat which had formed his disguise, he packed them away in a hand-bag.

" Have you seen the morning paper, Watson ? "

" No."

" You haven't seen about Baker Street, then ? "

" Baker Street ? "

" They set fire to our rooms last night. No great harm was done."

547

" Good heavens, Holmes ! This is intolerable."

" They must have lost my track completely after their bludgeon-man was arrested. Otherwise they could not have imagined that I had returned to my rooms. They have evidently taken the precaution of watching you, however, and that is what has brought Moriarty to Victoria. You could not have made any slip in coming ? "

" I did exactly what you advised."

" Did you find your brougham ? "

" Yes, it was waiting."

" Did you recognize your coachman ? "

" No."

" It was my brother Mycroft. It is an advantage to get about in such a case without taking a mercenary into your confidence. But we must plan what we are to do about Moriarty now."

" As this is an express, and as the boat runs in connection with it, I should think we have shaken him off very effectively."

" My dear Watson, you evidently did not realize my meaning when I said that this man may be taken as being quite on the same intellectual plane as myself. You do not imagine that if I were the pursuer I should allow myself to be baffled by so slight an obstacle. Why, then, should you think so meanly of him ? "

" What will he do ? "

" What I should do."

" What would you do, then ? "

" Engage a special."

" But it must be late."

" By no means. This train stops at Canterbury ; and there is always at least a quarter of an hour's delay at the boat. He will catch us there."

" One would think that we were the criminals. Let us have him arrested on his arrival."

" It would be to ruin the work of three months. We should get the big fish, but the smaller would dart right

548

and left out of the net. On Monday we should have them all. No, an arrest is inadmissible."

"What then?"

"We shall get out at Canterbury."

"And then?"

"Well, then we must make a cross-country journey to Newhaven, and so over to Dieppe. Moriarty will again do what I should do. He will get on to Paris, mark down our luggage, and wait for two days at the depot. In the meantime we shall treat ourselves to a couple of carpet bags, encourage the manufactures of the countries through which we travel, and make our way at our leisure into Switzerland, via Luxembourg and Basle."

I am too old a traveller to allow myself to be seriously inconvenienced by the loss of my luggage, but I confess that I was annoyed at the idea of being forced to dodge and hide before a man whose record was black with unutterable infamies. It was evident, however, that Holmes understood the situation more clearly than I did. At Canterbury, therefore, we alighted, only to find that we should have to wait an hour before we could get a train to Newhaven.

I was still looking rather ruefully after the rapidly disappearing luggage van which contained my wardrobe, when Holmes pulled my sleeve and pointed up the line.

"Already, you see," said he.

Far away from among the Kentish woods there arose a thin spray of smoke. A minute later a carriage and engine could be seen flying along the open curve which leads to the station. We had hardly time to take our places behind a pile of luggage when it passed with a rattle and a roar, beating a blast of hot air into our faces.

"There he goes," said Holmes, as we watched the carriage swing and rock over the points. "There are limits, you see, to our friend's intelligence. It would have been a *coup de maître* had he deduced what I would deduce and acted accordingly."

"And what would he have done had he overtaken us?"

" There cannot be the least doubt that he would have made a murderous attack upon me. It is, however, a game at which two may play. The question now is whether we should take a premature lunch here, or run our chance of starving before we reach the buffet at Newhaven."

We made our way to Brussels that night and spent two days there, moving on upon the third day as far as Strasburg. On the Monday morning Holmes had telegraphed to the London police, and in the evening we found a reply waiting for us at our hotel. Holmes tore it open, and then with a bitter curse hurled it into the grate.

" I might have known it," he groaned. " He has escaped ! "

" Moriarty ! "

" They have secured the whole gang with the exception of him. He has given them the slip. Of course, when I had left the country there was no one to cope with him. But I did think that I had put the game in their hands. I think that you had better return to England, Watson."

" Why ? "

" Because you will find me a dangerous companion now. This man's occupation is gone. He is lost if he returns to London. If I read his character right he will devote his whole energies to revenging himself upon me. He said as much in our short interview, and I fancy that he meant it. I should certainly recommend you to return to your practice."

It was hardly an appeal to be successful with one who was an old campaigner as well as an old friend. We sat in the Strasburg *salle-à-manger* arguing the question for half an hour, but the same night we had resumed our journey and were well on our way to Geneva.

For a charming week we wandered up the Valley of the Rhone, and then, branching off at Leuk, we made our way over the Gemmi Pass, still deep in snow, and so, by way of Interlaken, to Meiringen. It was a lovely trip, the dainty green of the spring below, the virgin white of the winter above ; but it was clear to me that never for one instant did Holmes forget the shadow which lay across him. In the homely Alpine villages or in the lonely mountain passes, I could still tell, by his quick glancing eyes and his sharp scrutiny of every face that passed us, that he was well convinced that, walk where we would, we could not walk ourselves clear of the danger which was dogging our footsteps.

Once, I remember, as we passed over the Gemmi, and walked along the border of the melancholy Daubensee, a large rock which had been dislodged from the ridge upon our right clattered down and roared into the lake behind us. In an instant Holmes had raced up on to the ridge, and, standing upon a lofty pinnacle, craned his neck in every direction. It was in vain that our guide assured him that a fall of stones was a common chance in the spring-time at that spot. He said nothing, but he smiled at me with the air of a man who sees the fulfilment of that which he had expected.

And yet for all his watchfulness he was never depressed. On the contrary, I can never recollect having seen him in such exuberant spirits. Again and again he recurred to the fact that if he could be assured that society was freed from Professor Moriarty, he would cheerfully bring his own career to a conclusion.

" I think that I may go so far as to say, Watson, that I have not lived wholly in vain," he remarked. " If my record were closed to-night I could still survey it with equanimity. The air of London is the sweeter for my presence. In over a thousand cases I am not aware that I have ever used my powers upon the wrong side. Of late I have been tempted to look into the problems furnished by Nature rather than those more superficial ones for which our artificial state of society is responsible. Your memoirs will draw to an end, Watson, upon the day that I crown my career by the capture or extinction of the most dangerous and capable criminal in Europe."

I shall be brief, and yet exact, in the little which remains for me to tell. It is not a subject on which I would willingly dwell, and yet I am conscious that a duty devolves upon me to omit no detail.

It was upon the 3rd of May that we reached the little village of Meiringen, where we put up at the 'Englischer Hof, then kept by Peter Steiler the elder. Our landlord was an intelligent man, and spoke excellent English, having served for three years as waiter at the Grosvenor Hotel in London. At his advice, upon the afternoon of the 4th we set off together with the intention of crossing the hills and spending the night at the Hamlet of Rosen-laui. We had strict injunctions, however, on no account to pass the falls of Reichenbach, which are about half-way up the hill, without making a small detour to see them.

It is, indeed, a fearful place. The torrent, swollen by the melting snow, plunges into a tremendous abyss, from which the spray rolls up like the smoke from a burning house. The shaft into which the river hurls itself is an immense chasm, lined by glistening, coal-black rock, and narrowing into a creaming, boiling pit of incalculable depth, which brims over and shoots the stream onward over its jagged lip. The long sweep of green water roaring for ever down, and the thick flickering curtain of spray hissing for ever upwards, turn a man giddy with their constant whirl and clamour. We stood near the edge peering down at the gleam of the breaking water far below us against the black rocks, and listening to the half-human shout which came booming up with the spray out of the abyss.

The path has been cut half-way round the fall to afford a complete view, but it ends abruptly, and the traveller has to return as he came. We had turned to do so, when we saw a Swiss lad come running along it with a letter in his hand. It bore the mark of the hotel which we had just left, and was addressed to me by the landlord. It appeared that within a very few minutes of our leaving, an English lady had arrived who was in the last stage of consumption. She had wintered at Davos Platz, and was journeying now to join her friends at Lucerne, when a sudden hæmorrhage had overtaken her. It was thought that she could hardly live a few hours, but it would be a great consolation to her to see an English doctor, and, if I would only return, etc. etc. The good Steiler assured me in a postscript that he would himself look upon my compliance as a very great favour, since the lady absolutely refused to see a Swiss physician, and he could not but feel that he was incurring a great responsibility.

The appeal was one which could not be ignored. It was impossible to refuse the request of a fellow-countrywoman dying in a strange land. Yet I had my scruples about leaving Holmes. It was finally agreed, however, that he should retain the young Swiss messenger with him as guide and companion while I returned to Meiringen. My friend would stay some little time at the fall, he said, and would then walk slowly over the hill to Rosenlaui, where I was to rejoin him in the evening. As I turned away I saw Holmes with his back against a rock and his arms folded, gazing down at the rush of the waters. It was the last that I was ever destined to see of him in this world.

When I was near the bottom of the descent I looked back. It was impossible, from that position, to see the fall, but I could see the curving path which winds over the shoulder of the hill and leads to it. Along this a man was, I remember, walking very rapidly. I could see his black figure clearly outlined against the green behind him. I noted him, and the energy with which he walked, but he passed from my mind again as I hurried on upon my errand.

It may have been a little over an hour before I reached Meiringen. Old Steiler was standing at the porch of his hotel.

"Well," said I, as I came hurrying up, "I trust that she is no worse?"

A look of surprise passed over his face, and at the first

quiver of his eyebrows my heart turned to lead in my breast.

" You did not write this ? " I said, pulling the letter from my pocket. " There is no sick Englishwoman in the hotel ? "

" Certainly not," he cried. " But it has the hotel mark upon it ! Ha ! it must have been written by that tall Englishman who came in after you had gone. He said——"

But I waited for none of the landlord's explanations. In a tingle of fear I was already running down the village street, and making for the path which I had so lately descended. It had taken me an hour to come down. For all my efforts, two more had passed before I found myself at the fall of Reichenbach once more. There was Holmes' alpenstock still leaning against the rock by which I had left him. But there was no sign of him, and it was in vain that I shouted. My only answer was my own voice reverberating in a rolling echo from the cliffs around me.

It was the sight of that alpenstock which turned me cold and sick. He had not gone to Rosenlaui, then. He had remained on that three-foot path, with sheer wall on one side and sheer drop upon the other, until his enemy had overtaken him. The young Swiss had gone too. He had probably been in the pay of Moriarty, and had left the two men together. And then what had happened ? Who was to tell us what had happened then ?

I stood for a minute or two to collect myself, for I was dazed with the horror of the thing. Then I began to think of Holmes' own methods and to try to practise them in reading this tragedy. It was, alas ! only too easy to do. During our conversation we had not gone to the end of the path, and the alpenstock marked the place where we had stood. The blackish soil is kept for ever soft by the incessant drift of spray, and a bird would leave its tread upon it. Two lines of footmarks were clearly marked along the further end of the path, both leading away from me. There were none returning. A few yards from the end the soil was all ploughed up into a patch of mud, and the brambles and ferns which fringed the chasm were torn and bedraggled. I lay upon my face and peered over, with the spray spouting up all around me. It had darkened since I had left, and now I could only see here and there the glistening of moisture upon the black walls, and far away down at the end of the shaft the gleam of the broken water. I shouted ; but only that same half-human cry of the fall was borne back to my ears.

But it was destined that I should after all have a last word of greeting from my friend and comrade. I have said that his alpenstock had been left leaning against a rock which jutted on to the path. From the top of this boulder the gleam of something bright caught my eye, and, raising my hand, I found that it came from the silver cigarette-case which he used to carry. As I took it up a small square of paper upon which it had lain fluttered down on to the ground. Unfolding it I found that it consisted of three pages torn from his notebook and addressed to me. It was characteristic of the man that the direction was as precise, and the writing as firm and clear, as though it had been written in his study.

"MY DEAR WATSON," he said, " I write these few lines through the courtesy of Mr. Moriarty, who awaits my convenience for the final discussion of those questions which lie between us. He has been giving me a sketch of the methods by which he avoided the English police and kept himself informed of our movements. They certainly confirm the very high opinion which I had formed of his abilities. I am pleased to think that I shall be able to free society from any further effects of his presence, though I fear that it is at a cost which will give pain to my friends, and especially, my dear Watson, to you. I have already explained to you, however, that my career had in any case reached its crisis, and that no possible conclusion to it could be more congenial to me than this. Indeed, if I may make a full confession to you, I was quite convinced that the letter from Meiringen was a hoax, and I allowed you to depart on that errand under the persuasion that some development of this sort would follow. Tell Inspector Patterson that the papers which he needs to convict the gang are in pigeon-hole M., done up in a blue envelope and inscribed ' Moriarty.' I made every disposition of my property before leaving England, and handed it to my brother Mycroft. Pray give my greetings to Mrs. Watson, and believe me to be, my dear fellow,

" Very sincerely yours,
" SHERLOCK HOLMES."

A few words may suffice to tell the little that remains. An examination by experts leaves little doubt that a personal contest between the two men ended, as it could hardly fail to end in such a situation, in their reeling over, locked in each other's arms. Any attempt at recovering the bodies was absolutely hopeless, and there, deep down in that dreadful cauldron of swirling water and seething foam, will lie for all time the most dangerous criminal and the foremost champion of the law of their generation. The Swiss youth was never found again, and there can be no doubt that he was one of the numerous agents whom Moriarty kept in his employ. As to the gang, it will be within the memory of the public how completely the evidence which Holmes had accumulated exposed their organization, and how heavily the hand of the dead man weighed upon them. Of their terrible chief few details came out during the proceeding, and if I have now been compelled to make a clear statement of his career, it is due to those injudicious champions who have endeavoured to clear his memory by attacks upon him whom I shall ever regard as the best and the wisest man whom I have ever known.

THE RETURN OF
SHERLOCK HOLMES

24. *The Empty House*

IT was in the spring of the year 1894 that all London was interested, and the fashionable world dismayed, by the murder of the Honourable Ronald Adair, under most unusual and inexplicable circumstances. The public has already learned those particulars of the crime which came out in the police investigation ; but a good deal was suppressed upon that occasion, since the case for the prosecution was so overwhelmingly strong that it was not necessary to bring forward all the facts. Only now, at the end of nearly ten years, am I allowed to supply those missing links which make up the whole of that remarkable chain. The crime was of interest in itself, but that interest was as nothing to me compared to the inconceivable sequel, which afforded me the greatest shock and surprise of any event in my adventurous life. Even now, after this long interval, I find myself thrilling as I think of it, and feeling once more that sudden flood of joy, amazement, and incredulity which utterly submerged my mind. Let me say to that public which has shown some interest in those glimpses which I have occasionally given them of the thoughts and actions of a very remarkable man that they are not to blame me if I have not shared my knowledge with them, for I should have considered it my first duty to have done so had I not been barred by a positive prohibition from his own lips, which was only withdrawn upon the third of last month.

It can be imagined that my close intimacy with Sherlock Holmes had interested me deeply in crime, and that after his disappearance I never failed to read with care the various problems which came before the public, and I even attempted more than once for my own private satisfaction to employ his methods in their solution, though with indifferent success. There was none, however, which appealed to me like this tragedy of Ronald Adair. As I read the evidence at the inquest, which led up to a verdict of wilful murder against some person or persons unknown, I realized more clearly than I had ever done the loss which the community had sustained by the death of Sherlock Holmes. There were points about this strange business which would, I was sure, have specially appealed to him, and the efforts of the police would have been supplemented, or more probably anticipated, by the trained observation and the alert mind of the first criminal agent in Europe. All day as I drove upon my round I turned over the case in my mind, and found no explanation which appeared to me to be adequate. At the risk of telling a twice-told tale I will recapitulate the facts as they were known to the public at the conclusion of the inquest.

The Honourable Robert Adair was the second son of the Earl of Maynooth, at that time Governor of one of the Australian colonies. Adair's mother had returned from Australia to undergo an operation for cataract, and she, her son Ronald, and her daughter Hilda were living together at 427 Park Lane. The youth moved in the best society, had, so far as was known, no enemies, and no particular vices. He had been engaged to Miss Edith Woodley, of Carstairs, but the engagement had been broken off by mutual consent some months before, and there was no sign that it had left any very profound feeling behind it. For the rest, the man's life moved in a narrow and conventional circle, for his habits were quiet and his nature unemotional. Yet it was upon this easy-going young aristocrat that death came in most strange and unexpected form between the hours of ten and eleven-twenty on the night of March 30, 1894.

Ronald Adair was fond of cards, playing continually,

but never for such stakes as would hurt him. He was a member of the Baldwin, the Cavendish, and the Bagatelle Card Clubs. It was shown that after dinner on the day of his death he had played a rubber of whist at the latter club. He had also played there in the afternoon. The evidence of those who had played with him—Mr. Murray, Sir John Hardy, and Colonel Moran—showed that the game was whist, and that there was a fairly equal fall of the cards. Adair might have lost five pounds, but not more. His fortune was a considerable one, and such a loss could not in any way affect him. He had played nearly every day at one club or other, but he was a cautious player, and usually rose a winner. It came out in evidence that in partnership with Colonel Moran he had actually won as much as £420 in a sitting some weeks before from Godfrey Milner and Lord Balmoral. So much for his recent history, as it came out at the inquest.

On the evening of the crime he returned from the club exactly at ten. His mother and sister were out spending the evening with a relation. The servant deposed that she heard him enter the front room on the second floor, generally used as his sitting-room. She had lit a fire there, and as it smoked she had opened the window. No sound was heard from the room until eleven-twenty, the hour of the return of Lady Maynooth and her daughter. Desiring to say good night, she had attempted to enter her son's room. The door was locked on the inside, and no answer could be got to their cries and knocking. Help was obtained, and the door forced. The unfortunate young man was found lying near the table. His head had been horribly mutilated by an expanded revolver bullet, but no weapon of any sort was to be found in the room. On the table lay two bank-notes for £10 each and £17 10s. in silver and gold, the money arranged in little piles of varying amount. There were some figures also upon a sheet of paper with the names of some club friends opposite to them, from which it was conjectured that before his death he was endeavouring to make out his losses or winnings at cards.

A minute examination of the circumstances served only to make the case more complex. In the first place, no reason could be given why the young man should have fastened the door upon the inside. There was the possibility that the murderer had done this and had afterwards escaped by the window. The drop was at least twenty feet, however, and a bed of crocuses in full bloom lay beneath. Neither the flowers nor the earth showed any sign of having been disturbed, nor were there any marks upon the narrow strip of grass which separated the house from the road. Apparently, therefore, it was the young man himself who had fastened the door. But how did he come by his death? No one could have climbed up to the window without leaving traces. Suppose a man had fired through the window, it would indeed be a remarkable shot who could with a revolver inflict so deadly a wound. Again, Park Lane is a frequented thoroughfare, and there is a cab-stand within a hundred yards of the house. No one had heard a shot. And yet there was the dead man, and there the revolver bullet, which had mushroomed out, as soft-nosed bullets will, and so inflicted a wound which must have caused instantaneous death. Such were the circumstances of the Park Lane Mystery, which were further complicated by entire absence of motive, since, as I have said, young Adair was not known to have any enemy, and no attempt had been made to remove the money or valuables in the room.

All day I turned these facts over in my mind, endeavouring to hit upon some theory which could reconcile them all, and to find that line of least resistance which my poor friend had declared to be the starting-point of every investigation. I confess that I made little progress. In the evening I strolled across the Park, and found myself about six o'clock at the Oxford Street end of Park Lane. A group of loafers upon the pavements, all staring up at a particular window, directed me to the house which I had come to see. A tall, thin man with coloured glasses, whom I strongly suspected of being a plain-clothes detective, was pointing out some theory of his own, while the others crowded round to listen to what he said. I got as near as I could, but his observations seemed to me to be absurd, so I withdrew again in some disgust. As I did so I struck against an elderly deformed man, who had been behind me, and I knocked down several books which he was carrying. I remember that as I picked them up I observed the title of one of them, *The Origin of Tree Worship*, and it struck me that the fellow must be some poor bibliophile who, either as a trade or as a hobby, was a collector of obscure volumes. I endeavoured to apologize for the accident, but it was evident that these books which I had so unfortunately maltreated were very precious objects in the eyes of their owner. With a snarl of contempt he turned upon his heel, and I saw his curved back and white side-whiskers disappear among the throng.

My observations of No. 427 Park Lane did little to clear up the problem in which I was interested. The house was separated from the street by a low wall and railing, the whole not more than five feet high. It was perfectly easy, therefore, for anyone to get into the garden ; but the window was entirely inaccessible, since there was no water-pipe or anything which could help the most active man to climb it. More puzzled than ever, I retraced my steps to Kensington. I had not been in my study five minutes when the maid entered to say that a person desired to see me. To my astonishment, it was none other than my strange old book-collector, his sharp, wizened face peering out from a frame of white hair, and his precious volumes, a dozen of them at least, wedged under his right arm.

" You're surprised to see me, sir," said he, in a strange, croaking voice.

I acknowledged that I was.

"Well, I've a conscience, sir, and when I chanced to see you go into this house, as I came hobbling after you, I thought to myself, I'll just step in and see that kind gentleman, and tell him that if I was a bit gruff in my manner there was not any harm meant, and that I am much obliged to him for picking up my books."

"You make too much of a trifle," said I. "May I ask how you knew who I was?"

"Well, sir, if it isn't too great a liberty, I am a neighbour of yours, for you'll find my little bookshop at the corner of Church Street, and very happy to see you, I am sure. Maybe you collect yourself, sir; here's *British Birds*, and *Catullus*, and *The Holy War*—a bargain every one of them. With five volumes you could just fill that gap on that second shelf. It looks untidy, does it not, sir?"

I moved my head to look at the cabinet behind me. When I turned again Sherlock Holmes was standing smiling at me across my study table. I rose to my feet, stared at him for some seconds in utter amazement, and then it appears that I must have fainted for the first and the last time in my life. Certainly a grey mist swirled before my eyes, and when it cleared I found my collar-ends undone and the tingling after-taste of brandy upon my lips. Holmes was bending over my chair, his flask in his hand.

"My dear Watson," said the well-remembered voice, "I owe you a thousand apologies. I had no idea that you would be so affected."

I gripped him by the arm.

"Holmes!" I cried. "Is it really you? Can it indeed be that you are alive? Is it possible that you succeeded in climbing out of that awful abyss?"

"Wait a moment!" said he. "Are you sure that you are really fit to discuss things? I have given you a serious shock by my unnecessarily dramatic appearance."

"I am all right; but indeed, Holmes, I can hardly believe my eyes. Good heavens, to think that you—you

564

of all men—should be standing in my study!" Again I gripped him by the sleeve and felt the thin, sinewy arm beneath it. "Well, you're not a spirit, anyhow," said I. "My dear chap, I am overjoyed to see you. Sit down, and tell me how you came alive out of that dreadful chasm."

He sat opposite to me and lit a cigarette in his old nonchalant manner. He was dressed in the seedy frock-coat of the book merchant, but the rest of that individual lay in a pile of white hair and old books upon the table. Holmes looked even thinner and keener than of old, but there was a dead-white tinge in his aquiline face which told me that his life recently had not been a healthy one.

"I am glad to stretch myself, Watson," said he. "It is no joke when a tall man has to take a foot off his stature for several hours on end. Now, my dear fellow, in the matter of these explanations we have, if I may ask for your co-operation, a hard and dangerous night's work in front of us. Perhaps it would be better if I gave you an account of the whole situation when that work is finished."

"I am full of curiosity. I should much prefer to hear now."

"You'll come with me to-night?"

"When you like and where you like."

"This is indeed like the old days. We shall have time for a mouthful of dinner before we need go. Well, then, about that chasm. I had no serious difficulty in getting out of it, for the very simple reason that I never was in it."

"You never were in it?"

"No, Watson, I never was in it. My note to you was absolutely genuine. I had little doubt that I had come to the end of my career when I perceived the somewhat sinister figure of the late Professor Moriarty standing upon the narrow pathway which led to safety. I read an inexorable purpose in his grey eyes. I exchanged some remarks with him, therefore, and obtained his courteous permission to write the short note which you afterwards received. I left it with my cigarette-box and my stick, and I walked along the pathway, Moriarty still at my heels. When I reached the end I stood at bay. He drew no weapon, but he rushed at me and threw his long arms around me. He knew that his own game was up, and was only anxious to revenge himself upon me. We tottered together upon the brink of the fall. I have some knowledge, however, of baritsu, or the Japanese system of wrestling, which has more than once been very useful to me. I slipped through his grip, and he with a horrible scream kicked madly for a few seconds and clawed the air with both his hands. But for all his efforts he could not get his balance, and over he went. With my face over the brink I saw him fall for a long way. Then he struck a rock, bounded off, and splashed into the water."

I listened with amazement to this explanation, which Holmes delivered between the puffs of his cigarette.

" But the tracks ! " I cried. " I saw with my own eyes that two went down the path and none returned."

" It came about in this way. The instant that the professor had disappeared it struck me what a really extraordinarily lucky chance Fate had placed in my way. I knew that Moriarty was not the only man who had sworn my death. There were at least three others whose desire for vengeance upon me would only be increased by the death of their leader. They were all most dangerous men. One or other would certainly get me. On the other hand, if all the world was convinced that I was dead they would take liberties, these men ; they would lay themselves open, and sooner or later I could destroy them. Then it would be time for me to announce that I was still in the land of the living. So rapidly does the brain act that I believe I had thought this all out before Professor Moriarty had reached the bottom of the Reichenbach Fall.

" I stood up and examined the rocky wall behind me.

In your picturesque account of the matter, which I read with great interest some months later, you assert that the wall was sheer. This was not literally true. A few small footholds presented themselves, and there was some indication of a ledge. The cliff is so high that to climb it all was an obvious impossibility, and it was equally impossible to make my way along the wet path without leaving some tracks. I might, it is true, have reversed my boots, as I have done on similar occasions, but the sight of three sets of tracks in one direction would certainly have suggested a deception. On the whole, then, it was best that I should risk the climb. It was not a pleasant business, Watson. The fall roared beneath me. I am not a fanciful person, but I give you my word that I seemed to hear Moriarty's voice screaming at me out of the abyss. A mistake would have been fatal. More than once, as tufts of grass came out in my hand or my foot slipped in the wet notches of the rock, I thought that I was gone. But I struggled upwards, and at last I reached a ledge several feet deep and covered with soft green moss, where I could lie unseen in the most perfect comfort. There I was stretched when you, my dear Watson, and all your following were investigating in the most sympathetic and inefficient manner the circumstances of my death.

" At last, when you had all formed your inevitable and totally erroneous conclusions, you departed for the hotel, and I was left alone. I had imagined that I had reached the end of my adventures, but a very unexpected occurrence showed me that there were surprises still in store for me. A huge rock, falling from above, boomed past me, struck the path, and bounded over into the chasm. For an instant I thought that it was an accident ; but a moment later, looking up, I saw a man's head against the darkening sky, and another stone struck the very ledge upon which I was stretched, within a foot of my head. Of course, the meaning of this was obvious. Moriarty had not been alone. A confederate—and even that one glance had told me how dangerous a man that confederate was—had kept guard while the professor had attacked me. From a distance, unseen by me, he had been a witness of his friend's death and of my escape. He had waited, and then, making his way round to the top of the cliff, he had endeavoured to succeed where his comrade had failed.

"I did not take long to think about it, Watson. Again I saw that grim face look over the cliff, and I knew that it was the precursor of another stone. I scrambled down on to the path. I don't think I could have done it in cold blood. It was a hundred times more difficult than getting up. But I had no time to think of the danger, for another stone sang past me as I hung by my hands from the edge of the ledge. Half-way down I slipped, but by the blessing of God I landed, torn and bleeding, upon the path. I took to my heels, did ten miles over the mountains in the darkness, and a week later I found myself in Florence, with the certainty that no one in the world knew what had become of me.

"I had only one confidant—my brother Mycroft. I owe you many apologies, my dear Watson, but it was all-important that it should be thought I was dead, and it is quite certain that you would not have written so convincing an account of my unhappy end had you not yourself thought that it was true. Several times during the last three years I have taken up my pen to write to you, but always I feared lest your affectionate regard for me should tempt you to some indiscretion which would betray my secret. For that reason I turned away from you this evening when you upset my books, for I was in danger at the time, and any show of surprise and emotion upon your part might have drawn attention to my identity and led to the most deplorable and irreparable results. As to Mycroft, I had to confide in him in order to obtain the money which I needed. The course of events in London did not run so well as I had hoped, for the trial of the Moriarty gang left two of its most dangerous members, my own most vindictive enemies, at liberty. I travelled for two years in Tibet, therefore, and amused myself by visiting Lhassa and spending some days with the head Llama. You may have read of the remarkable explorations of a Norwegian named Sigerson, but I am sure that it never occurred to you that you were receiving news of your friend. I then passed through Persia, looked in at Mecca, and paid a short but interesting visit to the Khalifa at Khartoum, the results of which I have communicated to the Foreign Office. Returning to France, I spent some months in a research into the coal-tar derivatives, which I conducted in a laboratory at Montpelier, in the south of France. Having concluded this to my satisfaction, and learning that only one of my enemies was now left in London, I was about to return, when my movements were hastened by the news of this remarkable Park Lane Mystery, which not only appealed to me by its own merits, but which seemed to offer some most peculiar personal opportunities. I came over at once to London, called in my own person at Baker Street, threw Mrs. Hudson into violent hysterics, and found that Mycroft had preserved my rooms and my papers exactly as they had always been. So it was, my dear Watson, that at two o'clock to-day I found myself in my old arm-chair in my own old room, and only wishing that I could have seen my old friend Watson in the other chair which he has so often adorned."

Such was the remarkable narrative to which I listened on that April evening—a narrative which would have been utterly incredible to me had it not been confirmed by the actual sight of the tall, spare figure and the keen, eager face which I had never thought to see again. In some manner he had learned of my own sad bereavement, and his sympathy was shown in his manner rather than in his words. "Work is the best antidote to sorrow, my dear Watson," said he, "and I have a piece of work for us both to-night which, if we can bring it to a successful conclusion, will in itself justify a man's life on this planet." In vain I begged him to tell me more. "You will hear and see enough before morning," he answered. "We have three years of the past to discuss. Let that suffice until half-past nine, when we start upon the notable adventure of the empty house."

It was indeed like old times when, at that hour, I found myself seated beside him in a hansom, my revolver in my pocket and the thrill of adventure in my heart. Holmes was cold and stern and silent. As the gleam of the street-lamps flashed upon his austere features, I saw that his brows were drawn down in thought and his thin lips compressed. I knew not what wild beast we were about to hunt down in the dark jungle of criminal London, but I was well assured from the bearing of this master huntsman that the adventure was a most grave one, while the sardonic smile which occasionally broke through his ascetic gloom boded little good for the object of our quest.

I had imagined that we were bound for Baker Street, but Holmes stopped the cab at the corner of Cavendish Square. I observed that as he stepped out he gave a most searching glance to right and left, and at every subsequent street corner he took the utmost pains to assure that he was not followed. Our route was certainly a singular one. Holmes' knowledge of the by-ways of London was extraordinary, and on this occasion he passed rapidly, and with an assured step, through a network of mews and stables the very existence of which I had never known. We emerged at last into a small road, lined with old, gloomy houses, which led us into Manchester Street, and so to Blandford Street. Here he turned swiftly down a narrow passage, passed through a wooden gate into a deserted yard, and then opened with a key the back door of a house. We entered together, and he closed it behind us.

The place was pitch dark, but it was evident to me that it was an empty house. Our feet creaked and crackled over the bare planking, and my outstretched hand touched a wall from which the paper was hanging in ribbons. Holmes' cold, thin fingers closed round my wrist and led me forward down a long hall, until I dimly saw the murky fanlight over the door. Here Holmes turned suddenly to the right, and we found ourselves in a large, square, empty room, heavily shadowed in the corners, but faintly lit in the centre from the lights of the street beyond. There was no lamp near, and the window was thick with dust, so that we could only just discern each other's figures within. My companion put his hand upon my shoulder, and his lips close to my ear.

" Do you know where we are ? " he whispered.

" Surely that is Baker Street," I answered, staring through the dim window.

" Exactly. We are in Camden House, which stands opposite to our own old quarters."

" But why are we here ? "

" Because it commands so excellent a view of that picturesque pile. Might I trouble you, my dear Watson, to draw a little nearer to the window, taking every precaution not to show yourself, and then to look up at our old rooms—the starting-point of so many of our little adventures ? We will see if my three years of absence have entirely taken away my power to surprise you."

I crept forward and looked across at the familiar window. As my eyes fell upon it I gave a gasp and a cry of amazement. The blind was down, and a strong light was burning in the room. The shadow of a man who was seated in a chair within was thrown in hard, black outline upon the luminous screen of the window. There was no mistaking the poise of the head, the squareness of the shoulders, the sharpness of the features. The face was turned half-round, and the effect was that of one of those black silhouettes which our grandparents loved to frame. It was a perfect reproduction of Holmes. So amazed was I that I threw out my hand to make sure that the man himself was standing beside me. He was quivering with silent laughter.

" Well ? " said he.

" Good heavens ! " I cried. " It's marvellous."

" I trust that age doth not wither nor custom stale my infinite variety," said he, and I recognized in his voice the joy and pride which the artist takes in his own creation. " It really is rather like me, is it not ? "

" I should be prepared to swear that it was you."

" The credit of the execution is due to Monsieur Oscar Meunier, of Grenoble, who spent some days in doing the moulding. It is a bust in wax. The rest I arranged myself during my visit to Baker Street this afternoon."

" But why ? "

" Because, my dear Watson, 1 had the strongest possible reason for wishing certain people to think that I was there when I was really elsewhere."

" And you thought the rooms were watched ? "

" I *knew* that they were watched."

" By whom ? "

" By my old enemies, Watson. By the charming society whose leader lies in the Reichenbach Fall. You must remember that they knew, and only they knew, that I was still alive. Sooner or later they believed that I should come back to my rooms. They watched them continuously, and this morning they saw me arrive."

" How do you know ? "

" Because I recognized their sentinel when I glanced out of my window. He is a harmless enough fellow, Parker by name, a garrotter by trade, and a remarkable performer upon the jews' harp. I cared nothing for him. But I cared a great deal for the much more formidable person who was behind him, the bosom friend of Moriarty, the man who dropped the rocks over the cliff, the most cunning and dangerous criminal in London. That is the man who is after me to-night, Watson, and that is the man who is quite unaware that we are after *him.*"

My friend's plans were gradually revealing themselves. From this convenient retreat the watchers were being watched and the trackers tracked. That angular shadow up yonder was the bait, and we were the hunters. In silence we stood together in the darkness and watched the hurrying figures who passed and repassed in front of us. Holmes was silent and motionless ; but I could tell that he was keenly alert, and that his eyes were fixed intently upon the stream of passers-by. It was a bleak and boisterous night, and the wind whistled shrilly down the long street. Many people were moving to and fro, most of them muffled in their coats and cravats. Once or twice it seemed to me that I had seen the same figure before, and I especially noticed two men who appeared to be sheltering themselves from the wind in the doorway of a house some distance up the street. I tried to draw my companion's attention to them, but he gave a little ejaculation of impatience, and continued to stare into the street. More than once he fidgeted with his feet and tapped rapidly with his fingers upon the wall. It was evident to me that he was becoming uneasy, and that his plans were not working out altogether as he had hoped. At last, as midnight approached and the street gradually cleared, he paced up and down the room in uncontrollable agitation. I was about to make some remark to him, when I raised my eyes to the lighted window, and again experienced almost as great a surprise as before. I clutched Holmes' arm and pointed upwards.

" The shadow has moved ! " I cried.

It was, indeed, no longer the profile, but the back which was turned towards us.

Three years had certainly not smoothed the asperities of his temper, or his impatience with a less active intelligence than his own.

" Of course it has moved," said he. " Am I such a farcical bungler, Watson, that I should erect an obvious dummy and expect that some of the sharpest men in Europe would be deceived by it ? We have been in this room two hours, and Mrs. Hudson has made some change in that figure eight times, or once every quarter of an hour. She works it from the front, so that her shadow may never be seen. Ah!" He drew in his breath with a shrill, excited intake. In the dim light I saw his head thrown forward, his whole attitude rigid with attention. Those two men might still be crouching in the doorway, but I could no longer see them. All was still and dark, save only that brilliant yellow screen in front of us with the black figure outlined upon its centre. Again in the utter silence I heard that thin, sibilant note which spoke of intense suppressed excitement. An instant later he pulled me back into the blackest corner of the room, and I felt his warning hand upon my lips. The fingers which clutched me were quivering. Never had I known my friend more moved, and yet the dark street still stretched lonely and motionless before us.

But suddenly I was aware of that which his keener senses had already distinguished. A low, stealthy sound came to my ears, not from the direction of Baker Street, but from the back of the very house in which we lay concealed. A door opened and shut. An instant later steps crept down the passage—steps which were meant to be silent, but which reverberated harshly through the empty house. Holmes crouched back against the wall, and I did the same, my hand closing upon the handle of my revolver. Peering through the gloom, I saw the vague outline of a man a shade blacker than the blackness of the open door. He stood for an instant, and then he crept forward, crouching, menacing, into the room. He was within three yards of us, this sinister figure, and I had braced myself to meet his spring, before I realized that he had no idea of our presence. He passed close beside us, stole over to the window, and very softly and noiselessly raised it for half a foot. As he sank to the level of this opening the light of the street, no longer dimmed by the dusty glass, fell full upon his face. The man seemed to be beside himself with excitement. His two eyes shone like stars, and his features were working convulsively. He was an elderly man, with a thin projecting nose, a high, bald forehead, and a huge grizzled moustache. An opera-hat was pushed to the back of his head, and an evening dress shirt-front gleamed out through his open overcoat. His face was gaunt and swarthy, scored with deep, savage lines. In his hand he carried what appeared to be a stick, but as he laid it down upon the floor it gave a metallic clang. Then from the pocket of his overcoat he drew a bulky object, and he busied himself in some task which ended with a loud, sharp click, as if a spring or bolt had fallen into its place. Still kneeling upon the floor, he bent forward and threw all his weight and strength upon some lever, with the result that there came a long, whirling, grinding noise, ending once more in a powerful click. He straightened himself then, and I saw that what he held in his hand was a sort of a gun, with a curiously misshapen butt. He opened it at the breech, put something in, and snapped the breech-block. Then, crouching down, he rested the end of the barrel upon the ledge of the open window, and I saw his long moustache droop over the stock and his eye gleam as it peered along the sights. I heard a little sigh of satisfaction as he cuddled the butt into his shoulder, and saw that amazing target, the black man on the yellow ground, standing clear at the end of his foresight. For an instant he was rigid and motionless. Then his finger tightened on the trigger. There was a strange, loud whiz and a long, silvery tinkle of broken glass. At that instant Holmes sprang like a tiger on to the marksman's back and hurled him flat upon his face. He was up again at a moment, and with convulsive strength he seized Holmes by the throat; but I struck him on the head with the butt of my revolver, and he dropped again upon the floor. I fell upon him, and as I held him my comrade blew a shrill call upon a whistle. There was the clatter of running feet upon the pavement, and two policemen in uniform, with one plain-clothes detective, rushed through the front entrance and into the room.

" That you, Lestrade ? " said Holmes.

" Yes, Mr. Holmes. I took the job myself. It's good to see you back in London, sir."

" I think you want a little unofficial help. Three undetected murders in one year won't do, Lestrade. But you handled the Molesey Mystery with less than your usual—that's to say, you handled it fairly well."

We had all risen to our feet, our prisoner breathing hard, with a stalwart constable on each side of him. Already a few loiterers had begun to collect in the street. Holmes stepped up to the window, closed it, and dropped the blinds. Lestrade had produced two candles, and the policemen had uncovered their lanterns. I was able at last to have a good look at our prisoner.

It was a tremendously virile and yet sinister face which was turned towards us. With the brow of a philosopher above and the jaw of a sensualist below, the man must have started with great capacities for good or for evil. But one could not look upon his cruel blue eyes, with their drooping, cynical lids, or upon the fierce, aggressive nose and the threatening, deep-lined brow, without reading Nature's plainest danger-signals. He took no heed of any of us, but his eyes were fixed upon Holmes' face with an expression in which hatred and amazement were equally blended. " You fiend ! " he kept on muttering —" you clever, clever fiend ! "

" Ah, colonel," said Holmes, arranging his rumpled collar, " ' journeys end in lovers' meetings,' as the old play says. I don't think I have had the pleasure of seeing you since you favoured me with those attentions as I lay on the ledge above the Reichenbach Fall."

The colonel still stared at my friend like a man in a trance. " You cunning, cunning fiend ! " was all that he could say.

" I have not introduced you yet," said Holmes. " This, gentlemen, is Colonel Sebastian Moran, once of

Her Majesty's Indian Army, and the best heavy game shot that our Eastern Empire has ever produced. I believe I am correct, colonel, in saying that your bag of tigers still remain unrivalled ? "

The fierce old man said nothing, but still glared at my companion ; with his savage eyes and bristling moustache, he was wonderfully like a tiger himself.

" I wonder that my very simple stratagem could deceive so old a shikari," said Holmes. " It must be very familiar to you. Have you not tethered a young kid under a tree, lain above it with your rifle, and waited for the bait to bring up your tiger ? This empty house is my tree, and you are my tiger. You have possibly had other guns in reserve in case there should be several tigers, or in the unlikely supposition of your own aim failing you. These," he pointed around, " are my other guns. The parallel is exact."

Colonel Moran sprang forward with a snarl of rage, but the constables dragged him back. The fury upon his face was terrible to look at.

" I confess that you had one small surprise for me," said Holmes. " I did not anticipate that you would yourself make use of this empty house and this convenient front window. I had imagined you as operating from the street, where my friend Lestrade and his merry men were awaiting you. With that exception, all has gone as I expected."

Colonel Moran turned to the official detective.

" You may or may not have just cause for arresting me," said he, " but at least there can be no reason why I should submit to the gibes of this person. If I am in the hands of the law, let things be done in a legal way."

" Well, that's reasonable enough," said Lestrade. " Nothing further you have to say, Mr. Holmes, before we go ? "

Holmes had picked up the powerful air-gun from the floor, and was examining its mechanism.

" An admirable and unique weapon," said he, " noiseless and of tremendous power. I knew Von Herder, the blind German mechanic, who constructed it to the order of the late Professor Moriarty. For years I have been aware of its existence, though I have never before had an opportunity of handling it. I commend it very specially to your attention, Lestrade, and also the bullets which fit it."

"You can trust us to look after that, Mr. Holmes," said Lestrade, as the whole party moved towards the door. "Anything further to say?"

"Only to ask what charge you intend to prefer?"

"What charge, sir? Why, of course, the attempted murder of Mr. Sherlock Holmes."

"Not so, Lestrade. I do not propose to appear in the matter at all. To you, and to you only, belongs the credit of the remarkable arrest which you have effected. Yes, Lestrade, I congratulate you! With your usual happy mixture of cunning and audacity you have got him."

"Got him! Got whom, Mr. Holmes?"

"The man whom the whole Force has been seeking in vain—Colonel Sebastian Moran, who shot the Honourable Ronald Adair with an expanding bullet from an air-gun through the open window of the second-floor front of No. 427 Park Lane, upon the 30th of last month. That's the charge, Lestrade. And now, Watson, if you can endure the draught from a broken window, I think that half an hour in my study over a cigar may afford you some profitable amusement."

Our old chambers had been left unchanged, through the supervision of Mycroft Holmes and the immediate care of Mrs. Hudson. As I entered I saw, it is true, an unwonted tidiness, but the old landmarks were all in their places. There were the chemical corner and the acid-stained deal-topped table. There upon a shelf was the row of formidable scrap-books and books of reference which many of our fellow-citizens would have been so glad to burn. The diagrams, the violin-case, and the pipe-rack—even the Persian slipper which contained the tobacco—all met my eye as I glanced round me. There were two occupants of the room—one Mrs. Hudson, who beamed upon us both as we entered; the other, the strange dummy which had played so important a part in the evening's adventures. It was a wax-coloured model of my friend, so admirably done that it was a perfect facsimile. It stood on a small pedestal table with an old dressing-gown of Holmes' so draped round it that the illusion from the street was absolutely perfect.

"I hope you preserved all precautions, Mrs. Hudson?" said Holmes.

"I went to it on my knees, sir, just as you told me."

"Excellent. You carried the thing out very well. Did you observe where the bullet went?"

"Yes, sir. I'm afraid it has spoilt your beautiful bust, for it passed right through the head and flattened itself on the wall. I picked it up from the carpet. Here it is!"

Holmes held it out to me. "A soft revolver bullet, as you perceive, Watson. There's genius in that—for who would expect to find such a thing fired from an air-gun? All right, Mrs. Hudson, I am much obliged for your assistance. And now, Watson, let me see you in your old seat once more, for there are several points which I should like to discuss with you."

He had thrown off the seedy frock-coat, and now he was the Holmes of old, in the mouse-coloured dressing-gown which he took from his effigy.

"The old shikari's nerves have not lost their steadiness nor his eyes their keenness," said he, with a laugh, as he inspected the shattered forehead of his bust.

"Plumb in the middle of the back of the head and smack through the brain. He was the best shot in India, and I expect that there are few better in London. Have you heard the name?"

"No, I have not."

"Well, well, such is fame! But then, if I remember aright, you had not heard the name of Professor James Moriarty, who had one of the great brains of the century. Just give me down my index of biographies from the shelf."

He turned over the pages lazily, leaning back in his chair and blowing great clouds of smoke from his cigar.

"My collection of M's is a fine one," said he. "Moriarty himself is enough to make any letter illustrious, and here is Morgan the poisoner, and Merridew of abominable memory, and Mathews, who knocked out my left canine in the waiting-room at Charing Cross, and, finally, here is our friend of to-night."

He handed over the book, and I read: "*Moran, Sebastian, Colonel*. Unemployed. Formerly 1st Bengalore Pioneers. Born London, 1840. Son of Sir Augustus Moran, C.B., once British Minister to Persia. Educated Eton and Oxford. Served in Jowaki Campaign, Afghan Campaign, Charasiab (dispatches), Sherpur, and Cabul. Author of *Heavy Game of the Western Himalayas*, 1881; *Three Months in the Jungle*, 1884. Address: Conduit Street. Clubs: The Anglo-Indian, the Tankerville, the Bagatelle Card Club."

On the margin was written in Holmes' precise hand: "The second most dangerous man in London."

"This is astonishing," said I, as I handed back the volume. "The man's career is that of an honourable soldier."

"It is true," Holmes answered. "Up to a certain point he did well. He was always a man of iron nerve, and the story is still told in India how he crawled down a drain after a wounded man-eating tiger. There are some trees, Watson, which grow to a certain height and then suddenly develop some unsightly eccentricity. You will see it often in humans. I have a theory that the individual represents in his development the whole procession of his ancestors, and that such a sudden turn to good or evil stands for some strong influence which came into the line of his pedigree. The person becomes, as it were, the epitome of the history of his own family."

"It is surely rather fanciful."

"Well, I don't insist upon it. Whatever the cause, Colonel Moran began to go wrong. Without any open scandal, he still made India too hot to hold him. He retired, came to London, and again acquired an evil name. It was at this time that he was sought out by Professor Moriarty, to whom for a time he was chief of the staff. Moriarty supplied him liberally with money, and used him only in one or two very high-class jobs which no ordinary criminal could have undertaken. You may have some recollection of the death of Mrs. Stewart, of Lauder, in 1887. Not? Well, I am sure Moran was at the bottom of it; but nothing could be proved. So cleverly was the colonel concealed that even when the Moriarty gang was broken up we could not incriminate him. You remember at that date, when I called upon you in your rooms, how I put up the shutters for fear of air-guns? No doubt you thought me fanciful. I knew exactly what I was doing, for I knew of the existence of this remarkable gun, and I knew also that one of the best shots in the world would be behind it. When we were in Switzerland he followed us with Moriarty, and it was undoubtedly he who gave me that evil five minutes on the Reichenbach ledge.

"You may think that I read the papers with some attention during my sojourn in France, on the look-out for any chance of laying him by the heels. So long as he was free in London my life would really not have been worth living. Night and day the shadow would have been over me, and sooner or later his chance must have come. What could I do? I could not shoot him at sight, or I should myself be in the dock. There was no use appealing to a magistrate. They cannot interfere on the strength of what would appear to them to be a wild suspicion. So I could do nothing. But I watched the criminal news, knowing that sooner or later I should

get him. Then came the death of this Ronald Adair.
My chance had come at last! Knowing what I did,
was it not certain that Colonel Moran had done it? He
had played cards with the lad; he had followed him
home from the club; he had shot him through the open
window. There was not a doubt of it. The bullets
alone are enough to put his head in a noose. I came
over at once. I was seen by the sentinel, who would, I
knew, direct the colonel's attention to my presence.
He could not fail to connect my sudden return with his
crime, and to be terribly alarmed. I was sure that
he would make an attempt to get me out of the way *at
once*, and would bring round his murderous weapon for
that purpose. I left him an excellent mark in the window, and, having warned the police that they might be
needed—by the way, Watson, you spotted their presence
in that doorway with unerring accuracy—I took up what
seemed to me to be a judicious post for observation, never
dreaming that he would choose the same spot for his
attack. Now, my dear Watson, does anything remain
for me to explain?"

"Yes," said I. "You have not made it clear what was
Colonel Moran's motive in murdering the Honourable
Ronald Adair."

"Ah! my dear Watson, there we come into those
realms of conjecture where the most logical mind may be
at fault. Each may form his own hypothesis upon the
present evidence, and yours is as likely to be correct as
mine."

"You have formed one, then?"

"I think that is not difficult to explain the facts. It
came out in evidence that Colonel Moran and young
Adair had between them won a considerable amount of
money. Now, Moran undoubtedly played foul—of that
I have long been aware. I believe that on the day of the
murder, Adair had discovered that Moran was cheating.
Very likely he had spoken to him privately, and had
threatened to expose him unless he voluntarily resigned

his membership of the club and promised not to play cards again. It is unlikely that a youngster like Adair would at once make a hideous scandal by exposing a well-known man so much older than himself. Probably he acted as I suggest. The exclusion from his clubs would mean ruin to Moran, who lived by his ill-gotten card gains. He therefore murdered Adair, who at the time was endeavouring to work out how much money he should himself return, since he could not profit by his partner's foul play. He locked the door, lest the ladies should surprise him and insist upon knowing what he was doing with these names and coins. Will it pass ? "

" I have no doubt that you have hit upon the truth."

" It will be verified or disproved at the trial. Meanwhile, come what may, Colonel Moran will trouble us no more, the famous air-gun of Von Herder will embellish the Scotland Yard Museum, and once again Mr. Sherlock Holmes is free to devote his life to examining those interesting little problems which the complex life of London so plentifully presents."

25. *The Norwood Builder*

" FROM the point of view of the criminal expert," said Mr. Sherlock Holmes, " London has become a singularly uninteresting city since the death of the late lamented Professor Moriarty."

" I can hardly think that you would find many decent citizens to agree with you," I answered.

" Well, well, I must not be selfish," said he, with a smile, as he pushed back his chair from the breakfast-table. " The community is certainly the gainer, and no one the loser, save the poor out-of-work specialist, whose occupation has gone. With that man in the field one's morning paper presented infinite possibilities. Often it was only the smallest trace, Watson, the faintest indication, and yet it was enough to tell me that the great malignant brain was there, as the gentlest tremors of the edges of the web remind one of the foul spider which lurks in the centre. Petty thefts, wanton assaults, purposeless outrage—to the man who held the clue all could be worked into one connected whole. To the scientific student of the higher criminal world no capital in Europe offered the advantages which London then possessed. But now——" He shrugged his shoulders in humorous deprecation of the state of things which he had himself done so much to produce.

At the time of which I speak, Holmes had been back for some months, and I, at his request, had sold my practice and returned to share the old quarters in Baker Street. A young doctor, named Verner, had purchased my small Kensington practice, and given with astonishingly little demur the highest price that I ventured to ask—an incident which only explained itself some years later, when I found that Verner was a distant relation of Holmes', and that it was my friend who had really found the money.

Our months of partnership had not been so uneventful as he had stated, for I find, on looking over my notes, that this period includes the case of the papers of ex-President Murillo, and also the shocking affair of the Dutch steamship, *Friesland*, which so nearly cost us both our lives. His cold and proud nature was always averse, however, to anything in the shape of public applause, and he bound me in the most stringent terms to say no further word of himself, his methods, or his successes—a prohibition which, as I have explained, has only now been removed.

Mr. Sherlock Holmes was leaning back in his chair after his whimsical protest, and was unfolding his morning paper in a leisurely fashion, when our attention was arrested by a tremendous ring at the bell, followed immediately by a hollow drumming sound, as if someone were beating on the outer door with his fist. As it opened there came a tumultuous rush into the hall, rapid feet clattered up the stair, and an instant later a wild-eyed and frantic young man, pale, dishevelled, and palpitating, burst into the room. He looked from one to the other of us, and under our gaze of inquiry he became conscious that some apology was needed for this unceremonious entry.

"I'm sorry, Mr. Holmes," he cried. "You mustn't blame me. I am nearly mad. Mr. Holmes, I am the unhappy John Hector McFarlane."

He made the announcement as if the name alone would explain both his visit and its manner, but I could see by my companion's unresponsive face that it meant no more to him than to me.

"Have a cigarette, Mr. McFarlane," said he, pushing his case across. "I am sure that with your symptoms my friend Dr. Watson here would prescribe a sedative. The weather has been so very warm these last few days. Now, if you feel a little more composed, I should be glad if you would sit down in that chair and tell us very slowly and quietly who you are and what it is that you want. You mentioned your name as if I should recognize it, but I assure you that, beyond obvious facts that you are a bachelor, a solicitor, a Freemason, and an asthmatic, I know nothing whatever about you."

Familiar as I was with my friend's methods, it was not difficult for me to follow his deductions, and to observe the untidiness of attire, the sheaf of legal papers, the watch-charm, and the breathing which had prompted them. Our client, however, stared in amazement.

"Yes, I am all that, Mr. Holmes, and in addition I am the most unfortunate man at this moment in London. For Heaven's sake don't abandon me, Mr. Holmes! If they come to arrest me before I have finished my story, make them give me time, so that I may tell you the whole truth. I could go to gaol happy if I knew that you were working for me outside."

"Arrest you!" said Holmes. "This is really most grati—most interesting. On what charge do you expect to be arrested?"

"Upon the charge of murdering Mr. Jonas Oldacre, of Lower Norwood."

My companion's expressive face showed a sympathy which was not, I am afraid, unmixed with satisfaction.

"Dear me!" said he; "it was only this moment at breakfast that I was saying to my friend, Dr. Watson, that sensational cases had disappeared out of our papers."

Our visitor stretched forward a quivering hand and picked up the *Daily Telegraph*, which still lay upon Holmes' knee.

"If you had looked at it, sir, you would have seen at a glance what the errand is on which I have come to you this morning. I feel as if my name and my misfortune must be in every man's mouth." He turned it over to expose the central page. "Here it is, and with your permission I will read it to you. Listen to this, Mr. Holmes. The headlines are: 'Mysterious affair at Lower Norwood. Disappearance of a Well-known Builder. Suspicion of Murder and Arson. A Clue to the Criminal.' That is the clue which they are already following, Mr. Holmes, and I know that it leads infallibly to me. I have been followed from London Bridge Station, and I am sure that they are only waiting for the warrant to arrest me. It will break my mother's heart—it will break her heart!" He wrung his hands in an agony of apprehension, and swayed backwards and forwards in his chair.

I looked with interest upon this man, who was accused of being the perpetrator of a crime of violence. He was flaxen-haired and handsome in a washed-out negative fashion, with frightened blue eyes and a clean-shaven face, with a weak, sensitive mouth. His age may have been about twenty-seven; his dress and bearing, that of a gentleman. From the pocket of his light summer overcoat protruded the bundle of endorsed papers which proclaimed his profession.

"We must use what time we have," said Holmes.

" Watson, would you have the kindness to take the paper and to read me the paragraph in question ? "

Underneath the vigorous headlines which our client had quoted I read the following suggestive narrative :

Late last night, or early this morning, an incident occurred at Lower Norwood which points, it is feared, to a serious crime. Mr. Jonas Oldacre is a well-known resident of that suburb, where he has carried on his business as a builder for many years. Mr. Oldacre is a bachelor, fifty-two years of age, and lives in Deep Dene House, at the Sydenham end of the road of that name. He has had the reputation of being a man of eccentric habits, secretive and retiring. For some years he has practically withdrawn from the business, in which he is said to have amassed considerable wealth. A small timber-yard still exists, however, at the back of the house, and last night, about twelve o'clock, an alarm was given that one of the stacks was on fire. The engines were soon upon the spot, but the dry wood burned with great fury, and it was impossible to arrest the conflagration until the stack had been entirely consumed. Up to this point the incident bore the appearance of an ordinary accident, but fresh indications seem to point to serious crime. Surprise was expressed at the absence of the master of the establishment from the scene of the fire, and an inquiry followed which showed that he had disappeared from the house. An examination of his room revealed that the bed had not been slept in, that a safe which stood in it was open, that a number of important papers were scattered about the room, and, finally, that there were signs of a murderous struggle, slight traces of blood being found within the room, and an oaken walking-stick which also showed stains of blood upon the handle. It is known that Mr. Jonas Oldacre had received a late visitor in his bedroom upon that night, and the stick found has been identified as the property of this person, who is a young London solicitor named John Hector McFarlane, junior partner of Graham & McFarlane, of 426 Gresham Buildings, E.C. The police believe that they have evidence in their possession which supplies a very convincing motive for the crime, and altogether it cannot be doubted that sensational developments will follow.

LATER.—It is rumoured as we go to press that Mr. John Hector McFarlane has actually been arrested on the charge of the murder of Mr. Jonas Oldacre. It is at least certain that a warrant has been issued. There have been further and sinister developments in the investigation at Norwood.

Besides the signs of a struggle in the room of the unfortunate builder, it is now known that the French windows of his bedroom (which is on the ground floor) were found to be open, that there were marks as if some bulky object had been dragged across to the wood-pile, and, finally, it is asserted that charred remains have been found among the charcoal ashes of the fire. The police theory is that a most sensational crime has been committed, that the victim was clubbed to death in his own bedroom, his papers rifled, and his dead body dragged across to the wood-stack, which was then ignited so as to hide all traces of the crime. The conduct of the criminal investigation has been left in the experienced hands of Inspector Lestrade, of Scotland Yard, who is following up the clues with his accustomed energy and sagacity.

Sherlock Holmes listened with closed eyes and finger-tips together to this remarkable account.

"The case has certainly some points of interest," said he, in his languid fashion. "May I ask, in the first place, Mr. McFarlane, how it is that you are still at liberty, since there appears to be enough evidence to justify your arrest?"

"I live at Torrington Lodge, Blackheath, with my parents, Mr. Holmes; but last night, having to do business very late with Mr. Jonas Oldacre, I stayed at an hotel in Norwood, and came to my business from there. I knew nothing of this affair until I was in the train, when I read what you have just heard. I at once saw the horrible danger of my position, and I hurried to put the case into your hands. I have no doubt that I should have been arrested either at my City office or at my home. A man followed me from London Bridge Station, and I have no doubt—— Great heaven, what is that?"

It was a clang of the bell, followed instantly by heavy steps upon the stair. A moment later our old friend Lestrade appeared in the doorway. Over his shoulder I caught a glimpse of one or two uniformed policemen outside.

"Mr. John Hector McFarlane," said Lestrade.

Our unfortunate client rose with a ghastly face.

"I arrest you for the wilful murder of Mr. Jonas Oldacre, of Lower Norwood."

McFarlane turned to us with a gesture of despair, and sank into his chair once more like one who is crushed.

"One moment, Lestrade," said Holmes. "Half an hour more or less can make no difference to you, and the gentleman was about to give us an account of this very interesting affair, which might aid us in clearing it up."

"I think there will be no difficulty in clearing it up," said Lestrade grimly.

"None the less, with your permission, I should be much interested to hear his account."

"Well, Mr. Holmes, it is difficult for me to refuse you anything, for you have been of use to the Force once or twice in the past, and we owe you a good turn at Scotland Yard," said Lestrade. "At the same time, I must remain with my prisoner, and I am bound to warn him that anything he may say will appear in evidence against him."

"I wish nothing better," said our client. "All I ask is that you should hear and recognize the absolute truth."

Lestrade looked at his watch. "I'll give you half an hour," said he.

"I must explain first," said McFarlane, "that I knew nothing of Mr. Jonas Oldacre. His name was familiar to me; for many years ago my parents were acquainted with him, but they drifted apart. I was very much surprised, therefore, when yesterday, about three o'clock in the afternoon, he walked into my office in the City. But I was still more astonished when he told me the object of his visit. He had in his hand several sheets of a note-book, covered with scribbled writing—here they are—and he laid them on my table.

"'Here is my will,' said he. 'I want you, Mr. Mc-Farlane, to cast it into proper legal shape. I will sit here while you do so.'"

" I set myself to copy it, and you can imagine my astonishment when I found that, with some reservations, he had left all his property to me. He was a strange, little, ferret-like man, with white eyelashes, and when I looked up at him I found his keen grey eyes fixed upon me with an amused expression. I could hardly believe my own senses as I read the terms of the will; but he explained that he was a bachelor with hardly any living relation, that he had known my parents in his youth, and that he had always heard of me as a very deserving young man, and was assured that his money would be in worthy hands. Of course, I could only stammer out my thanks. The will was duly finished, signed, and witnessed by my clerk. This is it on the blue paper, and these slips, as I have explained, are the rough draft. Mr. Jonas Oldacre then informed me that there were a number of documents—building leases, title-deeds, mortgages, scrip, and so forth—which it was necessary that I should see and understand. He said that his mind would not be easy until the whole thing was settled, and he begged me to come out to his house at Norwood that night, bringing the will with me, and to arrange matters. ' Remember, my boy, not one word to your parents about the affair until everything is settled. We will keep it as a little surprise for them.' He was very insistent upon this point, and made me promise it faithfully.

" You can imagine, Mr. Holmes, that I was not in a humour to refuse him anything that he might ask. He was my benefactor, and all my desire was to carry out his wishes in every particular. I sent a telegram home, therefore, to say that I had important business on hand, and that it was impossible for me to say how late I might be. Mr. Oldacre had told me that he would like me to have supper with him at nine, as he might not be home before that hour. I had some difficulty in finding his house, however, and it was nearly half-past before I reached it. I found him——"

" One moment ! " said Holmes. " Who opened the door ? "

" A middle-aged woman, who was, I suppose, his housekeeper."

" And it was she, I presume, who mentioned your name ? "

" Exactly," said McFarlane.

" Pray proceed."

Mr. McFarlane wiped his damp brow, and then continued his narrative :

" I was shown by this woman into a sitting-room, where a frugal supper was laid out. Afterwards Mr. Jonas Oldacre led me into his bedroom, in which there stood a heavy safe. This he opened and took out a mass of documents, which we went over together. It was between eleven and twelve when we finished. He remarked that we must not disturb the housekeeper. He showed me out through his own French window, which had been open all this time."

" Was the blind down ? " asked Holmes.

" I will not be sure, but I believe that it was only half down. Yes, I remember how he pulled it up in order to swing open the window. I could not find my stick, and he said, ' Never mind, my boy ; I shall see a good deal of you now, I hope, and I will keep your stick until you come back to claim it.' I left him there, the safe open, and the papers made up in packets upon the table. It was so late that I could not get back to Blackheath, so I spent the night at the ' Anerley Arms,' and I knew nothing more until I read of this horrible affair in the morning."

" Anything more that you would like to ask, Mr. Holmes ? " said Lestrade, whose eyebrows had gone up once or twice during this remarkable explanation.

" Not until I have been to Blackheath."

" You mean to Norwood," said Lestrade.

" Oh, yes ; no doubt that is what I must have meant," said Holmes, with his enigmatical smile. Lestrade had learned by more experiences than he would care to acknowledge that that razor-like brain could cut through that which was impenetrable to him. I saw him look curiously at my companion.

"I think I should like to have a word with you presently, Mr. Sherlock Holmes," said he. "Now, Mr. McFarlane, two of my constables are at the door, and there is a four-wheeler waiting." The wretched young man arose, and with a last beseeching glance at us he walked from the room. The officers conducted him to the cab, but Lestrade remained.

Holmes had picked up the pages which formed the rough draft of the will, and was looking at them with the keenest interest upon his face.

"There are some points about that document, Lestrade, are there not?" said he pushing them over.

The official looked at them with a puzzled expression.

"I can read the first few lines, and these in the middle of the second page, and one or two at the end. Those are as clear as print," said he; "but the writing in between is very bad, and there are three places where I cannot read it at all."

"What do you make of that?" said Holmes.

"Well, what do *you* make of it?"

"That it was written in a train; the good writing represents stations, the bad writing movement, and the very bad writing passing over points. A scientific expert would pronounce at once that this was drawn up on a suburban line, since nowhere save in the immediate vicinity of a great city could there be so quick a succession of points. Granting that his whole journey was occupied in drawing up the will, then the train was an express, only stopping once between Norwood and London Bridge."

Lestrade began to laugh.

"You are too many for me when you begin to get on your theories, Mr. Holmes," said he. "How does this bear on the case?"

"Well, it corroborates the young man's story to the extent that the will was drawn up by Jonas Oldacre in his journey yesterday. It is curious—is it not?—that a man should draw up so important a document in so haphazard a fashion. It suggests that he did not think it was going to be of much practical importance. If a man drew up a will which he did not intend ever to be effective he might do it so."

"Well, he drew up his own death-warrant at the same time," said Lestrade.

"Oh, you think so?"

"Don't you?"

"Well, it is quite possible; but the case is not clear to me yet."

"Not clear? Well, if that isn't clear, what *could* be clearer? Here is a young man who learns suddenly that if a certain older man dies he will succeed to a fortune. What does he do? He says nothing to anyone but he arranges that he shall go out on some pretext to see his client that night; he waits until the only other person in the house is in bed, and then in the solitude of the man's room he murders him, burns his body in the wood-pile, and departs to a neighbouring hotel. The blood-stains in the room and also on the stick are very slight. It is probable that he imagined his crime to be a bloodless one, and hoped that if the body were consumed it would hide all traces of the method of his death—traces which for some reason must have pointed to him. Is all this not obvious?"

"It strikes me, my good Lestrade, as being just a trifle too obvious," said Holmes. "You do not add imagination to your other great qualities; but if you could for one moment put yourself in the place of this young man, would you choose the very night after the will had been made to commit your crime? Would it not seem dangerous to you to make so very close a relation between the two incidents? Again, would you choose an occasion when you are known to be in the house, when a servant

has let you in ? And, finally, would you take the great
pains to conceal the body and yet leave your own stick as
a sign that you were the criminal ? Confess, Lestrade,
that all this is very unlikely."

" As to the stick, Mr. Holmes, you know as well as I do
that a criminal is often flurried and does things which a
cool man would avoid. He was very likely afraid to go
back to the room. Give me another theory that would fit
the facts."

" I could very easily give you half a dozen," said
Holmes. " Here, for example, is a very possible and even
probable one. I make you a free present of it. The
older man is showing documents which are of evident
value. A passing tramp sees them through the window,
the blind of which is only half down. Exit the solicitor.
Enter the tramp ! He seizes a stick, which he observes
there, kills Oldacre, and departs after burning the body."

" Why should the tramp burn the body ? "

" For the matter of that, why should McFarlane ? "

" To hide some evidence."

" Possibly the tramp wanted to hide that any murder
at all had been committed."

" And why did the tramp take nothing ? "

" Because they were papers that he could not negotiate."

Lestrade shook his head, though it seemed to me that his
manner was less absolutely assured than before.

" Well, Mr. Sherlock Holmes, you may look for your
tramp, and while you are finding him we will hold on to
our man. The future will show which is right. Just
notice this point, Mr. Holmes—that so far as we know
none of the papers were removed, and that the prisoner
is the one man in the world who had no reason for
removing them since he was heir-at-law and would
come into them in any case."

My friend seemed struck by this remark.

" I don't mean to deny that the evidence is in some ways
very strongly in favour of your theory," said he. " I only

wish to point out that there are other theories possible. As you say, the future will decide. Good morning ! I dare say that in the course of the day I shall drop in at Norwood and see how you are getting on."

When the detective departed my friend rose and made his preparations for the day's work with the alert air of a man who has a congenial task before him.

" My first movement, Watson," said he, as he bustled into his frock-coat, " must, as I said, be in the direction of Blackheath."

" And why not Norwood ? "

" Because we have in this case one singular incident coming close to the heels of another singular incident. The police are making the mistake of concentrating their attention upon the second because it happens to be the one which is actually criminal. But it is evident to me that the logical way to approach the case is to begin by trying to throw some light upon the first incident—the curious will, so suddenly made, and to so unexpected an heir. It may do something to simplify what followed. No, my dear fellow, I don't think you can help me. There is no prospect of danger, or I should not dream of stirring out without you. I trust that when I see you in the evening I will be able to report that I have been able to do something for this unfortunate youngster who has thrown himself upon my protection."

It was late when my friend returned, and I could see by a glance at his haggard and anxious face that the high hopes with which he had started had not been fulfilled. For an hour he droned away upon his violin, endeavouring to soothe his own ruffled spirits. At last he flung down the instrument and plunged into a detailed account of his misadventures.

" It's all going wrong, Watson—all as wrong as it can go. I kept a bold face before Lestrade, but, upon my soul, I believe that for once the fellow is on the right track and we are on the wrong. All my instincts are one way, and all the facts are the other, and I much

fear that British juries have not yet attained that pitch
of intelligence when they will give the preference to
my theories over Lestrade's facts."

" Did you go to Blackheath ? "

" Yes, Watson, I went there, and I found very quickly
that the late lamented Oldacre was a pretty considerable
blackguard. The father was away in search of his son.
The mother was at home—a little, fluffy, blue-eyed
person, in a tremor of fear and indignation. Of course,
she would not admit even the possibility of his guilt.
But she would not express either surprise or regret over
the fate of Oldacre. On the contrary, she spoke of him
with such bitterness that she was unconsciously considerably strengthening the case of the police ; for, of course,
if her son had heard her speak of the man in that fashion
it would predispose him towards hatred and violence.
' He was more like a malignant and cunning ape than
a human being,' said she, ' and he always was, ever
since he was a young man.'

" ' You knew him at the time ? ' said I.

" ' Yes, I knew him well ; in fact, he was an old suitor
of mine. Thank Heaven that I had the sense to turn
away from him and to marry a better, if a poorer, man.
I was engaged to him, Mr. Holmes, when I heard a
shocking story of how he had turned a cat loose in an
aviary, and I was so horrified at his brutal cruelty that
I would have nothing more to do with him.' She
rummaged in a bureau, and presently she produced a
photograph of a woman, shamefully defaced and mutilated with a knife. ' That is my own photograph,' said
she. ' He sent it to me in that state, with his curse,
upon my wedding morning.'

" ' Well,' said I, ' at least he has forgiven you now,
since he has left all his property to your son.'

" ' Neither my son nor I want anything from Jonas
Oldacre, dead or alive,' she cried, with a proper spirit.
' There is a God in heaven, Mr. Holmes, and that same
God who has punished that wicked man will show in

His own good time that my son's hands are guiltless of his blood.'

" Well, I tried one or two leads, but could get at nothing which would help our hypothesis, and several points which would make against it. I gave it up at last, and off I went to Norwood.

" This place, Deep Dene House, is a big modern villa of staring brick, standing back in its own grounds, with a laurel-clumped lawn in front of it. To the right and some distance back from the road was the timber-yard which had been the scene of the fire. Here's a rough plan on a leaf of my notebook. This window on the left is the one which opens into Oldacre's room. You can look into it from the road, you see. That is about the only bit of consolation I have had to-day. Lestrade was not there, but his head constable did the honours. They had just made a great treasure-trove. They had spent the morning raking among the ashes of the burned wood-pile, and besides the charred organic remains they had secured several discoloured metal discs. I examined them with care, and there was no doubt that they were trouser buttons. I even distinguished that one of them was marked with the name of ' Hyams,' who was Oldacre's tailor. I then worked the lawn very carefully for signs and traces, but this drought has made everything as hard as iron. Nothing was to be seen save that somebody or a bundle had been dragged through a low privet hedge which is in a line with the wood-pile. All that, of course, fits in with the official theory. I crawled about the lawn with an August sun on my back. But I got up at the end of an hour no wiser than before.

" Well, after this fiasco I went into the bedroom and examined that also. The blood-stains were very slight, mere smears and discolorations, but undoubtedly fresh. The stick had been removed, but there also the marks were slight. There is no doubt about the stick belonging to our client. He admits it. Footmarks of both men could be made out on the carpet, but none of any third person, .

which again is a trick for the other side. They were piling up their score all the time, and we were at a standstill.

" Only one little gleam of hope did I get—and yet it amounted to nothing. I examined the contents of the safe, most of which had been taken out and left on the table. The papers had been made up into sealed envelopes, one or two of which had been opened by the police. They were not, so far as I could judge, of any great value, nor did the bank book show that Mr. Oldacre was in such very affluent circumstances. But it seemed to me that all the papers were not there. There were allusions to some deeds—possibly the more valuable —which I could not find. This, of course, if we could definitely prove it, would turn Lestrade's argument against himself, for who would steal a thing if he knew that he would shortly inherit it ?

" Finally, having drawn every other cover and picked up no scent, I tried my luck with the housekeeper. Mrs. Lexington is her name, a little, dark, silent person, with suspicious and sidelong eyes. She could tell us something if she would—I am convinced of it. But she was as close as wax. Yes, she had let Mr. McFarlane in at half-past nine. She wished her hand had withered before she had done so. She had gone to bed at half-past ten. Her room was at the other end of the house, and she could hear nothing of what passed. Mr. McFarlane had left his hat, and to the best of her belief his stick, in the hall. She had been awakened by the alarm of fire. Her poor, dear master had certainly been murdered. Had he any enemies ? Well, every man had enemies, but Mr. Oldacre kept himself very much to himself, and only met people in the way of business. She had seen the buttons, and was sure that they belonged to the clothes which he had worn last night. The wood-pile was very dry, for it had not rained for a month. It burned like a tinder, and by the time she reached the spot nothing could be seen but flames.

She and all the firemen smelled the burned flesh from inside it. She knew nothing of the papers, nor of Mr. Oldacre's private affairs.

"So, my dear Watson, there's my report of a failure. And yet—and yet"—he clenched his thin hands in a paroxysm of conviction—"I *know* it's all wrong. I feel it in my bones. There is something that has not come out, and that housekeeper knows it. There was a sort of sulky defiance in her eyes which only goes with guilty knowledge. However, there's no good talking any more about it, Watson; but unless some lucky chance comes our way I fear that the Norwood Disappearance Case will not figure in that chronicle of our successes which I foresee that a patient public will sooner or later have to endure."

"Surely," said I, "the man's appearance would go far with any jury?"

"That is a dangerous argument, my dear Watson. You remember that terrible murderer, Bert Stevens, who wanted us to get him off in '87? Was there ever a more mild-mannered, Sunday-school young man?"

"It is true."

"Unless we succeed in establishing an alternative theory, this man is lost. You can hardly find a flaw in the case which can now be presented against him, and all further investigation has served to strengthen it. By the way, there is one curious little point about those papers which may serve us as the starting-point for an inquiry. On looking over the bank book I found that the low state of the balance was principally due to large cheques which have been made out during the last year to Mr. Cornelius. I confess that I should be interested to know who this Mr. Cornelius may be with whom a retired builder has such very large transactions. Is it possible that he has had a hand in the affair? Cornelius might be a broker, but we have found no scrip to correspond with these large payments. Failing any other indication, my researches must now take the direction of an inquiry at the bank for the gentleman who has cashed these cheques. But I fear, my dear fellow, that our case will end ingloriously by Lestrade hanging our client, which will certainly be a triumph for Scotland Yard."

I do not know how far Sherlock Holmes took any sleep that night, but when I came down to breakfast I found him pale and harassed, his bright eyes the brighter for the dark shadows round them. The carpet round his chair was littered with cigarette ends, and with the early editions of the morning papers. An open telegram lay upon the table.

"What do you think of this, Watson?" he asked, tossing it across.

It was from Norwood, and ran as follows:

"Important fresh evidence to hand. McFarlane's guilt definitely established. Advise you to abandon case.—LESTRADE."

"This sounds serious," said I.

"It is Lestrade's little cock-a-doodle of victory," Holmes answered with a bitter smile. "And yet it may be premature to abandon the case. After all, important fresh evidence is a two-edged thing, and may possibly cut in a very different direction to that which Lestrade imagines. Take your breakfast, Watson, and we will go out together and see what we can do. I feel as if I shall need your company and your moral support to-day."

My friend had no breakfast himself, for it was one of his peculiarities that in his more intense moments he would permit himself no food, and I have known him presume upon his iron strength until he has fainted from pure inanition. "At present I cannot spare energy and nerve force for digestion," he would say, in answer to my medical remonstrances. I was not surprised, therefore, when this morning he left his untouched meal behind him and started with me for Norwood. A crowd of morbid sightseers were still gathered round Deep Dene House, which was just such a suburban villa as I had pictured. Within the gates Lestrade met us, his face flushed with victory, his manner grossly triumphant.

" Well, Mr. Holmes, have you proved us to be wrong yet ? Have you found your tramp ? " he cried.

" I have formed no conclusion whatever," my companion answered.

" But we formed ours yesterday, and now it proves to be correct ; so you must acknowledge that we have been a little in front of you this time, Mr. Holmes."

" You certainly have the air of something unusual having occurred," said Holmes.

Lestrade laughed loudly.

" You don't like being beaten any more than the rest of us do," said he. " A man can't expect always to have it his own way—can he, Dr. Watson ? Step this way, if you please, gentlemen, and I think I can convince you once for all that it was John McFarlane who did this crime."

He led us through the passage and out into a dark hall beyond.

" This is where young McFarlane must have come out to get his hat after the crime was done," said he. " Now look at this." With dramatic suddenness he struck a match, and by its light exposed a stain of blood upon the whitewashed wall. As he held the match nearer I saw that it was more than a stain. It was the well-marked print of a thumb.

" Look at that with your magnifying glass, Mr. Holmes."

" Yes, I am doing so."

" You are aware that no two thumb-marks are alike ? "

" I have heard something of the kind."

" Well, then, will you please compare that print with this wax impression of young McFarlane's right thumb, taken by my orders this morning ? "

As he held the waxen print close to the blood-stain it

did not take a magnifying glass to see that the two were undoubtedly from the same thumb. It was evident to me that our unfortunate client was lost.

"That is final," said Lestrade.

"Yes, that is final," I voluntarily echoed.

"It is final," said Holmes.

Something in his tone caught my ear, and I turned to look at him. An extraordinary change had come over his face. It was writhing with inward merriment. His two eyes were shining like stars. It seemed to me that he was making desperate efforts to restrain a convulsive attack of laughter.

"Dear me! Dear me!" he said at last. "Well, now, who would have thought it? And how deceptive appearances may be, to be sure! Such a nice young man to look at! It is a lesson to us not to trust our own judgment—is it not, Lestrade?"

"Yes, some of us are a little too much inclined to be cocksure, Mr. Holmes," said Lestrade. The man's insolence was maddening, but we could not resent it.

"What a providential thing that this young man should press his right thumb against the wall in taking his hat from the peg! Such a very natural action, too, if you come to think of it." Holmes was outwardly calm, but his whole body gave a wriggle of suppressed excitement as he spoke. "By the way, Lestrade, who made this remarkable discovery?"

"It was the housekeeper, Mrs. Lexington, who drew the night constable's attention to it?"

"Where was the night constable?"

"He remained on guard in the bedroom where the crime was committed, so as to see that nothing was touched."

"But why didn't the police see this mark yesterday?"

"Well, we had no particular reason to make a careful examination of the hall. Besides, it's not in a very prominent place, as you see."

"No, no, of course not. I suppose there is no doubt that the mark was there yesterday?"

Lestrade looked at Holmes as if he thought he was going out of his mind. I confess that I was myself surprised both at his hilarious manner and at his rather wild observation.

"I don't know whether you think that McFarlane came out of gaol in the dead of the night in order to strengthen the evidence against himself," said Lestrade. "I leave it to any expert in the world whether that is not the mark of his thumb."

"It is unquestionably the mark of his thumb."

"There, that's enough," said Lestrade. "I am a practical man, Mr. Holmes, and when I have got my evidence I come to my conclusions. If you have anything to say you will find me writing my report in the sitting-room."

Holmes had recovered his equanimity, though I still seemed to detect gleams of amusement in his expression.

"Dear me, this is a very sad development, Watson, is it not?" said he. "And yet there are singular points about it which hold out some hopes for our client."

"I am delighted to hear it," said I heartily. "I was afraid it was all up with him."

"I would hardly go so far as to say that, my dear Watson. The fact is that there is one really serious flaw in this evidence to which our friend attaches so much importance."

"Indeed, Holmes! What is it?"

"Only this—that I *know* that that mark was not there when I examined the hall yesterday. And now, Watson, let us have a little stroll round in the sunshine."

With a confused brain, but with a heart into which some warmth of hope was returning, I accompanied my friend in a walk round the garden. Holmes took each face of the house in turn and examined it with great interest. He then led the way inside, and went over the whole building from basement to attics. Most of the rooms were unfurnished, but none the less Holmes inspected them all minutely. Finally, on the top corridor, which ran outside three untenanted bedrooms, he again was seized with a spasm of merriment.

" There are really some very unique features about this case, Watson," said he. " I think it is time now that we took our friend Lestrade into our confidence. He has had his little smile at our expense, and perhaps we may do as much by him if my reading of this problem proves to be correct. Yes, yes; I think I see how we should approach it."

The Scotland Yard inspector was still writing in the parlour when Holmes interrupted him.

" I understood that you were writing a report of this case," said he.

" So I am."

" Don't you think it may be a little premature ? I can't help thinking that your evidence is not complete."

Lestrade knew my friend too well to disregard his words. He laid down his pen and looked curiously at him.

" What do you mean, Mr. Holmes ? "

" Only that there is an important witness whom you have not seen."

" Can you produce him ? "

" I think I can."

" Then do so."

" I will do my best. How many constables have you ? "

" There are three within call."

" Excellent ! " said Holmes. " May I ask if they are all large, able-bodied men with powerful voices ? "

" I have no doubt they are, though I fail to see what their voices have to do with it."

" Perhaps I can help you to see that, and one or two other things as well," said Holmes. " Kindly summon your men, and I will try."

Five minutes later three policemen had assembled in the hall.

"In the outhouse you will find a considerable quantity of straw," said Holmes. "I will ask you to carry in two bundles of it. I think it will be of the greatest assistance in producing the witness whom I require. Thank you very much. I believe you have some matches in your pocket, Watson. Now, Mr. Lestrade, I will ask you all to accompany me to the top landing."

As I have said, there was a broad corridor there, which ran outside three empty bedrooms. At one end of the corridor we were all marshalled by Sherlock Holmes, the constables grinning, and Lestrade staring at my friend with amazement, expectation, and derision chasing each other across his features. Holmes stood before us with an air of a conjurer who is performing a trick.

"Would you kindly send one of your constables for two buckets of water? Put the straw on the floor here, free from the wall on either side. Now I think that we are all ready."

Lestrade's face had begun to grow red and angry.

"I don't know whether you are playing a game with us, Mr. Sherlock Holmes," said he. "If you know anything, you can surely say it without all this tom-foolery."

"I assure you, my good Lestrade, that I have an excellent reason for everything that I do. You may possibly remember that you chaffed me a little some hours ago, when the sun seemed on your side of the hedge, so you must not grudge me a little pomp and ceremony now. Might I ask you, Watson, to open that window, and then to put a match to the edge of the straw?"

I did so, and, driven by the draught, a coil of grey smoke swirled down the corridor, while the dry straw crackled and flamed.

"Now we must see if we can find this witness for you, Lestrade. Might I ask you all to join in the cry of 'Fire'? Now, then: one, two, three——"

" Fire ! " we all yelled.

" Thank you. I will trouble you once again."

" Fire ! "

" Just once more, gentlemen, and all together."

" Fire ! " The shout must have rung over Norwood.

It had hardly died away when an amazing thing happened. A door suddenly flew open out of what appeared to be solid wall at the end of the corridor, and a little wizened man darted out of it, like a rabbit out of its burrow.

" Capital ! " said Holmes calmly. " Watson, a bucket of water over the straw. That will do ! Lestrade, allow me to present you with your principal missing witness, Mr. Jonas Oldacre."

The detective stared at the new-comer with blank amazement. The latter was blinking in the bright light of the corridor, and peering at us and at the smouldering fire. It was an odious face—crafty, vicious, malignant, with shifty, light-grey eyes and white eyelashes.

" What's this, then ? " said Lestrade at last. " What have you been doing all this time, eh ? "

Oldacre gave an uneasy laugh, shrinking back from the furious red face of the angry detective.

" I have done no harm."

" No harm ? You have done your best to get an innocent man hanged. If it wasn't for this gentleman here, I am not sure that you would not have succeeded."

The wretched creature began to whimper.

" I am sure, sir, it was only my practical joke."

" Oh ! a joke, was it ? You won't find the laugh on your side, I promise you. Take him down and keep him in the sitting-room until I come. Mr. Holmes," he continued, when they had gone, " I could not speak before the constables, but I don't mind saying, in the presence of Dr. Watson, that this is the brightest thing that you have done yet, though it is a mystery to me how you did it. You have saved an innocent man's life, and you have prevented a very grave scandal, which would have ruined my reputation in the Force."

Holmes smiled and clapped Lestrade upon the shoulder.

" Instead of being ruined, my good sir, you will find that your reputation has been enormously enhanced. Just make a few alterations in that report which you were writing, and they will understand how hard it is to throw dust in the eyes of Inspector Lestrade."

"And you don't want your name to appear ? "

" Not at all. The work is its own reward. Perhaps I shall get the credit also at some distant day when I permit my zealous historian to lay out his foolscap once more —eh, Watson ? Well, now, let us see where this rat has been lurking."

A lath-and-plaster partition had been run across the passage six feet from the end, with a door cunningly concealed in it. It was lit within by slits under the eaves. A few articles of furniture and a supply of food and water were within, together with a number of books and papers.

" There's the advantage of being a builder," said Holmes as we came out. " He was able to fix up his own little hiding-place without any confederate—save, of course, that precious housekeeper of his, whom I should lose no time in adding to your bag, Lestrade."

" I will take your advice. But how did you know of this place, Mr. Holmes ? "

" I made up my mind that the fellow was in hiding in the house. When I paced one corridor and found it six feet shorter than the corresponding one below, it was pretty clear where he was. I thought he had not the nerve to lie quiet before an alarm of fire. We could, of course, have gone in and taken him, but it amused me to make him reveal himself ; besides, I owed you a little mystification, Lestrade, for your chaff in the morning."

" Well, sir, you certainly got equal with me on that. But how in the world did you know that he was in the house at all ? "

"The thumb-mark, Lestrade. You said it was final ; and so it was, in a very different sense. I knew it had not been there the day before. I pay a good deal of attention to matters of detail, as you may have observed, and I had examined the hall, and was sure that the wall was clear. Therefore, it had been put on during the night."

"But how ? "

"Very simply. When those packets were sealed up, Jonas Oldacre got McFarlane to secure one of the seals by putting his thumb upon the soft wax. It would be done so quickly and so naturally that I dare say the young man himself has no recollection of it. Very likely it just so happened, and Oldacre had himself no notion of the use he would put it to. Brooding over the case in that den of his, it suddenly struck him what absolutely damning evidence he could make against McFarlane by using that thumb-mark. It was the simplest thing in the world for him to take a wax impression from the seal, to moisten it in as much blood as he could get from a pin-prick, and to put the mark upon the wall during the night, either with his own hand or with that of his housekeeper. If you examine among these documents which he took with him into his retreat, I will lay you a wager that you find the seal with the thumb-mark upon it."

"Wonderful ! " said Lestrade. "Wonderful ! It's all as clear as crystal, as you put it. But what is the object of this deep deception, Mr. Holmes ? "

It was amusing to me to see how the detective's overbearing manner had changed suddenly to that of a child asking questions of its teacher.

"Well, I don't think that is very hard to explain. A very deep, malicious, vindictive person is the gentleman who is now awaiting us downstairs. You know that he was once refused by McFarlane's mother ? You don't ! I told you that you should go to Blackheath first and Norwood afterwards. Well, this injury, as he would consider it, has rankled in his wicked, scheming brain, and all his life he has longed for vengeance, but never seen his chance. During the last year or two things have gone against him—secret speculation, I think—and he finds himself in a bad way. He determines to swindle his creditors, and for this purpose he pays large cheques to a certain Mr. Cornelius, who is, I imagine, himself under another name. I have not traced these cheques yet, but I have no doubt that they were banked under that name at some provincial town where Oldacre from time to time led a double existence. He intended to change his name altogether, draw this money, and vanish, starting life again elsewhere."

" Well, that's likely enough."

" It would strike him that in disappearing he might throw all pursuit off his track, and at the same time have an ample and crushing revenge upon his old sweetheart, if he could give the impression that he had been mur- dered by her only child. It was a masterpiece of vil- lainy, and he carried it out like a master. The idea of the will, which would give an obvious motive for the crime, the secret visit unknown to his own parents, the retention of the stick, the blood, and the animal remains and buttons in the wood-pile, all were admirable. It was a net from which it seemed to me a few hours ago that there was no possible escape. But he had not that supreme gift of the artist, the knowledge of when to stop. He wished to improve that which was already perfect—to draw the rope tighter yet round the neck of his unfor- tunate victim—and so he ruined all. Let us descend, Lestrade. There are just one or two questions that I would ask him."

The malignant creature was seated in his own parlour with a policeman upon each side of him.

" It was a joke, my good sir ; a practical joke, nothing more," he whined incessantly. " I assure you, sir, that I simply concealed myself in order to see the effect of my disappearance, and I am sure that you would not be so unjust as to imagine that I would have allowed any harm to befall poor young Mr. McFarlane."

"That's for the jury to decide," said Lestrade. "Anyhow, we shall have you on a charge of conspiracy, if not for attempted murder."

"And you'll probably find that your creditors will impound the banking account of Mr. Cornelius," said Holmes.

The little man started and turned his malignant eyes upon my friend.

"I have to thank you for a good deal," said he. "Perhaps I'll pay my debt some day."

Holmes smiled indulgently.

"I fancy that for some few years you will find your time very fully occupied," said he. "By the way, what was it you put into the wood-pile besides your old trousers? A dead dog, or rabbits, or what? You won't tell? Dear me, how very unkind of you! Well, well, I dare say that a couple of rabbits would account both for the blood and for the charred ashes. If ever you write an account, Watson, you can make rabbits serve your turn."

26. *The Dancing Men*

HOLMES had been seated for some hours in silence, with his long, thin back curved over a chemical vessel in which he was brewing a particularly malodorous product. His head was sunk upon his breast, and he looked from my point of view like a strange, lank bird, with dull grey plumage and a black top-knot.

"So, Watson," said he suddenly, "you do not propose to invest in South African securities?"

I gave a start of astonishment. Accustomed as I was to Holmes' curious faculties, this sudden intrusion into my most intimate thoughts was utterly inexplicable.

"How on earth do you know that?" I asked.

He wheeled round upon his stool, with a steaming test-

tube in his hand and a gleam of amusement in his deep-set
eyes.

"Now, Watson, confess yourself utterly taken aback,"
said he.

"I am."

"I ought to make you sign a paper to that effect."

"Why?"

"Because in five minutes you will say that it is all so
absurdly simple."

"I am sure that I shall say nothing of the kind."

"You see, my dear Watson"—he propped his test-
tube in the rack and began to lecture with the air of a
professor addressing his class—"it is not really difficult
to construct a series of inferences, each dependent upon
its predecessor and each simple in itself. If, after doing
so, one simply knocks out all the central inferences and
presents one's audience with the starting-point and the
conclusion, one may produce a startling, though possibly
a meretricious, effect. Now, it was not really difficult,
by an inspection of the groove between your left forefinger and thumb, to feel sure that you did *not* propose
to invest your small capital in the goldfields."

"I see no connection."

"Very likely not; but I can quickly show you a close
connection. Here are the missing links of the very
simple chain: 1. You had chalk between your left
finger and thumb when you returned from the club
last night. 2. You put chalk there when you play
billiards to steady the cue. 3. You never play billiards except with Thurston. 4. You told me four
weeks ago that Thurston had an option on some South
African property which would expire in a month, and
which he desired you to share with him. 5. Your
cheque-book is locked in my drawer, and you have
not asked for the key. 6. You do not propose to invest
your money in this manner."

"How absurdly simple!" I cried.

"Quite so!" said he, a little nettled. "Every problem

becomes very childish when once it is explained to you. Here is an unexplained one. See what you can make of that, friend Watson." He tossed a sheet of paper upon the table, and turned once more to his chemical analysis.

I looked with amazement at the absurd hieroglyphics upon the paper.

"Why, Holmes, it is a child's drawing!" I cried.

"Oh, that's your idea!"

"What else should it be?"

"That is what Mr. Hilton Cubitt, of Ridling Thorpe Manor, Norfolk, is very anxious to know. This little conundrum came by the first post, and he was to follow by the next train. There's a ring at the bell, Watson. I should not be very much surprised if this were he."

A heavy step was heard upon the stairs, and an instant later there entered a tall, ruddy, clean-shaven gentleman, whose clear eyes and florid cheeks told of a life led far from the fogs of Baker Street. He seemed to bring a whiff of his strong, fresh, bracing, east-coast air with him as he entered. Having shaken hands with each of us, he was about to sit down, when his eye rested upon the paper with the curious markings, which I had just examined and left upon the table.

"Well, Mr. Holmes, what do you make of these?" he cried. "They told me that you were fond of queer mysteries, and I don't think you can find a queerer one than that. I sent the paper on ahead so that you might have time to study it before I came."

"It is certainly rather a curious production," said Holmes. "At first sight it would appear to be some childish prank. It consists of a number of absurd little figures dancing across the paper upon which they are drawn. Why should you attribute any importance to so grotesque an object?"

"I never should, Mr. Holmes. But my wife does. It is frightening her to death. She says nothing, but I can see terror in her eyes. That's why I want to sift the matter to the bottom."

Holmes held up the paper so that the sunlight shone full upon it. It was a page torn from a notebook. The markings were done in pencil, and ran in this way :

Holmes examined it for some time, and then, folding it carefully up, he placed it in his pocket-book.

"This promises to be a most interesting and unusual case," said he. "You gave me a few particulars in your letter, Mr. Hilton Cubitt, but I should be very much obliged if you would kindly go over it all again for the benefit of my friend, Dr. Watson."

"I'm not much of a story-teller," said our visitor, nervously clasping and unclasping his great, strong hands. "You'll just ask me anything that I don't make clear. I'll begin at the time of my marriage last year ; but I want to say first of all that, though I'm not a rich man, my people have been at Ridling Thorpe for a matter of five centuries, and there is no better-known family in the county of Norfolk. Last year I came up to London for the Jubilee, and I stopped at a boarding-house in Russell Square, because Parker, the vicar of our parish, was staying in it. There was an American young lady there—Patrick was the name—Elsie Patrick. In some way we became friends, until before my month was up I was as much in love as a man could be. We were quietly married at a registry office, and we returned to Norfolk a wedded couple. You'll think it very mad, Mr. Holmes, that a man of a good old family should marry a wife in this fashion, knowing nothing of her past or of her people ; but if you saw her and knew her it would help you to understand.

"She was very straight about it, was Elsie. I can't say that she did not give me every chance of getting out of it if I wished to do so. 'I have had some very disagreeable associations in my life,' said she ; ' I wish to forget all about them. I would rather never allude to the past, for it is very painful to me. If you take me, Hilton, you will take a woman who has nothing that she need be personally ashamed of ; but you will have to be content with my word for it, and to allow me to be silent as to all that passed up to the time when I became yours. If these conditions are too hard, then go back to Norfolk and leave me to the lonely life in which you found me.' It was only the day before our wedding that she said those very words to me. I told her that I was content to take her on her own terms, and I have been as good as my word.

" Well, we have been married now for a year, and very happy we have been. But about a month ago, at the end of June, I saw for the first time signs of trouble. One day my wife received a letter from America. I saw the American stamp. She turned deadly white, read the letter, and threw it into the fire. She made no allusion to it afterwards, and I made none, for a promise is a promise ; but she has never known an easy hour from that moment. There is always a look of fear upon her face —a look as if she were waiting and expecting. She would do better to trust me. She would find that I was her best friend. But until she speaks I can say nothing. Mind you, she is a truthful woman, Mr. Holmes, and whatever trouble there may have been in her past life, it has been no fault of hers. I am only a simple Norfolk squire, but there is not a man in England who ranks his family honour more highly than I do. She knows it well, and she knew it well before she married me. She would never bring any stain upon it—of that I am sure.

" Well, now I come to the queer part of my story. About a week ago—it was the Tuesday of last week—I found on one of the window-sills a number of absurd little dancing figures, like these upon the paper. They were scrawled with chalk. I thought that it was the stable-boy who had drawn them, but the lad swore he knew nothing about it. Anyhow, they had come there during the night. I had them washed out, and I only mentioned the matter to my wife afterwards. To my surprise she took it very seriously, and begged me if any more came to let her see them. None did come for a week, and then yesterday morning I found this paper lying on the sundial in the garden. I showed it to Elsie, and down she dropped in a dead faint. Since then she has looked like a woman in a dream, half dazed, and with terror always lurking in her eyes. It was then that I wrote and sent the paper to you, Mr. Holmes. It was not a thing that I could take to the police, for they would have laughed at me, but you will tell me what to do. I am not a rich man ; but if there is any danger threatening my little woman, I would spend my last copper to shield her."

He was a fine creature, this man of the old English soil, simple, straight, and gentle, with his great, earnest blue eyes and broad, comely face. His love for his wife and his trust in her shone in his features. Holmes had listened to his story with the utmost attention, and now he sat for some time in silent thought.

" Don't you think, Mr. Cubitt," said he at last, " that your best plan would be to make a direct appeal to your wife, and to ask her to share her secret with you ? "

Hilton Cubitt shook his massive head.

" A promise is a promise, Mr. Holmes. If Elsie wished to tell me, she would. If not, it is not for me to force her confidence. But I am justified in taking my own line —and I will."

" Then I will help you with all my heart. In the first place, have you heard of any strangers being seen in your neighbourhood ? "

" No."

" I presume that it is a very quiet place. Any fresh face would cause comment ? "

" In the immediate neighbourhood, yes. But we have several small watering-places not very far away. And the farmers take in lodgers."

"These hieroglyphics have evidently a meaning. If it is a purely arbitrary one, it may be impossible for us to solve it. If, on the other hand, it is systematic, I have no doubt that we shall get to the bottom of it. But this particular sample is so short that I can do nothing, and the facts which you have brought me are so indefinite that we have no basis for an investigation. I would suggest that you return to Norfolk, that you keep a keen look-out, and that you take an exact copy of any fresh dancing men which may appear. It is a thousand pities that we have not a reproduction of those which were done in chalk upon the window-sill. Make a discreet inquiry, also, as to any strangers in the neighbourhood. When you have collected some fresh evidence, come to me again. That is the best advice which I can give you, Mr. Hilton Cubitt. If there are any pressing fresh developments, I shall be always ready to run down and see you in your Norfolk home."

The interview left Sherlock Holmes very thoughtful, and several times in the next few days I saw him take his slip of paper from his notebook and look long and earnestly at the curious figures inscribed upon it. He made no allusion to the affair, however, until one afternoon a fortnight or so later. I was going out, when he called me back.

"You had better stay here, Watson."

"Why?"

"Because I had a wire from Hilton Cubitt this morning—you remember Hilton Cubitt, of the dancing men? He was to reach Liverpool Street at one-twenty. He may be here at any moment. I gather from his wire that there have been some new incidents of importance."

We had not long to wait, for our Norfolk squire came straight from the station as fast as a hansom could bring him. He was looking worried and depressed, with tired eyes and a lined forehead.

"It's getting on my nerves, this business, Mr. Holmes,"

said he, as he sank, like a wearied man, into an arm-chair.
" It's bad enough to feel that you are surrounded by unseen, unknown folk, who have some kind of design upon
you ; but when, in addition to that, you know that it is
just killing your wife by inches, then it becomes as much
as flesh and blood can endure. She's wearing away under
it—just wearing away before my eyes."

" Has she said anything yet ? "

" No, Mr. Holmes, she has not. And yet there have
been times when the poor girl has wanted to speak,
and yet could not quite bring herself to take the plunge.
I have tried to help her ; but I dare say I did it clumsily,
and scared her off from it. She has spoken about my
old family, and our reputation in the county, and our pride
in our unsullied honour, and I always felt it was leading
to the point ; but somehow it turned off before we got
there."

" But you have found out something for yourself ? "

" A good deal, Mr. Holmes. I have several fresh
dancing men pictures for you to examine, and, what is
more important, I have seen the fellow."

" What—the man who draws them ? "

" Yes, I saw him at his work. But I will tell you everything in order. When I got back after my visit to you, the
very first thing I saw next morning was a fresh crop of
dancing men. They had been drawn in chalk upon the
black wooden door of the tool-house, which stands beside
the lawn in full view of the front windows. I took an
exact copy, and here it is." He unfolded a paper and
laid it upon the table. Here is a copy of the hieroglyphics :

" Excellent ! " said Holmes. " Excellent ! Pray continue."

" When I had taken the copy I rubbed out the marks ;

but two mornings later a fresh inscription had appeared. I have a copy of it here ":

Holmes rubbed his hands and chuckled with delight. "Our material is rapidly accumulating," said he.

"Three days later a message was left scrawled upon paper, and placed under a pebble upon the sundial. Here it is. The characters are, as you see, exactly the same as the last one. After that I determined to lie in wait ; so I got out my revolver and I sat up in my study, which overlooks the lawn and garden. About two in the morning I was seated by the window, all being dark save for the moonlight outside, when I heard steps behind me, and there was my wife in her dressing-gown. She implored me to come to bed. I told her frankly that I wished to see who it was who played such absurd tricks upon us. She answered that it was some senseless practical joke, and that I should not take any notice of it.

" ' If it really annoys you, Hilton, we might go and travel, you and I, and so avoid this nuisance.'

" ' What, be driven out of our own house by a practical joker ? ' said I. ' Why, we should have the whole county laughing at us ! '

" ' Well, come to bed,' said she, ' and we can discuss it in the morning.'

"Suddenly, as she spoke, I saw her white face grow whiter yet in the moonlight, and her hand tightened upon my shoulder. Something was moving in the shadow of the tool-house. I saw a dark, creeping figure which crawled round the corner and squatted in front of the door. Seizing my pistol I was rushing out, when my wife threw her arms round me and held me with convulsive strength. I tried to throw her off, but she clung to me most desperately. At last I got clear, but by the time I had opened the door and reached the house the creature was gone. He had left a trace of his presence, however, for there on the door was the very same arrangement of dancing men which had already twice appeared, and which I have copied on that paper. There was no other sign of the fellow anywhere, though I ran all over the grounds. And yet the amazing thing is that he must have been there all the time, for when I examined the door again in the morning he had scrawled some more of his pictures under the line which I had already seen."

" Have you that fresh drawing ? "

" Yes ; it is very short, but I made a copy of it, and here it is."

Again he produced a paper. The new dance was in this form :

" Tell me," said Holmes—and I could see by his eyes that he was much excited—" was this a mere addition to the first, or did it appear to be entirely separate ? "

" It was on a different panel of the door."

" Excellent ! This is far the most important of all for our purpose. It fills me with hopes. Now, Mr. Hilton Cubitt, please continue your most interesting statement."

" I have nothing more to say, Mr. Holmes, except that I was angry with my wife that night for having held me back when I might have caught the skulking rascal. She said that she feared that I might come to harm. For an instant it had crossed my mind that perhaps what she really feared was that *he* might come to harm, for I could not doubt that she knew who this man was and what he meant by these strange signals. But there is a tone in my wife's voice, Mr. Holmes, and a look in her eyes which forbid doubt, and I am sure that it was indeed my own safety that was in her mind. There's the whole case, and now I want your advice as to what I ought to do. My own inclination is to put half a dozen of my farm lads in the shrubbery, and when this fellow comes again to give him such a hiding that he will leave us in peace for the future."

" I fear it is too deep a case for such simple remedies," said Holmes. " How long can you stop in London ? "

" I must go back to-day. I would not leave my wife alone at night for anything. She is very nervous and begged me to come back."

" I dare say you are right. But if you could have stopped I might possibly have been able to return with you in a day or two. Meanwhile, you will leave me these papers, and I think that it is very likely that I shall be able to pay you a visit shortly and to throw some light upon your case."

Sherlock Holmes preserved his calm professional manner until our visitor had left us, although it was easy for me, who knew him so well, to see that he was profoundly excited. The moment that Hilton Cubitt's broad back had disappeared through the door my comrade rushed to the table, laid out all the slips of paper containing dancing men in front of him, and threw himself into an intricate and elaborate calculation.

For two hours I watched him as he covered sheet after sheet of paper with figures and letters, so completely absorbed in his task that he had evidently forgotten my presence. Sometimes he was making progress, and whistled and sang at his work ; sometimes he was puzzled and would sit for a long spell with a furrowed brow and a vacant eye. Finally he sprang from his chair with a cry of satisfaction, and walked up and down the room rubbing his hands together. Then he wrote a long telegram upon a cable form. " If my answer to this is as I hope, you will have a very pretty case to add to your collection, Watson," said he. " I expect that we shall be able to go down to Norfolk to-morrow, and to take our friend some very definite news as to the secret of his annoyance."

I confess that I was filled with curiosity, but I was aware that Holmes liked to make his disclosures at his own time and in his own way ; so I waited until it should suit him to take me into his confidence.

But there was a delay in that answering telegram, and two days of impatience followed, during which Holmes pricked up his ears at every ring of the bell. On the evening of the second there came a letter from Hilton Cubitt. All was quiet with him, save that a long inscription had appeared that morning upon the pedestal of the sundial. He enclosed a copy of it, which is here reproduced :

Holmes bent over this grotesque frieze for some minutes and then suddenly sprang to his feet with an exclamation of surprise and dismay. His face was haggard with anxiety.

"We have let this affair go far enough," said he. "Is there a train to North Walsham to-night ? "

I turned up the time-table. The last had just gone.

"Then we shall breakfast early and take the very first in the morning," said Holmes. "Our presence is most urgently needed. Ah, here is our expected cablegram. One moment, Mrs. Hudson—there may be an answer. No, that is quite as I expected. This message makes it even more essential that we should not lose an hour in letting Hilton Cubitt know how matters stand, for it is a singular and dangerous web in which our simple Norfolk squire is entangled."

So, indeed, it proved, and as I come to the dark conclusion of a story which had seemed to me to be only childish and bizarre, I experience once again the dismay and horror with which I was filled. Would that I had

some brighter ending to communicate to my readers;
but these are the chronicles of facts, and I must follow
to their dark crisis the strange chain of events which for
some days made Ridling Thorpe Manor a household
word through the length and breadth of England.

We had hardly alighted at North Walsham, and mentioned the name of our destination, when the station-
master hurried towards us. " I suppose that you are the
detectives from London ? " said he.

A look of annoyance passed over Holmes' face.

" What makes you think such a thing ? "

" Because Inspector Martin from Norwich has just
passed through. But maybe you are the surgeons. She's
not dead—or wasn't by last accounts. You may be in
time to save her yet—though it be for the gallows."

Holmes' brow was dark with anxiety.

" We are going to Ridling Thorpe Manor," said he,
" but we have heard nothing of what has passed there."

" It's a terrible business," said the station-master.
" They are shot, both Mr. Hilton Cubitt and his wife.
She shot him and then herself—so the servants say.
He's dead, and her life is despaired of. Dear, dear !
one of the oldest families in the county of Norfolk, and
one of the most honoured."

Without a word Holmes hurried to a carriage, and
during the long seven-miles drive he never opened his
mouth. Seldom have I seen him so utterly despondent.
He had been uneasy during all our journey from town,
and I had observed that he had turned over the morning
papers with anxious attention ; but now this sudden
realization of his worst fears left him in a blank melancholy. He leaned back in his seat, lost in gloomy
speculation. Yet there was much around us to interest
us, for we were passing through as singular a country-
side as any in England, where a few scattered cottages
represented the population of to-day, while on every hand
enormous square-towered churches bristled up from the
flat, green landscape and told of the glory and prosperity

of old East Anglia. At last the violet rim of the German Ocean appeared over the green edge of the Norfolk coast, and the driver pointed with his whip to two old brick-and-timber gables which projected from a grove of trees. " That's Ridling Thorpe Manor," said he.

As we drove up to the porticoed front door I observed in front of it, beside the tennis lawn, the black tool-house and the pedestalled sundial with which we had such strange associations. A dapper little man, with a quick, alert manner and a waxed moustache, had just descended from a high dog-cart. He introduced himself as Inspector Martin, of the Norfolk Constabulary, and he was considerably astonished when he heard the name of my companion.

" Why, Mr. Holmes, the crime was only committed at three this morning ! How could you hear of it in London and get to the spot as soon as I ? "

" I anticipated it. I came in the hope of preventing it."

" Then you must have important evidence of which we are ignorant, for they were said to be a most united couple."

" I have only the evidence of the dancing men," said Holmes. " I will explain the matter to you later. Meanwhile, since it is too late to prevent this tragedy, I am very anxious that I should use the knowledge which I possess in order to ensure that justice be done. Will you associate me in your investigation, or will you prefer that I should act independently ? "

" I should be proud to feel that we were acting together, Mr. Holmes," said the Inspector earnestly.

" In that case I should be glad to hear the evidence and to examine the premises without an instant of unnecessary delay."

Inspector Martin had the good sense to allow my friend to do things in his own fashion, and contented himself with carefully noting the results. The local surgeon, an old, white-haired man, had just come down from Mrs.

Hilton Cubitt's room, and he reported that her injuries
were serious, but not necessarily fatal. The bullet had
passed through the front of her brain, and it would
probably be some time before she could regain consciousness. On the question of whether she had been
shot or had shot herself he would not venture to express
any decided opinion. Certainly the bullet had been discharged at very close quarters. There was only the one
pistol found in the room, two barrels of which had been
emptied. Mr. Hilton Cubitt had been shot through the
heart. It was equally conceivable that he had shot her
and then himself, or that she had been the criminal, for
the revolver lay upon the floor midway between them.

" Has he been moved ? " asked Holmes.

" We have moved nothing except the lady. We
could not leave her lying wounded upon the floor."

" How long have you been here, doctor ? "

" Since four o'clock."

" Anyone else ? "

" Yes, the constable here."

" And you have touched nothing ? "

" Nothing."

" You have acted with great discretion. Who sent for
you ? "

" The housemaid, Saunders."

" Was it she who gave the alarm ? "

" She and Mrs. King, the cook."

" Where are they now ? "

" In the kitchen, I believe."

" Then I think we had better hear their story at
once."

The old hall, oak-panelled and high-windowed, had
been turned into a court of investigation. Holmes sat
in a great, old-fashioned chair, his inexorable eyes gleaming out of his haggard face. I could read in them a
set purpose to devote his life to this quest until the client
whom he had failed to save should at last be avenged.
The trim Inspector Martin, the old grey-bearded country

doctor, myself, and a stolid village policeman made up the rest of that strange company.

The two women told their story clearly enough. They had been aroused from their sleep by the sound of an explosion, which had been followed a minute later by a second one. They slept in adjoining rooms, and Mrs. King had rushed in to Saunders. Together they had descended the stairs. The door of the study was open and a candle was burning upon the table. Their master lay upon his face in the centre of the room. He was quite dead. Near the window his wife was crouching, her head leaning against the wall. She was horribly wounded, and the side of the face was red with blood. She breathed heavily, but was incapable of saying any-thing. The passage, as well as the room, was full of smoke and the smell of powder. The window was certainly shut and fastened upon the inside. Both women were positive upon the point. They had at once sent for the doctor and for the constable. Then, with the aid of the groom and the stable-boy, they had con-veyed their injured mistress to her room. Both she and her husband had occupied the bed. She was clad in her dress—he in his dressing-gown, over his night-clothes. Nothing had been moved in the study. So far as they knew, there had never been any quarrel between hus-band and wife. They had always looked upon them as a very united couple.

These were the main points of the servants' evidence. In answer to Inspector Martin they were clear that every door was fastened upon the inside and that no one could have escaped from the house. In answer to Holmes, they both remembered that they were conscious of the smell of powder from the moment that they ran out of their rooms upon the top floor. "I commend that fact very carefully to your attention," said Holmes to his professional col-league. " And now I think that we are in a position to undertake a thorough examination of the room."

The study proved to be a small chamber, lined on three

sides with books, and with a writing-table facing an ordinary window, which looked out upon the garden. Our first attention was given to the body of the unfortunate squire, whose huge frame lay stretched across the room. His disordered dress showed that he had been hastily aroused from sleep. The bullet had been fired at him from the front, and had remained in his body after penetrating the heart. His death had certainly been instantaneous and painless. There was no powder-marking either upon his dressing-gown or on his hands. According to the country surgeon, the lady had stains upon her face, but none upon her hand.

" The absence of the latter means nothing, though its presence may mean everything," said Holmes. " Unless the powder from a badly fitting cartridge happens to spurt backwards, one may fire many shots without leaving a sign. I would suggest that Mr. Cubitt's body may now be removed. I suppose, doctor, you have not recovered the bullet which wounded the lady ? "

" A serious operation will be necessary before that can be done. But there are still four cartridges in the revolver. Two have been fired and two wounds inflicted, so that each bullet can be accounted for."

" So it would seem," said Holmes. " Perhaps you can account also for the bullet which has so obviously struck the edge of the window ? "

He had turned suddenly, and his long, thin finger was pointing to a hole which had been drilled right through the lower window-sash about an inch above the bottom.

" By George ! " cried the Inspector. " How ever did you see that ? "

" Because I looked for it."

" Wonderful ! " said the country doctor. " You are certainly right, sir. Then a third shot has been fired, and therefore a third person must have been present. But who could that have been, and how could he have got away ? "

" That is the problem which we are now about to solve," said Sherlock Holmes. " You remember, Inspector Martin, when the servants said that on leaving their room they were at once conscious of a smell of powder, I remarked that the point was an extremely important one ? "

" Yes, sir ; but I confess I did not quite follow you."

" It suggested that at the time of the firing the window as well as the door of the room had been open. Otherwise the fumes of powder could not have been blown so rapidly through the house. A draught in the room was necessary for that. Both door and window were only open for a short time, however."

" How do you prove that ? "

" Because the candle has not gutted."

" Capital ! " cried the Inspector. " Capital ! "

" Feeling sure that the window had been open at the time of the tragedy, I conceived that there might have been a third person in the affair, who stood outside this opening and fired through it. Any shot directed at this person might hit the sash. I looked, and there, sure enough, was the bullet mark ! "

" But how came the window to be shut and fastened ? "

" The woman's first instinct would be to shut and fasten the window. But, halloa ! what is this ? "

It was a lady's hand-bag which stood upon the study table—a trim little hand-bag of crocodile-skin and silver. Holmes opened it and turned the contents out. There were twenty fifty-pound notes of the Bank of England, held together by an india-rubber band—nothing else.

" This must be preserved, for it will figure in the trial," said Holmes, as he handed the bag with its contents to the Inspector. " It is now necessary that we should try to throw some light upon this third bullet, which has clearly, from the splintering of the wood, been fired from inside the room. I should like to see Mrs. King, the cook, again. . . . You said, Mrs. King, that you were awakened by a *loud* explosion. When you said that, did you mean that it seemed to you to be louder than the second one ? "

" Well, sir, it wakened me from my sleep, and so it is hard to judge. But it did seem very loud."

" You don't think that it might have been two shots fired almost at the same instant ? "

" I am sure I couldn't say, sir."

" I believe that it was undoubtedly so. I rather think, Inspector Martin, that we have now exhausted all that this room can teach us. If you will kindly step round with me we shall see what fresh evidence the garden has to offer."

A flower-bed extended up to the study window, and we all broke into an exclamation as we approached it. The flowers were trampled down, and the soft soil was imprinted all over with footmarks. Large, masculine feet they were, with peculiarly long, sharp toes. Holmes hunted about among the grass and leaves like a retriever after a wounded bird. Then, with a cry of satisfaction, bent forward and picked up a little brazen cylinder.

" I thought so," said he ; " the revolver had an ejector, and here is the third cartridge. I really think, Inspector Martin, that our case is almost complete."

The country inspector's face had shown his intense amazement at the rapid and masterful progress of Holmes' investigations. At first he had shown some disposition to assert his own position ; but now he was overcome with admiration, and ready to follow without question wherever Holmes led.

" Whom do you suspect ? " he asked.

" I'll go into that later. There are several points in this problem which I have not been able to explain to you yet. Now that I have got so far I had best proceed on my own lines, and then clear the whole matter up once and for all."

" Just as you wish, Mr. Holmes, so long as we get our man."

" I have no desire to make mysteries, but it is impossible at the moment of action to enter into long and complex explanations. I have the threads of this affair all in my hand. Even if this lady should never recover consciousness we can still reconstruct the events of last night and ensure that justice be done. First of all I wish to know whether there is any inn in this neighbourhood known as ' Elrige's ' ? "

The servants were cross-questioned, but none of them had heard of such a place. The stable-boy threw a light upon the matter by remembering that a farmer of that name lived miles off in the direction of East Ruston.

" Is it a lonely farm ? "

" Very lonely, sir."

" Perhaps they have not heard yet of all that happened here during the night ? "

" Maybe not, sir."

Holmes thought for a little, and then a curious smile played over his face.

" Saddle a horse, my lad," said he. " I shall wish you to take a note to Elrige's Farm."

He took from his pocket the various slips of the dancing men. With these in front of him he worked for some time at the study table. Finally he handed a note to the boy, with directions to put it into the hands of the person to whom it was addressed, and especially to answer no questions of any sort which might be put to him. I saw the outside of the note, addressed in straggling, irregular characters, very unlike Holmes' usual precise hand. It was consigned to Mr. Abe Slaney, Elrige's Farm, East Ruston, Norfolk.

" I think, Inspector," Holmes remarked, " that you would do well to telegraph for an escort, as, if my calculations prove to be correct, you may have a particularly dangerous prisoner to convey to the county gaol. The boy who takes this note could no doubt forward your telegram. If there is an afternoon train to town, Watson, I think we should do well to take it, as I have a chemical analysis of some interest to finish, and this investigation draws rapidly to a close."

When the youth had been despatched with the note, Sherlock Holmes gave his instructions to the servants. If any visitor were to call asking for Mrs. Hilton Cubitt no information should be given as to her condition, but he was to be shown at once into the drawing-room. He impressed these points upon them with the utmost earnestness. Finally he led the way into the drawing-room, with the remark that the business was now out of our hands, and that we must while away the time as best we might until we could see what was in store for us. The doctor had departed to his patients, and only the Inspector and myself remained.

" I think I can help you to pass an hour in an interesting and profitable manner," said Holmes, drawing his chair up to the table and spreading out in front of him the various papers upon which were recorded the antics of the dancing men. " As to you, friend Watson, I owe you every atonement for having allowed your natural curiosity to remain so long unsatisfied. To you, Inspector, the whole incident may appeal as a remarkable professional study. I must tell you first of all the interesting circumstances connected with the previous consultations which Mr. Hilton Cubitt has had with me in Baker Street." He then shortly recapitulated the facts which have already been recorded.

" I have here in front of me these singular productions, at which one might smile had they not proved themselves to be the forerunners of so terrible a tragedy. I am fairly familiar with all forms of secret writings, and am myself the author of a trifling monograph upon the subject, in which I analyse one hundred and sixty separate ciphers ; but I confess that this is entirely new to me. The object of those who invented the system has apparently been to conceal that these characters convey a message, and to give the idea that they are the mere random sketches of children.

" Having once recognized, however, that the symbols

stood for letters, and having applied the rules which guide us in all forms of secret writings, the solution was easy enough. The first message submitted to me was so short that it was impossible for me to do more than to say with some confidence that the symbol stood for E. As you are aware, E is the most common letter in the English alphabet and it predominat e s to so marked an extent that even in a short sentence one would expect to find it most often. Out of fifteen symbols in the first message four were the same, so it was reasonable to set this down as E. It is true that in some cases the figure was bearing a flag, and in some cases not, but it was probable from the way in which the flags were distributed that they were used to break the sentence up into words. I accepted this as an hypothesis, and noted that E was represented by

"But now came the real difficulty of the inquiry. The order of the English letters after E is by no means well-marked, and any preponderance which may be shown in an average of a printed sheet may be reversed in a single short sentence. Speaking roughly, T, A, O, I, N, S, H, R, D, and L are the numerical order in which letters occur ; but T, A, O, and I are very nearly abreast of each other, and it would be an endless task to try each combination until a meaning was arrived at. I, therefore, waited for fresh material. In my second interview with Mr. Hilton Cubitt he was able to give me two other short sentences and one message, which appeared—since there was no flag—to be a single word. Here are the symbols. Now, in the single word I have already got the two E's coming second and fourth in a word of five letters. It might be ' sever,' or ' lever,' or ' never.' There can be no question that the latter as a reply to an appeal is far the most probable, and the circumstances pointed to its being a reply written by the lady. Accepting it as correct, we are now able to say that the symbols stand respectively for N, V, and R.

"Even now I was in considerable difficulty, but a happy thought put me in possession of several other letters. It occurred to me that if these appeals came, as I expected, from someone who had been intimate with the lady in her early life, a combination which contained two E's with three letters between might very well stand for the name 'ELSIE.' On examination I found that such a combination formed the termination of the message which was three times repeated. It was certainly some appeal to 'Elsie.' In this way I had got my L, S, and I. But what appeal could it be? There were only four letters in the word which preceded 'Elsie,' and it ended in E. Surely the word must be 'COME.' I tried all other four letters ending in E, but could find none to fit the case. So now I was in possession of C, O, and M, and I was in a position to attack the first message once more, dividing it into words and putting dots for each symbol which was still unknown. So treated it worked out in this fashion:

. M . ERE . . E SL . NE .

"Now, the first letter can only be A, which is a most useful discovery, since it occurs no fewer than three times in this short sentence, and the H is also apparent in the second word. Now it becomes:

AM HERE A . E SLANE .

Or, filling in the obvious vacancies in the name:

AM HERE A . E SLANEY.

I had so many letters now that I could proceed with considerable confidence to the second message, which worked out in this fashion:

A . ELRI . ES.

Here I could only make sense by putting T and G for the missing letters, and supposing that the name was that of some house or inn at which the writer was staying."

Inspector Martin and I had listened with the utmost

interest to the full and clear account of how my friend had produced results which had led to so complete a command over our difficulties.

" What did you do then, sir ? " asked the Inspector.

" I had every reason to suppose that this Abe Slaney was an American, since Abe is an American contraction, and since a letter from America had been the starting-point of all the trouble. I had also every cause to think that there was some criminal secret in the matter. The lady's allusions to her past and her refusal to take her husband into her confidence both pointed in that direction. I therefore cabled to my friend, Wilson Hargreave, of the New York Police Bureau, who has more than once made use of my knowledge of London crime. I asked him whether the name of Abe Slaney was known to him. Here is his reply : ' The most dangerous crook in Chicago.' On the very evening upon which I had his answer Hilton Cubitt sent me the last message from Slaney. Working with known letters it took this form :

ELSIE . RE . ARE TO MEET THY GO .

The addition of a P and a D completed a message which showed me that the rascal was proceeding from persuasion to threats, and my knowledge of the crooks of Chicago prepared me to find that he might very rapidly put his words into action. I at once came to Norfolk with my friend and colleague, Dr. Watson, but, unhappily, only in time to find that the worst had already occurred."

" It is a privilege to be associated with you in the handling of a case," said the Inspector warmly. " You will excuse me, however, if I speak frankly to you. You are only answerable to yourself, but I have to answer to my superiors. If this Abe Slaney, living at Elrige's, is indeed the murderer, and if he has made his escape while I am seated here, I should certainly get into serious trouble."

" You need not be uneasy. He will not try to escape."

" How do you know ? "

" To fly would be a confession of guilt."

633

" Then let us go to arrest him."

" I expect him here every instant."

" But why should he come ? "

" Because I have written and asked him."

" But this is incredible, Mr. Holmes ! Why should he come because you have asked him ? Would not such a request rather rouse his suspicions and cause him to fly ? "

" I think I have known how to frame the letter," said Sherlock Holmes. " In fact, if I am not very much mistaken, here is the gentleman himself coming up the drive."

A man was striding up the path which led to the door. He was a tall, handsome, swarthy fellow, clad in a suit of grey flannel, with a Panama hat, a bristling black beard, and a great, aggressive, hooked nose, and flourishing a cane as he walked. He swaggered up the path as if the place belonged to him, and we heard his loud, confident peal at the bell.

" I think, gentlemen," said Holmes quietly, " that we had best take up our position behind the door. Every precaution is necessary when dealing with such a fellow. You will need your handcuffs, Inspector. You can leave the talking to me."

We waited in silence for a minute—one of those minutes which one can never forget. Then the door opened, and the man stepped in. In an instant Holmes clapped a pistol to his head, and Martin slipped the handcuffs over his wrists. It was all done so swiftly and deftly that the fellow was helpless before he knew that he was attacked. He glared from one to the other of us with a pair of blazing black eyes. Then he burst into a bitter laugh.

" Well, gentlemen, you have the drop on me this time. I seem to have knocked up against something hard. But I came here in answer to a letter from Mrs. Hilton Cubitt. Don't tell me that she is in this ? Don't tell me that she helped to set a trap for me ? "

" Mrs. Hilton Cubitt was seriously injured, and is at death's door."

The man gave a hoarse cry of grief which rang through the house.

"You're crazy!" he cried fiercely. "It was he that was hurt, not she. Who would have hurt little Elsie? I may have threatened her, God forgive me, but I would not have touched a hair of her pretty head. Take it back—you! Say that she is not hurt!"

"She was found badly wounded by the side of her dead husband."

He sank with a deep groan on to the settee, and buried his face in his manacled hands. For five minutes he was silent. Then he raised his face once more, and spoke with the cold composure of despair.

"I have nothing to hide from you, gentlemen," said he. "If I shot the man he had his shot at me, and there's no murder in that. But if you think I could have hurt that woman, then you don't know either me or her. I tell you there was never a man in this world loved a woman more than I loved her. I had a right to her. She was pledged to me years ago. Who was this Englishman that he should come between us? I tell you that I had the first right to her, and that I was only claiming my own."

"She broke away from your influence when she found the man that you are," said Holmes sternly. "She fled from America to avoid you, and she married an honourable gentleman in England. You dogged her and followed her, and made her life a misery to her in order to induce her to abandon the husband whom she loved and respected in order to fly with you, whom she feared and hated. You have ended by bringing about the death of a noble man and driving his wife to suicide. That is your record in this business, Mr. Abe Slaney, and you will answer for it to the law."

"If Elsie dies I care nothing what becomes of me," said the American. He opened one of his hands and looked at a note crumpled up in his palm. "See here, mister," he cried, with a gleam of suspicion in his eyes,

" you're not trying to scare me over this, are you ? If the lady is hurt as bad as you say, who was it that wrote this note ? " He tossed it forward on to the table.

" I wrote it to bring you here."

" You wrote it ? There was no one on earth outside the Joint who knew the secret of the dancing men. How came you to write it ? "

" What one man can invent another can discover," said Holmes. " There is a cab coming to convey you to Norwich, Mr. Slaney. But, meanwhile, you have time to make some small reparation for the injury you have wrought. Are you aware that Mrs. Hilton Cubitt has herself lain under grave suspicion of the murder of her husband, and that it was only my presence here and the knowledge which I happened to possess which has saved her from the accusation ? The least that you owe her is to make it clear to the whole world that she was in no way directly or indirectly responsible for his tragic end."

" I ask nothing better," said the American. " I guess the very best case I can make for myself is the absolute naked truth."

" It is my duty to warn you that it will be used against you," cried the Inspector, with the magnificent fair-play of the British criminal law.

Slaney shrugged his shoulders.

" I'll chance that," said he. " First of all, I want you gentlemen to understand that I have known this lady since she was a child. There were seven of us in a gang in Chicago, and Elsie's father was the boss of the Joint. He was a clever man, was old Patrick. It was he who invented that writing, which would pass as a child's scrawl unless you just happened to have the key to it. Well, Elsie learned some of our ways ; but she couldn't stand the business, and she had a bit of honest money of her own, so she gave us all the slip and got away to London. She had been engaged to me, and she would have married me, I believe, if I had taken over another profession ; but she would have nothing to do with anything on the cross. It was only after her marriage to this Englishman that I was able to find out where she was. I wrote to her, but got no answer. After that I came over, and, as letters were of no use, I put my messages where she could read them.

"Well, I have been here a month now. I lived in that farm, where I had a room down below, and could get in and out every night, and no one the wiser. I tried all I could to coax Elsie away. I knew that she read the messages, for once she wrote an answer under one of them. Then my temper got the better of me, and I began to threaten her. She sent me a letter then, imploring me to go away, and saying that it would break her heart if any scandal should come upon her husband. She said that she would come down when her husband was asleep at three in the morning, and speak with me through the end window, if I would go away afterwards and leave her in peace. She came down and brought money with her, trying to bribe me to go. This made me mad, and I caught her arm and tried to pull her through the window. At that moment in rushed the husband with his revolver in his hand. Elsie had sunk down upon the floor, and we were face to face. I was heeled also, and I held up my gun to scare him off and let me get away. He fired and missed me. I pulled off almost at the same instant, and down he dropped. I made away across the garden, and as I went I heard the window shut behind me. That's God's truth, gentlemen, every word of it, and I heard no more about it until that lad came riding up with a note which made me walk in here, like a jay, and give myself into your hands."

A cab had driven up whilst the American had been talking. Two uniformed policemen sat inside. Inspector Martin rose and touched his prisoner on the shoulder.

"It is time for us to go."

"Can I see her first ? "

" No, she is not conscious. Mr. Sherlock Holmes, I only hope that if ever again I have an important case I shall have the good fortune to have you by my side."

We stood at the window and watched the cab drive away. As I turned back my eye caught the pellet of paper which the prisoner had tossed upon the table. It was the note with which Holmes had decoyed him.

" See if you can read it, Watson," said he, with a smile.

It contained no word, but this little line of dancing men :

" If you use the code which I have explained," said Holmes, " you will find that it simply means ' Come here at once.' I was convinced that it was an invitation which he would not refuse, since he could never imagine that it could come from anyone but the lady. And so, my dear Watson, we have ended by turning the dancing men to good when they have so often been the agents of evil, and I think that I have fulfilled my promise of giving you something unusual for your notebook. Three-forty is our train, and I fancy we should be back in Baker Street for dinner."

Only one word of epilogue.

The American, Abe Slaney, was condemned to death at the winter assizes at Norwich ; but his penalty was changed to penal servitude in consideration of mitigating circumstances, and the certainty that Hilton Cubitt had fired the first shot.

Of Mrs. Hilton Cubitt I only know that I have heard she recovered entirely, and that she still remains a widow, devoting her whole life to the care of the poor and to the administration of her husband's estate.

27. *The Solitary Cyclist*

FROM the years 1894 to 1901 inclusive, Mr. Sherlock Holmes was a very busy man. It is safe to say that there was no public case of any difficulty in which he was not consulted during those eight years, and there were hundreds of private cases, some of them of the most intricate and extraordinary character, in which he played a prominent part. Many startling successes and a few unavoidable failures were the outcome of this long period of continuous work. As I have preserved very full notes of all these cases, and was myself personally engaged in many of them, it may be imagined that it is no easy task to know which I should select to lay before the public. I shall, however, preserve my former rule, and give the preference to those cases which derive their interest not so much from the brutality of the crime as from the ingenuity and dramatic quality of the solution. For this reason I will now lay before the reader the facts connected with Miss Violet Smith, the solitary cyclist of Charlington, and the curious sequel of our investigation, which culminated in unexpected tragedy. It is true that the circumstances did not permit of any striking illustration of those powers for which my friend was famous, but there were some points about the case which made it stand out in those long records of crime from which I gather the material for these little narratives.

On referring to my notebook for the year 1895, I find that it was upon Saturday, April 23, that we first heard of Miss Violet Smith. Her visit was, I remember, extremely unwelcome to Holmes, for he was immersed at the moment in a very abstruse and complicated problem concerning the peculiar persecution to which John Vincent Harden, the well-known tobacco millionaire, had been subjected. My friend, who loved above all things precision and concentration of thought, resented anything which distracted his attention from the matter in hand. And yet without harshness which was foreign to his nature it was impossible to refuse to listen to the story of the young and beautiful woman, tall, graceful, and queenly, who presented herself at Baker Street late in the evening and implored his assistance and advice. It was vain to urge that his time was already fully occupied, for the young lady had come with the determination to tell her story, and it was evident that nothing short of force could get her out of the room until she had done so. With a resigned air and a somewhat weary smile, Holmes begged the beautiful intruder to take a seat and to inform us what it was that was troubling her.

"At least it cannot be your health," said he, as his keen eyes darted over her; "so ardent a bicyclist must be full of energy."

She glanced down in surprise at her own feet, and I observed the slight roughening of the side of the sole caused by the friction of the edge of the pedal.

"Yes, I bicycle a good deal, Mr. Holmes, and that has something to do with my visit to you to-day."

My friend took the lady's ungloved hand and examined it with as close an attention and as little sentiment as a scientist would show to a specimen.

"You will excuse me, I am sure. It is my business," said he, as he dropped it. "I nearly fell into the error of supposing that you were typewriting. Of course, it is obvious that it is music. You observe the spatulate finger-end, Watson, which is common to both professions? There is a spirituality about the face, however"
—he gently turned it towards the light—"which the typewriter does not generate. This lady is a musician."

"Yes, Mr. Holmes, I teach music."

"In the country, I presume, from your complexion."

"Yes, sir; near Farnham, on the borders of Surrey."

"A beautiful neighbourhood, and full of the most interesting associations. You remember, Watson, that it was near there that we took Archie Stamford, the forger.

Now, Miss Violet, what has happened to you near Farnham, on the borders of Surrey?"

The young lady, with great clearness and composure, made the following curious statement:

"My father is dead, Mr. Holmes. He was James Smith, who conducted the orchestra at the old Imperial Theatre. My mother and I were left without a relation in the world except one uncle, Ralph Smith, who went to Africa twenty-five years ago, and we have never had a word from him since. When father died we were left very poor, but one day we were told that there was an advertisement in *The Times* inquiring for our whereabouts. You can imagine how excited we were, for we thought that someone had left us a fortune. We went at once to the lawyer whose name was given in the paper. There we met two gentlemen, Mr. Carruthers and Mr. Woodley, who were home on a visit from South Africa. They said that my uncle was a friend of theirs, that he died some months before in poverty in Johannesburg, and that he had asked them with his last breath to hunt up his relations and see that they were in no want. It seemed strange to us that Uncle Ralph, who took no notice of us when he was alive, should be so careful to look after us when he was dead; but Mr. Carruthers explained that the reason was that my uncle had just heard of the death of his brother, and so felt responsible for our fate."

"Excuse me," said Holmes; "when was this interview?"

"Last December—four months ago."

"Pray proceed."

"Mr. Woodley seemed to me to be a most odious person. He was for ever making eyes at me—a coarse, puffy-faced, red-moustached young man, with his hair plastered down on each side of his forehead. I thought that he was perfectly hateful—and I was sure that Cyril would not wish me to know such a person."

"Oh, Cyril is his name!" said Holmes, smiling.

The young lady blushed and laughed.

" Yes, Mr. Holmes ; Cyril Morton, an electrical engineer, and we hope to be married at the end of the summer. Dear me, how *did* I get talking about him ? What I wished to say was that Mr. Woodley was perfectly odious, but that Mr. Carruthers, who was a much older man, was more agreeable. He was a dark, sallow, clean-shaven, silent person ; but he had polite manners and a pleasant smile. He inquired how we were left, and on finding that we were very poor he suggested that I should come and teach music to his only daughter, aged ten. I said that I did not like to leave my mother, on which he suggested that I should go home to her every week-end, and he offered me a hundred a year, which was certainly splendid pay. So it ended by my accepting, and I went down to Chiltern Grange, about six miles from Farnham. Mr. Carruthers was a widower, but he had engaged a lady-housekeeper, a very respectable, elderly person, called Mrs. Dixon, to look after his establishment. The child was a dear, and everything promised well. Mr. Carruthers was very kind and very musical, and we had most pleasant evenings together. Every week-end I went home to my mother in town.

" The first flaw in my happiness was the arrival of the red-moustached Mr. Woodley. He came for a visit of a week, and oh, it seemed three months to me ! He was a dreadful person, a bully to everyone else, but to me something infinitely worse. He made odious love to me, boasted of his wealth, said that if I married him I would have the finest diamonds in London, and finally, when I would have nothing to do with him, he seized me in his arms one day after dinner—he was hideously strong— and he swore that he would not let me go until I had kissed him. Mr. Carruthers came in, and tore him off from me, on which he turned upon his own host, knocking him down and cutting his face open. That was the end of his visit, as you can imagine. Mr. Carruthers apologized to me next day, and assured me that I should never be exposed to such an insult again. I have not seen Mr. Woodley since.

"And now, Mr. Holmes, I come at last to the special thing which has caused me to ask your advice to-day. You must know that every Saturday forenoon I ride on my bicycle to Farnham Station in order to get the 12.22 to town. The road from Chiltern Grange is a lonely one, and at one spot it is particularly so, for it lies for over a mile between Charlington Heath upon one side and the woods which lie round Charlington Hall upon the other. You could not find a more lonely tract of road anywhere, and it is quite rare to meet so much as a cart, or a peasant, until you reach the high-road near Crooksbury Hill. Two weeks ago I was passing this place when I chanced to look back over my shoulder, and about two hundred yards behind me I saw a man, also on a bicycle. He seemed to be a middle-aged man, with a short, dark beard. I looked back before I reached Farnham, but the man was gone, so I thought no more about it. But you can imagine how surprised I was, Mr. Holmes, when on my return on the Monday I saw the same man on the same stretch of road. My astonishment was increased when the incident occurred again, exactly as before, on the following Saturday and Monday. He always kept his distance, and did not molest me in any way, but still it certainly was very odd. I mentioned it to Mr. Carruthers, who seemed interested in what I said, and told me that he had ordered a horse and trap, so that in future I should not pass over these lonely roads without some companion.

"The horse and trap were to have come this week, but for some reason they were not delivered, and again I had to cycle to the station. That was this morning. You can think that I looked out when I came to Charlington Heath, and there, sure enough, was the man, exactly as he had been the two weeks before. He always kept so far from me that I could not clearly see his face, but it was certainly someone whom I did not know. He was dressed in a dark suit with a cloth cap. The only thing about his face that I could clearly see was his dark beard. To-day I was not alarmed, but I was filled with curiosity, and I determined to find out who he was and what he wanted. I slowed down my machine, but he slowed down his. Then I stopped altogether, but he stopped also. Then I laid a trap for him. There is a sharp turning of the road, and I pedalled very quickly round this, and then I stopped and waited. I expected him to shoot round and pass me before he could stop. But he never appeared. Then I went back and looked round the corner. I could see a mile of road, but he was not on it. To make it the more extraordinary there was no sideroad at this point down which he could have gone."

Holmes chuckled and rubbed his hands.

" This case certainly presents some features of its own," said he. " How much time elapsed between your turning the corner and your discovery that the road was clear ? "

" Two or three minutes."

" Then he could not have retreated down the road, and you say that there are no side-roads ? "

" None."

" Then he certainly took a footpath on one side or the other."

" It could not have been on the side of the heath or I should have seen him."

" So by the process of exclusion we arrive at the fact that he made his way towards Charlington Hall, which, as I understand, is situated in its own grounds on one side of the road. Anything else ? "

" Nothing, Mr. Holmes, save that I was so perplexed that I felt I should not be happy until I had seen you and had your advice."

Holmes sat in silence for some little time.

" Where is the gentleman to whom you are engaged ? " he asked at last.

" He is in the Midland Electric Company, at Coventry."

" He would not pay you a surprise visit ? "

" Oh, Mr. Holmes ! As if I should not know him ! "

" Have you had any other admirers ? "

" Several before I knew Cyril."

" And since ? "

" There was this dreadful man, Woodley, if you can call him an admirer."

" No one else ? "

Our fair client seemed a little confused.

" Who was he ? " asked Holmes.

" Oh, it may be a mere fancy of mine ; but it has seemed to me sometimes that my employer, Mr. Carruthers, takes a great deal of interest in me. We are thrown rather together. I play his accompaniments in the evening. He has never said anything. He is a perfect gentleman. But a girl always knows."

" Ha ! " Holmes looked grave. " What does he do for a living ? "

" He is a rich man."

" No carriages or horses ? "

" Well, at least he is fairly well-to-do. But he goes into the city two or three times a week. He is deeply interested in South African gold shares."

" You will let me know any fresh development, Miss Smith. I am very busy just now, but I will find time to make some inquiries into your case. In the meantime, take no step without letting me know. Good-bye, and I trust that we shall have nothing but good news from you."

" It is part of the settled order of Nature that such a girl should have followers," said Holmes, as he pulled at his meditative pipe, " but for choice not on bicycles in lonely country roads. Some secretive lover, beyond all doubt. But there are curious and suggestive details about the case, Watson."

" That he should appear only at that point ? "

" Exactly. Our first effort must be to find who are the tenants of Charlington Hall. Then, again, how about the connection between Carruthers and Woodley, since they appear to be men of such different types? How came they *both* to be so keen upon looking up Ralph Smith's relations? One more point. What sort of a *ménage* is it which pays double the market price for a governess, but does not keep a horse although six miles from the station? Odd, Watson—very odd."

" You will go down? "

" No, my dear fellow, *you* will go down. This may be some trifling intrigue, and I cannot break my other important research for the sake of it. On Monday you will arrive early at Farnham; you will conceal yourself near Charlington Heath; you will observe these facts for yourself, and act as your own judgment advises. Then, having inquired as to the occupants of the Hall, you will come back to me and report. And now, Watson, not another word of the matter until we have a few solid stepping-stones on which we may hope to get across to our solution."

We had ascertained from the lady that she went down upon the Monday by the train which leaves Waterloo at 9.50, so I started early and caught the 9.13. At Farnham Station I had no difficulty in being directed to Charlington Heath. It was impossible to mistake the scene of the young lady's adventure, for the road runs between the open heath on one side, and an old yew hedge upon the other, surrounding a park which is studded with magnificent trees. There was a main gateway of lichen-studded stone, each side-pillar surmounted by mouldering heraldic emblems; but besides this central carriage-drive I observed several points where there were gaps in the hedge and paths leading through them. The house was invisible from the road, but the surroundings all spoke of gloom and decay.

The heath was covered with golden patches of flowering gorse, gleaming magnificently in the light of the bright spring sunshine. Behind one of these clumps I took up my position, so as to command both the gateway of the

Hall and a long stretch of the road upon either side. It had been deserted when I left it, but now I saw a cyclist riding down it from the opposite direction to that in which I had come. He was clad in a dark suit, and I saw that he had a black beard. On reaching the end of the Charlington grounds he sprang from his machine and led it through a gap in the hedge, disappearing from my view.

A quarter of an hour passed and then a second cyclist appeared. This time it was the young lady coming from the station. I saw her look about her as she came to the Charlington hedge. An instant later the man emerged from his hiding-place, sprang upon his bicycle, and followed her. In all the broad landscape those were the only moving figures, the graceful girl sitting very straight upon her machine, and the man behind her bending low over his handle-bar, with a curiously furtive suggestion in every movement. She looked back at him and slowed her pace. He slowed also. She stopped. He at once stopped, too, keeping two hundred yards behind her. Her next movement was as unexpected as it was spirited. She suddenly whisked her wheels round and dashed straight at him ! He was as quick as she, however, and darted off in desperate flight. Presently she came back up the road again, her head haughtily in the air, not deigning to take further notice of her silent attendant. He had turned also, and still kept his distance until the curve of the road hid them from my sight.

I remained in my hiding-place, and it was well that I did so, for presently the man reappeared cycling slowly back. He turned in at the Hall gates and dismounted from his machine. For some few minutes I could see him standing among the trees. His hands were raised, and he seemed to be settling his necktie. Then he mounted his bicycle and rode away from me down the drive towards the Hall. I ran across the heath and peered through the trees. Far away I could catch glimpses of the old grey building with its bristling Tudor chimneys, but the drive ran through a dense shrubbery, and I saw no more of my man.

However, it seemed to me that I had done a fairly good morning's work, and I walked back in high spirits to Farnham. The local house agent could tell me nothing about Charlington Hall, and referred me to a well-known firm in Pall Mall. There I halted on my way home, and met with courtesy from the representative. No, I could not have Charlington Hall for the summer. I was just too late. It had been let about a month ago. Mr. Williamson was the name of the tenant. He was a respectable elderly gentleman. The polite agent was afraid he could say no more, as the affairs of his clients were not matters which he could discuss.

Mr. Sherlock Holmes listened with attention to the long report which I was able to present to him that evening, but it did not elicit that word of curt praise which I had hoped for and should have valued. On the contrary, his austere face was even more severe than usual as he commented upon the things that I had done and the things that I had not.

"Your hiding-place, my dear Watson, was very faulty. You should have been behind the hedge ; then you would have had a close view of this interesting person. As it is you were some hundreds of yards away, and can tell me even less than Miss Smith. She thinks she does not know the man ; I am convinced she does. Why, otherwise, should he be so desperately anxious that she should not get so near him as to see his features ? You describe him as bending over the handle-bar. Concealment again, you see. You really have done remarkably badly. He returns to the house, and you want to find out who he is. You come to a London house agent !"

"What should I have done ? " I cried, with some heat.

"Gone to the nearest public-house. That is the centre of country gossip. They would have told you every name, from the master to the scullery-maid. William-son ! It conveys nothing to my mind. If he is an elderly man he is not this active cyclist who sprints away from that athletic young lady's pursuit. What have we gained by your expedition ? The knowledge that the girl's story is true. I never doubted it. That there is a connection between the cyclist and the Hall. I never doubted that either. That the Hall is tenanted by Williamson. Who's the better for that ? Well, well, my dear sir, don't look so depressed. We can do little more until next Saturday, and in the meantime I may make one or two inquiries myself."

Next morning we had a note from Miss Smith, recounting shortly and accurately the very incidents which I had seen, but the pith of the letter lay in the postscript :

" I am sure that you will respect my confidence, Mr. Holmes, when I tell you that my place here has become difficult owing to the fact that my employer has proposed marriage to me. I am convinced that his feelings are most deep and most honourable. At the same time my promise is, of course, given. He took my refusal very seriously, but also very gently. You can understand, however, that the situation is a little strained."

" Our young friend seems to be getting into deep waters," said Holmes thoughtfully, as he finished the letter. " The case certainly presents more features of interest and more possibility of development than I had originally thought. I should be none the worse for a quiet, peaceful day in the country, and I am inclined to run down this afternoon and test one or two theories which I have formed."

Holmes' quiet day in the country had a singular termination, for he arrived at Baker Street late in the evening with a cut lip and a discoloured lump upon his forehead, besides a general air of dissipation which would have made his own person the fitting object of a Scotland Yard investigation. He was immensely tickled by his own adventures, and laughed heartily as he recounted them.

"I get so little active exercise that it is always a treat," said he. "You are aware that I have some proficiency in the good old British sport of boxing. Occasionally it is of service. To-day, for example, I should have come to very ignominious grief without it."

I begged him to tell me what had occurred.

"I found that country pub which I had already recommended to your notice, and there I made my discreet inquiries. I was in the bar, and a garrulous landlord was giving me all that I wanted. Williamson is a white-bearded man, and he lives alone with a small staff of servants at the Hall. There is some rumour that he is or has been a clergyman; but one or two incidents of his short residence at the Hall struck me as peculiarly unecclesiastical. I have already made some inquiries at a clerical agency, and they tell me that there *was* a man of that name in orders whose career has been a singularly dark one. The landlord further informed me that there are usually week-end visitors—'a warm lot, sir'—at the Hall, and especially one gentleman with a red moustache, Mr. Woodley by name, who was always there. We had got as far as this when who should walk in but the gentleman himself, who had been drinking his beer in the tap-room, and had heard the whole conversation. Who was I? What did I want? What did I mean by asking questions? He had a fine flow of language, and his adjectives were very vigorous. He ended a string of abuse by a vicious back-hander, which I failed to entirely avoid. The next few minutes were delicious. It was a straight left against a slogging ruffian. I emerged as you see me. Mr. Woodley went home in a cart. So ended my country trip, and it must be confessed that, however enjoyable, my day on the Surrey border has not been much more profitable than your own."

The Thursday brought us another letter from our client.

"You will not be surprised, Mr. Holmes (said she),

to hear that I am leaving Mr. Carruthers' employment. Even the high pay cannot reconcile me to the discomforts of my situation. On Saturday I come up to town, and I do not intend to return. Mr. Carruthers has got a trap, and so the dangers of the lonely road, if there ever were any dangers, are now over.

" As to the special cause of my leaving, it is not merely the strained situation with Mr. Carruthers, but it is the reappearance of that odious man, Mr. Woodley. He was always hideous, but he looks more awful than ever now, for he appears to have had an accident and he is much disfigured. I saw him out of the window, but I am glad to say I did not meet him. He had a long talk with Mr. Carruthers, who seemed much excited afterwards. Woodley must be staying in the neighbourhood, for he did not sleep here, and yet I caught a glimpse of him again this morning slinking about in the shrubbery. I would sooner have a savage wild animal loose about the place. I loathe and fear him more than I can say. How *can* Mr. Carruthers endure such a creature for a moment? However, all my troubles will be over on Saturday."

" So I trust, Watson, so I trust,"said Holmes gravely. " There is some deep intrigue going on round that little woman, and it is our duty to see that no one molests her upon that last journey. I think, Watson, that we must spare time to run down together on Saturday morning, and make sure that this curious and inconclusive investigation has no untoward ending."

I confess that I had not up to now taken a very serious view of the case, which had seemed to me rather grotesque and bizarre than dangerous. That a man should lie in wait for and follow a very handsome woman is no un-heard-of thing, and if he had so little audacity that he not only dared not address her, but even fled from her approach, he was not a very formidable assailant. The ruffian Woodley was a very different person, but, except on the one occasion, he had not molested our client, and now he visited the house of Carruthers without intruding upon her presence. The man on the bicycle was doubtless a member of those week-end parties at the Hall of which the publican had spoken ; but who he was or what he wanted was as obscure as ever. It was the severity of Holmes' manner and the fact that he slipped a revolver into his pocket before leaving our rooms which impressed me with the feeling that tragedy might prove to lurk behind this curious train of events.

A rainy night had been followed by a glorious morning, and the heath-covered country-side, with the glowing clumps of flowering gorse, seemed all the more beautiful to eyes which were weary of the duns and drabs and slate-greys of London. Holmes and I walked along the broad, sandy road inhaling the fresh morning air, and rejoicing in the music of the birds and the fresh breath of the spring. From a rise of the road on the shoulder of Crooksbury Hill we could see the grim Hall bristling out from amidst the ancient oaks, which, old as they were, were still younger than the building which they surrounded. Holmes pointed down the long tract of road which wound, a reddish-yellow band, between the brown of the heath and the budding green of the woods. Far away, a black dot, we could see a vehicle moving in our direction. Holmes gave an exclamation of impatience.

" I had given a margin of half an hour," said he. " If that is her trap she must be making for the earlier train. I fear, Watson, that she will be past Charlington before we can possibly meet her."

From the instant that we passed the rise we could no longer see the vehicle, but we hastened onwards at such a pace that my sedentary life began to tell upon me, and I was compelled to fall behind. Holmes, however, was always in training, for he had inexhaustible stores of nervous energy upon which to draw. His springy step never slowed, until suddenly, when he was a hundred yards in front of me, he halted, and I saw him throw up his hand with a gesture of grief and despair. At the same instant an empty dog-cart, the horse cantering, the reins trailing, appeared round the curve of the road and rattled swiftly towards us.

"Too late, Watson; too late!" cried Holmes, as I ran panting to his side. "Fool that I was not to allow for the earlier train! It's abduction, Watson—abduction! Murder! Heaven knows what! Block the road! Stop the horse! That's right. Now jump in, and let us see if I can repair the consequences of my own blunder."

We had sprung into the dog-cart, and Holmes, after turning the horse, gave it a sharp cut with the whip, and we flew back along the road. As we turned the curve the whole stretch of road between the Hall and the heath was opened up. I grasped Holmes' arm.

"That's the man!" I gasped.

A solitary cyclist was coming towards us. His head was down and his shoulders rounded as he put every ounce of energy that he possessed on to the pedals. He was flying like a racer. Suddenly he raised his bearded face, saw us close to him, and pulled up, springing from his machine. That coal-black beard was in singular contrast to the pallor of his face, and his eyes were as bright as if he had a fever. He stared at us and at the dog-cart. Then a look of amazement came over his face.

"Halloa! Stop there!" he shouted, holding his bicycle to block our road. "Where did you get that dog-cart? Pull up, man!" he yelled, drawing a pistol from his side-pocket. "Pull up, I say, or, by George, I'll put a bullet into your horse!"

Holmes threw the reins into my lap and sprang down from the cart.

"You're the man we want to see. Where is Miss Violet Smith?" he said in his quick, clear way.

"That's what I am asking you. You're in her dog-cart. You ought to know where she is."

"We met the dog-cart on the road. There was no one in it. We drove back to help the young lady."

"Good Lord! Good Lord! What shall I do?"
cried the stranger, in an ecstasy of despair. "They've
got her. that hellhound Woodley and the blackguard
parson. Come, man, come, if you really are her friend.
Stand by me and we'll save her, if I have to leave my
carcass in Charlington Wood."

He ran distractedly, his pistol in his hand, towards a
gap in the hedge. Holmes followed him, and I, leaving
the horse grazing beside the road, followed Holmes.

"This is where they came through," said he, pointing to the marks of several feet upon the muddy path.
"Halloa! Stop a minute! Who's this in the bush?"

It was a young fellow about seventeen, dressed like an
ostler, with leather cords and gaiters. He lay upon his
back, his knees drawn up, a terrible cut upon his head.
He was insensible, but alive. A glance at his wound
told me that it had not penetrated the bone.

"That's Peter, the groom," cried the stranger. "He
drove her. The beasts have pulled him off and clubbed
him. Let him lie; we can't do him any good, but we
may save her from the worst fate that can befall a woman."

We ran frantically down the path, which wound among
the trees. We had reached the shrubbery which surrounded the house when Holmes pulled up.

"They didn't go to the house. Here are their marks
on the left—here, beside the laurel bushes! Ah, I said
so!"

As he spoke a woman's shrill scream—a scream which
vibrated with a frenzy of horror—burst from the thick
green clump of bushes in front of us. It ended suddenly on its highest note with a choke and a gurgle.

"This way! This way! They are in the bowling
alley," cried the stranger, darting through the bushes.
"Ah, the cowardly dogs! Follow me, gentlemen! Too
late! too late! by the living Jingo!"

We had broken suddenly into a lovely glade of greens-
ward surrounded by ancient trees. On the farther side of
it, under the shadow of a mighty oak, there stood a

singular group of three people. One was a woman, our client, drooping and faint, a handkerchief round her mouth. Opposite her stood a brutal, heavy-faced, red-moustached young man, his gaitered legs parted wide, one arm akimbo, the other waving a riding-crop, his whole attitude suggestive of triumphant bravado. Between them an elderly, grey-bearded man, wearing a short surplice over a light tweed suit, had evidently just completed the wedding service, for he pocketed his Prayer Book as we appeared, and slapped the sinister bridegroom upon the back in jovial congratulation.

" They're married ! " I gasped.

" Come on ! " cried our guide; " come on ! " He rushed across the glade, Holmes and I at his heels. As we approached, the lady staggered against the trunk of the tree for support. Williamson, the ex-clergyman, bowed to us with mock politeness, and the bully Woodley advanced with a shout of brutal and exultant laughter.

" You can take your beard off, Bob," said he. " I know you right enough. Well, you and your pals have just come in time for me to be able to introduce you to Mrs. Woodley."

Our guide's answer was a singular one. He snatched off the dark beard which had disguised him and threw it on the ground, disclosing a long, sallow, clean-shaven face below it. Then he raised his revolver and covered the young ruffian, who was advancing upon him with his dangerous riding-crop swinging in his hand.

" Yes," said our ally, " I *am* Bob Carruthers, and I'll see this woman righted if I have to swing for it. I told you what I'd do if you molested her, and, by the Lord, I'll be as good as my word ! "

" You're too late. She's my wife ! "

" No, she's your widow."

His revolver cracked, and I saw the blood spurt from the front of Woodley's waistcoat. He spun round with a scream and fell upon his back, his hideous red face turning suddenly to a dreadful mottled pallor. The old man, still clad in his surplice, burst into such a string of foul oaths as I have never heard, and pulled out a revolver of his own, but before he could raise it he was looking down the barrel of Holmes' weapon.

" Enough of this," said my friend coldly. " Drop that pistol ! Watson, pick it up ! Hold it to his head ! Thank you. You, Carruthers, give me that revolver. We'll have no more violence. Come, hand it over ! "

" Who are you, then ? "

" My name is Sherlock Holmes."

" Good Lord ! "

" You have heard of me, I see. I will represent the official police until their arrival. Here, you ! " he shouted to the frightened groom, who had appeared at the edge of the glade. " Come here. Take this note as hard as you can ride to Farnham." He scribbled a few words upon a leaf from his notebook. " Give it to the super-intendent at the police-station. Until he comes, I must detain you all under my personal custody."

The strong, masterful personality of Holmes domin-ated the tragic scene, and all were equally puppets in his hands. Williamson and Carruthers found themselves carrying the wounded Woodley into the house, and I gave my arm to the frightened girl. The injured man was laid on his bed, and at Holmes' request I examined him. I carried my report to where he sat in the old tapestry-hung dining-room with his two prisoners before him.

" He will live," said I.

" What ! " cried Carruthers, springing out of his chair. " I'll go upstairs and finish him first. Do you tell me that that girl, that angel, is to be tied to Roaring Jack Woodley for life ? "

" You need not concern yourself about that," said Holmes. " There are two very good reasons why she should under no circumstances be his wife. In the first place, we are very safe in questioning Mr. Williamson's right to solemnize a marriage."

" I have been ordained," cried the old rascal.

" And also unfrocked."

" Once a clergyman, always a clergyman."

" I think not. How about the licence ? "

" We had a licence for the marriage. I have it here in my pocket."

" Then you got it by a trick. But in any case a forced marriage is no marriage, but it is a very serious felony, as you will discover before you have finished. You'll have time to think the point out during the next ten years or so, unless I am mistaken. As to you, Carruthers, you would have done better to keep your pistol in your pocket."

" I begin to think so, Mr. Holmes ; but when I thought of all the precaution I had taken to shield this girl—for I loved her, Mr. Holmes, and it is the only time that ever I knew what love was—it fairly drove me mad to think that she was in the power of the greatest brute and bully in South Africa, a man whose name is a holy terror from Kimberley to Johannesburg. Why, Mr. Holmes, you'll hardly believe it, but ever since that girl has been in my employment I never once let her go past this house, where I knew these rascals were lurking, without following her on my bicycle just to see that she came to no harm. I kept my distance from her, and I wore a beard so that she should not recognize me, for she is a good and high-spirited girl, and she wouldn't have stayed in my employment long if she had thought that I was following her about the country roads."

" Why didn't you tell her of her danger ? "

" Because then, again, she would have left me, and I couldn't bear to face that. Even if she couldn't love me it was a great deal to me just to see her dainty form about the house, and to hear the sound of her voice."

" Well," said I, " you call that love, Mr. Carruthers, but I should call it selfishness."

" Maybe the two things go together. Anyhow, I couldn't let her go. Besides, with this crowd about, it was well that she should have someone near to look after

her. Then when the cable came I knew they were bound
to make a move."

" What cable ? "

Carruthers took a telegram from his pocket.

" That's it ! " said he. It was short and concise :

" The old man is dead."

" Hum ! " said Holmes. " I think I see how things
worked, and I can understand how this message would, as
you say, bring them to a head. But while we wait, you
might tell me what you can."

The old reprobate with the surplice burst into a volley
of bad language.

" By Heaven," said he, " if you squeal on us, Bob Carruthers, I'll serve you as you served Jack Woodley ! You
can bleat about the girl to your heart's content, for that's
your own affair, but if you round on your pals to this
plain-clothes copper it will be the worst day's work that
ever you did "

" Your reverence need not be excited," said Holmes,
lighting a cigarette. " The case is clear enough against
you, and all I ask is a few details for my private curiosity. However, if there's any difficulty in your telling
me I'll do the talking, and then you will see how far
you have a chance of holding back your secrets. In the
first place, three of you came from South Africa on this
game—you, Williamson, you, Carruthers, and Woodley."

" Lie number one," said the old man ; " I never saw
either of them until two months ago, and I have never
been in Africa in my life, so you can put that in your
pipe and smoke it, Mr. Busybody Holmes ! "

" What he says is true," said Carruthers.

" Well, well, two of you came over. His reverence is
our own home-made article. You had known Ralph
Smith in South Africa. You had reason to believe he
would not live long. You found out that his niece would
inherit his fortune. How's that—eh ? "

Carruthers nodded, and Williamson swore.

" She was next-of-kin, no doubt, and you were aware that the old fellow would make no will."

" Couldn't read or write," said Carruthers.

" So you came over, the two of you, and hunted up the girl. The idea was that one of you was to marry her, and the other have a share of the plunder. For some reason Woodley was chosen as the husband. Why was that ? "

" We played cards for her on the voyage. He won."

" I see. You got the young lady into your service, and there Woodley was to do the courting. She recognized the drunken brute that he was, and would have nothing to do with him. Meanwhile, your arrangement was rather upset by the fact that you had yourself fallen in love with the lady. You could no longer bear the idea of this ruffian owning her."

" No, by George, I couldn't ! "

" There was a quarrel between you. He left you in a rage, and began to make his own plans independently of you."

" It strikes me, Williamson, there isn't very much that we can tell this gentleman," cried Carruthers, with a bitter laugh. " Yes, we quarrelled, and he knocked me down. I am level with him on that, anyhow. Then I lost sight of him. That was when he picked up with this cast padre here. I found that they had set up housekeeping together at this place on the line that she had to pass for the station. I kept my eye on her after that, for I knew there was some devilry in the wind. I saw them from time to time, for I was anxious to know what they were after. Two days ago Woodley came up to my house with this cable, which showed that Ralph Smith was dead. He asked me if I would stand by the bargain. I said I would not. He asked me if I would marry the girl myself and give him a share. I said I would willingly do so, but that she would not have me. He said, ' Let us get her married first, and after a week or two she may see things a bit different.' I said I would have nothing to do with violence. So he went off cursing, like the foul-mouthed blackguard that he was, and swearing that he would have her yet. She was leaving me this week-end, and I had got a trap to take her to the station, but I was so uneasy in my mind that I followed her on my bicycle. She had got a start, however, and before I could catch her the mischief was done. The first thing I knew about it was when I saw you two gentlemen driving back in her dog-cart."

Holmes rose and tossed the end of his cigarette into the grate. " I have been very obtuse, Watson," said he. " When in your report you said that you had seen the cyclist as you thought arrange his necktie in the shrubbery, that alone should have told me all. However, we may congratulate ourselves upon a curious and in some respects a unique case. I perceive three of the county constabulary in the drive, and I am glad to see that the little ostler is able to keep pace with them ; so it is likely that neither he nor the interesting bridegroom will be permanently damaged by their morning's adventures. I think, Watson, that in your medical capacity you might wait upon Miss Smith and tell her that if she is sufficiently recovered we shall be happy to escort her to her mother's home. If she is not quite convalescent you will find that a hint that we were about to telegraph to a young electrician in the Midlands would probably complete the cure. As to you, Mr. Carruthers, I think that you have done what you could to make amends for your share in an evil plot. There is my card, sir, and if my evidence can be of help to you in your trial it shall be at your disposal."

In the whirl of our incessant activity it has often been difficult for me, as the reader has probably observed, to round off my narratives, and to give those final details which the curious might expect. Each case has been the prelude to another, and the crisis once over, the actors have passed for ever out of our busy lives. I find, however, a short note at the end of my manuscripts dealing with this case, in which I have put it upon record that

Miss Violet Smith did indeed inherit a large fortune, and that she is now the wife of Cyril Morton, the senior partner of Morton and Kennedy, the famous Westminster electricians. Williamson and Woodley were both tried for abduction and assault, the former getting seven years and the latter ten. Of the fate of Carruthers I have no record, but I am sure that his assault was not viewed very gravely by the Court, since Woodley had the reputation of being a most dangerous ruffian, and I think that a few months were sufficient to satisfy the demands of justice.

28. *The Priory School*

WE have had some dramatic entrances and exits upon our small stage at Baker Street, but I cannot recollect anything more sudden and startling than the first appearance of Dr. Thorneycroft Huxtable, M.A., Ph.D., etc. His card, which seemed too small to carry the weight of his academic distinctions, preceded him by a few seconds, and then he entered himself—so large, so pompous, and so dignified that he was the very embodiment of self-possession and solidity. And yet his first action when the door had closed behind him was to stagger against the table, whence he slipped down upon the floor, and there was that majestic figure prostrate and insensible upon our bearskin hearthrug.

We had sprung to our feet, and for a few moments we stared in silent amazement at this ponderous piece of wreckage, which told of some sudden and fatal storm far out on the ocean of life. Then Holmes hurried with a cushion for his head, and I with brandy for his lips. The heavy white face was seamed with lines of trouble, the hanging pouches under the closed eyes were leaden in colour, the loose mouth drooped dolorously at the corners, the rolling chins were unshaven. Collar and shirt bore the grime of a long journey, and the hair bristled unkempt from the well-shaped head. It was a sorely stricken man who lay before us.

" What is it, Watson ? " asked Holmes.

" Absolute exhaustion—possibly mere hunger and fatigue," said I, with my finger on the thready pulse, where the stream of life trickled thin and small.

" Return ticket from Mackleton, in the North of England," said Holmes, drawing it from the watch-pocket. " It is not twelve o'clock yet. He has certainly been an early starter."

The puckered eyelids had begun to quiver, and now a pair of vacant grey eyes looked up at us. An instant later the man had scrambled on to his feet, his face crimson with shame.

" Forgive this weakness, Mr. Holmes ; I have been a little overwrought. Thank you, if I might have a glass of milk and a biscuit I have no doubt that I should be better. I came personally, Mr. Holmes, in order to ensure that you would return with me. I feared that no telegram would convince you of the absolute urgency of the case."

" When you are quite restored——"

" I am quite well again. I cannot imagine how I came to be so weak. I wish you, Mr. Holmes, to come to Mackleton with me by the next train."

My friend shook his head.

" My colleague, Dr. Watson, could tell you that we are very busy at present. I am retained in this case of the Ferrers Documents, and the Abergavenny murder is coming up for trial. Only a very important issue could call me from London at present."

" Important ! " Our visitor threw up his hands. " Have you heard nothing of the abduction of the only son of the Duke of Holdernesse ? "

" What ! the late Cabinet Minister ? "

" Exactly. We had tried to keep it out of the papers, but there was some rumour in the *Globe* last night. I thought it might have reached your ears."

Holmes shot out his long, thin arm and picked out Volume " H " in his encyclopædia of reference.

" ' Holdernesse, sixth Duke, K.G., P.C.'—half the alphabet ! ' Baron Beverley, Earl of Carston '—dear me, what a list ! ' Lord-Lieutenant of Hallamshire since 1900. Married Edith, daughter of Sir Charles Appledore, 1888. Heir and only child, Lord Saltire. Owns about two hundred and fifty thousand acres. Minerals in Lancashire and Wales. Address : Carlton House Terrace ; Holdernesse Hall, Hallamshire ; Carston Castle, Bangor, Wales. Lord of the Admiralty, 1872 ; Chief Secretary of State for——' Well, well, this man is certainly one of the greatest subjects of the Crown ! "

" The greatest and perhaps the wealthiest. I am aware, Mr. Holmes, that you take a very high line in professional matters, and that you are prepared to work for the work's sake. I may tell you, however, that his Grace has already intimated that a cheque for five thousand pounds will be handed over to the person who can tell him where his son is, and another thousand to him who can name the man, or men, who have taken him."

" It is a princely offer," said Holmes. " Watson, I think that we shall accompany Dr. Huxtable back to the North of England. And now, Dr. Huxtable, when you have consumed that milk you will kindly tell me what has happened, when it happened, how it happened, and, finally, what Dr. Thorneycroft Huxtable, of the Priory School, near Mackleton, has to do with the matter, and why he comes three days after an event—the state of your chin gives the date—to ask for my humble services."

Our visitor had consumed his milk and biscuits. The light had come back to his eyes and the colour to his cheeks as he set himself with great vigour and lucidity to explain the situation.

" I must inform you, gentlemen, that the Priory is a preparatory school, of which I am the founder and principal. *Huxtable's Sidelights on Horace* may possibly recall my name to your memories. The Priory is, without exception, the best and most select preparatory school in England. Lord Leverstoke, the Earl of Blackwater, Sir Cathcart Soames—they all have entrusted their sons to me. But I felt that my school had reached its zenith when, three weeks ago, the Duke of Holdernesse sent Mr. James Wilder, his secretary, with the intimation that young Lord Saltire, ten years old, his only son and heir, was about to be committed to my charge. Little did I think that this would be the prelude to the most crushing misfortune of my life.

"On May 1 the boy arrived, that being the beginning of the summer term. He was a charming youth, and he soon fell into our ways. I may tell you—I trust that I am not indiscreet; half-confidences are absurd in such a case—that he was not entirely happy at home. It is an open secret that the duke's married life had not been a peaceful one, and the matter had ended in a separation by mutual consent, the duchess taking up her residence in the South of France. This had occurred very shortly before, and the boy's sympathies are known to have been strongly with his mother. He moped after her departure from Holdernesse Hall, and it was for this reason that the duke desired to send him to my establishment. In a fortnight the boy was quite at home with us, and was apparently absolutely happy.

"He was last seen on the night of May 13—that is, the night of last Monday. His room was on the second floor, and was approached through another larger room in which two boys were sleeping. These boys saw and heard nothing, so that it is certain that young Saltire did not pass out that way. His window was open, and there is a stout ivy plant leading to the ground. We could trace no footmarks below, but it is sure that this is the only possible exit.

"His absence was discovered at seven o'clock on Tuesday morning. His bed had been slept in. He had dressed himself fully before going off in his usual school suit of black Eton jacket and dark grey trousers. There were no signs that anyone had entered the room, and it is quite certain that anything in the nature of cries or a struggle would have been heard, since Caunter, the elder boy in the inner room, is a very light sleeper.

" When Lord Saltire's disappearance was discovered I at once called a roll of the whole establishment—boys, masters, and servants. It was then that we ascertained that Lord Saltire had not been alone in his flight. Heidegger, the German master, was missing. His room was on the second floor, at the farther end of the building, facing the same way as Lord Saltire's. His bed had also been slept in ; but he had apparently gone away partly dressed, since his shirt and socks were lying on the floor. He had undoubtedly let himself down by the ivy, for we could see the marks of his feet where he had landed on the lawn. His bicycle was kept in a small shed beside this lawn, and it also was gone.

" He had been with me for two years, and came with the best references ; but he was a silent, morose man, not very popular either with masters or boys. No trace could be found of the fugitives, and now on Thursday morning we are as ignorant as we were on Tuesday. Inquiry was, of course, made at once at Holdernesse Hall. It is only a few miles away, and we imagined that in some sudden attack of home-sickness he had gone back to his father ; but nothing had been heard of him. The duke is greatly agitated—and as to me, you have seen yourselves the state of nervous prostration to which the suspense and the responsibility have reduced me. Mr. Holmes, if ever you put forward your full powers, I implore you to do so now, for never in your life could you have a case which is more worthy of them."

Sherlock Holmes had listened with the utmost intentness to the statement of the unhappy schoolmaster. His drawn brows and the deep furrow between them showed that he needed no exhortation to concentrate all his attention upon a problem which, apart from the tremendous interests involved, must appeal so directly to his love of the complex and the unusual. He now drew out his notebook and jotted down one or two memoranda.

" You have been very remiss in not coming to me sooner," said he severely. " You start me on my investigation with a very serious handicap. It is inconceivable, for example, that this ivy and this lawn would have yielded nothing to an expert observer."

" I am not to blame, Mr. Holmes. His Grace was extremely desirous to avoid all public scandal. He was afraid of his family unhappiness being dragged before the world. He has a deep horror of anything of the kind."

" But there has been some official investigation ? "

" Yes, sir, and it has proved most disappointing. An apparent clue was at once obtained, since a boy and a young man were reported to have been seen leaving a neighbouring station by an early train. Only last night we had news that the couple had been hunted down in Liverpool, and they prove to have no connection whatever with the matter in hand. Then it was that in my despair and disappointment, after a sleepless night, I came straight to you by the early train."

" I suppose the local investigation was relaxed while this false clue was being followed up ? "

" It was entirely dropped."

" So that three days have been wasted. The affair has been most deplorably handled."

" I feel it, and admit it."

" And yet the problem should be capable of ultimate solution. I shall be very happy to look into it. Have you been able to trace any connection between the missing boy and this German master ? "

" None at all."

" Was he in the master's class ? "

" No ; he never exchanged a word with him, so far as I know."

" That is certainly very singular. Had the boy a bicycle ? "

"No."

"Was any other bicycle missing?"

"No."

"Is that certain?"

"Quite."

"Well, now, you do not mean to seriously suggest that this German rode off upon a bicycle in the dead of the night bearing the boy in his arms?"

"Certainly not."

"Then what is the theory in your mind?"

"The bicycle may have been a blind. It may have been hidden somewhere, and the pair gone off on foot."

"Quite so; but it seems rather an absurd blind, does it not? Were there other bicycles in this shed?"

"Several."

"Would he not have hidden a *couple* had he desired to give the idea that they had gone off upon them?"

"I suppose he would."

"Of course he would. The blind theory won't do. But the incident is an admirable starting-point for an investigation. After all, a bicycle is not an easy thing to conceal or to destroy. One other question. Did anyone call to see the boy on the day before he disappeared?"

"No."

"Did he get any letters?"

"Yes; one letter."

"From whom?"

"From his father."

"Do you open the boys' letters?"

"No."

"How do you know it was from the father?"

"The coat-of-arms was on the envelope, and it was addressed in the duke's peculiar stiff hand. Besides, the duke remembers having written."

"When had he a letter before that?"

"Not for several days."

"Had he ever one from France?"

"No; never."

" You see the point of my questions, of course. Either the boy was carried off by force or he went of his own free will. In the latter case you would expect that some prompting from outside would be needed to make so young a lad do such a thing. If he has had no visitors, that prompting must have come in letters. Hence I try to find out who were his correspondents."

" I fear I cannot help you much. His only correspondent, so far as I know, was his own father."

" Who wrote to him on the very day of his disappearance. Were the relations between father and son very friendly ? "

" His Grace is never very friendly with anyone. He is completely immersed in large public questions, and is rather inaccessible to all ordinary emotions. But he was always kind to the boy in his own way."

" But the sympathies of the latter were with the mother ? "

" Yes."

" Did he say so ? "

" No."

" The duke, then ? "

" Good heavens, no ! "

" Then how could you know ? "

" I have had some confidential talk with Mr. James Wilder, his Grace's secretary. It was he who gave me the information about Lord Saltire's feelings."

" I see. By the way, that last letter of the duke's—was it found in the boy's room after he was gone ? "

" No ; he had taken it with him. I think, Mr. Holmes, it is time that we were leaving for Euston."

" I will order a four-wheeler. In a quarter of an hour we shall be at your service. If you are telegraphing home, Mr. Huxtable, it would be well to allow the people in your neighbourhood to imagine that the inquiry is still going on in Liverpool, or wherever else that red herring led your pack. In the meantime, I will do a little quiet work at your own doors, and perhaps the scent is not so cold but that two old hounds like Watson and myself may get a sniff of it."

That evening found us in the cold, bracing atmosphere of the Peak country, in which Dr. Huxtable's famous school is situated. It was already dark when we reached it. A card was lying on the hall table, and the butler whispered something to his master, who turned to us with agitation in every heavy feature.

"The duke is here," said he. "The duke and Mr. Wilder are in the study. Come, gentlemen, and I will introduce you."

I was, of course, familiar with the pictures of the famous statesman, but the man himself was very different from his representation. He was a tall and stately person, scrupulously dressed, with a drawn, thin face, and a nose which was grotesquely curved and long. His complexion was of a dead pallor, which was more startling by contrast with a long, dwindling beard of vivid red, which flowed down over his white waistcoat, with his watch-chain gleaming through its fringe. Such was the stately presence who looked stonily at us from the centre of Dr. Huxtable's hearthrug. Beside him stood a very young man, whom I understood to be Wilder, the private secretary. He was small, nervous, alert, with intelligent, light blue eyes and mobile features. It was he who at once, in an incisive and positive tone, opened the conversation.

"I called this morning, Dr. Huxtable, too late to prevent you from starting for London. I learned that your object was to invite Mr. Sherlock Holmes to undertake the conduct of this case. His Grace is surprised, Dr. Huxtable, that you should have taken such a step without consulting him."

"When I learned the police had failed——"

"His Grace is by no means convinced that the police have failed."

"But surely, Mr. Wilder——"

669

" You are well aware, Dr. Huxtable, that his Grace is particularly anxious to avoid all public scandal. He prefers to take as few people as possible into his confidence."

" The matter can be easily remedied," said the browbeaten doctor. " Mr. Sherlock Holmes can return to London by the morning train."

" Hardly that, doctor, hardly that," said Holmes, in his blandest voice. " This northern air is invigorating and pleasant, so I propose to spend a few days upon your moors, and to occupy my mind as best I may. Whether I have the shelter of your roof or of the village inn is, of course, for you to decide."

I could see that the unfortunate doctor was in the last stage of indecision, from which he was rescued by the deep, sonorous voice of the red-bearded duke, which boomed out like a dinner-gong.

" I agree with Mr. Wilder, Dr. Huxtable, that you would have done wisely to consult me. But since Mr. Holmes has already been taken into your confidence, it would indeed be absurd that we should not avail ourselves of his services. Far from going to the inn, Mr. Holmes, I should be pleased if you would come and stay with me at Holdernesse Hall ? "

" I thank your Grace. For the purposes of my investigation I think that it would be wiser for me to remain at the scene of the mystery."

" Just as you like, Mr. Holmes. Any information which Mr. Wilder or I can give you is, of course, at your disposal."

" It will probably be necessary for me to see you at the Hall," said Holmes. " I would only ask you now, sir, whether you have formed any explanation in your own mind as to the mysterious disappearance of your son ? "

" No, sir, I have not."

" Excuse me if I allude to that which is painful to you, but I have no alternative. Do you think that the duchess had anything to do with the matter ? "

The great minister showed perceptible hesitation.

" I do not think so," he said at last.

" The other most obvious explanation is that the child had been kidnapped for the purpose of levying ransom. You have not had any demand of the sort ? "

" No, sir."

" One more question, your Grace. I understand that you wrote to your son upon the day when this incident occurred."

" No ; I wrote upon the day before."

" Exactly. But he received it on that day ? "

" Yes."

" Was there anything in your letter which might have unbalanced him or induced him to take such a step ? "

" No, sir, certainly not."

" Did you post that letter yourself ? "

The nobleman's reply was interrupted by his secretary, who broke in with some heat.

" His Grace is not in the habit of posting letters himself," said he. " This letter was laid with others upon the study table, and I myself put them in the post-bag."

" You are sure this one was among them ? "

" Yes ; I observed it."

" How many letters did your Grace write that day ? "

" Twenty or thirty. I have a large correspondence. But surely this is somewhat irrelevant ? "

" Not entirely," said Holmes.

" For my own part," the duke continued, " I have advised the police to turn their attention to the South of France. I have already said that I do not believe that the duchess would encourage so monstrous an action, but the lad had the most wrong-headed opinions, and it is possible that he may have fled to her, aided and abetted by this German. I think, Dr. Huxtable, that we will now return to the Hall."

I could see that there were other questions which Holmes would have wished to put ; but the nobleman's abrupt manner showed that the interview was at an end.

It was evident that to his intensely aristocratic nature this discussion of his intimate family affairs with a stranger was most abhorrent, and that he feared lest every fresh question would throw a fiercer light into the discreetly shadowed corners of his ducal history.

When the nobleman and his secretary had left, my friend flung himself at once with characteristic eagerness into the investigation.

The boy's chamber was carefully examined, and yielded nothing save the absolute conviction that it was only through the window that he could have escaped. The German master's room and effects gave no further clue. In his case a trailer of ivy had given way under his weight, and we saw by the light of a lantern the mark on the lawn where his heels had come down. That one dent in the short green grass was the only material witness left of this inexplicable nocturnal flight.

Sherlock Holmes left the house alone, and only returned after eleven. He had obtained a large ordnance map of the neighbourhood, and this he brought into my room, where he laid it out on the bed, and, having balanced the lamp in the middle of it, he began to smoke over it, and occasionally to point out objects of interest with the reeking amber of his pipe.

" This case grows upon me, Watson," said he. " There are decidedly some points of interest in connection with it. In this early stage I want you to realize these geographical features, which may have a good deal to do with our investigation.

" Look at this map. This dark square is the Priory School. I'll put a pin in it. Now, this line is the main road. You see that it runs east and west past the school, and you see also there is no side-road for a mile either way. If these two folk passed away by road it was *this* road."

" Exactly."

" By a singular and happy chance we are able to some extent to check what passed along this road during the night in question. At this point, where my pipe is now resting, a country constable was on duty from twelve to six. It is, as you perceive, the first cross-road on the east side. This man declares that he was not absent from his post for an instant, and he is positive that neither boy nor man could have gone that way unseen. I have

SKETCH MAP SHOWING THE LOCALITY.

spoken with this policeman to-night, and he appears to me to be a perfectly reliable person. That blocks this end. We have now to deal with the other. There is an inn here, the 'Red Bull,' the landlady of which was ill. She had sent to Mackleton for a doctor, but he did not arrive until morning, being absent at another case.

The people at the inn were alert all night, awaiting his coming, and one or other of them seems to have continually had an eye upon the road. They declare that no one passed. If their evidence is good, then we are fortunate enough to be able to block the west, and also to be able to say that the fugitives did *not* use the road at all."

" But the bicycle ? " I objected.

" Quite so. We will come to the bicycle presently. To continue our reasoning : if these people did not go by the road, they must have traversed the country to the north of the house or to the south of the house. That is certain. Let us weigh the one against the other. On the south of the house is, as you perceive, a large district of arable land, cut up into small fields, with stone walls between them. There, I admit that a bicycle is impossible. We can dismiss the idea. We turn to the country on the north. Here there lies a grove of trees, marked as the ' Ragged Shaw,' and on the farther side stretches a great rolling moor, Lower Gill Moor, extending for ten miles, and sloping gradually upwards. Here, at one side of this wilderness, is Holdernesse Hall, ten miles by road, but only six across the moor. It is a peculiarly desolate plain. A few moor farmers have small holdings, where they rear sheep and cattle. Except these, the plover and the curlew are the only inhabitants until you come to the Chesterfield high road. There is a church there, you see, a few cottages, and an inn. Beyond that the hills become precipitous. Surely it is here to the north that our quest must lie."

" But the bicycle ? " I persisted.

" Well, well ! " said Holmes impatiently. " A good cyclist does not need a high road. The moor is inter-sected with paths, and the moon was at the full. Halloa ! What is this ? "

There was an agitated knock at the door, and an instant afterwards Dr. Huxtable was in the room. In his hand he held a blue cricket-cap, with a white chevron on the peak.

"At last we have a clue!" he cried. "Thank Heaven, at last we are on the dear boy's track! It is his cap."

"Where was it found?"

"In the van of the gipsies who camped on the moor. They left on Tuesday. To-day the police traced them down and examined their caravan. This was found."

"How do they account for it?"

"They shuffled and lied—said that they found it on the moor on Tuesday morning. They know where he is, the rascals! Thank goodness, they are all safe under lock and key. Either the fear of the law or the duke's purse will certainly get out of them all that they know."

"So far, so good," said Holmes, when the doctor had at last left the room. "It at least bears out the theory that it is on the side of the Lower Gill Moor that we must hope for results. The police have really done nothing locally, save the arrest of these gipsies. Look here, Watson! There is a watercourse across the moor. You see it marked here in the map. In some parts it widens into a morass. This is particularly so in the region between Holdernesse Hall and the school. It is vain to look elsewhere for tracks in this dry weather; but at *that* point there is certainly a chance of some record being left. I will call you early to-morrow morning, and you and I will try if we can throw some light upon the mystery."

The day was just breaking when I woke to find the long, thin form of Holmes by my bedside. He was fully dressed, and had apparently already been out.

"I have done the lawn and the bicycle shed," said he. "I have also had a ramble through the Ragged Shaw. Now, Watson, there is cocoa ready in the next room. I must beg you to hurry, for we have a great day before us."

His eyes shone, and his cheek was flushed with the exhilaration of the master workman who sees his work lies ready before him. A very different Holmes, this active, alert man, from the introspective and pallid dreamer of Baker Street. I felt, as I looked upon that supple figure, alive with nervous energy, that it was indeed a strenuous day that awaited us.

And yet it opened in the blackest disappointment. With high hopes we struck across the peaty, russet moor, intersected with a thousand sheep-paths, until we came to the broad light green-belt which marked the morass between us and Holdernesse. Certainly, if the lad had gone homewards, he must have passed this, and he would not pass it without leaving his trace. But no sign of him or the German could be seen. With a darkening face my friend strode along the margin, eagerly observant of every muddy stain upon the mossy surface. Sheep-marks there were in profusion, and at one place, some miles down, cows had left their tracks. Nothing more.

" Check number one," said Holmes, looking gloomily over the rolling expanse of the moor. " There is another morass down yonder, and a narrow neck between. Halloa ! halloa ! halloa ! What have we here ? "

We had come on a small black ribbon of pathway. In the middle of it, clearly marked on the sodden soil, was the track of a bicycle.

" Hurrah ! " I cried. " We have it."

But Holmes was shaking his head, and his face was puzzled and expectant rather than joyous.

" A bicycle certainly, but not *the* bicycle," said he. " I am familiar with forty-two different impressions left by tyres. This, as you perceive, is a Dunlop, with a patch upon the outer cover. Heidegger's tyres were Palmer's, leaving longitudinal stripes. Aveling, the mathematical master, was sure upon the point. Therefore it is not Heidegger's track."

" The boy's, then ? "

" Possibly, if we could prove a bicycle to have been in his possession. But this we have utterly failed to do. This track, as you perceive, was made by a rider who was going from the direction of the school."

" Or towards it ? "

"No, no, my dear Watson. The more deeply sunk impression is, of course, the hind wheel, upon which the weight rests. You perceive several places where it has passed across and obliterated the more shallow mark of the front one. It was undoubtedly heading away from the school. It may or may not be connected with our inquiry, but we will follow it backwards before we go any farther."

We did so, and at the end of a few hundred yards lost the tracks as we emerged from the boggy portion of the moor. Following the path backwards, we picked out another spot, where a spring trickled across it. Here, once again, was the mark of the bicycle, though nearly obliterated by the hoofs of cows. After that there was no sign, but the path ran right on into Ragged Shaw, the wood which backed on to the school. From this wood the cycle must have emerged. Holmes sat down on a boulder and rested his chin in his hands. I had smoked two cigarettes before he moved.

"Well, well," said he at last. "It is, of course, possible that a cunning man might change the tyre of his bicycle in order to leave unfamiliar tracks. A criminal who was capable of such a thought is a man whom I should be proud to do business with. We will leave this question undecided and hark back to our morass again, for we have left a good deal unexplored."

We continued our systematic survey of the edge of the sodden portion of the moor, and soon our perseverance was gloriously rewarded.

Right across the lower part of the bog lay a miry path. Holmes gave a cry of delight as he approached it. An impression like a fine bundle of telegraph wires ran down the centre of it. It was the Palmer tyre.

"Here is Herr Heidegger, sure enough!" cried Holmes exultantly. "My reasoning seems to have been pretty sound, Watson."

"I congratulate you."

"But we have a long way still to go. Kindly walk clear

677

of the path. Now let us follow the trail. I fear that it will not lead very far."

We found, however, as we advanced, that this portion of the moor is intersected with soft patches, and, though we frequently lost sight of the track, we always succeeded in picking it up once more.

"Do you observe," said Holmes, "that the rider is now undoubtedly forcing the pace? There can be no doubt of it. Look at this impression, where you get both tyres clear. The one is as deep as the other. That can only mean that the rider is throwing his weight on to the handle-bar as a man does when he is sprinting. By Jove! he has had a fall."

There was a broad, irregular smudge covering some yards of the track. Then there were a few footmarks, and the tyre reappeared once more.

"A side-slip," I suggested.

Holmes held up a crumpled branch of flowering gorse. To my horror I perceived that the yellow blossoms were all dabbled with crimson. On the path, too, and among the heather were dark stains of clotted blood.

"Bad!" said Holmes. "Bad! Stand clear, Watson! Not an unnecessary footstep! What do I read here? He fell wounded, he stood up, he remounted, he proceeded. But there is no other track. Cattle on this side-path. He was surely not gored by a bull? Impossible! But I see no traces of anyone else. We must push on, Watson. Surely, with stains as well as the track to guide us, he cannot escape us now."

Our search was not a very long one. The tracks of the tyre began to curve fantastically upon the wet and shining path. Suddenly, as I looked ahead, the gleam of metal caught my eye from amid the thick gorse bushes. Out of them we dragged a bicycle, Palmer-tyred, one pedal bent, and the whole front of it horribly smeared and slob-bered with blood. On the other side of the bushes a shoe was projecting. We ran round, and there lay the unfor-tunate rider. He was a tall man, full bearded, with spectacles, one glass of which had been knocked out. The cause of his death was a frightful blow upon the head, which had crushed in part of his skull. That he could have gone on after receiving such an injury said much for the vitality and courage of the man. He wore shoes, but no socks, and his open coat disclosed a night-shirt beneath it. It was undoubtedly the German master.

Holmes turned the body over reverently, and examined it with great attention. He then sat in deep thought for a time, and I could see by his ruffled brow that this grim discovery had not, in his opinion, advanced us much in our inquiry.

" It is a little difficult to know what to do, Watson," said he, at last. " My own inclinations are to push this inquiry on, for we have already lost so much time that we cannot afford to waste another hour. On the other hand, we are bound to inform the police of this discovery, and to see that this poor fellow's body is looked after."

" I could take a note back."

" But I need your company and assistance. Wait a bit ! There is a fellow cutting peat up yonder. Bring him over here, and he will guide the police."

I brought the peasant across, and Holmes despatched the frightened man with a note to Dr. Huxtable.

" Now, Watson," said he, " we have picked up two clues this morning. One is the bicycle with the Palmer tyre, and we see what that has led to. The other is the bicycle with the patched Dunlop. Before we start to investigate that, let us try to realize what we *do* know, so as to make the most of it, and to separate the essential from the accidental.

" First of all, I wish to impress upon you that the boy certainly left of his own free will. He got down from his window and he went off, either alone or with someone. That is sure."

I assented.

" Well, now, let us turn to this unfortunate German master. The boy was fully dressed when he fled. Therefore he foresaw what he would do. But the German went without his socks. He certainly acted on very short notice."

" Undoubtedly."

" Why did he go ? Because, from his bedroom window, he saw the flight of the boy. Because he wished to overtake him and bring him back. He seized his bicycle, pursued the lad, and in pursuing him met his death."

" So it would seem."

" Now I come to the critical part of my argument. The natural action of a man in pursuing a little boy would be to run after him. He would know that he could overtake him. But the German does not do so. He turns to his bicycle. I am told that he was an excellent cyclist. He would not do this if he did not see that the boy had some swift means of escape."

" The other bicycle."

" Let us continue our reconstruction. He meets his death five miles from the school—not by a bullet, mark you, which even a lad might conceivably discharge, but by a savage blow dealt by a vigorous arm. The lad, then, *had* a companion in his flight. And the flight was a swift one, since it took five miles before an expert cyclist could overtake them. Yet we survey the ground round the scene of the tragedy. What do we find ? A few cattle tracks, nothing more. I took a wide sweep round, and there is no path within fifty yards. Another cyclist could have had nothing to do with the actual murder. Nor were there any human footmarks."

" Holmes," I cried, " this is impossible."

" Admirable ! " he said. " A most illuminating remark. It *is* impossible as I state it, and therefore I must in some respect have stated it wrong. Yet you saw for yourself. Can you suggest any fallacy ? "

" He could not have fractured his skull in a fall ? "

" In a morass, Watson ? "

" I am at my wits' end."

" Tut, tut ; we have solved some worse problems. At

least we have plenty of material, if we can only use it. Come, then, and, having exhausted the Palmer, let us see what the Dunlop with the patched cover has to offer us."

We picked up the track and followed it onwards for some distance; but soon the moor rose into a long, heather-tufted curve, and we left the watercourse behind us. No further help from tracks could be hoped for. At the spot where we saw the last of the Dunlop tyre it might equally have led to Holdernesse Hall, the stately towers of which rose some miles to our left, or to a low, grey village which lay in front of us, and marked the position of the Chesterfield high-road.

As we approached the forbidding and squalid inn, with the sign of a game-cock above the door, Holmes gave a sudden groan and clutched me by the shoulder to save himself from falling. He had had one of those violent strains of the ankle which leave a man helpless. With difficulty he limped up to the door, where a squat, dark, elderly man was smoking a black clay pipe.

"How are you, Mr. Reuben Hayes?" said Holmes.

"Who are you, and how do you get my name so pat?" the countryman answered, with a suspicious flash of a pair of cunning eyes.

"Well, it's printed on the board above your head. It's easy to see a man who is master of his own house. I suppose you haven't such a thing as a carriage in your stables?"

"No; I have not."

"I can hardly put my foot to the ground."

"Don't put it to the ground."

"But I can't walk."

"Well, then, hop."

Mr. Reuben Hayes' manner was far from gracious, but Holmes took it with admirable good humour.

"Look here, my man," said he. "This is really rather an awkward fix for me. I don't mind how I get on."

"Neither do I," said the morose landlord.

" The matter is very important. I would offer you a sovereign for the use of a bicycle."

The landlord pricked up his ears.

" Where do you want to go ? "

" To Holdernesse Hall."

" Pals of the dook, I suppose ? " said the landlord, surveying our mud-stained garments with ironical eyes.

Holmes laughed good-naturedly.

" He'll be glad to see us, anyhow."

" Why ? "

" Because we bring him news of his lost son."

The landlord gave a very visible start.

" What, you're on his track ? "

" He has been heard of in Liverpool. They expect to get him every hour."

Again a swift change passed over the heavy, unshaven face. His manner was suddenly genial.

" I've less reason to wish the dook well than most men," said he, " for I was his head coachman once, and cruel bad he treated me. It was him that sacked me without a character on the word of a lying corn-chandler. But I'm glad to hear that the young lord was heard of in Liverpool, and I'll help you to take the news to the Hall."

" Thank you," said Holmes. " We'll have some food first. Then you can bring round the bicycle."

" I haven't got a bicycle."

Holmes held up a sovereign.

" I tell you, man, that I haven't got one. I'll let you have two horses as far as the Hall."

" Well, well," said Holmes, " we'll talk about it when we've had something to eat."

When we were left alone in the stone-flagged kitchen it was astonishing how rapidly that sprained ankle recovered. It was nearly nightfall, and we had eaten nothing since early morning, so that we spent some time over our meal. Holmes was lost in thought, and once or twice he walked over to the window and stared earnestly out. It opened on to a squalid courtyard. In the far corner was a smithy, where a grimy lad was at work. On the other side were the stables. Holmes had sat down again after one of these excursions, when he suddenly sprang out of his chair with a loud exclamation.

"By Heaven, Watson, I believe that I've got it!" he cried. "Yes, yes, it must be so. Watson, do you remember seeing any cow-tracks to-day?"

"Yes, several."

"Where?"

"Well, everywhere. They were at the morass, and again on the path, and again near where poor Heidegger met his death."

"Exactly. Well, now, Watson, how many cows did you see on the moor?"

"I don't remember seeing any."

"Strange, Watson, that we should see tracks all along our line, but never a cow on the whole moor; very strange, Watson, eh?"

"Yes, it is strange."

"Now, Watson, make an effort; throw your mind back! Can you see those tracks upon the path?"

"Yes, I can."

"Can you recall that the tracks were sometimes like that, Watson"—he arranged a number of breadcrumbs in this fashion—: : : : :—"and sometimes like this"—: · : · : · : ·—"and occasionally like this—. · · · · ·

"Can you remember that?"

"No, I cannot."

"But I can. I could swear to it. However, we will go back at our leisure and verify it. What a blind beetle I have been not to draw my conclusion?"

"And what is your conclusion?"

"Only that it is a remarkable cow which walks, canters, and gallops. By George, Watson, it was no brain of a country publican that thought out such a blind as that! The coast seems to be clear, save for that lad in the smithy. Let us slip out and see what we can see."

There were two rough-haired, unkempt horses in the tumble-down stable. Holmes raised the hind-leg of one of them and laughed aloud.

"Old shoes, but newly shod—old shoes, but new nails. This case deserves to be a classic. Let us go across to the smithy."

The lad continued his work without regarding us. I saw Holmes' eye darting to right and left among the litter of iron and wood, which was scattered about the floor. Suddenly, however, we heard a step behind us, and there was the landlord, his heavy eyebrows drawn down over his savage eyes, his swarthy features convulsed with passion.

He held a short metal-headed stick in his hand, and he advanced in so menacing a fashion that I was right glad to feel the revolver in my pocket.

"You infernal spies!" the man cried. "What are you doing there?"

"Why, Mr. Reuben Hayes," said Holmes coolly, "one might think that you were afraid of our finding something out."

The man mastered himself with a violent effort, and his grim mouth loosened into a false laugh, which was more menacing than his frown.

"You're welcome to all you can find out in my smithy," said he. "But look here, mister, I don't care for folk poking about my place without my leave, so the sooner you pay your score and get out of this the better I shall be pleased."

"All right, Mr. Hayes—no harm meant," said Holmes. "We have been having a look at your horses; but I think I'll walk after all. It's not far, I believe."

"Not more than two miles to the Hall gates. That's the road to the left." He watched us with sullen eyes until we had left his premises.

We did not go very far along the road, for Holmes stopped the instant that the curve hid us from the landlord's view.

"We were warm, as the children say, at that inn," said he. "I seem to grow colder every step that I take away from it. No, no; I can't possibly leave it."

"I am convinced," said I, "that this Reuben Hayes knows all about it. A more self-evident villain I never saw."

"Oh! he impressed you in that way, did he? There are the horses, there is the smithy. Yes, it is an interesting place, this 'Fighting Cock.' I think we shall have another look at it in an unobtrusive way."

A long, sloping hill-side, dotted with grey limestone boulders, stretched behind us. We had turned off the road, and were making our way up the hill, when, looking in the direction of Holdernesse Hall, I saw a cyclist coming swiftly along.

"Get down, Watson!" cried Holmes, with a heavy hand upon my shoulder. We had hardly sunk from view when the man flew past us on the road. Amid a rolling cloud of dust I caught a glimpse of a pale, agitated face—a face with horror in every lineament, the mouth open, the eyes staring wildly in front. It was like some strange caricature of the dapper James Wilder whom we had seen the night before.

"The duke's secretary!" cried Holmes. "Come, Watson, let us see what he does."

We scrambled from rock to rock until in a few moments we had made our way to a point from which we could see the front door of the inn. Wilder's bicycle was leaning against the wall beside it. No one was moving about the house, nor could we catch a glimpse of any faces at the windows. Slowly the twilight crept down as the sun sank behind the high towers of Holdernesse Hall. Then in the gloom we saw the two side-lamps of a trap light up in the stable-yard of the inn, and shortly afterwards heard the rattle of hoofs, as it wheeled out into the road and tore off at a furious pace in the direction of Chesterfield.

"What do you make of that, Watson?" Holmes whispered.

"It looks like a flight."

"A single man in a dog-cart, so far as I could see. Well, it certainly was not Mr. James Wilder, for there he is at the door."

A red square of light had sprung out of the darkness. In the middle of it was the black figure of the secretary, his head advanced, peering out into the night. It was evident that he was expecting some one. Then at last there were steps in the road, a second figure was visible for an instant against the light, the door shut, and all was black once more. Five minutes later a lamp was lit in a room upon the first floor.

"It seems to be a curious class of custom that is done by the 'Fighting Cock,'" said Holmes.

"The bar is on the other side."

"Quite so. These are what one may call the private guests. Now, what in the world is Mr. James Wilder doing in that den at this hour of night, and who is the companion who comes to meet him there? Come, Watson, we must really take a risk and try to investigate this a little more closely."

Together we stole down to the road and crept across to the door of the inn. The bicycle still leaned against the wall. Holmes struck a match and held it to the back wheel, and I heard him chuckle as the light fell upon a patched Dunlop tyre. Up above us was the lighted window.

"I must have a peep through that, Watson. If you bend your back and support yourself upon the wall, I think that I can manage."

An instant later his feet were on my shoulders. But he was hardly up before he was down again.

"Come, my friend," said he, "our day's work has been quite long enough. I think that we have gathered all that we can. It's a long walk to the school, and the sooner we get started the better."

He hardly opened his lips during that weary trudge across the moor, nor would he enter the school when he reached it, but went on to Mackleton Station, whence he could send some telegrams. Late at night I heard him consoling Dr. Huxtable, prostrated by the tragedy of his master's death, and later still he entered my room as alert and vigorous as he had been when he started in the morning. " All goes well, my friend," said he. " I promise that before to-morrow evening we shall have reached the solution of the mystery."

At eleven o'clock next morning my friend and I were walking up the famous yew avenue of Holdernesse Hall. We were ushered through the magnificent Elizabethan doorway and into his Grace's study. There we found Mr. James Wilder, demure and courtly, but with some trace of that wild terror of the night before still lurking in his furtive eyes and in his twitching features.

" You have come to see his Grace ? I am sorry ; but the fact is that the duke is far from well. He has been very much upset by the tragic news. We received a telegram from Dr. Huxtable yesterday afternoon, which told us of your discovery."

" I must see the duke, Mr. Wilder."

" But he is in his room."

" Then I must go to his room."

" I believe he is in his bed."

" I will see him there."

Holmes' cold and inexorable manner showed the secretary that it was useless to argue with him.

" Very good, Mr. Holmes ; I will tell him that you are here."

After half an hour's delay the great nobleman appeared. His face was more cadaverous than ever, his shoulders had rounded, and he seemed to me to be an altogether older man than he had been the morning before. He greeted us with a stately courtesy, and seated himself at his desk, his red beard streaming down on to the table.

" Well, Mr. Holmes ? " said he.

But my friend's eyes were fixed upon the secretary, who stood by his master's chair.

" I think, your Grace, that I could speak more freely in Mr. Wilder's absence."

The man turned a shade paler and cast a malignant glance at Holmes.

" If your Grace wishes——"

" Yes, yes ; you had better go. Now, Mr. Holmes, what have you to say ? "

My friend waited until the door had closed behind the retreating secretary.

" The fact is, your Grace," said he, " that my colleague, Dr. Watson, and myself had an assurance from Dr. Hux-table that a reward had been offered in this case. I should like to have this confirmed from your own lips."

" Certainly, Mr. Holmes."

" It amounted, if I am correctly informed, to five thousand pounds to anyone who will tell you where your son is ? "

" Exactly."

" And another thousand to the man who will name the person or persons who keep him in custody ? "

" Exactly."

" Under the latter heading is included, no doubt, not only those who may have taken him away, but also those who conspire to keep him in his present position ? "

" Yes, yes," cried the duke impatiently. " If you do your work well, Mr. Sherlock Holmes, you will have no reason to complain of niggardly treatment."

My friend rubbed his thin hands together with an appearance of avidity which was a surprise to me, who knew his frugal tastes.

" I fancy that I see your Grace's cheque-book upon the table," said he. " I should be glad if you would make me out a cheque for six thousand pounds. It would be as well, perhaps, for you to cross it. The Capital and Counties Bank, Oxford Street branch, are my agents."

His Grace sat very stern and upright in his chair, and looked stonily at my friend.

"Is this a joke, Mr. Holmes? It is hardly a subject for pleasantry."

"Not at all, your Grace. I was never more earnest in my life."

"What do you mean, then?"

"I mean that I have earned the reward. I know where your son is, and I know some, at least, of those who are holding him."

The duke's beard had turned more aggressively red than ever against his ghastly white face.

"Where is he?" he gasped.

"He is, or was last night, at the Fighting Cock Inn, about two miles from your park gate."

The duke fell back in his chair.

"And whom do you accuse?"

Sherlock Holmes' answer was an astounding one. He stepped swiftly forward and touched the duke upon the shoulder.

"I accuse *you*," said he. "And now, your Grace, I'll trouble you for that cheque."

Never shall I forget the duke's appearance as he sprang up and clawed with his hand like one who is sinking into an abyss. Then, with an extraordinary effort of aristocratic self-command, he sat down and sank his face in his hands. It was some minutes before he spoke.

"How much do you know?" he asked at last, without raising his head.

"I saw you together last night."

"Does anyone else besides your friend know?"

"I have spoken to no one."

The duke took a pen in his quivering fingers and opened his cheque-book.

"I shall be as good as my word, Mr. Holmes. I am about to write your cheque, however unwelcome the information which you have gained may be to me. When the offer was first made I little thought the turn which events would take. But you and your friend are men of discretion, Mr. Holmes?"

" I hardly understand your Grace."

" I must put it plainly, Mr. Holmes. If only you two know of the incident, there is no reason why it should go any farther. I think twelve thousand pounds is the sum that I owe you, is it not ? "

But Holmes smiled, and shook his head.

" I fear, your Grace, that matters can hardly be arranged so easily. There is the death of this school-master to be accounted for."

" But James knew nothing of that. You cannot hold him responsible for that. It was the work of this brutal ruffian whom he had the misfortune to employ."

" I must take the view, your Grace, that when a man embarks upon a crime he is morally guilty of any other crime which may spring from it."

" Morally, Mr. Holmes. No doubt you are right. But surely not in the eyes of the law. A man cannot be con-demned for a murder at which he was not present, and which he loathes and abhors as much as you do. The instant that he heard of it he made a complete confession to me, so filled was he with horror and remorse. He lost not an hour in breaking entirely with the murderer. Oh, Mr. Holmes, you must save him—you must save him ! I tell you that you must save him ! " The duke had dropped the last attempt at self-command, and was pacing the room with a convulsed face and with his clenched hands raving in the air. At last he mastered himself and sat down once more at his desk. " I appre-ciate your conduct in coming here before you spoke to anyone else," said he. " At least we may take counsel how far we can minimize this hideous scandal."

" Exactly," said Holmes. " I think, your Grace, that this can only be done by absolute and complete frankness between us. I am disposed to help your Grace to the best of my ability ; but in order to do so I must under-stand to the last detail how the matter stands. I realize that your words applied to Mr. James Wilder, and that he is not the murderer."

" No ; the murderer has escaped."

Sherlock Holmes smiled demurely.

" Your Grace can hardly have heard of any small
reputation which I possess, or you would not imagine
that it is so easy to escape me. Mr. Reuben Hayes was
arrested at Chesterfield on my information at eleven
o'clock last night. I had a telegram from the head of
the local police before I left the school this morning."

The duke leaned back in his chair and stared with
amazement at my friend.

" You seem to have powers that are hardly human,"
said he. " So Reuben Hayes is taken ? I am right
glad to hear it, if it will not react upon the fate of James."

" Your secretary ? "

" No, sir ; my son."

It was Holmes' turn to look astonished.

" I confess that this is entirely new to me, your Grace.
I must beg of you to be more explicit."

" I will conceal nothing from you. I agree with you
that complete frankness, however painful it may be to me,
is the best policy in this desperate situation to which
James' folly and jealousy have reduced us. When I was
a young man, Mr. Holmes, I loved with such a love as
comes only once in a lifetime. I offered the lady marriage, but she refused it on the grounds that such a match
might mar my career. Had she lived I would certainly
never have married anyone else. She died, and left this
one child, whom for her sake I have cherished and cared
for. I could not acknowledge the paternity to the world ;
but I gave him the best of educations, and since he came
to manhood I have kept him near my person. He
surprised my secret, and has presumed ever since upon
the claim which he has upon me and upon his power of
provoking a scandal, which would be abhorrent to me.
His presence had something to do with the unhappy issue
of my marriage. Above all, he hated my young legitimate
heir from the first with a persistent hatred. You may
well ask me why, under these circumstances, I still kept

James under my roof. I answer that it was because I could see his mother's face in his, and that for her dear sake there was no end to my long-suffering. All her pretty ways, too—there was not one of them which he could not suggest and bring back to my memory. I *could* not send him away. But I feared so lest he should do Arthur—that is, Lord Saltire—a mischief that I despatched him for safety to Dr. Huxtable's school.

"James came into contact with this fellow Hayes because the man was a tenant of mine, and James acted as agent. The fellow was a rascal from the beginning; but in some extraordinary way James became intimate with him. He had always a taste for low company. When James determined to kidnap Lord Saltire it was of this man's service that he availed himself. You remember that I wrote to Arthur upon that last day. Well, James opened the letter and inserted a note asking Arthur to meet him in a little wood called the Ragged Shaw which is near to the school. He used the duchess' name, and in that way got the boy to come. That evening James cycled over—I am telling you what he has himself confessed to me—and he told Arthur, whom he met in the wood, that his mother longed to see him, that she was awaiting him on the moor, and that if he would come back into the wood at midnight he would find a man with a horse, who would take him to her. Poor Arthur fell into the trap. He came to the appointment, and found this fellow Hayes with a led pony. Arthur mounted, and they set off together. It appears—though this James only heard yesterday—that they were pursued, that Hayes struck the pursuer with his stick, and that the man died of his injuries. Hayes brought Arthur to his public-house, the 'Fighting Cock,' where he was confined in an upper room, under the care of Mrs. Hayes, who is a kindly woman, but entirely under the control of her brutal husband.

"Well, Mr. Holmes, that was the state of affairs when I first saw you two days ago. I had no more idea of the truth than you. You will ask me what was James' motive in doing such a deed. I answer that there was a great deal which was unreasoning and fanatical in the hatred which he bore my heir. In his view he should himself have been heir of all my estates, and he deeply resented those social laws which made it impossible. At the same time, he had a definite motive also. He was eager that I should break the entail, and he was of opinion that it lay in my power to do so. He intended to make a bargain with me—to restore Arthur if I would break the entail, and so make it possible for the estate to be left to him by will. He knew well that I should never willingly invoke the aid of the police against him. I say that he would have proposed such a bargain to me, but he did not actually do so, for events moved too quickly for him, and he had not time to put his plans into practice.

" What brought all his wicked scheme to wreck was your discovery of this man Heidegger's dead body. James was seized with horror at the news. It came to us yesterday as we sat together in this study. Dr. Huxtable had sent a telegram. James was so overwhelmed with grief and agitation that my suspicions, which had never been entirely absent, rose instantly to a certainty, and I taxed him with the deed. He made a complete voluntary confession. Then he implored me to keep his secret for three days longer, so as to give his wretched accomplice a chance of saving his guilty life. I yielded—as I have always yielded—to his prayers, and instantly James hurried off to the ' Fighting Cock ' to warn Hayes and give him the means of flight. I could not go there by daylight without provoking comment, but as soon as night fell I hurried off to see my dear Arthur. I found him safe and well, but horrified beyond expression by the dreadful deed he had witnessed. In deference to my promise, and much against my will, I consented to leave him there for three days under the charge of Mrs. Hayes, since it was evident that it was impossible to inform the police where he was without telling them also who was the murderer, and I could not see how that murderer could be punished without ruin to my unfortunate James. You asked for frankness, Mr. Holmes, and I have taken you at your word, for I have now told you everything without an attempt at circumlocution or concealment. Do you in your turn be as frank with me."

" I will," said Holmes. " In the first place, your Grace, I am bound to tell you that you have placed yourself in a most serious position in the eyes of the law. You have condoned a felony, and you have aided the escape of a murderer ; for I cannot doubt that any money which was taken by James Wilder to aid his accomplice in his flight came from your Grace's purse."

The duke bowed his assent.

" This is indeed a most serious matter. Even more culpable, in my opinion, your Grace, is your attitude towards your younger son. You leave him in this den for three days."

" Under solemn promises——"

" What are promises to such people as these ? You have no guarantee that he will not be spirited away again. To humour your guilty elder son you have exposed your innocent younger son to imminent and unnecessary danger. It was a most unjustifiable action."

The proud lord of Holdernesse was not accustomed to be so rated in his own ducal hall. The blood flushed into his high forehead, but his conscience held him dumb.

" I will help you, but on one condition only. It is that you ring for the footman and let me give such orders as I like."

Without a word the duke pressed the electric button. A servant entered.

" You will be glad to hear," said Holmes, " that your young master is found. It is the duke's desire that the carriage shall go at once to the Fighting Cock Inn to bring Lord Saltire home."

" Now," said Holmes, when the rejoicing lackey had

disappeared, " having secured the future we can afford to be more lenient with the past. I am not in an official position, and there is no reason, so long as the ends of justice are served, why I should disclose all that I know. As to Hayes I say nothing. The gallows awaits him, and I would do nothing to save him from it. What he will divulge I cannot tell, but I have no doubt that your Grace could make him understand that it is to his interest to be silent. From the police point of view he will have kidnapped the boy for the purpose of ransom. If they do not themselves find it out I see no reason why I should prompt them to take a broader view. I would warn your Grace, however, that the continued presence of Mr. James Wilder in your household can only lead to misfortune."

" I understand that, Mr. Holmes, and it is already settled that he shall leave me for ever and go to seek his fortune in Australia."

" In that case, your Grace, since you have yourself stated that any unhappiness in your married life was caused by his presence, I would suggest that you make such amends as you can to the duchess, and that you try to resume those relations which have been so unhappily interrupted."

" That also I have arranged, Mr. Holmes. I wrote to the duchess this morning."

" In that case," said Holmes, rising, " I think that my friend and I can congratulate ourselves upon several most happy results from our little visit to the North. There is one other small point upon which I desire some light. This fellow Hayes had shod his horses with shoes which counterfeited the tracks of cows. Was it from Mr. Wilder that he learned so extraordinary a device ? "

The duke stood in thought for a moment, with a look of intense surprise on his face. Then he opened a door and showed us into a large room furnished as a museum. He led the way to a glass case in a corner, and pointed to the inscription.

"These shoes," it ran, "were dug up in the moat of Holdernesse Hall. They are for the use of horses ; but they are shaped below with a cloven foot of iron, so as to throw pursuers off the track. They are supposed to have belonged to some of the marauding Barons of Holdernesse in the Middle Ages."

Holmes opened the case, and, moistening his finger, he passed it along the shoe. A thin film of recent mud was left upon his skin.

"Thank you," said he, as he replaced the glass. "It is the second most interesting object that I have seen in the North."

"And the first ? "

Holmes folded up his cheque, and placed it carefully in his notebook. "I am a poor man," said he, as he patted it affectionately, and thrust it into the depths of his inner pocket.

29. *Black Peter*

I HAVE never known my friend to be in better form, both mental and physical, than in the year '95. His increasing fame had brought with it an immense practice, and I should be guilty of an indiscretion if I were even to hint at the identity of some of the illustrious clients who crossed our humble threshold in Baker Street. Holmes, however, like all great artists, lived for his art's sake, and, save in the case of the Duke of Holdernesse, I have seldom known him claim any large reward for his inestimable services. So unworldly was he—or so capricious—that he frequently refused his help to the powerful and wealthy where the problem made no appeal to his sympathies, while he would devote weeks of most intense application to the affairs of some humble client whose case presented those strange and dramatic qualities which appealed to his imagination and challenged his ingenuity.

In this memorable year '95 a curious and incongruous

succession of cases had engaged his attention, ranging from his famous investigation of the sudden death of Cardinal Tosca—an inquiry which was carried out by him at the express desire of his Holiness the Pope—down to his arrest of Wilson, the notorious canary-trainer, which removed a plague-spot from the East End of London. Close on the heels of these two famous cases came the tragedy of Woodman's Lee, and the very obscure circumstances which surrounded the death of Captain Peter Carey. No record of the doings of Mr. Sherlock Holmes would be complete which did not include some account of this very unusual affair.

During the first week of July my friend had been absent so often and so long from our lodgings that I knew he had something on hand. The fact that several rough-looking men called during that time and inquired for Captain Basil made me understand that Holmes was working somewhere under one of the numerous disguises and names with which he concealed his own formidable identity. He had at least five small refuges in different parts of London in which he was able to change his personality. He said nothing of his business to me, and it was not my habit to force a confidence. The first positive sign which he gave me of the direction which his investigation was taking was an extraordinary one. He had gone out before breakfast, and I had sat down to mine, when he strode into the room, his hat upon his head, and a huge, barb-headed spear tucked like an umbrella under his arm.

" Good gracious, Holmes ! " I cried. " You don't mean to say that you have been walking about London with that thing ? "

" I drove to the butcher's and back."

" The butcher's ? "

" And I return with an excellent appetite. There can be no question, my dear Watson, of the value of exercise before breakfast. But I am prepared to bet that you will not guess the form that my exercise has taken."

" I will not attempt it."

He chuckled as he poured out the coffee.

" If you could have looked into Allardyce's back shop you would have seen a dead pig swung from a hook in the ceiling, and a gentleman in his shirt-sleeves furiously stabbing at it with this weapon. I was that energetic person, and I have satisfied myself that by no exertion of my strength can I transfix the pig with a single blow. Perhaps you would care to try ? "

" Not for worlds. But why were you doing this ? "

" Because it seemed to me to have an indirect bearing upon the mystery of Woodman's Lee. Ah, Hopkins, I got your wire last night, and I have been expecting you. Come and join us."

Our visitor was an exceedingly alert man, thirty years of age, dressed in a quiet tweed suit, but retaining the erect bearing of one who was accustomed to official uniform. I recognized him at once as Stanley Hopkins, a young police inspector for whose future Holmes had high hopes, while he in turn professed the admiration and respect of a pupil for the scientific methods of the famous amateur. Hopkins' brow was clouded and he sat down with an air of deep dejection.

" No, thank you, sir. I breakfasted before I came round. I spent the night in town, for I came up yesterday to report."

" And what had you to report ? "

" Failure, sir—absolute failure."

" You have made no progress ? "

" None."

" Dear me ! I must have a look at the matter."

" I .wish to heavens that you would, Mr. Holmes. It's my first big chance, and I am at my wits' end. For goodness' sake come down and lend me a hand."

" Well, well, it happens that I have already read all the available evidence, including the report of the inquest, with some care. By the way, what do you make of that tobacco-pouch found on the scene of the crime ? Is there no clue there ? "

Hopkins looked surprised.

" It was the man's own pouch, sir. His initials were inside it. And it was of sealskin—and he an old sealer."

" But he had no pipe."

" No, sir, we could find no pipe ; indeed, he smoked very little. And yet he might have kept some tobacco for his friends."

" No doubt. I only mention it because if I had been handling the case I should have been inclined to make that the starting-point of my investigation. However, my friend Dr. Watson knows nothing of this matter, and I should be none the worse for hearing the sequence of events once more. Just give us some short sketch of the essentials."

Stanley Hopkins drew a slip of paper from his pocket.

" I have a few dates here which will give you the career of the dead man, Captain Peter Carey. He was born in '45—fifty years of age. He was a most daring and successful seal and whale fisher. In 1883 he commanded the steam sealer *Sea Unicorn*, of Dundee. He had then had several successful voyages in succession, and in the following year, 1884, he retired. After that he travelled for some years, and finally he bought a small place called Woodman's Lee, near Forest Row, in Sussex. There he has lived for six years, and there he died just a week ago to-day.

" There were some most singular points about the man. In ordinary life he was a strict Puritan—a silent, gloomy fellow. His household consisted of his wife, his daughter, aged twenty, and two female servants. These last were continually changing, for it was never a very cheery situation, and sometimes it became past all bearing. The man was an intermittent drunkard, and when he had the fit on him he was a perfect fiend. He has been known to drive his wife and his daughter out of doors in the middle of the night, and flog them through the park until the whole village outside the gates was aroused by their screams.

" He was summoned once for a savage assault upon the old vicar, who had called upon him to remonstrate with him upon his conduct. In short, Mr. Holmes, you would go far before you found a more dangerous man than Peter Carey, and I have heard that he bore the same character when he commanded his ship. He was known in the trade as Black Peter, and the name was given him, not only on account of his swarthy features and the colour of his huge beard, but for the humours which were the terror of all around him I need not say that he was loathed and avoided by every one of his neighbours, and that I have not heard one single word of sorrow about his terrible end.

" You must have read in the account of the inquest about the man's cabin, Mr. Holmes ; but perhaps your friend here has not heard of it. He had built himself a wooden outhouse—he always called it ' the cabin '—a few hundred yards from his house, and it was here that he slept every night. It was a little, single-roomed hut, sixteen feet by ten. He kept the key in his pocket, made his own bed, cleaned it himself, and allowed no other foot to cross the threshold. There are small windows on each side, which were covered by curtains, and never opened. One of these windows was turned towards the high-road, and when the light burned in it at night the folk used to point it out to each other, and wonder what Black Peter was doing in there. That's the window, Mr. Holmes, which gave us one of the few bits of positive evidence that came out at the inquest.

" You remember that a stonemason, named Slater, walking from Forest Row about one o'clock in the morning —two days before the murder—stopped as he passed the grounds and looked at the square of light still shining among the trees. He swears that the shadow of a man's head turned sideways was clearly visible on the blind, and that this shadow was certainly not that of Peter Carey, whom he knew well. It was that of a bearded man, but the beard was short, and bristled forwards in a way very different from that of the captain. So he says, but he had been two hours in the public-house, and it is some distance from the road to the window. Besides, this refers to the Monday, and the crime was done upon the Wednesday.

" On the Tuesday Peter Carey was in one of his blackest moods, flushed with drink and as savage as a dangerous wild beast. He roamed about the house, and the women ran for it when they heard him coming. Late in the evening he went down to his own hut. About two o'clock the following morning his daughter, who slept with her window open, heard a most fearful yell from that direction, but it was no unusual thing for him to bawl and shout when he was in drink, so no notice was taken. On rising at seven one of the maids noticed that the door of the hut was open, but so great was the terror which the man caused that it was midday before anyone would venture down to see what had become of him. Peeping into the open door, they saw a sight which sent them flying with white faces into the village. Within an hour I was on the spot, and had taken over the case.

" Well, I have fairly steady nerves, as you know, Mr. Holmes, but I give you my word that I got a shake when I put my head into that little house. It was droning like a harmonium with the flies and bluebottles, and the floor and walls were like a slaughter-house. He had called it a cabin, and a cabin it was, sure enough, for you would have thought that you were in a ship. There was a bunk at one end, a sea-chest, maps and charts, a picture of the *Sea Unicorn*, a line of log-books on a shelf, all exactly as one would expect to find it in a captain's room. And there in the middle of it was the man himself, his face twisted like a lost soul in torment, and his great brindled beard stuck upwards in his agony. Right through his broad breast a steel harpoon had been driven, and it had sunk deep into the wood of the wall behind him. He was pinned like a beetle on a card. Of course, he was quite dead, and had been so from the instant that he uttered that last yell of agony.

" I know your methods, sir, and I applied them. Before I permitted anything to be moved I examined most carefully the ground outside, and also the floor of the room. There were no footmarks."

" Meaning that you saw none ? "

" I assure you, sir, that there were none."

" My good Hopkins, I have investigated many crimes, but I have never yet seen one which was committed by a flying creature. As long as the criminal remains upon two legs so long must there be some indentation, some abrasion, some trifling displacement which can be detected by the scientific searcher. It is incredible that this blood-bespattered room contained no trace which could have aided us. I understand, however, from the inquest that there were some objects which you failed to overlook ? "

The young inspector winced at my companion's ironical comments.

" I was a fool not to call you in at the time, Mr. Holmes. However, that's past praying for now. Yes, there were several objects in the room which called for special attention. One was the harpoon with which the deed was committed. It had been snatched down from a rack on the wall. Two others remained there, and there was a vacant place for the third. On the stock was engraved ' S.s. *Sea Unicorn*, Dundee.' This seemed to establish that the crime had been done in a moment of fury, and that the murderer had seized the first weapon which came in his way. The fact that the crime was committed at two in the morning, and yet Peter Carey was fully dressed, suggested that he had an appointment with the murderer, which is borne out by the fact that a bottle of rum and two dirty glasses stood upon the table."

" Yes," said Holmes ; " I think that both inferences

are permissible. Was there any other spirit but rum in the room ? "

" Yes ; there was a tantalus containing brandy and whisky on the sea-chest. It is of no importance to us, however, since the decanters were full and it had therefore not been used."

" For all that its presence has some significance," said Holmes. " However, let us hear some more about the objects which do seem to you to bear upon the case."

" There was this tobacco-pouch upon the table."

" What part of the table ? "

" It lay in the middle. It was of coarse sealskin—the straight-haired skin, with a leather thong to bind it. Inside was ' P. C.' on the flap. There was half an ounce of strong ship's tobacco in it."

" Excellent ! What more ? "

Stanley Hopkins drew from his pocket a drab-covered notebook. The outside was rough and worn, the leaves were discoloured. On the first page were written the initials " J. H. N." and the date " 1883." Holmes laid it on the table and examined it in his minute way, while Hopkins and I gazed over each shoulder. On the second page were printed the letters " C. P. R.," and then came several sheets of numbers. Another heading was Argentine, another Costa Rica, and another San Paulo, each with pages of signs and figures after it.

" What do you make of these ? " asked Holmes.

" They appear to be lists of Stock Exchange securities. I thought that ' J. H. N.' were the initials of a broker, and that ' C. P. R.' may have been his client."

" Try Canadian Pacific Railway," said Holmes.

Stanley Hopkins swore between his teeth, and struck his thigh with his clenched hand.

" What a fool I have been ! " he cried. " Of course it is as you say. Then ' J. H. N.' are the only initials we have to solve. I have already examined the old Stock Exchange lists, and I can find no one in 1883 either in the House or among the outside brokers whose initials correspond with these. Yet I feel that the clue is the most important one that I hold. You will admit, Mr. Holmes, that there is a possibility that these initials are those of the second person who was present—in other words, of the murderer. I would also urge that the introduction into the case of a document relating to large masses of valuable securities gives us for the first time some indication of a motive for the crime."

Sherlock Holmes' face showed that he was thoroughly taken aback by this new development.

" I must admit both your points," said he. " I confess that the notebook, which did not appear at the inquest, modifies any views which I may have formed. I had come to a theory of the crime in which I can find no place for this. Have you endeavoured to trace any of the securities here mentioned ? "

" Inquiries are now being made at the offices, but I fear that the complete register of the stock-holders of these South American concerns is in South America, and that some weeks must elapse before we can trace the shares."

Holmes had been examining the cover of the notebook with his magnifying lens.

" Surely there is some discoloration here," said he.

" Yes, sir, it is a blood-stain. I told you that I picked the book off the floor."

" Was the blood-stain above or below ? "

" On the side next the boards."

" Which proves, of course, that the book was dropped after the crime was committed."

" Exactly, Mr. Holmes. I appreciated that point, and I conjectured that it was dropped by the murderer on his hurried flight. It lay near the door."

" I suppose that none of these securities have been found among the property of the dead man ? "

" No, sir."

" Have you any reason to suspect robbery ? "

" No, sir. Nothing seemed to have been touched."

704

" Dear me, it is certainly a very interesting case. Then there was a knife, was there not ? "

" A sheath-knife, still in its sheath. It lay at the feet of the dead man. Mrs. Carey has identified it as being her husband's property."

Holmes was lost in thought for some time.

" Well," said he at last, " I suppose I shall have to come out and have a look at it."

Stanley Hopkins gave a cry of joy.

" Thank you, sir. That will indeed be a weight off my mind."

Holmes shook his finger at the Inspector.

" It would have been an easier task a week ago," said he. " But even now my visit may not be entirely fruitless. Watson, if you can spare the time, I should be very glad of your company. If you will call a four-wheeler, Hopkins, we shall be ready to start for Forest Row in a quarter of an hour."

Alighting at the small wayside station, we drove for some miles through the remains of widespread woods, which were once part of that great forest which for so long held the Saxon invaders at bay—the impenetrable " weald," for sixty years the bulwark of Britain. Vast sections of it have been cleared, for this is the seat of the first ironworks of the country, and the trees have been felled to smelt the ore. Now the richer fields of the North have absorbed the trade, and nothing save these ravaged groves and great scars in the earth show the work of the past. Here in a clearing upon the green slope of a hill stood a long, low stone house, approached by a curving drive running through the fields. Nearer the road, and surrounded on three sides by bushes, was a small outhouse, one window and the door facing in our direction. It was the scene of the murder.

Stanley Hopkins led us first to the house, where he introduced us to a haggard, grey-haired woman, the widow of the murdered man, whose gaunt and deep-lined face, with the furtive look of terror in the depths of her red-rimmed eyes, told of the years of hardship and ill-usage which she had endured. With her was her daughter, a pale, fair-haired girl, whose eyes blazed defiantly at us as she told us that she was glad that her father was dead, and that she blessed the hand which had struck him down. It was a terrible household that Black Peter Carey had made for himself, and it was with a sense of relief that we found ourselves in the sunlight again and making our way along the path which had been worn across the fields by the feet of the dead man.

The outhouse was the simplest of dwellings, wooden-walled, single-roofed, one window beside the door, and one on the farther side. Stanley Hopkins drew the key from his pocket, and had stooped to the lock, when he paused with a look of attention and surprise upon his face.

" Someone has been tampering with it," he said.

There could be no doubt of the fact. The woodwork was cut, and the scratches showed white through the paint, as if they had been that instant done. Holmes had been examining the window.

" Someone has tried to force this also. Whoever it was has failed to make his way in. He must have been a very poor burglar."

" This is a most extraordinary thing," said the Inspector ; " I could swear that these marks were not here yesterday evening."

" Some curious person from the village, perhaps," I suggested.

" Very unlikely. Few of them would dare to set foot in the grounds, far less try to force their way into the cabin. What do you think of it, Mr. Holmes ? "

" I think that fortune is very kind to us."

" You mean that the person will come again ? "

" It is very probable. He came expecting to find the door open. He tried to get in with the blade of a very small penknife. He could not manage it. What would he do ? "

706

" Come again next night with a more useful tool."

" So I should say. It will be our fault if we are not there to receive him. Meanwhile, let me see the inside of the cabin."

The traces of the tragedy had been removed, but the furniture of the little room still stood as it had been on the night of the crime. For two hours, with the most intense concentration, Holmes examined every object in turn, but his face showed that his quest was not a successful one. Once only he paused in his patient investigation.

" Have you taken anything off this shelf, Hopkins ? "

" No ; I have moved nothing."

" Something has been taken. There is less dust in this corner of the shelf than elsewhere. It may have been a book lying on its side. It may have been a box. Well, well, I can do nothing more. Let us walk in these beautiful woods, Watson, and give a few hours to the birds and the flowers. We shall meet you here later, Hopkins, and see if we can come to closer quarters with the gentleman who has paid this visit in the night."

It was past eleven o'clock when we formed our little ambuscade. Hopkins was for leaving the door of the hut open, but Holmes was of opinion that this would rouse the suspicions of the stranger. The lock was a perfectly simple one, and only a strong blade was needed to push it back. Holmes also suggested that we should wait, not inside the hut, but outside it among the bushes which grew round the farther window. In this way we should be able to watch our man if he struck a light, and see what his object was in this stealthy nocturnal visit.

It was a long and melancholy vigil, and yet it brought with it something of the thrill which the hunter feels when he lies beside the water-pool and waits for the coming of the thirsty beast of prey. What savage creature was it which might steal upon us out of the darkness ? Was it a fierce tiger of crime, which could only be taken fighting hard with flashing fang and claw, or would it prove to be some skulking jackal, dangerous only to the weak and unguarded ? In absolute silence we crouched amongst the bushes, waiting for whatever might come. At first the steps of a few belated villagers, or the sound of voices from the village, lightened our vigil ; but one by one these interruptions died away, and an absolute stillness fell upon us, save for the chimes of the distant church, which told us of the progress of the night, and for the rustle and whisper of a fine rain falling amid the foliage which roofed us in.

Half-past two had chimed, and it was the darkest hour which precedes the dawn, when we all started as a low but sharp click came from the direction of the gate. Some-one had entered the drive. Again there was a long silence, and I had begun to fear that it was a false alarm, when a stealthy step was heard upon the other side of the hut, and a moment later a metallic scraping and clicking. The man was trying to force the lock ! This time his skill was greater or his tool was better, for there was a sudden snap and the creak of the hinges. Then a match was struck, and next instant the steady light from a candle filled the interior of the hut. Through the gauze curtain our eyes were all riveted upon the scene within.

The nocturnal visitor was a young man, frail and thin, with black moustache which intensified the deadly pallor of his face. He could not have been much above twenty years of age. I have never seen any human being who appeared to be in such a pitiable fright, for his teeth were visibly chattering, and he was shaking in every limb. He was dressed like a gentleman, in Norfolk jacket and knickerbockers, with a cloth cap upon his head. We watched him staring round with frightened eyes. Then he laid the candle-end upon the table and disappeared from our view into one of the corners. He returned with a large book, one of the log-books which formed a line upon the shelves. Leaning on the table, he rapidly turned over the leaves of this volume until he came to the entry which he sought. Then, with an angry gesture of his clenched hand, he closed the book, replaced it in the corner, and put out the light. He had hardly turned to leave the hut when Hopkins' hand was on the fellow's collar, and I heard his loud gasp of terror as he understood that he was taken. The candle was relit, and there was our wretched captive shivering and cowering in the grasp of the detective. He sank down upon the sea-chest, and looked helplessly from one of us to the other.

"Now, my fine fellow," said Stanley Hopkins, "who are you, and what do you want here?"

The man pulled himself together and faced us with an effort at self-composure.

"You are detectives, I suppose?" said he. "You imagine I am connected with the death of Captain Peter Carey. I assure you that I am innocent."

"We'll see about that," said Hopkins. "First of all, what is your name?"

"It is John Hopley Neligan."

I saw Holmes and Hopkins exchange a quick glance.

"What are you doing here?"

"Can I speak confidentially?"

"No, certainly not."

"Why should I tell you?"

"If you have no answer it may go badly with you at the trial."

The young man winced.

"Well, I will tell you," he said. "Why should I not? And yet I hate to think of this old scandal gaining a new lease of life. Did you ever hear of Dawson & Neligan?"

I could see from Hopkins' face that he never had; but Holmes was keenly interested.

"You mean the West Country bankers," said he. "They failed for a million, ruined half the county families of Cornwall, and Neligan disappeared."

"Exactly. Neligan was my father."

At last we were getting something positive, and yet it

seemed a long gap between an absconding banker and Captain Peter Carey pinned against the wall with one of his own harpoons. We all listened intently to the young man's words.

" It was my father who was really concerned. Dawson had retired. I was only ten years of age at the time, but I was old enough to feel the shame and horror of it all. It has always been said that my father stole all the securities and fled. It is not true. It was his belief that if he were given time in which to realize them all would be well, and every creditor paid in full. He started in his little yacht for Norway just before the warrant was issued for his arrest. I can remember that last night when he bade farewell to my mother. He left us a list of the securities he was taking, and he swore that he would come back with his honour cleared, and that none who had trusted him would suffer. Well, no word was ever heard from him again. Both the yacht and he vanished utterly. We believed, my mother and I, that he and it, with the securities that he had taken with him, were at the bottom of the sea. We had a faithful friend, however, who is a business man, and it was he who discovered some time ago that some of the securities which my father had with him have reappeared on the London market. You can imagine our amazement. I spent months in trying to trace them, and at last, after many doublings and difficulties, I discovered that the original seller had been Captain Peter Carey, the owner of this hut.

" Naturally I made some inquiries about the man. I found that he had been in command of a whaler which was due to return from the Arctic seas at the very time when my father was crossing to Norway. The autumn of that year was a stormy one, and there was a long succession of southerly gales. My father's yacht may well have been blown to the north, and there met by Captain Peter Carey's ship. If that were so, what had become of my father? In any case, if I could prove from Peter Carey's evidence how these securities came on the market, it would be a proof that my father had not sold them, and that he had no view to personal profit when he took them.

" I came down to Sussex with the intention of seeing the captain, but it was at this moment that his terrible death occurred. I read at the inquest a description of his cabin, in which it stated that the old log-books of his vessel were preserved in it. It struck me that if I could see what occurred in the month of August, 1883, on board the *Sea Unicorn*, I might settle the mystery of my father's fate. I tried last night to get at these log-books, but was unable to open the door. To-night I tried again, and succeeded ; but I find that the pages which deal with that month have been torn from the book. It was at that moment I found myself a prisoner in your hands."

" Is that all ? " asked Hopkins.

" Yes, that is all." His eyes shifted as he said it.

" You have nothing else to tell us ? "

He hesitated.

" No ; there is nothing."

" You have not been here before last night ? "

" No."

" Then how do you account for *that* ? " cried Hopkins, as he held up the damning notebook, with the initials of our prisoner on the first leaf, and the blood-stain on the cover.

The wretched man collapsed. He sank his face in his hands and trembled all over.

" Where did you get it ? " he groaned. " I did not know. I thought I had lost it at the hotel."

" That is enough," said Hopkins sternly. " Whatever else you have to say you must say in court. You will walk down with me now to the police-station. Well, Mr. Holmes, I am very much obliged to you and to your friend for coming down to help me. As it turns out your presence was unnecessary, and I would have brought the case to this successful issue without you ; but none the less I am very grateful. Rooms have been reserved for

711

you at the Brambletye Hotel, so we can all walk down to the village together."

"Well, Watson, what do you think of it?" asked Holmes as we travelled back next morning.

"I can see that you are not satisfied."

"Oh, yes, my dear Watson, I am perfectly satisfied. At the same time Stanley Hopkins' methods do not commend themselves to me. I am disappointed in Stanley Hopkins. I had hoped for better things from him. One should always look for a possible alternative and provide against it. It is the first rule of criminal investigation."

"What, then, is the alternative?"

"The line of investigation which I have myself been pursuing. It may give nothing. I cannot tell. But at least I shall follow it to the end."

Several letters were waiting for Holmes at Baker Street. He snatched one of them up, opened it, and burst out into a triumphant chuckle of laughter.

"Excellent, Watson. The alternative develops. Have you telegraph forms? Just write a couple of messages for me : ' Sumner, Shipping Agent, Ratcliff Highway. Send three men on, to arrive ten to-morrow morning.— Basil.' That's my name in those parts. The other is ' Inspector .Stanley Hopkins, 46 Lord Street, Brixton. Come breakfast to-morrow at nine-thirty. Important. Wire if unable to come.—Sherlock Holmes.' There, Watson, this infernal case had haunted me for ten days. I hereby banish it completely from my presence. To-morrow I trust that we shall hear the last of it for ever."

Sharp at the hour named Inspector Stanley Hopkins appeared, and we sat down together to the excellent breakfast which Mrs. Hudson had prepared. The young detective was in high spirits at his success.

"You really think that your solution must be correct?" asked Holmes.

"I could not imagine a more complete case."

"It did not seem to me conclusive."

"You astonish me, Mr. Holmes. What more could one ask for?"

"Does your explanation cover every point?"

"Undoubtedly. I find that young Neligan arrived at the Brambletye Hotel on the very day of the crime. He came on the pretence of playing golf. His room was on the ground floor, and he could get out when he liked. That very night he went down to Woodman's Lee, saw Peter Carey at the hut, quarrelled with him, and killed him with the harpoon. Then, horrified by what he had done, he fled out of the hut, dropping the notebook which he had brought with him in order to question Peter Carey about these different securities. You may have observed that some of them were marked with ticks, and the others—the great majority—were not. Those which are ticked have been traced on the London market; but the others presumably were still in the possession of Carey, and young Neligan, according to his own account, was anxious to recover them in order to do the right thing by his father's creditors. After his flight he did not dare to approach the hut again for some time; but at last he forced himself to do so in order to obtain the information which he needed. Surely that is all simple and obvious?"

Holmes smiled and shook his head.

"It seems to me to have only one drawback, Hopkins, and that is that it is intrinsically impossible. Have you tried to drive a harpoon through a body? No? Tut, tut, my dear sir, you must really pay attention to these details My friend Watson could tell you that I spent a whole morning in that exercise. It is no easy matter, and requires a strong and practised arm. But this blow was delivered with such violence that the head of the weapon sank deep into the wall. Do you imagine that this anæmic youth was capable of so frightful an assault? Is he the man who hob-nobbed in rum and water with Black Peter in the dead of the night? Was it his profile that was seen on the blind two nights before? No, no,

Hopkins ; it is another and a more formidable person for whom we must seek."

The detective's face had grown longer and longer during Holmes' speech. His hopes and his ambitions were all crumbling about him. But he would not abandon his position without a struggle.

" You can't deny that Neligan was present that night, Mr. Holmes. The book will prove that. I fancy that I have evidence enough to satisfy a jury, even if you are able to pick a hole in it. Besides, Mr. Holmes, I have laid my hand upon *my* man. As to this terrible person of yours, where is he ? "

" I rather fancy that he is on the stair," said Holmes serenely. " I think, Watson, that you would do well to put that revolver where you can reach it." He rose, and laid a written paper upon a side-table. " Now we are ready," said he.

There had been some talking in gruff voices outside, and now Mrs. Hudson opened the door to say that there were three men inquiring for Captain Basil.

" Show them in one by one," said Holmes.

The first who entered was a little ribston-pippin of a man, with ruddy cheeks and fluffy white side-whiskers. Holmes had drawn a letter from his pocket.

" What name ? " he asked.

" James Lancaster."

" I am sorry, Lancaster, but the berth is full. Here is half a sovereign for your trouble. Just step into this room and wait there for a few minutes."

The second man was a long, dried-up creature, with lank hair and sallow cheeks. His name was Hugh Pattins. He also received his dismissal, his half-sovereign, and the order to wait.

The third applicant was a man of remarkable appearance. A fierce, bull-dog face was framed in a tangle of hair and beard, and two bold dark eyes gleamed behind the cover of thick, tufted, overhung eyebrows. He saluted and stood sailor-fashion, turning his cap round in his hands.

"Your name ?" asked Holmes.

"Patrick Cairns."

"Harpooner ?"

"Yes, sir. Twenty-six voyages."

"Dundee, I suppose ?"

"Yes, sir."

"And ready to start with an exploring ship ?"

"Yes, sir."

"What wages ?"

"Eight pounds a month."

"Could you start at once ?"

"As soon as I get my kit."

"Have you your papers ?"

"Yes, sir." He took a sheaf of worn and greasy forms from his pocket. Holmes glanced over them and returned them.

"You are just the man I want," said he. "Here's the agreement on the side-table. If you sign it the whole matter will be settled."

The seaman lurched across the room and took up the pen.

"Shall I sign here ?" he asked, stooping over the table.

Holmes leaned over his shoulder and passed both hands over his neck.

"This will do," said he.

I heard a click of steel and a bellow like an enraged bull. The next instant Holmes and the seaman were rolling on the ground together. He was a man of such gigantic strength that, even with the handcuffs which Holmes had so deftly fastened upon his wrists, he would have quickly overpowered my friend had Hopkins and I not rushed to his rescue. Only when I pressed the cold muzzle of the revolver to his temple did he at last understand that resistance was vain. We lashed his ankles with cord and rose breathless from the struggle.

"I must really apologize, Hopkins," said Sherlock Holmes; "I fear that the scrambled eggs are cold. However, you will enjoy the rest of your breakfast all the better, will you not, for the thought that you have brought your case to a triumphant conclusion?"

Stanley Hopkins was speechless with amazement.

"I don't know what to say, Mr. Holmes," he blurted out at last, with a very red face. "It seems to me that I have been making a fool of myself from the beginning. I understand now, what I should never have forgotten, that I am the pupil and you are the master. Even now I see what you have done, but I don't know how you did it, or what it signifies."

"Well, well," said Holmes good-humouredly. "We all learn by experience, and your lesson this time is that you should never lose sight of the alternative. You were so absorbed in young Neligan that you could not spare a thought to Patrick Cairns, the true murderer of Peter Carey."

The hoarse voice of the seaman broke in on our conversation.

"See here, mister," said he, "I make no complaint of being man-handled in this fashion, but I would have you call things by their right names. You say I murdered Peter Carey; I say I *killed* Peter Carey, and there's all the difference. Maybe you don't believe what I say. Maybe you think I am just slinging you a yarn."

"Not at all," said Holmes. "Let us hear what you have to say."

"It's soon told, and, by the Lord, every word of it is truth. I knew Black Peter, and when he pulled out his knife I whipped a harpoon through him sharp, for I knew that it was him or me. That's how he died. You can call it murder. Anyhow, I'd as soon die with a rope round my neck as with Black Peter's knife in my heart."

"How came you there?" asked Holmes.

"I'll tell it you from the beginning. Just sit me up a little so as I can speak easy. It was in '83 that it happened—August of that year. Peter Carey was master of the *Sea Unicorn*, and I was spare harpooner. We were coming out of the ice-pack on our way home, with head winds and a week's southerly gale, when we picked up a little craft that had been blown north. There was one man on her—a landsman. The crew had thought she would founder, and had made for the Norwegian coast in the dinghy. I guess they were all drowned. Well, we took him on board, this man, and he and the skipper had some long talks in the cabin. All the baggage we took off with him was one tin box. So far as I know the man's name was never mentioned, and on the second night he disappeared as if he had never been. It was given out that he had either thrown himself overboard or fallen overboard in the heavy weather that we were having. Only one man knew what had happened to him, and that was me, for with my own eyes I saw the skipper tip up his heels and put him over the rail in the middle watch of a dark night, two days before we sighted the Shetland lights.

" Well, I kept my knowledge to myself and waited to see what would come of it. When we got back to Scotland it was easily hushed up, and nobody asked any questions. A stranger died by an accident, and it was nobody's business to inquire. Shortly after Peter Carey gave up the sea, and it was long years before I could find where he was. I guessed that he had done the deed for the sake of what was in that tin box, and that he could afford now to pay me well for keeping my mouth shut.

" I found out where he was through a sailor man that had met him in London, and down I went to squeeze him. The first night he was reasonable enough, and was ready to give me what would make me free of the sea for life. We were to fix it all two nights later. When I came I found him three-parts drunk and in a vile temper. We sat down and we drank and we yarned about old times, but the more he drank the less I liked the look on his face. I spotted that harpoon upon the wall, and I thought I might need it before I was through. Then at last he broke out at me, spitting and cursing, with murder in his eyes and a great clasp-knife in his hand. He had not time to get it from the sheath before I had the harpoon through him. Heavens! what a yell he gave; and his face gets between me and my sleep! I stood there, with his blood splashing round me, and I waited for a bit; but all was quiet, so I took heart once more. I looked round, and there was the tin box on a shelf. I had as much right to it as Peter Carey, anyhow, so I took it with me and left the hut. Like a fool I left my baccy-pouch upon the table.

"Now I'll tell you the queerest part of the whole story. I had hardly got outside the hut when I heard someone coming, and I hid among the bushes. A man came slinking along, went into the hut, gave a cry as if he had seen a ghost, and legged it as hard as he could run until he was out of sight. Who he was or what he wanted is more than I can tell. For my part, I walked ten miles, got a train at Tunbridge Wells, and so reached London, and no one the wiser.

"Well, when I came to examine the box I found there was no money in it, and nothing but papers that I would not dare to sell. I had lost my hold on Black Peter, and was stranded in London without a shilling. There was only my trade left. I saw these advertisements about harpooners and high wages, so I went to the shipping agents, and they sent me here. That's all I know, and I say again that if I killed Black Peter the law should give me thanks, for I saved them the price of a hempen rope."

"A very clear statement," said Holmes, rising and lighting his pipe. "I think, Hopkins, that you should lose no time in conveying your prisoner to a place of safety. This room is not well adapted for a cell, and Mr. Patrick Cairns occupies too large a portion of our carpet."

"Mr. Holmes," said Hopkins, "I do not know how to

express my gratitude. Even now I do not understand how you attained this result."

" Simply by having the good fortune to get the right clue from the beginning. It is very possible that if I had known about this notebook it might have led away my thoughts, as it did yours. But all I heard pointed in the one direction. The amazing strength, the skill in the use of the harpoon, the rum and water, the sealskin tobacco-pouch, with the coarse tobacco—all these pointed to a seaman, and one who had been a whaler. I was convinced that the initials ' P. C.' upon the pouch were a coincidence, and not those of Peter Carey, since he seldom smoked, and no pipe was found in his cabin. You remember that I asked whether whisky and brandy were in the cabin. You said they were. How many landsmen are there who would drink rum when they could get these other spirits ? Yes, I was certain it was a seaman."

" And how did you find him ? "

" My dear sir, the problem had become a very simple one. If it were a seaman, it could only be a seaman who had been with him on the *Sea Unicorn*. So far as I could learn, he had sailed in no other ship. I spent three days in wiring to Dundee, and at the end of that time I had ascertained the names of the crew of the *Sea Unicorn* in 1883. When I found Patrick Cairns among the harpooners my research was nearing its end. I argued that the man was probably in London, and that he would desire to leave the country for a time. I therefore spent some days in the East End, devised an Arctic expedition, put forward tempting terms for harpooners who would serve under Captain Basil—and behold the result ! "

" Wonderful ! " cried Hopkins. " Wonderful ! "

" You must obtain the release of young Neligan as soon as possible," said Holmes. " I confess that I think you owe him some apology. The tin box must be returned to him, but, of course, the securities which Peter Carey has sold are lost for ever. There's the cab, Hopkins, and you can remove your man. If you want me for the trial, my address and that of Watson will be somewhere in Norway—I'll send particulars later."

30. *Charles Augustus Milverton*

IT is years since the incidents of which I speak took place, and yet it is with diffidence that I allude to them. For a long time, even with the utmost discretion and reticence, it would have been impossible to make the facts public ; but now the principal person concerned is beyond the reach of human law, and with due suppression the story may be told in such fashion as to injure no one. It records an absolutely unique experience in the career both of Mr. Sherlock Holmes and of myself. The reader will excuse me if I conceal the date or any other fact by which he might trace the actual occurrence.

We had been out for one of our evening rambles, Holmes and I, and had returned about six o'clock on a cold, frosty winter's evening. As Holmes turned up the lamp the light fell upon a card on the table. He glanced at it, and then, with an ejaculation of disgust, threw it on the floor. I picked it up and read :

CHARLES AUGUSTUS MILVERTON,
APPLEDORE TOWERS,
HAMPSTEAD.
Agent.

" Who is he ? " I asked.

" The worst man in London," Holmes answered, as he sat down and stretched his legs before the fire. " Is anything on the back of the card ? "

I turned it over.

" Will call at 6.30.—C. A. M.," I read.

" Hum ! He's about due. Do you feel a creeping, shrinking sensation, Watson, when you stand before the serpents in the Zoo and see the slithery, gliding, venomous creatures, with their deadly eyes and wicked, flattened faces ? Well, that's how Milverton impresses me. I've had to do with fifty murderers in my career, but the worst of them never gave me the repulsion which I have for this fellow. And yet I can't get out of doing business with him—indeed, he is here at my invitation."

"But who is he ? "

"I'll tell you, Watson. He is the king of all the blackmailers. Heaven help the man, and still more the woman, whose secret and reputation come into the power of Milverton. With a smiling face and a heart of marble he will squeeze and squeeze until he has drained them dry. The fellow is a genius in his way, and would have made his mark in some more savoury trade. His method is as follows : He allows it to be known that he is prepared to pay very high sums for letters which compromise people of wealth or position. He receives these wares not only from treacherous valets or maids, but frequently from genteel ruffians who have gained the confidence and affection of trusting women. He deals with no niggard hand. I happen to know that he paid seven hundred pounds to a footman for a note two lines in length, and that the ruin of a noble family was the result. Everything which is in the market goes to Milverton, and there are hundreds in this great city who turn white at his name. No one knows where his grip may fall, for he is far too rich and far too cunning to work from hand to mouth. He will hold a card back for years in order to play it at the moment when the stake is best worth winning. I have said that he is the worst man in London, and I would ask you how could one compare the ruffian who in hot blood bludgeons his mate with this man, who methodically and at his leisure tortures the soul and wrings the nerves in order to add to his already swollen money-bags ? "

I had seldom heard my friend speak with such intensity of feeling.

"But surely," said I, "the fellow must be within the grasp of the law ? "

"Technically, no doubt, but practically not. What would it profit a woman, for example, to get him a few months' imprisonment if her own ruin must immediately follow ? His victims dare not hit back. If ever he blackmailed an innocent person, then, indeed, we should have him ; but he is as cunning as the Evil One. No, no ; we must find other ways to fight him."

"And why is he here ? "

"Because an illustrious client has placed her piteous case in my hands. It is the Lady Eva Brackwell, the most beautiful *débutante* of last season. She is to be married in a fortnight to the Earl of Dovercourt. This fiend has several imprudent letters—imprudent, Watson, nothing worse—which were written to an impecunious young squire in the country. They would suffice to break off the match. Milverton will send the letters to the earl unless a large sum of money is paid him. I have been commissioned to meet him, and—to make the best terms I can."

At that instant there was a clatter and a rattle in the street below. Looking down I saw a stately carriage and pair, the brilliant lamps gleaming on the glossy haunches of the noble chestnuts. A footman opened the door, and a small, stout man in a shaggy astrachan overcoat descended. A minute later he was in the room.

Charles Augustus Milverton was a man of fifty, with a large, intellectual head, a round, plump, hairless face, a perpetual frozen smile, and two keen grey eyes, which gleamed brightly from behind broad, golden-rimmed glasses. There was something of Mr. Pickwick's benevolence in his appearance, marred only by the insincerity of the fixed smile and by the hard glitter of those restless and penetrating eyes. His voice was as smooth and suave as his countenance, as he advanced with a plump little hand extended, murmuring his regret for having missed us at his first visit.

Holmes disregarded the outstretched hand and looked at him with a face of granite. Milverton's smile broadened ; he shrugged his shoulders, removed his overcoat, folded it with great deliberation over the back of a chair, and then took a seat.

" This gentleman," said he, with a wave in my direction. " Is it discreet ? Is it right ? "

" Dr. Watson is my friend and partner."

" Very good, Mr. Holmes. It is only in your client's interests that I protested. The matter is so very delicate——"

" Dr. Watson has already heard of it."

" Then we can proceed to business. You say that you are acting for Lady Eva. Has she empowered you to accept my terms ? "

" What are your terms ? "

" Seven thousand pounds."

" And the alternative ? "

" My dear sir, it is painful to me to discuss it ; but if the money is not paid on the 14th there certainly will be no marriage on the 18th." His insufferable smile was more complacent than ever. Holmes thought for a little.

" You appear to me," he said at last, " to be taking matters too much for granted. I am, of course, familiar with the contents of these letters. My client will certainly do what I may advise. I shall counsel her to tell her future husband the whole story and to trust to his generosity."

Milverton chuckled.

" You evidently do not know the earl," said he.

From the baffled look upon Holmes' face I could clearly see that he did.

" What harm is there in the letters ? " he asked.

" They are sprightly—very sprightly," Milverton answered. " The lady was a charming correspondent. But I can assure you that the Earl of Dovercourt would fail to appreciate them. However, since you think otherwise, we will let it rest at that. It is purely a matter of business. If you think that it is in the best interests of your client that these letters should be placed in the hands of the earl, then you would indeed be foolish to pay so large a sum of money to regain them." He rose and seized his astrachan coat.

Holmes was grey with anger and mortification.

" Wait a little," he said. " You go too fast. We would certainly make every effort to avoid scandal in so delicate a matter."

Milverton relapsed into his chair.

" I was sure that you would see it in that light," he purred.

" At the same time," Holmes continued, " Lady Eva is not a wealthy woman. I assure you that two thousand pounds would be a drain upon her resources, and that the sum you name is utterly beyond her power. I beg, therefore, that you will moderate your demands, and that you will return the letters at the price I indicate, which is, I assure you, the highest that you can get."

Milverton's smile broadened and his eyes twinkled humorously.

" I am aware that what you say is true about the lady's resources," said he. " At the same time, you must admit that the occasion of a lady's marriage is a very suitable time for her friends and relatives to make some little effort upon her behalf. They may hesitate as to an acceptable wedding present. Let me assure them that this little bundle of letters would give more joy than all the candelabra and butter-dishes in London."

" It is impossible," said Holmes.

" Dear me, dear me, how unfortunate ! " cried Milverton, taking out a bulky pocket-book. " I cannot help thinking that ladies are ill-advised in not making an effort. Look at this ! " He held up a little note with a coat-of-arms upon the envelope. " That belongs to—well, perhaps it is hardly fair to tell the name until to-morrow morning. But at that time it will be in the hands of the lady's husband. And all because she will not find a beggarly sum which she could get in an hour by turning her diamonds into paste. It *is* such a pity. Now, you remember the sudden end of the engagement between the Honourable Miss Miles and Colonel Dorking? Only two days before the wedding there was a paragraph in the *Morning Post* to say that it was all off. And why? It is almost incredible, but the absurd sum of twelve hundred pounds would have settled the whole question. Is it not pitiful? And there I find you, a man of sense, boggling about terms when your client's future and honour are at stake. You surprise me, Mr. Holmes."

"What I say is true," Holmes answered. "The money cannot be found. Surely it is better for you to take the substantial sum which I offer than to ruin this woman's career, which can profit you in no way?"

"There you make a mistake, Mr. Holmes. An exposure would profit me indirectly to a considerable extent. I have eight or ten similar cases maturing. If it was circulated among them that I had made a severe example of the Lady Eva I should find all of them much more open to reason. You see my point?"

Holmes sprang from his chair.

"Get behind him, Watson. Don't let him out! Now, sir, let us see the contents of that notebook."

Milverton had glided as quick as a rat to the side of the room, and stood with his back against the wall.

"Mr. Holmes, Mr. Holmes!" he said, turning the front of his coat and exhibiting the butt of a large revolver, which projected from the inside pocket. "I have been expecting you to do something original. This has been done so often, and what good has ever come from it? I assure you that I am armed to the teeth, and I am perfectly prepared to use my weapon, knowing that the law will support me. Besides, your supposition that I would bring the letters here in a notebook is entirely mistaken. I would do nothing so foolish. And now, gentlemen, I have one or two little interviews this evening, and it is a long drive to Hampstead." He stepped forward, took up his coat, laid his hand on his revolver, and turned to the door. I picked up a chair, but Holmes shook his head, and I laid it down again. With a bow, a smile, and a twinkle Milverton was out of the room, and a few moments after we heard the slam of the carriage door and the rattle of the wheels as he drove away.

Holmes sat motionless by the fire, his hands buried deep in his trouser pockets, his chin sunk upon his breast, his eyes fixed upon the glowing embers. For half an hour he was silent and still. Then, with the gesture of a man who has taken his decision, he sprang to his feet and passed into his bedroom. A little later a rakish young workman with a goatee beard and a swagger lit his clay pipe at the lamp before descending into the street. " I'll be back some time, Watson," said he, and vanished into the night. I understood that he had opened his campaign against Charles Augustus Milverton ; but I little dreamed the strange shape which that campaign was destined to take.

For some days Holmes came and went at all hours in this attire, but beyond a remark that his time was spent at Hampstead, and that it was not wasted, I knew nothing of what he was doing. At last, however, on a wild, tempestuous evening, when the wind screamed and rattled against the windows, he returned from his last expedition, and, having removed his disguise, he sat before the fire and laughed heartily in his silent, inward fashion.

" You would not call me a marrying man, Watson ? "

" No, indeed ! "

" You will be interested to hear that I am engaged."

" My dear fellow ! I congrat——"

" To Milverton's housemaid."

" Good heavens, Holmes ! "

" I wanted information, Watson."

" Surely you have gone too far ? "

" It was a most necessary step. I am a plumber with a rising business, Escott by name. I have walked out with her each evening, and I have talked with her.

Good heavens, those talks ! However, I have got all I wanted. I know Milverton's house as I know the palm of my hand."

" But the girl, Holmes ? "

He shrugged his shoulders.

" You can't help it, my dear Watson. You must play your cards as best you can when such a stake is on the table. However, I rejoice to say that I have a hated rival who will certainly cut me out the instant that my back is turned. What a splendid night it is ! "

" You like this weather ? "

" It suits my purpose. Watson, I mean to burgle Milverton's house to-night."

I had a catching of the breath, and my skin went cold at the words, which were slowly uttered in a tone of concentrated resolution. As a flash of lightning in the night shows up in an instant every detail of a wide landscape, so at one glance I seemed to see every possible result of such an action—the detection, the capture, the honoured career ending in irreparable failure and disgrace, my friend himself lying at the mercy of the odious Milverton.

" For Heaven's sake, Holmes, think what you are doing ! " I cried.

" My dear fellow, I have given it every consideration. I am never precipitate in my actions, nor would I adopt so energetic and indeed so dangerous a course if any other were possible. Let us look at the matter clearly and fairly. I suppose that you will admit that the action is morally justifiable, though technically criminal. To burgle his house is no more than to forcibly take his pocket-book—an action in which you were prepared to aid me."

I turned it over in my mind.

" Yes," I said ; " it is morally justifiable so long as our object is to take no articles save those which are used for an illegal purpose."

" Exactly. Since it is morally justifiable, I have only to consider the question of personal risk. Surely a gentleman should not lay much stress upon this when a lady is in most desperate need of his help ? "

" You will be in such a false position."

" Well, that is part of the risk. There is no other possible way of regaining these letters. The unfortunate lady has not the money, and there are none of her people in whom she could confide. To-morrow is the last day of grace, and unless we can get the letters to-night this villain will be as good as his word, and will bring about her ruin. I must, therefore, abandon my client to her fate, or I must play this last card. Between ourselves, Watson, it's a sporting duel between this fellow Milverton and me. He had, as you saw, the best of the first exchanges ; but my self-respect and my reputation are concerned to fight it to a finish."

" Well, I don't like it ; but I suppose it must be," said I. " When do we start ? "

" You are not coming."

" Then you are not going," said I. " I give you my word of honour—and I never broke it in my life—that I will take a cab straight to the police-station and give you away unless you let me share this adventure with you."

" You can't help me."

" How do you know that ? You can't tell what may happen. Anyway, my resolution is taken. Other people besides you have self-respect and even reputations."

Holmes had looked annoyed, but his brow cleared, and he clapped me on the shoulder.

" Well, well, my dear fellow, be it so. We have shared the same room for some years, and it would be amusing if we ended by sharing the same cell. You know, Watson, I don't mind confessing to you that I have always had an idea that I would have made a highly efficient criminal. This is the chance of my lifetime in that direction. See here ! " He took a neat little leather case out of a drawer, and opening it he exhibited a number of shining instruments. " This is a first-class, up-to-date burgling kit, with nickel-plated jemmy, diamond-tipped glass cutter, adaptable keys, and every modern improvement which the march of civilization demands. Here, too, is my dark lantern. Everything is in order. Have you a pair of silent shoes ? "

" I have rubber-soled tennis shoes."

" Excellent. And a mask ? "

" I can make a couple out of black silk."

" I can see that you have a strong natural turn for this sort of thing. Very good ; do you make the masks. We shall have some cold supper before we start. It is now nine-thirty. At eleven we shall drive as far as Church Row. It is a quarter of an hour's walk from there to Appledore Towers. We shall be at work before midnight. Milverton is a heavy sleeper, and retires punctually at ten-thirty. With any luck we should be back here by two, with the Lady Eva's letters in my pocket."

Holmes and I put on our dress-clothes, so that we might appear to be two theatre-goers homeward bound. In Oxford Street we picked up a hansom and drove to an address in Hampstead. Here we paid off our cab, and with our greatcoats buttoned up—for it was bitterly cold, and the wind seemed to blow through us—we walked along the edge of the Heath.

" It's a business that needs delicate treatment," said Holmes. " These documents are contained in a safe in the fellow's study, and the study is the ante-room of his bedchamber. On the other hand, like all these stout, little men who do themselves well, he is a plethoric sleeper. Agatha—that's my fiancée—says it is a joke in the servants' hall that it's impossible to wake the master. He has a secretary who is devoted to his interests, and never budges from the study all day. That's why we are going at night. Then he has a beast of a dog which roams the garden. I met Agatha late the last two evenings, and she locks the brute up so as to give me a clear run. This is the house, this big one in its own grounds. Through the gate—now to the right among the laurels.

We might put on our masks here, I think. You see, there is not a glimmer of light in any of the windows, and everything is working splendidly."

With our black silk face-coverings, which turned us into two of the most truculent figures in London, we stole up to the silent, gloomy house. A sort of tiled veranda extended along one side of it, lined by several windows and two doors.

" That's his bedroom," Holmes whispered. " This door opens straight into the study. It would suit us best, but it is bolted as well as locked, and we should make too much noise getting in. Come round here. There's a greenhouse which opens into the drawing-room."

The place was locked, but Holmes removed a circle of glass and turned the key from the inside. An instant afterwards he had closed the door behind us, and we had become felons in the eyes of the law. The thick warm air of the conservatory and the rich, choking fragrance of exotic plants took us by the throat. He seized my hand in the darkness and led me swiftly past banks of shrubs which brushed against our faces. Holmes had remarkable powers, carefully cultivated, of seeing in the dark. Still holding my hand in one of his, he opened a door, and I was vaguely conscious that we had entered a large room in which a cigar had been smoked not long before. He felt his way among the furniture, opened another door, and closed it behind us. Putting out my hand I felt several coats hanging from the wall, and I understood that I was in a passage. We passed along it, and Holmes very gently opened a door upon the right-hand side. Something rushed out at us, and my heart sprang into my mouth, but I could have laughed when I realized that it was the cat. A fire was burning in this new room, and again the air was heavy with tobacco smoke. Holmes entered on tiptoe, waited for me to follow, and then very gently closed the door. We were in Milverton's study, and a *portière* at the farther side showed the entrance to his bedroom.

It was a good fire, and the room was illuminated by it. Near the door I saw the gleam of an electric switch, but it was unnecessary, even if it had been safe, to turn it on. At one side of the fireplace was a heavy curtain, which covered the bay window we had seen from outside. On the other side was the door which communicated with the veranda. A desk stood in the centre, with a turning chair of shining red leather. Opposite was a large bookcase, with a marble bust of Athene on the top. In the corner between the bookcase and the wall there stood a tall green safe, the firelight flashing back from the polished brass knobs upon its face. Holmes stole across and looked at it. Then he crept to the door of the bedroom, and stood with slanting head listening intently. No sound came from within. Meanwhile it had struck me that it would be wise to secure our retreat through the outer door, so I examined it. To my amazement it was neither locked nor bolted ! I touched Holmes on the arm, and he turned his masked face in that direction. I saw him start, and he was evidently as surprised as I.

" I don't like it," he whispered, putting his lips to my very ear. " I can't quite make it out. Anyhow, we have no time to lose."

" Can I do anything ? "

" Yes ; stand by the door. If you hear anyone come, bolt it on the inside, and we can get away as we came. If they come the other way, we can get through the door if our job is done, or hide behind these window curtains if it is not. Do you understand ? "

I nodded and stood by the door. My first feeling of fear had passed away, and I thrilled now with a keener zest than I had ever enjoyed when we were the defenders of the law instead of its defiers. The high object of our mission, the consciousness that it was unselfish and chivalrous, the villainous character of our opponent, all added to the sporting interest of the adventure. Far from feeling guilty, I rejoiced and exulted in our dangers. With a glow of admiration I watched Holmes

unrolling his case of instruments and choosing his tool
with the calm, scientific accuracy of a surgeon who per-
forms a delicate operation. I knew that the opening of
safes was a particular hobby with him, and I understood
the joy which it gave him to be confronted with this
green and gold monster, the dragon which held in its
maw the reputations of many fair ladies. Turning up the
cuffs of his dress-coat—he had placed his overcoat on a
chair—Holmes laid out two drills, a jemmy, and several
skeleton keys. I stood at the centre door with my eyes
glancing at each of the others, ready for any emergency ;
though, indeed, my plans were somewhat vague as to what
I should do if we were interrupted. For half an hour
Holmes worked with concentrated energy, laying down
one tool, picking up another, handling each with the
strength and delicacy of the trained mechanic. Finally
I heard a click, the broad green door swung open, and
inside I had a glimpse of a number of paper packets, each
tied, sealed, and inscribed. Holmes picked one out, but
it was hard to read by the flickering fire, and he drew
out his little dark lantern, for it was too dangerous, with
Milverton in the next room, to switch on the electric light.
Suddenly I saw him halt, listen intently, and then in an
instant he had swung the door of the safe to, picked up
his coat, stuffed his tools into the pockets, and darted
behind the window curtain, motioning me to do the
same.

It was only when I had joined him there that I heard
what had alarmed his quicker senses. There was a noise
somewhere within the house. A door slammed in the
distance. Then a confused, dull murmur broke itself
into the measured thud of heavy footsteps rapidly
approaching. They were in the passage outside the
room. They paused at the door. The door opened.
There was a sharp snick as the electric light was turned
on. The door closed once more, and the pungent reek
of a strong cigar was borne to our nostrils. Then
the footsteps continued backwards and forwards, back-

wards and forwards, within a few yards of us. Finally, there was a creak from a chair, and the footsteps ceased. Then a key clicked in a lock, and I heard the rustle of papers. So far I had not dared to look out, but now I gently parted the division of the curtains in front of me and peeped through. From the pressure of Holmes' shoulder against mine I knew that he was sharing my observations. Right in front of us, and almost within our reach, was the broad, rounded back of Milverton. It was evident that we had entirely miscalculated his movements, that he had never been to his bedroom, but that he had been sitting up in some smoking- or billiard-room in the farther wing of the house, the windows of which we had not seen. His broad, grizzled head, with its shining patch of baldness, was in the immediate foreground of our vision. He was leaning far back in the red leather chair, his legs outstretched, a long black cigar projecting at an angle from his mouth. He wore a semi-military smoking-jacket, claret-coloured, with a black velvet collar. In his hand he held a long legal document, which he was reading in an indolent fashion, blowing rings of tobacco smoke from his lips as he did so. There was no promise of a speedy departure in his composed bearing and his comfortable attitude.

I felt Holmes' hand steal into mine and give me a reassuring shake, as if to say that the situation was within his powers, and that he was easy in his mind. I was not sure whether he had seen what was only too obvious from my position—that the door of the safe was imperfectly closed, and that Milverton might at any moment observe it. In my own mind I had determined that if I were sure, from the rigidity of his gaze, that it had caught his eye, I would at once spring out, throw my greatcoat over his head, pinion him, and leave the rest to Holmes. But Milverton never looked up. He was languidly interested by the papers in his hand, and page after page was turned as he followed the argument of the lawyer. At least, I thought, when he has finished the document

733

and the cigar he will go to his room ; but before he had reached the end of either there came a remarkable development which turned our thoughts into quite another channel.

Several times I had observed that Milverton looked at his watch, and once he had risen and sat down again, with a gesture of impatience. The idea, however, that he might have an appointment at so strange an hour never occurred to me until a faint sound reached my ears from the veranda outside. Milverton dropped his papers and sat rigid in his chair. The sound was repeated, and then there came a gentle tap at the door. Milverton rose and opened it.

" Well," said he curtly, " you are nearly half an hour late."

So this was the explanation of the unlocked door and of the nocturnal vigil of Milverton. There was the gentle rustle of a woman's dress. I had closed the slit between the curtains as Milverton's face turned in our direction, but now I ventured very carefully to open it once more. He had resumed his seat, the cigar still projecting at an insolent angle from the corner of his mouth. In front of him, in the full glare of the electric light, there stood a tall, slim, dark woman, a veil over her face, a mantle drawn round her chin. Her breath came quick and fast, and every inch of the lithe figure was quivering with strong emotion.

" Well," said Milverton, " you've made me lose a good night's rest, my dear. I hope you'll prove worth it. You couldn't come any other time—eh ? "

The woman shook her head.

" Well, if you couldn't you couldn't. If the countess is a hard mistress you have your chance to get level with her now. Bless the girl, what are you shivering about ? That's right ! Pull yourself together ! Now, let us get down to business." He took a note from the drawer of his desk. " You say that you have five letters which compromise the Countess d'Albert. You want to sell

734

them. I want to buy them. So far so good. It only remains to fix a price. I should want to inspect the letters, of course. If they are really good specimens—— Great heavens, is it you ? "

The woman without a word had raised her veil and dropped the mantle from her chin. It was a dark, handsome, clear-cut face which confronted Milverton, a face with a curved nose, strong, dark eyebrows, shading hard, glittering eyes, and a straight, thin-lipped mouth set in a dangerous smile.

" It is I," she said—" the woman whose life you have ruined."

Milverton laughed, but fear vibrated in his voice. " You were so very obstinate," said he. " Why did you drive me to such extremities ? I assure you I wouldn't hurt a fly of my own accord, but every man has his business, and what was I to do ? I put the price well within your means. You would not pay."

" So you sent the letters to my husband, and he—the noblest gentleman that ever lived, a man whose boots I was never worthy to lace—he broke his gallant heart and died. You remember that last night when I came through that door I begged and prayed you for mercy, and you laughed in my face as you are trying to laugh now, only your coward heart cannot keep your lips from twitching ? Yes ; you never thought to see me here again, but it was that night which taught me how I could meet you face to face, and alone. Well, Charles Milverton, what have you to say ? "

" Don't imagine that you can bully me," said he, rising to his feet. " I have only to raise my voice, and I could call my servants and have you arrested. But I will make allowance for your natural anger. Leave the room at once as you came, and I will say no more."

The woman stood with her hand buried in her bosom, and the same deadly smile on her thin lips.

" You will ruin no more lives as you ruined mine. You will wring no more hearts as you wrung mine. I will free the world of a poisonous thing. Take that, you hound, and that !—and that !—and that !—and that ! "

She had drawn a little gleaming revolver, and emptied barrel after barrel into Milverton's body, the muzzle within two feet of his shirt-front. He shrank away, and then fell forward upon the table, coughing furiously and clawing among the papers. Then he staggered to his feet, received another shot, and rolled upon the floor. " You've done me," he cried, and lay still. The woman looked at him intently and ground her heel into his upturned face. She looked again, but there was no sound or movement. I heard a sharp rustle, the night air blew into the heated room, and the avenger was gone.

No interference upon our part could have saved the man from his fate ; but as the woman poured bullet after bullet into Milverton's shrinking body, I was about to spring out, when I felt Holmes' cold, strong grasp upon my wrist. I understood the whole argument of that firm, restraining grip—that it was no affair of ours ; that justice had overtaken a villain ; that we had our own duties and our own objects which were not to be lost sight of. But hardly had the woman rushed from the room when Holmes, with swift, silent steps, was over at the other door. He turned the key in the lock. At the same instant we heard voices in the house and the sound of hurrying feet. The revolver shots had roused the household. With perfect coolness Holmes slipped across to the safe, filled his two arms with bundles of letters, and poured them all into the fire. Again and again he did it, until the safe was empty. Someone turned the handle and beat upon the outside of the door. Holmes looked swiftly round. The letter which had been the messenger of death for Milverton lay, all mottled with his blood, upon the table. Holmes tossed it in among the blazing papers. Then he drew the key from the outer door, passed through after me, and locked it on the outside. " This way, Watson," said he ; " we can scale the garden wall in this direction."

I could not have believed that an alarm could have

spread so swiftly. Looking back, the huge house was one blaze of light. The front door was open, and figures were rushing down the drive. The whole garden was alive with people, and one fellow raised a view-halloa as we emerged from the veranda and followed hard at our heels. Holmes seemed to know the ground perfectly, and he threaded his way swiftly among a plantation of small trees, I close at his heels, and our foremost pursuer panting behind us. It was a six-foot wall which barred our path, but he sprang to the top and over. As I did the same I felt the hand of the man behind me grab at my ankle; but I kicked myself free, and scrambled over a glass-strewn coping. I fell upon my face among some bushes; but Holmes had me on my feet in an instant, and together we dashed away across the huge expanse of Hampstead Heath. We had run two miles, I suppose, before Holmes at last halted and listened intently. All was absolutely silence behind us. We had shaken off our pursuers, and were safe.

We had breakfasted and were smoking our morning pipe, on the day after the remarkable experience which I have recorded, when Mr. Lestrade, of Scotland Yard, very solemn and impressive, was ushered into our modest sitting-room.

"Good morning, Mr. Holmes," said he—"good morning. May I ask if you are very busy just now?"

"Not too busy to listen to you."

"I thought that, perhaps, if you had nothing particular on hand, you might care to assist us in a most remarkable case which occurred only last night at Hampstead."

"Dear me!" said Holmes. "What was that?"

"A murder—a most dramatic and remarkable murder. I know how keen you are upon these things, and I would take it as a great favour if you would step down to Appledore Towers and give us the benefit of your advice. It is no ordinary crime. We have had our eyes upon this Mr. Milverton for some time, and, between ourselves, he was a bit of a villain. He is known to have held papers which he used for blackmailing purposes. These papers have all been burned by the murderers. No article of value was taken, as it is probable that the criminals were men of good position, whose sole object was to prevent social exposure."

" Criminals ! " exclaimed Holmes. " Plural ! "

" Yes, there were two of them. They were, as nearly as possible, captured red-handed. We have their foot-marks, we have their description ; it's ten to one that we trace them. The first fellow was a bit too active, but the second was caught by the under-gardener, and only got away after a struggle. He was a middle-sized, strongly built man—square jaw, thick neck, moustache, a mask over his eyes."

" That's rather vague," said Sherlock Holmes. " Why, it might be a description of Watson ! "

" It's true," said the Inspector, with much amusement. " It might be a description of Watson."

" Well, I am afraid I can't help you, Lestrade," said Holmes. " The fact is that I knew this fellow Milverton, that I considered him one of the most dangerous men in London, and that I think there are certain crimes which the law cannot touch, and which therefore, to some extent, justify private revenge. No, it's no use arguing. I have made up my mind. My sympathies are with the criminals rather than with the victim, and I will not handle this case."

Holmes had not said one word to me about the tragedy which we had witnessed, but I observed all the morning that he was in the most thoughtful mood, and he gave me the impression, from his vacant eyes and his abstracted manner, of a man who is striving to recall something to his memory. We were in the middle of our lunch, when he suddenly sprang to his feet. " By Jove, Watson ! I've got it ! " he cried. " Take your hat ! Come with me ! " He hurried at his top speed down Baker

Street and along Oxford Street, until we had almost reached Regent Circus. Here on the left hand there stands a shop window filled with photographs of the celebrities and beauties of the day. Holmes' eyes fixed themselves upon one of them, and following his gaze I saw the picture of a regal and stately lady in Court dress, with a high diamond tiara upon her noble head. I looked at that delicately curved nose, at the marked eyebrows, at the straight mouth, and the strong little chin beneath it. Then I caught my breath as I read the time-honoured title of the great nobleman and statesman whose wife she had been. My eyes met those of Holmes, and he put his finger to his lips as we turned away from the window.

31. *The Six Napoleons*

IT was no very unusual thing for Mr. Lestrade, of Scotland Yard, to look in upon us of an evening, and his visits were welcome to Sherlock Holmes, for they enabled him to keep in touch with all that was going on at the police headquarters. In return for the news which Lestrade would bring, Holmes was always ready to listen with attention to the details of any case upon which the detective was engaged, and was able occasionally, without any active interference, to give some hint or suggestion drawn from his own vast knowledge and experience.

On this particular evening Lestrade had spoken of the weather and the newspapers. Then he had fallen silent, puffing thoughtfully at his cigar. Holmes looked keenly at him.

" Anything remarkable on hand ? " he asked.

" Oh, no, Mr. Holmes, nothing very particular."

" Then tell me all about it."

Lestrade laughed.

" Well, Mr. Holmes, there is no use denying that there *is* something on my mind. And yet it is such an absurd business that I hesitated to bother you about it. On the other hand, although it is trivial, it is undoubtedly queer, and I know that you have a taste for all that is out of the common. But in my opinion it comes more in Dr. Watson's line than ours."

" Disease ? " said I.

" Madness, anyhow. And a queer madness too ! You wouldn't think there was anyone living at this time of day who had such a hatred of Napoleon the First that he would break any image of him that he could see."

Holmes sank back in his chair.

" That's no business of mine," said he.

" Exactly. That's what I said. But then, when the man commits burglary in order to break images which are not his own, that brings it away from the doctor and on to the policeman."

Holmes sat up again.

" Burglary ! This is more interesting. Let me hear the details."

Lestrade took out his official notebook and refreshed his memory from its pages.

" The first case reported was four days ago," said he. " It was at the shop of Morse Hudson, who has a place for the sale of pictures and statues in the Kennington Road. The assistant had left the front shop for an instant, when he heard a crash, and, hurrying in, found a plaster bust of Napoleon, which stood with several other works of art upon the counter, lying shivered into fragments. He rushed out into the road, but, although several passers-by declared that they had noticed a man run out of the shop, he could neither see anyone nor could he find any means of identifying the rascal. It seemed to be one of those senseless acts of hooliganism which occur from time to time, and it was reported to the constable on the beat as such. The plaster cast was not worth more than a few shillings, and the whole affair appeared to be too childish for any particular investigation.

" The second case, however, was more serious and also more singular. It occurred only last night.

" In Kennington Road, and within a few hundred yards of Morse Hudson's shop, there lives a well-known medical practitioner, named Dr. Barnicot, who has one of the largest practices upon the south side of the Thames. His residence and principal consulting-room is at Kennington Road, but he has a branch surgery and dispensary at Lower Brixton Road, two miles away. This Dr. Barnicot is an enthusiastic admirer of Napoleon, and his house is full of books, pictures, and relics of the French Emperor. Some little time ago he purchased from Morse Hudson two duplicate plaster casts of the famous head of Napoleon by the French sculptor Devine. One of these he placed in his hall in the house at Kennington Road, and the other on the mantelpiece of the surgery at Lower Brixton. Well, when Dr. Barnicot came down this morning he was astonished to find that his house had been burgled during the night, but that nothing had been taken save the plaster head from the hall. It had been carried out, and had been dashed savagely against the garden wall, under which its splintered fragments were discovered."

Holmes rubbed his hands.

" This is certainly very novel," said he.

" I thought it would please you. But I have not got to the end yet. Dr. Barnicot was due at his surgery at twelve o'clock, and you can imagine his amazement when, on arriving there, he found that the window had been opened in the night, and that the broken pieces of his second bust were strewn all over the room. It had been smashed to atoms where it stood. In neither case were there any signs which could give us a clue as to the criminal or lunatic who had done the mischief. Now, Mr. Holmes, you have got the facts."

" They are singular, not to say grotesque," said Holmes. " May I ask whether the two busts smashed in Dr. Barnicot's rooms were the exact duplicates of the one which was destroyed in Morse Hudson's shop ? "

" They were taken from the same mould."

" Such a fact must tell against the theory that the man who breaks them is influenced by any general hatred of Napoleon. Considering how many hundreds of statues of the great Emperor must exist in London, it is too much to suppose such a coincidence as that a promiscuous iconoclast should chance to begin upon three specimens of the same bust."

" Well, I thought as you do," said Lestrade. " On the other hand, this Morse Hudson is the purveyor of busts in that part of London, and these three were the only ones which had been in his shop for years. So although, as you say, there are many hundreds of statues in London, it is very probable that these three were the only ones in that district. Therefore a local fanatic would begin with them. What do you think, Dr. Watson ? "

" There are no limits to the possibilities of mono-mania," I answered. " There is the condition which the modern French psychologists have called the ' idée fixe,' which may be trifling in character, and accompanied by complete sanity in every other way. A man who had read deeply about Napoleon, or who had possibly re-ceived some hereditary family injury through the great war, might conceivably form such an ' idée fixe,' and under its influence be capable of any fantastic outrage."

" That won't do, my dear Watson," said Holmes, shaking his head ; " for no amount of ' idée fixe ' would enable your interesting monomaniac to find out where these busts were situated."

" Well, how do you explain it ? "

" I don't attempt to do so. I would only observe that there is a certain method in the gentleman's eccentric proceedings. For example, in Dr. Barnicot's hall where a sound might arouse the family, the bust was taken outside before being broken, whereas in the surgery, where there was less danger of an alarm, it was smashed where it stood. The affair seems absurdly trifling, and yet I dare call nothing trivial when I reflect that some of my most classic cases have had the least promising commencement. You will remember, Watson, how the dreadful business of the Abernetty family was first brought to my notice by the depth which the parsley had sunk into the butter upon a hot day. I can't afford, therefore, to smile at your three broken busts, Lestrade, and I shall be very much obliged to you if you will let me hear of any fresh developments of so singular a chain of events."

The development for which my friend had asked came in a quicker and an infinitely more tragic form than he could have imagined. I was still dressing in my bedroom next morning, when there was a tap at the door, and Holmes entered, a telegram in his hand. He read it aloud :

"Come instantly, 131 Pitt Street, Kensington.— LESTRADE."

"What is it, then ? " I asked.

"Don't know—may be anything. But I suspect it is the sequel of the story of the statues. In that case our friend the image-breaker has begun operations in another quarter of London. There's coffee on the table, Watson, and I have a cab at the door."

In half an hour we had reached Pitt Street, a quiet little backwater just beside one of the briskest currents of London life. No. 131 was one of a row, all flat-chested, respectable, and most unromantic dwellings. As we drove up we found the railings in front of the house lined by a curious crowd. Holmes whistled.

"By George ! it's attempted murder at the least. Nothing less will hold the London message boy. There's a deed of violence indicated in that fellow's round shoulders and outstretched neck. What's this, Watson ? The top step swilled down and the other ones dry. Footsteps enough, anyhow l Well, well, there's Lestrade at the front window, and we shall soon know all about it."

The official received us with a very grave face and showed us into a sitting-room, where an exceedingly unkempt and agitated elderly man, clad in a flannel dressing-gown, was pacing up and down. He was introduced to us as the owner of the house—Mr. Horace Harker, of the Central Press Syndicate.

" It's the Napoleon bust business again," said Lestrade. " You seemed interested last night, Mr. Holmes, so I thought perhaps you would be glad to be present now that the affair has taken a very much graver turn."

" What has it turned to, then ? "

" To murder. Mr. Harker, will you tell these gentlemen exactly what has occurred ? "

The man in the dressing-gown turned upon us with a most melancholy face.

" It's an extraordinary thing," said he, " that all my life I have been collecting other people's news, and now that a real piece of news has come my own way I am so confused and bothered that I can't put two words together. If I had come in here as a journalist I should have interviewed myself and had two columns in every evening paper. As it is, I am giving away valuable copy by telling my story over and over to a string of different people, and I can make no use of it myself. However, I've heard your name, Mr. Sherlock Holmes, and if you'll only explain this queer business I shall be paid for my trouble in telling you the story."

Holmes sat down and listened.

" It all seems to centre round that bust of Napoleon which I bought for this very room about four months ago. I picked it up cheap from Harding Brothers, two doors from the High Street Station. A great deal of my journalistic work is done at night, and I often write until the early morning. So it was to-day. I was sitting in my den, which is at the back of the top of the house, about three o'clock, when I was convinced that I heard some sounds downstairs. I listened, but they were not repeated, and I concluded that they came from outside. Then suddenly, about five minutes later, there came a most horrible yell—the most dreadful sound, Mr. Holmes, that ever I heard. It will ring in my ears as long as I live. I sat frozen with horror for a minute or two. Then I seized the poker and went downstairs. When I entered this room I found the window wide open, and I at once observed that the bust was gone from the mantel-piece. Why any burglar should take such a thing passes my understanding, for it was only a plaster cast, and of no real value whatever.

"You can see for yourself that anyone going out through that open window could reach the front doorstep by taking a long stride. This was clearly what the burglar had done, so I went round and opened the door. Stepping out into the dark I nearly fell over a dead man who was lying there. I ran back for a light, and there was the poor fellow, a great gash in his throat and the whole place swimming in blood. He lay on his back, his knees drawn up, and his mouth horribly open. I shall see him in my dreams. I had just time to blow on my police whistle, and then I must have fainted, for I knew nothing more until I found the policeman standing over me in the hall."

"Well, who was the murdered man?" asked Holmes.

"There's nothing to show who he was," said Lestrade. "You shall see the body at the mortuary, but we have made nothing of it up to now. He is a tall man, sunburnt, very powerful, not more than thirty. He is poorly dressed, and yet does not appear to be a labourer. A horn-handled clasp-knife was lying in a pool of blood beside him. Whether it was the weapon which did the deed, or whether it belonged to the dead man, I do not know. There was no name on his clothing, and nothing in his pockets save an apple, some string, a shilling map of London, and a photograph. Here it is."

It was evidently taken by a snap-shot from a small camera. It represented an alert, sharp-featured simian man with thick eyebrows, and a very peculiar projection of the lower part of the face like the muzzle of a baboon.

" And what became of the bust ? " asked Holmes, after a careful study of this picture.

" We had news of it just before you came. It has been found in the front garden of an empty house in Campden House Road. It was broken into fragments. I am going round now to see it. Will you come ? "

" Certainly. I must just take one look round." He examined the carpet and the window. " The fellow had either very long legs or was a most active man," said he. " With an area beneath it was no mean feat to reach that window-ledge and open that window. Getting back was comparatively simple. Are you coming with us to see the remains of your bust, Mr. Harker ? "

The disconsolate journalist had seated himself at a writing-table.

" I must try and make something of it," said he, " though I have no doubt that the first editions of the evening papers are out already with full details. It's like my luck ! You remember when the stand fell at Doncaster ! Well, I was the only journalist in the stand, and my journal the only one that had no account of it, for I was too shaken to write it. And now I'll be too late with a murder done on my own doorstep."

As we left the room we heard his pen travelling shrilly over the foolscap.

The spot where the fragments of the bust had been found was only a few hundred yards away. For the first time our eyes rested upon this presentment of the great Emperor, which seemed to raise such frantic and destructive hatred in the mind of the unknown. It lay scattered in splintered shards upon the grass. Holmes picked up several of them and examined them carefully. I was convinced from his intent face and his purposeful manner that at last he was upon a clue.

" Well ? " asked Lestrade.

Holmes shrugged his shoulders.

" We have a long way to go yet," said he. " And yet —and yet—well, we have some suggestive facts to act upon. The possession of this trifling bust was worth more in the eyes of this strange criminal than a human life. That is one point. Then there is the singular fact that he did not break it in the house, or immediately outside the house, if to break it was his sole object."

" He was rattled and bustled by meeting this other fellow. He hardly knew what he was doing."

" Well, that's likely enough. But I wish to call your attention very particularly to the position of this house in the garden of which the bust was destroyed."

Lestrade looked about him.

" It was an empty house, and so he knew that he would not be disturbed in the garden."

" Yes, but there is another empty house farther up the street which he must have passed before he came to this one. Why did he not break it there, since it is evident that every yard that he carried it increased the risk of someone meeting him ? "

" I give it up," said Lestrade.

Holmes pointed to the street lamp above our heads.

" He could see what he was doing here, and he could not there. That was the reason."

" By Jove ! that's true," said the detective. " Now that I come to think of it, Mr. Barnicot's bust was broken not far from his red lamp. Well, Mr. Holmes, what are we to do with that fact ? "

" To remember it—to docket it. We may come on something later which will bear upon it. What steps do you propose to take now, Lestrade ? "

" The most practical way of getting at it, in my opinion, is to identify the dead man. There should be no difficulty about that. When we have found who he is and who his associates are, we should have a good start in learning what he was doing in Pitt Street last night, and who it was who met him and killed him on the doorstep of Mr. Horace Harker. Don't you think so ? "

" No doubt ; and yet it is not quite the way in which I should approach the case."

" What would you do then ? "

" Oh, you must not let me influence you in any way. I suggest that you go on your line and I on mine. We can compare notes afterwards, and each will supplement the other."

" Very good," said Lestrade.

" If you are going back to Pitt Street you might see Mr. Horace Harker. Tell him from me that I have quite made up my mind, and that it is certain that a dangerous homicidal lunatic with Napoleonic delusions was in his house last night. It will be useful for his article."

Lestrade stared.

" You don't seriously believe that ? "

Holmes smiled.

" Don't I ? Well, perhaps I don't. But I am sure that it will interest Mr. Horace Harker and the subscribers of the Central Press Syndicate. Now, Watson, I think that we shall find that we have a long and rather complex day's work before us. I should be glad, Lestrade, if you could make it convenient to meet us at Baker Street at six o'clock this evening. Until then I should like to keep this photograph found in the dead man's pocket. It is possible that I may have to ask your company and assistance upon a small expedition which will have to be undertaken to-night, if my chain of reasoning should prove to be correct. Until then, good-bye, and good luck."

Sherlock Holmes and I walked together to the High Street, where he stopped at the shop of Harding Brothers, whence the bust had been purchased. A young assistant informed us that Mr. Harding would be absent until afternoon, and that he was himself a new-comer, who could give us no information. Holmes' face showed his disappointment and annoyance.

" Well, well, we can't expect to have it all our own way, Watson," he said at last. " We must come back in the afternoon, if Mr. Harding will not be here until then. I am, as you have no doubt surmised, endeavouring to trace these busts to their source, in order to find if there is not something peculiar which may account for their remarkable fate. Let us make for Mr. Morse Hudson, of the Kennington Road, and see if he can throw any light upon the problem."

A drive of an hour brought us to the picture-dealer's establishment. He was a small, stout man with a red face and a peppery manner.

" Yes, sir. On my very counter, sir," said he. " What we pay rates and taxes for I don't know, when any ruffian can come in and break one's goods. Yes, sir, it was I who sold Dr. Barnicot his two statues. Disgraceful, sir ! A Nihilist plot, that's what I make it. No one but an Anarchist would go about breaking statues. Red republicans, that's what I call 'em. Who did I get the statues from ? I don't see what that has to do with it. Well, if you really want to know, I got them from Gelder & Co., in Church Street, Stepney. They are a well-known house in the trade, and have been this twenty years. How many had I ? Three—two and one are three— two of Dr. Barnicot's and one smashed in broad daylight on my own counter. Do I know that photograph ? No, I don't. Yes, I do, though. Why, it's Beppo ! He was a kind of Italian piecework man, who made himself useful in the shop. He could carve a bit, and gild a frame, and do odd jobs. The fellow left me last week, and I've heard nothing of him since. No, I don't know where he came from nor where he went to. I have nothing against him while he was here. He was gone two days before the bust was smashed."

" Well, that's all we could reasonably expect to get from Morse Hudson," said Holmes, as we emerged from the shop. " We have this Beppo as a common factor, both in Kennington and in Kensington, so that is worth a ten-mile drive. Now, Watson, let us make for Gelder & Co., of Stepney, the source and origin of busts. I shall be surprised if we don't get some help down there."

In rapid succession we passed through the fringe of fashionable London, hotel London, theatrical London, literary London, commercial London, and, finally, maritime London, till we came to a river-side city of a hundred thousand souls, where the tenement houses swelter and reek with the outcasts of Europe. Here, in a broad thoroughfare, once the abode of wealthy city merchants, we found the sculptor works for which we searched. Outside was a considerable yard full of monumental masonry. Inside was a large room in which fifty workers were carving or moulding. The manager, a big blond German, received us civilly, and gave a clear answer to all Holmes' questions. A reference to his books showed that hundreds of casts had been taken from a marble copy of Devine's head of Napoleon, but that the three which had been sent to Morse Hudson a year or so before had been half of a batch of six, the other three being sent to Harding Brothers, of Kensington. There was no reason why those six should be different to any of the other casts. He could suggest no possible cause why anyone should wish to destroy them—in fact, he laughed at the idea. Their wholesale price was six shillings, but the retailer would get twelve or more. The cast was taken in two moulds from each side of the face, and then these two profiles of plaster of Paris were joined together to make the complete bust. The work was usually done by Italians in the room we were in. When finished the busts were put on a table in the passage to dry, and afterwards stored. That was all he could tell us.

But the production of the photograph had a remarkable effect upon the manager. His face flushed with anger, and his brows knotted over his blue Teutonic eyes.

"Ah, the rascal!" he cried. "Yes, indeed, I know

him very well. This has always been a respectable establishment, and the only time that we have ever had the police in it was over this very fellow. It was more than a year ago now. He knifed another Italian in the street, and then he came to the works with the police on his heels, and he was taken here. Beppo was his name—his second name I never knew. Serve me right for engaging a man with such a face. But he was a good workman—one of the best."

" What did he get ? "

" The man lived, and he got off with a year. I have no doubt he is out now ; but he has not dared to show his nose here. We have a cousin of his here, and I dare say he could tell you where he is."

" No, no," cried Holmes, " not a word to the cousin ---not a word, I beg you. The matter is very important, and the farther I go with it the more important it seems to grow. When you referred in your ledger to the sale of those casts I observed that the date was June 3 of last year. Could you give me the date when Beppo was arrested ? "

" I could tell you roughly by the pay-list," the manager answered. " Yes," he continued, after some turning over of pages, " he was paid last on May 20."

" Thank you," said Holmes. " I don't think that I need intrude upon your time and patience any more." With a last word of caution that he should say nothing as to our researches we turned our faces westward once more.

The afternoon was far advanced before we were able to snatch a hasty luncheon at a restaurant. A news-bill at the entrance announced " Kensington Outrage. Murder by a Madman," and the contents of the paper showed that Mr. Horace Harker had got his account into print after all. Two columns were occupied with a highly sensational and flowery rendering of the whole incident. Holmes propped it against the cruet-stand and read it while he ate. Once or twice he chuckled.

751

"This is all right, Watson," said he. "Listen to this: 'It is satisfactory to know that there can be no difference of opinion upon this case, since Mr. Lestrade, one of the most experienced members of the official force, and Mr. Sherlock Holmes, the well-known consulting expert, have each come to the conclusion that the grotesque series of incidents, which have ended in so tragic a fashion, arise from lunacy rather than from deliberate crime. No explanation save mental aberration can cover the facts.' The Press, Watson, is a most valuable institution, if you only know how to use it. And now, if you have quite finished, we will hark back to Kensington, and see what the manager of Harding Brothers has to say to the matter."

The founder of that great emporium proved to be a brisk, crisp little person, very dapper and quick, with a clear head and a ready tongue.

"Yes, sir, I have already read the account in the evening papers. Mr. Horace Harker is a customer of ours. We supplied him with the busts some months ago. We ordered three busts of that sort from Gelder & Co., of Stepney. They are all sold now. To whom? Oh, I dare say by consulting our sales book we could very easily tell you. Yes, we have the entries here. One to Mr. Harker, you see, and one to Mr. Josiah Brown, of Laburnum Lodge, Laburnum Vale, Chiswick, and one to Mr. Sandeford, of Lower Grove Road, Reading. No, I have never seen this face which you show me in the photograph. You would hardly forget it—would you, sir?—for I've seldom seen an uglier. Have we any Italians on the staff? Yes, sir, we have several among our workpeople and cleaners. I dare say they might get a peep at that sales book if they wanted to. There is no particular reason for keeping a watch upon that book. Well, well, it's a very strange business, and I hope that you'll let me know if anything comes of your inquiries."

Holmes had taken several notes during Mr. Harding's evidence, and I could see that he was thoroughly satisfied by the turn which affairs were taking. He made no remark, however, save that, unless we hurried, we should be late for our appointment with Lestrade. Sure enough, when we reached Baker Street the detective was already there, and we found him pacing up and down in a fever of impatience. His look of importance showed that his day's work had not been in vain.

" Well ? " he asked. " What luck, Mr. Holmes ? "

" We have had a very busy day, and not entirely a wasted one," my friend explained. " We have seen both the retailers and also the wholesale manufacturers. I can trace each of the busts now from the beginning."

" The busts ! " cried Lestrade. " Well, well, you have your own methods, Mr. Sherlock Holmes, and it is not for me to say a word against them, but I think I have done a better day's work than you. I have identified the dead man."

" You don't say so ! "

" And found a cause for the crime."

" Splendid ! "

" We have an inspector who makes a speciality of Saffron Hill and the Italian quarter. Well, this dead man had some Catholic emblem round his neck, and that, along with his colour, made me think he was from the South. Inspector Hill knew him the moment he caught sight of him. His name is Pietro Venucci, from Naples, and he is one of the greatest cut-throats in London. He is connected with the Mafia, which, as you know, is a secret political society, enforcing its decrees by murder. Now you see how the affair begins to clear up. The other fellow is probably an Italian also, and a member of the Mafia. He has broken the rules in some fashion. Pietro is set upon his track. Probably the photograph we found in his pocket is the man himself, so that he may not knife the wrong person. He dogs the fellow, he sees him enter a house, he waits outside for him, and in the scuffle he receives his own death-wound. How is that, Mr. Sherlock Holmes ? "

Holmes clapped his hands approvingly.

" Excellent, Lestrade, excellent ! " he cried. " But I didn't quite follow your explanation of the destruction of the busts."

" The busts ! You never can get those busts out of your head. After all, that is nothing ; petty larceny, six months at the most. It is the murder that we are really investigating, and I tell you that I am gathering all the threads into my hands."

" And the next stage ? "

" Is a very simple one. I shall go down with Hill to the Italian quarter, find the man whose photograph we have got, and arrest him on the charge of murder. Will you come with us ? "

" I think not. I fancy we can attain our end in a simpler way. I can't say for certain, because it all depends—well, it all depends upon a factor which is completely outside our control. But I have great hopes—in fact, the betting is exactly two to one—that if you will come with us to-night I shall be able to help you to lay him by the heels."

" In the Italian quarter ? "

" No ; I fancy Chiswick is an address which is more likely to find him. If you will come with me to Chiswick to-night, Lestrade, I'll promise to go to the Italian quarter with you to-morrow, and no harm will be done by the delay. And now I think that a few hours' sleep would do us all good, for I do not propose to leave before eleven o'clock, and it is unlikely that we shall be back before morning. You'll dine with us, Lestrade, and then you are welcome to the sofa until it is time for us to start. In the meantime, Watson, I should be glad if you would ring for an express messenger, for I have a letter to send, and it is important that it should go at once."

Holmes spent the evening in rummaging among the files of the old daily papers with which one of our lumber-rooms was packed. When at last he descended it was with triumph in his eyes, but he said nothing to either of us as to the result of his researches. For my own part, I had followed step by step the methods by which he had traced the various windings of this complex case, and, though I could not yet perceive the goal which we would reach, I understood clearly that Holmes expected this grotesque criminal to make an attempt upon the two remaining busts, one of which, I remember, was at Chiswick. No doubt the object of our journey was to catch him in the very act, and I could not but admire the cunning with which my friend had inserted a wrong clue in the evening paper so as to give the fellow the idea that he could continue his scheme with impunity. I was not surprised when Holmes suggested that I should take my revolver with me. He had himself picked up the loaded hunting-crop which was his favourite weapon.

A four-wheeler was at the door at eleven, and in it we drove to a spot at the other side of Hammersmith Bridge. Here the cabman was directed to wait. A short walk brought us to a secluded road fringed with pleasant houses, each standing in its own grounds. In the light of a street lamp we read " Laburnum Villa " upon the gate-post of one of them. The occupants had evidently retired to rest, for all was dark save for a fanlight over the hall door, which shed a single blurred circle on to the garden path. The wooden fence which separated the grounds from the road threw a dense black shadow upon the inner side, and here it was that we crouched.

" I fear that you'll have a long time to wait," Holmes whispered. " We may thank our stars that it is not raining. I don't think we can even venture to smoke to pass the time. However, it's a two to one chance that we get something to pay us for our trouble."

It proved, however, that our vigil was not to be so long as Holmes had led us to fear, and it ended in a very sudden and singular fashion. In an instant, without the least sound to warn us of his coming, the garden gate swung open, and a lithe, dark figure, as swift and active

e, rushed up the garden path. We saw it whisk
light thrown from over the door and disappear
st the black shadow of the house. There was a
long pause, during which we held our breath, and then
a very gentle creaking sound came to our ears. The
window was being opened. The noise ceased, and again
there was a long silence. The fellow was making his
way into the house. We saw the sudden flash of a dark
lantern inside the room. What he sought was evidently
not there, for again we saw the flash through another
blind, and then through another.

" Let us get to the open window. We will nab him
as he climbs out," Lestrade whispered.

But before we could move the man had emerged again.
As he came out into the glimmering patch of light we saw
that he carried something white under his arm. He
looked stealthily all round him. The silence of the
deserted street reassured him. Turning his back upon
us, he laid down his burden, and the next instant there
was the sound of a sharp tap, followed by a clatter and
rattle. The man was so intent upon what he was doing
that he never heard our steps as we stole across the grass
plot. With the bound of a tiger Holmes was on his
back, and an instant later Lestrade and I had him by
either wrist, and the handcuffs had been fastened. As
we turned him over I saw a hideous, sallow face, with
writhing, furious features glaring up at us, and I knew
that it was indeed the man of the photograph whom
we had secured.

But it was not our prisoner to whom Holmes was giving
his attention. Squatted on the doorstep, he was engaged
in most carefully examining that which the man had
brought from the house. It was a bust of Napoleon
like the one which we had seen that morning, and it had
been broken into similar fragments. Carefully Holmes
held each separate shard to the light, but in no way did it
differ from any other shattered piece of plaster. He
had just completed his examination, when the hall lights

flew up, the door opened, and the owner of the house, a jovial, rotund figure in shirt and trousers, presented himself.

" Mr. Josiah Brown, I suppose ? " said Holmes.

"Yes, sir ; and you no doubt are Mr. Sherlock Holmes ? I had the note which you sent by the express messenger, and I did exactly what you told me. We locked every door on the inside and awaited developments. Well, I'm very glad to see that you have got the rascal. I hope, gentlemen, that you will come in and have some refreshment."

However, Lestrade was anxious to get his man into safe quarters, so within a few minutes our cab had been summoned and we were all four upon our way to London. Not a word would our captive say ; but he glared at us from the shadow of his matted hair, and once, when my hand seemed within his reach, he snapped at it like a hungry wolf. We stayed long enough at the police-station to learn that a search of his clothing revealed nothing save a few shillings and a long sheath knife, the handle of which bore copious traces of recent blood.

" That's all right," said Lestrade, as we parted. " Hill knows all these gentry, and he will give a name to him. You'll find that my theory of the Mafia will work out all right. But I'm sure I am exceedingly obliged to you, Mr. Holmes, for the workmanlike way in which you laid hands upon him. I don't quite understand it all yet."

" I fear it is rather too late an hour for explanations," said Holmes. " Besides, there are one or two details which are not finished off, and it is one of those cases which are worth working out to the very end. If you will come round once more to my rooms at six o'clock to-morrow I think I shall be able to show you that even now you have not grasped the entire meaning of this business, which presents some features which make it absolutely original in the history of crime. If ever I permit you to chronicle any more of my little problems,

Watson, I foresee that you will enliven your pages by an account of the singular adventure of the Napoleonic busts."

When we met again next evening, Lestrade was furnished with much information concerning our prisoner. His name, it appeared, was Beppo, second name unknown. He was a well-known ne'er-do-well among the Italian colony. He had once been a skilful sculptor and had earned an honest living, but he had taken to evil courses, and had twice already been in gaol—once for a petty theft and once, as we had already heard, for stabbing a fellow-countryman. He could talk English perfectly well. His reasons for destroying the busts were still unknown, and he refused to answer any questions upon the subject ; but the police had discovered that these same busts might very well have been made by his own hands, since he was engaged in this class of work at the establishment of Gelder & Co. To all this information, much of which we already knew, Holmes listened with polite attention ; but I, who knew him so well, could clearly see that his thoughts were elsewhere, and I detected a mixture of mingled uneasiness and expectation beneath that mask which he was wont to assume. At last he started in his chair and his eyes brightened. There had been a ring at the bell. A minute later we heard steps upon the stairs, and an elderly, red-faced man with grizzled side-whiskers was ushered in. In his right hand he carried an old-fashioned carpet-bag, which he placed upon the table.

" Is Mr. Sherlock Holmes here ? "

My friend bowed and smiled. " Mr. Sandeford, of Reading, I suppose ? " said he.

" Yes, sir. I fear that I am a little late ; but the trains were awkward. You wrote to me about a bust that is in my possession."

" Exactly."

" I have your letter here. You said, ' I desire to

possess a copy of Devine's Napoleon, and am prepared to pay you ten pounds for the one which is in your possession.' Is that right ? "

" Certainly."

" I was very much surprised at your letter, for I could not imagine how you knew that I owned such a thing."

" Of course you must have been surprised, but the explanation is very simple. Mr. Harding, of Harding Brothers, said that they had sold you their last copy, and he gave me your address."

" Oh, that was it, was it ? Did he tell you what I paid for it ? "

" No, he did not."

" Well, I am an honest man, though not a very rich one. I only gave fifteen shillings for the bust, and I think you ought to know that before I take ten pounds from you."

" I am sure the scruple does you honour, Mr. Sandeford. But I have named that price, so I intend to stick to it."

" Well, it is very handsome of you, Mr. Holmes. I brought the bust up with me, as you asked me to do. Here it is ! "

He opened his bag, and at last we saw placed upon our table a complete specimen of that bust which we had already seen more than once in fragments.

Holmes took a paper from his pocket and laid a ten-pound note upon the table.

" You will kindly sign that paper, Mr. Sandeford, in the presence of these witnesses. It is simply to say that you transfer every possible right that you ever had in the bust to me. I am a methodical man, you see, and you never know what turn events might take afterwards. Thank you, Mr. Sandeford ; here is your money, and I wish you a very good evening."

When our visitor had disappeared Sherlock Holmes' movements were such as to rivet our attention. He began by taking a clean white cloth from a drawer and laying it over the table. Then he placed his newly acquired bust in the centre of the cloth. Finally he picked up his hunting-crop and struck Napoleon a sharp blow on the top of the head. The figure broke into fragments, and Holmes bent eagerly over the shattered remains. Next instant, with a loud shout of triumph, he held up one splinter, in which a round, dark object was fixed like a plum in a pudding.

"Gentlemen," he cried, "let me introduce you to the famous black pearl of the Borgias!"

Lestrade and I sat silent for a moment, and then, with a spontaneous impulse, we both broke out clapping as at the well-wrought crisis of a play. A flush of colour sprang to Holmes' pale cheeks, and he bowed to us like the master dramatist who receives the homage of his audience. It was at such moments that for an instant he ceased to be a reasoning machine, and betrayed his human love for admiration and applause. The same singularly proud and reserved nature which turned away with disdain from popular notoriety was capable of being moved to its depths by spontaneous wonder and praise from a friend.

"Yes, gentlemen," said he, "it is the most famous pearl now existing in the world, and it has been my good fortune by a connected chain of inductive reasoning, to trace it from the Prince of Colonna's bedroom at the Dacre Hotel, where it was lost, to the interior of this, the last of the six busts of Napoleon which were manufactured by Gelder & Co., of Stepney. You will remember, Lestrade, the sensation caused by the disappearance of this valuable jewel, and the vain efforts of the London police to recover it. I was myself consulted upon the case; but I was unable to throw any light upon it. Suspicion fell upon the maid of the Princess, who was an Italian, and it was proved that she had a brother in London, but we failed to trace any connection between them. The maid's name was Lucretia Venucci, and there is no doubt in my mind that this Pietro who was murdered two nights ago was the brother. I have been looking up the dates in the old files of the paper, and I find that the disappearance of the pearl was exactly two days before the arrest of Beppo for some crime of violence—an event which took place in the factory of Gelder & Co., at the very moment when these busts were being made. Now you clearly see the sequence of events, though you see them, of course, in the inverse order to the way in which they presented themselves to me. Beppo had the pearl in his possession. He may have stolen it from Pietro, he may have been Pietro's confederate, he may have been the go-between of Pietro and his sister. It is of no consequence to us which is the correct solution.

" The main fact is that he *had* the pearl, and at that moment, when it was on his person, he was pursued by the police. He made for the factory in which he worked, and he knew that he had only a few minutes in which to conceal this enormously valuable prize, which would otherwise be found on him when he was searched. Six plaster casts of Napoleon were drying in the passage. One of them was still soft. In an instant Beppo, a skilful workman, made a small hole in the wet plaster, dropped in the pearl, and with a few touches covered over the aperture once more. It was an admirable hiding-place. No one could possibly find it. But Beppo was condemned to a year's imprisonment, and in the meanwhile his six busts were scattered over London. He could not tell which contained his treasure. Only by breaking them could he see. Even shaking would tell him nothing for as the plaster was wet it was probable that the pearl would adhere to it—as, in fact, it has done. Beppo did not despair, and he conducted his search with considerable ingenuity and perseverance. Through a cousin who works with Gelder he found out the retail firms who had bought the busts. He managed to find employment with Morse Hudson, and in that way tracked down three of them. The pearl was not there. Then with the help of some Italian employé, he succeeded in finding out where the other three busts had gone. The first was at

Harker's. There he was dogged by his confederate, who held Beppo responsible for the loss of the pearl, and he stabbed him in the scuffle which followed."

" If he was his confederate, why should he carry his photograph ? " I asked.

" As a means of tracing him if he wished to inquire about him from any third person. That was the obvious reason. Well, after the murder I calculated that Beppo would probably hurry rather than delay his movements. He would fear that the police would read his secret, and so he hastened on before they should get ahead of him. Of course, I could not say that he had not found the pearl in Harker's bust. I had not even concluded for certain that it was the pearl ; but it was evident to me that he was looking for something, since he carried the bust past the other houses in order to break it in the garden which had a lamp overlooking it. Since Harker's bust was one in three, the chances were exactly as I told you—two to one against the pearl being inside it. There remained two busts, and it was obvious that he would go for the London one first. I warned the inmates of the house, so as to avoid a second tragedy, and we went down, with the happiest results. By that time, of course, I knew for certain that it was the Borgia pearl that we were after. The name of the murdered man linked the one event with the other. There only remained a single bust —the Reading one—and the pearl must be there. I bought it in your presence from the owner—and there it lies."

We sat in silence for a moment.

" Well," said Lestrade, " I've seen you handle a good many cases, Mr. Holmes, but I don't know that I ever knew a more workmanlike one than that. We're not jealous of you at Scotland Yard. No, sir, we are very proud of you, and if you come down to-morrow there's not a man, from the oldest inspector to the youngest constable, who wouldn't be glad to shake you by the hand."

" Thank you ! " said Holmes. " Thank you ! " and as he turned away it seemed to me that he was more nearly moved by the softer human emotions than I had ever seen him. A moment later he was the cold and practical thinker once more. " Put the pearl in the safe, Watson," said he, " and get out the papers of the Conk-Singleton forgery case. Good-bye, Lestrade. If any little problem comes your way I shall be happy, if I can, to give you a hint or two as to its solution."

32. *The Three Students*

IT was in the year '95 that a combination of events, into which I need not enter, caused Mr. Sherlock Holmes and myself to spend some weeks in one of our great University towns, and it was during this time that the small but instructive adventure which I am about to relate befell us. It will be obvious that any details which would help the reader to exactly identify the college or the criminal would be injudicious and offensive. So painful a scandal may well be allowed to die out. With due discretion the incident itself may, however, be described, since it serves to illustrate some of those qualities for which my friend was remarkable. I will endeavour in my statement to avoid such terms as would serve to limit the events to any particular place, or give a clue as to the people concerned.

We were residing at the time in furnished lodgings close to a library where Sherlock Holmes was pursuing some laborious researches in Early English charters—researches which led to results so striking that they may be the subject of one of my future narratives. Here it was that one evening we received a visit from an acquaintance, Mr. Hilton Soames, tutor and lecturer at the College of St. Luke's. Mr. Soames was a tall, spare man, of a nervous and excitable temperament. I had always known him to be restless in his manner, but on this particular occasion he was in such a state of uncontrollable agitation that it was clear something very unusual had occurred.

" I trust, Mr. Holmes, that you can spare me a few hours of your valuable time. We have had a very painful incident at St. Luke's, and really, but for the happy chance of your being in the town, I should have been at a loss what to do."

" I am very busy just now, and I desire no distractions," my friend answered. " I should much prefer that you called in the aid of the police."

" No, no, my dear sir ; such a course is utterly impossible. When once the law is evoked it cannot be stayed again, and this is just one of those cases where, for the credit of the college, it is most essential to avoid scandal. Your discretion is as well known as your powers, and you are the one man in the world who can help me. I beg you, Mr. Holmes, to do what you can."

My friend's temper had not improved since he had been deprived of the congenial surroundings of Baker Street. Without his scrap-books, his chemicals, and his homely untidiness, he was an uncomfortable man. He shrugged his shoulders in ungracious acquiescence, while our visitor in hurried words and with much excitable gesticulation poured forth his story.

" I must explain to you, Mr. Holmes, that to-morrow is the first day of the examination for the Fortescue Scholarship. I am one of the examiners. My subject is Greek, and the first of the papers consists of a large passage of Greek translation which the candidate has not seen. This passage is printed on the examination paper, and it would naturally be an immense advantage if the candidate could prepare it in advance. For this reason great care is taken to keep the paper secret.

" To-day about three o'clock the proofs of this paper arrived from the printers. The exercise consists of half a chapter of Thucydides. I had to read it over carefully, as the text must be absolutely correct. At four-thirty my task was not yet completed. I had, however, promised to take tea in a friend's rooms, so I left the proof upon my desk. I was absent rather more than an hour. You are aware, Mr. Holmes, that our college doors are double—a green baize one within and a heavy oak one without. As I approached my outer door I was amazed to see a key in it. For an instant I imagined that I had left my own there, but on feeling in my pocket I found that it was all right. The only duplicate which existed, so far as I knew, was that which belonged to my servant, Bannister, a man who has looked after my room for ten years, and whose honesty is absolutely above suspicion. I found that the key was indeed his, that he had entered my room to know if I wanted tea, and that he had very carelessly left the key in the door when he came out. His visit to my room must have been within a very few minutes of my leaving it. His forgetfulness about the key would have mattered little upon any other occasion, but on this one day it has produced the most deplorable consequences.

"The moment I looked at my table I was aware that some one had rummaged among my papers. The proof was in three long slips. I had left them all together. Now I found that one of them was lying on the floor, one was on the side-table near the window, and the third was where I had left it."

Holmes stirred for the first time.

"The first page on the floor, the second in the window, and the third where you left it," said he.

"Exactly, Mr. Holmes. You amaze me. How could you possibly know that?"

"Pray continue your very interesting statement."

"For an instant I imagined that Bannister had taken the unpardonable liberty of examining my papers. He denied it, however, with the utmost earnestness, and I am convinced that he was speaking the truth. The alternative was that someone passing had observed the key in the door, had known that I was out, and had entered to look at the papers. A large sum of money is at stake, for the scholarship is a very valuable one, and an unscrupulous man might very well run a risk in order to gain advantage over his fellows.

" Bannister was very much upset by the incident. He had nearly fainted when we found that the papers had undoubtedly been tampered with. I gave him a little brandy and left him collapsed in a chair while I made a most careful examination of the room. I soon saw that the intruder had left other traces of his presence besides the rumpled papers. On the table in the window were several shreds from a pencil which had been sharpened. A broken tip of lead was lying there also. Evidently the rascal had copied the paper in a great hurry, had broken his pencil, and had been compelled to put a fresh point to it."

" Excellent ! " said Holmes, who was recovering his good humour as his attention became more engrossed by the case. " Fortune has been your friend."

" This was not all. I have a new writing-table with a fine surface of red leather. I am prepared to swear, and so is Bannister, that it was smooth and unstained. Now I found a clean cut in it about three inches long—not a mere scratch, but a positive cut. Not only this, but on the table I found a small ball of black dough, or clay, with specks of something which looks like sawdust in it. I am convinced that these marks were left by the man who rifled the papers. There were no footmarks and no other evidence as to his identity. I was at my wits' end, when suddenly the happy thought occurred to me that you were in the town, and I came straight round to put the matter into your hands. Do help me, Mr. Holmes ! You see my dilemma. Either I must find the man, or else the examination must be postponed until fresh papers are prepared, and since this cannot be done without explanation, there will ensue a hideous scandal, which will throw a cloud not only on the college but on the University. Above all things, I desire to settle the matter quietly and discreetly."

"I shall be happy to look into it and to give you such advice as I can," said Holmes, rising and putting on his overcoat. "This case is not entirely devoid of interest. Had anyone visited you in your room after the papers came to you?"

"Yes; young Daulat Ras, an Indian student who lives on the same stair, came in to ask me some particulars about the examination."

"For which he was entered?"

"Yes."

"And the papers were on your table?"

"To the best of my belief they were rolled up."

"But might be recognized as proofs?"

"Possibly."

"No one else in your room?"

"No."

"Did anyone know that these proofs would be there?"

"No one save the printer?"

"Did this man Bannister know?"

"No, certainly not. No one knew."

"Where is Bannister now?"

"He was very ill, poor fellow! I left him collapsed in the chair. I was in such a hurry to come to you."

"You left your door open?"

"I locked the papers up first."

"Then it amounts to this, Mr. Soames, that unless the Indian student recognized the roll as being proofs, the man who tampered with them came upon them accidentally without knowing that they were there."

"So it seems to me."

Holmes gave an enigmatic smile.

"Well," said he, "let us go round. Not one of your cases, Watson—mental, not physical. All right; come if you want to. Now, Mr. Soames—at your disposal!"

The sitting-room of our client opened by a long, low, latticed window on to the ancient lichen-tinted court of the old college. A Gothic arched door led to a worn stone staircase. On the ground floor was the tutor's room. Above were three students, one on each story. It was already twilight when we reached the scene of our problem. Holmes halted and looked earnestly at the window. Then he approached it, and, standing on tiptoe, with his neck craned, he looked into the room.

"He must have entered through the door. There is no opening except the one pane," said our learned guide.

"Dear me!" said Holmes, and he smiled in a singular way as he glanced at our companion. "Well, if there is nothing to be learned here we had best go inside."

The lecturer unlocked the outer door and ushered us into his room. We stood at the entrance while Holmes made an examination of the carpet.

"I am afraid there are no signs here," said he. "One could hardly hope for any upon so dry a day. Your servant seems to have quite recovered. You left him in a chair, you say; which chair?"

"By the window there."

"I see. Near this little table. You can come in now. I have finished with the carpet. Let us take the little table first. Of course, what has happened is very clear. The man entered and took the papers, sheet by sheet, from the central table. He carried them over to the window table, because from there he could see if you came across the courtyard, and so could effect an escape."

"As a matter of fact, he could not," said Soames, "for I entered by the side-door."

"Ah, that's good! Well, anyhow, that was in his mind. Let me see the three strips. No finger impressions—no! Well, he carried over this one first and he copied it. How long would it take him to do that, using every possible contraction? A quarter of an hour, not less. Then he tossed it down and seized the next. He was in the midst of that when your return caused him to make a very hurried retreat—*very* hurried, since he had not time to replace the papers which would tell you that he

had been there. You were not aware of any hurrying
feet on the stair as you entered the outer door ? "

" No, I can't say I was."

" Well, he wrote so furiously that he broke his pencil,
and had, as you observe, to sharpen it again. This is of
interest, Watson. The pencil was not an ordinary one.
It was about the usual size with a soft lead ; the outer
colour was dark blue, the maker's name was printed in
silver lettering, and the piece remaining is only about an
inch and a half long. Look for such a pencil, Mr.
Soames, and you have got your man. When I add that
he possesses a large and very blunt knife, you have an
additional aid."

Mr. Soames was somewhat overwhelmed by this flood
of information. " I can follow the other points," said
he, " but really in this matter of the length——"

Holmes held out a small chip with the letters NN and a
space of clear wood after them.

" You see ? "

" No, I fear that even now——"

" Watson, I have always done you an injustice. There
are others. What could this NN be ? It is at the end
of a word. You are aware that Johann Faber is the most
common maker's name. Is it not clear that there is just
as much of the pencil left as usually follows the Johann ? "
He held the small table sideways to the electric light. " I
was hoping that if the paper on which he wrote was thin
some trace of it might come through upon this polished
surface. No, I see nothing. I don't think there is anything more to be learned here. Now for the central
table. This small pellet is, I presume, the black doughy
mass you spoke of. Roughly pyramidal in shape and
hollowed out, I perceive. As you say, there appear to
be grains of sawdust in it. Dear me, this is very interesting. And the cut—a positive tear, I see. It began
with a thin scratch and ended in a jagged hole. I am
much indebted to you for directing my attention to
this case, Mr. Soames. Where does that door lead to ? "

"To my bedroom."

"Have you been in it since your adventure?"

"No; I came straight away for you."

"I should like to have a glance round. What a charming, old-fashioned room! Perhaps you will kindly wait a minute until I have examined the floor. No, I see nothing. What about this curtain? You hang your clothes behind it. If anyone were forced to conceal himself in this room he must do it there, since the bed is too low and the wardrobe too shallow. No one there, I suppose?"

As Holmes drew the curtain I was aware, from some little rigidity and alertness of his attitude, that he was prepared for an emergency. As a matter of fact the drawn curtain disclosed nothing but three or four suits of clothes hanging from a line of pegs. Holmes turned away, and stooped suddenly to the floor.

"Halloa! What's this?" said he.

It was a small pyramid of black, putty-like stuff, exactly like the one upon the table of the study. Holmes held it out on his open palm in the glare of the electric light.

"Your visitor seems to have left traces in your bedroom as well as in your sitting-room, Mr. Soames."

"What could he have wanted there?"

"I think it is clear enough. You came back by an unexpected way, and so he had no warning until you were at the very door. What could he do? He caught up everything which would betray him, and he rushed into your bedroom to conceal himself."

"Good gracious, Mr. Holmes, do you mean to tell me that all the time I was talking to Bannister in this room we had the man prisoner if we had only known it?"

"So I read it."

"Surely there is another alternative, Mr. Holmes? I don't know whether you observed my bedroom window."

"Lattice-paned, lead framework, three separate windows, one swinging on hinge and large enough to admit a man."

"Exactly. And it looks out on an angle of the courtyard so as to be partly invisible. The man might have effected his entrance there, left traces as he passed through the bedroom, and, finally, finding the door open, have escaped that way."

Holmes shook his head impatiently.

"Let us be practical," said he. "I understand you to say that there are three students who use this stair and are in the habit of passing your door?"

"Yes, there are."

"And they are all in for this examination?"

"Yes."

"Have you any reason to suspect any one of them more than the others?"

Soames hesitated.

"It is a very delicate question," said he. "One hardly likes to throw suspicion where there are no proofs."

"Let us hear the suspicions. I will look after the proofs."

"I will tell you, then, in a few words, the character of the three men who inhabit these rooms. The lower of the three is Gilchrist, a fine scholar and athlete; plays in the Rugby team and the cricket team for the college, and got his Blue for the hurdles and the long lump. He is a fine, manly fellow. His father was the notorious Sir Jabez Gilchrist, who ruined himself on the Turf. My scholar has been left very poor, but he is hard-working and industrious. He will do well.

"The second floor is inhabited by Daulat Ras, the Indian. He is a quiet, inscrutable fellow, as most of those Indians are. He is well up in his work, though his Greek is his weak subject. He is steady and methodical.

"The top floor belongs to Miles McLaren. He is a brilliant fellow when he chooses to work—one of the brightest intellects of the University; but he is wayward, dissipated, and unprincipled. He was nearly expelled over a card scandal in his first year. He has been idling all this term, and he must look forward with dread to the examination."

" Then it is he whom you suspect ? "

" I dare not go so far as that. But of the three he is perhaps the least unlikely."

" Exactly. Now, Mr. Soames, let us have a look at your servant, Bannister."

He was a little, white-faced, clean-shaven, grizzly haired fellow of fifty. He was still suffering from this sudden disturbance of the quiet routine of his life. His plump face was twitching with his nervousness, and his fingers could not keep still.

" We are investigating this unhappy business, Bannister," said his master.

" Yes, sir."

" I understand," said Holmes, " that you left your key in the door ? "

" Yes, sir."

" Was it not very extraordinary that you should do this on the very day when there were these papers inside ? "

" It was most unfortunate, sir. But I have occasionally done the same thing at other times."

" When did you enter the room ? "

" It was about half-past four. That is Mr. Soames' tea-time."

" How long did you stay ? "

" When I saw that he was absent I withdrew at once."

" Did you look at these papers on the table ? "

" No, sir ; certainly not."

" How came you to leave the key in the door ? "

" I had the tea-tray in my hand. I thought I would come back for the key. Then I forgot."

" Has the outer door a spring lock ? "

" No, sir."

" Then it was open all the time ? "

" Yes, sir."

" Any one in the room could get out ? "

" Yes, sir."

" When Mr. Soames returned and called for you, you were very much disturbed ? "

" Yes, sir. Such a thing has never happened during the many years that I have been here. I nearly fainted, sir."

" So I understand. Where were you when you began to feel bad ? "

" Where was I, sir ? Why, here, near the door."

" That is singular, because you sat down in that chair over yonder near the corner. Why did you pass these other chairs ? "

" I don't know, sir. It didn't matter to me where I sat."

" I really don't think he knew much about it, Mr. Holmes. He was looking very bad—quite ghastly."

" You stayed here when your master left ? "

" Only for a minute or so. Then I locked the door and went to my room."

" Whom do you suspect ? "

" Oh, I would not venture to say, sir. I don't believe there is any gentleman in this University who is capable of profiting by such an action. No, sir, I'll not believe it."

" Thank you ; that will do," said Holmes. " Oh, one more word. You have not mentioned to any of the three gentlemen whom you attend that anything is amiss ? "

" No, sir ; not a word."

" You haven't seen any of them ? "

" No, sir."

" Very good. Now, Mr. Soames, we will take a walk in the quadrangle, if you please."

Three yellow squares of light shone above us in the gathering gloom.

" Your three birds are all in their nests," said Holmes, looking up. " Halloa ! What's that ? One of them seems restless enough."

It was the Indian, whose dark silhouette appeared suddenly upon the blind. He was pacing swiftly up and down his room.

"I should like to have a peep at each of them," said Holmes. "Is it possible?"

"No difficulty in the world," Soames answered. "This set of rooms is quite the oldest in the college, and it is not unusual for visitors to go over them. Come along, and I will personally conduct you."

"No names, please!" said Holmes, as we knocked at Gilchrist's door. A tall, flaxen-haired, slim young fellow opened it, and made us welcome when he understood our errand. There were some really curious pieces of mediæval domestic architecture within. Holmes was so charmed with one of them that he insisted on drawing it on his notebook, broke his pencil, had to borrow one from our host, and finally borrowed a knife to sharpen his own. The same curious accident happened to him in the rooms of the Indian—a silent little hook-nosed fellow, who eyed us askance and was obviously glad when Holmes' architectural studies had come to an end. I could not see that in either case Holmes had come upon the clue for which he was searching. Only at the third did our visit prove abortive. The outer door would not open to our knock, and nothing more substantial than a torrent of bad language came from behind it. "I don't care who you are. You can go to blazes!" roared the angry voice. "To-morrow's the exam., and I won't be drawn by anyone."

"A rude fellow," said our guide, flushing with anger as we withdrew down the stair. "Of course, he did not realize that it was I who was knocking, but none the less his conduct was very uncourteous, and, indeed, under the circumstances, rather suspicious."

Holmes' response was a curious one.

"Can you tell me his exact height?" he asked.

"Really, Mr. Holmes, I cannot undertake to say. He is taller than the Indian, not so tall as Gilchrist. I suppose five foot six would be about it."

"That is very important," said Holmes. "And now, Mr. Soames, I wish you good night."

Our guide cried aloud in his astonishment and dismay. "Good gracious, Mr. Holmes, you are surely not going to leave me in this abrupt fashion! You don't seem to realize the position. To-morrow is the examination. I must take some definite action to-night. I cannot allow the examination to be held if one of the papers has been tampered with. The situation must be faced."

"You must leave it as it is. I shall drop round early to-morrow morning and chat the matter over. It is possible that I may be in a position then to indicate some course of action. Meanwhile you change nothing—nothing at all."

"Very good, Mr. Holmes."

"You can be perfectly easy in your mind. We shall certainly find some way out of your difficulties. I will take the black clay with me, also the pencil cuttings. Good-bye."

When we were out in the darkness of the quadrangle we again looked up at the windows. The Indian still paced his room. The others were invisible.

"Well, Watson, what do you think of it?" Holmes asked as we came out into the main street. "Quite a little parlour game—sort of three-card trick, is it not? There are your three men. It must be one of them. You take your choice. Which is yours?"

"The foul-mouthed fellow at the top. He is the one with the worst record. And yet that Indian was a sly fellow also. Why should he be pacing his room all the time?"

"There is nothing in that. Many men do it when they are trying to learn anything by heart."

"He looked at us in a queer way."

"So would you if a flock of strangers came in on you when you were preparing for an examination next day, and every moment was of value. No, I see nothing in that. Pencils, too, and knives—all was satisfactory. But that fellow *does* puzzle me."

"Who ? "

"Why, Bannister, the servant. What's his game in the matter ? "

"He impressed me as being a perfectly honest man."

"So he did me. That's the puzzling part. Why should a perfectly honest man—well, well, here's a large stationer's. We shall begin our researches here."

There were only four stationers of any consequence in the town, and at each Holmes produced his pencil chips and bid high for a duplicate. All were agreed that one could be ordered, but that it was not a usual size of pencil, and that it was seldom kept in stock. My friend did not appear to be depressed by his failure, but shrugged his shoulders in half-humorous resignation.

"No good, my dear Watson. This, the best and only final clue, has run to nothing. But, indeed, I have little doubt that we can build up a sufficient case without it. By Jove ! my dear fellow, it is nearly nine, and the land-lady babbled of green peas at seven-thirty. What with your eternal tobacco, Watson, and your irregularity at meals, I expect that you will get notice to quit, and that I shall share your downfall—not, however, before we have solved the problem of the nervous tutor, the careless servant, and the three enterprising students."

Holmes made no further allusion to the matter that day, though he sat lost in thought for a long time after our belated dinner. At eight in the morning he came into my room just as I finished my toilet.

"Well, Watson," said he, "it is time we went down to St. Luke's. Can you do without breakfast ? "

"Certainly."

"Soames will be in a dreadful fidget until we are able to tell him something positive."

"Have you anything positive to tell him ? "

"I think so."

"You have formed a conclusion ? "

"Yes, my dear Watson ; I have solved the mystery."

" But what fresh evidence could you have got ? "

" Aha ! It is not for nothing that I have turned myself out of bed at the untimely hour of six. I have put in two hours' hard work and covered at least five miles, with something to show for it. Look at that ! "

He held out his hand. On the palm were three little pyramids of black, doughy clay.

" Why, Holmes, you had only two yesterday ! "

" And one more this morning. It is a fair argument, that wherever No. 3 came from is also the source of Nos. 1 and 2. Eh, Watson ? Well, come along and put friend Soames out of his pain."

The unfortunate tutor was certainly in a state of pitiable agitation when we found him in his chambers. In a few hours the examinations would commence and he was still in the dilemma between making the facts public and allowing the culprit to compete for the valuable scholarship. He could hardly stand still, so great was his mental agitation, and he ran towards Holmes with two eager hands outstretched.

" Thank Heaven that you have come ! I feared that you had given it up in despair. What am I to do ? Shall the examination proceed ? "

" Yes ; let it proceed, by all means."

" But this rascal—— ? "

" He shall not compete."

" You know him ? "

" I think so. If this matter is not to become public we must give ourselves certain powers, and resolve ourselves into a small private court-martial. You there, if you please, Soames ! Watson, you here ! I'll take the arm-chair in the middle. I think that we are now sufficiently imposing to strike terror into a guilty breast. Kindly ring the bell ! "

Bannister entered, and shrank back in evident surprise and fear at our judicial appearance.

" You will kindly close the door," said Holmes.

" Now, Bannister, will you please tell us the truth about yesterday's incident ? "

The man turned white to the roots of his hair.

" I have told you everything, sir."

" Nothing to add ? "

" Nothing at all, sir."

" Well, then, I must make some suggestions to you. When you sat down on that chair yesterday, did you do so in order to conceal some object which would have shown who had been in the room ? "

Bannister's face was ghastly.

" No, sir ; certainly not."

" It is only a suggestion," said Holmes suavely. " I frankly admit that I am unable to prove it. But it seems probable enough, since the moment that Mr. Soames' back was turned you released the man who was hiding in that bedroom."

Bannister licked his dry lips.

" There was no man, sir."

" Ah, that's a pity, Bannister. Up to now you may have spoken the truth, but now I know that you have lied."

The man's face set in sullen defiance.

" There was no man, sir."

" Come, come, Bannister."

" No, sir ; there was no one."

" In that case you can give us no further information. Would you please remain in the room ? Stand over there near the bedroom door. Now, Soames, I am going to ask you to have the great kindness to go up to the room of young Gilchrist, and to ask him to step down into yours."

An instant later the tutor returned, bringing with him the student. He was a fine figure of a man, tall, lithe, and agile, with a springy step and a pleasant, open face. His troubled blue eyes glanced at each of us, and finally rested with an expression of blank dismay upon Bannister in the farther corner.

" Just close the door," said Holmes. " Now, Mr. Gilchrist, we are all quite alone here, and no one need ever know one word of what passes between us. We can be perfectly frank with each other. We want to know, Mr. Gilchrist, how you, an honourable man, ever came to commit such an action as that of yesterday?"

The unfortunate young man staggered back, and cast a look full of horror and reproach at Bannister.

"No, no, Mr. Gilchrist, sir; I never said a word— never one word!" cried the servant.

"No, but you have now," said Holmes. "Now, sir, you must see that after Bannister's words your position is hopeless, and that your only chance lies in a frank confession."

For a moment Gilchrist, with upraised hand, tried to control his writhing features. The next he had thrown himself on his knees beside the table, and, burying his face in his hands, he burst into a storm of passionate sobbing.

"Come, come," said Holmes kindly; "it is human to err, and at least no one can accuse you of being a callous criminal. Perhaps it would be easier for you if I were to tell Mr. Soames what occurred, and you can check me where I am wrong. Shall I do so? Well, well, don't trouble to answer. Listen, and see that I do you no injustice.

"From the moment, Mr. Soames, that you said to me that no one, not even Bannister, could have told that the papers were in your room, the case began to take a definite shape in my mind. The printer one could, of course, dismiss. He could examine the papers in his own office. The Indian I also thought nothing of. If the proofs were in roll he could not possibly know what they were. On the other hand, it seemed an unthinkable coincidence that a man should dare to enter the room, and that by chance on that very day the papers were on the table. I dismissed that. The man who entered knew that the papers were there. How did he know?

"When I approached your room I examined the window. You amused me by supposing that I was contemplating the possibility of someone having in broad daylight, under the eyes of all these opposite rooms, forced himself through it. Such an idea was absurd. I was measuring how tall a man would need to be in order to see as he passed what papers were on the central table. I am six feet high, and I could do it with an effort. No one less than that would have a chance. Already, you see, I had reason to think that if one of your three students was a man of unusual height he was the most worth watching of the three.

" I entered, and I took you into my confidence as to the suggestions of the side-table. Of the centre table I could make nothing, until in your description of Gilchrist you mentioned that he was a long-distance jumper. Then the whole thing came to me in an instant, and I only needed certain corroborative proofs, which I speedily obtained.

" What happened was this. This young fellow had employed his afternoon at the athletic grounds, where he had been practising the jump. He returned carrying his jumping-shoes, which are provided, as you are aware, with several spikes. As he passed your window he saw, by means of his great height, these proofs upon your table, and conjectured what they were. No harm would have been done had it not been that as he passed your door he perceived the key which had been left by the carelessness of your servant. A sudden impulse came over him to enter and see if they were indeed the proofs. It was not a dangerous exploit, for he could always pretend that he had simply looked in to ask a question.

" Well, when he saw that they were indeed the proofs, it was then that he yielded to temptation. He put his shoes on the table. What was it you put on that chair near the window ? "

" Gloves," said the young man.

Holmes looked triumphantly at Bannister.

" He put his gloves on the chair, and he took the proofs, sheet by sheet, to copy them. He thought the tutor must return by the main gate, and that he would see him. As we know, he came back by the side-gate. Suddenly he heard him at the very door. There was no possible escape. He forgot his gloves, but he caught up his shoes and darted into the bedroom. You observe that the scratch on that table is slight at one side, but deepens in the direction of the bedroom door. That in itself is enough to show us that the shoes had been drawn in that direction, and that the culprit had taken refuge there. The earth round the spike had been left on the table, and a second sample was loosened and fell in the bedroom. I may add that I walked out to the athletic grounds this morning, saw that tenacious black clay is used in the jumping-pit, and carried away a specimen of it, together with some of the fine tan or sawdust which is strewn over it to prevent the athlete from slipping. Have I told the truth, Mr. Gilchrist ? "

The student had drawn himself erect.

" Yes, sir, it is true," said he.

" Good heavens, have you nothing to add ?" cried Soames.

" Yes, sir, I have, but the shock of this disgraceful exposure has bewildered me. I have a letter here, Mr. Soames, which I wrote to you early this morning in the middle of a restless night. It was before I knew that my sin had found me out. Here it is, sir. You will see that I have said, ' I have determined not to go in for the examination. I have been offered a commission in the Rhodesian Police, and I am going out to South Africa at once.' "

" I am indeed pleased to hear that you did not intend to profit by your unfair advantage," said Soames. " But why did you change your purpose ? "

Gilchrist pointed to Bannister.

" There is the man who sent me in the right path," said he.

" Come now, Bannister," said Holmes. " It will be clear to you from what I have said that only you could have let this young man out, since you were left in the

781

room and must have locked the door when you went out. As to his escaping by that window, it was incredible. Can you not clear up the last point in this mystery, and tell us the reason for your action ? "

" It was simple enough, sir, if you only had known ; but with all your cleverness it was impossible that you could know. Time was, sir, when I was butler to old Sir Jabez Gilchrist, this young gentleman's father. When he was ruined I come to the college as servant, but I never forgot my old employer because he was down in the world. I watched his son all I could for the sake of the old days. Well, sir, when I came into this room yesterday when the alarm was given, the first thing I saw was Mr. Gilchrist's tan gloves a-lying in that chair. I knew those gloves well, and I understood their message. If Mr. Soames saw them the game was up. I flopped down into that chair, and nothing would budge me until Mr. Soames he went for you. Then out came my poor young master, whom I had dandled on my knee, and confessed it all to me. Wasn't it natural, sir, that I should save him, and wasn't it natural also that I should try to speak to him as his dead father would have done, and make him understand that he could not profit by such a deed ? Could you blame me, sir ? "

" No, indeed ! " said Holmes heartily, springing to his feet. " Well, Soames, I think we have cleared your little problem up, and our breakfast awaits us at home. Come, Watson ! As to you, sir, I trust that a bright future awaits you in Rhodesia. For once you have fallen low. Let us see in the future how high you can rise."

33. *The Golden Pince-Nez*

WHEN I look at the three massive manuscript volumes which contain our work for the year 1894 I confess that it is very difficult for me, out of such a wealth of material, to select the cases which are most interesting in themselves and at the same time most conducive to a display of those peculiar powers for which my friend was famous. As I turn over the pages I see my notes upon the repulsive story of the red leech and the terrible death of Crosby the banker. Here also I find an account of the Addleton tragedy and the singular contents of the ancient British barrow. The famous Smith-Mortimer succession case comes also within this period, and so does the tracking and arrest of Huret, the Boulevard assassin—an exploit which won for Holmes an autograph letter of thanks from the French President and the Order of the Legion of Honour. Each of these would furnish a narrative, but on the whole I am of opinion that none of them unite so many singular points of interest as the episode of Yoxley Old Place, which includes, not only the lamentable death of young Willoughby Smith, but also those subsequent developments which threw so curious a light upon the causes of the crime.

It was a wild, tempestuous night towards the close of November. Holmes and I sat together in silence all the evening, he engaged with a powerful lens deciphering the remains of the original inscription upon a palimpsest, I deep in a recent treatise upon surgery. Outside the wind howled down Baker Street, while the rain beat fiercely against the windows. It was strange there in the very depths of the town, with ten miles of man's handiwork on every side of us, to feel the iron grip of Nature, and to be conscious that to the huge elemental forces all London was no more than the molehills that dot the fields. I walked to the window and looked out on the deserted street. The occasional lamps gleamed on the expanse of muddy road and shining pavement. A single cab was splashing its way from the Oxford Street end.

"Well, Watson, it's as well we have not to turn out tonight," said Holmes, laying aside his lens and rolling up the palimpsest. "I've done enough for one sitting. It is trying work for the eyes. So far as I can make out, it is nothing more exciting than an Abbey's accounts dating from the second half of the fifteenth century. Halloa ! halloa ! halloa ! What's this ? "

Amid the droning of the wind there had come the stamping of a horse's hoofs and the long grind of a wheel as it rasped against the kerb. The cab which I had seen had pulled up at our door.

" What can he want ? " I ejaculated, as a man stepped out of it.

" Want ! He wants us. And we, my poor Watson, want overcoats and cravats and goloshes, and every aid that man ever invented to fight the weather. Wait a bit, though ! There's the cab off again ! There's hope yet. He'd have kept it if he had wanted us to come. Run down, my dear fellow, and open the door, for all virtuous folk have been long in bed."

When the light of the hall lamp fell upon our midnight visitor, I had no difficulty in recognizing him. It was young Stanley Hopkins, a promising detective, in whose career Holmes had several times shown a very practical interest.

" Is he in ? " he asked eagerly.

" Come up, my dear sir," said Holmes' voice from above. " I hope you have no designs upon us on such a night as this."

The detective mounted the stairs, and our lamp gleamed upon his shining waterproof. I helped him out of it, while Holmes knocked a blaze out of the logs in the grate.

" Now, my dear Hopkins, draw up and warm your toes," said he. " Here's a cigar, and the doctor has a prescription containing hot water and a lemon which is good medicine on a night like this. It must be something important which has brought you out in such a gale."

" It is indeed, Mr. Holmes. I've had a bustling afternoon, I promise you. Did you see anything of the Yoxley case in the latest editions ? "

" I've seen nothing later than the fifteenth century to-day."

" Well, it was only a paragraph, and all wrong at

that, so you have not missed anything. I haven't let the grass grow under my feet. It's down in Kent, seven miles from Chatham and three from the railway line. I was wired for at three-fifteen, reached Yoxley Old Place at five, conducted my investigation, was back at Charing Cross by the last train and straight to you by cab."

"Which means, I suppose, that you are not quite clear about your case ? "

" It means that I can make neither head nor tail of it. So far as I can see it is just as tangled a business as ever I handled, and yet at first it seemed so simple that one couldn't go wrong. There's no motive, Mr. Holmes. That's what bothers me—I can't put my hand on a motive. Here's a man dead—there's no denying that —but, so far as I can see, no reason on earth why anyone should wish him harm."

Holmes lit his cigar and leaned back in his chair.

"Let us hear about it," said he.

" I've got my facts pretty clear," said Stanley Hopkins. " All I want now is to know what they all mean. The story, so far as I can make it out, is like this. Some years ago this country house, Yoxley Old Place, was taken by an elderly man, who gave the name of Professor Coram. He was an invalid, keeping his bed half the time, and the other half hobbling round the house with a stick, or being pushed about the grounds by the gardener in a bath-chair. He was well liked by the few neighbours who called upon him, and he has the reputation down there of being a very learned man. His household used to consist of an elderly housekeeper, Mrs. Marker, and of a maid, Susan Tarlton. These have both been with him since his arrival, and they seem to be women of excellent character. The professor is writing a learned book, and he found it necessary about a year ago to engage a secretary. The first two that he tried were not successes ; but the third, Mr. Willoughby Smith, a very young man straight from the University, seems to have been just what his employer wanted. His work consisted in writing all the morning to the professor's dictation, and he usually spent the evening in hunting up references and passages which bore upon the next day's work. This Willoughby Smith has nothing against him either as a boy at Uppingham or as a young man at Cambridge. I have seen his testimonials, and from the first he was a decent, quiet, hard-working fellow, with no weak spot in him at all. And yet this is the lad who has met his death this morning in the professor's study under circumstances which can point only to murder."

The wind howled and screamed at the windows. Holmes and I drew closer to the fire while the young inspector slowly and point by point developed his singular narrative.

" If you were to search all England," said he, " I don't suppose you could find a household more self-contained or free from outside influences. Whole weeks would pass and not one of them go past the garden gate. The professor was buried in his work, and existed for nothing else. Young Smith knew nobody in the neighbourhood, and lived very much as his employer did. The two women had nothing to take them from the house. Mortimer, the gardener, who wheels the bath-chair, is an Army pensioner—an old Crimean man of excellent character. He does not live in the house, but in a three-roomed cottage at the other end of the garden. Those are the only people that you would find within the grounds of Yoxley Old Place. At the same time, the gate of the garden is a hundred yards from the main London to Chatham road. It opens with a latch, and there is nothing to prevent anyone from walking in.

" Now I will give you the evidence of Susan Tarlton, who is the only person who can say anything positive about the matter. It was in the forenoon, between eleven and twelve. She was engaged at the moment in hanging some curtains in the upstairs front bedroom. Professor Coram was still in bed, for when the weather is bad

786

he seldom rises before midday. The housekeeper was busied with some work in the back of the house. Willoughby Smith had been in his bedroom, which he uses as a sitting-room ; but the maid heard him at that moment pass along the passage and descend to the study immediately below her. She did not see him, but she says that she could not be mistaken in his quick, firm tread. She did not hear the study door close, but a minute or so later there was a dreadful cry in the room below. It was a wild, hoarse scream, so strange and unnatural that it might have come either from a man or a woman. At the same instant there was a heavy thud, which shook the whole house, and then all was silence. The maid stood petrified for a moment, and then, recovering her courage, she ran downstairs. The study door was shut, and she opened it. Inside young Mr. Willoughby Smith was stretched upon the floor. At first she could see no injury, but as she tried to raise him she saw that blood was pouring from the under side of his neck. It was pierced by a very small but very deep wound, which had divided the carotid artery. The instrument with which the injury had been inflicted lay upon the carpet beside him. It was one of those small sealing-wax knives to be found on old-fashioned writing-tables, with an ivory handle and a stiff blade. It was part of the fittings of the professor's own desk.

" At first the maid thought that young Smith was already dead, but on pouring some water from the carafe over his forehead, he opened his eyes for an instant. ' The professor,' he murmured—' it was she.' The maid is prepared to swear that those were the exact words. He tried desperately to say something else, and he held his right hand up in the air. Then he fell back dead.

" In the meantime the housekeeper had also arrived upon the scene, but she was just too late to catch the young man's dying words. Leaving Susan with the body, she hurried to the professor's room. He was sitting up in bed, horribly agitated, for he had heard enough to convince him that something terrible had occurred. Mrs. Marker is prepared to swear that the professor was still in his night-clothes, and, indeed, it was impossible for him to dress without the help of Mortimer, whose orders were to come at twelve o'clock. The professor declares that he heard the distant cry, but that he knows nothing more. He can give no explanation of the young man's last words, 'The professor—it was she,' but imagines that they were the outcome of delirium. He believes that Willoughby Smith had not an enemy in the world, and can give no reason for the crime. His first action was to send Mortimer, the gardener, for the local police. A little later the chief constable sent for me. Nothing was moved before I got there, and strict orders were given that no one should walk upon the paths leading to the house. It was a splendid chance of putting your theories into practice, Mr. Sherlock Holmes. There was really nothing wanting."

"Except Mr. Sherlock Holmes!" said my companion, with a somewhat bitter smile. "Well, let us hear about it. What sort of job did you make of it?"

"I must ask you first, Mr. Holmes, to glance at this rough plan, which will give you a general idea of the position of the professor's study and the various points of the case. It will help you in following my investigations."

He unfolded the rough chart, which I here reproduce, and he laid it across Holmes' knee. I rose, and, standing behind Holmes, I studied it over his shoulder.

"It is very rough, of course, and it only deals with the points which seem to me to be essential. All the rest you will see later for yourself. Now, first of all, presuming that the assassin entered the house, how did he or she come in? Undoubtedly by the garden path and the back door, from which there is direct access to the study. Any other way would have been exceedingly complicated. The escape must also have been made along that line, for of the two other exits from the room one was blocked by Susan as she ran downstairs, and the other leads straight to the professor's bedroom. I therefore directed my attention at once to the garden path, which was saturated with recent rain and would certainly show any footmarks.

"My examination showed me that I was dealing with a cautious and expert criminal. No footmarks were to be found on the path. There could be no question, however, that someone had passed along the grass border which lines the path, and that he had done so in order to avoid leaving a track. I could not find anything in the nature of a distinct impression, but the grass was trodden down and someone had undoubtedly passed. It could only have been the murderer, since neither the gardener nor anyone else had been there that morning, and the rain had only begun during the night."

"One moment," said Holmes. "Where does this path lead to?"

"To the road."

"How long is it?"

"A hundred yards or so."

"At the point where the path passes through the gate you could surely pick up the tracks?"

"Unfortunately the path was tiled at that point."

"Well, on the road itself?"

"No; it was all trodden into mire."

"Tut-tut! Well, then, these tracks upon the grass—were they coming or going?"

"It was impossible to say. There was never any outline."

"A large foot or a small?"

"You could not distinguish."

Holmes gave an ejaculation of impatience. "It has been pouring rain and blowing a hurricane ever since," said he. "It will be harder to read now than that palimpsest. Well, well, it can't be helped. What did you do, Hopkins, after you had made certain that you had made certain of nothing?"

"I think I made certain of a good deal, Mr. Holmes. I knew that someone had entered the house cautiously from without. I next examined the corridor. It is lined with coconut matting, and had taken no impression of any kind. This brought me into the study itself. It is a scantily furnished room. The main article is a large writing-table with a fixed bureau. This bureau consists of a double column of drawers with a central small cupboard between them. The drawers were open, the cupboard locked. The drawers, it seems, were always open, and nothing of value was kept in them. There were some papers of importance in the cupboard, but there were no signs that this had been tampered with, and the professor assures me that nothing was missing. It is certain that no robbery had been committed.

"I come now to the body of the young man. It was found near the bureau, and just to the left of it, as marked upon that chart. The stab was on the right side of the neck and from behind forwards, so that it is almost impossible that it could have been self-inflicted."

"Unless he fell upon the knife," said Holmes.

"Exactly. The idea crossed my mind. But we found the knife some feet away from the body, so that seems impossible. Then, of course, there are the man's own dying words. And, finally, there was this very important piece of evidence which was found clasped in the dead man's right hand."

From his pocket Stanley Hopkins drew a small paper packet. He unfolded it, and disclosed a golden pince-nez, with two broken ends of black silk cord dangling from the end of it. "Willoughby Smith had excellent sight," he added. "There can be no question that this was snatched from the face or the person of the assassin."

Sherlock Holmes took the glasses into his hand and examined them with the utmost attention and interest. He held them on his nose, endeavoured to read through them, went to the window and stared up the street with them, looked at them most minutely in the full light of the lamp, and finally, with a chuckle, seated himself at the table and wrote a few lines upon a sheet of paper, which he tossed across to Stanley Hopkins.

"That's the best I can do for you," said he. "It may prove to be of some use."

The astonished detective read the note aloud. It ran as follows :

"Wanted, a woman of good address, attired like a lady. She has a remarkably thick nose, with eyes which are set close upon either side of it. She has a puckered forehead, a peering expression, and probably rounded shoulders. There are indications that she has had recourse to an optician at least twice during the last few months. As her glasses are of remarkable strength, and as opticians are not very numerous, there should be no difficulty in tracing her."

Holmes smiled at the astonishment of Hopkins, which must have been reflected upon my features.

"Surely my deductions are simplicity itself," said he. "It would be difficult to name any articles which afford a

791

finer field for inference than a pair of glasses, especially so remarkable a pair as these. That they belong to a woman I infer from their delicacy, and also, of course, from the last words of the dying man. As to her being a person of refinement and well dressed, they are, as you perceive, handsomely mounted in solid gold, and it is inconceivable that anyone who wore such glasses could be slatternly in other respects. You will find that the clips are too wide for your nose, showing that the lady's nose was very broad at the base. This sort of nose is usually a short and coarse one, but there are a sufficient number of exceptions to prevent me from being dogmatic or from insisting upon this point in my description. My own face is a narrow one, and yet I find that I cannot get my eyes into the centre, or near the centre, of these glasses. Therefore, the lady's eyes are set very near to the sides of the nose. You will perceive, Watson, that the glasses are concave and of unusual strength. A lady whose vision has been so extremely contracted all her life is sure to have the physical characteristics of such vision, which are seen in the forehead, the eyelids, and the shoulders."

" Yes," I said, " I can follow each of your arguments. I confess, however, that I am unable to understand how you arrive at the double visit to the optician."

Holmes took the glasses into his hand.

" You will perceive," he said, " that the clips are lined with tiny bands of cork to soften the pressure upon the nose. One of these is discoloured and worn to some slight extent, but the other is new. Evidently one has fallen off and been replaced. I should judge that the older of them has not been there more than a few months. They exactly correspond, so I gather that the lady went back to the same establishment for the second."

" By George, it's marvellous ! " cried Hopkins, in an ecstasy of admiration. " To think that I had all that evidence in my hand and never knew it ! I had intended, however, to go the round of the London opticians."

" Of course you would. Meanwhile, have you anything more to tell us about the case ? "

" Nothing, Mr. Holmes. I think that you know as much as I do now—probably more. We have had inquiries made as to any stranger seen on the country roads or at the railway station. We have heard of none. What beats me is the utter want of all object in the crime. Not a ghost of a motive can anyone suggest."

" Ah ! there I am not in a position to help you. But I suppose you want us to come out to-morrow ? "

" If it is not asking too much, Mr. Holmes. There's a train from Charing Cross to Chatham at six in the morning, and we should be at Yoxley Old Place between eight and nine."

" Then we shall take it. Your case has certainly some features of great interest, and I shall be delighted to look into it. Well, it's nearly one, and we had best get a few hours' sleep. I dare say you can manage all right on the sofa in front of the fire. I'll light my spirit-lamp and give you a cup of coffee before we start."

The gale had blown itself out next day, but it was a bitter morning when we started upon our journey. We saw the cold winter sun rise over the dreary marshes of the Thames and the long, sullen reaches of the river, which I shall ever associate with our pursuit of the Andaman Islander in the earlier days of our career. After a long and weary journey we alighted at a small station some miles from Chatham. While a horse was being put into a trap at the local inn we snatched a hurried breakfast, and so we were all ready for business when we at last arrived at Yoxley Old Place. A constable met us at the garden gate.

" Well, Wilson, any news ? "

" No, sir, nothing."

" No reports of any stranger seen ? "

" No, sir. Down at the station they are certain that no stranger either came or went yesterday."

" Have you had inquiries made at inns and lodgings ? "

" Yes, sir ; there is no one that we cannot account for."

" Well, it's only a reasonable walk to Chatham. Anyone might stay there, or take a train without being observed. This is the garden path of which I spoke, Mr. Holmes. I'll pledge my word there was no mark on it yesterday."

" On which side were the marks on the grass ? "

" This side, sir. This narrow margin of grass between the path and the flower-bed. I can't see the traces now, but they were clear to me then."

" Yes, yes ; someone has passed along," said Holmes, stooping over the grass border. " Our lady must have picked her steps carefully, must she not, since on the one side she would leave a track on the path, and on the other an even clearer one on the soft bed ? "

" Yes, sir, she must have been a cool hand."

I saw an intent look pass over Holmes' face.

" You say that she must have come back this way ? "

" Yes, sir ; there is no other."

" On this strip of grass ? "

" Certainly, Mr. Holmes."

" Hum ! It was a very remarkable performance— very remarkable. Well, I think we have exhausted the path. Let us go farther. This garden door is usually kept open, I suppose ? Then this visitor had nothing to do but to walk in. The idea of murder was not in her mind, or she would have provided herself with some sort of weapon, instead of having to pick this knife off the writing-table. She advanced along this corridor, leaving no traces upon the coconut matting. Then she found herself in this study. How long was she there ? We have no means of judging."

" Not more than a few minutes, sir. I forgot to tell you that Mrs. Marker, the housekeeper, had been in there tidying not very long before—about a quarter of an hour she says."

"Well, that gives us a limit. Our lady enters this room, and what does she do ? She goes over to the writing-table. What for ? Not for anything in the drawers. If there had been anything worth her taking it would scarcely have been locked up. No ; it was for something in that wooden bureau. Halloa ! what is that scratch upon the face of it ? Just hold a match, Watson. Why did you not tell me of this, Hopkins ? "

The mark which he was examining began upon the brasswork on the right-hand side of the keyhole, and extended for about four inches, where it had scratched the varnish from the surface.

" I noticed it, Mr. Holmes. But you'll always find scratches round a keyhole."

" This is recent—quite recent. See how the brass shines where it is cut. An old scratch would be the same colour as the surface. Look at it through my lens. There's the varnish, too, like earth on each side of a furrow. Is Mrs. Marker there ? "

A sad-faced, elderly woman came into the room.

" Did you dust this bureau yesterday morning ? "

" Yes, sir."

" Did you notice this scratch ? "

" No, sir, I did not."

" I am sure you did not, for a duster would have swept away these shreds of varnish. Who has the key of this bureau ? "

" The professor keeps it on his watch-chain."

" Is it a simple key ? "

" No, sir ; it is a Chubb's key."

" Very good. Mrs. Marker, you can go. Now we are making a little progress. Our lady enters the room, advances to the bureau, and either opens it or tries to do so. While she is thus engaged young Willoughby Smith enters the room. In her hurry to withdraw the key she makes this scratch upon the door. He seizes her, and she, snatching up the nearest object, which happens to be this knife, strikes at him in order to make him let go his hold.

The blow is a fatal one. He falls and she escapes, either with or without the object for which she has come. Is Susan the maid there? Could anyone have got away through that door after the time that you heard the cry, Susan?"

"No, sir; it is impossible. Before I got down the stair I'd have seen anyone in the passage. Besides, the door never opened, for I would have heard it."

"That settles this exit. Then no doubt the lady went out the way she came. I understand that this other passage leads only to the professor's room. There is no exit that way?"

"No, sir."

"We shall go down it and make the acquaintance of the professor. Halloa, Hopkins! this is very important, very important indeed. The professor's corridor is also lined with coconut matting."

"Well, sir, what of that?"

"Don't you see any bearing upon the case? Well, well, I don't insist upon it. No doubt I am wrong. And yet it seems to me to be suggestive. Come with me and introduce me."

We passed down the passage, which was of the same length as that which led to the garden. At the end was a short flight of steps ending in a door. Our guide knocked, and then ushered us into the professor's bedroom.

It was a very large chamber, lined with innumerable volumes, which had overflowed from the shelves and lay in piles in the corners, or were stacked all round at the base of the cases. The bed was in the centre of the room, and in it, propped up with pillows, was the owner of the house. I have seldom seen a more remarkable-looking person. It was a gaunt, aquiline face which was turned towards us, with piercing dark eyes, which lurked in deep hollows under overhung and tufted brows. His hair and beard were white, save that the latter was curiously stained with yellow around his mouth. A cigarette glowed amid the tangle of white hair, and the air of the room was fetid with stale tobacco smoke. As he held out his hand to Holmes I perceived that it also was stained yellow with nicotine.

" A smoker, Mr. Holmes ? " said he, speaking well-chosen English with a curious little mincing accent. " Pray take a cigarette. And you, sir ? I can recommend them, for I have them especially prepared by Ionides of Alexandria. He sends me a thousand at a time, and I grieve to say that I have to arrange for a fresh supply every fortnight. Bad, sir, very bad ; but an old man has few pleasures. Tobacco and my work—that is all that is left to me."

Holmes had lit a cigarette, and was shooting little darting glances all over the room.

" Tobacco and my work, but now only tobacco," the old man exclaimed. " Alas, what a fatal interruption ! Who could have foreseen such a terrible catastrophe ? So estimable a young man ! I assure you that after a few months' training he was an admirable assistant. What do you think of the matter, Mr. Holmes ? "

" I have not yet made up my mind."

" I shall indeed be indebted to you if you can throw a light where all is so dark to us. To a poor bookworm and invalid like myself such a blow is paralysing. I seem to have lost the faculty of thought. But you are a man of action—you are a man of affairs. It is part of the every-day routine of your life. You can preserve your balance in every emergency. We are fortunate indeed in having you at our side."

Holmes was pacing up and down on one side of the room whilst the old professor was talking. I observed that he was smoking with extraordinary rapidity. It was evident that he shared our host's liking for the fresh Alexandrian cigarettes.

" Yes, sir, it is a crushing blow," said the old man. " That is my *magnum opus*—the pile of papers on the side-table yonder. It is my analysis of the documents found in the Coptic monasteries of Syria and Egypt, a work which will cut deep at the very foundations of revealed religion. With my enfeebled health I do not know whether I shall ever be able to complete it now that my assistant has been taken from me. Dear me, Mr. Holmes ; why, you are even a quicker smoker than I am myself."

Holmes smiled.

" I am a connoisseur," said he, taking another cigarette from the box—his fourth—and lighting it from the stub of that which he had finished. " I will not trouble you with any lengthy cross-examination, Professor Coram, since I gather that you were in bed at the time of the crime and could know nothing about it. I would only ask this—What do you imagine that this poor fellow meant by his last words : ' The professor—it was she ' ? "

The professor shook his head.

" Susan is a country girl," said he, " and you know the incredible stupidity of that class. I fancy that the poor fellow murmured some incoherent, delirious words, and that she twisted them into this meaningless message."

" I see. You have no explanation yourself of the tragedy ? "

" Possibly an accident ; possibly—I only breathe it among ourselves—a suicide. Young men have their hidden troubles—some affair of the heart, perhaps, which we have never known. It is a more probable supposition than murder."

" But the eyeglasses ? "

" Ah ! I am only a student—a man of dreams. I cannot explain the practical things of life. But still, we are aware, my friend, that love-gages may take strange shapes. By all means take another cigarette. It is a pleasure to see anyone appreciate them so. A fan, a glove, glasses—who knows what article may be carried as a token or treasured when a man puts an end to his life ? This gentleman speaks of footsteps on the grass ; but, after all, it is easy to be mistaken on such a point. As to the knife, it might well be thrown far from the unfortunate man as he fell. It is possible that I speak as a child, but to me it seems that Willoughby Smith has met his fate by his own hand."

Holmes seemed struck by the theory thus put forward, and he continued to walk up and down for some time, lost in thought and consuming cigarette after cigarette.

" Tell me, Professor Coram," he said at last, " what is in that cupboard in the bureau ? "

" Nothing that would help a thief. Family papers, letters from my poor wife, diplomas of Universities which have done me honour. Here is the key. You can look for yourself."

Holmes picked up the key and looked at it for an instant ; then he handed it back.

" No ; I hardly think that it would help me," said he. " I should prefer to go quietly down to your garden and turn the whole matter over in my head. There is something to be said for the theory of suicide which you have put forward. We must apologize for having intruded upon you, Professor Coram, and I promise that we won't disturb you until after lunch. At two o'clock we will come again and report to you anything which may have happened in the interval."

Holmes was curiously distrait, and we walked up and down the garden path for some time in silence.

" Have you a clue ? " I asked at last.

" It depends upon those cigarettes that I smoked," said he. " It is possible that I am utterly mistaken. The cigarettes will show me."

" My dear Holmes," I exclaimed, " how on earth——"

" Well, well, you may see for yourself. If not, there's no harm done. Of course, we always have the optician clue to fall back upon, but I take a short cut when I can get it. Ah, here is the good Mrs. Marker ! Let us enjoy five minutes of instructive conversation with her."

I may have remarked before that Holmes had, when he liked, a peculiarly ingratiating way with women, and that he very readily established terms of confidence with them.

In half the time which he had named he had captured the housekeeper's goodwill, and was chatting with her as if he had known her for years.

"Yes, Mr. Holmes, it is as you say, sir. He does smoke something terrible. All day and sometimes all night, sir. I've seen that room of a morning—well, sir, you'd have thought it was a London fog. Poor young Mr. Smith, he was a smoker also, but not as bad as the professor. His health—well, I don't know that it's better nor worse for the smoking."

"Ah!" said Holmes, "but it kills the appetite."

"Well, I don't know about that, sir."

"I suppose the professor eats hardly anything?"

"Well, he is variable. I'll say that for him."

"I'll wager he took no breakfast this morning, and won't face his lunch after all the cigarettes I saw him consume."

"Well, you're out there, sir, as it happens, for he ate a remarkably big breakfast this morning. I don't know when I've known him make a better one, and he's ordered a good dish of cutlets for his lunch. I'm surprised myself, for since I came into that room yesterday and saw young Mr. Smith lying there on the floor I couldn't bear to look at food. Well, it takes all sorts to make a world, and the professor hasn't let it take his appetite away."

We loitered the morning away in the garden. Stanley Hopkins had gone down to the village to look into some rumours of a strange woman who had been seen by some children on the Chatham road the previous morning. As to my friend, all his usual energy seemed to have deserted him. I had never known him handle a case in such a half-hearted fashion. Even the news brought back by Hopkins that he had found the children and that they had undoubtedly seen a woman exactly corresponding with Holmes' description, and wearing either spectacles or eyeglasses, failed to rouse any sign of keen interest. He was more attentive when Susan, who waited upon us at lunch, volunteered the information that she believed Mr. Smith had been out for a walk yesterday morning, and that he had only returned half an hour before the tragedy occurred. I could not myself see the bearing of this incident, but I clearly perceived that Holmes was weaving it into the general scheme which he had formed in his brain. Suddenly he sprang from his chair, and glanced at his watch. "Two o'clock, gentlemen," said he. "We must go up and have it out with our friend the professor."

The old man had just finished his lunch, and certainly his empty dish bore evidence to the good appetite with which his housekeeper had credited him. He was, indeed, a weird figure as he turned his white mane and his glowing eyes towards us. The eternal cigarette smouldered in his mouth. He had been dressed and was seated in an arm-chair by the fire.

"Well, Mr. Holmes, have you solved this mystery yet?" He shoved the large tin of cigarettes which stood on a table beside him towards my companion. Holmes stretched out his hand at the same moment, and between them they tipped the box over the edge. For a minute or two we were all on our knees retrieving stray cigarettes from impossible places. When we rose again I observed that Holmes' eyes were shining and his cheeks tinged with colour. Only at a crisis have I seen those battle-signals flying.

"Yes," said he, "I have solved it."

Stanley Hopkins and I stared in amazement. Something like a sneer quivered over the gaunt features of the old professor.

"Indeed! In the garden?"

"No, here."

"Here! When?"

"This instant."

"You are surely joking, Mr. Sherlock Holmes. You compel me to tell you that this is too serious a matter to be treated in such a fashion."

"I have forged and tested every link of my chain,

Professor Coram, and I am sure that it is sound. What your motives are, or what exact part you play in this strange business, I am not yet able to say. In a few minutes I shall probably hear it from your own lips. Meanwhile, I will reconstruct what is past for your benefit, so that you may know the information which I still require.

" A lady yesterday entered your study. She came with the intention of possessing herself of certain documents which were in your bureau. She had a key of her own. I have had an opportunity of examining yours, and I do not find that slight discoloration which the scratch made upon the varnish would have produced. You were not an accessory, therefore, and she came, so far as I can read the evidence, without your knowledge to rob you."

The professor blew a cloud from his lips.

" This is most interesting and instructive," said he. " Have you no more to add ? Surely, having traced this lady so far, you can also say what has become of her."

" I will endeavour to do so. In the first place, she was seized by your secretary, and stabbed him in order to escape. This catastrophe I am inclined to regard as an unhappy accident, for I am convinced that the lady had no intention of inflicting so grievous an injury. An assassin does not come unarmed. Horrified by what she had done, she rushed wildly away from the scene of the tragedy. Unfortunately for her she had lost her glasses in the scuffle, and as she was extremely short-sighted she was really helpless without them. She ran down a corridor, which she imagined to be that by which she had come—both were lined with coconut matting—and it was only when it was too late that she understood that she had taken the wrong passage and that her retreat was cut off behind her. What was she to do ? She could not go back. She could not remain where she was. She must go on. She went on. She mounted a stair, pushed open a door, and found herself in your room."

The old man sat with his mouth open staring wildly at

Holmes. Amazement and fear were stamped upon his expressive features. Now, with an effort, he shrugged his shoulders and burst into insincere laughter.

"All very fine, Mr. Holmes," said he. "But there is one little flaw in a splendid theory. I was myself in my room, and I never left it during the day."

"I am aware of that, Professor Coram."

"And you mean to say that I could lie upon that bed and not be aware that a woman had entered my room?"

"I never said so. You *were* aware of it. You spoke with her. You recognized her. You aided her to escape."

Again the professor burst into high-keyed laughter. He had risen to his feet, and his eyes glowed like embers.

"You are mad!" he cried. "You are talking insanely. I helped her to escape? Where is she now?"

"She is there," said Holmes, and he pointed to a high bookcase in the corner of the room.

I saw the old man throw up his arms, a terrible convulsion passed over his grim face, and he fell back in his chair. At the same instant the bookcase at which Holmes pointed swung round upon a hinge, and a woman rushed out into the room.

"You are right," she cried, in a strange foreign voice. "You are right! I am here."

She was brown with the dust and draped with the cobwebs which had come from the walls of her hiding-place. Her face, too, was streaked with grime, and at the best she could have never been handsome, for she had the exact physical characteristics which Holmes had divined, with, in addition, a long and obstinate chin. What with her natural blindness, and what with the change from dark to light, she stood as one dazed, blinking about her to see where and who we were. And yet, in spite of all these disadvantages, there was a certain nobility in the woman's bearing, a gallantry in the defiant chin and in the upraised head, which compelled something of respect and admiration. Stanley Hopkins had laid his hand upon her arm and claimed her as his prisoner, but she waved him aside gently, and yet with an overmastering dignity which compelled obedience. The old man lay back in his chair, with a twitching face, and stared at her with brooding eyes.

"Yes, sir, I am your prisoner," she said. "From where I stood I could hear everything, and I know that you have learned the truth. I confess it all. It was I who killed the young man. But you are right, you who say that it was an accident. I did not even know that it was a knife which I held in my hand, for in my despair I snatched anything from the table and struck at him to make him let me go. It is the truth that I tell."

"Madame," said Holmes, "I am sure that it is the truth. I fear that you are far from well."

She had turned a dreadful colour, the more ghastly under the dark dust-streaks upon her face. She seated herself on the side of the bed; then she resumed.

"I have only a little time here," she said, "but I would have you to know the whole truth. I am this man's wife. He is not an Englishman. He is a Russian. His name I will not tell."

For the first time the old man stirred. "God bless you, Anna!" he cried. "God bless you!"

She cast a look of the deepest disdain in his direction. "Why should you cling so hard to that wretched life of yours, Sergius?" said she. "It has done harm to many and good to none—not even to yourself. However, it is not for me to cause the frail thread to be snapped before God's time. I have enough already upon my soul since I crossed the threshold of this cursed house. But I must speak, or I shall be too late.

"I have said, gentlemen, that I am this man's wife. He was fifty and I a foolish girl of twenty when we married. It was in a city of Russia, a University—I will not name the place."

"God bless you, Anna!" murmured the old man again.

"We were reformers—revolutionists—Nihilists, you

804

understand. He and I and many more. Then there came a time of trouble, a police officer was killed, many were arrested, evidence was wanted, and in order to save his own life and to earn a great reward my husband betrayed his own wife and his companions. Yes ; we were all arrested upon his confession. Some of us found our way to the gallows and some to Siberia. I was among these last but my term was not for life. My husband came to England with his ill-gotten gains, and has lived in quiet ever since, knowing well that if the Brotherhood knew where he was not a week would pass before justice would be done."

The old man reached out a trembling hand and helped himself to a cigarette. " I am in your hands, Anna," said he. " You were always good to me."

" I have not yet told you the height of his villainy ! " said she. " Among our comrades of the Order there was one who was the friend of my heart. He was noble, unselfish, loving—all that my husband was not. He hated violence. We were all guilty—if that is guilt—but he was not. He wrote for ever dissuading me from such a course. These letters would have saved him. So would my diary, in which from day to day I had entered both my feelings towards him and the view which each of us had taken. My husband found and kept both diary and letters. He hid them, and he tried hard to swear away the young man's life. In this he failed, but Alexis was sent a convict to Siberia, where now, at this moment, he works in a salt mine. Think of that, you villain, you villain ; now, now, at this very moment, Alexis, a man whose name you are not worthy to speak, works and lives like a slave, and yet I have your life in my hands and I let you go ! "

" You were always a noble woman, Anna," said the old man, puffing at his cigarette.

She had risen, but she fell back again with a little cry of pain.

" I must finish," she said. " When my term was over

805

I set myself to get the diary and letters, which if sent to the Russian Government, would procure my friend's release. I knew that my husband had come to England. After months of searching I discovered where he was. I knew that he still had the diary, for when I was in Siberia I had a letter from him once reproaching me and quoting some passages from its pages. Yet I was sure that with his revengeful nature he would never give it to me of his own free will. I must get it for myself. With this object I engaged an agent from a private detective firm, who entered my husband's house as secretary—it was your second secretary, Sergius, the one who left you so hurriedly. He found that papers were kept in the cupboard, and he got an impression of the key. He would not go farther. He furnished me with a plan of the house, and he told me that in the forenoon the study was always empty, as the secretary was employed up here. So at last I took my courage in both hands and I came down to get the papers for myself. I succeeded, but at what a cost!

" I had just taken the papers and was locking the cupboard when the young man seized me. I had seen him already that morning. He had met me in the road, and I had asked him to tell me where Professor Coram lived, not knowing that he was in his employ."

" Exactly! exactly! " said Holmes. " The secretary came back and told his employer of the woman he had met. Then in his last breath he tried to send a message that it was she—the she whom he had just discussed with him."

" You must let me speak," said the woman, in an imperative voice, and her face contracted as if in pain. " When he had fallen I rushed from the room, chose the wrong door, and found myself in my husband's room. He spake of giving me up. I showed him that if he did so his life was in my hands. If he gave me to the law I could give him to the Brotherhood. It was not that I wished to live for my own sake, but it was that I desired to accomplish my purpose. He knew that I would do what I said—that his own fate was involved in mine. For that reason, and for no other, he shielded me. He thrust me into that dark hiding-place, a relic of old days, known only to himself. He took his meals in his own room, and so was able to give me part of his food. It was agreed that when the police left the house I should slip away by night and come back no more. But in some way you have read our plans." She tore from the bosom of her dress a small packet. "These are my last words," said she; "here is the packet which will save Alexis. I confide it to your honour and to your love of justice. Take it! You will deliver it at the Russian Embassy. Now I have done my duty, and——"

"Stop her!" cried Holmes. He had bounded across the room and had wrenched a small phial from her hand.

"Too late!" she said, sinking back on the bed. "Too late! I took the poison before I left my hiding-place. My head swims! I am going! I charge you, sir, to remember the packet."

"A simple case, and yet in some ways an instructive one," Holmes remarked as we travelled back to town. "It hinged from the outset upon the pince-nez. But for the fortunate chance of the dying man having seized these I am not sure that we could ever have reached our solution. It was clear to me from the strength of the glasses that the wearer must have been very blind and helpless when deprived of them. When you asked me to believe that she walked along a narrow strip of grass without once making a false step I remarked, as you may remember, that it was a noteworthy performance. In my mind, I set it down as an impossible performance, save in the unlikely case that she had a second pair of glasses. I was forced, therefore, to seriously consider the hypothesis that she had remained within the house. On perceiving the similarity of the two corridors, it became clear that she might very easily have made such a mistake, and in that case it was evident that she must have entered the professor's room. I was keenly on the alert, therefore, for whatever would bear out this supposition, and I examined the room narrowly for anything in the shape of a hiding-place. The carpet seemed continuous and firmly nailed, so I dismissed the idea of a trap-door. There might well be a recess behind the books. As you are aware, such devices are common in old libraries. I observed that books were piled on the floor at all other points, but that one bookcase was left clear. This, then, might be the door. I could see no marks to guide me, but the carpet was of a dun colour, which lends itself very well to examination. I therefore smoked a great number of those excellent cigarettes, and I dropped the ash all over the space in front of the suspected bookcase. It was a simple trick, but exceedingly effective. I then went downstairs, and I ascertained in your presence, Watson, without your quite perceiving the drift of my remarks, that Professor Coram's consumption of food had increased—as one would expect when he is supplying a second person. We then ascended to the room again, when, by upsetting the cigarette-box, I obtained a very excellent view of the floor, and was able to see quite clearly, from the traces upon the cigarette ash, that the prisoner had, in our absence, come out from her retreat. Well, Hopkins, here we are at Charing Cross, and I congratulate you on having brought your case to a successful conclusion. You are going to headquarters, no doubt. I think, Watson, you and I will drive together to the Russian Embassy."

34. *The Missing Three-Quarter*

WE were fairly accustomed to receive weird telegrams at Baker Street, but I have a particular recollection of one which reached us on a gloomy February morning some seven or eight years ago, and gave Mr. Sherlock Holmes a puzzled quarter of an hour. It was addressed to him, and ran thus :

" Please await me. Terrible misfortune. Right wing three-quarter missing ; indispensable to-morrow.—OVERTON."

" Strand postmark, and despatched ten thirty-six," said Holmes, reading it over and over. " Mr. Overton was evidently considerably excited when he sent it, and somewhat incoherent in consequence. Well, well, he will be here, I dare say, by the time I have looked through *The Times*, and then we shall know all about it. Even the most insignificant problem would be welcome in these stagnant days."

Things had indeed been very slow with us, and I had learned to dread such periods of inaction, for I knew by experience that my companion's brain was so abnormally active that it was dangerous to leave it without material upon which to work. For years I had gradually weaned him from that drug mania which had threatened once to check his remarkable career. Now I knew that under ordinary conditions he no longer craved for this artificial stimulus ; but I was well aware that the fiend was not dead, but sleeping ; and I have known that the sleep was a light one and the waking near when in periods of idleness I have seen the drawn look upon Holmes' ascetic face, and the brooding of his deep-set and inscrutable eyes. Therefore I blessed this Mr. Overton, whoever he might be, since he had come with his enigmatic message to break that dangerous calm which brought more peril to my friend than all the storms of his tempestuous life.

As we expected, the telegram was soon followed by its sender, and the card of Mr. Cyril Overton, of Trinity College, Cambridge, announced the arrival of an enormous young man, sixteen stone of solid bone and muscle, who spanned the doorway with his broad shoulders and looked from one of us to the other with a comely face which was haggard with anxiety.

" Mr. Sherlock Holmes ? "

My companion bowed.

" I've been down to Scotland Yard, Mr. Holmes. I saw Inspector Stanley Hopkins. He advised me to come to you. He said the case, so far as he could see, was more in your line than in that of the regular police."

" Pray sit down and tell me what is the matter."

" It's awful, Mr. Holmes, simply awful ! I wonder my hair isn't grey. Godfrey Staunton—you've heard of him, of course ? He's simply the hinge that the whole team turns on. I'd rather spare two from the pack and have Godfrey for my three-quarter line. Whether it's passing, or tackling, or dribbling, there's no one to touch him ; and then, he's got the head and can hold us all together. What am I to do ? That's what I ask you, Mr. Holmes. There's Moorhouse, first reserve, but he is trained as a half, and he always edges right in on to the scrum instead of keeping out on the touch-line. He's a fine place-kick, it's true, but, then, he has no judgment, and he can't sprint for nuts. Why, Morton or Johnson, the Oxford fliers, could romp round him. Stevenson is fast enough, but he couldn't drop from the twenty-five line, and a three-quarter who can't either punt or drop isn't worth a place for pace alone. No, Mr. Holmes, we are done unless you can help me to find Godfrey Staunton."

My friend had listened with amused surprise to this long speech, which was poured forth with extraordinary vigour and earnestness, every point being driven home by the slapping of a brawny hand upon the speaker's knee. When our visitor was silent Holmes stretched out his hand and took down letter " S " of his commonplace book. For once he dug in vain into that mine of varied information.

" There is Arthur H. Staunton, the rising young forger," said he, " and there was Henry Staunton, whom

I helped to hang, but Godfrey Staunton is a new name to me."

It was our visitor's turn to look surprised.

"Why, Mr. Holmes, I thought you knew things," said he. "I suppose, then, if you have never heard of Godfrey Staunton you don't know Cyril Overton either ? "

Holmes shook his head good-humouredly.

"Great Scott ! " cried the athlete. "Why, I was first reserve for England against Wales, and I've skippered the 'Varsity all this year. But that's nothing. I didn't think there was a soul in England who didn't know Godfrey Staunton, the crack three-quarter, Cambridge, Blackheath, and five Internationals. Good Lord ! Mr. Holmes, where *have* you lived ? "

Holmes laughed at the young giant's naïve astonishment.

"You live in a different world to me, Mr. Overton, a sweeter and healthier one. My ramifications stretch out into many sections of society, but never, I am happy to say, into amateur sport, which is the best and soundest thing in England. However, your unexpected visit this morning shows me that even in that world of fresh air and fair play there may be work for me to do ; so now, my good sir, I beg you to sit down and to tell me slowly and quietly exactly what it is that has occurred, and how you desire that I should help you."

Young Overton's face assumed the bothered look of the man who is more accustomed to using his muscles than his wits ; but by degrees, with many repetitions and obscurities which I may omit from his narrative, he laid his strange story before us.

"It's this way, Mr. Holmes. As I have said, I am the skipper of the Rugger team of Cambridge 'Varsity, and Godfrey Staunton is my best man. To-morrow we play Oxford. Yesterday we all came up and we settled at Bentley's private hotel. At ten o'clock I went round and saw that all the fellows had gone to roost, for I believe in strict training and plenty of sleep to keep a team fit. I

had a word or two with Godfrey before he turned in.
He seemed to me to be pale and bothered. I asked him
what was the matter. He said he was all right—just a
touch of headache. I bade him good night and left him.
Half an hour later the porter tells me that a rough-looking
man with a beard called with a note for Godfrey. He
had not gone to bed, and the note was taken to his room.
Godfrey read it and fell back in a chair as if he had been
pole-axed. The porter was so scared that he was going
to fetch me, but Godfrey stopped him, had a drink of
water, and pulled himself together. Then he went
downstairs, said a few words to the man who was waiting
in the hall, and the two of them went off together. The
last that the porter saw of them, they were almost running down the street in the direction of the Strand.
This morning Godfrey's room was empty, his bed had
never been slept in, and his things were all just as I had
seen them the night before. He had gone off at a moment's
notice with this stranger, and no word has come from
him since. I don't believe he will ever come back.
He was a sportsman, was Godfrey, down to his marrow,
and he wouldn't have stopped his training and let in his
skipper if it were not for some cause that was too strong
for him. No ; I feel as if he were gone for good and
we should never see him again."

Sherlock Holmes listened with the deepest attention to
this singular narrative.

" What did you do ? " he asked.

" I wired to Cambridge to learn if anything had been
heard of him there. I have had an answer. No one
has seen him."

" Could he have got back to Cambridge ? "

" Yes, there is a late train—quarter-past eleven."

" But, so far as you can ascertain, he did not take it ? "

" No, he has not been seen."

" What did you do next ? "

" I wired to Lord Mount-James."

" Why to the Lord Mount-James ? "

" Godfrey is an orphan, and Lord Mount-James is his nearest relative—his uncle, I believe."

" Indeed. This throws new light upon the matter. Lord Mount-James is one of the richest men in England."

" So I've heard Godfrey say."

" And your friend was closely related ? "

" Yes, he was his heir, and the old boy is nearly eighty —cram full of gout, too. They say he could chalk his billiard-cue with his knuckles. He never allowed Godfrey a shilling in his life, for he is an absolute miser, but it will all come to him right enough."

" Have you heard from Lord Mount-James ? "

" No."

" What motive could your friend have in going to Lord Mount-James ? "

" Well, something was worrying him the night before, and if it was to do with money it is possible that he would make for his nearest relative who had so much of it, though from all I have heard he would not have much chance of getting it. Godfrey was not fond of the old man. He would not go if he could help it."

" Well, we can soon determine that. If your friend was going to his relative Lord Mount-James, you have then to explain the visit of this rough-looking fellow at so late an hour, and the agitation that was caused by his coming."

Cyril Overton pressed his hands to his head. " I can make nothing of it ! " said he.

" Well, well, I have a clear day, and I shall be happy to look into the matter," said Holmes. " I should strongly recommend you to make your preparations for your match without reference to this young gentleman. It must, as you say, have been an overpowering necessity which tore him away in such a fashion, and the same necessity is likely to hold him away. Let us step round together to this hotel, and see if the porter can throw any fresh light upon the matter."

Sherlock Holmes was a past master in the art of putting a humble witness at his ease, and very soon, in the privacy of Godfrey Staunton's abandoned room, he had extracted all that the porter had to tell. The visitor of the night before was not a gentleman, neither was he a working man. He was simply what the porter described as a "medium-looking chap"; a man of fifty, beard grizzled, pale face, quietly dressed. He seemed himself to be agitated. The porter had observed his hand trembling when he had held out the note. Godfrey Staunton had crammed the note into his pocket. Staunton had not shaken hands with the man in the hall. They had exchanged a few sentences, of which the porter had only distinguished the one word "time." Then they had hurried off in the manner described. It was just half-past ten by the hall clock.

"Let me see," said Holmes, seating himself on Staunton's bed. "You are the day porter, are you not?"

"Yes, sir; I go off duty at eleven."

"The night porter saw nothing, I suppose?"

"No, sir; one theatre party came in late. No one else."

"Were you on duty all day yesterday?"

"Yes, sir."

"Did you take any message to Mr. Staunton?"

"Yes, sir; one telegram."

"Ah! that is interesting. What o'clock was this?"

"About six."

"Where was Mr. Staunton when he received it?"

"Here in his room."

"Were you present when he opened it?"

"Yes, sir; I waited to see if there was an answer."

"Well, was there?"

"Yes, sir. He wrote an answer."

"Did you take it?"

"No; he took it himself."

"But he wrote it in your presence?"

"Yes, sir. I was standing by the door, and he with

814

his back turned at that table. When he had written it he said, ' All right, porter, I will take this myself.' "

" What did he write it with ? "

" A pen, sir."

" Was the telegraphic form one of these on the table ? "

" Yes, sir ; it was the top one."

Holmes rose. Taking the forms, he carried them over to the window and carefully examined that which was uppermost.

" It is a pity he did not write in pencil," said he, throwing them down again with a shrug of disappointment. " As you have no doubt frequently observed, Watson, the impression usually goes through—a fact which has dissolved many a happy marriage. However, I can find no trace here. I rejoice, however, to perceive that he wrote with a broad-pointed quill pen, and I can hardly doubt that we will find some impression upon this blotting-pad. Ah, yes, surely this is the very thing ! "

He tore off a strip of the blotting-paper and turned towards us the following hieroglyphic :

Cyril Overton was much excited. " Hold it to the glass," he cried.

" That is unnecessary," said Holmes. " The paper is thin, and the reverse will give the message. Here it is." He turned it over, and we read :

" So that is the tail end of the telegram which Godfrey Staunton despatched within a few hours of his disappearance. There are at least six words of the message which have escaped us ; but what remains—' Stand by us for

God's sake!'—proves that this young man saw a formidable danger which approached him, and from which someone else could protect him. '*Us*,' mark you! Another person was involved. Who should it be but the pale-faced, bearded man who seemed himself in so nervous a state? What, then, is the connection between Godfrey Staunton and the bearded man? And what is the third source from which each of them sought for help against pressing danger? Our inquiry has already narrowed down to that."

"We have only to find to whom that telegram is addressed," I suggested.

"Exactly, my dear Watson. Your reflection, though profound, had already crossed my mind. But I dare say it may have come to your notice that if you walk into a post-office and demand to see the counterfoil of another man's message there may be some disinclination on the part of the officials to oblige you. There is so much red tape in these matters! However, I have no doubt that with a little delicacy and finesse the end may be attained. Meanwhile, I should like in your presence, Mr. Overton, to go through these papers which have been left upon the table."

There were a number of letters, bills, and notebooks, which Holmes turned over and examined with quick, nervous fingers and darting, penetrating eyes. "Nothing here," he said at last. "By the way, I suppose your friend was a healthy young fellow—nothing amiss with him?"

"Sound as a bell."

"Have you ever known him ill?"

"Not a day. He has been laid up with a hack, and once he slipped his knee-cap, but that was nothing."

"Perhaps he was not so strong as you suppose. I should think he may have had some secret trouble. With your assent I will put one or two of these papers in my pocket, in case they should bear upon our future inquiry."

"One moment, one moment!" cried a querulous voice, and we looked up to find a queer little old man jerking and twitching in the doorway. He was dressed in rusty black, with a very broad-brimmed top-hat and a loose white necktie—the whole effect being that of a very rustic parson or of an undertaker's mute. Yet, in spite of his shabby and even absurd appearance, his voice had a sharp crackle, and his manner a quick intensity which commanded attention.

"Who are you, sir, and by what right do you touch this gentleman's papers?" he asked.

"I am a private detective, and I am endeavouring to explain his disappearance."

"Oh, you are, are you? And who instructed you, eh?"

"This gentleman, Mr. Staunton's friend, was referred to me by Scotland Yard."

"Who are you, sir?"

"I am Cyril Overton."

"Then it is you who sent me a telegram. My name is Lord Mount-James. I came round as quickly as the Bayswater bus would bring me. So you have instructed a detective?"

"Yes, sir."

"And are you prepared to meet the cost?"

"I have no doubt, sir, that my friend Godfrey, when we find him, will be prepared to do that."

"But if he is never found, eh? Answer me that?"

"In that case no doubt his family——"

"Nothing of the sort, sir!" screamed the little man. "Don't look to me for a penny—not a penny! You understand that, Mr. Detective! I am all the family that this young man has got, and I tell you that I am not responsible. If he has any expectations it is due to the fact that I have never wasted money, and I do not propose to begin to do so now. As to those papers with which you are making so free, I may tell you that in case there should be anything of any value among them you

817

will be held strictly to account for what you do with
them."

"Very good, sir," said Sherlock Holmes. "May I ask
in the meanwhile whether you have yourself any theory
to account for this young man's disappearance?"

"No, sir, I have not. He is big enough and old enough
to look after himself, and if he is so foolish as to lose
himself I entirely refuse to accept the responsibility of
hunting for him."

"I quite understand your position," said Holmes, with
a mischievous twinkle in his eyes. "Perhaps you don't
quite understand mine. Godfrey Staunton appears to
have been a poor man. If he has been kidnapped it could
not have been for anything which he himself possesses.
The fame of your wealth has gone abroad, Lord Mount-
James, and it is entirely possible that a gang of thieves
has secured your nephew in order to gain from him
some information as to your house, your habits, and your
treasure."

The face of our unpleasant little visitor turned as white
as his neckcloth.

"Heavens, sir, what an idea! I never thought of such
villainy! What inhuman rogues there are in the world!
But Godfrey is a fine lad—a staunch lad. Nothing would
induce him to give his old uncle away. I'll have the plate
moved over to the bank this evening. In the meantime
spare no pains, Mr. Detective. I beg you to leave no
stone unturned to bring him safely back. As to money,
well, so far as a fiver, or even a tenner, goes, you can always
look to me."

Even in his chastened frame of mind the noble miser
could give us no information which could help us, for he
knew little of the private life of his nephew. Our only
clue lay in the truncated telegram, and with a copy of this
in his hand Holmes set forth to find a second link for his
chain. We had shaken off Lord Mount-James, and
Overton had gone to consult with the other members of
his team over the misfortune which had befallen them.

There was a telegraph office at a short distance from the hotel. We halted outside it.

"It's worth trying, Watson," said Holmes. "Of course, with a warrant we could demand to see the counterfoils, but we have not reached that stage yet. I don't suppose they remember faces in so busy a place. Let us venture it."

"I am sorry to trouble you," said he in his blandest manner to the young woman behind the grating; "there is some small mistake about a telegram I sent yesterday. I have had no answer, and I very much fear that I must have omitted to put my name at the end. Could you tell me if this was so?"

The young lady turned over a sheaf of counterfoils.

"What o'clock was it?" she asked.

"A little after six."

"Whom was it to?"

Holmes put his finger to his lips and glanced at me. "The last words in it were ' for God's sake,' " he whispered confidentially; "I am very anxious at getting no answer."

The young woman separated one of the forms.

"This is it. There is no name," said she, smoothing it out upon the counter.

"Then that, of course, accounts for my getting no answer," said Holmes. "Dear me, how very stupid of me, to be sure! Good morning, miss, and many thanks for having relieved my mind." He chuckled and rubbed his hands when we found ourselves in the street once more.

"Well?" I asked.

"We progress, my dear Watson, we progress. I had seven different schemes for getting a glimpse of that telegram, but I could hardly hope to succeed the very first time."

"And what have you gained?"

"A starting-point for our investigation." He hailed a cab. "King's Cross Station," said he.

"We have a journey, then?"

"Yes, I think we must run down to Cambridge together. All the indications seem to point in that direction."

"Tell me," I asked as we rattled up Gray's Inn Road, "have you any suspicion yet as to the cause of the disappearance? I don't think that among all our cases I have known one where the motives were more obscure. Surely you don't really imagine that he may be kidnapped in order to give information against his wealthy uncle?"

"I confess, my dear Watson, that that does not appeal to me as a very probable explanation. It struck me, however, as being the one which was most likely to interest that exceedingly unpleasant old person."

"It certainly did that. But what are your alternatives?"

"I could mention several. You must admit that it is curious and suggestive that this incident should occur on the eve of this important match, and should involve the only man whose presence seems essential to the success of the side. It may, of course, be coincidence, but it is interesting. Amateur sport is free from betting, but a good deal of outside betting goes on among the public, and it is possible that it might be worth someone's while to get at a player as the ruffians of the Turf get at a race-horse. There is one explanation. A second very obvious one is that this young man really is the heir of a great property, however modest his means may be at present, and it is not impossible that a plot to hold him for ransom might be concocted."

"These theories take no account of the telegram."

"Quite true, Watson. The telegram still remains the only solid thing with which we have to deal, and we must not permit our attention to wander away from it. It is to gain light upon the purpose of this telegram that we are now upon our way to Cambridge. The path of our investigation is at present obscure, but I shall be very much surprised if before evening we have not cleared it up or made a considerable advance along it."

It was already dark when we reached the old University city. Holmes took a cab at the station, and ordered the man to drive to the house of Dr. Leslie Armstrong. A few minutes later we had stopped at a large mansion in the busiest thoroughfare. We were shown in, and after a long wait were admitted into the consulting-room, where we found the doctor seated behind his table.

It argues the degree in which I had lost touch with my profession that the name of Leslie Armstrong was unknown to me. Now I am aware that he is not only one of the heads of the medical school of the University, but a thinker of European reputation in more than one branch of science. Yet even without knowing his brilliant record one could not fail to be impressed by a mere glance at the man—the square, massive face, the brooding eyes under the thatched brows, and the granite moulding of the inflexible jaw. A man of deep character, a man with an alert mind, grim, ascetic, self-contained, formidable—so I read Dr. Leslie Armstrong. He held my friend's card in his hand, and he looked up with no very pleased expression upon his dour features.

" I have heard your name, Mr. Sherlock Holmes, and I am aware of your profession, one of which I by no means approve."

" In that, doctor, you will find yourself in agreement with every criminal in the country," said my friend quietly.

" So far as your efforts are directed towards the suppression of crime, sir, they must have the support of every reasonable member of the community, though I cannot doubt that the official machinery is amply sufficient for the purpose. Where your calling is more open to criticism is when you pry into the secrets of private individuals, when you rake up family matters which are better hidden, and when you incidentally waste the time of men who are more busy than yourself. At the present moment, for example, I should be writing a treatise instead of conversing with you."

" No doubt, doctor ; and yet the conversation may prove more important than the treatise. Incidentally I may tell you that we are doing the reverse of what you very justly blame, and that we are endeavouring to prevent anything like public exposure of private matters which must necessarily follow when once the case is fairly in the hands of the official police. You may look upon me simply as an irregular pioneer who goes in front of the regular force of the country. I have come to ask you about Mr. Godfrey Staunton."

" What about him ? "

" You know him, do you not ? "

" He is an intimate friend of mine."

" You are aware that he has disappeared ? "

" Ah, indeed ! " There was no change of expression in the rugged features of the doctor.

" He left his hotel last night. He has not been heard of."

" No doubt he will return."

" To-morrow is the 'Varsity football match."

" I have no sympathy with these childish games. The young man's fate interests me deeply, since I know him and like him. The football match does not come within my horizon at all."

" I claim your sympathy, then, in my investigation of Mr. Staunton's fate. Do you know where he is ? "

" Certainly not."

" You have not seen him since yesterday ? "

" No, I have not."

" Was Mr. Staunton a healthy man ? "

" Absolutely."

" Did you ever know him ill ? "

" Never."

Holmes popped a sheet of paper before the doctor's eyes. " Then perhaps you will explain this receipted bill for thirteen guineas, paid by Mr. Godfrey Staunton last month to Dr. Leslie Armstrong, of Cambridge. I picked it out from among the papers upon his desk."

The doctor flushed with anger.

" I do not feel that there is any reason why I should render an explanation to you, Mr. Holmes."

Holmes replaced the bill in his notebook.

" If you prefer a public explanation it must come sooner or later," said he. " I have already told you that I can hush up that which others will be bound to publish, and you would really be wiser to take me into your complete confidence."

" I know nothing about it."

" Did you hear from Mr. Staunton in London ? "

" Certainly not."

" Dear me, dear me !—the post office again ! " Holmes sighed wearily. " A most urgent telegram was despatched to you from London by Godfrey Staunton at six-fifteen yesterday evening—a telegram which is undoubtedly associated with his disappearance—and yet you have not had it. It is most culpable. I shall certainly go down to the office here and register a complaint."

Dr. Leslie Armstrong sprang up from behind his desk, and his dark face was crimson with fury.

" I'll trouble you to walk out of my house, sir," said he. " You can tell your employer, Lord Mount-James, that I do not wish to have anything to do either with him or with his agents. No, sir, not another word ! " He rang the bell furiously. " John, show these gentlemen out." A pompous butler ushered us severely to the door, and we found ourselves in the street. Holmes burst out laughing.

" Dr. Leslie Armstrong is certainly a man of energy and character," said he. " I have not seen a man who, if he turned his talents that way, was more calculated to fill the gap left by the illustrious Moriarty. And now, my poor Watson, here we are, stranded and friendless, in this inhospitable town, which we cannot leave without abandoning our case. This little inn just opposite Armstrong's house is singularly adapted to our needs. If you would engage a front room and purchase the necessaries for the night, I may have time to make a few inquiries."

These few inquiries proved, however, to be a more lengthy proceeding than Holmes had imagined, for he did not return to the inn until nearly nine o'clock. He was pale and dejected, stained with dust, and exhausted with hunger and fatigue. A cold supper was ready upon the table, and when his needs were satisfied and his pipe alight he was ready to take that half-comic and wholly philosophic view which was natural to him when his affairs were going awry. The sound of carriage wheels caused him to rise and glance out of the window. A brougham and pair of greys under the glare of a gas-lamp stood before the doctor's door.

"It's been out three hours," said Holmes ; "started at half-past six, and here it is back again. That gives a radius of ten or twelve miles, and he does it once, or sometimes twice, a day."

"No unusual thing for a doctor in practice."

"But Armstrong is not really a doctor in practice. He is a lecturer and a consultant, but he does not care for general practice, which distracts him from his literary work. Why, then, does he make these long journeys, which must be exceedingly irksome to him, and who is it that he visits ? "

"His coachman——"

"My dear Watson, can you doubt that it was to him that I first applied ? I do not know whether it came from his own innate depravity or from the promptings of his master, but he was rude enough to set a dog at me. Neither dog nor man liked the look of my stick, however, and the matter fell through. Relations were strained after that, and further inquiries out of the question. All that I have learned I got from a friendly native in the yard of our own inn. It was he who told me of the doctor's habits and of his daily journey. At that instant, to give point to his words, the carriage came round to the door."

"Could you not follow it?"

"Excellent, Watson! You are scintillating this evening. The idea did cross my mind. There is, as you may have observed, a bicycle shop next to our inn. Into this I rushed, engaged a bicycle, and was able to get started before the carriage was quite out of sight. I rapidly overtook it, and then, keeping at a discreet distance of a hundred yards or so, I followed its lights until we were clear of the town. He had got well out on the country road when a somewhat mortifying incident occurred. The carriage stopped, the doctor alighted, walked swiftly back to where I had also halted, and told me in an excellent sardonic fashion that he feared the road was narrow, and that he hoped his carriage did not impede the passage of my bicycle. Nothing could have been more admirable than his way of putting it. I at once rode past the carriage, and, keeping to the main road, I went on for a few miles, and then halted in a convenient place to see if the carriage passed. There was no sign of it, however, and so it became evident that it had turned down one of several side-roads which I had observed. I rode back, but again saw nothing of the carriage, and now, as you perceive, it has returned after me. Of course, I had at the outset no particular reason to connect these journeys with the disappearance of Godfrey Staunton, and was only inclined to investigate them on the general grounds that everything which concerns Dr. Armstrong is at present of interest to us; but, now that I find he keeps so keen a lookout upon anyone who may follow him on these excursions, the affair appears more important, and I shall not be satisfied until I have made the matter clear."

"We can follow him to-morrow."

"Can we? It is not so easy as you seem to think. You are not familiar with Cambridgeshire scenery, are you ? It does not lend itself to concealment. All this country that I passed over to-night is as flat and clean as the palm of your hand, and the man we are following is no fool, as he very clearly showed to-night. I have wired to Overton to let us know any fresh London developments at this address, and in the meantime we can only concentrate our attention upon Dr. Armstrong, whose name the obliging young lady at the office allowed me to read upon the counterfoil of Staunton's urgent message. He knows where that young man is—to that I'll swear—and if he knows, then it must be our own fault if we cannot manage to know also. At present it must be admitted that the odd trick is in his possession, and, as you are aware, Watson, it is not my habit to leave the game in that condition."

And yet the next day brought us no nearer to the solution of the mystery. A note was handed in after breakfast, which Holmes passed across to me with a smile.

SIR [it ran],—I can assure you that you are wasting your time in dogging my movements. I have, as you discovered last night, a window at the back of my brougham, and if you desire a twenty-mile ride which will lead you to the spot from which you started, you have only to follow me. Meanwhile, I can inform you that no spying upon me can in any way help Mr. Godfrey Staunton, and I am convinced that the best service you can do to that gentleman is to return at once to London and to report to your employer that you are unable to trace him. Your time in Cambridge will certainly be wasted.—Yours faithfully,

" LESLIE ARMSTRONG."

" An outspoken, honest antagonist is the doctor," said Holmes. " Well, well, he excites my curiosity, and I must really know more before I leave him."

" His carriage is at his door now," said I. " There he

is stepping into it. I saw him glance up at our window as he did so. Suppose I try my luck upon the bicycle ? "

" No, no, my dear Watson ! With all respect for your natural acumen, I do not think that you are quite a match for the worthy doctor. I think that possibly I can attain our end by some independent explorations of my own. I am afraid that I must leave you to your own devices, as the appearance of *two* inquiring strangers upon a sleepy country-side might excite more gossip than I care for. No doubt you will find some sights to amuse you in this venerable city, and I hope to bring back a more favourable report to you before evening."

Once more, however, my friend was destined to be disappointed. He came back at night weary and unsuccessful.

" I have had a blank day, Watson. Having got the doctor's general direction, I spent the day in visiting all the villages upon that side of Cambridge, and comparing notes with publicans and other local news agencies. I have covered some ground : Chesterton, Histon, Waterbeach, and Oakington have each been explored, and have each proved disappointing. The daily appearance of a brougham and pair could hardly have been overlooked in such Sleepy Hollows. The doctor has scored once more. Is there a telegram for me ? "

" Yes ; I opened it. Here it is : ' Ask for Pompey from Jeremy Dixon, Trinity College.' I don't understand it."

" Oh, it is clear enough. It is from our friend Overton, and is in answer to a question from me. I'll just send round a note to Mr. Jeremy Dixon, and then I have no doubt that our luck will turn. By the way, is there any news of the match ? "

" Yes, the local evening paper has an excellent account in its last edition. Oxford won by a goal and two tries. The last sentences of the description say : ' The defeat of the Light Blues may be entirely attributed to the unfortunate absence of the crack International, Godfrey

Staunton, whose want was felt at every instant of the game. The lack of combination in the three-quarter line and their weakness both in attack and defence more than neutralized the efforts of a heavy and hard-working pack.' "

" Then our friend Overton's forebodings have been justified," said Holmes. " Personally I am in agreement with Dr. Armstrong, and football does not come within my horizon. Early to bed to-night, Watson, for I foresee that to-morrow may be an eventful day."

I was horrified by my first glimpse of Holmes next morning, for he sat by the fire holding his tiny hypodermic syringe. I associated that with the single weakness of his nature, and I feared the worst when I saw it glittering in his hand. He laughed at my expression of dismay, and laid it upon the table.

" No, no, my dear fellow, there is no cause for alarm. It is not upon this occasion the instrument of evil, but it will rather prove to be the key which will unlock our mystery. On this syringe I base all my hopes. I have just returned from a small scouting expedition, and everything is favourable. Eat a good breakfast, Watson, for I propose to get upon Dr. Armstrong's trail to-day, and once on it I will not stop for rest or food until I run him to his burrow."

" In that case," said I, " we had best carry our breakfast with us, for he is making an early start. His carriage is at the door."

" Never mind. Let him go. He will be clever if he can drive where I cannot follow him. When you have finished come downstairs with me, and I will introduce you to a detective who is a very eminent specialist in the work that lies before us."

When we descended I followed Holmes into the stableyard, where he opened the door of a loose-box and led out a squat, lop-eared, white-and-tan dog, something between a beagle and a foxhound.

" Let me introduce you to Pompey," said he. " Pompey is the pride of the local draghounds, no very great flier, as his build will show, but a staunch hound on a scent. Well, Pompey, you may not be fast, but I expect you will be too fast for a couple of middle-aged London gentlemen, so I will take the liberty of fastening this leather leash to your collar. Now, boy, come along, and show what you can do." He led him across to the doctor's door. The dog sniffed round for an instant, and then with a shrill whine of excitement started off down the street, tugging at his leash in his efforts to go faster. In half an hour we were clear of the town and hastening down a country road.

" What have you done, Holmes ? " I asked.

" A threadbare and venerable device, but useful upon occasion. I walked into the doctor's yard this morning and shot my syringe full of aniseed over the hind wheel. A draghound will follow aniseed from here to John o' Groats, and our friend Armstrong would have to drive through the Cam before he would shake Pompey off his trail. Oh, the cunning rascal ! This is how he gave me the slip the other night."

The dog had suddenly turned out of the main road into a grass-grown lane. Half a mile farther this opened into another broad road, and the trail turned hard to the right in the direction of the town, which we had just quitted. The road took a sweep to the south of the town and continued in the opposite direction to that in which we started.

" This detour has been entirely for our benefit, then ? " said Holmes. " No wonder that my inquiries among those villages led to nothing. The doctor has certainly played the game for all it is worth, and one would like to know the reason for such elaborate deception. This should be the village of Trumpington to the right of us. And, by Jove ! here is the brougham coming round the corner ! Quick, Watson, quick, or we are done ! "

He sprang through a gate into a field, dragging the reluctant Pompey after him. We had hardly got under the shelter of the hedge when the carriage rattled past. I caught a glimpse of Dr. Armstrong within, his shoulders bowed, his head sunk on his hands, the very image of distress. I could tell by my companion's graver face that he also had seen.

" I fear there is some dark ending to our quest," said he. " It cannot be long before we know it. Come, Pompey ! Ah, it is the cottage in the field."

There could be no doubt that we had reached the end of our journey. Pompey ran about and whined eagerly outside the gate, where the marks of the brougham's wheels were still to be seen. A footpath led across to the lonely cottage. Holmes tied the dog to the hedge, and we hastened onwards. My friend knocked at the little rustic door, and knocked again without response. And yet the cottage was not deserted, for a low sound came to our ears—a kind of drone of misery and despair, which was indescribably melancholy. Holmes paused irresolute, and then he glanced back at the road which we had just traversed. A brougham was coming down it, and there could be no mistaking those grey horses.

" By Jove, the doctor is coming back ! " cried Holmes. " That settles it. We are bound to see what it means before he comes."

He opened the door, and we stepped into the hall. The droning sound swelled louder upon our ears, until it became one long, deep wail of distress. It came from upstairs. Holmes darted up, and I followed him. He pushed open a half-closed door, and we both stood appalled at the sight before us.

A woman, young and beautiful, was lying dead upon the bed. Her calm, pale face, with dim, wide-opened blue eyes, looked upwards from amid a great tangle of golden hair. At the foot of the bed, half sitting, half kneeling, his face buried in the clothes, was a young man, whose frame was racked by his sobs. So absorbed was he by his bitter grief that he never looked up until Holmes' hand was on his shoulder.

" Are you Mr. Godfrey Staunton ? "

" Yes, yes ; I am—but you are too late. She is dead."

The man was so dazed that he could not be made to understand that we were anything but doctors who had been sent to his assistance. Holmes was endeavouring to utter a few words of consolation, and to explain the alarm which had been caused to his friends by his sudden disappearance, when there was a step upon the stairs, and there was the heavy, stern, questioning face of Dr. Armstrong at the door.

" So, gentlemen," said he, " you have attained your end, and have certainly chosen a particularly delicate moment for your intrusion. I would not brawl in the presence of death, but I can assure you that if I were a younger man your monstrous conduct would not pass with impunity."

" Excuse me, Dr. Armstrong, I think we are a little at cross purposes," said my friend with dignity. " If you could step downstairs with us we may each be able to give some light to the other upon this miserable affair."

A minute later the grim doctor and ourselves were in the sitting-room below.

" Well, sir ? " said he.

" I wish you to understand, in the first place, that I am not employed by Lord Mount-James, and that my sympathies in this matter are entirely against that nobleman. When a man is lost it is my duty to ascertain his fate, but having done so the matter ends so far as I am concerned ; and so long as there is nothing criminal, I am much more anxious to hush up private scandals than to give them publicity. If, as I imagine, there is no breach of the law in this matter, you can absolutely depend upon my discretion and my co-operation in keeping the facts out of the papers ! "

Dr. Armstrong took a quick step forward and wrung Holmes by the hand.

" You are a good fellow," said he. " I had misjudged you. I thank Heaven that my compunction at leaving poor Staunton all alone in this plight caused me to turn my carriage back, and so to make your acquaintance. Knowing as much as you do, the situation is very easily explained. A year ago Godfrey Staunton lodged in London for a time, and became passionately attached to his landlady's daughter, whom he married. She was as good as she was beautiful, and as intelligent as she was good. No man need be ashamed of such a wife. But Godfrey was the heir to this crabbed old nobleman, and it was quite certain that the news of his marriage would have been the end of his inheritance. I knew the lad well, and I loved him for his many excellent qualities. I did all I could to help him to keep things straight. We did our very best to keep the thing from everyone, for when once such a whisper gets about it is not long before everyone has heard it. Thanks to this lonely cottage and his own discretion, Godfrey has up to now succeeded. Their secret was known to no one save to me and to one excellent servant who has at present gone for assistance to Trumpington. But at last there came a terrible blow in the shape of dangerous illness to his wife. It was consumption of the most virulent kind. The poor boy was half crazed with grief, and yet he had to go to London to play this match, for he could not get out of it without explanations which would expose the secret. I tried to cheer him up by a wire, and he sent me one in reply imploring me to do all I could. This was the telegram which you appear in some inexplicable way to have seen. I did not tell him how urgent the danger was, for I knew that he could do no good here, but I sent the truth to the girl's father, and he very injudiciously communicated to Godfrey. The result was that he came straight away in a state bordering on frenzy, and has remained in the same state, kneeling at the end of her bed, until this morning death put an end to her sufferings. That is all, Mr. Holmes, and I am sure that I can rely upon your discretion and that of your friend."

Holmes grasped the doctor's hand.

"Come, Watson," said he, and we passed from that house of grief into the pale sunlight of the winter day.

35. *The Abbey Grange*

IT was on a bitterly cold and frosty morning during the winter of '97 that I was wakened by a tugging at my shoulder. It was Holmes. The candle in his hand shone upon his eager, stooping face, and told me at a glance that something was amiss.

"Come, Watson, come!" he cried. "The game is afoot. Not a word! Into your clothes and come!"

Ten minutes later we were both in a cab and rattling through the silent streets on our way to Charing Cross Station. The first faint winter's dawn was beginning to appear, and we could dimly see the occasional figure of an early workman as he passed us, blurred and indistinct in the opalescent London reek. Holmes nestled in silence into his heavy coat, and I was glad to do the same, for the air was most bitter, and neither of us had broken our fast. It was not until we had consumed some hot tea at the station, and taken our places in the Kentish train, that we were sufficiently thawed, he to speak and I to listen. Holmes drew a note from his pocket and read it aloud:

"ABBEY GRANGE, MARSHAM, KENT, 3.30 a.m.

"MY DEAR MR. HOLMES,—I should be very glad of your immediate assistance in what promises to be a most remarkable case. It is something quite in your line. Except for releasing the lady I will see that everything is kept exactly as I have found it, but I beg you not to lose an instant, as it is difficult to leave Sir Eustace there.—Yours faithfully,

"STANLEY HOPKINS.

" Hopkins has called me in seven times, and on each occasion his summons has been entirely justified," said Holmes. " I fancy that every one of his cases has found its way into your collection, and I must admit, Watson, that you have some power of selection which atones for much which I deplore in your narratives. Your fatal habit of looking at everything from the point of view of a story instead of as a scientific exercise has ruined what might have been an instructive and even classical series of demonstrations. You slur over work of the utmost finesse and delicacy in order to dwell upon sensational details which may excite but cannot possibly instruct the reader."

" Why do you not write them yourself ? " I said, with some bitterness.

" I will, my dear Watson, I will. At present I am, as you know, fairly busy, but I propose to devote my declining years to the composition of a textbook which shall focus the whole art of detection into one volume. Our present research appears to be a case of murder."

" You think this Sir Eustace is dead, then ? "

" I should say so. Hopkins' writing shows considerable agitation, and he is not an emotional man. Yes, I gather there has been violence, and that the body is left for our inspection. A mere suicide would not have caused him to send for me. As to the release of the lady, it would appear that she has been locked in her room during the tragedy. We are moving in high life, Watson—crackling paper, ' E.B.' monogram, coat-of-arms, picturesque address. I think that friend Hopkins will live up to his reputation, and that we shall have an interesting morning. The crime was committed before twelve last night."

" How can you possibly tell ? "

" By an inspection of the trains and by reckoning the time. The local police had to be called in, they had to communicate with Scotland Yard, Hopkins had to go out, and he in turn had to send for me. All that makes a fair night's work. Well, here we are at Chislehurst Station, and we shall soon set our doubts at rest."

A drive of a couple of miles through narrow country lanes brought us to a park gate, which was opened for us by an old lodge-keeper, whose haggard face bore the reflection of some great disaster. The avenue ran through a noble park, between lines of ancient elms, and ended in a low, widespread house, pillared in front after the fashion of Palladio. The central part was evidently of a great age and shrouded in ivy, but the large windows showed that modern changes had been carried out, and one wing of the house appeared to be entirely new. The youthful figure and alert, eager face of Inspector Stanley Hopkins confronted us in the open doorway.

" I'm very glad you have come, Mr. Holmes. And you, too, Dr. Watson! But, indeed, if I had my time over again I should not have troubled you, for since the lady has come to herself she has given so clear an account of the affair that there is not much left for us to do. You remember that Lewisham gang of burglars ? "

" What, the three Randalls ? "

" Exactly ; the father and two sons. It's their work. I have not a doubt of it. They did a job at Sydenham a fortnight ago, and were seen and described. Rather cool to do another so soon and so near ; but it is they, beyond all doubt. It's a hanging matter this time."

" Sir Eustace is dead, then ? "

" Yes ; his head was knocked in with his own poker."

" Sir Eustace Brackenstall, the driver tells me."

" Exactly—one of the richest men in Kent. Lady Brackenstall is in the morning-room. Poor lady, she has had a most dreadful experience. She seemed half dead when I saw her first. I think you had best see her and hear her account of the facts. Then we will examine the dining-room together."

Lady Brackenstall was no ordinary person. Seldom have I seen so graceful a figure, so womanly a presence, and so beautiful a face. She was a blonde, golden-haired, blue-eyed, and would, no doubt, have had the perfect complexion which goes with such colouring had not her recent experience left her drawn and haggard. Her sufferings were physical as well as mental, for over one eye rose a hideous, plum-coloured swelling, which her maid, a tall, austere woman, was bathing assiduously with vinegar and water. The lady lay back exhausted upon a couch, but her quick, observant gaze as we entered the room, and the alert expression of her beautiful features, showed that neither her wits nor her courage had been shaken by her terrible experience. She was enveloped in a loose dressing-gown of blue and silver, but a black sequin-covered dinner-dress was hung upon the couch beside her.

" I have told you all that happened, Mr. Hopkins," she said wearily ; " could you not repeat it for me ? Well, if you think it necessary, I will tell these gentlemen what occurred. Have they been in the dining-room yet ? "

" I thought they had better hear your ladyship's story first."

" I shall be glad when you can arrange matters. It is horrible to me to think of him still lying there." She shuddered and buried her face for a moment in her hands. As she did so the loose gown fell back from her forearm. Holmes uttered an exclamation.

" You have other injuries, madam ! What is this ? " Two vivid red spots stood out on one of the white, round limbs. She hastily covered it.

" It is nothing. It has no connection with the hideous business of last night. If you and your friend will sit down I will tell you all I can.

" I am the wife of Sir Eustace Brackenstall. I have been married about a year. I suppose that it is no use my attempting to conceal that our marriage has not been a happy one. I fear that all our neighbours would tell you that, even if I were to attempt to deny it. Perhaps the fault may be partly mine. I was brought up in the freer, less conventional atmosphere of South Australia, and this English life, with its proprieties and its primness, is not congenial to me. But the main reason lies in the one fact which is notorious to everyone, and that is that Sir Eustace was a confirmed drunkard. To be with such a man for an hour is unpleasant. Can you imagine what it means for a sensitive and high-spirited woman to be tied to him for day and night ? It is a sacrilege, a crime, a villainy to hold that such a marriage is binding. I say that these monstrous laws of yours will bring a curse upon the land—Heaven will not let such wickedness endure." For an instant she sat up, her cheeks flushed, and her eyes blazing from under the terrible mark upon her brow. Then the strong, soothing hand of the austere maid drew her head down on to the cushion, and the wild anger died away into passionate sobbing. At last she continued :

"I will tell you about last night. You are aware, perhaps, that in this house all servants sleep in the modern wing. This central block is made up of the dwelling-rooms, with the kitchen behind and our bedroom above. My maid Theresa sleeps above my room. There is no one else, and no sound could alarm those who are in the farther wing. This must have been well known to the robbers, or they would not have acted as they did.

"Sir Eustace retired about half-past ten. The servants had already gone to their quarters. Only my maid was up, and she had remained in her room at the top of the house until I needed her services. I sat until after eleven in this room, absorbed in a book. Then I walked round to see that all was right before I went upstairs. It was my custom to do this myself, for, as I have explained, Sir Eustace was not always to be trusted. I went into the kitchen, the butler's pantry, the gun-room, the billiard-room, the drawing-room, and finally the dining-room. As I approached the window, which is covered with thick curtains, I suddenly felt the wind blow upon my face, and realized that it was open. I

flung the curtain aside, and found myself face to face
with a broad-shouldered, elderly man who had just
stepped into the room. The window is a long French
one, which really forms a door leading to the lawn. I
held my bedroom candle lit in my hand, and, by its light,
behind the first man I saw two others, who were in the
act of entering. I stepped back, but the fellow was on
me in an instant. He caught me first by the wrist and
then by the throat. I opened my mouth to scream, but
he struck me a savage blow with his fist over the eye,
and felled me to the ground. I must have been unconscious for a few minutes, for when I came to myself I
found that they had torn down the bell-rope and had
secured me tightly to the oaken chair which stands at the
head of the dining-room table. I was so firmly bound
that I could not move, and a handkerchief round my
mouth prevented me from uttering any sound. It was
at this instant that my unfortunate husband entered
the room. He had evidently heard some suspicious
sounds, and he came prepared for such a scene as he
found. He was dressed in his shirt and trousers, with
his favourite blackthorn cudgel in his hand. He rushed
at one of the burglars, but another—it was the elderly
man—stooped, picked the poker out of the grate, and
struck him a terrible blow as he passed. He fell without
a groan, and never moved again. I fainted once more,
but again it could only have been a very few minutes
during which I was insensible. When I opened my
eyes I found that they had collected the silver from the
sideboard, and they had drawn a bottle of wine which
stood there. Each of them had a glass in his hand. I
have already told you, have I not, that one was elderly,
with a beard, and the others young, hairless lads. They
might have been a father with his two sons. They talked
together in whispers. Then they came over and made
sure that I was still securely bound. Finally they withdrew, closing the window after them. It was quite a
quarter of an hour before I got my mouth free. When

I did so my screams brought the maid to my assistance. The other servants were soon alarmed, and we sent for the local police, who instantly communicated with London. That is really all I can tell you, gentlemen, and I trust that it will not be necessary for me to go over so painful a story again."

" Any questions, Mr. Holmes ? " asked Hopkins.

" I will not impose any further tax upon Lady Brackenstall's patience and time," said Holmes. " Before I go into the dining-room I should be glad to hear your experience." He looked at the maid.

" I saw the men before ever they came into the house," said she. " As I sat by my bedroom window I saw three men in the moonlight down by the lodge gate yonder, but I thought nothing of it at the time. It was more than an hour after that I heard my mistress scream, and down I ran, to find her, poor lamb, just as she says, and him on the floor with his blood and brains over the room. It was enough to drive a woman out of her wits, tied there, and her very dress spotted with him ; but she never wanted courage, did Miss Mary Fraser of Adelaide, and Lady Brackenstall of Abbey Grange hasn't learned new ways. You've questioned her long enough, you gentlemen, and now she is coming to her own room, just with her old Theresa, to get the rest that she badly needs."

With a motherly tenderness the gaunt woman put her arm round her mistress and led her from the room.

" She has been with her all her life," said Hopkins. " Nursed her as a baby, and came with her to England when they first left Australia eighteen months ago. Theresa Wright is her name, and the kind of maid you don't pick up nowadays. This way, Mr. Holmes, if you please ! "

The keen interest had passed out of Holmes' expressive face, and I knew that with the mystery all the charm of the case had departed. There still remained an arrest to be effected, but what were these commonplace rogues

that he should soil his hands with them ? An abstruse
and learned specialist who finds that he has been called
in for a case of measles would experience something of the
annoyance which I read in my friend's eyes. Yet the
scene in the dining-room of the Abbey Grange was
sufficiently strange to arrest his attention and to recall his
waning interest.

It was a very large and high chamber, with carved oak
ceiling, oaken panelling, and a fine array of deers' heads
and ancient weapons around the walls. At the farther
end from the door was the high French window of which
we had heard. Three smaller windows on the right-hand
side filled the apartment with cold winter sunshine. On
the left was a large, deep fireplace, with a massive overhanging oak mantelpiece. Beside the fireplace was a
heavy oaken chair with arms and cross-bars at the bottom. In and out through the open woodwork was woven
a crimson cord, which was secured at each side to the
crosspiece below. In releasing the lady the cord had
been slipped off her, but the knots with which it had
been secured still remained. These details only struck
our attention afterwards, for our thoughts were entirely
absorbed by the terrible object which lay spread upon the
tiger-skin hearthrug in front of the fire.

It was the body of a tall, well-made man, about forty
years of age. He lay upon his back, his face upturned,
with his white teeth grinning through his short, black
beard. His two clenched hands were raised above his
head, and a heavy blackthorn stick lay across them. His
dark, handsome, aquiline features were convulsed into a
spasm of vindictive hatred, which had set his dead face
in a terribly fiendish expression. He had evidently been
in his bed when the alarm had broken out, for he wore
a foppish, embroidered night-shirt, and his bare feet
projected from his trousers. His head was horribly
injured, and the whole room bore witness to the savage
ferocity of the blow which had struck him down. Beside him lay the heavy poker, bent into a curve by the

concussion. Holmes examined both it and the indescribable wreck which it had wrought.

"He must be a powerful man, this elder Randall," he remarked.

"Yes," said Hopkins. "I have some record of the fellow, and he is a rough customer."

"You should have no difficulty in getting him."

"Not the slightest. We have been on the look-out for him, and there was some idea that he had got away to America. Now that we know the gang are here I don't see how they can escape. We have the news at every seaport already, and a reward will be offered before evening. What beats me is how they could have done so mad a thing, knowing that the lady would describe them, and that we could not fail to recognize the description."

"Exactly. One would have expected that they would have silenced Lady Brackenstall as well."

"They may not have realized," I suggested, "that she had recovered from her faint."

"That is likely enough. If she seemed to be senseless they would not take her life. What about this poor fellow, Hopkins? I seem to have heard some queer stories about him."

"He was a good-hearted man when he was sober, but a perfect fiend when he was drunk, or rather when he was half drunk, for he seldom really went the whole way. The devil seemed to be in him at such times, and he was capable of anything. From what I hear, in spite of all his wealth and his title, he very nearly came our way once or twice. There was a scandal about his drenching a dog with petroleum and setting it on fire—her ladyship's dog, to make the matter worse—and that was only hushed up with difficulty. Then he threw a decanter at that maid Theresa Wright; there was trouble about that. On the whole, and between ourselves, it will be a brighter house without him. What are you looking at now?"

Holmes was down on his knees examining with great attention the knots upon the red cord with which the lady had been secured. Then he carefully scrutinized the broken and frayed end where it had snapped off when the burglar had dragged it down.

" When this was pulled down the bell in the kitchen must have rung loudly," he remarked.

" No one could hear it. The kitchen stands right at the back of the house."

" How did the burglar know no one would hear it ? How dare he pull at a bell-rope in that reckless fashion ? "

" Exactly, Mr. Holmes, exactly. You put the very question which I have asked myself again and again. There can be no doubt that this fellow must have known the house and its habits. He must have perfectly understood that the servants would all be in bed at that comparatively early hour, and that no one could possibly hear a bell ring in the kitchen. Therefore he must have been in close league with one of the servants. Surely that is evident. But there are eight servants, and all of good character."

" Other things being equal," said Holmes, " one would suspect the one at whose head the master threw a decanter. And yet that would involve treachery towards the mistress to whom this woman seems devoted. Well, well, the point is a minor one, and when you have Randall you will probably find no difficulty in securing his accomplices. The lady's story certainly seems to be corroborated, if it needed corroboration, by every detail which we see before us." He walked to the French window and threw it open. " There are no signs here, but the ground is iron hard, and one would not expect them. I see that these candles on the mantelpiece have been lighted."

" Yes, it was by their light and that of the lady's bedroom candle that the burglars saw their way about."

" And what did they take ? "

" Well, they did not take much—only half a dozen

articles of plate off the sideboard. Lady Brackenstall thinks that they were themselves so disturbed by the death of Sir Eustace that they did not ransack the house as they would otherwise have done."

" No doubt that is true. And yet they drank some wine, I understand."

" To steady their own nerves."

" Exactly. These three glasses upon the sideboard have been untouched, I suppose ? "

" Yes ; and the bottle stands as they left it."

" Let us look at it. Halloa, halloa ! what is this ? "

The three glasses were grouped together, all of them tinged with wine, and one of them containing some dregs of beeswing. The bottle stood near them, two-thirds full, and beside it lay a long, deeply stained cork. Its appearance and the dust upon the bottle showed that it was no common vintage which the murderers had enjoyed.

A change had come over Holmes' manner. He had lost his listless expression, and again I saw an alert light of interest in his keen deep-set eyes. He raised the cork and examined it minutely.

" How did they draw it ? " he asked.

Hopkins pointed to a half-opened drawer. In it lay some table linen and a large corkscrew.

" Did Lady Brackenstall say that screw was used ? "

" No ; you remember that she was senseless at the moment when the bottle was opened."

" Quite so. As a matter of fact, that screw was *not* used. This bottle was opened by a pocket-screw, probably contained in a knife, and not more than an inch and a half long. If you examine the top of the cork you will observe that the screw was driven in three times before the cork was extracted. It has never been transfixed. This long screw would have transfixed it and drawn it with a single pull. When you catch this fellow you will find that he has one of these multiplex knives in his possession."

" Excellent ! " said Hopkins.

" But these glasses do puzzle me, I confess. Lady Brackenstall actually *saw* the three men drinking, did she not ? "

" Yes ; she was clear about that."

" Then there is an end of it. What more is to be said ? And yet you must admit that the three glasses are very remarkable, Hopkins. What, you see nothing remarkable ! Well, well, let it pass. Perhaps when a man has special knowledge and special powers like my own it rather encourages him to seek a complex explanation when a simpler one is at hand. Of course, it must be a mere chance about the glasses. Well, good morning, Hopkins. I don't see that I can be of any use to you, and you appear to have your case very clear. You will let me know when Randall is arrested, and any further developments which may occur. I trust that I shall soon have to congratulate you upon a successful conclusion. Come, Watson, I fancy that we may employ ourselves more profitably at home."

During our return journey I could see by Holmes' face that he was much puzzled by something which he had observed. Every now and then, by an effort, he would throw off the impression and talk as if the matter were clear, but then his doubts would settle down upon him again, and his knitted brows and abstracted eyes would show that his thoughts had gone back once more to the great dining-room of the Abbey Grange in which this midnight tragedy had been enacted. At last, by a sudden impulse, just as our train was crawling out of a suburban station, he sprang on to the platform and pulled me out after him.

" Excuse me, my dear fellow," said he, as we watched the rear carriages of our train disappearing round a curve ; " I am sorry to make you the victim of what may seem a mere whim, but on my life, Watson, I simply *can't* leave that case in this condition. Every instinct that I possess cries out against it. It's wrong—it's all wrong—I'll swear that it's wrong. And yet the lady's story was complete, the maid's corroboration was sufficient, the detail was fairly exact. What have I to put against that? Three wine-glasses, that is all. But if I had not taken things for granted, if I had examined everything with the care which I would have shown had we approached the case *de novo* and had no cut-and-dried story to warp my mind, would I not then have found something more definite to go upon? Of course I should. Sit down on this bench, Watson, until a train for Chislehurst arrives, and allow me to lay the evidence before you, imploring you in the first instance to dismiss from your mind the idea that anything which the maid or mistress may have said must necessarily be true. The lady's charming personality must not be permitted to warp our judgment.

" Surely there are details in her story which, if we look at it in cold blood, would excite our suspicion. These burglars made a considerable haul at Sydenham a fortnight ago. Some account of them and their appearance was in the papers, and would naturally occur to anyone who wished to invent a story in which imaginary robbers should play a part. As a matter of fact, burglars who have done a good stroke of business are, as a rule, only too glad to enjoy the proceeds in peace and quiet without embarking on another perilous undertaking. Again, it is unusual for burglars to operate at so early an hour ; it is unusual for burglars to strike a lady to prevent her screaming, since one would imagine that was the sure way to make her scream ; it is unusual for them to commit murder when their numbers are sufficient to overpower one man ; it is unusual for them to be content with a limited plunder when there is much more within their reach ; and, finally, I should say that it was very unusual for such men to leave a bottle half empty. How do all these unusuals strike you, Watson ? "

" Their cumulative effect is certainly considerable, and yet each of them is quite possible in itself. The most unusual thing of all, as it seems to me, is that the lady should be tied to the chair."

" Well, I am not so sure about that, Watson, for it is evident that they must either kill her or else secure her in such a way that she could not give immediate notice of their escape. But at any rate I have shown, have I not, that there is a certain element of improbability about the lady's story ? And now on the top of this comes the incident of the wine-glasses."

" What about the wine-glasses ? "

" Can you see them in your mind's eye ? "

" I see them clearly."

" We are told that three men drank from them. Does that strike you as likely ? "

" Why not ? There was wine in each glass."

" Exactly ; but there was beeswing only in one glass. You must have noticed that fact. What does that suggest to your mind ? "

" The last glass filled would be most likely to contain beeswing."

" Not at all. The bottle was full of it, and it is inconceivable that the first two glasses were clear and the third heavily charged with it. There are two possible explanations, and only two. One is that after the second glass was filled the bottle was violently agitated, and so the third glass received the beeswing. That does not appear probable. No, no ; I am sure that I am right."

" What, then, do you suppose ? "

" That only two glasses were used, and that the dregs of both were poured into a third glass, so as to give the false impression that three people had been there. In that way all the beeswing would be in the last glass, would it not ? Yes, I am convinced that this is so. But if I have hit upon the true explanation of this one small phenomenon, then in an instant the case rises from the commonplace to the exceedingly remarkable, for it can only mean that Lady Brackenstall and her maid have deliberately lied to us, that not one word of their story is to be believed, that they have some very strong reason for covering the real criminal, and that we must construct our case for ourselves without any help from them. That is the mission which now lies before us, and here, Watson, is the Chislehurst train."

The household of the Abbey Grange were much surprised at our return, but Sherlock Holmes, finding that Stanley Hopkins had gone off to report to headquarters, took possession of the dining-room, locked the door upon the inside and devoted himself for two hours to one of those minute and laborious investigations which formed the solid basis on which his brilliant edifices of deduction were reared. Seated in a corner like an interested student who observes the demonstration of his professor, I followed every step of that remarkable research. The window, the curtains, the carpet, the chair, the rope—each in turn was minutely examined and duly pondered. The body of the unfortunate baronet had been removed, but all else remained as we had seen it in the morning. Then, to my astonishment, Holmes climbed up on to the massive mantelpiece. Far above his head hung the few inches of red cord which were still attached to the wire. For a long time he gazed upwards at it, and then in an attempt to get nearer to it he rested his knee upon a wooden bracket on the wall. This brought his hand within a few inches of the broken end of the rope ; but it was not this so much as the bracket itself which seemed to engage his attention. Finally he sprang down with an ejaculation of satisfaction.

" It's all right, Watson," said he. " We have got our case—one of the most remarkable in our collection. But, dear me, how slow-witted I have been, and how nearly I have committed the blunder of my lifetime ! Now, I think that with a few missing links my chain is almost complete."

" You have got your men ? "

" Man, Watson, man. Only one, but a very formidable person. Strong as a lion—witness the blow which bent that poker. Six foot three in height, active as a squirrel, dexterous with his fingers ; finally, remarkably quick-witted, for this whole ingenious story is of his concoction. Yes, Watson, we have come upon the handiwork of a very remarkable individual. And yet in that bell-rope he has given us a clue which should not have left us a doubt."

" Where was the clue ? "

" Well, if you were to pull down a bell-rope, Watson, where would you expect it to break ? Surely at the spot where it is attached to the wire. Why should it break three inches from the top as this one has done ? "

" Because it is frayed there ? "

" Exactly. This end, which we can examine, is frayed. He was cunning enough to do that with his knife. But the other end is not frayed. You could not observe that from here, but if you were on the mantelpiece you would see that it is cut clean off without any mark of fraying whatever. You can reconstruct what occurred. The man needed the rope. He would not tear it down for fear of giving the alarm by ringing the bell. What did he do ? He sprang up on the mantelpiece, could not quite reach it, put his knee on the bracket—you will see the impression in the dust—and got his knife to bear upon the cord. I could not reach the place by at least three inches, from which I infer that he is at least three inches a bigger man than I. Look at that mark upon the seat of the oaken chair ! What is it ? "

" Blood."

" Undoubtedly it is blood. This alone puts the lady's story out of court. If she were seated on the chair when the crime was done, how comes that mark ? No, no ; she was placed in the chair *after* the death of her husband. I'll wager that the black dress shows a corresponding mark to this. We have not yet met our Waterloo, Watson, but this is our Marengo, for it begins in defeat and ends in victory. I should like now to have a few words with the nurse Theresa. We must be wary for a while, if we are to get the information which we want."

She was an interesting person, this stern Australian nurse. Taciturn, suspicious, ungracious, it took some time before Holmes' pleasant manner and frank acceptance of all that she said thawed her into a corresponding amiability. She did not attempt to conceal her hatred for her late employer.

"Yes, sir, it is true that he threw the decanter at me. I heard him call my mistress a name, and I told him that he would not dare to speak so if her brother had been there. Then it was that he threw it at me. He might have thrown a dozen if he had but left my bonny bird alone. He was for ever ill-treating her, and she was too proud to complain. She will not even tell me all that he has done to her. She never told me of those marks on her arm that you saw this morning, but I know very well that they come from a stab with a hat-pin. The sly fiend—Heaven forgive me that I should speak of him so, now that he is dead, but a fiend he was if ever one walked the earth. He was all honey when first we met him, only eighteen months ago, and we both feel as if it were eighteen years. She had only just arrived in London. Yes, it was her first voyage—she had never been from home before. He won her with his title and his money and his false London ways. If she made a mistake she has paid for it, if ever a woman did. What month did we meet him? Well, I tell you it was just after we arrived. We arrived in June, and it was July. They were married in January of last year. Yes, she is down in the morning-room again, and I have no doubt she will see you, but you must not ask too much of her, for she has gone through all that flesh and blood will stand."

Lady Brackenstall was reclining on the same couch, but looked brighter than before. The maid had entered with us, and began once more to foment the bruise upon her mistress's brow.

"I hope," said the lady, "that you have not come to cross-examine me again?"

" No," Holmes answered, in his gentlest voice, " I will not cause you any unnecessary trouble, Lady Brackenstall, and my whole desire is to make things easy for you, for I am convinced that you are a much-tried woman. If you will treat me as a friend and trust me, you may find that I will justify your trust."

" What do you want me to do ? "

" To tell me the truth."

" Mr. Holmes ! "

" No, no, Lady Brackenstall, it is no use. You may have heard of any little reputation which I possess. I will stake it all on the fact that your story is an absolute fabrication."

Mistress and maid were both staring at Holmes with pale faces and frightened eyes.

" You are an impudent fellow ! " cried Theresa. " Do you mean to say that my mistress has told a lie ? "

Holmes rose from his chair.

" Have you nothing to tell me ? "

" I have told you everything."

" Think once more, Lady Brackenstall. Would it not be better to be frank ? "

For an instant there was hesitation in her beautiful face. Then some new strong thought caused it to set like a mask.

" I have told you all I know."

Holmes took his hat and shrugged his shoulders. " I am sorry," he said, and without another word we left the room and the house. There was a pond in the park, and to this my friend led the way. It was frozen over, but a single hole was left for the convenience of a solitary swan. Holmes gazed at it, and then passed on to the lodge gate. There he scribbled a short note for Stanley Hopkins, and left it with the lodge-keeper.

" It may be a hit, or it may be a miss, but we are bound to do something for friend Hopkins, just to justify this second visit," said he. " I will not quite take him into my confidence yet. I think our next scene of operations

850

must be the shipping office of the Adelaide-Southampton line, which stands at the end of Pall Mall, if I remember right. There is a second line of steamers which connect South Australia with England, but we will draw the larger cover first."

Holmes' card sent in to the manager ensured instant attention, and he was not long in acquiring all the information which he needed. In June of '95 only one of their line had reached a home port. It was the *Rock of Gibraltar*, their largest and best boat. A reference to the passenger list showed that Miss Fraser of Adelaide, with her maid, had made the voyage in her. The boat was now on her way to Australia, somewhere to the south of the Suez Canal. Her officers were the same as in '95, with one exception. The first officer, Mr. Jack Croker, had been made a captain, and was to take charge of their new ship, the *Bass Rock*, sailing in two days' time from Southampton. He lived at Sydenham, but he was likely to be in that morning for instructions, if we cared to wait for him.

No; Mr. Holmes had no desire to see him, but would be glad to know more about his record and character.

His record was magnificent. There was not an officer in the fleet to touch him. As to his character, he was reliable on duty, but a wild, desperate fellow off the deck of his ship, hot-headed, excitable, but loyal, honest, and kind-hearted. That was the pith of the information with which Holmes left the office of the Adelaide-Southampton Company. Thence he drove to Scotland Yard, but instead of entering he sat in his cab, with his brows drawn down, lost in profound thought. Finally he drove round to the Charing Cross telegraph office, sent off a message, and then, at last, we made for Baker Street once more.

"No, I couldn't do it, Watson," said he, as we re-entered our room. "Once that warrant was made out nothing on earth would save him. Once or twice in my career I feel that I have done more real harm by my discovery of the criminal than ever he had done by his crime. I have learned caution now, and I had rather play tricks with the law of England than with my own conscience. Let us know a little more before we act."

Before evening we had a visit from Inspector Stanley Hopkins. Things were not going very well with him.

"I believe that you are a wizard, Mr. Holmes. I really do sometimes think that you have powers that are not human. Now, how on earth could you know that the stolen silver was at the bottom of that pond?"

"I didn't know it."

"But you told me to examine it."

"You got it then?"

"Yes, I got it."

"I am very glad if I have helped you."

"But you haven't helped me. You have made the affair far more difficult. What sort of burglars are they who steal silver and then throw it into the nearest pond?"

"It was certainly rather eccentric behaviour. I was merely going on the idea that if the silver had been taken by persons who did not want it, who merely took it for a blind, as it were, then they would naturally be anxious to get rid of it."

"But why should such an idea cross your mind?"

"Well, I thought it was possible. When they came out through the French window there was the pond, with one tempting little hole in the ice right in front of their noses. Could there be a better hiding-place?"

"Ah, a hiding-place—that is better!" cried Stanley Hopkins. "Yes, yes, I see it all now! It was early, there were folk upon the roads, they were afraid of being seen with the silver, so they sank it in the pond, intending to return for it when the coast was clear. Excellent, Mr. Holmes—that is better than your idea of a blind."

"Quite so; you have got an admirable theory. I have no doubt that my own ideas were quite wild, but you must admit that they have ended in discovering the silver."

"Yes, sir; yes. It was all your doing. But I have had a bad set-back."

"A set-back?"

"Yes, Mr. Holmes. The Randall gang were arrested in New York this morning."

"Dear me, Hopkins. That is certainly rather against your theory that they committed a murder in Kent last night."

"It is fatal, Mr. Holmes, absolutely fatal. Still, there are other gangs of three besides the Randalls, or it may be some new gang of which the police have never heard."

"Quite so; it is perfectly possible. What, are you off?"

"Yes, Mr. Holmes; there is no rest for me until I have got to the bottom of the business. I suppose you have no hint to give me?"

"I have given you one."

"Which?"

"Well, I suggested a blind."

"But why, Mr. Holmes, why!"

"Ah, that's the question, of course. But I commend the idea to your mind. You might possibly find that there was something in it. You won't stop for dinner? Well, good-bye, and let us know how you get on."

Dinner was over and the table cleared before Holmes alluded to the matter again. He had lit his pipe, and held his slippered feet to the cheerful blaze of the fire. Suddenly he looked at his watch.

"I expect developments, Watson."

"When?"

"Now—within a few minutes. I dare say you thought I acted rather badly to Stanley Hopkins just now?"

"I trust your judgment."

"A very sensible reply, Watson. You must look at it this way: what I know is unofficial; what he knows is official. I have the right to private judgment, but he has none. He must disclose all, or he is a traitor to his service. In a doubtful case I would not put him in so painful a position, and so I reserve my information until my own mind is clear upon the matter."

" But when will that be ? "

" The time has come. You will now be present at the last scene of a remarkable little drama."

There was a sound upon the stairs, and our door was opened to admit as fine a specimen of manhood as ever passed through it. He was a very tall young man, golden-moustached, blue-eyed, with a skin which had been burned by tropical suns, and a springy step which showed that the huge frame was as active as it was strong. He closed the door behind him, and then he stood with clenched hands and heaving breast, choking down some overmastering emotion.

" Sit down, Captain Croker. You got my telegram ? "

Our visitor sank into an arm-chair and looked from one to the other of us with questioning eyes.

" I got your telegram, and I came at the hour you said. I heard that you had been down to the office. There was no getting away from you. Let's hear the worst. What are you going to do with me ? Arrest me ? Speak out, man ! You can't sit there and play with me like a cat with a mouse."

" Give him a cigar," said Holmes. " Bite on that, Captain Croker, and don't let your nerves run away with you. I should not sit here smoking with you if I thought that you were a common criminal, you may be sure of that. Be frank with me, and we may do some good. Play tricks with me, and I'll crush you."

" What do you wish me to do ? "

" To give me a true account of all that happened at the Abbey Grange last night—a *true* account, mind you, with nothing added and nothing taken off. I know so much already that if you go one inch off the straight I'll blow this police whistle from my window and the affair goes out of my hands for ever."

The sailor thought for a little. Then he struck his leg with his great sunburnt hand.

" I'll chance it," he cried. " I believe you are a man of your word, and a white man, and I'll tell you the whole story. But one thing I will say first. So far as I am concerned, I regret nothing and I fear nothing, and I would do it all again and be proud of the job. Curse the beast—if he had as many lives as a cat he would owe them all to me ! But it's the lady, Mary—Mary Fraser—for never will I call her by that accursed name. When I think of getting her into trouble, I who would give my life just to bring one smile to her dear face, it's that that turns my soul into water. And yet—and yet—what less could I do ? I'll tell you my story, gentlemen, and then I'll ask you as man to man what less could I do.

" I must go back a bit. You seem to know everything, so I expect that you know that I met her when she was a passenger and I was first officer of the *Rock of Gibraltar*. From the first day I met her she was the only woman to me. Every day of that voyage I loved her more, and many a time since have I kneeled down in the darkness of the night watch and kissed the deck of that ship because I knew her dear feet had trod it. She was never engaged to me. She treated me as fairly as ever a woman treated a man. I have no complaint to make. It was all love on my side, and all good comradeship and friendship on hers. When we parted she was a free woman, but I could never again be a free man.

" Next time I came back from sea I heard of her marriage. Well, why shouldn't she marry whom she liked ? Title and money—who could carry them better than she ? She was born for all that is beautiful and dainty. I didn't grieve over her marriage. I was not such a selfish hound as that. I just rejoiced that good luck had come her way, and that she had not thrown herself away on a penniless sailor. That's how I loved Mary Fraser.

" Well, I never thought to see her again ; but last voyage I was promoted, and the new boat was not yet launched, so I had to wait for a couple of months with my people at Sydenham. One day out in a country lane I met Theresa Wright, her old maid. She told me about her, about him, about everything. I tell you, gentlemen, it nearly drove me mad. This drunken hound, that he should dare to raise his hand to her whose boots he was not worthy to lick! I met Theresa again. Then I met Mary herself—and met her again. Then she would meet me no more. But the other day I had a notice that I was to start on my voyage within a week, and I determined that I would see her once before I left. Theresa was always my friend, for she loved Mary and hated this villain almost as much as I did. From her I learned the ways of the house. Mary used to sit up reading in her own little room downstairs. I crept round there last night and scratched at the window. At first she would not open to me, but in her heart I know that now she loves me, and she could not leave me in the frosty night. She whispered to me to come round to the big front window, and I found it open before me so as to let me into the dining-room. Again I heard from her own lips things that made my blood boil, and again I cursed this brute who mishandled the woman that I loved. Well, gentlemen, I was standing with her just inside the window, in all innocence, as Heaven is my judge, when he rushed like a madman into the room, called her the vilest name that a man could use to a woman, and welted her across the face with the stick he had in his hand. I had sprung for the poker, and it was a fair fight between us. See here on my arm where his first blow fell. Then it was my turn, and I went through him as if he had been a rotten pumpkin. Do you think I was sorry? Not I! It was his life or mine; but far more than that—it was his life or hers, for how could I leave her in the power of this madman? That was how I killed him. Was I wrong? Well, then, what would either of you gentlemen have done if you had been in my position?

" She had screamed when he struck her, and that brought old Theresa down from the room above. There was a bottle of wine on the sideboard, and I opened it and poured a little between Mary's lips, for she was half dead with the shock. Then I took a drop myself. Theresa was as cool as ice, and it was her plot as much as mine. We must make it appear that burglars had done the thing. Theresa kept on repeating our story to her mistress, while I swarmed up and cut the rope of the bell. Then I lashed her in her chair, and frayed out the end of the rope to make it look natural, else they would wonder how in the world a burglar could have got up there to cut it. Then I gathered up a few plates and pots of silver, to carry out the idea of a robbery, and there I left them, with orders to give the alarm when I had a quarter of an hour's start. I dropped the silver into the pond and made off for Sydenham, feeling that for once in my life I had done a real good night's work. And that's the truth and the whole truth, Mr. Holmes, if it costs me my neck."

Holmes smoked for some time in silence. Then he crossed the room and shook our visitor by the hand.

" That's what I think," said he. " I know that every word is true, for you have hardly said a word which I did not know. No one but an acrobat or a sailor could have got up to that bell-rope from the bracket, and no one but a sailor could have made the knots with which the cord was fastened to the chair. Only once had this lady been brought into contact with sailors, and that was on her voyage, and it was someone of her own class of life, since she was trying hard to shield him and so showing that she loved him. You see how easy it was for me to lay my hands upon you when once I had started upon the right trail."

" I thought the police never could have seen through our dodge."

" And the police haven't ; nor will they, to the best of my belief. Now, look here, Captain Croker, this is a very serious matter, though I am willing to admit that you acted under the most extreme provocation to which any man could be subjected. I am not sure that in defence of your own life your action will not be pronounced legitimate. However, that is for a British jury to decide. Meanwhile I have so much sympathy for you that if you choose to disappear in the next twenty-four hours I will promise you that no one will hinder you."

" And then it will all come out ? "

" Certainly it will come out."

The sailor flushed with anger.

" What sort of proposal is that to make to a man ? I know enough of law to understand that Mary would be had as accomplice. Do you think I would leave her alone to face the music while I slunk away ? No, sir ; let them do their worst upon me, but for Heaven's sake, Mr. Holmes, find some way of keeping my poor Mary out of the courts."

Holmes for the second time held out his hand to the sailor.

" I was only testing you, and you ring true every time. Well, it is a great responsibility that I take upon myself, but I have given Hopkins an excellent hint, and if he can't avail himself of it I can do no more. See here, Captain Croker, we'll do this in due form of law. You are the prisoner. Watson, you are a British jury, and I never met a man who was more eminently fitted to represent one. I am the judge. Now, gentlemen of the jury, you have heard the evidence. Do you find the prisoner guilty or not guilty ? "

" Not guilty, my lord," said I.

" *Vox populi, vox Dei*. You are acquitted, Captain Croker. So long as the law does not find some other victim, you are safe from me. Come back to this lady in a year, and may her future and yours justify us in the judgment which we have pronounced this night."

858

36. *The Second Stain*

I HAD intended the " Adventure of the Abbey Grange " to be the last of those exploits of my friend, Mr. Sherlock Holmes, which I should ever communicate to the public. This resolution of mine was not due to any lack of material, since I have notes of many hundreds of cases to which I have never alluded, nor was it caused by any waning interest on the part of my readers in the singular personality and unique methods of this remarkable man. The real reason lay in the reluctance which Mr. Holmes has shown to the continued publication of his experiences. So long as he was in actual professional practice the records of his successes were of some practical value to him ; but since he has definitely retired from London and betaken himself to study and bee-farming on the Sussex Downs, notoriety has become hateful to him, and he has peremptorily requested that his wishes in this matter should be strictly observed. It was only upon my representing to him that I had given a promise that " The Adventure of the Second Stain " should be published when the time was ripe, and pointed out to him that it was only appropriate that this long series of episodes should culminate in the most important international case which he has ever been called upon to handle, that I at last succeeded in obtaining his consent that a carefully guarded account of the incident should at last be laid before the public. If in telling the story I seem to be somewhat vague in certain details the public will readily understand that there is an excellent reason for my reticence.

It was, then, in a year, and even in a decade, that shall be nameless, that upon one Tuesday morning in autumn we found two visitors of European fame within the walls of our humble room in Baker Street. The one, austere, high-nosed, eagle-eyed, and dominant, was none other than the illustrious Lord Bellinger, twice Premier of Britain. The other, dark, clear-cut, and elegant, hardly yet of middle age, and endowed with every beauty of body and of mind, was the Right Honourable Trelawney Hope, Secretary for European Affairs, and the most rising statesman in the country. They sat side by side upon our paper-littered settee, and it was easy to see from their worn and anxious faces that it was business of the most pressing importance which had brought them. The Premier's thin, blue-veined hands were clasped tightly over the ivory head of his umbrella, and his gaunt, ascetic face looked gloomily from Holmes to me. The European Secretary pulled nervously at his moustache and fidgeted with the seals of his watch-chain.

"When I discovered my loss, Mr. Holmes, which was at eight o'clock this morning, I at once informed the Prime Minister. It was at his suggestion that we have both come to you."

"Have you informed the police?"

"No, sir," said the Prime Minister, with the quick, decisive manner for which he was famous. "We have not done so, nor is it possible that we should do so. To inform the police must, in the long run, mean to inform the public. This is what we particularly desire to avoid."

"And why, sir?"

"Because the document in question is of such immense importance that its publication might very easily—I might almost say probably—lead to European complications of the utmost moment. It is not too much to say that peace or war may hang upon the issue. Unless its recovery can be attended with the utmost secrecy, then it may as well not be recovered at all, for all that is aimed at by those who have taken it is that its contents should be generally known."

"I understand. Now, Mr. Trelawney Hope, I should be much obliged if you would tell me exactly the circumstances under which this document disappeared."

" That can be done in a very few words, Mr. Holmes. The letter—for it was a letter from a foreign potentate— was received six days ago. It was of such importance that I have never left it in my safe, but I have taken it across each evening to my house in Whitehall Terrace, and kept it in my bedroom in a locked dispatch-box. It was there last night. Of that I am certain. I actually opened the box while I was dressing for dinner, and saw the document inside. This morning it was gone. The dispatch-box had stood beside the glass upon my dressing-table all night. I am a light sleeper, and so is my wife. We are both prepared to swear that no one could have entered the room during the night. And yet I repeat that the paper is gone."

" What time did you dine ? "

" Half-past seven."

" How long was it before you went to bed ? "

" My wife had gone to the theatre. I waited up for her. It was half-past eleven before we went to our room."

" Then for four hours the dispatch-box had lain unguarded ? "

" No one is ever permitted to enter that room save the housemaid in the morning, and my valet, or my wife's maid, during the rest of the day. They are both trusty servants who have been with us for some time. Besides, neither of them could possibly have known that there was anything more valuable than the ordinary departmental papers in my dispatch-box."

" Who did know of the existence of that letter ? "

" No one in the house."

" Surely your wife knew ? "

" No, sir ; I had said nothing to my wife until I missed the paper this morning."

The Premier nodded approvingly.

" I have long known, sir, how high is your sense of

861

public duty," said he. " I am convinced that in the case of a secret of this importance it would rise superior to the most intimate domestic ties."

The European Secretary bowed.

" You do me no more than justice, sir. Until this morning I have never breathed one word to my wife upon this matter."

" Could she have guessed ? "

" No, Mr. Holmes, she could not have guessed—nor could anyone have guessed."

" Have you lost any documents before ? "

" No, sir."

" Who is there in England who did know of the existence of this letter ? "

" Each member of the Cabinet was informed of it yesterday ; but the pledge of secrecy which attends every Cabinet meeting was increased by the solemn warning which was given by the Prime Minister. Good heavens, to think that within a few hours I should myself have lost it ! " His handsome face was distorted with a spasm of despair, and his hands tore at his hair. For a moment we caught a glimpse of the natural man— impulsive, ardent, keenly sensitive. The next the aristocratic mask was replaced, and the gentle voice had returned. " Besides the members of the Cabinet there are two, or possibly three, departmental officials who know of the letter. No one else in England, Mr. Holmes, I assure you."

" But abroad ? "

" I believe that no one abroad has seen it save the man who wrote it. I am well convinced that his ministers —that the usual official channels have not been employed."

Holmes considered for some little time.

" Now, sir, I must ask you more particularly what this document is, and why its disappearance should have such momentous consequences ? "

The two statesmen exchanged a quick glance, and the Premier's shaggy eyebrows gathered in a frown.

" Mr. Holmes, the envelope is a long, thin one of pale blue colour. There is a seal of red wax stamped with a crouching lion. It is addressed in large, bold hand-writing to——"

" I fear," said Holmes, " that, interesting and indeed essential as these details are, my inquiries must go more to the root of things. What *was* the letter ? "

" That is a State secret of the utmost importance, and I fear that I cannot tell you, nor do I see that it is necessary. If by the aid of the powers which you are said to possess you can find such an envelope as I describe with its enclosure, you will have deserved well of your country, and earned any reward which it lies in our power to bestow."

Sherlock Holmes rose with a smile.

" You are two of the most busy men in the country," said he, " and in my own small way I have also a good many calls upon me. I regret exceedingly that I cannot help you in this matter, and any continuation of this interview would be a waste of time."

The Premier sprang to his feet with that quick, fierce gleam of his deep-set eyes before which a Cabinet had cowered. " I am not accustomed——" he began, but mastered his anger and resumed his seat. For a minute or more we all sat in silence. Then the old statesman shrugged his shoulders.

" We must accept your terms, Mr. Holmes. No doubt you are right, and it is unreasonable for us to expect you to act unless we give you our entire confidence."

" I agree with you, sir," said the younger statesman.

" Then I will tell you, relying entirely upon your hon-our and that of your colleague, Dr. Watson. I may appeal to your patriotism also, for I could not imagine a greater misfortune for the country than that this affair should come out."

" You may safely trust us."

" The letter, then, is from a certain foreign potentate who has been ruffled by some recent colonial developments of this country. It has been written hurriedly and upon his own responsibility entirely. Inquiries have shown that his ministers know nothing of the matter. At the same time it is couched in so unfortunate a manner, and certain phrases in it are of so provocative a character, that its publication would undoubtedly lead to a most dangerous state of feeling in this country. There would be such a ferment, sir, that I do not hesitate to say that within a week of the publication of that letter this country would be involved in a great war."

Holmes wrote a name upon a slip of paper and handed it to the Premier.

"Exactly. It was he. And it is this letter—this letter which may well mean the expenditure of a thousand millions and the lives of a hundred thousand men—which has become lost in this unaccountable fashion."

"Have you informed the sender?"

"Yes, sir, a cipher telegram has been despatched."

"Perhaps he desires the publication of the letter."

"No, sir, we have strong reason to believe that he already understands that he has acted in an indiscreet and hot-headed manner. It would be a greater blow to him and to his country than to us if this letter were to come out."

"If this is so, whose interest is it that the letter should come out? Why should anyone desire to steal it or to publish it?"

"There, Mr. Holmes, you take me into regions of high international politics. But if you consider the European situation you will have no difficulty in perceiving the motive. The whole of Europe is an armed camp. There is a double league which makes a fair balance of military power. Great Britain holds the scales. If Britain were driven into war with one confederacy, it would assure the supremacy of the other confederacy, whether they joined in the war or not. Do you follow?"

"Very clearly. It is then the interest of the enemies of this potentate to secure and publish this letter, so as to make a breach between his country and ours?"

"Yes, sir."

"And to whom would this document be sent if it fell into the hands of an enemy?"

"To any of the great Chancelleries of Europe. It is probably speeding on its way thither at the present instant as fast as steam can take it."

Mr. Trelawney Hope dropped his head on his chest and groaned aloud. The Premier placed his hand kindly upon his shoulder.

"It is your misfortune, my dear fellow. No one can blame you. There is no precaution which you have neglected. Now, Mr. Holmes, you are in full possession of the facts. What course do you recommend?"

Holmes shook his head mournfully.

"You think, sir, that unless this document is recovered there will be war?"

"I think it is very probable."

"Then, sir, prepare for war."

"That is a hard saying, Mr. Holmes."

"Consider the facts, sir. It is inconceivable that it was taken after eleven-thirty at night, since I understand that Mr. Hope and his wife were both in the room from that hour until the loss was found out. It was taken, then, yesterday evening between seven-thirty and eleven-thirty, probably near the earlier hour, since whoever took it evidently knew that it was there, and would naturally secure it as early as possible. Now, sir, if a document of this importance were taken at that hour, where can it be now? No one has any reason to retain it. It has been passed rapidly on to those who need it. What chance have we now to overtake or even to trace it? It is beyond our reach."

The Prime Minister rose from the settee.

"What you say is perfectly logical, Mr. Holmes. I feel that the matter is indeed out of our hands."

" Let us presume, for argument's sake, that the document was taken by the maid or by the valet——"

" They are both old and tried servants."

" I understand you to say that your room is on the second floor, that there is no entrance from without, and that from within no one could go up unobserved. It must, then, be somebody in the house who has taken it. To whom would the thief take it? To one of several international spies and secret agents, whose names are tolerably familiar to me. There are three who may be said to be the heads of their profession. I will begin my research by going round and finding if each of them is at his post. If one is missing—especially if he has disappeared since last night—we will have some indication as to where the document has gone."

" Why should he be missing? " asked the European Secretary. " He would take the letter to an Embassy in London, as likely as not."

" I fancy not. These agents work independently, and their relations with the Embassies are often strained."

The Prime Minister nodded his acquiescence.

" I believe you are right, Mr. Holmes. He would take so valuable a prize to headquarters with his own hands. I think that your course of action is an excellent one. Meanwhile, Hope, we cannot neglect our other duties on account of this one misfortune. Should there be any fresh developments during the day we shall communicate with you, and you will no doubt let us know the results of your own inquiries."

The two statesmen bowed and walked gravely from the room.

When our illustrious visitors had departed, Holmes lit his pipe in silence, and sat for some time lost in the deepest thought. I had opened the morning paper and was immersed in a sensational crime which had occurred in London the night before, when my friend gave an exclamation, sprang to his feet, and laid his pipe down upon the mantelpiece.

"Yes," said he, " there is no better way of approaching it. The situation is desperate, but not hopeless. Even now, if we could be sure which of them has taken it, it is just possible that it has not yet passed out of his hands. After all, it is a question of money with these fellows, and I have the British Treasury behind me. If it's on the market I'll buy it—if it means another penny on the income tax. It is conceivable that the fellow might hold it back to see what bids come from this side before he tries his luck on the other. There are only those three capable of playing so bold a game ; there are Oberstein, La Rothiere, and Eduardo Lucas. I will see each of them."

I glanced at my morning paper.

" Is that Eduardo Lucas of Godolphin Street ? "

" Yes."

" You will not see him."

" Why not ? "

" He was murdered in his house last night."

My friend has so often astonished me in the course of our adventures that it was with a sense of exultation that I realized how completely I had astonished him. He stared in amazement, and then snatched the paper from my hands. This was the paragraph which I had been engaged in reading when he rose from his chair :

MURDER IN WESTMINSTER.

A crime of a mysterious character was committed last night at 16 Godolphin Street, one of the old-fashioned and secluded rows of eighteenth-century houses which lie between the river and the Abbey, almost in the shadow of the great tower of the Houses of Parliament. This small but select mansion has been inhabited for some years by Mr. Eduardo Lucas, well known in society circles both on account of his charming personality and because he has the well-deserved reputation of being one of the best amateur tenors in the country. Mr. Lucas is an unmarried man, thirty-four years of age, and his establishment consists of Mrs. Pringle, an elderly housekeeper, and of Mitton, his valet. The former retires early and sleeps at the top of the house. The valet was out for the evening, visiting a friend at Hammersmith. From ten o'clock onwards Mr. Lucas had the house to himself. What occurred during that time has not yet transpired, but at a quarter to twelve Police-constable Barrett, passing along Godolphin Street, observed that the door of No. 16 was ajar. He knocked, but received no answer. Perceiving a light in the front room he advanced into the passage and again knocked, but without reply. He then pushed open the door and entered. The room was in a state of wild disorder, the furniture being all swept to one side, and one chair lying on its back in the centre. Beside this chair, and still grasping one of its legs, lay the unfortunate tenant of the house. He had been stabbed to the heart, and must have died instantly. The knife with which the crime had been committed was a curved Indian dagger, plucked down from a trophy of Oriental arms which adorned one of the walls. Robbery does not appear to have been the motive of the crime, for there had been no attempt to remove the valuable contents of the room. Mr. Eduardo Lucas was so well known and popular that his violent and mysterious fate will arouse painful interest and intense sympathy in a widespread circle of friends.

" Well, Watson, what do you make of this ? " asked Holmes, after a long pause.

" It is an amazing coincidence."

" A coincidence ! Here is one of three men whom we had named as possible actors in this drama, and he meets a violent death during the very hours when we know that that drama was being enacted. The odds are enormous against its being coincidence. No figures could express them. No, my dear Watson, the two events are connected—*must* be connected. It is for us to find the connection."

" But now the official police must know all."

" Not at all. They know all they see at Godolphin Street. They know—and shall know—nothing of Whitehall Terrace. Only *we* know of both events, and can trace the relation between them. There is one obvious point which would, in any case, have turned my suspicions against Lucas. Godolphin Street, Westminster, is only a few minutes' walk from Whitehall Terrace. The other secret agents whom I have named live in the extreme

West End. It was easier, therefore, for Lucas than for the others to establish a connection or receive a message from the European Secretary's household—a small thing, and yet where events are compressed into a few hours it may prove essential. Halloa ! what have we here ? "

Mrs. Hudson had appeared with a lady's card upon her salver. Holmes glanced at it, raised his eyebrows, and handed it over to me.

" Ask Lady Hilda Trelawney Hope if she will be kind enough to step up," said he.

A moment later our modest apartment, already so distinguished that morning, was further honoured by the entrance of the most lovely woman in London. I had often heard of the beauty of the youngest daughter of the Duke of Belminster, but no description of it, and no contemplation of colourless photographs, had prepared me for the subtle, delicate charm and the beautiful colouring of that exquisite head. And yet as we saw it that autumn morning it was not its beauty which would be the first thing to impress the observer. The cheek was lovely, but it was paled with emotion ; the eyes were bright, but it was the brightness of fever ; the sensitive mouth was tight and drawn in an effort after self-command. Terror—not beauty—was what sprang first to the eye as our fair visitor stood framed for an instant in the open door.

" Has my husband been here, Mr. Holmes ? "

" Yes, madam, he has been here."

" Mr. Holmes, I implore you not to tell him that I came here." Holmes bowed coldly and motioned the lady to a chair.

" Your ladyship places me in a very delicate position. I beg that you will sit down and tell me what you desire ; but I fear that I cannot make any unconditional promise."

She swept across the room and seated herself with her back to the window. It was a queenly presence—tall, graceful, and intensely womanly.

" Mr. Holmes," she said—and her white-gloved hands

869

clasped and unclasped as she spoke—" I will speak frankly to you in the hope that it may induce you to speak frankly in return. There is complete confidence between my husband and me on all matters save one. That one is politics. On this his lips are sealed. He tells me nothing. Now, I am aware that there was a most deplorable occurrence in our house last night. I know that a paper has disappeared. But because the matter is political my husband refuses to take me into his complete confidence. Now it is essential—essential, I say—that I should thoroughly understand it. You are the only other person, save these politicians, who knows the true facts. I beg you, then, Mr. Holmes, to tell me exactly what has happened and what it will lead to. Tell me all, Mr. Holmes. Let no regard for your client's interests keep you silent, for I assure you that his interests, if he would only see it, would be best served by taking me into his complete confidence. What was this paper that was stolen ? "

" Madam, what you ask me is really impossible."

She groaned and sank her face in her hands.

" You must see that this is so, madam. If your husband thinks fit to keep you in the dark over this matter, is it for me, who have only learned the true facts under the pledge of professional secrecy, to tell what he has withheld ? It is not fair to ask it. It is him whom you must ask."

" I have asked him. I come to you as a last resource. But without your telling me anything definite, Mr. Holmes, you may do a great service if you would enlighten me on one point."

" What is it, madam ? "

" Is my husband's political career likely to suffer through this incident ? "

" Well, madam, unless it is set right it may certainly have a very unfortunate effect."

" Ah ! " She drew in her breath sharply as one whose doubts are resolved.

" One more question, Mr. Holmes. From an expression which my husband dropped in the first shock of this disaster I understood that terrible public consequences might arise from the loss of this document."

" If he said so, I certainly cannot deny it."

" Of what nature are they ? "

" Nay, madam, there again you ask me more than I can possibly answer."

" Then I will take up no more of your time. I cannot blame you, Mr. Holmes, for having refused to speak more freely, and you on your side will not, I am sure, think the worse of me because I desire, even against his will, to share my husband's anxieties. Once more I beg that you will say nothing of my visit." She looked back at us from the door, and I had a last impression of that beautiful, haunted face, the startled eyes, and the drawn mouth. Then she was gone.

" Now, Watson, the fair sex is your department," said Holmes, with a smile, when the dwindling *frou-frou* of skirts had ended in the slam of the door. " What was the fair lady's game ? What did she really want ? "

" Surely her own statement is clear and her anxiety very natural."

" Hum ! Think of her appearance, Watson, her manner, her suppressed excitement, her restlessness, her tenacity in asking questions. Remember that she comes of a caste who do not lightly show emotion."

" She was certainly much moved."

" Remember also the curious earnestness with which she assured us that it was best for her husband that she should know all. What did she mean by that ? And you must have observed, Watson, how she manœuvred to have the light at her back. She did not wish us to read her expression."

" Yes ; she chose the one chair in the room."

" And yet the motives of women are so inscrutable. You remember the woman at Margate whom I suspected for the same reason. No powder on her nose—that proved to be the correct solution. How can you build on such a quicksand ? Their most trivial action may mean volumes, or their most extraordinary conduct may depend upon a hairpin or a curling-tongs. Good morning, Watson."

" You are off ? "

" Yes ; I will while away the morning at Godolphin Street with our friends of the regular establishment. With Eduardo Lucas lies the solution of our problem, though I must admit that I have not an inkling as to what form it may take. It is a capital mistake to theorize in advance of the facts. Do you stay on guard, my good Watson, and receive any fresh visitors. I'll join you at lunch if I am able."

All that day and the next and the next Holmes was in a mood which his friends would call taciturn, and others morose. He ran out and ran in, smoked incessantly, played snatches on his violin, sank into reveries, devoured sandwiches at irregular hours, and hardly answered the casual questions which I put to him. It was evident to me that things were not going well with him or his quest. He would say nothing of the case, and it was from the papers that I learned the particulars of the inquest, and the arrest with the subsequent release of John Mitton, the valet of the deceased. The coroner's jury brought in the obvious " Wilful murder," but the parties remained as unknown as ever. No motive was suggested. The room was full of articles of value, but none had been taken. The dead man's papers had not been tampered with. They were carefully examined, and showed that he was a keen student of international politics, an indefatigable gossip, a remarkable linguist, and an untiring letter-writer. He had been on intimate terms with the leading politicians of several countries. But nothing sensational was discovered among the documents which filled his drawers. As to his relations with women, they appeared to have been promiscuous but superficial. He had many acquaintances among them, but few friends, and no one whom he loved. His habits were regular, his conduct inoffensive. His death was an absolute mystery, and likely to remain so.

As to the arrest of John Mitton, the valet, it was a counsel of despair as an alternative to absolute inaction. But no case could be sustained against him. He had visited friends in Hammersmith that night. The *alibi* was complete. It is true that he started home at an hour which should have brought him to Westminster before the time when the crime was discovered, but his own explanation that he had walked part of the way seemed probable enough in view of the fineness of the night. He had actually arrived at twelve o'clock, and appeared to be overwhelmed by the unexpected tragedy. He had always been on good terms with his master. Several of the dead man's possessions—notably a small case of razors—had been found in the valet's boxes, but he explained that they had been presents from the deceased, and the housekeeper was able to corroborate the story. Mitton had been in Lucas's employment for three years. It was noticeable that Lucas did not take Mitton on the Continent with him. Sometimes he visited Paris for three months on end, but Mitton was left in charge of the Godolphin Street house. As to the housekeeper, she had heard nothing on the night of the crime. If her master had a visitor, he had himself admitted him.

So for three mornings the mystery remained, so far as I could follow it in the papers. If Holmes knew more he kept his own counsel, but, as he told me that Inspector Lestrade had taken him into his confidence in the case, I knew that he was in close touch with every development. Upon the fourth day there appeared a long telegram from Paris which seemed to solve the whole question.

A discovery has just been made by the Parisian police (said the *Daily Telegraph*) which raises the veil which hung round the tragic fate of Mr. Eduardo Lucas, who met his death by violence last Monday night at Godolphin Street, Westminster.

Our readers will remember that the deceased gentleman was found stabbed in his room, and that some suspicion attached to his valet, but that the case broke down on an *alibi*. Yesterday a lady, who has been known as Mme. Henri Fournaye, occupying a small villa in the Rue Austerlitz, was reported to the authorities by her servants as being insane. An examination showed that she had indeed developed mania of a dangerous and permanent form. On inquiry the police have discovered that Mme. Henri Fournaye only returned from a journey to London on Tuesday last, and there is evidence to connect her with the crime at Westminster. A comparison of photographs has proved conclusively that M. Henri Fournaye and Eduardo Lucas were really one and the same person, and that the deceased had for some reason lived a double life in London and Paris. Mme. Fournaye, who is of creole origin, is of an extremely excitable nature, and has suffered in the past from attacks of jealousy which have amounted to frenzy. It is conjectured that it was in one of these that she committed the terrible crime which has caused such a sensation in London. Her movements upon the Monday night have not yet been traced, but it is undoubted that a woman answering to her description attracted much attention at Charing Cross Station on Tuesday morning by the wildness of her appearance and the violence of her gestures. It is probable, therefore, that the crime was either committed when insane, or that its immediate effect was to drive the unhappy woman out of her mind. At present she is unable to give any coherent account of the past, and the doctors hold out no hopes of the re-establishment of her reason. There is evidence that a woman, who might have been Mme. Fournaye, was seen for some hours on Monday night watching the house in Godolphin Street.

" What do you think of that, Holmes ? " I had read the account aloud to him, while he finished his breakfast.

" My dear Watson," said he, as he rose from the table and paced up and down the room, " you are most long-suffering, but if I have told you nothing in the last three days it is because there is nothing to tell. Even now this report from Paris does not help us much."

" Surely it is final as regards the man's death."

" The man's death is a mere incident—a trivial episode —in comparison with our real task, which is to trace this document and save a European catastrophe. Only one important thing has happened in the last three days, and that is that nothing has happened. I get reports almost hourly from the Government, and it is certain that nowhere in Europe is there any sign of trouble. Now, if this letter were loose—no, it *can't* be loose—but if it isn't loose, where can it be ? Who has it ? Why is it held back ? That's the question that beats in my brain like a hammer. Was it, indeed, a coincidence that Lucas should meet his death on the night when the letter disappeared ? Did the letter ever reach him ? If so, why is it not among his papers ? Did this mad wife of his carry it off with her ? If so, is it in her house in Paris ? How could I search for it without the French police having their suspicions aroused ? It is a case, my dear Watson, where the law is as dangerous to us as the criminals are. Every man's hand is against us, and yet the interests at stake are colossal. Should I bring it to a successful conclusion, it will certainly represent the crowning glory of my career. Ah, here is my latest from the front ! " He glanced hurriedly at the note which had been handed in. " Halloa ! Lestrade seems to have observed something of interest. Put on your hat, Watson, and we will stroll down together to Westminster."

It was my first visit to the scene of the crime—a high, dingy, narrow-chested house, prim, formal, and solid, like the century which gave it birth. Lestrade's bulldog features gazed out at us from the front window, and he greeted us warmly when a big constable had opened the door and let us in. The room into which we were shown was that in which the crime had been committed, but no trace of it now remained, save an ugly, irregular stain upon the carpet. This carpet was a small square drugget in the centre of the room, surrounded by a broad expanse of beautiful, old-fashioned, wood flooring in square blocks highly polished. Over the fireplace was a magnificent trophy of weapons, one of which had been used on that tragic night. In the window was a sumptuous writing-desk, and every detail of the apartment, the pictures, the rugs, and the hangings, all pointed to a taste which was luxurious to the verge of effeminacy.

" Seen the Paris news ? " asked Lestrade.

Holmes nodded.

" Our French friends seem to have touched the spot this time. No doubt it's just as they say. She knocked at the door—surprise visit, I guess, for he kept his life in watertight compartments. He let her in—couldn't keep her in the street. She told him how she had traced him, reproached him, one thing led to another, and then with that dagger so handy the end soon came. It wasn't all done in an instant, though, for these chairs were all swept over yonder, and he had one in his hand as if he had tried to hold her off with it. We've got it all as clear as if we had seen it."

Holmes raised his eyebrows.

" And yet you have sent for me ? "

" Ah, yes, that's another matter—a mere trifle, but the sort of thing you take an interest in—queer, you know, and what you might call freakish. It has nothing to do with the main fact—can't have, on the face of it."

" What is it, then ? "

" Well, you know after a crime of this sort we are very careful to keep things in their position. Nothing has been moved. Officer in charge here day and night. This morning, as the man was buried and the investigation over—so far as this room is concerned—we thought we could tidy up a bit. This carpet. You see, it is not fastened down ; only just laid there. We had occasion to raise it. We found——"

" Yes ? You found——"

Holmes' face grew tense with anxiety.

" Well, I'm sure you would never guess in a hundred years what we did find. You see that stain on the carpet ? Well, a great deal must have soaked through, must it not ? "

"Undoubtedly it must."

" Well, you will be surprised to hear that there is no stain on the white woodwork to correspond."

" No stain ! But there must——"

" Yes ; so you would say. But the fact remains that there isn't."

He took the corner of the carpet in his hand and, turning it over, he showed that it was indeed as he said.

" But the under side is as stained as the upper. It must have left a mark."

Lestrade chuckled with delight at having puzzled the famous expert.

" Now I'll show you the explanation. There *is* a second stain, but it does not correspond with the other. See for yourself." As he spoke he turned over another portion of the carpet, and there, sure enough, was a great crimson spill upon the square white facing of the old-fashioned floor. " What do you make of that, Mr. Holmes ? "

" Why, it is simple enough. The two stains did correspond, but the carpet has been turned round. As it was square and unfastened, it was easily done."

" The official police don't need you, Mr. Holmes, to tell them that the carpet must have been turned round. That's clear enough, for the stains lie above each other —if you lay it over this way. But what I want to know is, who shifted the carpet, and why ? "

I could see from Holmes' rigid face that he was vibrating with inward excitement.

" Look here, Lestrade ! " said he. " Has that constable in the passage been in charge of the place all the time ? "

" Yes, he has."

" Well, take my advice. Examine him carefully. Don't do it before us. We'll wait here. You take him into the back room. You'll be more likely to get a confession out of him alone. Ask him how he dare to admit people and leave them alone in this room. Don't ask him if he has done it. Take it for granted. Tell him you *know* someone has been here. Press him. Tell him that a full confession is his only chance of forgiveness. Do exactly what I tell you ! "

" By George, if he knows I'll have it out of him ! " cried Lestrade. He darted into the hall, and a few moments later his bullying voice sounded from the back room.

" Now, Watson, now ! " cried Holmes, with frenzied eagerness. All the demoniacal force of the man masked behind that listless manner burst out in a paroxysm of energy. He tore the drugget from the floor, and in an instant was down on his hands and knees clawing at each of the squares of wood beneath it. One turned sideways as he dug his nails into the edge of it. It hinged back like the lid of a box. A small black cavity opened beneath it. Holmes plunged his eager hand into it, and drew it out with a bitter snarl of anger and disappointment. It was empty.

" Quick, Watson, quick ! Get it back again ! " The wooden lid was replaced, and the drugget had only just been drawn straight, when Lestrade's voice was heard in the passage. He found Holmes leaning languidly against the mantelpiece, resigned and patient, endeavouring to conceal his irrepressible yawns.

" Sorry to keep you waiting, Mr. Holmes. I can see that you are bored to death with the whole affair. Well, he has confessed all right. Come in here, Mac-Pherson. Let these gentlemen hear of your most inexcusable conduct."

The big constable, very hot and penitent, sidled into the room.

" I meant no harm, sir, I'm sure. The young woman came to the door last evening—mistook the house, she did. And then we got talking. It's lonesome, when you're on duty here all day."

" Well, what happened then ? "

" She wanted to see where the crime was done—had

878

read about it in the papers, she said. She was a very respectable, well-spoken young woman, sir, and I saw no harm in letting her have a peep. When she saw that mark on the carpet, down she dropped on the floor, and lay as if she were dead. I ran to the back and got some water, but I could not bring her to. Then I went round the corner to the ' Ivy Plant ' for some brandy, and by the time I had brought it back the young woman had recovered and was off—ashamed of herself, I dare say, and dared not face me."

" How about moving that drugget ? "

" Well, sir, it was a bit rumpled, certainly, when I came back. You see, she fell on it, and it lies on a polished floor with nothing to keep it in place. I straightened it out afterwards."

" It's a lesson to you that you can't deceive me, Constable MacPherson," said Lestrade, with dignity. " No doubt you thought that your breach of duty could never be discovered, and yet a mere glance at that drugget was enough to convince me that someone had been admitted to the room. It's lucky for you, my man, that nothing is missing, or you would find yourself in Queer Street. I'm sorry to have to call you down over such a petty business, Mr. Holmes, but I thought the point of the second stain not corresponding with the first would interest you."

" Certainly it was most interesting. Has this woman only been here once, constable ? "

" Yes, sir, only once."

" Who was she ? "

" Don't know the name, sir. Was answering an advertisement about typewriting, and came to the wrong number—very pleasant, genteel young woman, sir."

" Tall ? Handsome ? "

" Yes, sir ; she was a well-grown young woman. I suppose you might say she was handsome. Perhaps some would say she was very handsome. ' Oh, officer, do let me have a peep ! ' says she. She had pretty, coaxing ways, as you might say, and I thought there was no harm in letting her just put her head through the door."

" How was she dressed ? "

" Quiet, sir—a long mantle down to her feet."

" What time was it ? "

" It was just growing dusk at the time. They were lighting the lamps as I came back with the brandy."

" Very good," said Holmes. " Come, Watson, I think that we have more important work elsewhere."

As we left the house Lestrade remained in the front room, while the repentant constable opened the door to let us out. Holmes turned on the step and held up something in his hand. The constable stared intently.

" Good Lord, sir ! " he cried, with amazement on his face. Holmes put his finger on his lips, replaced his hand in his breast-pocket, and burst out laughing as we turned down the street. " Excellent ! " said he. " Come, friend Watson, the curtain rings up for the last act. You will be relieved to hear that there will be no war, that the Right Honourable Trelawney Hope will suffer no set-back in his brilliant career, that the indiscreet Sovereign will receive no punishment for his indiscretion, that the Prime Minister will have no European complication to deal with, and that with a little tact and management upon our part nobody will be a penny the worse for what might have been a very ugly accident."

My mind filled with admiration for this extraordinary man.

" You have solved it ! " I cried.

" Hardly that, Watson. There are some points which are as dark as ever. But we have so much that it will be our own fault if we cannot get the rest. We will go straight to Whitehall Terrace and bring the matter to a head."

When we arrived at the residence of the European Secretary it was for Lady Hilda Trelawney Hope that Sherlock Holmes inquired. We were shown into the morning-room.

" Mr. Holmes ! " said the lady, and her face was pink with indignation, " this is surely most unfair and ungenerous upon your part. I desired, as I have explained, to keep my visit to you a secret, lest my husband should think that I was intruding into his affairs. And yet you compromise me by coming here, and so showing that there are business relations between us."

" Unfortunately, madam, I had no possible alternative. I have been commissioned to recover this immensely important paper. I must therefore ask you, madam, to be kind enough to place it in my hands."

The lady sprang to her feet, with the colour all dashed in an instant from her beautiful face. Her eyes glazed—she tottered—I thought that she would faint. Then with a grand effort she rallied from the shock, and a supreme astonishment and indignation chased every other expression from her features.

" You—you insult me, Mr. Holmes."

" Come, come, madam, it is useless. Give up the letter."

She darted to the bell.

" The butler shall show you out."

" Do not ring, Lady Hilda. If you do, then all my earnest efforts to avoid a scandal will be frustrated. Give up the letter, and all will be set right. If you will work with me, I can arrange everything. If you work against me, I must expose you."

She stood grandly defiant, a queenly figure, her eyes fixed upon his as if she would read his very soul. Her hand was on the bell, but she had forborne to ring it.

" You are trying to frighten me. It is not a very manly thing, Mr. Holmes, to come here and browbeat a woman. You say that you know something. What is it that you know ? "

" Pray sit down, madam. You will hurt yourself there if you fall. I will not speak until you sit down. Thank you."

" I give you five minutes, Mr. Holmes."

" One is enough, Lady Hilda. I know of your visit to Eduardo Lucas, and of your giving him this document, of your ingenious return to the room last night, and of the manner in which you took the letter from the hiding-place under the carpet."

She stared at him with an ashen face, and gulped twice before she could speak.

" You are mad, Mr. Holmes—you are mad ! " she cried at last.

He drew a small piece of cardboard from his pocket. It was the face of a woman cut out of a portrait.

" I have carried this because I thought it might be useful," said he. " The policeman has recognized it."

She gave a gasp, and her head dropped back in her chair.

" Come, Lady Hilda. You have the letter. The matter may still be adjusted. I have no desire to bring trouble to you. My duty ends when I have returned the lost letter to your husband. Take my advice and be frank with me ; it is your only chance."

Her courage was admirable. Even now she would not own defeat.

" I tell you again, Mr. Holmes, that you are under some absurd illusion."

Holmes rose from his chair.

" I am sorry for you, Lady Hilda. I have done my best for you ; I can see that it is all in vain."

He rang the bell. The butler entered.

" Is Mr. Trelawney Hope at home ? "

" He will be home, sir, at a quarter to one."

Holmes glanced at his watch.

" Still a quarter of an hour," said he. " Very good, I shall wait."

The butler had hardly closed the door behind him when Lady Hilda was down on her knees at Holmes' feet, her hands outstretched, her beautiful face upturned and wet with her tears.

" Oh, spare me, Mr. Holmes ! Spare me ! " she

pleaded, in a frenzy of supplication. " For Heaven's sake don't tell him ! I love him so ! I would not bring one shadow on his life, and this I know would break his noble heart."

Holmes raised the lady. " I am thankful, madam, that you have come to your senses even at this last moment ! There is not an instant to lose. Where is the letter ? "

She darted across to a writing-desk, unlocked it, and drew out a long blue envelope.

" Here it is, Mr. Holmes. Would to Heaven I had never seen it ! "

" How can we return it ? " Holmes muttered. " Quick, quick, we must think of some way ! Where is the dispatch-box ? "

" Still in his bedroom."

" What a stroke of luck ! Quick, madam, bring it here."

A moment later she had appeared with a red flat box in her hand.

" How did you open it before ? You have a duplicate key ? Yes, of course you have. Open it ! "

From out of her bosom Lady Hilda had drawn a small key. The box flew open. It was stuffed with papers. Holmes thrust the blue envelope deep down into the heart of them, between the leaves of some other document. The box was shut, locked, and returned to his bedroom.

" Now we are ready for him," said Holmes ; " we have still ten minutes. I am going far to screen you, Lady Hilda. In return you will spend the time in telling me frankly the real meaning of this extraordinary affair."

" Mr. Holmes, I will tell you everything," cried the lady. " Oh, Mr. Holmes, I would cut off my right hand before I gave him a moment of sorrow ! There is no woman in all London who loves her husband as I do, and yet if he knew how I have acted—how I have been compelled to act—he would never forgive me. For his own honour stands so high that he could not forget or pardon a lapse in another. Help me, Mr. Holmes! My happiness, his happiness, our very lives are at stake!"

"Quick, madam, the time grows short!"

"It was a letter of mine, Mr. Holmes, an indiscreet letter written before my marriage—a foolish letter, a letter of an impulsive, loving girl. I meant no harm, and yet he would have thought it criminal. Had he read that letter his confidence would have been for ever destroyed. It is years since I wrote it. I had thought that the whole matter was forgotten. Then at last I heard from this man, Lucas, that it had passed into his hands, and that he would lay it before my husband. I implored his mercy. He said that he would return my letter if I would return him a certain document which he described in my husband's dispatch-box. He had some spy in the office who had told him of its existence. He assured me that no harm could come to my husband. Put yourself in my position, Mr. Holmes! What was I to do?"

"Take your husband into your confidence."

"I could not, Mr. Holmes, I could not! On the one side seemed certain ruin; on the other, terrible as it seemed to take my husband's papers, still in a matter of politics I could not understand the consequences, while in a matter of love and trust they were only too clear to me. I did it, Mr. Holmes! I took an impression of his key; this man Lucas furnished a duplicate. I opened his dispatch-box, took the paper, and conveyed it to Godolphin Street."

"What happened there, madam?"

"I tapped at the door, as agreed. Lucas opened it. I followed him into his room, leaving the hall door ajar behind me, for I feared to be alone with the man. I remembered that there was a woman outside as I entered. Our business was soon done. He had my letter on his desk; I handed him the document. He gave me the letter. At this instant there was a sound at the door.

There were steps in the passage. Lucas quickly turned back the drugget, thrust the document into some hiding-place there, and covered it over.

" What happened after that is like some fearful dream. I have a vision of a dark, frantic face, of a woman's voice, which screamed in French, ' My waiting is not in vain. At last, at last I have found you with her ! ' There was a savage struggle. I saw him with a chair in his hand, a knife gleamed in hers. I rushed from the horrible scene, ran from the house, and only next morning in the paper did I learn the dreadful result. That night I was happy, for I had my letter, and I had not seen yet what the future would bring.

" It was next morning that I realized that I had only exchanged one trouble for another. My husband's anguish at the loss of his paper went to my heart. I could hardly prevent myself from there and then kneeling down at his feet and telling him what I had done. But that again would mean a confession of the past. I came to you that morning in order to understand the full enormity of my offence. From the instant that I grasped it my whole mind was turned to the one thought of getting back my husband's paper. It must still be where Lucas had placed it, for it was concealed before this dreadful woman entered the room. If it had not been for her coming, I should not have known where his hiding-place was. How was I to get into the room ? For two days I watched the place, but the door was never left open. Last night I made a last attempt. What I did and how I succeeded, you have already learned. I brought the paper back with me, and thought of destroying it, since I could see no way of returning it without confessing my guilt to my husband. Heavens, I hear his step upon the stair ! "

The European Secretary burst excitedly into the room.

" Any news, Mr. Holmes, any news ? " he cried.

" I have some hopes."

" Ah, thank Heaven ! " His face became radiant.

" The Prime Minister is lunching with me. May he share your hopes ? He has nerves of steel, and yet I know that he has hardly slept since this terrible event. Jacobs, will you ask the Prime Minister to come up ? As to you, dear, I fear that this is a matter of politics. We will join you in a few minutes in the dining-room."

The Prime Minister's manner was subdued, but I could see by the gleam of his eyes and the twitchings of his bony hands that he shared the excitement of his young colleague.

" I understand that you have something to report, Mr. Holmes ? "

" Purely negative as yet," my friend answered. " I have inquired at every point where it might be, and I am sure that there is no danger to be apprehended."

" But that is not enough, Mr. Holmes. We cannot live for ever on such a volcano. We must have something definite."

" I am in hopes of getting it. That is why I am here. The more I think of the matter the more convinced I am that the letter has never left this house."

" Mr. Holmes ! "

" If it had it would certainly have been public by now."

" But why should anyone take it in order to keep it in this house ? "

" I am not convinced that anyone did take it."

" Then how could it leave the dispatch-box ? "

" I am not convinced that it ever did leave the dispatch-box."

" Mr. Holmes, this joking is very ill-timed. You have my assurance that it left the box."

" Have you examined the box since Tuesday morning ? "

" No ; it was not necessary."

" You may conceivably have overlooked it."

" Impossible, I say."

" But I am not convinced of it ; I have known such

886

things happen. I presume there are other papers there. Well, it may have got mixed with them."

" It was on the top."

" Someone may have shaken the box and displaced it."

" No, no ; I had everything out."

" Surely it is easily decided, Hope ! " said the Premier. " Let us have the dispatch-box brought in."

The Secretary rang the bell.

" Jacobs, bring down my dispatch-box. This is a farcical waste of time, but still, if nothing else will satisfy you, it shall be done. Thank you, Jacobs ; put it here. I have always had the key on my watch-chain. Here are the papers, you see. Letter from Lord Merrow, report from Sir Charles Hardy, memorandum from Belgrade, note on the Russo-German grain taxes, letter from Madrid, note from Lord Flowers—good heavens ! what is this ? Lord Bellinger ! Lord Bellinger ! "

The Premier snatched the blue envelope from his hand.

" Yes, it is it—and the letter intact. Hope, I congratulate you ! "

" Thank you ! Thank you ! What a weight from my heart ! But this is inconceivable—impossible ! Mr. Holmes, you are a wizard, a sorcerer ! How did you know it was there ? "

" Because I knew it was nowhere else."

" I cannot believe my eyes ! " He ran wildly to the door. " Where is my wife ? I must tell her that all is well. Hilda ! Hilda ! " we heard his voice on the stairs.

The Premier looked at Holmes with twinkling eyes.

" Come, sir," said he. " There is more in this than meets the eye. How came the letter back in the box ? "

Holmes turned away smiling from the keen scrutiny of those wonderful eyes.

" We also have our diplomatic secrets," said he, and picking up his hat he turned to the door.

HIS LAST BOW

37. *Wisteria Lodge*

I—The Singular Experience of Mr. John Scott Eccles

I FIND it recorded in my notebook that it was a bleak and windy day towards the end of March in the year 1892. Holmes had received a telegram whilst we sat at our lunch, and he had scribbled a reply. He made no remark, but the matter remained in his thoughts, for he stood in front of the fire afterwards with a thoughtful face, smoking his pipe, and casting an occasional glance at the message. Suddenly he turned upon me with a mischievous twinkle in his eyes.

" I suppose, Watson, we must look upon you as a man of letters," said he. " How do you define the word ' grotesque ' ? "

" Strange—remarkable," I suggested.

He shook his head at my definition.

" There is surely something more than that," said he ; " some underlying suggestion of the tragic and the terrible. If you cast your mind back to some of those narratives with which you have afflicted a long-suffering public, you will recognize how often the grotesque has deepened into the criminal. Think of that little affair of the red-headed men. That was grotesque enough in the outset, and yet it ended in a desperate attempt at robbery. Or, again, there was that most grotesque affair of the five orange pips, which led straight to a murderous conspiracy. The word puts me on the alert."

" Have you it there ? " I asked.

He read the telegram aloud.

" Have just had most incredible and grotesque experience. May I consult you ?—Scott Eccles, Post Office, Charing Cross."

" Man or woman ? " I asked.

" Oh, man, of course. No woman would ever send a reply-paid telegram. She would have come."

" Will you see him ? "

" My dear Watson, you know how bored I have been since we locked up Colonel Carruthers. My mind is like a racing engine, tearing itself to pieces because it is not connected up with the work for which it was built. Life is commonplace, the papers are sterile ; audacity and romance seem to have passed for ever from the criminal world. Can you ask me, then, whether I am ready to look into any new problem, however trivial it may prove ? But here, unless I am mistaken, is our client."

A measured step was heard upon the stairs, and a moment later a stout, tall, grey-whiskered and solemnly respectable person was ushered into the room. His life history was written in his heavy features and pompous manner. From his spats to his gold-rimmed spectacles he was a Conservative, a Churchman, a good citizen, orthodox and conventional to the last degree. But some amazing experience had disturbed his native composure and left its traces in his bristling hair, his flushed, angry cheeks, and his flurried, excited manner. He plunged instantly into his business.

" I have had a most singular and unpleasant experience, Mr. Holmes," said he. " Never in my life have I been placed in such a situation. It is most improper—most outrageous. I must insist upon some explanation." He swelled and puffed in his anger.

" Pray sit down, Mr. Scott Eccles," said Holmes, in a soothing voice. " May I ask, in the first place, why you came to me at all ? "

" Well, sir, it did not appear to be a matter which concerned the police, and yet, when you have heard the facts, you must admit that I could not leave it where it was.

Private detectives are a class with whom I have absolutely no sympathy, but none the less, having heard your name ——"

" Quite so. But, in the second place, why did you not come at once ? "

" What do you mean ? "

Holmes glanced at his watch.

" It is a quarter past two," he said. " Your telegram was dispatched about one. But no one can glance at your toilet and attire without seeing that your disturbance dates from the moment of your waking."

Our client smoothed down his unbrushed hair and felt his unshaven chin.

" You are right, Mr. Holmes. I never gave a thought to my toilet. I was only too glad to get out of such a house. But I have been running round making inquiries before I came to you. I went to the house agents, you know, and they said that Mr. Garcia's rent was paid up all right and that everything was in order at Wisteria Lodge."

" Come, come, sir," said Holmes, laughing. " You are like my friend Dr. Watson, who has a bad habit of telling his stories wrong end foremost. Please arrange your thoughts and let me know, in their due sequence, exactly what those events are which have sent you out unbrushed and unkempt, with dress-boots and waistcoat buttoned awry, in search of advice and assistance."

Our client looked down with a rueful face at his own unconventional appearance.

" I'm sure it must look very bad, Mr. Holmes, and I am not aware that in my whole life such a thing has ever happened before. But I will tell you the whole queer business, and when I have done so you will admit, I am sure, that there has been enough to excuse me."

But his narrative was nipped in the bud. There was a bustle outside, and Mrs. Hudson opened the door to usher in two robust and official-looking individuals, one of whom was well known to us as Inspector Gregson of Scotland Yard, an energetic, gallant, and, within his limitations, a capable officer. He shook hands with Holmes, and introduced his comrade as Inspector Baynes of the Surrey Constabulary.

"We are hunting together, Mr. Holmes, and our trail lay in this direction." He turned his bulldog eyes upon our visitor. "Are you Mr. John Scott Eccles, of Popham House, Lee?"

"I am."

"We have been following you about all the morning."

"You traced him through the telegram, no doubt," said Holmes.

"Exactly, Mr. Holmes. We picked up the scent at Charing Cross Post Office and came on here."

"But why do you follow me? What do you want?"

"We wish a statement, Mr. Scott Eccles, as to the events which led up to the death last night of Mr. Aloysius Garcia, of Wisteria Lodge, near Esher."

Our client had sat up with staring eyes and every tinge of colour struck from his astonished face.

"Dead? Did you say he was dead?"

"Yes, sir, he is dead."

"But how? An accident?"

"Murder, if ever there was one upon earth."

"Good God! This is awful! You don't mean—you don't mean that I am suspected?"

"A letter of yours was found in the dead man's pocket, and we know by it that you had planned to pass last night at his house."

"So I did."

"Oh, you did, did you?"

Out came the official notebook.

"Wait a bit, Gregson," said Sherlock Holmes. "All you desire is a plain statement, is it not?"

"And it is my duty to warn Mr. Scott Eccles that it may be used against him."

"Mr. Eccles was going to tell us about it when you entered the room. I think, Watson, a brandy and soda would do him no harm. Now, sir, I suggest that you take no notice of this addition to your audience, and that you proceed with your narrative exactly as you would have done had you never been interrupted."

Our visitor had gulped off the brandy and the colour had returned to his face. With a dubious glance at the inspector's notebook, he plunged at once into his extraordinary statement.

" I am a bachelor," said he, " and, being of a sociable turn, I cultivate a large number of friends. Among these are the family of a retired brewer called Melville, living at Albemarle Mansion, Kensington. It was at his table that I met some weeks ago a young fellow named Garcia. He was, I understood, of Spanish descent and connected in some way with the Embassy. He spoke perfect English, was pleasing in his manners, and as good-looking a man as ever I saw in my life.

" In some way we struck up quite a friendship, this young fellow and I. He seemed to take a fancy to me from the first, and within two days of our meeting he came to see me at Lee. One thing led to another, and it ended in his inviting me out to spend a few days at his house, Wisteria Lodge, between Esher and Oxshott. Yesterday evening I went to Esher to fulfil this engagement.

" He had described his household to me before I went there. He lived with a faithful servant, a countryman of his own, who looked after all his needs. This fellow could speak English and did his housekeeping for him. Then there was a wonderful cook, he said, a half-breed whom he had picked up in his travels, who could serve an excellent dinner. I remember that he remarked what a queer household it was to find in the heart of Surrey, and that I agreed with him, though it has proved a good deal queerer than I thought.

" I drove to the place—about two miles on the south side of Esher. The house was a fair-sized one, standing back from the road, with a curving drive which was banked with high evergreen shrubs. It was an old, tumble-down building in a crazy state of disrepair. When the trap

pulled up on the grass-grown drive in front of the blotched
and weather-stained door, I had doubts as to my wisdom
in visiting a man whom I knew so slightly. He opened the
door himself, however, and greeted me with a great show
of cordiality. I was handed over to the man-servant, a
melancholy, swarthy individual, who led the way, my bag
in his hand, to my bedroom. The whole place was depressing. Our dinner was *tête-à-tête*, and though my host did
his best to be entertaining, his thoughts seemed to continually wander, and he talked so vaguely and wildly that
I could hardly understand him. He continually drummed
his fingers on the table, gnawed his nails, and gave other
signs of nervous impatience. The dinner itself was
neither well served nor well cooked, and the gloomy presence of the taciturn servant did not help to enliven us. I
can assure you that many times in the course of the evening I wished that I could invent some excuse which would
take me back to Lee.

" One thing comes back to my memory which may have
a bearing upon the business that you two gentlemen are
investigating. I thought nothing of it at the time. Near
the end of dinner a note was handed in by the servant. I
noticed that after my host had read it he seemed even more
distrait and strange than before. He gave up all pretence
at conversation and sat, smoking endless cigarettes, lost in
his own thoughts, but he made no remark as to the contents. About eleven I was glad to go to bed. Some time
later Garcia looked in at my door—the room was dark at
the time—and asked me if I had rung. I said that I had
not. He apologized for having disturbed me so late, saying that it was nearly one o'clock. I dropped off after this
and slept soundly all night.

" And now I come to the amazing part of my tale.
When I woke it was broad daylight. I glanced at my
watch, and the time was nearly nine. I had particularly
asked to be called at eight, so I was very much astonished
at this forgetfulness. I sprang up and rang for the servant. There was no response. I rang again and again,

with the same result. Then I came to the conclusion that the bell was out of order. I huddled on my clothes and hurried downstairs in an exceedingly bad temper to order some hot water. You can imagine my surprise when I found that there was no one there. I shouted in the hall. There was no answer. Then I ran from room to room. All were deserted. My host had shown me which was his bedroom the night before, so I knocked at the door. No reply. I turned the handle and walked in. The room was empty, and the bed had never been slept in. He had gone with the rest. The foreign host, the foreign footman, the foreign cook, all had vanished in the night ! That was the end of my visit to Wisteria Lodge."

Sherlock Holmes was rubbing his hands and chuckling as he added this bizarre incident to his collection of strange episodes.

" Your experience is, so far as I know, perfectly unique," said he. " May I ask, sir, what you did then ? "

" I was furious. My first idea was that I had been the victim of some absurd practical joke. I packed my things, banged the hall door behind me, and set off for Esher, with my bag in my hand. I called at Allan Brothers', the chief land agents in the village, and found that it was from this firm that the villa had been rented. It struck me that the whole proceeding could hardly be for the purpose of making a fool of me, and that the main object must be to get out of the rent. It is late in March, so quarter-day is at hand. But this theory would not work. The agent was obliged to me for my warning, but told me that the rent had been paid in advance. Then I made my way to town and called at the Spanish Embassy. The man was unknown there. After this I went to see Melville, at whose house I had first met Garcia, but I found that he really knew rather less about him than I did. Finally, when I got your reply to my wire I came out to you, since I understand that you are a person who gives advice in difficult cases. But now, Mr. Inspector, I gather, from what you said when you entered the room, that you can carry the story on, and that some tragedy has occurred. I can assure you that every word I have said is the truth, and that, outside of what I have told you, I know absolutely nothing about the fate of this man. My only desire is to help the law in every possible way."

" I am sure of it, Mr. Scott Eccles—I am sure of it," said Inspector Gregson, in a very amiable tone. " I am bound to say that everything which you have said agrees very closely with the facts as they have come to our notice. For example, there was that note which arrived during dinner. Did you chance to observe what became of it ? "

" Yes, I did. Garcia rolled it up and threw it into the fire."

" What do you say to that, Mr. Baynes ? "

The country detective was a stout, puffy, red man, whose face was only redeemed from grossness by two extra-ordinarily bright eyes, almost hidden behind the heavy creases of cheek and brow. With a slow smile he drew a folded and discoloured scrap of paper from his pocket.

" It was a dog-grate, Mr. Holmes, and he over-pitched it. I picked this out unburned from the back of it."

Holmes smiled his appreciation.

" You must have examined the house very carefully to find a single pellet of paper."

" I did, Mr. Holmes. It's my way. Shall I read it, Mr. Gregson ? "

The Londoner nodded.

" The note is written upon ordinary cream-laid paper without watermark. It is a quarter-sheet. The paper is cut off in two snips with a short-bladed scissors. It has been folded over three times and sealed with purple wax, put on hurriedly and pressed down with some flat, oval object. It is addressed to Mr. Garcia, Wisteria Lodge. It says : ' Our own colours, green and white. Green open, white shut. Main stair, first corridor, seventh right, green baize. God speed. D.' It is a woman's writing, done with a sharp-pointed pen, but the address is

898

either done with another pen or by someone else. It is thicker and bolder, as you see."

"A very remarkable note," said Holmes, glancing it over. "I must compliment you, Mr. Baynes, upon your attention to detail in your examination of it. A few trifling points might perhaps be added. The oval seal is undoubtedly a plain sleeve-link—what else is of such a shape ? The scissors were bent nail-scissors. Short as the two snips are, you can distinctly see the same slight curve in each."

The country detective chuckled.

"I thought I had squeezed all the juice out of it, but I see there was a little over," he said. "I'm bound to say that I make nothing of the note except that there was something on hand, and that a woman, as usual, was at the bottom of it."

Mr. Scott Eccles had fidgeted in his seat during this conversation.

"I am glad you found the note, since it corroborates my story," said he. "But I beg to point out that I have not yet heard what has happened to Mr. Garcia, nor what has become of his household."

"As to Garcia," said Gregson, "that is easily answered. He was found dead this morning upon Oxshott Common, nearly a mile from his home. His head had been smashed to pulp by heavy blows of a sand-bag or some such instrument, which had crushed rather than wounded. It is a lonely corner, and there is no house within a quarter of a mile of the spot. He had apparently been struck down first from behind, but his assailant had gone on beating him long after he was dead. It was a most furious assault. There are no footsteps nor any clue to the criminals."

"Robbed ?"

"No, there was no attempt at robbery."

"This is very painful—very painful and terrible," said Mr. Scott Eccles, in a querulous voice ; "but it is really uncommonly hard upon me. I had nothing to do with my host going off upon a nocturnal excursion and meeting so sad an end. How do I come to be mixed up with the case ? "

" Very simply, sir," Inspector Baynes answered. " The only document found in the pocket of the deceased was a letter from you saying that you would be with him on the night of his death. It was the envelope of this letter which gave us the dead man's name and address. It was after nine this morning when we reached his house and found neither you nor anyone else inside it. I wired to Mr. Gregson to run you down in London while I examined Wisteria Lodge. Then I came into town, joined Mr. Gregson, and here we are."

" I think now," said Gregson, rising, " we had best put this matter into an official shape. You will come round with us to the station, Mr. Scott Eccles, and let us have your statement in writing."

" Certainly, I will come at once. But I retain your services, Mr. Holmes. I desire you to spare no expense and no pains to get at the truth."

My friend turned to the country inspector.

" I suppose that you have no objection to my collaborating with you, Mr. Baynes ? "

" Highly honoured, sir, I am sure."

" You appear to have been very prompt and business-like in all that you have done. Was there any clue, may I ask, as to the exact hour that the man met his death ? "

" He had been there since one o'clock. There was rain about that time, and his death had certainly been before the rain."

" But that is perfectly impossible, Mr. Baynes," cried our client. " His voice is unmistakable. I could swear to it that it was he who addressed me in my bedroom at that very hour."

" Remarkable, but by no means impossible," said Holmes, smiling.

" You have a clue ? " asked Gregson.

" On the face of it the case is not a very complex one, though it certainly presents some novel and interesting features. A further knowledge of facts is necessary before I would venture to give a final and definite opinion. By the way, Mr. Baynes, did you find anything remarkable besides this note in your examination of the house ? "

The detective looked at my friend in a singular way.

" There were," said he, " one or two *very* remarkable things. Perhaps when I have finished at the police-station you would care to come out and give me your opinion of them."

" I am entirely at your service," said Sherlock Holmes, ringing the bell. " You will show these gentlemen out, Mrs. Hudson, and kindly send the boy with this telegram. He is to pay a five-shilling reply."

We sat for some time in silence after our visitors had left. Holmes smoked hard, with his brows drawn down over his keen eyes, and his head thrust forward in the eager way characteristic of the man.

" Well, Watson," he asked, turning suddenly upon me, " what do you make of it ? "

" I can make nothing of this mystification of Scott Eccles."

" But the crime ? "

" Well, taken with the disappearance of the man's com-panions, I should say that they were in some way con-cerned in the murder and had fled from justice."

" That is certainly a possible point of view. On the face of it you must admit, however, that it is very strange that his two servants should have been in a conspiracy against him and should have attacked him on the one night when he had a guest. They had him alone at their mercy every other night in the week."

" Then why did they fly ? "

" Quite so. Why did they fly ? There is a big fact. Another big fact is the remarkable experience of our client, Scott Eccles. Now, my dear Watson, is it beyond the limits of human ingenuity to furnish an explanation which would cover both these big facts ? If it were one which would also admit of the mysterious note with its very curious phraseology, why, then it would be worth accepting as a temporary hypothesis. If the fresh facts which come to our knowledge all fit themselves into the scheme, then our hypothesis may gradually become a solution."

" But what is our hypothesis ? "

Holmes leaned back in his chair with half-closed eyes.

" You must admit, my dear Watson, that the idea of a joke is impossible. There were grave events afoot, as the sequel showed, and the coaxing of Scott Eccles to Wisteria Lodge had some connection with them."

" But what possible connection ? "

" Let us take it link by link. There is, on the face of it, something unnatural about this strange and sudden friendship between the young Spaniard and Scott Eccles. It was the former who forced the pace. He called upon Eccles at the other end of London on the very day after he first met him, and he kept in close touch with him until he got him down to Esher. Now, what did he want with Eccles ? What could Eccles supply ? I see no charm in the man. He is not particularly intelligent—not a man likely to be congenial to a quick-witted Latin. Why, then, was he picked out from all the other people whom Garcia met as particularly suited to his purpose ? Has he any one outstanding quality ? I say that he has. He is the very type of conventional British respectability, and the very man as a witness to impress another Briton. You saw yourself how neither of the inspectors dreamed of questioning his statement, extraordinary as it was."

" But what was he to witness ? "

" Nothing, as things turned out, but everything had they gone another way. That is how I read the matter."

" I see, he might have proved an alibi."

" Exactly, my dear Watson ; he might have proved an alibi. We will suppose, for argument's sake, that the household of Wisteria Lodge are confederates in some design. The attempt, whatever it may be, is to come off, we will say, before one o'clock. By some juggling of the clocks it is quite possible that they may have got Scott

Eccles to bed earlier than he thought, but in any case it is likely that when Garcia went out of his way to tell him that it was one it was really not more than twelve. If Garcia could do whatever he had to do and be back by the hour mentioned he had evidently a powerful reply to any accusation. Here was this irreproachable Englishman ready to swear in any court of law that the accused was in his house all the time. It was an insurance against the worst."

"Yes, yes, I see that. But how about the disappearance of the others ? "

" I have not all my facts yet, but I do not think there are any insuperable difficulties. Still, it is an error to argue in front of your data. You find yourself insensibly twisting them round to fit your theories."

" And the message ? "

" How did it run ? ' Our own colours, green and white.' Sounds like racing. ' Green open, white shut.' That is clearly a signal. ' Main stair, first corridor, seventh right, green baize.' This is an assignation. We may find a jealous husband at the bottom of it all. It was clearly a dangerous quest. She would not have said ' God speed ' had it not been so. ' D '—that should be a guide."

" The man was a Spaniard. I suggest that ' D ' stands for Dolores, a common female name in Spain."

" Good, Watson, very good—but quite inadmissible. A Spaniard would write to a Spaniard in Spanish. The writer of this note is certainly English. Well, we can only possess our souls in patience, until this excellent inspector comes back for us. Meanwhile we can thank our lucky fate which has rescued us for a few short hours from the insufferable fatigues of idleness."

An answer had arrived to Holmes' telegram before our Surrey officer had returned. Holmes read it, and was about to place it in his notebook when he caught a glimpse of my expectant face. He tossed it across with a laugh.

" We are moving in exalted circles," said he.

The telegram was a list of names and addresses : " Lord Harringby, The Dingle ; Sir George Ffolliott, Oxshott Towers ; Mr. Hynes Hynes, J.P., Purdey Place ; Mr. James Baker Williams, Forton Old Hall ; Mr. Henderson, High Gable ; Rev. Joshua Stone, Nether Walsling."

" This is a very obvious way of limiting our field of operations," said Holmes. " No doubt Baynes, with his methodical mind, has already adopted some similar plan."

" I don't quite understand."

" Well, my dear fellow, we have already arrived at the conclusion that the message received by Garcia at dinner was an appointment or an assignation. Now, if the obvious reading of it is correct, and in order to keep this tryst one has to ascend a main stair and seek the seventh door in a corridor, it is perfectly clear that the house is a very large one. It is equally certain that this house cannot be more than a mile or two from Oxshott, since Garcia was walking in that direction, and hoped, according to my reading of the facts, to be back in Wisteria Lodge in time to avail himself of an alibi, which would only be valid up to one o'clock. As the number of large houses close to Oxshott must be limited, I adopted the obvious method of sending to the agents mentioned by Scott Eccles and obtaining a list of them. Here they are in this telegram, and the other end of our tangled skein must lie among them."

It was nearly six o'clock before we found ourselves in the pretty Surrey village of Esher, with Inspector Baynes as our companion.

Holmes and I had taken things for the night, and found comfortable quarters at the Bull. Finally we set out in the company of the detective on our visit to Wisteria Lodge. It was a cold, dark March evening, with a sharp wind and a fine rain beating upon our faces, a fit setting for the wild common over which our road passed and the tragic goal to which it led us.

II—THE TIGER OF SAN PEDRO

A cold and melancholy walk of a couple of miles brought us to a high wooden gate, which opened into a gloomy avenue of chestnuts. The curved and shadowed drive led us to a low, dark house, pitch-black against a slate-coloured sky. From the front window upon the left of the door there peeped a glimmer of a feeble light.

" There's a constable in possession," said Baynes. " I'll knock at the window." He stepped across the grass plot and tapped with his hand on the pane. Through the fogged glass I dimly saw a man spring up from a chair beside the fire, and heard a sharp cry from within the room. An instant later a white-faced, hard-breathing policeman had opened the door, the candle wavering in his trembling hand.

" What's the matter, Walters ? " asked Baynes, sharply.

The man mopped his forehead with his handkerchief and gave a long sigh of relief.

" I am glad you have come, sir. It has been a long evening and I don't think my nerve is as good as it was."

" Your nerve, Walters ? I should not have thought you had a nerve in your body."

" Well, sir, it's this lonely, silent house and the queer thing in the kitchen. Then when you tapped at the window I thought it had come again."

" That what had come again ? "

" The devil, sir, for all I know. It was at the window."

" What was at the window, and when ? "

" It was just about two hours ago. The light was just fading. I was sitting reading in the chair. I don't know what made me look up, but there was a face looking in at me through the lower pane. Lord, sir, what a face it was ! I'll see it in my dreams."

" Tut, tut, Walters ! This is not talk for a police-constable."

" I know, sir, I know ; but it shook me, sir, and there's no use to deny it. It wasn't black, sir, nor was it white, nor any colour that I know, but a kind of queer shade like clay with a splash of milk in it. Then there was the size of it—it was twice yours, sir. And the look of it—the great staring goggle eyes, and the line of white teeth like a hungry beast. I tell you, sir, I couldn't move a finger, nor get my breath, till it whisked away and was gone. Out I ran and through the shrubbery, but thank God there was no one there."

" If I didn't know you were a good man, Walters, I should put a black mark against you for this. If it were the devil himself a constable on duty should never thank God that he could not lay his hands upon him. I suppose the whole thing is not a vision and a touch of nerves ? "

" That, at least, is very easily settled," said Holmes, lighting his little pocket lantern. " Yes," he reported, after a short examination of the grass bed, " a number twelve shoe, I should say. If he was all on the same scale as his foot he must certainly have been a giant."

" What became of him ? "

" He seems to have broken through the shrubbery and made for the road."

" Well," said the inspector, with a grave and thoughtful face, " whoever he may have been, and whatever he may have wanted, he's gone for the present, and we have more immediate things to attend to. Now, Mr. Holmes, with your permission, I will show you round the house."

The various bedrooms and sitting-rooms had yielded nothing to a careful search. Apparently the tenants had brought little or nothing with them, and all the furniture down to the smallest details had been taken over with the house. A good deal of clothing with the stamp of Marx & Co., High Holborn, had been left behind. Telegraphic inquiries had been already made which showed that Marx knew nothing of his customer save that he was a good payer. Odds and ends, some pipes, a few novels, two of them in Spanish, an old-fashioned pinfire revolver, and a guitar were amongst the personal property.

" Nothing in all this," said Baynes, stalking, candle in

hand, from room to room. " But now, Mr. Holmes, I invite your attention to the kitchen."

It was a gloomy, high-ceilinged room at the back of the house, with a straw litter in one corner, which served apparently as a bed for the cook. The table was piled with half-eaten dishes and dirty plates, the debris of last night's dinner.

" Look at this," said Baynes. " What do you make of it ? "

He held up his candle before an extraordinary object which stood at the back of the dresser. It was so wrinkled and shrunken and withered that it was difficult to say what it might have been. One could but say that it was black and leathery and that it bore some resemblance to a dwarfish human figure. At first, as I examined it, I thought that it was a mummified negro baby, and then it seemed a very twisted and ancient monkey. Finally I was left in doubt as to whether it was animal or human. A double band of white shells was strung round the centre of it.

" Very interesting — very interesting indeed ! " said Holmes peering at this sinister relic. " Anything more ? "

In silence Baynes led the way to the sink and held forward his candle. The limbs and body of some large white bird, torn savagely to pieces with the feathers still on, were littered all over it. Holmes pointed to the wattles on the severed head.

" A white cock," said he ; " most interesting ! It is really a very curious case."

But Mr. Baynes had kept his most sinister exhibit to the last. From under the sink he drew a zinc pail which contained a quantity of blood. Then from the table he took a platter heaped with small pieces of charred bone.

" Something has been killed and something has been burned. We raked all these out of the fire. We had a doctor in this morning. He says that they are not human."

Holmes smiled and rubbed his hands.

" I must congratulate you, inspector, on handling so distinctive and instructive a case. Your powers, if I may say so without offence, seem superior to your opportunities."

Inspector Baynes' small eyes twinkled with pleasure.

" You're right, Mr. Holmes. We stagnate in the provinces. A case of this sort gives a man a chance, and I hope that I shall take it. What do you make of these bones ? "

" A lamb, I should say, or a kid."

" And the white cock ? "

" Curious, Mr. Baynes, very curious. I should say almost unique."

" Yes, sir, there must have been some very strange people with some very strange ways in this house. One of them is dead. Did his companions follow him and kill him ? If they did we should have them, for every port is watched. But my own views are different. Yes, sir, my own views are very different."

" You have a theory, then ? "

" And I'll work it myself, Mr. Holmes. It's only due to my own credit to do so. Your name is made, but I have still to make mine. I should be glad to be able to say afterwards that I had solved it without your help."

Holmes laughed good-humouredly.

" Well, well, inspector," said he. " Do you follow your path and I will follow mine. My results are always very much at your service if you care to apply to me for them. I think that I have seen all that I wish in this house, and that my time may be more profitably employed elsewhere. *Au revoir* and good luck ! "

I could tell by numerous subtle signs, which might have been lost upon anyone but myself, that Holmes was on a hot scent. As impassive as ever to the casual observer, there were none the less a subdued eagerness and suggestion of tension in his brightened eyes and brisker manner which assured me that the game was afoot. After his habit he said nothing, and after mine I asked no questions. Sufficient for me to share the sport and lend my humble help to the capture without distracting that intent brain

"I assure you I speak for your good."

It seemed to me that something like a wink quivered for an instant over one of Mr. Baynes' tiny eyes.

"We agreed to work on our own lines, Mr. Holmes. That's what I am doing."

"Oh, very good," said Holmes. "Don't blame me."

"No, sir; I believe you mean well by me. But we all have our own systems, Mr. Holmes. You have yours, and maybe I have mine."

"Let us say no more about it."

"You're welcome always to my news. This fellow is a perfect savage, as strong as a cart-horse and as fierce as the devil. He chewed Downing's thumb nearly off before they could master him. He hardly speaks a word of English, and we can get nothing out of him but grunts."

"And you think you have evidence that he murdered his late master?"

"I didn't say so, Mr. Holmes; I didn't say so. We all have our little ways. You try yours and I will try mine. That's the agreement."

Holmes shrugged his shoulders as we walked away together. "I can't make the man out. He seems to be riding for a fall. Well, as he says, we must each try our own way and see what comes of it. But there's something in Inspector Baynes which I can't quite understand."

"Just sit down in that chair, Watson," said Sherlock Holmes, when we had returned to our apartment at the Bull. "I want to put you in touch with the situation, as I may need your help to-night. Let me show you the evolution of this case, so far as I have been able to follow it. Simple as it has been in its leading features, it has none the less presented surprising difficulties in the way of an arrest. There are gaps in that direction which we have still to fill.

"We will go back to the note which was handed in to Garcia upon the evening of his death. We may put aside this idea of Baynes' that Garcia's servants were concerned in the matter. The proof of this lies in the fact that it was *he* who had arranged for the presence of Scott Eccles, which could only have been done for the purpose of an alibi. It was Garcia, then, who had an enterprise, and apparently a criminal enterprise, in hand that night, in the course of which he met his death. I say criminal because only a man with a criminal enterprise desires to establish an alibi. Who, then, is most likely to have taken his life? Surely the person against whom the criminal enterprise was directed. So far it seems to me that we are on safe ground.

" We can now see a reason for the disappearance of Garcia's household. They were *all* confederates in the same unknown crime. If it came off then Garcia returned, any possible suspicion would be warded off by the Englishman's evidence, and all would be well. But the attempt was a dangerous one, and if Garcia did *not* return by a certain hour it was probable that his own life had been sacrificed. It had been arranged, therefore, that in such a case his two subordinates were to make for some pre-arranged spot, where they could escape investigation and be in a position afterwards to renew their attempt. That would fully explain the facts, would it not? "

The whole inexplicable tangle seemed to straighten out before me. I wondered, as I always did, how it had not been obvious to me before.

" But why should one servant return? "

" We can imagine that, in the confusion of flight, something precious, something which he could not bear to part with, had been left behind. That would explain his persistence, would it not? "

" Well, what is the next step? "

" The next step is the note received by Garcia at the dinner. It indicates a confederate at the other end. Now, where was the other end? I have already shown you that it could only lie in some large house, and that the number of large houses is limited. My first days in this village were devoted to a series of walks, in which in the intervals of my botanical researches I made a reconnaissance of all the large houses and an examination of the family history of the occupants. One house, and only one, riveted my attention. It is the famous old Jacobean grange of High Gable, one mile on the farther side of Oxshott, and less than half a mile from the scene of the tragedy. The other mansions belonged to prosaic and respectable people who live far aloof from romance. But Mr. Henderson, of High Gable, was by all accounts a curious man, to whom curious adventures might befall. I concentrated my attention, therefore, upon him and his household.

" A singular set of people, Watson—the man himself the most singular of them all. I managed to see him on a plausible pretext, but I seemed to read in his dark, deep-set, brooding eyes that he was perfectly aware of my true business. He is a man of fifty, strong, active, with iron-grey hair, great bunched black eyebrows, the step of a deer, and the air of an emperor—a fierce, masterful man, with a red-hot spirit behind his parchment face. He is either a foreigner or has lived long in the Tropics, for he is yellow and sapless, but tough as whipcord. His friend and secretary, Mr. Lucas, is undoubtedly a foreigner, chocolate brown, wily, suave and cat-like with a poisonous gentleness of speech. You see, Watson, we have come already upon two sets of foreigners—one at Wisteria Lodge and one at High Gable—so our gaps are beginning to close.

" These two men, close and confidential friends, are the centre of the household ; but there is one other person, who for our immediate purpose may be even more important. Henderson has two children—girls of eleven and thirteen. Their governess is a Miss Burnet, an Englishwoman of forty or thereabouts. There is also one confidential man-servant. This little group forms the real family, for they travel about together, and Henderson is a great traveller, always on the move. It is only within the last few weeks that he has returned, after a year's absence, to High Gable. I may add that he is enormously rich, and whatever his whims may be he can very easily satisfy them. For the rest, his house is full of butlers, footmen, maid-servants, and the usual overfed, underworked staff of a large English country-house.

" So much I learned partly from village gossip and partly from my own observation. There are no better instruments than discharged servants with a grievance, and I was lucky enough to find one. I call it luck, but it would not have come my way had I not been looking out for it. As Baynes remarks, we all have our systems. It was my system which enabled me to find John Warner, late gardener of High Gable, sacked in a moment of temper by his imperious employer. He in turn had friends among the indoor servants, who unite in their fear and dislike of their master. So I had my key to the secrets of the establishment.

" Curious people, Watson ! I don't pretend to understand it all yet, but very curious people anyway. It's a double-winged house, and the servants live on one side, the family on the other. There's no link between the two save for Henderson's own servant, who serves the family's meals. Everything is carried to a certain door, which forms the one connection. Governess and children hardly go out at all, except into the garden. Henderson never by any chance walks alone. His dark secretary is like his shadow. The gossip among the servants is that their master is terribly afraid of something. ' Sold his soul to the devil in exchange for money,' says Warner, ' and expects his creditor to come up and claim his own.' Where they came from, or who they are, nobody has an idea. They are very violent. Twice Henderson has lashed at folk with his dog-whip, and only his long purse and heavy compensation have kept him out of the courts.

" Well, now, Watson, let us judge the situation by this new information. We may take it that the letter came out of this strange household, and was an invitation to Garcia to carry out some attempt which had already been planned. Who wrote the note ? It was someone within the citadel, and it was a woman. Who then, but Miss Burnet, the governess ? All our reasoning seems to point that way.

At any rate, we may take it as a hypothesis, and see what consequences it would entail. I may add that Miss Burnet's age and character make it certain that my first idea that there might be a love interest in our story is out of the question.

" If she wrote the note she was presumably the friend and confederate of Garcia. What, then, might she be expected to do if she heard of his death ? If he met it in some nefarious enterprise her lips might be sealed. Still, in her heart she must retain bitterness and hatred against those who had killed him, and would presumably help so far as she could to have revenge upon them. Could we see her, then, and try to use her ? That was my first thought. But now we come to a sinister fact. Miss Burnet has not been seen by any human eye since the night of the murder. From that evening she has utterly vanished. Is she alive ? Has she perhaps met her end on the same night as the friend whom she had summoned ? Or is she merely a prisoner ? There is the point which we still have to decide.

" You will appreciate the difficulty of the situation, Watson. There is nothing upon which we can apply for a warrant. Our whole scheme might seem fantastic if laid before a magistrate. The woman's disappearance counts for nothing, since in that extraordinary household any member of it might be invisible for a week. And yet she may at the present moment be in danger of her life. All I can do is to watch the house and leave my agent, Warner, on guard at the gates. We can't let such a situation continue. If the law can do nothing we must take the risk ourselves."

" What do you suggest ? "

" I know which is her room. It is accessible from the top of an outhouse. My suggestion is that you and I go to-night and see if we can strike at the very heart of the mystery."

It was not, I must confess, a very alluring prospect. The old house with its atmosphere of murder, the singular and formidable inhabitants, the unknown dangers of the approach, and the fact that we were putting ourselves legally in a false position, all combined to damp my ardour. But there was something in the ice-cold reasoning of Holmes which made it impossible to shrink from any adventure which he might recommend. One knew that thus, and only thus, could a solution be found. I clasped his hand in silence, and the die was cast.

But it was not destined that our investigation should have so adventurous an ending. It was about five o'clock, and the shadows of the March evening were beginning to fall, when an excited rustic rushed into our room.

" They've gone, Mr. Holmes. They went by the last train. The lady broke away, and I've got her in a cab downstairs."

" Excellent, Warner ! " cried Holmes, springing to his feet. " Watson, the gaps are closing rapidly."

In the cab was a woman, half-collapsed from nervous exhaustion. She bore upon her aquiline and emaciated face the traces of some recent tragedy. Her head hung listlessly upon her breast, but as she raised it and turned her dull eyes upon us, I saw that her pupils were dark dots in the centre of the broad grey iris. She was drugged with opium.

" I watched at the gate, same as you advised, Mr. Holmes," said our emissary, the discharged gardener. " When the carriage came out I followed it to the station. She was like one walking in her sleep ; but when they tried to get her into the train she came to life and struggled. They pushed her into the carriage. She fought her way out again. I took her part, got her into a cab, and here we are. I shan't forget the face at the carriage window as I led her away. I'd have a short life if he had his way— the black-eyed, scowling, yellow devil."

We carried her upstairs, laid her on the sofa, and a couple of cups of the strongest coffee soon cleared her brain from the mists of the drug. Baynes had been summoned by Holmes, and the situation rapidly explained to him.

" Why, sir, you've got me the very evidence I want," said the inspector, warmly, shaking my friend by the hand. " I was on the same scent as you from the first."

" What ! You were after Henderson ? "

" Why, Mr. Holmes, when you were crawling in the shrubbery at High Gable I was up one of the trees in the plantation and saw you down below. It was just who would get his evidence first."

" Then why did you arrest the mulatto ? "

Baynes chuckled.

" I was sure Henderson, as he calls himself, felt that he was suspected, and that he would lie low and make no move so long as he thought he was in any danger. I arrested the wrong man to make him believe that our eyes were off him. I knew he would be likely to clear off then and give us a chance of getting at Miss Burnet."

Holmes laid his hand upon the inspector's shoulder.

" You will rise high in your profession. You have instinct and intuition," said he.

Baynes flushed with pleasure.

" I've had a plain-clothes man waiting at the station all the week. Wherever the High Gable folk go he will keep them in sight. But he must have been hard put to it when Miss Burnet broke away. However, your man picked her up, and it all ends well. We can't arrest without her evidence, that is clear, so the sooner we get a statement the better."

" Every minute she gets stronger," said Holmes, glancing at the governess. " But tell me, Baynes, who is this man Henderson ? "

" Henderson," the inspector answered, "is Don Murillo, once called the Tiger of San Pedro."

The Tiger of San Pedro ! The whole history of the man came back to me in a flash. He had made his name as the most lewd and bloodthirsty tyrant that had ever governed any country with a pretence to civilization. Strong, fearless, and energetic, he had sufficient virtue to enable him to impose his odious vices upon a cowering people for ten or twelve years. His name was a terror through all Central America. At the end of that time there was a universal rising against him. But he was as cunning as he was cruel, and at the first whisper of coming trouble he had secretly conveyed his treasures aboard a ship which was manned by devoted adherents. It was an empty palace which was stormed by the insurgents next day. The Dictator, his two children, his secretary, and his wealth had all escaped them. From that moment he had vanished from the world, and his identity had been a frequent subject for comment in the European Press.

" Yes, sir ; Don Murillo, the Tiger of San Pedro," said Baynes. " If you look it up you will find that the San Pedro colours are green and white, same as in the note, Mr. Holmes. Henderson he called himself, but I traced him back, Paris and Rome and Madrid to Barcelona, where his ship came in in '86. They've been looking for him all the time for their revenge, but it is only now that they have begun to find him out."

" They discovered him a year ago," said Miss Burnet, who had sat up and was now intently following the conversation. " Once already his life has been attempted ; but some evil spirit shielded him. Now, again, it is the noble, chivalrous Garcia who has fallen, while the monster goes safe. But another will come, and yet another, until some day justice will be done ; that is as certain as the rise of to-morrow's sun." Her thin hands clenched, and her worn face blanched with the passion of her hatred.

" But how come you into this matter, Miss Burnet ? " asked Holmes. " How can an English lady join in such a murderous affair ? "

" I join in it because there is no other way in the world by which justice can be gained. What does the law of England care for the rivers of blood shed years ago in San Pedro, or for the ship-load of treasure which this man has stolen ? To you they are like crimes committed in some other planet. But *we* know. We have learned the truth in sorrow and in suffering. To us there is no fiend in hell like Juan Murillo, and no peace in life while his victims still cry for vengeance."

"No doubt," said Holmes, "he was as you say. I have heard that he was atrocious. But how are you affected ? "

"I will tell you it all. This villain's policy was to murder, on one pretext or another, every man who showed such promise that he might in time come to be a dangerous rival. My husband—yes, my real name is Signora Victor Durando—was the San Pedro Minister in London. He met me and married me there. A nobler man never lived upon earth. Unhappily, Murillo heard of his excellence, recalled him on some pretext, and had him shot. With a premonition of his fate he had refused to take me with him. His estates were confiscated, and I was left with a pittance and a broken heart.

"Then came the downfall of the tyrant. He escaped as you have just described. But the many whose lives he had ruined, whose nearest and dearest had suffered torture and death at his hands, would not let the matter rest. They banded themselves into a society which should never be dissolved until the work was done. It was my part after we had discovered in the transformed Henderson the fallen despot, to attach myself to his household and keep the others in touch with his movements. This I was able to do by securing the position of governess in his family. He little knew that the woman who faced him at every meal was the woman whose husband he had hurried at an hour's notice into eternity. I smiled on him, did my duty to his children, and bided my time. An attempt was made in Paris, and failed. We zigzagged swiftly here and there over Europe, to throw off the pursuers, and finally returned to this house, which he had taken upon his first arrival in England.

"But here also the ministers of justice were waiting. Knowing that he would return there, Garcia, who is the son of the former highest dignitary in San Pedro, was waiting with two trusty companions of humble station, all three fired with the same reasons for revenge. He could do little during the day, for Murillo took every precaution, and never went out save with his satellite Lucas, or Lopez as he was known in the days of his greatness. At night, however, he slept alone, and the avenger might find him. On a certain evening, which had been prearranged, I sent my friend final instructions, for the man was for ever on the alert, and continually changed his room. I was to see that the doors were open and the signal of a green or white light in a window which faced the drive was to give notice if all was safe, or if the attempt had better be postponed.

" But everything went wrong with us. In some way I had excited the suspicion of Lopez, the secretary. He crept up behind me, and sprang upon me just as I had finished the note. He and his master dragged me to my room, and held judgment upon me as a convicted traitress. Then and there they would have plunged their knives into me, could they have seen how to escape the consequence of the deed. Finally, after much debate, they concluded that my murder was too dangerous. But they determined to get rid for ever of Garcia. They had gagged me, and Murillo twisted my arm round until I gave him the address. I swear that he might have twisted it off had I understood what it would mean to Garcia. Lopez addressed the note which I had written, sealed it with his sleeve-link, and sent it by the hand of the servant, José. How they murdered him I do not know, save that it was Murillo's hand who struck him down, for Lopez had remained to guard me. I believe he must have waited among the gorse bushes through which the path winds and struck him down as he passed. At first they were of a mind to let him enter the house and to kill him as a detected burglar ; but they argued that if they were mixed up in an inquiry their own identity would at once be publicly disclosed and they would be open to further attacks. With the death of Garcia the pursuit might cease, since such a death might frighten others from the task.

" All would now have been well for them had it not been for my knowledge of what they had done. I have no doubt that there were times when my life hung in the balance. I was confined to my room, terrorized by the most horrible threats, cruelly ill-used to break my spirit—see this stab on my shoulder and the bruises from end to end of my arms—and a gag was thrust into my mouth on the one occasion when I tried to call from the window. For five days this cruel imprisonment continued, with hardly enough food to hold body and soul together. This afternoon a good lunch was brought me, but the moment after I took it I knew that I had been drugged. In a sort of dream I remember being half-led, half-carried to the carriage ; in the same state I was conveyed to the train. Only then, when the wheels were almost moving did I suddenly realize that my liberty lay in my own hands. I sprang out, they tried to drag me back, and had it not been for the help of this good man, who led me to the cab, I should never have broken away. Now, thank God, I am beyond their power for ever."

We had all listened intently to this remarkable statement. It was Holmes who broke the silence.

" Our difficulties are not over," he remarked, shaking his head. " Our police work ends, but our legal work begins."

" Exactly," said I. " A plausible lawyer could make it out as an act of self-defence. There may be a hundred crimes in the background, but it is only on this one that they can be tried."

" Come, come," said Baynes, cheerily ; " I think better of the law than that. Self-defence is one thing. To entice a man in cold blood with the object of murdering him is another, whatever danger you may fear from him. No, no ; we shall all be justified when we see the tenants of High Gable at the next Guildford Assizes."

It is a matter of history, however, that a little time was still to elapse before the Tiger of San Pedro should meet with his deserts. Wily and bold, he and his companion threw their pursuer off their track by entering a lodging-house in Edmonton Street and leaving by the back-gate into Curzon Square. From that day they were seen no more in England. Some six months afterwards the Marquess of Montalva and Signor Rulli, his secretary, were both murdered in their rooms at the Hotel Escurial at Madrid. The crime was ascribed to Nihilism, and the murderers were never arrested. Inspector Baynes visited us at Baker Street with a printed description of the dark face of the secretary, and of the masterful features, the magnetic black eyes, and the tufted brows of his master. We could not doubt that justice, if belated, had come at last.

" A chaotic case, my dear Watson," said Holmes, over an evening pipe. " It will not be possible for you to present it in that compact form which is dear to your heart. It covers two continents, concerns two groups of mysterious persons, and is further complicated by the highly respectable presence of our friend Scott Eccles, whose inclusion shows me that the deceased Garcia had a scheming mind and a well-developed instinct of self-preservation. It is remarkable only for the fact that amid a perfect jungle of possibilities we, with our worthy collaborator the inspector, have kept our close hold on the essentials and so been guided along the crooked and winding path. Is there any point which is not quite clear to you ? "

" The object of the mulatto cook's return ? "

" I think that the strange creature in the kitchen may account for it. The man was a primitive savage from the backwoods of San Pedro, and this was his fetish. When his companion and he had fled to some prearranged retreat —already occupied, no doubt, by a confederate—the companion had persuaded him to leave so compromising an article of furniture. But the mulatto's heart was with it, and he was driven back to it next day, when, on reconnoitring through the window, he found policeman Walters in possession. He waited three days longer, and then his piety or his superstition drove him to try once more.

Inspector Baynes, who, with his usual astuteness, had minimized the incident before me, had really recognized its importance, and had left a trap into which the creature walked. Any other point, Watson ? "

" The torn bird, the pail of blood, the charred bones, all the mystery of that weird kitchen ? "

Holmes smiled as he turned up an entry in his notebook.

" I spent a morning in the British Museum reading up that and other points. Here is a quotation from Eckermann's *Voodooism and the Negroid Religions* :

> " The true Voodoo-worshipper attempts nothing of importance without certain sacrifices which are intended to propitiate his unclean gods. In extreme cases these rites take the form of human sacrifices followed by cannibalism. The more usual victims are a white cock, which is plucked in pieces alive, or a black goat, whose throat is cut and body burned.

" So you see our savage friend was very orthodox in his ritual. It is grotesque, Watson," Holmes added, as he slowly fastened his notebook ; " but, as I have had occasion to remark, there is but one step from the grotesque to the horrible."

38. *The Cardboard Box*

IN choosing a few typical cases which illustrate the remarkable mental qualities of my friend, Sherlock Holmes, I have endeavoured, so far as possible, to select those which presented the minimum of sensationalism, while offering a fair field for his talents. It is, however, unfortunately, impossible entirely to separate the sensational from the criminal, and a chronicler is left in the dilemma that he must either sacrifice details which are essential to his statement, and so give a false impression of the problem, or he must use matter which chance, and not choice, has provided him with. With this short preface I shall turn to my notes of what proved to be a strange, though a peculiarly terrible, chain of events.

It was a blazing hot day in August. Baker Street was

like an oven, and the glare of the sunlight upon the yellow brickwork of the house across the road was painful to the eye. It was hard to believe that these were the same walls which loomed so gloomily through the fogs of winter. Our blinds were half-drawn, and Holmes lay curled upon the sofa, reading and re-reading a letter which he had received by the morning post. For myself, my term of service in India had trained me to stand heat better than cold, and a thermometer at 90 was no hardship. But the morning paper was uninteresting. Parliament had risen. Everybody was out of town, and I yearned for the glades of the New Forest or the shingle of Southsea. A depleted bank account had caused me to postpone my holiday, and as to my companion, neither the country nor the sea presented the slightest attraction to him. He loved to lie in the very centre of five millions of people, with his filaments stretching out and running through them, responsive to every little rumour or suspicion of unsolved crime. Appreciation of nature found no place among his many gifts, and his only change was when he turned his mind from the evil-doer of the town to track down his brother of the country.

Finding that Holmes was too absorbed for conversation I had tossed aside the barren paper and, leaning back in my chair, I fell into a brown study. Suddenly my companion's voice broke in upon my thoughts.

" You are right, Watson," said he. " It does seem a most preposterous way of settling a dispute."

" Most preposterous ! " I exclaimed, and then suddenly realizing how he had echoed the inmost thought of my soul, I sat up in my chair and stared at him in blank amazement.

" What is this, Holmes ? " I cried. " This is beyond anything which I could have imagined."

He laughed heartily at my perplexity.

" You remember," said he, " that some little time ago when I read you the passage in one of Poe's sketches in which a close reasoner follows the unspoken thoughts of his companion, you were inclined to treat the matter as a mere *tour-de-force* of the author. On my remarking that I was constantly in the habit of doing the same thing you expressed incredulity."

"Oh, no !"

"Perhaps not with your tongue, my dear Watson, but certainly with your eyebrows. So when I saw you throw down your paper and enter upon a train of thought, I was very happy to have the opportunity of reading it off, and eventually of breaking into it, as a proof that I had been *en rapport* with you."

But I was still far from satisfied. "In the example which you read to me," said I, "the reasoner drew his conclusions from the actions of the man whom he observed. If I remember right, he stumbled over a heap of stones, looked up at the stars, and so on. But I have been seated quietly in my chair, and what clues can I have given you ? "

"You do yourself an injustice. The features are given to man as the means by which he shall express his emotions, and yours are faithful servants."

"Do you mean to say that you read my train of thoughts from my features ? "

"Your features, and especially your eyes. Perhaps you cannot yourself recall how your reverie commenced ? "

"No, I cannot."

"Then I will tell you. After throwing down your paper, which was the action which drew my attention to you, you sat for half a minute with a vacant expression. Then your eyes fixed themselves upon your newly framed picture of General Gordon, and I saw by the alteration in your face that a train of thought had been started. But it did not lead very far. Your eyes flashed across to the unframed portrait of Henry Ward Beecher which stands upon the top of your books. Then you glanced up at the wall, and of course your meaning was obvious. You were thinking that if the portrait were framed, it would just cover that bare space and correspond with Gordon's picture over there."

"You have followed me wonderfully!" I exclaimed.

"So far I could hardly have gone astray. But now your thoughts went back to Beecher, and you looked hard across as if you were studying the character in his features. Then your eyes ceased to pucker, but you continued to look across, and your face was thoughtful. You were recalling the incidents of Beecher's career. I was well aware that you could not do this without thinking of the mission which he undertook on behalf of the North at the time of the Civil War, for I remember your expressing your passionate indignation at the way in which he was received by the more turbulent of our people. You felt so strongly about it, that I knew you could not think of Beecher without thinking of that also. When a moment later I saw your eyes wander away from the picture, I suspected that your mind had now turned to the Civil War, and when I observed that your lips set, your eyes sparkled, and your hands clenched, I was positive that you were indeed thinking of the gallantry which was shown by both sides in that desperate struggle. But then, again, your face grew sadder ; you shook your head. You were dwelling upon the sadness and horror and useless waste of life. Your hand stole towards your own old wound and a smile quivered on your lips, which showed me that the ridiculous side of this method of settling international questions had forced itself upon your mind. At this point I agreed with you that it was preposterous, and was glad to find that all my deductions had been correct."

"Absolutely!" said I. "And now that you have explained it, I confess that I am as amazed as before."

"It was very superficial, my dear Watson, I assure you. I should not have intruded it upon your attention had you not shown some incredulity the other day. But I have in my hands here a little problem which may prove to be more difficult of solution than my small essay in thought-reading. Have you observed in the paper a short paragraph referring to the remarkable contents of a packet sent

through the post to Miss Cushing, of Cross Street, Croydon ? "

" No, I saw nothing."

" Ah ! then you must have overlooked it. Just toss it
over to me. Here it is, under the financial column. Perhaps you would be good enough to read it aloud."

I picked up the paper which he had thrown back to me,
and read the paragraph indicated. It was headed, " A
Gruesome Packet."

" Miss Susan Cushing, living at Cross Street, Croydon, has
been made the victim of what must be regarded as a peculiarly
revolting practical joke, unless some more sinister meaning
should prove to be attached to the incident. At two o'clock
yesterday afternoon a small packet, wrapped in brown paper,
was handed in by the postman. A cardboard box was inside,
which was filled with coarse salt. On emptying this, Miss
Cushing was horrified to find two human ears, apparently quite
freshly severed. The box had been sent by parcel post from
Belfast upon the morning before. There is no indication
as to the sender, and the matter is the more mysterious as Miss
Cushing, who is a maiden lady of fifty, has led a most retired
life, and has so few acquaintances or correspondents that it is a
rare event for her to receive anything through the post. Some
years ago, however, when she resided at Penge, she let apart-
ments in her house to three young medical students, whom
she was obliged to get rid of on account of their noisy and
irregular habits. The police are of opinion that this outrage
may have been perpetrated upon Miss Cushing by these youths,
who owed her a grudge, and who hoped to frighten her by
sending her these relics of the dissecting-rooms. Some probability is lent to the theory by the fact that one of these students
came from the North of Ireland, and, to the best of Miss Cushing's belief, from Belfast. In the meantime, the matter is
being actively investigated, Mr. Lestrade, one of the very
smartest of our detective officers, being in charge of the case."

" So much for the *Daily Chronicle*," said Holmes, as I
finished reading. " Now for our friend Lestrade. I had
a note from him this morning, in which he says : ' I think
that this case is very much in your line. We have every
hope of clearing the matter up, but we find a little difficulty
in getting anything to work upon. We have, of course,

wired to the Belfast post office, but a large number of parcels were handed in upon that day, and they have no means of identifying this particular one, or of remembering the sender. The box is a half-pound box of honeydew tobacco, and does not help us in any way. The medical-student theory still appears to me to be the most feasible, but if you should have a few hours to spare, I should be very happy to see you out here. I shall be either at the house or in the police-station all day.' What say you, Watson? Can you rise superior to the heat, and run down to Croydon with me on the off chance of a case for your annals?"

"I was longing for something to do."

"You shall have it then. Ring for our boots, and tell them to order a cab. I'll be back in a moment, when I have changed my dressing-gown and filled my cigar-case."

A shower of rain fell while we were in the train, and the heat was far less oppressive in Croydon than in town. Holmes had sent on a wire, so that Lestrade, as wiry, as dapper, and as ferret-like as ever, was waiting for us at the station. A walk of five minutes took us to Cross Street, where Miss Cushing resided.

It was a very long street of two-story brick houses, neat and prim, with whitened stone steps and little groups of aproned women gossiping at the doors. Half-way down, Lestrade stopped and tapped at a door, which was opened by a small servant girl. Miss Cushing was sitting in the front room, into which we were ushered. She was a placid-faced woman, with large, gentle eyes, and grizzled hair curving down over her temples on each side. A worked antimacassar lay upon her lap and a basket of coloured silks stood upon a stool beside her.

"They are in the outhouse, those dreadful things," said she, as Lestrade entered. "I wish that you would take them away altogether."

"So I shall, Miss Cushing. I only kept them here until my friend, Mr. Holmes, should have seen them in your presence."

" Why in my presence, sir ? "

" In case he wished to ask any questions."

" What is the use of asking me questions, when I tell you I know nothing whatever about it ? "

" Quite so, madam," said Holmes, in his soothing way. " I have no doubt that you have been annoyed more than enough already over this business."

" Indeed, I have, sir. I am a quiet woman and live a retired life. It is something new for me to see my name in the papers and to find the police in my house. I won't have those things in here, Mr. Lestrade. If you wish to see them you must go to the outhouse."

It was a small shed in the narrow garden which ran behind the house. Lestrade went in and brought out a yellow cardboard box, with a piece of brown paper and some string. There was a bench at the end of the path, and we all sat down while Holmes examined, one by one, the articles which Lestrade had handed to him.

" The string is exceedingly interesting," he remarked, holding it up to the light and sniffing at it. " What do you make of this string, Lestrade ? "

" It has been tarred."

" Precisely. It is a piece of tarred twine. You have also, no doubt, remarked that Miss Cushing has cut the cord with a scissors, as can be seen by the double fray on each side. This is of importance."

" I cannot see the importance," said Lestrade.

" The importance lies in the fact that the knot is left intact, and that this knot is of a peculiar character."

" It is very neatly tied. I had already made a note to that effect," said Lestrade, complacently.

" So much for the string, then," said Holmes, smiling ; " now for the box wrapper. Brown paper, with a distinct smell of coffee. What, did not observe it ? I think there can be no doubt of it. Address printed in rather straggling characters : ' Miss S. Cushing, Cross Street, Croydon.' Done with a broad-pointed pen, probably a J, and with very inferior ink. The word Croydon has been originally spelt with an *i*, which has been changed to *y*. The parcel was directed then by a man—the printing is distinctly masculine—of limited education and unacquainted with the town of Croydon. So far, so good! The box is a yellow, half-pound honeydew box, with nothing distinctive save two thumb marks at the left bottom corner. It is filled with rough salt of the quality used for preserving hides and other of the coarser commercial purposes. And embedded in it are these very singular enclosures."

He took out the two ears as he spoke, and laying a board across his knee, he examined them minutely, while Lestrade and I, bending forward on each side of him, glanced alternately at these dreadful relics and at the thoughtful, eager face of our companion. Finally he returned them to the box once more, and sat for a while in deep meditation.

" You have observed, of course," said he at last, " that the ears are not a pair."

" Yes, I have noticed that. But if this were the practical joke of some students from the dissecting-rooms, it would be as easy for them to send two odd ears as a pair."

" Precisely. But this is not a practical joke."

" You are sure of it ? "

" The presumption is strongly against it. Bodies in the dissecting-rooms are injected with preservative fluid. These ears bear no signs of this. They are fresh too. They have been cut off with a blunt instrument, which would hardly happen if a student had done it. Again, carbolic or rectified spirits would be the preservatives which would suggest themselves to the medical mind, certainly not rough salt. I repeat that there is no practical joke here, but that we are investigating a serious crime."

A vague thrill ran through me as I listened to my companion's words and saw the stern gravity which had hardened his features. This brutal preliminary seemed to shadow forth some strange and inexplicable horror in the background. Lestrade, however, shook his head like a man who is only half convinced.

"There are objections to the joke theory, no doubt," said he ; " but there are much stronger reasons against the other. We know that this woman has led a most quiet and respectable life at Penge and here for the last twenty years. She has hardly been away from her home for a day during that time. Why on earth, then, should any criminal send her the proofs of his guilt, especially as, unless she is a most consummate actress, she understands quite as little of the matter as we do ? "

"That is the problem which we have to solve," Holmes answered, "and for my part I shall set about it by presuming that my reasoning is correct, and that a double murder has been committed. One of these ears is a woman's, small, finely formed, and pierced for an ear-ring. The other is a man's, sun-burned, discoloured, and also pierced for an ear-ring. These two people are presumably dead, or we should have heard their story before now. To-day is Friday. The packet was posted on Thursday morning. The tragedy, then, occurred on Wednesday or Tuesday, or earlier. If the two people were murdered, who but their murderer would have sent this sign of his work to Miss Cushing ? We may take it that the sender of the packet is the man whom we want. But he must have some strong reason for sending Miss Cushing this packet. What reason then ? It must have been to tell her that the deed was done ; or to pain her, perhaps. But in that case she knows who it is. Does she know ? I doubt it. If she knew, why should she call the police in ? She might have buried the ears, and no one would have been the wiser. That is what she would have done if she had wished to shield the criminal. But if she does not wish to shield him she would give his name. There is a tangle here which needs straightening out." He had been talking in a high, quick voice, staring blankly up over the garden fence, but now he sprang briskly to his feet and walked towards the house.

"I have a few questions to ask Miss Cushing," said he.

"In that case I may leave you here," said Lestrade, "for I have another small business on hand. I think that I have nothing further to learn from Miss Cushing. You will find me at the police-station."

"We shall look in on our way to the train," answered Holmes. A moment later he and I were back in the front room, where the impassive lady was still quietly working away at her antimacassar. She put it down on her lap as we entered, and looked at us with her frank, searching blue eyes.

"I am convinced, sir," she said, "that this matter is a mistake, and that the parcel was never meant for me at all. I have said this several times to the gentleman from Scotland Yard, but he simply laughs at me. I have not an enemy in the world, as far as I know, so why should anyone play me such a trick?"

"I am coming to be of the same opinion, Miss Cushing," said Holmes, taking a seat beside her. "I think that it is more than probable . . ." He paused, and I was surprised, on glancing round, to see that he was staring with singular intentness at the lady's profile. Surprise and satisfaction were both for an instant to be read upon his eager face, though when she glanced round to find out the cause of his silence he had become as demure as ever. I stared hard myself at her flat, grizzled hair, her trim cap, her little gilt ear-rings, her placid features; but I could see nothing which could account for my companion's evident excitement.

"There were one or two questions——"

"Oh, I am weary of questions!" cried Miss Cushing, impatiently.

"You have two sisters, I believe."

"How could you know that?"

"I observed the very instant that I entered the room that you have a portrait group of three ladies upon the mantelpiece, one of whom is undoubtedly yourself, while the others are so exceedingly like you that there could be no doubt of the relationship."

" Yes, you are quite right. Those are my sisters, Sarah and Mary."

" And here at my elbow is another portrait, taken at Liverpool, of your younger sister, in the company of a man who appears to be a steward by his uniform. I observe that she was unmarried at the time."

" You are very quick at observing."

" That is my trade."

" Well, you are quite right. But she was married to Mr. Browner a few days afterwards. He was on the South American line when that was taken, but he was so fond of her that he couldn't abide to leave her for so long, and he got into the Liverpool and London boats."

" Ah, the *Conqueror*, perhaps ? "

" No, the *May Day*, when last I heard. Jim came down here to see me once. That was before he broke the pledge ; but afterwards he would always take drink when he was ashore, and a little drink would send him stark, staring mad. Ah ! it was a bad day that ever he took a glass in his hand again. First he dropped me, then he quarrelled with Sarah, and now that Mary has stopped writing we don't know how things are going with them."

It was evident that Miss Cushing had come upon a subject on which she felt very deeply. Like most people who lead a lonely life, she was shy at first, but ended by becoming extremely communicative. She told us many details about her brother-in-law the steward, and then wandering off on to the subject of her former lodgers, the medical students, she gave us a long account of their delinquencies, with their names and those of their hospitals. Holmes listened attentively to everything, throwing in a question from time to time.

" About your second sister, Sarah," said he. " I wonder, since you are both maiden ladies, that you do not keep house together."

" Ah ! you don't know Sarah's temper, or you would

wonder no more. I tried it when I came to Croydon, and we kept on until about two months ago, when we had to part. I don't want to say a word against my own sister, but she was always meddlesome and hard to please, was Sarah."

"You say that she quarrelled with your Liverpool relations."

"Yes, and they were the best of friends at one time. Why, she went up there to live in order to be near them. And now she has no word hard enough for Jim Browner. The last six months that she was here she would speak of nothing but his drinking and his ways. He had caught her meddling, I suspect, and given her a bit of his mind, and that was the start of it."

"Thank you, Miss Cushing," said Holmes, rising and bowing. "Your sister Sarah lives, I think you said, at New Street, Wallington? Good-bye, and I am very sorry that you should have been troubled over a case with which, as you say, you have nothing whatever to do."

There was a cab passing as we came out, and Holmes hailed it.

"How far to Wallington?" he asked.

"Only about a mile, sir."

"Very good. Jump in, Watson. We must strike while the iron is hot. Simple as the case is, there have been one or two very instructive details in connection with it. Just pull up at a telegraph office as you pass, cabby."

Holmes sent off a short wire, and for the rest of the drive lay back in the cab with his hat tilted over his nose to keep the sun from his face. Our driver pulled up at a house which was not unlike the one which we had just quitted. My companion ordered him to wait, and had his hand upon the knocker, when the door opened and a grave young gentleman in black, with a very shiny hat, appeared on the step.

"Is Miss Cushing at home?" asked Holmes.

"Miss Sarah Cushing is extremely ill," said he. "She has been suffering since yesterday from brain symptoms of great severity. As her medical adviser, I cannot possibly take the responsibility of allowing anyone to see her. I should recommend you to call again in ten days." He drew on his gloves, closed the door, and marched off down the street.

"Well, if we can't, we can't," said Holmes, cheerfully. "Perhaps she could not, or would not have told you much."

"I did not wish her to tell me anything. I only wanted to look at her. However, I think that I have got all that I want. Drive us to some decent hotel, cabby, where we may have some lunch, and afterwards we shall drop down upon friend Lestrade at the police-station."

We had a pleasant little meal together, during which Holmes would talk about nothing but violins, narrating with great exultation how he had purchased his own Stradivarius, which was worth at least five hundred guineas, at a Jew broker's in Tottenham Court Road for fifty-five shillings. This led him to Paganini, and we sat for an hour over a bottle of claret while he told me anecdote after anecdote of that extraordinary man. The afternoon was far advanced and the hot glare had softened into a mellow glow before we found ourselves at the police-station. Lestrade was waiting for us at the door.

"A telegram for you, Mr. Holmes," said he.

"Ha! It is the answer!" He tore it open, glanced his eyes over it, and crumpled it into his pocket. "That's all right," said he.

"Have you found out anything?"

"I have found out everything!"

"What!" Lestrade stared at him in amazement. "You are joking."

"I was never more serious in my life. A shocking crime has been committed, and I think I have now laid bare every detail of it."

"And the criminal?"

Holmes scribbled a few words upon the back of one of his visiting-cards and threw it over to Lestrade.

935

"That is the name," he said. "You cannot effect an arrest until to-morrow night at the earliest. I should prefer that you do not mention my name at all in connection with the case, as I choose to be only associated with those crimes which present some difficulty in their solution. Come on, Watson." We strode off together to the station, leaving Lestrade still staring with a delighted face at the card which Holmes had thrown him.

"The case," said Sherlock Holmes, as we chatted over our cigars that night in our rooms at Baker Street, "is one where, as in the investigations which you have chronicled under the names of the 'Study in Scarlet' and of the 'Sign of Four,' we have been compelled to reason backward from effects to causes. I have written to Lestrade asking him to supply us with the details which are now wanting, and which he will only get after he has secured his man. That he may be safely trusted to do, for although he is absolutely devoid of reason, he is as tenacious as a bulldog when he once understands what he has to do, and indeed, it is just this tenacity which has brought him to the top at Scotland Yard."

"Your case is not complete, then?" I asked.

"It is fairly complete in essentials. We know who the author of the revolting business is, although one of the victims still escapes us. Of course, you have formed your own conclusions."

"I presume that this Jim Browner, the steward of a Liverpool boat, is the man whom you suspect?"

"Oh! it is more than a suspicion."

"And yet I cannot see anything save very vague indications."

"On the contrary, to my mind nothing could be more clear. Let me run over the principal steps. We approached the case, you remember, with an absolutely blank mind, which is always an advantage. We had formed no theories. We were simply there to observe and to draw inferences from our observations. What did we see first ? A very placid and respectable lady, who seemed quite innocent of any secret, and a portrait which showed me that she had two younger sisters. It instantly flashed across my mind that the box might have been meant for one of these. I set the idea aside as one which could be disproved or confirmed at our leisure. Then we went to the garden, as you remember, and we saw the very singular contents of the little yellow box.

"The string was of the quality which is used by sailmakers aboard ship, and at once a whiff of the sea was perceptible in our investigation. When I observed that the knot was one which is popular with sailors, that the parcel had been posted at a port, and that the male ear was pierced for an ear-ring which is so much more common among sailors than landsmen, I was quite certain that all the actors in the tragedy were to be found among our seafaring classes.

"When I came to examine the address of the packet I observed that it was to Miss S. Cushing. Now, the oldest sister would, of course, be Miss Cushing, and although her initial was ' S ' it might belong to one of the others as well. In that case we should have to commence our investigation from a fresh basis altogether. I therefore went into the house with the intention of clearing up this point. I was about to assure Miss Cushing that I was convinced that a mistake had been made, when you may remember that I came suddenly to a stop. The fact was that I had just seen something which filled me with surprise, and at the same time narrowed the field of our inquiry immensely.

"As a medical man, you are aware, Watson, that there is no part of the body which varies so much as the human ear. Each ear is as a rule quite distinctive, and differs from all other ones. In last year's *Anthropological Journal* you will find two short monographs from my pen upon the subject. I had, therefore, examined the ears in the box with the eyes of an expert, and had carefully noted their anatomical peculiarities. Imagine my surprise then, when, on looking at Miss Cushing, I perceived that her ear corresponded exactly with the female ear which I had just inspected. The matter was entirely beyond coincidence. There was the same shortening of the pinna, the same broad curve of the upper lobe, the same convolution of the inner cartilage. In all essentials it was the same ear.

" Of course, I at once saw the enormous importance of the observation. It was evident that the victim was a blood relation, and probably a very close one. I began to talk to her about her family, and you remember that she at once gave us some exceedingly valuable details.

" In the first place, her sister's name was Sarah, and her address had, until recently, been the same, so that it was quite obvious how the mistake had occurred, and for whom the packet was meant. Then we heard of this steward, married to the third sister, and learned that he had at one time been so intimate with Miss Sarah that she had actually gone up to Liverpool to be near the Browners, but a quarrel had afterwards divided them. This quarrel had put a stop to all communications for some months, so that if Browner had occasion to address a packet to Miss Sarah, he would undoubtedly have done so to her old address.

" And now the matter had begun to straighten itself out wonderfully. We had learned of the existence of this steward, an impulsive man, of strong passions—you remember that he threw up what must have been a very superior berth, in order to be nearer to his wife—subject, too, to occasional fits of hard drinking. We had reason to believe that his wife had been murdered, and that a man— presumably a seafaring man—had been murdered at the same time. Jealousy, of course, at once suggests itself as the motive for the crime. And why should these proofs of the deed be sent to Miss Sarah Cushing ? Probably because during her residence in Liverpool she had some hand in bringing about the events which led to the tragedy. You will observe that this line of boats calls at Belfast, Dublin, and Waterford ; so that, presuming that Browner had committed the deed, and had embarked at once upon his steamer, the *May Day*, Belfast would be the first place at which he could post his terrible packet.

"A second solution was at this stage obviously possible, and although I thought it exceedingly unlikely, I was determined to elucidate it before going further. An unsuccessful lover might have killed Mr. and Mrs. Browner, and the male ear might have belonged to the husband. There were many grave objections to this theory, but it was conceivable. I therefore sent off a telegram to my friend Algar, of the Liverpool Force, and asked him to find out if Mrs. Browner were at home, and if Browner had departed in the *May Day*. Then we went on to Wallington to visit Miss Sarah.

"I was curious, in the first place, to see how far the family ear had been reproduced in her. Then, of course, she might give us very important information, but I was not sanguine that she would. She must have heard of the business the day before, since all Croydon was ringing with it, and she alone could have understood for whom the packet was meant. If she had been willing to help justice she would probably have communicated with the police already. However, it was clearly our duty to see her, so we went. We found that the news of the arrival of the packet—for her illness dated from that time—had such an effect upon her as to bring on brain fever. It was clearer than ever that she understood its full significance, but equally clear that we should have to wait some time for any assistance from her.

"However, we were really independent of her help. Our answers were waiting for us at the police-station, where I had directed Algar to send them. Nothing could be more conclusive. Mrs. Browner's house had been closed for more than three days, and the neighbours were of opinion that she had gone south to see her relatives. It had been ascertained at the shipping offices that Browner had left aboard of the *May Day*, and I calculate that she is due in the Thames to-morrow night. When he arrives he will be met by the obtuse but resolute Lestrade, and I have no doubt that we shall have all our details filled in."

Sherlock Holmes was not disappointed in his expectations. Two days later he received a bulky envelope, which contained a short note from the detective, and a typewritten document, which covered several pages of foolscap.

"Lestrade has got him all right," said Holmes, glancing up at me. "Perhaps it would interest you to hear what he says."

"MY DEAR MR. HOLMES,—

"In accordance with the scheme which we had formed in order to test our theories"—"the 'we' is rather fine, Watson, is it not?"—"I went down to the Albert Dock yesterday at 6 p.m., and boarded the s.s. *May Day*, belonging to the Liverpool, Dublin, and London Steam Packet Company. On inquiry, I found that there was a steward on board of the name of James Browner and that he had acted during the voyage in such an extraordinary manner that the captain had been compelled to relieve him of his duties. On descending to his berth, I found him seated upon a chest with his head sunk upon his hands, rocking himself to and fro. He is a big, powerful chap, clean-shaven, and very swarthy—something like Aldridge, who helped us in the bogus laundry affair. He jumped up when he heard my business, and I had my whistle to my lips to call a couple of river police, who were round the corner, but he seemed to have no heart in him, and he held out his hands quietly enough for the darbies. We brought him along to the cells, and his box as well, for we thought there might be something incriminating; but, bar a big sharp knife such as most sailors have, we got nothing for our trouble. However, we find that we shall want no more evidence, for on being brought before the inspector at the station, he asked leave to make a statement, which was, of course, taken down, just as he made it, by our shorthand man. We had three copies typewritten, one of which I enclose. The affair proves, as I always thought it would, to be an extremely simple one, but I am obliged to you for assisting me in my investigation. With kind regards, yours very truly, "G. LESTRADE."

"Hum! The investigation really was a very simple one," remarked Holmes; "but I don't think it struck him in that light when he first called us in. However, let us see what Jim Browner has to say for himself. This is his statement, as made before Inspector Montgomery at the Shadwell Police Station, and it has the advantage of being verbatim."

"Have I anything to say? Yes, I have a deal to say. I have to make a clean breast of it all. You can hang me, or you can leave me alone. I don't care a plug which you do. I tell you I've not shut an eye in sleep since I did it, and I don't believe I ever will again until I get past all waking. Sometimes it's his face, but most generally it's hers. I'm never without one or the other before me. He looks frowning and black-like, but she has a kind o' surprise upon her face. Aye, the white lamb, she might well be surprised when she read death on a face that had seldom looked anything but love upon her before.

"But it was Sarah's fault, and may the curse of a broken man put a blight on her and set the blood rotting in her veins! It's not that I want to clear myself. I know that I went back to drink, like the beast that I was. But she would have forgiven me; she would have stuck as close to me as a rope to a block if that woman had never darkened our door. For Sarah Cushing loved me—that's the root of the business—she loved me, until all her love turned to poisonous hate when she knew that I thought more of my wife's foot-mark in the mud than I did of her whole body and soul.

"There were three sisters altogether. The old one was just a good woman, the second was a devil, and the third was an angel. Sarah was thirty-three, and Mary was

twenty-nine when I married. We were just as happy as
the day was long when we set up house together, and in all
Liverpool there was no better woman than my Mary.
And then we asked Sarah up for a week, and the week grew
into a month, and one thing led to another, until she was
just one of ourselves.

" I was blue ribbon at that time, and we were putting a
little money by, and all was as bright as a new dollar. My
God, whoever would have thought that it could have come
to this ? Whoever would have dreamed it ?

" I used to be home for the week-ends very often, and
sometimes if the ship were held back for cargo I would
have a whole week at a time, and in this way I saw a deal
of my sister-in-law, Sarah. She was a fine tall woman,
black and quick and fierce, with a proud way of carrying
her head, and a glint from her eye like a spark from a flint.
But when little Mary was there I had never a thought of
her, and that I swear as I hope for God's mercy.

" It had seemed to me sometimes that she liked to be
alone with me, or to coax me out for a walk with her, but
I had never thought anything of that. But one evening
my eyes were opened. I had come up from the ship and
found my wife out, but Sarah at home. 'Where's Mary ?'
I asked. 'Oh, she has gone to pay some accounts.' I
was impatient and paced up and down the room. 'Can't
you be happy for five minutes without Mary, Jim ?' says
she. 'It's a bad compliment to me that you can't be contented with my society for so short a time.' 'That's all
right, my lass,' said I, putting out my hand towards her
in a kindly way, but she had it in both hers in an instant,
and they burned as if they were in a fever. I looked into
her eyes and I read it all there. There was no need for
her to speak, nor for me either. I frowned and drew my
hand away. Then she stood by my side in silence for a
bit, and then put up her hand and patted me on the shoulder. 'Steady, old Jim !' said she ; and with a kind o'
mocking laugh, she ran out of the room.

" Well, from that time Sarah hated me with her whole

heart and soul, and she is a woman who can hate too. I was a fool to let her go on biding with us—a besotted fool—but I never said a word to Mary, for I knew it would grieve her. Things went on much as before, but after a time I began to find that there was a bit of a change in Mary herself. She had always been so trusting and so innocent, but now she became queer and suspicious, wanting to know where I had been and what I had been doing, and whom my letters were from, and what I had in my pockets, and a thousand such follies. Day by day she grew queerer and more irritable, and we had causeless rows about nothing. I was fairly puzzled by it all. Sarah avoided me now, but she and Mary were just inseparable. I can see now how she was plotting and scheming and poisoning my wife's mind against me, but I was such a blind beetle that I could not understand it at the time. Then I broke my blue ribbon and began to drink again, but I think I should not have done it if Mary had been the same as ever. She had some reason to be disgusted with me now, and the gap between us began to be wider and wider. And then this Alec Fairbairn chipped in, and things became a thousand times blacker.

" It was to see Sarah that he came to my house first, but soon it was to see us, for he was a man with winning ways, and he made friends wherever he went. He was a dashing, swaggering chap, smart and curled, who had seen half the world, and could talk of what he had seen. He was good company, I won't deny it, and he had wonderful polite ways with him for a sailor man, so that I think there must have been a time when he knew more of the poop than the forecastle. For a month he was in and out of my house, and never once did it cross my mind that harm might come of his soft, tricky ways. And then at last something made me suspect, and from that day my peace was gone for ever.

" It was only a little thing too. I had come into the parlour unexpected, and as I walked in at the door I saw a light of welcome on my wife's face. But as she saw who it was it faded again, and she turned away with a look of disappointment. That was enough for me. There was no one but Alec Fairbairn whose step she could have mistaken for mine. If I could have seen him then I should have killed him, for I have always been like a madman when my temper gets loose. Mary saw the devil's light in my eyes, and she ran forward with her hands on my sleeve. 'Don't, Jim, don't!' says she. 'Where's Sarah?' I asked. 'In the kitchen,' says she. 'Sarah,' says I, as I went in, 'this man Fairbairn is never to darken my door again.' 'Why not?' says she. 'Because I order it.' 'Oh!' says she, 'if my friends are not good enough for this house then I am not good enough for it either.' 'You can do what you like,' says I, 'but if Fairbairn shows his face here again, I'll send you one of his ears for a keepsake.' She was frightened by my face, I think, for she never answered a word, and the same evening she left my house.

" Well, I don't know now whether it was pure devilry on the part of this woman, or whether she thought that she could turn me against my wife by encouraging her to misbehave. Anyway, she took a house just two streets off, and let lodgings to sailors. Fairbairn used to stay there, and Mary would go round to have tea with her sister and him. How often she went I don't know, but I followed her one day, and as I broke in at the door, Fairbairn got away over the back garden wall, like the cowardly skunk that he was. I swore to my wife that I would kill her if I found her in his company again, and I led her back with me, sobbing and trembling, and as white as a piece of paper. There was no trace of love between us any longer. I could see that she hated me and feared me, and when the thought of it drove me to drink then she despised me as well.

" Well, Sarah found that she could not make a living in Liverpool, so she went back, as I understand, to live with her sister in Croydon, and things jogged on much the same as ever at home. And then came this last week and all the misery and ruin.

" It was in this way. We had gone on the *May Day* for a round voyage of seven days, but a hogshead got loose and started one of our plates, so that we had to put back into port for twelve hours. I left the ship and came home, thinking what a surprise it would be for my wife, and hoping that maybe she would be glad to see me so soon. The thought was in my head as I turned into my own street, and at that moment a cab passed me, and there she was, sitting by the side of Fairbairn, the two chatting and laughing, with never a thought for me as I stood watching them from the footpath.

" I tell you, and I give you my word for it, that from that moment I was not my own master, and it is all like a dim dream when I look back on it. I had been drinking hard of late, and the two things together fairly turned my brain. There's something throbbing in my head now, like a docker's hammer, but that morning I seemed to have all Niagara whizzing and buzzing in my ears.

" Well, I took to my heels, and I ran after the cab. I had a heavy oak stick in my hand, and I tell you I saw red from the first ; but as I ran I got cunning, too, and hung back a little to see them without being seen. They pulled up soon at the railway station. There was a good crowd round the booking-office, so I got quite close to them without being seen. They took tickets for New Brighton. So did I, but I got in three carriages behind them. When we reached it they walked along the Parade, and I was never more than a hundred yards from them. At last I saw them hire a boat and start for a row, for it was a very hot day, and they thought no doubt that it would be cooler on the water.

" It was just as if they had been given into my hands. There was a bit of a haze, and you could not see more than a few hundred yards. I hired a boat for myself, and I pulled after them. I could see the blurr of their craft, but they were going nearly as fast as I, and they must have been a long mile from the shore before I caught them up. The haze was like a curtain all round us, and there were

we three in the middle of it. My God, shall I ever forget
their faces when they saw who was in the boat that was
closing in upon them? She screamed out. He swore
like a madman, and jabbed at me with an oar, for he must
have seen death in my eyes. I got past it and got one in
with my stick, that crushed his head like an egg. I would
have spared her, perhaps, for all my madness, but she
threw her arms round him, crying out to him, and calling
him 'Alec.' I struck again, and she lay stretched beside
him. I was like a wild beast then that had tasted blood.
If Sarah had been there, by the Lord, she should have
joined them. I pulled out my knife, and—well, there!
I've said enough. It gave me a kind of savage joy when I
thought how Sarah would feel when she had such signs as
these of what her meddling had brought about. Then
I tied the bodies into the boat, stove a plank, and stood by
until they had sunk. I knew very well that the owner
would think that they had lost their bearings in the haze,
and had drifted off out to sea. I cleaned myself up, got
back to land, and joined my ship without a soul having a
suspicion of what had passed. That night I made up the
packet for Sarah Cushing, and next day I sent it from
Belfast.

"There you have the whole truth of it. You can hang
me, or do what you like with me, but you cannot punish
me as I have been punished already. I cannot shut my
eyes but I see those two faces staring at me—staring at me
as they stared when my boat broke through the haze. I
killed them quick, but they are killing me slow; and if I
have another night of it I shall be either mad or dead
before morning. You won't put me alone into a cell, sir?
For pity's sake don't, and may you be treated in your day
of agony as you treat me now."

"What is the meaning of it, Watson?" said Holmes,
solemnly, as he laid down the paper. "What object is
served by this circle of misery and violence and fear? It
must tend to some end, or else our universe is ruled by

chance, which is unthinkable. But what end? There is the great standing perennial problem to which human reason is as far from an answer as ever."

39. *The Red Circle*

I

"WELL, Mrs. Warren, I cannot see that you have any particular cause for uneasiness, nor do I understand why I, whose time is of some value, should interfere in the matter. I really have other things to engage me." So spoke Sherlock Holmes, and turned back to the great scrap-book in which he was arranging and indexing some of his recent material.

But the landlady had the pertinacity, and also the cunning, of her sex. She held her ground firmly.

"You arranged an affair for a lodger of mine last year," she said—"Mr. Fairdale Hobbs."

"Ah, yes—a simple matter."

"But he would never cease talking of it—your kindness, sir, and the way in which you brought light into the darkness. I remembered his words when I was in doubt and darkness myself. I know you could if you only would."

Holmes was accessible upon the side of flattery, and also, to do him justice, upon the side of kindliness. The two forces made him lay down his gum-brush with a sigh of resignation and push back his chair.

"Well, well, Mrs. Warren, let us hear about it, then. You don't object to tobacco, I take it? Thank you, Watson—the matches! You are uneasy, as I understand, because your new lodger remains in his rooms and you cannot see him. Why, bless you, Mrs. Warren, if I were your lodger you often would not see me for weeks on end."

"No doubt, sir; but this is different. It frightens me, Mr. Holmes. I can't sleep for fright. To hear his quick step moving here and moving there from early morning to late at night, and yet never to catch so much as a glimpse of him—it's more than I can stand. My husband is as nervous over it as I am, but he is out at his work all day, while I get no rest from it. What is he hiding for? What has he done? Except for the girl, I am all alone in the house with him, and it's more than my nerves can stand."

Holmes leaned forward and laid his long, thin fingers upon the woman's shoulder. He had an almost hypnotic power of soothing when he wished. The scared look faded from her eyes, and her agitated features smoothed into their usual commonplace. She sat down in the chair which he had indicated.

"If I take it up I must understand every detail," said he. "Take time to consider. The smallest point may be the most essential. You say that the man came ten days ago, and paid you for a fortnight's board and lodging?"

"He asked my terms, sir. I said fifty shillings a week. There is a small sitting-room and bedroom, and all complete, at the top of the house."

"Well?"

"He said, 'I'll pay you five pounds a week if I can have it on my own terms.' I'm a poor woman, sir, and Mr. Warren earns little, and the money meant much to me. He took out a ten-pound note, and he held it out to me then and there. 'You can have the same every fortnight for a long time to come if you keep the terms,' he said. 'If not, I'll have no more to do with you.'"

"What were the terms?"

"Well, sir, they were that he was to have a key of the house. That was all right. Lodgers often have them. Also, that he was to be left entirely to himself, and never, upon any excuse, to be disturbed."

"Nothing wonderful in that, surely?"

"Not in reason, sir. But this is out of all reason. He has been there for ten days, and neither Mr. Warren, nor I, nor the girl has once set eyes upon him. We can hear that quick step of his pacing up and down, up and down, night, morning, and noon ; but except on that first night he has never once gone out of the house."

" Oh, he went out the first night, did he ? "

" Yes, sir, and returned very late—after we were all in bed. He told me after he had taken the rooms that he would do so, and asked me not to bar the door. I heard him come up the stair after midnight."

" But his meals ? "

" It was his particular direction that we should always, when he rang, leave his meal upon a chair, outside his door. Then he rings again when he has finished, and we take it down from the same chair. If he wants anything else he prints it on a slip of paper and leaves it."

" Prints it ? "

" Yes, sir ; prints it in pencil. Just the word, nothing more. Here's one I brought to show you—SOAP. Here's another—MATCH. This is one he left the first morning—DAILY GAZETTE. I leave that paper with his breakfast every morning."

" Dear me, Watson," said Holmes, staring with great curiosity at the slips of foolscap which the landlady had handed to him, " this is certainly a little unusual. Seclusion I can understand ; but why print ? Printing is a clumsy process. Why not write ? What would it suggest, Watson ? "

" That he desired to conceal his handwriting."

" But why ? What can it matter to him that his landlady should have a word of his writing ? Still, it may be as you say. Then, again, why such laconic messages ? "

" I cannot imagine."

" It opens a pleasing field for intelligent speculation. The words are written with a broad-pointed, violet-tinted pencil of a not unusual pattern. You will observe that the paper is torn away at the side here after the printing was done, so that the ' S ' of ' SOAP ' is partly gone. Suggestive, Watson, is it not ? "

" Of caution ? "

" Exactly. There was evidently some mark, some

thumb-print, something which might give a clue to the person's identity. Now, Mrs. Warren, you say that the man was of middle size, dark, and bearded. What age would he be ? "

" Youngish, sir—not over thirty."

" Well, can you give me no further indications ? "

" He spoke good English, sir, and yet I thought he was a foreigner by his accent."

" And he was well dressed ? "

" Very smartly dressed, sir—quite the gentleman. Dark clothes—nothing you would note."

" He gave no name ? "

" No, sir."

" And has had no letters or callers ? "

" None."

" But surely you or the girl enter his room of a morning ? "

" No, sir ; he looks after himself entirely."

" Dear me ! that is certainly remarkable. What about his luggage ? "

" He had one big brown bag with him—nothing else."

" Well, we don't seem to have much material to help us. Do you say nothing has come out of that room—absolutely nothing ? "

The landlady drew an envelope from her bag ; from it she shook out two burnt matches and a cigarette-end upon the table.

" They were on his tray this morning. I brought them because I had heard that you can read great things out of small ones."

Holmes shrugged his shoulders.

" There is nothing here," said he. " The matches have, of course, been used to light cigarettes. That is obvious from the shortness of the burnt end. Half the match is consumed in lighting a pipe or cigar. But, dear me ! this cigarette stub is certainly remarkable. The gentleman was bearded and moustached, you say ? "

" Yes, sir."

" I don't understand that. I should say that only a clean-shaven man could have smoked this. Why, Watson, even your modest moustache would have been singed."

" A holder ? " I suggested.

" No, no ; the end is matted. I suppose there could not be two people in your rooms, Mrs. Warren ? "

" No, sir. He eats so little that I often wonder it can keep life in one."

" Well, I think we must wait for a little more material. After all, you have nothing to complain of. You have received your rent, and he is not a troublesome lodger, though he is certainly an unusual one. He pays you well, and if he chooses to lie concealed it is no direct business of yours. We have no excuse for an intrusion upon his privacy until we have some reason to think that there is a guilty reason for it. I've taken up the matter, and I won't lose sight of it. Report to me if anything fresh occurs, and rely upon my assistance if it should be needed."

" There are certainly some points of interest in this case, Watson," he remarked, when the landlady had left us. " It may, of course, be trivial—individual eccentricity ; or it may be very much deeper than appears on the surface. The first thing that strikes one is the obvious possibility that the person now in the rooms may be entirely differen* from the one who engaged them."

" Why should you think so ? "

" Well, apart from this cigarette-end, was it not sugges tive that the only time the lodger went out was immediately after his taking the rooms ? He came back—or someone came back—when all witnesses were out of the way. We have no proof that the person who came back was the person who went out. Then, again, the man who took the rooms spoke English well. This other, however, prints ' match ' when it should have been ' matches.' I can imagine that the word was taken out of a dictionary, which would give the noun but not the plural. The laconic style may be to conceal the absence of knowledge of English. Yes, Watson, there are good reasons to suspect that there has been a substitution of lodgers."

" But for what possible end ? "

" Ah ! there lies our problem. There is one rather obvious line of investigation." He took down the great book in which, day by day, he filed the agony columns of the various London journals. " Dear me ! " said he, turning over the pages, " what a chorus of groans, cries, and bleatings ! What a rag-bag of singular happenings ! But surely the most valuable hunting-ground that ever was given to a student of the unusual ! This person is alone, and cannot be approached by letter without a breach of that absolute secrecy which is desired. How is any news or any message to reach him from without ? Obviously by advertisement through a newspaper. There seems no other way, and fortunately we need concern ourselves with the one paper only. Here are the *Daily Gazette* extracts of the last fortnight. ' Lady with a black boa at Prince's Skating Club '—that we may pass. ' Surely Jimmy will not break his mother's heart '—that appears to be irrelevant. ' If the lady who fainted in the Brixton bus '—she does not interest me. ' Every day my heart longs——' Bleat, Watson—unmitigated bleat ! Ah ! this is a little more possible. Listen to this : ' Be patient. Will find some sure means of communication. Meanwhile, this column.—G.' That is two days after Mrs. Warren's lodger arrived. It sounds plausible, does it not ? The mysterious one could understand English, even if he could not print it. Let us see if we can pick up the trace again. Yes, here we are—three days later. ' Am making successful arrangements. Patience and prudence. The clouds will pass.—G.' Nothing for a week after that. Then comes something much more definite : ' The path is clearing. If I find chance signal message remember code agreed—one A, two B, and so on. You will hear soon.—G.' That was in yesterday's paper, and there is nothing in to-day's. It's all very appropriate to Mrs. Warren's lodger. If we wait a little, Watson, I don't doubt that the affair will grow more intelligible."

So it proved; for in the morning I found my friend standing on the hearthrug with his back to the fire, and a smile of complete satisfaction upon his face.

"How's this, Watson?" he cried, picking up the paper from the table. "'High red house with white stone facings. Third floor. Second window left. After dusk. —G.' That is definite enough. I think after breakfast we must make a little reconnaissance of Mrs. Warren's neighbourhood. Ah, Mrs. Warren! what news do you bring us this morning?"

Our client had suddenly burst into the room with an explosive energy which told of some new and momentous development.

"It's a police matter, Mr. Holmes!" she cried. "I'll have no more of it! He shall pack out of that with his baggage. I would have gone straight up and told him so, only I thought it was but fair to you to take your opinion first. But I'm at the end of my patience, and when it comes to knocking my old man about——"

"Knocking Mr. Warren about?"

"Using him roughly, anyway."

"But who used him roughly?"

"Ah! that's what we want to know! It was this morning, sir. Mr. Warren is a timekeeper at Morton & Waylight's, in Tottenham Court Road. He has to be out of the house before seven. Well, this morning he had not got ten paces down the road when two men came up behind him, threw a coat over his head, and bundled him into a cab that was beside the kerb. They drove him an hour, and then opened the door and shot him out. He lay in the roadway so shaken in his wits that he never saw what became of the cab. When he picked himself up he found he was on Hampstead Heath; so he took a bus home, and there he lies now on the sofa, while I came straight round to tell you what had happened."

"Most interesting," said Holmes. "Did he observe

the appearance of these men—did he hear them talk ? "

" No ; he is clean dazed. He just knows that he was lifted up as if by magic and dropped as if by magic. Two at least were in it, and maybe three."

" And you connect this attack with your lodger ? "

" Well, we've lived there fifteen years and no such happenings ever came before. I've had enough of him. Money's not everything. I'll have him out of my house before the day is done."

" Wait a bit, Mrs. Warren. Do nothing rash. I begin to think that this affair may be very much more important than appeared at first sight. It is clear now that some danger is threatening your lodger. It is equally clear that his enemies, lying in wait for him near your door, mistook your husband for him in the foggy morning light. On discovering their mistake they released him. What they would have done had it not been a mistake, we can only conjecture."

" Well, what am I to do, Mr. Holmes ? "

" I have a great fancy to see this lodger of yours, Mrs. Warren."

" I don't see how that is to be managed, unless you break in the door. I always hear him unlock it as I go down the stair after I leave the tray."

" He has to take the tray in. Surely we could conceal ourselves and see him do it."

The landlady thought for a moment.

" Well, sir, there's the box-room opposite. I could arrange a looking-glass, maybe, and if you were behind the door——"

" Excellent ! " said Holmes. " When does he lunch ? "

" About one, sir."

" Then Dr. Watson and I will come round in time. For the present, Mrs. Warren, good-bye."

At half-past twelve we found ourselves upon the steps of Mrs. Warren's house—a high, thin, yellow-brick edifice in Great Orme Street, a narrow thoroughfare at the north-

east side of the British Museum. Standing as it does near
the corner of the street, it commands a view down Howe
Street, with its more pretentious houses. Holmes pointed
with a chuckle to one of these, a row of residential flats,
which projected so that they could not fail to catch the eye.

"See, Watson!" said he. "'High red house with
stone facings.' There is the signal station all right. We
know the place, and we know the code; so surely our task
should be simple. There's a 'To Let' card in that window. It is evidently an empty flat to which the confederate has access. Well, Mrs. Warren, what now?"

"I have it all ready for you. If you will both come up
and leave your boots below on the landing, I'll put you
there now."

It was an excellent hiding-place which she had arranged.
The mirror was so placed that, seated in the dark, we could
very plainly see the door opposite. We had hardly settled
down in it, and Mrs. Warren left us, when a distant tinkle
announced that our mysterious neighbour had rung.
Presently the landlady appeared with the tray, laid it down
upon a chair beside the closed door, and then, treading
heavily, departed. Crouching together in the angle of
the door, we kept our eyes fixed upon the mirror. Suddenly, as the landlady's footsteps died away, there was the
creak of a turning key, the handle revolved, and two thin
hands darted out and lifted the tray from the chair. An
instant later it was hurriedly replaced, and I caught a
glimpse of a dark, beautiful, horrified face glaring at the
narrow opening of the box-room. Then the door crashed
to, the key turned once more, and all was silence. Holmes
twitched my sleeve, and together we stole down the
stair.

"I will call again in the evening," said he to the expectant landlady. "I think, Watson, we can discuss this
business better in our own quarters."

"My surmise, as you saw, proved to be correct," said
he, speaking from the depths of his easy-chair. "There
has been a substitution of lodgers. What I did not fore-

see is that we should find a woman, and no ordinary
woman, Watson."

" She saw us."

" Well, she saw something to alarm her. That is certain. The general sequence of events is pretty clear, is it
not ? A couple seek refuge in London from a very terrible
and instant danger. The measure of that danger is the
rigour of their precautions. The man, who has some
work which he must do, desires to leave the woman in
absolute safety while he does it. It is not an easy problem,
but he solved it in an original fashion, and so effectively
that her presence was not even known to the landlady who
supplies her with food. The printed messages, as is now
evident, were to prevent her sex being discovered by her
writing. The man cannot come near the woman, or he
will guide their enemies to her. Since he cannot communicate with her direct, he has recourse to the agony
column of a paper. So far all is clear."

" But what is at the root of it ? "

" Ah, yes, Watson—severely practical, as usual ! What
is at the root of it all ? Mrs. Warren's whimsical problem
enlarges somewhat and assumes a more sinister aspect as
we proceed. This much we can say : that it is no ordinary
love escapade. You saw the woman's face at the sign of
danger. We have heard, too, of the attack upon the landlord, which was undoubtedly meant for the lodger. These
alarms, and the desperate need for secrecy, argue that the
matter is one of life or death. The attack upon Mr.
Warren further shows that the enemy, whoever they are,
are themselves not aware of the substitution of the female
lodger for the male. It is very curious and complex,
Watson."

" Why should you go further in it ? What have you to
gain from it ? "

" What, indeed ? It is Art for Art's sake, Watson. I
suppose when you doctored you found yourself studying
cases without thought of a fee ? "

" For my education, Holmes."

"Education never ends, Watson. It is a series of lessons, with the greatest for the last. This is an instructive case. There is neither money nor credit in it, and yet one would wish to tidy it up. When dusk comes we should find ourselves one stage advanced in our investigation."

When we returned to Mrs. Warren's rooms, the gloom of a London winter evening had thickened into one grey curtain, a dead monotone of colour, broken only by the sharp yellow squares of the windows and the blurred haloes of the gas-lamps. As we peered from the darkened sitting-room of the lodging-house, one more dim light glimmered high up through the obscurity.

"Someone is moving in that room," said Holmes in a whisper, his gaunt and eager face thrust forward to the window-pane. "Yes, I can see his shadow. There he is again! He has a candle in his hand. Now he is peering across. He wants to be sure that she is on the look-out. Now he begins to flash. Take the message also, Watson, that we may check each other. A single flash—that is 'A,' surely. Now, then. How many did you make it? Twenty. So did I. That should mean 'T.' A T— that's intelligible enough! Another 'T.' Surely this is the beginning of a second word. Now, then—TENTA. Dead stop. That can't be all, Watson? 'ATTENTA' gives no sense. Nor is it any better as three words— 'AT. TEN. TA,' unless 'T.A.' are a person's initials. There it goes again! What's that? ATTE—why, it is the same message over again. Curious, Watson, very curious! Now he is off once more! AT—why, he is repeating it for the third time. 'ATTENTA' three times! How often will he repeat it? No, that seems to be the finish. He has withdrawn from the window. What do you make of it, Watson?"

"A cipher message, Holmes."

My companion gave a sudden chuckle of comprehension. "And not a very obscure cipher, Watson," said he. "Why, of course, it is Italian! The 'A' means that it

is addressed to a woman. ' Beware ! Beware ! Beware ' '
How's that, Watson ? "

" I believe you have hit it."

" Not a doubt of it. It is a very urgent message, thrice
repeated to make it more so. But beware of what ? Wait
a bit ; he is coming to the window once more."

Again we saw the dim silhouette of a crouching man and
the whisk of the small flame across the window, as the
signals were renewed. They came more rapidly than
before—so rapid that it was hard to follow them.

" ' PERICOLO '—' Pericolo '—Eh, what's that, Watson ? Danger, isn't it ? Yes, by Jove ! it's a danger signal.
There he goes again !' PERI.' Halloa, what on earth——"

The light had suddenly gone out, the glimmering square
of window had disappeared, and the third floor formed a
dark band round the lofty building, with its tiers of shining
casements. That last warning cry had been suddenly cut
short. How, and by whom ? The same thought occurred
on the instant to us both. Holmes sprang up from where
he crouched by the window.

" This is serious, Watson," he cried. " There is some
devilry going forward ! Why should such a message stop
in such a way ? I should put Scotland Yard in touch with
this business—and yet, it is too pressing for us to leave."

" Shall I go for the police ? "

" We must define the situation a little more clearly. It
may bear some more innocent interpretation. Come,
Watson, let us go across ourselves and see what we can
make of it."

II

As we walked rapidly down Howe Street I glanced back
at the building which we had left. There, dimly outlined
at the top window, I could see the shadow of a head, a
woman's head, gazing tensely, rigidly, out into the night,
waiting with breathless suspense for the renewal of that
interrupted message. At the doorway of the Howe Street
flats a man, muffled in a cravat and greatcoat, was leaning

958

against the railing. He started as the hall-light fell upon
our faces.

" Holmes ! " he cried.

" Why, Gregson ! " said my companion, as he shook
hands with the Scotland Yard detective. " Journeys end
with lovers' meetings. What brings you here ? "

" The same reasons that bring you, I expect," said
Gregson. " How you got on to it I can't imagine."

" Different threads, but leading up to the same tangle.
I've been taking the signals."

" Signals ? "

" Yes, from that window. They broke off in the
middle. We came over to see the reason. But since it is
safe in your hands I see no object in continuing the business."

" Wait a bit ! " cried Gregson, eagerly. " I'll do you
this justice, Mr. Holmes, that I was never in a case yet
that I didn't feel stronger for having you on my side.
There's only the one exit to these flats, so we have him
safe."

" Who is he ? "

" Well, well, we score over you for once, Mr. Holmes.
You must give us best this time." He struck his stick
sharply upon the ground, on which a cabman, his whip in
his hand, sauntered over from a four-wheeler which stood
on the far side of the street. " May I introduce you to
Mr. Sherlock Holmes ? " he said to the cabman. " This is
Mr. Leverton, of Pinkerton's American Agency."

" The hero of the Long Island Cave mystery ? " said
Holmes. " Sir, I am pleased to meet you."

The American, a quiet, business-like young man, with a
clean-shaven, hatchet face, flushed up at the words of
commendation. " I am on the trail of my life now, Mr.
Holmes," said he. " If I can get Gorgiano——"

" What ! Gorgiano of the Red Circle ? "

" Oh, he has a European fame, has he ? Well, we've
learned all about him in America. We *know* he is at the
bottom of fifty murders, and yet we have nothing positive

we can take him on. I tracked him over from New York, and I've been close to him for a week in London, waiting some excuse to get my hand on his collar. Mr. Gregson and I ran him to ground in that big tenement house, and there's only the one door, so he can't slip us. There's three folk come out since he went in, but I'll swear he wasn't one of them."

" Mr. Holmes talks of signals," said Gregson. " I expect, as usual, he knows a good deal that we don't."

In a few clear words Holmes explained the situation as it had appeared to us. The American struck his hands together with vexation.

" He's on to us ! " he cried.

" Why do you think so ? "

" Well, it figures out that way, does it not ? Here he is, sending out messages to an accomplice—there are several of his gang in London. Then suddenly, just as by your own account he was telling them that there was danger, he broke short off. What could it mean except that from the window he had suddenly either caught sight of us in the street, or in some way come to understand how close the danger was, and that he must act right away, if he was to avoid it ? What do you suggest, Mr. Holmes ? "

" That we go up at once and see for ourselves."

" But we have no warrant for his arrest."

" He is in unoccupied premises under suspicious circumstances," said Gregson. " That is good enough for the moment. When we have him by the heels we can see if New York can't help us to keep him. I'll take the responsibility of arresting him now."

Our official detectives may blunder in the matter of intelligence, but never in that of courage. Gregson climbed the stair to arrest this desperate murderer with the same absolutely quiet and business-like bearing with which he would have ascended the official staircase of Scotland Yard. The Pinkerton man had tried to push past him, but Gregson had firmly elbowed him back. London dangers were the privilege of the London force.

The door of the left-hand flat upon the third landing was standing ajar. Gregson pushed it open. Within all was absolute silence and darkness. I struck a match, and lit the detective's lantern. As I did so, and as the flicker steadied into a flame, we all gave a gasp of surprise. On the deal boards of the carpetless floor there was outlined a fresh track of blood. The red steps pointed towards us, and led away from an inner room, the door of which was closed. Gregson flung it open and held his light full blaze in front of him, whilst we all peered eagerly over his shoulders.

In the middle of the floor of the empty room was huddled the figure of an enormous man, his clean-shaven, swarthy face grotesquely horrible in its contortion, and his head encircled by a ghastly crimson halo of blood, lying in a broad wet circle upon the white woodwork. His knees were drawn up, his hands thrown out in agony, and from the centre of his broad, brown, upturned throat there projected the white haft of a knife driven blade-deep into his body. Giant as he was, the man must have gone down like a pole-axed ox before that terrific blow. Beside his right hand a most formidable horn-handled, two-edged dagger lay upon the floor, and near it a black kid glove.

" By George ! it's Black Gorgiano himself ! " cried the American detective. " Someone has got ahead of us this time."

" Here is the candle in the window, Mr. Holmes," said Gregson. " Why, whatever are you doing ? "

Holmes had stepped across, had lit the candle, and was passing it backwards and forwards across the window-panes. Then he peered into the darkness, blew the candle out, and threw it on the floor.

" I rather think that will be helpful," said he. He came over and stood in deep thought while the two professionals were examining the body. " You say that three people came out from the flat while you were waiting downstairs," said he, at last. " Did you observe them closely ? "

"Yes, I did."

"Was there a fellow about thirty, black-bearded, dark, of middle size?"

"Yes; he was the last to pass me."

"That is your man, I fancy. I can give you his description, and we have a very excellent outline of his footmark. That should be enough for you."

"Not much, Mr. Holmes, among the millions of London."

"Perhaps not. That is why I thought it best to summon this lady to your aid."

We all turned round at the words. There, framed in the doorway, was a tall and beautiful woman—the mysterious lodger of Bloomsbury. Slowly she advanced, her face pale and drawn with a frightful apprehension, her eyes fixed and staring, her terrified gaze riveted upon the dark figure on the floor.

"You have killed him!" she muttered. "Oh, *Dio mio*, you have killed him!" Then I heard a sudden sharp intake of her breath, and she sprang into the air with a cry of joy. Round and round the room she danced, her hands clapping, her dark eyes gleaming with delighted wonder, and a thousand pretty Italian exclamations pouring from her lips. It was terrible and amazing to see such a woman so convulsed with joy at such a sight. Suddenly she stopped and gazed at us all with a questioning stare.

"But you! You are police, are you not? You have killed Giuseppe Gorgiano. Is it not so?"

"We are police, madam."

She looked round into the shadows of the room.

"But where, then, is Gennaro?" she asked. "He is my husband, Gennaro Lucca. I am Emilia Lucca, and we are both from New York. Where is Gennaro? He called me this moment from this window, and I ran with all my speed."

"It was I who called," said Holmes.

"You! How could you call?"

"Your cipher was not difficult, madam. Your pres-

962

ence here was desirable. I knew that I had only to flash ' *Vieni* ' and you would surely come."

The beautiful Italian looked with awe at my companion. " I do not understand how you know these things," she said. " Giuseppe Gorgiano—how did he——" She paused, and then suddenly her face lit up with pride and delight. " Now I see it ! My Gennaro ! My splendid, beautiful Gennaro, who has guarded me safe from all harm, he did it, with his own strong hand he killed the monster ! Oh, Gennaro, how wonderful you are ! What woman could ever be worthy of such a man ? "

" Well, Mrs. Lucca," said the prosaic Gregson, laying his hand upon the lady's sleeve with as little sentiment as if she were a Notting Hill hooligan, " I am not very clear yet who you are or what you are ; but you've said enough to make it very clear that we shall want you at the Yard."

" One moment, Gregson," said Holmes. " I rather fancy that this lady may be as anxious to give us information as we can be to get it. You understand, madam, that your husband will be arrested and tried for the death of the man who lies before us ? What you say may be used in evidence. But if you think that he has acted from motives which are not criminal, and which he would wish to have known, then you cannot serve him better than by telling us the whole story."

" Now that Gorgiano is dead we fear nothing," said the lady. " He was a devil and a monster, and there can be no judge in the world who would punish my husband for having killed him."

" In that case," said Holmes, " my suggestion is that we lock this door, leave things as we found them, go with this lady to her room, and form our opinion after we have heard what it is that she has to say to us."

Half an hour later we were seated, all four, in the small sitting-room of Signora Lucca, listening to her remarkable narrative of those sinister events, the ending of which we had chanced to witness. She spoke in rapid and fluent but very unconventional English, which, for the sake of clearness, I will make grammatical.

" I was born in Posilippo, near Naples," said she, " and was the daughter of Augusto Barelli, who was the chief lawyer and once the deputy of that part. Gennaro was in my father's employment, and I came to love him, as any woman must. He had neither money nor position—nothing but his beauty and strength and energy—so my father forbade the match. We fled together, were married at Bari, and sold my jewels to gain the money which would take us to America. This was four years ago, and we have been in New York ever since.

" Fortune was very good to us at first. Gennaro was able to do a service to an Italian gentleman—he saved him from some ruffians in the place called the Bowery, and so made a powerful friend. His name was Tito Castalotte, and he was the senior partner of the great firm of Castalotte & Zamba, who are the chief fruit importers of New York. Signor Zamba is an invalid, and our new friend Castalotte has all power within the firm, which employs more than three hundred men. He took my husband into his employment, made him head of a department, and showed his goodwill towards him in every way. Signor Castalotte was a bachelor, and I believe that he felt as if Gennaro was his son, and both my husband and I loved him as if he were our father. We had taken and furnished a little house in Brooklyn, and our whole future seemed assured, when that black cloud appeared which was soon to overspread our sky.

" One night, when Gennaro returned from his work, he brought a fellow-countryman back with him. His name was Gorgiano, and he had come also from Posilippo. He was a huge man, as you can testify, for you have looked upon his corpse. Not only was his body that of a giant, but everything about him was grotesque, gigantic, and terrifying. His voice was like thunder in our little house. There was scarce room for the whirl of his great arms as he talked. His thoughts, his emotions, his passions, all were exaggerated and monstrous. He talked, or rather roared, with such energy that others could but sit and listen, cowed with the mighty stream of words. His eyes blazed at you and held you at his mercy. He was a terrible and wonderful man. I thank God that he is dead !

" He came again and again. Yet I was aware that Gennaro was no more happy than I was in his presence. My poor husband would sit pale and listless, listening to the endless raving upon politics and upon social questions which made up our visitor's conversation. Gennaro said nothing, but I who knew him so well could read in his face some emotion which I had never seen there before. At first I thought that it was dislike. And then, gradually, I understood that it was more than dislike. It was fear—a deep, secret, shrinking fear. That night—the night that I read his terror—I put my arms round him and I implored him by his love for me and by all that he held dear to hold nothing from me, and to tell me why this huge man overshadowed him so.

" He told me, and my own heart grew cold as ice as I listened. My poor Gennaro, in his wild and fiery days, when all the world seemed against him and his mind was driven half mad by the injustices of life, had joined a Neapolitan society, the Red Circle, which was allied to the old Carbonari. The oaths and secrets of this brotherhood were frightful ; but once within its rule no escape was possible. When we had fled to America Gennaro thought that he had cast it all off for ever. What was his horror one evening to meet in the streets the very man who had initiated him in Naples, the giant Gorgiano, a man who had earned the name of ' Death ' in the South of Italy, for he was red to the elbow in murder ! He had come to New York to avoid the Italian police, and he had already planted a branch of this dreadful society in his new home. All this Gennaro told me, and showed me a summons which he had received that very day, a Red Circle drawn upon the head of it, telling him that a lodge would be held upon a certain date, and that his presence at it was required and ordered.

"That was bad enough, but worse was to come. I had noticed for some time that when Gorgiano came to us, as he constantly did, in the evening, he spoke much to me ; and even when his words were to my husband those terrible, glaring, wild-beast eyes of his were always turned upon me. One night his secret came out. I had awakened what he called ' love ' within him—the love of a brute—a savage. Gennaro had not yet returned when he came. He pushed his way in, seized me in his mighty arms, hugged me in his bear's embrace, covered me with kisses, and implored me to come away with him. I was struggling and screaming when Gennaro entered and attacked him. He struck Gennaro senseless and fled from the house which he was never more to enter. It was a deadly enemy that we made that night.

" A few days later came the meeting. Gennaro returned from it with a face which told me that something dreadful had occurred. It was worse than we could have imagined possible. The funds of the society were raised by blackmailing rich Italians and threatening them with violence should they refuse the money. It seems that Castalotte, our dear friend and benefactor, had been approached. He had refused to yield to threats, and he had handed the notices to the police. It was resolved now that such an example should be made of him as would prevent any other victim from rebelling. At the meeting it was arranged that he and his house should be blown up with dynamite. There was a drawing of lots as to who should carry out the deed. Gennaro saw our enemy's cruel face smiling at him as he dipped his hand in the bag. No doubt it had been prearranged in some fashion, for it was the fatal disc with the Red Circle upon it, the mandate for murder, which lay upon his palm. He was to kill his best friend, or he was to expose himself and me to the vengeance of his comrades. It was part of their fiendish system to punish those whom they feared or hated by injuring not only their own persons, but those whom they loved, and it was the knowledge of this which hung as a terror over my poor Gennaro's head and drove him nearly crazy with apprehension.

"All that night we sat together, our arms round each other, each strengthening each for the troubles that lay before us. The very next evening had been fixed for the attempt. By midday my husband and I were on our way to London, but not before he had given our benefactor full warning of his danger, and had also left such information for the police as would safeguard his life for the future.

"The rest, gentlemen, you know for yourselves. We were sure that our enemies would be behind us like our own shadows. Gorgiano had his private reasons for vengeance, but in any case we knew how ruthless, cunning, and untiring he could be. Both Italy and America are full of stories of his dreadful powers. If ever they were exerted it would be now. My darling made use of the few clear days which our start had given us in arranging for a refuge for me in such a fashion that no possible danger could reach me. For his own part, he wished to be free that he might communicate both with the American and with the Italian police. I do not myself know where he lived, or how. All that I learned was through the columns of a newspaper. But once, as I looked through my window, I saw two Italians watching the house, and I understood that in some way Gorgiano had found out our retreat. Finally Gennaro told me, through the paper, that he would signal to me from a certain window, but when the signals came they were nothing but warnings, which were suddenly interrupted. It is very clear to me now that he knew Gorgiano to be close upon him, and that, thank God ! he was ready for him when he came. And now, gentlemen, I would ask you whether we have anything to fear from the Law, or whether any judge upon earth would condemn my Gennaro for what he has done ? "

"Well, Mr. Gregson," said the American, looking

across at the official, " I don't know what your British point of view may be, but I guess that in New York this lady's husband will receive a pretty general vote of thanks."

" She will have to come with me and see the Chief," Gregson answered. " If what she says is corroborated, I do not think she or her husband has much to fear. But what I can't make head or tail of, Mr. Holmes, is how on earth *you* got yourself mixed up in the matter."

" Education, Gregson, education. Still seeking knowledge at the old university. Well, Watson, you have one more specimen of the tragic and grotesque to add to your collection. By the way, it is not eight o'clock, and a Wagner night at Covent Garden ! If we hurry, we might be in time for the second act."

40. *The Bruce-Partington Plans*

IN the third week of November, in the year 1895, a dense yellow fog settled down upon London. From the Monday to the Thursday I doubt whether it was ever possible from our windows in Baker Street to see the loom of the opposite houses. The first day Holmes had spent in cross-indexing his huge book of references. The second and third had been patiently occupied upon a subject which he had recently made his hobby—the music of the Middle Ages. But when, for the fourth time, after pushing back our chairs from breakfast we saw the greasy, heavy brown swirl still drifting past us and condensing in oily drops upon the window-panes, my comrade's impatient and active nature could endure this drab existence no longer. He paced restlessly about our sitting-room in a fever of suppressed energy, biting his nails, tapping the furniture, and chafing against inaction.

" Nothing of interest in the paper, Watson ? " he said.

I was aware that by anything of interest, Holmes meant anything of criminal interest. There was the news of a revolution, of a possible war, and of an impending change of Government ; but these did not come within the horizon of my companion. I could see nothing recorded in the shape of crime which was not commonplace and futile. Holmes groaned and resumed his restless meanderings.

"The London criminal is certainly a dull fellow," said he, in the querulous voice of the sportsman whose game has failed him. "Look out of this window, Watson. See how the figures loom up, are dimly seen, and then blend once more into the cloud-bank. The thief or the murderer could roam London on such a day as the tiger does the jungle, unseen until he pounces, and then evident only to his victim."

"There have," said I, "been numerous petty thefts." Holmes snorted his contempt.

"This great and sombre stage is set for something more worthy than that," said he. "It is fortunate for this community that I am not a criminal."

"It is, indeed!" said I, heartily.

"Suppose that I were Brooks or Woodhouse, or any of the fifty men who have good reason for taking my life, how long could I survive against my own pursuit? A summons, a bogus appointment, and all would be over. It is well they don't have days of fog in the Latin countries —the countries of assassination. By Jove! here comes something at last to break our dead monotony."

It was the maid with a telegram. Holmes tore it open and burst out laughing.

"Well, well! What next?" said he. "Brother Mycroft is coming round."

"Why not?" I asked.

"Why not? It is as if you met a tram-car coming down a country lane. Mycroft has his rails and he runs on them. His Pall Mall lodgings, the Diogenes Club, Whitehall—that is his cycle. Once, and only once, he has been here. What upheaval can possibly have derailed him?"

"Does he not explain?"

Holmes handed me his brother's telegram.

" Must see you over Cadogan West. Coming at once.
MYCROFT."

" Cadogan West ? I have heard the name."

" It recalls nothing to my mind. But that Mycroft
should break out in this erratic fashion ! A planet might
as well leave its orbit. By the way, do you know what
Mycroft is ? "

I had some vague recollection of an explanation at the
time of the Adventure of the Greek Interpreter.

" You told me that he had some small office under the
British Government."

Holmes chuckled.

" I did not know you quite so well in those days. One
has to be discreet when one talks of high matters of state.
You are right in thinking that he is under the British
Government. You would also be right in a sense if you
said that occasionally he *is* the British Government."

" My dear Holmes ! "

" I thought I might surprise you. Mycroft draws four
hundred and fifty pounds a year, remains a subordinate,
has no ambitions of any kind, will receive neither honour
nor title, but remains the most indispensable man in the
country."

" But how ? "

" Well, his position is unique. He has made it for
himself. There has never been anything like it before, nor
will be again. He has the tidiest and most orderly brain,
with the greatest capacity for storing facts, of any man
living. The same great powers which I have turned to
the detection of crime he has used for this particular business. The conclusions of every department are passed to
him, and he is the central exchange, the clearing-house,
which makes out the balance. All other men are special-
ists, but his specialism is omniscience. We will suppose
that a Minister needs information as to a point which
involves the Navy, India, Canada and the bi-metallic question ; he could get his separate advices from various

departments upon each, but only Mycroft can focus them all, and say off-hand how each factor would affect the other. They began by using him as a short-cut, a convenience ; now he has made himself an essential. In that great brain of his everything is pigeon-holed, and can be handed out in an instant. Again and again his word has decided the national policy. He lives in it. He thinks of nothing else save when, as an intellectual exercise, he unbends if I call upon him and ask him to advise me on one of my little problems. But Jupiter is descending to-day. What on earth can it mean ? Who is Cadogan West, and what is he to Mycroft ? "

" I have it," I cried, and plunged among the litter of papers upon the sofa. " Yes, yes, here he is, sure enough ! Cadogan West was the young man who was found dead on the Underground on Tuesday morning."

Holmes sat up at attention, his pipe half-way to his lips.

" This must be serious, Watson. A death which has caused my brother to alter his habits can be no ordinary one. What in the world can he have to do with it ? The case was featureless as I remember it. The young man had apparently fallen out of the train and killed himself. He had not been robbed, and there was no particular reason to suspect violence. Is that not so ? "

" There has been an inquest," said I, " and a good many fresh facts have come out. Looked at more closely, I should certainly say that it was a curious case."

" Judging by its effect upon my brother, I should think it must be a most extraordinary one." He snuggled down in his arm-chair. " Now, Watson, let us have the facts."

" The man's name was Arthur Cadogan West. He was twenty-seven years of age, unmarried, and a clerk at Woolwich Arsenal."

" Government employ. Behold the link with brother Mycroft ! "

" He left Woolwich suddenly on Monday night. Was last seen by his fiancée, Miss Violet Westbury, whom he left abruptly in the fog about 7.30 that evening. There was no quarrel between them and she can give no motive for his action. The next thing heard of him was when his dead body was discovered by a platelayer named Mason, just outside Aldgate Station on the Underground system in London."

" When ? "

" The body was found at six on the Tuesday morning. It was lying wide of the metals upon the left hand of the track as one goes eastward, at a point close to the station, where the line emerges from the tunnel in which it runs. The head was badly crushed—an injury which might well have been caused by a fall from the train. The body could only have come on the line in that way. Had it been carried down from any neighbouring street, it must have passed the station barriers, where a collector is always standing. This point seems absolutely certain."

" Very good. The case is definite enough. The man, dead or alive, either fell or was precipitated from a train. So much is clear to me. Continue."

" The trains which traverse the lines of rail beside which the body was found are those which run from west to east, some being purely Metropolitan, and some from Willesden and outlying junctions. It can be stated for certain that this young man, when he met his death, was travelling in this direction at some late hour of the night, but at what point he entered the train it is impossible to state."

" His ticket, of course, would show that."

" There was no ticket in his pockets."

" No ticket ! Dear me, Watson, this is really very singular. According to my experience it is not possible to reach the platform of a Metropolitan train without exhibiting one's ticket. Presumably, then, the young man had one. Was it taken from him in order to conceal the station from which he came ? It is possible. Or did he drop it in the carriage ? That also is possible. But the point is of curious interest. I understand that there was no sign of robbery ? "

" Apparently not. There is a list here of his possessions. His purse contained two pounds fifteen. He had also a cheque-book on the Woolwich branch of the Capital and Counties Bank. Through this his identity was established. There were also two dress-circle tickets for the Woolwich Theatre, dated for that very evening. Also a small packet of technical papers."

Holmes gave an exclamation of satisfaction.

"There we have it at last, Watson! British Government—Woolwich Arsenal—Technical papers—Brother Mycroft, the chain is complete. But here he comes, if I am not mistaken, to speak for himself."

A moment later the tall and portly form of Mycroft Holmes was ushered into the room. Heavily built and massive, there was a suggestion of uncouth physical inertia in the figure, but above this unwieldy frame there was perched a head so masterful in its brow, so alert in its steel-grey, deep-set eyes, so firm in its lips, and so subtle in its play of expression, that after the first glance one forgot the gross body and remembered only the dominant mind.

At his heels came our old friend Lestrade, of Scotland Yard—thin and austere. The gravity of both their faces foretold some weighty quest. The detective shook hands without a word. Mycroft Holmes struggled out of his overcoat and subsided into an arm-chair.

"A most annoying business, Sherlock," said he. "I extremely dislike altering my habits, but the powers that be would take no denial. In the present state of Siam it is most awkward that I should be away from the office. But it is a real crisis. I have never seen the Prime Minister so upset. As to the Admiralty—it is buzzing like an overturned beehive. Have you read up the case?"

"We have just done so. What were the technical papers?"

"Ah, there's the point! Fortunately, it has not come out. The Press would be furious if it did. The papers which this wretched youth had in his pocket were the plans of the Bruce-Partington submarine."

Mycroft Holmes spoke with a solemnity which showed his sense of the importance of the subject. His brother and I sat expectant.

"Surely you have heard of it? I thought everyone had heard of it."

"Only as a name."

"Its importance can hardly be exaggerated. It has been the most jealously guarded of all Government secrets. You may take it from me that naval warfare becomes impossible within the radius of a Bruce-Partington's operation. Two years ago a very large sum was smuggled through the Estimates and was expended in acquiring a monopoly of the invention. Every effort has been made to keep the secret. The plans, which are exceedingly intricate, comprising some thirty separate patents, each essential to the working of the whole, are kept in an elaborate safe in a confidential office adjoining the Arsenal, with burglar-proof doors and windows. Under no conceivable circumstances were the plans to be taken from the office. If the Chief Constructor of the Navy desired to consult them, even he was forced to go to the Woolwich office for the purpose. And yet here we find them in the pockets of a dead junior clerk in the heart of London. From an official point of view it's simply awful."

"But you have recovered them?"

"No, Sherlock, no! That's the pinch. We have not. Ten papers were taken from Woolwich. There were seven in the pockets of Cadogan West. The three most essential are gone—stolen, vanished. You must drop everything, Sherlock. Never mind your usual petty puzzles of the police-court. It's a vital international problem that you have to solve. Why did Cadogan West take the papers, where are the missing ones, how did he die, how came his body where it was found, how can the evil be set right? Find an answer to all these questions, and you will have done good service for your country."

"Why do you not solve it yourself, Mycroft? You can see as far as I."

974

"Possibly, Sherlock. But it is a question of getting details. Give me your details, and from an arm-chair I will return you an excellent expert opinion. But to run here and run there, to cross-question railway guards, and lie on my face with a lens to my eye—it is not my *métier*. No, you are the one man who can clear the matter up. If you have a fancy to see your name in the next honours list——"

My friend smiled and shook his head.

"I play the game for the game's own sake," said he. "But the problem certainly presents some points of interest, and I shall be very pleased to look into it. Some more facts, please."

"I have jotted down the more essential ones upon this sheet of paper, together with a few addresses which you will find of service. The actual official guardian of the papers is the famous Government expert, Sir James Walter, whose decorations and sub-titles fill two lines of a book of reference. He has grown grey in the service, is a gentleman, a favoured guest in the most exalted houses, and above all a man whose patriotism is beyond suspicion. He is one of two who have a key of the safe. I may add that the papers were undoubtedly in the office during working hours on Monday, and that Sir James left for London about three o'clock taking his key with him. He was at the house of Admiral Sinclair at Barclay Square during the whole of the evening when this incident occurred."

"Has the fact been verified?"

"Yes; his brother, Colonel Valentine Walter, has testified to his departure from Woolwich, and Admiral Sinclair to his arrival in London; so Sir James is no longer a direct factor in the problem."

"Who was the other man with a key?"

"The senior clerk and draughtsman, Mr. Sidney Johnson. He is a man of forty, married, with five children. He is a silent, morose man, but he has, on the whole, an excellent record in the public service. He is unpopular with his colleagues, but a hard worker. According to his own account, corroborated only by the word of his wife, he was at home the whole of Monday evening after office hours, and his key has never left the watch-chain upon which it hangs."

" Tell us about Cadogan West."

" He has been ten years in the Service, and has done good work. He has the reputation of being hot-headed and impetuous, but a straight, honest man. We have nothing against him. He was next Sidney Johnson in the office. His duties brought him into daily personal contact with the plans. No one else had the handling of them."

" Who locked the plans up that night ? "

" Mr. Sidney Johnson, the senior clerk."

" Well, it is surely perfectly clear who took them away. They are actually found upon the person of this junior clerk, Cadogan West. That seems final, does it not ? "

" It does, Sherlock, and yet it leaves so much unexplained. In the first place, why did he take them ? "

" I presume they were of value ? "

" He could have got several thousands for them very easily."

" Can you suggest any possible motive for taking the papers to London except to sell them ? "

" No, I cannot."

" Then we must take that as our working hypothesis. Young West took the papers. Now this could only be done by having a false key——"

" Several false keys. He had to open the building and the room."

" He had, then, several false keys. He took the papers to London to sell the secret, intending, no doubt, to have the plans themselves back in the safe next morning before they were missed. While in London on this treasonable mission he met his end."

" How ? "

" We will suppose that he was travelling back to Woolwich when he was killed and thrown out of the compartment."

"Aldgate, where the body was found, is considerably past the station for London Bridge, which would be his route to Woolwich."

"Many circumstances could be imagined under which he would pass London Bridge. There was someone in the carriage, for example, with whom he was having an absorbing interview. This interview led to a violent scene, in which he lost his life. Possibly he tried to leave the carriage, fell out on the line, and so met his end. The other closed the door. There was a thick fog, and nothing could be seen."

"No better explanation can be given with our present knowledge ; and yet consider, Sherlock, how much you leave untouched. We will suppose, for argument's sake, that young Cadogan West *had* determined to convey these papers to London. He would naturally have made an appointment with the foreign agent and kept his evening clear. Instead of that he took two tickets for the theatre, escorted his fiancée half-way there, and then suddenly disappeared."

"A blind," said Lestrade, who had sat listening with some impatience to the conversation.

"A very singular one. That is objection No. 1. Objection No. 2 : We will suppose that he reaches London and sees the foreign agent. He must bring back the papers before morning or the loss will be discovered. He took away ten. Only seven were in his pocket. What had become of the other three ? He certainly would not leave them of his own free will. Then, again, where is the price of his treason ? One would have expected to find a large sum of money in his pocket."

"It seems to me perfectly clear," said Lestrade. "I have no doubt at all as to what occurred. He took the papers to sell them. He saw the agent. They could not agree as to price. He started home again, but the agent went with him. In the train the agent murdered him, took the more essential papers, and threw his body from the carriage. That would account for everything, would it not ? "

" Why had he no ticket ? "

" The ticket would have shown which station was nearest the agent's house. Therefore he took it from the murdered man's pocket."

" Good, Lestrade, very good," said Holmes. " Your theory holds together. But if this is true, then the case is at an end. On the one hand the traitor is dead. On the other the plans of the Bruce-Partington submarine are presumably already on the Continent. What is there for us to do ? "

" To act, Sherlock—to act ! " cried Mycroft, springing to his feet. " All my instincts are against this explanation. Use your powers ! Go to the scene of the crime ! See the people concerned ! Leave no stone unturned ! In all your career you have never had so great a chance of serving your country."

" Well, well ! " said Holmes, shrugging his shoulders. " Come, Watson ! And you, Lestrade, could you favour us with your company for an hour or two ? We will begin our investigation by a visit to Aldgate Station. Good-bye, Mycroft. I shall let you have a report before evening, but I warn you in advance that you have little to expect."

An hour later, Holmes, Lestrade and I stood upon the underground railroad at the point where it emerges from the tunnel immediately before Aldgate Station. A courteous red-faced old gentleman represented the railway company.

" This is where the young man's body lay," said he, indicating a spot about three feet from the metals. " It could not have fallen from above, for these, as you see, are all blank walls. Therefore, it could only have come from a train, and that train, so far as we can trace it, must have passed about midnight on Monday."

" Have the carriages been examined for any sign of violence ? "

" There are no such signs, and no ticket has been found."

" No record of a door being found open ? "

" None."

" We have had some fresh evidence this morning," said Lestrade. " A passenger who passed Aldgate in an ordinary Metropolitan train about 11.40 on Monday night declares that he heard a heavy thud, as of a body striking the line, just before the train reached the station. There was dense fog, however, and nothing could be seen. He made no report of it at the time. Why, whatever is the matter with Mr. Holmes ? "

My friend was standing with an expression of strained intensity upon his face, staring at the railway metals where they curved out of the tunnel. Aldgate is a junction, and there was a network of points. On these his eager, questioning eyes were fixed, and I saw on his keen, alert face that tightening of the lips, that quiver of the nostrils, and concentration of the heavy tufted brows which I knew so well.

" Points," he muttered ; " the points."

" What of it ? What do you mean ? "

" I suppose there are no great number of points on a system such as this ? "

" No ; there are very few."

" And a curve, too. Points, and a curve. By Jove ! if it were only so."

" What is it, Mr. Holmes ? Have you a clue ? "

" An idea—an indication, no more. But the case certainly grows in interest. Unique, perfectly unique, and yet why not ? I do not see any indications of bleeding on the line."

" There were hardly any."

" But I understand that there was a considerable wound."

" The bone was crushed, but there was no great external injury."

"And yet one would have expected some bleeding. Would it be possible for me to inspect the train which contained the passenger who heard the thud of a fall in the fog?"

"I fear not, Mr. Holmes. The train has been broken up before now, and the carriages redistributed."

"I can assure you, Mr. Holmes," said Lestrade, "that every carriage has been carefully examined. I saw to it myself."

It was one of my friend's most obvious weaknesses that he was impatient with less alert intelligences than his own.

"Very likely," said he, turning away. "As it happens, it was not the carriages which I desired to examine. Watson, we have done all we can here. We need not trouble you any further, Mr. Lestrade. I think our investigations must now carry us to Woolwich."

At London Bridge, Holmes wrote a telegram to his brother, which he handed to me before dispatching it. It ran thus:

"See some light in the darkness, but it may possibly flicker out. Meanwhile, please send by messenger, to await return at Baker Street, a complete list of all foreign spies or international agents known to be in England, with full address.—SHERLOCK."

"That should be helpful, Watson," he remarked, as we took our seats in the Woolwich train. "We certainly owe brother Mycroft a debt for having introduced us to what promises to be a really very remarkable case."

His eager face still wore that expression of intense and high-strung energy, which showed me that some novel and suggestive circumstance had opened up a stimulating line of thought. See the foxhound with hanging ears and drooping tail as it lolls about the kennels, and compare it with the same hound as, with gleaming eyes and straining muscles, it runs upon a breast-high scent—such was the change in Holmes since the morning. He was a different man to the limp and lounging figure in the mouse-coloured dressing-gown who had prowled so restlessly only a few hours before round the fog-girt room.

"There is material here. There is scope," said he. "I am dull indeed not to have understood its possibilities."

"Even now they are dark to me."

"The end is dark to me also, but I have hold of one idea which may lead us far. The man met his death elsewhere, and his body was on the *roof* of a carriage."

"On the roof!"

"Remarkable, is it not? But consider the facts. Is it a coincidence that it is found at the very point where the train pitches and sways as it comes round on the points? Is not that the place where an object upon the roof might be expected to fall off? The points would affect no object inside the train. Either the body fell from the roof, or a very curious coincidence has occurred. But now consider the question of the blood. Of course, there was no bleeding on the line if the body had bled elsewhere. Each fact is suggestive in itself. Together they have a cumulative force."

"And the ticket, too!" I cried.

"Exactly. We could not explain the absence of a ticket. This would explain it. Everything fits together."

"But suppose it were so, we are still as far as ever from unravelling the mystery of his death. Indeed, it becomes not simpler, but stranger."

"Perhaps," said Holmes, thoughtfully; "perhaps." He relapsed into a silent reverie, which lasted until the slow train drew up at last in Woolwich Station. There he called a cab and drew Mycroft's paper from his pocket.

"We have quite a little round of afternoon calls to make," said he. "I think that Sir James Walter claims our first attention."

The house of the famous official was a fine villa with green lawns stretching down to the Thames. As we reached it the fog was lifting, and a thin, watery sunshine was breaking through. A butler answered our ring.

" Sir James, sir ! " said he, with solemn face. " Sir James died this morning."

" Good heavens ! " cried Holmes, in amazement. " How did he die ? "

" Perhaps you would care to step in, sir, and see his brother, Colonel Valentine ? "

" Yes, we had best do so."

We were ushered into a dim-lit drawing-room, where an instant later we were joined by a very tall, handsome, light-bearded man of fifty, the younger brother of the dead scientist. His wild eyes, stained cheeks, and unkempt hair all spoke of the sudden blow which had fallen upon the household. He was hardly articulate as he spoke of it.

" It was this horrible scandal," said he. " My brother, Sir James, was a man of very sensitive honour, and he could not survive such an affair. It broke his heart. He was always so proud of the efficiency of his department, and this was a crushing blow."

" We had hoped that he might have given us some indications which would have helped us to clear the matter up."

" I assure you that it was all a mystery to him as it is to you and to all of us. He had already put all his knowledge at the disposal of the police. Naturally, he had no doubt that Cadogan West was guilty. But all the rest was inconceivable."

" You cannot throw any new light upon the affair ? "

" I know nothing myself save what I have read or heard. I have no desire to be discourteous, but you can understand, Mr. Holmes, that we are much disturbed at present, and I must ask you to hasten this interview to an end."

" This is indeed an unexpected development," said my friend when we had regained the cab. " I wonder if the death was natural, or whether the poor old fellow killed himself ! If the latter, may it be taken as some sign of self-reproach for duty neglected ? We must leave that question to the future. Now we shall turn to the Cadogan Wests."

A small but well-kept house in the outskirts of the town sheltered the bereaved mother. The old lady was too dazed with grief to be of any use to us, but at her side was a white-faced young lady, who introduced herself as Miss Violet Westbury, the fiancée of the dead man, and the last to see him upon that fatal night.

" I cannot explain it, Mr. Holmes," she said. " I have not shut an eye since the tragedy, thinking, thinking, thinking, night and day, what the true meaning of it can be. Arthur was the most single-minded, chivalrous, patriotic man upon earth. He would have cut his right hand off before he would sell a State secret confided to his keeping. It is absurd, impossible, preposterous to anyone who knew him."

" But the facts, Miss Westbury ? "

" Yes, yes ; I admit I cannot explain them."

" Was he in any want of money ? "

" No ; his needs were very simple and his salary ample. He had saved a few hundreds, and we were to marry at the New Year."

" No signs of any mental excitement ? Come, Miss Westbury, be absolutely frank with us."

The quick eye of my companion had noted some change in her manner. She coloured and hesitated.

" Yes," she said, at last. " I had a feeling that there was something on his mind."

" For long ? "

" Only for the last week or so. He was thoughtful and worried. Once I pressed him about it. He admitted that there was something, and that it was concerned with his official life. ' It is too serious for me to speak about, even to you,' said he. I could get nothing more."

Holmes looked grave.

" Go on, Miss Westbury. Even if it seems to tell against him, go on. We cannot say what it may lead to."

" Indeed I have nothing more to tell. Once or twice it seemed to me that he was on the point of telling me something. He spoke one evening of the importance of the secret, and I have some recollection that he said that no doubt foreign spies would pay a great deal to have it."

My friend's face grew graver still.

" Anything else ? "

" He said that we were slack about such matters—that it would be easy for a traitor to get the plans."

" Was it only recently that he made such remarks ? "

" Yes, quite recently."

" Now tell us of that last evening."

" We were to go to the theatre. The fog was so thick that a cab was useless. We walked, and our way took us close to the office. Suddenly he darted away into the fog."

" Without a word ? "

" He gave an exclamation ; that was all. I waited but he never returned. Then I walked home. Next morning, after the office opened, they came to inquire. About twelve o'clock we heard the terrible news. Oh, Mr. Holmes, if you could only, only save his honour ! It was so much to him."

Holmes shook his head sadly.

" Come, Watson," said he, " our ways lie elsewhere. Our next station must be the office from which the papers were taken."

" It was black enough before against this young man, but our inquiries make it blacker," he remarked, as the cab lumbered off. " His coming marriage gives a motive for the crime. He naturally wanted money. The idea was in his head, since he spoke about it. He nearly made the girl an accomplice in the treason by telling her his plans. It is all very bad."

" But surely, Holmes, character goes for something ? Then, again, why should he leave the girl in the street and dart away to commit a felony ? "

" Exactly ! There are certainly objections. But it is a formidable case which they have to meet."

Mr. Sidney Johnson, the senior clerk, met us at the office, and received us with that respect which my companion's card always commanded. He was a thin, gruff, bespectacled man of middle age, his cheeks haggard, and his hands twitching from the nervous strain to which he had been subjected.

" It is bad, Mr. Holmes, very bad ! Have you heard of the death of the Chief ? "

" We have just come from his house."

" The place is disorganized. The Chief dead, Cadogan West dead, our papers stolen. And yet, when we closed our door on Monday evening we were as efficient an office as any in the Government service. Good God, it's dreadful to think of ! That West, of all men, should have done such a thing ! "

" You are sure of his guilt, then ? "

" I can see no other way out of it. And yet I would have trusted him as I trust myself."

" At what hour was the office closed on Monday ? "

" At five."

" Did you close it ? "

" I am always the last man out."

" Where were the plans ? "

" In that safe. I put them there myself."

" Is there no watchman to the building ? "

" There is ; but he has other departments to look after as well. He is an old soldier and a most trustworthy man. He saw nothing that evening. Of course, the fog was very thick."

" Suppose that Cadogan West wished to make his way into the building after hours ; he would need three keys, would he not, before he could reach the papers ? "

" Yes, he would. The key of the outer door, the key of the office, and the key of the safe."

" Only Sir James Walter and you had those keys ? "

" I had no keys of the doors—only of the safe."

" Was Sir James a man who was orderly in his habits ? "

" Yes, I think he was. I know that so far as those three keys are concerned he kept them on the same ring. I have often seen them there."

"And that ring went with him to London?"

"He said so."

"And your key never left your possession?"

"Never."

"Then West, if he is the culprit, must have had a duplicate. And yet none was found upon his body. One other point: if a clerk in this office desired to sell the plans, would it not be simpler to copy the plans for himself than to take the originals, as was actually done?"

"It would take considerable technical knowledge to copy the plans in an effective way."

"But I suppose either Sir James, or you, or West had that technical knowledge?"

"No doubt we had, but I beg you won't try to drag me into the matter, Mr. Holmes. What is the use of our speculating in this way when the original plans were actually found on West?"

"Well, it is certainly singular that he should run the risk of taking originals, if he could safely have taken copies, which would have equally served his turn."

"Singular, no doubt—and yet he did so."

"Every inquiry in this case reveals something inexplicable. Now there are three papers still missing. They are, as I understand, the vital ones."

"Yes, that is so."

"Do you mean to say that anyone holding these three papers, and without the seven others, could construct a Bruce-Partington submarine?"

"I reported to that effect to the Admiralty. But to-day I have been over the drawings again, and I am not so sure of it. The double valves with the automatic self-adjusting slots are drawn in one of the papers which have been returned. Until the foreigners had invented that for themselves they could not make the boat. Of course, they might soon get over the difficulty."

"But the three missing drawings are the most important?"

"Undoubtedly."

986

" I think, with your permission, I will now take a stroll round the premises. I do not recall any other question which I desired to ask."

He examined the lock of the safe, the door of the room, and finally the iron shutters of the window. It was only when we were on the lawn outside that his interest was strongly excited. There was a laurel bush outside the window, and several of the branches bore signs of having been twisted or snapped. He examined them carefully with his lens, and then some dim and vague marks upon the earth beneath. Finally he asked the chief clerk to close the iron shutters, and he pointed out to me that they hardly met in the centre, and that it would be possible for anyone outside to see what was going on within the room.

" The indications are ruined by the three days' delay. They may mean something or nothing. Well, Watson, I do not think that Woolwich can help us further. It is a small crop which we have gathered. Let us see if we can do better in London."

Yet we added one more sheaf to our harvest before we left Woolwich Station. The clerk in the ticket office was able to say with confidence that he saw Cadogan West—whom he knew well by sight—upon the Monday night, and that he went to London by the 8.15 to London Bridge. He was alone, and took a single third-class ticket. The clerk was struck at the time by his excited and nervous manner. So shaky was he that he could hardly pick up his change, and the clerk had helped him with it. A reference to the time-table showed that the 8.15 was the first train which it was possible for West to take after he had left the lady about 7.30.

" Let us reconstruct, Watson," said Holmes, after half an hour of silence. " I am not aware that in all our joint researches we have ever had a case which was more difficult to get at. Every fresh advance which we make only reveals a fresh ridge beyond. And yet we have surely made some appreciable progress.

"The effect of our inquiries at Woolwich has in the main been against young Cadogan West; but the indications at the window would lend themselves to a more favourable hypothesis. Let us suppose, for example, that he had been approached by some foreign agent. It might have been done under such pledges as would have prevented him from speaking of it, and yet would have affected his thoughts in the direction indicated by his remarks to his fiancée. Very good. We will now suppose that as he went to the theatre with the young lady he suddenly, in the fog, caught a glimpse of this same agent going in the direction of the office. He was an impetuous man, quick in his decisions. Everything gave way to his duty. He followed the man, reached the window, saw the abstraction of the documents, and pursued the thief. In this way we get over the objection that no one would take originals when he could make copies. This outsider had to take originals. So far it holds together."

"What is the next step?"

"Then we come into difficulties. One would imagine that under such circumstances the first act of young Cadogan West would be to seize the villain and raise the alarm. Why did he not do so? Could it have been an official superior who took the papers? That would explain West's conduct. Or could the Chief have given West the slip in the fog, and West started at once to London to head him off from his own rooms, presuming that he knew where the rooms were? The call must have been very pressing, since he left his girl standing in the fog, and made no effort to communicate with her. Our scent runs cold here, and there is a vast gap between either hypothesis and the laying of West's body, with seven papers in his pocket, on the roof of a Metropolitan train. My instinct now is to work from the other end. If Mycroft has given us the list of addresses we may be able to pick our man, and follow two tracks instead of one."

Surely enough, a note awaited us at Baker Street.

A Government messenger had brought it post-haste. Holmes glanced at it and threw it over to me.

"There are numerous small fry, but few who would handle so big an affair. The only men worth considering are Adolph Meyer, of 13 Great George Street, Westminster; Louis La Rothière, of Campden Mansions, Notting Hill; and Hugo Oberstein, 13 Caulfield Gardens, Kensington. The latter was known to be in town on Monday, and is now reported as having left. Glad to hear you have seen some light. The Cabinet awaits your final report with the utmost anxiety. Urgent representations have arrived from the very highest quarter. The whole force of the State is at your back if you should need it.—MYCROFT."

"I'm afraid," said Holmes, smiling, "that all the Queen's horses and all the Queen's men cannot avail in this matter." He had spread out his big map of London, and leaned eagerly over it. "Well, well," said he presently, with an exclamation of satisfaction, "things are turning a little in our direction at last. Why, Watson, I do honestly believe that we are going to pull it off after all." He slapped me on the shoulder with a sudden burst of hilarity. "I am going out now. It is only a reconnaissance. I will do nothing serious without my trusted comrade and biographer at my elbow. Do you stay here, and the odds are that you will see me again in an hour or two. If time hangs heavy get foolscap and a pen, and begin your narrative of how we saved the State."

I felt some reflection of his elation in my own mind, for I knew well that he would not depart so far from his usual austerity of demeanour unless there was good cause for exultation. All the long November evening I waited, filled with impatience for his return. At last, shortly after nine o'clock there arrived a messenger with a note:

"Am dining at Goldini's Restaurant, Gloucester Road,

Kensington. Please come at once and join me there. Bring with you a jemmy, a dark lantern, a chisel, and a revolver.—S.H."

It was a nice equipment for a respectable citizen to carry through the dim, fog-draped streets. I stowed them all discreetly away in my overcoat, and drove straight to the address given. There sat my friend at a little round table near the door of the garish Italian restaurant.

" Have you had something to eat ? Then join me in a coffee and curaçao. Try one of the proprietor's cigars. They are less poisonous than one would expect. Have you the tools ? "

" They are here, in my overcoat."

" Excellent. Let me give you a short sketch of what I have done, with some indication of what we are about to do. Now it must be evident to you, Watson, that this young man's body was *placed* on the roof of the train. That was clear from the instant that I determined the fact that it was from the roof, and not from a carriage, that he had fallen."

" Could it not have been dropped from a bridge ? "

" I should say it was impossible. If you examine the roofs you will find that they are slightly rounded, and there is no railing round them. Therefore, we can say for certain that young Cadogan West was placed on it."

" How could he be placed there ? "

" That was the question which we had to answer. There is only one possible way. You are aware that the Underground runs clear of tunnels at some points in the West End. I had a vague memory that as I have travelled by it I have occasionally seen windows just above my head. Now, suppose that a train halted under such a window, would there be any difficulty in laying a body upon the roof ? "

" It seems most improbable."

" We must fall back upon the old axiom that when all other contingencies fail, whatever remains, however improbable, must be the truth. Here all other contingencies *have* failed. When I found that the leading international agent, who had just left London, lived in a row of houses which abutted upon the Underground, I was so pleased that you were a little astonished at my sudden frivolity."

" Oh, that was it, was it ? "

" Yes, that was it. Mr. Hugo Oberstein, of 13 Caulfield Gardens, had become my objective. I began my operations at Gloucester Road Station, where a very helpful official walked with me along the track, and allowed me to satisfy myself, not only that the back-stair windows of Caulfield Gardens open on the line, but the even more essential fact that, owing to the intersection of one of the larger railways, the Underground trains are frequently held motionless for some minutes at that very spot."

" Splendid, Holmes ! You have got it ! "

" So far—so far, Watson. We advance, but the goal is afar. Well, having seen the back of Caulfield Gardens, I visited the front and satisfied myself that the bird was indeed flown. It is a considerable house, unfurnished, so far as I could judge, in the upper rooms. Oberstein lived there with a single valet, who was probably a confederate entirely in his confidence. We must bear in mind that Oberstein has gone to the Continent to dispose of his booty, but not with any idea of flight ; for he had no reason to fear a warrant, and the idea of an amateur domiciliary visit would certainly never occur to him. Yet that is precisely what we are about to make."

" Could we not get a warrant and legalize it ? "

" Hardly on the evidence."

" What can we hope to do ? "

" We cannot tell what correspondence may be there."

" I don't like it, Holmes."

" My dear fellow, you shall keep watch in the street. I'll do the criminal part. It's not a time to stick at trifles. Think of Mycroft's note, of the Admiralty, the Cabinet, the exalted person who waits for news. We are bound to go."

My answer was to rise from the table.

"You are right, Holmes. We are bound to go."

He sprang up and shook me by the hand.

"I knew you would not shrink at the last," said he, and for a moment I saw something in his eyes which was nearer to tenderness than I had ever seen. The next instant he was his masterful, practical self once more.

"It is nearly half a mile, but there is no hurry. Let us walk," said he. "Don't drop the instruments, I beg. Your arrest as a suspicious character would be a most unfortunate complication."

Caulfield Gardens was one of those lines of flat-faced, pillared, and porticoed houses which are so prominent a product of the middle Victorian epoch in the West End of London. Next door there appeared to be a children's party, for the merry buzz of young voices and the clatter of a piano resounded through the night. The fog still hung about and screened us with its friendly shade. Holmes had lit his lantern and flashed it upon the massive door.

"This is a serious proposition," said he. "It is certainly bolted as well as locked. We would do better in the area. There is an excellent archway down yonder in case a too zealous policeman should intrude. Give me a hand, Watson, and I'll do the same for you."

A minute later we were both in the area. Hardly had we reached the dark shadows before the step of the policeman was heard in the fog above. As its soft rhythm died away, Holmes set to work upon the lower door. I saw him stoop and strain until with a sharp crash it flew open. We sprang through into the dark passage, closing the area door behind us. Holmes led the way up the curving, uncarpeted stair. His little fan of yellow light shone upon a low window.

"Here we are, Watson—this must be the one." He threw it open, and as he did so there was a low, harsh murmur, growing steadily into a loud roar as a train dashed past us in the darkness. Holmes swept his light along the window-sill. It was thickly coated with soot from the passing engines, but the black surface was blurred and rubbed in places.

"You can see where they rested the body. Halloa, Watson! what is this? There can be no doubt that it is a blood mark." He was pointing to faint discolorations along the woodwork of the window. "Here it is on the stone of the stair also. The demonstration is complete. Let us stay here until a train stops."

We had not long to wait. The very next train roared from the tunnel as before, but slowed in the open, and then, with a creaking of brakes, pulled up immediately beneath us. It was not four feet from the window-ledge to the roof of the carriages. Holmes softly closed the window.

"So far we are justified," said he. "What do you think of it, Watson?"

"A masterpiece. You have never risen to a greater height."

"I cannot agree with you there. From the moment that I conceived the idea of the body being upon the roof, which surely was not a very abstruse one, all the rest was inevitable. If it were not for the grave interests involved the affair up to this point would be insignificant. Our difficulties are still before us. But perhaps we may find something here which may help us."

We had ascended the kitchen stair and entered the suite of rooms upon the first floor. One was a dining-room, severely furnished and containing nothing of interest. A second was a bedroom, which also drew blank. The remaining room appeared more promising, and my companion settled down to a systematic examination. It was littered with books and papers, and was evidently used as a study. Swiftly and methodically Holmes turned over the contents of drawer after drawer and cupboard after cupboard, but no gleam of success came to brighten his austere face. At the end of an hour he was no further than when he started.

" The cunning dog has covered his tracks," said he. " He has left nothing to incriminate him. His dangerous correspondence has been destroyed or removed. This is our last chance."

It was a small tin cash-box which stood upon the writing-desk. Holmes prised it open with his chisel. Several rolls of paper were within, covered with figures and calculations, without any note to show to what they referred. The recurring words, " Water pressure," and " Pressure to the square inch " suggested some possible relation to a submarine. Holmes tossed them all impatiently aside. There only remained an envelope with some small newspaper slips inside it. He shook them out on the table, and at once I saw by his eager face that his hopes had been raised.

" What's this, Watson ? Eh ? What's this ? Record of a series of messages in the advertisements of a paper. *Daily Telegraph* agony column by the print and paper. Right-hand top corner of a page. No dates—but messages arrange themselves. This must be the first :

" ' Hoped to hear sooner. Terms agreed to. Write fully to address given on card.—Pierrot.'

" Next comes : ' Too complex for description. Must have full report. Stuff awaits you when goods delivered. —Pierrot.'

" Then comes : ' Matter presses. Must withdraw offer unless contract completed. Make appointment by letter. Will confirm by advertisement.—Pierrot.'

" Finally : ' Monday night after nine. Two taps. Only ourselves. Do not be so suspicious. Payment in hard cash when goods delivered.—Pierrot.'

" A fairly complete record, Watson ! If we could only get at the man at the other end ! " He sat lost in thought, tapping his fingers on the table. Finally he sprang to his feet.

" Well, perhaps it won't be so difficult after all. There

is nothing more to be done here, Watson. I think we might drive round to the offices of the *Daily Telegraph*, and so bring a good day's work to a conclusion."

Mycroft Holmes and Lestrade had come round by appointment after breakfast next day and Sherlock Holmes had recounted to them our proceedings of the day before. The professional shook his head over our confessed burglary.

"We can't do these things in the force, Mr. Holmes," said he. "No wonder you get results that are beyond us. But some of these days you'll go too far, and you'll find yourself and your friend in trouble."

"For England, home and beauty—eh, Watson? Martyrs on the altar of our country. But what do you think of it, Mycroft?"

"Excellent, Sherlock! Admirable! But what use will you make of it?"

Holmes picked up the *Daily Telegraph* which lay upon the table.

"Have you seen Pierrot's advertisement to-day?"

"What! Another one?"

"Yes, here it is: 'To-night. Same hour. Same place. Two taps. Most vitally important. Your own safety at stake.—Pierrot.'"

"By George!" cried Lestrade. "If he answers that we've got him!"

"That was my idea when I put it in. I think if you could both make it convenient to come with us about eight o'clock to Caulfield Gardens we might possibly get a little nearer to a solution."

One of the most remarkable characteristics of Sherlock Holmes was his power of throwing his brain out of action and switching all his thoughts on to lighter things whenever he had convinced himself that he could no longer work to advantage. I remember that during the whole of that memorable day he lost himself in a monograph which he had undertaken upon the Polyphonic Motets of Lassus. For my own part I had none of this power of detachment, and the day, in consequence, appeared to be interminable. The great national importance of the issue, the suspense in high quarters, the direct nature of the experiment which we were trying—all combined to work upon my nerve. It was a relief to me when at last, after a light dinner, we set out upon our expedition. Lestrade and Mycroft met us by appointment at the outside of Gloucester Road Station. The area door of Oberstein's house had been left open the night before, and it was necessary for me, as Mycroft Holmes absolutely and indignantly declined to climb the railings, to pass in and open the hall door. By nine o'clock we were all seated in the study, waiting patiently for our man.

An hour passed and yet another. When eleven struck, the measured beat of the great church clock seemed to sound the dirge of our hopes. Lestrade and Mycroft were fidgeting in their seats and looking twice a minute at their watches. Holmes sat silent and composed, his eyelids half shut, but every sense on the alert. He raised his head with a sudden jerk.

" He is coming," said he.

There had been a furtive step past the door. Now it returned. We heard a shuffling sound outside, and then two sharp taps with the knocker. Holmes rose, motioning to us to remain seated. The gas in the hall was a mere point of light. He opened the outer door, and then as a dark figure slipped past him he closed and fastened it. " This way ! " we heard him say, and a moment later our man stood before us. Holmes had followed him closely, and as the man turned with a cry of surprise and alarm he caught him by the collar and threw him back into the room. Before our prisoner had recovered his balance the door was shut and Holmes standing with his back against it. The man glared round him, staggered, and fell senseless upon the floor. With the shock, his broad-brimmed hat flew from his head, his cravat slipped down from his lips, and there was the long light beard and the soft, handsome delicate features of Colonel Valentine Walter.

Holmes gave a whistle of surprise.

"You can write me down an ass this time, Watson," said he. "This was not the bird that I was looking for."

"Who is he?" asked Mycroft eagerly.

"The younger brother of the late Sir James Walter, the head of the Submarine Department. Yes, yes; I see the fall of the cards. He is coming to. I think that you had best leave his examination to me."

We had carried the prostrate body to the sofa. Now our prisoner sat up, looked round him with a horror-stricken face, and passed his hand over his forehead, like one who cannot believe his own senses.

"What is this?" he asked. "I came here to visit Mr. Oberstein."

"Everything is known, Colonel Walter," said Holmes. "How an English gentleman could behave in such a manner is beyond my comprehension. But your whole correspondence and relations with Oberstein are within our knowledge. So also are the circumstances connected with the death of young Cadogan West. Let me advise you to gain at least the small credit for repentance and confession, since there are still some details which we can only learn from your lips."

The man groaned and sank his face in his hands. We waited, but he was silent.

"I can assure you," said Holmes, "that every essential is already known. We know that you were pressed for money; that you took an impress of the keys which your brother held; and that you entered into a correspondence with Oberstein, who answered your letters through the advertisement columns of the *Daily Telegraph*. We are aware that you went down to the office in the fog on Monday night, but that you were seen and followed by young Cadogan West, who had probably some previous reason to suspect you. He saw your theft, but could not give the alarm, as it was just possible that you were taking the papers to your brother in London. Leaving all his private concerns, like the good citizen that he was, he followed you closely in the fog, and kept at your heels until you reached this very house. There he intervened, and then it was, Colonel Walter, that to treason you added the more terrible crime of murder."

" I did not ! I did not ! Before God I swear that I did not ! " cried our wretched prisoner.

" Tell us, then, how Cadogan West met his end before you laid him upon the roof of a railway carriage."

" I will. I swear to you that I will. I did the rest. I confess it. It was just as you say. A Stock Exchange debt had to be paid. I needed the money badly. Oberstein offered me five thousand. It was to save myself from ruin. But as to murder, I am as innocent as you."

" What happened then ? "

" He had his suspicions before, and he followed me as you describe. I never knew it until I was at the very door. It was thick fog, and one could not see three yards. I had given two taps and Oberstein had come to the door. The young man rushed up and demanded to know what we were about to do with the papers. Oberstein had a short life-preserver. He always carried it with him. As West forced his way after us into the house Oberstein struck him on the head. The blow was a fatal one. He was dead within five minutes. There he lay in the hall, and we were at our wits' end what to do. Then Oberstein had this idea about the trains which halted under his back window. But first he examined the papers which I had brought. He said that three of them were essential, and that he must keep them. ' You cannot keep them,' said I. ' There will be a dreadful row at Woolwich if they are not returned.' ' I must keep them,' said he, ' for they are so technical that it is impossible in the time to make copies.' ' Then they must all go back together to-night,' said I. He thought for a little, and then he cried out that he had it. ' Three I will keep,' said he. ' The others we will stuff into the pocket of this young man. When he is found the whole business will assuredly be put to his account. I could see no other way out of it, so we did as he suggested. We waited half an hour at the window before a train stopped. It was so thick that nothing could be seen, and we had no difficulty in lowering West's body on to the train. That was the end of the matter so far as I was concerned."

"And your brother?"

"He said nothing, but he had caught me once with his keys, and I think that he suspected. I read in his eyes that he suspected. As you know, he never held up his head again."

There was silence in the room. It was broken by Mycroft Holmes.

"Can you not make reparation? It would ease your conscience, and possibly your punishment."

"What reparation can I make?"

"Where is Oberstein with the papers?"

"I do not know."

"Did he give you no address?"

"He said that letters to the Hôtel du Louvre, Paris, would eventually reach him."

"Then reparation is still within your power," said Sherlock Holmes.

"I will do anything I can. I owe this fellow no particular goodwill. He has been my ruin and my downfall."

"Here are paper and pen. Sit at this desk and write to my dictation. Direct the envelope to the address given. That is right. Now the letter : ' Dear Sir,—With regard to our transaction, you will no doubt have observed by now that one essential detail is missing. I have a tracing which will make it complete. This has involved me in extra trouble, however, and I must ask you for a further advance of five hundred pounds. I will not trust it to the post, nor will I take anything but gold or notes. I would come to you abroad, but it would excite remark if I left the country at present. Therefore I shall expect to meet you in the smoking-room of the Charing Cross Hotel at noon on Saturday. Remember that only English notes, or gold, will be taken.' That will do very well. I shall be very much surprised if it does not fetch our man."

And it did! It is a matter of history—that secret history of a nation which is often so much more intimate and interesting than its public chronicles—that Oberstein, eager to complete the coup of his lifetime, came to the lure and was safely engulfed for fifteen years in a British prison. In his trunk were found the invaluable Bruce-Partington plans, which he had put up for auction in all the naval centres of Europe.

Colonel Walter died in prison towards the end of the second year of his sentence. As to Holmes, he returned refreshed to his monograph upon the Polyphonic Motets of Lassus, which has since been printed for private circulation, and is said by experts to be the last word upon the subject. Some weeks afterwards I learned incidentally that my friend spent a day at Windsor, whence he returned with a remarkably fine emerald tie-pin. When I asked him if he had bought it, he answered that it was a present from a certain gracious lady in whose interests he had once been fortunate enough to carry out a small commission. He said no more; but I fancy that I could guess at that lady's august name, and I have little doubt that the emerald pin will for ever recall to my friend's memory the adventure of the Bruce-Partington plans.

41. *The Dying Detective*

MRS. HUDSON, the landlady of Sherlock Holmes, was a long-suffering woman. Not only was her first-floor flat invaded at all hours by throngs of singular and often undesirable characters, but her remarkable lodger showed an eccentricity and irregularity in his life which must have sorely tried her patience. His incredible untidiness, his addiction to music at strange hours, his occasional revolver practice within doors, his weird and often malodorous scientific experiments, and the atmosphere of violence and danger which hung around him made him the very worst tenant in London. On the other hand, his payments were princely. I have no doubt that the house might have been purchased at the price which Holmes paid for his rooms during the years that I was with him.

The landlady stood in the deepest awe of him, and never dared to interfere with him, however outrageous his proceedings might seem. She was fond of him, too, for he had a remarkable gentleness and courtesy in his dealings with women. He disliked and distrusted the sex, but he was always a chivalrous opponent. Knowing how genuine was her regard for him, I listened earnestly to her story when she came to my rooms in the second year of my married life and told me of the sad condition to which my poor friend was reduced.

" He's dying, Dr. Watson," said she. " For three days he has been sinking, and I doubt if he will last the day. He would not let me get a doctor. This morning when I saw his bones sticking out of his face and his great bright eyes looking at me I could stand no more of it. ' With your leave or without it, Mr. Holmes, I am going for a doctor this very hour,' said I. ' Let it be Watson, then,' said he. I wouldn't waste an hour in coming to him, sir, or you may not see him alive."

I was horrified, for I had heard nothing of his illness. I need not say that I rushed for my coat and my hat. As we drove back I asked for the details.

" There is little I can tell you, sir. He has been working at a case down at Rotherhithe, in an alley near the river, and he has brought this illness back with him. He took to his bed on Wednesday afternoon and has never moved since. For these three days neither food nor drink has passed his lips."

" Good God ! Why did you not call in a doctor ? "

" He wouldn't have it, sir. You know how masterful he is. I didn't dare to disobey him. But he's not long for this world, as you'll see for yourself the moment that you set eyes on him."

He was indeed a deplorable spectacle. In the dim light of a foggy November day the sick-room was a gloomy spot, but it was that gaunt, wasted face staring at me from the bed which sent a chill to my heart. His eyes had the brightness of fever, there was a hectic flush upon either cheek, and dark crusts clung to his lips ; the thin hands upon the coverlet twitched incessantly, his voice was croaking and spasmodic. He lay listlessly as I entered the room, but the sight of me brought a gleam of recognition to his eyes.

"Well, Watson, we seem to have fallen upon evil days," said he, in a feeble voice, but with something of his old carelessness of manner.

"My dear fellow !" I cried, approaching him.

"Stand back ! Stand right back !" said he, with the sharp imperiousness which I had associated only with moments of crisis. "If you approach me, Watson, I shall order you out of the house."

"But why ?"

"Because it is my desire. Is that not enough ?"

Yes, Mrs. Hudson was right. He was more masterful than ever. It was pitiful, however, to see his exhaustion.

"I only wished to help," I explained.

"Exactly ! You will help best by doing what you are told."

"Certainly, Holmes."

He relaxed the austerity of his manner.

"You are not angry ?" he asked, gasping for breath.

Poor devil, how could I be angry when I saw him lying in such a plight before me ?

"It's for your own sake, Watson," he croaked.

"For *my* sake ?"

"I know what is the matter with me. It is a coolie disease from Sumatra—a thing that the Dutch know more about than we, though they have made little of it up to date. One thing only is certain. It is infallibly deadly, and it is horribly contagious."

He spoke now with a feverish energy, the long hands twitching and jerking as he motioned me away.

"Contagious by touch, Watson—that's it, by touch. Keep your distance and all is well."

"Good heavens, Holmes! Do you suppose that such a consideration weighs with me for an instant? It would not affect me in the case of a stranger. Do you imagine it would prevent me from doing my duty to so old a friend?"

Again I advanced, but he repulsed me with a look of furious anger.

"If you will stand there I will talk. If you do not you must leave the room."

I have so deep a respect for the extraordinary qualities of Holmes that I have always deferred to his wishes, even when I least understood them. But now all my professional instincts were aroused. Let him be my master elsewhere, I at least was his in a sick-room.

"Holmes," said I, "you are not yourself. A sick man is but a child, and so I will treat you. Whether you like it or not, I will examine your symptoms and treat you for them."

He looked at me with venomous eyes.

"If I am to have a doctor whether I will or not, let me at least have someone in whom I have confidence," said he.

"Then you have none in me?"

"In your friendship, certainly. But facts are facts, Watson, and after all you are only a general practitioner with very limited experience and mediocre qualifications. It is painful to have to say these things, but you leave me no choice."

I was bitterly hurt.

"Such a remark is unworthy of you, Holmes. It shows me very clearly the state of your own nerves. But if you have no confidence in me I would not intrude my services.

Let me bring Sir Jasper Meek or Penrose Fisher, or any of the best men in London. But someone you *must* have, and that is final. If you think that I am going to stand here and see you die without either helping you myself or bringing anyone else to help you, then you have mistaken your man."

" You mean well, Watson," said the sick man, with something between a sob and a groan. " Shall I demonstrate your own ignorance ? What do you know, pray, of Tapanuli fever ? What do you know of the black Formosa corruption ? "

" I have never heard of either."

" There are many problems of disease, many strange pathological possibilities, in the East, Watson." He paused after each sentence to collect his failing strength. " I have learned so much during some recent researches which have a medico-criminal aspect. It was in the course of them that I contracted this complaint. You can do nothing."

" Possibly not. But I happen to know that Dr. Ainstree, the greatest living authority upon tropical disease, is now in London. All remonstrance is useless, Holmes. I am going this instant to fetch him." I turned resolutely to the door.

Never have I had such a shock ! In an instant, with a tiger-spring, the dying man had intercepted me. I heard the sharp snap of a twisted key. The next moment he had staggered back to his bed, exhausted and panting after his one tremendous outflame of energy.

" You won't take the key from me by force, Watson. I've got you, my friend. Here you are, and here you will stay until I will otherwise. But I'll humour you." (All this in little gasps, with terrible struggles for breath between.) " You've only my own good at heart. Of course I know that very well. You shall have your way, but give me time to get my strength. Not now, Watson, not now. It's four o'clock. At six you can go."

" This is insanity, Holmes."

"Only two hours, Watson. I promise you will go at six. Are you content to wait ?"

"I seem to have no choice."

"None in the world, Watson. Thank you, I need no help in arranging the clothes. You will please keep your distance. Now, Watson, there is one other condition that I would make. You will seek help, not from the man you mention, but from the one that I choose."

"By all means."

"The first three sensible words that you have uttered since you entered this room, Watson. You will find some books over there. I am somewhat exhausted ; I wonder how a battery feels when it pours electricity into a non-conductor ? At six, Watson, we resume our conversation."

But it was destined to be resumed long before that hour, and in circumstances which gave me a shock hardly second to that caused by his spring to the door. I had stood for some minutes looking at the silent figure in the bed. His face was almost covered by the clothes and he appeared to be asleep. Then, unable to settle down to reading, I walked slowly round the room, examining the pictures of celebrated criminals with which every wall was adorned. Finally, in my aimless perambulation, I came to the mantelpiece. A litter of pipes, tobacco-pouches, syringes, pen-knives, revolver cartridges, and other *débris* was scattered over it. In the midst of these was a small black and white ivory box with a sliding lid. It was a neat little thing, and I had stretched out my hand to examine it more closely, when——

It was a dreadful cry that he gave—a yell which might have been heard down the street. My skin went cold and my hair bristled at that horrible scream. As I turned I caught a glimpse of a convulsed face and frantic eyes. I stood paralysed, with the little box in my hand.

"Put it down ! Down, this instant, Watson—this instant, I say ! " His head sank back upon the pillow and he gave a deep sigh of relief as I replaced the box upon the mantelpiece. " I hate to have my things touched, Watson. You know that I hate it. You fidget me beyond endurance. You, a doctor—you are enough to drive a patient into an asylum. Sit down, man, and let me have my rest ! "

The incident left a most unpleasant impression upon my mind. The violent and causeless excitement, followed by this brutality of speech, so far removed from his usual suavity, showed me how deep was the disorganization of his mind. Of all ruins, that of a noble mind is the most deplorable. I sat in silent dejection until the stipulated time had passed. He seemed to have been watching the clock as well as I, for it was hardly six before he began to talk with the same feverish animation as before.

" Now, Watson," said he. " Have you any change in your pocket ? "

" Yes."

" Any silver ? "

" A good deal."

" How many half-crowns ? "

" I have five."

" Ah, too few ! Too few ! How very unfortunate, Watson ! However, such as they are you can put them in your watch-pocket. And all the rest of your money in your left trouser-pocket. Thank you. It will balance you so much better like that."

This was raving insanity. He shuddered, and again made a sound between a cough and a sob.

" You will now light the gas, Watson, but you will be very careful that not for one instant shall it be more than half on. I implore you to be careful, Watson. Thank you, that is excellent. No, you need not draw the blind. Now you will have the kindness to place some letters and papers upon this table within my reach. Thank you. Now some of that litter from the mantelpiece. Excellent, Watson ! There is a sugar-tongs there. Kindly raise that small ivory box with its assistance. Place it here among the papers. Good ! You can now go and fetch Mr. Culverton Smith, of 13 Lower Burke Street."

To tell the truth, my desire to fetch a doctor had somewhat weakened, for poor Holmes was so obviously delirious that it seemed dangerous to leave him. However, he was as eager now to consult the person named as he had been obstinate in refusing.

"I never heard the name," said I.

"Possibly not, my good Watson. It may surprise you to know that the man upon earth who is best versed in this disease is not a medical man, but a planter. Mr. Culverton Smith is a well-known resident of Sumatra, now visiting London. An outbreak of the disease upon his plantation, which was distant from medical aid, caused him to study it himself, with some rather far-reaching consequences. He is a very methodical person, and I did not desire you to start before six because I was well aware that you would not find him in his study. If you could persuade him to come here and give us the benefit of his unique experience of this disease, the investigation of which has been his dearest hobby, I cannot doubt that he could help me."

I give Holmes's remarks as a consecutive whole, and will not attempt to indicate how they were interrupted by gaspings for breath and those clutchings of his hands which indicated the pain from which he was suffering. His appearance had changed for the worse during the few hours that I had been with him. Those hectic spots were more pronounced, the eyes shone more brightly out of darker hollows, and a cold sweat glimmered upon his brow. He still retained, however, the jaunty gallantry of his speech. To the last gasp he would always be the master.

"You will tell him exactly how you have left me," said he. "You will convey the very impression which is in your own mind—a dying man—a dying and delirious man. Indeed, I cannot think why the whole bed of the ocean is not one solid mass of oysters, so prolific the creatures seem. Ah, I am wandering! Strange how the brain controls the brain. What was I saying, Watson ? "

" My directions for Mr. Culverton Smith."

" Ah, yes, I remember. My life depends upon it. Plead with him, Watson. There is no good feeling between us. His nephew, Watson—I had suspicions of foul play and I allowed him to see it. The boy died horribly. He has a grudge against me. You will soften him, Watson. Beg him, pray him, get him here by any means. He can save me—only he ! "

" I will bring him in a cab, if I have to carry him down to it."

" You will do nothing of the sort. You will persuade him to come. And then you will return in front of him. Make any excuse so as not to come with him. Don't forget, Watson. You won't fail me. You never did fail me. No doubt there are natural enemies which limit the increase of the creatures. You and I, Watson, we have done our part. Shall the world, then, be overrun by oysters ? No, no ; horrible ! You'll convey all that is in your mind."

I left him, full of the image of this magnificent intellect babbling like a foolish child. He had handed me the key, and with a happy thought I took it with me lest he should lock himself in. Mrs. Hudson was waiting, trembling and weeping, in the passage. Behind me as I passed from the flat I heard Holmes's high, thin voice in some delirious chant. Below, as I stood whistling for a cab, a man came on me through the fog.

" How is Mr. Holmes, sir ? " he asked.

It was an old acquaintance, Inspector Morton, of Scotland Yard, dressed in unofficial tweeds.

" He is very ill," I answered.

He looked at me in a most singular fashion. Had it not been too fiendish, I could have imagined that the gleam of the fanlight showed exultation in his face.

" I heard some rumour of it," said he.

The cab had driven up, and I left him.

Lower Burke Street proved to be a line of fine houses lying in the vague borderland between Notting Hill and

Kensington. The particular one at which my cabman pulled up had an air of smug and demure respectability in its old-fashioned iron railings, its massive folding-door, and its shining brasswork. All was in keeping with a solemn butler who appeared framed in the pink radiance of a tinted electric light behind him.

"Yes, Mr. Culverton Smith is in. Dr. Watson! Very good, sir, I will take up your card."

My humble name and title did not appear to impress Mr. Culverton Smith. Through the half-open door I heard a high, petulant, penetrating voice.

"Who is this person? What does he want? Dear me, Staples, how often have I said that I am not to be disturbed in my hours of study?"

There came a gentle flow of soothing explanation from the butler.

"Well, I won't see him, Staples. I can't have my work interrupted like this. I am not at home. Say so. Tell him to come in the morning if he really must see me."

Again the gentle murmur.

"Well, well, give him that message. He can come in the morning, or he can stay away. My work must not be hindered."

I thought of Holmes tossing upon his bed of sickness, and counting the minutes, perhaps, until I could bring help to him. It was not a time to stand upon ceremony. His life depended upon my promptness. Before the apologetic butler had delivered his message I had pushed past him and was in the room.

With a shrill cry of anger a man rose from a reclining chair beside the fire. I saw a great yellow face, coarse-grained and greasy, with heavy double-chin, and two sullen, menacing grey eyes which glared at me from under tufted and sandy brows. A high bald head had a small velvet smoking-cap poised coquettishly upon one side of its pink curve. The skull was of enormous capacity, and yet, as I looked down I saw to my amazement that the figure of the man was small and frail, twisted in the shoulders and back like one who has suffered from rickets in his childhood.

"What's this?" he cried, in a high, screaming voice. "What is the meaning of this intrusion? Didn't I send you word that I would see you to-morrow morning?"

"I am sorry," said I, "but the matter cannot be delayed. Mr. Sherlock Holmes——"

The mention of my friend's name had an extraordinary effect upon the little man. The look of anger passed in an instant from his face. His features became tense and alert.

"Have you come from Holmes?" he asked.

"I have just left him."

"What about Holmes? How is he?"

"He is desperately ill. That is why I have come."

The man motioned me to a chair, and turned to resume his own. As he did so I caught a glimpse of his face in the mirror over the mantelpiece. I could have sworn that it was set in a malicious and abominable smile. Yet I persuaded myself that it must have been some nervous contraction which I had surprised, for he turned to me an instant later with genuine concern upon his features.

"I am sorry to hear this," said he. "I only know Mr. Holmes through some business dealings which we have had, but I have every respect for his talents and his character. He is an amateur of crime, as I am of disease. For him the villain, for me the microbe. There are my prisons," he continued, pointing to a row of bottles and jars which stood upon a side table. "Among those gelatine cultivations some of the very worst offenders in the world are now doing time."

"It was on account of your special knowledge that Mr. Holmes desired to see you. He has a high opinion of you, and thought that you were the one man in London who could help him."

The little man started, and the jaunty smoking-cap slid to the floor.

" Why ? " he asked. " Why should Mr. Holmes think that I could help him in his trouble ? "

" Because of your knowledge of Eastern diseases."

" But why should he think that this disease which he has contracted is Eastern ? "

" Because, in some professional inquiry, he has been working among Chinese sailors down in the docks."

Mr. Culverton Smith smiled pleasantly and picked up his smoking-cap.

" Oh, that's it—is it ? " said he. " I trust the matter is not so grave as you suppose. How long has he been ill ? "

" About three days."

" Is he delirious ? "

" Occasionally."

" Tut, tut ! This sounds serious. It would be in-human not to answer his call. I very much resent any interruption to my work, Dr. Watson, but this case is certainly exceptional. I will come with you at once."

I remembered Holmes's injunction.

" I have another appointment," said I.

" Very good. I will go alone. I have a note of Mr. Holmes's address. You can rely upon my being there within half an hour at most."

It was with a sinking heart that I re-entered Holmes's bedroom. For all that I knew the worst might have happened in my absence. To my enormous relief, he had improved greatly in the interval. His appearance was as ghastly as ever, but all trace of delirium had left him and he spoke in a feeble voice, it is true, but with even more than his usual crispness and lucidity.

" Well, did you see him, Watson ? "

" Yes ; he is coming."

" Admirable, Watson ! Admirable ! You are the best of messengers."

" He wished to return with me."

" That would never do, Watson. That would be obvi-ously impossible. Did he ask what ailed me ? "

"I told him about the Chinese in the East End."

"Exactly! Well, Watson, you have done all that a good friend could. You can now disappear from the scene."

"I must wait and hear his opinion, Holmes."

"Of course you must. But I have reasons to suppose that this opinion would be very much more frank and valuable if he imagines that we are alone. There is just room behind the head of my bed, Watson."

"My dear Holmes!"

"I fear there is no alternative, Watson. The room does not lend itself to concealment, which is as well, as it is the less likely to arouse suspicion. But just there, Watson, I fancy that it could be done." Suddenly he sat up with a rigid intentness upon his haggard face. "There are the wheels, Watson. Quick, man, if you love me! And don't budge, whatever happens—whatever happens, do you hear? Don't speak! Don't move! Just listen with all your ears." Then in an instant his sudden access of strength departed, and his masterful, purposeful talk droned away into the low, vague murmurings of a semi-delirious man.

From the hiding-place into which I had been so swiftly hustled I heard the footfalls upon the stair, with the opening and the closing of the bedroom door. Then, to my surprise, there came a long silence, broken only by the heavy breathings and gaspings of the sick man. I could imagine that our visitor was standing by the bedside and looking down at the sufferer. At last that strange hush was broken.

"Holmes!" he cried. "Holmes!" in the insistent tone of one who awakens a sleeper. "Can't you hear me, Holmes?" There was a rustling, as if he had shaken the sick man roughly by the shoulder.

"Is that you, Mr. Smith?" Holmes whispered. "I hardly dared hope that you would come."

The other laughed.

"I should imagine not," he said. "And yet, you see, I am here. Coals of fire, Holmes—coals of fire!"

"It is very good of you—very noble of you. I appreciate your special knowledge."

Our visitor sniggered.

"You do. You are, fortunately, the only man in London who does. Do you know what is the matter with you?"

"The same," said Holmes.

"Ah! You recognize the symptoms?"

"Only too well."

"Well, I shouldn't be surprised, Holmes. I shouldn't be surprised if it *were* the same. A bad look-out for you if it is. Poor Victor was a dead man on the fourth day—a strong, hearty young fellow. It was certainly, as you said, very surprising that he should have contracted an out-of-the-way Asiatic disease in the heart of London—a disease, too, of which I had made such a very special study. Singular coincidence, Holmes. Very smart of you to notice it, but rather uncharitable to suggest that it was cause and effect."

"I knew that you did it."

"Oh, you did, did you? Well, you couldn't prove it, anyhow. But what do you think of yourself spreading reports about me like that, and then crawling to me for help the moment you are in trouble? What sort of a game is that—eh?"

I heard the rasping, laboured breathing of the sick man. "Give me the water!" he gasped.

"You're precious near your end, my friend, but I don't want you to go till I have had a word with you. That's why I give you water. There, don't slop it about! That's right. Can you understand what I say?"

Holmes groaned.

"Do what you can for me. Let bygones be bygones," he whispered. "I'll put the words out of my head—I swear I will. Only cure me, and I'll forget it."

"Forget what?"

"Well, about Victor Savage's death. You as good as admitted just now that you had done it. I'll forget it."

" You can forget it or remember it, just as you like. I don't see you in the witness-box. Quite another shaped box, my good Holmes, I assure you. It matters nothing to me that you should know how my nephew died. It's not him we are talking about. It's you."

" Yes, yes."

" The fellow who came for me—I've forgotten his name —said that you contracted it down in the East End among the sailors."

" I could only account for it so."

" You are proud of your brains, Holmes, are you not ? Think yourself smart, don't you ?   You came across some-one who was smarter this time.   Now cast your mind back, Holmes.   Can you think of no other way you could have got this thing ? "

" I can't think.   My mind is gone.   For Heaven's sake help me ! "

" Yes, I will help you.   I'll help you to understand just where you are and how you got there.   I'd like you to know before you die."

" Give me something to ease my pain."

" Painful, is it ?   Yes, the coolies used to do some squealing towards the end.   Takes you as cramp, I fancy."

" Yes, yes ; it is cramp."

" Well, you can hear what I say, anyhow.   Listen now ! Can you remember any unusual incident in your life just about the time your symptoms began ? "

" No, no ; nothing."

" Think again."

" I'm too ill to think."

" Well, then, I'll help you.   Did anything come by post ? "

" By post ? "

" A box by chance ? "

" I'm fainting—I'm gone ! "

" Listen, Holmes ! "   There was a sound as if he was shaking the dying man, and it was all that I could do to hold myself quiet in my hiding-place.   " You must hear me. You *shall* hear me. Do you remember a box—an ivory box ? It came on Wednesday. You opened it—do you remember ? "

" Yes, yes, I opened it. There was a sharp spring inside it. Some joke——"

" It was no joke, as you will find to your cost. You fool, you would have it and you have got it. Who asked you to cross my path ? If you had left me alone I would not have hurt you."

" I remember," Holmes gasped. " The spring ! It drew blood. This box—this on the table."

" The very one, by George ! And it may as well leave the room in my pocket. There goes your last shred of evidence. But you have the truth now, Holmes, and you can die with the knowledge that I killed you. You knew too much of the fate of Victor Savage, so I have sent you to share it. You are very near your end, Holmes. I will sit here and I will watch you die."

Holmes's voice had sunk to an almost inaudible whisper.

" What is that ? " said Smith. " Turn up the gas ? Ah, the shadows begin to fall, do they ? Yes, I will turn it up, that I may see you the better." He crossed the room and the light suddenly brightened. " Is there any other little service that I can do you, my friend ? "

" A match and a cigarette."

I nearly called out in my joy and my amazement. He was speaking in his natural voice—a little weak, perhaps, but the very voice I knew. There was a long pause, and I felt that Culverton Smith was standing in silent amazement looking down at his companion.

" What's the meaning of this ? " I heard him say at last, in a dry, rasping tone.

" The best way of successfully acting a part is to be it," said Holmes. " I give you my word that for three days I have tasted neither food nor drink until you were good enough to pour me out that glass of water. But it is the tobacco which I find most irksome. Ah, here *are* some cigarettes." I heard the striking of a match. " That is very much better. Halloa ! halloa ! Do I hear the step of a friend ? "

There were footfalls outside, the door opened, and Inspector Morton appeared.

" All is in order and this is your man," said Holmes. The officer gave the usual cautions.

" I arrest you on the charge of the murder of one Victor Savage," he concluded.

" And you might add the attempted murder of one Sherlock Holmes," remarked my friend with a chuckle. " To save an invalid trouble, inspector, Mr. Culverton Smith was good enough to give our signal by turning up the gas. By the way, the prisoner has a small box in the right-hand pocket of his coat which it would be as well to remove. Thank you. I would handle it gingerly if I were you. Put it down here. It may play its part in the trial."

There was a sudden rush and a scuffle, followed by the clash of iron and a cry of pain.

" You'll only get yourself hurt," said the inspector. " Stand still, will you ? " There was the click of the closing handcuffs.

" A nice trap ! " cried the high, snarling voice. " It will bring *you* into the dock, Holmes, not me. He asked me to come here to cure him. I was sorry for him and I came. Now he will pretend, no doubt, that I have said anything which he may invent which will corroborate his insane suspicions. You can lie as you like, Holmes. My word is always as good as yours."

" Good heavens ! " cried Holmes. " I had totally forgotten him. My dear Watson, I owe you a thousand apologies. To think that I should have overlooked you ! I need not introduce you to Mr. Culverton Smith, since I understand that you met somewhat earlier in the evening. Have you the cab below ? I will follow you when I am dressed, for I may be of some use at the station."

" I never needed it more," said Holmes, as he refreshed himself with a glass of claret and some biscuits in the intervals of his toilet. "However, as you know, my habits are irregular, and such a feat means less to me than to most men. It was very essential that I should impress Mrs. Hudson with the reality of my condition, since she was to convey it to you, and you in turn to him. You won't be offended, Watson? You will realize that among your many talents dissimulation finds no place, and that if you had shared my secret you would never have been able to impress Smith with the urgent necessity of his presence, which was the vital point of the whole scheme. Knowing his vindictive nature, I was perfectly certain that he would come to look upon his handiwork."

"But your appearance, Holmes—your ghastly face?"

"Three days of absolute fast does not improve one's beauty, Watson. For the rest, there is nothing which a sponge may not cure. With vaseline upon one's forehead, belladonna in one's eyes, rouge over the cheek-bones, and crusts of beeswax round one's lips, a very satisfying effect can be produced. Malingering is a subject upon which I have sometimes thought of writing a monograph. A little occasional talk about half-crowns, oysters, or any other extraneous subject produces a pleasing effect of delirium."

"But why would you not let me near you, since there was in truth no infection?"

"Can you ask, my dear Watson? Do you imagine that I have no respect for your medical talents? Could I fancy that your astute judgment would pass a dying man who, however weak, had no rise of pulse or temperature? At four yards, I could deceive you. If I failed to do so, who would bring my Smith within my grasp? No, Watson, I would not touch that box. You can just see if you look at it sideways where the sharp spring like a viper's tooth emerges as you open it. I dare say it was by some such device that poor Savage, who stood between this monster and a reversion, was done to death. My correspondence, however, is, as you know, a varied one, and I am somewhat upon my guard against any packages which reach me. It was clear to me, however, that by pretending that he had really succeeded in his design I might surprise a confession. That pretence I have carried out with the thoroughness of the true artist. Thank you, Watson, you must help me on with my coat. When we have finished at the police-station I think that something nutritious at Simpson's would not be out of place."

42. *The Disappearance of Lady Frances Carfax*

"BUT why Turkish ? " asked Mr. Sherlock Holmes, gazing fixedly at my boots. I was reclining in a cane-backed chair at the moment, and my protruded feet had attracted his ever-active attention.

" English," I answered, in some surprise. " I got them at Latimer's, in Oxford Street."

Holmes smiled with an expression of weary patience.

" The bath ! " he said ; " the bath ! Why the relaxing and expensive Turkish rather than the invigorating home-made article ? "

" Because for the last few days I have been feeling rheumatic and old. A Turkish bath is what we call an alterative in medicine—a fresh starting-point, a cleanser of the system.

" By the way, Holmes," I added, " I have no doubt the connection between my boots and a Turkish bath is a perfectly self-evident one to a logical mind, and yet I should be obliged to you if you would indicate it."

" The train of reasoning is not very obscure, Watson," said Holmes, with a mischievous twinkle. " It belongs to the same elementary class of deduction which I should illustrate if I were to ask you who shared your cab in your drive this morning."

" I don't admit that a fresh illustration is an explanation," said I, with some asperity.

" Bravo, Watson ! A very dignified and logical remonstrance. Let me see, what were the points ? Take the last one first—the cab. You observe that you have some splashes on the left sleeve and shoulder of your coat. Had you sat in the centre of a hansom you would probably have had no splashes, and if you had they would certainly have been symmetrical. Therefore it is clear that you sat at the side. Therefore it is equally clear that you had a companion."

"That is very evident."

"Absurdly commonplace, is it not ?"

"But the boots and the bath ?"

"Equally childish. You are in the habit of doing up your boots in a certain way. I see them on this occasion fastened with an elaborate double bow, which is not your usual method of tying them. You have, therefore, had them off. Who has tied them ? A bootmaker—or the boy at the bath. It is unlikely that it is the bootmaker, since your boots are nearly new. Well, what remains ? The bath. Absurd, is it not ? But, for all that, the Turkish bath has served a purpose."

"What is that ?"

"You say that you have had it because you need a change. Let me suggest that you take one. How would Lausanne do, my dear Watson—first-class tickets and all expenses paid on a princely scale ?"

"Splendid ! But why ?"

Holmes leaned back in his arm-chair and took his notebook from his pocket.

"One of the most dangerous classes in the world," said he, " is the drifting and friendless woman. She is the most harmless, and often the most useful of mortals, but she is the inevitable inciter of crime in others. She is helpless. She is migratory. She has sufficient means to take her from country to country and from hotel to hotel. She is lost, as often as not, in a maze of obscure *pensions* and boarding-houses. She is a stray chicken in a world of foxes. When she is gobbled up she is hardly missed. I much fear that some evil has come to the Lady Frances Carfax."

I was relieved at this sudden descent from the general to the particular. Holmes consulted his notes.

"Lady Frances," he continued, "is the sole survivor of the direct family of the late Earl of Rufton. The estates went, as you may remember, in the male line. She was left with limited means, but with some very remarkable old Spanish jewellery of silver and curiously-cut diamonds to which she was fondly attached—too attached, for she refused to leave them with her banker and always carried them about with her. A rather pathetic figure, the Lady Frances, a beautiful woman, still in fresh middle age, and yet, by a strange chance, the last derelict of what only twenty years ago was a goodly fleet."

"What has happened to her, then ? "

"Ah, what has happened to the Lady Frances ? Is she alive or dead ? There is our problem. She is a lady of precise habits, and for four years it has been her invariable custom to write every second week to Miss Dobney, her old governess, who has long retired, and lives in Camberwell. It is this Miss Dobney who has consulted me. Nearly five weeks have passed without a word. The last letter was from the Hôtel National at Lausanne. Lady Frances seems to have left there and given no address. The family are anxious, and, as they are exceedingly wealthy, no sum will be spared if we can clear the matter up."

"Is Miss Dobney the only source of information ? Surely she had other correspondents ? "

"There is one correspondent who is a sure draw, Watson. That is the bank. Single ladies must live, and their pass-books are compressed diaries. She banks at Silvester's. I have glanced over her account. The last cheque but one paid her bill at Lausanne, but it was a large one and probably left her with cash in hand. Only one cheque has been drawn since."

"To whom, and where ? "

"To Miss Marie Devine. There is nothing to show where the cheque was drawn. It was cashed at the Crédit

Lyonnais at Montpelier less than three weeks ago. The sum was fifty pounds."

"And who is Miss Marie Devine ? "

"That also I have been able to discover. Miss Marie Devine was the maid of Lady Frances Carfax. Why she should have paid her this cheque we have not yet determined. I have no doubt, however, that your researches will soon clear the matter up."

" *My* researches ! "

"Hence the health-giving expedition to Lausanne. You know that I cannot possibly leave London while old Abrahams is in such mortal terror of his life. Besides, on general principles it is best that I should not leave the country. Scotland Yard feels lonely without me, and it causes an unhealthy excitement among the criminal classes. Go, then, my dear Watson, and if my humble counsel can ever be valued at so extravagant a rate as twopence a word, it waits your disposal night and day at the end of the Continental wire."

Two days later found me at the National Hotel at Lausanne, where I received every courtesy at the hands of M. Moser, the well-known manager. Lady Frances, as he informed me, had stayed there for several weeks. She had been much liked by all who met her. Her age was not more than forty. She was still handsome, and bore every sign of having in her youth been a very lovely woman. M. Moser knew nothing of any valuable jewellery, but it had been remarked by the servants that the heavy trunk in the lady's bedroom was always scrupulously locked. Marie Devine, the maid, was as popular as her mistress. She was actually engaged to one of the head waiters in the hotel, and there was no difficulty in getting her address. It was 11 Rue de Trajan, Montpelier. All this I jotted down, and felt that Holmes himself could not have been more adroit in collecting his facts.

Only one corner still remained in the shadow. No light which I possessed could clear up the cause for the lady's sudden departure. She was very happy at Lausanne. There was every reason to believe that she intended to remain for the season in her luxurious rooms overlooking the lake. And yet she had left at a single day's notice, which involved her in the useless payment of a week's rent. Only Jules Vibart, the lover of the maid, had any suggestion to offer. He connected the sudden departure with the visit to the hotel a day or two before of a tall, dark, bearded man. " *Un sauvage—un véritable sauvage!* " cried Jules Vibart. The man had rooms somewhere in the town. He had been seen talking earnestly to madame on the promenade by the lake. Then he had called. She had refused to see him. He was English, but of his name there was no record. Madame had left the place immediately afterwards. Jules Vibart, and, what was of more importance, Jules Vibart's sweetheart, thought that this call and this departure were cause and effect. Only one thing Jules could not discuss. That was the reason why Marie had left her mistress. Of that he could or would say nothing. If I wished to know, I must go to Montpelier and ask her.

So ended the first chapter of my inquiry. The second was devoted to the place which Lady Frances Carfax had sought when she left Lausanne. Concerning this there had been some secrecy, which confirmed the idea that she had gone with the intention of throwing someone off her track. Otherwise why should not her luggage have been openly labelled for Baden ? Both she and it reached the Rhenish spa by some circuitous route. Thus much I gathered from the manager of Cook's local office. So to Baden I went, after dispatching to Holmes an account of all my proceedings, and receiving in reply a telegram of half-humorous commendation.

At Baden the track was not difficult to follow. Lady Frances had stayed at the Englischer Hof for a fortnight. Whilst there she had made the acquaintance of a Dr. Shlessinger and his wife, a missionary from South America. Like most lonely ladies, Lady Frances found her comfort and occupation in religion. Dr. Shlessinger's remarkable personality, his whole-hearted devotion, and the fact that he was recovering from a disease contracted in the exercise of his apostolic duties, affected her deeply. She had helped Mrs. Shlessinger in the nursing of the convalescent saint. He spent his day, as the manager described it to me, upon a lounge-chair on the verandah, with an attendant lady upon either side of him. He was preparing a map of the Holy Land, with special reference to the kingdom of the Midianites, upon which he was writing a monograph. Finally, having improved much in health, he and his wife had returned to London, and Lady Frances had started thither in their company. This was just three weeks before, and the manager had heard nothing since. As to the maid, Marie, she had gone off some days beforehand in floods of tears, after informing the other maids that she was leaving service for ever. Dr. Shlessinger had paid the bill of the whole party before his departure.

" By the way," said the landlord, in conclusion, " you are not the only friend of Lady Frances Carfax who is inquiring after her just now. Only a week or so ago we had a man here upon the same errand."

" Did he give a name ? " I asked.

" None ; but he was an Englishman, though of an unusual type."

" A savage ? " said I, linking my facts after the fashion of my illustrious friend.

" Exactly. That describes him very well. He is a bulky, bearded, sunburned fellow, who looks as if he would be more at home in a farmers' inn than in a fashionable hotel. A hard, fierce man, I should think, and one whom I should be sorry to offend."

Already the mystery began to define itself, as figures grow clearer with the lifting of a fog. Here was this good and pious lady pursued from place to place by a sinister and unrelenting figure. She feared him, or she would not have fled from Lausanne. He had still followed. Sooner or later he would overtake her. Had he already overtaken her ? Was *that* the secret of her continued silence ? Could the good people who were her companions not screen her from his violence or his blackmail ? What horrible purpose, what deep design, lay behind this long pursuit ? There was the problem which I had to solve.

To Holmes I wrote showing how rapidly and surely I had got down to the roots of the matter. In reply I had a telegram asking for a description of Dr. Shlessinger's left ear. Holmes' ideas of humour are strange and occasionally offensive, so I took no notice of his ill-timed jest—indeed, I had already reached Montpelier in my pursuit of the maid, Marie, before his message came.

I had no difficulty in finding the ex-servant and in learning all that she could tell me. She was a devoted creature, who had only left her mistress because she was sure that she was in good hands, and because her own approaching marriage made a separation inevitable in any case. Her mistress had, as she confessed with distress, shown some irritability of temper towards her during their stay in Baden, and had even questioned her once as if she had suspicions of her honesty, and this had made the parting easier than it would otherwise have been. Lady Frances had given her fifty pounds as a wedding-present. Like me, Marie viewed with deep distrust the stranger who had driven her mistress from Lausanne. With her own eyes she had seen him seize the lady's wrist with great violence on the public promenade by the lake. He was a fierce and terrible man. She believed that it was out of dread of him that Lady Frances had accepted the escort of the Shlessingers to London. She had never spoken to Marie about it, but many little signs had convinced the maid that her mistress lived in a state of continual nervous apprehension. So far she had got in her narrative, when suddenly she sprang from her chair and her face was convulsed with surprise and fear. " See ! " she cried. " The miscreant follows still ! There is the very man of whom I speak."

Through the open sitting-room window I saw a huge, swarthy man with a bristling black beard walking slowly down the centre of the street and staring eagerly at the numbers of the houses. It was clear that, like myself, he was on the track of the maid. Acting upon the impulse of the moment, I rushed out and accosted him.

" You are an Englishman," I said.

" What if I am ? " he asked, with a most villainous scowl.

" May I ask what your name is ? "

" No, you may not," said he, with decision.

The situation was awkward, but the most direct way is often the best.

" Where is the Lady Frances Carfax ? " I asked.

He stared at me in amazement.

" What have you done with her ? Why have you pursued her ? I insist upon an answer ! " said I.

The fellow gave a bellow of anger and sprang upon me like a tiger. I have held my own in many a struggle, but the man had a grip of iron and the fury of a fiend. His hand was on my throat and my senses were nearly gone before an unshaven French *ouvrier*, in a blue blouse, darted out from a *cabaret* opposite, with a cudgel in his hand, and struck my assailant a sharp crack over the forearm, which made him leave go his hold. He stood for an instant fuming with rage and uncertain whether he should not renew his attack. Then, with a snarl of anger, he left me and entered the cottage from which I had just come. I turned to thank my preserver, who stood beside me in the roadway.

" Well, Watson," said he, " a very pretty hash you have made of it ! I rather think you had better come back with me to London by the night express."

An hour afterwards Sherlock Holmes, in his usual garb and style, was seated in my private room at the hotel. His explanation of his sudden and opportune appearance was simplicity itself, for, finding that he could get away from London, he determined to head me off at the next obvious point of my travels. In the disguise of a working-man he had sat in the *cabaret* waiting for my appearance.

" And a singularly consistent investigation you have made, my dear Watson," said he. " I cannot at the moment recall any possible blunder which you have omitted. The total effect of your proceedings has been to give the alarm everywhere and yet to discover nothing."

" Perhaps you would have done no better," I answered, bitterly.

" There is no ' perhaps ' about it. I *have* done better. Here is the Hon. Philip Green, who is a fellow-lodger with you in this hotel, and we may find in him the starting-point for a more successful investigation."

A card had come up on a salver, and it was followed by the same bearded ruffian who had attacked me in the street. He started when he saw me.

" What is this, Mr. Holmes ? " he asked. " I had your note and I have come. But what has this man to do with the matter ? "

" This is my old friend and associate, Dr. Watson, who is helping us in this affair."

The stranger held out a huge, sunburned hand, with a few words of apology.

" I hope I didn't harm you. When you accused me of hurting her I lost my grip of myself. Indeed, I'm not responsible in these days. My nerves are like live wires. But this situation is beyond me. What I want to know, in the first place, Mr. Holmes, is, how in the world you came to hear of my existence at all."

" I am in touch with Miss Dobney, Lady Frances' governess."

" Old Susan Dobney with the mob cap ! I remember her well."

" And she remembers you. It was in the days before— before you found it better to go to South Africa."

" Ah, I see you know my whole story. I need hide nothing from you. I swear to you, Mr. Holmes, that there never was in this world a man who loved a woman with a more whole-hearted love than I had for Frances. I was a wild youngster, I know—not worse than others of my class. But her mind was pure as snow. She could not bear a shadow of coarseness. So, when she came to hear of things that I had done, she would have no more to say to me. And yet she loved me—that is the wonder of it!—loved me well enough to remain single all her sainted days just for my sake alone. When the years had passed and I had made my money at Barberton I thought perhaps I could seek her out and soften her. I had heard that she was still unmarried. I found her at Lausanne, and tried all I knew. She weakened, I think, but her will was strong, and when next I called she had left the town. I traced her to Baden, and then after a time heard that her maid was here. I'm a rough fellow, fresh from a rough life, and when Dr. Watson spoke to me as he did I lost hold of myself for a moment. But for God's sake tell me what has become of the Lady Frances."

" That is for us to find out," said Sherlock Holmes, with peculiar gravity. " What is your London address, Mr. Green ? "

" The Langham Hotel will find me."

" Then may I recommend that you return there and be on hand in case I should want you ? I have no desire to encourage false hopes, but you may rest assured that all that can be done will be done for the safety of Lady Frances. I can say no more for the instant. I will leave you this card so that you may be able to keep in touch with us. Now, Watson, if you will pack your bag I will cable to Mrs. Hudson to make one of her best efforts for two hungry travellers at seven-thirty to-morrow."

A telegram was awaiting us when we reached our Baker Street rooms, which Holmes read with an exclamation of interest and threw across to me. " Jagged or torn," was the message, and the place of origin Baden.

" What is this ? " I asked.

" It is everything," Holmes answered. " You may

remember my seemingly irrelevant question as to this clerical gentleman's left ear. You did not answer it."

" I had left Baden, and could not inquire."

" Exactly. For this reason I sent a duplicate to the manager of the Englischer Hof, whose answer lies here."

" What does it show ? "

" It shows, my dear Watson, that we are dealing with an exceptionally astute and dangerous man. The Rev. Dr. Shlessinger, missionary from South America, is none other than Holy Peters, one of the most unscrupulous rascals that Australia has ever evolved—and for a young country it has turned out some very finished types. His particular speciality is the beguiling of lonely ladies by playing upon their religious feelings, and his so-called wife, an Englishwoman named Fraser, is a worthy help-mate. The nature of his tactics suggested his identity to me, and this physical peculiarity—he was badly bitten in a saloon-fight at Adelaide in '89—confirmed my suspicion. This poor lady is in the hands of a most infernal couple, who will stick at nothing, Watson. That she is already dead is a very likely supposition. If not, she is undoubtedly in some sort of confinement, and unable to write to Miss Dobney or her other friends. It is always possible that she never reached London, or that she has passed through it, but the former is improbable, as, with their system of registration, it is not easy for foreigners to play tricks with the Continental police ; and the latter is also unlikely, as these rogues could not hope to find any other place where it would be as easy to keep a person under restraint. All my instincts tell me that she is in London, but, as we have at present no possible means of telling where, we can only take the obvious steps, eat our dinner, and possess our souls in patience. Later in the evening I will stroll down and have a word with friend Lestrade at Scotland Yard."

But neither the official police nor Holmes' own small, but very efficient, organization sufficed to clear away the mystery. Amid the crowded millions of London the three persons we sought were as completely obliterated as if they had never lived. Advertisements were tried, and failed. Clues were followed, and led to nothing. Every criminal resort which Shlessinger might frequent was drawn in vain. His old associates were watched, but they kept clear of him. And then suddenly, after a week of helpless suspense, there came a flash of light. A silver-and-brilliant pendant of old Spanish design had been pawned at Bevington's, in Westminster Road. The pawner was a large, clean-shaven man of clerical appearance. His name and address were demonstrably false. The ear had escaped notice, but the description was surely that of Shlessinger.

Three times had our bearded friend from the Langham called for news—the third time within an hour of this fresh development. His clothes were getting looser on his great body. He seemed to be wilting away in his anxiety. " If you will only give me something to do ! " was his constant wail. At last Holmes could oblige him.

" He has begun to pawn the jewels. We should get him now."

" But does this mean that any harm has befallen the Lady Frances ? "

Holmes shook his head very gravely.

" Supposing that they have held her prisoner up to now, it is clear that they cannot let her loose without their own destruction. We must prepare for the worst."

" What can I do ? "

" These people do not know you by sight ? "

" No."

" It is possible that he will go to some other pawnbroker in the future. In that case, we must begin again. On the other hand, he has had a fair price and no questions asked, so if he is in need of ready money he will probably come back to Bevington's. I will give you a note to them, and they will let you wait in the shop. If the fellow comes you will follow him home. But no indiscretion, and, above all, no violence. I put you on your honour that you will take no step without my knowledge and consent."

For two days the Hon. Philip Green (he was, I may mention, the son of the famous admiral of that name who commanded the Sea of Azof fleet in the Crimean War) brought us no news. On the evening of the third he rushed into our sitting-room, pale, trembling, with every muscle of his powerful frame quivering with excitement.

"We have him! We have him!" he cried.

He was incoherent in his agitation. Holmes soothed him with a few words, and thrust him into an arm-chair.

"Come, now, give us the order of events," said he.

"She came only an hour ago. It was the wife, this time, but the pendant she brought was the fellow of the other. She is a tall, pale woman, with ferret eyes."

"That is the lady," said Holmes.

"She left the office and I followed her. She walked up the Kennington Road, and I kept behind her. Presently she went into a shop. Mr. Holmes, it was an undertaker's."

My companion started. "Well?" he asked, in that vibrant voice which told of the fiery soul behind the cold, grey face.

"She was talking to the woman behind the counter. I entered as well. 'It is late,' I heard her say, or words to that effect. The woman was excusing herself. 'It should be there before now,' she answered. 'It took longer, being out of the ordinary.' They both stopped and looked at me, so I asked some question and then left the shop."

"You did excellently well. What happened next?"

"The woman came out, but I had hid myself in a doorway. Her suspicions had been aroused, I think, for she looked round her. Then she called a cab and got in. I was lucky enough to get another and so to follow her. She got down at last at No. 36 Poultney Square, Brixton. I drove past, left my cab at the corner of the square, and watched the house."

"Did you see anyone?"

"The windows were all in darkness save one on the lower floor. The blind was down, and I could not see in. I was standing there, wondering what I should do next, when a covered van drove up with two men in it. They descended, took something out of the van, and carried it up the steps to the hall door. Mr. Holmes, it was a coffin."

"Ah!"

"For an instant I was on the point of rushing in. The door had been opened to admit the men and their burden. It was the woman who had opened it. But as I stood there she caught a glimpse of me, and I think that she recognized me. I saw her start, and she hastily closed the door. I remembered my promise to you, and here I am."

"You have done excellent work," said Holmes, scribbling a few words upon a half-sheet of paper. "We can do nothing legal without a warrant, and you can serve the cause best by taking this note down to the authorities and getting one. There may be some difficulty, but I should think that the sale of the jewellery should be sufficient. Lestrade will see to all details."

"But they may murder her in the meanwhile. What could the coffin mean, and for whom could it be but for her?"

"We will do all that can be done, Mr. Green. Not a moment will be lost. Leave it in our hands. Now, Watson," he added, as our client hurried away, "he will set the regular forces on the move. We are, as usual, the irregulars, and we must take our own line of action. The situation strikes me as so desperate that the most extreme measures are justified. Not a moment is to be lost in getting to Poultney Square."

"Let us try to reconstruct the situation," said he, as we drove swiftly past the Houses of Parliament and over Westminster Bridge. "These villains have coaxed this unhappy lady to London, after first alienating her from her faithful maid. If she has written any letters they have been intercepted. Through some confederate they have engaged a furnished house. Once inside it, they have made her a prisoner, and they have become possessed of the valuable jewellery which has been their object from the first. Already they have begun to sell part of it, which seems safe enough to them, since they have no reason to think that anyone is interested in the lady's fate. When she is released she will, of course, denounce them. Therefore, she must not be released. But they cannot keep her under lock and key for ever. So murder is their only solution."

" That seems very clear."

" Now we will take another line of reasoning. When you follow two separate chains of thought, Watson, you will find some point of intersection which should approximate to the truth. We will start now, not from the lady, but from the coffin, and argue backwards. That incident proves, I fear, beyond all doubt that the lady is dead. It points also to an orthodox burial with proper accompaniment of medical certificate and official sanction. Had the lady been obviously murdered, they would have buried her in a hole in the back garden. But here all is open and regular. What does that mean ? Surely that they have done her to death in some way which has deceived the doctor, and simulated a natural end—poisoning, perhaps. And yet how strange that they should ever let a doctor approach her unless he were a confederate, which is hardly a credible proposition."

" Could they have forged a medical certificate ? "

" Dangerous, Watson, very dangerous. No, I hardly see them doing that. Pull up, cabby ! This is evidently the undertaker's, for we have just passed the pawnbroker's. Would you go in, Watson ? Your appearance inspires confidence. Ask what hour the Poultney Square funeral takes place to-morrow."

The woman in the shop answered me without hesitation that it was to be at eight o'clock in the morning.

" You see, Watson, no mystery ; everything above-board! In some way the legal forms have undoubtedly been complied with, and they think that they have little to fear. Well, there's nothing for it now but a direct frontal attack. Are you armed?"

"My stick!"

"Well, well, we shall be strong enough. 'Thrice is he armed who hath his quarrel just.' We simply can't afford to wait for the police, or to keep within the four corners of the law. You can drive off, cabby. Now, Watson, we'll just take our luck together, as we have occasionally done in the past."

He had rung loudly at the door of a great dark house in the centre of Poultney Square. It was opened immediately, and the figure of a tall woman was outlined against the dim-lit hall.

"Well, what do you want?" she asked, sharply, peering at us through the darkness.

"I want to speak to Dr. Shlessinger," said Holmes.

"There is no such person here," she answered, and tried to close the door, but Holmes had jammed it with his foot.

"Well, I want to see the man who lives here, whatever he may call himself," said Holmes, firmly.

She hesitated. Then she threw open the door. "Well, come in!" said she. "My husband is not afraid to face any man in the world." She closed the door behind us, and showed us into a sitting-room on the right side of the hall, turning up the gas as she left us. "Mr. Peters will be with you in an instant," she said.

Her words were literally true, for we had hardly time to look round the dusty and moth-eaten apartment in which we found ourselves before the door opened and a big, clean-shaven, bald-headed man stepped lightly into the room. He had a large red face, with pendulous cheeks, and a general air of superficial benevolence which was marred by a cruel, vicious mouth.

"There is surely some mistake here, gentlemen," he

said, in an unctuous, make-everything-easy voice. " I fancy that you have been misdirected. Possibly if you tried farther down the street——"

" That will do ; we have no time to waste," said my companion, firmly. " You are Henry Peters, of Adelaide, late the Rev. Dr. Shlessinger, of Baden and South America. I am as sure of that as that my own name is Sherlock Holmes."

Peters, as I will now call him, started and stared hard at his formidable pursuer. " I guess your name does not frighten me, Mr. Holmes," said he, coolly. " When a man's conscience is easy you can't rattle him. What is your business in my house ? "

" I want to know what you have done with the Lady Frances Carfax, whom you brought away with you from Baden."

" I'd be very glad if you could tell me where that lady may be," Peters answered, coolly. " I've a bill against her for nearly a hundred pounds, and nothing to show for it but a couple of trumpery pendants that the dealer would hardly look at. She attached herself to Mrs. Peters and me at Baden (it is a fact that I was using another name at the time), and she stuck on to us until we came to London. I paid her bill and her ticket. Once in London, she gave us the slip, and, as I say, left these out-of-date jewels to pay her bills. You find her, Mr. Holmes, and I'm your debtor."

" *I mean* to find her," said Sherlock Holmes. " I'm going through this house till I do find her."

" Where is your warrant ? "

Holmes half drew a revolver from his pocket. " This will have to serve till a better one comes."

" Why, you are a common burglar."

" So you might describe me," said Holmes, cheerfully. " My companion is also a dangerous ruffian. And together we are going through your house."

Our opponent opened the door.

" Fetch a policeman, Annie ! " said he. There was a

whisk of feminine skirts down the passage, and the hall
door was opened and shut.

"Our time is limited, Watson," said Holmes. "If you
try to stop us, Peters, you will most certainly get hurt.
Where is that coffin which was brought into your house ?"

"What do you want with the coffin ? It is in use.
There is a body in it."

"I must see that body."

"Never with my consent."

"Then without it." With a quick movement Holmes
pushed the fellow to one side and passed into the hall. A
door half-open stood immediately before us. We entered.
It was the dining-room. On the table, under a half-lit
chandelier, the coffin was lying. Holmes turned up the
gas and raised the lid. Deep down in the recesses of the
coffin lay an emaciated figure. The glare from the lights
above beat down upon an aged and withered face. By no
possible process of cruelty, starvation, or disease could
this worn-out wreck be the still beautiful Lady Frances.
Holmes' face showed his amazement, and also his relief.

"Thank God !" he muttered. "It's someone else."

"Ah, you've blundered badly for once, Mr. Sherlock
Holmes," said Peters, who had followed us into the room.

"Who is this dead woman ?"

"Well, if you really must know, she is an old nurse
of my wife's, Rose Spender her name, whom we found
in the Brixton Workhouse Infirmary. We brought her
round here, called in Dr. Horsom, of 13 Firbank Villas—
mind you take the address, Mr. Holmes—and had her
carefully tended, as Christian folk should. On the third
day she died—certificate says senile decay—but that's only
the doctor's opinion, and, of course, you know better.
We ordered her funeral to be carried out by Stimson &
Co., of the Kennington Road, who will bury her at eight
o'clock to-morrow morning. Can you pick any hole in
that, Mr. Holmes ? You've made a silly blunder, and
you may as well own up to it. I'd give something for a
photograph of your gaping, staring face when you pulled

aside that lid expecting to see the Lady Frances Carfax, and only found a poor old woman of ninety."

Holmes' expression was as impassive as ever under the jeers of his antagonist, but his clenched hands betrayed his acute annoyance.

" I am going through your house," said he.

" Are you, though ! " cried Peters, as a woman's voice and heavy steps sounded in the passage. " We'll soon see about that. This way, officers, if you please. These men have forced their way into my house, and I cannot get rid of them. Help me to put them out."

A sergeant and a constable stood in the doorway. Holmes drew his card from his case.

" This is my name and address. This is my friend, Dr. Watson."

" Bless you, sir, we know you very well," said the sergeant, " but you can't stay here without a warrant."

" Of course not. I quite understand that."

" Arrest him ! " cried Peters.

" We know where to lay our hands on this gentleman if he is wanted," said the sergeant, majestically ; " but you'll have to go, Mr. Holmes."

" Yes, Watson, we shall have to go."

A minute later we were in the street once more. Holmes was as cool as ever, but I was hot with anger and humiliation. The sergeant had followed us.

" Sorry, Mr. Holmes, but that's the law."

" Exactly, sergeant ; you could not do otherwise."

" I expect there was good reason for your presence there. If there is anything I can do——"

" It's a missing lady, sergeant, and we think she is in that house. I expect a warrant presently."

" Then I'll keep my eye on the parties, Mr. Holmes. If anything comes along, I will surely let you know."

It was only nine o'clock, and we were off full cry upon the trail at once. First we drove to Brixton Workhouse Infirmary, where we found that it was indeed the truth that a charitable couple had called some days before, that they had claimed an imbecile old woman as a former servant, and that they had obtained permission to take her away with them. No surprise was expressed at the news that she had since died.

The doctor was our next goal. He had been called in, had found the woman dying of pure senility, had actually seen her pass away, and had signed the certificate in due form. "I assure you that everything was perfectly normal and there was no room for foul play in the matter," said he. Nothing in the house had struck him as suspicious, save that for people of their class it was remarkable that they should have no servant. So far and no farther went the doctor.

Finally, we found our way to Scotland Yard. There had been difficulties of procedure in regard to the warrant. Some delay was inevitable. The magistrate's signature might not be obtained until next morning. If Holmes would call about nine he could go down with Lestrade and see it acted upon. So ended the day, save that near midnight our friend, the sergeant, called to say that he had seen flickering lights here and there in the windows of the great dark house, but that no one had left it and none had entered. We could but pray for patience, and wait for the morrow.

Sherlock Holmes was too irritable for conversation and too restless for sleep. I left him smoking hard, with his heavy, dark brows knotted together, and his long, nervous fingers tapping upon the arms of his chair, as he turned over in his mind every possible solution of the mystery. Several times in the course of the night I heard him prowling about the house. Finally, just after I had been called in the morning, he rushed into my room. He was in his dressing-gown, but his pale, hollow-eyed face told me that his night had been a sleepless one.

"What time was the funeral? Eight, was it not?" he asked, eagerly. "Well, it is seven-twenty now. Good heavens, Watson, what has become of any brains that God has given me? Quick, man, quick! It's life or death—a

hundred chances on death to one on life. I'll never forgive myself, never, if we are too late ! "

Five minutes had not passed before we were flying in a
hansom down Baker Street. But even so it was twenty-
five to eight as we passed Big Ben, and eight struck as we
tore down the Brixton Road. But others were late as well
as we. Ten minutes after the hour the hearse was still
standing at the door of the house, and even as our foaming
horse came to a halt the coffin, supported by three men,
appeared on the threshold. Holmes darted forward and
barred their way.

" Take it back ! " he cried, laying his hand on the breast
of the foremost. " Take it back this instant ! "

" What the devil do you mean ? Once again I ask you,
where is your warrant ? " shouted the furious Peters, his
big red face glaring over the farther end of the coffin.

" The warrant is on its way. This coffin shall remain
in the house until it comes."

The authority in Holmes' voice had its effect upon the
bearers. Peters had suddenly vanished into the house,
and they obeyed these new orders. " Quick, Watson,
quick ! Here is a screw-driver ! " he shouted, as the coffin
was replaced upon the table. " Here's one for you, my
man : a sovereign if the lid comes off in a minute ! Ask
no questions—work away ! That's good ! Another !
And another ! Now pull all together ! It's giving ! It's
giving ! Ah, that does it at last ! "

With a united effort we tore off the coffin-lid. As we
did so there came from the inside a stupefying and overpowering smell of chloroform. A body lay within, its
head all wreathed in cotton-wool, which had been soaked
in the narcotic. Holmes plucked it off and disclosed the
statuesque face of a handsome and spiritual woman of
middle age. In an instant he had passed his arm round
the figure and raised her to a sitting position.

" Is she gone, Watson ? Is there a spark left ? Surely
we are not too late ! "

For half an hour it seemed that we were. What with

actual suffocation, and what with the poisonous fumes of the chloroform, the Lady Frances seemed to have passed the last point of recall. And then, at last, with artificial respiration, with injected ether, with every device that science could suggest, some flutter of life, some quiver of the eyelids, some dimming of a mirror, spoke of the slowly returning life. A cab had driven up, and Holmes, parting the blind, looked out at it. " Here is Lestrade with his warrant," said he. " He will find that his birds have flown. And here," he added, as a heavy step hurried along the passage, " is someone who has a better right to nurse this lady than we have. Good morning, Mr. Green ; I think that the sooner we can move the Lady Frances the better. Meanwhile, the funeral may proceed, and the poor old woman who still lies in that coffin may go to her last resting-place alone."

" Should you care to add the case to your annals, my dear Watson," said Holmes that evening, " it can only be as an example of that temporary eclipse to which even the best-balanced mind may be exposed. Such slips are common to all mortals, and the greatest is he who can recognize and repair them. To this modified credit I may, perhaps, make some claim. My night was haunted by the thought that somewhere a clue, a strange sentence, a curious observation, had come under my notice and had been too easily dismissed. Then, suddenly, in the grey of the morning, the words came back to me. It was the remark of the undertaker's wife, as reported by Philip Green. She had said, ' It should be there before now. It took longer, being out of the ordinary.' It was the coffin of which she spoke. It had been out of the ordinary. That could only mean that it had been made to some special measurement. But why ? Why ? Then in an instant I remembered the deep sides, and the little wasted figure at the bottom. Why so large a coffin for so small a body ? To leave room for another body. Both would be buried under the one certificate. It had all been so clear, if only my own sight had not been dimmed. At eight the Lady Frances would be buried. Our one chance was to stop the coffin before it left the house.

"It was a desperate chance that we might find her alive, but it *was* a chance, as the result showed. These people had never, to my knowledge, done a murder. They might shrink from actual violence at the last. They could bury her with no sign of how she met her end, and even if she were exhumed there was a chance for them. I hoped that such considerations might prevail with them. You can reconstruct the scene well enough. You saw the horrible den upstairs, where the poor lady had been kept so long. They rushed in and overpowered her with their chloroform, carried her down, poured more into the coffin to ensure against her waking, and then screwed down the lid. A clever device, Watson. It is new to me in the annals of crime. If our ex-missionary friends escape the clutches of Lestrade, I shall expect to hear of some brilliant incidents in their future career."

43. *The Devil's Foot*

IN recording from time to time some of the curious experiences and interesting recollections which I associate with my long and intimate friendship with Mr. Sherlock Holmes, I have continually been faced by difficulties caused by his own aversion to publicity. To his sombre and cynical spirit all popular applause was always abhorrent, and nothing amused him more at the end of a successful case than to hand over the actual exposure to some orthodox official, and to listen with a mocking smile to the general chorus of misplaced congratulation. It was indeed, this attitude upon the part of my friend, and certainly not any lack of interesting material which has caused me of late years to lay very few of my records before the public. My participation in some of his adventures was always a privilege which entailed discretion and reticence upon me.

It was, then, with considerable surprise that I received a telegram from Holmes last Tuesday—he has never been known to write where a telegram would serve—in the following terms : " Why not tell them of the Cornish horror—strangest case I have handled." I have no idea what backward sweep of memory had brought the matter fresh to his mind, or what freak had caused him to desire that I should recount it ; but I hasten, before another cancelling telegram may arrive, to hunt out the notes which give me the exact details of the case, and to lay the narrative before my readers.

It was, then, in the spring of the year 1897 that Holmes' iron constitution showed some symptoms of giving way in the face of constant hard work of a most exacting kind, aggravated, perhaps, by occasional indiscretions of his own. In March of that year Dr. Moore Agar, of Harley Street, whose dramatic introduction to Holmes I may some day recount, gave positive injunctions that the famous private agent would lay aside all his cases and surrender himself to complete rest if he wished to avert an absolute break-down. The state of his health was not a matter in which he himself took the faintest interest, for his mental detachment was absolute, but he was induced at last, on the threat of being permanently disqualified from work, to give himself a complete change of scene and air. Thus it was that in the early spring of that year we found ourselves together in a small cottage near Poldhu Bay, at the further extremity of the Cornish peninsula.

It was a singular spot, and one peculiarly well suited to the grim humour of my patient. From the windows of our little whitewashed house, which stood high upon a grassy headland, we looked down upon the whole sinister semicircle of Mounts Bay, that old death trap of sailing vessels, with its fringe of black cliffs and surge-swept reefs on which innumerable seamen have met their end. With a northerly breeze it lies placid and sheltered, inviting the storm-tossed craft to tack into it for rest and protection. Then comes the sudden swirl round of the wind, the blustering gale from the south-west, the dragging anchor, the lee shore, and the last battle in the creaming breakers. The wise mariner stands far out from that evil place.

On the land side our surroundings were as sombre as on the sea. It was a country of rolling moors, lonely and dun-coloured, with an occasional church tower to mark the site of some old-world village. In every direction upon these moors there were traces of some vanished race which had passed utterly away, and left as its sole record strange monuments of stone, irregular mounds which contained the burned ashes of the dead, and curious earthworks which hinted at prehistoric strife. The glamour and mystery of the place, with its sinister atmosphere of forgotten nations, appealed to the imagination of my friend, and he spent much of his time in long walks and solitary meditations upon the moor. The ancient Cornish language had also arrested his attention, and he had, I remember, conceived the idea that it was akin to the Chaldean, and had been largely derived from the Phœnician traders in tin. He had received a consignment of books upon philology and was settling down to develop this thesis, when suddenly, to my sorrow and to his unfeigned delight, we found ourselves, even in that land of dreams, plunged into a problem at our very doors which was more intense, more engrossing, and infinitely more mysterious than any of those which had driven us from London. Our simple life and peaceful, healthy routine were violently interrupted, and we were precipitated into the midst of a series of events which caused the utmost excitement not only in Cornwall, but throughout the whole West of England. Many of my readers may retain some recollection of what was called at the time " The Cornish Horror," though a most imperfect account of the matter reached the London Press. Now, after thirteen years, I will give the true details of this inconceivable affair to the public.

I have said that scattered towers marked the villages which dotted this part of Cornwall. The nearest of these was the hamlet of Tredannick Wollas, where the cottages of a couple of hundred inhabitants clustered round an ancient, moss-grown church. The vicar of the parish, Mr. Roundhay, was something of an archæologist, and as such Holmes had made his acquaintance. He was a middle-aged man, portly and affable, with a considerable fund of local lore. At his invitation we had taken tea at the vicarage, and had come to know, also, Mr. Mortimer Tregennis, an independent gentleman, who increased the clergyman's scanty resources by taking rooms in his large straggling house. The vicar, being a bachelor, was glad to come to such an arrangement, though he had little in common with his lodger, who was a thin, dark, spectacled man, with a stoop which gave the impression of actual physical deformity. I remember that during our short visit we found the vicar garrulous, but his lodger strangely reticent, a sad-faced, introspective man, sitting with averted eyes, brooding apparently upon his own affairs.

These were the two men who entered abruptly into our little sitting-room on Tuesday, March the 16th, shortly after our breakfast hour, as we were smoking together, preparatory to our daily excursion upon the moors.

"Mr. Holmes," said the vicar, in an agitated voice, "the most extraordinary and tragic affair has occurred during the night. It is the most unheard-of business. We can only regard it as a special Providence that you should chance to be here at the time, for in all England you are the one man we need."

I glared at the intrusive vicar with no very friendly eyes; but Holmes took his pipe from his lips and sat up in his chair like an old hound who hears the view-holloa. He waved his hand to the sofa, and our palpitating visitor with his agitated companion sat side by side upon it. Mr. Mortimer Tregennis was more self-contained than the clergyman, but the twitching of his thin hands and the brightness of his dark eyes showed that they shared a common emotion.

"Shall I speak or you?" he asked of the vicar.

"Well, as you seem to have made the discovery, whatever it may be, and the vicar to have had it second-hand, perhaps you had better do the speaking," said Holmes.

I glanced at the hastily-clad clergyman, with the formally-dressed lodger seated beside him, and was amused at the surprise which Holmes' simple deduction had brought to their faces.

"Perhaps I had best say a few words first," said the vicar, "and then you can judge if you will listen to the details from Mr. Tregennis, or whether we should not hasten at once to the scene of this mysterious affair. I may explain, then, that our friend here spent last evening in the company of his two brothers, Owen and George, and of his sister Brenda, at their house of Tredannick Wartha, which is near the old stone cross upon the moor. He left them shortly after ten o'clock, playing cards round the dining-room table, in excellent health and spirits. This morning, being an early riser, he walked in that direction before breakfast, and was overtaken by the carriage of Dr. Richards, who explained that he had just been sent for on a most urgent call to Tredannick Wartha. Mr. Mortimer Tregennis naturally went with him. When he arrived at Tredannick Wartha he found an extraordinary state of things. His two brothers and his sister were seated round the table exactly as he had left them, the cards still spread in front of them and the candles burned down to their sockets. The sister lay back stone-dead in her chair, while the two brothers sat on each side of her laughing, shouting, and singing, the senses stricken clean out of them. All three of them, the dead woman and the two demented men, retained upon their faces an expression of the utmost horror—a convulsion of terror which was dreadful to look upon. There was no sign of the presence of anyone in the house, except Mrs. Porter, the old cook and housekeeper, who declared that she had slept deeply and heard no sound during the night. Nothing had been stolen or disarranged, and there is absolutely no explanation of what the horror can be which has frightened a woman to death and two strong men out of their senses. There is the situation, Mr. Holmes, in a nutshell and if you can help us to clear it up you will have done a great work."

I had hoped that in some way I could coax my companion back into the quiet which had been the object of our journey ; but one glance at his intense face and contracted eyebrows told me how vain was now the expectation. He sat for some little time in silence, absorbed in the strange drama which had broken in upon our peace.

" I will look into this matter," he said at last. " On the face of it, it would appear to be a case of a very exceptional nature. Have you been there yourself, Mr. Roundhay ? "

" No, Mr. Holmes. Mr. Tregennis brought back the account to the vicarage, and I at once hurried over with him to consult you."

" How far is it to the house where this singular tragedy occurred ? "

" About a mile inland."

" Then we shall walk over together. But, before we start, I must ask you a few questions, Mr. Mortimer Tregennis."

The other had been silent all this time, but I had observed that his more controlled excitement was even greater than the obtrusive emotion of the clergyman. He sat with a pale, drawn face, his anxious gaze fixed upon Holmes, and his thin hands clasped convulsively together. His pale lips quivered as he listened to the dreadful experience which had befallen his family, and his dark eyes seemed to reflect something of the horror of the scene.

" Ask what you like, Mr. Holmes," said he eagerly. " It is a bad thing to speak of, but I will answer you the truth."

" Tell me about last night."

" Well, Mr. Holmes, I supped there, as the vicar has said, and my elder brother George proposed a game of whist afterwards. We sat down about nine o'clock. It was a quarter-past ten when I moved to go. I left them all round the table, as merry as could be."

"Who let you out?"

"Mrs. Porter had gone to bed, so I let myself out. I shut the hall door behind me. The window of the room in which they sat was closed, but the blind was not drawn down. There was no change in door or window this morning, nor any reason to think that any stranger had been to the house. Yet there they sat, driven clean mad with terror, and Brenda lying dead of fright, with her head hanging over the arm of the chair. I'll never get the sight of that room out of my mind so long as I live."

"The facts, as you state them, are certainly most remarkable," said Holmes. "I take it that you have no theory yourself which can in any way account for them?"

"It's devilish, Mr. Holmes; devilish!" cried Mortimer Tregennis. "It is not of this world. Something has come into that room which has dashed the light of reason from their minds. What human contrivance could do that?"

"I fear," said Holmes, "that if the matter is beyond humanity it is certainly beyond me. Yet we must exhaust all natural explanations before we fall back upon such a theory as this. As to yourself, Mr. Tregennis, I take it you were divided in some way from your family, since they lived together and you had rooms apart?"

"That is so, Mr. Holmes, though the matter is past and done with. We were a family of tin-miners at Redruth, but we sold out our venture to a company, and so retired with enough to keep us. I won't deny that there was some feeling about the division of the money and it stood between us for a time, but it was all forgiven and forgotten, and we were the best of friends together."

"Looking back at the evening which you spent together, does anything stand out in your memory as throwing any possible light upon the tragedy? Think carefully, Mr. Tregennis, for any clue which can help me."

"There is nothing at all, sir."

" Your people were in their usual spirits ? "

" Never better."

" Were they nervous people ? Did they ever show any apprehension of coming danger ? "

" Nothing of the kind."

" You have nothing to add then, which could assist me ? "

Mortimer Tregennis considered earnestly for a moment.

" There is one thing occurs to me," said he at last. " As we sat at the table my back was to the window, and my brother George, he being my partner at cards, was facing it. I saw him once look hard over my shoulder, so I turned round and looked also. The blind was up and the window shut, but I could just make out the bushes on the lawn, and it seemed to me for a moment that I saw something moving among them. I couldn't even say if it were man or animal, but I just thought there was something there. When I asked him what he was looking at, he told me that he had the same feeling. That is all that I can say."

" Did you not investigate ? "

" No ; the matter passed as unimportant."

" You left them, then, without any premonition of evil ? "

" None at all."

" I am not clear how you came to hear the news so early this morning."

" I am an early riser, and generally take a walk before breakfast. This morning I had hardly started when the doctor in his carriage overtook me. He told me that old Mrs. Porter had sent a boy down with an urgent message. I sprang in beside him and we drove on. When we got there we looked into that dreadful room. The candles and the fire must have burned out hours before, and they had been sitting there in the dark until dawn had broken. The doctor said Brenda must have been dead at least six hours. There were no signs of violence. She just lay across the arm of the chair with that look on her face.

George and Owen were singing snatches of songs and gibbering like two great apes. Oh, it was awful to see ! I couldn't stand it, and the doctor was as white as a sheet. Indeed, he fell into a chair in a sort of faint, and we nearly had him on our hands as well."

"Remarkable—most remarkable !" said Holmes, rising and taking his hat. "I think, perhaps, we had better go down to Tredannick Wartha without further delay. I confess that I have seldom known a case which at first sight presented a more singular problem."

Our proceedings of that first morning did little to advance the investigation. It was marked, however, at the outset by an incident which left the most sinister impression upon my mind. The approach to the spot at which the tragedy occurred is down a narrow winding country lane. While we made our way along it we heard the rattle of a carriage coming towards us, and stood aside to let it pass. As it drove by us I caught a glimpse through the closed window of a horribly contorted, grinning face glaring out at us. Those staring eyes and gnashing teeth flashed past us like a dreadful vision.

"My brothers !" cried Mortimer Tregennis, white to his lips. "They are taking them to Helston."

We looked with horror after the black carriage, lumbering upon its way. Then we turned our steps towards this ill-omened house in which they had met their strange fate. It was a large and bright dwelling, rather a villa than a cottage, with a considerable garden which was already, in that Cornish air, well filled with spring flowers. Towards this garden the window of the sitting-room fronted, and from it, according to Mortimer Tregennis, must have come that thing of evil which had by sheer horror in a single instant blasted their minds. Holmes walked slowly and thoughtfully among the flower-pots and along the path before we entered the porch. So absorbed was he in his thoughts, I remember, that he stumbled over the watering-pot, upset its contents, and deluged both our feet and the garden path. Inside the house we were met by the elderly Cornish housekeeper, Mrs. Porter, who, with the aid of a young girl, looked after the wants of the family. She readily answered all Holmes' questions. She had heard nothing in the night. Her employers had all been in excellent spirits lately, and she had never known them more cheerful and prosperous. She had fainted with horror upon entering the room in the morning and seeing that dreadful company round the table. She had, when she recovered, thrown open the window to let the morning air in, and had run down to the lane, whence she sent a farm-lad for the doctor. The lady was on her bed upstairs, if we cared to see her. It took four strong men to get the brothers into the asylum carriage. She would not herself stay in the house another day, and was starting that very afternoon to rejoin her family at St. Ives.

We ascended the stairs and viewed the body. Miss Brenda Tregennis had been a very beautiful girl, though now verging upon middle age. Her dark, clear-cut face was handsome, even in death, but there still lingered upon it something of that convulsion of horror which had been her last human emotion. From her bedroom we descended to the sitting-room where this strange tragedy had actually occurred. The charred ashes of the overnight fire lay in the grate. On the table were the four guttered and burned-out candles, with the cards scattered over its surface. The chairs had been moved back against the walls, but all else was as it had been the night before. Holmes paced with light, swift steps about the room ; he sat in the various chairs, drawing them up and reconstructing their positions. He tested how much of the garden was visible ; he examined the floor, the ceiling, and the fireplace ; but never once did I see that sudden brightening of his eyes and tightening of his lips which would have told me that he saw some gleam of light in this utter darkness.

"Why a fire ? " he asked once. " Had they always a fire in this small room on a spring evening ? "

Mortimer Tregennis explained that the night was cold and damp. For that reason, after his arrival, the fire was lit. " What are you going to do now, Mr. Holmes ? " he asked.

My friend smiled and laid his hand upon my arm. " I think, Watson, that I shall resume that course of tobacco-poisoning which you have so often and so justly condemned," said he. " With your permission, gentlemen, we will now return to our cottage, for I am not aware that any new factor is likely to come to our notice here. I will turn the facts over in my mind, Mr. Tregennis, and should anything occur to me I will certainly communicate with you and the vicar. In the meantime I wish you both good morning."

It was not until long after we were back in Poldhu Cottage that Holmes broke his complete and absorbed silence. He sat coiled in his arm-chair, his haggard and ascetic face hardly visible amid the blue swirl of his tobacco smoke, his black brows drawn down, his forehead contracted, his eyes vacant and far away. Finally, he laid down his pipe and sprang to his feet.

" It won't do, Watson ! " said he, with a laugh. " Let us walk along the cliffs together and search for flint arrows. We are more likely to find them than clues to this problem. To let the brain work without sufficient material is like racing an engine. It racks itself to pieces. The sea air, sunshine, and patience, Watson—all else will come.

" Now, let us calmly define our position, Watson," he continued, as we skirted the cliffs together. " Let us get a firm grip of the very little which we *do* know, so that when fresh facts arise we may be ready to fit them into their places. I take it, in the first place, that neither of us is prepared to admit diabolical intrusions into the affairs of men. Let us begin by ruling that entirely out of our minds. Very good. There remain three persons who have been grievously stricken by some conscious or unconscious human agency. That is firm ground. Now, when did this occur ? Evidently, assuming his narrative to be true, it was immediately after Mr. Mortimer Tregennis had left the room. That is a very important point. The presumption is that it was within a few minutes afterwards. The cards still lay upon the table. It was already past their usual hour for bed. Yet they had not changed their position or pushed back their chairs. I repeat, then, that the occurrence was immediately after his departure, and not later than eleven o'clock last night.

"Our next obvious step is to check, so far as we can, the movements of Mortimer Tregennis after he left the room. In this there is no difficulty, and they seem to be above suspicion. Knowing my methods as you do, you were, of course, conscious of the somewhat clumsy water-pot expedient by which I obtained a clearer impress of his foot than might otherwise have been possible. The wet sandy path took it admirably. Last night was also wet, you will remember, and it was not difficult—having obtained a sample print—to pick out his track among others and to follow his movements. He appears to have walked away swiftly in the direction of the vicarage.

"If, then, Mortimer Tregennis disappeared from the scene, and yet some outside person affected the card-players, how can we reconstruct that person, and how was such an impression of horror conveyed? Mrs. Porter may be eliminated. She is evidently harmless. Is there any evidence that someone crept up to the garden window and in some manner produced so terrific an effect that he drove those who saw it out of their senses? The only suggestion in this direction comes from Mortimer Tregennis himself, who says that his brother spoke about some movement in the garden. That is certainly remarkable, as the night was rainy, cloudy, and dark. Anyone who had the design to alarm these people would be compelled to place his very face against the glass before he could be seen. There is a three-foot flower-border outside this window, but no indication of a footmark. It is difficult to imagine, then, how an outsider could have made so terrible an impression upon the company, nor have we found any possible motive for so strange and elaborate an attempt. You perceive our difficulties, Watson ? "

" They are only too clear," I answered, with conviction.

" And yet, with a little more material, we may prove that they are not insurmountable," said Holmes. " I fancy that among your extensive archives, Watson, you may find some which were nearly as obscure. Meanwhile, we shall put the case aside until more accurate data are available, and devote the rest of our morning to the pursuit of neolithic man."

I may have commented upon my friend's power of mental detachment, but never have I wondered at it more than upon that spring morning in Cornwall when for two hours he discoursed upon celts, arrowheads, and shards, as lightly as if no sinister mystery was waiting for his solution. It was not until we had returned in the afternoon to our cottage that we found a visitor awaiting us, who soon brought our minds back to the matter in hand. Neither of us needed to be told who that visitor was. The huge body, the craggy and deeply-seamed face with the fierce eyes and hawk-like nose, the grizzled hair which nearly brushed our cottage ceiling, the beard—golden at the fringes and white near the lips, save for the nicotine stain from his perpetual cigar—all these were as well known in London as in Africa, and could only be associated with the tremendous personality of Dr. Leon Sterndale, the great lion-hunter and explorer.

We had heard of his presence in the district, and had once or twice caught sight of his tall figure upon the moorland paths. He made no advances to us, however, nor would we have dreamed of doing so to him, as it was well known that it was his love of seclusion which caused him to spend the greater part of the intervals between his journeys in a small bungalow buried in the lonely wood of Beauchamp Arriance. Here, amid his books and his maps, he lived an absolutely lonely life, attending to his own simple wants, and paying little apparent heed to the affairs of his neighbours. It was a surprise to me, therefore, to hear him asking Holmes in an eager voice, whether he had made any advance in his reconstruction of this mysterious episode. "The county police are utterly at fault," said he; "but perhaps your wider experience has suggested some conceivable explanation. My only claim to being taken into your confidence is that during my many residences here I have come to know this family of Tregennis very well—indeed, upon my Cornish mother's side I could call them cousins—and their strange fate has naturally been a great shock to me. I may tell you that I had got as far as Plymouth upon my way to Africa, but the news reached me this morning, and I came straight back again to help in the inquiry."

Holmes raised his eyebrows.

"Did you lose your boat through it?"

"I will take the next."

"Dear me! that is friendship indeed."

"I tell you they were relatives."

"Quite so—cousins of your mother. Was your baggage aboard the ship?"

"Some of it, but the main part at the hotel."

"I see. But surely this event could not have found its way into the Plymouth morning papers?"

"No, sir; I had a telegram."

"Might I ask from whom?"

A shadow passed over the gaunt face of the explorer.

"You are very inquisitive, Mr. Holmes."

"It is my business."

With an effort, Dr. Sterndale recovered his ruffled composure.

"I have no objection to telling you," he said. "It was Mr. Roundhay, the vicar, who sent me the telegram which recalled me."

"Thank you," said Holmes. "I may say in answer to your original question, that I have not cleared my mind entirely on the subject of this case, but that I have every hope of reaching some conclusion. It would be premature to say more."

"Perhaps you would not mind telling me if your suspicions point in any particular direction?"

"No, I can hardly answer that."

"Then I have wasted my time, and need not prolong my visit." The famous doctor strode out of our cottage in considerable ill-humour, and within five minutes Holmes had followed him. I saw him no more until the evening, when he returned with a slow step and haggard face which assured me that he had made no great progress with his investigation. He glanced at a telegram which awaited him, and threw it into the grate.

"From the Plymouth hotel, Watson," he said. "I learned the name of it from the vicar, and I wired to make certain that Dr. Leon Sterndale's account was true. It appears that he did indeed spend last night there, and that he has actually allowed some of his baggage to go on to Africa, while he returned to be present at this investigation. What do you make of that, Watson?"

"He is deeply interested."

"Deeply interested—yes. There is a thread here which we have not yet grasped, and which might lead us through the tangle. Cheer up, Watson, for I am very sure that our material has not yet all come to hand. When it does, we may soon leave our difficulties behind us."

Little did I think how soon the words of Holmes would be realized, or how strange and sinister would be that new development which opened up an entirely fresh line of investigation. I was shaving at my window in the morning when I heard the rattle of hoofs, and, looking up, saw a dog-cart coming at a gallop down the road. It pulled up at our door, and our friend the vicar sprang from it and rushed up our garden path. Holmes was already dressed, and we hastened down to meet him.

Our visitor was so excited that he could hardly articulate, but at last in gasps and bursts his tragic story came out of him.

"We are devil-ridden, Mr. Holmes! My poor parish is devil-ridden!" he cried. "Satan himself is loose in

it ! We are given over into his hands ! " He danced
about in his agitation, a ludicrous object if it were not for
his ashy face and startled eyes. Finally he shot out his
terrible news.

" Mr. Mortimer Tregennis died during the night, and
with exactly the same symptoms as the rest of his family."

Holmes sprang to his feet, all energy in an instant.

" Can you fit us both into your dog-cart ? "

" Yes, I can."

" Then, Watson, we will postpone our breakfast. Mr.
Roundhay, we are entirely at your disposal. Hurry—
hurry, before things get disarranged."

The lodger occupied two rooms at the vicarage, which
were in an angle by themselves, the one above the other.
Below was a large sitting-room ; above, his bedroom.
They looked out upon a croquet lawn which came up to
the windows. We had arrived before the doctor or the
police, so that everything was absolutely undisturbed.
Let me describe exactly the scene as we saw it upon that
misty March morning. It has left an impression which
can never be effaced from my mind.

The atmosphere of the room was of a horrible and depressing stuffiness. The servant who had first entered had
thrown up the window, or it would have been even more
intolerable. This might partly be due to the fact
that a lamp stood flaring and smoking on the centre
table. Beside it sat the dead man, leaning back in his
chair, his thin beard projecting, his spectacles pushed up
on to his forehead, and his lean, dark face turned towards
the window and twisted into the same distortion of terror
which had marked the features of his dead sister. His
limbs were convulsed and his fingers contorted as though
he had died in a very paroxysm of fear. He was fully
clothed, though there were signs that his dressing had been
done in a hurry. We had already learned that his bed
had been slept in, and that the tragic end had come to him
in the early morning.

One realized the red-hot energy which underlay Holmes'

phlegmatic exterior when one saw the sudden change which came over him from the moment that he entered the fatal apartment. In an instant he was tense and alert, his eyes shining, his face set, his limbs quivering with eager activity. He was out on the lawn, in through the window, round the room, and up into the bedroom, for all the world like a dashing foxhound drawing a cover. In the bedroom he made a rapid cast around, and ended by throwing open the window, which appeared to give him some fresh cause for excitement, for he leaned out of it with loud ejaculations of interest and delight. Then he rushed down the stair, out through the open window, threw himself upon his face on the lawn, sprang up and into the room once more, all with the energy of the hunter who is at the very heels of his quarry. The lamp, which was an ordinary standard, he examined with minute care, making certain measurements upon its bowl. He carefully scrutinized with his lens the talc shield which covered the top of the chimney, and scraped off some ashes which adhered to its upper surface, putting some of them into an envelope, which he placed in his pocket-book. Finally, just as the doctor and the official police put in an appearance, he beckoned to the vicar and we all three went out upon the lawn.

" I am glad to say that my investigation has not been entirely barren," he remarked. " I cannot remain to discuss the matter with the police, but I should be exceedingly obliged, Mr. Roundhay, if you would give the inspector my compliments and direct his attention to the bedroom window and to the sitting-room lamp. Each is suggestive, and together they are almost conclusive. If the police would desire further information I shall be happy to see any of them at the cottage. And now, Watson, I think that, perhaps, we shall be better employed elsewhere."

It may be that the police resented the intrusion of an amateur, or that they imagined themselves to be upon some hopeful line of investigation ; but it is certain that we heard nothing from them for the next two days. During this time Holmes spent some of his time smoking and dreaming in the cottage ; but a greater portion in country walks which he undertook alone, returning after many hours without remark as to where he had been. One experiment served to show me the line of his investigation. He had bought a lamp which was the duplicate of the one which had burned in the room of Mortimer Tregennis on the morning of the tragedy. This he filled with the same oil as that used at the vicarage, and he carefully timed the period which it would take to be exhausted. Another experiment which he made was of a more unpleasant nature, and one which I am not likely ever to forget.

" You will remember, Watson," he remarked one afternoon, " that there is a single common point of resemblance in the varying reports which have reached us. This concerns the effect of the atmosphere of the room in each case upon those who had first entered it. You will recollect that Mortimer Tregennis, in describing the episode of his last visit to his brothers' house, remarked that the doctor on entering the room fell into a chair ? You had forgotten ? Well, I can answer for it that it was so. Now, you will remember also that Mrs. Porter, the housekeeper, told us that she herself fainted upon entering the room and had afterwards opened the window. In the second case—that of Mortimer Tregennis himself—you cannot have forgotten the horrible stuffiness of the room when we arrived, though the servant had thrown open the window. That servant, I found upon inquiry, was so ill that she had gone to her bed. You will admit, Watson, that these facts are very suggestive. In each case there is evidence of a poisonous atmosphere. In each case, also, there is combustion going on in the room—in the one case a fire, in the other a lamp. The fire was needed, but the lamp was lit—as a comparison of the oil consumed will show—long after it was broad daylight. Why ? Surely because there is some connection between three things—the burning, the stuffy atmosphere, and, finally, the madness or death of those unfortunate people. That is clear. is it not ? "

" It would appear so."

" At least we may accept it as a working hypothesis. We will suppose, then, that something was burned in each case which produced an atmosphere causing strange toxic effects. Very good. In the first instance—that of the Tregennis family—this substance was placed in the fire. Now the window was shut, but the fire would naturally carry fumes to some extent up the chimney. Hence one would expect the effects of the poison to be less than in the second case, where there was less escape for the vapour. The result seems to indicate that it was so, since in the first case only the woman, who had presumably the more sensitive organism, was killed, the others exhibiting that temporary or permanent lunacy which is evidently the first effect of the drug. In the second case the result was complete. The facts, therefore, seem to bear out the theory of a poison which worked by combustion.

" With this train of reasoning in my head I naturally looked about in Mortimer Tregennis' room to find some remains of this substance. The obvious place to look was the talc shield or smoke-guard of the lamp. There, sure enough, I perceived a number of flaky ashes, and round the edges a fringe of brownish powder, which had not yet been consumed. Half of this I took, as you saw, and I placed it in an envelope."

" Why half, Holmes ? "

" It is not for me, my dear Watson, to stand in the way of the official police force. I leave them all the evidence which I found. The poison still remained upon the talc, had they the wit to find it. Now, Watson, we will light our lamp ; we will, however, take the precaution to open our window to avoid the premature decease of two deserving members of society, and you will seat yourself near that open window in an arm-chair, unless, like a sensible man, you determine to have nothing to do with the affair. Oh, you will see it out, will you ? I thought I knew my

Watson. This chair I will place opposite yours, so that we may be the same distance from the poison, and face to face. The door we will leave ajar. Each is now in a position to watch the other and to bring the experiment to an end should the symptoms seem alarming. Is that all clear? Well, then, I take our powder—or what remains of it—from the envelope, and I lay it above the burning lamp. So! Now, Watson, let us sit down and await developments."

They were not long in coming. I had hardly settled in my chair before I was conscious of a thick, musky odour, subtle and nauseous. At the very first whiff of it my brain and my imagination were beyond all control. A thick, black cloud swirled before my eyes, and my mind told me that in this cloud, unseen as yet, but about to spring out upon my appalled senses, lurked all that was vaguely horrible, all that was monstrous and inconceivably wicked in the universe. Vague shapes swirled and swam amid the dark cloud-bank, each a menace and a warning of something coming, the advent of some unspeakable dweller upon the threshold, whose very shadow would blast my soul. A freezing horror took possession of me. I felt that my hair was rising, that my eyes were protruding, that my mouth was opened, and my tongue like leather. The turmoil within my brain was such that something must surely snap. I tried to scream, and was vaguely aware of some hoarse croak which was my own voice, but distant and detached from myself. At the same moment, in some effort of escape, I broke through that cloud of despair, and had a glimpse of Holmes' face, white, rigid, and drawn with horror—the very look which I had seen upon the features of the dead. It was that vision which gave me an instant of sanity and of strength. I dashed from my chair, threw my arms round Holmes, and together we lurched through the door, and an instant afterwards had thrown ourselves down upon the grass plot and were lying side by side, conscious only of the glorious sunshine which was bursting its way through the hellish cloud of terror which had girt us in. Slowly it rose from our souls like the mists from a landscape, until peace and reason had returned, and we were sitting upon the grass, wiping our clammy foreheads, and looking with apprehension at each other to mark the last traces of that terrific experience which we had undergone.

" Upon my word, Watson ! " said Holmes at last, with an unsteady voice ; " I owe you both my thanks and an apology. It was an unjustifiable experiment even for oneself, and doubly so for a friend. I am really very sorry."

" You know," I answered, with some emotion, for I had never seen so much of Holmes' heart before, " that it is my greatest joy and privilege to help you."

He relapsed at once into the half-humorous, half-cynical vein which was his habitual attitude to those about him. " It would be superfluous to drive us mad, my dear Watson," said he. " A candid observer would certainly declare that we were so already before we embarked upon so wild an experiment. I confess that I never imagined that the effect could be so sudden and so severe." He dashed into the cottage, and reappearing with the burning lamp held at full arm's length, he threw it among a bank of brambles. " We must give the room a little time to clear. I take it, Watson, that you have no longer a shadow of a doubt as to how these tragedies were produced ? "

" None whatever."

" But the cause remains as obscure as before. Come into the arbour here, and let us discuss it together. That villainous stuff seems still to linger round my throat. I think we must admit that all the evidence points to this man, Mortimer Tregennis, having been the criminal in the first tragedy, though he was the victim in the second one. We must remember, in the first place, that there is some story of a family quarrel, followed by a reconciliation. How bitter that quarrel may have been, or how hollow the reconciliation we cannot tell. When I think of Mortimer Tregennis, with the foxy face and the small shrewd, beady eyes behind the spectacles, he is not a man whom I should judge to be of a particularly forgiving disposition. Well, in the next place, you will remember that this idea of someone moving in the garden, which took our attention for a moment from the real cause of the tragedy, emanated from him. He had a motive in misleading us. Finally, if he did not throw this substance into the fire at the moment of leaving the room, who did do so? The affair happened immediately after his departure. Had anyone else come in, the family would certainly have risen from the table. Besides, in peaceful Cornwall, visitors do not arrive after ten o'clock at night. We may take it, then, that all the evidence points to Mortimer Tregennis as the culprit."

"Then his own death was suicide!"

"Well, Watson, it is on the face of it a not impossible supposition. The man who had the guilt upon his soul of having brought such a fate upon his own family might well be driven by remorse to inflict it upon himself. There are, however, some cogent reasons against it. Fortunately, there is one man in England who knows all about it, and I have made arrangements by which we shall hear the facts this afternoon from his own lips. Ah! he is a little before his time. Perhaps you would kindly step this way, Dr. Leon Sterndale. We have been conducting a chemical experiment indoors which has left our little room hardly fit for the reception of so distinguished a visitor."

I had heard the click of the garden gate, and now the majestic figure of the great African explorer appeared upon the path. He turned in some surprise towards the rustic arbour in which we sat.

"You sent for me, Mr. Holmes. I had your note about an hour ago, and I have come, though I really do not know why I should obey your summons."

"Perhaps we can clear the point up before we separate," said Holmes. "Meanwhile, I am much obliged to you for your courteous acquiescence. You will excuse this informal reception in the open air, but my friend Watson and I have nearly furnished an additional chapter to what the papers call the 'Cornish Horror,' and we prefer a clear atmosphere for the present. Perhaps, since the matters which we have to discuss will affect you personally in a very intimate fashion, it is as well that we should talk where there can be no eavesdropping."

The explorer took his cigar from his lips and gazed sternly at my companion.

" I am at a loss to know, sir," he said, " what you can have to speak about which affects me personally in a very intimate fashion."

" The killing of Mortimer Tregennis," said Holmes.

For a moment I wished that I were armed. Sterndale's fierce face turned to a dusky red, his eyes glared, and the knotted, passionate veins started out in his forehead, while he sprang forward with clenched hands towards my companion. Then he stopped, and with a violent effort he resumed a cold, rigid calmness which was, perhaps, more suggestive of danger than his hot-headed outburst.

" I have lived so long among savages and beyond the law," said he, " that I have got into the way of being a law to myself. You would do well, Mr. Holmes, not to forget it, for I have no desire to do you an injury."

" Nor have I any desire to do you an injury, Dr. Sterndale. Surely the clearest proof of it is that, knowing what I know, I have sent for you and not for the police."

Sterndale sat down with a gasp, overawed for, perhaps, the first time in his adventurous life. There was a calm assurance of power in Holmes' manner which could not be withstood. Our visitor stammered for a moment, his great hands opening and shutting in his agitation.

" What do you mean ? " he asked, at last. " If this is bluff upon your part, Mr. Holmes, you have chosen a bad man for your experiment. Let us have no more beating about the bush. What *do* you mean ? "

" I will tell you," said Holmes, " and the reason why I tell you is that I hope frankness may beget frankness.

What my next step may be will depend entirely upon the
nature of your own defence."

" My defence ? "

" Yes, sir."

" My defence against what ? "

" Against the charge of killing Mortimer Tregennis."

Sterndale mopped his forehead with his handkerchief.
" Upon my word, you are getting on," said he. " Do all
your successes depend upon this prodigious power of
bluff ? "

" The bluff," said Holmes, sternly, " is upon your side,
Dr. Leon Sterndale, and not upon mine. As a proof I
will tell you some of the facts upon which my conclusions
are based. Of your return from Plymouth, allowing much
of your property to go on to Africa, I will say nothing save
that it first informed me that you were one of the factors
which had to be taken into account in reconstructing this
drama——"

" I came back——"

" I have heard your reasons and regard them as uncon-
vincing and inadequate. We will pass that. You came
down here to ask me whom I suspected. I refused to
answer you. You then went to the vicarage, waited outside it for some time, and finally returned to your cottage."

" How do you know that ? "

" I followed you."

" I saw no one."

" That is what you may expect to see when I follow
you. You spent a restless night at your cottage, and you
formed certain plans, which in the early morning you proceeded to put into execution. Leaving your door just as
day was breaking, you filled your pocket with some reddish
gravel that was lying heaped beside your gate."

Sterndale gave a violent start and looked at Holmes in
amazement.

" You then walked swiftly for the mile which separated
you from the vicarage. You were wearing, I may remark,
the same pair of ribbed tennis shoes which are at the present

moment upon your feet. At the vicarage you passed through the orchard and the side hedge, coming out under the window of the lodger Tregennis. It was now daylight, but the household was not yet stirring. You drew some of the gravel from your pocket, and you threw it up at the window above you."

Sterndale sprang to his feet.

" I believe that you are the devil himself ! " he cried.

Holmes smiled at the compliment. " It took two, or possibly three, handfuls before the lodger came to the window. You beckoned him to come down. He dressed hurriedly and descended to his sitting-room. You entered by the window. There was an interview—a short one— during which you walked up and down the room. Then you passed out and closed the window, standing on the lawn outside smoking a cigar and watching what occurred. Finally, after the death of Tregennis, you withdrew as you had come. Now, Dr. Sterndale, how do you justify such conduct, and what were the motives for your actions ? If you prevaricate or trifle with me, I give you my assurance that the matter will pass out of my hands for ever."

Our visitor's face had turned ashen grey as he listened to the words of his accuser. Now he sat for some time in thought with his face sunk in his hands. Then with a sudden impulsive gesture he plucked a photograph from his breast-pocket and threw it on the rustic table before us.

" That is why I have done it," said he.

It showed the bust and face of a very beautiful woman. Holmes stooped over it.

" Brenda Tregennis," said he.

" Yes, Brenda Tregennis," repeated our visitor. " For years I have loved her. For years she has loved me. There is the secret of that Cornish seclusion which people have marvelled at. It has brought me close to the one thing on earth that was dear to me. I could not marry her, for I have a wife who has left me for years and yet whom, by the deplorable laws of England, I could not divorce. For years Brenda waited. For years I waited.

And this is what we have waited for." A terrible sob shook his great frame, and he clutched his throat under his brindled beard. Then with an effort he mastered himself and spoke on.

"The vicar knew. He was in our confidence. He would tell you that she was an angel upon earth. That was why he telegraphed to me and I returned. What was my baggage or Africa to me when I learned that such a fate had come upon my darling? There you have the missing clue to my action, Mr. Holmes."

"Proceed," said my friend.

Dr. Sterndale drew from his pocket a paper packet and laid it upon the table. On the outside was written, "*Radix pedis diaboli*" with a red poison label beneath it. He pushed it towards me. "I understand that you are a doctor, sir. Have you ever heard of this preparation?"

"Devil's-foot root! No, I have never heard of it."

"It is no reflection upon your professional knowledge," said he, "for I believe that, save for one sample in a laboratory at Buda, there is no other specimen in Europe. It has not yet found its way either into the pharmacopœia or into the literature of toxicology. The root is shaped like a foot, half human, half goat-like; hence the fanciful name given by a botanical missionary. It is used as an ordeal poison by the medicine-men in certain districts of West Africa, and is kept as a secret among them. This particular specimen I obtained under very extraordinary circumstances in the Ubanghi country." He opened the paper as he spoke, and disclosed a heap of reddish-brown, snuff-like powder.

"Well, sir?" asked Holmes sternly.

"I am about to tell you, Mr. Holmes, all that actually occurred, for you already know so much that it is clearly to my interest that you should know all. I have already explained the relationship in which I stood to the Tregennis family. For the sake of the sister I was friendly with the brothers. There was a family quarrel about money which estranged this man Mortimer, but it was supposed to be made up, and I afterwards met him as I did the others. He was a sly, subtle, scheming man, and several things arose which gave me a suspicion of him, but I had no cause for any positive quarrel.

" One day, only a couple of weeks ago, he came down to my cottage and I showed him some of my African curiosities. Among other things I exhibited this powder, and I told him of its strange properties, how it stimulates those brain centres which control the emotion of fear, and how either madness or death is the fate of the unhappy native who is subjected to the ordeal by the priest of his tribe. I told him also how powerless European science would be to detect it. How he took it I cannot say, for I never left the room, but there is no doubt that it was then, while I was opening cabinets and stooping to boxes, that he managed to abstract some of the devil's-foot root. I well remember how he plied me with questions as to the amount and the time that was needed for its effect, but I little dreamed that he could have a personal reason for asking.

" I thought no more of the matter until the vicar's telegram reached me at Plymouth. This villain had thought that I would be at sea before the news could reach me, and that I should be lost for years in Africa. But I returned at once. Of course, I could not listen to the details without feeling assured that my poison had been used. I came round to see you on the chance that some other explanation had suggested itself to you. But there could be none. I was convinced that Mortimer Tregennis was the murderer ; that for the sake of money, and with the idea, perhaps, that if the other members of his family were all insane he would be the sole guardian of their joint property, he had used the devil's-foot powder upon them, driven two of them out of their senses, and killed his sister Brenda, the one human being whom I have ever loved or who has ever loved me. There was his crime ; what was to be his punishment ?

" Should I appeal to the law ? Where were my proofs ?

I knew that the facts were true, but could I help to make a jury of countrymen believe so fantastic a story ? I might or I might not. But I could not afford to fail. My soul cried out for revenge. I have said to you once before, Mr. Holmes, that I have spent much of my life outside the law, and that I have come at last to be a law to myself. So it was now. I determined that the fate which he had given to others should be shared by himself. Either that or I would do justice upon him with my own hand. In all England there can be no man who sets less value upon his own life than I do at the present moment.

"Now I have told you all. You have yourself supplied the rest. I did, as you say, after a restless night, set off early from my cottage. I foresaw the difficulty of arousing him, so I gathered some gravel from the pile which you have mentioned, and I used it to throw up to his window. He came down and admitted me through the window of the sitting-room. I laid his offence before him. I told him that I had come both as judge and executioner. The wretch sank into a chair paralysed at the sight of my revolver. I lit the lamp, put the powder above it, and stood outside the window, ready to carry out my threat to shoot him should he try to leave the room. In five minutes he died. My God ! how he died ! But my heart was flint, for he endured nothing which my innocent darling had not felt before him. There is my story, Mr. Holmes. Perhaps, if you loved a woman, you would have done as much yourself. At any rate, I am in your hands. You can take what steps you like. As I have already said, there is no man living who can fear death less than I do."

Holmes sat for some little time in silence.

"What were your plans ? " he asked, at last.

"I had intended to bury myself in Central Africa. My work there is but half finished."

"Go and do the other half," said Holmes. "I, at least, am not prepared to prevent you."

Dr. Sterndale raised his giant figure, bowed gravely, and

walked from the arbour. Holmes lit his pipe and handed me his pouch.

"Some fumes which are not poisonous would be a welcome change," said he. "I think you must agree, Watson, that it is not a case in which we are called upon to interfere. Our investigation has been independent, and our action shall be so also. You would not denounce the man?"

"Certainly not," I answered.

"I have never loved, Watson, but if I did and if the woman I loved had met such an end, I might act even as our lawless lion-hunter has done. Who knows? Well, Watson, I will not offend your intelligence by explaining what is obvious. The gravel upon the window-sill was, of course, the starting-point of my research. It was unlike anything in the vicarage garden. Only when my attention had been drawn to Dr. Sterndale and his cottage did I find its counterpart. The lamp shining in broad daylight and the remains of powder upon the shield were successive links in a fairly obvious chain. And now, my dear Watson, I think we may dismiss the matter from our mind, and go back with a clear conscience to the study of those Chaldean roots which are surely to be traced in the Cornish branch of the great Celtic speech."

44. *His Last Bow*

AN EPILOGUE OF SHERLOCK HOLMES

IT was nine o'clock at night upon the second of August —the most terrible August in the history of the world. One might have thought already that God's curse hung heavy over a degenerate world, for there was an awesome hush and a feeling of vague expectancy in the sultry and stagnant air. The sun had long set, but one blood-red gash like an open wound lay low in the distant west. Above, the stars were shining brightly; and below, the lights of the shipping glimmered in the bay. The two famous Germans stood beside the stone parapet of the garden walk, with the long, low, heavily gabled house behind them, and they looked down upon the broad sweep of the beach at the foot of the great chalk cliff on which Von Bork, like some wandering eagle, had perched himself four years before. They stood with their heads close together, talking in low, confidential tones. From below the two glowing ends of their cigars might have been the smouldering eyes of some malignant fiend looking down in the darkness.

A remarkable man this Von Bork—a man who could hardly be matched among all the devoted agents of the Kaiser. It was his talents which had first recommended him for the English mission, the most important mission of all, but since he had taken it over, those talents had become more and more manifest to the half-dozen people in the world who were really in touch with the truth. One of these was his present companion, Baron Von Herling, the chief secretary of the legation, whose huge 100-horse-power Benz car was blocking the country lane as it waited to waft its owner back to London.

"So far as I can judge the trend of events, you will probably be back in Berlin within the week," the secretary was saying. "When you get there, my dear Von Bork, I think you will be surprised at the welcome you will receive. I happen to know what is thought in the highest quarters of your work in this country." He was a huge man, the secretary, deep, broad, and tall, with a slow, heavy fashion of speech which had been his main asset in his political career.

Von Bork laughed.

"They are not very hard to deceive," he remarked. "A more docile, simple folk could not be imagined."

"I don't know about that," said the other thoughtfully. "They have strange limits and one must learn to observe them. It is that surface simplicity of theirs which makes a trap for the stranger. One's first impression is that they are entirely soft. Then one comes suddenly upon something very hard and you know that you have reached the limit, and must adapt yourself to the fact. They have, for example, their insular conventions which simply *must* be observed."

"Meaning, 'good form' and that sort of thing?" Von Bork sighed, as one who had suffered much.

"Meaning British prejudice in all its queer manifestations. As an example I may quote one of my own worst blunders—I can afford to talk of my blunders, for you know my work well enough to be aware of my successes. It was on my first arrival. I was invited to a week-end gathering at the country house of a Cabinet Minister. The conversation was amazingly indiscreet."

Von Bork nodded. "I've been there," said he dryly.

"Exactly. Well, I naturally sent a résumé of the information to Berlin. Unfortunately our good Chancellor is a little heavy-handed in these matters, and he transmitted a remark which showed that he was aware of what had been said. This, of course, took the trail straight up to me. You've no idea the harm that it did me. There was nothing soft about our British hosts on that occasion, I can assure you. I was two years living it down. Now you, with this sporting pose of yours."

"No, no, don't call it a pose. A pose is an artificial thing. This is quite natural. I am a born sportsman. I enjoy it."

"Well, that makes it the more effective. You yacht against them, you hunt with them, you play polo, you match them in every game, your four-in-hand takes the prize at Olympia. I have even heard that you go the length of boxing with the young officers. What is the result? Nobody takes you seriously. You are a 'good old sport,' 'quite a decent fellow for a German,' a hard-drinking, night-club, knock-about-town, devil-may-care young fellow. And all the time this quiet country house of yours is the centre of half the mischief in England, and the sporting squire the most astute Secret Service man in Europe. Genius, my dear Von Bork—genius!"

" You flatter me, Baron. But certainly I may claim that my four years in this country have not been unproductive. I've never shown you my little store. Would you mind stepping in for a moment ? "

The door of the study opened straight on to the terrace. Von Bork pushed it back, and, leading the way, he clicked the switch of the electric light. He then closed the door behind the bulky form which followed him, and carefully adjusted the heavy curtain over the latticed window. Only when all these precautions had been taken and tested did he turn his sunburned aquiline face to his guest.

" Some of my papers have gone," said he ; " when my wife and the household left yesterday for Flushing they took the less important with them. I must, of course, claim the protection of the Embassy for the others."

" Your name has already been filed as one of the personal suite. There will be no difficulties for you or your baggage. Of course, it is just possible that we may not have to go. England may leave France to her fate. We are sure that there is no binding treaty between them."

" And Belgium ? "

" Yes, and Belgium, too."

Von Bork shook his head. " I don't see how that could be. There is a definite treaty there. She could never recover from such a humiliation."

" She would at least have peace for the moment."

" But her honour ? "

" Tut, my dear sir, we live in a utilitarian age. Honour is a mediæval conception. Besides England is not ready. It is an inconceivable thing, but even our special war tax of fifty millions, which one would think made our purpose as clear as if we had advertised it on the front page of *The Times*, has not roused these people from their slumbers. Here and there one hears a question. It is my business to find an answer. Here and there also there is an irritation. It is my business to soothe it. But I can assure you that so far as the essentials go—the storage of munitions, the preparation for submarine attack, the arrangements for making high explosives—nothing is prepared. How then can England come in, especially when we have stirred her up such a devil's brew of Irish civil war, window-breaking Furies, and God knows what to keep her thoughts at home ? "

" She must think of her future."

" Ah, that is another matter. I fancy that in the future, we have our own very definite plans about England, and that your information will be very vital to us. It is to-day or to-morrow with Mr. John Bull. If he prefers to-day we are perfectly ready. If it is to-morrow we shall be more ready still. I should think they would be wiser to fight with allies than without them, but that is their own affair. This week is their week of destiny. But you were speaking of your papers." He sat in the arm-chair with the light shining upon his broad bald head, while he puffed sedately at his cigar.

The large oak-panelled book-lined room had a curtain hung in the further corner. When this was drawn it disclosed a large brass-bound safe. Von Bork detached a small key from his watch-chain, and after some considerable manipulation of the lock he swung open the heavy door.

" Look ! " said he, standing clear, with a wave of his hand.

The light shone vividly into the opened safe, and the secretary of the Embassy gazed with an absorbed interest at the rows of stuffed pigeon-holes with which it was furnished. Each pigeon-hole had its label, and his eyes as he glanced along them read a long series of such titles as " Fords," " Harbour-defences," " Aeroplanes," " Ireland," " Egypt," " Portsmouth forts," " The Channel," " Rosyth," and a score of others. Each compartment was bristling with papers and plans.

" Colossal ! " said the secretary. Putting down his cigar he softly clapped his fat hands.

" And all in four years, Baron. Not such a bad show for the hard-drinking, hard-riding country squire. But the gem of my collection is coming and there is the setting all ready for it." He pointed to a space over which " Naval Signals " was printed.

" But you have a good dossier there already."

" Out of date and waste paper. The Admiralty in some way got the alarm and every code has been changed. It was a blow, Baron—the worst set-back in my whole campaign. But thanks to my cheque-book and the good Altamont all will be well to-night."

The Baron looked at his watch, and gave a guttural exclamation of disappointment.

" Well, I really can wait no longer. You can imagine that things are moving at present in Carlton Terrace and that we have all to be at our posts. I had hoped to be able to bring news of your great coup. Did Altamont name no hour ? "

Von Bork pushed over a telegram.

" Will come without fail to-night and bring new sparking plugs.—ALTAMONT."

" Sparking plugs, eh ? "

" You see he poses as a motor expert and I keep a full garage. In our code everything likely to come up is named after some spare part. If he talks of a radiator it is a battleship, of an oil-pump a cruiser, and so on. Sparking plugs are naval signals."

" From Portsmouth at midday," said the secretary, examining the superscription. " By the way, what do you give him ? "

" Five hundred pounds for this particular job. Of course he has a salary as well."

" The greedy rogue. They are useful, these traitors, but I grudge them their blood-money."

" I grudge Altamont nothing. He is a wonderful worker. If I pay him well, at least he delivers the goods, to use his own phrase. Besides he is not a traitor. I assure you that our most pan-Germanic Junker is a sucking dove in his feelings towards England as compared with a real bitter Irish-American."

" Oh, an Irish-American ? "

" If you heard him talk you would not doubt it. Sometimes I assure you I can hardly understand him. He seems to have declared war on the King's English as well as on the English King. Must you really go ? He may be here any moment."

" No. I'm sorry, but I have already overstayed my time. We shall expect you early to-morrow, and when you get that signal-book through the little door on the Duke of York's steps you can put a triumphant Finis to your record in England. What ! Tokay ! " He indicated a heavily sealed dust-covered bottle which stood with two high glasses upon a salver.

" May I offer you a glass before your journey ? "

" No, thanks. But it looks like revelry."

" Altamont has a nice taste in wines, and he took a fancy to my Tokay. He is a touchy fellow, and needs humouring in small things. I have to study him, I assure you." They had strolled out on to the terrace again, and along it to the further end where at a touch from the Baron's chauffeur the great car shivered and chuckled. " Those are the lights of Harwich, I suppose," said the secretary, pulling on his dust coat. " How still and peaceful it all seems. There may be other lights within the week, and the English coast a less tranquil place ! The heavens, too, may not be quite so peaceful if all that the good Zeppelin promises us comes true. By the way, who is that ? "

Only one window showed a light behind them ; in it there stood a lamp, and beside it, seated at a table, was a dear old ruddy-faced woman in a country cap. She was bending over her knitting and stopping occasionally to stroke a large black cat upon a stool beside her.

" That is Martha, the only servant I have left."

The secretary chuckled.

" She might almost personify Britannia," said he, " with her complete self-absorption and general air of comfortable somnolence. Well, au revoir, Von Bork!"—with a final wave of his hand he sprang into the car, and a moment later the two golden cones from the headlights shot forward through the darkness. The secretary lay back in the cushions of the luxurious limousine, with his thoughts so full of the impending European tragedy that he hardly observed that as his car swung round the village street it nearly passed over a little Ford coming in the opposite direction.

Von Bork walked slowly back to the study when the last gleams of the motor lamps had faded into the distance. As he passed he observed that his old housekeeper had put out her lamp and retired. It was a new experience to him, the silence and darkness of his widespread house, for his family and household had been a large one. It was a relief to him, however, to think that they were all in safety and that, but for that one old woman who had lingered in the kitchen, he had the whole place to himself. There was a good deal of tidying up to do inside his study and he set himself to do it, until his keen, handsome face was flushed with the heat of the burning papers. A leather valise stood beside his table, and into this he began to pack very neatly and systematically the precious contents of his safe. He had hardly got started with the work, however, when his quick ears caught the sound of a distant car. Instantly he gave an exclamation of satisfaction, strapped up the valise, shut the safe, locked it, and hurried out on to the terrace. He was just in time to see the lights of a small car come to a halt at the gate. A passenger sprang out and advanced swiftly towards him, while the chauffeur, a heavily built, elderly man, with a grey moustache, settled down, like one who resigns himself to a long vigil.

"Well?" asked Von Bork eagerly, running forward to meet his visitor.

For answer the man waved a small brown-paper parcel triumphantly above his head.

"You can give me the glad hand to-night, Mister," he cried. "I'm bringing home the bacon at last."

" The signals ? "

" Same as I said in my cable. Every last one of them, semaphore, lamp code, Marconi—a copy, mind you, not the original. That was too dangerous. But it's the real goods, and you can lay to that." He slapped the German upon the shoulder with a rough familiarity from which the other winced.

" Come in," he said. " I'm all alone in the house. I was only waiting for this. Of course a copy is better than the original. If an original were missing they would change the whole thing. You think it's all safe about the copy ? "

The Irish-American had entered the study and stretched his long limbs from the arm-chair. He was a tall, gaunt man of sixty, with clear-cut features and a small goatee beard which gave him a general resemblance to the caricatures of Uncle Sam. A half-smoked, sodden cigar hung from the corner of his mouth, and as he sat down he struck a match and relit it. " Making ready for a move ? " he remarked as he looked round him. " Say, Mister," he added, as his eyes fell upon the safe from which the curtain was now removed, " you don't tell me you keep your papers in that ? "

" Why not ? "

" Gosh, in a wide-open contraption like that ! And they reckon you to be some spy. Why a Yankee crook would be into that with a can-opener. If I'd known that any letter of mine was goin' to lie loose in a thing like that I'd have been a mug to write to you at all."

" It would puzzle any crook to force that safe," Von Bork answered. " You won't cut that metal with any tool."

" But the lock ? "

" No, it's a double combination lock. You know what that is ? "

" Search me," said the American.

" Well, you need a word as well as a set of figures before you can get the lock to work." He rose and showed a double-radiating disc round the keyhole. "This outer one is for the letters, the inner one for the figures."

"Well, well, that's fine."

"So it's not quite as simple as you thought. It was four years ago that I had it made, and what do you think I chose for the word and figures?"

"It's beyond me."

"Well, I chose August for the word, and 1914 for the figures, and here we are."

The American's face showed his surprise and admiration.

"My, but that was smart! You had it down to a fine thing."

"Yes, a few of us even then could have guessed the date. Here it is, and I'm shutting down to-morrow morning."

"Well, I guess you'll have to fix me up also. I'm not staying in this goldarned country all on my lonesome. In a week or less from what I see, John Bull will be on his hind legs and fair ramping. I'd rather watch him from over the water."

"But you're an American citizen?"

"Well, so was Jack James an American citizen, but he's doing time in Portland all the same. It cuts no ice with a British copper to tell him you're an American citizen. 'It's British law and order over here,' says he. By the way, Mister, talking of Jack James, it seems to me you don't do much to cover your men."

"What do you mean?" Von Bork asked sharply.

"Well, you are their employer, ain't you? It's up to you to see that they don't fall down. But they do fall down, and when did you ever pick them up? There's James——"

"It was James' own fault. You know that yourself. He was too self-willed for the job."

"James was a bonehead—I give you that. Then there was Hollis."

"The man was mad."

" Well, he went a bit woozy towards the end. It's enough to make a man bughouse when he has to play a part from morning to night with a hundred guys all ready to set the coppers wise to him. But now there is Steiner ——"

Von Bork started violently, and his ruddy face turned a shade paler.

" What about Steiner ? "

" Well, they've got him, that's all. They raided his store last night, and he and his papers are all in Portsmouth gaol. You'll go off and he, poor devil, will have to stand the racket, and lucky if he gets off with his life. That's why I want to get over the water as soon as you do."

Von Bork was a strong, self-contained man, but it was easy to see that the news had shaken him.

" How could they have got on to Steiner ? " he muttered. " That's the worst blow yet."

" Well, you nearly had a worse one, for I believe they are not far off me."

" You don't mean that ! "

" Sure thing. My landlady down Fratton way had some inquiries, and when I heard of it I guessed it was time for me to hustle. But what I want to know, Mister, is how the coppers know these things ? Steiner is the fifth man you've lost since I signed on with you, and I know the name of the sixth if I don't get a move on. How do you explain it, and ain't you ashamed to see your men go down like this ? "

Von Bork flushed crimson.

" How dare you speak in such a way ! "

" If I didn't dare things, Mister, I wouldn't be in your service. But I'll tell you straight what is in my mind. I've heard that with you German politicians when an agent has done his work you are not sorry to see him put away."

Von Bork sprang to his feet.

" Do you dare to suggest that I have given away my own agents ! "

" I don't stand for that, Mister, but there's a stool pigeon or a cross somewhere, and it's up to you to find out where it is. Anyhow I am taking no more chances. It's me for little Holland, and the sooner the better."

Von Bork had mastered his anger.

" We have been allies too long to quarrel now at the very hour of victory," he said. " You've done splendid work and taken risks and I can't forget it. By all means go to Holland, and you can get a boat from Rotterdam to New York. No other line will be safe a week from now. I'll take that book and pack it with the rest."

The American held the small parcel in his hand, but made no motion to give it up.

" What about the dough ? " he asked.

" The what ? "

" The boodle. The reward. The £500. The gunner turned damned nasty at the last, and I had to square him with an extra hundred dollars or it would have been nitsky for you and me. ' Nothin' doin' ! ' says he, and he meant it too, but the last hundred did it. It's cost me two hundred pound from first to last, so it isn't likely I'd give it up without gettin' my wad."

Von Bork smiled with some bitterness. " You don't seem to have a very high opinion of my honour," said he, " you want the money before you give up the book."

" Well, Mister, it is a business proposition."

" All right. Have your way." He sat down at the table and scribbled a cheque, which he tore from the book, but he refrained from handing it to his companion. " After all, since we are to be on such terms, Mr. Altamont," said he, " I don't see why I should trust you any more than you trust me. Do you understand ? " he added, looking back over his shoulder at the American. " There's the cheque upon the table. I claim the right to examine that parcel before you pick the money up."

The American passed it over without a word. Von Bork undid a winding of string and two wrappers of paper. Then he sat gazing for a moment in silent amazement at a small blue book which lay before him. Across the cover was printed in golden letters *Practical Handbook of Bee Culture.* Only for one instant did the master spy glare at this strangely irrelevant inscription. The next he was gripped at the back of his neck by a grasp of iron, and a chloroformed sponge was held in front of his writhing face.

" Another glass, Watson ! " said Mr. Sherlock Holmes, as he extended the bottle of Imperial Tokay.

The thick-set chauffeur, who had seated himself by the table, pushed forward his glass with some eagerness.

" It is a good wine, Holmes."

" A remarkable wine, Watson. Our friend upon the sofa has assured me that it is from Franz Joseph's special cellar at the Schoenbrunn Palace. Might I trouble you to open the window, for chloroform vapour does not help the palate."

The safe was ajar, and Holmes standing in front of it was removing dossier after dossier, swiftly examining each, and then packing it neatly in Von Bork's valise. The German lay upon the sofa sleeping stertorously with a strap round his upper arms and another round his legs.

" We need not hurry ourselves, Watson. We are safe from interruption. Would you mind touching the bell. There is no one in the house except old Martha, who has played her part to admiration. I got her the situation here when first I took the matter up. Ah, Martha, you will be glad to hear that all is well."

The pleasant old lady had appeared in the doorway. She curtseyed with a smile to Mr. Holmes, but glanced with some apprehension at the figure upon the sofa.

" It is all right, Martha. He has not been hurt at all."

" I am glad of that, Mr. Holmes. According to his lights he has been a kind master. He wanted me to go with his wife to Germany yesterday, but that would hardly have suited your plans, would it, sir ? "

" No, indeed, Martha. So long as you were here I was easy in my mind. We waited some time for your signal to-night."

" It was the secretary, sir."

" I know. His car passed ours."

" I thought he would never go. I knew that it would not suit your plans, sir, to find him here."

" No, indeed. Well, it only meant that we waited half an hour or so until I saw your lamp go out and knew that the coast was clear. You can report to me to-morrow in London, Martha, at Claridge's Hotel."

" Very good, sir."

" I suppose you have everything ready to leave."

" Yes, sir. He posted seven letters to-day. I have the addresses as usual."

" Very good, Martha. I will look into them to-morrow. Good night. These papers," he continued, as the old lady vanished, " are not of very great importance, for, of course, the information which they represent has been sent off long ago to the German Government. These are the originals which could not safely be got out of the country."

" Then they are of no use."

" I should not go so far as to say that, Watson. They will at least show our people what is known and what is not. I may say that a good many of these papers have come through me, and I need not add are thoroughly untrustworthy. It would brighten my declining years to see a German cruiser navigating the Solent according to the minefield plans which I have furnished. But you, Watson," he stopped his work and took his old friend by the shoulders ; " I've hardly seen you in the light yet. How have the years used you ? You look the same blithe boy as ever."

" I feel twenty years younger, Holmes. I have seldom felt so happy as when I got your wire asking me to meet you at Harwich with the car. But you, Holmes—you have changed very little—save for that horrible goatee."

" These are the sacrifices one makes for one's country, Watson," said Holmes, pulling at his little tuft. " To-morrow it will be but a dreadful memory. With my hair cut and a few other superficial changes I shall no doubt reappear at Claridge's to-morrow as I was before this American stunt—I beg your pardon, Watson, my well of English seems to be permanently defiled—before this American job came my way."

" But you had retired, Holmes. We heard of you as living the life of a hermit among your bees and your books in a small farm upon the South Downs."

" Exactly, Watson. Here is the fruit of my leisured ease, the *magnum opus* of my latter years !" He picked up the volume from the table and read out the whole title, *Practical Handbook of Bee Culture, with some Observations upon the Segregation of the Queen.* Alone I did it. Behold the fruit of pensive nights and laborious days, when I watched the little working gangs as once I watched the criminal world of London."

" But how did you get to work again ? "

" Ah, I have often marvelled at it myself. The Foreign Minister alone I could have withstood, but when the Premier also deigned to visit my humble roof——! The fact is, Watson, that this gentleman upon the sofa was a bit too good for our people. He was in a class by himself. Things were going wrong, and no one could understand why they were going wrong. Agents were suspected or even caught, but there was evidence of some strong and secret central force. It was absolutely necessary to expose it. Strong pressure was brought upon me to look into the matter. It has cost me two years, Watson, but they have not been devoid of excitement. When I say that I started my pilgrimage at Chicago, graduated in an Irish secret society at Buffalo, gave serious trouble to the constabulary at Skibbareen and so eventually caught the eye of a sub-ordinate agent of Von Bork, who recommended me as a likely man, you will realize that the matter was complex. Since then I have been honoured by his confidence, which has not prevented most of his plans going subtly wrong and five of his best agents being in prison. I watched them, Watson, and I picked them as they ripened. Well, sir, I hope that you are none the worse ! "

The last remark was addressed to Von Bork himself, who after much gasping and blinking had lain quietly listening to Holmes' statement. He broke out now into a furious stream of German invective, his face convulsed with passion. Holmes continued his swift investigation of documents while his prisoner cursed and swore.

"Though unmusical, German is the most expressive of all languages," he observed, when Von Bork had stopped from pure exhaustion. "Hullo! Hullo!" he added, as he looked hard at the corner of a tracing before putting it in the box. "This should put another bird in the cage. I had no idea that the paymaster was such a rascal, though I have long had an eye upon him. Mister Von Bork, you have a great deal to answer for."

The prisoner had raised himself with some difficulty upon the sofa and was staring with a strange mixture of amazement and hatred at his captor.

"I shall get level with you, Altamont," he said, speaking with slow deliberation, "if it takes me all my life I shall get level with you!"

"The old sweet song," said Holmes. "How often have I heard it in days gone by. It was a favourite ditty of the late lamented Professor Moriarty. Colonel Sebastian Moran has also been known to warble it. And yet I live and keep bees upon the South Downs."

"Curse you, you double traitor!" cried the German, straining against his bonds and glaring murder from his furious eyes.

"No, no, it is not so bad as that," said Holmes, smiling. "As my speech surely shows you, Mr. Altamont of Chicago had no existence in fact. I used him and he is gone."

"Then who are you?"

"It is really immaterial who I am, but since the matter seems to interest you, Mr. Von Bork, I may say that this is not my first acquaintance with the members of your family. I have done a good deal of business in Germany in the past, and my name is probably familiar to you."

"I would wish to know it," said the Prussian grimly.

" It was I who brought about the separation between Irene Adler and the late King of Bohemia when your cousin Heinrich was the Imperial Envoy. It was I also who saved from murder, by the Nihilist Klopman, Count Von und Zu Grafenstein, who was your mother's elder brother. It was I——"

Von Bork sat up in amazement.

" There is only one man," he cried.

" Exactly," said Holmes.

Von Bork groaned and sank back on the sofa. " And most of that information came through you," he cried. " What is it worth ? What have I done ? It is my ruin for ever ! "

" It is certainly a little untrustworthy," said Holmes. " It will require some checking, and you have little time to check it. Your admiral may find the new guns rather larger than he expects, and the cruisers perhaps a trifle faster."

Von Bork clutched at his own throat in despair.

" There are a good many other points of detail which will, no doubt, come to light in good time. But you have one quality which is very rare in a German, Mr. Von Bork, you are a sportsman and you will bear me no ill-will when you realize that you, who have outwitted so many other people, have at last been outwitted yourself. After all, you have done your best for your country, and I have done my best for mine, and what could be more natural ? Besides," he added, not unkindly, as he laid his hand upon the shoulder of the prostrate man, " it is better than to fall before some more ignoble foe. These papers are now ready, Watson. If you will help me with our prisoner, I think that we may get started for London at once."

It was no easy task to move Von Bork, for he was a strong and a desperate man. Finally, holding either arm, the two friends walked him very slowly down the garden walk which he had trod with such proud confidence when he received the congratulations of the famous diplomatist only a few hours before. After a short, final struggle he was hoisted, still bound hand and foot, into the spare seat of the little car. His precious valise was wedged in beside him.

"I trust that you are as comfortable as circumstances permit," said Holmes, when the final arrangements were made. "Should I be guilty of a liberty if I lit a cigar and placed it between your lips?"

But all amenities were wasted upon the angry German.

"I suppose you realize, Mr. Sherlock Holmes," said he, "that if your Government bears you out in this treatment it becomes an act of war."

"What about your Government and all this treatment?" said Holmes, tapping the valise.

"You are a private individual. You have no warrant for my arrest. The whole proceeding is absolutely illegal and outrageous."

"Absolutely," said Holmes.

"Kidnapping a German subject."

"And stealing his private papers."

"Well, you realize your position, you and your accomplice here. If I were to shout for help as we pass through the village——"

"My dear sir, if you did anything so foolish you would probably enlarge the too limited titles of our village inns by giving us 'The Dangling Prussian' as a sign-post. The Englishman is a patient creature, but at present his temper is a little inflamed and it would be as well not to try him too far. No, Mr. Von Bork, you will go with us in a quiet, sensible fashion to Scotland Yard, whence you can send for your friend Baron Von Herling and see if even now you may not fill that place which he has reserved for you in the ambassadorial suite. As to you, Watson, you are joining us with your old service, as I understand, so London won't be out of your way. Stand with me here upon the terrace, for it may be the last quiet talk that we shall ever have."

The two friends chatted in intimate converse for a few minutes, recalling once again the days of the past whilst their prisoner vainly wriggled to undo the bonds that held him. As they turned to the car, Holmes pointed back to the moonlit sea, and shook a thoughtful head.

" There's an east wind coming, Watson."

" I think not, Holmes. It is very warm."

" Good old Watson ! You are the one fixed point in a changing age. There's an east wind coming all the same, such a wind as never blew on England yet. It will be cold and bitter, Watson, and a good many of us may wither before its blast. But it's God's own wind none the less, and a cleaner, better, stronger land will lie in the sunshine when the storm has cleared. Start her up, Watson, for it's time that we were on our way. I have a cheque for five hundred pounds which should be cashed early, for the drawer is quite capable of stopping it, if he can."

THE CASE-BOOK OF
SHERLOCK HOLMES

45. *The Illustrious Client*

"IT can't hurt now," was Mr. Sherlock Holmes'
comment when, for the tenth time in as many
years, I asked his leave to reveal the following
narrative. So it was that at last I obtained permission
to put on record what was, in some ways, the supreme
moment of my friend's career.

Both Holmes and I had a weakness for the Turkish
Bath. It was over a smoke in the pleasant lassitude of the
drying-room that I have found him less reticent and more
human than anywhere else. On the upper floor of the
Northumberland Avenue establishment there is an
isolated corner where two couches lie side by side, and
it was on these that we lay upon September 3, 1902, the
day when my narrative begins. I had asked him whether
anything was stirring, and for answer he had shot his
long, thin, nervous arm out of the sheets which enveloped
him and had drawn an envelope from the inside pocket
of the coat which hung beside him.

"It may be some fussy, self-important fool, it may be
a matter of life or death," said he, as he handed me the
note. "I know no more than this message tells me."

It was from the Carlton Club, and dated the evening
before. This is what I read :

"Sir James Damery presents his compliments to Mr.
Sherlock Holmes, and will call upon him at 4.30 to-morrow. Sir James begs to say that the matter upon which
he desires to consult Mr. Holmes is very delicate, and
also very important. He trusts, therefore, that Mr.

Holmes will make every effort to grant this interview, and that he will confirm it over the telephone to the Carlton Club."

" I need not say that I have confirmed it, Watson," said Holmes, as I returned the paper. " Do you know anything of this man Damery ? "

" Only that his name is a household word in Society."

" Well, I can tell you a little more than that. He has rather a reputation for arranging delicate matters which are to be kept out of the papers. You may remember his negotiations with Sir George Lewis over the Hammerford Will case. He is a man of the world with a natural turn for diplomacy. I am bound, therefore, to hope that it is not a false scent and that he has some real need for our assistance."

" Our ? "

" Well, if you will be so good, Watson."

" I shall be honoured."

" Then you have the hour—four-thirty. Until then we can put the matter out of our heads."

I was living in my own rooms in Queen Anne Street at the time, but I was round at Baker Street before the time named. Sharp to the half-hour, Colonel Sir James Damery was announced. It is hardly necessary to describe him, for many will remember that large, bluff, honest personality, that broad, clean-shaven face, above all, that pleasant, mellow voice. Frankness shone from his grey Irish eyes, and good humour played round his mobile, smiling lips. His lucent top-hat, his dark frock-coat, indeed, every detail, from the pearl pin in the black satin cravat to the lavender spats over the varnished shoes, spoke of the meticulous care in dress for which he was famous. The big, masterful aristocrat dominated the little room.

" Of course, I was prepared to find Dr. Watson," he remarked, with a courteous bow. " His collaboration may be very necessary, for we are dealing on this occasion, Mr. Holmes, with a man to whom violence is familiar and who will, literally, stick at nothing. I should say that there is no more dangerous man in Europe."

"I have had several opponents to whom that flattering term has been applied," said Holmes, with a smile. "Don't you smoke? Then you will excuse me if I light my pipe. If your man is more dangerous than the late Professor Moriarty, or than the living Colonel Sebastian Moran, then he is indeed worth meeting. May I ask his name?"

"Have you ever heard of Baron Gruner?"

"You mean the Austrian murderer?"

Colonel Damery threw up his kid-gloved hands with a laugh. "There is no getting past you, Mr. Holmes! Wonderful! So you have already sized him up as a murderer?"

"It is my business to follow the details of Continental crime. Who could possibly have read what happened at Prague and have any doubts as to the man's guilt! It was a purely technical legal point and the suspicious death of a witness that saved him! I am as sure that he killed his wife when the so-called ' accident ' happened in the Splügen Pass as if I had seen him do it. I knew, also, that he had come to England, and had a presentiment that sooner or later he would find me some work to do. Well, what has Baron Gruner been up to? I presume it is not this old tragedy which has come up again?"

"No, it is more serious than that. To revenge crime is important, but to prevent it is more so. It is a terrible thing, Mr. Holmes, to see a dreadful event, an atrocious situation, preparing itself before your eyes, to clearly understand whither it will lead and yet to be utterly unable to avert it. Can a human being be placed in a more trying position?"

"Perhaps not."

"Then you will sympathize with the client in whose interests I am acting."

" I did not understand that you were merely an intermediary. Who is the principal ? "

" Mr. Holmes, I must beg you not to press that question. It is important that I should be able to assure him that his honoured name has been in no way dragged into the matter. His motives are, to the last degree, honourable and chivalrous, but he prefers to remain unknown. I need not say that your fees will be assured and that you will be given a perfectly free hand. Surely the actual name of your client is immaterial ? "

" I am sorry," said Holmes. " I am accustomed to have mystery at one end of my cases, but to have it at both ends is too confusing. I fear, Sir James, that I must decline to act."

Our visitor was greatly disturbed. His large, sensitive face was darkened with emotion and disappointment.

" You hardly realize the effect of your own action, Mr. Holmes," said he. " You place me in a most serious dilemma, for I am perfectly certain that you would be proud to take over the case if I could give you the facts, and yet a promise forbids me from revealing them all. May I, at least, lay all that I can before you ? "

" By all means, so long as it is understood that I commit myself to nothing."

" That is understood. In the first place, you have no doubt heard of General de Merville ? "

" De Merville of Khyber fame ? Yes, I have heard of him."

" He has a daughter, Violet de Merville, young, rich, beautiful, accomplished, a wonder-woman in every way. It is this daughter, this lovely, innocent girl, whom we are endeavouring to save from the clutches of a fiend."

" Baron Gruner has some hold over her, then ? "

" The strongest of all holds where a woman is concerned—the hold of love. The fellow is, as you may have heard, extraordinarily handsome, with a most fascinating manner, a gentle voice, and that air of romance and mystery which means so much to a woman. He is said to have the whole sex at his mercy and to have made ample use of the fact."

" But how came such a man to meet a lady of the standing of Miss Violet de Merville ? "

" It was on a Mediterranean yachting voyage. The company, though select, paid their own passages. No doubt the promoters hardly realized the Baron's true character until it was too late. The villain attached himself to the lady, and with such effect that he has completely and absolutely won her heart. To say that she loves him hardly expresses it. She dotes upon him, she is obsessed by him. Outside of him there is nothing on earth. She will not hear one word against him. Everything has been done to cure her of her madness, but in vain. To sum up, she proposes to marry him next month. As she is of age and has a will of iron, it is hard to know how to prevent her."

" Does she know about the Austrian episode ? "

" The cunning devil has told her every unsavoury public scandal of his past life, but always in such a way as to make himself out to be an innocent martyr. She absolutely accepts his version and will listen to no other."

" Dear me ! But surely you have inadvertently let out the name of your client ? It is no doubt General de Merville."

Our visitor fidgeted in his chair.

" I could deceive you by saying so, Mr. Holmes, but it would not be true. De Merville is a broken man. The strong soldier has been utterly demoralized by this incident. He has lost the nerve which never failed him on the battlefield and has become a weak, doddering old man, utterly incapable of contending with a brilliant, forceful rascal like this Austrian. My client, however, is an old friend, one who has known the General intimately for many years and taken a paternal interest in this young girl since she wore short frocks. He cannot see this tragedy consummated without some attempt to stop it.

There is nothing in which Scotland Yard can act. It was his own suggestion that you should be called in, but it was, as I have said, on the express stipulation that he should not be personally involved in the matter. I have no doubt, Mr. Holmes, with your great powers you could easily trace my client back through me, but I must ask you, as a point of honour, to refrain from doing so, and not to break in upon his incognito."

Holmes gave a whimsical smile.

" I think I may safely promise that," said he. " I may add that your problem interests me, and that I shall be prepared to look into it. How shall I keep in touch with you ? "

" The Carlton Club will find me. But, in case of emergency, there is a private telephone call, ' XX.31.' "

Holmes noted it down and sat, still smiling, with the open memorandum-book upon his knee.

" The Baron's present address, please ? "

" Vernon Lodge, near Kingston. It is a large house. He has been fortunate in some rather shady speculations and is a rich man, which, naturally, makes him a more dangerous antagonist."

" Is he at home at present ? "

" Yes."

" Apart from what you have told me, can you give me any further information about the man ? "

" He has expensive tastes. He is a horse fancier. For a short time he played polo at Hurlingham, but then this Prague affair got noised about and he had to leave. He collects books and pictures. He is a man with a considerable artistic side to his nature. He is, I believe, a recognized authority upon Chinese pottery, and has written a book upon the subject."

" A complex mind," said Holmes. " All great criminals have that. My old friend Charlie Peace was a violin virtuoso. Wainwright was no mean artist. I could quote many more. Well, Sir James, you will inform your client that I am turning my mind upon

Baron Gruner. I can say no more. I have some sources of information of my own, and I dare say we may find some means of opening the matter up."

When our visitor had left us, Holmes sat so long in deep thought that it seemed to me that he had forgotten my presence. At last, however, he came briskly back to earth.

" Well, Watson, any views ? " he asked.

" I should think you had better see the young lady herself."

" My dear Watson, if her poor old broken father cannot move her, how shall I, a stranger, prevail ? And yet there is something in the suggestion if all else fails. But I think we must begin from a different angle. I rather fancy that Shinwell Johnson might be a help."

I have not had occasion to mention Shinwell Johnson in these memoirs because I have seldom drawn my cases from the latter phases of my friend's career. During the first years of the century he became a valuable assistant. Johnson, I grieve to say, made his name first as a very dangerous villain and served two terms at Parkhurst. Finally, he repented and allied himself to Holmes, acting as his agent in the huge criminal underworld of London, and obtaining information which often proved to be of vital importance. Had Johnson been a " nark " of the police he would soon have been exposed, but as he dealt with cases which never came directly into the courts, his activities were never realized by his companions. With the glamour of his two convictions upon him, he had the *entrée* of every night-club, doss-house, and gambling-den in the town, and his quick observation and active brain made him an ideal agent for gaining information. It was to him that Sherlock Holmes now proposed to turn.

It was not possible for me to follow the immediate steps taken by my friend, for I had some pressing professional business of my own, but I met him by appointment that evening at Simpson's, where, sitting at a small table in the front window, and looking down at the rushing stream of life in the Strand, he told me something of what had passed.

"Johnson is on the prowl," said he. "He may pick up some garbage in the darker recesses of the underworld, for it is down there, amid the black roots of crime, that we must hunt for this man's secrets."

"But, if the lady will not accept what is already known, why should any fresh discovery of yours turn her from her purpose?"

"Who knows, Watson? Woman's heart and mind are insoluble puzzles to the male. Murder might be condoned or explained, and yet some smaller offence might rankle. Baron Gruner remarked to me——"

"He remarked to you!"

"Oh, to be sure, I had not told you of my plans! Well, Watson, I love to come to close grips with my man. I like to meet him eye to eye and read for myself the stuff that he is made of. When I had given Johnson his instructions, I took a cab out to Kingston and found the Baron in a most affable mood."

"Did he recognize you?"

"There was no difficulty about that, for I simply sent in my card. He is an excellent antagonist, cool as ice, silky voiced and soothing as one of your fashionable consultants and poisonous as a cobra. He has breed in him, a real aristocrat of crime, with a superficial suggestion of afternoon tea and all the cruelty of the grave behind it. Yes, I am glad to have had my attention called to Baron Adelbert Gruner."

"You say he was affable?"

"A purring cat who thinks he sees prospective mice. Some people's affability is more deadly than the violence of coarser souls. His greeting was characteristic. 'I rather thought I should see you sooner or later, Mr. Holmes,' said he. 'You have been engaged, no doubt, by General de Merville to endeavour to stop my marriage with his daughter, Violet. That is so, is it not ? '

" I acquiesced.

" ' My dear man,' said he, ' you will only ruin your own well-deserved reputation. It is not a case in which you can possibly succeed. You will have barren work, to say nothing of incurring some danger. Let me very strongly advise you to draw off at once.'

" ' It is curious,' I answered, ' but that was the very advice which I had intended to give you. I have a respect for your brains, Baron, and the little which I have seen of your personality has not lessened it. Let me put it to you as man to man. No one wants to rake up your past and make you unduly uncomfortable. It is over, and you are now in smooth waters, but if you persist in this marriage you will raise up a swarm of powerful enemies who will never leave you alone until they have made England too hot to hold you. Is the game worth it ? Surely you would be wiser if you left the lady alone. It would not be pleasant for you if these facts of your past were brought to her notice.'

" The Baron has little waxed tips of hair under his nose, like the short antennæ of an insect. These quivered with amusement as he listened, and he finally broke into a gentle chuckle.

" ' Excuse my amusement, Mr. Holmes,' said he, ' but it is really funny to see you trying to play a hand with no cards in it. I don't think anyone could do it better, but it is rather pathetic, all the same. Not a colour card there, Mr. Holmes, nothing but the smallest of the small.'

" ' So you think.'

" ' So I know. Let me make the thing clear to you, for my own hand is so strong that I can afford to show it. I have been fortunate enough to win the entire affection of this lady. This was given to me in spite of the fact that I told her very clearly of all the unhappy incidents in my past life. I also told her that certain wicked and designing persons—I hope you recognize yourself—would come to her and tell her these things, and I warned her how to treat them. You have heard of post-hypnotic suggestion, Mr. Holmes? Well, you will see how it works, for a man of personality can use hypnotism without any vulgar passes or tomfoolery. So she is ready for you and, I have no doubt, would give you an appointment, for she is quite amenable to her father's will—save only in the one little matter.'

" Well, Watson, there seemed to be no more to say, so I took my leave with as much cold dignity as I could summon, but, as I had my hand on the door-handle, he stopped me.

" ' By the way, Mr. Holmes,' said he, ' did you know Le Brun, the French agent ? '

" ' Yes,' said I.

" ' Do you know what befell him ? '

" ' I heard that he was beaten by some Apaches in the Montmartre district and crippled for life.'

" ' Quite true, Mr. Holmes. By a curious coincidence he had been inquiring into my affairs only a week before. Don't do it, Mr. Holmes ; it's not a lucky thing to do. Several have found that out. My last word to you is, go your own way and let me go mine. Good-bye ! '

" So there you are, Watson. You are up to date now."

" The fellow seems dangerous."

" Mighty dangerous. I disregard the blusterer, but this is the sort of man who says rather less than he means."

" Must you interfere ? Does it really matter if he marries the girl ? "

" Considering that he undoubtedly murdered his last wife, I should say it mattered very much. Besides, the client ! Well, well, we need not discuss that. When you have finished your coffee you had best come home with me, for the blithe Shinwell will be there with his report."

We found him sure enough, a huge, coarse, red-faced,

scorbutic man, with a pair of vivid black eyes which were the only external sign of the very cunning mind within. It seems that he had dived down into what was peculiarly his kingdom, and beside him on the settee was a brand which he had brought up in the shape of a slim, flame-like young woman with a pale, intense face, youthful, and yet so worn with sin and sorrow that one read the terrible years which had left their leprous mark upon her.

"This is Miss Kitty Winter," said Shinwell Johnson, waving his fat hand as an introduction. "What she don't know—well, there, she'll speak for herself. Put my hand right on her, Mr. Holmes, within an hour of your message."

"I'm easy to find," said the young woman. "Hell, London, gets me every time. Same address for Porky Shinwell. We're old mates, Porky, you and I. But, by Cripes! there is another who ought to be down in a lower hell than we if there was any justice in the world! That is the man you are after, Mr. Holmes."

Holmes smiled. "I gather we have your good wishes, Miss Winter."

"If I can help to put him where he belongs, I'm yours to the rattle," said our visitor, with fierce energy. There was an intensity of hatred in her white, set face and her blazing eyes such as woman seldom and man never can attain. "You needn't go into my past, Mr. Holmes. That's neither here nor there. But what I am Adelbert Gruner made me. If I could pull him down!" She clutched frantically with her hands into the air. "Oh, if I could only pull him into the pit where he has pushed so many!"

"You know how the matter stands?"

"Porky Shinwell has been telling me. He's after some other poor fool and wants to marry her this time. You want to stop it. Well, you surely know enough about this devil to prevent any decent girl in her senses wanting to be in the same parish with him."

"She is not in her senses. She is madly in love. She has been told all about him. She cares nothing."

"Told about the murder?"

"Yes."

"My Lord, she must have a nerve!"

"She puts them all down as slanders."

"Couldn't you lay proofs before her silly eyes?"

"Well, can you help us do so?"

"Ain't I a proof myself? If I stood before her and told her how he used me——"

"Would you do this?"

"Would I? Would I not!"

"Well, it might be worth trying. But he has told her most of his sins and had pardon from her, and I understand she will not reopen the question."

"I'll lay he didn't tell her all," said Miss Winter. "I caught a glimpse of one or two murders besides the one that made such a fuss. He would speak of someone in his velvet way and then look at me with a steady eye and say: 'He died within a month.' It wasn't hot air, either. But I took little notice—you see, I loved him myself at that time. Whatever he did went with me, same as with this poor fool! There was just one thing that shook me. Yes, by Cripes! if it had not been for his poisonous, lying tongue that explains and soothes, I'd have left him that very night. It's a book he has—a brown leather book with a lock, and his arms in gold on the outside. I think he was a bit drunk that night, or he would not have shown it to me."

"What was it, then?"

"I tell you, Mr. Holmes, this man collects women, and takes a pride in his collection, as some men collect moths or butterflies. He had it all in that book. Snapshot photographs, names, details, everything about them. It was a beastly book—a book no man, even if he had come from the gutter, could have put together. But it was Adelbert Gruner's book all the same. 'Souls I have ruined.' He could have put that on the outside if he had been so minded. However, that's neither here nor there, for the book would not serve you, and, if it would, you can't get it."

" Where is it ? "

" How can I tell you where it is now ? It's more than a year since I left him. I know where he kept it then. He's a precise, tidy cat of a man in many of his ways, so maybe it is still in the pigeon-hole of the old bureau in the inner study. Do you know his house ? "

" I've been in the study," said Holmes.

" Have you, though ? You haven't been slow on the job if you only started this morning. Maybe dear Adelbert has met his match this time. The outer study is the one with the Chinese crockery in it—big glass cupboard between the windows. Then behind his desk is the door that leads to the inner study—a small room where he keeps papers and things."

" Is he not afraid of burglars ? "

" Adelbert is no coward. His worst enemy couldn't say that of him. He can look after himself. There's a burglar alarm at night. Besides, what is there for a burglar—unless they got away with all this fancy crockery ? "

" No good," said Shinwell Johnson, with the decided voice of the expert. " No fence wants stuff of that sort that you can neither melt nor sell."

" Quite so," said Holmes. " Well, now, Miss Winter, if you would call here to-morrow evening at five, I would consider in the meanwhile whether your suggestion of seeing this lady personally may not be arranged. I am exceedingly obliged to you for your co-operation. I need not say that my clients will consider liberally——"

" None of that, Mr. Holmes," cried the young woman. " I am not out for money. Let me see this man in the mud, and I've got all I worked for—in the mud with my foot on his cursed face. That's my price. I'm with you to-morrow or any other day so long as you are on his track. Porky here can tell you always where to find me."

I did not see Holmes again until the following evening, when we dined once more at our Strand restaurant. He shrugged his shoulders when I asked him what luck he had had in his interview. Then he told the story, which I would repeat in this way. His hard, dry statement needs some little editing to soften it into the terms of real life.

"There was no difficulty at all about the appointment," said Holmes, "for the girl glories in showing abject filial obedience in all secondary things in an attempt to atone for her flagrant breach of it in her engagement. The General 'phoned that all was ready and the fiery Miss W. turned up according to schedule, so that at half-past five a cab deposited us outside 104 Berkeley Square, where the old soldier resides—one of those awful grey London castles which would make a church seem frivolous. A footman showed us into a great yellow-curtained drawing-room, and there was the lady awaiting us, demure, pale, self-contained, as inflexible and remote as a snow image on a mountain.

"I don't quite know how to make her clear to you, Watson. Perhaps you may meet her before we are through, and you can use your own gift of words. She is beautiful, but with the ethereal other-world beauty of some fanatic whose thoughts are set on high. I have seen such faces in the pictures of the old masters of the Middle Ages. How a beast-man could have laid his vile paws upon such a being of the beyond I cannot imagine. You may have noticed how extremes call to each other, the spiritual to the animal, the cave-man to the angel. You never saw a worse case than this.

"She knew what we had come for, of course—that villain had lost no time in poisoning her mind against us. Miss Winter's advent rather amazed her, I think, but she waved us into our respective chairs like a reverend abbess receiving two rather leprous mendicants. If your head is inclined to swell, my dear Watson, take a course of Miss Violet de Merville.

" ' Well, sir,' said she, in a voice like the wind from an iceberg, ' your name is familiar to me. You have called, as I understand, to malign my fiancé, Baron Gruner. It is only by my father's request that I see you at all, and I warn you in advance that anything you can say could not possibly have the slightest effect upon my mind.'

" I was sorry for her, Watson. I thought of her for the moment as I would have thought of a daughter of my own. I am not often eloquent. I use my head, not my heart. But I really did plead with her with all the warmth of words that I could find in my nature. I pictured to her the awful position of the woman who only wakes to a man's character after she is his wife— a woman who has to submit to be caressed by bloody hands and lecherous lips. I spared her nothing—the shame, the fear, the agony, the hopelessness of it all. All my hot words could not bring one tinge of colour to those ivory cheeks or one gleam of emotion to those abstracted eyes. I thought of what the rascal had said about a post-hypnotic influence. One could really believe that she was living above the earth in some ecstatic dream. Yet there was nothing indefinite in her replies.

" ' I have listened to you with patience, Mr. Holmes,' said she. ' The effect upon my mind is exactly as predicted. I am aware that Adelbert, that my fiancé, has had a stormy life in which he has incurred bitter hatreds and most unjust aspersions. You are only the last of a series who have brought their slanders before me. Possibly you mean well, though I learn that you are a paid agent who would have been equally willing to act for the Baron as against him. But in any case I wish you to understand once for all that I love him and that he loves me, and that the opinion of all the world is no more to me than the twitter of those birds outside the window. If his noble nature has ever for an instant fallen, it may be that I have been specially sent to raise it to its true and lofty level. I am not clear,' here she turned her eyes upon my companion, ' who this young lady may be.'

" I was about to answer when the girl broke in like a whirlwind. If ever you saw flame and ice face to face, it was those two women.

" ' I'll tell you who I am,' she cried, springing out of her chair, her mouth all twisted with passion—' I am his last mistress. I am one of a hundred that he has tempted and used and ruined and thrown into the refuse heap, as he will you also. *Your* refuse heap is more likely to be a grave, and maybe that's the best. I tell you, you foolish woman, if you marry this man he'll be the death of you. It may be a broken heart or it may be a broken neck, but he'll have you one way or the other. It's not out of love for you I'm speaking. I don't care a tinker's curse whether you live or die. It's out of hate for him and to spite him and to get back on him for what he did to me. But it's all the same, and you needn't look at me like that, my fine lady, for you may be lower than I am before you are through with it.'

" ' I should prefer not to discuss such matters,' said Miss de Merville coldly. ' Let me say once for all that I am aware of three passages in my fiancé's life in which he became entangled with designing women, and that I am assured of his hearty repentance for any evil that he may have done.'

" ' Three passages ! ' screamed my companion. ' You fool ! You unutterable fool ! '

" ' Mr. Holmes, I beg that you will bring this interview to an end,' said the icy voice. ' I have obeyed my father's wish in seeing you, but I am not compelled to listen to the ravings of this person.'

" With an oath Miss Winter darted forward, and if I had not caught her wrist she would have clutched this maddening woman by the hair. I dragged her towards the door, and was lucky to get her back into the cab without a public scene, for she was beside herself with rage. In a cold way I felt pretty furious myself, Watson, for there was something indescribably annoying in the calm aloofness and supreme self-complaisance of the woman whom we were trying to save. So now once again you know exactly how we stand, and it is clear that I must plan some fresh opening move, for this gambit won't work. I'll keep in touch with you, Watson, for it is more than likely that you will have your part to play, though it is just possible that the next move may lie with them rather than with us."

And it did. Their blow fell—or his blow rather, for never could I believe that the lady was privy to it. I think I could show you the very paving-stone upon which I stood when my eyes fell upon the placard, and a pang of horror passed through my very soul. It was between the Grand Hotel and Charing Cross Station, where a one-legged newsvendor displayed his evening papers. The date was just two days after the last conversation. There, black upon yellow, was the terrible news-sheet :

MURDEROUS
ATTACK
UPON
SHERLOCK
HOLMES.

I think I stood stunned for some moments. Then I have a confused recollection of snatching at a paper, of the remonstrance of the man, whom I had not paid, and, finally, of standing in the doorway of a chemist's shop while I turned up the fateful paragraph. This was how it ran :

" We learn with regret that Mr. Sherlock Holmes. the well-known private detective, was the victim this morning of a murderous assault which has left him in a precarious position. There are no exact details to hand, but the event seems to have occurred about twelve o'clock in Regent Street, outside the Café Royal. The attack was made by two men armed with sticks, and Mr. Holmes was beaten about the head and body, receiving injuries which the doctors describe as most serious. He was carried to Charing Cross Hospital, and afterwards insisted upon being taken to his rooms in Baker Street. The miscreants who attacked him appear to have been respectably dressed men, who escaped from the bystanders by passing through the Café Royal and out into Glasshouse Street behind it. No doubt they belonged to that criminal fraternity which has so often had occasion to bewail the activity and ingenuity of the injured man."

I need not say that my eyes had hardly glanced over the paragraph before I had sprung into a hansom and was on my way to Baker Street. I found Sir Leslie Oakshott, the famous surgeon, in the hall and his brougham waiting at the kerb.

" No immediate danger," was his report. " Two lacerated scalp wounds and some considerable bruises. Several stitches have been necessary. Morphine has been injected and quiet is essential, but an interview of a few minutes would not be absolutely forbidden."

With this permission I stole into the darkened room. The sufferer was wide awake, and I heard my name in a hoarse whisper. The blind was three-quarters down, but one ray of sunlight slanted through and struck the bandaged head of the injured man. A crimson patch had soaked through the white linen compress. I sat beside him and bent my head.

" All right, Watson. Don't look so scared," he muttered in a very weak voice. " It's not as bad as it seems."

" Thank God for that ! "

" I'm a bit of a single-stick expert, as you know. I took most of them on my guard. It was the second man that was too much for me."

" What can I do, Holmes ? Of course, it was that damned fellow who set them on. I'll go and thrash the hide off him if you give the word."

" Good old Watson ! No, we can do nothing there

unless the police lay their hands on the men. But their get-away had been well prepared. We may be sure of that. Wait a little. I have my plans. The first thing is to exaggerate my injuries. They'll come to you for news. Put it on thick, Watson. Lucky if I live the week out—concussion—delirium—what you like! You can't overdo it."

" But Sir Leslie Oakshott ? "

" Oh, he's all right. He shall see the worst side of me. I'll look after that."

" Anything else ? "

" Yes. Tell Shinwell Johnson to get that girl out of the way. Those beauties will be after her now. They know, of course, that she was with me in the case. If they dared to do me in it is not likely they will neglect her. That is urgent. Do it to-night."

" I'll go now. Anything more ? "

" Put my pipe on the table—and the tobacco-slipper. Right ! Come in each morning and we will plan our campaign."

I arranged with Johnson that evening to take Miss Winter to a quiet suburb and see that she lay low until the danger was past.

For six days the public were under the impression that Holmes was at the door of death. The bulletins were very grave and there were sinister paragraphs in the papers. My continual visits assured me that it was not so bad as that. His wiry constitution and his determined will were working wonders. He was recovering fast, and I had suspicions at times that he was really finding himself faster than he pretended, even to me. There was a curious secretive streak in the man which led to many dramatic effects, but left even his closest friend guessing as to what his exact plans might be. He pushed to an extreme the axiom that the only safe plotter was he who plotted alone. I was nearer him than anyone else, and yet I was always conscious of the gap between.

On the seventh day the stitches were taken out, in spite of which there was a report of erysipelas in the evening papers. The same evening papers had an announcement which I was bound, sick or well, to carry to my friend. It was simply that among the passengers on the Cunard boat *Ruritania*, starting from Liverpool on Friday, was the Baron Adelbert Gruner, who had some important financial business to settle in the States before his impending wedding to Miss Violet de Merville, only daughter of, etc., etc. Holmes listened to the news with a cold, concentrated look upon his pale face, which told me that it hit him hard.

"Friday!" he cried. "Only three clear days. I believe the rascal wants to put himself out of danger's way. But he won't, Watson! By the Lord Harry, he won't! Now, Watson, I want you to do something for me."

"I am here to be used, Holmes."

"Well, then, spend the next twenty-four hours in an intensive study of Chinese pottery."

He gave no explanations and I asked for none. By long experience I had learned the wisdom of obedience. But when I had left his room I walked down Baker Street, revolving in my head how on earth I was to carry out so strange an order. Finally I drove to the London Library in St. James' Square, put the matter to my friend Lomax, the sub-librarian, and departed to my rooms with a goodly volume under my arm.

It is said that the barrister who crams up a case with such care that he can examine an expert witness upon the Monday has forgotten all his forced knowledge before the Saturday. Certainly I should not like now to pose as an authority upon ceramics. And yet all that evening, and all that night with a short interval for rest, and all next morning I was sucking in knowledge and committing names to memory. There I learned of the hall-marks of the great artist-decorators, of the mystery of cyclical dates, the marks of the Hung-wu and the beauties of the Yung-lo, the writings of Tang-ying, and the glories of the primitive period of the Sung and the Yuan. I was charged with all this information when I called upon Holmes next evening. He was out of bed now, though you would not have guessed it from the published reports, and he sat with his much-bandaged head resting upon his hand in the depth of his favourite arm-chair.

" Why, Holmes," I said, " if one believed the papers you are dying."

" That," said he, " is the very impression which I intended to convey. And now, Watson, have you learned your lessons ? "

" At least I have tried to."

" Good. You could keep up an intelligent conversation on the subject ? "

" I believe I could."

" Then hand me that little box from the mantelpiece."

He opened the lid and took out a small object most carefully wrapped in some fine Eastern silk. This he unfolded, and disclosed a delicate little saucer of the most beautiful deep-blue colour.

" It needs careful handling, Watson. This is the real egg-shell pottery of the Ming dynasty. No finer piece ever passed through Christie's. A complete set of this would be worth a king's ransom—in fact, it is doubtful if there is a complete set outside the Imperial palace of Peking. The sight of this would drive a real connoisseur wild."

" What am I to do with it ? "

Holmes handed me a card upon which was printed : " Dr. Hill Barton, 369 Half Moon Street."

" That is your name for the evening, Watson. You will call upon Baron Gruner. I know something of his habits, and at half-past eight he would probably be disengaged. A note will tell him in advance that you are about to call, and you will say that you are bringing him a specimen of an absolutely unique set of Ming china. You may as well be a medical man, since that is a part which you can play without duplicity. You are a collector, this set has come your way, you have heard of the Baron's interest in the subject, and you are not averse to selling at a price."

" What price ? "

" Well asked, Watson. You would certainly fall down badly if you did not know the value of your own wares. This saucer was got for me by Sir James, and comes, I understand, from the collection of his client. You will not exaggerate if you say that it could hardly be matched in the world."

" I could perhaps suggest that the set should be valued by an expert."

" Excellent, Watson ! You scintillate to-day. Suggest Christie or Sotheby. Your delicacy prevents your putting a price for yourself."

" But if he won't see me ? "

" Oh, yes, he will see you. He has the collection mania in its most acute form—and especially on this subject, on which he is an acknowledged authority. Sit down, Watson, and I will dictate the letter. No answer needed. You will merely say that you are coming, and why."

It was an admirable document, short, courteous, and stimulating to the curiosity of the connoisseur. A district messenger was duly dispatched with it. On the same evening, with the precious saucer in my hand and the card of Dr. Hill Barton in my pocket, I set off on my own adventure.

The beautiful house and grounds indicated that Baron Gruner was, as Sir James had said, a man of considerable wealth. A long winding drive, with banks of rare shrubs on either side, opened out into a great gravelled square adorned with statues. The place had been built by a South African gold king in the days of the great boom, and the long, low house with the turrets at the corners, though an architectural nightmare, was imposing in its size and solidity. A butler who would have adorned a bench of bishops showed me in, and handed me over to a plush-clad footman, who ushered me into the Baron's presence.

He was standing at the open front of a great case which stood between the windows, and which contained part of his Chinese collection. He turned as I entered, with a small brown vase in his hand.

"Pray sit down, doctor," said he. "I was looking over my own treasures and wondering whether I could really afford to add to them. This little Tang specimen, which dates from the seventh century, would probably interest you. I am sure you never saw finer workmanship or a richer glaze. Have you the Ming saucer with you of which you spoke?"

I carefully unpacked it and handed it to him. He seated himself at his desk, pulled over the lamp, for it was growing dark, and set himself to examine it. As he did so the yellow light beat upon his own features, and I was able to study them at my ease.

He was certainly a remarkably handsome man. His European reputation for beauty was fully deserved. In figure he was not more than of middle size, but was built upon graceful and active lines. His face was swarthy, almost Oriental, with large, dark, languorous eyes which might easily hold an irresistible fascination for women. His hair and moustache were raven black: the latter short, pointed, and carefully waxed. His features were regular and pleasing, save only his straight, thin-lipped mouth. If ever I saw a murderer's mouth it was there—a cruel, hard gash in the face, compressed, inexorable, and terrible. He was ill-advised to train his moustache away from it, for it was Nature's danger-signal, set as a warning to his victims. His voice was engaging and his manners perfect. In age I should have put him at little over thirty, though his record afterwards showed that he was forty-two.

" Very fine—very fine indeed ! " he said at last. " And you say you have a set of six to correspond. What puzzles me is that I should not have heard of such magnificent specimens. I only know of one in England to match this, and it is certainly not likely to be in the market. Would it be indiscreet if I were to ask you, Dr. Hill Barton, how you obtained this ? "

" Does it really matter ? " I asked, with as careless an air as I could muster. " You can see that the piece is genuine, and, as to the value, I am content to take an expert's valuation."

" Very mysterious," said he, with a quick, suspicious flash of his dark eyes. " In dealing with objects of such value, one naturally wishes to know all about the transaction. That the piece is genuine is certain. I have no doubts at all about that. But suppose—I am bound to take every possibility into account—that it should prove afterwards that you had no right to sell ? "

" I would guarantee you against any claim of the sort."

" That, of course, would open up the question as to what your guarantee was worth."

" My bankers would answer that."

" Quite so. And yet the whole transaction strikes me as rather unusual."

" You can do business or not," said I, with indifference. " I have given you the first offer, as I understood that you were a connoisseur, but I shall have no difficulty in other quarters."

" Who told you I was a connoisseur ? "

" I was aware that you had written a book upon the subject."

" Have you read the book ? "

" No."

" Dear me, this becomes more and more difficult for me to understand ! You are a connoisseur and collector with a very valuable piece in your collection, and yet you have never troubled to consult the one book which would have told you of the real meaning and value of what you held. How do you explain that ? "

" I am a very busy man. I am a doctor in practice."

" That is no answer. If a man has a hobby he follows it up, whatever his other pursuits may be. You said in your note that you were a connoisseur."

" So I am."

" Might I ask you a few questions to test you ? I am obliged to tell you, doctor—if you are indeed a doctor—that the incident becomes more and more suspicious. I would ask you what do you know of the Emperor Shomu and how do you associate him with the Shoso-in near Nara ? Dear me, does that puzzle you ? Tell me a little about the Northern Wei dynasty and its place in the history of ceramics."

I sprang from my chair in simulated anger.

" This is intolerable, sir," said I. " I came here to do you a favour, and not to be examined as if I were a schoolboy. My knowledge on these subjects may be second only to your own, but I certainly shall not answer questions which have been put in so offensive a way."

He looked at me steadily. The languor had gone from his eyes. They suddenly glared. There was a gleam of teeth from between those cruel lips.

" What is the game ? You are here as a spy. You are an emissary of Holmes. This is a trick that you are playing upon me. The fellow is dying, I hear, so he sends his tools to keep watch upon me. You've made your way in here without leave, and, by God ! you may find it harder to get out than to get in."

He had sprung to his feet, and I stepped back, bracing myself for an attack, for the man was beside himself with rage. He may have suspected me from the first ; certainly this cross-examination had shown him the truth ; but it was clear that I could not hope to deceive him. He dived his hand into a side-drawer and rummaged furiously. Then something struck upon his ear, for he stood listening intently.

"Ah!" he cried. "Ah!" and dashed into the room behind him.

Two steps took me to the open door, and my mind will ever carry a clear picture of the scene within. The window leading out to the garden was wide open. Beside it, looking like some terrible ghost, his head girt with bloody bandages, his face drawn and white, stood Sherlock Holmes. The next instant he was through the gap, and I heard the crash of his body among the laurel bushes outside. With a howl of rage the master of the house rushed after him to the open window.

And then! It was done in an instant, and yet I clearly saw it. An arm—a woman's arm—shot out from among the leaves. At the same instant the Baron uttered a horrible cry—a yell which will always ring in my memory. He clapped his two hands to his face and rushed round the room, beating his head horribly against the walls. Then he fell upon the carpet, rolling and writhing, while scream after scream resounded through the house.

"Water! For God's sake, water!" was his cry.

I seized a carafe from a side-table and rushed to his aid. At the same moment the butler and several footmen ran in from the hall. I remember that one of them fainted as I knelt by the injured man and turned that awful face to the light of the lamp. The vitriol was eating into it everywhere and dripping from the ears and the chin. One eye was already white and glazed. The other was red and inflamed. The features which I had admired a few minutes before were now like some beautiful painting over which the artist has passed a wet and foul sponge. They were blurred, discoloured, inhuman, terrible.

In a few words I explained exactly what had occurred, so far as the vitriol attack was concerned. Some had climbed through the window and others had rushed out on to the lawn, but it was dark and it had begun to rain. Between his screams the victim raged and raved against the avenger. "It was that hell-cat, Kitty Winter!" he cried. "Oh, the she-devil! She shall pay for it! She shall pay! Oh, God in heaven, this pain is more than I can bear!"

I bathed his face in oil, put cotton wadding on the raw surfaces, and administered a hypodermic of morphia. All suspicion of me had passed from his mind in the presence of this shock, and he clung to my hands as if I might have the power even yet to clear those dead-fish eyes which gazed up at me. I could have wept over the ruin had I not remembered very clearly the vile life which had led up to so hideous a change. It was loath-some to feel the pawing of his burning hands, and I was relieved when his family surgeon, closely followed by a specialist, came to relieve me of my charge. An inspector of police had also arrived, and to him I handed my real card. It would have been useless as well as foolish to do otherwise, for I was nearly as well known by sight at the Yard as Holmes himself. Then I left that house of gloom and terror. Within an hour I was at Baker Street.

Holmes was seated in his familiar chair, looking very pale and exhausted. Apart from his injuries, even his iron nerves had been shocked by the events of the even-ing, and he listened with horror to my account of the Baron's transformation.

"The wages of sin, Watson—the wages of sin!" said he. "Sooner or later it will always come. God knows, there was sin enough," he added, taking up a brown volume from the table. "Here is the book the woman talked of. If this will not break off the marriage, nothing ever could. But it will, Watson. It must. No self-respecting woman could stand it."

"It is his love diary?"

"Or his lust diary. Call it what you will. The moment the woman told us of it I realized what a tre-mendous weapon was there, if we could but lay our hands on it. I said nothing at the time to indicate my thoughts, for this woman might have given it away. But I brooded over it. Then this assault upon me gave me the chance of letting the Baron think that no precautions need be taken against me. That was all to the good. I would have waited a little longer, but his visit to America forced my hand. He would never have left so compromising a document behind him. Therefore we had to act at once. Burglary at night is impossible. He takes precautions. But there was a chance in the evening if I could only be sure that his attention was engaged. That was where you and your blue saucer came in. But I had to be sure of the position of the book, and I knew I had only a few minutes in which to act, for my time was limited by your knowledge of Chinese pottery. Therefore I gathered the girl up at the last moment. How could I guess what the little packet was that she carried so carefully under her cloak ? I thought she had come altogether on my business, but it seems she had some of her own."

"He guessed I came from you."

"I feared he would. But you held him in play just long enough for me to get the book, though not long enough for an unobserved escape. Ah, Sir James, I am very glad you have come ! "

Our courtly friend had appeared in answer to a previous summons. He listened with the deepest attention to Holmes' account of what had occurred.

"You have done wonders—wonders ! " he cried, when he had heard the narrative. "But if these injuries are as terrible as Dr. Watson describes, then surely our purpose of thwarting the marriage is sufficiently gained without the use of this horrible book."

Holmes shook his head.

"Women of the de Merville type do not act like that. She would love him the more as a disfigured martyr. No, no. It is his moral side, not his physical, which we have to destroy. That book will bring her back to earth—and I know nothing else that could. It is in his own writing. She cannot get past it."

Sir James carried away both it and the precious saucer. As I was myself overdue, I went down with him into the street. A brougham was waiting for him. He sprang in, gave a hurried order to the cockaded coachman, and drove swiftly away. He flung his overcoat half out of the window to cover the armorial bearings upon the panel, but I had seen them in the glare of our fanlight none the less. I gasped with surprise. Then I turned back and ascended the stair to Holmes' room.

" I have found out who our client is," I cried, bursting with my great news. "Why, Holmes, it is——"

" It is a loyal friend and a chivalrous gentleman," said Holmes, holding up a restraining hand. " Let that now and for ever be enough for us."

I do not know how the incriminating book was used. Sir James may have managed it. Or it is more probable that so delicate a task was entrusted to the young lady's father. The effect, at any rate, was all that could be desired. Three days later appeared a paragraph in the *Morning Post* to say that the marriage between Baron Adelbert Gruner and Miss Violet de Merville would not take place. The same paper had the first police-court hearing of the proceedings against Miss Kitty Winter on the grave charge of vitriol-throwing. Such extenuating circumstances came out in the trial that the sentence, as will be remembered, was the lowest that was possible for such an offence. Sherlock Holmes was threatened with a prosecution for burglary, but when an object is good and a client is sufficiently illustrious, even the rigid British law becomes human and elastic. My friend has not yet stood in the dock.

46. *The Blanched Soldier*

THE ideas of my friend Watson, though limited are exceedingly pertinacious. For a long time he has worried me to write an experience of my own. Perhaps I have rather invited this persecution, since I have often had occasion to point out to him how superficial are his own accounts and to accuse him of pandering to popular taste instead of confining himself rigidly to facts and figures. " Try it yourself, Holmes ! " he has retorted, and I am compelled to admit that, having taken my pen in my hand, I do begin to realize that the matter must be presented in such a way as may interest the reader. The following case can hardly fail to do so, as it is among the strangest happenings in my collection, though it chanced that Watson had no note of it in his collection. Speaking of my old friend and biographer, I would take this opportunity to remark that if I burden myself with a companion in my various little inquiries it is not done out of sentiment or caprice, but it is that Watson has some remarkable characteristics of his own, to which in his modesty he has given small attention amid his exaggerated estimates of my own performances. A confederate who foresees your conclusions and course of action is always dangerous, but one to whom each development comes as a perpetual surprise, and to whom the future is always a closed book, is, indeed, an ideal helpmate.

I find from my notebook that it was in January, 1903, just after the conclusion of the Boer War, that I had my visit from Mr. James M. Dodd, a big, fresh, sunburned, upstanding Briton. The good Watson had at that time deserted me for a wife, the only selfish action which I can recall in our association. I was alone.

It is my habit to sit with my back to the window and to place my visitors in the opposite chair, where the light falls full upon them. Mr. James M. Dodd seemed somewhat at a loss how to begin the interview. I did not attempt to help him, for his silence gave me more time for observation. I have found it wise to impress clients with a sense of power, and so I gave him some of my conclusions.

" From South Africa, sir, I perceive."

" Yes, sir," he answered, with some surprise.

" Imperial Yeomanry, I fancy."

" Exactly."

" Middlesex Corps, no doubt."

" That is so. Mr. Holmes, you are a wizard."

I smiled at his bewildered expression.

" When a gentleman of virile appearance enters my room with such tan upon his face as an English sun could never give, and with his handkerchief in his sleeve instead of in his pocket, it is not difficult to place him. You wear a short beard, which shows that you were not a regular. You have the cut of a riding-man. As to Middlesex, your card has already shown me that you are a stockbroker from Throgmorton Street. What other regiment would you join ? "

" You see everything."

" I see no more than you, but I have trained myself to notice what I see. However, Mr. Dodd, it was not to discuss the science of observation that you called upon me this morning. What has been happening at Tuxbury Old Park ? "

" Mr. Holmes—— ! "

" My dear sir, there is no mystery. Your letter came with that heading, and as you fixed this appointment in very pressing terms it was clear that something sudden and important had occurred."

" Yes, indeed. But the letter was written in the afternoon, and a good deal has happened since then. If Colonel Emsworth had not kicked me out——"

" Kicked you out ! "

" Well, that was what it amounted to. He is a hard nail, is Colonel Emsworth. The greatest martinet in the Army in his day, and it was a day of rough language, too. I couldn't have stuck the Colonel if it had not been for Godfrey's sake."

I lit my pipe and leaned back in my chair.

" Perhaps you will explain what you are talking about."

My client grinned mischievously.

" I had got into the way of supposing that you knew everything without being told," said he. " But I will give you the facts, and I hope to God that you will be able to tell me what they mean. I've been awake all night puzzling my brain, and the more I think the more incredible does it become.

" When I joined up in January, 1901—just two years ago—young Godfrey Emsworth had joined the same squadron. He was Colonel Emsworth's only son— Emsworth, the Crimean V.C.—and he had the fighting blood in him, so it is no wonder he volunteered. There was not a finer lad in the regiment. We formed a friend-ship—the sort of friendship which can only be made when one lives the same life and shares the same joys and sorrows. He was my mate—and that means a good deal in the Army. We took the rough and the smooth together for a year of hard fighting. Then he was hit with a bullet from an elephant gun in the action near Diamond Hill outside Pretoria. I got one letter from the hospital at Cape Town and one from Southampton. Since then not a word—not one word, Mr. Holmes, for six months and more, and he my closest pal.

" Well, when the war was over, and we all got back, I wrote to his father and asked where Godfrey was. No answer. I waited a bit and then I wrote again. This time I had a reply, short and gruff. Godfrey had gone on a voyage round the world, and it was not likely that he would be back for a year. That was all.

" I wasn't satisfied, Mr. Holmes. The whole thing seemed to me so damned unnatural. He was a good lad and he would not drop a pal like that. It was not like him. Then, again, I happened to know that he was heir to a lot of money, and also that his father and he did not always hit it off too well. The old man was sometimes a bully, and young Godfrey had too much spirit to stand it. No, I wasn't satisfied, and I deter-mined that I would get to the root of the matter. It happened, however, that my own affairs needed a lot

of straightening out, after two years' absence, and so it
is only this week that I have been able to take up Godfrey's
case again. But since I have taken it up I mean to drop
everything in order to see it through."

Mr. James M. Dodd appeared to be the sort of person
whom it would be better to have as a friend than as an
enemy. His blue eyes were stern and his square jaw
had set hard as he spoke.

"Well, what have you done ? " I asked.

"My first move was to get down to his home, Tuxbury Old Park, near Bedford, and to see for myself how
the ground lay. I wrote to the mother, therefore—I
had had quite enough of the curmudgeon of a father—and
I made a clean frontal attack : Godfrey was my chum,
I had a great deal of interest which I might tell her of
our common experiences, I should be in the neighbourhood, would there be any objection, et cetera ? In reply
I had quite an amiable answer from her and an offer to
put me up for the night. That was what took me down
on Monday.

"Tuxbury Old Hall is inaccessible—five miles from
anywhere. There was no trap at the station, so I had
to walk, carrying my suit-case, and it was nearly dark
before I arrived. It is a great wandering house, standing
in a considerable park. I should judge it was of all
sorts of ages and styles, starting on a half-timbered
Elizabethan foundation and ending in a Victorian portico.
Inside it was all panelling and tapestry and half-effaced
old pictures, a house of shadows and mystery. There
was a butler, old Ralph, who seemed about the same
age as the house, and there was his wife, who might have
been older. She had been Godfrey's nurse, and I had
heard him speak of her as second only to his mother in
his affections, so I was drawn to her in spite of her queer
appearance. The mother I liked also—a gentle little
white mouse of a woman. It was only the Colonel
himself whom I barred.

"We had a bit of a barney right away, and I should

have walked back to the station if I had not felt that it might be playing his game for me to do so. I was shown straight into his study, and there I found him, a huge, bow-backed man with a smoky skin and a straggling grey beard, seated behind his littered desk. A red-veined nose jutted out like a vulture's beak, and two fierce grey eyes glared at me from under tufted brows. I could understand now why Godfrey seldom spoke of his father.

" ' Well, sir,' said he in a rasping voice. ' I should be interested to know the real reasons for this visit.'

" I answered that I had explained them in my letter to his wife.

" ' Yes, yes ; you said that you had known Godfrey in Africa. We have, of course, only your word for that.'

" ' I have his letters to me in my pocket.'

" ' Kindly let me see them.'

" He glanced at the two which I handed him, and then he tossed them back.

" ' Well, what then ? ' he asked.

" ' I was fond of your son Godfrey, sir. Many ties and memories united us. Is it not natural that I should wonder at his sudden silence and should wish to know what has become of him ? '

" ' I have some recollection, sir, that I had already corresponded with you and had told you what had become of him. He has gone upon a voyage round the world. His health was in a poor way after his African experiences, and both his mother and I were of opinion that complete rest and change were needed. Kindly pass that explanation on to any other friends who may be interested in the matter.'

" ' Certainly,' I answered. ' But perhaps you would have the goodness to let me have the name of the steamer and of the line by which he sailed, together with the date. I have no doubt that I should be able to get a letter through to him.'

" My request seemed both to puzzle and to irritate

my host. His great eyebrows came down over his eyes and he tapped his fingers impatiently on the table. He looked up at last with the expression of one who has seen his adversary make a dangerous move at chess, and has decided how to meet it.

" ' Many people, Mr. Dodd,' said he, ' would take offence at your infernal pertinacity and would think that this insistence had reached the point of damned impertinence.'

" ' You must put it down, sir, to my real love for your son.'

" ' Exactly. I have already made every allowance upon that score. I must ask you, however, to drop these inquiries. Every family has its own inner knowledge and its own motives, which cannot always be made clear to outsiders, however well-intentioned. My wife is anxious to hear something of Godfrey's past which you are in a position to tell her, but I would ask you to let the present and the future alone. Such inquiries serve no useful purpose, sir, and place us in a delicate and difficult position.'

" So I came to a dead end, Mr. Holmes. There was no getting past it. I could only pretend to accept the situation and register a vow inwardly that I would never rest until my friend's fate had been cleared up. It was a dull evening. We dined quietly, the three of us, in a gloomy, faded old room. The lady questioned me eagerly about her son, but the old man seemed morose and depressed. I was so bored by the whole proceeding that I made an excuse as soon as I decently could and retired to my bedroom. It was a large, bare room on the ground floor, as gloomy as the rest of the house, but after a year of sleeping upon the veldt, Mr. Holmes, one is not too particular about one's quarters. I opened the curtains and looked out into the garden, remarking that it was a fine night with a bright half-moon. Then I sat down by the roaring fire with the lamp on a table beside me, and endeavoured to distract my mind with a novel. I was interrupted, however, by Ralph, the old butler, who came in with a fresh supply of coals.

" ' I thought you might run short in the night-time, sir. It is bitter weather and these rooms are cold.'

" He hesitated before leaving the room, and when I looked round he was standing facing me with a wistful look upon his wrinkled face.

" ' Beg your pardon, sir, but I could not help hearing what you said of young Master Godfrey at dinner. You know, sir, that my wife nursed him, and so I may say I am his foster-father. It's natural we should take an interest. And you say he carried himself well, sir ? '

" ' There was no braver man in the regiment. He pulled me out once from under the rifles of the Boers, or maybe I should not be here.'

" The old butler rubbed his skinny hands.

" ' Yes, sir, yes, that is Master Godfrey all over. He was always courageous. There's not a tree in the park, sir, that he has not climbed. Nothing would stop him. He was a fine boy—and oh, sir, he was a fine man.'

" I sprang to my feet.

" ' Look here ! ' I cried. ' You say he *was*. You speak as if he were dead. What is all this mystery ? What has become of Godfrey Emsworth ? '

" I gripped the old man by the shoulder, but he shrank away.

" ' I don't know what you mean, sir. Ask the master about Master Godfrey. He knows. It is not for me to interfere.'

" He was leaving the room, but I held his arm.

" ' Listen,' I said. ' You are going to answer one question before you leave if I have to hold you all night. Is Godfrey dead ? '

" He could not face my eyes. He was like a man hypnotized. The answer was dragged from his lips. It was a terrible and unexpected one.

" ' I wish to God he was ! ' he cried, and, tearing himself free, he dashed from the room.

" You will think, Mr. Holmes, that I returned to my chair in no very happy state of mind. The old man's words seemed to me to bear only one interpretation. Clearly my poor friend had become involved in some criminal, or, at the least, disreputable, transaction which touched the family honour. That stern old man had sent his son away and hidden him from the world lest some scandal should come to light. Godfrey was a reckless fellow. He was easily influenced by those around him. No doubt he had fallen into bad hands and been misled to his ruin. It was a piteous business, if it was indeed so, but even now it was my duty to hunt him out and see if I could aid him. I was anxiously pondering the matter when I looked up, and there was Godfrey Emsworth standing before me."

My client had paused as one in deep emotion.

" Pray continue," I said. " Your problem presents some very unusual features."

" He was outside the window, Mr. Holmes, with his face pressed against the glass. I have told you that I looked out at the night. When I did so, I left the curtains partly open. His figure was framed in this gap. The window came down to the ground and I could see the whole length of it, but it was his face which held my gaze. He was deadly pale—never have I seen a man so white. I reckon ghosts may look like that ; but his eyes met mine, and they were the eyes of a living man. He sprang back when he saw that I was looking at him, and he vanished into the darkness.

" There was something shocking about the man, Mr. Holmes. It wasn't merely that ghastly face glimmering as white as cheese in the darkness. It was more subtle than that—something slinking, something furtive, something guilty—something very unlike the frank, manly lad that I had known. It left a feeling of horror in my mind.

" But when a man has been soldiering for a year or two with brother Boer as a playmate, he keeps his nerve and acts quickly. Godfrey had hardly vanished before I was at the window. There was an awkward catch, and I was some little time before I could throw it up. Then I nipped through and ran down the garden path in the direction that I thought he might have taken.

" It was a long path and the light was not very good, but it seemed to me something was moving ahead of me. I ran on and called his name, but it was no use. When I got to the end of the path there were several others branching in different directions to various outhouses. I stood hesitating, and as I did so I heard distinctly the sound of a closing door. It was not behind me in the house, but ahead of me, somewhere in the darkness. That was enough, Mr. Holmes, to assure me that what I had seen was not a vision. Godfrey had run away from me and he had shut a door behind him. Of that I was certain.

" There was nothing more I could do, and I spent an uneasy night turning the matter over in my mind and trying to find some theory which would cover the facts. Next day I found the Colonel rather more conciliatory, and as his wife remarked that there were some places of interest in the neighbourhood, it gave me an opening to ask whether my presence for one more night would incommode them. A somewhat grudging acquiescence from the old man gave me a clear day in which to make my observations. I was already perfectly convinced that Godfrey was in hiding somewhere near, but where and why remained to be solved.

" The house was so large and so rambling that a regiment might be hid away in it and no one the wiser. If the secret lay there, it was difficult for me to penetrate it. But the door which I had heard close was certainly not in the house. I must explore the garden and see what I could find. There was no difficulty in the way, for the old people were busy in their own fashion and left me to my own devices.

"There were several small outhouses, but at the end of the garden there was a detached building of some size—large enough for a gardener's or a game-keeper's residence. Could this be the place whence the sound of that shutting door had come ? I approached it in a careless fashion, as though I were strolling aimlessly round the grounds. As I did so, a small, brisk, bearded man in a black coat and bowler hat—not at all the gardener type—came out of the door. To my surprise, he locked it after him and put the key in his pocket. Then he looked at me with some surprise on his face.

" ' Are you a visitor here ? ' he asked.

" I explained that I was and that I was a friend of Godfrey's.

" ' What a pity that he should be away on his travels, for he would have so liked to see me,' I continued.

" ' Quite so. Exactly,' said he, with a rather guilty air. ' No doubt you will renew your visit at some more propitious time.' He passed on, but when I turned I observed that he was standing watching me, half-concealed by the laurels at the far end of the garden.

" I had a good look at the little house as I passed it, but the windows were heavily curtained, and, so far as one could see, it was empty. I might spoil my own game, and even be ordered off the premises, if I were too audacious, for I was still conscious that I was being watched. Therefore, I strolled back to the house and waited for night before I went on with my inquiry. When all was dark and quiet, I slipped out of my window and made my way as silently as possible to the mysterious lodge.

" I have said that it was heavily curtained, but now I found that the windows were shuttered as well. Some light, however, was breaking through one of them, so I concentrated my attention upon this. I was in luck, for the curtain had not been quite closed, and there was a crack in the shutter so that I could see the inside of the room. It was a cheery place enough, a bright lamp and a blazing fire. Opposite to me was seated the little man whom I had seen in the morning. He was smoking a pipe and reading a paper——"

"What paper?" I asked.

My client seemed annoyed at the interruption of his narrative.

"Can it matter?" he asked.

"It is most essential."

"I really took no notice."

"Possibly you observed whether it was a broad-leafed paper or of that smaller type which one associates with weeklies."

"Now that you mention it, it was not large. It might have been the *Spectator*. However, I had little thought to spare upon such details, for a second man was seated with his back to the window, and I could swear that this second man was Godfrey. I could not see his face, but I knew the familiar slope of his shoulders. He was leaning upon his elbow in an attitude of great melancholy, his body turned towards the fire. I was hesitating as to what I should do when there was a sharp tap on my shoulder, and there was Colonel Emsworth beside me.

" ' This way, sir ! ' said he in a low voice. He walked in silence to the house and I followed him into my own bedroom. He had picked up a time-table in the hall.

" ' There is a train to London at eight-thirty,' said he. ' The trap will be at the door at eight.'

" He was white with rage, and, indeed, I felt myself in so difficult a position that I could only stammer out a few incoherent apologies, in which I tried to excuse myself by urging my anxiety for my friend.

" ' The matter will not bear discussion,' said he abruptly. ' You have made a most damnable intrusion into the privacy of our family. You were here as a guest and you have become a spy. I have nothing more to say, sir, save that I have no wish ever to see you again.'

"At this I lost my temper, Mr. Holmes, and I spoke with some warmth.

"'I have seen your son, and I am convinced that for some reason of your own you are concealing him from the world. I have no idea what your motives are in cutting him off in this fashion, but I am sure that he is no longer a free agent. I warn you, Colonel Emsworth, that until I am assured as to the safety and well-being of my friend I shall never desist in my efforts to get to the bottom of the mystery, and I shall certainly not allow myself to be intimidated by anything which you may say or do.'

"The old fellow looked diabolical, and I really thought he was about to attack me. I have said that he was a gaunt, fierce old giant, and though I am no weakling I might have been hard put to it to hold my own against him. However, after a long glare of rage he turned upon his heel and walked out of the room. For my part, I took the appointed train in the morning, with the full intention of coming straight to you and asking for your advice and assistance at the appointment for which I had already written."

Such was the problem which my visitor laid before me. It presented, as the astute reader will have already perceived, few difficulties in its solution, for a very limited choice of alternatives must get to the root of the matter. Still, elementary as it was, there were points of interest and novelty about it which may excuse my placing it upon record. I now proceeded, using my familiar method of logical analysis, to narrow down the possible solutions.

"The servants," I asked; "how many were in the house?"

"To the best of my belief there were only the old butler and his wife. They seemed to live in the simplest fashion."

" There was no servant, then, in the detached house ? "

" None, unless the little man with the beard acted as such. He seemed, however, to be quite a superior person."

" That seems very suggestive. Had you any indication that food was conveyed from the one house to the other ? "

" Now that you mention it, I did see old Ralph carrying a basket down the garden walk and going in the direction of this house. The idea of food did not occur to me at the moment."

" Did you make any local inquiries ? "

" Yes, I did. I spoke to the station-master and also to the innkeeper in the village. I simply asked if they knew anything of my old comrade, Godfrey Emsworth. Both of them assured me that he had gone for a voyage round the world. He had come home and then had almost at once started off again. The story was evidently universally accepted."

" You said nothing of your suspicions ? "

" Nothing."

" That was very wise. The matter should certainly be inquired into. I will go back with you to Tuxbury Old Park."

" To-day ? "

It happened that at the moment I was clearing up the case which my friend Watson has described as that of the Abbey School, in which the Duke of Greyminster was so deeply involved. I had also a commission from the Sultan of Turkey which called for immediate action, as political consequences of the gravest kind might arise from its neglect. Therefore it was not until the beginning of the next week, as my diary records, that I was able to start forth on my mission to Bedfordshire in company with Mr. James M. Dodd. As we drove to Euston we picked up a grave and taciturn gentleman of iron-grey aspect, with whom I had made the necessary arrangements.

" This is an old friend," said I to Dodd. " It is possible that his presence may be entirely unnecessary, and, on the other hand, it may be essential. It is not necessary at the present stage to go further into the matter."

The narratives of Watson have accustomed the reader, no doubt, to the fact that I do not waste words or disclose my thoughts while a case is actually under consideration. Dodd seemed surprised, but nothing more was said and the three of us continued our journey together. In the train I asked Dodd one more question which I wished our companion to hear.

" You say that you saw your friend's face quite clearly at the window, so clearly that you are sure of his identity ? "

" I have no doubt about it whatever. His nose was pressed against the glass. The lamplight shone full upon him."

" It could not have been someone resembling him ? "

" No, no ; it was he."

" But you say he was changed ? "

" Only in colour. His face was—how shall I describe it ?—it was of a fish-belly whiteness. It was bleached."

" Was it equally pale all over ? "

" I think not. It was his brow which I saw so clearly as it was pressed against the window."

" Did you call to him ? "

" I was too startled and horrified for the moment. Then I pursued him, as I have told you, but without result."

My case was practically complete, and there was only one small incident needed to round it off. When, after a considerable drive, we arrived at the strange old rambling house which my client had described, it was Ralph, the elderly butler, who opened the door. I had requisitioned the carriage for the day and had asked my elderly friend to remain within it unless we should summon him. Ralph, a little wrinkled old fellow, was in the conventional costume of black coat and pepper-

and-salt trousers, with only one curious variant. He wore brown leather gloves, which at sight of us he instantly shuffled off, laying them down on the hall-table as we passed in. I have, as my friend Watson may have remarked, an abnormally acute set of senses, and a faint but incisive scent was apparent. It seemed to centre on the hall-table. I turned, placed my hat there, knocked it off, stooped to pick it up, and contrived to bring my nose within a foot of the gloves. Yes, it was undoubtedly from them that the curious tarry odour was oozing. I passed on into the study with my case complete. Alas, that I should have to show my hand so when I tell my own story! It was by concealing such links in the chain that Watson was enabled to produce his meretricious finales.

Colonel Emsworth was not in his room, but he came quickly enough on receipt of Ralph's message. We heard his quick, heavy step in the passage. The door was flung open and he rushed in with bristling beard and twisted features, as terrible an old man as ever I have seen. He held our cards in his hand, and he tore them up and stamped on the fragments.

"Have I not told you, you infernal busybody, that you are warned off the premises? Never dare to show your damned face here again. If you enter again without my leave I shall be within my rights if I use violence. I'll shoot you, sir! By God, I will! As to you, sir," turning upon me, "I extend the same warning to you. I am familiar with your ignoble profession, but you must take your reputed talents to some other field. There is no opening for them here."

"I cannot leave here," said my client firmly, "until I hear from Godfrey's own lips that he is under no restraint."

Our involuntary host rang the bell.

"Ralph," he said, "telephone down to the county police and ask the inspector to send up two constables. Tell him there are burglars in the house."

"One moment," said I. "You must be aware, Mr. Dodd, that Colonel Emsworth is within his rights and that we have no legal status within his house. On the other hand, he should recognize that your action is prompted entirely by solicitude for his son. I venture to hope that, if I were allowed to have five minutes' conversation with Colonel Emsworth, I could certainly alter his view of the matter."

"I am not so easily altered," said the old soldier. "Ralph, do what I have told you. What the devil are you waiting for? Ring up the police!"

"Nothing of the sort," I said, putting my back to the door. "Any police interference would bring about the very catastrophe which you dread." I took out my notebook and scribbled one word upon a loose sheet. "That," said I, as I handed it to Colonel Emsworth, "is what has brought us here."

He stared at the writing with a face from which every expression save amazement had vanished.

"How do you know?" he gasped, sitting down heavily in his chair.

"It is my business to know things. That is my trade."

He sat in deep thought, his gaunt hand tugging at his straggling beard. Then he made a gesture of resignation.

"Well, if you wish to see Godfrey, you shall. It is no doing of mine, but you have forced my hand. Ralph, tell Mr. Godfrey and Mr. Kent that in five minutes we shall be with them."

At the end of that time we passed down the garden path and found ourselves in front of the mystery house at the end. A small bearded man stood at the door with a look of considerable astonishment upon his face.

"This is very sudden, Colonel Emsworth," said he. "This will disarrange all our plans."

"I can't help it, Mr. Kent. Our hands have been forced. Can Mr. Godfrey see us?"

"Yes; he is waiting inside." He turned and led us into a large, plainly furnished front room. A man was standing with his back to the fire, and at the sight of him my client sprang forward with outstretched hand.

"Why, Godfrey, old man, this is fine!"

But the other waved him back.

"Don't touch me, Jimmie. Keep your distance. Yes, you may well stare! I don't quite look the smart Lance-Corporal Emsworth, of B Squadron, do I?"

His appearance was certainly extraordinary. One could see that he had indeed been a handsome man with clear-cut features sunburned by an African sun, but mottled in patches over this darker surface were curious whitish patches which had bleached his skin.

"That's why I don't court visitors," said he. "I don't mind you, Jimmie, but I could have done without your friend. I suppose there is some good reason for it, but you have me at a disadvantage."

"I wanted to be sure that all was well with you, Godfrey. I saw you that night when you looked into my window, and I could not let the matter rest till I had cleared things up."

"Old Ralph told me you were there, and I couldn't help taking a peep at you. I hoped you would not have seen me, and I had to run to my burrow when I heard the window go up."

"But what in Heaven's name is the matter?"

"Well, it's not a long story to tell," said he, lighting a cigarette. "You remember that morning fight at Buffelsspruit, outside Pretoria, on the Eastern railway line? You heard I was hit?"

"Yes, I heard that, but I never got particulars."

"Three of us got separated from the others. It was very broken country, you may remember. There was Simpson—the fellow we called Baldy Simpson—and Anderson, and I. We were clearing brother Boer, but he lay low and got the three of us. The other two were killed. I got an elephant bullet through my shoulder. I stuck on to my horse, however, and he galloped several miles before I fainted and rolled off the saddle.

" When I came to myself it was nightfall, and I raised myself up, feeling very weak and ill. To my surprise there was a house close beside me, a fairly large house with a broad stoep and many windows. It was deadly cold. You remember the kind of numb cold which used to come at evening, a deadly, sickening sort of cold, very different from a crisp healthy frost. Well, I was chilled to the bone, and my only hope seemed to lie in reaching that house. I staggered to my feet and dragged myself along, hardly conscious of what I did. I have a dim memory of slowly ascending the steps, entering a wide-opened door, passing into a large room which contained several beds, and throwing myself down with a gasp of satisfaction upon one of them. It was unmade, but that troubled me not at all. I drew the clothes over my shivering body and in a moment I was in a deep sleep.

" It was morning when I wakened, and it seemed to me that instead of coming out into a world of sanity I had emerged into some extraordinary nightmare. The African sun flooded through the big, curtainless windows, and every detail of the great, bare, white-washed dormitory stood out hard and clear. In front of me was standing a small, dwarf-like man with a huge bulbous head, who was jabbering excitedly in Dutch, waving two horrible hands which looked to me like brown sponges. Behind him stood a group of people who seemed to be intensely amused by the situation, but a chill came over me as I looked at them. Not one of them was a normal human being. Every one was twisted or swollen or disfigured in some strange way. The laughter of these strange monstrosities was a dreadful thing to hear.

" It seemed that none of them could speak English,

but the situation wanted clearing up, for the creature with the big head was growing furiously angry and, uttering wild-beast cries, he had laid his deformed hands upon me and was dragging me out of bed, regardless of the fresh flow of blood from my wound. The little monster was as strong as a bull, and I don't know what he might have done to me had not an elderly man who was clearly in authority been attracted to the room by the hubbub. He said a few stern words in Dutch, and my persecutor shrank away. Then he turned upon me, gazing at me in the utmost amazement.

" ' How in the world did you come here ? ' he asked, in amazement. ' Wait a bit ! I see that you are tired out and that wounded shoulder of yours wants looking after. I am a doctor, and I'll soon have you tied up. But, man alive ! you are in far greater danger here than ever you were on the battlefield. You are in the Leper Hospital, and you have slept in a leper's bed.'

" Need I tell you more, Jimmie ? It seems that in view of the approaching battle all these poor creatures had been evacuated the day before. Then, as the British advanced, they had been brought back by this, their medical superintendent, who assured me that, though he believed he was immune to the disease, he would none the less never have dared to do what I had done. He put me in a private room, treated me kindly, and within a week or so I was removed to the general hospital at Pretoria.

" So there you have my tragedy. I hoped against hope, but it was not until I had reached home that the terrible signs which you see upon my face told me that I had not escaped. What was I to do ? I was in this lonely house. We had two servants whom we could utterly trust. There was a house where I could live. Under pledge of secrecy, Mr. Kent, who is a surgeon, was prepared to stay with me. It seemed simple enough on those lines. The alternative was a dreadful one—segregation for life among strangers with never a hope of release. But absolute secrecy was necessary, or even in this quiet country-side there would have been an outcry, and I should have been dragged to my horrible doom. Even you, Jimmie—even you had to be kept in the dark. Why my father has relented I cannot imagine."

Colonel Emsworth pointed to me.

"This is the gentleman who forced my hand." He unfolded the scrap of paper on which I had written the word "Leprosy." "It seemed to me that if he knew so much as that it was safer that he should know all."

"And so it was," said I. "Who knows but good may come of it? I understand that only Mr. Kent has seen the patient. May I ask, sir, if you are an authority on such complaints, which are, I understand, tropical or semi-tropical in their nature?"

"I have the ordinary knowledge of the educated medical man," he observed, with some stiffness.

"I have no doubt, sir, that you are fully competent, but I am sure that you will agree that in such a case a second opinion is valuable. You have avoided this, I understand, for fear that pressure should be put upon you to segregate the patient."

"That is so," said Colonel Emsworth.

"I foresaw this situation," I explained, "and I have brought with me a friend whose discretion may absolutely be trusted. I was able once to do him a professional service, and he is ready to advise as a friend rather than as a specialist. His name is Sir James Saunders."

The prospect of an interview with Lord Roberts would not have excited greater wonder and pleasure in a raw subaltern than was now reflected upon the face of Mr. Kent.

"I shall indeed be proud," he murmured.

"Then I will ask Sir James to step this way. He is at present in the carriage outside the door. Meanwhile, Colonel Emsworth, we may perhaps assemble in your study, where I could give the necessary explanations."

And here it is that I miss my Watson. By cunning questions and ejaculations of wonder he could elevate my simple art, which is but systematized common sense, into a prodigy. When I tell my own story I have no such aid. And yet I will give my process of thought even as I gave it to my small audience, which included Godfrey's mother, in the study of Colonel Emsworth.

"That process," said I, "starts upon the supposition that when you have eliminated all which is impossible, then whatever remains, however improbable, must be the truth. It may well be that several explanations remain, in which case one tries test after test until one or other of them has a convincing amount of support. We will now apply this principle to the case in point. As it was first presented to me, there were three possible explanations of the seclusion or incarceration of this gentleman in an outhouse of his father's mansion. There was the explanation that he was in hiding for a crime, or that he was mad and that they wished to avoid an asylum, or that he had some disease which caused his segregation. I could think of no other adequate solutions. These, then, had to be sifted and balanced against each other.

"The criminal solution would not bear inspection. No unsolved crime had been reported from that district. I was sure of that. If it were some crime not yet discovered, then clearly it would be to the interest of the family to get rid of the delinquent and send him abroad rather than keep him concealed at home. I could see no explanation for such a line of conduct.

"Insanity was more plausible. The presence of the second person in the outhouse suggested a keeper. The fact that he locked the door when he came out strengthened the supposition and gave the idea of constraint. On the other hand, this constraint could not be severe or the young man could not have got loose and come down to have a look at his friend. You will remember, Mr. Dodd, that I felt round for points, asking you, for example, about the paper which Mr. Kent was reading. Had it been the *Lancet* or the *British Medical Journal* it would have helped me. It is not illegal, however, to keep a lunatic upon private premises so long as there is a qualified person in attendance and that the authorities have been duly notified. Why, then, all this desperate desire for secrecy? Once again I could not get the theory to fit the facts.

"There remained the third possibility, into which, rare and unlikely as it was, everything seemed to fit. Leprosy is not uncommon in South Africa. By some extraordinary chance this youth might have contracted it. His people would be placed in a very dreadful position, since they would desire to save him from segregation. Great secrecy would be needed to prevent rumours from getting about and subsequent interference by the authorities. A devoted medical man, if sufficiently paid, would easily be found to take charge of the sufferer. There would be no reason why the latter should not be allowed freedom after dark. Bleaching of the skin is a common result of the disease. The case was a strong one—so strong that I determined to act as if it were actually proved. When on arriving here I noticed that Ralph, who carries out the meals, had gloves which are impregnated with disinfectants, my last doubts were removed. A single word showed you, sir, that your secret was discovered, and if I wrote rather than said it, it was to prove to you that my discretion was to be trusted."

I was finishing this little analysis of the case when the door was opened and the austere figure of the great dermatologist was ushered in. But for once his sphinx-like features had relaxed and there was a warm humanity in his eyes. He strode up to Colonel Emsworth and shook him by the hand.

"It is often my lot to bring ill-tidings, and seldom

good," said he. " This occasion is the more welcome. It is not leprosy."

" What ? "

" A well-marked case of pseudo-leprosy or ichthyosis, a scale-like affection of the skin, unsightly, obstinate, but possibly curable, and certainly non-infective. Yes, Mr. Holmes, the coincidence is a remarkable one. But is it coincidence ? Are there not subtle forces at work of which we know little ? Are we assured that the apprehension, from which this young man has no doubt suffered terribly since his exposure to its contagion, may not produce a physical effect which simulates that which it fears ? At any rate, I pledge my professional reputation—— But the lady has fainted ! I think that Mr. Kent had better be with her until she recovers from this joyous shock."

47. *The Mazarin Stone*

IT was pleasant to Dr. Watson to find himself once more in the untidy room of the first floor in Baker Street which had been the starting-point of so many remarkable adventures. He looked round him at the scientific charts upon the wall, the acid-charred bench of chemicals, the violin-case leaning in the corner, the coal-scuttle, which contained of old the pipes and tobacco. Finally, his eyes came round to the fresh and smiling face of Billy, the young but very wise and tactful page, who had helped a little to fill up the gap of loneliness and isolation which surrounded the saturnine figure of the great detective.

" It all seems very unchanged, Billy. You don't change, either. I hope the same can be said of him ? "

Billy glanced, with some solicitude, at the closed door of the bedroom.

" I think he's in bed and asleep," he said.

It was seven in the evening of a lovely summer's day, but Dr. Watson was sufficiently familiar with the irregularity of his old friend's hours to feel no surprise at the idea.

" That means a case, I suppose ? "

" Yes, sir ; he is very hard at it just now. I'm frightened for his health. He gets paler and thinner, and he eats nothing. ' When will you be pleased to dine, Mr. Holmes ? ' Mrs. Hudson asked. ' Seven-thirty, the day after to-morrow,' said he. You know his way when he is keen on a case."

" Yes, Billy, I know."

" He's following someone. Yesterday he was out as a workman looking for a job. To-day he was an old woman. Fairly took me in, he did, and I ought to know his ways by now." Billy pointed with a grin to a very baggy parasol which leaned against the sofa. " That's part of the old woman's outfit," he said.

" But what is it all about, Billy ? "

Billy sank his voice, as one who discusses great secrets of State. " I don't mind telling you, sir, but it should go no farther. It's this case of the Crown diamond."

" What—the hundred-thousand-pound burglary ? "

" Yes, sir. They must get it back, sir. Why, we had the Prime Minister and the Home Secretary both sitting on that very sofa. Mr. Holmes was very nice to them. He soon put them at their ease and promised he would do all he could. Then there is Lord Cantlemere——"

" Ah ! "

" Yes, sir ; you know what that means. He's a stiff 'un, sir, if I may say so. I can get along with the Prime Minister, and I've nothing against the Home Secretary, who seemed a civil, obliging sort of man, but I can't stand his lordship. Neither can Mr. Holmes, sir. You see, he don't believe in Mr. Holmes and he was against employing him. He'd *rather* he failed."

" And Mr. Holmes knows it ? "

" Mr. Holmes always knows whatever there is to know."

" Well, we'll hope he won't fail and that Lord Cantlemere will be confounded. But I say, Billy, what is that curtain for across the window ? "

" Mr. Holmes had it put up there three days ago. We've got something funny behind it."

Billy advanced and drew away the drapery which screened the alcove of the bow window.

Dr. Watson could not restrain a cry of amazement. There was a facsimile of his old friend, dressing-gown and all, the face turned three-quarters towards the window and downwards, as though reading an invisible book, while the body was sunk deep in an arm-chair. Billy detached the head and held it in the air.

" We put it at different angles, so that it may seem more life-like. I wouldn't dare touch it if the blind were not down. But when it's up you can see this from across the way."

" We used something of the sort once before."

" Before my time," said Billy. He drew the window curtains apart and looked out into the street. " There are folk who watch us from over yonder. I can see a fellow now at the window. Have a look for yourself."

Watson had taken a step forward when the bed-room door opened, and the long, thin form of Holmes emerged, his face pale and drawn, but his step and bear-ing as active as ever. With a single spring he was at the window, and had drawn the blind once more.

" That will do, Billy," said he. " You were in danger of your life then, my boy, and I can't do without you just yet. Well, Watson, it is good to see you in your old quarters once again. You come at a critical moment."

" So I gather."

" You can go, Billy. That boy is a problem, Watson. How far am I justified in allowing him to be in danger ? "

" Danger of what, Holmes ? "

" Of sudden death. I'm expecting something this evening."

" Expecting what ? "

" To be murdered, Watson."

" No, no ; you are joking, Holmes ! "

" Even my limited sense of humour could evolve a better joke than that. But we may be comfortable in the meantime, may we not ? Is alcohol permitted ? The gasogene and cigars are in the old place. Let me see you once more in the customary arm-chair. You have not, I hope, learned to despise my pipe and my lamentable tobacco ? It has to take the place of food these days."

" But why not eat ? "

" Because the faculties become refined when you starve them. Why, surely, as a doctor, my dear Watson, you must admit that what your digestion gains in the way of blood supply is so much lost to the brain. I am a brain, Watson. The rest of me is a mere appendix. Therefore, it is the brain I must consider."

" But this danger, Holmes ? "

" Ah, yes ; in case it should come off, it would perhaps be as well that you should burden your memory with the name and address of the murderer. You can give it to Scotland Yard, with my love and a parting blessing. Sylvius is the name—Count Negretto Sylvius. Write it down, man, write it down ! 136 Moorside Gardens, N.W. Got it ? "

Watson's honest face was twitching with anxiety. He knew only too well the immense risks taken by Holmes, and was well aware that what he said was more likely to be under-statement than exaggeration. Watson was always the man of action, and he rose to the occasion.

" Count me in, Holmes. I have nothing to do for a day or two."

" Your morals don't improve, Watson. You have added fibbing to your other vices. You bear every sign of the busy medical man, with calls on him every hour."

" Not such important ones. But can't you have this fellow arrested ? "

"Yes, Watson, I could. That's what worries him so."

"But why don't you?"

"Because I don't know where the diamond is."

"Ah! Billy told me—the missing Crown jewel!"

"Yes, the great yellow Mazarin stone. I've cast my net and I have my fish. But I have not got the stone. What is the use of taking *them*? We can make the world a better place by laying them by the heels. But that is not what I am out for. It's the stone I want."

"And is this Count Sylvius one of your fish?"

"Yes, and he's a shark. He bites. The other is Sam Merton, the boxer. Not a bad fellow, Sam, but the Count has used him. Sam's not a shark. He is a great big silly bull-headed gudgeon. But he is flopping about in my net all the same."

"Where is this Count Sylvius?"

"I've been at his very elbow all the morning. You've seen me as an old lady, Watson. I was never more convincing. He actually picked up my parasol for me once. 'By your leave, madame,' said he—half-Italian, you know, and with the Southern graces of manner when in the mood, but a devil incarnate in the other mood. Life is full of whimsical happenings, Watson."

"It might have been tragedy."

"Well, perhaps it might. I followed him to old Straubenzee's workshop in the Minories. Straubenzee made the air-gun—a very pretty bit of work, as I understand, and I rather fancy it is in the opposite window at the present moment. Have you seen the dummy? Of course, Billy showed it to you. Well, it may get a bullet through its beautiful head at any moment. Ah, Billy, what is it?"

The boy had reappeared in the room with a card upon a tray. Holmes glanced at it with raised eyebrows and an amused smile.

"The man himself. I had hardly expected this.

Grasp the nettle, Watson! A man of nerve. Possibly you have heard of his reputation as a shooter of big game. It would indeed be a triumphant ending to his excellent sporting record if he added me to his bag. This is a proof that he feels my toe very close behind his heel."

"Send for the police."

"I probably shall. But not just yet. Would you glance carefully out of the window, Watson, and see if anyone is hanging about in the street?"

Watson looked warily round the edge of the curtain.

"Yes, there is one rough fellow near the door."

"That will be Sam Merton—the faithful but rather fatuous Sam. Where is this gentleman, Billy?"

"In the waiting-room, sir."

"Show him up when I ring."

"Yes, sir."

"If I am not in the room, show him in all the same."

"Yes, sir."

Watson waited until the door was closed, and then he turned earnestly to his companion.

"Look here, Holmes, this is simply impossible. This is a desperate man, who sticks at nothing. He may have come to murder you."

"I should not be surprised."

"I insist upon staying with you."

"You would be horribly in the way."

"In *his* way?"

"No, my dear fellow—in my way."

"Well, I can't possibly leave you."

"Yes, you can, Watson. And you will, for you have never failed to play the game. I am sure you will play it to the end. This man has come for his own purpose, but he may stay for mine." Holmes took out his notebook and scribbled a few lines. "Take a cab to Scotland Yard and give this to Youghal of the C.I.D. Come back with the police. The fellow's arrest will follow."

"I'll do that with joy."

"Before you return I may have just time enough to find out where the stone is." He touched the bell. "I think we will go out through the bedroom. This second exit is exceedingly useful. I rather want to see my shark without his seeing me, and I have, as you will remember, my own way of doing it."

It was, therefore, an empty room into which Billy, a minute later, ushered Count Sylvius. The famous game-shot, sportsman, and man-about-town was a big, swarthy fellow, with a formidable dark moustache, shading a cruel, thin-lipped mouth, and surmounted by a long, curved nose, like the beak of an eagle. He was well dressed, but his brilliant necktie, shining pin, and glittering rings were flamboyant in their effect. As the door closed behind him he looked round him with fierce, startled eyes, like one who suspects a trap at every turn. Then he gave a violent start as he saw the impassive head and the collar of the dressing-gown which projected above the arm-chair in the window. At first his expression was one of pure amazement. Then the light of a horrible hope gleamed in his dark, murderous eyes. He took one more glance round to see that there were no witnesses, and then, on tiptoe, his thick stick half raised, he approached the silent figure. He was crouching for his final spring and blow when a cool, sardonic voice greeted him from the open bedroom door:

"Don't break it, Count! Don't break it!"

The assassin staggered back, amazement in his convulsed face. For an instant he half raised his loaded cane once more, as if he would turn his violence from the effigy to the original; but there was something in that steady grey eye and mocking smile which caused his hand to sink to his side.

"It's a pretty little thing," said Holmes, advancing towards the image. "Tavernier, the French modeller, made it. He is as good at wax-works as your friend Straubenzee is at air-guns."

"Air-guns, sir! What do you mean?"

" Put your hat and stick on the side-table. Thank you ! Pray take a seat. Would you care to put your revolver out also ? Oh, very good, if you prefer to sit upon it. Your visit is really most opportune, for I wanted badly to have a few minutes' chat with you."

The Count scowled, with heavy, threatening eyebrows.

" I, too, wished to have some words with you, Holmes. That is why I am here. I won't deny that I intended to assault you just now."

Holmes swung his leg on the edge of the table.

" I rather gathered that you had some idea of the sort in your head," said he. " But why these personal attentions ? "

" Because you have gone out of your way to annoy me. Because you have put your creatures upon my track."

" My creatures ! I assure you no ! "

" Nonsense ! I have had them followed. Two can play at that game, Holmes."

" It is a small point, Count Sylvius, but perhaps you would kindly give me my prefix when you address me. You can understand that, with my routine of work, I should find myself on familiar terms with half the rogues' gallery, and you will agree that exceptions are invidious."

" Well, *Mr*. Holmes, then."

" Excellent ! But I assure you you are mistaken about my alleged agents."

Count Sylvius laughed contemptuously.

" Other people can observe as well as you. Yesterday there was an old sporting man. To-day it was an elderly woman. They held me in view all day."

" Really, sir, you compliment me. Old Baron Dowson said the night before he was hanged that in my case what the law had gained the stage had lost. And now you give my little impersonations your kindly praise ! "

" It was you—you yourself ? "

Holmes shrugged his shoulders. "You can see in the corner the parasol which you so politely handed to me in the Minories before you began to suspect."

"If I had known, you might never——"

"Have seen this humble home again. I was well aware of it. We all have neglected opportunities to deplore. As it happens, you did not know, so here we are!"

The Count's knotted brows gathered more heavily over his menacing eyes. "What you say only makes the matter worse. It was not your agents, but your play-acting, busybody self! You admit that you have dogged me. Why?"

"Come now, Count. You used to shoot lions in Algeria."

"Well?"

"But why?"

"Why? The sport—the excitement—the danger!"

"And, no doubt, to free the country from a pest?"

"Exactly!"

"My reasons in a nutshell!"

The Count sprang to his feet, and his hand involuntarily moved back to his hip-pocket.

"Sit down, sir, sit down! There was another, more practical, reason. I want that yellow diamond!"

Count Sylvius lay back in his chair with an evil smile.

"Upon my word!" said he.

"You knew that I was after you for that. The real reason why you are here to-night is to find out how much I know about the matter and how far my removal is absolutely essential. Well, I should say that, from your point of view, it *is* absolutely essential, for I know all about it, save only one thing, which you are about to tell me."

"Oh, indeed! And, pray, what is this missing fact?"

"Where the Crown diamond now is."

The Count looked sharply at his companion. "Oh,

you want to know that, do you ? How the devil should I be able to tell you where it is ? "

" You can, and you will."

" Indeed ! "

" You can't bluff me, Count Sylvius." Holmes' eyes, as he gazed at him, contracted and lightened until they were like two menacing points of steel. " You are absolute plate-glass. I see to the very back of your mind."

" Then, of course, you see where the diamond is ! "

Holmes clapped his hands with amusement, and then pointed a derisive finger. " Then you do know. You have admitted it ! "

" I admit nothing."

" Now, Count, if you will be reasonable we can do business. If not, you will get hurt."

Count Sylvius threw up his eyes to the ceiling. " And you talk about bluff ! " said he.

Holmes looked at him thoughtfully, like a master chess-player who meditates his crowning move. Then he threw open the table drawer and drew out a squat notebook.

" Do you know what I keep in this book ? "

" No, sir, I do not ! "

" You ! "

" Me ? "

" Yes, sir, *you* ! You are all here—every action of your vile and dangerous life."

" Damn you, Holmes ! " cried the Count, with blazing eyes. " There are limits to my patience ! "

" It's all here, Count. The real facts as to the death of old Mrs. Harold, who left you the Blymer estate, which you so rapidly gambled away."

" You are dreaming ! "

" And the complete life history of Miss Minnie War-render."

" Tut ! You will make nothing of that ! "

" Plenty more here, Count. Here is the robbery

in the train-de-luxe to the Riviera on February 13, 1892. Here is the forged cheque in the same year on the Crédit Lyonnais."

" No ; you're wrong there."

" Then I am right on the others ! Now, Count, you are a card-player. When the other fellow has all the trumps, it saves time to throw down your hand."

" What has all this talk to do with the jewel of which you spoke ? "

" Gently, Count. Restrain that eager mind ! Let me get to the points in my own humdrum fashion. I have all this against you ; but, above all, I have a clear case against both you and your fighting bully in the case of the Crown diamond."

" Indeed ! "

" I have the cabman who took you to Whitehall and the cabman who brought you away. I have the Commissionaire who saw you near the case. I have Ikey Sanders, who refused to cut it up for you. Ikey has peached, and the game is up."

The veins stood out on the Count's forehead. His dark, hairy hands were clenched in a convulsion of restrained emotion. He tried to speak, but the words would not shape themselves.

" That's the hand I play from," said Holmes. " I put it all upon the table. But one card is missing. It's the King of Diamonds. I don't know where the stone is."

" You never shall know."

" No ? Now, be reasonable, Count. Consider the situation. You are going to be locked up for twenty years. So is Sam Merton. What good are you going to get out of your diamond ? None in the world. But if you hand it over—well, I'll compound a felony. We don't want you or Sam. We want the stone. Give that up, and so far as I am concerned you can go free so long as you behave yourself in the future. If you make another slip—well, it will be the last. But this time my commission is to get the stone, not you."

" But if I refuse ? "

" Why, then—alas !—it must be you and not the stone."

Billy had appeared in answer to a ring.

" I think, Count, that it would be as well to have your friend Sam at this conference. After all, his interests should be represented. Billy, you will see a large and ugly gentleman outside the front door. Ask him to come up."

" If he won't come, sir ? "

" No violence, Billy. Don't be rough with him. If you tell him that Count Sylvius wants him he will certainly come."

" What are you going to do now ? " asked the Count, as Billy disappeared.

" My friend Watson was with me just now. I told him that I had a shark and a gudgeon in my net ; now I am drawing the net and up they come together."

The Count had risen from his chair, and his hand was behind his back. Holmes held something half protruding from the pocket of his dressing-gown.

" You won't die in your bed, Holmes."

" I have often had the same idea. Does it matter very much ? After all, Count, your own exit is more likely to be perpendicular than horizontal. But these anticipations of the future are morbid. Why not give ourselves up to the unrestrained enjoyment of the present?"

A sudden wild-beast light sprang up in the dark, menacing eyes of the master criminal. Holmes' figure seemed to grow taller as he grew tense and ready.

" It is no use your fingering your revolver, my friend," he said, in a quiet voice. " You know perfectly well that you dare not use it, even if I gave you time to draw it. Nasty, noisy things, revolvers, Count. Better stick to air-guns. Ah ! I think I hear the fairy footstep of your estimable partner. Good day, Mr. Merton. Rather dull in the street, is it not ? "

The prize-fighter, a heavily built young man with

a stupid, obstinate, slab-sided face, stood awkwardly at the door, looking about him with a puzzled expression. Holmes' debonair manner was a new experience, and though he vaguely felt that it was hostile, he did not know how to counter it. He turned to his more astute comrade for help.

"What's the game now, Count? What's this fellow want? What's up?" His voice was deep and raucous.

The Count shrugged his shoulders and it was Holmes who answered.

"If I may put it in a nutshell, Mr. Merton, I should say it was *all* up."

The boxer still addressed his remarks to his associate.

"Is this cove trying to be funny, or what? I'm not in the funny mood myself."

"No, I expect not," said Holmes. "I think I can promise you that you will feel even less humorous as the evening advances. Now, look here, Count Sylvius. I'm a busy man and I can't waste time. I'm going into that bedroom. Pray make yourselves quite at home in my absence. You can explain to your friend how the matter lies without the restraint of my presence. I shall try over the Hoffmann Barcarolle upon my violin. In five minutes I shall return for your final answer. You quite grasp the alternative, do you not? Shall we take you, or shall we have the stone?"

Holmes withdrew, picking up his violin from the corner as he passed. A few moments later the long-drawn, wailing notes of that most haunting of tunes came faintly through the closed door of the bedroom.

"What is it, then?" asked Merton anxiously, as his companion turned to him. "Does he know about the stone?"

"He knows a damned sight too much about it. I'm not sure that he doesn't know all about it."

"Good Lord!" The boxer's sallow face turned a shade whiter.

"Ikey Sanders has split on us."

" He has, has he ? I'll do him down a thick 'un for that if I swing for it."

" That won't help us much. We've got to make up our minds what to do."

" Half a mo'," said the boxer, looking suspiciously at the bedroom door. " He's a leary cove that wants watching. I suppose he's not listening ? "

" How can he be listening with that music going ? "

" That's right. Maybe somebody's behind a curtain. Too many curtains in this room." As he looked round he suddenly saw for the first time the effigy in the window, and stood staring and pointing, too amazed for words.

" Tut ! it's only a dummy," said the Count.

" A fake, is it ? Well, strike me ! Madame Tussaud ain't in it. It's the living spit of him, gown and all. But them curtains, Count ! "

" Oh, confound the curtains ! We are wasting our time, and there is none too much. He can lag us over this stone."

" The deuce he can ! "

" But he'll let us slip if we only tell him where the swag is."

" What ! Give it up ? Give up a hundred thousand quid ? "

" It's one or the other."

Merton scratched his short-cropped pate.

" He's alone in there. Let's do him in. If his light were out we should have nothing to fear."

The Count shook his head.

" He is armed and ready. If we shot him we could hardly get away in a place like this. Besides, it's likely enough that the police know whatever evidence he has got. Hallo ! What was that ? "

There was a vague sound which seemed to come from the window. Both men sprang round, but all was quiet. Save for the one strange figure seated in the chair, the room was certainly empty.

"Something in the street," said Merton. " Now look here, guv'nor, you've got the brains. Surely you can think a way out of it. If slugging is no use then it's up to you."

" I've fooled better men than he," the Count answered. " The stone is here in my secret pocket. I take no chances leaving it about. It can be out of England to-night and cut into four pieces in Amsterdam before Sunday. He knows nothing of Van Seddar."

" I thought Van Seddar was going next week."

" He *was*. But now he must get off by the next boat. One or other of us must slip round with the stone to Lime Street and tell him."

" But the false bottom ain't ready."

" Well, he must take it as it is and chance it. There's not a moment to lose." Again, with the sense of danger which becomes an instinct with the sportsman, he paused and looked hard at the window. Yes, it was surely from the street that the faint sound had come.

" As to Holmes," he continued, " we can fool him easily enough. You see, the damned fool won't arrest us if he can get the stone. Well, we'll promise him the stone. We'll put him on the wrong track about it, and before he finds that it *is* the wrong track it will be in Holland and we out of the country."

" That sounds good to me ! " cried Sam Merton, with a grin.

" You go on and tell the Dutchman to get a move on him. I'll see this sucker and fill him up with a bogus confession. I'll tell him that the stone is in Liverpool. Confound that whining music ; it gets on my nerves ! By the time he finds it isn't in Liverpool it will be in quarters and we on the blue water. Come back here, out of a line with that keyhole. Here is the stone."

" I wonder you dare carry it."

" Where could I have it safer ? If we could take it out of Whitehall someone else could surely take it out of my lodgings."

" Let's have a look at it."

Count Sylvius cast a somewhat unflattering glance at his associate, and disregarded the unwashed hand which was extended towards him.

" What—d'ye think I'm going to snatch it off you ? See here, mister, I'm getting a bit tired of your ways."

" Well, well ; no offence, Sam. We can't afford to quarrel. Come over to the window if you want to see the beauty properly. Now hold it to the light ! Here ! "

" Thank you ! "

With a single spring Holmes had leaped from the dummy's chair and had grasped the precious jewel. He held it now in one hand, while his other pointed a revolver at the Count's head. The two villains staggered back in utter amazement. Before they had recovered Holmes had pressed the electric bell.

" No violence, gentlemen—no violence, I beg of you ! Consider the furniture ! It must be very clear to you that your position is an impossible one. The police are waiting below."

The Count's bewilderment overmastered his rage and fear.

" But how the deuce—— ? " he gasped.

" Your surprise is very natural. You are not aware that a second door from my bedroom leads behind that curtain. I fancied that you must have heard me when I displaced the figure, but luck was on my side. It gave me a chance of listening to your racy conversation which would have been painfully constrained had you been aware of my presence."

The Count gave a gesture of resignation.

" We give you best, Holmes. I believe you are the devil himself."

" Not far from him, at any rate," Holmes answered, with a polite smile.

Sam Merton's slow intellect had only gradually appreciated the situation. Now, as the sound of heavy steps came from the stairs outside, he broke silence at last.

"A fair cop!" said he. "But, I say, what about that bloomin' fiddle! I hear it yet."

"Tut, tut!" Holmes answered. "You are perfectly right. Let it play! These modern gramophones are a remarkable invention."

There was an inrush of police, the handcuffs clicked and the criminals were led to the waiting cab. Watson lingered with Holmes, congratulating him upon this fresh leaf added to his laurels. Once more their conversation was interrupted by the imperturbable Billy with his card-tray.

"Lord Cantlemere, sir."

"Show him up, Billy. This is the eminent peer who represents the very highest interests," said Holmes. "He is an excellent and loyal person, but rather of the old regime. Shall we make him unbend? Dare we venture upon a slight liberty? He knows, we may conjecture, nothing of what has occurred."

The door opened to admit a thin, austere figure with a hatchet face and drooping mid-Victorian whiskers of a glossy blackness which hardly corresponded with the rounded shoulders and feeble gait. Holmes advanced affably, and shook an unresponsive hand.

"How-do-you-do, Lord Cantlemere? It is chilly, for the time of year, but rather warm indoors. May I take your overcoat?"

"No, I thank you; I will not take it off."

Holmes laid his hand insistently upon the sleeve.

"Pray allow me! My friend Dr. Watson would assure you that these changes of temperature are most insidious."

His lordship shook himself free with some impatience.

"I am quite comfortable, sir. I have no need to stay. I have simply looked in to know how your self-appointed task was progressing."

"It is difficult—very difficult."

" I feared that you would find it so."

There was a distinct sneer in the old courtier's words and manner.

" Every man finds his limitations, Mr. Holmes, but at least it cures us of the weakness of self-satisfaction."

" Yes, sir, I have been much perplexed."

" No doubt."

" Especially upon one point. Possibly you could help me upon it ? "

" You apply for my advice rather late in the day. I thought that you had your own all-sufficient methods. Still, I am ready to help you."

" You see, Lord Cantlemere, we can no doubt frame a case against the actual thieves."

" When you have caught them."

" Exactly. But the question is—how shall we proceed against the receiver ? "

" Is this not rather premature ? "

" It is as well to have our plans ready. Now, what would you regard as final evidence against the receiver ? "

" The actual possession of the stone."

" You would arrest him upon that ? "

" Most undoubtedly."

Holmes seldom laughed, but he got as near it as his old friend Watson could remember.

" In that case, my dear sir, I shall be under the painful necessity of advising your arrest."

Lord Cantlemere was very angry. Some of the ancient fires flickered up into his sallow cheeks.

" You take a great liberty, Mr. Holmes. In fifty years of official life I cannot recall such a case. I am a busy man, sir, engaged upon important affairs, and I have no time or taste for foolish jokes. I may tell you frankly, sir, that I have never been a believer in your powers, and that I have always been of the opinion that the matter was far safer in the hands of the regular police force. Your conduct confirms all my conclusions. I have the honour, sir, to wish you good evening."

Holmes had swiftly changed his position and was between the peer and the door.

"One moment, sir," said he. "To actually go off with the Mazarin stone would be a more serious offence than to be found in temporary possession of it."

"Sir, this is intolerable ! Let me pass."

"Put your hand in the right-hand pocket of your overcoat."

"What do you mean, sir ? "

"Come—come ; do what I ask."

An instant later the amazed peer was standing, blinking and stammering, with the great yellow stone on his shaking palm.

"What ! What ! How is this, Mr. Holmes ? "

"Too bad, Lord Cantlemere, too bad ! " cried Holmes. "My old friend here will tell you that I have an impish habit of practical joking. Also that I can never resist a dramatic situation. I took the liberty—the very great liberty, I admit—of putting the stone into your pocket at the beginning of our interview."

The old peer stared from the stone to the smiling face before him.

"Sir, I am bewildered. But—yes—it is indeed the Mazarin stone. We are greatly your debtors, Mr. Holmes. Your sense of humour may, as you admit, be somewhat perverted, and its exhibition remarkably untimely, but at least I withdraw any reflection I have made upon your amazing professional powers. But how——"

"The case is but half finished ; the details can wait. No doubt, Lord Cantlemere, your pleasure in telling of this successful result in the exalted circle to which you return will be some small atonement for my practical joke. Billy, you will show his lordship out, and tell Mrs. Hudson that I should be glad if she would send up dinner for two as soon as possible."

48. *The Three Gables*

I DON'T think that any of my adventures with Mr. Sherlock Holmes opened quite so abruptly, or so dramatically, as that which I associate with The Three Gables. I had not seen Holmes for some days, and had no idea of the new channel into which his activities had been directed. He was in a chatty mood that morning, however, and had just settled me into the well-worn low arm-chair on one side of the fire, while he had curled down with his pipe in his mouth upon the opposite chair, when our visitor arrived. If I had said that a mad bull had arrived, it would give a clearer impression of what occurred.

The door had flown open and a huge negro had burst into the room. He would have been a comic figure if he had not been terrific, for he was dressed in a very loud grey check suit with a flowing salmon-coloured tie. His broad face and flattened nose were thrust forward, as his sullen dark eyes, with a smouldering gleam of malice in them, turned from one of us to the other.

"Which of you genelmen is Masser Holmes?" he asked.

Holmes raised his pipe with a languid smile.

"Oh! it's you, is it?" said our visitor, coming with an unpleasant, stealthy step round the angle of the table. "See here, Masser Holmes, you keep your hands out of other folks' business. Leave folks to manage their own affairs. Got that, Masser Holmes?"

"Keep on talking," said Holmes. "It's fine."

"Oh! it's fine, is it?" growled the savage. "It won't be so damn fine if I have to trim you up a bit. I've handled your kind before now, and they didn't look fine when I was through with them. Look at that, Masser Holmes!"

He swung a huge knotted lump of a fist under my friend's nose. Holmes examined it closely with an air

1159

of great interest. "Were you born so?" he asked. "Or did it come by degrees?"

It may have been the icy coolness of my friend, or it may have been the slight clatter which I made as I picked up the poker. In any case, our visitor's manner became less flamboyant.

"Well, I've given you fair warnin'," said he. "I've a friend that's interested out Harrow way—you know what I'm meaning—and he don't intend to have no buttin' in by you. Got that? You ain't the law, and I ain't the law either, and if you come in I'll be on hand also. Don't you forget it."

"I've wanted to meet you for some time," said Holmes. "I won't ask you to sit down, for I don't like the smell of you, but aren't you Steve Dixie, the bruiser?"

"That's my name, Masser Holmes, and you'll get put through it for sure if you give me any lip."

"It is certainly the last thing you need," said Holmes, staring at our visitor's hideous mouth. "But it was the killing of young Perkins outside the Holborn Bar—— What! you're not going?"

The negro had sprung back, and his face was leaden. "I won't listen to no such talk," said he. "What have I to do with this 'ere Perkins, Masser Holmes? I was trainin' at the Bull Ring in Birmingham when this boy done gone get into trouble."

"Yes, you'll tell the magistrate about it, Steve," said Holmes. "I've been watching you and Barney Stockdale——"

"So help me the Lord! Masser Holmes——"

"That's enough. Get out of it. I'll pick you up when I want you."

"Good mornin', Masser Holmes. I hope there ain't no hard feelin's about this 'ere visit?"

"There will be unless you tell me who sent you."

"Why, there ain't no secret about that, Masser Holmes. It was that same genelman that you have just done gone mention."

" And who set him on to it ? "

" S'elp me. I don't know, Masser Holmes. He just say, ' Steve, you go see Mr. Holmes, and tell him his life ain't safe if he go down Harrow way.' That's the whole truth."

Without waiting for any further questioning, our visitor bolted out of the room almost as precipitately as he had entered. Holmes knocked out the ashes of his pipe with a quiet chuckle.

" I am glad you were not forced to break his woolly head, Watson. I observed your manœuvres with the poker. But he is really rather a harmless fellow, a great muscular, foolish, blustering baby, and easily cowed, as you have seen. He is one of the Spencer John gang and has taken part in some dirty work of late which I may clear up when I have time. His immediate principal, Barney, is a more astute person. They specialize in assaults, intimidation, and the like. What I want to know is, who is at the back of them on this particular occasion ? "

" But why do they want to intimidate you ? "

" It is this Harrow Weald case. It decides me to look into the matter, for if it is worth anyone's while to take so much trouble, there must be something in it."

" But what is it ? "

" I was going to tell you when we had this comic interlude. Here is Mrs. Maberley's note. If you care to come with me we will wire her and go out at once."

DEAR MR. SHERLOCK HOLMES, (I read)—
I have had a succession of strange incidents occur to me in connection with this house, and I should much value your advice. You would find me at home any time to-morrow. The house is within a short walk of the Weald Station. I believe that my late husband, Mortimer Maberley, was one of your early clients.

Yours faithfully,
MARY MABERLEY.

The address was " The Three Gables, Harrow Weald."

" So that's that ! " said Holmes. " And now, if you can spare the time, Watson, we will get upon our way."

A short railway journey, and a shorter drive, brought us to the house, a brick and timber villa, standing in its own acre of undeveloped grassland. Three small projections above the upper windows made a feeble attempt to justify its name. Behind was a grove of melancholy, half-grown pines, and the whole aspect of the place was poor and depressing. None the less, we found the house to be well furnished, and the lady who received us was a most engaging elderly person, who bore every mark of refinement and culture.

" I remember your husband well, madam," said Holmes, " though it is some years since he used my services in some trifling matter."

" Probably you would be more familiar with the name of my son Douglas."

Holmes looked at her with great interest.

" Dear me ! Are you the mother of Douglas Maberley ? I knew him slightly. But, of course, all London knew him. What a magnificent creature he was ! Where is he now ? "

" Dead, Mr. Holmes, dead ! He was Attaché at Rome, and he died there of pneumonia last month."

" I am sorry. One could not connect death with such a man. I have never known anyone so vitally alive. He lived intensely—every fibre of him ! "

" Too intensely, Mr. Holmes. That was the ruin of him. You remember him as he was—debonair and splendid. You did not see the moody, morose, brooding creature into which he developed. His heart was broken. In a single month I seemed to see my gallant boy turn into a worn-out cynical man."

" A love-affair—a woman ? "

" Or a fiend. Well, it was not to talk of my poor lad that I asked you to come, Mr. Holmes."

" Dr. Watson and I are at your service."

" There have been some very strange happenings. I

1162

have been in this house more than a year now, and as I wished to lead a retired life I have seen little of my neighbours. Three days ago I had a call from a man who said that he was a house agent. He said that this house would exactly suit a client of his and that if I would part with it money would be no object. It seemed to me very strange, as there are several empty houses on the market which appear to be equally eligible, but naturally I was interested in what he said. I therefore named a price which was five hundred pounds more than I gave. He at once closed with the offer, but added that his client desired to buy the furniture as well and would I put a price upon it. Some of this furniture is from my old home, and it is, as you see, very good, so that I named a good round sum. To this also he at once agreed. I had always wanted to travel, and the bargain was so good a one that it really seemed that I should be my own mistress for the rest of my life.

"Yesterday the man arrived with the agreement all drawn out. Luckily I showed it to Mr. Sutro, my lawyer, who lives in Harrow. He said to me, ' This is a very strange document. Are you aware that if you sign it you could not legally take *anything* out of the house —not even your own private possessions ? ' When the man came again in the evening I pointed this out, and I said that I meant only to sell the furniture.

" ' No, no ; everything,' said he.

" ' But my clothes ? My jewels ?

" ' Well, well, some concession might be made for your personal effects. But nothing shall go out of the house unchecked. My client is a very liberal man, but he has his fads and his own way of doing things. It is everything or nothing with him.'

" ' Then it must be nothing,' said I. And there the matter was left, but the whole thing seemed to me to be so unusual that I thought——"

Here we had a very extraordinary interruption.

Holmes raised his hand for silence. Then he strode

across the room, flung open the door, and dragged in a great gaunt woman whom he had seized by the shoulder. She entered with ungainly struggles, like some huge awkward chicken, torn squawking out of its coop.

" Leave me alone ! What are you a-doin' of ? " she screeched.

" Why, Susan, what is this ? "

" Well, ma'am, I was comin' in to ask if the visitors was stayin' for lunch when this man jumped out at me."

" I have been listening to her for the last five minutes, but did not wish to interrupt your most interesting narrative. Just a little wheezy, Susan, are you not ? You breathe too heavily for that kind of work."

Susan turned a sulky but amazed face upon her captor. " Who be you, anyhow, and what right have you a-pullin' me about like this ? "

" It was merely that I wished to ask a question in your presence. Did you, Mrs. Maberley, mention to anyone that you were going to write to me and consult me ? "

" No, Mr. Holmes, I did not."

" Who posted your letter ? "

" Susan did."

" Exactly. Now, Susan, to whom was it that you wrote or sent a message to say that your mistress was asking advice from me ? "

" It's a lie. I sent no message."

" Now, Susan, wheezy people may not live long, you know. It's a wicked thing to tell fibs. Whom did you tell ? "

" Susan ! " cried her mistress, " I believe you are a bad, treacherous woman. I remember now that I saw you speaking to someone over the hedge."

" That was my own business," said the woman sullenly.

" Suppose I tell you that it was Barney Stockdale to whom you spoke ? " said Holmes.

" Well, if you know, what do you want to ask for ? "

" I was not sure, but I know now. Well now, Susan, it will be worth ten pounds to you if you will tell me who is at the back of Barney."

" Someone that could lay down a thousand pounds for every ten you have in the world."

" So, a rich man ? No ; you smiled—a rich woman. Now we have got so far, you may as well give the name and earn the tenner."

" I'll see you in hell first."

" Oh, Susan ! Language ! "

" I am clearing out of here. I've had enough of you all. I'll send for my box to-morrow." She flounced for the door.

" Good-bye, Susan. Paregoric is the stuff. . . . Now," he continued, turning suddenly from lively to severe when the door had closed behind the flushed and angry woman, " this gang means business. Look how close they play the game. Your letter to me had the 10 p.m. postmark. And yet Susan passes the word to Barney. Barney has time to go to his employer and get instructions ; he or she—I incline to the latter from Susan's grin when she thought I had blundered—forms a plan. Black Steve is called in, and I am warned off by eleven o'clock next morning. That's quick work, you know."

" But what do they want ? "

" Yes, that's the question. Who had the house before you ? "

" A retired sea captain, called Ferguson."

" Anything remarkable about him ? "

" Not that ever I heard of."

" I was wondering whether he could have buried something. Of course, when people bury treasure nowadays they do it in the Post Office bank. But there are always some lunatics about. It would be a dull world without them. At first I thought of some buried valuable. But why, in that case, should they want your furniture ?

You don't happen to have a Raphael or a First Folio Shakespeare without knowing it ? "

" No, I don't think I have anything rarer than a Crown Derby tea-set."

" That would hardly justify all this mystery. Besides, why should they not openly state what they want ? If they covet your tea-set, they can surely offer a price for it without buying you out, lock, stock, and barrel. No, as I read it, there is something which you do not know that you have, and which you would not give up if you did know."

" That is how I read it," said I.

" Dr. Watson agrees, so that settles it."

" Well, Mr. Holmes, what can it be ? "

" Let us see whether by this purely mental analysis we can get it to a finer point. You have been in this house a year."

" Nearly two."

" All the better. During this long period no one wants anything from you. Now suddenly within three or four days you have urgent demands. What would you gather from that ? "

" It can only mean," said I, " that the object, whatever it may be, has only just come into the house."

" Settled once again," said Holmes. " Now, Mrs. Maberley, has any object just arrived ? "

" No ; I have bought nothing new this year."

" Indeed ! That is very remarkable. Well, I think we had best let matters develop a little further until we have clearer data. Is that lawyer of yours a capable man ? "

" Mr. Sutro is most capable."

" Have you another maid, or was the fair Susan, who has just banged your front door, alone ? "

" I have a young girl."

" Try and get Sutro to spend a night or two in the house. You might possibly want protection."

" Against whom ? "

"Who knows? The matter is certainly obscure. If I can't find what they are after, I must approach the matter from the other end, and try to get at the principal. Did this house-agent man give any address?"

"Simply his card and occupation. Haines-Johnson, Auctioneer and Valuer."

"I don't think we shall find him in the Directory. Honest business men don't conceal their place of business. Well, you will let me know any fresh development. I have taken up your case, and you may rely upon it that I shall see it through."

As we passed through the hall Holmes' eyes, which missed nothing, lighted upon several trunks and cases which were piled in the corner. The labels shone out upon them.

"'Milano.' 'Lucerne.' These are from Italy."

"They are poor Douglas' things."

"You have not unpacked them? How long have you had them?"

"They arrived last week."

"But you said—why, surely this might be the missing link. How do we know that there is not something of value there?"

"There could not possibly be, Mr. Holmes. Poor Douglas had only his pay and a small annuity. What could he have of value?"

Holmes was lost in thought.

"Delay no longer, Mrs. Maberley," he said at last. "Have these things taken upstairs to your bedroom. Examine them as soon as possible and see what they contain. I will come to-morrow and hear your report."

It was quite evident that The Three Gables was under very close surveillance, for as we came round the high hedge at the end of the lane there was the negro prize-fighter standing in the shadow. We came on him quite suddenly, and a grim and menacing figure he looked in that lonely place. Holmes clapped his hand to his pocket.

" Lookin' for your gun, Masser Holmes ? "

" No ; for my scent-bottle, Steve."

" You are funny, Masser Holmes, ain't you ? "

" It won't be funny for you, Steve, if I get after you. I gave you fair warning this morning."

" Well, Masser Holmes, I done gone think over what you said, and I don't want no more talk about that affair of Masser Perkins. S'pose I can help you, Masser Holmes, I will."

" Well, then, tell me who is behind you on this job ? "

" So help me the Lord ! Masser Holmes, I told you the truth before. I don't know. My boss Barney gives me orders and that's all."

" Well, just bear in mind, Steve, that the lady in that house, and everything under that roof, is under my protection. Don't you forget it."

" All right, Masser Holmes. I'll remember."

" I've got him thoroughly frightened for his own skin, Watson," Holmes remarked as we walked on. " I think he would double-cross his employer if he knew who he was. It was lucky I had some knowledge of the Spencer John crowd, and that Steve was one of them. Now, Watson, this is a case for Langdale Pike, and I am going to see him now. When I get back I may be clearer in the matter."

I saw no more of Holmes during the day, but I could well imagine how he spent it, for Langdale Pike was his human book of reference upon all matters of social scandal. This strange, languid creature spent his waking hours in the bow window of a St. James' Street club, and was the receiving-station, as well as the transmitter, for all the gossip of the Metropolis. He made, it was said, a four-figure income by the paragraphs which he contributed every week to the garbage papers which cater for an inquisitive public. If ever, far down in the turbid depths of London life, there was some strange swirl or eddy, it was marked with automatic exactness by this human dial upon the surface. Holmes discreetly helped Langdale to knowledge, and on occasion was helped in turn.

When I met my friend in his room early next morning, I was conscious from his bearing that all was well, but none the less a most unpleasant surprise was awaiting us. It took the shape of the following telegram :

"Please come out at once. Client's house burgled in the night. Police in possession.

"SUTRO."

Holmes whistled. "The drama has come to a crisis, and quicker than I had expected. There is a great driving-power at the back of this business, Watson, which does not surprise me after what I have heard. This Sutro, of course, is her lawyer. I made a mistake, I fear, in not asking you to spend the night on guard. This fellow has clearly proved a broken reed. Well, there is nothing for it but another journey to Harrow Weald."

We found The Three Gables a very different establishment to the orderly household of the previous day. A small group of idlers had assembled at the garden gate, while a couple of constables were examining the windows and the geranium beds. Within we met a grey old gentleman, who introduced himself as the lawyer, together with a bustling, rubicund Inspector, who greeted Holmes as an old friend.

"Well, Mr. Holmes, no chance for you in this case, I'm afraid. Just a common, ordinary burglary, and well within the capacity of the poor old police. No experts need apply."

"I am sure the case is in very good hands," said Holmes. "Merely a common burglary, you say ? "

"Quite so. We know pretty well who the men are and where to find them. It is that gang of Barney Stockdale, with the big nigger in it—they've been seen about here."

"Excellent! What did they get?"

"Well, they don't seem to have got much. Mrs. Maberley was chloroformed and the house was—— Ah! here is the lady herself."

Our friend of yesterday, looking very pale and ill, had entered the room, leaning upon a little maid-servant.

"You gave me good advice, Mr. Holmes," said she, smiling ruefully. "Alas, I did not take it! I did not wish to trouble Mr. Sutro, and so I was unprotected."

"I only heard of it this morning," the lawyer explained.

"Mr. Holmes advised me to have some friend in the house. I neglected his advice, and I have paid for it."

"You look wretchedly ill," said Holmes. "Perhaps you are hardly equal to telling me what occurred."

"It is all here," said the Inspector, tapping a bulky notebook.

"Still, if the lady is not too exhausted——"

"There is really so little to tell. I have no doubt that wicked Susan had planned an entrance for them. They must have known the house to an inch. I was conscious for a moment of the chloroform rag which was thrust over my mouth, but I have no notion how long I may have been senseless. When I woke, one man was at the bedside and another was rising with a bundle in his hand from among my son's baggage, which was partially opened and littered over the floor. Before he could get away I sprang up and seized him."

"You took a big risk," said the Inspector.

"I clung to him, but he shook me off, and the other may have struck me, for I can remember no more. Mary the maid heard the noise and began screaming out of the window. That brought the police, but the rascals had got away."

"What did they take?"

"Well, I don't think there is anything of value missing. I am sure there was nothing in my son's trunks."

"Did the men leave no clue?"

" There was one sheet of paper which I may have torn from the man that I grasped. It was lying all crumpled on the floor. It is in my son's handwriting."

" Which means that it is not of much use," said the Inspector. " Now if it had been in the burglar's——"

" Exactly," said Holmes. " What rugged common sense ! None the less, I should be curious to see it."

The Inspector drew a folded sheet of foolscap from his pocket-book.

" I never pass anything, however trifling," said he, with some pomposity. " That is my advice to you, Mr. Holmes. In twenty-five years' experience I have learned my lesson. There is always the chance of finger-marks or something."

Holmes inspected the sheet of paper.

" What do you make of it, Inspector ? "

" Seems to be the end of some queer novel, so far as I can see."

" It may certainly prove to be the end of a queer tale," said Holmes. " You have noticed the number on the top of the page. It is two hundred and forty-five. Where are the odd two hundred and forty-four pages ? "

" Well, I suppose the burglars got those. Much good may it do them ! "

" It seems a queer thing to break into a house in order to steal such papers as that. Does it suggest anything to you, Inspector ? "

" Yes, sir ; it suggests that in their hurry the rascals just grabbed at what came first to hand. I wish them joy of what they got."

" Why should they go to my son's things ? " asked Mrs. Maberley.

" Well, they found nothing valuable downstairs, so they tried their luck upstairs. That is how I read it. What do you make of it, Mr. Holmes ? "

" I must think it over, Inspector. Come to the window, Watson." Then, as we stood together, he read over the fragment of paper. It began in the middle of a sentence and ran like this :

" . . . face bled considerably from the cuts and blows, but it was nothing to the bleeding of his heart as he saw that lovely face, the face for which he had been prepared to sacrifice his very life, looking out at his agony and humiliation. She smiled—yes, by Heaven ! she smiled, like the heartless fiend she was, as he looked up at her. It was at that moment that love died and hate was born. Man must live for something. If it is not for your embrace, my lady, then it shall surely be for your undoing and my complete revenge."

" Queer grammar ! " said Holmes, with a smile, as he handed the paper back to the Inspector. " Did you notice how the ' he ' suddenly changed to ' my.' The writer was so carried away by his own story that he imagined himself at the supreme moment to be the hero."

" It seemed mighty poor stuff," said the Inspector, as he replaced it in his book. " What ! are you off, Mr. Holmes ? "

" I don't think there is anything more for me to do now that the case is in such capable hands. By the way, Mrs. Maberley, did you say you wished to travel ? "

" It has always been my dream, Mr. Holmes."

" Where would you like to go—Cairo, Madeira, the Riviera ? "

" Oh ! if I had the money I would go round the world."

" Quite so. Round the world. Well, good morning. I may drop you a line in the evening." As we passed the window I caught a glimpse of the Inspector's smile and shake of the head. " These clever fellows have always a touch of madness." That was what I read in the Inspector's smile.

" Now, Watson, we are at the last lap of our little journey," said Holmes, when we were back in the roar of Central London once more. "I think we had best clear the matter up at once, and it would be well that you should come with me, for it is safer to have a witness when you are dealing with such a lady as Isadora Klein."

We had taken a cab and were speeding to some address in Grosvenor Square. Holmes had been sunk in thought, but he roused himself suddenly.

"By the way, Watson, I suppose you see it all clearly ? "

"No, I can't say that I do. I only gather that we are going to see the lady who is behind all this mischief."

"Exactly ! But does the name Isadora Klein convey nothing to you ? She was, of course, *the* celebrated beauty. There was never a woman to touch her. She is pure Spanish, the real blood of the masterful Conquistadors, and her people have been leaders in Pernambuco for generations. She married the aged German sugar king, Klein, and presently found herself the richest as well as the most lovely widow upon earth. Then there was an interval of adventure when she pleased her own tastes. She had several lovers, and Douglas Maberley, one of the most striking men in London, was one of them.

"It was by all accounts more than an adventure with him. He was not a Society butterfly, but a strong, proud man who gave and expected all. But she is the '*belle dame sans merci*' of fiction. When her caprice is satisfied, the matter is ended, and if the other party in the matter can't take her word for it, she knows how to bring it home to him."

"Then that was his own story——"

"Ah ! you are piecing it together now. I hear that she is about to marry the young Duke of Lomond, who might almost be her son. His Grace's ma might overlook the age, but a big scandal would be a different matter, so it is imperative—— Ah ! here we are."

It was one of the finest corner-houses of the West End. A machine-like footman took up our cards and returned with word that the lady was not at home.

" Then we shall wait until she is," said Holmes cheerfully.

The machine broke down.

" Not at home means not at home to *you*," said the footman.

" Good," Holmes answered. " That means that we shall not have to wait. Kindly give this note to your mistress."

He scribbled three or four words upon a sheet of his notebook, folded it, and handed it to the man.

" What did you say, Holmes ? " I asked.

" I simply wrote ' Shall it be the police, then ? ' I think that should pass us in."

It did—with amazing celerity. A minute later we were in an Arabian Nights' drawing-room, vast and wonderful, in a half gloom, picked out with an occasional pink electric light. The lady had come, I felt, to that time of life when even the proudest beauty finds the half-light more welcome. She rose from a settee as we entered : tall, queenly, a perfect figure, a lovely mask-like face, with two wonderful Spanish eyes which looked murder at us both.

" What is this intrusion—and this insulting message ? " she asked, holding up the slip of paper.

" I need not explain, madame. I have too much respect for your intelligence to do so—though I confess that intelligence has been surprisingly at fault of late."

" How so, sir ? "

" By supposing that your hired bullies could frighten me from my work. Surely no man would take up my profession if it were not that danger attracts him. It was you, then, who forced me to examine the case of young Maberley."

" I have no idea what you are talking about. What have I to do with hired bullies ? "

Holmes turned away wearily.

" Yes, I have underrated your intelligence. Well, good afternoon ! "

" Stop ! Where are you going ? "

" To Scotland Yard."

We had not got half-way to the door before she had overtaken us and was holding his arm. She had turned in a moment from steel to velvet.

" Come and sit down, gentlemen. Let us talk this matter over. I feel that I may be frank with you, Mr. Holmes. You have the feelings of a gentleman. How quick a woman's instinct is to find it out. I will treat you as a friend."

" I cannot promise to reciprocate, madame. I am not the law, but I represent justice so far as my feeble powers go. I am ready to listen, and then I will tell you how I will act."

" No doubt it was foolish of me to threaten a brave man like yourself."

" What was really foolish, madame, is that you have placed yourself in the power of a band of rascals who may blackmail or give you away."

" No, no ! I am not so simple. Since I have promised to be frank, I may say that no one, save Barney Stockdale and Susan, his wife, have the least idea who their employer is. As to them, well, it is not the first——" She smiled and nodded, with a charming coquettish intimacy.

" I see. You've tested them before."

" They are good hounds who run silent."

" Such hounds have a way sooner or later of biting the hand that feeds them. They will be arrested for this burglary. The police are already after them."

" They will take what comes to them. That is what they are paid for. I shall not appear in the matter."

" Unless I bring you into it."

" No, no ; you would not. You are a gentleman. It is a woman's secret."

" In the first place you must give back this manuscript."

She broke into a ripple of laughter, and walked to the fire-place. There was a calcined mass which she broke up with the poker. " Shall I give this back ? " she asked. So roguish and exquisite did she look as she stood before us with a challenging smile that I felt of all Holmes' criminals this was the one whom he would find it hardest to face. However, he was immune from sentiment.

" That seals your fate," he said coldly. " You are very prompt in your actions, madame, but you have overdone it on this occasion."

She threw the poker down with a clatter.

" How hard you are ! " she cried. " May I tell you the whole story ? "

" I fancy I could tell it to you."

" But you must look at it with my eyes, Mr. Holmes. You must realize it from the point of view of a woman who sees all her life's ambition about to be ruined at the last moment. Is such a woman to be blamed if she protects herself ? "

" The original sin was yours."

" Yes, yes ! I admit it. He was a dear boy, Douglas, but it so chanced that he could not fit into my plans. He wanted marriage—marriage, Mr. Holmes—with a penniless commoner. Nothing less would serve him. Then he became pertinacious. Because I had given he seemed to think that I still must give, and to him only. It was intolerable. At last I had to make him realize it."

" By hiring ruffians to beat him under your own window."

" You do indeed seem to know everything. Well, it is true. Barney and the boys drove him away, and were, I admit, a little rough in doing so. But what did he do then ? Could I have believed that a gentleman would do such an act ? He wrote a book in which he described his own story. I, of course, was the wolf ; he the lamb. It was all there, under different names, of course ; but who in all London would have failed to recognize it ? What do you say to that, Mr. Holmes ? "

" Well, he was within his rights."

" It was as if the air of Italy had got into his blood

1176

and brought with it the old cruel Italian spirit. He wrote to me and sent me a copy of his book that I might have the torture of anticipation. There were two copies, he said—one for me, one for his publisher."

" How did you know the publisher's had not reached him ? "

" I knew who his publisher was. It is not his only novel, you know. I found out that he had not heard from Italy. Then came Douglas' sudden death. So long as that other manuscript was in the world there was no safety for me. Of course, it must be among his effects, and these would be returned to his mother. I set the gang at work. One of them got into the house as servant. I wanted to do the thing honestly. I really and truly did. I was ready to buy the house and everything in it. I offered any price she cared to ask. I only tried the other way when everything else had failed. Now, Mr. Holmes, granting that I was too hard on Douglas —and, God knows, I am sorry for it !—what else could I do with my whole future at stake ? "

Sherlock Holmes shrugged his shoulders.

" Well, well," said he, " I suppose I shall have to compound a felony as usual. How much does it cost to go round the world in first-class style ? "

The lady stared in amazement.

" Could it be done on five thousand pounds ? "

" Well, I should think so, indeed ! "

" Very good. I think you will sign me a cheque for that, and I will see that it comes to Mrs. Maberley. You owe her a little change of air. Meantime, lady " —he wagged a cautionary forefinger—" have a care ! Have a care ! You can't play with edged tools for ever without cutting those dainty hands."

49. *The Sussex Vampire*

HOLMES had read carefully a note which the last post had brought him. Then, with the dry chuckle which was his nearest approach to a laugh, he tossed it over to me.

"For a mixture of the modern and the mediæval, of the practical and of the wildly fanciful, I think this is surely the limit," said he. "What do you make of it, Watson?"

I read as follows:

46 OLD JEWRY,
Nov. 19th.

Re Vampires.

SIR,—

Our client, Mr. Robert Ferguson, of Ferguson & Muirhead, tea brokers, of Mincing Lane, has made some inquiry from us in a communication of even date concerning vampires. As our firm specializes entirely upon the assessment of machinery the matter hardly comes within our purview, and we have therefore recommended Mr. Ferguson to call upon you and lay the matter before you. We have not forgotten your successful action in the case of Matilda Briggs.

We are, Sir, faithfully yours,
MORRISON, MORRISON, AND DODD.
per E. J. C.

"Matilda Briggs was not the name of a young woman, Watson," said Holmes, in a reminiscent voice. "It was a ship which is associated with the giant rat of Sumatra, a story for which the world is not yet prepared. But what do we know about vampires? Does it come within our purview either? Anything is better than stagnation, but really we seem to have been switched on to a Grimm's fairy tale. Make a long arm, Watson, and see what V has to say."

I leaned back and took down the great index volume to which he referred. Holmes balanced it on his knee and his eyes moved slowly and lovingly over the record of old cases, mixed with the accumulated information of a lifetime.

" Voyage of the *Gloria Scott*," he read. " That was a bad business. I have some recollection that you made a record of it, Watson, though I was unable to congratulate you upon the result. Victor Lynch, the forger. Venomous lizard or gila. Remarkable case, that ! Vittoria, the circus belle. Vanderbilt and the Yeggman. Vipers. Vigor, the Hammersmith wonder. Hullo ! Hullo ! Good old index. You can't beat it. Listen to this, Watson. Vampirism in Hungary. And again, Vampires in Transylvania." He turned over the pages with eagerness, but after a short intent perusal he threw down the great book with a snarl of disappointment.

" Rubbish, Watson, rubbish ! What have we to do with walking corpses who can only be held in their grave by stakes driven through their hearts ? It's pure lunacy."

" But surely," said I, " the vampire was not necessarily a dead man ? A living person might have the habit. I have read, for example, of the old sucking the blood of the young in order to retain their youth."

" You are right, Watson. It mentions the legend in one of these references. But are we to give serious attention to such things ? This Agency stands flat-footed upon the ground, and there it must remain. The world is big enough for us. No ghosts need apply. I fear that we cannot take Mr. Robert Ferguson very seriously. Possibly this note may be from him, and may throw some light upon what is worrying him."

He took up a second letter which had lain unnoticed upon the table whilst he had been absorbed with the first. This he began to read with a smile of amusement upon his face which gradually faded away into an expression of intense interest and concentration. When he had finished he sat for some little time lost in thought with the letter dangling from his fingers. Finally, with a start, he aroused himself from his reverie.

" Cheeseman's, Lamberley. Where is Lamberley, Watson ? "

" It is in Sussex, south of Horsham."

" Not very far, eh ? And Cheeseman's ? "

" I know that country, Holmes. It is full of old houses which are named after the men who built them centuries ago. You get Odley's and Harvey's and Carriton's—the folk are forgotten but their names live in their houses."

" Precisely," said Holmes coldly. It was one of the peculiarities of his proud, self-contained nature that, though he docketed any fresh information very quickly and accurately in his brain, he seldom made any acknowledgment to the giver. " I rather fancy we shall know a good deal more about Cheeseman's, Lamberley, before we are through. The letter is, as I had hoped, from Robert Ferguson. By the way, he claims acquaintance with you."

" With me ! "

" You had better read it."

He handed the letter across. It was headed with the address quoted.

DEAR MR. HOLMES, (it said)—I have been recommended to you by my lawyers, but indeed the matter is so extraordinarily delicate that it is most difficult to discuss. It concerns a friend for whom I am acting. This gentleman married some five years ago a Peruvian lady, the daughter of a Peruvian merchant, whom he had met in connection with the importation of nitrates. The lady was very beautiful, but the fact of her foreign birth and of her alien religion always caused a separation of interests and of feelings between husband and wife, so that after a time his love may have cooled towards her and he may have come to regard their union as a mistake. He felt there were sides of her character which he could never explore or understand. This was the more painful as she was as loving a wife as a man could have—to all appearance absolutely devoted.

Now for the point which I will make more plain when we meet. Indeed, this note is merely to give you a general idea of the situation and to ascertain whether you would care to interest yourself in the matter. The lady began to show some curious traits, quite alien to her ordinarily sweet and gentle disposition. The gentleman had been married twice and he had one son by the first wife. This boy was now fifteen, a very charming and affectionate youth, though unhappily injured through an accident in childhood. Twice the wife was caught in the act of assaulting this poor lad in the most unprovoked way. Once she struck him with a stick and left a great weal on his arm.

This was a small matter, however, compared with her conduct to her own child, a dear boy just under one year of age. On one occasion about a month ago this child had been left by its nurse for a few minutes. A loud cry from the baby, as of pain, called the nurse back. As she ran into the room she saw her employer, the lady, leaning over the baby and apparently biting his neck. There was a small wound in the neck, from which a stream of blood had escaped. The nurse was so horrified that she wished to call the husband, but the lady implored her not to do so, and actually gave her five pounds as a price for her silence. No explanation was ever given, and for the moment the matter was passed over.

It left, however, a terrible impression upon the nurse's mind, and from that time she began to watch her mistress closely, and to keep a closer guard upon the baby, whom she tenderly loved. It seemed to her that even as she watched the mother, so the mother watched her, and that every time she was compelled to leave the baby alone the mother was waiting to get at it. Day and night the nurse covered the child, and day and night the silent, watchful mother seemed to be lying in wait as a wolf waits for a lamb. It must read most incredible to you, and yet I beg you to take it seriously, for a child's life and a man's sanity may depend upon it.

At last there came one dreadful day when the facts could no longer be concealed from the husband. The nurse's nerve had given way; she could stand the strain no longer, and she made a clean breast of it all to the man. To him it seemed as wild a tale as it may now seem to you. He knew his wife to be a loving wife, and, save for the assaults upon her stepson, a loving mother. Why, then, should she wound her own dear little baby? He told the nurse that she was dreaming, that her suspicions were those of a lunatic, and that such libels upon her mistress were not to be tolerated. Whilst they were talking, a sudden cry of pain was heard. Nurse and master rushed together to the nursery. Imagine his feelings, Mr. Holmes, as he saw his wife rise from a kneeling position beside the cot, and saw blood upon the child's exposed neck and upon the sheet. With a cry of horror, he turned his wife's face to the light and saw blood all round her lips. It was she—she beyond all question—who had drunk the poor baby's blood.

So the matter stands. She is now confined to her room. There has been no explanation. The husband is half demented. He knows, and I know, little of Vampirism beyond the name. We had thought it was some wild tale of foreign parts. And yet here in the very heart of the English Sussex—well, all this can be discussed with you in the morning. Will you see me? Will you use your great powers in aiding a distracted man? If so, kindly wire to Ferguson, Cheeseman's, Lamberley, and I will be at your rooms by ten o'clock.

Yours faithfully,

ROBERT FERGUSON.

PS.—I believe your friend Watson played Rugby for Blackheath when I was three-quarter for Richmond. It is the only personal introduction which I can give.

"Of course I remember him," said I, as I laid down the letter. "Big Bob Ferguson, the finest three-quarter Richmond ever had. He was always a good-natured chap. It's like him to be so concerned over a friend's case."

Holmes looked at me thoughtfully and shook his head.

"I never get your limits, Watson," said he. "There are unexplored possibilities about you. Take a wire down, like a good fellow. 'Will examine your case with pleasure.'"

"*Your* case!"

"We must not let him think that this Agency is a home for the weak-minded. Of course it is his case. Send him that wire and let the matter rest till morning."

Promptly at ten o'clock next morning Ferguson strode into our room. I had remembered him as a long, slab-sided man with loose limbs and a fine turn of speed, which had carried him round many an opposing back. There is surely nothing in life more painful than to meet the wreck of a fine athlete whom one has known in his prime. His great frame had fallen in, his flaxen hair was scanty, and his shoulders were bowed. I fear that I roused corresponding emotions in him.

"Hullo, Watson," said he, and his voice was still deep and hearty. "You don't look quite the man you did when I threw you over the ropes into the crowd at the Old Deer Park. I expect I have changed a bit also. But it's this last day or two that has aged me. I see by your telegram, Mr. Holmes, that it is no use my pretending to be anyone's deputy."

"It is simpler to deal direct," said Holmes.

"Of course it is. But you can imagine how difficult it is when you are speaking of the one woman whom you are bound to protect and help. What can I do?

How am I to go to the police with such a story? And yet the kiddies have got to be protected. Is it madness, Mr. Holmes? Is it something in the blood? Have you any similar case in your experience? For God's sake, give me some advice, for I am at my wits' end."

"Very naturally, Mr. Ferguson. Now sit here and pull yourself together and give me a few clear answers. I can assure you that I am very far from being at my wits' end, and that I am confident we shall find some solution. First of all, tell me what steps you have taken. Is your wife still near the children?"

"We had a dreadful scene. She is a most loving woman, Mr. Holmes. If ever a woman loved a man with all her heart and soul, she loves me. She was cut to the heart that I should have discovered this horrible, this incredible, secret. She would not even speak. She gave no answer to my reproaches, save to gaze at me with a sort of wild, despairing look in her eyes. Then she rushed to her room and locked herself in. Since then she has refused to see me. She has a maid who was with her before her marriage, Dolores by name —a friend rather than a servant. She takes her food to her."

"Then the child is in no immediate danger?"

"Mrs. Mason, the nurse, has sworn that she will not leave it night or day. I can absolutely trust her. I am more uneasy about poor little Jack, for, as I told you in my note, he has twice been assaulted by her."

"But never wounded?"

"No; she struck him savagely. It is the more terrible as he is a poor little inoffensive cripple." Ferguson's gaunt features softened as he spoke of his boy. "You would think that the dear lad's condition would soften anyone's heart. A fall in childhood and a twisted spine, Mr. Holmes. But the dearest, most loving heart within."

Holmes had picked up the letter of yesterday and

was reading it over. "What other inmates are there in your house, Mr. Ferguson?"

"Two servants who have not been long with us. One stable-hand, Michael, who sleeps in the house. My wife, myself, my boy Jack, baby, Dolores, and Mrs. Mason. That is all."

"I gather that you did not know your wife well at the time of your marriage?"

"I had only known her a few weeks."

"How long had this maid Dolores been with her?"

"Some years."

"Then your wife's character would really be better known by Dolores than by you?"

"Yes, you may say so."

Holmes made a note.

"I fancy," said he, "that I may be of more use at Lamberley than here. It is eminently a case for personal investigation. If the lady remains in her room, our presence could not annoy or inconvenience her. Of course, we would stay at the inn."

Ferguson gave a gesture of relief.

"It is what I hoped, Mr. Holmes. There is an excellent train at two from Victoria, if you could come."

"Of course we could come. There is a lull at present. I can give you my undivided energies. Watson, of course, comes with us. But there are one or two points upon which I wish to be very sure before I start. This unhappy lady, as I understand it, has appeared to assault both the children, her own baby and your little son?"

"That is so."

"But the assaults take different forms, do they not? She has beaten your son."

"Once with a stick and once very savagely with her hands."

"Did she give no explanation why she struck him?"

"None, save that she hated him. Again and again she said so."

" Well, that is not unknown among stepmothers. A posthumous jealousy, we will say. Is the lady jealous by nature ? "

" Yes, she is very jealous—jealous with all the strength of her fiery tropical love."

" But the boy—he is fifteen, I understand, and probably very developed in mind, since his body has been circumscribed in action. Did he give you no explanation of these assaults ? "

" No ; he declared there was no reason."

" Were they good friends at other times ? "

" No ; there was never any love between them."

" Yet you say he is affectionate ? "

" Never in the world could there be so devoted a son. My life is his life. He is absorbed in what I say or do."

Once again Holmes made a note. For some time he sat lost in thought.

" No doubt you and the boy were great comrades before this second marriage. You were thrown very close together, were you not ? "

" Very much so."

" And the boy, having so affectionate a nature, was devoted, no doubt, to the memory of his mother ? "

" Most devoted."

" He would certainly seem to be a most interesting lad. There is one other point about these assaults. Were the strange attacks upon the baby and the assaults upon your son at the same period ? "

" In the first case it was so. It was as if some frenzy had seized her, and she had vented her rage upon both. In the second case it was only Jack who suffered. Mrs. Mason had no complaint to make about the baby."

" That certainly complicates matters."

" I don't quite follow you, Mr. Holmes."

" Possibly not. One forms provisional theories and waits for time or fuller knowledge to explode them. A bad habit, Mr. Ferguson ; but human nature is weak.

I fear that your old friend here has given an exaggerated view of my scientific methods. However, I will only say at the present stage that your problem does not appear to me to be insoluble, and that you may expect to find us at Victoria at two o'clock."

It was evening of a dull, foggy November day when, having left our bags at the "Chequers," Lamberley, we drove through the Sussex clay of a long winding lane, and finally reached the isolated and ancient farm-house in which Ferguson dwelt. It was a large, straggling building, very old in the centre, very new at the wings, with towering Tudor chimneys and a lichen-spotted, high-pitched roof of Horsham slabs. The doorsteps were worn into curves, and the ancient tiles which lined the porch were marked with the rebus of a cheese and a man, after the original builder. Within, the ceilings were corrugated with heavy oaken beams, and the uneven floors sagged into sharp curves. An odour of age and decay pervaded the whole crumbling building.

There was one very large central room, into which Ferguson led us. Here, in a huge old-fashioned fireplace with an iron screen behind it dated 1670, there blazed and spluttered a splendid log fire.

The room, as I gazed round, was a most singular mixture of dates and of places. The half-panelled walls may well have belonged to the original yeoman farmer of the seventeenth century. They were ornamented, however, on the lower part by a line of well-chosen modern water-colours; while above, where yellow plaster took the place of oak, there was hung a fine collection of South American utensils and weapons, which had been brought, no doubt, by the Peruvian lady upstairs. Holmes rose, with that quick curiosity which sprang from his eager mind, and examined them with some care. He returned with his eyes full of thought.

" Hullo ! " he cried. " Hullo ! "

A spaniel had lain in a basket in the corner. It came

slowly forward towards its master, walking with difficulty. Its hind-legs moved irregularly and its tail was on the ground. It licked Ferguson's hand.

" What is it, Mr. Holmes ? "

" The dog. What's the matter with it ? "

" That's what puzzled the vet. A sort of paralysis. Spinal meningitis, he thought. But it is passing. He'll be all right soon—won't you, Carlo ? "

A shiver of assent passed through the drooping tail. The dog's mournful eyes passed from one of us to the other. He knew that we were discussing his case.

" Did it come on suddenly ? "

" In a single night."

" How long ago ? "

" It may have been four months ago."

" Very remarkable. Very suggestive."

" What do you see in it, Mr. Holmes ? "

" A confirmation of what I had already thought."

" For God's sake, what *do* you think, Mr. Holmes ? It may be a mere intellectual puzzle to you, but it is life and death to me ! My wife a would-be murderer —my child in constant danger ! Don't play with me, Mr. Holmes. It is too terribly serious."

The big Rugby three-quarter was trembling all over. Holmes put his hand soothingly upon his arm.

" I fear that there is pain for you, Mr. Ferguson, what-ever the solution may be," said he. " I would spare you all I can. I cannot say more for the instant, but before I leave this house I hope I may have something definite."

" Please God you may ! If you will excuse me, gentlemen, I will go up to my wife's room and see if there has been any change."

He was away some minutes, during which Holmes resumed his examination of the curiosities upon the wall. When our host returned it was clear from his downcast face that he had made no progress. He brought with him a tall, slim, brown-faced girl.

"The tea is ready, Dolores," said Ferguson. "See that your mistress has everything she can wish."

"She verra ill," cried the girl, looking with indignant eyes at her master. "She no ask for food. She verra ill. She need doctor. I frightened stay alone with her without doctor."

Ferguson looked at me with a question in his eyes.

"I should be so glad if I could be of use."

"Would your mistress see Dr. Watson?"

"I take him. I no ask leave. She needs doctor."

"Then I'll come with you at once."

I followed the girl, who was quivering with strong emotion, up the staircase and down an ancient corridor. At the end was an iron-clamped and massive door. It struck me as I looked at it that if Ferguson tried to force his way to his wife he would find it no easy matter. The girl drew a key from her pocket, and the heavy oaken planks creaked upon their old hinges. I passed in and she swiftly followed, fastening the door behind her.

On the bed a woman was lying who was clearly in a high fever. She was only half conscious, but as I entered she raised a pair of frightened but beautiful eyes and glared at me in apprehension. Seeing a stranger, she appeared to be relieved, and sank back with a sigh upon the pillow. I stepped up to her with a few reassuring words, and she lay still while I took her pulse and temperature. Both were high, and yet my impression was that the condition was rather that of mental and nervous excitement than of any actual seizure.

"She lie like that one day, two day. I 'fraid she die," said the girl.

The woman turned her flushed and handsome face towards me.

"Where is my husband?"

"He is below, and would wish to see you."

"I will not see him. I will not see him." Then

1189

she seemed to wander off into delirium. " A fiend !
A fiend ! Oh, what shall I do with this devil ? "

" Can I help you in any way ? "

" No. No one can help. It is finished. All is
destroyed. Do what I will, all is destroyed."

The woman must have some strange delusion. I
could not see honest Bob Ferguson in the character of
fiend or devil.

" Madame," I said, " your husband loves you dearly.
He is deeply grieved at this happening."

Again she turned on me those glorious eyes.

" He loves me. Yes. But do I not love him ? Do
I not love him even to sacrifice myself rather than break
his dear heart. That is how I love him. And yet he
could think of me—he could speak of me so."

" He is full of grief, but he cannot understand."

" No, he cannot understand. But he should trust."

" Will you not see him ? " I suggested.

" No, no ; I cannot forget those terrible words nor
the look upon his face. I will not see him. Go now.
You can do nothing for me. Tell him only one thing.
I want my child. I have a right to my child. That is the
only message I can send him." She turned her face
to the wall and would say no more.

I returned to the room downstairs, where Ferguson
and Holmes still sat by the fire. Ferguson listened
moodily to my account of the interview.

" How can I send her the child ? " he said. " How
do I know what strange impulse might come upon her ?
How can I ever forget how she rose from beside it with
its blood upon her lips ? " He shuddered at the recollection. " The child is safe with Mrs. Mason, and there
he must remain."

A smart maid, the only modern thing which we had
seen in the house, had brought in some tea. As she was
serving it the door opened and a youth entered the room.
He was a remarkable lad, pale-faced and fair-haired, with
excitable light blue eyes which blazed into a sudden

flame of emotion and joy as they rested upon his father. He rushed forward and threw his arms round his neck with the abandon of a loving girl.

"Oh, daddy," he cried, "I did not know that you were due yet. I should have been here to meet you. Oh, I am so glad to see you!"

Ferguson gently disengaged himself from the embrace with some little show of embarrassment.

"Dear old chap," said he, patting the flaxen head with a very tender hand. "I came early because my friends, Mr. Holmes and Dr. Watson, have been persuaded to come down and spend an evening with us."

"Is that Mr. Holmes, the detective?"

"Yes."

The youth looked at us with a very penetrating and, as it seemed to me, unfriendly gaze.

"What about your other child, Mr. Ferguson?" asked Holmes. "Might we make the acquaintance of the baby?"

"Ask Mrs. Mason to bring baby down," said Ferguson. The boy went off with a curious, shambling gait which told my surgical eyes that he was suffering from a weak spine. Presently he returned, and behind him came a tall, gaunt woman bearing in her arms a very beautiful child, dark-eyed, golden-haired, a wonderful mixture of the Saxon and the Latin. Ferguson was evidently devoted to it, for he took it into his arms and fondled it most tenderly.

"Fancy anyone having the heart to hurt him," he muttered, as he glanced down at the small, angry red pucker upon the cherub throat.

It was at this moment that I chanced to glance at Holmes, and saw a most singular intentness in his expression. His face was as set as if it had been carved out of old ivory, and his eyes, which had glanced for a moment at father and child, were now fixed with eager curiosity upon something at the other side of the room. Following his gaze I could only guess that he was looking out through the window at the melancholy, dripping garden. It is true that a shutter had half closed outside and obstructed the view, but none the less it was certainly at the window that Holmes was fixing his concentrated attention. Then he smiled, and his eyes came back to the baby. On its chubby neck there was this small puckered mark. Without speaking, Holmes examined it with care. Finally he shook one of the dimpled fists which waved in front of him.

"Good-bye, little man. You have made a strange start in life. Nurse, I should wish to have a word with you in private."

He took her aside and spoke earnestly for a few minutes. I only heard the last words, which were : " Your anxiety will soon, I hope, be set at rest." The woman, who seemed to be a sour, silent kind of creature, withdrew with the child.

"What is Mrs. Mason like ? " asked Holmes.

" Not very prepossessing externally, as you can see, but a heart of gold, and devoted to the child."

" Do you like her, Jack ? " Holmes turned suddenly upon the boy. His expressive mobile face shadowed over, and he shook his head.

" Jacky has very strong likes and dislikes," said Ferguson, putting his arm round the boy. " Luckily I am one of his likes."

The boy cooed and nestled his head upon his father's breast. Ferguson gently disengaged him.

" Run away, little Jacky," said he, and he watched his son with loving eyes until he disappeared. " Now, Mr. Holmes," he continued, when the boy was gone, " I really feel that I have brought you on a fool's errand, for what can you possibly do, save give me your sympathy ? It must be an exceedingly delicate and complex affair from your point of view."

" It is certainly delicate," said my friend, with an amused smile, " but I have not been struck up to now with its complexity. It has been a case for intellectual deduction, but when this original intellectual deduction is confirmed point by point by quite a number of independent incidents, then the subjective becomes objective and we can say confidently that we have reached our goal. I had, in fact, reached it before we left Baker Street, and the rest has merely been observation and confirmation."

Ferguson put his big hand to his furrowed forehead.

"For Heaven's sake, Holmes," he said hoarsely, "if you can see the truth in this matter, do not keep me in suspense. How do I stand ? What shall I do ? I care nothing as to how you have found your facts so long as you have really got them."

"Certainly I owe you an explanation, and you shall have it. But you will permit me to handle the matter in my own way ? Is the lady capable of seeing us, Watson ? "

"She is ill, but she is quite rational."

"Very good. It is only in her presence that we can clear the matter up. Let us go up to her."

"She will not see me," cried Ferguson.

"Oh, yes, she will," said Holmes. He scribbled a few lines upon a sheet of paper. "You at least have the *entrée*, Watson. Will you have the goodness to give the lady this note ? "

I ascended again and handed the note to Dolores, who cautiously opened the door. A minute later I heard a cry from within, a cry in which joy and surprise seemed to be blended. Dolores looked out.

"She will see them. She will leesten," said she.

At my summons Ferguson and Holmes came up. As we entered the room Ferguson took a step or two towards his wife, who had raised herself in the bed, but she held out her hand to repulse him. He sank into an arm-chair, while Holmes seated himself beside him, after bowing to the lady, who looked at him with wide-eyed amazement.

"I think we can dispense with Dolores," said Holmes.

" Oh, very well, madame, if you would rather she stayed I can see no objection. Now, Mr. Ferguson, I am a busy man with many calls, and my methods have to be short and direct. The swiftest surgery is the least painful. Let me first say what will ease your mind. Your wife is a very good, a very loving, and a very ill-used woman."

Ferguson sat up with a cry of joy.

" Prove that, Mr. Holmes, and I am your debtor for ever."

" I will do so, but in doing so I must wound you deeply in another direction."

" I care nothing so long as you clear my wife. Everything on earth is insignificant compared to that."

" Let me tell you, then, the train of reasoning which passed through my mind in Baker Street. The idea of a vampire was to me absurd. Such things do not happen in criminal practice in England. And yet your observation was precise. You had seen the lady rise from beside the child's cot with the blood upon her lips."

" I did."

" Did it not occur to you that a bleeding wound may be sucked for some other purpose than to draw the blood from it ? Was there not a Queen in English history who sucked such a wound to draw poison from it ? "

" Poison ! "

" A South American household. My instinct felt the presence of those weapons upon the wall before my eyes ever saw them. It might have been other poison, but that was what occurred to me. When I saw that little empty quiver beside the small bird-bow, it was just what I expected to see. If the child were pricked with one of those arrows dipped in curare or some other devilish drug, it would mean death if the venom were not sucked out.

" And the dog ! If one were to use such a poison, would one not try it first in order to see that it had not lost its power ? I did not foresee the dog, but at least

I understood him and he fitted into my reconstruction.

"Now do you understand? Your wife feared such an attack. She saw it made and saved the child's life, and yet she shrank from telling you all the truth, for she knew how you loved the boy and feared lest it break your heart."

"Jacky!"

"I watched him as you fondled the child just now. His face was clearly reflected in the glass of the window where the shutter formed a background. I saw such jealousy, such cruel hatred, as I have seldom seen in a human face."

"My Jacky!"

"You have to face it, Mr. Ferguson. It is the more painful because it is a distorted love, a maniacal exaggerated love for you, and possibly for his dead mother, which has prompted his action. His very soul is consumed with hatred for this splendid child, whose health and beauty are a contrast to his own weakness."

"Good God! It is incredible!"

"Have I spoken the truth, madame?"

The lady was sobbing, with her face buried in the pillows. Now she turned to her husband.

"How could I tell you, Bob? I felt the blow it would be to you. It was better that I should wait and that it should come from some other lips than mine. When this gentleman, who seems to have powers of magic, wrote that he knew all, I was glad."

"I think a year at sea would be my prescription for Master Jacky," said Holmes, rising from his chair. "Only one thing is still clouded, madame. We can quite understand your attacks upon Master Jacky. There is a limit to a mother's patience. But how did you dare to leave the child these last two days?"

"I had told Mrs. Mason. She knew."

"Exactly. So I imagined."

Ferguson was standing by the bed, choking, his hands outstretched and quivering.

"This, I fancy, is the time for our exit, Watson," said Holmes in a whisper. "If you will take one elbow of the too faithful Dolores, I will take the other. There, now," he added, as he closed the door behind him. "I think we may leave them to settle the rest among themselves."

I have only one further note of this case. It is the letter which Holmes wrote in final answer to that with which the narrative begins. It ran thus :

BAKER STREET,
Nov. 21st.

Re Vampires.

SIR,—

Referring to your letter of the 19th, I beg to state that I have looked into the inquiry of your client, Mr. Robert Ferguson, of Ferguson & Muirhead, tea brokers, of Mincing Lane, and that the matter has been brought to a satisfactory conclusion. With thanks for your recommendation,

I am, Sir,
Faithfully yours,
SHERLOCK HOLMES.

50. *The Three Garridebs*

IT may have been a comedy, or it may have been a tragedy. It cost one man his reason, it cost me a blood-letting, and it cost yet another man the penalties of the law. Yet there was certainly an element of comedy. Well, you shall judge for yourselves.

I remember the date very well, for it was in the same month that Holmes refused a knighthood for services which may perhaps some day be described. I only refer to the matter in passing, for in my position of partner and confidant I am obliged to be particularly careful to avoid any indiscretion. I repeat, however, that this enables me to fix the date, which was the latter end of June, 1902, shortly after the conclusion of the South African War. Holmes had spent several days in bed, as was his habit from time to time, but he emerged that morning with a long foolscap document in his hand and a twinkle of amusement in his austere grey eyes.

"There is a chance for you to make some money, friend Watson," said he. "Have you ever heard the name of Garrideb ? "

I admitted that I had not.

"Well, if you can lay your hand upon a Garrideb, there's money in it."

"Why ? "

"Ah, that's a long story—rather a whimsical one, too. I don't think in all our explorations of human complexities we have ever come upon anything more singular. The fellow will be here presently for cross-examination, so I won't open the matter up till he comes. But meanwhile, that's the name we want."

The telephone directory lay on the table beside me, and I turned over the pages in a rather hopeless quest. But to my amazement there was this strange name in its due place. I gave a cry of triumph.

"Here you are, Holmes ! Here it is ! "

Holmes took the book from my hand.

"' Garrideb, N.,'" he read, "' 136 Little Ryder Street, W.' Sorry to disappoint you, my dear Watson, but this is the man himself. That is the address upon his letter. We want another to match him."

Mrs. Hudson had come in with a card upon a tray. I took it up and glanced at it.

"Why, here it is ! " I cried in amazement. "This is a different initial. John Garrideb, Counsellor at Law, Moorville, Kansas, U.S.A."

Holmes smiled as he looked at the card. "I am afraid you must make yet another effort, Watson," said he. " This gentleman is also in the plot already, though I certainly did not expect to see him this morning. However, he is in a position to tell us a good deal which I want to know."

A moment later he was in the room. Mr. John Garrideb, Counsellor at Law, was a short, powerful man with the round, fresh, clean-shaven face characteristic of so many American men of affairs. The general effect was chubby and rather childlike, so that one received the impression of quite a young man with a broad set smile upon his face. His eyes, however, were arresting. Seldom in any human head have I seen a pair which bespoke a more intense inward life, so bright were they, so alert, so responsive to every change of thought. His accent was American, but was not accompanied by any eccentricity of speech.

" Mr. Holmes ? " he asked, glancing from one to the other. " Ah, yes ! Your pictures are not unlike you, sir, if I may say so. I believe you have had a letter from my namesake, Mr. Nathan Garrideb, have you not ? "

" Pray sit down," said Sherlock Holmes. " We shall, I fancy, have a good deal to discuss." He took up his sheets of foolscap. " You are, of course, the Mr. John Garrideb mentioned in this document. But surely you have been in England some time ? "

" Why do you say that, Mr. Holmes ? " I seemed to read sudden suspicion in those expressive eyes.

" Your whole outfit is English."

Mr. Garrideb forced a laugh. " I've read of your tricks, Mr. Holmes, but I never thought I would be the subject of them. Where do you read that ? "

" The shoulder cut of your coat, the toes of your boots ---could anyone doubt it ? "

" Well, well, I had no idea I was so obvious a Britisher. But business brought me over here some time ago, and so, as you say, my outfit is nearly all London. However, I guess your time is of value, and we did not meet to talk about the cut of my socks. What about getting down to that paper you hold in your hand ? "

Holmes had in some way ruffled our visitor, whose chubby face had assumed a far less amiable expression.

" Patience ! Patience, Mr. Garrideb ! " said my friend in a soothing voice. " Dr. Watson would tell you that these little digressions of mine sometimes prove in the end to have some bearing on the matter. But why did Mr. Nathan Garrideb not come with you ? "

" Why did he ever drag you into it at all ? " asked our visitor, with a sudden outflame of anger. " What in thunder had you to do with it ? Here was a bit of professional business between two gentlemen, and one of them must needs call in a detective ! I saw him this morning, and he told me this fool-trick he had played me, and that's why I am here. But I feel bad about it, all the same."

" There was no reflection upon you, Mr. Garrideb. It was simply zeal upon his part to gain your end—an end which is, I understand, equally vital for both of you. He knew that I had means of getting information, and, therefore, it was very natural that he should apply to me."

Our visitor's angry face gradually cleared.

" Well, that puts it different," said he. " When I went to see him this morning and he told me he had sent to a detective, I just asked for your address and came right away. I don't want police butting into a private matter. But if you are content just to help us find the man, there can be no harm in that."

" Well, that is just how it stands," said Holmes. " And now, sir, since you are here, we had best have a clear account from your own lips. My friend here knows nothing of the details."

Mr. Garrideb surveyed me with not too friendly a gaze.

" Need he know ? " he asked.

" We usually work together."

" Well, there's no reason it should be kept a secret.
I'll give you the facts as short as I can make them. If
you came from Kansas I would not need to explain to
you who Alexander Hamilton Garrideb was. He made
his money in real estate, and afterwards in the wheat
pit at Chicago, but he spent it in buying up as much
land as would make one of your counties, lying along
the Arkansas River, west of Fort Dodge. It's grazing-
land and lumber-land and arable-land and mineralized-
land, and just every sort of land that brings dollars to the
man that owns it.

" He had no kith nor kin—or, if he had, I never heard
of it. But he took a kind of pride in the queerness of his
name. That was what brought us together. I was in the
law at Topeka, and one day I had a visit from the old
man, and he was tickled to death to meet another man
with his own name. It was his pet fad, and he was
dead set to find out if there were any more Garridebs in
the world. ' Find me another ! ' said he. I told him
I was a busy man and could not spend my life hiking
round the world in search of Garridebs. ' None the
less,' said he, ' that is just what you will do if things
pan out as I planned them.' I thought he was joking,
but there was a powerful lot of meaning in the words, as
I was soon to discover.

" For he died within a year of saying them, and he
left a will behind him. It was the queerest will that
has ever been filed in the State of Kansas. His property
was divided into three parts, and I was to have one on
condition that I found two Garridebs who would share
the remainder. It's five million dollars for each if it is a
cent, but we can't lay a finger on it until we all three
stand in a row.

" It was so big a chance that I just let my legal practice
slide and I set forth looking for Garridebs. There is
not one in the United States. I went through it, sir,
with a fine-toothed comb and never a Garrideb could I
catch. Then I tried the old country. Sure enough

there was the name in the London Telephone Directory.
I went after him two days ago and explained the whole
matter to him. But he is a lone man, like myself, with
some women relations, but no men. It says three adult
men in the will. So you see we still have a vacancy, and
if you can help to fill it we will be very ready to pay
your charges."

"Well, Watson," said Holmes, with a smile, "I said
it was rather whimsical, did I not? I should have
thought, sir, that your obvious way was to advertise in
the agony columns of the papers."

"I have done that, Mr. Holmes. No replies."

"Dear me! Well, it is certainly a most curious
little problem. I may take a glance at it in my leisure.
By the way, it is curious that you should have come
from Topeka. I used to have a correspondent—he is
dead now—old Dr. Lysander Starr, who was Mayor in
1890."

"Good old Dr. Starr!" said our visitor. "His name
is still honoured. Well, Mr. Holmes, I suppose all we
can do is to report to you and let you know how we
progress. I reckon you will hear within a day or two."
With this assurance our American bowed and departed.

Holmes had lit his pipe, and he sat for some time with
a curious smile upon his face.

"Well?" I asked at last.

"I am wondering, Watson—just wondering!"

"At what?"

Holmes took his pipe from his lips.

"I was wondering, Watson, what on earth could be
the object of this man in telling us such a rigmarole of
lies. I nearly asked him so—for there are times when a
brutal frontal attack is the best policy—but I judged
it better to let him think he had fooled us. Here is a
man with an English coat frayed at the elbow and trousers
bagged at the knee with a year's wear, and yet by this
document and by his own account he is a provincial
American lately landed in London. There have been

no advertisements in the agony columns. You know that I miss nothing there. They are my favourite covert for putting up a bird, and I would never have overlooked such a cock pheasant as that. I never knew a Dr. Lysander Starr of Topeka. Touch him where you would he was false. I think the fellow is really an American, but he has worn his accent smooth with years of London. What is his game, then, and what motive lies behind this preposterous search for Garridebs ? It's worth our attention, for, granting that the man is a rascal, he is certainly a complex and ingenious one. We must now find out if our other correspondent is a fraud also. Just ring him up, Watson."

I did so, and heard a thin, quavering voice at the other end of the line.

"Yes, yes, I am Mr. Nathan Garrideb. Is Mr. Holmes there ? I should very much like to have a word with Mr. Holmes."

My friend took the instrument and I heard the usual syncopated dialogue.

"Yes, he has been here. I understand that you don't know him. . . . How long ? . . . Only two days ! . . . Yes, yes, of course, it is a most captivating prospect. Will you be at home this evening ? I suppose your namesake will not be there ? . . . Very good, we will come then, for I would rather have a chat without him. . . . Dr. Watson will come with me. . . . I understood from your note that you did not go out often. . . . Well, we shall be round about six. You need not mention it to the American lawyer. . . . Very good. Goodbye ! "

It was twilight of a lovely spring evening, and even Little Ryder Street, one of the smaller offshoots from the Edgware Road, within a stone-cast of old Tyburn Tree of evil memory, looked golden and wonderful in the slanting rays of the setting sun. The particular house to which we were directed was a large, old-fashioned, Early Georgian edifice with a flat brick face broken only by two deep bay windows on the ground floor. It was on this ground floor that our client lived, and, indeed, the low windows proved to be the front of the huge room in which he spent his waking hours. Holmes pointed as we passed to the small brass plate which bore the curious name.

"Up some years, Watson," he remarked, indicating its discoloured surface. "It's *his* real name, anyhow, and that is something to note."

The house had a common stair, and there were a number of names painted in the hall, some indicating offices and some private chambers. It was not a collection of residential flats, but rather the abode of Bohemian bachelors. Our client opened the door for us himself and apologized by saying that the woman in charge left at four o'clock. Mr. Nathan Garrideb proved to be a very tall, loose-jointed, round-backed person, gaunt and bald, some sixty-odd years of age. He had a cadaverous face, with the dull dead skin of a man to whom exercise was unknown. Large round spectacles and a small projecting goat's beard combined with his stooping attitude to give him an expression of peering curiosity. The general effect, however, was amiable, though eccentric.

The room was as curious as its occupant. It looked like a small museum. It was both broad and deep, with cupboards and cabinets all round, crowded with specimens, geological and anatomical. Cases of butterflies and moths flanked each side of the entrance. A large table in the centre was littered with all sorts of debris, while the tall brass tube of a powerful microscope bristled up amongst them. As I glanced round I was surprised at the universality of the man's interests. Here was a case of ancient coins. There was a cabinet of flint instruments. Behind his central table was a large cupboard of fossil bones. Above was a line of plaster skulls with such names as " Neanderthal," " Heidelberg," " Cromagnon " printed beneath them. It was clear that he was a student of many subjects. As he stood in front of us now, he held a piece of chamois leather in his right hand with which he was polishing a coin.

" Syracusan—of the best period," he explained, holding it up. " They degenerated greatly towards the end. At their best I hold them supreme, though some prefer the Alexandrian school. You will find a chair here, Mr. Holmes. Pray allow me to clear these bones. And you, sir—ah, yes, Dr. Watson—if you would have the goodness to put the Japanese vase to one side. You see round me my little interests in life. My doctor lectures me about never going out, but why should I go out when I have so much to hold me here ? I can assure you that the adequate cataloguing of one of those cabinets would take me three good months."

Holmes looked round him with curiosity.

" But do you tell me that you *never* go out ? " he said.

" Now and again I drive down to Sotheby's or Christie's. Otherwise I very seldom leave my room. I am not too strong, and my researches are very absorbing. But you can imagine, Mr. Holmes, what a terrific shock— pleasant but terrific—it was for me when I heard of this unparalleled good fortune. It only needs one more Garrideb to complete the matter, and surely we can find one. I had a brother, but he is dead, and female relatives are disqualified. But there must surely be others in the world. I had heard that you handled strange cases, and that was why I sent to you. Of course, this American gentleman is quite right, and I should have taken his advice first, but I acted for the best."

" I think you acted very wisely indeed," said Holmes. " But are you really anxious to acquire an estate in America ? "

" Certainly not, sir. Nothing would induce me to leave my collection. But this gentleman has assured me that he will buy me out as soon as we have established our claim. Five million dollars was the sum named. There are a dozen specimens in the market at the present moment which fill gaps in my collection, and which I am unable to purchase for want of a few hundred pounds. Just think what I could do with five million dollars. Why, I have the nucleus of a national collection. I shall be the Hans Sloane of my age."

His eyes gleamed behind his great spectacles. It was very clear that no pains would be spared by Mr. Nathan Garrideb in finding a namesake.

"I merely called to make your acquaintance, and there is no reason why I should interrupt your studies," said Holmes. "I prefer to establish personal touch with those with whom I do business. There are few questions I need ask, for I have your very clear narrative in my pocket, and I filled up the blanks when this American gentleman called. I understand that up to this week you were unaware of his existence."

"That is so. He called last Tuesday."

"Did he tell you of our interview to-day?"

"Yes, he came straight back to me. He had been very angry."

"Why should he be angry?"

"He seemed to think it was some reflection on his honour. But he was quite cheerful again when he returned."

"Did he suggest any course of action?"

"No, sir, he did not."

"Has he had, or asked for, any money from you?"

"No, sir, never!"

"You see no possible object he has in view?"

"None, except what he states."

"Did you tell him of our telephone appointment?"

"Yes, sir, I did."

Holmes was lost in thought. I could see that he was puzzled.

"Have you any articles of great value in your collection?"

"No, sir. I am not a rich man. It is a good collection, but not a very valuable one."

" You have no fear of burglars ? "

" Not the least."

" How long have you been in these rooms ? "

" Nearly five years."

Holmes' cross-examination was interrupted by an imperative knocking at the door. No sooner had our client unlatched it than the American lawyer burst excitedly into the room.

" Here you are ! " he cried, waving a paper over his head. " I thought I should be in time to get you. Mr. Nathan Garrideb, my congratulations ! You are a rich man, sir. Our business is happily finished and all is well. As to you, Mr. Holmes, we can only say we are sorry if we have given you any useless trouble."

He handed over the paper to our client, who stood staring at a marked advertisement. Holmes and I leaned forward and read it over his shoulder. This is how it ran :

HOWARD GARRIDEB.

Constructor of Agricultural Machinery.

Binders, reapers' steam and hand plows, drills, harrows, farmers' carts, buckboards, and all other appliances.
Estimates for Artesian Wells.

Apply Grosvenor Buildings, Aston.

" Glorious ! " gasped our host. " That makes our third man."

" I had opened up inquiries in Birmingham," said the American, " and my agent there has sent me this advertisement from a local paper. We must hustle and put the thing through. I have written to this man and told him that you will see him in his office to-morrow afternoon at four o'clock."

" You want *me* to see him ? "

"What do you say, Mr. Holmes? Don't you think it would be wiser? Here am I, a wandering American with a wonderful tale. Why should he believe what I tell him? But you are a Britisher with solid references, and he is bound to take notice of what you say. I would go with you if you wished, but I have a very busy day to-morrow, and I could always follow you if you are in any trouble."

"Well, I have not made such a journey for years."

"It is nothing, Mr. Garrideb. I have figured out your connections. You leave at twelve and should be there soon after two. Then you can be back the same night. All you have to do is to see this man, explain the matter, and get an affidavit of his existence. By the Lord!" he added hotly, "considering I've come all the way from the centre of America, it is surely little enough if you go a hundred miles in order to put this matter through."

"Quite so," said Holmes. "I think what this gentleman says is very true."

Mr. Nathan Garrideb shrugged his shoulders with a disconsolate air. "Well, if you insist I shall go," said he. "It is certainly hard for me to refuse you anything, considering the glory of hope that you have brought into my life."

"Then that is agreed," said Holmes, "and no doubt you will let me have a report as soon as you can."

"I'll see to that," said the American. "Well," he added, looking at his watch, "I'll have to get on. I'll call to-morrow, Mr. Nathan, and see you off to Birmingham. Coming my way, Mr. Holmes? Well, then, good-bye, and we may have good news for you to-morrow night."

I noticed that my friend's face cleared when the American left the room, and the look of thoughtful perplexity had vanished.

"I wish I could look over your collection, Mr. Garrideb," said he. "In my profession all sorts of odd knowledge comes useful, and this room of yours is a storehouse of it."

Our client shone with pleasure and his eyes gleamed from behind his big glasses.

"I had always heard, sir, that you were a very intelligent man," said he. "I could take you round now, if you have the time."

"Unfortunately, I have not. But these specimens are so well labelled and classified that they hardly need your personal explanation. If I should be able to look in to-morrow, I presume that there would be no objection to my glancing over them?"

"None at all. You are most welcome. The place will, of course, be shut up, but Mrs. Saunders is in the basement up to four o'clock and would let you in with her key."

"Well, I happen to be clear to-morrow afternoon. If you would say a word to Mrs. Saunders it would be quite in order. By the way, who is your house-agent?"

Our client was amazed at the sudden question.

"Holloway and Steele, in the Edgware Road. But why?"

"I am a bit of an archæologist myself when it comes to houses," said Holmes, laughing. "I was wondering if this was Queen Anne or Georgian."

"Georgian, beyond doubt."

"Really. I should have thought a little earlier. However, it is easily ascertained. Well, good-bye, Mr. Garrideb, and may you have every success in your Birmingham journey."

The house-agent's was close by, but we found that it was closed for the day, so we made our way back to Baker Street. It was not till after dinner that Holmes reverted to the subject.

"Our little problem draws to a close," said he. "No doubt you have outlined the solution in your own mind."

"I can make neither head nor tail of it."

"The head is surely clear enough and the tail we

should see to-morrow. Did you notice nothing curious about that advertisement ? "

" I saw that the word ' plough ' was mis-spelt."

" Oh, you did notice that, did you ? Come, Watson, you improve all the time. Yes, it was bad English but good American. The printer had set it up as received. Then the buckboards. That is American also. And artesian wells are commoner with them than with us. It was a typical American advertisement, but purporting to be from an English firm. What do you make of that ? "

" I can only suppose that this American lawyer put it in himself. What his object was I fail to understand."

" Well, there are alternative explanations. Anyhow, he wanted to get this good old fossil up to Birmingham. That is very clear. I might have told him that he was clearly going on a wild-goose chase, but, on second thoughts, it seemed better to clear the stage by letting him go. To-morrow, Watson—well, to-morrow will speak for itself."

Holmes was up and out early. When he returned at lunch-time I noticed that his face was very grave.

" This is a more serious matter than I had expected, Watson," said he. " It is fair to tell you so, though I know it will only be an additional reason to you for running your head into danger. I should know my Watson by now. But there is danger, and you should know it."

" Well, it is not the first we have shared, Holmes I hope it may not be the last. What is the particular danger this time ? "

" We are up against a very hard case. I have identified Mr. John Garrideb, Counsellor at Law. He is none other than ' Killer ' Evans, of sinister and murderous reputation."

" I fear I am none the wiser."

" Ah, it is not part of your profession to carry about

a portable Newgate Calendar in your memory. I have
been down to see friend Lestrade at the Yard. There
may be an occasional want of imaginative intuition down
there, but they lead the world for thoroughness and
method. I had an idea that we might get on the track
of our American friend in their records. Sure enough,
I found his chubby face smiling up at me from the
Rogues' Portrait Gallery. James Winter, *alias* More-
croft, *alias* Killer Evans, was the inscription below."
Holmes drew an envelope from his pocket. "I scribbled
down a few points from his dossier. Aged forty-four.
Native of Chicago. Known to have shot three men in the
States. Escaped from penitentiary through political
influence. Came to London in 1893. Shot a man
over cards in a night club in the Waterloo Road in
January, 1895. Man died, but he was shown to have
been the aggressor in the row. Dead man was identified
as Rodger Prescott, famous as forger and coiner in Chicago.
Killer Evans released in 1901. Has been under police
supervision since, but so far as known has led an honest
life. Very dangerous man, usually carries arms and is
prepared to use them. That is our bird, Watson—
a sporting bird, as you must admit."

"But what is his game?"

"Well, it begins to define itself. I have been to the
house-agents. Our client, as he told us, has been there
five years. It was unlet for a year before then. The
previous tenant was a gentleman at large named Waldron.
Waldron's appearance was well remembered at the office.
He had suddenly vanished and nothing more been heard
of him. He was a tall, bearded man with very dark
features. Now, Prescott, the man whom Killer Evans
had shot, was, according to Scotland Yard, a tall, dark
man with a beard. As a working hypothesis, I think
we may take it that Prescott, the American criminal,
used to live in the very room which our innocent friend
now devotes to his museum. So at last we get a link,
you see."

" And the next link ? "

" Well, we must go now and look for that."

He took a revolver from the drawer and handed it to me.

" I have my old favourite with me. If our Wild West friend tries to live up to his nickname, we must be ready for him. I'll give you an hour for a siesta, Watson, and then I think it will be time for our Ryder Street adventure."

It was just four o'clock when we reached the curious apartment of Nathan Garrideb. Mrs. Saunders, the caretaker, was about to leave, but she had no hesitation in admitting us, for the door shut with a spring lock and Holmes promised to see that all was safe before we left. Shortly afterwards the outer door closed, her bonnet passed the bow window, and we knew that we were alone in the lower floor of the house. Holmes made a rapid examination of the premises. There was one cupboard in a dark corner which stood out a little from the wall. It was behind this that we eventually crouched, while Holmes in a whisper outlined his intentions.

" He wanted to get our amiable friend out of his room —that is very clear, and, as the collector never went out, it took some planning to do it. The whole of this Garrideb invention was apparently for no other end. I must say, Watson, that there is a certain devilish ingenuity about it even if the queer name of the tenant did give him an opening which he could hardly have expected. He wove his plot with remarkable cunning."

" But what did he want ? "

" Well, that is what we are here to find out. It has nothing whatever to do with our client, so far as I can read the situation. It is something connected with the man he murdered—the man who may have been his confederate in crime. There is some guilty secret in the room. That is how I read it. At first I thought our friend might have something in his collection more valuable than he knew—something worth the attention of a big criminal. But the fact that Rodger Prescott of evil memory inhabited these rooms points to some deeper reason. Well, Watson, we can but possess our souls in patience and see what the hour may bring."

That hour was not long in striking. We crouched closer in the shadow as we heard the outer door open and shut. Then came the sharp, metallic snap of a key, and the American was in the room. He closed the door softly behind him, took a sharp glance around him to see that all was safe, threw off his overcoat, and walked up to the central table with the brisk manner of one who knows exactly what he has to do and how to do it. He pushed the table to one side, tore up the square of carpet on which it rested, rolled it completely back, and then, drawing a jemmy from his inside pocket, he knelt down and worked vigorously upon the floor. Presently we heard the sound of sliding boards, and an instant later a square had opened in the planks. Killer Evans struck a match, lit a stump of candle, and vanished from our view.

Clearly our moment had come. Holmes touched my wrist as a signal, and together we stole across to the open trap-door. Gently as we moved, however, the old floor must have creaked under our feet, for the head of our American, peering anxiously round, emerged suddenly from the open space. His face turned upon us with a glare of baffled rage, which gradually softened into a rather shamefaced grin as he realized that two pistols were pointed at his head.

" Well, well ! " said he, coolly, as he scrambled to the surface. " I guess you have been one too many for me, Mr. Holmes. Saw through my game, I suppose, and played me for a sucker from the first. Well, sir, I hand it to you ; you have me beat and——"

In an instant he had whisked out a revolver from his breast and had fired two shots. I felt a sudden hot sear as if a red-hot iron had been pressed to my thigh.

There was a crash as Holmes' pistol came down on the man's head. I had a vision of him sprawling upon the floor with blood running down his face while Holmes rummaged him for weapons. Then my friend's wiry arms were round me and he was leading me to a chair.

"You're not hurt, Watson? For God's sake, say that you are not hurt!"

It was worth a wound—it was worth many wounds —to know the depth of loyalty and love which lay behind that cold mask. The clear, hard eyes were dimmed for a moment, and the firm lips were shaking. For the one and only time I caught a glimpse of a great heart as well as of a great brain. All my years of humble but single-minded service culminated in that moment of revelation.

"It's nothing, Holmes. It's a mere scratch."

He had ripped up my trousers with his pocket-knife.

"You are right," he cried, with an immense sigh of relief. "It is quite superficial." His face set like flint as he glared at our prisoner, who was sitting up with a dazed face. "By the Lord, it is as well for you. If you had killed Watson, you would not have got out of this room alive. Now, sir, what have you to say for yourself?"

He had nothing to say for himself. He only lay and scowled. I leaned on Holmes' arm, and together we looked down into the small cellar which had been disclosed by the secret flap. It was still illuminated by the candle which Evans had taken down with him. Our eyes fell upon a mass of rusted machinery, great rolls of paper, a litter of bottles, and, neatly arranged upon a small table, a number of neat little bundles.

"A printing press—a counterfeiter's outfit," said Holmes.

"Yes, sir," said our prisoner, staggering slowly to his feet and then sinking into the chair. "The greatest counterfeiter London ever saw. That's Prescott's machine, and those bundles on the table are two thousand of Prescott's notes worth a hundred each and fit to pass anywhere. Help yourselves, gentlemen. Call it a deal and let me beat it."

Holmes laughed.

" We don't do things like that, Mr. Evans. There is no bolt-hole for you in this country. You shot this man Prescott, did you not ? "

" Yes, sir, and got five years for it, though it was he who pulled on me. Five years—when I should have had a medal the size of a soup plate. No living man could tell a Prescott from a Bank of England, and if I hadn't put him out he would have flooded London with them. I was the only one in the world who knew where he made them. Can you wonder that I wanted to get to the place ? And can you wonder that when I found this crazy boob of a bug-hunter with the queer name squatting right on the top of it, and never quitting his room, I had to do the best I could to shift him ? Maybe I would have been wiser if I had put him away. It would have been easy enough, but I'm a soft-hearted guy that can't begin shooting unless the other man has a gun also. But say, Mr. Holmes, what have I done wrong, anyhow ? I've not used this plant. I've not hurt this old stiff. Where do you get me ? "

" Only attempted murder, so far as I can see," said Holmes. " But that's not our job. They take that at the next stage. What we wanted at present was just your sweet self. Please give the Yard a call, Watson. It won't be entirely unexpected."

So those were the facts about Killer Evans and his remarkable invention of the three Garridebs. We heard later that our poor old friend never got over the shock of his dissipated dreams. When his castle in the air fell down, it buried him beneath the ruins. He was last heard of at a nursing-home in Brixton. It was a glad day at the Yard when the Prescott outfit was discovered, for, though they knew that it existed, they had never been able, after the death of the man, to find out where it was. Evans had indeed done great service and caused several worthy C.I.D. men to sleep the sounder, for the counterfeiter stands in a class by himself as a public danger. They would willingly have subscribed to that soup-plate medal of which the criminal had spoken, but an unappreciative Bench took a less favourable view, and the Killer returned to those shades from which he had just emerged.

51. *Thor Bridge*

SOMEWHERE in the vaults of the bank of Cox & Co., at Charing Cross, there is a travel-worn and battered tin dispatch-box with my name, John H. Watson, M.D., Late Indian Army, painted upon the lid. It is crammed with papers, nearly all of which are records of cases to illustrate the curious problems which Mr. Sherlock Holmes had at various times to examine. Some, and not the least interesting, were complete failures, and as such will hardly bear narrating, since no final explanation is forthcoming. A problem without a solution may interest the student, but can hardly fail to annoy the casual reader. Among these unfinished tales is that of Mr. James Phillimore, who, stepping back into his own house to get his umbrella, was never more seen in this world. No less remarkable is that of the cutter *Alicia*, which sailed one spring morning into a small patch of mist from where she never again emerged, nor was anything further ever heard of herself and her crew. A third case worthy of note is that of Isadora Persano, the well-known journalist and duellist, who was found stark staring mad with a match-box in front of him which contained a remarkable worm, said to be unknown to science. Apart from these unfathomed cases, there are some which involve the secrets of private families to an extent which would mean consternation in many exalted quarters if it were thought possible that they might find their way into print. I need not say that such a breach of confidence is unthinkable, and that these records will be separated and destroyed now that my friend has time to turn his energies to the matter. There remain a considerable residue of cases of greater or less interest which I might have edited before had I not feared to give the public a surfeit which might react upon the reputation of the man whom above all others I revere. In some I was myself concerned and can speak as an eye-witness, while in others I was either not present or played so small a part that they could only be told as by a third person. The following narrative is drawn from my own experience.

It was a wild morning in October, and I observed as I was dressing how the last remaining leaves were being whirled from the solitary plane tree which graces the yard behind our house. I descended to breakfast prepared to find my companion in depressed spirits, for, like all great artists, he was easily impressed by his surroundings. On the contrary, I found that he had nearly finished his meal, and that his mood was particularly bright and joyous, with that somewhat sinister cheerfulness which was characteristic of his lighter moments.

" You have a case, Holmes ? " I remarked.

" The faculty of deduction is certainly contagious, Watson," he answered. " It has enabled you to probe my secret. Yes, I have a case. After a month of trivialities and stagnation the wheels move once more."

" Might I share it ? "

" There is little to share, but we may discuss it when you have consumed the two hard-boiled eggs with which our new cook has favoured us. Their condition may not be unconnected with the copy of the *Family Herald* which I observed yesterday upon the hall-table. Even so trivial a matter as cooking an egg demands an attention which is conscious of the passage of time, and incompatible with the love romance in that excellent periodical."

A quarter of an hour later the table had been cleared

and we were face to face. He had drawn a letter from his pocket.

" You have heard of Neil Gibson, the Gold King ? " he said.

" You mean the American Senator ? "

" Well, he was once Senator for some Western State, but is better known as the greatest gold-mining magnate in the world."

" Yes, I know of him. He has surely lived in England for some time. His name is very familiar."

" Yes ; he bought a considerable estate in Hampshire some five years ago. Possibly you have already heard of the tragic end of his wife ? "

" Of course. I remember it now. That is why the name is familiar. But I really know nothing of the details."

Holmes waved his hand towards some papers on a chair. " I had no idea that the case was coming my way or I should have had my extracts ready," said he. " The fact is that the problem, though exceedingly sensational, appeared to present no difficulty. The interesting personality of the accused does not obscure the clearness of the evidence. That was the view taken by the coroner's jury and also in the police-court proceedings. It is now referred to the Assizes at Winchester. I fear it is a thankless business. I can discover facts, Watson, but I cannot change them. Unless some entirely new and unexpected ones come to light I do not see what my client can hope for."

" Your client ? "

" Ah, I forgot I had not told you. I am getting into your involved habit, Watson, of telling a story backwards. You had best read this first."

The letter which he handed to me, written in a bold, masterful hand, ran as follows :

CLARIDGE'S HOTEL, *October 3rd.*
DEAR MR. SHERLOCK HOLMES,—
I can't see the best woman God ever made go to

her death without doing all that is possible to save her. I can't explain things—I can't even try to explain them, but I know beyond all doubt that Miss Dunbar is innocent. You know the facts—who doesn't ? It has been the gossip of the country. And never a voice raised for her ! It's the damned injustice of it all that makes me crazy. That woman has a heart that wouldn't let her kill a fly. Well, I'll come at eleven to-morrow and see if you can get some ray of light in the dark. Maybe I have a clue and don't know it. Anyhow, all I know and all I have and all I am are for your use if only you can save her. If ever in your life you showed your powers, put them now into this case.

Yours faithfully,
J. NEIL GIBSON.

" There you have it," said Sherlock Holmes, knocking out the ashes of his after-breakfast pipe and slowly refilling it. " That is the gentleman I await. As to the story, you have hardly time to master all these papers, so I must give it to you in a nutshell if you are to take an intelligent interest in the proceedings. This man is the greatest financial power in the world, and a man, as I understand, of most violent and formidable character. He married a wife, the victim of this tragedy, of whom I know nothing save that she was past her prime, which was the more unfortunate as a very attractive governess superintended the education of two young children. These are the three people concerned, and the scene is a grand old manor-house, the centre of an historical English estate. Then as to the tragedy. The wife was found in the grounds nearly half a mile from the house, late at night, clad in her dinner dress, with a shawl over her shoulders and a revolver bullet through her brain. No weapon was found near her and there was no local clue as to the murder. No weapon near her, Watson— mark that ! The crime seems to have been committed late in the evening, and the body was found by a gamekeeper about eleven o'clock, when it was examined by the police and by a doctor before being carried up to the house. Is this too condensed, or can you follow it clearly ? "

" It is all very clear. But why suspect the governess ? "

" Well, in the first place there is some very direct evidence. A revolver with one discharged chamber and a calibre which corresponded with the bullet was found on the floor of her wardrobe." His eyes fixed and he repeated in broken words, " On—the—floor—of—her—wardrobe." Then he sank into silence, and I saw that some train of thought had been set moving which I should be foolish to interrupt. Suddenly with a start he emerged into brisk life once more. " Yes, Watson, it was found. Pretty damning, eh ? So the two juries thought. Then the dead woman had a note upon her making an appointment at that very place and signed by the governess. How's that ? Finally, there is the motive. Senator Gibson is an attractive person. If his wife dies, who more likely to succeed her than the young lady who had already by all accounts received pressing attentions from her employer. Love, fortune, power, all depending upon one middle-aged life. Ugly, Watson—very ugly ! "

" Yes, indeed, Holmes."

" Nor could she prove an alibi. On the contrary, she had to admit that she was down near Thor Bridge —that was the scene of the tragedy—about that hour. She couldn't deny it, for some passing villager had seen her there."

" That really seems final."

" And yet, Watson—and yet ! This bridge—a single broad span of stone with balustraded sides—carries the drive over the narrowest part of a long, deep, reed-girt sheet of water. Thor Mere it is called. In the mouth of the bridge lay the dead woman. Such are the main facts. But here, if I mistake not, is our client, considerably before his time."

Billy had opened the door, but the name which he announced was an unexpected one. Mr. Marlow Bates was a stranger to both of us. He was a thin, nervous wisp of a man with frightened eyes, and a twitching, hesitating manner—a man whom my own professional eye would judge to be on the brink of an absolute nervous breakdown.

"You seem agitated, Mr. Bates," said Holmes. "Pray sit down. I fear I can only give you a short time, for I have an appointment at eleven."

"I know you have," our visitor gasped, shooting out short sentences like a man who is out of breath. "Mr. Gibson is coming. Mr. Gibson is my employer. I am manager of his estate. Mr. Holmes, he is a villain —an infernal villain."

"Strong language, Mr. Bates."

"I have to be emphatic, Mr. Holmes, for the time is so limited. I would not have him find me here for the world. He is almost due now. But I was so situated that I could not come earlier. His secretary, Mr. Ferguson, only told me this morning of his appointment with you."

"And you are his manager?"

"I have given him notice. In a couple of weeks I shall have shaken off his accursed slavery. A hard man, Mr. Holmes, hard to all about him. Those public charities are a screen to cover his private iniquities. But his wife was his chief victim. He was brutal to her—yes, sir, brutal! How she came by her death I do not know, but I am sure that he had made her life a misery to her. She was a creature of the Tropics, a Brazilian by birth, as no doubt you know?"

"No; it had escaped me."

"Tropical by birth and tropical by nature. A child of the sun and of passion. She had loved him as such women can love, but when her own physical charms had faded—I am told that they once were great—there was nothing to hold him. We all liked her and felt for her and nated him for the way that he treated her. But he is plausible and cunning. That is all I have to say to you. Don't take him at his face value. There is more behind. Now I'll go. No, no, don't detain me! He is almost due."

With a frightened look at the clock our strange visitor literally ran to the door and disappeared.

"Well! Well!" said Holmes, after an interval of silence. "Mr. Gibson seems to have a nice loyal household. But the warning is a useful one, and now we can only wait till the man himself appears."

Sharp at the hour we heard a heavy step upon the stairs and the famous millionaire was shown into the room. As I looked upon him I understood not only the fears and dislike of his manager, but also the execrations which so many business rivals have heaped upon his head. If I were a sculptor and desired to idealize the successful man of affairs, iron of nerve and leathery of conscience, I should choose Mr. Neil Gibson as my model. His tall, gaunt craggy figure had a suggestion of hunger and rapacity. An Abraham Lincoln keyed to base uses instead of high ones would give some idea of the man. His face might have been chiselled in granite, hard-set, craggy, remorseless, with deep lines upon it, the scars of many a crisis. Cold grey eyes, looking shrewdly out from under bristling brows, surveyed us each in turn. He bowed in perfunctory fashion as Holmes mentioned my name, and then with a masterful air of possession he drew a chair up to my companion and seated himself with his bony knees almost touching him.

"Let me say right here, Mr. Holmes," he began, "that money is nothing to me in this case. You can burn it if it's any use in lighting you to the truth. This woman is innocent and this woman has to be cleared, and it's up to you to do it. Name your figure!"

"My professional charges are upon a fixed scale," said Holmes coldly. "I do not vary them, save when I remit them altogether."

"Well, if dollars make no difference to you, think of the reputation. If you pull this off every paper in England and America will be booming you. You'll be the talk of two continents."

"Thank you, Mr. Gibson, I do not think that I am in need of booming. It may surprise you to know that I prefer to work anonymously, and that it is the problem itself which attracts me. But we are wasting time. Let us get down to the facts."

"I think that you will find all the main ones in the Press reports. I don't know that I can add anything which will help you. But if there is anything you would wish more light upon—well, I am here to give it."

"Well, there is just one point."

"What is it ? "

"What were the exact relations between you and Miss Dunbar ? "

The Gold King gave a violent start, and half rose from his chair. Then his massive calm came back to him.

"I suppose you are within your rights—and maybe doing your duty—in asking such a question, Mr. Holmes."

"We will agree to suppose so," said Holmes.

"Then I can assure you that our relations were entirely and always those of an employer towards a young lady whom he never conversed with, or ever saw, save when she was in the company of his children."

Holmes rose from his chair.

"I am a rather busy man, Mr. Gibson," said he, "and I have no time or taste for aimless conversations. I wish you good morning."

Our visitor had risen also and his great loose figure towered above Holmes. There was an angry gleam from under those bristling brows and a tinge of colour in the sallow cheeks.

"What the devil do you mean by this, Mr. Holmes ? Do you dismiss my case ? "

"Well, Mr. Gibson, at least I dismiss you. I should have thought my words were plain."

"Plain enough, but what's at the back of it? Raising the price on me, or afraid to tackle it, or what? I've a right to a plain answer."

"Well, perhaps you have," said Holmes. "I'll give you one. This case is quite sufficiently complicated to start with, without the further difficulty of false information."

"Meaning that I lie."

"Well, I was trying to express it as delicately as I could, but if you insist upon the word I will not contradict you."

I sprang to my feet, for the expression upon the millionaire's face was fiendish in its intensity, and he had raised his great knotted fist. Holmes smiled languidly, and reached his hand out for his pipe.

"Don't be noisy, Mr. Gibson. I find that after breakfast even the smallest argument is unsettling. I suggest that a stroll in the morning air and a little quiet thought will be greatly to your advantage."

With an effort the Gold King mastered his fury. I could not but admire him, for by a supreme self-command he had turned in a minute from a hot flame of anger to a frigid and contemptuous indifference.

"Well, it's your choice. I guess you know how to run your own business. I can't make you touch the case against your will. You've done yourself no good this morning, Mr. Holmes, for I have broken stronger men than you. No man ever crossed me and was the better for it."

"So many have said so, and yet here I am," said Holmes, smiling. "Well, good morning, Mr. Gibson. You have a good deal yet to learn."

Our visitor made a noisy exit, but Holmes smoked in imperturbable silence with dreamy eyes fixed upon the ceiling.

"Any views, Watson?" he asked at last.

" Well, Holmes, I must confess that when I consider that this is a man who would certainly brush any obstacle from his path, and when I remember that his wife may have been an obstacle and an object of dislike, as that man Bates plainly told us, it seems to me——"

" Exactly. And to me also."

" But what were his relations with the governess, and how did you discover them ? "

" Bluff, Watson, bluff ! When I considered the passionate, unconventional, unbusiness-like tone of his letter, and contrasted it with his self-contained manner and appearance, it was pretty clear that there was some deep emotion which centred upon the accused woman rather than upon the victim. We've got to understand the exact relations of those three people if we are to reach the truth. You saw the frontal attack which I made upon him and how imperturbably he received it. Then I bluffed him by giving him the impression that I was absolutely certain, when in reality I was only extremely suspicious."

" Perhaps he will come back ? "

" He is sure to come back. He *must* come back. He can't leave it where it is Ha ! isn't that a ring ? Yes, there is his footstep. Well, Mr. Gibson, I was just saying to Dr. Watson that you were somewhat overdue."

The Gold King had re-entered the room in a more chastened mood than he had left it. His wounded pride still showed in his resentful eyes, but his common sense had shown him that he must yield if he would attain his end.

" I've been thinking it over, Mr. Holmes, and I feel that I have been hasty in taking your remarks amiss. You are justified in getting down to the facts, whatever they may be, and I think the more of you for it. I can assure you, however, that the relations between Miss Dunbar and me don't really touch this case."

" That is for me to decide, is it not ? "

"Yes, I guess that is so. You're like a surgeon who wants every symptom before he can give his diagnosis."

"Exactly. That expresses it. And it is only a patient who has an object in deceiving his surgeon who would conceal the facts of his case."

"That may be so, but you will admit, Mr. Holmes, that most men would shy off a bit when they are asked point-blank what their relations with a woman may be —if there is really some serious feeling in the case. I guess most men have a little private reserve of their own in some corner of their souls where they don't welcome intruders. And you burst suddenly into it. But the object excuses you, since it was to try and save her. Well, the stakes are down and the reserve open and you can explore where you will. What is it you want?"

"The truth."

The Gold King paused for a moment, as one who marshals his thoughts. His grim, deep-lined face had become even sadder and more grave.

"I can give it to you in a very few words, Mr. Holmes," said he at last. "There are some things that are painful as well as difficult to say, so I won't go deeper than is needful. I met my wife when I was gold-hunting in Brazil. Maria Pinto was the daughter of a Government official at Manaos, and she was very beautiful. I was young and ardent in those days, but even now, as I look back with colder blood and a more critical eye, I can see that she was rare and wonderful in her beauty. It was a deep rich nature, too, passionate, wholehearted, tropical, ill-balanced, very different from the American women whom I had known. Well, to make a long story short, I loved her and I married her. It was only when the romance had passed—and it lingered for years —that I realized that we had nothing—absolutely nothing—in common. My love faded. If hers had faded also it might have been easier. But you know the wonderful way of women! Do what I might nothing could turn her from me. If I have been harsh to her, even brutal as some have said, it has been because I knew that if I could kill her love, or if it turned to hate, it would be easier for both of us. But nothing changed her. She adored me in those English woods as she had adored me twenty years ago on the banks of the Amazon. Do what I might, she was as devoted as ever.

" Then came Miss Grace Dunbar. She answered our advertisement and became governess to our two children. Perhaps you have seen her portrait in the papers. The whole world has proclaimed that she also is a very beautiful woman. Now, I make no pretence to be more moral than my neighbours, and I will admit to you that I could not live under the same roof with such a woman and in daily contact with her without feeling a passionate regard for her. Do you blame me, Mr. Holmes ? "

" I do not blame you for feeling it. I should blame you if you expressed it, since this young lady was in a sense under your protection."

" Well, maybe so," said the millionaire, though for a moment the reproof had brought the old angry gleam into his eyes. " I'm not pretending to be any better than I am. I guess all my life I've been a man that reached out his hand for what he wanted, and I never wanted anything more than the love and possession of that woman. I told her so."

" Oh, you did, did you ? "

Holmes could look very formidable when he was moved.

" I said to her that if I could marry her I would, but that it was out of my power. I said that money was no object and that all I could do to make her happy and comfortable would be done."

" Very generous, I am sure," said Holmes, with a sneer.

" See here, Mr. Holmes. I came to you on a question of evidence, not on a question of morals. I'm not asking for your criticism."

"It is only for the young lady's sake that I touch your case at all," said Holmes sternly. "I don't know that anything she is accused of is really worse than what you have yourself admitted, that you have tried to ruin a defenceless girl who was under your roof. Some of you rich men have to be taught that all the world cannot be bribed into condoning your offences."

To my surprise the Gold King took the reproof with equanimity.

"That's how I feel myself about it now. I thank God that my plans did not work out as I intended. She would have none of it, and she wanted to leave the house instantly."

"Why did she not ?"

"Well, in the first place, others were dependent upon her, and it was no light matter for her to let them all down by sacrificing her living. When I had sworn —as I did—that she should never be molested again, she consented to remain. But there was another reason. She knew the influence she had over me, and that it was stronger than any other influence in the world. She wanted to use it for good."

"How ?"

"Well, she knew something of my affairs. They are large, Mr. Holmes—large beyond the belief of an ordinary man. I can make or break—and it is usually break. It wasn't individuals only. It was communities, cities, even nations. Business is a hard game, and the weak go to the wall. I played the game for all it was worth. I never squealed myself and I never cared if the other fellow squealed. But she saw it different. I guess she was right. She believed and said that a fortune for one man that was more than he needed should not be built on ten thousand ruined men who were left without the means of life. That was how she saw it, and I guess she could see past the dollars to something that was more lasting. She found that I listened to what she said, and she believed she was serving the world by influencing my actions. So she stayed—and then this came along."

"Can you throw any light upon that?"

The Gold King paused for a minute or more, his head sunk in his hands, lost in deep thought.

"It's very black against her. I can't deny that. And women lead an inward life and may do things beyond the judgment of a man. At first I was so rattled and taken aback that I was ready to think she had been led away in some extraordinary fashion that was clean against her usual nature. One explanation came into my head. I give it to you, Mr. Holmes, for what it is worth. There is no doubt that my wife was bitterly jealous. There is a soul-jealousy that can be as frantic as any body-jealousy, and though my wife had no cause —and I think she understood this—for the latter, she was aware that this English girl exerted an influence upon my mind and my acts that she herself never had. It was an influence for good, but that did not mend the matter. She was crazy with hatred, and the heat of the Amazon was always in her blood. She might have planned to murder Miss Dunbar—or we will say to threaten her with a gun and so frighten her into leaving us. Then there might have been a scuffle and the gun gone off and shot the woman who held it."

"That possibility had already occurred to me," said Holmes. "Indeed, it is the only obvious alternative to deliberate murder."

"But she utterly denies it."

"Well, that is not final—is it? One can understand that a woman placed in so awful a position might hurry home still in her bewilderment holding the revolver. She might even throw it down among her clothes, hardly knowing what she was doing, and when it was found she might try to lie her way out by a total denial, since all explanation was impossible. What is against such a supposition?"

"Miss Dunbar herself."

"Well, perhaps."

Holmes looked at his watch. "I have no doubt we can get the necessary permits this morning and reach Winchester by the evening train. When I have seen this young lady, it is very possible that I may be of more use to you in the matter, though I cannot promise that my conclusions will necessarily be such as you desire."

There was some delay in the official pass, and instead of reaching Winchester that day we went down to Thor Place, the Hampshire estate of Mr. Neil Gibson. He did not accompany us himself, but we had the address of Sergeant Coventry, of the local police, who had first examined into the affair. He was a tall, thin, cadaverous man, with a secretive and mysterious manner, which conveyed the idea that he knew or suspected a very great deal more than he dared say. He had a trick, too, of suddenly sinking his voice to a whisper as if he had come upon something of vital importance, though the information was usually commonplace enough. Behind these tricks of manner he soon showed himself to be a decent, honest fellow who was not too proud to admit that he was out of his depth and would welcome any help.

"Anyhow, I'd rather have you than Scotland Yard, Mr. Holmes," said he. "If the Yard gets called into a case, then the local loses all credit for success and may be blamed for failure. Now, you play straight, so I've heard."

"I need not appear in the matter at all," said Holmes, to the evident relief of our melancholy acquaintance. "If I can clear it up I don't ask to have my name mentioned."

"Well, it's very handsome of you, I am sure. And your friend, Dr. Watson, can be trusted, I know. Now, Mr. Holmes, as we walk down to the place there is one question I should like to ask you. I'd breathe it to no soul but you." He looked round as though he hardly dare utter the words. "Don't you think there might be a case against Mr. Neil Gibson himself?"

" I have been considering that."

" You've not seen Miss Dunbar. She is a wonderfully fine woman in every way. He may well have wished his wife out of the road. And these Americans are readier with pistols than our folk are. It was *his* pistol, you know."

" Was that clearly made out ? "

" Yes, sir. It was one of a pair that he had."

" One of a pair ? Where is the other ? "

" Well, the gentleman has a lot of fire-arms of one sort and another. We never quite matched that particular pistol—but the box was made for two."

" If it was one of a pair you should surely be able to match it."

" Well, we have them all laid out at the house if you would care to look them over."

" Later, perhaps. I think we will walk down together and have a look at the scene of the tragedy."

This conversation had taken place in the little front room of Sergeant Coventry's humble cottage which served as the local police-station. A walk of half a mile or so across a wind-swept heath, all gold and bronze with the fading ferns, brought us to a side-gate opening into the grounds of the Thor Place estate. A path led us through the pheasant preserves, and then from a clearing we saw the widespread, half-timbered house, half Tudor and half Georgian, upon the crest of the hill. Beside us there was a long, reedy pool, constricted in the centre where the main carriage drive passed over a stone bridge, but swelling into small lakes on either side. Our guide paused at the mouth of this bridge, and he pointed to the ground.

" That was where Mrs. Gibson's body lay. I marked it by that stone."

" I understand that you were there before it was moved ? "

" Yes ; they sent for me at once."

" Who did ? "

" Mr. Gibson himself. The moment the alarm was given and he had rushed down with others from the house, he insisted that nothing should be moved until the police should arrive."

" That was sensible. I gathered from the newspaper report that the shot was fired from close quarters."

" Yes, sir, very close."

" Near the right temple ? "

" Just behind it, sir."

" How did the body lie ? "

" On the back, sir. No trace of a struggle. No marks. No weapon. The short note from Miss Dunbar was clutched in her left hand."

" Clutched, you say ? "

" Yes, sir ; we could hardly open the fingers."

" That is of great importance. It excludes the idea that anyone could have placed the note there after death in order to furnish a false clue. Dear me ! The note, as I remember, was quite short. ' I will be at Thor Bridge at nine o'clock.—G. Dunbar.' Was that not so ? "

" Yes, sir."

" Did Miss Dunbar admit writing it ? "

" Yes, sir."

" What was her explanation ? "

" Her defence was reserved for the Assizes. She would say nothing."

" The problem is certainly a very interesting one. The point of the letter is very obscure, is it not ? "

" Well, sir," said the guide, " it seemed, if I may be so bold as to say so, the only really clear point in the whole case."

Holmes shook his head.

" Granting that the letter is genuine and was really written, it was certainly received some time before— say one hour or two. Why, then, was this lady still clasping it in her left hand ? Why should she carry it so carefully ? She did not need to refer to it in the interview. Does it not seem remarkable ? "

"Well, sir, as you put it, perhaps it does."

"I think I should like to sit quietly for a few minutes and think it out." He seated himself upon the stone ledge of the bridge, and I could see his quick grey eyes darting their questioning glances in every direction. Suddenly he sprang up again and ran across to the opposite parapet, whipped his lens from his pocket, and began to examine the stonework.

"This is curious," said he.

"Yes, sir ; we saw the chip on the ledge. I expect it's been done by some passer-by."

The stonework was grey, but at this one point it showed white for a space not larger than a sixpence. When examined closely one could see that the surface was chipped as by a sharp blow.

"It took some violence to do that," said Holmes thoughtfully. With his cane he struck the ledge several times without leaving a mark. "Yes, it was a hard knock. In a curious place, too. It was not from above but from below, for you see that it is on the *lower* edge of the parapet."

"But it is at least fifteen feet from the body."

"Yes, it is fifteen feet from the body. It may have nothing to do with the matter, but it is a point worth noting. I do not think that we have anything more to learn here. There were no footsteps, you say ? "

"The ground was iron hard, sir. There were no traces at all."

"Then we can go. We will go up to the house first and look over these weapons of which you speak. Then we shall get on to Winchester, for I should desire to see Miss Dunbar before we go farther."

Mr. Neil Gibson had not returned from town, but we saw in the house the neurotic Mr. Bates who had called upon us in the morning. He showed us with a sinister relish the formidable array of fire-arms of various shapes and sizes which his employer had accumulated in the course of an adventurous life.

"Mr. Gibson has his enemies, as anyone would expect who knew him and his methods," said he. "He sleeps with a loaded revolver in the drawer beside his bed He is a man of violence, sir, and there are times when all of us are afraid of him. I am sure that the poor lady who has passed was often terrified."

"Did you ever witness physical violence towards her?"

"No, I cannot say that. But I have heard words which were nearly as bad—words of cold, cutting contempt, even before the servants."

"Our millionaire does not seem to shine in private life," remarked Holmes, as we made our way to the station. "Well, Watson, we have come on a good many facts, some of them new ones, and yet I seem some way from my conclusion. In spite of the very evident dislike which Mr. Bates has to his employer, I gather from him that when the alarm came he was undoubtedly in his library. Dinner was over at eight-thirty and all was normal up to then. It is true that the alarm was somewhat late in the evening, but the tragedy certainly occurred about the hour named in the note. There is no evidence at all that Mr. Gibson had been out of doors since his return from town at five o'clock. On the other hand, Miss Dunbar, as I understand it, admits that she had made an appointment to meet Mrs. Gibson at the bridge. Beyond this she would say nothing, as her lawyer had advised her to reserve her defence. We have several very vital questions to ask that young lady, and my mind will not be easy until we have seen her. I must confess that the case would seem to me to be very black against her if it were not for one thing."

"And what is that, Holmes?"

"The finding of the pistol in her wardrobe."

"Dear me, Holmes!" I cried, "that seemed to me to be the most damning incident of all."

"Not so, Watson. It had struck me even at my first perfunctory reading as very strange, and now that

I am in closer touch with the case it is my only firm ground for hope. We must look for consistency. Where there is a want of it we must suspect deception."

" I hardly follow you."

" Well now, Watson, suppose for a moment that we visualize you in the character of a woman who, in a cold, premeditated fashion, is about to get rid of a rival. You have planned it. A note has been written. The victim has come. You have your weapon. The crime is done. It has been workmanlike and complete. Do you tell me that after carrying out so crafty a crime you would now ruin your reputation as a criminal by forgetting to fling your weapon into those adjacent reed-beds which would for ever cover it, but you must needs carry it carefully home and put it in your own wardrobe, the very first place that would be searched ? Your best friends would hardly call you a schemer, Watson, and yet I could not picture you doing anything so crude as that."

" In the excitement of the moment——"

" No, no, Watson, I will not admit that it is possible. Where a crime is coolly premeditated, then the means of covering it are coolly premeditated also. I hope, therefore, that we are in the presence of a serious mis-conception."

" But there is so much to explain."

" Well, we shall set about explaining it. When once your point of view is changed, the very thing which was so damning becomes a clue to the truth. For example, there is this revolver. Miss Dunbar disclaims all knowledge of it. On our new theory she is speaking truth when she says so. Therefore, it was placed in her wardrobe. Who placed it there ? Someone who wished to incriminate her. Was not that person the actual criminal ? You see how we come at once upon a most fruitful line of inquiry."

We were compelled to spend the night at Winchester, as the formalities had not yet been completed, but next morning, in the company of Mr. Joyce Cummings, the rising barrister who was entrusted with the defence, we were allowed to see the young lady in her cell. I had expected from all that we had heard to see a beautiful woman, but I can never forget the effect which Miss Dunbar produced upon me. It was no wonder that even the masterful millionaire had found in her something more powerful than himself—something which could control and guide him. One felt, too, as one looked at that strong, clear-cut, and yet sensitive face, that even should she be capable of some impetuous deed, none the less there was an innate nobility of character which would make her influence always for the good. She was a brunette, tall, with a noble figure and commanding presence, but her dark eyes had in them the appealing, helpless expression of the hunted creature who feels the nets around it, but can see no way out from the toils. Now, as she realized the presence and the help of my famous friend, there came a touch of colour in her wan cheeks and a light of hope began to glimmer in the glance which she turned upon us.

" Perhaps Mr. Neil Gibson has told you something of what occurred between us ? " she asked, in a low, agitated voice.

" Yes," Holmes answered ; " you need not pain yourself by entering into that part of the story. After seeing you, I am prepared to accept Mr. Gibson's statement both as to the influence which you had over him and as to the innocence of your relations with him. But why was the whole situation not brought out in court ? "

" It seemed to me incredible that such a charge could be sustained. I thought that if we waited the whole thing must clear itself up without our being compelled to enter into painful details of the inner life of the family. But I understand that far from clearing it has become even more serious."

" My dear young lady," cried Holmes earnestly, " I beg you to have no illusions upon the point. Mr.

Cummings here would assure you that all the cards are at present against us, and that we must do everything that is possible if we are to win clear. It would be a cruel deception to pretend that you are not in very great danger. Give me all the help you can, then, to get at the truth."

" I will conceal nothing."

" Tell us, then, of your true relations with Mr. Gibson's wife."

" She hated me, Mr. Holmes. She hated me with all the fervour of her tropical nature. She was a woman who would do nothing by halves, and the measure of her love for her husband was the measure also of her hatred for me. It is probable that she misunderstood our relations. I would not wish to wrong her, but she loved so vividly in a physical sense that she could hardly understand the mental, and even spiritual, tie which held her husband to me, or imagine that it was only my desire to influence his power to good ends which kept me under his roof. I can see now that I was wrong. Nothing could justify me in remaining where I was a cause of unhappiness, and yet it is certain that the unhappiness would have remained even if I had left the house."

" Now, Miss Dunbar," said Holmes, " I beg you to tell us exactly what occurred that evening."

" I can tell you the truth so far as I know it, Mr. Holmes, but I am in a position to prove nothing, and there are points—the most vital points—which I can neither explain nor can I imagine any explanation."

" If you will find the facts, perhaps others may find the explanation."

" With regard, then, to my presence at Thor Bridge that night, I received a note from Mrs. Gibson in the morning. It lay on the table of the schoolroom, and it may have been left there by her own hand. It implored me to see her there after dinner, said she had something important to say to me, and asked me to leave an answer on the sundial in the garden, as she desired no one to be in our confidence. I saw no reason for such secrecy, but I did as she asked, accepting the appointment. She asked me to destroy her note and I burned it in the schoolroom grate. She was very much afraid of her husband, who treated her with a harshness for which I frequently reproached him, and I could only imagine that she acted in this way because she did not wish him to know of our interview."

" Yet she kept your reply very carefully ? "

" Yes. I was surprised to hear that she had it in her hand when she died."

" Well, what happened then ? "

" I went down as I had promised. When I reached the bridge she was waiting for me. Never did I realize till that moment how this poor creature hated me. She was like a mad woman—indeed, I think she *was* a mad woman, subtly mad with the deep power of deception which insane people may have. How else could she have met me with unconcern every day and yet had so raging a hatred of me in her heart ? I will not say what she said. She poured her whole wild fury out in burning and horrible words. I did not even answer—I could not. It was dreadful to see her. I put my hands to my ears and rushed away. When I left her she was standing still shrieking out her curses at me, in the mouth of the bridge."

" Where she was afterwards found ? "

" Within a few yards from the spot."

" And yet, presuming that she met her death shortly after you left her, you heard no shot ? "

" No, I heard nothing. But, indeed, Mr. Holmes, I was so agitated and horrified by this terrible outbreak that I rushed to get back to the peace of my own room, and I was incapable of noticing anything which happened."

" You say that you returned to your room. Did you leave it again before next morning ? "

" Yes ; when the alarm came that the poor creature had met her death I ran out with the others."

" Did you see Mr. Gibson ? "

" Yes ; he had just returned from the bridge when I saw him. He had sent for the doctor and the police."

" Did he seem to you much perturbed ? "

" Mr. Gibson is a very strong, self-contained man. I do not think that he would ever show his emotions on the surface. But I, who knew him so well, could see that he was deeply concerned."

" Then we come to the all-important point. This pistol that was found in your room. Had you ever seen it before ? "

" Never, I swear it."

" When was it found ? "

" Next morning, when the police made their search."

" Among your clothes ? "

" Yes ; on the floor of my wardrobe under my dresses."

" You could not guess how long it had been there ? "

" It had not been there the morning before."

" How do you know ? "

" Because I tidied out the wardrobe."

" That is final. Then someone came into your room and placed the pistol there in order to inculpate you."

" It must have been so."

" And when ? "

" It could only have been at meal-time, or else at the hours when I would be in the schoolroom with the children."

" As you were when you got the note ? "

" Yes ; from that time onwards for the whole morning."

" Thank you, Miss Dunbar. Is there any other point which could help me in the investigation ? "

" I can think of none."

" There was some sign of violence on the stonework of the bridge—a perfectly fresh chip just opposite the body. Could you suggest any possible explanation of that ? "

" Surely it must be a mere coincidence."

" Curious, Miss Dunbar, very curious. Why should

it appear at the very time of the tragedy and why at the very place ? "

" But what could have caused it ? Only great violence could have such an effect."

Holmes did not answer. His pale, eager face had suddenly assumed that tense, far-away expression which I had learned to associate with the supreme manifestations of his genius. So evident was the crisis in his mind that none of us dared to speak, and we sat, barrister, prisoner, and myself, watching him in a concentrated and absorbed silence. Suddenly he sprang from his chair, vibrating with nervous energy and the pressing need for action.

" Come, Watson, come ! " he cried.

" What is it, Mr. Holmes ? "

" Never mind, my dear lady. You will hear from me, Mr. Cummings. With the help of the God of justice I will give you a case which will make England ring. You will get news by to-morrow, Miss Dunbar, and meanwhile take my assurance that the clouds are lifting and that I have every hope that the light of truth is breaking through."

It was not a long journey from Winchester to Thor Place, but it was long to me in my impatience, while for Holmes it was evident that it seemed endless ; for, in his nervous restlessness, he could not sit still, but paced the carriage or drummed with his long, sensitive fingers upon the cushions beside him. Suddenly, however, as we neared our destination he seated himself opposite to me—we had a first-class carriage to ourselves—and laying a hand upon each of my knees he looked into my eyes with the peculiarly mischievous gaze which was characteristic of his more imp-like moods.

" Watson," said he, " I have some recollection that you go armed upon these excursions of ours."

It was as well for him that I did so, for he took little care for his own safety when his mind was once absorbed by a problem, so that more than once my revolver had been a good friend in need. I reminded him of the fact.

" Yes, yes, I am a little absent-minded in such matters. But have you your revolver on you ? "

I produced it from my hip-pocket, a short, handy, but very serviceable little weapon. He undid the catch, shook out the cartridges, and examined it with care.

" It's heavy—remarkably heavy," said he.

" Yes, it is a solid bit of work."

He mused over it for a minute.

" Do you know, Watson," said he, " I believe your revolver is going to have a very intimate connection with the mystery which we are investigating."

" My dear Holmes, you are joking."

" No, Watson, I am very serious. There is a test before us. If the test comes off, all will be clear. And the test will depend upon the conduct of this little weapon. One cartridge out. Now we will replace the other five and put on the safety-catch. So ! That increases the weight and makes it a better reproduction."

I had no glimmer of what was in his mind nor did he enlighten me, but sat lost in thought until we pulled up in the little Hampshire station. We secured a ramshackle trap and in a quarter of an hour were at the house of our confidential friend, the sergeant.

" A clue, Mr. Holmes ? What is it ? "

" It all depends upon the behaviour of Dr. Watson's revolver," said my friend. " Here it is. Now, officer, can you give me ten yards of string ? "

The village shop provided a ball of stout twine.

" I think that this is all we will need," said Holmes. " Now, if you please, we will get off on what I hope is the last stage of our journey."

The sun was setting and turning the rolling Hampshire moor into a wonderful autumnal panorama. The sergeant, with many critical and incredulous glances, which showed his deep doubts of the sanity of my companion, lurched along beside us. As we approached the scene of the crime I could see that my friend under all his habitual coolness was in truth deeply agitated.

" Yes," he said, in answer to my remark, " you have seen me miss my mark before, Watson. I have an instinct for such things, and yet it has sometimes played me false. It seemed a certainty when first it flashed across my mind in the cell at Winchester, but one drawback of an active mind is that one can always conceive alternative explanations which would make our scent a false one. And yet—and yet—— Well, Watson, we can but try."

As he walked he had firmly tied one end of the string to the handle of the revolver. We had now reached the scene of the tragedy. With great care he marked out under the guidance of the policeman the exact spot where the body had been stretched. He then hunted among the heather and the ferns until he found a considerable stone. This he secured to the other end of his line of string, and he hung it over the parapet of the bridge so that it swung clear above the water. He then stood on the fatal spot, some distance from the edge of the bridge, with my revolver in his hand, the string being taut between the weapon and the heavy stone on the farther side.

" Now for it ! " he cried.

At the words he raised the pistol to his head, and then let go his grip. In an instant it had been whisked away by the weight of the stone, had struck with a sharp crack against the parapet and had vanished over the side into the water. It had hardly gone before Holmes was kneeling beside the stonework, and a joyous cry showed that he had found what he expected.

" Was there ever a more exact demonstration ? " he cried. " See, Watson, your revolver has solved the problem ! " As he spoke he pointed to a second chip of the exact size and shape of the first which had appeared on the under edge of the stone balustrade.

" We'll stay at the inn to-night," he continued, as he

rose and faced the astonished sergeant. " You will, of course, get a grappling-hook and you will easily restore my friend's revolver. You will also find beside it the revolver, string and weight with which this vindictive woman attempted to disguise her own crime and to fasten a charge of murder upon an innocent victim. You can let Mr. Gibson know that I will see him in the morning, when steps can be taken for Miss Dunbar's vindication."

Late that evening, as we sat together smoking our pipes in the village inn, Holmes gave me a brief review of what had passed.

" I fear, Watson," said he, " that you will not improve any reputation which I may have acquired by adding the Case of the Thor Bridge Mystery to your annals. I have been sluggish in mind and wanting in that mixture of imagination and reality which is the basis of my art. I confess that the chip in the stonework was a sufficient clue to suggest the true solution, and that I blame myself for not having attained it sooner.

" It must be admitted that the workings of this unhappy woman's mind were deep and subtle, so that it was no very simple matter to unravel her plot. I do not think that in our adventures we have ever come across a stranger example of what perverted love can bring about. Whether Miss Dunbar was her rival in a physical or in a merely mental sense seems to have been equally unforgivable in her eyes. No doubt she blamed this innocent lady for all those harsh dealings and unkind words with which her husband tried to repel her too demonstrative affection. Her first resolution was to end her own life. Her second was to do it in such a way as to involve her victim in a fate which was worse far than any sudden death could be.

" We can follow the various steps quite clearly, and they show a remarkable subtlety of mind. A note was extracted very cleverly from Miss Dunbar which would make it appear that she had chosen the scene of the crime. In her anxiety that it should be discovered she somewhat overdid it, by holding it in her hand to the last. This alone should have excited my suspicions earlier than it did.

"Then she took one of her husband's revolvers—there was, as you saw, an arsenal in the house—and kept it for her own use. A similar one she concealed that morning in Miss Dunbar's wardrobe after discharging one barrel, which she could easily do in the woods without attracting attention. She then went down to the bridge where she had contrived this exceedingly ingenious method for getting rid of her weapon. When Miss Dunbar appeared she used her last breath in pouring out her hatred, and then, when she was out of hearing, carried out her terrible purpose. Every link is now in its place and the chain is complete. The papers may ask why the mere was not dragged in the first instance, but it is easy to be wise after the event, and in any case the expanse of a reed-filled lake is no easy matter to drag unless you have a clear perception of what you are looking for, and where. Well, Watson, we have helped a remarkable woman, and also a formidable man. Should they in the future join their forces, as seems not unlikely, the financial world may find that Mr. Neil Gibson has learned something in that schoolroom of Sorrow where our earthly lessons are taught."

52. *The Creeping Man*

MR. SHERLOCK HOLMES was always of opinion that I should publish the singular facts connected with Professor Presbury, if only to dispel once for all the ugly rumours which some twenty years ago agitated the University and were echoed in the learned societies of London. There were, however, certain obstacles in the way, and the true history of this curious case remained entombed in the tin box which contains so many records of my friend's adventures. Now we have at last obtained permission to ventilate the facts which formed one of the very last cases handled by Holmes before his retirement from practice. Even now a certain reticence and discretion have to be observed in laying the matter before the public.

It was one Sunday evening early in September of the year 1903 that I received one of Holmes' laconic messages : " Come at once if convenient—if inconvenient come all the same.—S. H." The relations between us in those latter days were peculiar. He was a man of habits, narrow and concentrated habits, and I had become one of them. As an institution I was like the violin, the shag tobacco, the old black pipe, the index books, and others perhaps less excusable. When it was a case of active work and a comrade was needed upon whose nerve he could place some reliance, my rôle was obvious. But apart from this I had uses. I was a whetstone for his mind. I stimulated him. He liked to think aloud in my presence. His remarks could hardly be said to be made to me—many of them would have been as appropriately addressed to his bedstead—but none the less, having formed the habit, it had become in some way helpful that I should register and interject. If I irritated him by a certain methodical slowness in my mentality, that irritation served only to make his own flame-like intuitions and impressions flash up the more vividly and swiftly. Such was my humble rôle in our alliance.

When I arrived at Baker Street I found him huddled up in his arm-chair with updrawn knees, his pipe in his mouth and his brow furrowed with thought. It was clear that he was in the throes of some vexatious problem. With a wave of his hand he indicated my old arm-chair, but otherwise for half an hour he gave no sign that he was aware of my presence. Then with a start he seemed to come from his reverie, and, with his usual whimsical smile, he greeted me back to what had once been my home.

"You will excuse a certain abstraction of mind, my dear Watson," said he. "Some curious facts have been submitted to me within the last twenty-four hours, and they in turn have given rise to some speculations of a more general character. I have serious thoughts of writing a small monograph upon the uses of dogs in the work of the detective."

"But surely, Holmes, this has been explored," said I. "Bloodhounds—sleuth-hounds——"

"No, no, Watson; that side of the matter is, of course, obvious. But there is another which is far more subtle. You may recollect that in the case which you, in your sensational way, coupled with the Copper Beeches, I was able, by watching the mind of the child, to form a deduction as to the criminal habits of the very smug and respectable father."

"Yes, I remember it well."

"My line of thoughts about dogs is analogous. A dog reflects the family life. Whoever saw a frisky dog in a gloomy family, or a sad dog in a happy one ? Snarling people have snarling dogs, dangerous people have dangerous ones. And their passing moods may reflect the passing moods of others."

I shook my head. "Surely, Holmes, this is a little far-fetched," said I.

He had refilled his pipe and resumed his seat, taking no notice of my comment.

"The practical application of what I have said is very close to the problem which I am investigating. It is a tangled skein, you understand, and I am looking for a loose end. One possible loose end lies in the question : Why does Professor Presbury's faithful wolf-hound, Roy, endeavour to bite him ? "

I sank back in my chair in some disappointment. Was it for so trivial a question as this that I had been summoned from my work ? Holmes glanced across at me.

"The same old Watson!" said he. "You never learn that the gravest issues may depend upon the smallest things. But is it not on the face of it strange that a staid, elderly philosopher—you've heard of Presbury, of course, the famous Camford physiologist?—that such a man, whose friend has been his devoted wolf-hound, should now have been twice attacked by his own dog? What do you make of it?"

"The dog is ill."

"Well, that has to be considered. But he attacks no one else, nor does he apparently molest his master, save on very special occasions. Curious, Watson—very curious. But young Mr. Bennett is before his time, if that is his ring. I had hoped to have a longer chat with you before he came."

There was a quick step on the stairs, a sharp tap at the door, and a moment later the new client presented himself. He was a tall, handsome youth about thirty, well dressed and elegant, but with something in his bearing which suggested the shyness of the student rather than the self-possession of the man of the world. He shook hands with Holmes, and then looked with some surprise at me.

"This matter is very delicate, Mr. Holmes," he said. "Consider the relation in which I stand to Professor Presbury, both privately and publicly. I really can hardly justify myself if I speak before any third person."

"Have no fear, Mr. Bennett. Dr. Watson is the very soul of discretion, and I can assure you that this is a matter in which I am very likely to need an assistant."

"As you like, Mr. Holmes. You will, I am sure, understand my having some reserves in the matter."

"You will appreciate it, Watson, when I tell you that this gentleman, Mr. Trevor Bennett, is professional assistant to the great scientist, lives under his roof, and is engaged to his only daughter. Certainly we must agree that the Professor has every claim upon his loyalty and devotion. But it may best be shown by taking the necessary steps to clear up this strange mystery."

"I hope so, Mr. Holmes. That is my one object. Does Dr. Watson know the situation?"

"I have not had time to explain it."

"Then perhaps I had better go over the ground again before explaining some fresh developments."

"I will do so myself," said Holmes, "in order to show that I have the events in their due order. The Professor, Watson, is a man of European reputation. His life has been academic. There has never been a breath of scandal. He is a widower with one daughter, Edith. He is, I gather, a man of very virile and positive, one might almost say combative, character. So the matter stood until a very few months ago.

"Then the current of his life was broken. He is sixty-one years of age, but he became engaged to the daughter of Professor Morphy, his colleague in the chair of Comparative Anatomy. It was not, as I understand, the reasoned courting of an elderly man, but rather the passionate frenzy of youth, for no one could have shown himself a more devoted lover. The lady, Alice Morphy, was a very perfect girl both in mind and body, so that there was every excuse for the Professor's infatuation. None the less, it did not meet with full approval in his own family."

"We thought it rather excessive," said our visitor.

"Exactly. Excessive and a little violent and unnatural. Professor Presbury was rich, however, and there was no objection upon the part of the father. The daughter, however, had other views, and there were already several candidates for her hand, who, if they were less eligible from a worldly point of view, were at least more of an age. The girl seemed to like the Professor in spite of his eccentricities. It was only age which stood in the way.

"About this time a little mystery suddenly clouded the normal routine of the Professor's life. He did what he had never done before. He left home and gave no indication where he was going. He was away a fortnight, and returned looking rather travel-worn. He made no allusion to where he had been, although he was usually the frankest of men. It chanced, however, that our client here, Mr. Bennett, received a letter from a fellow-student in Prague, who said that he was glad to have seen Professor Presbury there, although he had not been able to talk to him. Only in this way did his own household learn where he had been.

" Now comes the point. From that time onwards a curious change came over the Professor. He became furtive and sly. Those around him had always the feeling that he was not the man that they had known, but that he was under some shadow which had darkened his higher qualities. His intellect was not affected. His lectures were as brilliant as ever. But always there was something new, something sinister and unexpected. His daughter, who was devoted to him, tried again and again to resume the old relations and to penetrate this mask which her father seemed to have put on. You, sir, as I understand, did the same—but all was in vain. And now, Mr. Bennett, tell in your own words the incident of the letters."

" You must understand, Dr. Watson, that the Professor had no secrets from me. If I were his son or his younger brother, I could not have more completely enjoyed his confidence. As his secretary I handled every paper which came to him, and I opened and subdivided his letters. Shortly after his return all this was changed. He told me that certain letters might come to him from London which would be marked by a cross under the stamp. These were to be set aside for his own eyes only. I may say that several of these did pass through my hands, that they had the E.C. mark, and were in an illiterate handwriting. If he answered them at all the answers did not pass through my hands nor into the letter-basket in which our correspondence was collected."

" And the box," said Holmes.

" Ah, yes, the box. The Professor brought back a little wooden box from his travels. It was the one thing which suggested a Continental tour, for it was one of those quaint carved things which one associates with Germany. This he placed in his instrument cupboard. One day, in looking for a cannula, I took up the box. To my surprise he was very angry, and reproved me in words which were quite savage for my curiosity. It was the first time such a thing had happened, and I was deeply hurt. I endeavoured to explain that it was a mere accident that I had touched the box, but all the evening I was conscious that he looked at me harshly and that the incident was rankling in his mind." Mr. Bennett drew a little diary book from his pocket. " That was on July 2," said he.

" You are certainly an admirable witness," said Holmes. " I may need some of these dates which you have noted."

" I learned method among other things from my great teacher. From the time that I observed abnormality in his behaviour I felt that it was my duty to study his case. Thus I have it here that it was on that very day, July 2, that Roy attacked the Professor, as he came from his study into the hall. Again on July 11, there was a scene of the same sort and then I have a note of yet another upon July 20. After that we had to banish Roy to the stables. He was a dear, affectionate animal —but I fear I weary you."

Mr. Bennett spoke in a tone of reproach, for it was very clear that Holmes was not listening. His face was rigid and his eyes gazed abstractedly at the ceiling. With an effort he recovered himself.

" Singular ! Most singular ! " he murmured. " These details were new to me, Mr. Bennett. I think we have now fairly gone over the old ground, have we not ? But you spoke of some fresh developments."

The pleasant, open face of our visitor clouded over, shadowed by some grim remembrance. " What I speak

of occurred the night before last," said he. " I was
lying awake about two in the morning, when I was aware
of a dull muffled sound coming from the passage. I
opened my door and peeped out. I should explain
that the Professor sleeps at the end of the passage——"

" The date being—— ? " asked Holmes.

Our visitor was clearly annoyed at so irrelevant an
interruption.

" I have said, sir, that it was the night before last—that
is, September 4."

Holmes nodded and smiled.

" Pray continue," said he.

" He sleeps at the end of the passage, and would have
to pass my door in order to reach the staircase. It was a
really terrifying experience, Mr. Holmes. I think that
I am as strong-nerved as my neighbours, but I was
shaken by what I saw. The passage was dark save that
one window half-way along it threw a patch of light.
I could see that something was coming along the passage, something dark and crouching. Then suddenly it
emerged into the light, and I saw that it was he. He was
crawling, Mr. Holmes—crawling ! He was not quite on
his hands and knees. I should rather say on his hands
and feet, with his face sunk between his hands. Yet he
seemed to move with ease. I was so paralysed by the
sight that it was not until he had reached my door that
I was able to step forward and ask if I could assist him.
His answer was extraordinary. He sprang up, spat out
some atrocious word at me, and hurried on past me, and
down the staircase. I waited about for an hour, but
he did not come back. It must have been daylight
before he regained his room."

" Well, Watson, what make you of that ? " asked
Holmes, with the air of the pathologist who presents a
rare specimen.

" Lumbago, possibly. I have known a severe attack
make a man walk in just such a way, and nothing would
be more trying to the temper."

" Good, Watson ! You always keep us flat-footed on the ground. But we can hardly accept lumbago, since he was able to stand erect in a moment."

" He was never better in health," said Bennett. " In fact, he is stronger than I have known him for years. But there are the facts, Mr. Holmes. It is not a case in which we can consult the police, and yet we are utterly at our wits' end as to what to do, and we feel in some strange way that we are drifting towards disaster. Edith —Miss Presbury—feels as I do, that we cannot wait passively any longer."

" It is certainly a very curious and suggestive case. What do you think, Watson ? "

" Speaking as a medical man," said I, " it appears to be a case for an alienist. The old gentleman's cerebral processes were disturbed by the love affair. He made a journey abroad in the hope of breaking himself of the passion. His letters and the box may be connected with some other private transaction—a loan, perhaps, or share certificates, which are in the box."

" And the wolf-hound no doubt disapproved of the financial bargain. No, no, Watson, there is more in it than this. Now, I can only suggest——"

What Sherlock Holmes was about to suggest will never be known, for at this moment the door opened and a young lady was shown into the room. As she appeared Mr. Bennett sprang up with a cry and ran forward with his hands out to meet those which she had herself outstretched.

" Edith, dear ! Nothing the matter, I hope ? "

" I felt I must follow you. Oh, Jack, I have been so dreadfully frightened ! It is awful to be there alone."

" Mr. Holmes, this is the young lady I spoke of. This is my fiancée."

" We were gradually coming to that conclusion, were we not, Watson ? " Holmes answered, with a smile. " I take it, Miss Presbury, that there is some fresh development in the case, and that you thought we should know ? "

Our new visitor, a bright, handsome girl of a conventional English type, smiled back at Holmes as she seated herself beside Mr. Bennett.

" When I found Mr. Bennett had left his hotel I thought I should probably find him here. Of course, he had told me that he would consult you. But, oh, Mr. Holmes, can you do nothing for my poor father ? "

" I have hopes, Miss Presbury, but the case is still obscure. Perhaps what you have to say may throw some fresh light upon it."

" It was last night, Mr. Holmes. He had been very strange all day. I am sure that there are times when he has no recollection of what he does. He lives as in a strange dream. Yesterday was such a day. It was not my father with whom I lived. His outward shell was there, but it was not really he."

" Tell me what happened."

" I was awakened in the night by the dog barking most furiously. Poor Roy, he is chained now near the stable. I may say that I always sleep with my door locked ; for, as Jack—as Mr. Bennett—will tell you, we all have a feeling of impending danger. My room is on the second floor. It happened that the blind was up in my window, and there was bright moonlight outside. As I lay with my eyes fixed upon the square of light, listening to the frenzied barkings of the dog, I was amazed to see my father's face looking in at me. Mr. Holmes, I nearly died of surprise and horror. There it was pressed against the window-pane, and one hand seemed to be raised as if to push up the window. If that window had opened, I think I should have gone mad. It was no delusion, Mr. Holmes. Don't deceive yourself by thinking so. I dare say it was twenty seconds or so that I lay paralysed and watched the face. Then it vanished, but I could not—I could not spring out of bed and look out after it. I lay cold and shivering till morning. At breakfast he was sharp and fierce in manner, and made no allusion to the adventure of the night. Neither did I, but I gave an excuse for coming to town—and here I am."

Holmes looked thoroughly surprised at Miss Presbury's narrative.

"My dear young lady, you say that your room is on the second floor. Is there a long ladder in the garden?"

"No, Mr. Holmes; that is the amazing part of it. There is no possible way of reaching the window—and yet he was there."

"The date being September 5," said Holmes. "That certainly complicates matters."

It was the young lady's turn to look surprised. "This is the second time that you have alluded to the date, Mr. Holmes," said Bennett. "Is it possible that it has any bearing upon the case?"

"It is possible—very possible—and yet I have not my full material at present."

"Possibly you are thinking of the connection between insanity and phases of the moon?"

"No, I assure you. It was quite a different line of thought. Possibly you can leave your notebook with me and I will check the dates. Now I think, Watson, that our line of action is perfectly clear. This young lady has informed us—and I have the greatest confidence in her intuition—that her father remembers little or nothing which occurs upon certain dates. We will therefore call upon him as if he had given us an appointment upon such a date. He will put it down to his own lack of memory. Thus we will open our campaign by having a good close view of him."

"That is excellent," said Mr. Bennett. "I warn you, however, that the Professor is irascible and violent at times."

Holmes smiled. "There are reasons why we should come at once—very cogent reasons if my theories hold good. To-morrow, Mr. Bennett, will certainly see us in Camford. There is, if I remember right, an inn called the ' Chequers ' where the port used to be above mediocrity, and the linen was above reproach. I think, Watson, that our lot for the next few days might lie in less pleasant places."

Monday morning found us on our way to the famous University town—an easy effort on the part of Holmes, who had no roots to pull up, but one which involved frantic planning and hurrying on my part, as my practice was by this time not inconsiderable. Holmes made no allusion to the case until after we had deposited our suit-cases at the ancient hostel of which he had spoken.

" I think, Watson, that we can catch the Professor just before lunch. He lectures at eleven, and should have an interval at home."

" What possible excuse have we for calling ? "

Holmes glanced at his notebook.

" There was a period of excitement upon August 26. We will assume that he is a little hazy as to what he does at such times. If we insist that we are there by appointment I think he will hardly venture to contradict us. Have you the effrontery necessary to put it through ? "

" We can but try."

" Excellent, Watson ! Compound of the Busy Bee and Excelsior. We can but try—the motto of the firm. A friendly native will surely guide us."

Such a one on the back of a smart hansom swept us past a row of ancient colleges, and finally turning into a tree-lined drive pulled up at the door of a charming house, girt round with lawns and covered with purple wistaria. Professor Presbury was certainly surrounded with every sign not only of comfort but of luxury. Even as we pulled up a grizzled head appeared at the front window, and we were aware of a pair of keen eyes from under shaggy brows which surveyed us through large horn glasses. A moment later we were actually in his sanctum, and the mysterious scientist, whose vagaries had brought us from London, was standing before us. There was certainly no sign of eccentricity either in his manner or appearance, for he was a portly, large-featured man, grave, tall, and frock-coated, with the dignity of bearing which a lecturer needs. His eyes were his most remarkable feature, keen, observant, and clever to the verge of cunning.

He looked at our cards. " Pray sit down, gentlemen. What can I do for you ? "

Mr. Holmes smiled amiably.

" It was the question which I was about to put to you, Professor."

" To me, sir ! "

" Possibly there is some mistake. I heard through a second person that Professor Presbury of Camford had need of my services."

" Oh, indeed ! " It seemed to me that there was a malicious sparkle in the intense grey eyes. " You heard that, did you ? May I ask the name of your informant ? "

" I am sorry, Professor, but the matter was rather confidential. If I have made a mistake there is no harm done. I can only express my regret."

" Not at all. I should wish to go further into this matter. It interests me. Have you any scrap of writing, any letter or telegram, to bear out your assertion ? "

" No, I have not."

" I presume that you do not go so far as to assert that I summoned you ? "

" I would rather answer no questions," said Holmes.

" No, I dare say not," said the Professor, with asperity. " However, that particular one can be answered very easily without your aid."

He walked across the room to the bell. Our London friend, Mr. Bennett, answered the call.

" Come in, Mr. Bennett. These two gentlemen have

come from London under the impression that they
have been summoned. You handle all my correspondence. Have you a note of anything going to a person
named Holmes ? "

" No, sir," Bennett answered, with a flush.

" That is conclusive," said the Professor, glaring
angrily at my companion. " Now, sir "—he leaned
forward with his two hands upon the table—" it seems
to me that your position is a very questionable one."

Holmes shrugged his shoulders.

" I can only repeat that I am sorry that we have made
a needless intrusion."

" Hardly enough, Mr. Holmes ! " the old man cried,
in a high screaming voice, with extraordinary malignancy
upon his face. He got between us and the door as he
spoke, and he shook his two hands at us with furious
passion. " You can hardly get out of it so easily as that."
His face was convulsed and he grinned and gibbered at
us in his senseless rage. I am convinced that we should
have had to fight our way out of the room if Mr. Bennett
had not intervened.

" My dear Professor," he cried, " consider your position ! Consider the scandal at the University ! Mr.
Holmes is a well-known man. You cannot possibly
treat him with such discourtesy."

Sulkily our host—if I may call him so—cleared the
path to the door. We were glad to find ourselves outside the house, and in the quiet of the tree-lined drive.
Holmes seemed greatly amused by the episode.

" Our learned friend's nerves are somewhat out of
order," said he. " Perhaps our intrusion was a little
crude, and yet we have gained that personal contact
which I desired. But, dear me, Watson, he is surely at
our heels. The villain still pursues us."

There were the sounds of running feet behind, but
it was, to my relief, not the formidable Professor but
his assistant who appeared round the curve of the drive.
He came panting up to us.

" I am so sorry, Mr. Holmes. I wished to apologize."

" My dear sir, there is no need. It is all in the way of professional experience."

" I have never seen him in a more dangerous mood. But he grows more sinister. You can understand now why his daughter and I are alarmed. And yet his mind is perfectly clear."

" Too clear ! " said Holmes. " That was my miscalculation. It is evident that his memory is much more reliable than I had thought. By the way, can we, before we go, see the window of Miss Presbury's room ? "

Mr. Bennett pushed his way through some shrubs and we had a view of the side of the house.

" It is there. The second on the left."

" Dear me, it seems hardly accessible. And yet you will observe that there is a creeper below and a water-pipe above which give some foothold."

" I could not climb it myself," said Mr. Bennett.

" Very likely. It would certainly be a dangerous exploit for any normal man."

" There was one other thing I wished to tell you, Mr. Holmes. I have the address of the man in London to whom the Professor writes. He seems to have written this morning and I got it from his blotting-paper. It is an ignoble position for a trusted secretary, but what else can I do ? "

Holmes glanced at the paper and put it into his pocket.

" Dorak—a curious name. Slavonic, I imagine. Well, it is an important link in the chain. We return to London this afternoon, Mr. Bennett. I see no good purpose to be served by our remaining. We cannot arrest the Professor, because he has done no crime, nor can we place him under constraint, for he cannot be proved to be mad. No action is as yet possible."

" Then what on earth are we to do ? "

" A little patience, Mr. Bennett. Things will soon develop. Unless I am mistaken next Tuesday may mark a crisis. Certainly we shall be in Camford on that day.

Meanwhile, the general position is undeniably unpleasant, and if Miss Presbury can prolong her visit——"

" That is easy."

" Then let her stay till we can assure her that all danger is past. Meanwhile, let him have his way and do not cross him. So long as he is in a good humour all is well."

" There he is ! " said Bennett, in a startled whisper. Looking between the branches we saw the tall, erect figure emerge from the hall door and look around him. He stood leaning forward, his hands swinging straight before him, his head turning from side to side. The secretary with a last wave slipped off among the trees, and we saw him presently rejoin his employer, the two entering the house together in what seemed to be animated and even excited conversation.

" I expect the old gentleman has been putting two and two together," said Holmes, as we walked hotelwards. " He struck me as having a particularly clear and logical brain, from the little I saw of him. Explosive, no doubt, but then from his point of view he has something to explode about if detectives are put on his track and he suspects his own household of doing it. I rather fancy that friend Bennett is in for an uncomfortable time."

Holmes stopped at a post office and sent off a telegram on our way. The answer reached us in the evening, and he tossed it across to me. " Have visited the Commercial Road and seen Dorak. Suave person, Bohemian, elderly. Keeps large general store.—Mercer."

" Mercer is since your time," said Holmes. " He is my general utility man who looks up routine business. It was important to know something of the man with whom our Professor was so secretly corresponding. His nationality connects up with the Prague visit."

" Thank goodness that something connects with something," said I. " At present we seem to be faced by a long series of inexplicable incidents with no bearing upon each other. For example, what possible connection can there be between an angry wolf-hound and a visit to Bohemia, or either of them with a man crawling down a passage at night ? As to your dates, that is the biggest mystification of all."

Holmes smiled and rubbed his hands. We were, I may say, seated in the old sitting-room of the ancient hotel, with a bottle of the famous vintage of which Holmes had spoken on the table between us.

"Well, now, let us take the dates first," said he, his finger-tips together and his manner as if he were addressing a class. "This excellent young man's diary shows that there was trouble upon July 2, and from then onwards it seems to have been at nine-day intervals, with, so far as I remember, only one exception. Thus the last outbreak upon Friday was on September 3, which also falls into the series, as did August 26, which preceded it. The thing is beyond coincidence."

I was forced to agree.

"Let us, then, form the provisional theory that every nine days the Professor takes some strong drug which has a passing but highly poisonous effect. His naturally violent nature is intensified by it. He learned to take this drug while he was in Prague, and is now supplied with it by a Bohemian intermediary in London. This all hangs together, Watson ! "

"But the dog, the face at the window, the creeping man in the passage ? "

"Well, well, we have made a beginning. I should not expect any fresh developments until next Tuesday. In the meantime we can only keep in touch with friend Bennett and enjoy the amenities of this charming town."

In the morning Mr. Bennett slipped round to bring us the latest report. As Holmes had imagined, times had not been easy with him. Without exactly accusing him of being responsible for our presence, the Professor had been very rough and rude in his speech, and evidently felt some strong grievance. This morning he was quite himself again, however, and had delivered his usual brilliant lecture to a crowded class. "Apart from his queer fits," said Bennett, "he has actually more energy and vitality than I can ever remember, nor was his brain ever clearer. But it's not he—it's never the man whom we have known."

"I don't think you have anything to fear now for a week at least," Holmes answered. "I am a busy man, and Dr. Watson has his patients to attend to. Let us agree that we meet here at this hour next Tuesday, and I shall be surprised if before we leave you again we are not able to explain, even if we cannot perhaps put an end to, your troubles. Meanwhile, keep us posted in what occurs."

I saw nothing of my friend for the next few days, but on the following Monday evening I had a short note asking me to meet him next day at the train. From what he told me as we travelled up to Camford all was well, the peace of the Professor's house had been un-ruffled, and his own conduct perfectly normal. This also was the report which was given us by Mr. Bennett himself when he called upon us that evening at our old quarters in the "Chequers." "He heard from his London correspondent to-day. There was a letter and there was a small packet, each with the cross under the stamp which warned me not to touch them. There has been nothing else."

"That may prove quite enough," said Holmes grimly. "Now, Mr. Bennett, we shall, I think, come to some conclusion to-night. If my deductions are correct we should have an opportunity of bringing matters to a head. In order to do so it is necessary to hold the Professor under observation. I would suggest, therefore, that you remain awake and on the look-out. Should you hear him pass your door do not interrupt him, but follow him as discreetly as you can. Dr. Watson and I will not be far off. By the way, where is the key of that little box of which you spoke ? "

" Upon his watch-chain."

" I fancy our researches must lie in that direction. At the worst the lock should not be very formidable. Have you any other able-bodied man on the premises ? "

" There is the coachman, Macphail."

" Where does he sleep ? "

" Over the stables."

" We might possibly want him. Well, we can do no more until we see how things develop. Good-bye—but I expect that we shall see you before morning."

It was nearly midnight before we took our station among some bushes immediately opposite the hall door of the Professor. It was a fine night, but chilly, and we were glad of our warm overcoats. There was a breeze, and clouds were scudding across the sky, obscuring from time to time the half-moon. It would have been a dismal vigil were it not for the expectation and excitement which carried us along, and the assurance of my comrade that we had probably reached the end of the strange sequence of events which had engaged our attention.

" If the cycle of nine days holds good, then we shall have the Professor at his worst to-night," said Holmes. " The fact that these strange symptoms began after his visit to Prague, that he is in secret correspondence with a Bohemian dealer in London, who presumably represents someone in Prague, and that he received a packet from him this very day, all point in one direction. What he takes and why he takes it are still beyond our ken, but that it emanates in some way from Prague is clear enough. He takes it under definite directions which regulate this ninth-day system, which was the first point which attracted my attention. But his symptoms are most remarkable. Did you observe his knuckles ? "

I had to confess that I did not.

" Thick and horny in a way which is quite new in my experience. Always look at the hands first, Watson.

Then cuffs, trouser-knees, and boots. Very curious knuckles which can only be explained by the mode of progression observed by——" Holmes paused, and suddenly clapped his hand to his forehead. " Oh, Watson, Watson, what a fool I have been ! It seems incredible, and yet it must be true. All points in one direction. How could I miss seeing the connection of ideas ? Those knuckles—how could I have passed those knuckles ? And the dog ! And the ivy ! It's surely time that I disappeared into that little farm of my dreams. Look out, Watson ! Here he is ! We shall have the chance of seeing for ourselves."

The hall door had slowly opened, and against the lamp-lit background we saw the tall figure of Professor Presbury. He was clad in his dressing-gown. As he stood outlined in the doorway he was erect but leaning forward with dangling arms, as when we saw him last.

Now he stepped forward into the drive, and an extraordinary change came over him. He sank down into a crouching position, and moved along upon his hands and feet, skipping every now and then as if he were overflowing with energy and vitality. He moved along the face of the house and then round the corner. As he disappeared Bennett slipped through the hall door and softly followed him.

" Come, Watson, come ! " cried Holmes, and we stole as softly as we could through the bushes until we had gained a spot whence we could see the other side of the house, which was bathed in the light of the half-moon. The Professor was clearly visible crouching at the foot of the ivy-covered wall. As we watched him he suddenly began with incredible agility to ascend it. From branch to branch he sprang, sure of foot and firm of grasp, climbing apparently in mere joy at his own powers, with no definite object in view. With his dressing-gown flapping on each side of him he looked like some huge bat glued against the side of his own house, a great square dark patch upon the moonlit wall. Presently he tired of this amusement, and, dropping from branch to branch, he squatted down into the old attitude and moved towards the stables, creeping along in the same strange way as before. The wolf-hound was out now, barking furiously, and more excited than ever when it actually caught sight of its master. It was straining on its chain, and quivering with eagerness and rage. The Professor squatted down very deliberately just out of reach of the hound, and began to provoke it in every possible way. He took handfuls of pebbles from the drive and threw them in the dog's face, prodded him with a stick which he had picked up, flicked his hands about only a few inches from the gaping mouth, and endeavoured in every way to increase the animal's fury, which was already beyond all control. In all our adventures I do not know that I have ever seen a more strange sight than this impassive and still dignified figure crouching frog-like upon the ground and goading to a wilder exhibition of passion the maddened hound, which ramped and raged in front of him, by all manner of ingenious and calculated cruelty.

And then in a moment it happened! It was not the chain that broke, but it was the collar that slipped, for it had been made for a thick-necked Newfoundland. We heard the rattle of falling metal, and the next instant dog and man were rolling on the ground together, the one roaring in rage, the other screaming in a strange shrill falsetto of terror. It was a very narrow thing for the Professor's life. The savage creature had him fairly by the throat, its fangs had bitten deep, and he was senseless before we could reach them and drag the two apart. It might have been a dangerous task for us, but Bennett's voice and presence brought the great wolf-hound instantly to reason. The uproar had brought the sleepy and astonished coachman from his room above the stables. "I'm not surprised," said he, shaking his head. "I've seen him at it before. I knew the dog would get him sooner or later."

The hound was secured, and together we carried the Professor up to his room, where Bennett, who had a medical degree, helped me to dress his torn throat. The sharp teeth had passed dangerously near the carotid artery, and the hæmorrhage was serious. In half an hour the danger was past, I had given the patient an injection of morphia, and he had sunk into deep sleep. Then, and only then, were we able to look at each other and to take stock of the situation.

"I think a first-class surgeon should see him," said I.

"For God's sake, no!" cried Bennett. "At present the scandal is confined to our own household. It is safe with us. If it gets beyond these walls it will never stop. Consider his position at the University, his European reputation, the feelings of his daughter."

"Quite so," said Holmes. "I think it may be quite possible to keep the matter to ourselves, and also to prevent its recurrence now that we have a free hand. The key from the watch-chain, Mr. Bennett. Macphail will guard the patient and let us know if there is any change. Let us see what we can find in the Professor's mysterious box."

There was not much, but there was enough—an empty phial, another nearly full, a hypodermic syringe, several letters in a crabbed, foreign hand. The marks on the envelopes showed that they were those which had disturbed the routine of the secretary, and each was dated from the Commercial Road and signed "A. Dorak." They were mere invoices to say that a fresh bottle was being sent to Professor Presbury, or receipts to acknowledge money. There was one other envelope, however, in a more educated hand and bearing the Austrian stamp with the postmark of Prague. "Here we have our material!" cried Holmes, as he tore out the enclosure.

"HONOURED COLLEAGUE," it ran. "Since your esteemed visit I have thought much of your case, and though in your circumstances there are some special reasons for the treatment, I would none the less enjoin caution, as my results have shown that it is not without danger of a kind.

"It is possible that the Serum of Anthropoid would have been better. I have, as I explained to you, used black-faced Langur because a specimen was accessible. Langur is, of course, a crawler and climber, while Anthropoid walks erect, and is in all ways nearer.

"I beg you to take every possible precaution that there be no premature revelation of the process. I have one other client in England, and Dorak is my agent for both.

"Weekly reports will oblige.

"Yours with high esteem,
"H. LOWENSTEIN."

Lowenstein! The name brought back to me the memory of some snippet from a newspaper which spoke of an obscure scientist who was striving in some unknown way for the secret of rejuvenescence and the elixir of life. Lowenstein of Prague! Lowenstein with the wondrous strength-giving serum, tabooed by the profession because he refused to reveal its source. In a few words I said what I remembered. Bennett had taken a manual of Zoology from the shelves. " 'Langur,' " he read, " 'the great black-faced monkey of the Himalayan slopes, biggest and most human of climbing monkeys.' Many details are added. Well, thanks to you, Mr. Holmes, it is very clear that we have traced the evil to its source."

"The real source," said Holmes, "lies, of course, in that untimely love affair which gave our impetuous Professor the idea that he could only gain his wish by turning himself into a younger man. When one tries to rise above Nature one is liable to fall below it. The highest type of man may revert to the animal if he leaves the straight road of destiny." He sat musing for a little with the phial in his hand, looking at the clear liquid within. " When I have written to this man and told him that I hold him criminally responsible for the poisons which he circulates, we will have no more trouble. But it may recur. Others may find a better way. There is danger there—a very real danger to humanity. Consider, Watson, that the material, the sensual, the worldly would all prolong their worthless lives. The spiritual would not avoid the call to something higher. It would be the survival of the least fit. What sort of cesspool may not our poor world become ? " Suddenly the dreamer disappeared, and Holmes, the man of action, sprang from his chair. " I think there is nothing more to be said, Mr. Bennett. The various incidents will now fit themselves easily into the general scheme. The dog, of course, was aware of the change far more quickly than you. His smell would ensure that. It was the monkey, not the Professor, whom Roy attacked, just as it was the monkey who teased Roy. Climbing was a joy to the creature, and it was a mere chance, I take it, that the pastime brought him to the young lady's window. There is an early train to town, Watson, but I think we shall just have time for a cup of tea at the ' Chequers ' before we catch it."

53. *The Lion's Mane*

IT is a most singular thing that a problem which was certainly as abstruse and unusual as any which I have faced in my long professional career should have come to me after my retirement ; and be brought, as it were, to my very door. It occurred after my withdrawal to my little Sussex home, when I had given myself up entirely to that soothing life of Nature for which I had so often yearned during the long years spent amid the gloom of London. At this period of my life the good Watson had passed almost beyond my ken. An occasional week-end visit was the most that I ever saw of him. Thus I must act as my own chronicler. Ah ! had he but been with me, how much he might have made of so wonderful a happening and of my eventual triumph against every difficulty ! As it is, however, I must needs tell my tale in my own plain way, showing by my words each step upon the difficult road which lay before me as I searched for the mystery of the Lion's Mane.

My villa is situated upon the southern slope of the Downs, commanding a great view of the Channel. At this point the coast-line is entirely of chalk cliffs, which can only be descended by a single, long, tortuous path, which is steep and slippery. At the bottom of the path lie a hundred yards of pebbles and shingle, even when the tide is at full. Here and there, however, there are curves and hollows which make splendid swimming-pools filled afresh with each flow. This admirable beach extends for some miles in each direction, save only at one point where the little cove and village of Fulworth break the line.

My house is lonely. I, my old housekeeper, and my bees have the estate all to ourselves. Half a mile off, however, is Harold Stackhurst's well-known coaching establishment, The Gables, quite a large place, which contains some score of young fellows preparing for various professions, with a staff of several masters. Stackhurst himself was a well-known rowing Blue in his day, and an excellent all-round scholar. He and I were always friendly from the day I came to the coast, and he was the one man who was on such terms with me that we could drop in on each other in the evenings without an invitation.

Towards the end of July, 1907, there was a severe gale, the wind blowing up-Channel, heaping the seas to the base of the cliffs, and leaving a lagoon at the turn of the tide. On the morning of which I speak the wind had abated, and all Nature was newly washed and fresh. It was impossible to work upon so delightful a day, and I strolled out before breakfast to enjoy the exquisite air. I walked along the cliff path which led to the steep descent to the beach. As I walked I heard a shout behind me, and there was Harold Stackhurst waving his hand in cheery greeting.

" What a morning, Mr. Holmes ! I thought I should see you out."

" Going for a swim, I see."

" At your old tricks again," he laughed, patting his bulging pocket. " Yes. McPherson started early, and I expect I may find him there."

Fitzroy McPherson was the science master, a fine upstanding young fellow whose life had been crippled by heart trouble following rheumatic fever. He was a natural athlete, however, and excelled in every game which did not throw too great a strain upon him. Summer and winter he went for his swim, and, as I am a swimmer myself, I have often joined him.

At this moment we saw the man himself. His head showed above the edge of the cliff where the path ends. Then his whole figure appeared at the top, staggering like a drunken man. The next instant he threw up his hands, and, with a terrible cry, fell upon his face. Stackhurst and I rushed forward—it may have been fifty yards —and turned him on his back. He was obviously dying. Those glazed sunken eyes and dreadful livid cheeks could mean nothing else. One glimmer of life came into his face for an instant, and he uttered two or three words with an eager air of warning. They were slurred and indistinct, but to my ear the last of them, which burst in a shriek from his lips, were " the lion's mane." It was utterly irrelevant and unintelligible, and yet I could twist the sound into no other sense. Then he half raised himself from the ground, threw his arms into the air and fell forward on his side. He was dead.

My companion was paralysed by the sudden horror of it, but I, as may well be imagined, had every sense on the alert. And I had need, for it was speedily evident that we were in the presence of an extraordinary case. The man was dressed only in his Burberry overcoat, his

trousers, and an unlaced pair of canvas shoes   A
fell over, his Burberry, which had been simply thro
round his shoulders, slipped off, exposing his trur
We stared at it in amazement. His back was covere
with dark red lines as though he had been terribly flogge
by a thin wire scourge.   The instrument with which this
punishment had been inflicted was clearly flexible, for
the long, angry weals curved round his shoulders and ribs.
There was blood dripping down his chin, for he had
bitten through his lower lip in the paroxysm of his
agony.   His drawn and distorted face told how terrible
that agony had been.

I was kneeling and Stackhurst standing by the body
when a shadow fell across us, and we found that Ian
Murdoch was by our side.   Murdoch was the mathematical coach at the establishment, a tall, dark, thin man,
so taciturn and aloof that none can be said to have been
his friend. He seemed to live in some high, abstract
region of surds and conic sections with little to connect
him with ordinary life.   He was looked upon as an oddity
by the students, and would have been their butt, but there
was some strange outlandish blood in the man, which
showed itself not only in his coal-black eyes and swarthy
face, but also in occasional outbreaks of temper which
could only be described as ferocious.   On one occasion,
being plagued by a little dog belonging to McPherson,
he had caught the creature up and hurled it through
the plate-glass window, an action for which Stackhurst
would certainly have given him his dismissal had he not
been a very valuable teacher.   Such was the strange,
complex man who now appeared beside us.   He seemed
to be honestly shocked at the sight before him, though
the incident of the dog may show that there was no
great sympathy between the dead man and himself.

" Poor fellow !   Poor fellow !   What can I do ?   How
can I help ? "

" Were you with him ?   Can you tell us what has
happened ? "

"No, no, I was late this morning. I was not on the beach at all. I have come straight from The Gables. What can I do?"

"You can hurry to the police-station at Fulworth. Report the matter at once."

Without a word he made off at top speed, and I proceeded to take the matter in hand, while Stackhurst, dazed at this tragedy, remained by the body. My first task naturally was to note who was on the beach. From the top of the path I could see the whole sweep of it, and it was absolutely deserted save that two or three dark figures could be seen far away moving towards the village of Fulworth. Having satisfied myself upon this point, I walked slowly down the path. There was clay or soft marl mixed with the chalk, and every here and there I saw the same footstep, both ascending and descending. No one else had gone down to the beach by this track that morning. At one place I observed the print of an open hand with the fingers towards the incline. This could only mean that poor McPherson had fallen as he ascended. There were rounded depressions, too, which suggested that he had come down upon his knees more than once. At the bottom of the path was the considerable lagoon left by the retreating tide. At the side of it McPherson had undressed, for there lay his towel on a rock. It was folded and dry, so that it would seem that after all he had never entered the water. Once or twice as I hunted round amid the hard shingle I came on little patches of sand where the print of his canvas shoe, and also of his naked foot, could be seen. The latter fact proved that he had made all ready to bathe, though the towel indicated that he had not actually done so.

And here was the problem clearly defined—as strange a one as had ever confronted me. The man had not been on the beach more than a quarter of an hour at the most. Stackhurst had followed him from The Gables, so there could be no doubt about that. He had gone to bathe and had stripped, as the naked footsteps showed.

Then he had suddenly huddled on his clothes again—they were all dishevelled and unfastened—and he had returned without bathing, or at any rate without drying himself. And the reason for his change of purpose had been that he had been scourged in some savage, inhuman fashion, tortured until he bit his lip through in his agony, and was left with only strength enough to crawl away and to die. Who had done this barbarous deed ? There were, it is true, small grottos and caves in the base of the cliffs, but the low sun shone directly into them, and there was no place for concealment. Then, again, there were those distant figures on the beach. They seemed too far away to have been connected with the crime, and the broad lagoon in which McPherson had intended to bathe lay between him and them, lapping up to the rocks. On the sea two or three fishing-boats were at no great distance. Their occupants might be examined at our leisure. There were several roads for inquiry, but none which led to any very obvious goal.

When I at last returned to the body I found that a little group of wandering folk had gathered round it. Stackhurst was, of course, still there, and Ian Murdoch had just arrived with Anderson, the village constable, a big, ginger-moustached man of the slow, solid Sussex breed—a breed which covers much good sense under a heavy, silent exterior. He listened to everything, took note of all we said, and finally drew me aside.

" I'd be glad of your advice, Mr. Holmes. This is a big thing for me to handle, and I'll hear of it from Lewes if I go wrong."

I advised him to send for his immediate superior, and for a doctor ; also to allow nothing to be moved, and as few fresh footmarks as possible to be made, until they came. In the meantime I searched the dead man's pockets. There were his handkerchief, a large knife, and a small folding card-case. From this projected a slip of paper, which I unfolded and handed to the constable. There was written on it in a scrawling, feminine

hand : " I will be there, you may be sure.—Maudie."
It read like a love affair, an assignation, though when
and where were a blank. The constable replaced it in
the card-case and returned it with the other things to the
pockets of the Burberry. Then, as nothing more suggested itself, I walked back to my house for breakfast,
having first arranged that the base of the cliffs should be
thoroughly searched.

Stackhurst was round in an hour or two to tell me that
the body had been removed to The Gables, where the
inquest would be held. He brought with him some
serious and definite news. As I expected, nothing had
been found in the small caves below the cliff, but he had
examined the papers in McPherson's desk, and there were
several which showed an intimate correspondence with a
certain Miss Maud Bellamy, of Fulworth. We had then
established the identity of the writer of the note.

" The police have the letters," he explained. " I
could not bring them. But there is no doubt that it was a
serious love affair. I see no reason, however, to connect
it with that horrible happening save, indeed, that the
lady had made an appointment with him."

" But hardly at a bathing-pool which all of you were
in the habit of using," I remarked.

" It is mere chance," said he, " that several of the
students were not with McPherson."

" *Was* it mere chance ? "

Stackhurst knit his brows in thought.

" Ian Murdoch held them back," said he ; " he would
insist upon some algebraic demonstration before breakfast. Poor chap, he is dreadfully cut up about it
all."

" And yet I gather that they were not friends."

" At one time they were not. But for a year or more
Murdoch has been as near to McPherson as he ever could
be to anyone. He is not of a very sympathetic disposition
by nature."

" So I understand. I seem to remember your telling me once about a quarrel over the ill-usage of a dog."

" That blew over all right."

" But left some vindictive feeling, perhaps."

" No, no ; I am sure they were real friends."

" Well, then, we must explore the matter of the girl. Do you know her ? "

" Everyone knows her. She is the beauty of the neighbourhood—a real beauty, Holmes, who would draw attention everywhere. I knew that McPherson was attracted by her, but I had no notion that it had gone so far as these letters would seem to indicate."

" But who is she ? "

" She is the daughter of old Tom Bellamy, who owns all the boats and bathing-cots at Fulworth. He was a fisherman to start with, but is now a man of some substance. He and his son William run the business."

" Shall we walk into Fulworth and see them ? "

" On what pretext ? "

" Oh, we can easily find a pretext. After all, this poor man did not ill-use himself in this outrageous way. Some human hand was on the handle of that scourge, if indeed it was a scourge which inflicted the injuries. His circle of acquaintances in this lonely place was surely limited. Let us follow it up in every direction and we can hardly fail to come upon the motive, which in turn should lead us to the criminal."

It would have been a pleasant walk across the thyme-scented Downs had our minds not been poisoned by the tragedy we had witnessed. The village of Fulworth lies in a hollow curving in a semicircle round the bay. Behind the old-fashioned hamlet several modern houses have been built upon the rising ground. It was to one of these that Stackhurst guided me.

" That's The Haven, as Bellamy called it. The one with the corner tower and slate roof. Not bad for a man who started with nothing but—— By Jove, look at that ! "

The garden gate of The Haven had opened and a man had emerged. There was no mistaking that tall, angular, straggling figure. It was Ian Murdoch, the mathematician. A moment later we confronted him upon the road.

"Hullo!" said Stackhurst. The man nodded, gave us a sideways glance from his curious dark eyes, and would have passed us, but his principal pulled him up.

"What were you doing there?" he asked.

Murdoch's face flushed with anger. "I am your subordinate, sir, under your roof. I am not aware that I owe you any account of my private actions."

Stackhurst's nerves were near the surface after all he had endured. Otherwise, perhaps, he would have waited. Now he lost his temper completely.

"In the circumstances your answer is pure impertinence, Mr. Murdoch."

"Your own question might perhaps come under the same heading."

"This is not the first time that I have had to overlook your insubordinate ways. It will certainly be the last. You will kindly make fresh arrangements for your future as speedily as you can."

"I had intended to do so. I have lost to-day the only person who made The Gables habitable."

He strode off upon his way, while Stackhurst, with angry eyes, stood glaring after him. "Is he not an impossible, intolerable man?" he cried.

The one thing that impressed itself forcibly upon my mind was that Mr. Ian Murdoch was taking the first chance to open a path of escape from the scene of the crime. Suspicion, vague and nebulous, was now beginning to take outline in my mind. Perhaps the visit to the Bellamys might throw some further light upon the matter. Stackhurst pulled himself together and we went forward to the house.

Mr. Bellamy proved to be a middle-aged man with

a flaming red beard. He seemed to be in a very angry mood, and his face was soon as florid as his hair.

" No, sir, I do not desire any particulars. My son here "—indicating a powerful young man, with a heavy, sullen face, in the corner of the sitting-room—" is of one mind with me that Mr. McPherson's attentions to Maud were insulting. Yes, sir, the word ' marriage ' was never mentioned, and yet there were letters and meetings, and a great deal more of which neither of us could approve. She has no mother, and we are her only guardians. We are determined——"

But the words were taken from his mouth by the appearance of the lady herself. There was no gain-saying that she would have graced any assembly in the world. Who could have imagined that so rare a flower would grow from such a root and in such an atmosphere ? Women have seldom been an attraction to me, for my brain has always governed my heart, but I could not look upon her perfect clear-cut face, with all the soft freshness of the Downlands in her delicate colouring, without realizing that no young man would cross her path unscathed. Such was the girl who had pushed open the door and stood now, wide-eyed and intense, in front of Harold Stackhurst.

" I know already that Fitzroy is dead," she said. " Do not be afraid to tell me the particulars."

" This other gentleman of yours let us know the news," explained the father.

" There is no reason why my sister should be brought into the matter," growled the younger man.

The sister turned a sharp, fierce look upon him. " This is my business, William. Kindly leave me to manage it in my own way. By all accounts there has been a crime committed. If I can help to show who did it, it is the least I can do for him who is gone."

She listened to a short account from my companion, with a composed concentration which showed me that she possessed strong character as well as great beauty.

Maud Bellamy will always remain in my memory as a most complete and remarkable woman. It seems that she already knew me by sight, for she turned to me at the end.

"Bring them to justice, Mr. Holmes. You have my sympathy and my help, whoever they may be." It seemed to me that she glanced defiantly at her father and brother as she spoke.

"Thank you," said I. "I value a woman's instinct in such matters. You use the word 'they.' You think that more than one was concerned?"

"I knew Mr. McPherson well enough to be aware that he was a brave and a strong man. No single person could ever have inflicted such an outrage upon him."

"Might I have one word with you alone?"

"I tell you, Maud, not to mix yourself up in the matter," cried her father angrily.

She looked at me helplessly. "What can I do?"

"The whole world will know the facts presently, so there can be no harm if I discuss them here," said I. "I should have preferred privacy, but if your father will not allow it, he must share the deliberations." Then I spoke of the note which had been found in the dead man's pocket. "It is sure to be produced at the inquest. May I ask you to throw any light upon it that you can?"

"I see no reason for mystery," she answered. "We were engaged to be married, and we only kept it secret because Fitzroy's uncle, who is very old and said to be dying, might have disinherited him if he had married against his wish. There was no other reason."

"You could have told us," growled Mr. Bellamy.

"So I would, father, if you had ever shown sympathy."

"I object to my girl picking up with men outside her own station."

"It was your prejudice against him which prevented us from telling you. As to this appointment "—she

fumbled in her dress and produced a crumpled note—
" it was in answer to this."

" DEAREST," ran the message : " The old place on
the beach just after sunset on Tuesday. It is the only
time I can get away.—F. M."

" Tuesday was to-day, and I had meant to meet him
to-night."

I turned over the paper. " This never came by post.
How did you get it ? "

" I would rather not answer that question. It has
really nothing to do with the matter which you are
investigating. But anything which bears upon that I
will most freely answer."

She was as good as her word, but there was nothing
which was helpful in our investigation. She had no
reason to think that her fiancé had any hidden enemy,
but she admitted that she had had several warm admirers.

" May I ask if Mr. Ian Murdoch was one of them ? "

She blushed and seemed confused.

" There was a time when I thought he was. But that
was all changed when he understood the relations between
Fitzroy and myself."

Again the shadow round this strange man seemed
to me to be taking more definite shape. His record
must be examined. His rooms must be privately searched.
Stackhurst was a willing collaborator, for in his mind
also suspicions were forming. We returned from our
visit to The Haven with the hope that one free end
of this tangled skein was already in our hands.

A week passed. The inquest had thrown no light
upon the matter and had been adjourned for further
evidence. Stackhurst had made discreet inquiry about
his subordinate, and there had been a superficial search of
his room, but without result. Personally, I had gone over
the whole ground again, both physically and mentally,
but with no new conclusions. In all my chronicles the

reader will find no case which brought me so completely to the limit of my powers. Even my imagination could conceive no solution to the mystery. And then there came the incident of the dog.

It was my old housekeeper who heard of it first by that strange wireless by which such people collect the news of the country-side.

"Sad story this, sir, about Mr. McPherson's dog," said she one evening.

I do not encourage such conversations, but the words arrested my attention.

"What of Mr. McPherson's dog?"

"Dead, sir. Died of grief for its master."

"Who told you this?"

"Why, sir, everyone is talking of it. It took on terrible, and has eaten nothing for a week. Then to-day two of the young gentlemen from The Gables found it dead—down on the beach, sir, at the very place where its master met his end."

"At the very place." The words stood out clear in my memory. Some dim perception that the matter was vital rose in my mind. That the dog should die was after the beautiful, faithful nature of dogs. But 'in the very place'! Why should this lonely beach be fatal to it? Was it possible that it also, had been sacrificed to some revengeful feud? Was it possible——? Yes, the perception was dim, but already something was building up in my mind. In a few minutes I was on my way to The Gables, where I found Stackhurst in his study. At my request he sent for Sudbury and Blount, the two students who had found the dog.

"Yes, it lay on the very edge of the pool," said one of them. "It must have followed the trail of its dead master."

I saw the faithful little creature, an Airedale terrier, laid out upon the mat in the hall. The body was stiff and rigid, the eyes projecting, and the limbs contorted. There was agony in every line of it.

From The Gables I walked down to the bathing-pool. The sun had sunk and the shadow of the great cliff lay black across the water, which glimmered dully like a sheet of lead. The place was deserted and there was no sign of life save for two sea-birds circling and screaming overhead. In the fading light I could dimly make out the little dog's spoor upon the sand round the very rock on which his master's towel had been laid. For a long time I stood in deep meditation while the shadows grew darker around me. My mind was filled with racing thoughts. You have known what it was to be in a nightmare in which you feel that there is some all-important thing for which you search and which you know is there, though it remains for ever just beyond your reach. That was how I felt that evening as I stood alone by that place of death. Then at last I turned and walked slowly homewards.

I had just reached the top of the path when it came to me. Like a flash, I remembered the thing for which I had so eagerly and vainly grasped. You will know, or Watson has written in vain, that I hold a vast store of out-of-the-way knowledge, without scientific system, but very available for the needs of my work. My mind is like a crowded box-room with packets of all sorts stowed away therein—so many that I may well have but a vague perception of what was there. I had known that there was something which might bear upon this matter. It was still vague, but at least I knew how I could make it clear. It was monstrous, incredible, and yet it was always a possibility. I would test it to the full.

There is a great garret in my little house which is stuffed with books. It was into this that I plunged and rummaged for an hour. At the end of that time I emerged with a little chocolate and silver volume. Eagerly I turned up the chapter of which I had a dim remembrance. Yes, it was indeed a far-fetched and unlikely proposition, and yet I could not be at rest until I had made sure if it might, indeed, be so. It was late when I retired, with my mind eagerly awaiting the work of the morrow.

But that work met with an annoying interruption. I had hardly swallowed my early cup of tea and was starting for the beach when I had a call from Inspector Bardle of the Sussex Constabulary—a steady, solid, bovine man with thoughtful eyes, which looked at me now with a very troubled expression.

" I know your immense experience, sir," said he. " This is quite unofficial, of course, and need go no further. But I am fairly up against it in this McPherson case. The question is, shall I make an arrest, or shall I not ? "

" Meaning Mr. Ian Murdoch ? "

" Yes, sir. There is really no one else when you come to think of it. That's the advantage of this solitude. We narrow it down to a very small compass. If he did not do it, then who did ? "

" What have you against him ? "

He had gleaned along the same furrows as I had. There was Murdoch's character and the mystery which seemed to hang round the man. His furious bursts of temper, as shown in the incident of the dog. The fact that he had quarrelled with McPherson in the past, and that there was some reason to think that he might have resented his attentions to Miss Bellamy. He had all my points, but no fresh ones, save that Murdoch seemed to be making every preparation for departure.

" What would my position be if I let him slip away with all this evidence against him ? " The burly, phlegmatic man was sorely troubled in his mind.

" Consider," I said, " all the essential gaps in your case. On the morning of the crime he can surely prove an alibi. He had been with his scholars till the last moment, and within a few minutes of McPherson's appearance he came upon us from behind. Then bear in mind the absolute impossibility that he could single-handed have inflicted this outrage upon a man quite as strong as himself. Finally, there is this question of the instrument with which these injuries were inflicted."

"What could it be but a scourge or flexible whip of some sort?"

"Have you examined the marks?" I asked.

"I have seen them. So has the doctor."

"But I have examined them very carefully with a lens. They have peculiarities."

"What are they, Mr. Holmes?"

I stepped to my bureau and brought out an enlarged photograph. "This is my method in such cases," I explained.

"You certainly do things thoroughly, Mr. Holmes."

"I should hardly be what I am if I did not. Now let us consider this weal which extends round the right shoulder. Do you observe nothing remarkable?"

"I can't say I do."

"Surely it is evident that it is unequal in its intensity. There is a dot of extravasated blood here, and another there. There are similar indications in this other weal down here. What can that mean?"

"I have no idea. Have you?"

"Perhaps I have. Perhaps I haven't. I may be able to say more soon. Anything which will define what made that mark will bring us a long way towards the criminal."

"It is, of course, an absurd idea," said the policeman, "but if a red-hot net of wire had been laid across the back, then these better-marked points would represent where the meshes crossed each other."

"A most ingenious comparison. Or shall we say a very stiff cat-o'-nine-tails with small hard knots upon it?"

"By Jove, Mr. Holmes, I think you have hit it."

"Or there may be some very different cause, Mr Bardle. But your case is far too weak for an arrest. Besides, we have those last words—'Lion's Mane.'"

"I have wondered whether Ian——"

"Yes, I have considered that. If the second word had borne any resemblance to Murdoch—but it did not.

He gave it almost in a shriek. I am sure that it was ' Mane.' "

" Have you no alternative, Mr. Holmes ? "

" Perhaps I have. But I do not care to discuss it until there is something more solid to discuss."

" And when will that be ? "

" In an hour—possibly less."

The Inspector rubbed his chin and looked at me with dubious eyes.

" I wish I could see what was in your mind, Mr. Holmes. Perhaps it's those fishing-boats."

" No, no ; they were too far out."

" Well, then, is it Bellamy and that big son of his ? They were not too sweet upon Mr. McPherson. Could they have done him a mischief ? "

" No, no ; you won't draw me until I am ready," said I with a smile. " Now, Inspector, we each have our own work to do. Perhaps if you were to meet me here at midday——? "

So far we had got when there came the tremendous interruption which was the beginning of the end.

My outer door was flung open, there were blundering footsteps in the passage, and Ian Murdoch staggered into the room, pallid, dishevelled, his clothes in wild disorder, clawing with his bony hands at the furniture to hold himself erect. " Brandy ! Brandy ! " he gasped, and fell groaning upon the sofa.

He was not alone. Behind him came Stackhurst, hatless and panting, almost as *distrait* as his companion.

" Yes, yes, brandy ! " he cried. " The man is at his last gasp. It was all I could do to bring him here. He fainted twice upon the way."

Half a tumbler of the raw spirit brought about a wondrous change. He pushed himself up on one arm and swung his coat from off his shoulders. " For God's sake ! oil, opium, morphia ! " he cried. " Anything to ease this infernal agony ! "

The Inspector and I cried out at the sight. There,

criss-crossed upon the man's naked shoulder, was the same strange reticulated pattern of red, inflamed lines which had been the death-mark of Fitzroy McPherson.

The pain was evidently terrible and was more than local, for the sufferer's breathing would stop for a time, his face would turn black, and then with loud gasps he would clap his hand to his heart, while his brow dropped beads of sweat. At any moment he might die. More and more brandy was poured down his throat, each fresh dose bringing him back to life. Pads of cotton-wool soaked in salad-oil seemed to take the agony from the strange wounds. At last his head fell heavily upon the cushion. Exhausted Nature had taken refuge in its last storehouse of vitality. It was half a sleep and half a faint, but at least it was ease from pain.

To question him had been impossible, but the moment we were assured of his condition Stackhurst turned upon me.

"My God!" he cried, "what is it, Holmes? What is it?"

"Where did you find him?"

"Down on the beach. Exactly where poor McPherson met his end. If this man's heart had been weak as McPherson's was, he would not be here now. More than once I thought he was gone as I brought him up. It was too far to The Gables, so I made for you."

"Did you see him on the beach?"

"I was walking on the cliff when I heard his cry. He was at the edge of the water, reeling about like a drunken man. I ran down, threw some clothes about him, and brought him up. For Heaven's sake, Holmes, use all the powers you have and spare no pains to lift the curse from this place, for life is becoming unendurable. Can you, with all your world-wide reputation, do nothing for us?"

"I think I can, Stackhurst. Come with me now! And you, Inspector, come along! We will see if we cannot deliver this murderer into your hands."

Leaving the unconscious man in the charge of my housekeeper, we all three went down to the deadly lagoon. On the shingle there was piled a little heap of towels and clothes, left by the stricken man. Slowly I walked round the edge of the water, my comrades in Indian file behind me. Most of the pool was quite shallow, but under the cliff where the beach was hollowed out it was four or five feet deep. It was to this part that a swimmer would naturally go, for it formed a beautiful pellucid green pool as clear as crystal. A line of rocks lay above it at the base of the cliff, and along this I led the way, peering eagerly into the depths beneath me. I had reached the deepest and stillest pool when my eyes caught that for which they were searching, and I burst into a shout of triumph.

" Cyanea ! " I cried. " Cyanea ! Behold the Lion's Mane ! "

The strange object at which I pointed did indeed look like a tangled mass torn from the mane of a lion. It lay upon a rocky shelf some three feet under the water, a curious waving, vibrating, hairy creature with streaks of silver among its yellow tresses. It pulsated with a slow, heavy dilation and contraction.

" It has done mischief enough. Its day is over ! " I cried. " Help me, Stackhurst ! Let us end the murderer for ever."

There was a big boulder just above the ledge, and we pushed it until it fell with a tremendous splash into the water. When the ripples had cleared we saw that it had settled upon the ledge below. One flapping edge of yellow membrane showed that our victim was beneath it. A thick oily scum oozed out from below the stone and stained the water round, rising slowly to the surface.

" Well, this gets me ! " cried the Inspector. " What was it, Mr. Holmes ? I'm born and bred in these parts, but I never saw such a thing. It don't belong to Sussex."

" Just as well for Sussex," I remarked. " It may have been the south-west gale that brought it up. Come back to my house, both of you, and I will give you the terrible experience of one who has good reason to remember his own meeting with the same peril of the seas."

When we reached my study, we found that Murdoch was so far recovered that he could sit up. He was dazed in mind, and every now and then was shaken by a paroxysm of pain. In broken words he explained that he had no notion what had occurred to him, save that terrific pangs had suddenly shot through him, and that it had taken all his fortitude to reach the bank.

"Here is a book," I said, taking up the little volume, "which first brought light into what might have been for ever dark. It is *Out of Doors*, by the famous observer J. G. Wood. Wood himself very nearly perished from contact with this vile creature, so he wrote with a very full knowledge. *Cyanea Capillata* is the miscreant's full name, and he can be as dangerous to life as, and far more painful than, the bite of the cobra. Let me briefly give this extract.

"'If the bather should see a loose roundish mass of tawny membranes and fibres, something like very large handfuls of lion's mane and silver paper, let him beware, for this is the fearful stinger, *Cyanea Capillata*.' Could our sinister acquaintance be more clearly described?

"He goes on to tell his own encounter with one when swimming off the coast of Kent. He found that the creature radiated almost invisible filaments to the distance of fifty feet, and that anyone within that circumference from the deadly centre was in danger of death. Even at a distance the effect upon Wood was almost fatal. 'The multitudinous threads caused light scarlet lines upon the skin which on closer examination resolved into minute dots or pustules, each dot charged as it were with a red-hot needle making its way through the nerves.'

"The local pain was, as he explains, the least part of the exquisite torment. 'Pangs shot through the chest, causing me to fall as if struck by a bullet. The pulsation would cease, and then the heart would give six or seven leaps as if it would force its way through the chest.'

" It nearly killed him, although he had only been exposed to it in the disturbed ocean and not in the narrow calm waters of a bathing-pool. He says that he could hardly recognize himself afterwards, so white, wrinkled and shrivelled was his face. He gulped down brandy, a whole bottleful, and it seems to have saved his life. There is the book, Inspector. I leave it with you, and you cannot doubt that it contains a full explanation of the tragedy of poor McPherson."

" And incidentally exonerates me," remarked Ian Murdoch with a wry smile. " I do not blame you, Inspector, nor you, Mr. Holmes, for your suspicions were natural. I feel that on the very eve of my arrest I have only cleared myself by sharing the fate of my poor friend."

" No, Mr. Murdoch. I was already upon the track, and had I been out as early as I intended I might well have saved you from this terrific experience."

" But how did you know, Mr. Holmes ? "

" I am an omnivorous reader with a strangely retentive memory for trifles. That phrase ' Lion's Mane ' haunted my mind. I knew that I had seen it somewhere in an unexpected context. You have seen that it does describe the creature. I have no doubt that it was floating on the water when McPherson saw it, and that this phrase was the only one by which he could convey to us a warning as to the creature which had been his death."

" Then I, at least, am cleared," said Murdoch, rising slowly to his feet. " There are one or two words of explanation which I should give, for I know the direction in which your inquiries have run. It is true that I loved this lady, but from the day when she chose my friend McPherson my one desire was to help her to happiness. I was well content to stand aside and act as their go-between. Often I carried their messages, and it was because I was in their confidence and because she was so dear to me that I hastened to tell her of my friend's death, lest someone should forestall me in a more sudden and heartless manner. She would not tell you, sir, of our relations lest you should disapprove and I might suffer. But with your leave I must try to get back to The Gables, for my bed will be very welcome."

Stackhurst held out his hand. "Our nerves have all been at concert-pitch," said he. "Forgive what is past, Murdoch. We shall understand each other better in the future." They passed out together with their arms linked in friendly fashion. The Inspector remained, staring at me in silence with his ox-like eyes.

"Well, you've done it!" he cried at last. "I had read of you, but I never believed it. It's wonderful!"

I was forced to shake my head. To accept such praise was to lower one's own standards.

"I was slow at the outset—culpably slow. Had the body been found in the water I could hardly have missed it. It was the towel which misled me. The poor fellow had never thought to dry himself, and so I in turn was led to believe that he had never been in the water. Why, then, should the attack of any water creature suggest itself to me? That was where I went astray. Well, well, Inspector, I often ventured to chaff you gentlemen of the police force, but *Cyanea Capillata* very nearly avenged Scotland Yard."

54. *The Veiled Lodger*

WHEN one considers that Mr. Sherlock Holmes was in active practice for twenty-three years, and that during seventeen of these I was allowed to co-operate with him and to keep notes of his doings, it will be clear that I have a mass of material at my command. The problem has always been, not to find, but to choose. There is the long row of year-books which fill a shelf, and there are the dispatch-cases filled with documents, a perfect quarry for the student, not only of crime, but of the social and official scandals of the late Victorian era. Concerning these latter, I may say that the writers of agonized letters, who beg that the honour of their families or the reputation of famous forbears may not be touched, have nothing to fear. The discretion and high sense of professional honour which have always distinguished my friend are still at work in the choice of these memoirs, and no confidence will be abused. I deprecate, however, in the strongest way the attempts which have been made lately to get at and to destroy these papers. The source of these outrages is known, and if they are repeated I have Mr. Holmes' authority for saying that the whole story concerning the politician, the lighthouse and the trained cormorant will be given to the public. There is at least one reader who will understand.

It is not reasonable to suppose that every one of these cases gave Holmes the opportunity of showing those curious gifts of instinct and observation which I have endeavoured to set forth in these memoirs. Sometimes he had with much effort to pick the fruit, sometimes it fell easily into his lap. But the most terrible human tragedies were often involved in these cases which brought him the fewest personal opportunities, and it is one of these which I now desire to record. In telling it, I have made a slight change of name and place, but otherwise the facts are as stated.

One forenoon—it was late in 1896—I received a hurried note from Holmes asking for my attendance. When I arrived, I found him seated in a smoke-laden atmosphere, with an elderly, motherly woman of the buxom landlady type in the corresponding chair in front of him.

" This is Mrs. Merrilow, of South Brixton," said my friend, with a wave of the hand. " Mrs. Merrilow does not object to tobacco, Watson, if you wish to indulge your filthy habits. Mrs. Merrilow has an interesting story to tell which may well lead to further developments in which your presence may be useful."

" Anything I can do——"

" You will understand, Mrs. Merrilow, that if I come to Mrs. Ronder I should prefer to have a witness. You will make her understand that before we arrive."

" Lord bless you, Mr. Holmes," said our visitor ; " she is that anxious to see you that you might bring the whole parish at your heels ! "

" Then we shall come early in the afternoon. Let us see that we have our facts correct before we start. If we go over them it will help Dr. Watson to understand the situation. You say that Mrs. Ronder has been your lodger for seven years and that you have only once seen her face."

" And I wish to God I had not ! " said Mrs. Merrilow.

" It was, I understand, terribly mutilated."

" Well, Mr. Holmes, you would hardly say it was a face at all. That's how it looked. Our milkman got a glimpse of her once peeping out of the upper window, and he dropped his tin and the milk all over the front garden. That is the kind of face it is. When I saw her—I happened on her unawares—she covered up quick, and then she said, ' Now, Mrs. Merrilow, you know at last why it is that I never raise my veil.' "

" Do you know anything about her history ? "

" Nothing at all."

" Did she give references when she came ? "

" No, sir, but she gave hard cash, and plenty of it. A quarter's rent right down on the table in advance and no arguing about terms. In these times a poor woman like me can't afford to turn down a chance like that."

" Did she give any reason for choosing your house ? "

" Mine stands well back from the road and is more private than most. Then, again, I only take the one, and I have no family of my own. I reckon she had tried others and found that mine suited her best. It's privacy she is after, and she is ready to pay for it."

" You say that she never showed her face from first to last save on the one accidental occasion. Well, it is a very remarkable story, most remarkable, and I don't wonder that you want it examined."

" I don't, Mr. Holmes. I am quite satisfied so long as I get my rent. You could not have a quieter lodger or one who gives less trouble."

" Then what has brought matters to a head ? "

" Her health, Mr. Holmes. She seems to be wasting away. And there's something terrible on her mind. ' Murder ! ' she cries. ' Murder ! ' And once I heard her, ' You cruel beast ! You monster ! ' she cried. It was in the night, and it fair rang through the house and sent the shivers through me. So I went to her in the morning. ' Mrs. Ronder,' I says, ' if you have anything that is troubling your soul, there's the clergy,' I says, ' and there's the police. Between them you should get some help.' ' For God's sake, not the police ! ' says she, ' and the clergy can't change what is past. And yet,' she says, ' it would ease my mind if someone knew the truth before I died.' ' Well,' says I, ' if you won't have the regulars, there is this detective man what we read about '—beggin' your pardon, Mr. Holmes. And she, she fair jumped at it. ' That's the man,' says she. ' I wonder I never thought of it before. Bring him here, Mrs. Merrilow, and if he won't come, tell him I am the wife of Ronder's wild beast show. Say that, and give him the name Abbas Parva. Here it is as she wrote it, Abbas Parva. ' That will bring him, if he's the man I think he is.' "

" And it will, too," remarked Holmes. " Very good, Mrs. Merrilow. I should like to have a little chat with Dr. Watson. That will carry us till lunch-time. About three o'clock you may expect to see us at your house in Brixton."

Our visitor had no sooner waddled out of the room —no other verb can describe Mrs. Merrilow's method of progression—than Sherlock Holmes threw himself with fierce energy upon the pile of commonplace books in the corner. For a few minutes there was a constant swish of the leaves, and then with a grunt of satisfaction he came upon what he sought. So excited was he that he did not rise, but sat upon the floor like some strange Buddha, with crossed legs, the huge books all round him, and one open upon his knees.

" The case worried me at the time, Watson. Here are my marginal notes to prove it. I confess that I could make nothing of it. And yet I was convinced that the coroner was wrong. Have you no recollection of the Abbas Parva tragedy ? "

" None, Holmes."

" And yet you were with me then. But certainly my own impression was very superficial, for there was nothing to go by, and none of the parties had engaged my services. Perhaps you would care to read the papers ? "

" Could you not give me the points ? "

" That is very easily done. It will probably come back to your memory as I talk. Ronder, of course, was a household word. He was the rival of Wombwell, and of Sanger, one of the greatest showmen of his day. There is evidence, however, that he took to drink, and that both he and his show were on the down grade at the time of the great tragedy. The caravan had halted for the night at Abbas Parva, which is a small village in Berkshire, when this horror occurred. They were on their way to Wimbledon, travelling by road, and they were simply camping, and not exhibiting, as the place is so small a one that it would not have paid them to open.

" They had among their exhibits a very fine North African lion. Sahara King was its name, and it was the habit, both of Ronder and his wife, to give exhibitions inside its cage. Here, you see, is a photograph of the performance, by which you will perceive that Ronder was a huge porcine person and that his wife was a very magnificent woman. It was deposed at the inquest

that there had been some signs that the lion was dangerous, but, as usual, familiarity begat contempt, and no
notice was taken of the fact.

" It was usual for either Ronder or his wife to feed the
lion at night. Sometimes one went, sometimes both, but
they never allowed anyone else to do it, for they believed
that so long as they were the food-carriers he would
regard them as benefactors, and would never molest
them. On this particular night, seven years ago, they
both went, and a very terrible happening followed, the
details of which have never been made clear.

" It seems that the whole camp was roused near midnight by the roars of the animal and the screams of the
woman. The different grooms and *employés* rushed from
their tents, carrying lanterns, and by their light an awful
sight was revealed. Ronder lay, with the back of his
head crushed in and deep claw-marks across his scalp,
some ten yards from the cage, which was open. Close
to the door of the cage lay Mrs. Ronder, upon her back,
with the creature squatting and snarling above her. It
had torn her face in such a fashion that it was never
thought that she could live. Several of the circus men,
headed by Leonardo, the strong man, and Griggs, the
clown, drove the creature off with poles, upon which it
sprang back into the cage, and was at once locked in.
How it had got loose was a mystery. It was conjectured
that the pair intended to enter the cage, but that when
the door was loosed the creature bounded out upon them.
There was no other point of interest in the evidence,
save that the woman in a delirium of agony kept screaming, ' Coward ! Coward ! ' as she was carried back to
the van in which they lived. It was six months before
she was fit to give evidence, but the inquest was duly
held, with the obvious verdict of death from misadven-
ture."

" What alternative could be conceived ? " said I.

" You may well say so. And yet there were one or
two points which worried young Edmunds, of the Berk-

shire Constabulary. A smart lad that ! He was sent later to Allahabad. That was how I came into the matter, for he dropped in and smoked a pipe or two over it."

"A thin, yellow-haired man ? "

"Exactly. I was sure you would pick up the trail presently."

"But what worried him ? "

"Well, we were both worried. It was so deucedly difficult to reconstruct the affair. Look at it from the lion's point of view. He is liberated. What does he do ? He takes half a dozen bounds forward, which brings him to Ronder. Ronder turns to fly—the claw-marks were on the back of his head—but the lion strikes him down. Then, instead of bounding on and escaping, he returns to the woman, who was close to the cage, and he knocks her over and chews her face up. Then, again, those cries of hers would seem to imply that her husband had in some way failed her. What could the poor devil have done to help her ? You see the difficulty ? "

"Quite."

"And then there was another thing. It comes back to me now as I think it over. There was some evidence that, just at the time the lion roared and the woman screamed, a man began shouting in terror."

"This man Ronder, no doubt."

"Well, if his skull was smashed in you would hardly expect to hear from him again. There were at least two witnesses who spoke of the cries of a man being mingled with those of a woman."

"I should think the whole camp was crying out by then. As to the other points, I think I could suggest a solution."

"I should be glad to consider it."

"The two were together, ten yards from the cage, when the lion got loose. The man turned and was struck down. The woman conceived the idea of get-

ting into the cage and shutting the door. It was her
only refuge. She made for it, and just as she reached
it the beast bounded after her and knocked her over.
She was angry with her husband for having encouraged
the beast's rage by turning. If they had faced it, they
might have cowed it. Hence her cries of ' Coward ! ' "

" Brilliant, Watson ! Only one flaw in your diamond."

" What is the flaw, Holmes ? "

" If they were both ten paces from the cage, how came
the beast to get loose ? "

" Is it possible that they had some enemy who loosed
it ? "

" And why should it attack them savagely when it was
in the habit of playing with them, and doing tricks with
them inside the cage ? "

" Possibly the same enemy had done something to
enrage it."

Holmes looked thoughtful and remained in silence for
some moments.

" Well, Watson, there is this to be said for your theory.
Ronder was a man of many enemies. Edmunds told
me that in his cups he was horrible. A huge bully of a
man, he cursed and slashed at everyone who came in his
way. I expect those cries about a monster, of which our
visitor has spoken, were nocturnal reminiscences of the
dear departed. However, our speculations are futile
until we have all the facts. There is a cold partridge on
the sideboard, Watson, and a bottle of Montrachet.
Let us renew our energies before we make a fresh call
upon them."

When our hansom deposited us at the house of Mrs.
Merrilow, we found that plump lady blocking up the
open door of her humble but retired abode. It was
very clear that her chief preoccupation was lest she should
lose a valuable lodger, and she implored us, before showing us up, to say and do nothing which could lead to so
undesirable an end. Then, having reassured her, we

followed her up the straight, badly-carpeted staircase
and were shown into the room of the mysterious lodger.

It was a close, musty, ill-ventilated place, as might
be expected, since its inmate seldom left it. From
keeping beasts in a cage, the woman seemed, by some
retribution of Fate, to have become herself a beast in a
cage. She sat now in a broken arm-chair in the shadowy
corner of the room. Long years of inaction had coarsened
the lines of her figure, but at some period it must have
been beautiful, and was still full and voluptuous. A
thick dark veil covered her face, but it was cut off close
at her upper lip, and disclosed a perfectly-shaped mouth
and a delicately-rounded chin. I could well conceive
that she had indeed been a very remarkable woman.
Her voice, too, was well-modulated and pleasing.

"My name is not unfamiliar to you, Mr. Holmes,"
said she. "I thought that it would bring you."

"That is so, madam, though I do not know how you
are aware that I was interested in your case."

"I learned it when I had recovered my health and was
examined by Mr. Edmunds, the County detective. I
fear I lied to him. Perhaps it would have been wiser
had I told the truth."

"It is usually wiser to tell the truth. But why did
you lie to him?"

"Because the fate of someone else depended upon it.
I know that he was a very worthless being, and yet I
would not have his destruction upon my conscience.
We had been so close—so close!"

"But has this impediment been removed?"

"Yes, sir. The person that I allude to is dead."

"Then why should you not now tell the police anything you know?"

"Because there is another person to be considered.
That other person is myself. I could not stand the
scandal and publicity which would come from a police
examination. I have not long to live, but I wish to die
undisturbed. And yet I wanted to find one man of

judgment to whom I could tell my terrible story, so that when I am gone all might be understood."

"You compliment me, madam. At the same time, I am a responsible person. I do not promise you that when you have spoken I may not myself think it my duty to refer the case to the police."

"I think not, Mr. Holmes. I know your character and methods too well, for I have followed your work for some years. Reading is the only pleasure which Fate has left me, and I miss little which passes in the world. But in any case, I will take my chance of the use which you may make of my tragedy. It will ease my mind to tell it."

"My friend and I would be glad to hear it."

The woman rose and took from a drawer the photograph of a man. He was clearly a professional acrobat, a man of magnificent physique, taken with his huge arms folded across his swollen chest and a smile breaking from under his heavy moustache—the self-satisfied smile of the man of many conquests.

"That is Leonardo," she said.

"Leonardo, the strong man, who gave evidence?"

"The same. And this—this is my husband."

It was a dreadful face—a human pig, or rather a human wild boar, for it was formidable in its bestiality. One could imagine that vile mouth champing and foaming in its rage, and one could conceive those small, vicious eyes darting pure malignancy as they looked forth upon the world. Ruffian, bully, beast—it was all written on that heavy-jowled face.

"Those two pictures will help you, gentlemen, to understand the story. I was a poor circus girl brought up on the sawdust, and doing springs through the hoop before I was ten. When I became a woman this man loved me, if such lust as his can be called love, and in an evil moment I became his wife. From that day I was in hell, and he the devil who tormented me. There was no one in the show who did not know of his treatment.

He deserted me for others. He tied me down and lashed me with his riding-whip when I complained. They all pitied me and they all loathed him, but what could they do? They feared him, one and all. For he was terrible at all times, and murderous when he was drunk. Again and again he was had for assault, and for cruelty to the beasts, but he had plenty of money and the fines were nothing to him. The best men all left us and the show began to go downhill. It was only Leonardo and I who kept it up—with little Jimmy Griggs, the clown. Poor devil, he had not much to be funny about, but he did what he could to hold things together.

"Then Leonardo came more and more into my life. You see what he was like. I know now the poor spirit that was hidden in that splendid body, but compared to my husband he seemed like the Angel Gabriel. He pitied me and helped me, till at last our intimacy turned to love—deep, deep, passionate love, such love as I had dreamed of but never hoped to feel. My husband suspected it, but I think that he was a coward as well as a bully, and that Leonardo was the one man that he was afraid of. He took revenge in his own way by torturing me more than ever. One night my cries brought Leonardo to the door of our van. We were near tragedy that night, and soon my lover and I understood that it could not be avoided. My husband was not fit to live. We planned that he should die.

"Leonardo had a clever, scheming brain. It was he who planned it. I do not say that to blame him, for I was ready to go with him every inch of the way. But I should never have had the wit to think of such a plan. We made a club—Leonardo made it—and in the leaden head he fastened five long steel nails, the points outwards, with just such a spread as the lion's paw. This was to give my husband his death-blow, and yet to leave the evidence that it was the lion which we would loose who had done the deed.

"It was a pitch-dark night when my husband and

I went down, as was our custom, to feed the beast. We carried with us the raw meat in a zinc pail. Leonardo was waiting at the corner of the big van which we should have to pass before we reached the cage. He was too slow, and we walked past him before he could strike, but he followed us on tiptoe and I heard the crash as the club smashed my husband's skull. My heart leaped with joy at the sound. I sprang forward, and I undid the catch which held the door of the great lion's cage.

" And then the terrible thing happened. You may have heard how quick these creatures are to scent human blood, and how it excites them. Some strange instinct had told the creature in one instant that a human being had been slain. As I slipped the bars it bounded out, and was on me in an instant. Leonardo could have saved me. If he had rushed forward and struck the beast with his club he might have cowed it. But the man lost his nerve. I heard him shout in his terror, and then I saw him turn and fly. At the same instant the teeth of the lion met in my face. Its hot, filthy breath had already poisoned me and I was hardly conscious of pain. With the palms of my hands I tried to push the great steaming, blood-stained jaws away from me, and I screamed for help. I was conscious that the camp was stirring, and then dimly I remember a group of men, Leonardo, Griggs and others, dragging me from under the creature's paws. That was my last memory, Mr. Holmes, for many a weary month. When I came to myself, and saw myself in the mirror, I cursed that lion—oh, how I cursed him !—not because he had torn away my beauty, but because he had not torn away my life. I had but one desire, Mr. Holmes, and I had enough money to gratify it. It was that I should cover myself so that my poor face should be seen by none, and that I should dwell where none whom I had ever known should find me. That was all that was left to me to do—and that is what I have done. A poor wounded beast that has crawled into its hole to die—that is the end of Eugenia Ronder."

We sat in silence for some time after the unhappy woman had told her story. Then Holmes stretched out his long arm and patted her hand with such a show of sympathy as I had seldom known him to exhibit.

"Poor girl!" he said. "Poor girl! The ways of Fate are indeed hard to understand. If there is not some compensation hereafter, then the world is a cruel jest. But what of this man Leonardo?"

"I never saw him or heard from him again. Perhaps I have been wrong to feel so bitterly against him. He might as soon have loved one of the freaks whom we carried round the country as the thing which the lion had left. But a woman's love is not so easily set aside. He had left me under the beast's claws, he had deserted me in my need, and yet I could not bring myself to give him to the gallows. For myself, I cared nothing what became of me. What could be more dreadful than my actual life? But I stood between Leonardo and his fate."

"And he is dead?"

"He was drowned last month when bathing near Margate. I saw his death in the paper."

"And what did he do with this five-clawed club, which is the most singular and ingenious part of all your story?"

"I cannot tell, Mr. Holmes. There is a chalk-pit by the camp, with a deep green pool at the base of it. Perhaps in the depths of that pool——"

"Well, well, it is of little consequence now. The case is closed."

"Yes," said the woman, "the case is closed."

We had risen to go, but there was something in the woman's voice which arrested Holmes' attention. He turned swiftly upon her.

"Your life is not your own," he said. "Keep your hands off it."

"What use is it to anyone?"

" How can you tell ? The example of patient suffering is in itself the most precious of all lessons to an impatient world."

The woman's answer was a terrible one. She raised her veil and stepped forward into the light.

" I wonder if you would bear it," she said.

It was horrible. No words can describe the framework of a face when the face itself is gone. Two living and beautiful brown eyes looking sadly out from that grisly ruin did but make the view more awful. Holmes held up his hand in a gesture of pity and protest, and together we left the room.

Two days later, when I called upon my friend, he pointed with some pride to a small blue bottle upon his mantelpiece. I picked it up. There was on it a red poison label. A pleasant almondy odour rose when I opened it.

" Prussic acid ? " said I.

" Exactly. It came by post. ' I send you my temptation. I will follow your advice.' That was the message. I think, Watson, we can guess the name of the brave woman who sent it."

55. *Shoscombe Old Place*

SHERLOCK HOLMES had been bending for a long time over a low-power microscope. Now he straightened himself up and looked round at me in triumph.

" It is glue, Watson," said he. " Unquestionably it is glue. Have a look at these scattered objects in the field ! "

I stooped to the eyepiece and focused for my vision.

" Those hairs are threads from a tweed coat. The irregular grey masses are dust. There are epithelial scales on the left. Those brown blobs in the centre are undoubtedly glue."

"Well," I said, laughing, "I am prepared to take your word for it. Does anything depend upon it ? "

"It is a very fine demonstration," he answered. "In the St. Pancras case you may remember that a cap was found beside the dead policeman. The accused man denies that it is his. But he is a picture-frame maker who habitually handles glue."

"Is it one of your cases ? "

"No ; my friend, Merivale of the Yard, asked me to look into the case. Since I ran down that coiner by the zinc and copper filings in the seam of his cuff they have begun to realize the importance of the microscope." He looked impatiently at his watch. "I had a new client calling, but he is overdue. By the way, Watson, you know something of racing ? "

"I ought to. I pay for it with about half my wound pension."

"Then I'll make you my ' Handy Guide to the Turf.' What about Sir Robert Norberton ? Does the name recall anything ? "

"Well, I should say so. He lives at Shoscombe Old Place, and I know it well, for my summer quarters were down there once. Norberton nearly came within your province once."

"How was that ? "

"It was when he horsewhipped Sam Brewer, the well-known Curzon Street moneylender, on Newmarket Heath. He nearly killed the man."

"Ah, he sounds interesting ! Does he often indulge in that way ? "

"Well, he has the name of being a dangerous man. He is about the most daredevil rider in England—second in the Grand National a few years back. He is one of those men who have overshot their true generation. He should have been a buck in the days of the Regency —a boxer, an athlete, a plunger on the Turf, a lover of fair ladies, and, by all account, so far down Queer Street that he may never find his way back again."

" Capital, Watson ! A thumb-nail sketch. I seem to know the man. Now, can you give me some idea of Shoscombe Old Place ? "

" Only that it is in the centre of Shoscombe Park, and that the famous Shoscombe stud and training quarters are to be found there."

" And the head trainer," said Holmes, " is John Mason. You need not look surprised at my knowledge, Watson, for this is a letter from him which I am unfolding. But let us have some more about Shoscombe. I seem to have struck a rich vein."

" There are the Shoscombe spaniels," said I. " You hear of them at every dog show. The most exclusive breed in England. They are the special pride of the lady of Shoscombe Old Place."

" Sir Robert Norberton's wife, I presume ! "

" Sir Robert has never married. Just as well, I think, considering his prospects. He lives with his widowed sister, Lady Beatrice Falder."

" You mean that she lives with him ? "

" No, no. The place belonged to her late husband, Sir James. Norberton has no claim on it at all. It is only a life interest and reverts to her husband's brother. Meantime, she draws the rents every year."

" And brother Robert, I suppose, spends the said rents ? "

" That is about the size of it. He is a devil of a fellow and must lead her a most uneasy life. Yet I have heard that she is devoted to him. But what is amiss at Shoscombe ? "

" Ah, that is just what I want to know. And here, I expect, is the man who can tell us."

The door had opened and the page had shown in a tall, clean-shaven man with the firm, austere expression which is only seen upon those who have to control horses or boys. Mr. John Mason had many of both under his sway, and he looked equal to the task. He bowed with cold self-possession and seated himself upon the chair to which Holmes had waved him.

" You had my note, Mr. Holmes ? "

" Yes, but it explained nothing."

" It was too delicate a thing for me to put the details on paper. And too complicated. It was only face to face I could do it."

" Well, we are at your disposal."

" First of all, Mr. Holmes, I think that my employer, Sir Robert, has gone mad."

Holmes raised his eyebrows. " This is Baker Street, not Harley Street," said he. " But why do you say so ? "

" Well, sir, when a man does one queer thing, or two queer things, there may be a meaning to it, but when everything he does is queer, then you begin to wonder. I believe Shoscombe Prince and the Derby have turned his brain."

" That is a colt you are running ? "

" The best in England, Mr. Holmes. I should know, if anyone does. Now, I'll be plain with you, for I know you are gentlemen of honour and that it won't go beyond the room. Sir Robert has got to win this Derby. He's up to the neck, and it's his last chance. Everything he could raise or borrow is on the horse—and at fine odds, too ! You can get forties now, but it was nearer the hundred when he began to back him."

" But how is that, if the horse is so good ? "

" The public don't know how good he is. Sir Robert has been too clever for the touts. He has the Prince's half-brother out for spins. You can't tell 'em apart. But there are two lengths in a furlong between them when it comes to a gallop. He thinks of nothing but the horse and the race. His whole life is on it. He's hold-ing off the Jews till then. If the Prince fails him, he is done."

" It seems a rather desperate gamble, but where does the madness come in ? "

" Well, first of all, you have only to look at him. I don't believe he sleeps at night. He is down at the

1303

stables at all hours. His eyes are wild. It has all been too much for his nerves. Then there is his conduct to Lady Beatrice ! "

" Ah ! what is that ? "

" They have always been the best of friends. They had the same tastes, the two of them, and she loved the horses as much as he did. Every day at the same hour she would drive down to see them—and, above all, she loved the Prince. He would prick up his ears when he heard the wheels on the gravel, and he would trot out each morning to the carriage to get his lump of sugar. But that's all over now."

" Why ? "

" Well, she seems to have lost all interest in the horses. For a week now she has driven past the stables with never so much as ' good morning ' ! "

" You think there has been a quarrel ? "

" And a bitter, savage, spiteful quarrel at that. Why else would he give away her pet spaniel that she loved as if he were her child ? He gave it a few days ago to old Barnes, what keeps the ' Green Dragon,' three miles off, at Crendall."

" That certainly did seem strange."

" Of course, with her weak heart and dropsy one couldn't expect that she could get about with him, but he spent two hours every evening in her room. He might well do what he could, for she has been a rare good friend to him. But that's all over, too. He never goes near her. And she takes it to heart. She is brooding and sulky and drinking, Mr. Holmes—drinking like a fish."

" Did she drink before this estrangement ? "

" Well, she took her glass, but now it is often a whole bottle of an evening. So Stephens, the butler, told me. It's all changed, Mr. Holmes, and there is something damned rotten about it. But then, again, what is master doing down at the old church crypt at night ? And who is the man that meets him there ? "

Holmes rubbed his hands.

" Go on, Mr. Mason. You get more and more interesting."

" It was the butler who saw him go. Twelve o'clock
at night and raining hard. So next night I was up at the
house and, sure enough, master was off again. Stephens
and I went after him, but it was jumpy work, for it would
have been a bad job if he had seen us. He's a terrible
man with his fists if he gets started, and no respecter of
persons. So we were shy of getting too near, but we
marked him down all right. It was the haunted crypt
that he was making for, and there was a man waiting for
him there."

" What is this haunted crypt ? "

" Well, sir, there is an old ruined chapel in the park.
It is so old that nobody could fix its date. And under it
there's a crypt which has a bad name among us. It's a
dark, damp, lonely place by day, but there are few in that
county that would have the nerve to go near it at night.
But master's not afraid. He never feared anything in
his life. But what is he doing there in the night-time ? "

" Wait a bit ! " said Holmes. " You say there is
another man there. It must be one of your own stable-
men, or someone from the house ! Surely you have
only to spot who it is and question him ? "

" It's no one I know."

" How can you say that ? "

" Because I have seen him, Mr. Holmes. It was on
that second night. Sir Robert turned and passed us—
me and Stephens, quaking in the bushes like two bunny-
rabbits, for there was a bit of moon that night. But
we could hear the other moving about behind. We were
not afraid of him. So we up when Sir Robert was gone
and pretended we were just having a walk like in the moonlight, and so we came right on him as casual and innocent
as you please. ' Hullo, mate ! who may you be ? ' says I.
I guess he had not heard us coming, so he looked over
his shoulder with a face as if he had seen the Devil
coming out of Hell. He let out a yell, and away he went

as hard as he could lick it in the darkness. He could run !—I'll give him that. In a minute he was out of sight and hearing, and who he was, or what he was, we never found."

" But you saw him clearly in the moonlight ? "

" Yes, I would swear to his yellow face—a mean dog, I should say. What could he have in common with Sir Robert ? "

Holmes sat for some time lost in thought.

" Who keeps Lady Beatrice Falder company ? " he asked at last.

" There is her maid, Carrie Evans. She has been with her this five years."

" And is, no doubt, devoted ? "

Mr. Mason shuffled uncomfortably.

" She's devoted enough," he answered at last. " But I won't say to whom."

" Ah ! " said Holmes.

" I can't tell tales out of school."

" I quite understand, Mr. Mason. Of course, the situation is clear enough. From Dr. Watson's description of Sir Robert I can realize that no woman is safe from him. Don't you think the quarrel between brother and sister may lie there ? "

" Well, the scandal has been pretty clear for a long time."

" But she may not have seen it before. Let us suppose that she has suddenly found it out. She wants to get rid of the woman. Her brother will not permit it. The invalid, with her weak heart and inability to get about, has no means of enforcing her will. The hated maid is still tied to her. The lady refuses to speak, sulks, takes to drink. Sir Robert in his anger takes her pet spaniel away from her. Does not all this hang together ? "

" Well, it might do—so far as it goes."

" Exactly ! As far as it goes. How would all that bear upon the visits by night to the old crypt ? We can't fit that into our plot."

" No, sir, and there is something more that I can't fit in. Why should Sir Robert want to dig up a dead body ? "

Holmes sat up abruptly.

" We only found it out yesterday—after I had written to you. Yesterday Sir Robert had gone to London, so Stephens and I went down to the crypt. It was all in order, sir, except that in one corner was a bit of a human body."

" You informed the police, I suppose ? "

Our visitor smiled grimly.

" Well, sir, I think it would hardly interest them. It was just the head and a few bones of a mummy. It may have been a thousand years old. But it wasn't there before. That I'll swear, and so will Stephens. It had been stowed away in a corner and covered over with a board, but that corner had always been empty before."

" What did you do with it ? "

" Well, we just left it there."

" That was wise. You say Sir Robert was away yesterday. Has he returned ? "

" We expect him back to-day."

" When did Sir Robert give away his sister's dog ? "

" It was just a week ago to-day. The creature was howling outside the old well-house, and Sir Robert was in one of his tantrums that morning. He caught it up and I thought he would have killed it. Then he gave it to Sandy Bain, the jockey, and told him to take the dog to old Barnes at the ' Green Dragon,' for he never wished to see it again."

Holmes sat for some time in silent thought. He had lit the oldest and foulest of his pipes.

" I am not clear yet what you want me to do in this matter, Mr. Mason," he said at last. " Can't you make it more definite ? "

" Perhaps this will make it more definite, Mr. Holmes," said our visitor.

He took a paper from his pocket and, unwrapping it carefully, he exposed a charred fragment of bone.

Holmes examined it with interest.

" Where did you get it ? "

" There is a central heating furnace in the cellar under Lady Beatrice's room. It's been off for some time, but Sir Robert complained of cold and had it on again. Harvey runs it—he's one of my lads. This very morning he came to me with this which he found raking out the cinders. He didn't like the look of it."

" Nor do I," said Holmes. " What do you make of it, Watson ? "

It was burned to a black cinder, but there could be no question as to its anatomical significance.

" It's the upper condyle of a human femur," said I.

" Exactly ! " Holmes had become very serious. " When does this lad attend to the furnace ? "

" He makes it up every evening and then leaves it."

" Then anyone could visit it during the night ? "

" Yes, sir."

" Can you enter it from outside ? "

" There is one door from outside. There is another which leads up by a stair to the passage in which Lady Beatrice's room is situated."

" These are deep waters, Mr. Mason ; deep and rather dirty. You say that Sir Robert was not at home last night ?"

" No, sir."

" Then, whoever was burning bones, it was not he."

" That's true, sir."

" What is the name of that inn you spoke of ? "

" The ' Green Dragon.' "

" Is there good fishing in that part of Berkshire ? "

The honest trainer showed very clearly upon his face that he was convinced that yet another lunatic had come into his harassed life.

" Well, sir, I've heard there are trout in the mill-stream and pike in the Hall lake."

" That's good enough. Watson and I are famous

fishermen—are we not, Watson? You may address us in future at the ' Green Dragon.' We should reach it to-night. I need not say that we don't want to see you, Mr. Mason, but a note will reach us, and no doubt I could find you if I want you. When we have gone a little further into the matter I will let you have a considered opinion."

Thus it was that on a bright May evening Holmes and I found ourselves alone in a first-class carriage and bound for the little " halt-on-demand " station of Shoscombe. The rack above us was covered with a formidable litter of rods, reels and baskets. On reaching our destination a short drive took us to an old-fashioned tavern, where a sporting host, Josiah Barnes, entered eagerly into our plans for the extirpation of the fish of the neighbourhood.

" What about the Hall lake and the chance of a pike ? " said Holmes.

The face of the innkeeper clouded.

" That wouldn't do, sir. You might chance to find yourself in the lake before you were through."

" How's that, then ? "

" It's Sir Robert, sir. He's terrible jealous of touts. If you two strangers were as near his training quarters as that he'd be after you as sure as fate. He ain't taking no chances, Sir Robert ain't."

" I've heard he has a horse entered for the Derby."

" Yes, and a good colt, too. He carries all our money for the race, and all Sir Robert's into the bargain. By the way "—he looked at us with thoughtful eyes—" I suppose you ain't on the Turf yourselves ? "

" No, indeed. Just two weary Londoners who badly need some good Berkshire air."

" Well, you are in the right place for that. There is a deal of it lying about. But mind what I have told you about Sir Robert. He's the sort that strikes first and speaks afterwards. Keep clear of the park."

" Surely, Mr. Barnes ! We certainly shall. By the way, that was a most beautiful spaniel that was whining in the hall."

" I should say it was. That was the real Shoscombe breed. There ain't a better in England."

" I am a dog-fancier myself," said Holmes. " Now, if it is a fair question, what would a prize dog like that cost ? "

" More than I could pay, sir. It was Sir Robert himself who gave me this one. That's why I have to keep it on a lead. It would be off to the Hall in a jiffy if I gave it its head."

" We are getting some cards in our hand, Watson," said Holmes, when the landlord had left us. " It's not an easy one to play, but we may see our way in a day or two. By the way, Sir Robert is still in London, I hear. We might, perhaps, enter the sacred domain to-night without fear of bodily assault. There are one or two points on which I should like reassurance."

" Have you any theory, Holmes ? "

" Only this, Watson, that something happened a week or so ago which has cut deep into the life of the Shoscombe household. What is that something ? We can only guess at it from its effects. They seem to be of a curiously mixed character. But that should surely help us. It is only the colourless, uneventful case which is hopeless."

" Let us consider our data. The brother no longer visits the beloved invalid sister. He gives away her favourite dog. Her dog, Watson ! Does that suggest nothing to you ? "

" Nothing but the brother's spite."

" Well, it might be so. Or—well, there is an alternative. Now to continue our review of the situation from the time that the quarrel, if there is a quarrel, began. The lady keeps her room, alters her habits, is not seen save when she drives out with her maid, refuses to stop at the stables to greet her favourite horse, and apparently takes to drink. That covers the case, does it not ? "

" Save for the business in the crypt."

" That is another line of thought. There are two, and I beg you will not tangle them. Line A, which concerns Lady Beatrice, has a vaguely sinister flavour, has it not ? "

" I can make nothing of it."

" Well, now, let us take up line B, which concerns Sir Robert. He is mad keen upon winning the Derby. He is in the hands of the Jews, and may at any moment be sold up and his racing stables seized by his creditors. He is a daring and desperate man. He derives his income from his sister. His sister's maid is his willing tool. So far we seem to be on fairly safe ground, do we not ? "

" But the crypt ? "

" Ah, yes, the crypt ! Let us suppose, Watson—it is merely a scandalous supposition, a hypothesis put forward for argument's sake—that Sir Robert has done away with his sister."

" My dear Holmes, it is out of the question."

" Very possibly, Watson. Sir Robert is a man of an honourable stock. But you do occasionally find a carrion crow among the eagles. Let us for a moment argue upon this supposition. He could not fly the country until he had realized his fortune, and that fortune could only be realized by bringing off this coup with Shoscombe Prince. Therefore, he has still to stand his ground. To do this he would have to dispose of the body of his victim, and he would also have to find a substitute who would impersonate her. With the maid as his confidante that would not be impossible. The woman's body might be conveyed to the crypt, which is a place so seldom visited, and it might be secretly destroyed at night in the furnace, leaving behind it such evidence as we have already seen. What say you to that, Watson ? "

" Well, it is all possible if you grant the original monstrous supposition."

" I think that there is a small experiment which we may

try to-morrow, Watson, in order to throw some light on the matter. Meanwhile, if we mean to keep up our characters, I suggest that we have our host in for a glass of his own wine and hold some high converse upon eels and dace, which seems to be the straight road to his affections. We may chance to come upon some useful local gossip in the process."

In the morning Holmes discovered that we had come without our spoon-bait for jack, which absolved us from fishing for the day. About eleven o'clock we started for a walk, and he obtained leave to take the black spaniel with us.

" This is the place," said he, as we came to two high park gates with heraldic griffins towering above them. " About midday, Mr. Barnes informs me, the old lady takes a drive, and the carriage must slow down while the gates are opened. When it comes through, and before it gathers speed, I want you, Watson, to stop the coachman with some question. Never mind me. I shall stand behind this holly-bush and see what I can see."

It was not a long vigil. Within a quarter of an hour we saw the big open yellow barouche coming down the long avenue, with two splendid, high-stepping grey carriage horses in the shafts. Holmes crouched behind his bush with the dog. I stood unconcernedly swinging a cane in the roadway. A keeper ran out and the gates swung open.

The carriage had slowed to a walk and I was able to get a good look at the occupants. A highly-coloured young woman with flaxen hair and impudent eyes sat on the left. At her right was an elderly person with rounded back and a huddle of shawls about her face and shoulders which proclaimed the invalid. When the horses reached the high road I held up my hand with an authoritative gesture, and as the coachman pulled up I inquired if Sir Robert was at Shoscombe Old Place.

At the same moment Holmes stepped out and released the spaniel. With a joyous cry it dashed forward to the carriage and sprang upon the step. Then in a moment its eager greeting changed to furious rage, and it snapped at the black skirt above it.

" Drive on ! Drive on ! " shrieked a harsh voice. The coachman lashed the horses, and we were left standing in the roadway.

" Well, Watson, that's done it," said Holmes, as he fastened the lead to the neck of the excited spaniel. " He thought it was his mistress and he found it was a stranger. Dogs don't make mistakes."

" But it was the voice of a man ! " I cried.

" Exactly ! We have added one card to our hand, Watson, but it needs careful playing, all the same."

My companion seemed to have no further plans for the day, and we did actually use our fishing tackle in the mill-stream, with the result that we had a dish of trout for our supper. It was only after that meal that Holmes showed signs of renewed activity. Once more we found ourselves upon the same road as in the morning, which led us to the park gates. A tall, dark figure was awaiting us there, who proved to be our London acquaintance, Mr. John Mason, the trainer.

" Good evening, gentlemen," said he. " I got your note, Mr. Holmes. Sir Robert has not returned yet, but I hear that he is expected to-night."

" How far is this crypt from the house ? " asked Holmes.

" A good quarter of a mile."

" Then I think we can disregard him altogether."

" I can't afford to do that, Mr. Holmes. The moment he arrives he will want to see me to get the last news of Shoscombe Prince."

" I see ! In that case we must work without you, Mr. Mason. You can show us the crypt and then leave us."

It was pitch-dark and without a moon, but Mason led us over the grass-lands until a dark mass loomed up in front of us which proved to be the ancient chapel.

We entered the broken gap which was once the porch, and our guide, stumbling among heaps of loose masonry, picked his way to the corner of the building, where a steep stair led down into the crypt. Striking a match, he illuminated the melancholy place—dismal and evil-smelling, with ancient crumbling walls of rough-hewn stone, and piles of coffins, some of lead and some of stone, extending upon one side right up to the arched and groined roof which lost itself in the shadows above our heads. Holmes had lit his lantern, which shot a tiny tunnel of vivid yellow light upon the mournful scene. Its rays were reflected back from the coffin-plates, many of them adorned with the griffin and coronet of this old family which carried its honours even to the gate of Death.

" You spoke of some bones, Mr. Mason. Could you show them before you go ? "

" They are here in this corner." The trainer strode across and then stood in silent surprise as our light was turned upon the place. " They are gone," said he.

" So I expected," said Holmes, chuckling. " I fancy the ashes of them might even now be found in that oven which had already consumed a part."

" But why in the world would anyone want to burn the bones of a man who has been dead a thousand years ? " asked John Mason.

" That is what we are here to find out," said Holmes. " It may mean a long search, and we need not detain you. I fancy that we shall get our solution before morning."

When John Mason had left us, Holmes set to work making a very careful examination of the graves, ranging from a very ancient one, which appeared to be Saxon, in the centre, through a long line of Norman Hugos and Odos, until we reached the Sir William and Sir Denis Falder of the eighteenth century. It was an hour or more before Holmes came to a leaden coffin standing on end before the entrance to the vault. I heard his little cry of satisfaction, and was aware from his hurried but purposeful movements that he had reached a goal. With his lens he was eagerly examining the edges of the heavy lid. Then he drew from his pocket a short jemmy, a box-opener, which he thrust into a chink, levering back the whole front, which seemed to be secured by only a couple of clamps. There was a rending, tearing sound as it gave way, but it had hardly hinged back and partly revealed the contents before we had an unforeseen interruption.

Someone was walking in the chapel above. It was the firm, rapid step of one who came with a definite purpose and knew well the ground upon which he walked. A light streamed down the stairs, and an instant later the man who bore it was framed in the Gothic archway. He was a terrible figure, huge in stature and fierce in manner. A large stable-lantern which he held in front of him shone upwards upon a strong, heavily-moustached face and angry eyes, which glared round him into every recess of the vault, finally fixing themselves with a deadly stare upon my companion and myself.

"Who the devil are you?" he thundered. "And what are you doing upon my property?" Then, as Holmes returned no answer, he took a couple of steps forward and raised a heavy stick which he carried. "Do you hear me?" he cried. "Who are you? What are you doing here?" His cudgel quivered in the air.

But instead of shrinking, Holmes advanced to meet him.

"I also have a question to ask you, Sir Robert," he said in his sternest tone. "Who is this? And what is it doing here?"

He turned and tore open the coffin-lid behind him. In the glare of the lantern I saw a body swathed in a sheet from head to foot, with dreadful, witch-like features, all nose and chin, projecting at one end, the dim, glazed eyes staring from a discoloured and crumbling face.

The Baronet had staggered back with a cry and supported himself against a stone sarcophagus.

" How came you to know of this ? " he cried. And then, with some return of his truculent manner : " What business is it of yours ? "

" My name is Sherlock Holmes," said my companion. " Possibly it is familiar to you. In any case, my business is that of every other good citizen—to uphold the law. It seems to me that you have much to answer for."

Sir Robert glared for a moment, but Holmes' quiet voice and cool, assured manner had their effect.

" 'Fore God, Mr. Holmes, it's all right," said he. " Appearances are against me, I'll admit, but I could act no otherwise."

" I should be happy to think so, but I fear your explanations must be for the police."

Sir Robert shrugged his broad shoulders.

" Well, if it must be, it must. Come up to the house and you can judge for yourself how the matter stands."

Quarter of an hour later we found ourselves in what I judge, from the lines of polished barrels behind glass covers, to be the gun-room of the old house. It was comfortably furnished, and here Sir Robert left us for a few moments. When he returned he had two companions with him ; the one, the florid young woman whom we had seen in the carriage ; the other, a small rat-faced man with a disagreeably furtive manner. These two wore an appearance of utter bewilderment, which showed that the Baronet had not yet had time to explain to them the turn events had taken.

" There," said Sir Robert, with a wave of his hand, " are Mr. and Mrs. Norlett. Mrs. Norlett, under her maiden name of Evans, has for some years been my sister's confidential maid. I have brought them here because I feel that my best course is to explain the true position to you, and they are the two people upon earth who can substantiate what I say."

" Is this necessary, Sir Robert ? Have you thought what you are doing ? " cried the woman.

" As to me, I entirely disclaim all responsibility," said her husband.

Sir Robert gave him a glance of contempt. " I will take all responsibility," said he. " Now, Mr. Holmes, listen to a plain statement of the facts.

" You have clearly gone pretty deeply into my affairs or I should not have found you where I did. There-fore, you know already, in all probability, that I am running a dark horse for the Derby and that everything depends upon my success. If I win, all is easy. If I lose—well, I dare not think of that ! "

" I understand the position," said Holmes.

" I am dependent upon my sister, Lady Beatrice, for everything. But it is well known that her interest in the estate is for her own life only. For myself, I am deeply in the hands of the Jews. I have always known that if my sister were to die my creditors would be on to my estate like a flock of vultures. Everything would be seized ; my stables, my horses—everything. Well, Mr. Holmes, my sister *did* die just a week ago."

" And you told no one ! "

" What could I do ? Absolute ruin faced me. If I could stave things off for three weeks all would be well. Her maid's husband—this man here—is an actor. It came into our heads—it came into my head—that he could for that short period personate my sister. It was but a case of appearing daily in the carriage, for no one need enter her room save the maid. It was not difficult to arrange. My sister died of the dropsy which had long afflicted her."

" That will be for a coroner to decide."

" Her doctor would certify that for months her symp-toms have threatened such an end."

" Well, what did you do ? "

" The body could not remain there. On the first night Norlett and I carried it out to the old well-house, which is now never used. We were followed, however, by her pet spaniel, which yapped continually at the door, so I felt some safer place was needed. I got rid of the spaniel and we carried the body to the crypt of the church. There was no indignity or irreverence, Mr. Holmes. I do not feel that I have wronged the dead."

" Your conduct seems to me inexcusable, Sir Robert."

The Baronet shook his head impatiently. " It is easy to preach," said he. " Perhaps you would have felt differently if you had been in my position. One cannot see all one's hopes and all one's plans shattered at the last moment and make no effort to save them. It seemed to me that it would be no unworthy resting-place if we put her for the time in one of the coffins of her husband's ancestors lying in what is still consecrated ground. We opened such a coffin, removed the contents, and placed her as you have seen her. As to the old relics which we took out, we could not leave them on the floor of the crypt. Norlett and I removed them, and he descended at night and burned them in the central furnace. There is my story, Mr. Holmes, though how you forced my hand so that I have to tell it is more than I can say."

Holmes sat for some time lost in thought.

" There is one flaw in your narrative, Sir Robert," he said at last. " Your bets on the race, and therefore your hopes for the future, would hold good even if your creditors seized your estate."

" The horse would be part of the estate. What do they care for my bets ? As likely as not they would not run him at all. My chief creditor is, unhappily, my most bitter enemy—a rascally fellow, Sam Brewer, whom I was once compelled to horsewhip on Newmarket Heath. Do you suppose that he would try to save me ? "

" Well, Sir Robert," said Holmes, rising, " this matter must, of course, be referred to the police. It was my duty to bring the facts to light and there I must leave it. As to the morality or decency of your own conduct, it is not for me to express an opinion. It is nearly midnight, Watson, and I think we may make our way back to our humble abode."

It is generally known now that this singular episode ended upon a happier note than Sir Robert's actions deserved. Shoscombe Prince did win the Derby, the sporting owner did net eighty thousand pounds in bets, and the creditors did hold their hand until the race was over, when they were paid in full, and enough was left to re-establish Sir Robert in a fair position in life. Both police and coroner took a lenient view of the transaction, and beyond a mild censure for the delay in registering the lady's decease, the lucky owner got away scatheless from this strange incident in a career which has now outlived its shadows and promises to end in an honoured old age.

56. *The Retired Colourman*

SHERLOCK HOLMES was in a melancholy and philosophic mood that morning. His alert practical nature was subject to such reactions.

" Did you see him ? " he asked.

" You mean the old fellow who has just gone out ? "

" Precisely."

" Yes, I met him at the door."

" What did you think of him ? "

" A pathetic, futile, broken creature."

" Exactly, Watson. Pathetic and futile. But is not all life pathetic and futile ? Is not his story a microcosm of the whole ? We reach. We grasp. And what is left in our hands at the end ? A shadow. Or worse than a shadow—misery."

" Is he one of your clients ? "

" Well, I suppose I may call him so. He has been sent on by the Yard. Just as medical men occasionally send their incurables to a quack. They argue that they can do nothing more, and that whatever happens the patient can be no worse than he is."

"What is the matter?"

Holmes took a rather soiled card from the table. "Josiah Amberley. He says he was junior partner of Brickfall & Amberley, who are manufacturers of artistic materials. You will see their names upon paint-boxes. He made his little pile, retired from business at the age of sixty-one, bought a house at Lewisham, and settled down to rest after a life of ceaseless grind. One would think his future was tolerably assured."

"Yes, indeed."

Holmes glanced over some notes which he had scribbled upon the back of an envelope.

"Retired in 1896, Watson. Early in 1897 he married a woman twenty years younger than himself—a good-looking woman, too, if the photograph does not flatter. A competence, a wife, leisure—it seemed a straight road which lay before him. And yet within two years he is, as you have seen, as broken and miserable a creature as crawls beneath the sun."

"But what has happened?"

"The old story, Watson. A treacherous friend and a fickle wife. It would appear that Amberley has one hobby in life, and it is chess. Not far from him at Lewisham there lives a young doctor who is also a chess-player. I have noted his name as Dr. Ray Ernest. Ernest was frequently in the house, and an intimacy between him and Mrs. Amberley was a natural sequence, for you must admit that our unfortunate client has few outward graces, whatever his inner virtues may be. The couple went off together last week—destination untraced. What is more, the faithless spouse carried off the old man's deed-box as her personal luggage with a good part of his life's savings within. Can we find the lady? Can we save the money? A commonplace problem so far as it has developed, and yet a vital one for Josiah Amberley."

"What will you do about it?"

"Well, the immediate question, my dear Watson, happens to be, What will *you* do?—if you will be good enough to understudy me. You know that I am preoccupied with this case of the two Coptic Patriarchs, which should come to a head to-day. I really have not time to go out to Lewisham, and yet evidence taken on the spot has a special value. The old fellow was quite insistent that I should go, but I explained my difficulty. He is prepared to meet a representative."

"By all means," I answered. "I confess I don't see that I can be of much service, but I am willing to do my best." And so it was that on a summer afternoon I set forth to Lewisham, little dreaming that within a week the affair in which I was engaging would be the eager debate of all England.

It was late that evening before I returned to Baker Street and gave an account of my mission. Holmes lay with his gaunt figure stretched in his deep chair, his pipe curling forth slow wreaths of acrid tobacco, while his eyelids drooped over his eyes so lazily that he might almost have been asleep were it not that at any halt or questionable passage of my narrative they half lifted, and two grey eyes, as bright and keen as rapiers, transfixed me with their searching glance.

"The Haven is the name of Mr. Josiah Amberley's house," I explained. "I think it would interest you, Holmes. It is like some penurious patrician who has sunk into the company of his inferiors. You know that particular quarter, the monotonous brick streets, the weary suburban highways. Right in the middle of them, a little island of ancient culture and comfort, lies this old home, surrounded by a high sun-baked wall mottled with lichens and topped with moss, the sort of wall——"

"Cut out the poetry, Watson," said Holmes severely. "I note that it was a high brick wall."

" Exactly. I should not have known which was The Haven had I not asked a lounger who was smoking in the street. I have a reason for mentioning him. He was a tall, dark, heavily-moustached, rather military-looking man. He nodded in answer to my inquiry and gave me a curiously questioning glance, which came back to my memory a little later.

" I had hardly entered the gateway before I saw Mr. Amberley coming down the drive. I only had a glimpse of him this morning, and he certainly gave me the impression of a strange creature, but when I saw him in full light his appearance was even more abnormal."

" I have, of course, studied it, and yet I should be interested to have your impression," said Holmes.

" He seemed to me like a man who was literally bowed down by care. His back was curved as though he carried a heavy burden. Yet he was not the weakling that I had at first imagined, for his shoulders and chest have the framework of a giant, though his figure tapers away into a pair of spindled legs."

" Left shoe wrinkled, right one smooth."

" I did not observe that."

" No, you wouldn't. I spotted his artificial limb. But proceed."

" I was struck by the snaky locks of grizzled hair which curled from under his old straw hat, and his face with its fierce, eager expression and the deeply-lined features."

" Very good, Watson. What did he say ? "

" He began pouring out the story of his grievances. We walked down the drive together, and of course I took a good look round. I have never seen a worse-kept place. The garden was all running to seed, giving me an impression of wild neglect in which the plants had been allowed to find the way of nature rather than of art. How any decent woman could have tolerated such a state of things, I don't know. The house, too, was slatternly to the last degree, but the poor man seemed himself to be aware of it and to be trying to remedy it,

for a great pot of green paint stood in the centre of the
hall and he was carrying a thick brush in his left hand.
He had been working on the woodwork.

"He took me into his dingy sanctum, and we had a
long chat. Of course, he was disappointed that you had
not come yourself. ' I hardly expected,' he said, ' that
so humble an individual as myself, especially after my
heavy financial loss, could obtain the complete attention
of so famous a man as Mr. Sherlock Holmes.'

"I assured him that the financial question did not
arise. ' No, of course, it is art for art's sake with him,'
said he ; ' but even on the artistic side of crime he might
have found something here to study. And human
nature, Dr. Watson—the black ingratitude of it all !
When did I ever refuse one of her requests ? Was
ever a woman so pampered ? And that young man—he
might have been my own son. He had the run of my
house. And yet see how they have treated me ! Oh,
Dr. Watson, it is a dreadful, dreadful world ! '

"That was the burden of his song for an hour or more.
He had, it seems, no suspicion of an intrigue. They
lived alone save for a woman who comes in by the day
and leaves every evening at six. On that particular
evening old Amberley, wishing to give his wife a treat,
had taken two upper circle seats at the Haymarket
Theatre. At the last moment she had complained of a
headache and had refused to go. He had gone alone.
There seemed to be no doubt about the fact, for he
produced the unused ticket which he had taken for his
wife."

"That is remarkable—most remarkable," said Holmes,
whose interest in the case seemed to be rising. "Pray
continue, Watson. I find your narrative most arresting.
Did you personally examine this ticket ? You did not,
perchance, take the number ? "

"It so happens that I did," I answered with some
pride. "It chanced to be my old school number, thirty-
one, and so it stuck in my head."

"Excellent, Watson ! His seat, then, was either thirty or thirty-two."

"Quite so," I answered, with some mystification.
"And on B row."

"That is most satisfactory. What else did he tell you ? "

"He showed me his strong-room, as he called it. It really is a strong-room—like a bank—with iron door and shutter—burglar-proof, as he claimed. However, the woman seems to have had a duplicate key, and between them they had carried off some seven thousand pounds' worth of cash and securities."

"Securities ! How could they dispose of those ? "

"He said that he had given the police a list and that he hoped they would be unsaleable. He had got back from the theatre about midnight, and found the place plundered, the door and window open and the fugitives gone. There was no letter or message, nor has he heard a word since. He at once gave the alarm to the police."

Holmes brooded for some minutes.

"You say he was painting. What was he painting ? "

"Well, he was painting the passage. But he had already painted the door and woodwork of this room I spoke of."

"Does it not strike you as a strange occupation in the circumstances ? "

" 'One must do something to ease an aching heart.' That was his own explanation. It was eccentric, no doubt, but he is clearly an eccentric man. He tore up one of his wife's photographs in my presence—tore it up furiously in a tempest of passion. 'I never wish to see her damned face again,' he shrieked."

"Anything more, Watson ? "

"Yes, one thing which struck me more than anything else. I had driven to the Blackheath Station and had caught my train there, when just as it was starting I saw a man dart into the carriage next to my own. You know that I have a quick eye for faces, Holmes. It was undoubtedly the tall, dark man whom I had addressed in the street. I saw him once more at London Bridge, and then I lost him in the crowd. But I am convinced that he was following me."

"No doubt! No doubt!" said Holmes. "A tall, dark, heavily-moustached man, you say, with grey-tinted sun-glasses?"

"Holmes, you are a wizard. I did not say so, but he *had* grey-tinted sun-glasses."

"And a Masonic tie-pin?"

"Holmes!"

"Quite simple, my dear Watson. But let us get down to what is practical. I must admit to you that the case, which seemed to me to be so absurdly simple as to be hardly worth my notice, is rapidly assuming a very different aspect. It is true that though in your mission you have missed everything of importance, yet even those things which have obtruded themselves upon your notice give rise to serious thought."

"What have I missed?"

"Don't be hurt, my dear fellow. You know that I am quite impersonal. No one else would have done better. Some possibly not so well. But clearly you have missed some vital points. What is the opinion of the neighbours about this man Amberley and his wife? That surely is of importance. What of Dr. Ernest? Was he the gay Lothario one would expect? With your natural advantages, Watson, every lady is your helper and accomplice. What about the girl at the post office, or the wife of the greengrocer? I can picture you whispering soft nothings with the young lady at the 'Blue Anchor,' and receiving hard somethings in exchange. All this you have left undone."

"It can still be done."

"It has been done. Thanks to the telephone and the help of the Yard, I can usually get my essentials without leaving this room. As a matter of fact, my information confirms the man's story. He has the local repute of being a miser as well as a harsh and exacting husband. That he had a large sum of money in that strong-room of his is certain. So also is it that young Dr. Ernest, an unmarried man, played chess with Amberley, and probably played the fool with his wife. All this seems plain sailing, and one would think that there was no more to be said—and yet !—and yet ! "

" Where lies the difficulty ? "

" In my imagination, perhaps. Well, leave it there, Watson. Let us escape from this weary workaday world by the side door of music. Carina sings to-night at the Albert Hall, and we still have time to dress, dine and enjoy."

In the morning I was up betimes, but some toast crumbs and two empty egg-shells told me that my companion was earlier still. I found a scribbled note upon the table.

DEAR WATSON,—

There are one or two points of contact which I should wish to establish with Mr. Josiah Amberley. When I have done so we can dismiss the case—or not. I would only ask you to be on hand about three o'clock, as I conceive it possible that I may want you.

S. H.

I saw nothing of Holmes all day, but at the hour named he returned, grave, preoccupied and aloof. At such times it was wiser to leave him to himself.

" Has Amberley been here yet ? "

" No."

" Ah ! I am expecting him."

He was not disappointed, for presently the old fellow arrived with a very worried and puzzled expression upon his austere face.

" I've had a telegram, Mr. Holmes. I can make nothing of it." He handed it over, and Holmes read it aloud.

"Come at once without fail. Can give you information as to your recent loss.—ELMAN. The Vicarage."

"Dispatched at two-ten from Little Purlington," said
Holmes. "Little Purlington is in Essex, I believe, not
far from Frinton. Well, of course you will start at once.
This is evidently from a responsible person, the vicar of
the place. Where is my Crockford? Yes, here we have
him. J. C. Elman, M.A., Living of Mossmoor-cum-
Little Purlington. Look up the trains, Watson."

"There is one at five-twenty from Liverpool Street."

"Excellent. You had best go with him, Watson.
He may need help or advice. Clearly we have come to a
crisis in this affair."

But our client seemed by no means eager to start.

"It's perfectly absurd, Mr. Holmes," he said. "What
can this man possibly know of what has occurred? It
is waste of time and money."

"He would not have telegraphed to you if he did not
know something. Wire at once that you are coming."

"I don't think I shall go."

Holmes assumed his sternest aspect.

"It would make the worst possible impression both
on the police and upon myself, Mr. Amberley, if when so
obvious a clue arose you should refuse to follow it up.
We should feel that you were not really in earnest in this
investigation."

Our client seemed horrified at the suggestion.

"Why, of course I shall go if you look at it in that
way," said he. "On the face of it, it seems absurd to
suppose that this parson knows anything, but if you
think——"

"I do think," said Holmes, with emphasis, and so we
were launched upon our journey. Holmes took me aside
before we left the room and gave me one word of counsel
which showed that he considered the matter to be of
importance. "Whatever you do, see that he really does
go," said he. "Should he break away or return, get to

the nearest telephone exchange and send the single word 'Bolted.' I will arrange here that it shall reach me wherever I am."

Little Purlington is not an easy place to reach, for it is on a branch line. My remembrance of the journey is not a pleasant one, for the weather was hot, the train slow, and my companion sullen and silent, hardly talking at all, save to make an occasional sardonic remark as to the futility of our proceedings. When we at last reached the little station it was a two-mile drive before we came to the Vicarage, where a big, solemn, rather pompous clergyman received us in his study. Our telegram lay before him.

"Well, gentlemen," he asked, "what can I do for you?"

"We came," I explained, "in answer to your wire."

"My wire! I sent no wire."

"I mean the wire which you sent to Mr. Josiah Amberley about his wife and his money."

"If this is a joke, sir, it is a very questionable one," said the vicar angrily. "I have never heard of the gentleman you name, and I have not sent a wire to anyone."

Our client and I looked at each other in amazement.

"Perhaps there is some mistake," said I; "are there perhaps two vicarages? Here is the wire itself, signed Elman, and dated from the Vicarage."

"There is only one vicarage, sir, and only one vicar, and this wire is a scandalous forgery, the origin of which shall certainly be investigated by the police. Meanwhile, I can see no possible object in prolonging this interview."

So Mr. Amberley and I found ourselves on the roadside in what seemed to me to be the most primitive village in England. We made for the telegraph office, but it was already closed. There was a telephone, however, at the little 'Railway Arms,' and by it I got into touch with Holmes, who shared in our amazement at the result of our journey.

"Most singular!" said the distant voice. "Most remarkable! I much fear, my dear Watson, that there is no return train to-night. I have unwittingly condemned you to the horrors of a country inn. However, there is always Nature, Watson—Nature and Josiah Amberley—you can be in close commune with both." I heard his dry chuckle as he turned away.

It was soon apparent to me that my companion's reputation as a miser was not undeserved. He had grumbled at the expense of the journey, had insisted upon travelling third-class, and was now clamorous in his objections to the hotel bill. Next morning, when we did at last arrive in London, it was hard to say which of us was in the worse humour.

"You had best take Baker Street as we pass," said I. "Mr. Holmes may have some fresh instructions."

"If they are not worth more than the last ones they are not of much use," said Amberley, with a malevolent scowl. None the less, he kept me company. I had already warned Holmes by telegram of the hour of our arrival, but we found a message waiting that he was at Lewisham, and would expect us there. That was a surprise, but an even greater one was to find that he was not alone in the sitting-room of our client. A stern-looking, impassive man sat beside him, a dark man with grey-tinted glasses and a large Masonic pin projecting from his tie.

"This is my friend Mr. Barker," said Holmes. "He has been interesting himself also in your business, Mr. Josiah Amberley, though we have been working independently. But we both have the same question to ask you!"

Mr. Amberley sat down heavily. He sensed impending danger. I read it in his straining eyes and his twitching features.

"What is the question, Mr. Holmes?"

" Only this : What did you do with the bodies ? "

The man sprang to his feet with a hoarse scream. He clawed into the air with his bony hands. His mouth was open, and for the instant he looked like some horrible bird of prey. In a flash we got a glimpse of the real Josiah Amberley, a misshapen demon with a soul as distorted as his body. As he fell back into his chair he clapped his hand to his lips as if to stifle a cough. Holmes sprang at his throat like a tiger, and twisted his face towards the ground. A white pellet fell from between his gasping lips.

" No short cuts, Josiah Amberley. Things must be done decently and in order. What about it, Barker ? "

" I have a cab at the door," said our taciturn companion.

" It is only a few hundred yards to the station. We will go together. You can stay here, Watson. I shall be back within half an hour."

The old colourman had the strength of a lion in that great trunk of his, but he was helpless in the hands of the two experienced man-handlers. Wriggling and twisting he was dragged to the waiting cab, and I was left to my solitary vigil in the ill-omened house. In less time than he had named, however, Holmes was back, in company with a smart young police inspector.

" I've left Barker to look after the formalities," said Holmes. " You had not met Barker, Watson. He is my hated rival upon the Surrey shore. When you said a tall, dark man it was not difficult for me to complete the picture. He has several good cases to his credit, has he not, Inspector ? "

" He has certainly interfered several times," the Inspector answered with reserve.

" His methods are irregular, no doubt, like my own. The irregulars are useful sometimes, you know. You, for example, with your compulsory warning about whatever he said being used against him, could never have bluffed this rascal into what is virtually a confession."

" Perhaps not. But we get there all the same, Mr. Holmes. Don't imagine that we had not formed our own views of this case, and that we would not have laid our hands on our man. You will excuse us for feeling sore when you jump in with methods which we cannot use, and so rob us of the credit."

" There shall be no such robbery, MacKinnon. I assure you that I efface myself from now onwards, and as to Barker, he has done nothing save what I told him."

The Inspector seemed considerably relieved.

" That is very handsome of you, Mr. Holmes. Praise or blame can matter little to you, but it is very different to us when the newspapers begin to ask questions."

" Quite so. But they are pretty sure to ask questions anyhow, so it would be as well to have answers. What will you say, for example, when the intelligent and enterprising reporter asks you what the exact points were which aroused your suspicion, and finally gave you a certain conviction as to the real facts ? "

The Inspector looked puzzled.

" We don't seem to have got any real facts yet, Mr. Holmes. You say that the prisoner, in the presence of three witnesses, practically confessed, by trying to commit suicide, that he had murdered his wife and her lover. What other facts have you ? "

" Have you arranged for a search ? "

" There are three constables on their way."

" Then you will soon get the clearest fact of all. The bodies cannot be far away. Try the cellars and the garden. It should not take long to dig up the likely places. This house is older than the water-pipes. There must be a disused well somewhere. Try your luck there."

" But how did you know of it, and how was it done ? "

" I'll show you first how it was done, and then I will give the explanation which is due to you, and even more to my long-suffering friend here, who has been invaluable throughout. But, first, I would give you an insight into this man's mentality. It is a very unusual one—so much so that I think his destination is more likely to be Broadmoor than the scaffold. He has, to a high degree, the sort of mind which one associates with the mediæval Italian nature rather than with the modern Briton. He was a miserable miser who made his wife so wretched by his niggardly ways that she was a ready prey for any adventurer. Such a one came upon the scene in the person of this chess-playing doctor. Amberley excelled at chess—one mark, Watson, of a scheming mind. Like all misers, he was a jealous man, and his jealousy became a frantic mania. Rightly or wrongly, he suspected an intrigue. He determined to have his revenge, and he planned it with diabolical cleverness. Come here ! "

Holmes led us along the passage with as much certainty as if he had lived in the house, and halted at the open door of the strong-room.

" Pooh ! What an awful smell of paint ! " cried the Inspector.

" That was our first clue," said Holmes. " You can thank Dr. Watson's observation for that, though he failed to draw the inference. It set my foot upon the trail. Why should this man at such a time be filling his house with strong odours ? Obviously, to cover some other smell which he wished to conceal—some guilty smell which would suggest suspicions. Then came the idea of a room such as you see here with iron door and shutter —a hermetically sealed room. Put those two facts together, and whither do they lead ? I could only determine that by examining the house myself. I was already certain that the case was serious, for I had examined the box-office chart at the Haymarket Theatre—another of Dr. Watson's bull's-eyes—and ascertained that neither B thirty nor thirty-two of the upper circle had been occupied that night. Therefore, Amberley had not been to the theatre, and his alibi fell to the ground. He made a bad slip when he allowed my astute friend to notice the number of the seat taken for his wife. The question now arose how I might be able to examine the house. I sent an agent to the most impossible village I could think of, and summoned my man to it at such an hour that he could not possibly get back. To prevent any miscarriage, Dr. Watson accompanied him. The good vicar's name I took, of course, out of my Crockford. Do I make it all clear to you ? "

" It is masterly," said the Inspector, in an awed voice.

" There being no fear of interruption I proceeded to burgle the house. Burglary has always been an alternative profession, had I cared to adopt it, and I have little doubt that I should have come to the front. Observe what I found. You see the gas-pipe along the skirting here. Very good. It rises in the angle of the wall, and there is a tap here in the corner. The pipe runs out into the strong-room, as you can see, and ends in that plaster rose in the centre of the ceiling, where it is concealed by the ornamentation. That end is wide open. At any moment by turning the outside tap the room could be flooded with gas. With door and shutter closed and the tap full on I would not give two minutes of conscious sensation to anyone shut up in that little chamber. By what devilish device he decoyed them there I do not know, but once inside the door they were at his mercy."

The Inspector examined the pipe with interest. " One of our officers mentioned the smell of gas," said he, " but, of course, the window and door were open then, and the paint—or some of it—was already about. He had begun the work of painting the day before, according to his story. But what next, Mr. Holmes ? "

" Well, then came an incident which was rather unexpected to myself. I was slipping through the pantry window in the early dawn when I felt a hand inside my collar, and a voice said : ' Now, you rascal, what are you doing in there ? ' When I could twist my head round I looked into the tinted spectacles of my friend and rival,

Mr. Barker. It was a curious forgathering, and set us both smiling. It seems that he had been engaged by Dr. Ray Ernest's family to make some investigations, and had come to the same conclusion as to foul play. He had watched the house for some days, and had spotted Dr. Watson as one of the obviously suspicious characters who had called there. He could hardly arrest Watson, but when he saw a man actually climbing out of the pantry window there came a limit to his restraint. Of course, I told him how matters stood and we continued the case together."

" Why him ? Why not us ? "

" Because it was in my mind to put that little test which answered so admirably. I fear you would not have gone so far."

The Inspector smiled.

" Well, maybe not. I understand that I have your word, Mr. Holmes, that you step right out of the case now and that you turn all your results over to us."

" Certainly, that is always my custom."

" Well, in the name of the Force I thank you. It seems a clear case, as you put it, and there can't be much difficulty over the bodies."

" I'll show you a grim little bit of evidence," said Holmes, " and I am sure Amberley himself never observed it. You'll get results, Inspector, by always putting yourself in the other fellow's place, and thinking what you would do yourself. It takes some imagination, but it pays. Now, we will suppose that you were shut up in this little room, had not two minutes to live, but wanted to get even with the fiend who was probably mocking at you from the other side of the door. What would you do ? "

" Write a message."

" Exactly. You would like to tell people how you died. No use writing on paper. That would be seen. If you wrote on the wall some eye might rest upon it. Now, look here ! Just above the skirting is scribbled with a purple indelible pencil : ' We we——' That's all."

" What do you make of that ? "

" Well, it's only a foot above the ground. The poor devil was on the floor and dying when he wrote it. He lost his senses before he could finish."

" He was writing, ' We were murdered.' "

" That's how I read it. If you find an indelible pencil on the body——"

" We'll look out for it, you may be sure. But those securities ? Clearly there was no robbery at all. And yet he *did* possess those bonds. We verified that."

" You may be sure he has them hidden in a safe place. When the whole elopement had passed into history he would suddenly discover them, and announce that the guilty couple had relented and sent back the plunder or had dropped it on the way."

" You certainly seem to have met every difficulty," said the Inspector. " Of course, he was bound to call us in, but why he should have gone to you I can't understand."

" Pure swank ! " Holmes answered. " He felt so clever and so sure of himself that he imagined no one could touch him. He could say to any suspicious neighbour, ' Look at the steps I have taken. I have consulted not only the police, but even Sherlock Holmes.' "

The Inspector laughed.

" We must forgive you your ' even,' Mr. Holmes," said he ; " it's as workmanlike a job as I can remember."

A couple of days later my friend tossed across to me a copy of the bi-weekly *North Surrey Observer*. Under a series of flaming headlines, which began with " The Haven Horror " and ended with " Brilliant Police Investigation," there was a packed column of print which gave the first consecutive account of the affair. The concluding paragraph is typical of the whole. It ran thus :

" The remarkable acumen by which Inspector Mac-Kinnon deduced from the smell of paint that some other smell, that of gas, for example, might be concealed ; the bold deduction that the strong-room might also be the death-chamber, and the subsequent inquiry which led to the discovery of the bodies in a disused well, cleverly concealed by a dog-kennel, should live in the history of crime as a standing example of the intelligence of our professional detectives."

" Well, well, MacKinnon is a good fellow," said Holmes, with a tolerant smile. " You can file it in our archives, Watson. Some day the true story may be told."

BY SIR ARTHUR CONAN DOYLE

CENTENARY VOLUME

GREAT STORIES

SELECTED BY JOHN DICKSON CARR

This collection has been made to celebrate the hundredth anniversary of Sir Arthur Conan Doyle's birth. It is representative of him at his best in all the styles of which he was a master: science fiction, mystery and adventure, the sporting world, horror, historical adventure, and detection with his inimitable Sherlock Holmes.

THE

SHERLOCK HOLMES

LONG STORIES

4 Volumes in 1

A Study in Scarlet : The Sign of Four
The Hound of the Baskervilles
The Valley of Fear

" The creator of the greatest detective in all fiction need not fear that the younger generation will be less sensitive to the thrills that are latent on nearly every one of these pages than were those of us who read them as children in the 'nineties. Excitement is less susceptible to the wear and tear of time than humour."—*The Daily Telegraph.*

THE
CONAN DOYLE
STORIES

6 Volumes in 1
The Ring and the Camp
Pirates and Blue Water
Terror and Mystery
Twilight and the Unseen
Adventure and Medical Life
Tales of Long Ago

THE COMPLETE
PROFESSOR
CHALLENGER
STORIES

5 Volumes in 1

The Lost World   The Poison Belt
The Land of Mist   When the World
Screamed
The Disintegration Machine

'He had the two necessary qualities for a writer of adventure: he could describe suspense and he could describe, wonderfully, the action that follows'—*Time and Tide*.

THE
CONAN DOYLE
HISTORICAL ROMANCES

The White Company
Sir Nigel
Micah Clarke
The Refugees

Opinions of the Press

'If this is not value for money, we do not know what is!
In every way a most noteworthy publication.'—*Church of
England Newspaper*.

'A triumph of publishing enterprise.'—*Sunday Referee*.

'The men who were boys when I was a boy will surely,
as one man, welcome these. What a thrill the mere names
conjure up.'—Gerald Gould in *The Observer*.

THE COMPLETE
NAPOLEONIC
STORIES

Uncle Bernac
Adventures of Gerard
Exploits of Brigadier Gerard
The Great Shadow

'Sir Arthur could never resist an adventurous bit of
history, and in one volume we have four whole romances,
and of course Brigadier Gerard whom some, at least, would
not exchange for Sherlock Holmes himself.'—*Glasgow Herald*.

THE LIFE OF

SIR ARTHUR
CONAN DOYLE

BY JOHN DICKSON CARR

This is the first biography for which access has been granted to all Doyle's private letters and papers. John Dickson Carr has made excellent use of his material and solves all those mysteries which surround the great creator of Sherlock Holmes.

Opinions of the Press

" His story, from its struggling and impecunious beginning to its wealthy and honoured close, is the adventure of an eager, chivalrous and courageous nature, accepting life in all its manifestations with an enormous gusto. Mr. John Dickson Carr has made good use of the abundant material —much of it hitherto inedited. His biography is admirably complete."—Dorothy Sayers in *The Sunday Times*.

" Mr. Dickson Carr is to be congratulated on the skill with which he has composed the official 'Life of Sir Arthur Conan Doyle.' As a fellow biographer, I recognise and praise Mr. Dickson Carr's taste and cunning."—Harold Nicolson in *The Daily Telegraph*.

" Let me say at once it is worth every farthing of its cost. Mr. Dickson Carr has written a fine, bustling book with enough sheer stingo in it to fill a dozen thrillers. It is full of fascinating new facts and fresh stories."—Ian Mackay in *The News Chronicle*.